MASTERS OF SF:
THE SCIENCE FICTION HALL OF FAME

by W. Fraser Sandercombe

Please note: Certain sections of this volume are not meant to approach any sort of complete listing - their purpose is to give a good cross-section of examples. These are: Awards; Radio; and Related. The other sections, Film and Television, Novels and Collections, Anthologies, and Non-Fiction, are as complete as possible.

My thanks to Robert Graber of Sunrise Books in Guelph, Ontario for his help with the research. And my thanks to bookseller Leonard Shoup of Burlington, Ontario for *his* help with the research.

This one is for Rob McIntyre and Chris Pappas and all those years ago when guys like Asimov and Bradbury and Clarke and Heinlein, et al, all seemed so new and so fresh... Hell, I guess they almost *were* new and fresh back then - at least, the newness hadn't worn off yet.

All rights reserved under article two of the Berne Copyright Convention (1971). No part of this book may be reproduced or transmitted in any form or by any means, electronic or mechanical, including photocopying, recording, or by any information storage and retrieval system without permission in writing from the publisher.
We acknowledge the financial support of the Government of Canada through the Book Publishing Industry Development Program for our publishing activities.
Published by Collector's Guide Publishing Inc., Box 62034, Burlington, Ontario, Canada, L7R 4K2
Printed and bound in Canada

Masters of SF The Science Fiction Hall of Fame /W. Fraser Sandercombe © 2010 CG Publishing Inc/W. Fraser Sandercombe ISBN 9781-897350-28-7

CONTENTS

1996 - John W. Campbell, Jr.	5
1996 - Hugo Gernsback	11
1996 - A. E. van Vogt	14
1996 - Jack Williamson	19
1997 - Isaac Asimov	24
1997 - Sir Arthur C. Clarke	63
1997 - Andre Norton	71
1997 - H. G. Wells	81
1998 - Hal Clement	95
1998 - Robert A. Heinlein	97
1998 - C.L. Moore	104
1998 - Frederik Pohl	109
1999 - Ray Bradbury	121
1999 - Abraham Merritt	144
1999 - Robert Silverberg	146
1999 - Jules Verne	174
2000 - Poul Anderson	188
2000 - Gordon R. Dickson	197
2000 - Eric Frank Russell	203
2000 - Theodore Sturgeon	205
2001 - Alfred Bester	211
2001 - Ursula K. Le Guin	214
2001 - Fritz Leiber	221
2001 - Jack Vance	228
2002 - James Blish	234
2002 - Samuel R. Delany	239
2002 - Michael Moorcock	243
2002 - Donald Allen Wollheim	256
2003 - Edgar Rice Burroughs	267
2003 - Damon Knight	276
2003 - Wilson Tucker	285
2003 - Kate Wilhelm	287
2004 - Brian W. Aldiss	290
2004 - Harry Harrison	302
2004 - Mary W. Shelley	313
2004 - E. E. Doc Smith	318
2005 - Chesley Bonestell	320
2005 - Philip K. Dick	323
2005 - Ray Harryhausen	330
2005 - Steven Spielberg	334
2006 - Frank Kelly Freas	343
2006 - Frank Herbert	345
2006 - George Lucas	349
2006 - Anne McCaffrey	355
2007 - Ed Emshwiller	360
2007 - Gene Roddenberry	362
2007 - Ridley Scott	367
2007 - Gene Wolfe	371
2008 - Betty Ballantine	375
2008 - Ian Ballantine	376
2008 - William Gibson	377
2008 - Richard M. Powers	379
2008 - Rod Serling	380
2009 - Edward L. Ferman	397
2009 - Michael Whelan	402
2009 - Frank R. Paul	403
2009 - Connie Willis	405
2010 – Octavia E. Butler	407
2010 – Richard Matheson	409
2010 – Douglas Trumbull	421
2010 – Roger Zelazny	423
Appendix: The Futurians	430
Bibliography	430

INTRODUCTION - SCIENCE FICTION

One of the great quandaries for fans and scholars alike has been defining the constituency of science fiction.

What is plainly evident in the historical record is that science and religion have not always been the sole sources of revelation. Frequently it is purely the faculty of unbridled imagination that has led to our species' enlightenment. As much as the stars of philosophy—both scientific and spiritual—have grappled to bring us into our modern world, it is sometimes at the hands of the fantasist, whose sole intention is to entertain, that we have been led to a myriad of important insights.

In 1851 an English poet called William Wilson became the earliest known critic to recognize the value of fiction as a method of dispensing scientific fact. Wilson was the first person to string together the words science and fiction consecutively in his book of poetry and reviews, called *A Little Earnest Book Upon a Great Old Subject*. Although a book of poetry may, at first glance, seem to be an incongruous place for such a term to appear, Wilson actually applied the term in exactly the same way as we do today. He was discussing a short story he had read by R.H.Horne called *The Poor Artist; or Seven Eyesights, One Object*. Horne had described how a gold coin covered in water drops might appear as viewed by a human, a bee, an ant, a spider, a perch, a robin and a cat. Wilson noted how much he had enjoyed the book and then stated:

"Fiction has lately been chosen as a means of familiarizing science...We hope it will not be long before we may have other works of Science-Fiction, as we believe such books likely to fulfil a good purpose, and create an interest, where, unhappily, science alone might fail."

Wilson understood and elaborated in detail how old-fashioned fairy tales were beginning to pale in the glow of new scientific discoveries. He also clearly understood that fiction was a legitimate vehicle for conveying scientific truth to the general reader. Horne's book is from an era when fiction had reached a crossroads between the superstitions of the past and the revelations of the new science. The most successful parables, handed down from generation to generation, usually included an explicit moral lesson. This is also true of Horne's story, but although it is in the vein of the most familiar of fables, it includes a scientific component. The author weaves together biology and philosophy with the moral. The title even states "Science as Fable." Although Horne's book was certainly not the first to take this approach, it seems to be the first to actually be called science fiction, and Horne must thus be counted in an illustrious list of early writers who projected what they thought was scientifically possible into a work of fiction.

In Brian Aldiss's worthwhile analysis of science fiction, *The Billion Year Spree*, attention is drawn to Mary Shelley's *Frankenstein*. Aldiss proposed that Shelley's 1818 masterpiece should be credited as the first science fiction novel. It is certainly recognised by many scholars to be as good a place as any to begin the saga of modern science fiction. Aldiss gets all the credit for suggesting that Frankenstein was the first science fiction novel, but the idea probably originally came from an article in the British newspapers in May of 1896, shortly after H.G. Wells' *Time Machine* had elevated him to the level of superstar. In this early article an anonymous scribe made lengthy comparisons between Wells and Shelley while giving due credit to Shelley's father, William Godwin, for his story *St Leon* as being one possible inspiration for Frankenstein. This same article even refers to "scientific-fictionists."

Aldiss acknowledged that no new form of literature comes from a vacuum and that Frankenstein was no exception. Mary Shelley had built upon the current trend of Gothic novels, with their strange settings and stranger characters. However, while her father's story relied on the supernatural Philosopher's Stone, she injected her own story with the latest in hard scientific possibility, having just acquainted herself with the works of Luigi Galvani and Erasmus Darwin (Charles' grandfather). Shelley also tackled the larger issue of human identity, by granting the tortured Victor Frankenstein the ability to create life. By removing the monopoly on this precious gift from the divine to the mundane, Shelley was reflecting the teachings of Darwin and introducing her audience to evolution and the potential pitfalls of future technology.

With the benefit of hindsight we can see the inevitability of this new form of literature. The world was undergoing profound changes in every walk of society. Industry had arrived and with it came the notion of free-time and workers' rights. The new technology changed perceptions of what tomorrow might bring. People could no longer anticipate the future with any sense of reliability. Life began to accelerate. Anticipation of the future evolved to incorporate scientific principles and slowly fairy tales and astrology were jointly consigned to the realms of quaint nostalgia.

Today we are living in a science fiction world. We are surrounded with the trappings of the fantastic. The overall picture has never really been predicted with any accuracy by these scientific fictionists, but the details are everywhere. Our world bleeds science fiction.

Here in Fraser's book is a remarkably comprehensive overview of the works of the most important purveyors of this most significant form of communication. The inductees of the Science Fiction Hall of Fame represent a mesmerising array of talents. Editors, writers, artists and film-makers. Notably all of them, at one level or another, have exhibited a fascination with technology and its potential impact on our future. Whether it be Mary Shelley's interest in Galvani's experiments, Wells' prognostications on the fourth dimension and genetics, Verne's and Trumbull's love of hardware, Gernsback's gadgets, Asimov's robots, Campbell's and Smith's giant interstellar spacecraft, Moorcock's multiverses, Lucas and Heinlein's space wars, Gibson's computers, Whelan's, Paul's and Bonestell's spaceships and planetary bases, Harrison, Matheson and Zelazny's distopias caused by over-population or biological or nuclear warfare, or the introspective insights of Bradbury, Serling, Dick and Clarke. Science fiction represents the only form of communication that makes us examine the future. Whether it be the future of our species or the future of an individual, it paints a fantastic picture of what might be. Contrary to popular opinion it doesn't need to get it right. As someone once pointed out, science fiction is a rhetorical strategy. It doesn't have to be prophetic it doesn't even have to be close. What it does need to do, is make us contemplate the consequences of our actions.

Imagination is a singularly human trait. Not only does it guide us to realise our potential, it is the well-spring for empathy and compassion. Those of us with proficient imaginations have sovereignty of the future. The 61 individuals in the pages ahead may not have divined the true nature of our future, but they do represent some of the best prognosticators of the last 200 years and for their efforts we should all be grateful.

Robert Godwin (2010)

John W. Campbell, Jr.

-1996-

John W. Campbell, Jr.

John Wood Campbell Jr. was born in Newark, New Jersey on June 8th, 1910 and died at home in New Jersey on July 11th, 1971. His university education was started at the Massachusetts Institute of Technology (MIT) but he was invited to leave after failing German; he moved on to Duke University, graduating in 1932 with a Bachelor of Science in physics.

As a serious fan of the Science Fiction magazines, Campbell started writing early and sold his first short story to Amazing Stories when he was 18. The story was Invaders from the Infinite but the editor, T. O'Conor Sloane, lost the manuscript so it was Campbell's second sale to Amazing that became his first published story: When the Atoms Failed, Amazing Stories, January 1930. Also in that issue were: The Hungry Guinea Pig by Miles J. Breuer; Air Lines by David H. Keller; The Sword and the Atopen by Taylor H. Greenfield; The First Ornithopter by Jack Winks; The Corpse that Lived by E. D. Skinner; and Fourth Dimensional Space Penetrator by Julian Kendig; along with the usual features.

In 1937, Campbell was hired by F. Orlin Tremaine as the editor of Astounding Stories, which, in March 1938, became Astounding Science Fiction. As a writer, Campbell was reasonably successful. His early work was compared to the writing of **E. E. Doc Smith** and had a strong following in the magazines. His more esoteric stuff was written under the byline Don A. Stuart, and much of that, including Who Goes There? - filmed as The Thing - was well received. His fiction still sells well in the secondary markets. But it was as an editor that Campbell truly shone. Provocative, challenging and astute, he revolutionized the science fiction world.

The first issue edited by Campbell was December, 1937. It contained: Angel in the Dust Bowl by Spencer Lane; City of the Rocket Horde by Nat Schachner; Dark Eternity by John Russell Fearn; From the Vacuum of Space by J. Harvey Haggard; Galactic Patrol - Part 4 - by **E. E. Doc Smith**; Mana by **Eric Frank Russell**; The Mind Master by Amelia Reynolds Long; The Secret of the Rocks by R. R. Winterbotham; Space Signals by A. B. L. MacFadyen Jr.; and The Time Contractor by Eando Binder.

That first issue still had some leftovers from Tremaine, the previous editor. But by May 1938, Campbell was fully in charge at Astounding and his first solo issue featured: The Brain-Storm Vibration by M. Schere; Incredible Visitor by Clifton B. Kruse; Island of the Individualists by Nat Schachner; The Legion of Time - Part 1 - by **Jack Williamson**; Niedbalski's Mutant by Spencer Lane; Procession of Suns by R. R. Winterbotham; Ra for the Rajah by John Victor Peterson; Static by Kent Casey; and Three Thousand Years - Part 2 - by Thomas Calvert McClary.

With that issue, Campbell had begun to put together the stable of writers that formed the focal point of what was later known as the Golden Age of Science Fiction: **Isaac Asimov**; Lester Del Rey; **Arthur C. Clarke**; **Robert A. Heinlein**; **Theodore Sturgeon**; **A. E. van Vogt**; L. Sprague de Camp; L. Ron Hubbard; Clifford D. Simak; **Jack Williamson**; Manly Wade Wellman; Edmond Hamilton; Henry Kuttner; and **C. L. Moore**; among others.

In 1939, Campbell started the fantasy magazine, Unknown, which survived for four years and went out of business in 1943 because of a war-time paper shortage. That first issue, March 1939 included: Sinister Barrier by **Eric Frank Russell**; Who Wants Power? by Mona Farnsworth; Dark Vision by Frank Belknap Long; Where Angels Fear... by Manly Wade Wellman; Closed Doors by A. Macfadyen; and Death Sentence by Robert Moore Williams.

Campbell's influence changed science fiction from stock slop riddled with clichés into something far more literary and original. Astounding evolved into Analog in 1960, and Campbell remained at the helm until his death.

The highest price book of Campbell's for collectors is usually Who Goes There?, from Shasta Publishers, 1948. Decent copies sell for between $1,500.00 and $2,000.00.

Pen names used: Don A. Stuart; Arthur McCann; Karl van Campen.

***

AWARDS

The awards were all Hugos and were presented for Best Professional Magazine but it was the editor who made the magazine and therefore, the editor was the one responsible for winning the award. In 1973, this award was replaced by the Hugo Award for Best Professional Editor.

1953. Astounding Science Fiction tied with Galaxy Science Fiction
1955. Astounding Science Fiction
1956. Astounding Science Fiction
1957. Astounding Science Fiction won in the U.S. while New Worlds was presented with a Hugo in the UK
1961. Analog Science Fiction
1962. Analog Science Fiction
1964. Analog Science Fiction
1965. Analog Science Fiction
1968. Skylark, Edward E. Smith Memorial Award for Imaginative Fiction.
1996. Inducted into The Science Fiction Hall of Fame.
1996. Retro Hugo for Best Professional Editor.
2001. Retro Hugo for Best Professional Editor.

***

FILM AND TELEVISION

1. The Thing. This was from the **John W. Campbell** story, Who Goes There? which was written under the name Don. A. Stuart. The longer title was The Thing from Another World but it was shortened for U.S. audiences. It was released in April 1951, directed by Christian Nyby. The film starred: Kenneth Tobey as Captain Patrick Hendry; Margaret Sheridan as Nikki Nicholson; James Young as Lt. Eddie Dykes; Dewey Martin as Sgt. Bob; and James Arness as The Thing.

2. The Machine. This short story, from 1935, was featured on the television series Tales of Tomorrow, Season Two, Episode Sixteen. The show aired on December 19th, 1952 and starred Georgann Johnson and Gene Lockhart.

3. John Carpenter's The Thing. Still from Campbell's story. Released in June 1982, directed by John Carpenter and starring: Kurt Russell; Wilford Brimley; T. K. Carter; David Clennon; Richard Dysart; and Charles Hallahan.

4. The Thing. With thanks to **John W. Campbell** for the original story. An animated feature produced by Chris Hadley and Peter Wanat, released in September 2002 and starring the voices of: Per Solli; Michael J. Shea; Kevin Moore; Jesse O'Connell; Kathryn Cressida; et al.

5. John W. Campbell's Golden Age of Science Fiction. A film by Eric Solstein and Digital Media Zone, 2002. This started with a short documentary made by James Gunn in 1971, a lunch meeting between Campbell, **Harry Harrison** and **Gordon Dickson**. Sadly, Campbell died just a few weeks after the film was shot. But Solstein restored it and then surrounded it with interviews of authors who knew Campbell, and balanced it with some critical insights. Among the authors were: Thomas Disch; **Robert Silverberg**; William Tenn; Philip Jose Farmer; Ben Bova; Stanley Schmidt; **Michael Moorcock**; **Brian Aldiss**; Greg Bear; **Jack Williamson** - and even **Isaac Asimov**, obviously from older footage.

***

RADIO

From December 11th, 1957 to June 13th, 1958, **John W. Campbell** hosted and narrated the science fiction radio show Exploring Tomorrow, featuring stories by **Gordon R. Dickson**, **Robert Silverberg**, **Poul Anderson**, **Isaac Asimov**, **Philip K. Dick** and many others. The show was billed as the "first science fiction old time radio show of science-fictioneers, by science-fictioneers, and for science-fictioneers."

***

NOVELS AND COLLECTIONS

1. The Mightiest Machine. Published by the Hadley Publishing Company of Providence, Rhode Island, 1947. Hardcover.

2. Who Goes There? Published by Shasta Publishers of Chicago, 1948. Hardcover. This story collection contains: Who Goes There?, 1938; Blindness, 1935; Frictional Losses, 1936; Dead Knowledge, 1938; Elimination, 1936; Twilight, 1934; and Night, 1935.

3. The Incredible Planet. Published by Fantasy Press of Reading, Pennsylvania, 1949. Hardcover. This contains: The Interstellar Search, 1949; and The Incredible Planet, 1949.

4. The Moon Is Hell! Published by Fantasy Press of Reading, Pennsylvania, 1951. Hardcover. This also contained The Elder Gods, 1939.

5. Empire. Actually written by Clifford D. Simak, based on a story that Campbell had done as a teenager. When Campbell couldn't find a publisher for it, he asked Simak to re-write it for Astounding but then rejected Simak's version. It was published by World Editions of New York, 1951, in softcover digest format as Galaxy Science Fiction Novel No. 7.

6. Cloak of Aesir. Published by Shasta Publishers of Chicago, 1952. Hardcover. This story collection contained: Introduction by Campbell; Forgetfulness, 1937; The Escape, 1935; The Machine, 1935; The Invaders, 1935; Rebellion, 1935; Out of Night, 1937; and Cloak of Aesir, 1939.

7. The Thing and Other Stories. Published by Fantasy Books of London, 1952. Softcover. A story collection:: Who Goes There?, 1938; Blindness, 1935; Frictional Losses, 1936; Dead Knowledge, 1938; Elimination, 1936; Twilight, 1934; and Night, 1935.

8. The Black Star Passes. Published by Fantasy Press of Reading, Pennsylvania, 1953. Hardcover. This collection contains: Introduction by Campbell; The Black Star Passes, 1930; Piracy Preferred, 1930; and Solarite, 1930.

9. Who Goes There - and Other Stories. Published in paperback by Dell Books, New York City, 1955. Gathering stories from Who Goes There?, 1952, and The Cloak of Aesir, 1948, this contained: Twilight, 1934; Night, 1935; Blindness, 1935; The Story of Aesir, 1952; Out of Night, 1937; Cloak of Aesir, 1939; and Who Goes There?, 1938.

10. Islands of Space. Published by Fantasy Press of reading, Pennsylvania, 1956. Hardcover.

11. Invaders from the Infinite. Published by Gnome Press of Hicksville, New York, 1961. Hardcover.

12. The Planeteers. Published by Ace Books, New York City, 1966. This was a paperback original, Ace Double G-585, presented with The Ultimate Weapon, also by Campbell.

13. The Ultimate Weapon. Published by Ace Books, New York City, 1966. This was a paperback original, Ace Double G-585, presented with The Planeteers, also by Campbell.

14. The Thing from Outer Space. Published by Tandem Books, London, 1966. This was a paperback reprint of Who Goes There?, Tandem Book T75, containing: Twilight, 1934; Night, 1935; Blindness, 1935; The Story of Aesir, 1952; Out of Night, 1937; Cloak of Aesir, 1939; and Who Goes There?, 1938.

John W. Campbell, Jr.

15. The Best of John W. Campbell. Published by Sidgwick and Jackson of London, 1973. Hardcover. This collection contained: Introduction by **James Blish**; Double Minds, 1937; Forgetfulness, 1937; Who Goes There?, 1938; Out of Night, 1937; and The Cloak of Aesir, 1939; along with a bibliography.

16. John W. Campbell Anthology. Published by Doubleday & Company, Garden City, New York, 1973. This collected: The Black Star Passes, 1930; Islands of Space, 1931; and Invaders from the Infinite, 1935; along with introductions by Lester del Rey, Of Destiny and Wonder; and **Isaac Asimov**, The Sense of Wonder.

17. The Best of John W. Campbell. Published by Nelson Doubleday of Garden City, New York, 1976. Hardcover. Released by the Science Fiction Book Club. This collection contained: The Three Careers of **John W. Campbell** by Lester del Rey; The Last Evolution, 1932; Twilight, 1934; The Machine, 1935; The Invaders, 1935; Rebellion, 1935; Blindness, 1935; Forgetfulness, 1937; Out of Night, 1937; Cloak of Aesir, 1939; Who Goes There?, 1938; and Space for Industry, an essay by Campbell, 1960; along with an afterword: Postscriptum by Mrs. John Campbell.

18. The Space Beyond. Published by Pyramid Books, New York City, 1976. A paperback original, Pyramid Book M3742. A collection: Big, Big, Big - an essay by **Isaac Asimov**, 1976; Marooned, 1976; All, 1976; The Space Beyond, 1976; and an Afterword by George Zebrowski.

19. A New Dawn: The Complete Don A. Stuart Stories. Edited by James A. Mann and Published by the NESFA Press in Framingham, Massachusetts, 2003. Hardcover. This collection contains: The Man Who Lost the Sea, an essay by Barry Malzberg; Twilight, 1934; Atomic Power, 1934; The Machine, 1935; The Invaders, 1935; Rebellion, 1935; Blindness, 1935; The Escape, 1935; Night, 1935; Elimination, 1936; Frictional Losses, 1936; Forgetfulness, 1937; Out of Night, 1937; Cloak of Aesir, 1939; Dead Knowledge, 1938; Who Goes There?, 1938; and The Elder Gods - written with Arthur J. Burks, 1939; along with a pair of essays by Campbell: Strange Worlds, 2003; and Wouldst Write, Wee One?, 2003.

***

ANTHOLOGIES

1. From Unknown Worlds. Published by Street and Smith Publications, New York City, 1948. Softcover. Editing and foreword by Campbell. This contains: The Compleat Werewolf by Anthony Boucher, 1942; Yesterday Was Monday by **Theodore Sturgeon**, 1941; Trouble with Water by H. L. Gold, 1939; The Cloak by Robert Bloch, 1939; The Summons by Don Evans, 1939; The Hexer by Howard Wandrei writing as H. W. Guernsey, 1939; Nothing in the Rules by L. Sprague de Camp, 1939; Anything by Lester del Rey writing as Philip St. John, 1939; Jesus Shoes by Allan R. Bosworth; The Psychomorph by E. A. Grosser; The Devil We Know by Henry Kuttner, 1941; The Refugee by Jane Rice, 1943; and The Enchanted Weekend by John MacCormac.

2. From Unknown Worlds. Published by Atlas Publishing and Distributing, London, 1952. First hardcover edition. Editing and foreword by Campbell. This contains: The Compleat Werewolf by Anthony Boucher, 1942; Yesterday Was Monday by **Theodore Sturgeon**, 1941; Trouble with Water by H. L. Gold, 1939; The Cloak by Robert Bloch, 1939; The Summons by Don Evans, 1939; The Hexer by Howard Wandrei writing as H. W. Guernsey, 1939; Nothing in the Rules by L. Sprague de Camp, 1939; Anything by Lester del Rey writing as Philip St. John, 1939; Jesus Shoes by Allan R. Bosworth; The Psychomorph by E. A. Grosser; The Devil We Know by Henry Kuttner, 1941; The Refugee by Jane Rice, 1943; and The Enchanted Weekend by John MacCormac.

3. The Astounding Science Fiction Anthology. Published by Simon and Schuster, New York City, 1952. Hardcover. Introduced and edited by Campbell. This contains: Blowups Happen by **Robert A. Heinlein**, 1940; Hindsight by **Jack Williamson**, 1940; Vault of the Beast by **A. E. van Vogt**, 1940; The Exalted by L. Sprague de Camp, 1940; Nightfall by **Isaac Asimov**, 1941; When the Bough Breaks by Henry Kuttner and **C. L. Moore** writing as Lewis Padgett, 1944; Clash by Night by Henry Kuttner and **C. L. Moore** writing as Lawrence O'Donnell, 1943; Invariant by John R. Pierce, 1944; First Contact by Murray Leinster, 1945; Meihem in ce Klasrum, an essay by Dolton Edwards, 1946; Hobbyist by **Eric Frank Russell**, 1947; E for Effort by T. L. Sherred, 1947; Child's Play by William Tenn, 1947; Thunder and Roses by **Theodore Sturgeon**, 1947; Late Night Final by **Eric Frank Russell**, 1948; Cold War by Kris Neville, 1949; Eternity Lost by Clifford D. Simak, 1949; The Witches of Karres by James L. Schmitz, 1949; Over the Top by Lester del Rey, 1949; Meteor by William T. Powers, 1950; Last Enemy by H. Beam Piper, 1950; Historical Note by Murray Leinster, 1951; and Protected Species by H. B. Fyfe, 1951.

4. The First Astounding Science Fiction Anthology. Published by Grayson and Grayson, London, 1954. Hardcover. Issued seven of the stories from The Astounding Science Fiction Anthology, 1952: Thunder and Roses by **Theodore Sturgeon**, 1947; Hobbyist by **Eric Frank Russell**, 1947; First Contact by Murray Leinster, 1945; Blowups Happen by **Robert A. Heinlein**, 1940; Child's Play by William Tenn, 1947; The Witches of Karres by James L. Schmitz, 1949; and Invariant by John R. Pierce, 1944.

5. The Second Astounding Science Fiction Anthology. Published by Grayson and Grayson, London, 1954. Hardcover. Issued eight of the stories from The Astounding Science Fiction Anthology, 1952: Vault of the Beast by **A. E. van Vogt**, 1940; E for Effort by T. L. Sherred, 1947; Clash by Night by Henry Kuttner and **C. L. Moore** writing as Lawrence O'Donnell, 1943; Cold War by Kris Neville, 1949; Protected Species by H. B. Fyfe, 1951; Historical Note by Murray Leinster, 1951; Late Night Final by **Eric Frank Russell**, 1948; and Meihem in ce Klasrum, an essay by Dolton Edwards, 1946.

6. Selections from The Astounding Science Fiction Anthology. Published in paperback by Berkley Publishing, New York City, 1956. Issued eight stories from the original hardcover anthology. Edited by Campbell.

7. Astounding Tales of Space and Time. Berkley Publishing, New York City, 1957. Paperback. Issued seven stories from The Astounding Science Fiction Anthology. Edited by Campbell. This contains: Hobbyist, 1947; and Late Night Final, 1948, by **Eric Frank Russell**; Hindsight by **Jack Williamson**, 1940; Thunder and Roses by **Theodore Sturgeon**, 1947; E for Effort by T. L. Sherred 1947; Protected Species by H. B. Fyfe, 1951; and Historical Note by Murray Leinster, 1951.

8. Prologue to Analog. Published by Doubleday & Company, Garden City, New York, 1962. Hardcover. Introduced and edited by Campbell. This contains: Belief by **Isaac Asimov**, 1953; Pandora's Planet by Christopher Anvil, 1956; Sound Decision by Randall Garrett and Robert Silverberg, 1956; Omnilingual by H. Beam Piper, 1957; Triggerman by J. F. Bone, 1958; A Filbert is a Nut by Rick Raphael, 1959; Business as Usual, During Alterations by Ralph Williams, 1958; Pushbutton War by Joseph P. Martino, 1960; We Didn't Do Anything Wrong, Hardly by Roger Kuykendall, 1959; and Minor Ingredient by **Eric Frank Russell**, 1956.

9. Analog I. Published by Doubleday & Company, Garden City, New York, 1963. Hardcover. Introduced and edited by Campbell. This contains: Join Our Gang by Sterling E. Lanier, 1961; Monument by Lloyd Biggle Jr.; The Plague by Teddy Keller, 1961; Remember the Alamo by T. R. Fehrenbach, 1961; The Hunch by Christopher Anvil, 1961; Barnacle Bull by **Poul Anderson** writing as Winston P. Sanders, 1960; Sleight of Wit by **Gordon R. Dickson**, 1961; and Prologue to an Analogue by Walt Richmond and Leigh Richmond, 1961.

10. Analog II. Published by Doubleday & Company, Garden City, New York, 1964. Hardcover. Edited, with a preface by Campbell. This contains: The Weather Man by Theodore L. Thomas, 1962; Good Indian by Mack Reynolds, 1962; Blind Man's Lantern by Allen Kim Lang, 1962; Junior Achievement by William Lee, 1962; Novice by James H. Schmitz, 1962; Ethical Quotient by John T. Phillifent, 1962; Philosopher's Stone by Christopher Anvil, 1963; and The Circuit Riders by R. C. FitzPatrick, 1962.

11. Analog 3. Published by Doubleday & Company, Garden City, New York, 1965. Hardcover. Introduced and edited by Campbell. This contains: Hilifter by **Gordon Dickson**, 1963; Not in the Literature by Christopher Anvil, 1963; Sonny by Rick Raphael, 1963; The Trouble with Telstar by John Berryman, 1963; New Folks' Home by Clifford D. Simak, 1963; Industrial Revolution by **Poul Anderson** writing as Winston P. Sanders, 1963; A World by the Tale by Randall Garrett writing as Seaton McKettrig, 1963; and Thin Edge by Jonathan Blake MacKenzie, 1963.

12. Analog Anthology. Published by Dennis Dobson, London, 1965. This puts together Prologue to Analog, Analog I and Analog II. Hardcover. Edited by Campbell. This contains: Belief by **Isaac Asimov**, 1953; Pandora's Planet by Christopher Anvil, 1956; Sound Decision by Randall Garrett and **Robert Silverberg**, 1956; Omnilingual by H. Beam Piper, 1957; Triggerman by J. F. Bone, 1958; A Filbert is a Nut by Rick Raphael, 1959; Business as Usual, During Alterations by Ralph Williams, 1958; Pushbutton War by Joseph P. Martino, 1960; We Didn't Do Anything Wrong, Hardly by Roger Kuykendall, 1959; and Minor Ingredient by **Eric Frank Russell**, 1956; Join Our Gang by Sterling E. Lanier, 1961; Monument by Lloyd Biggle Jr.; The Plague by Teddy Keller, 1961; Remember the Alamo by T. R. Fehrenbach, 1961; The Hunch by Christopher Anvil, 1961; Barnacle Bull by **Poul Anderson** writing as Winston P. Sanders, 1960; Sleight of Wit by **Gordon R. Dickson**, 1961; and Prologue to an Analogue by Walt Richmond and Leigh Richmond, 1961; The Weather Man by Theodore L. Thomas, 1962; Good Indian by Mack Reynolds, 1962; Blind Man's Lantern by Allen Kim Lang, 1962; Junior Achievement by William Lee, 1962; Novice by James H. Schmitz, 1962; Ethical Quotient by John T. Phillifent, 1962; Philosopher's Stone by Christopher Anvil, 1963; and The Circuit Riders by R. C. FitzPatrick, 1962.

13. Analog 4. Published by Doubleday & Company, Garden City, New York, 1966. Hardcover. Introduced and edited by Campbell: A Case of Identity by Randall Garrett, 1964; The Mary Celeste Move by **Frank Herbert**, 1964; The Permanent Implosion by Dean McLaughlin, 1964; A Day in the Life of Kelvin Throop by R. A. J. Phillips, 1964; Genus Traitor by Mack Reynolds, 1964; Sunjammer by **Poul Anderson** writing as Winston P. Sanders, 1964; and Subjectivity by Norman Spinrad, 1964.

14. Analog 5. Published by Doubleday & Company, Garden City, New York, 1967. Hardcover. Introduced and edited by Campbell: Computers Don't Argue by **Gordon R. Dickson**, 1965; The Adventure of the Extraterrestrial by Mack Reynolds, 1965; Say It with Flowers by **Poul Anderson** writing as Winston P. Sanders, 1965; Mission Red Clash by Joe Poyer, 1965; Countercommandment by Patrick Meadows, 1965; Coincidence Day by John Brunner, 1965; Balanced Ecology by James H. Schmitz, 1965; and Overproof by Jonathan Blake MacKenzie, 1965.

15. Selections from The Astounding Science Fiction Anthology. Published by Berkley Publishing, New York City, 1967. Paperback. Reissued Berkley's 1956 edition of The Astounding Science Fiction Anthology.

16. Analog 6. Published by Doubleday & Company, Garden City, New York, 1968. Hardcover. Introduced and edited by Campbell. This contains: 10:01 A. M. by Alexander B. Malec, 1966; Not a Prison Make by Joseph P. Martino, 1966; Letter from a Higher Critic by Stewart Robb, 1966; Something to Say by John Berryman, 1966; Light of Other Days by Bob Shaw, 1966; The Message by Piers Anthony and Frances Hall, 1966; Stranglehold by Christopher Anvil, 1966; CWACC Strikes Again by **Harry Harrison** writing as Hank Dempsey, 1966; Call Him Lord by **Gordon R. Dickson**, 1966; Early Warning by Robin Scott Wilson writing as Robin S. Scott, 1966; Giant Meteor Impact, an essay by J. E. Enever, 1966; The Easy Way Out by G. Harry Stine writing as Lee Correy,

John W. Campbell, Jr.

1966; Bookworm Run by Vernor Vinge, 1966; and Prototaph by Keith Laumer, 1966.

17. Analog 7. Published by Doubleday & Company, Garden City, New York, 1969. Hardcover. Introduced and edited by Campbell: Weyr Search by **Anne McCaffrey**, 1967; The Last Command by Keith Laumer, 1967; Elementary Mistake by **Poul Anderson** writing as Winston P. Sanders, 1967; There Is a Crooked Man by Jack Wodhams, 1967; Burden of Proof by Bob Shaw, 1967; Dead End by Mike Hodous, 1967; Aim for the Heel by John T. Phillifent, 1967; The Featherbedders by **Frank Herbert**, 1967; Fiesta Brava by Mack Reynolds, 1967; Lost Calling by Howard L. Myers writing as Verge Foray, 1967; and Free Vacation by W. Macfarlane, 1967.

18. A World by the Tale. Published by Curtis Books, New York City, 1970. Curtis Book 123-07060-075. A paperback reissue of Analog 3, introduced and edited by Campbell. This contains: Hilifter by **Gordon Dickson**, 1963; Not in the Literature by Christopher Anvil, 1963; Sonny by Rick Raphael, 1963; The Trouble with Telstar by John Berryman, 1963; New Folks' Home by Clifford D. Simak, 1963; Industrial Revolution by **Poul Anderson** writing as Winston P. Sanders, 1963; A World by the Tale by Randall Garrett writing as Seaton McKettrig, 1963; and Thin Edge by Jonathan Blake MacKenzie, 1963.

19. The Permanent Implosion. Published by Curtis Books, New York City, 1970. Curtis Book 123-07064-075. A paperback reissue of Analog 4, introduced and edited by Campbell: A Case of Identity by Randall Garrett, 1964; The Mary Celeste Move by **Frank Herbert**, 1964; The Permanent Implosion by Dean McLaughlin, 1964; A Day in the Life of Kelvin Throop by R. A. J. Phillips, 1964; Genus Traitor by Mack Reynolds, 1964; Sunjammer by **Poul Anderson** writing as Winston P. Sanders, 1964; and Subjectivity by Norman Spinrad, 1964.

20. Countercommandment and Other Stories. Published by Curtis Books, New York City, 1970. Curtis Book 123-07067-075. A paperback reissue of Analog 5, introduced and edited by Campbell: Computers Don't Argue by **Gordon R. Dickson**, 1965; The Adventure of the Extraterrestrial by Mack Reynolds, 1965; Say It with Flowers by **Poul Anderson** writing as Winston P. Sanders, 1965; Mission Red Clash by Joe Poyer, 1965; Countercommandment by Patrick Meadows, 1965; Coincidence Day by John Brunner, 1965; Balanced Ecology by James H. Schmitz, 1965; and Overproof by Jonathan Blake MacKenzie, 1965.

21. Analog 8. Published by Doubleday & Company, Garden City, New York, 1971. Hardcover. Edited by Campbell. This contains: Hawk Among the Sparrows by Dean McLaughlin, 1968; **The Powers of Observation** by Harry Harrison, 1968; In His Image by Robert Chilson, 1969; Jump by William Earls, 1969; The Hidden Ears by Lawrence A. Perkins, 1969; Womb to Tomb by Joseph Wesley, 1969; Testing... One... Two... Three... Four by Steve Chapman, 1969; and Winkin Blinkin by R. C. FitzPatrick, 1968.

22. Astounding Science Fiction July 1939. Published by Southern Illinois University Press, 1981. Hardcover. This contains: Foreword by Stanley Schmidt; Black Destroyer by **A. E. van Vogt**, 1939; City of the Cosmic Rays by Nat Schachner, 1939; Greater Than Gods by **C. L. Moore**, 1939; Trends by **Isaac Asimov**, 1939; Lightship, Ho! by Nelson S. Bond, 1939; The Moth by Ross Rocklynne, 1939; When the Half Gods Go by A. R. Long, 1939; Tools for Brains, an essay by Leo Vernon, 1939; Geography for Time Travelers, an essay by Willy Ley, 1939; On **John W. Campbell** and Science Fiction, an essay by Ross Rocklynne, 1981; Concerning Trends, an essay by **Isaac Asimov**, 1981; On Black Destroyer, an essay by **A. E. van Vogt**, 1981; Letter by P. Schuyler Miller, 1939; Letter by Casimir F. Pierog, 1939; Letter by D. R. Cummins, 1939; Letter by Donn Brazier, 1939; Letter by Grover Ables, 1939; Letter by **Damon Knight**, 1939; Letter by Arthur L. Widner, 1939; Letter by **Isaac Asimov**, 1939; Letter by Charles W. Jarvis, 1939; Letter by Ralph C. Hamilton, 1939; Numbers Without Meaning, an essay by **John W. Campbell** writing as Arthur McCann; and Addenda, an essay by Campbell, 1939.

***

NON-FICTION

1. The Atomic Story. Published by Henry Holt, New York City, 1947. Hardcover.

2. Collected Editorials from Analog. Published by Doubleday & Company, Garden City, New York, 1966. Selected and introduced by **Harry Harrison**.

3. The John W. Campbell Letters - Volume 1. Published by AC Projects, Franklin, Tennessee, 1985. Hardcover. Edited by Perry A Chapdelaine; Tony Chapdelaine; and George Hay.

4. The John W. Campbell Letters - Volume II with Isaac Asimov and A. E. van Vogt. Published by AC Projects, Franklin, Tennessee, 1991. Hardcover.

***

RELATED

1. A Requiem for Astounding. By Alva Rogers. Published by Advent Publishers, Chicago, 1964. Softcover.

2. Of Worlds Beyond: A Symposium by Edward E. Smith, Ph.D.; John W. Campbell; L. Sprague de Camp; Robert A. Heinlein; Jack Williamson; A. E. van Vogt; and John Taine. Edited by Lloyd Arthur Eschbach. Published by Advent Publishers, Chicago, 1964. Softcover.

3. Of Worlds Beyond: A Symposium by Edward E. Smith, Ph.D.; John W. Campbell; L. Sprague de Camp; Robert A. Heinlein; Jack Williamson; A. E. van Vogt; and John Taine. Edited by Lloyd Arthur Eschbach. Published by Dennis Dobson, London, 1965. First hardcover edition.

4. John W. Campbell: An Australian Tribute. By John Bangsund with a foreword by **Jack Williamson**. Published by Ronald E. Graham and John Bangsund,

Canberra, Australia, 1972. Softcover.

5. The John W. Campbell Memorial Anthology. Edited by **Harry Harrison** and published by Random House, New York City, 1973. Foreword: The Father of Science Fiction by **Isaac Asimov**, afterword by **Harry Harrison**. All the stories were by authors who had been previously published in Analog: Lodestar by **Poul Anderson**; Thiotimoline to the Stars by **Isaac Asimov**; Something Up There Likes Me by **Alfred Bester**; Lecture Demonstration by **Hal Clement**; Early Bird by Theodore R. Cogswell and Theodore L. Thomas; The Emperor's Fan by L. Sprague de Camp; Brothers by **Gordon R. Dickson**; The Mothballed Spaceship by **Harry Harrison**; Black Sheep Astray by Mack Reynolds; Epilog by Clifford D. Simak; Interlude by George O. Smith; Helix the Cat by **Theodore Sturgeon**; and Probability Zero! The Population Implosion by Theodore R. Cogswell.

6. Forgetfulness. A Campbell story adapted as a one-act play by Wayne Gordon and published as a softcover by Performance Publishing, Elgin, Illinois, 1973.

Hugo Gernsback.

He was born Hugo Gernsbacher in Luxembourg City, Luxembourg on August 16th, 1884, and died in New York City on August 19th, 1967. His father was a vintner but Gernsback had little interest in the family business. In Germany, at the Ecole Industrielle and the Technikum he studied science, and emigrated to the United States in 1904, enthralled with science and knowing it would be his life. His first plan was to sell his new invention, an improved dry cell battery, and take it from there.

Shortly after arriving in the U.S., he founded the Electric Importing Company, which he later claimed was the first radio supply house in the world - he was selling home radio kits.

Gernsback's first magazine, Modern Electrics, was started in 1908, and the following year, in 1909, he used the magazine to found the Wireless Association of America which, by 1912, had 10,000 members. Modern Electrics was where he published his novel Ralph 124C 41+, advertised as A Romance of the Year 2660 and serialised in twelve parts in 1911 and 1912.

Shortly after Ralph, Gernsback began publishing his Baron Munchausen Scientific Adventures. These were printed between 1915 and 1917, and languished in the pages of mouldering magazines until 2006 when Robert Godwin and Apogee Books published them as The Scientific Adventures of Baron Munchausen. This work, and Gernsback's devotion to this sort of work, more or less founded a genre, or perhaps a sub-genre: the serious scientific story set in the future - Science Fiction.

In 1913, he started the Electrical Experimenter which became Science and Invention in 1920. In 1925, he founded the radio station WRNY, and was soon involved in the first television broadcasts, tiny images received by scanners in and around New York City. Eventually, Gernsback the Inventor held 80 patents. His enthusiasm for all things scientific was limitless. And that extended deeply into fiction. He wanted futuristic, scientific fiction.

The August 1923 issue of Science and Invention was packed with what Gernsback named Scientific Fiction, which he later changed to Scientifiction. The success of this issue was enough to convince him that what the world needed was an entire magazine devoted to Scientifiction. He wanted to call it that but a reader's poll was overwhelmingly against Scientifiction as the name for a magazine.

So in April 1926, he launched Amazing Stories, the first magazine devoted to Scientifiction. That first issue, with the brilliant Frank R. Paul cover, was made up entirely of reprint of previously published stories. It included: The Facts in the Case of M. Valdemar by Edgar Allan Poe, which was first printed in American Review in 1845; The Man from the Atom - Part 1 - by G. Peyton Wertenbaker -originally published in Science and Invention in August 1923; The Man Who Saved the Earth by Austin Hall - originally published in All Story Magazine, December 1919; The New Accelerator by **H. G. Wells** from The Strand in 1901; Off on a Comet, or, Hector Servadac - Part 1 - by **Jules Verne**, which was published in France in 1877 as Hector Servadac. Voyages et aventures a travers le monde solaire - in 1911, Vincent Parke published an English version called Off on a Comet and the title stuck; and The Thing from "Outside" by George Allan England - originally from Science and Invention, April 1923.

Issue Two included: The Crystal Egg by **H. G. Wells**, from The New Review, 1897; The Infinite Vision by Charles C. Winn, originally printed in Science and Invention, May 1924; The Man from the Atom - Conclusion - by G. Peyton Wertenbaker, from Science and Invention, 1923; Mesmeric Revelation by Edgar Allan Poe, from Columbia Lady's and Gentleman's Magazine, August 1884; Off on a Comet - Conclusion - by **Jules Verne**; and A Trip to the Center of the Earth - Part 1 - by **Jules Verne**, originally published in France in 1864.

It wasn't until Issue Three, that Gernsback began to use original material for Amazing. That issue contained: The Coming of the Ice by G. Peyton Wertenbaker - original; Doctor Hackensaw's Secrets: Some Minor Inventions by Clement Fezandie - original; An Experiment in Gyro-Hats by Ellis Parker Butler from New Broadway Magazine, June 1920; The Malignant Entity by Otis Adelbert Kline, originally published in Weird Tales, 1924; Mr Fosdick Invents the Scidtzmobile by Jaque Morgan, from Modern Electrics, November 1912; The Runaway Skyscraper by Murray Leinster, originally in Argosy, February 22nd, 1919; The Star by **H. G. Wells**, from The Graphic, December 1897; A Trip to the Center of the Earth - Part 2 - by **Jules Verne** - France 1864; and Whispering Ether by Charles S. Wolfe, originally published in Electrical Experimenter, March 1920.

Gernsback's ideal was to publish stories that instructed in science while entertaining the reader. That ideal, of course, was impossible to maintain, which was how he came to publish **A. Merritt** and H. P. Lovecraft, among other non-scientific writers. But he tried. And, in trying, he forged a new genre, one that would never go away.

For as long as Gernsback managed Amazing, the contents page printed a picture of Jules Verne's grave with the words: "Extravagant Fiction Today - Cold Fact Tomorrow."

Amazing Stories, the first magazine devoted to Science Fiction later earned Gernsback the name "The Father of Science Fiction", bestowed by Sam Moskowitz in his essay **Hugo Gernsback**: The Father of Science Fiction, 1959. Within a decade, Scientifiction came to be known as Science Fiction. Also within that decade - in 1929 - Gernsback was forced into bankruptcy by a rival publisher, Bernarr Macfadden, and lost his first magazines. Almost immediately, he started a new company and founded four new magazines: Air Wonder Stories; Science Wonder Stories; Science Wonder Quarterly; and Scientific Detective Monthly. The year after their inauguration, Air Wonder Stories and Science Wonder Stories became Wonder Stories. But Gernsback's success as a science fiction publisher was waning. Scientific Detective Monthly, later known as Amazing Detective Tales, folded less than a year after it's birth. Science Wonder Quarterly, as Wonder Stories Quarterly, folded in 1933; and Wonder Stories was sold in 1936, becoming Thrilling Wonder Stories.

Gernsback's final attempt at publishing Science Fiction was in 1952/1953. He put out Science Fiction+, with Sam Moskowitz as managing editor even though Gernsback was *listed* as editor. It published some truly fine writers: Philip Jose Farmer; Eando Binder; Raymond Z. Gallun; Clifford D. Simak; Robert Bloch; Murray Leinster; Frank Belknap Long; Chad Oliver; Henry Hasse; **Anne McCaffrey**; **Eric Frank Russell**; James H. Schmitz; and many others. But Science Fiction+ only survived for seven issues, folding after the December 1953 issue.

Gernsback may have drifted away from science fiction, but no one was likely to forget him.

The Science Fiction Achievement Awards, started in 1955 and presented by the World Science Fiction Society - Worldcon, were named Hugo Awards, in his honour.

Even now, most science fictioneers know the name **Hugo Gernsback**. And to collectors, his most valuable book is Ralph 124C 41+: A Romance of the Year 2660. Printed in Boston in 1925, this sells for between $12,000.00 and $18,000.00.

Other names used: Greno Gashbuck; Gus N. Habergock; Dr Grego Banshuck.

***

AWARDS

1953. The Order of the Oak Crown, an award presented by the government of Luxembourg for outstanding achievement in an assortment of fields. The award was established on December 29th, 1841.
1960. Hugo Award. Gernsback was presented with a Worldcon Special Convention Award, his own Hugo.
1996. Inducted into The Science Fiction Hall of Fame.

***

MAGAZINES PUBLISHED

1. **Air Wonder Stories**
2. **Amazing Detective Stories**
3. **Amazing Stories**
4. **Aviation Mechanics**
5. **Electrical Experimenter** 1913 - 1920 - later known as Science and Invention
6. **Everyday Mechanics** - 1931 - later - Everyday Science and Mechanics - and still later - Science and Mechanics
7. **The Experimenter** 1924 - 1926
8. **Facts of Life**
9. **Flight**
10. **Fotocraft**
11. **French Humor** - later Tidbits
12. **Gadgets**
13. **High Sea Adventures**
14. **Know Yourself**
15. **Life Guide**
16. **Light**
17. **Luz**
18. **Milady**
19. **Modern Electrics** - 1908 - 1914
20. **Moneymaking**
21. **Motor Camper & Tourist**
22. **New Ideas for Everybody**
23. **Pirate Stories**
24. **Popular Medicine**
25. **Practical Electrics** - December 1921 to October 1924
26. **Radio Amateur News** - July 1919 to July 1920 - renamed Radio News
27. **Radio and Television**
28. **Radio Craft** - July 1929 to June 1948 - renamed Radio Electronics July 1948
29. **Radio Electronics Weekly Business Letter**
30. **Radio Listeners Guide and Call Book**
31. **Radio News** - July 1919 to July 1948
32. **Radio Program Weekly**
33. **Radio Review**
34. **Science and Invention** - August 1920 to August 1931
35. **Science Fiction Plus**
36. **Science Wonder Stories**
37. **Scientific Detective Monthly**
38. **Sexologia**
39. **Sexology**
40. **Short-Wave and Television**
41. **Short-Wave Craft** - later Radio-Craft
42. **Short-Wave Listener**
43. **Superworld Comics**
44. **Technocracy Review**
45. **Television**
46. **Television News**
47. **Tidbits** - originally French Humor
48. **Woman's Digest**
49. **Wonder Stories**
50. **Your Body**
51. **Your Dreams**

***

NOVELS AND COLLECTIONS

1. Ralph 124c 41+. (One to Foresee for One)
Published in Boston by The Stratford Company, 1925 with illustrations by Frank R. Paul. Hardcover. It was re-issued in 1950 by Frederick Fell of New York City, also in hardcover. Signed copies of this are actually available.

2. Ultimate World 1972. Edited by Sam Moskowitz. Published in New York City by Walker and Company, 1971. Dustjacket art by Frank R. Paul.

Hugo Gernsback

3. The Scientific Adventures of Baron Munchausen. Afterword by Robert Godwin. Published by Apogee Books in association with Black Cat Books, Burlington, Ontario, 2006. Paperback. This contained: I Make a Wireless Acquaintance; How Munchausen and the Allies Took Berlin; Munchausen on the Moon; The Earth as Viewed from the Moon; Munchausen Departs for the Planet Mars; Munchausen Lands on Mars; Munchausen is Taught Martian; Thought Transmission on Mars; The Cities of Mars; The Planets at Close Range; Martian Amusements; How the Martian Canals Are Built; and Martian Atmosphere Plants.

5. Hugo Gernsback and the Century of Science Fiction by Gary Westfahl. McFarland and Company, United States, 2007. Softcover. ISBN: 0786430796

***

NON-FICTION

1. Radio for All. Published by J. B. Lippincott, Philadelphia, 1922. Hardcover.

2. Evolution of Modern Science Fiction. Published in New York City by **Hugo Gernsback**, 1952. Softcover.

3. Concrete Science Fiction. This was an address by **Hugo Gernsback** to the Eastern Science Fiction Association on March 12, 1961 in Newark, New Jersey. Published by Hugo Gernsback in New York City, 1961. Stapled softcover.

4. Science Fiction vs. Reality. An address by **Hugo Gernsback** to the Massachusetts Institute of Technology Science Fiction Society on October 21, 1960. Published by **Hugo Gernsback** in New York City, 1960. Stapled softcover.

***

RELATED

1. Hugo Gernsback: The Father of Science Fiction by Sam Moskowitz. Published by Criterion in New York City in 1959. Softcover limited to 300 copies. This was later included in Explorers of the Infinite: Shapers of Science Fiction, World Publishing, New York City, 1963.

2. The Gernsback Days: The Evolution of Modern Science Fiction from 1911 - 1939 by Mike Ashley and Robert A. W. Lowndes. Published by Borgo Press, Los Angeles, 1997. Hardcover.

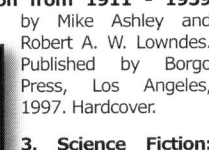

3. Science Fiction: The Gernsback Years by Everett F. Bleiler with Richard J. Bleiler. Published by The Kent State University Press, Kent, Ohio, 1998. Hardcover.

4. Hugo Gernsback: A Man Well Ahead of His Time by Larry Steckler. BookSurge Publishing, United States, 2007. Softcover. ISBN: 1419658573

A. E. van Vogt

Alfred Elton van Vogt was born on a farm on April 26th, 1912 near Gretna, Manitoba, Canada, and died on January 26th, 2000 in Los Angeles, California. He started his career writing confession stories for women's magazines but soon tired of that. Then he wrote plays for Canadian radio. That didn't take him anywhere, either. But by 1944, when he moved to the U.S., he was firmly established as a member of **John W. Campbell's** stable of writers for Astounding.

His first published science fiction story was Black Destroyer, released by Campbell in the July 1939 issue of Astounding Science Fiction. Campbell featured it on the cover. This issue also contained Trends, the first appearance by **Isaac Asimov** in Astounding, along with: City of Cosmic Rays by Nat Schachner; Lightship, Ho! By Nelson S. Bond; The Moth by Ross Rocklynne; When the Half Gods Go by Amelia R. Long; and Greater Than Gods by **C. L. Moore**.

Either consciously, or subconsciously, Black Destroyer was the inspiration for the Predator films, the Alien films, and a whole slew of other works. Later, van Vogt combined it with War of Nerves; Discord in Scarlet; and M33 in Andromeda to create the novel, The Voyage of the Space Beagle, 1950, a pre-cursor to Star Trek, a starship exploring the universe.

In 1939, he married E. (Edna) Mayne Hull and worked with her on a number of stories until she quit writing in 1950. That same year, 1950, van Vogt converted to Dianetics and also stopped writing for quite some time. It's a bit strange that he would have gotten involved with Hubbard's Dianetics. Legend has it that when Hubbard declared no one ever got rich writing for a penny a word, that the only way to get rich was to invent a religion, van Vogt was sitting right there in the bar with him, matching him pint for pint. He knew exactly what Hubbard was about to do. Although van Vogt himself said the reason he got into Hubbard's Dianetics was simply that it seemed like a good system, devoid of the mysticism that later invaded it - Scientology.

In any case, he wrote very little during the 1950s while he was involved in Dianetics. He worked on what he called fixups, piecing together series of short stories to form novels. But by the 1960s, he was back writing again and published his final novel in 1985. At the time of his death, though, he left behind an unfinished sequel to Slan called Slan Hunter. His second wife, Lydia, (his first wife had died of cancer in the 70s) and Kevin J. Anderson, completed the book. It was released on July 10th, 2007.

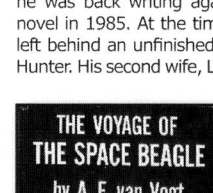

His highest priced books for collectors tend to be Slan and The Voyage of the Space Beagle. These both sell for between $450.00 and $750.00.

***

AWARDS

1980. The Casper Award for Lifetime Achievement in the field of Canadian Science Fiction and Fantasy. The awards began in 1980, and later became the Prix Aurora Awards. The first recipient was **A. E. van Vogt**.

1995. The Damon Knight Memorial Grand Master Award - aka Nebula Grand Master Award. He was presented with this by the Science Fiction Writers of America in 1995. It's interesting that he should be given an award that was named after **Damon Knight**. In 1945, Knight, not a fan of van Vogt's work, said, "van Vogt is not a giant as often maintained. He's only a pygmy using a giant typewriter."

1996. Inducted into The Science Fiction Hall of Fame.

1996. Special Award for Six Decades of Golden Age Science Fiction. This was awarded by The World Science Fiction Convention.

2005. Prometheus Hall of Fame Award for The Weapon Shops of Isher.

***

FILM AND TELEVISION

1. The Vault. A short story by **A. E. van Vogt** which was featured on the television series Tales of Tomorrow, Season Two, Episode Thirty-Six. The show aired on May 8th, 1953 and starred Dorothy Peterson and Cameron Prud'Homme.

2. The Witch. A 1943 short story, re-named Since Aunt Ada Came to Stay, and used on the television series Night Gallery, Season Two, Episode Nine, which aired on September 29th, 1971, starring: James Farentino; Jonathan Harris; Michele Lee; Jeanette Nolan; Alma Platt; Eldon Quick; Charles Seel; and Arnold F. Turner.

3. Amazing Worlds of Science Fiction and Fantasy. A 1991 film directed by Ray Ferry and written by Forrest J. Ackerman. It featured Ackerman as the host and he interviewed a number of people involved in SF and fantasy, including: **A. E. van Vogt**; **Ray Bradbury; Frank Kelly Freas**; **Ray Harryhausen**; **Gene Roddenberry**; et al.

4. Research Alpha. A 1965 short story written with James H. Schmitz, used on the television series Welcome to Paradox, Season One, Episode Two. The show aired on August 24th, 1998, starring Michael Philip; Roma Maffia; and Robert Wisden.

5. The Human Factor. A van Vogt story that was used on the television series, The Outer Limits, Season Seven, Episode Twenty-One. The Show aired on January 11th, 2001 and starred: Robert Duncan McNeil; Kevan Ohtsji; Talia Ranger; Laara Sadiq; Stephen Spender; and Zack Ward.

6. A Can of Paint. A van Vogt short story from 1944, made into a short film by Robi Michael in 2004 and starred: Jean Franzblau as the computer voice and Aaron Robson as Kilgour.

***

A. E. van Vogt

RADIO

1. Dear Pen Pal. This was produced for 2000X - Tales of the Next Millennia - Hollywood Theater of the Ear.

2. Far Centaurus. This was used on Challenge of Space.

***

NOVELS AND COLLECTIONS

1. Slan. Published by Arkham House in Sauk City, Wisconsin, 1946. Hardcover.

2. The Weapon Makers. Published by Hadley Publishing, Providence, Rhode Island, 1947. Hardcover.

3. The Book of Ptath. Published by Fantasy Press of Reading, Pennsylvania, 1947. Hardcover.

4. The World of A. Published by Simon and Schuster, New York City, 1948. Hardcover.

5. Out of the Unknown. With E. Mayne Hull. Published by the Fantasy Publishing Company of Los Angeles, 1948. This gathers three stories by **A. E. van Vogt**, and three by his wife, E. Mayne Hull: The Sea Thing, 1940; The Witch, 1943; and The Ghost, 1942, were by van Vogt. The Wishes We Make, 1943; The Patient, 1943; and The Ultimate Wish, 1943, were by Hull.

6. The Voyage of the Space Beagle. Published by Simon and Schuster, New York City, 1950. Hardcover. To create the novel, this gathered together: Black Destroyer, 1939; Discord in Scarlet, 1939; and M 33 in Andromeda, 1943.

7. The House That Stood Still. Published by Greenberg, New York City, 1950. Hardcover.

8. Masters of Time. Published by Fantasy Press of Reading, Pennsylvania, 1950. Hardcover. This put together Masters of Time, 1942; and The Changeling, 1944.

9. Slan. Revised edition of the 1946 Arkham House edition, published by Simon and Schuster, New York City, 1951. Hardcover.

10. The Weapon Shops of Isher. Published by Greenberg, New York City, 1951. Hardcover.

11. The Weapon Makers. Revised edition of the 1947 Hadley Publishing edition, published by Greenberg, New York City, 1952. Hardcover.

12. Away and Beyond. Published by Pellegrini and Cudahy, New York City, 1952. Hardcover. A story collection: Vault of the Beast, 1940; The Great Engine, 1943; The Great Judge, 1948; Secret Unattainable, 1942; The Harmonizer, 1944; Heir Unapparent, 1945; The Second Solution, 1942; Film Library, 1946; and Asylum, 1942.

13. Destination: Universe! Published by Pellegrini and Cudahy, New York City, 1952. Hardcover. A story collection: Far Centaurus, 1944; Dormant, 1948; The Monster, 1948; The Enchanted Village, 1950; A Can of Paint, 1944; Defense, 1947; The Rulers, 1944; Dear Pen Pal, 1949; The Sound, 1949; and The Search, 1942.

14. The Mixed Men. Published by Gnome Press, New York City, 1952. Hardcover. This collected the following stories to make a novel: The Mixed Men, 1945; Concealment, 1943; The Storm, 1943; and Lost: Fifty Suns, 1952.

15. Mission: Interplanetary. Published Signet Books - The New American Library, New York City, 1952. Paperback. Signet Book 914. A re-issue of Voyage of the Space Beagle, 1950. To create a novel, this gathered: Black Destroyer, 1939; Discord in Scarlet, 1939; and M 33 in Andromeda, 1943.

16. The Universe Maker. Published by Ace Books, New York City, 1953. Paperback. Presented with The World of Null-A, also by van Vogt. Ace Double D-31.

17. Planets for Sale. Published by Frederick Fell, New York City, 1954. Hardcover. This was a novelisation of five stories written by van Vogt's wife, E. Mayne Hull. Van Vogt novelised them: Competition, 1951; The Debt, 1951; The Contract, 1951; Enter the Professor, 1951; and Bankruptcy Proceedings, 1951.

18. Mission to the Stars. Published by Berkley Publishing, New York City, 1955. Paperback. Berkley Book 344. Re-issue of The Mixed Men, 1952. This collected the following stories to make a novel: The Mixed Men, 1945; Concealment, 1943; The Storm, 1943; and Lost: Fifty Suns, 1952.

19. One Against Eternity. Published by Ace Books, New York City, 1955. Paperback. A reprint of The Weapon Makers, the revised edition, 1952. Presented with The Other Side of Here by Murray Leinster. Ace Double D-94.

20. The Pawns of Null-A. Published by Ace Books, New York City, 1956. Paperback. Ace Book D-187.

21. Empire of the Atom. Published by Shasta Publishers of Chicago, 1957. Hardcover.

22. The Mind Cage. Published by Simon and Schuster, New York City, 1957. Hardcover.

23. The War Against the Rull. Published by Simon and Schuster, New York City, 1959. Hardcover.

24. Away and Beyond. Published by Berkley Books, New York City, 1959. A paperback version of the 1952 hardcover. Berkley Book G-215. It left out two of the stories from the original book, Vault of the Beast, 1940; and Heir Unapparent, 1945, keeping: The Great Engine, 1943; The Great Judge, 1948; Secret Unattainable, 1942; The Harmonizer, 1944; The Second Solution, 1942; Film Library, 1946; and Asylum, 1942.

25. Siege of the Unseen. Published by Ace Books, New York City, 1959. Paperback. Bound with The World Swappers by John Brunner. Ace Double D-391.

26. Triad. Published by Simon and Schuster and The Science Fiction Book Club, New York, 1959. Hardcover. This gathered The World of A, 1945, The Voyage of the Space Beagle, 1950, and Slan, 1946.

27. Earth's Last Fortress. Published by Ace Books, New York City, 1960. Paperback. A reprint of Masters in Time, 1950. Presented with Lost in Space by George O. Smith. Ace Double D-431.

28. The Mating Cry. This was a revision of The House That Stood Still, 1950, published in softcover digest format by Beacon Books, New York City, 1960 as Galaxy Novel 44.

29. The Violent Man. Published by Farrar, Straus and Cudahy, New York City, 1962. Hardcover.

30. The Wizard of Linn. Published by Ace Books, New York City, 1962. Paperback. Ace Book F-154.

31. The Beast. Published by Doubleday & Company, Garden City, New York, 1963. Hardcover.

32. The Twisted Men. Published by Ace Books, New York City, 1964. Paperback. Presented with One of Our Asteroids Is Missing by Calvin M. Knox. Ace Double F-253.

33. Two Hundred Million A.D. Published by Paperback Library, New York City, 1964. Paperback Library book 52-304. Re-issue of The Book of Ptath, 1947.

34. Rogue Ship. Published by Doubleday & Company, Garden City, New York, 1965. Hardcover. This tied three stories together to make a novel: Centauras II, 1947; Rogue Ship, 1950; and The Expendables, 1963.

35. The Winged Man. With E. Mayne Hull. Published by Doubleday & Company, Garden City, New York, 1966. Hardcover.

36. Monsters. Published by Paperback Library, New York City, 1965. Paperback Library book 52-515. The second printing from Berkley, in 1967, used the title Science Fiction Monsters: Not Only Dead Men, 1942; Final Command, 1949; War of Nerves, 1950; The Enchanted Village, 1950; Concealment, 1943; The Sea Thing, 1940; Resurrection, 1948; and Vault of the Beast, 1940.

37. The Players of Null-A. Published by Berkley Books, New York City, 1966. Paperback. Berkley Medallion F1195. A re-issue of The Pawns of Null-A.

38. Masters of Time. Published by Macfadden-Bartell, New York City, 1967. Paperback. Macfadden Book 50-334. Unlike the hardcover, 1950, this did not contain The Changeling, 1944.

39. The Changeling. Published by Macfadden-Bartell, New York City, 1967. Paperback. Macfadden Book 50-335. Originally published in Astounding in April 1944, this was used in 1950 first edition of Masters of Time.

40. A van Vogt Omnibus. Published by Sidgwick and Jackson, London, 1967. Hardcover. Gathers Planets for Sale - with E. Mayne Hull, 1954; The Beast, 1963; and The Book of Ptath, 1947.

41. The Far Out Worlds of A. E. van Vogt. Published by Ace Books, New York City, 1968. Paperback. Ace Book H-92. A story collection: The Replicators, 1965; The First Martian, 1939; The Purpose, 1945; The Earth Killers, 1949; The Cataaaa, 1947; Automaton, 1950; Itself, 1963; Process, 1950; Not the First, 1941; Fulfillment, 1951; Ship of Darkness, 1948; and The Ultra Man, 1966.

42. The Silkie. Published by Ace Books, New York City, 1969. Paperback. Ace Book 76500.

43. Moonbeast. Published by Panther Science Fiction, London, 1969. Paperback. Panther Book 586029370. Re-issue of The Beast.

44. Out of the Unknown. With E. Mayne Hull. Published by Powell Publications, Reseda, California, 1969. Paperback. Powell Book PP128. This added to the 1948 line-up The Wellwisher, 1970, by E. Mayne Hull and an introduction by van Vogt, along with: The Sea Thing, 1940; The Witch, 1943; and The Ghost, 1942, were by van Vogt. The Wishes We Make, 1943; The Patient, 1943; and The Ultimate Wish, 1943, were by Hull.

45. Out of the Unknown. With E. Mayne Hull. Published by New English Library, London, 1970. Paperback. NEL Book 2793. A reprint of the original 1948 book but dropping one of the van Vogt stories, The Witch, 1943.

46. The Sea Thing and Other Stories. With E. Mayne Hull. Published by Sidgwick and Jackson, London, 1970. A re-issue of Out of the Unknown, the 1969 Powel paperback edition: The Sea Thing, 1940; The Witch, 1943; and The Ghost, 1942, by van Vogt. The Wishes We Make, 1943; The Patient, 1943; The Ultimate Wish, 1943, and The Wellwisher, 1970, by Hull.

47. The Players of Null-A. First hardcover edition, published by Dennis Dobson, London, 1970. A re-issue of The Pawns of Null-A but with an introduction by van Vogt.

48. Children of Tomorrow. Published by Ace Books, New York City, 1970. Paperback. Ace Book 10410.

49. The World of Null-A. Revised edition of The World of A, 1948, with a new introduction by van Vogt, published by Berkley Books, New York City, 1970. Paperback. Berkley Medallion Book S1802.

50. Quest for the Future. Published by Ace Books, New York City, 1970. Paperback. Ace Book 69700.

51. Quest for the Future. Published by The Science Fiction Book Club, Garden City, New York, 1970. First hardcover edition.

52. van Vogt Omnibus 2. Published by Sidgwick and Jackson, London, 1971. This gathers The Mind Cage, 1957; The Winged Man - with E. Mayne Hull, 1966; and Slan, 1946.

53. The Proxy Intelligence and Other Mind Benders. Published by Paperback Library, New York City, 1971. Paperback Library book 64-512. A story collection: Problem Professor, 1949; Rebirth: Earth, 1942; The Gryb, 1940; Invisibility Gambit, written with E. Mayne Hull, 1943; Star-Saint, 1951; and Proxy Intelligence, 1968.

54. M 33 in Andromeda. Published by Paperback

A. E. van Vogt

Library, New York City, 1971. Paperback Library book 65-584. A story collection: Siege of the Unseen, 1959; Discord in Scarlet, 1939; The Expendables, 1963; Heir Unapparent, 1945; The Weapon Shop, 1943; M 33 in Andromeda, 1943.

55. More Than Superhuman. With Forrest J. Ackerman and James H. Schmitz. Published by Dell Books, New York City, 1971. Paperback. Dell Book 5818. A story collection: Humans Go Home, 1969; The Reflected Men, 1971; All the Loving Androids, 1971; Laugh, Clone, Laugh with Forrest J. Ackerman, 1969; Research Alpha with James H. Schmitz, 1965; and Him, 1969.

56. The Battle of Forever. Published by Ace Books, New York City, 1971. Paperback. Ace Book 04860.

57. The Battle of Forever. The first hardcover edition of the 1971 paperback original, published by Sidgwick and Jackson, London, 1972.

58. Children of Tomorrow. The first hardcover edition of the 1970 paperback original, published by Sidgwick and Jackson, London, 1972.

59. The Darkness on Diamondia. Published by Ace Books, New York City, 1972. Paperback. Ace Book 13798.

60. The Book of van Vogt. Published by DAW Books, New York City, 1972. Paperback. DAW Collector's Book 4 - UQ1004. A story collection: A Statement to Science Fiction Readers, introduction by Donald A. Wollheim; The Timed Clock, 1972; The Confession, 1972; The Rat and the Snake, 1971; The Barbarian, 1947; Ersatz Eternal, 1972; The Sound of Wild Laughter, 1972; and Lost: Fifty Suns, 1952.

61. The Far Out Worlds of A. E. van Vogt. The first hardcover edition of the 1968 paperback original, published by Sidgwick and Jackson, London, 1973. A story collection: The Replicators, 1965; The First Martian, 1939; The Purpose, 1945; The Earth Killers, 1949; The Cataaaa, 1947; Automaton, 1950; Itself, 1963; Process, 1950; Not the First, 1941; Fulfillment, 1951; Ship of Darkness, 1948; and The Ultra Man, 1966.

62. Future Glitter. Published by Ace Books, New York City, 1973. Paperback. Ace Book 25980.

63. Two Science Fiction Novels. The first hardcover edition, published by Sidgwick and Jackson, 1973. This gathered Earth's Last Fortress, 1960, and The Three Eyes of Evil - released in the U.S. in 1959 as Siege of the Unseen.

64. The Best of A. E. van Vogt. Published by Sphere Books, London, 1974. Softcover. This contains: Vault of the Beast, 1940; The Weapon Shop, 1942; The Storm, 1943; Juggernaut, 1944; Hand of the Gods, 1946; The Cataaaaa, 1947; The Monster, 1948; Dear Pen Pal, 1949; Three Green Forest, 1949; War of Nerves, 1950; The Expendables, 1963; Silkies in Space, 1966; The Proxy Intelligence, 1968; and a Bibliography.

65. The Best of A. E. van Vogt. The first hardcover edition of the 1974 paperback original, published by Sidgwick and Jackson, London, 1974. This contains: Vault of the Beast, 1940; The Weapon Shop, 1942; The Storm, 1943; Juggernaut, 1944; Hand of the Gods, 1946; The Cataaaaa, 1947; The Monster, 1948; Dear Pen Pal, 1949; Three Green Forest, 1949; War of Nerves, 1950; The Expendables, 1963; Silkies in Space, 1966; The Proxy Intelligence, 1968; and a Bibliography.

66. The Darkness on Diamondia. The first hardcover edition of the 1972 paperback original, published by Sidgwick and Jackson, London, 1974.

67. The Secret Galactics. Published by Prentice Hall of Englewood Cliffs, New Jersey, 1974. Paperback. Reward Book Science Fiction Original number 1.

68. The Secret Galactics. The first hardcover edition of the 1974 paperback original, published by Sidgwick and Jackson, London, 1975.

69. The Worlds of A. E. van Vogt. Published by Ace Books, New York City, 1974. Paperback. Ace Bok 22812. This contains: About the Author by Forrest J. Ackerman; The Replicators, 1965; The First Martian, 1939; The Purpose, 1945; The Earth Killers, 1949; The Cataaaaa, 1947; Automaton, 1950; Itself, 1963; Process, 1950; Not the First, 1941; Fulfillment, 1951; Ship of Darkness, 1948; The Ultra Man, 1966; The Storm, 1943; The Expendables, 1964; and The Reflected Men, 1971.

70. The Man with a Thousand Names. Published by DAW Books, New York City, 1975. Paperback. DAW Collector's Book 114 - UQ1125.

71. The Best of A. E. van Vogt. Published by Pocket Books, New York City, 1976. Paperback. Pocket Book 80546. The contents are not the same as the 1974 Sidgwick and Jackson and Sphere editions: Introduction by **A. E. van Vogt**; Ah, Careless, Rapturous van Vogt! By Barry N. Malzberg; Don't Hold Your Breath, 1973; All We Have on This Planet, 1974; War of Nerves, 1950; The Rull, 1948; The Semantics of Twenty-first-Century Science, an essay by van Vogt, 1976; Future Perfect, 1973; Home of the Gods, 1947; The Violent Male, an essay by van Vogt, 1965; Prologue to The Silkie, 1964; The Proxy Intelligence, 1968; Being an Examination of the Ponsian and Holmesian Secret Deductive Systems, an essay by van Vogt, 1971; and Final Comment, an essay by van Vogt, 1976.

72. Earth Factor X. Published by DAW Books, New York City, 1976. DAW Collector's Book 206 - UY1249. Paperback. A re-issue of The Secret Galactics, 1974.

73. Undercover Aliens. Published by Panther Books, London, 1976. Paperback. Panther Book 586 0432431. Re-issue of The House That Stood Still, 1950.

74. The Universe Maker and the Proxy Intelligence. Published by Sidgwick and Jackson, London, 1976. This puts together The Universe Maker, 1953, and The Proxy Intelligence, 1971. First hardcover printing of either title.

75. The Wizard of Linn. First hardcover edition of the 1962 paperback original, published by New English Library, London, 1976.

76. The Blal. Published by Zebra Books - Kensington Publishing, New York City, 1976. This was a re-issue of Monsters, 1965.

77. The Gryb. Published by Zebra Books - Kensington Publishing, New York City, 1976. A collection of short stories gathered from other collections: The Gryb, 1940; Humans, Go Home!, 1969; The Problem Professor, 1949; The Invisibility Gambit, written with E. Mayne Hull, 1943; Rebirth: Earth, written with E. Mayne Hull, 1942; and The Star-Saint, 1951.

78. The Anarchistic Colossus. Published by Ace Books, New York City, 1977, a paperback original. Ace 02255-3.

79. Supermind. Published by DAW Books, New York City, 1977. DAW Collector's Book 224 - UY1275.

80. The Players of Null-A. First American hardcover edition, published by Gregg Press, Boston, 1977. A re-issue of The Pawns of Null-A, 1956, but with an introduction by Charles Platt.

81. Tyranopolis. Published by Sphere Books, London, 1977. Paperback. Sphere ISBN 0722187343. Re-issue of Future Glitter, 1973.

82. Pendulum. Published by DAW Books, New York City, 1978. Paperback. DAW Collector's Book 316. A story collection: Pendulum, 1978; The Male Condition, 1978; Living with Jane, 1978; The First Rull, 1978; Footprint Farm, 1978; The Non-Aristotelian Detective, 1978; The Human Operators, written with **Harlan Ellison**, 1971; and The Launch of Apollo XVII, an essay, 1978.

83. The Enchanted Village. Published by The Misfit Press, Dearborn Heights, Michigan, 1979. Softcover.

84. Renaissance. Published by Pocket Books, New York City, 1979. Paperback. Pocket Book ISBN: 0671818597.

85. Cosmic Encounter. Published by Doubleday & Company, Garden City, New York, 1980. Hardcover.

86. Computerworld. Also released as Computer Eye. Published by DAW Books, New York City, 1983. Softcover. DAW Collector's Book 554.

87. Null-A Three. Published by DAW Books, New York City, 1985. Softcover. DAW Collector's Book 634.

88. Futures Past: The Best Short Fiction of A.E. Van Vogt. Published by Tachyon Publications, San Francisco, California, 1999. Hardcover. This contains: Van is Here, but Van is Gone by **Harlan Ellison**; The Enchanted Village, 1950; The First Martian, 1939; The Reflected Men, 1971; Cooperate or Else, 1942; The Second Solution, 1942; Fulfillment, 1951; The Replicators, 1965; and Vault of the Beast, 1940.

89. Transfinite: The Essential A. E. van Vogt. Published by NESFA Press, Framingham, Massachusetts, 2003. Hardcover. This contains: Introduction by **Hal Clement**; Foreword by Joe Rico; Black Destroyer, 1939; The Monster, 1948; Film Library, 1946; Enchanted Village, 1950; Asylum, 1942; Vault of the Beast, 1940; The Ghost, 1942; The Rull, 1948; Recruiting Station, 1942; A Can of Paint, 1944; The Search, 1943; Dear Pen Pal, 1949; The Harmonizer, 1944; The Great Judge, 1948; Far Centaurus, 1944; Secret Unattainable, 1942; Future Perfect, 1973; The Great Engine, 1943; Dormant, 1948; The Sound, 1950; The Rulers, 1944; Final Command, 1949; War of Nerves, 1950; Don't Hold Your Breath, 1973; and Discord in Scarlet, 1939; followed by an afterword by Rick Katze.

90. Transgalactic. Edited by Eric Flint and David Drake. Published by Baen Books, New York City, 2006. Softcover. This collection contains: Introduction by Eric Flint and David Drake; Child of the Gods, 1946; Hand of the Gods, 2006; A Son Is Born, 1946; Home of the Gods, 1947; The Barbarian, 1947; The Wizard of Linn, 1962; Co-Operate - Or Else!, 1942; The Second Solution, 1942; Concealment, 1943; The Storm, 1943; and The Mixed Men, 1945.

91. Slan Hunter. With Lydia van Vogt and Kevin J. Anderson. Tor Books - Tom Doherty Associates, New York City, 2007. Hardcover.

92. Slan - with - Slan Hunter. First edition thus, Science Fiction Book Club, Garden City, New York, 2007. Hardcover.

***

NON-FICTION

1. The Hypnotism Handbook. With Charles Edward Cooke. Published by Borden Publishing Company, Alhambra, California, 1956. Hardcover.

2. The Money Personality. Published by the Parker Publishing Company, West Nyack, New York, 1972. Hardcover.

3. Reflections of A. E. van Vogt. Published by Fictioneer Books, Lakemont, Georgia, 1975. Softcover.

4. A Report on the Violent Male. Introduction by Colin Wilson. Published by Pauper's Press, United Kingdom, 1992. Softcover.

***

RELATED

1. Of Worlds Beyond: A Symposium by Edward E. Smith, Ph.D.; John W. Campbell; L. Sprague de Camp; Robert A. Heinlein; Jack Williamson; A. E. van Vogt; and John Taine. Edited by Lloyd Arthur Eschbach. Published by Advent Publishers, Chicago, 1964. Softcover.

2. Of Worlds Beyond: A Symposium by Edward E. Smith, Ph.D.; John W. Campbell; L. Sprague de Camp; Robert A. Heinlein; Jack Williamson; A. E. van Vogt; and John Taine. Edited by Lloyd Arthur Eschbach. Published by Dennis Dobson, London, 1965. First hardcover edition.

3. A. E. van Vogt: Science Fantasy's Icon. By Harold L. Drake. Published by Booklocker, United States, 2002. Softcover.

Jack Williamson

Jack Williamson.

John Stewart Williamson was born on April 29th, 1908 in Bisbee, Arizona and died at the age of 98 on November 10th, 2006 in Portales, New Mexico. While growing up on a ranch in New Mexico, his first exposure to science fiction was through Amazing Stories - he answered an ad that promised a free issue of the magazine, which inspired him to write his own stories. At twenty years old, he sold his first story, The Metal Man, to **Hugo Gernsback**. It appeared in the December 1928 issue of Amazing Stories, along with: The Appendix and the Spectacles by Miles J. Breuer; Flight to Venus by Edwin K. Sloat; The World at Bay - part 2 of 2 by B. Wallis and Geo. C. Wallis; The Fifth Dimension by Clare Winger Harris; Before the Ice Age by Alfred Fritchey; Monorail by George McLociard; and The Space Bender by Edward L. Rementer. Williamson was on his way.

His first influence was **A. Merritt**, specifically, Merritt's novel The Moon Pool, which was serialized in Amazing in 1927. But his next influence was Miles J. Breuer, an SF-writing doctor who took to Williamson and helped him develop into an edgy writer. They collaborated on The Girl from Mars, 1929, and The Birth of a New Republic, 1931.

By the early 1930s, Williamson had established himself as a science fiction writer, which he pursued for the rest of his life, occasionally using the pen name Will Stewart, and, after 1954, occasionally collaborating with **Frederik Pohl**.

By the time **John W. Campbell** became editor of Astounding, **Jack Williamson** was a familiar name to Astounding's readers where his Legion of Space series had been running since 1934. And Campbell was smart enough to continue soliciting work from Williamson. His Seetee stories, as by Will Stewart, were published in Astounding during the 1940s, as were his Humanoids stories and others.

In the 1950s, Williamson received a Bachelor of Arts and a Master of Arts from Eastern New Mexico University, and he received his Ph.D. in English Lit from the University of Colorado. In 1960, he joined the faculty of Eastern New Mexico University and maintained his ties to the school for the rest of his life. During the 1980s, he donated a collection of books and manuscripts to the university library. They formed a Special Collections department to deal with the stuff. Now, The Jack Williamson Science Fiction Library has more than 30,000 volumes, including books, pulps, manuscripts, letters and assorted ephemera.

In 1976, Williamson became the second recipient of The Damon Knight Memorial Grand Master Award, preceded by **Robert A. Heinlein**. And the following year, he retired from teaching, although he did teach some evening classes, Creative Writing and Fantasy and Science Fiction.

Darker Than You Think, along with The Cometeers, tend to be the highest priced of his books for collectors, running around $900.00.

Pen names used: Will Stewart; Nils O. Sonderlund.

***

AWARDS

1975. The Damon Knight Memorial Grand Master Award - Nebula Grand Master Award, presented by the Science Fiction Writers of America.
1985. Hugo Award. For his autobiography, Wonder's Child: My Life in Science Fiction.
1985. The Skylark, Edward E. Smith Memorial Award for Imaginative Fiction.
1994. World Fantasy Life Achievement Award.
1996. Inducted into The Science Fiction Hall of Fame.
1997. Bram Stoker Life Achievement Award.
2001. Hugo Award for his novella, The Ultimate Earth.
2001. Nebula Award for his novella, The Ultimate Earth.
2002. John W. Campbell Memorial Award for Terraforming Earth.

***

FILM AND TELEVISION

1. The Creation of the Humanoids. This was a low budget film made in 1962, directed by Wesley Barry and based on Williamson's Humanoids series, although Williamson received no credit for it. The movie starred: Don Megowan as Captain Kenneth Cragis; Erica Elliott as Maxine Megan; Don Doolittle as Dr Raven; George Milan as Acto; Dudley Manlove as Lagan; Frances McCann as Esme Cragis Milos; David Cross as Pax; and many others.

***

RADIO

1. With Folded Hands. This aired on Dimension X on April 15th, 1950.

***

NOVELS AND COLLECTIONS

1. The Girl from Mars. Written with Dr. Miles J. Breuer. Stellar Publishing Corporation, New York City, 1929. Softcover.

2. Lady in Danger. Published by Utopian Publications, London, 1945. Softcover. Two versions exist. The first one, printed in Great Britain on yellow paper includes The Spanish Vampire by E. Hoffmann Price. The second one, printed in Ireland on white paper, includes the Price story as well as The Curse of the House by Robert Bloch.

3. The Legion of Space. Published by Fantasy Press, Reading, Pennsylvania, 1947. Hardcover. Five hundred copies of this were released with a signed and numbered insert by Williamson.

4. Darker Than You Think. Published by Fantasy Press, Reading, Pennsylvania, 1948. Hardcover.

5. The Humanoids. Published by Simon and Schuster, New York City, 1949. Hardcover.

6. The Cometeers. Published by Fantasy Press, Reading, Pennsylvania, 1950. Hardcover.

7. Seetee Shock. Writing as Will Stuart. Published by Simon and Schuster, New York City, 1950. Hardcover.

8. The Green Girl. Published by Avon Publishing, New York City, 1950. Paperback. Avon Fantasy Novel 2.

9. Dragon's Island. Published by Simon and Schuster, New York City, 1951. Hardcover.

10. Seetee Ship. Writing as Will Stuart. Published by Gnome Press, New York City, 1951. Hardcover.

11. The Legion of Time. Published by Fantasy Press, Reading, Pennsylvania, 1952. Hardcover. Includes the other Legion of Time story, After World's End.

12. Undersea Quest. With **Frederik Pohl**. Published by Gnome Press, New York City, 1954. Hardcover.

13. Dome Around America. Published by Ace Books, New York City, 1955. Paperback. Presented with The Paradox Men by Charles L. Harness. Ace Double D-118.

14. Star Bridge. With James E. Gunn. Gnome Press, New York City, 1955. Hardcover.

15. Undersea Fleet. With **Frederik Pohl**. Published by Gnome Press, New York City, 1956. Hardcover.

16. Undersea City. With **Frederik Pohl**. Published by Gnome Press, New York City, 1958. Hardcover.

17. The Legion of Time. Published by Brown Watson Limited - Digit Books, London, 1961. Paperback. Digit Book R 522. Unlike the hardcover edition, 1952, this does not include After World's End, which was printed separately.

18. After World's End. Published by Brown Watson Limited - Digit Books, London, 1961. Paperback. Digit Book R 538.

19. The Trial of Terra. Published by Ace Books, New York City, 1962. Paperback. Ace Book D-555.

20. The Legion of Time/After World's End. Published by Galaxy Publishing, New York City, 1963. Softcover. Megabook number 2.

21. The Reefs of Space. With **Frederik Pohl**. Published by Ballantine Books, New York City, 1964. Paperback. Ballantine Book U2172.

22. The Reign of Wizardry. Published by Lancer Books, New York City, 1964. Paperback. Lancer Book 72-761.

23. The Golden Blood. Published by Lancer Books, New York City, 1964. Paperback. Lancer Book 72-740.

24. The Reefs of Space. With **Frederik Pohl**. The first hardcover edition of the paperback original, 1964, published by Dennis Dobson, London, 1965.

25. Starchild. With **Frederik Pohl**. Published by Ballantine Books, New York City, 1965. Paperback. Ballantine Book U2176.

26. Starchild. With **Frederik Pohl**. The first hardcover edition of the paperback original, 1965, published by Dennis Dobson, London, 1966.

27. One Against the Legion. Published by Pyramid Books, New York City, 1967. Paperback. Pyramid Book X-1657. This also includes the first publication of Nowhere Near, 1967.

28. The Cometeers. Published by Pyramid Books, New York City, 1967. Paperback. This was an abridged edition, dropping One Against the Legion, 1939.

29. Bright New Universe. Published by Ace Books, New York City, 1967. Paperback. Ace Book G-641.

30. Bright New Universe. The first hardcover edition of the 1967 paperback original, published by Sidgwick and Jackson, London, 1969.

31. The Not-Men. Published by Tower Books, New York City, 1968. Paperback. Tower Book 43-957. A re-issue of Dragon's Island, 1951.

32. Trapped in Space. Published by Doubleday & Company, Garden City, New York, 1977. Hardcover.

33. Rogue Star. With **Frederik Pohl**. Published by Ballantine Books, New York City, 1969. Paperback. Ballantine book 01797-075.

34. The Pandora Effect. Published by Ace Books, New York City, 1969. Paperback. Ace Book 65125. A story collection: Introduction by Williamson; The Happiest Creature, 1953; The Cosmic Express, 1930; The Metal Man, 1928; The Cold Green Eye, 1953; Guinevere for Everybody, 1954; With Folded Hands, 1947; and The Equalizer, 1947.

35. The People Machines. Published by Ace Books, New York City, 1971. Paperback. Ace Book 65890. A story collection: Introduction - With Hints for Design and Assembly by Williamson; Star Bright, 1939; Non-Stop to Mars, 1939; Operation: Gravity, 1953; The Masked World, 1963; The Man from Outside, 1951; Hindsight, 1940; Jamboree, 1969; The Peddler's Nose, 1951; and Breakdown, 1942; followed by: Afterword about Theme by Williamson.

36. Seetee Ship/Seetee Shock. Published by Lancer Books, New York City, 1971. Paperback. Lancer Book 78706-125. Puts the two books together for the first time.

37. Rogue Star. With **Frederik Pohl**. The first hardcover edition of the paperback original, 1969, published by Dennis Dobson, London, 1972. On the title page, Pohl's name was spelled incorrectly: Frederick.

38. The Moon Children. Published by G. P. Putnam's Sons, New York City, 1972. Hardcover.

39. The Early Williamson. Published by Doubleday & Company, New York City, 1975. Hardcover. This story collection contains: Introduction by Williamson; The Metal Man, 1928; The Cosmic Express, 1930; Dead Star Station, 1933; Through the Purple Cloud, 1931; The Doom from Planet 4, 1931; We Ain't Beggars, 1933; Salvage in Space, 1933; The Plutonian Terror, 1933; Twelve Hours to Live!, 1931; The Meteor Girl, 1931; and an excerpt from The Girl from Mars, written with Miles J. Breuer, 1929.

40. Farthest Star. With **Frederik Pohl**. Published by Ballantine Books, New York City, 1975. Paperback. Ballantine Book: 24330.

Jack Williamson

41. The Power of Blackness. Published by Berkley Publishing, New York City, 1976. Paperback. Berkley Book D3260. ISBN: 0425032604.

42. Dreadful Sleep. Published by Robert Weinberg, Chicago, 1977. Softcover. Presented as Lost Fantasies number 7.

43. The Starchild Trilogy. With **Frederik Pohl**. Published by Nelson Doubleday, Garden City, New York, 1977. Hardcover. Released by the Science Fiction Book Club. Book Club Code H36. This gathered: The Reefs of Space, 1964; Starchild, 1965; and Rogue Star, 1969.

44. The Best of Jack Williamson. Published by Del Rey Books - Ballantine Publishing, New York City, 1978. Softcover. This collection contains: **Jack Williamson**: The Pathfinder by **Frederik Pohl**; The Metal Man, 1928; Dead Star Station, 1933; Nonstop to Mars, 1939; The Crucible of Power, 1939; Breakdown, 1942; With Folded Hands, 1947; The Equalizer, 1947; The Peddler's Nose, 1951; The Happiest Creature, 1953; The Cold Green Eye, 1953; Operation Gravity, 1953; Guinevere for Everybody, 1954; Jamboree, 1969; and The Highest Drive, 1976; followed by the Author's Afterword.

45. Brother to Demons, Brother to Gods. Published by Bobbs-Merrill, New York City and Indianapolis, 1979. Hardcover. This story collection contains: Brother to Demons, 1977; Brother to Gods, 1978; Kinsman to Lizards, 1978; Stepson to Creation, 1977; and Slave to Chaos, 1977.

46. The Humanoid Touch. Published by Holt Rinehart & Winston, New York City, 1980. Hardcover.

47. Three from the Legion. Published by Nelson Doubleday, Garden City, New York, 1980. Hardcover. Released by the Science Fiction Book Club. This gathered: The Legion of Space, 1947; The Cometeers, 1950; and One Against the Legion, 1967, along with: Nowhere Near, 1967.

48. The Alien Intelligence. Published by P.D.A. Enterprises, New Orleans, 1980. Softcover. This collection contains: The Prince of Space, 1931; The Second Shell, 1929; The Alien Intelligence, 1929; and As I Remember, 1980, an essay by Williamson.

49. Manseed. Published by Del Rey Books, Ballantine Publishing, New York City, 1982. Hardcover.

50. Wall Around a Star. With **Frederik Pohl**. Published by Del Rey Books, Ballantine Publishing, New York City, 1983. Paperback. ISBN: 0345289951.

51. The Saga of Cuckoo. With **Frederik Pohl**. Published by Nelson Doubleday, Garden City, New York, 1983. Hardcover. Released by the Science Fiction Book Club. Book Club Code N34. This gathers: Farthest Star, 1975; and Wall Around a Star, 1983.

52. Lifeburst. Published by Del Rey Books, Ballantine Publishing, New York City, 1984. Hardcover.

53. Firechild. Published by Bluejay Books, Gordonsville, Virginia, 1986. Hardcover.

54. Land's End. With **Frederik Pohl**. Published by Tor Books - Tom Doherty and Associates, New York City, 1988. Hardcover.

55. Mazeway. Published by Del Rey Books - Ballantine Published, New York City, 1990. Hardcover.

56. Into the Eighth Decade - Author's Choice Monthly 5. Published by Pulphouse Publishing, Eugene, Oregon, 1990. Signed and numbered hardcover, limited to three hundred copies. Author's Choice Monthly 5. This contains: Into the Eighth Decade - an introduction by Williamson; With Folded Hands, 1947; The Happiest Creature, 1953; Jamboree, 1969; and The Mental Man, 1988.

57. The Singers of Time. With **Frederik Pohl**. Published by Doubleday & Company, Garden City, New York. 1991. Hardcover.

58. Beachhead. Published by Tor Books - Tom Doherty and Associates, New York City, 1992. Hardcover.

59. The Undersea Trilogy. With **Frederik Pohl**. Published by Nelson Doubleday, Garden City, New York, 1992. Hardcover. Released by the Science Fiction Book Club. Book Club Code I01. This gathered: Undersea Quest, 1954; Undersea Fleet, 1955; Undersea City, 1958.

60. Demon Moon. Published by Tor Books - Tom Doherty and Associates, New York City, 1994. Hardcover.

61. The Black Sun. Published by Tor Books - Tom Doherty and Associates, New York City, 1997. Hardcover.

62. The Prince of Space - with - The Girl from Mars. Published by Gryphon Books, United States, 1998. Softcover.

63. The Silicon Dagger. Published by Tor Books - Tom Doherty and Associates, New York City, 1999. Hardcover.

64. The Metal Man and Others: The Collected Stories of Jack Williamson - Volume One. Published by Haffner Press, Royal Oak, Michigan, 1999. Hardcover. This contains: **Jack Williamson**, Speculator by **Hal Clement**; Scientifiction, Searchlight of Science, an essay, 1928; The Metal Man, 1928; The Girl from Mars, an excerpt, written with Miles J. Breuer, 1929; The Alien Intelligence, 1929; The Second Shell, 1929; The Green Girl, 1950; The Cosmic Express, 1930; The Birth of a New Republic, written with Miles J. Breuer, 1931; The Prince of Space, 1931; The Meteor Girl, 1931; and Afterword: The Metal Man and Others by Williamson; followed by Some Constructive Criticism, a letter to Amazing Stories, October 1927; Why I Want a Remington Noiseless Portable Typewriter, an essay; A Reader Who Wants Short Stories, a letter to Amazing Stories, June 1929; Tremendous Contribution to Civilization, an essay, 1929; The Amazing Work of Wells and Verne, an essay, 1930; and More Preferences, a letter to Astounding Stories, August 1930.

65. Wolves of Darkness: The Collected Stories of Jack Williamson - Volume Two. Published by Haffner Press, Royal Oak, Michigan, 1999. Hardcover. This contains: And Now, Ladies and Gentlemen, a Man Who Needs No Introduction by **Harlan Ellison**; The Lake of Light, 1931; Through the Purple Cloud, 1931; The Doom from Planet 4, 1931; Twelve Hours to Live!, 1931; The Stone from the Green Star, 1931; Wolves of Darkness, 1932; The Moon Era, 1932; The Pygmy Planet, 1932; Red Slag of Mars, written with Laurence

Schwartzman, 1932; and The Lady of Light, 1932; followed by: Afterword by Williamson; The Earth's Tail, a letter to Wonder Stories, June 1931; Prize Winning Letters - Contest Entries, Wonder Stories, November 1931, an essay by Walter L Dennis; M. Gittleman; and Frank M. Kelley; **Jack Williamson** to His Own Defense, a letter to Amazing Stories, June 1932; Pygmy Planet Science, a letter to Astounding Stories, November 1932; and Huge Skull Gazes Weirdly from Ad Building Window, an essay, 1933.

66. Wizard's Isle: The Collected Stories of Jack Williamson - Volume Three. Published by Haffner Press, Royal Oak, Michigan, 2000. Hardcover. Herein: **Jack Williamson**, Friend! by **Ray Bradbury**; The Electron Flame, 1932; The Wand of Doom, 1932; In the Scarlet Star, 1933; Salvage in Space, 1933; We Ain't Beggars, 1933; The Plutonian Terror, 1933; Dead Star Station, 1933; The Flame from Mars, 1934; Invaders of the Ice World, 1934; Born of the Sun, 1934; Xandulu, 1934; The Galactic Circle, 1935; Islands in the Sun, 1935; Grey Arms of Death, 1935; and Afterword by Williamson; followed by Cigarette Characterizations, an essay by R. F. Starzl; Donald Wandrei; Frank Belknap Long; P. Schuyler Miller; Arthur J. Burks; and **Jack Williamson**, 1934; and Preface from Invaders of the Ice World, previously unpublished.

67. Terraforming Earth. Published by Tor Books - Tom Doherty and Associates, New York City, 2001. Hardcover.

68. Spider Island: The Collected Stories of Jack Williamson - Volume Four. Published by Haffner Press, Royal Oak, Michigan, 2002. Hardcover. This contains: American Gods, American Dreaming by Edward Bryant; The Ruler of Fate, 1936; Death's Cold Daughter, 1936; The Great Illusion, with Eando Binder, Edmond Hamilton, Raymond Z. Gallun and John Russell Fearn, 1936; The Blue Spot, 1937; The Ice Entity, 1937; Spider Island, 1937; The Mark of the Monster, 1937; The Devil in Steel, 1937; Released Entropy, 1937; Dreadful Sleep, 1938; The Infinite Enemy, 1938; The Legion of Time, 1938; and Afterword by Williamson; followed by: Interview with **Jack Williamson**, 1936; Psychology and Characterization, an essay, 1936; Has Science Fiction a Future, an essay, 1937; Polar Catastrophe, an essay, 1937; Science in Science Fiction, a letter to Astounding Science Fiction, June 1937; Horror Yarns - Double Action, an essay, 1937; and The Inverse Universe, an essay, 1938.

69. Seventy-Five: The Diamond Anniversary of a Science Fiction Pioneer. Published by Haffner Press, Royal Oak, Michigan, 2003. Hardcover. This contains: 75 Years of Wonder by **Connie Willis**; Introduction by **Sir Arthur C. Clarke**; Scientifiction, Searchlight of Science, an essay, 1928; The Metal Man, 1928; The Crystal Years; Golden Blood - excerpt, 1933; The Legion of Space, excerpt, 1947; The Legion of Time, excerpt, 1938; Collision Orbit, 1942; With Folded Hands, 1947; Beyond Mars, 1952; A **Jack Williamson** Chronology, 2003; The Happiest Creature, 1953; Jamboree, 1969; The Next Century of Science Fiction, an essay, 1978; People Machines: Hints for Design and Assembly, an essay, 1971; Previews of Hell; Demon Moon, an excerpt, 1994; The Firefly Tree, 1997; The Ultimate Earth, 2000; and Afterword by Williamson; and throughout the pages there are biographical and bibliographical pieces.

70. The Crucible of Power: The Collected Stories of Jack Williamson - Volume Five. Published by Haffner Press, Royal Oak, Michigan, 2004. Hardcover. This contains: Foreword by Frank M. Robinson; The Chivaree, 1938; The Dead Spot, 1938; Nonstop to Mars, 1939; After World's End, 1939; The Crucible of Power, 1939; Passage to Saturn, 1939; Star Bright, 1939; The Fortress of Utopia, 1939; The Angel from Hell, 1939; As In the Beginning, 1940; Hindsight, 1940; Mistress of Machine-Age Madness, 1940; and an Afterword by Williamson.

71. The Stonehenge Gate. Published by Tor Books - Tom Doherty and Associates, New York City, 2005. Hardcover.

72. Gateway to Paradise: The Collected Stories of Jack Williamson - Volume Six. Published by Haffner Press, Royal Oak, Michigan, 2008. Hardcover. This contains: Foreword by **Frederick Pohl**; The Reign of Wizardry, 1940; The Sun-Maker, 1940; The Crystal of Death, 1940; The Girl in the Bottle, 1940; Racketeers in the Sky, 1940; Ashes of Iron, 1940; Darker Than You Think, 1940; The Star of Dreams, 1941; The Iron God, 1941; and Gateway to Paradise, 1941; followed by an Afterword by Williamson.

73. The Worlds of Jack Williamson: A Centennial Tribute 1908 - 2008. Published by Haffner Press, Royal Oak, Michigan, 2008. Hardcover. This contains: Jack by **Frederik Pohl**; Worlds of **Jack Williamson** by James Gunn; The Moon Bird, 1929; The Forbidden Window; The Golden Glass, 1939; Darker Than You Think, 1940; Darker Than He Thought: The Psychoanalysis of **Jack Williamson** by Alan C. Elms; Minus Sign, 1942; The Man from Outside, 1951; A Study of the Sense of Prophecy in Modern Science Fiction, an essay, 1957; The Planets Are Calling, 1957; **Jack Williamson**: The Comedy of Cosmic Evolution by Alfred D. Stewart; Tricentennial Century, 1975/1976; The Humanoid Universe, 1980; The Hole in the World, 1997; Afterlife, 2002; The Luck of the Legion, 2002; A Christmas Carol, 2000; Queens of Space: Women in the Work of Jack Williamson by Vicky Medley, 2003; and Collecting **Jack Williamson**: Master of Wonder by Ralph A. Hauptmann, 2004.

***

NON-FICTION

1. H. G. Wells: Critic of Progress. Published by Mirage Press, Baltimore, Maryland, 1973. Hardcover. Limited to 1500 copies.

2. Teaching Science Fiction: Education for Tomorrow. Published by Owlswick Press, Philadelphia, 1980. Hardcover.

3. Wonder's Child: My Life in Science fiction. Published by Bluejay Books, Gordonsville, Virginia, 1984. Hardcover.

4. Wonder's Child: My Life in Science fiction. Published by Benbella Books, Dallas, Texas, 2005. Softcover. Updated with more photographs and an Epilogue.

***

RELATED

1. Of Worlds Beyond: A Symposium by Edward E. Smith, Ph.D.; John W. Campbell; L. Sprague de

Jack Williamson

Camp; Robert A. Heinlein; Jack Williamson; A. E. van Vogt; and John Taine.** Edited by Lloyd Arthur Eschbach. Published by Advent Publishers, Chicago, 1964. Softcover.

2. Of Worlds Beyond: A Symposium by Edward E. Smith, Ph.D.; John W. Campbell; L. Sprague de Camp; Robert A. Heinlein; Jack Williamson; A. E. van Vogt; and John Taine. Edited by Lloyd Arthur Eschbach. Published by Dennis Dobson, London, 1965. First hardcover edition.

3. In Memory of Wonder's Child: Jack Williamson. Edited by Stephen Haffner. Haffner Press, Royal Oak, Michigan, 2007. Hardcover. A memorial volume with contributions from: Kevin J. Anderson; Greg Bear; David Brin; Charles N. Brown; Patrice Caldwell; John Clute; Stephen R. Donaldson; James Frenkel; James Gunn; Joe Haldeman; Rick Hauptmann; Elizabeth Anne Hull; Bradford Lyau; **Frederik Pohl**; Mike Resnick; Frank M. Robinson; Kristine Kathryn Rusch; **Robert Silverberg**; Michael Swanwick; Walter Jon Williams; Betty Williamson; and **Connie Willis**.

-1997-

Isaac Asimov.

For a man who considered writing an amusement and whose main hope for it was that it might pay off some of his college tuition, he appears to have done quite well for himself...

Isaac Asimov was born in Petrovichi in the Smolensk Oblast region of the Russian Soviet Federative Socialist Republic - Russia - sometime around January 2nd, 1920. The records of his birth were lost but Asimov celebrated it on January 2nd. He died in New York City on April 6th, 1992. His death was related to complications that arose from an HIV infection, a gift from his doctors during a 1983 heart-bypass operation when they pumped tainted blood into his veins. In other words, his own doctors killed him because no one in 1983 was intelligent enough to run disease tests on donated blood. The scientist who loved science, killed by a lack of it.

In 1923, when he was three years old, Asimov's family fled Russia for America and, five years later, young Isaac became a citizen. He grew up in Brooklyn and was educated at Columbia University, majoring in chemistry and graduating in 1939. Interrupted by World War Two, it wasn't until 1948 that Asimov earned his doctorate in biochemistry. He was then hired by the Boston University School of Medicine, where he taught until 1958, when he began to write full-time.

As the story goes, it was the science fiction magazines that his parents sold in their candy store that led him into science fiction... and science... and writing. He was nineteen when his first short story was published in the March 1939 issue of Amazing Stories. The story was Marooned Off Vesta. And the man who purchased it was Raymond A. Palmer, who had been hired as editor in June 1938 and lasted until January 1950. Also in that issue: The Strange Flight of Richard Clayton by Robert Bloch; The Raid from mars by Miles J. Breuer; The City That Walked by Ed Earl Repp; Trapped by Telepathy by Otto Binder writing as Eando Binder; Vengeance from the Void by Frederic Arnold Kummer; and Valley of Invisible Men by Edmond Hamilton.

Always, it has been understood that **John W. Campbell** was the editor who discovered **Isaac Asimov**. But Campbell rejected Marooned Off Vesta, which is how Palmer and Amazing Stories came to be Asimov's first publisher. His next story in Amazing was The Weapon Too Dreadful to Use - May 1939, along with: Secret of the Buried City by John Russell Fearn; Where Is Roger Davis? by David V. Reed; The City of Oblivion by Ed Earl Repp writing as Bradner Buckner; War with Jupiter by William Lawrence Hamling and Mark Reinsberg; The Curse of Montezuma by Ed Earl Repp; and The Foreign Legion of Mars by Frederic Arnold Kummer.

It wasn't until the July 1939 issue of Astounding Science Fiction that Campbell published a story by Asimov. The story was Trends and **A. E. van Vogt** shared the same issue with his first science fiction story, Black Destroyer. Asimov didn't have another story published in Astounding until September 1940 with Homo Sol. But it wasn't until September of 1941 that he really took off with Campbell and Astounding. Also in that issue were: Adam and Eve by Alfred Bester; Short-Circuited Probability by Norman L. Knight; Mission by Myer Krulfeld; Test of the Gods by Raymond F. Jones; Methuselah's Children - part 3 of 3 by **Robert A. Heinlein**; and Elsewhen by **Robert A. Heinlein** writing as Caleb Saunders.

Asimov's story was Nightfall. And he always considered it a landmark. He was twenty-one years old and had been getting stories published for a couple of years but no one was really noticing him. Then came Nightfall. Campbell liked it so much that he gave Asimov a little extra payment for it... and ran it as the lead story in the issue. It grabbed the attention of the readers as well.

And that was it. There was no turning back.

Asimov was truly on his way to becoming one of the most prolific authors ever. By the time his career was over, his books totalled at least 512, probably more*, and they ran from science fiction through mysteries, fantasy and history, on through religion, literature, general science, mathematics, astronomy, chemistry and biochemistry, earth sciences, physics and biology, along with some credible autobiographical books and some interesting humour.

He even did a film treatment for a former Beatle, Paul McCartney. In December 1974, McCartney told Asimov that he wanted to make a movie about a rock band that was being taken over by aliens. The film would, of course, star Paul and Wings. He asked Asimov to do the screenplay and Asimov wrote an outline, using Paul's idea as the core. Unfortunately, McCartney rejected Asimov's treatment, which now resides in the archives of Boston University. It was once said that the only thing Asimov never wrote about was animal husbandry.

For collector's,

Isaac Asimov

Asimov's most valuable books tend to be either the complete Gnome Press Foundation Trilogy, or I, Robot, also from Gnome Press. Both go for around $9,000.00.

Pen names used: Paul French; George E. Dale; H. B. Ogden; and Dr A.

Asimov's Three Laws of Robotics:
1. A robot may not injure a human being or, through inaction, allow a human being to come to harm.
2. A robot must obey orders given to it by human beings, except where such orders would conflict with the First Law.
3. A robot must protect its own existence as long as such protection does not conflict with the First or Second Law.

*Note: You will find 551 Asimov titles listed here, but whenever a book was re-titled, or re-issued, I have, for first edition purposes, given it a new listing. Interestingly, Robert Silverberg published 548 books, while Andre Norton published 236. But Norton did the most in the genre.

***

AWARDS

1957. Thomas Alva Edison Foundation Award presented for Building Blocks of the Universe.
1960. Howard W. Blakeslee Award from the American Heart Association for The Living River.
1962. Boston University's Publication Merit Award.
1963. Special Hugo Award for "adding science to science fiction" for essays used the Magazine of Fantasy and Science Fiction.
1965. James T. Grady Award presented by the American Chemical Society. The award is now known as the James T. Grady-James H. Stack Award for Interpreting Chemistry.
1966. Hugo Award for Best All-time Novel Series for the Foundation series.
1967. Skylark, Edward E. Smith Memorial Award for Imaginative Fiction.
1967. Westinghouse Science Writing Award.
1973. Hugo Award for Best Novel presented for The Gods Themselves.
1973. Locus Poll Best Novel Award for The Gods Themselves.
1973. Nebula Award for Best Novel presented for The Gods Themselves.
1973. Ditmar Award for Best International Long Fiction, The Gods Themselves.
1975. Locus Poll Best Reprint Anthology Award for Before the Golden Age.
1977. Hugo Award for Best Novelette presented for The Bicentennial Man - from Stellar 2, edited by Judy-Lynn del Rey.
1977. Nebula Award for Best Novelette presented for The Bicentennial Man - from Stellar 2, edited by Judy-Lynn del Rey.
1977. Locus Poll Best Novelette Award for The Bicentennial Man - from Stellar 2, edited by Judy-Lynn del Rey.
1981. Asteroid 5020 Asimov was named in his honour.
1981. Locus Poll Best Related Non-Fiction Book Award for In Joy Still Felt: The Autobiography of Isaac Asimov 1954 - 1978.
1983. Hugo Award for Best Novel presented for Foundation's Edge.
1983. Locus Poll Best Novel Award for Foundation's Edge.
1986. Nebula Grandmaster Award, a lifetime achievement award.
1987. Asimov Reader's Poll Best Short Story Award for Robot Dreams - Asimov's Science Fiction, Mid-December, 1986.
1987. Locus Poll Best Short Story Award for Robot Dreams - Asimov's Science Fiction, Mid-December, 1986.
1992. Hugo Award for Best Novelette presented for Gold - Analog, September 1991.
1995. Hugo Award for Best Nonfiction presented for I. Asimov: A Memoir.
1995. Locus Poll Award for Best Nonfiction presented for I. Asimov: A Memoir.
1996. A 1946 Hugo Award was presented retroactively for Best Novel of 1945 was given at the 1996 WorldCon to The Mule, a Foundation story published in the November and December issues of Astounding Science Fiction.
1997. Inducted into The Science Fiction Hall of Fame.

And in addition to all that, he managed to gather fourteen honorary doctorate degrees from an assortment of universities.

***

FILM AND TELEVISION

1. I, Tobor. A story by Asimov, used on the television series Captain Video and His Video Rangers. The show aired on November 2nd, 1953, starring: Al Hodge; Don Hastings; Ben Lackland; Hal Conklin; and Dave Ballard.

2. Little Lost Robot. A 1947 story used on the television series Out of This World, Season 1, Episode 3. The Show aired on July 7th, 1962, starring Boris Karloff as the host and Maxine Audley as Susan Calvin along with Clifford Evans, Murray Hayne, Gerald Flood, Hayden Jones, and Roger Snowden as the robot.

3. The Caves of Steel. A 1954 novel adapted for television in the UK, directed by Peter Sasdy with the teleplay by Terry Nation. It aired on June 5th, 1964, starring: Peter Cushing as Elijah Baley, along with: John Carson; Stanley Walsh; Ian Trigger; Kenneth J. Warren; Richard Beale; and many others.

4. Sucker Bait. A 1954 story used on the television series Out of the Unknown, Season 1, Episode 7. It aired on November 15th, 1965, starring: Del Baker; Tim Condren; Roger Croucher; Bill Dean; Peter Diamond; et al.

5. Satisfaction Guaranteed. From 1951, this was used on the television series Out of the Unknown, Season 2, Episode 12. It aired on December 29th, 1966, starring: Wendy Craig; Hal Hamilton; Ann Firbank; Helen Horton; Bruce Boa; and many others.

6. The Prophet. An Asimov story used on the

television series Out of the Unknown, Season 2, Episode 13. It aired on January 1st, 1967, starring Beatrix Lehmann as Dr Susan Calvin, along with: Tenniel Evans; David Healy; Brian Davies; Julie Allen; and many others.

7. Liar! A 1941 story used on the television series Out of the Unknown, Season 3, Episode 2. It aired on January 14th, 1969, starring: Paul Chapman; Rita Davies; Jumoke Debayo; Hamilton Dyce; Wendy Gifford; Ian Ogilvy; et al.

8. The Naked Sun. From 1957, this novel adapted for the television series Out of the Unknown, Season 3, Episode 7. It aired on February 18th, 1969, starring: Sheila Burrell; David Cargill; Erik Chitty; David Collings; Neil Hallett; Raymond Hardy; Trisha Noble; and many others.

9. The Nature of Things. Asimov was a guest on this Canadian show with David Suzuki. The episode aired December 31st, 1969.

10. The Dick Cavett Show. Asimov was Cavett's guest on an episode that aired February 13th, 1970.

11. A History of Science Fiction from 1938. A short film written by Asimov, produced by Denny McClatchey and Kyland Wakefield and released in 1971. The cast featured Asimov himself along with James Gunn.

12. The Ugly Little Boy. An **Isaac Asimov** story from 1958, adapted for Canadian television and released in 1977, starring Kate Reid, Barry Morse, Guy Big, Tim Burd and Sydney Sturgess.

13. The Magnificent Major. A 1977 television event, directed by Nick De Noia and featuring **Isaac Asimov** as the guest host.

14. Dark Island. The first episode from the television series Salvage 1, written by Ruel Fischmann and directed by Gene Nelson in 1979. Asimov was a special science advisor for that one episode.

15. Star Trek: The Motion Picture. Asimov acted as a special science consultant, 1979.

16. Target... Earth? A 95-minute documentary filmed in 1980 by Joost van Rees. Asimov was a guest.

17. Voyage to the Outer Planets and Beyond. A 1986 documentary that featured **Isaac Asimov** as the host.

18. Oltre New York. A 1986 exploration of Jewish American culture that featured **Isaac Asimov** as one of the guests.

19. Stranieri in America. A 1988 documentary that featured **Isaac Asimov** as one of the guests.

20. Feeling 109. A short film based on a story by Asimov, directed by Richard Kletter and released in 1988.

21. Computer Logic. A story by **Isaac Asimov** and Michael I. Wagner, used for the television series Probe, Season 1, Episode 1. It aired on March 7th, 1988, starring: Parker Stevenson; Ashley Crow; John Cypher; William Phipps; Andy Wood; and many others.

22. Untouched by Human Hands. A story based on the creation of Asimov and Michael I. Wagner, used for the television series Probe, Season 1, Episode 2. It aired on March 10th, 1988, starring: Parker Stevenson; Ashley Crow; John Cypher; Eileen Barnett; Christopher Thomas; Katherine Moffat; et al.

23. Robots. A short film based on Asimov's Robot stories, directed by Doug Smith and Kim Takal, released in 1988 and starring: Valerie Pettiford; Stephen Rowe; Richard Levine; Larry Block; Brent Barrett; John Henry Cox; and many others.

24. Gandahar. An animated film, directed by Rene Laloux from a novel by Jean-Pierre Andrevon. Asimov adapted the English version for the January 28th, 1988 American release.

25. Nightfall. A film based on Asimov's 1941 story, directed by Paul Mayersberg, released in April 1988, starring: David Birney; Sarah Douglas; Alexis Kanner; Andra Millian; Sarr Andreeff; Chuck Hayward; et al.

26. Teach 109. An Asimov story adapted by television and directed by Richard Kletter in 1990. It starred Lee Arenberg, Hart Bochner, Ron Campbell, Annabelle Burwitch, James Earl Jones, John Cameron Mitchell, Jason Patric, Elizabeth Perkins, and Tuesday Knight.

27. The Android Affair. An Asimov story adapted by television and directed by Richard Kletter in 1995. It starred: Harley Jane Kozak; Griffin Dunne; Ossie Davis; Saul Rubinek; Peter Outerbridge; Natalie Radford; Ron Hartman; and many others.

28. Bicentennial Man. A film based on Asimov's 1976 story, The Bicentennial Man, and on the Asimov and **Robert Silverberg** novel, The Positronic Man, 1992. it was directed by Chris Columbus and released in December 1999, starring: Robin Williams; Embeth Davidtz; Sam Neill; Oliver Platt; Kiersten Warren; Wendy Crewson; Hallie Kate Eisenberg; et al.

29. Nightfall. Another film based on Asimov's story, directed Gwyneth Gibby, released in 2000, starring Jennifer Burns, Winsome Brown, Joseph Hodge, David Carradine, Ashish Vidyarthi, and many others.

30. I, Robot. A film based on the stories by Asimov, which were published in 1950. It was directed by Alex Proyas and released in July 2004, starring: Will Smith; Bridget Moynahan; Alan Tudyk; James Cromwell; Bruce Greenwood; Adrian Ricard; Chi McBride; Jerry Wasserman; et al.

***

RADIO

1. A Pebble in the Sky. Asimov's first novel, published in 1950, this was used on Dimension X and broadcast on June 17th, 1951.

2. Nightfall. Published in 1941, this was used on Dimension X and broadcast on September 29th, 1951, the final show in the series.

3. Nightfall. Published in 1941, this was used on X Minus One and broadcast on December 7th, 1955.

4. C-Chute. Published in 1951, this was used on X Minus One and broadcast on February 8th, 1956.

5. Hostess. Published in 1951, this was used on X Minus One and broadcast on December 12th, 1956.

6. Liar! Published in 1941, this was used as The Liar on John W. Campbell's radio show, Exploring Tomorrow, which ran in 1957 and 1958.

7. The Caves of Steel. Published in 1954, this was produced for BBC Radio and broadcast on June 5th, 1964.

8. The Foundation Trilogy. Published between 1951 and 1953, this was adapted for BBC Radio and broadcast in 1973, starring Geoffrey Beevers; Lee Montague; Julian Glover; Dinsdale Landen; Angela Pleasence; Maurice Denham; and Prunella Scales.

9. The Caves of Steel. Published in 1954, this was produced for BBC Radio and broadcast in June, 1989, starring Ed Bishop and Sam Dastor.

***

NOVELS AND COLLECTIONS

1. Pebble in the Sky. Published by Doubleday & Company, Garden City, New York, 1950. Hardcover.

2. I, Robot. Published by Gnome Press, New York City, 1950. Hardcover. This collection contains: Introduction by **Isaac Asimov**; Robbie, 1940; Runaround, 1942; Reason, 1941; Catch That Rabbit, 1944; Liar!, 1941; Little Lost Robot, 1947; Escape!, 1945; Evidence, 1946; and The Evitable Conflict, 1950.

3. The Stars, Like Dust. Published by Doubleday & Company, Garden City, New York, 1951. Hardcover.

4. Foundation. Published by Gnome Press, New York City, 1951. Hardcover.

5. David Starr, Space Ranger. Writing as Paul French. Published by Doubleday & Company, Garden City, New York, 1952. Hardcover.

6. Foundation and Empire. Published by Gnome Press, New York City, 1952. Hardcover.

7. The Currents of Space. Published by Doubleday & Company, Garden City, New York, 1952. Hardcover.

8. Second Foundation. Published by Gnome Press, New York City, 1953. Hardcover.

9. Lucky Starr and the Pirates of the Asteroids. Writing as Paul French. Published by Doubleday & Company, Garden City, New York, 1953. Hardcover.

10. The Caves of Steel. Published by Doubleday & Company, Garden City, New York, 1954. Hardcover

11. Lucky Starr and the Oceans of Venus. Writing as Paul French. Published by Doubleday & Company, Garden City, New York, 1954. Hardcover.

12. The End of Eternity. Published by Doubleday & Company, Garden City, New York, 1955. Hardcover.

13. The Martian Way and Other Stories. Published by Doubleday & Company, Garden City, New York, 1955. Hardcover. Herein: The Martian Way, 1952; Youth, 1952; The Deep, 1942; Sucker Bait, 1954.

14. The 1,000 Year Plan. Published by Ace Books, New York City, 1955. Ace Double D-110. An abridged version of Foundation, bound with No World of Their Own by **Poul Anderson**.

15. The Man Who Upset the Universe. Published by Ace Books, New York City, 1955. Ace Book D-125. Foundation and Empire re-named.

16. Lucky Starr and the Big Sun of Mercury. Writing as Paul French. Published by Doubleday & Company, Garden City, New York, 1956. Hardcover.

17. The Naked Sun. Published by Doubleday & Company, Garden City, New York, 1957. Hardcover.

18. Earth Is Room Enough: Science Fiction Tales of Our Own Planet. Published by Doubleday & Company, Garden City, New York, 1957. Hardcover. This contains: The Dead Past, 1956; The Foundation of S.F. Success, a poem, 1954; Franchise, 1955; Gimmicks Three, 1956; Kid Stuff, 1953; The Watery Place, 1956; Living Space, 1956; The Message, 1956; Satisfaction Guaranteed, 1951; Hell-Fire, 1956; The Last Trump, 1955; The Fun They Had, 1951; Jokester, 1956; The Immortal Bard, 1954; Someday, 1956; The Author's Ordeal, a poem, 1957; and Dreaming is a Private Thing, 1955.

19. Lucky Starr and the Moons of Jupiter. Writing as Paul French. Published by Doubleday & Company, Garden City, New York, 1957. Hardcover.

20. Lucky Starr and the Rings of Saturn. Writing as Paul French. Published by Doubleday & Company, Garden City, New York, 1958. Hardcover.

21. The Death Dealers. Avon Books, New York City, 1958. Avon Book T-287. Paperback original. Reprinted later as A Whiff of Death.

22. Nine Tomorrows: Tales of the Near Future. Published by Doubleday & Company, Garden City, New York, 1959. Hardcover. This contains: I Just Make Them Up, See!, a poem, 1958; Rejection Slips, a poem, 1959; The Ugly Little Boy - also known as Lastborn, 1958; The Last Question, 1956; Spell My Name With an S, 1958; All the Troubles in the World, 1958; The Gentle Vultures, 1957; I'm in Marsport Without Hilda, 1957; The Dying Night, 1956; The Feeling of Power, 1958; Profession, 1957.

23. Triangle. Published by Doubleday & Company, Garden City, New York, 1961. Hardcover. An omnibus edition, this contains: The Currents of Space, 1952; Pebble in the Sky, 1950; and The Stars Like Dust, 1951.

24. The Foundation Trilogy. Published by Doubleday & Company, Garden City, New York, 1963. Hardcover.

25. The Rest of the Robots. Published by Doubleday & Company, Garden City, New York,

1964. Hardcover. This contains: Introduction by Asimov; The Naked Sun, 1957; The Caves of Steel, 1954; Robot AL-76 Goes Astray, 1942; Victory Unintentional, 1942; First Law, 1956; Let's Get Together, 1957; Satisfaction Guaranteed, 1951; Risk, 1955; Lenny, 1958; and Galley Slave, 1957.

26. Eight Stories from The Rest of the Robots. Published by Pyramid Books, New York City, 1966. Softcover. Pyramid Book R-1283. Herein: Introduction by Asimov; Robot AL-76 Goes Astray, 1942; Victory Unintentional, 1942; First Law, 1956; Let's Get Together, 1957; Satisfaction Guaranteed, 1951; Risk, 1955; Lenny, 1958; and Galley Slave, 1957.

27. Fantastic Voyage. Published by Houghton Mifflin, Boston, 1966. Hardcover.

28. An Isaac Asimov Omnibus. Published by Sidgwick and Jackson, London, 1966. Hardcover. This gathered Foundation, 1951, Foundation and Empire, 1952, and Second Foundation, 1953.

29. Through a Glass, Clearly. Published by Four Square, London, 1967. Softcover. Four Square Science Fiction Book 1866. Herein: It's Such a Beautiful Day, 1954; Belief, 1953; Breeds There a Man, 1951; and The C Chute, 1951.

30. A Whiff of Death. Published by Walker and Company, New York, 1968. First hardcover edition. Previously issued as The Death Dealers, 1958.

31. Asimov's Mysteries. Published by Doubleday & Company, Garden City, New York, 1968. Hardcover. This contains: Introduction by Asimov; The Singing Bell, 1955; The Talking Stone, 1955; What's in a Name, 1956; The Dying Night, 1956; Pate de Foie Gras, 1956; The Dust of Death, 1957; A Loint of Paw, 1957; I'm in Marsport Without Hilda, 1957; Marooned off Vesta, 1939; Anniversary, 1959; Obituary, 1959; Star Light, 1962; The Key, 1966; and The Billiard Ball, 1967.

32. An Isaac Asimov Second Omnibus. Published by Sidgwick and Jackson, London, 1969. Hardcover. This gathered The Currents of Space, 1952, Pebble in the Sky, 1950, and The Stars, Like Dust, 1951.

33. Nightfall and Other Stories. Published by Doubleday & Company, Garden City, New York, 1969. Hardcover. Herein: Introduction by Asimov; Green Patches, 1950; Hostess, 1951; Breeds There a Man, 1951; The C Chute, 1951; In a Good Cause, 1951; What If..., 1952; Sally, 1953; Flies, 1953; Nobody Here but..., 1953; It's Such a Beautiful Day, 1954; Strikebreaker, 1957; Insert Knob A in Hole B, 1957; The Up to Date Sorcerer, 1958; Unto the Fourth Generation, 1959; What is This Thing Called Love, 1961; The Machine that Won the War, 1961; My Son the Physicist, 1962; Eyes Do More Than See, 1965; Segregationist, 1968; and Nightfall, 1941.

34. The Best New Thing. The World Publishing Company, Cleveland and New York, 1971. Hardcover.

35. The Gods Themselves. Published by Doubleday & Company, Garden City, New York, 1972. Hardcover.

36. The Early Asimov. Published by Doubleday & Company, Garden City, New York, 1972. Hardcover. This contains: Introduction by Asimov; The Callistan Menace, 1940; Ring Around the Sun, 1940; The Magnificent Possession, 1940; Trends, 1939; The Weapon Too Dreadful to Use, 1939; Black Friar of the Flame, 1942; Half-Breed, 1940; The Secret Sense, 1941; Homo Sol, 1940; Half-Breeds on Venus, 1940; The Imaginary, 1942; Heredity, 1941; History, 1941; Christmas on Ganymede, 1942; The Little Man on the Subway, written with **Frederick Pohl** who wrote as James MacCreigh, 1950; The Hazing, 1942; Super Neutron, 1941; Not Final, 1941; Legal Rites, written with **Frederick Pohl** who wrote as James MacCreigh, 1950; Time Pussy, 1942; Author, Author, 1964; Death Sentence, 1943; Blind Alley, 1945; No Connection, 1948; The Endochronic Properties of Resublimated Thiotimoline, 1948; The Red Queen's Race, 1949; and Mother Earth, 1949.

37. An Isaac Asimov Double. Published by New English Library, London, 1972. Hardcover. This collected: David Starr, Space Ranger, 1952; and Lucky Starr and the Pirates of the Asteroids, 1953.

38. A Second Asimov Double. Published by New English Library, London, 1972. Hardcover. This collected: Lucky Starr and the Big Sun of Mercury, 1956; and Lucky Starr and the Oceans of Venus, 1954.

39. The Best of Isaac Asimov. Sidgwick and Jackson, London, 1973. Hardcover. This contains: Introduction by Asimov; Marooned off Vesta, 1939; Nightfall, 1941; The C Chute, 1951; The Martian Way, 1952; The Deep, 1952; The Fun They Had, 1951; The Last Question, 1956; The Dead Past, 1956; The Dying Night, 1956; Anniversary, 1959; The Billiard Ball, 1967; and Mirror Image, 1972; along with a bibliography by Gerald Bishop.

40. The Best of Isaac Asimov 1939 - 1952. Published by Sphere Books, London, 1973. Softcover. This contains: Marooned Off Vesta, 1939; Nightfall, 1941; The C Chute, 1951; The Martian Way, 1952; The Deep, 1952; and The Fun They Had, 1951.

41. The Third Isaac Asimov Double. Published by New English Library, London, 1972. Hardcover. This collected: Lucky Starr and the Rings of Saturn, 1958; and Lucky Starr and the Moons of Jupiter, 1957.

42. The Best of Isaac Asimov 1954 - 1972. Published by Sphere Books, London, 1973. Softcover. This contains: Anniversary, 1959; Mirror Image, 1972; The Billiard Ball, 1967; The Dead Past, 1956; The Dying Night, 1956; and The Last Question, 1956.

43. The Best of Isaac Asimov. Published by Doubleday & Company, Garden City, New York, 1974. Hardcover. Slightly different from the Sidgwick and Jackson edition: Part of the introduction, along with the Gerald Bishop bibliography, were omitted. Herein: Introduction by Asimov; Marooned off Vesta, 1939; Nightfall, 1941; The C Chute, 1951; The Martian Way, 1952; The Deep, 1952; The Fun They Had, 1951; The Last Question, 1956; The Dead Past, 1956; The Dying Night, 1956; Anniversary, 1959; The Billiard Ball, 1967; and Mirror Image, 1972.

Isaac Asimov

44. Have You Seen These? Published by The NESFA Press, Boston, 1974. Hardcover, limited to 500 numbered copies, all signed by Asimov. This contains: Introduction by Asimov; Silly Asses, 1958; Rain, Rain, Go Away, 1959; Blank!, 1957; The Pause, 1954; Everest, 1953; The Monkey's Fingers, 1953; Shah Guido G, 1951; and Day of the Hunters, 1950.

45. Tales of the Black Widowers. Published by Doubleday & Company, Garden City, New York, 1974. Hardcover. This contains: Introduction by Asimov; The Acquisitive Chuckle, 1972; PH as in Phony, 1972; Truth to Tell, 1972; Go, Little Book!, 1972; Early Sunday Morning, 1973; The Obvious Factor, 1973; The Pointing Finger, 1973; Miss What?, 1973; The Lullaby of Broadway, 1974; Yankee Doodle Went to Town, 1972; The Curious Omission, 1974; and Out of Sight, 1973.

46. Buy Jupiter and Other Stories. Published by Doubleday & Company, Garden City, New York, 1975. Hardcover. Herein: Introduction by Asimov; Darwinian Pool Room, 1950; Day of the Hunters, 1950; Shah Guido G, 1951; Button, Button, 1953; The Monkey's Finger, 1953; Everest, 1953; The Pause, 1954; Let's Not, 1954; Each an Explorer, 1956; Blank!, 1957; Does a Bee Care?, 1957; Silly Asses, 1958; Buy Jupiter!, 1958; A Statue for Father, 1959; Rain, Rain, Go Away, 1959; Founding Father, 1965; Exile to Hell, 1968; Key Item, 1968; The Proper Study, 1968; 2430 A.D., 1970; The Greatest Asset, 1972; Take a Match, 1972; Thiotimoline to the Stars, 1973; and Light Verse, 1973.

47. The Heavenly Host. Published by Walker and Company, New York City, 1975. Hardcover.

48. The Dream, Benjamin's Dream, and Benjamin's Bicentennial Blast - Three Short Stories. Private Printing, New York City, 1976. Hardcover. All three were first published in 1974.

49. More Tales of the Black Widowers. Published by Doubleday & Company, Garden City, New York, 1976. Hardcover. This contains: Introduction by Asimov; When No Man Pursueth, 1974; Quicker than the Eye, 1974; The Iron Gem, 1974; The Three Numbers, 1974; Nothing Like Murder, 1974; No Smoking, 1974; Season's Greetings, 1976; The One and Only East, 1975; Earthset and Evening Star, 1975; Friday the Thirteenth, 1975; The Unabridged, 1976; and The Ultimate Crime, 1976.

50. Murder at The ABA. Published by Doubleday & Company, Garden City, New York, 1976. Hardcover.

51. The Bicentennial Man and Other Stories. Published by Doubleday & Company, Garden City, New York, 1976. Hardcover. Herein: The Prime of Life, poem, 1966; Feminine Intuition, 1969; Waterclap, 1970; That Thou Art Mindful of Him, 1974; Stranger in Paradise, 1974; The Life and Times of Multivac, 1975; The Winnowing, 1976; Marching In, 1976; Old Fashioned, 1976; The Tercentenary Incident, 1976; Birth of a Notion, 1976; and The Bicentennial Man, 1976.

52. The Key Word and Other Mysteries. Published by Walker and Company, New York City, 1977. This contains: The Key Word, 1977; Santa Clause Gets a Coin, 1975; Sarah Tops, 1975; The Thirteenth Day of Christmas, 1977; and A Case of Need, 1975.

53. Good Taste: A Story. Published by Apocalypse Press, Topeka, Kansas, 1977. Softcover. Limited to 500 signed and numbered copies; and 500 numbered copies.

54. Through a Glass, Clearly. Published by Ian Henry Publications, Essex, England, 1977. First hardcover edition of the 1967 paperback original. This contains: It's Such a Beautiful Day, 1954; Belief, 1953; Breeds There a Man, 1951; and The C Chute, 1951.

55. Liar! Published by The Syndics of the Cambridge University Press, Cambridge, 1977. Softcover.

56. Little Lost Robot. Published by The Syndics of the Cambridge University Press, Cambridge, 1977. Softcover.

57. The Far Ends of Time and Earth. Published by Doubleday & Company, Garden City, New York, 1979. Hardcover. This contains: Introduction by Asimov; Pebble in the Sky, 1950; The Dead Past, 1956; The Foundation of Science Fiction Success, a poem, 1954; Franchise, 1955; Gimmicks Three, 1956; Kid Stuff, 1953; The Watery Place, 1956; Living Space, 1956; The Message, 1956; Satisfaction Guaranteed, 1951; Hell-Fire, 1956; The Last Trump, 1955; The Fun They Had, 1951; Jokester, 1956; The Immortal Bard, 1954; Someday, 1956; The Author's Ordeal, a poem, 1957; Dreaming Is a Private Thing, 1955; and The End of Eternity, 1955.

58. Prisoners of the Stars. Published by Doubleday & Company, Garden City, New York, 1980. Hardcover. Herein: Introduction by Asimov; The Martian Way and Other Stories, 1955: The Martian Way, 1952; Youth, 1952; The Deep, 1942; Sucker Bait, 1954; with: The Stars, Like Dust, 1951; and The Currents of Space, 1952.

59. Casebook of the Black Widowers. Published by Doubleday & Company, Garden City, New York, 1980. Hardcover. Herein: Introduction by Asimov; The Cross Lorraine, 1976; The Family Man, 1976; The Sports Page, 1977; Second Best, 1980; The Missing Item, 1980; The Next Day, 1978; Irrelevance!, 1979; The Backward Look, 1979; What Times Is It?, 1980; Middle Name, 1980; and To the Barest, 1979.

60. Three Science Fiction Tales. Published by Targ Editions, New York City, 1981. Hardcover. Limited to 250 copies signed by Asimov. Herein: True Love, 1977; Fair Exchange?, 1978; and The Last Answer, 1980.

61. Foundation's Edge. Published by Doubleday & Company, Garden City, New York, 1982. Hardcover.

62. The Complete Robot. Published by Doubleday & Company, Garden City, New York, 1982. Hardcover. Herein: Liar!, 1941; Evidence, 1946; The Bicentennial Man, 1976; True Love, 1977; Point of View, 1975; Robbie, 1940; Runaround, 1942; Reason, 1941; Paradoxical Escape, 1945; A Boy's Best Friend, 1975; Sally, 1953; Someday, 1956; Robot AL-76 Goes Astray, 1942; Victory

Unintentional, 1942; The Tercentenary Incident, 1976; First Law, 1956; Satisfaction Guaranteed, 1951; Lenny, 1958; Little Lost Robot, 1947; Galley Slave, 1957; Light Verse, 1973; Catch That Rabbit, 1944; That Thou Art Mindful of Him!, 1974; Mirror Image, 1972; The Evitable Conflict, 1950; Feminine Intuition, 1969; Segregationist, 1968; Stranger in Paradise, 1974; and Risk, 1955.

63. The Winds of Change and Other Stories. Published by Doubleday & Company, Garden City, New York, 1983. Hardcover. This contains: Introduction by Asimov; About Nothing, 1975; A Perfect Fit, 1981; Belief, 1953; Death of a Foy, 1980; Fair Exchange?, 1978; For the Birds, 1980; Found, 1978; Good Taste, 1976; How It Happened, 1979; Ideas Die Hard, 1957; Ignition Point!, 1981; It Is Coming, 1979; The Last Answer, 1980; The Last Shuttle, 1981; Lest We Remember, 1982; Nothing for Nothing, 1979; One Night of Song, 1982; The Smile That Loses, 1982; Sure Thing, 1977; To Tell at a Glance, 1981; and The Winds of Change, 1982.

64. The Robot Collection. Published by Doubleday & Company, Garden City, New York, 1983. Hardcover. Herein: The Naked Sun, 1957; The Caves of Steel, 1954; and The Complete Robot, 1982: Liar!, 1941; Evidence, 1946; The Bicentennial Man, 1976; True Love, 1977; Point of View, 1975; Robbie, 1940; Runaround, 1942; Reason, 1941; Paradoxical Escape, 1945; A Boy's Best Friend, 1975; Sally, 1953; Someday, 1956; Robot AL-76 Goes Astray, 1942; Victory Unintentional, 1942; The Tercentenary Incident, 1976; First Law, 1956; Satisfaction Guaranteed, 1951; Lenny, 1958; Little Lost Robot, 1947; Galley Slave, 1957; Light Verse, 1973; Catch That Rabbit, 1944; That Thou Art Mindful of Him!, 1974; Mirror Image, 1972; The Evitable Conflict, 1950; Feminine Intuition, 1969; Segregationist, 1968; Stranger in Paradise, 1974; and Risk, 1955.

65. The Union Club Mysteries. Published by Doubleday & Company, Garden City, New York, 1983. Hardcover. This contains: Foreword by Asimov; No Refuge Could Save, 1980; The Telephone Number, 1980; The Men Who Wouldn't Talk, 1980; A Clear Shot, 1980; Irresistible to Women, 1981; He Wasn't There, 1981; The Thin Line, 1981; Mystery Tune, 1981; Hide and Seek, 1981; Gift, 1981; Hot or Cold, 1981; The Thirteenth Page, 1981; 1 to 999, 1981; Twelve Years Old, 1981; Testing, Testing!, 1981; The Appleby Story, 1981; Dollars and Cents, 1982; Friends and Allies, 1982; Which is Which?, 1982; The Sign, 1982; Catching the Fox, 1982; Getting the Combination, 1982; The Library Book, 1982; The Three Goblets, 1982; Spell It!, 1982; Two Women, 1982; Sending a Signal, 1982; The Favorite Piece, 1982; Half a Ghost, 1983; and There Was a Young Lady, 1983; followed by an Afterword by Asimov.

66. Norby, the Mixed-up Robot. With Janet Asimov. Published by Walker and Company, New York City, 1983. Hardcover.

67. The Robots of Dawn. Published by Doubleday & Company, Garden City, New York, 1983. Hardcover.

68. Banquets of the Black Widowers. Published by Doubleday & Company, Garden City, New York, 1984. Hardcover. Herein: Introduction by Asimov; Neither Brute Nor Human, 1984; Sixty Million Trillion Combinations, 1980; The Woman in the Bar, 1980; The Driver, 1984; The Good Samaritan, 1980; The Year of the Action, 1980; Can You Prove It?, 1981; The Phoenician Bauble, 1982; A Monday in April, 1983; The Redhead, 1984; The Wrong House, 1984; and The Intrusion, 1984.

69. Norby's Other Secret. With Janet Asimov. Published by Walker and Company, New York City, 1984. Hardcover.

70. Norby and the Lost Princess. With Janet Asimov. Published by Walker and Company, New York City, 1985. Hardcover.

71. The Disappearing Man and Other Mysteries. Published by Walker and Company, New York City, 1985. Hardcover. This contains: The Disappearing Man; Lucky Seven; The Christmas Solution; The Twins; and The Man in the Park.

72. Robots and Empire. Published by Doubleday & Company, Garden City, New York, 1985. Hardcover.

73. Norby and the Invaders. With Janet Asimov. Published by Walker and Company, New York City, 1985. Hardcover.

74. The Edge of Tomorrow. Published by Tom Doherty Associates - Tor Books, New York City, 1985. Hardcover. This contains: Foreword by Ben Bova; Introduction by Asimov; Unique Is Where You Find It, 1985; The Eureka Phenomenon, an essay, 1971; The Feeling of Power, 1958; The Comet That Wasn't, an essay, 1976; Found, 1978; Twinkle, Twinkle Microwaves, an essay, 1977; Pate de Foie Gras, 1956; The Bridge of the Gods, an essay, 1975; Belief, 1953; Euclid's Fifth, an essay, 1971; The Plane Truth, an essay, 1971; The Billiard Ball, 1967; The Winds of Change, 1982; The Figure of the Fastest, an essay, 1973; The Dead Past, 1956; The Fateful Lightning, an essay, 1969; Breeds There a Man?, 1951; The Man Who Massed the Earth, an essay, 1969; Nightfall, 1941; The Planet That Wasn't, an essay, 1975; The Ugly Little Boy, 1958; The Three Who Died Too Soon, an essay, 1982; The Last Question, 1956; and The Nobel That Wasn't, an essay, 1970.

75. It's Such a Beautiful Day. Creative Education, North Mankato, Minnesota. 1985. Hardcover.

76. Foundation and Earth. Published by Doubleday & Company, Garden City, New York, 1986. Hardcover.

77. The Alternate Asimovs. Published by Doubleday & Company, Garden City, New York, 1986. Hardcover. This contains: Introduction by Asimov; Foreword: Grow Old Along With Me, an essay, 1986; Grow Old Along with Me (original version of the novel Pebble in the Sky, 1950); Foreword: The End of Eternity, an essay, 1986; The End of Eternity (original version of the novel The End of Eternity, 1955); Foreword: Belief - First Version, 1986; Belief (first version); Foreword: Belief - Published Version, 1986; and Belief (the published version, 1953)

78. The Best Science Fiction of Isaac Asimov. Published by Doubleday & Company, Garden City, New York, 1986. Hardcover. Herein: Introduction

Isaac Asimov

by Asimov; All the Troubles in the World, 1958; A Loint of Paw, 1957; The Dead Past, 1956; Death of a Foy, 1980; Dreaming Is a Private Thing, 1955; Dreamworld, 1955; Eyes Do More Than See, 1965; The Feeling of Power, 1958; Flies, 1953; Found!, 1978; The Foundation of Science Fiction Success, a poem, 1954; Franchise, 1955; The Fun They Had, 1951; How It Happened, 1979; I Just Make Them Up, See!, a poem, 1958; I'm in Marsport Without Hilda, 1957; The Immortal Bard, 1954; Jokester, 1956; The Last Answer, 1980; The Last Question, 1956; My Son, the Physicist!, 1962; Obituary, 1959; Spell My Name with an S, 1958; Strikebreaker, 1957; Sure Thing, 1977; The Ugly Little Boy - also known as Lastborn, 1958; and Unto the Fourth Generation, 1959.

79. The Best Mysteries of Isaac Asimov. Published by Doubleday & Company, Garden City, New York, 1986. Hardcover. This contains: The Obvious Factor, 1973; The Pointing Factor, 1986; Out of Sight, 1973; Yankee Doodle Went to Town, 1972; Quicker Than the Eye, 1974; The Three Numbers, 1974; The One and Only East, 1975; The Cross of Lorraine, 1976; The Next Day, 1978; What Time Is It?, 1980; Middle Name, 1980; Sixty Million Trillion Combinations, 1980; The Good Samaritan, 1980; Can You Prove It?, 1981; The Redhead, 1984; He Wasn't There, 1981; Hide and Seek, 1981; Dollars and Cents, 1982; The Sign, 1982; Getting the Combination, 1982; The Library Book, 1982; Never Out of Sight, 1986; The Magic Umbrella, 1986; The Speck, 1986; The Key, 1966; The Problem of Numbers, 1986; The Little Things, 1986; Halloween, 1975; The Thirteenth Day of Christmas, 1977; The Key Word, 1977; and Nothing Might Happen, 1986.

80. Robot Dreams. Published by Berkley Books, New York City, 1986. Hardcover. This contains: Introduction by Asimov; Little Lost Robot, 1947; Breeds There a Man?, 1951; Hostess, 1951; Sally, 1953; Strikebreaker, 1957; The Machine that Won the War, 1961; Eyes Do More Than See, 1965; The Martian Way, 1952; Franchise, 1955; Jokester, 1956; The Last Question, 1956; Does a Bee Care?, 1957; Light Verse, 1973; The Feeling of Power, 1958; Spell My Name with an S, 1958; The Ugly Little Boy - also known as Lastborn, 1958; The Billiard Ball, 1967; True Love, 1977; The Last Answer, 1980; Lest We Remember, 1982; and Robot Dreams, 1986.

81. Science Fiction by Asimov. Published by Davis Publications, New York City, 1986. Softcover. This contains: Introduction by Sheila Williams; More Things in Heaven and Earth, 1986; Rejection Slips, a poem, 1959; Death of a Foy, 1980; Dashing Through the Snow, 1984; Potential, 1983; Eyes Do More Than See, 1965; and The Dim Rumble, 1982.

82. Norby and the Queen's Necklace. With Janet Asimov. Published by Walker and Company, New York City, 1986. Hardcover.

83. The Norby Chronicles. With Janet Asimov. Ace Books, New York City, 1986. Softcover. An omnibus edition, this contains: Norby, the Mixed-up Robot, 1983; and Norby's Other Secret, 1984.

84. Norby Finds a Villain. With Janet Asimov. Published by Walker and Company, New York City, 1987. Hardcover.

85. Fantastic Voyage II: Destination Brain. Published by Doubleday & Company, Garden City, New York, 1987. Hardcover.

86. Other Worlds of Isaac Asimov. Published by Avenel Press, New Jersey, 1987. Hardcover. This collection contains: The C Chute, 1951; The Dead Past, 1956; Hostess, 1951; In a Good Cause, 1951; The Key, 1966; Lest We Remember, 1982; The Martian Way, 1952; Nightfall, 1941; Profession, 1957; Sucker Bait, 1954; The Ugly Little Boy - also known as Lastborn, 1958; and Youth, 1952.

87. Norby: Robot for Hire. With Janet Asimov. Published by Ace Books, New York City, 1987. Softcover. An omnibus edition, this contains: Norby and the Lost Princess, 1985; and Norby and the Invaders, 1985.

88. Prelude to Foundation. Published by Doubleday & Company, Garden City, New York, 1988. Hardcover.

89. Azazel. Published by Doubleday & Company, Garden City, New York, 1988. Hardcover. Herein: Introduction by Asimov; The Two-Centimeter Demon, 1988; One Night of Song, 1982; The Smile That Loses, 1982; To the Victor, 1982; The Dim Rumble, 1982; Saving Humanity, 1983; A Matter of Principle, 1984; The Evil Drink Does, 1984; Writing Time, 1984; Dashing Through the Snow, 1984; Logic is Logic, 1985; He Travels the Fastest, 1985; The Eye of the Beholder, 1986; More Things in Heaven and Earth, 1986; The Mind's Construction, 1986; The Flights of Spring, 1987; Galatea, 1987; and Flight of Fancy, 1988.

90. Norby Down to Earth. With Janet Asimov. Published by Walker and Company, New York City, 1988. Hardcover.

91. Norby Through Time and Space. With Janet Asimov. Published by Ace Books, New York City, 1988. Softcover. An omnibus edition, this contains: Norby and the Queen's Necklace, 1986; and Norby Finds a Villain, 1987.

92. Nemesis. Published by Doubleday & Company, Garden City, New York, 1989. Hardcover.

93. Norby and Yobo's Great Adventure. With Janet Asimov. Published by Walker and Company, New York City, 1989. Hardcover.

94. All the Troubles of the World. Creative Education, North Mankato, Minnesota. 1989. Hardcover.

95. Franchise. Creative Education, North Mankato, Minnesota. 1989. Hardcover.

96. Robbie. Creative Education, North Mankato, Minnesota. 1989. Hardcover.

97. Sally. Creative Education, North Mankato, Minnesota. 1989. Hardcover.

98. The Asimov Chronicles: Fifty Years of Isaac Asimov. Published by Dark Harvest, Arlington Heights, Illinois, 1989. Hardcover. Herein: The Ugly Little Boy, also known as Lastborn, 1958;

Found!, 1978; Marooned Off Vesta, 1939; Robbie, 1940; Nightfall, 1941; Runaround, 1942; Death Sentence, 1943; Catch That Rabbit, 1944; Blind Alley, 1945; Evidence, 1946; Little Lost Robot, 1947; No Connection, 1948; The Red Queen's Race, 1949; Green Patches, 1950; Breeds There a Man?, 1951; The Martian Way, 1952; Sally, 1953; The Fun They Had, 1951; Franchise, 1955; The Last Question, 1956; Profession, 1957; The Bicentennial Man, 1976; I Love Little Pussy, 1988; The Eye of the Beholder, 1986; Saving Humanity, 1983; Lest We Remember, 1982; True Love, 1977; For the Birds, 1980; Nothing for Nothing, 1979; Light Verse, 1973; Exile to Hell, 1968; Earthset and Evening Star, 1975; That Thou Art Mindful of Him!, 1974; Mirror Image, 1972; Feminine Intuition, 1969; The Key, 1966; Eyes Do More Than See, 1965; The Billiard Ball, 1967; Thiotimoline and the Space Age,1960; Unto the Fourth Generation, 1959; The Machine That Won the War, 1961; My Son, the Physicist!, 1962; T-Formation, an essay, 1963; Author! Author!, 1964; A Problem of Numbers, 1970; Ignition Point, 1981; Neither Brute Nor Human, 1984; The Fourth Homonym, 1985; The Quiet Place, 1988; and Bill and I, an essay, 1971.

99. Robot Visions. Published by Byron Preiss, New York City, 1990. Hardcover. This contains: Introduction by Asimov; STORIES: Robot Visions, 1990; Too Bad, 1989; Robbie, 1940; Reason, 1941; Liar!, 1941; Runaround, 1942; Evidence, 1946; Little Lost Robot, 1947; The Evitable Conflict, 1950; Feminine Intuition, 1969; The Bicentennial Man, 1976; Someday, 1956; Think!, 1977; Segregationist, 1968; Mirror Image, 1972; Lenny, 1958; Galley Slave, 1957; and Christmas Without Rodney, 1988. ESSAYS: Robots I Have Known, 1954; The New Teachers, 1976; Whatever You Wish, 1977; The Friends We Make, 1977; Our Intelligent Tools, 1977; The Laws of Robotics, 1979; Future Fantastic, 1989; The Machine and the Robot, 1978; The New Profession, 1979; The Robot as Enemy?, 1979; Intelligences Together, 1979; My Robots, 1987; The Laws of Humanics, 1987; Cybernetic Organism, 1987; The Sense of Humor, 1988; and Robots in Combination, 1988.

100. Norby and the Oldest Dragon. With Janet Asimov. Published by Walker and Company, New York City, 1990. Hardcover.

101. Puzzles of the Black Widowers. Published by Doubleday & Company, Garden City, New York, 1990. Hardcover. Herein: Introduction by Asimov; The Fourth Homonym, 1985; Unique Is Where You Find It, 1985; The Lucky Piece, 1990; Triple Devil, 1985; Sunset on the Water, 1986; Where Is He?, 1986; The Old Purse, 1987; The Quiet Place, 1988; The Four-Leaf Clover, 1990; The Envelope, 1989; The Alibi, 1989; and The Recipe, 1990.

102. Nightfall. With **Robert Silverberg**. Published by Doubleday & Company, Garden City, New York, 1990. Hardcover.

103. Cal: A Short Story Written Exclusively for Members of the Isaac Asimov Collection. Published by Doubleday & Company, Garden City, New York, 1990. Softcover.

104. The Complete Stories Volume 1. Published by Doubleday & Company, Garden City, New York, 1990. Hardcover. This collection contains: Introduction by Asimov; The Dead Past, 1956; The Foundation of SF Success, a poem, 1954; Franchise, 1955; Gimmicks Three, 1956; Kid Stuff, 1953; The Watery Place, 1956; Living Space, 1956; The Message, 1956; Satisfaction Guaranteed, 1951; Hell Fire, 1956; The Last Trump, 1955; The Fun They Had, 1951; Jokester, 1956; The Immortal Bard, 1954; Someday, 1956; The Author's Ordeal, a poem, 1957; Dreaming is a Private Thing, 1955; Profession, 1957; The Feeling of Power, 1958; The Dying Night, 1956; I'm in Marsport Without Hilda, 1957; The Gentle Vultures, 1957; All the Troubles of the World, 1958; Spell My Name with an S, 1958; The Last Question, 1968; The Ugly Little Boy - also known as Lastborn, 1958; Nightfall, 1941; Green Patches, 1950; Hostess, 1951; Breeds There a Man?, 1951; C Chute, 1951; In a Good Cause, 1951; What If..., 1952; Sally, 1953; Flies, 1951; Nobody Here but..., 1990; It's Such a Beautiful Day, 1954; Strikebreaker, 1957; Insert Knob A in Hole B, 1957; The Up-to-Date Sorcerer, 1958; Unto the Fourth Generation, 1959; What is This Thing Called Love?, 1961; The Machine that Won the War, 1961; My Son, the Physicist, 1962; Eyes Do More than See, 1965; Segregationist, 1968; I Just Make Them Up, See!, a poem, 1958; and Rejection Slips, a poem, 1959.

105. Norby and the Court Jester. With Janet Asimov. Published by Walker and Company, New York City, 1991. Hardcover.

106. The Complete Stories Volume 2. Published by Doubleday & Company, Garden City, New York, 1992. Hardcover. Herein: Not Final, 1941; The Hazing, 1942; Death Sentence, 1943; Blind Alley, 1945; Evidence, 1946; The Red Queen's Race, 1949; Day of the Hunters, 1950; The Deep, 1942; The Martian Way, 1952; The Monkey's Finger, 1953; The Singing Bell, 1955; The Talking Stone, 1955; Each an Explorer, 1956; Let's Get Together, 1957; Pate de Foie Gras, 1956; Galley Slave, 1957; Lenny, 1958; A Loint of Paw, 1957; A Statue for Father, 1959; Anniversary, 1959; Obituary, 1959; Rain, Rain Go Away, 1959; Star Light, 1962; Founding Father, 1965; The Key, 1966; The Billiard Ball, 1967; Exile to Hell, 1968; Key Item, 1968; Feminine Intuition, 1969; The Greatest Asset, 1972; Mirror Image, 1972; Take a Match, 1972; Light Verse, 1973; Stranger in Paradise, 1974; That Thou Are Mindful of Him, 1974; The Life and Times of Multivac, 1975; The Bicentennial Man, 1976; Marching In, 1976; Old Fashioned, 1976; and The Tercentenary Incident, 1976.

107. The Ugly Little Boy. With **Robert Silverberg**. Published by Doubleday & Company, Garden City, New York, 1992. Hardcover.

108. Forward the Foundation. Published by Doubleday & Company, Garden City, New York, 1993. Hardcover.

109. The Positronic Man. With **Robert Silverberg**. Published by Doubleday & Company, Garden City, New York, 1993. Hardcover.

110. I, Robot - The Illustrated Screenplay. With

Harlan Ellison. Published by Warner Books, New York City, 1994. Softcover.

111. Gold: The Final Science Fiction Collection. Published by Harper Prism, New York City, 1995. Hardcover. This contains: Introduction by John Silbersack; Cal, 1990; Left to Right, 1987; Frustration, 1991; Hallucination, 1985; The Instability, 1989; Alexander the God, 1995; In the Canyon, 1990; Good-bye to Earth, 1989; Battle-Hymn, 1995; Feghoot and the Courts, 1986; Fault-Intolerant, 1990; Kid Brother, 1990; The Nations in Space, 1995; The Smile of the Chipper, 1988; Gold, 1991; The Longest Voyage, an essay, 1983; Inventing a Universe, an essay, 1990; Flying Saucers and Science Fiction, an essay, 1982; Invasion, an essay, 1995; The Science Fiction Blowgun, an essay, 1995; The Robot Chronicles, an essay, 1990; Golden Age Ahead, an essay, 1979; The All-Human Galaxy, an essay, 1983; Psychohistory, an essay, 1988; Science Fiction Series, an essay, 1986; Survivors, an essay, 1987; Nowhere!, an essay, 1983; Outsiders, Insiders, an essay, 1986; Science Fiction Anthologies, an essay, 1981; The Influence of Science Fiction, an essay, 1981; Women and Science Fiction, an essay, 1983; Religion and Science Fiction, an essay, 1984; Time-Travel, an essay, 1984; Plotting, an essay, 1989; Metaphor, an essay, 1989; Ideas, an essay, 1990; Suspense, an essay, 1991; Serials, an essay, 1980; The Name of Our Field, an essay, 1978; Hints, an essay, 1979; Writing for Young People, an essay, 1986; Names, an essay, 1984; Originality, an essay, 1986; Book Reviews, an essay, 1981; What Writers Go Through, an essay, 1981; Revisions, an essay, 1982; Irony, an essay, 1984; Plagiarism, an essay, 1985; Symbolism, an essay, 1985; Prediction, an essay, 1989; Best Seller, an essay, 1983; Pseudonyms, an essay, 1984; and Dialog, an essay, 1985.

112. Magic: The Final Fantasy Collection. Published by Harper Prism, New York City, 1996. Hardcover. Herein: To Your Health, 1989; The Critic on the Hearth, 1992; It's a Job, 1991; Baby, it's Cold Outside, 1991; The Time Traveler, 1990; Wine is a Mocker, 1990; The Mad Scientist, 1989; The Fable of the Three Princes, 1987; March Against the Foe, 1994; Northwestward, 1989; Prince Delightful and the Flameless Dragon, 1991; Magic, an essay, 1985; Concerning Tolkien, an essay, 1991; Sword and Sorcery, an essay, 1985; In Days of Old, an essay, 1985; Giants in the Earth, an essay, 1985; When Fantasy Became Fantasy, an essay, 1982; The Reluctant Critic, an essay, 1978; The Unicorn, an essay, 1986; Unknown, an essay, 1987; Extraordinary Voyages, an essay, 1978; Fairy Tales, an essay, 1985; Dear Judy-Lynn, an essay, 1986; Fantasy, an essay, 1984; Reading and Writing, an essay, 1990; The Right Answer, an essay, 1996; Ignorance in America, an essay, 1989; Knock Plastic, an essay, 1989; Lost in Non-Translation, an essay, 1974; Look Long Upon a Monkey, an essay, 1974; and Thinking About Thinking, an essay, 1975.

113. Robots and Murder. Published by The Science Fiction Book Club, Garden City, New York, 1999. Hardcover. An omnibus edition, this contains: The Robots of Dawn, 1983; The Naked Sun, 1957; and The Caves of Steel, 1954.

114. The Complete Adventures of Lucky Starr. Published by The Science Fiction Book Club, New York, 2001. Hardcover. Herein: David Starr: Space Ranger, 1952; Lucky Starr and the Pirates of the Asteroids, 1953; Lucky Starr and the Oceans of Venus, 1954; Lucky Starr and the Big Sun of Mercury, 1956; Lucky Starr and the Moons of Jupiter, 1957; and Lucky Starr and the Rings of Saturn, 1958.

115. The Empire Novels. Published by The Science Fiction Book Club, New York, 2002. Hardcover. This collects: The Stars Like Dust, 1951; The Currents of Space, 1952; and Pebble in the Sky, 1950.

116. The Return of the Black Widowers. Published by Carroll and Graf, New York City, 2003. Hardcover. Edited by Charles Ardai. Introduction by **Harlan Ellison**; The Acquisitive Chuckle, 1972; Early Sunday Morning, 1973; The Obvious Factor, 1973; The Iron Gem, 1974; To the Barest, 1979; Sixty Million Trillion Combinations, 1980; The Wrong House, 1984; The Redhead, 1984; Triple Devil, 1985; The Men Who Read **Isaac Asimov** by William Brittain, 2003; Northwestward, 2003; Yes, but Why, 2003; Lost in a Space Warp, 2003; Police at the Door, 2003; The Haunted Cabin, 2003; The Guest's Guest, 2003; The Woman in the Bar, 1980; and The Last Story by Charles Ardai, 2003; followed by an afterword by Asimov.

***

ANTHOLOGIES

1. The Hugo Winners. Published by Doubleday & Company, Garden City, New York, 1962. Hardcover. This contains: The Darfsteller by Walter M. Miller Jr. 1955; Allamagoosa by **Eric Frank Russell**, 1955; Exploration Team by Murray Leinster, 156; The Star by **Arthur C. Clarke**, 1955; Or All the Seas with Oysters by Avram Davidson, 1958; The Big Front Yard by Clifford D. Simak, 1958; The Hell Bound Train by Robert Bloch, 1958; Flowers for Algernon by Daniel Keyes, 1959; and The Longest Voyage by **Poul Anderson**, 1960.

2. Fifty Short Science Fiction Tales. With Groff Conklin. Published by Collier, New York City, 1963. Softcover. This contains: Introduction by Asimov; Introduction by Groff Conklin; Men Are Different by Alan Bloch, 1954; The Ambassadors by Anthony Boucher, 1952; The Weapon by Fredric Brown, 1951; Random Sample by T. P. Caravan, 1953; Oscar by Cleve Cartmill, 1941; The Mist by Peter Grainger writing as Peter Cartur, 1952; Teething Ring by James Causey, 1953; The Haunted Space Suit by **Arthur C. Clarke**, 1958; Stair Trick by Mildred Clingerman, 1952; Unwelcome Tenant by Roger Dee, 1950; The Mathematicians by Arthur Feldman, 1953; The Third Level by Jack Finney, 1950; Beautiful, Beautiful, Beautiful by Stuart Friedman, 1952; The Figure by Edward Grendon, 1947; The Rag Thing by **Donald A. Wollheim** writing as David Grinnell, 1951; The Good Provider by Marion Gross, 1952; Columbus Was a Dope by **Robert A. Heinlein**, 1947; Texas Week by Albert Hernhuter, 1954; Hilda by H. B. Hickey, 1952; The Choice by W. Hilton-Young, 1952; Not with a Bang by **Damon Knight**, 1950; The Altar at Midnight by C. M. Kornbluth, 1952; A Bad Day for Sales by **Fritz Leiber**, 1953; Who's Cribbing by Jack Lewis, 1953; Spectator Sport by John D. MacDonald, 1950; The Cricket Ball by Avro Manhattan, 1963; Double-Take by Winston K. Marks, 1953; Prolog by John P. McKnight; The Available Data on the Worp Reaction by Lion Miller, 1953; Narapoia by Alan Nelson, 1948; Tiger by the Tail by Alan E. Nouse, 1951; Counter Charm by Peter Phillips, 1951; The Fly by Arthur Porges, 1952; The Business As Usual by Mack Reynolds, 1952; Two Weeks in August by Frank M. Robinson, 1951; See? by Edward G. Robles Jr., 1954; Appointment at Noon by **Eric Frank Russell**, 1954; We Don't Want Any Trouble by James H. Schmitz, 1953; Built Down Logically by Howard Schoenfeld, 1951; An Egg a Month from All Over by Margaret St. Clair writing as Idris Seabright, 1952; The Perfect Woman by Robert Sheckley, 1953; The Hunters by Walt Sheldon, 1952; The Martian and the Magician by Evelyn E. Smith, 1952; Barney by Will Stanton, 1951; Talent by **Theodore Sturgeon**, 1953; Project Hush by William Tenn, 1954; The Great Judge by **A. E. van Vogt**, 1948; Emergency Landing by Ralph Williams, 1940; and Obviously Suicide by S. Fowler Wright, 1951.

3. Tomorrow's Children: Eighteen Tales of Fantasy and Science Fiction. Published by Doubleday & Company, Garden City, New York, 1966. Hardcover. Herein: Introduction by Asimov; No Life of Their Own by Clifford D. Simak, 1959; The Accountant by Robert Sheckley, 1954; Novice by James H. Schmitz, 1962; Child of Void by Margaret St. Clair, 1949; When the Bough Breaks by Henry Kuttner and C. L. Moore writing as Lewis Padgett; A Pail of Air by **Fritz Leiber**, 1951; Junior Achievement by Williams S. Burroughs writing as William M. Lee, 1962; Cabin Boy by **Damon Knight**, 1951; The Little Terror by Will F. Jenkins - Murray Leinster, 1953; Gilead by Zenna Henderson, 1954; The Menace from Earth by **Robert A. Heinlein**, 1957; The Wayward Cravat by Gertrude Friedberg, 1958; The Father Thing by **Philip K. Dick**, 1954; Star Bright by Mark Clifton, 1952; All Summer in a Day by **Ray Bradbury**, 1954; It's a Good Life by Jerome Bixby, 1953; The Place of the Gods by Stephen Vincent Benet, 1937; and The Ugly Little Boy by **Isaac Asimov**, 1958.

4. Where Do We Go From Here? Published by Doubleday & Company, Garden City, New York, 1971. Hardcover. This contains: Introduction by Asimov; A Martian Odyssey by Stanley G. Weinbaum, 1934; And He Built a Crooked House by **Robert A. Heinlein**, 1941; Surface Tension by **James Blish**, 1956; The Big Bounce by Walter S. Tevis, 1958; Night by **John W. Campbell** writing as Don A. Stuart, 1935; Heavy Planet by Milton A. Rothman, 1939; Proof by **Hal Clement**, 1942; A Subway Named Mobius by A. J. Deutsch, 1950; Country Doctor by William Morrison, 1953; The Holes Around Mars by Jerome Bixby, 1954; The Deep Range by **Arthur C. Clarke**, 1954; The Cave of Night by James E. Gunn, 1955; Omnilingual by H. Beam Piper, 1957; Dust Rag by **Hal Clement**, 1956; Neutron Star by Larry Niven, 1966; and Pate de Foie Gras by **Isaac Asimov**, 1956.

5. The Hugo Winners - Volume II. Published by Doubleday & Company, Garden City, New York, 1971. Hardcover. This contains: Weyr Search by **Anne McCaffrey**, 1967; Riders of the Purple Wage by Philip Jose Farmer, 1967; Gonna Roll the Bones by **Fritz Leiber**, 1967; I Have No Mouth, and I Must Scream by **Harlan Ellison**, 1967; The Dragon Masters by **Jack Vance**, 1962; The Beast That Shouted Love at the Heart of the World by **Harlan Ellison**, 1968; Nightwings by **Robert Silverberg**, 1968; The Sharing of the Flesh by **Poul Anderson**, 1968; Time Considered as a Helix of Semi-Precious Stones by **Samuel R. Delany**, 1968; Soldier, Ask Not by **Gordon R. Dickson**, 1964; The Last Castle by **Jack Vance**, 1966; No Truce with Kings by **Poul Anderson**, 1963; Repent, Harlequin! Said the Ticktockman, by **Harlan Ellison**, 1965; Neutron Star by Larry Niven, 1966; and A Few Words-Unexpectedly: Here I Am Again, an essay by **Isaac Asimov**.

6. Nebula Award Stories Eight. Published by Harper and Row, New York City, 1973. Hardcover. This contains: So Why Aren't We Rich?, an essay by **Isaac Asimov**; A Meeting with Medusa by **Arthur C. Clarke**, 1971; Shaffery Among the Immortals by **Frederik Pohl**, 1972; Patron of the Arts by William Rotsler, 1972; When It Changed by Joanna Russ, 1972; On the Downhill Side by **Harlan Ellison**, 1972; The Fifth Head of Cerberus by **Gene Wolfe**, 1972; When We Went to See the End of the World by **Robert Silverberg**, 1972; and Goat Song by **Poul Anderson**, 1972.

7. Before the Golden Age: A Science Fiction Anthology of the 1930s. Published by Doubleday & Company, Garden City, New York, 1974. Hardcover. Herein: The Parasite Planet by Stanley G. Weinbaum, 1935; The Brain Stealers of Mars by **John W. Campbell**, 1936; Other Eyes Watching, as essay by **John W. Campbell**, 1937; He Who Shrank by Henry Hasse, 1936; The Human Pets of Mars by Leslie Frances Stone, 1936; The Man Who Evolved, 1931; The Accursed Galaxy, 1935; and Devolution, 1936, by Edmond Hamilton; The Jameson Satellite by Neil R. Jones, 1931; Submicroscopic, 1931; and Awlo of Ulm, 1931 by Captain S. P. Meek; Tetrahedra of Space by P. Schuyler Miller, 1931; The World of the Red Sun by Clifford D. Simak, 1931; Tumithak of the Corridors, 1932; and Tumithak in Shawm, 1933, by Charles R. Tanner; The Moon Era by **Jack Williamson**, 1932; The Man Who Awoke by Laurence Manning, 1933; Colossus by Donald Wandrei, 1934; Born of the Sun by **Jack Williamson**, 1934; Sidewise in Time by Murray Leinster, 1934; Old Faithful by Raymond Z. Gallun, 1934; Minus Planet by John D. Clark, 1937; Past Present and Future by Nat Schachner, 1937; The Men and the Mirror by Ross Rocklynne, 1938; and Big Game by **Isaac Asimov**, 1974.

8. The Hugo Winners - Volume III. Published by Doubleday & Company, Garden City, New York, 1977. Hardcover. This contains: Introduction: Third Time Around by Asimov; Ship of Shadows by **Fritz Leiber**, 1969; Ill Met in Lankhmar by **Fritz Leiber**, 1970; Slow Sculpture by **Theodore Sturgeon**, 1970; The Queen of Air and Darkness by **Poul Anderson**, 1971; Inconstant Moon by Larry Niven,

Isaac Asimov

1971; The Word for World is Forest by **Ursula K. Le Guin**, 1972; Goat Song by **Poul Anderson**, 1972; The Meeting by **Frederik Pohl** and C. M. Kornbluth, 1972; Eurema's Dam by R. A. Lafferty, 1972; The Girl Who Was Plugged In by James Tiptree Jr., 1973; The Deathbird by **Harlan Ellison**, 1973; The Ones Who Walk Away from Omelas by **Ursula K. Le Guin**, 1973; A Song for Lya by George R. R. Martin, 1974; Adrift Just Off the Islets of Langerhans: Latitude 38 54' N Longitude 77 00" 13" W by **Harlan Ellison**, 1974; and The Hole Man by Larry Niven, 1974; followed by an Afterword by Asimov.

9. One Hundred Great Science Fiction Short-Short Stories. With Martin H. Greenberg and Joseph D. Olander. Published by Doubleday & Company, Garden City, New York, 1978. Hardcover. Herein: Introduction: The Science Fiction Blowgun by **Isaac Asimov**; A Loint of Paw by **Isaac Asimov**, 1957; The Advent of Channel Twelve by C. M. Kornbluth, 1958; Plaything by Larry Niven, 1974; The Misfortune Cookie by Charles E. Fritch, 1970; I Wish I May I Wish I Might by Bill Pronzini, 1973; FTA by George R. R. Martin, 1974; Trace by Jerome Bixby, 1961; The Ingenious Patriot by Ambrose Bierce, 1891; Zoo by Edward D. Hoch, 1958; The Destiny of Milton Gomrath by Alexei Panshin, 1967; The Devil and the Trombone by Martin Gardner, 1948; Upstart by Steven Utley, 1977; How It All Went by Gregory Benford, 1976; Harry Protagonist, Brain-Drainer by Richard Wilson, 1965; Peeping Tommy by Robert F. Young, 1965; Starting from Scratch by Robert Sheckley, 1953; Corrida by Roger Zelazny, 1968; Shall the Dust Praise Thee by **Damon Knight**, 1967; Bug Getter by R. Bretnor, 1960; The Deadly Mission of Phineas Snodgrass, an essay by **Frederik Pohl**, 1962; Fire Sale by Laurence M. Janifer, 1964; Safe at Any Speed by Larry Niven, 1967; The Masks by **James Blish**, 1959; Innocence by Joanna Russ, 1975; Kin by Richard Wilson, 1956; The Long Night by Ray Russell, 1961; Sanity Clause by Edward Wellen, 1975; If At First You Don't Succeed To Hell With It by Charles E. Fritch, 1972; The Question by Laurence M. Janifer and Donald E. Westlake, 1963; The Perfect Woman by Robert Sheckley, 1953; The System by Ben Bova, 1968; Exile to Hell by **Isaac Asimov**, 1968; Inaugural by Barry N. Malzberg and Bill Pronzini, 1976; Martha by Fred Saberhagen, 1976; Kindergarten by **Fritz Leiber**, 1963; Landscape with Sphinxes by Karen Anderson, 1962; The Happiest Day of Your Life by Bob Shaw, 1970; The Worlds of Monty Willson by William F. Nolan, 1971; Punch by **Frederik Pohl**, 1961; Doctor by Henry Slesar, 1978; The Man From When by Dannie Plachta, 1966; Crying Willow by Edward Roger, 1973; January 1975 by Barry N. Malzberg, 1975; Mail Supremacy by Hayford Pierce, 1975; Mistake by Larry Niven, 1976; Half Baked Publisher's Delight by Jeffrey S. Hudson and **Isaac Asimov**, 1974; Far From Home by Walter Tevis, 1958; Swords of Ifthan by James Sutherland, 1973; Argent Blood by Joe L. Hensley, 1967; Collector's Fever by Roger Zelazny, 1964; Sign at the End of the Universe by Duane Ackerson, 1974; Stubborn by Stephen Goldin, 1972; The Re-creation by Robert E. Toomey Jr., 1972; The Better Man by Ray Russell, 1966; Oom by Martin Gardner, 1951; Merchant by Henry Slesar, 1978; Don't Fence Me In by Richard Wilson, 1956; The Die Hard by **Alfred Bester**, 1958; Eripmav by **Damon Knight**, 1958; Feeding Time by Robert Sheckley, 1953; The Voice from the Curious Cube by Nelson Bond, 1937; I'm Going to Get You by F. M. Busby, 1974; The Room by Ray Russell, 1961; Dry Spell by Bill Pronzini, 1970; Bohassian Learns by William Rotsler, 1971; Star Bride by Anthony Boucher, 1951; Latest Feature by Maggie Nadler, 1972; Chief by Henry Slesar, 1960; After You've Stood on the Log at the Center of the Universe What is There Left to Do? by Grant Carrington, 1974; Maid to Measure by **Damon Knight**, 1964; Eyes Do More Than See by **Isaac Asimov**, 1965; Thang by Martin Gardner, 1948; How Now Purple Cow by Bill Pronzini, 1969; Revival Meeting by Dannie Plachta, 1969; Prototaph by Keith Laumer, 1966; The Rocket of 1955 by C. M. Kornbluth, 1939; Science Fiction for Telepaths by E. Michael Blake, 1997; Kindergarten by James E. Gunn, 1970; A Little Knowledge by Paul Dellinger, 1975; A Cup of Hemlock by Lee Killough, 1978; Present Perfect by Thomas F. Monteleone, 1974; A Lot to Learn by Robert T. Kurosaka, 1978; The Amphibious Cavalry Gap by James E. Thompson, 1974; Not Counting Bridges by Robert L. Fish, 1963; The Man Inside by Bruce McAllister, 1969; The Mars Stone by Paul Bond, 1974; Source Material by Mildred Downey Broxon, 1974; The Compleat Consummators by Alan E. Nourse, 1964; Examination Day by Henry Slesar, 1958; The Man Who Could Turn Back the Clock by Ralph Milne Farley, 1950; Patent Rights by Daniel A. Darlington, 1974; The Sky's an Oyster, the Stars are Pearls by Dave Bischoff, 1975; Alien Cornucopia by Walt Liebscher, 1959; The Last Paradox by Edward D. Hoch, 1958; Course of Empire by Richard Wilson, 1956; Synchronicity by James E. Thompson, 1978; Sweet Dreams Melissa by Stephen Goldin, 1968; The Man on Top by R. Bretnor, 1951; and Rejection Slip by K. W. MacAnn, 1978.

10. Isaac Asimov Presents the Great SF Stories 1: 1939. With Martin H. Greenberg. Published by DAW Books, New York City, 1979. Softcover. DAW Collector's Book 329. Herein: Introduction by Martin H. Greenberg; I, Robot by Otto Binder writing as Eando Binder, 1939; The Strange Flight of Richard Clayton by Robert Bloch, 1939; Trouble with Water by H. L. Gold, 1939; Cloak of Aesir by **John W. Campbell** writing as Don A. Stuart, 1939; The Day Is Done by Lester del Rey, 1939; The Ultimate Catalyst by Eric Temple Bell writing as John Taine, 1939; The Gnarly Man by L. Sprague de Camp, 1939; Black Destroyer by **A. E. van Vogt**, 1939; Greater Than Gods by **C. L. Moore**, 1939; Trends by **Isaac Asimov**, 1939; The Blue Giraffe by L. Sprague de Camp, 1939; The Misguided Halo by Henry Kuttner, 1939; Heavy Planet by Milton A. Rothman, 1939; Life-Line by **Robert A. Heinlein**, 1939; Ether Breather by **Theodore Sturgeon**, 1939; Pilgrimage by Nelson Bond, 1939; Rust by Joseph E. Kelleam; The Four-Sided Triangle by William F. Temple, 1939; Star Bright by **Jack Williamson**, 1939; and Misfit by **Robert A. Heinlein**, 1939.

11. Isaac Asimov Presents the Great SF Stories 2: 1940. With Martin H. Greenberg. Published by DAW Books, New York City, 1979. Softcover. DAW Collector's Book 350. This contains: Introduction by Martin H. Greenberg; The Dwindling Sphere by Willard Hawkins, 1940; The Impossible Highway by Oscar J. Friend, 1940; Old Man Mulligan by P.

Schuyler Miller, 1940; Farewell to the Master by Harry Bates, 1940; The Automatic Pistol by **Fritz Leiber**, 1940; Hindsight by **Jack Williamson**, 1940; Postpaid to Paradise by Robert Arthur, 1940; Into the Darkness by Ross Rocklynne, 1940; Dark Mission by Lester del Rey, 1940; It; and Butyl and the Breather by **Theodore Sturgeon**, 1940; Vault of the Beast by **A. E. van Vogt**, 1940; The Warrior Race; and The Exalted by L. Sprague de Camp, 1940; and Strange Playfellow by **Isaac Asimov**, 1940.

12. The Science Fictional Solar System. With Martin H. Greenberg and Charles G. Waugh. Published by Harper and Row, New York City, 1979. Hardcover. This anthology contains: Introduction by Asimov; The Comet, the Cairn and the Capsule by Duncan Lunan, 1972; The Weather on the Sun by Theodore L. Thomas, 1970; Brightside Crossing by Alan E. Nourse, 1956; Prospector's Special by Robert Sheckley, 1959; Hop-Friend by Terry Carr, 1962; Barnacle Bull by **Poul Anderson** writing as Winston P. Sanders, 1960; Bridge by **James Blish**, 1952; Saturn Rising by **Arthur C. Clarke**, 1961; The Snowbank Orbit by **Fritz Leiber**, 1962; One Sunday on Neptune by Alexei Panshin, 1969; Wait It Out by Larry Niven, 1968; Nikita Eisenhower Jones by Robert F. Young, 1960; and Waterclap by **Isaac Asimov**, 1970.

13. The Thirteen Crimes of Science Fiction. With Martin H. Greenberg and Charles G. Waugh. Published by Doubleday & Company, Garden City, New York, 1979. Hardcover. Herein: The Universe of Science Fiction, an essay by **Isaac Asimov**; The Ipswich Phial by Randall Garrett, 1976; Coup de Grace by **Jack Vance**, 1958; War Game by **Philip K. Dick**, 1959; Time in Advance by William Tenn, 1956; The Detweiler Boy by Tom Reamy, 1977; Second Game by Charles V. deVet and Katherine MacLean, 1958; The Ceaseless Stone by Avram Davidson, 1975; The Green Car by William F. Temple, 1957; ARM by Larry Niven, 1975; Mouthpiece by Edward Wellen, 1974; Time Exposures by **Wilson Tucker**, 1971; How 2 by Clifford D. Simak, 1954; and The Singing Bell by **Isaac Asimov**, 1955.

14. The Future in Question. With Martin H. Greenberg and Joseph D. Olander. Published by Fawcett Crest, New York City, 1980. Softcover. This contains: The Nature of the Title, an introduction by Asimov; What's it Like Out There? by Edmond Hamilton, 1952; Who Can Replace a Man? by **Brian W. Aldiss**, 1958; What Have I Done? by Mark Clifton, 1952; Who's There? by **Arthur C. Clarke**, 1958; Can You Feel Anything When I Do This? by Robert Sheckley, 1969; What's Become of Screwloose? by Ron Goulart, 1970; Houston, Houston Do You Read? by James Tiptree Jr., 1976; Where Have You Been Billy Boy, Billy Boy? by **Kate Wilhelm**, 1971; If All Men Were Brothers Would You Let One Marry Your Sister? by **Theodore Sturgeon**, 1967; Will You Wait? by **Alfred Bester**, 1959; Who Goes There? by **John W. Campbell**, 1938; An Eye for a What? by **Damon Knight**, 1957; I Plingot Who You? by **Frederik Pohl**, 1959; Will You Walk a Little Faster? by William Tenn, 1951; Who's In Charge Here? by **James Blish**, 1962; The Last Question by **Isaac Asimov**, 1956; and Why? by **Robert Silverberg**, 1957.

15. Isaac Asimov Presents the Great SF Stories 3: 1941. With Martin H. Greenberg. Published by DAW Books, New York City, 1980. Softcover. DAW Collector's Book 377. Herein: Introduction by Martin H. Greenberg; Mechanical Mice by **Eric Frank Russell** writing as Maurice G. Hugi, 1941; Shottle Bop by **Theodore Sturgeon**, 1941; The Rocket of 1955 by C. M. Kornbluth, 1941; Microcosmic God by **Theodore Sturgeon**, 1941; Jay Score by **Eric Frank Russell**, 1941; Time Wants a Skeleton by Ross Rocklynne, 1941; The Words of Guru by C. M. Kornbluth, 1941; The Seesaw by **A. E. van Vogt**, 1941; Armageddon by Fredric Brown, 1941; Adam and Eve by **Alfred Bester**, 1941; Solar Plexus by **James Blish**, 1941; Nightfall by **Isaac Asimov**, 1941; A Gnome There Was by Henry Kuttner and **C. L. Moore** writing as Lewis Padgett, 1941; Snulbug by Anthony Boucher, 1941; and Hereafter, Inc. by Lester del Rey, 1941.

16. Who Done It? With Alice Laurance. Published by Houghton Mifflin, Boston, 1980. Hardcover. Stories by: John Ball; Robert Bloch; Dorothy Salisbury Davis; Rosemary Gatenby; Michael Gilbert; Elizabeth Gresham; Joe L. Hensley; Edward D. Hoch; R. A. Lafferty; John D. MacDonald; Florence Mayberry; Patricia Moyes; Ruth Rendell; Rachael Cosgrove Payes; Bill Pronzini; Lawrence Treat; and Janwillem van de Wetering.

17. Space Mail. With Martin H. Greenberg and Joseph D. Olander. Published by Fawcett Crest, New York City, 1980. Softcover. Herein: Introduction by Asimov; Letters for Laura by Mildred Clingerman, 1954; Itch on the Bull Run by Sharon Webb, 1979; Letter to a Phoenix by Fredric Brown, 1949; Letter to Ellen by Chan Davis, 1947; Flowers for Algernon by Daniel Keyes, 1959; The Second Kind of Loneliness by George R. R. Martin, 1972; The Prisoner by Christopher Anvil, 1956; One Rejection Too Many by Patricia Nurse, 1978; Space Opera by Ray Russell, 1961; The Invasion of the Terrible Titans by William Sambrot, 1959; That Only a Mother, 1948; and The Lonely, 1963 by Judith Merril; Who's Cribbing? by Jack Lewis, 1953; Computers Don't Argue by **Gordon R. Dickson**, 1965; Dear Pen Pal, 1949; and Secret Unattainable, 1942, by **A. E. van Vogt**; Damn Shame by Dean R. Lambe, 1979; The Trap by Howard Fast, 1960; Request for Proposal by Anthony R. Lewis, 1972; He Walked Around the Horses by H. Beam Piper, 1948; After the Great Space War by Barry N. Malzberg, 1974; I Never Ast No Favors by C. M. Kornbluth, 1954; and The Power by Murray Leinster, 1945.

18. Microcosmic Tales: 100 Wondrous Science Fiction Short-Short Stories. With Martin H. Greenberg and Joseph D. Olander. Published by Taplinger, New York City, 1980. Herein: Introduction: A Quick Dip by Asimov; Lost and Found by Phyllis Eisenstein, 1978; Pattern, 1954; Answer, 1954; Nightmare in Time, 1962; and Blood, 1955, by Fredric Brown; Renaissance Man by T.E.D. Klein, 1974; Nellthu, 1955; Mr. Lupescu, 1945; and A Shape in Time, 1970, by Anthony Boucher; Useful Phrases for the Tourist by Joanna Russ, 1972; Who Else Could I Count On by Manly Wade Wellman, 1963; Love Story, 1957; and Displaced Person,

Isaac Asimov

1948, by **Eric Frank Russell**; Mattie Harris, Galactic Spy by Rachel Cosgrove Payes, 1974; Changeover by Juleen Brantingham, 1980; Earthbound by Lester del Rey, 1963; Deflation 2001 by Bob Shaw, 1972; The Last Answer, 1980; Dreamworld, 1955; Buy Jupiter, 1958; and True Love, 1977, by **Isaac Asimov**; Package Deal, 1980; Shell Shock, 1974; and Taste of Battle, 1980, by Donald Franson; Lycanthrope by Norman E. Hartman, 1976; Gemini 74; Put Your Head Upon My Knee, 1967; and Upon My Soul, 1965, by Jack Ritchie; Geever's Flight by Charles E. Fritch, 1965; Discovering a New Earth by Robert Mattingly, 1980; Varieties of Technological Experience, 1978; and Linkage, 1973, by Barry N. Malzberg; Listen Love by George Zebrowski and Jack Dann, 1971; That Strain Again by Charles Sheffield, 1980; Take Me To Your Leader by George Henry Smith, 1980; The Big Fix by Robert F. Decker, 1980; Speed of the Cheetah, Roar of the Lion, 1975; A Fragment of Manuscript, 1980; The Final Battle, 1970; and The Finest Hunter in the World, 1970, by **Harry Harrison**; Just Call Me Irish, 1958; Hometown, 1957, by Richard Wilson; Pulpworld by R. K. Lyon, 1980; The Other Tiger, 1953; and Take a Deep Breath, 1957, by **Arthur C. Clarke**; Little William by Patricia Matthews, 1975; Steel by Alan Brennert, 1977; And So On and So On by James Tiptree Jr., 1971; Do Androids Dream of Electric Love by Walt Liebscher, 1972; Dog Star, 1956; Devil to Pay, 1957; and Dead End, 1957, by Mack Reynolds; The Great Judge, 1948; and The Rat and the Snake, 1971, by **A. E. van Vogt**; 2001: A Love Story by Paul Dellinger, 1976; Hadj, 1956; and The Voice in the Garden, 1967, by **Harlan Ellison**; Good Morning, This is the Future, 1962; The Old Man, 1980; The Penalty, 1962; and Speak, 1965, by Henry Slesar; Murder in the Nth Degree, 1980; and The Diana Syndrome, 1980, by R. A. Montana; The Burning, 1960; and Emergency Rations, 1953, by Theodore R. Cogswell; One Small Step by Eric Vinicoff and Marcia Martin, 1980; Paths by Edward Bryant, 1973; Woman's Work by Garen Drussai, 1956; Death Double by William F. Nolan, 1963; Tag by Helen Urban, 1980; The Nature of the Place by **Robert Silverberg**, 1963; The Game of the Name by Alice Laurance, 1980; Down the Digestive Tract by Robert Sheckley, 1971; Drawing Board by Charles Spano, 1980; Your Cruel Face by Craig Strete, 1976; The Best Laid Plans by Rick Conley, 1980; Life by Dennis R. Caro, 1980; Exile in Lakehurst by Robert Payes, 1980; The Bait, 1973; and X Marks the Pedwalk, 1963, by **Fritz Leiber**; The Humanic Complex by Ray Russell, 1978; Friends? by Roberta Ghidalia, 1973; The Quest of the Infidel by Sherwood Springer, 1980; Legal Rights for Germs by Joe Patrouch, 1977; Exile's Greeting by Roland Green, 1980; The Biography Project by H. L. Gold, 1951; The Grapes of the Rath by Jan Howard Finder, 1980; What I Did During My Park Vacation by Ruth Berman, 1980; The Boy with Five Fingers by James Gunn, 1953; The King of Beasts by Philip Jose Farmer, 1964; A Clone at Last by Bill Pronzini and Barry N. Malzberg, 1978; The Mission by Arthur Tofte, 1980; Proof by F. M. Busby, 1972; The Reunion by Paul J. Nahin, 1979; The Futile Flight of John Arthur Benn by Richard Wilson writing as Edward Halibut, 1956; Servants of the Lord by James Stevens, 1979; The Pill by Maggie Nadler, 1972; Rotating Cylinders and the Possibility of Global Causality Violation by Larry Niven, 1977; and If Eve Had Failed to Conceive by Edward Wellen, 1974.

19. Isaac Asimov Presents the Great SF Stories 4: 1942. With Martin H. Greenberg. Published by DAW Books, New York City, 1980. Softcover. DAW Collector's Book 405. Herein: The Star Mouse by Fredric Brown, 1942; The Wings of Night by Lester Del Rey, 1942; QRM -Interplanetary by George O. Smith, 1942; Asylum by **A. E. van Vogt**, 1942; Mimic by **Donald A. Wollheim**, 1942; Barrier by Anthony Boucher, 1942; Proof by **Hal Clement**, 1942; The Push of a Finger by **Alfred Bester**, 1942; Co-operate - or Else! by **A. E. van Vogt**, 1942; The Twonky by Henry Kuttner and **C. L. Moore** writing as Lewis Padgett, 1942; and Foundation by **Isaac Asimov**, 1942.

20. The Seven Deadly Sins of Science Fiction. With Martin H. Greenberg and Charles G. Waugh. Published by Fawcett Crest, New York City, 1980. Softcover. This contains: Introduction by Martin H. Greenberg; Sail 25 by **Jack Vance**, 1962; Divine Madness by Roger Zelazny, 1966; The Hook, the Eye and the Whip by Michael G. Coney, 1974; The Midas Plague, 1954; The Man Who Ate the World, 1956, by **Frederik Pohl**; Margin of Profit by **Poul Anderson**, 1956; Peeping Tom by Judith Merril, 1954; The Invisible Man Murder Case by Henry Slesar, 1958; and Galley Slave by **Isaac Asimov**, 1957.

21. Isaac Asimov's Science Fiction Treasury. With Martin H. Greenberg and Joseph D. Olander. Published by Bonanza Books, New York City, 1980. Hardcover. Herein: The Nature of the Title, an introduction by Asimov; What's it Like Out There? by Edmond Hamilton, 1952; Who Can Replace a Man? by **Brian W. Aldiss**, 1958; What Have I Done? by Mark Clifton, 1952; Who's There? by **Arthur C. Clarke**, 1958; Can You Feel Anything When I Do This? by Robert Sheckley, 1969; What's Become of Screwloose? by Ron Goulart, 1970; Houston, Houston Do You Read? by James Tiptree Jr., 1976; Where Have You Been Billy Boy, Billy Boy? by **Kate Wilhelm**, 1971; If All Men Were Brothers Would You Let One Marry Your Sister? by **Theodore Sturgeon**, 1967; Will You Wait? by **Alfred Bester**, 1959; Who Goes There? by **John W. Campbell**, 1938; An Eye for a What? by **Damon Knight**, 1957; I Plinglot Who You? by **Frederik Pohl**, 1959; Will You Walk a Little Faster? by William Tenn, 1951; Who's In Charge Here? by **James Blish**, 1962; The Last Question by **Isaac Asimov**, 1956; Why? by **Robert Silverberg**, 1957; Letters for Laura by Mildred Clingerman, 1954; Itch on the Bull Run by Sharon Webb, 1979; Letter to a Phoenix by Fredric Brown, 1949; Letter to Ellen by Chan Davis, 1947; Flowers for Algernon by Daniel Keyes, 1959; The Second Kind of Loneliness by George R. R. Martin, 1972; The Prisoner by Christopher Anvil, 1956; One Rejection Too Many by Patricia Nurse, 1978; Space Opera by Ray Russell, 1961; The Invasion of the Terrible Titans by William Sambrot, 1959; That Only a Mother, 1948; and The Lonely, 1963 by Judith Merril; Who's Cribbing? by Jack Lewis, 1953; Computers Don't Argue by **Gordon R. Dickson**, 1965; Dear Pen Pal, 1949; and Secret Unattainable, 1942, by **A. E. van Vogt**; Damn Shame by Dean R. Lambe, 1979; The

Trap by Howard Fast, 1960; Request for Proposal by Anthony R. Lewis, 1972; He Walked Around the Horses by H. Beam Piper, 1948; After the Great Space War by Barry N. Malzberg, 1974; I Never Ast No Favors by C. M. Kornbluth, 1954; and The Power by Murray Leinster, 1945.

22. The Future I. With Martin H. Greenberg and Joseph D. Olander. Published by Fawcett Crest, New York City, 1981. Softcover. Herein: Introduction: First Person by Asimov; Love is the Plan the Plan is Death by James Tiptree Jr., 1973; Closed Sicilian by Barry N. Malzberg, 1973; Transit of Earth by **Arthur C. Clarke**, 1971; Bernie the Faust by William Tenn, 1963; Ishmael in Love by **Robert Silverberg**, 1970; The Secret Place by Richard McKenna, 1966; The Large Ant by Howard Fast, 1960; Fear Hound by Katherine MacLean, 1968; Positively the Last Pact with the Devil by Janet Asimov writing as J. O. Jeppson, 1976; Rejoice, Rejoice, We Have No Choice by Terry Carr, 1974; Air Raid by John Varley writing as Herb Boehm, 1977; The Pi Man by **Alfred Bester**, 1959; Prototaph by Keith Laumer, 1966; Black Charlie by **Gordon R. Dickson**, 1954; With Morning Comes Mistfall by George R. R. Martin, 1973; End as a World by Floyd F. Wallace, 1955; The Mathenauts by Norman Kagan, 1964; How Can We Sink When We Can Fly by Alexei Panshin, 1971; and The Red Queen's Race by **Isaac Asimov**, 1949; followed by an afterword, Speaking from the Center by Barry N. Malzberg.

23. Isaac Asimov Presents the Great SF Stories 5: 1943. With Martin H. Greenberg. Published by DAW Books, New York City, 1981. Softcover. DAW Collector's Book 426. This contains: Introduction by Martin H. Greenberg; The Cave by P. Schuyler Miller, 1943; The Halfling by Leigh Brackett, 1943; Mimsy Were the Borogoves, 1943; The Proud Robot, 1943; and The Iron Standard, 1943, by Henry Kuttner and **C. L. Moore** writing as Lewis Padgett; Q.U.R. by Anthony Boucher, 1943; Clash by Night by **C. L. Moore** and Henry Kuttner writing as Lawrence O'Donnell, 1943; Exile by Edmond Hamilton, 1943; Daymare by Fredric Brown, 1943; Doorway into Time by **C. L. Moore**, 1943; The Storm by **A. E. Van Vogt**, 1943; and Symbiotica by **Eric Frank Russell**, 1943.

24. Catastrophes! With Martin H. Greenberg and Charles G. Waugh. Published by Fawcett Crest, New York City, 1981. Softcover. Herein: Foreword by Asimov; Universe Destroyed, an essay by Asimov, 1981; Sun Destroyed, an essay by Asimov, 1981; Earth Destroyed, an essay by Asimov, 1981; The Custodian by William Tenn, 1953; Phoenix by Clark Ashton Smith, 1954; King of the Hill by Chad Oliver; The New Atlantis by **Ursula K. Le Guin**; Dark Benediction by Walter M. Miller Jr.; No Other Gods by Edward Wellen, 1972; The Wine Has Been Left Open Too Long and the Memory Has Gone Flat by **Harlan Ellison**, 1976; Stars Won't You Hide Me by Ben Bova, 1966; Judgement Day by Lloyd Biggle Jr., 1958; Run from the Fire by **Harry Harrison**, 1975; Requiem by Edmond Hamilton, 1962; At the Core by Larry Niven, 1966; A Pail of Air by **Fritz Leiber**, 1951; History Lesson by **Arthur C. Clarke**, 1949; Seeds of the Dusk by Raymond Z. Gallun, 1938; Last Night of Summer by Alfred Coppel, 1954; **The**

Store of the Worlds by Robert Sheckley, 1959; How It Was When the Past Went Away by **Robert Silverberg**, 1969; Shark Ship - also known as Reap the Dark Tide by C. M. Kornbluth, 1958; and The Last Trump by **Isaac Asimov**, 1955; followed by an afterword by Asimov.

25. Isaac Asimov Presents the Best Science Fiction of the 19th Century. With Martin H. Greenberg and Charles G. Waugh. Published by Beaufort Books, New York City, 1981. Hardcover. This contains: The First Century of Science Fiction by Asimov; The Sandman by E. T. A. Hoffman, 1816; The Mortal Immortal by Mary Wollstonecraft Shelley, 1833; The Clock that Went Backward by Edward Page Mitchell, 1881; Into the Sun by Robert Duncan Milne, 1882; A Tale of Negative Gravity by Frank R. Stockton, 1884; The Shapes by J. H. Rosny aine, 1968; To Whom this May Come by Edward Bellamy, 1889; The Thames Valley Catastrophe by Grant Allen, 1897; The Lizard by C. J. Cutcliffe Hyne, 1898; A Thousand Deaths by Jack London, 1899; In the Abyss by **H. G. Wells**, 1896; The Great Keinplatz Experiment by Sir Arthur Conan Doyle, 1885; The Horla, or Modern Ghosts by Guy de Maupassant, 1886; Rappaccini's Daughter by Nathaniel Hawthorne, 1844; and A Descent into the Maelstrom by Edgar Allan Poe, 1841.

26. The Seven Cardinal Virtues of Science Fiction. With Martin H. Greenberg and Charles G. Waugh. Published by Fawcett Crest, New York City, 1981. Softcover. Herein: Introduction by Martin H. Greenberg; Superiority by **Arthur C. Clarke**, 1951; Whosawhatsa? by Jack Wodhams, 1967; Riding the Torch by Norman Spinrad, 1974; The Nail and the Oracle by **Theodore Sturgeon**, 1965; Jean Dupres by **Gordon R. Dickson**, 1970; Nuisance Value by **Eric Frank Russell**, 1957; The Sons of Prometheus by Alexei Panshin, 1966; and The Ugly Little Boy by **Isaac Asimov**, 1958.

27. Fantastic Creatures: An Anthology of Fantasy and Science Fiction. With Martin H. Greenberg and Charles G. Waugh. Published by Franklin Watts, New York City, 1981. Hardcover. This contains: Introduction by Asimov; The Smallest Dragonboy by **Anne McCaffrey**, 1973; The Botticelli Horror by Lloyd Biggle Jr., 1960; Kid Cardula by Jack Ritchie, 1978; The Man from P. I. G. by **Harry Harrison**, 1967; Flight Over XP-637 by Craig Sayre, 1980; The Bees from Borneo by Will H. Gray, 1931; The Anglers of Arz by Roger Dee, 1953; and The Game of Rat and Dragon by Cordwainer Smith.

28. Travels Through Time. With Martin H. Greenberg and Charles G. Waugh. Raintree Reading Series. Published by Raintree Publishers, Milwaukee, Wisconsin, 1981. Hardcover. Herein: Introduction by Asimov; The Assassin by **Robert Silverberg**, 1957; The Innocents' Refuge by Theodore L. Thomas, 1957; The Good Provider by Marion Gross, 1952; The Immortal Bard by **Isaac Asimov**, 1954; and The Figure by Edward Grendon, 1947.

29. Thinking Machines. With Martin H. Greenberg and Charles G. Waugh. Raintree Reading Series. Published by Raintree Publishers, Milwaukee, Wisconsin, 1981. Hardcover. This contains:

Isaac Asimov

Introduction by Asimov; Prototaph by Keith Laumer, 1966; A Bad Day for Sales by **Fritz Leiber**, 1953; Answer by Fredric Brown, 1954; Road Stop by David mason, 1963; and The Nine Billion Names of God by **Arthur C. Clarke**, 1953.

30. Wild Inventions. With Martin H. Greenberg and Charles G. Waugh. Raintree Reading Series. Published by Raintree Publishers, Milwaukee, Wisconsin, 1981. Hardcover. This contains: Introduction by Asimov; The Postponed Cure by Stan Nodvik, 1974; Man of Distinction by Michael Shaara, 1956; Speed of the Cheetah, Roar of the Lion by **Harry Harrison**, 1975; and Wapshott's Demon by **Frederik Pohl**, 1956.

31. After the End. With Martin H. Greenberg and Charles G. Waugh. Raintree Reading Series. Published by Raintree Publishers, Milwaukee, Wisconsin, 1981. Hardcover. This contains: Introduction by Asimov; The Wheel by John Wyndham, 1952; There Will Come Soft Rains by **Ray Bradbury**, 1950; Maybe We Got Something by Josef Berger, 1959; and If I Forget Thee, Oh Earth..., by **Arthur C. Clarke**, 1951.

32. The Twelve Crimes of Christmas. With Carol-Lynn Rossel Waugh and Martin H. Greenberg. Published by Avon Books, New York City, 1981. Softcover. Herein: Introduction: Noel, Noel by Asimov; Christmas Party by Rex Stout, 1956; Do Your Christmas Shoplifting Early by Robert Somerlott, 1965; The Necklace of Pearls by Dorothy L. Sayers, 1933; Father Chrumlish Celebrates Christmas by Alice Scanlan Reach, 1967; The Christmas Masque by S. S. Rafferty, 1976; The Dauphin's Doll by Ellery Queen, 1948; By the Chimney with Care by Nick O'Donohoe, 1978; The Problem of the Christmas Steeple by Edward D. Hoch, 1976; Death on Christmas Eve by Stanley Ellin, 1950; The Adventure of the Unique Dickensians by August Derleth, 1968; Blind Man's Hood by John Dickson Carr, 1940; and The Thirteenth Day of Christmas by **Isaac Asimov**, 1977.

33. Isaac Asimov Presents the Great SF Stories 6: 1944. With Martin H. Greenberg. Published by DAW Books, New York City, 1981. Softcover. DAW Collector's Book 461. Herein: Introduction by Martin H. Greenberg; Invariant by John R. Pierce, 1944; When the Bough Breaks by Henry Kuttner and **C. L. Moore** writing as Lewis Padgett, 1944; No Woman Born by **C. L. Moore**, 1944; Far Centaurus by **A. E. Van Vogt**, 1944; Deadline by Cleve Cartmill, 1944; The Veil of Astellar by Leigh Brackett, 1944; Sanity by **Fritz Leiber**, 1944; City, 1944; Huddling Place, 1944; and Desertion, 1944, by Clifford D. Simak; Arena by Fredric Brown, 1944; Kindness by Lester del Rey, 1944; and Killdozer by **Theodore Sturgeon**, 1944.

34. Miniature Mysteries: One Hundred Malicious Little Mystery Stories. With Martin H. Greenberg and Joseph D. Olander. Published by Taplinger, New York City, 1981. Hardcover. Herein: Six Words by Lew Gillis, 1978; The Little Things by **Isaac Asimov**, 1975; A Matter of Life and Death by Bill Pronzini and Barry N. Malzberg, 1974; Perfect Pigeon by Carroll Mayers, 1978; The Cop Who Hated Flowers by Henry Slesar, 1966; Trick or Treat by Judith Garner, 1975; Twice Around the Block by Lawrence Treat, 1956; An Easy Score by Al Nussbaum, 1973; The Good Lord Will Provide by Lawrence Treat and Charles M. Plotz, 1973; Boomerang by Harold Q. Masur, 1964; The Way It's Supposed to Be by Elsin Ann Graffam, 1976; Thank You, Mr. Thurston by Ed Dumonte, 1963; Funeral Music by Francis M. Nevins Jr., 1975; Murder Will Out by Edward Wellen, 1971; An Insignificant Crime by Maxine O'Callaghan, 1976; The Stray Bullet by Gary Brandner, 1971; A Night Out with the Boys by Elsin Ann Graffam, 1974; Office Party by Mary Bradford, 1976; Comes the Dawn by Michael Kurland, 1966; Acting Job by Richard Deming, 1960; The Last Smile by Henry Slesar, 1961; Grief Counselor by Julie Smith, 1978; The Best Place by A. F. Oreshnik, 1974; Dead End by Alvin S. Flick, 1977; Pure Rotten by John Lutz, 1977; Grounds for Divorce by James Holding, 1973; Inside Out by Barry N. Malzberg, 1978; The Bell, 1978; and The Box, 1976, by Isak Romun; The Physician and the Opium Fiend by Edward D. Hoch writing as R. L. Stevens, 1971; Over the Borderline by Jeff Sweet, 1973; It Could Happen to You by John Lutz, 1975; Class Reunion by Charles Boeckman, 1973; The Way It Is Now by Elaine Slater, 1967; The Hot Rock by James McKimmey, 1971; A Puff of Orange Smoke by Lael J. Littke, 1972; The Chicken Player by Joe L. Hensley, 1967; Nothing but Bad News by Henry Slesar, 1974; The Quick and the Dead by Helen McCloy, 1964; An Exercise in Insurance by James Holding, 1964; The Old Heap by Alvin S. Fick, 1977; As the Wheel Turns by Jane Speed, 1966; Knit One Purl Two by Thomasina Weber, 1970; The Paternal Instinct by Al Nussbaum, 1968; What Kind Person Are You by Bill Pronzini and Barry N. Malzberg, 1977; Shatter Proof by Jack Ritchie, 1960; Out of Order by Carl Henry Rathjen, 1963; The Handy Man by Marion M. Markham, 1976; Nightmare by Elaine Slater, 1963; Recipe for Revenge by Jane Speed, 1974; Sweet Fever by Bill Pronzini, 1976; Two Postludes by Isak Romun, 1976; The Magnum by Jack Ritchie, 1973; A Deal in Diamonds by Edward D. Hoch writing as R. L. Stevens, 1975; The Last Day of Shooting by Dion Henderson, 1967; Blisters in May by Jack Ritchie, 1965; The Collector by Patricia M. Mathews, 1975; House Call by Elsin Ann Graffam, 1970; The Adventure of the Blind Alley by Edward Wellen, 1978; The Unfriendly Neighbor by Al Nussbaum, 1972; A Feline Felony by Lael J. Littke, 1967; Don't I Know You by Henry Slesar, 1968; Meet Mr. Murder by Morris Hershman, 1968; Co-Incidence by Edward D. Hoch, 1956; Alma by Al Nussbaum, 1972; Grand Exit by Leo R. Ellis, 1969; Hunting Ground by A. F. Oreshnik, 1975; The Big Trip by Elsin Ann Graffam, 1971; Dutch by William F. Nolan, 1958; Loaded Quest by Thomasina Weber, 1973; Hand in Glove by James Holding, 1965; The Slantwise Scales of Justice by Phyllis Ann Karr, 1974; Child on a Journey by Fred S. Tobey, 1973; The Witches in the Closet by Anne Chamberlain, 1944; Setup by Jack Ritchie, 1972; A Very Rare Disease by Henry Slesar, 1958; Two Small Vials by Elsin Ann Graffam, 1977; Sweet Remembrance by Betty Ren Wright, 1968; A Dip in the Poole by Bill Pronzini, 1970; Doctor's Orders by John F. Suter, 1959; Mrs. Twiller Takes a Trip by Lael J. Littke, 1970; Such a Lovely Day by Penelope Wallace, 1964; Matinee by Ruth Wissmann, 1977; Big Mouth by Robert Edmond Alter, 1968; The

Weathered Board by Alvin S. Fick, 1977; Lot 721/XY258 by Edward D. Hoch writing as R. L. Stevens, 1972; Thirteen by Edward D. Hoch, 1971; Operative 375 by Gary Brandner, 1971; He'll Kill You by Richard Deming, 1950; Caveat Emptor by Kay Nolte Smith, 1976; The Facsimile Shop by Bill Pronzini and Jeffrey Wallman, 1970; A Corner of the Cellar by Michael Gilbert, 1959; Every Fifth Man by Edward D. Hoch, 1968; The Pro by Robert H. Curtis, 1978; Nobody That's Who, 1963; and Pigeon, 1957, by William F. Nolan; The Prisoner by Edward Wellen, 1973; The Sooey Pill by Elaine Slater, 1969; Backing Up by Barry N. Malzberg, 1979; and Wide O-- by Elsin Ann Graffam, 1968.

35. Space Mail II. With Martin H. Greenberg and Joseph D. Olander. Published by Fawcett Crest, New York City, 1982. Softcover. Herein: Introduction by Asimov; Adam's Diary (extracts) by Mark Twain, 1893; Aspic's Mystery by Arsen Darnay, 1976; Barney by Will Stanton, 1951; Evening Primrose by John Collier, 1940; View from a Height by Joan D. Vinge, 1978; First to Serve by Algis Budrys, 1954; The People's Choice by William Jon Watkins, 1974; Expedition by Anthony Boucher, 1943; Polity and Custom of the Camiroi, 1967; and Primary Education of the Camiroi, 1966, by R. A. Lafferty; The Shaker Revival by Gerald Jonas, 1970; Loophole by **Arthur C. Clarke**, 1946; Niche on the Bull Run, 1980; and Switch on the Bull Run, 1980, by Sharon Webb; Publish and Perish by Paul J. Nahin, 1978; Letters from Camp by Al Sarrantonio, 1982; The Several Murders of Roger Ackroyd, 1977; and A Delightful Comedic Premise, 1974, by Barry N. Malzberg; The Man from Not Yet by John Sladek, 1968; The Leader by Murray Leinster, 1960; Aristotle and the Gun by L. Sprague de Camp, 1958; and The Last Evolution by **John W. Campbell**, 1932.

36. Tantalizing Locked Room Mysteries. With Martin H. Greenberg and Charles G. Waugh. Published by Walker and Company, New York City, 1982. Hardcover. This contains: Introduction: No One Done It by Asimov; The Murders in the Rue Morgue by Edgar Allan Poe, 1841; The Adventure of the Speckled Band by Sir Arthur Conan Doyle, 1892; The Problem of Cell 13 by Jacques Futrell, 1905; The Light at Three O'Clock by MacKinlay Kantor, 1930; Murder at the Automat by Cornell Woolrich, 1937; The Exact Opposite by Erle Stanley Gardner, 1941; The Blind Spot by Barry Perowne, 1945; The Operator by Jack Wodhams; The Leopold Locked Room by Edward D. Hoch, 1971; and Vanishing Act by Bill Pronzini and Michael Kurland, 1976.

37. TV: 2000. With Martin H. Greenberg and Charles G. Waugh. Published by Fawcett Crest, New York City, 1982. Softcover. This contains: Introduction: It Changed the World by Asimov; Now Inhale by **Eric Frank Russell**, 1959; The Man Who Murdered Television by Joseph Patrouch, 1976; The Jester by William Tenn, 1951; The Man Who Came Back by **Robert Silverberg**, 1961; I See You by **Damon Knight**, 1976; The Prize of Peril by Robert Sheckley, 1958; Home Team Advantage by Jack C. Haldeman II, 1977; Mercenary by Mack Reynolds, 1962; Without Portfolio by James E. Gunn, 1955; The Idea by Barry N. Malzberg writing as K. M. O'Donnell, 1971; And Madly Teach by Lloyd Biggle Jr., 1966; Interview by Frank A. Javor, 1963; Cloak of Anarchy by Larry Niven, 1972; And Now the News by **Theodore Sturgeon**, 1956; Very Proper Charlies by Dean Ing, 1978; and Committee of the Whole by **Frank Herbert**, 1965.

38. Laughing Space. With J. O. Jeppson. Published by Houghton Mifflin, Boston, 1982. Hardcover. Herein: Introduction by Asimov; A Fuller Explanation of Original Sin, a poem by **Isaac Asimov** and Janet O. Jeppson; Et Tu, a poem by John Stallings, 1980; Creation, a poem by L. Sprague de Camp, 1970; Stag Night, Paleolithic, a poem by Ogden Nash, 1948; An Epicurean Fragment, a poem by Robert Hillyer, 1933; Spaced Out by Russell Baker, 1975; The Coffin Cure by Alan E. Nourse, 1957; Silenzia by Alan Nelson, 1953; The Agony of Defeat by Jack C. Haldeman II, 1978; Epitaph on Rigel XII, a poem by Sherwood Springer, 1977; The Snowball Effect by Katherine MacLean, 1952; Pate de Foie Gras by **Isaac Asimov**, 1956; The Available Data on the Worp Reaction by Lion Miller, 1953; Imaginary Numbers in a Real Garden, a poem by Gerald Jonas, 1965; The Mathenauts by Norman Kagan, 1964; Coffee Break by D. F. Jones, 1968; Putzi by Ludwig Bemelmans, 1935; All Things Come to Those Who Weight by Robert Gossenbach, 1980; Derm Fool by **Theodore Sturgeon**, 1940; The Heart on the Other Side by George Gamow, 1962; Blackmail by Fred Hoyle, 1967; A Slight Miscalculation by Ben Bova, 1971; A Subway Named Mobius by A. J. Deutsch, 1950; A Sinister Metamorphosis by Russell Baker, 1965; Something Up There Likes Me by **Alfred Bester**, 1973; A Prize for Edie by J. F. Bone, 1961; Isaac Asimov's The Caves of Steel, a poem by Randall Garrett, 1956; Neptune, a poem by Sansoucy North, 1977; Pluto, a poem by Sansoucy North, 1977; Jury-Rig by Avram Davidson, 1957; Protection by Robert Sheckley, 1956; The Self-Priming Solid-State Electronic Chicken by Jon Lucas, 1970; The Big Pat Boom by **Damon Knight**, 1963; The Night He Cried by **Fritz Leiber**, 1953; The Adventure of the Solitary Engineer by John M. Ford, 1979; Report on the Grand Central Terminal by Leo Szilard, 1952; Ad Astra, Al, a poem by Mary W. Stanton, 1979; They'll Do It Every Time by Cam Thornley, 1978; No Homelike Place by Dian Girard, 1978; Simworthy's Circus by Larry T. Shaw, 1950; A Growing Concern by Arnie Bateman, 1978; The Vilbar Party by Evelyn E. Smith, 1955; A Pestilence of Psychoanalysts by Janet Asimov writing as J. O. Jeppson, 1980; Death of a Foy by **Isaac Asimov**, 1980; The One Thing Lacking, a poem by **Isaac Asimov**, 1982; The Merchant of Stratford by Frank Ramirez, 1979; The Wheel of Time by Robert Arthur, 1950; Quit Zoomin' Those Hands Through the Air by Jack Finney, 1951; The Adventure of the Global Traveler or, The Global Consequences of How the Reichenbach Falls into the Wells of Iniquitie by Anne Lear, 1978; Pebble in Time by Avram Davidson and Cynthia Goldstone, 1970; Ahead of the Joneses by Al Sarrantonio, 1979; The Pinch Hitters by George Alec Effinger, 1979; Swift Completion, a poem by Brad Cahoon, 1979; A Skald's Lament, a poem by L. Sprague de Camp, 1955; The Stunning Science Fiction Caper by Thomas N. Scortia writing as Gerald Macdow, 1957; I, Claude by Charles Beaumont and Chad Oliver, 1956; Out of Control by Raylyn Moore, 1970; Slush by K. J. Snow, 1979; An Unsolicited Submission, a poem by Deborah Crawford, 1977;

Isaac Asimov

Judo and the Art of Self-Government by Kevin O'Donnell, Jr., 1980; Lulu by Clifford D. Simak, 1957; The Splendid Source by Richard Matheson, 1956; MS. Found in a Chinese Fortune Cookie by C. M. Kornbluth, 1957; The Several Murders of Roger Ackroyd by Barry N. Malzberg, 1977; The Critique of Impure Reason by **Poul Anderson**, 1962; One Rejection Too Many by Patricia Nurse, 1978; Bug-Getter by R. Bretnor, 1960; The Last Gothic by Jon L. Breen, 1979; A Benefactor of Humanity by James T. Farrell, 1958; The Silver Eggheads - excerpt - by **Fritz Leiber**, 1959; Adverbs, a poem by E. Y. Harburg, 1976; Dry Spell by Bill Pronzini, 1970; The Odds-on Favorite, a poem by E. Y. Harburg; and MS. Fnd in a Lbry by Hal Draper, 1961.

39. Speculations. With Alice Laurance. Published by Houghton Mifflin, Boston, 1982. Hardcover. Herein: 17 stories written especially for this volume by well-known science fiction authors but their names were concealed by a code and it was up to the reader to figure out who wrote what. The authors: **Isaac Asimov**; Scott Baker; Alan Dean Foster; Phyllis Gotlieb; Zenna Henderson; Joe L. Hensley; R. A. Lafferty; Alice Laurence and William K. Carlson; Jacqueline Lichtenberg; Roger Robert Lovin; Rachel Cosgrove Payes; Bill Pronzini and Barry Malzberg; Mack Reynolds; Joanna Russ; **Robert Silverberg**; **Jack Williamson**; and **Gene Wolfe**. The stories: Nor Iron Bars a Cage; Surfeit; The Winds of Change; Harpist; Great Tom Fool; The Hand of the Bard; The Man Who Floated in Time; Flee to the Mountains; Last Day; The Newest Profession; A Break for the Dinosaurs; Event at Holiday Rock; A Touch of Truth; Do I Dare to Eat a Peach?; Old... as a Garment; Flatsquid Thrills; and The Mystery of the Young Gentleman; followed by Biographies of the Authors; and To Break the Code.

40. Flying Saucers. With Martin H. Greenberg and Joseph D. Olander. Published by Fawcett Crest, New York City, 1982. Softcover. Herein: Flying Saucers and Science Fiction by Asimov; Exposure by **Eric Frank Russell**, 1950; Small Miracle by Randall Garrett, 1959; Fear Is a Business by **Theodore Sturgeon**, 1956; The Painter by Thomas Burnett Swann, 1960; The Junk Man Cometh by Robin Scott Wilson, 1966; The Deadly Ones by Floyd L. Wallace, 1954; Flying Pan by Robert F. Young, 1956; All the Universe in a Mason Jar by Joe Haldeman, 1977; Correspondence Course by Raymond F. Jones, 1945; Sam by Leo P. Kelly, 1971; The Mississippi Saucer by Frank Belknap Long, 1951; Posted by Mack Reynolds writing as Mark Mallory, 1957; Speak Up Melvin by Carol-Lynn Rossel Waugh writing as C. C. Rossel-Waugh, 1982; The Gumdrop King by Will Stanton, 1962; The Saucer of Loneliness by **Theodore Sturgeon**, 1953; Pagan by Algis Budrys, 1955; The Beholders, 1957; and Sense of Wonder, 1957, by A. Bertram Chandler; Trouble with the Natives by **Arthur C. Clarke**, 1951; The Lizard of Woz by Edmund Cooper, 1958; The Grantha Sighting by Avram Davidson, 1958; The Merchant by Larry Eisenberg, 1973; The Mouse by Howard Fast, 1969; The Time for Delusion by Donald Franson, 1958; and What is This Thing Called Love? by **Isaac Asimov**, 1961.

41. Earth Invaded. With Martin H. Greenberg and Charles G. Waugh. Raintree Reading Series II. Published by Raintree Publishers, Milwaukee, Wisconsin, 1982. Hardcover. This contains: Introduction by Asimov; Home Team Advantage by Jack C. Haldeman II, 1977; In the Arena by **Brian W. Aldiss**, 1963; Pattern by Fredric Brown, 1954; and Three Times Around by Jane Roberts, 1964.

42. Mad Scientists. With Martin H. Greenberg and Charles G. Waugh. Raintree Reading Series II. Published by Raintree Publishers, Milwaukee, Wisconsin, 1982. Hardcover. Herein: Introduction by Asimov; Von Goom's Gambit by Victor Contoski, 1966; The Weapon by Fredric Brown, 1951; Silence, Please! by **Arthur C. Clarke**, 1950; and The King of the Beasts by Philip Jose Farmer, 1964.

43. Mutants. With Martin H. Greenberg and Charles G. Waugh. Raintree Reading Series II. Published by Raintree Publishers, Milwaukee, Wisconsin, 1982. Hardcover. This contains: Introduction by Asimov; Prone by Mack Reynolds, 1954; The Better Choice by S. Fowler Wright, 1955; Barney by Will Stanton, 1951; and Lost Love by Algis Budrys writing as Paul Janvier, 1957.

44. Tomorrow's TV. With Martin H. Greenberg and Charles G. Waugh. Raintree Reading Series II. Published by Raintree Publishers, Milwaukee, Wisconsin, 1982. Hardcover. Herein: Introduction by Asimov; Eight O'Clock in the Morning by Ray Nelson, 1963; A Scientific Fact by Jack C. Haldeman II, 1979; The Pedestrian by **Ray Bradbury**, 1951; The Fun They Had by **Isaac Asimov**, 1951; and Crime Machine by Robert Bloch, 1961.

45. Dragon Tales. With Martin H. Greenberg and Charles G. Waugh. Published by Fawcett Crest, New York City, 1982. Softcover. Herein: Introduction by Asimov; Gerda by Evelyn E. Smith, 1954; Dragons' Teeth by David Drake, 1975; Two Yards of Dragon by L. Sprague de Camp, 1976; The King's Head and the Purple Dragon by L. Frank Baum, 1900; Soft Come the Dragons by Dean R. Koontz, 1967; Weyr Search by **Anne McCaffrey**, 1967; Demon and Demoiselle by Janet Fox, 1978; A Hiss of Dragon by Gregory Benford and Marc Laidlaw, 1978; The Dragon Fang Possessed by the Conjurer Piou Lu by Fitz-James O'Brien, 1856; The Bully and the Beast by Orson Scott Card, 1979; St. Dragon and the George by **Gordon R. Dickson**, 1957; and John Robert and the Dragon's Egg by Thomas N. Scortia, 1957.

46. The Big Apple Mysteries. With Carol-Lynn Rossel Waugh and Martin H. Greenberg. Published by Avon Books, New York City, 1982. Softcover.

47. Isaac Asimov Presents the Great SF Stories 7: 1945. With Martin H. Greenberg. Published by DAW Books, New York City, 1982. Softcover. DAW Collector's Book 489. Herein: Introduction by Greenberg; The Waveries, 1945; and Pi In The Sky, 1945, by Fredric Brown; The Piper's Son by Henry Kuttner and **C. L. Moore** writing as Lewis Padgett, 1945; Wanted An Enemy by **Fritz Leiber**, 1945; Correspondence Course by Raymond F. Jones, 1945; First Contact, 1945; The Power, 1945; and De Profundis, 1945, by Murray Leinster; The Vanishing Venusians by Leigh Brackett, 1945; Into Thy Hands by Lester Del Rey, 1945; Camouflage, 1945; and What You Need, 1945, by Henry Kuttner; Giant Killer by A. Bertram Chandler, 1945; and Blind Alley by **Isaac Asimov**, 1945.

48. The Last Man on Earth. With Martin H. Greenberg and Charles G. Waugh. Published by Fawcett Crest, New York City, 1982. Softcover. This contains: Introduction by Asimov; The New Reality by Charles L. Harness, 1950; Continuous Performance by Gordon Eklund, 1974; Day of Judgment, 1946; and In the World's Dusk, 1936, by Edmond Hamilton; Lucifer by Roger Zelazny, 1964; The Underdweller by William F. Nolan, 1957; The Coming of Ice by G. Peyton Wertenbaker, 1926; The Most Sentimental Man by Evelyn E. Smith, 1957; Knock by Fredric Brown, 1948; Eddie for Short by Wallace West; Original Sin by S. Fowler Wright; Kindness by Lester Del Rey, 1944; Resurrection by **A. E. Van Vogt**, 1948; The Second Class Citizen by **Damon Knight**, 1963; Trouble with Ants by Clifford D. Simak, 1982; A Man Spekith by Richard Wilson, 1969; and Flight to Forever by **Poul Anderson**, 1950.

49. Science Fiction A to Z: A Dictionary of Great Science Fiction Themes. With Martin H. Greenberg and Charles G. Waugh. Published by Houghton Mifflin, Boston, 1982. Hardcover. Herein: Dictionaries, an essay by Asimov; A Saucer of Loneliness by **Theodore Sturgeon**, 1953; There Will Come Soft Rains by **Ray Bradbury**, 1950; The Ship Who Sang by **Anne McCaffrey**, 1961; The Man with English by H. L. Gold, 1953; Let's Be Frank by **Brian W. Aldiss**, 1957; History Lesson by **Arthur C. Clarke**, 1949; The Game of Rat and Dragon by Cordwainer Smith, 1955; A Death in the House by Clifford D. Simak, 1959; The Cage by A. Bertram Chandler, 1957; Answer by Fredric Brown, 1954; Robbie by **Isaac Asimov**, 1940; The Easy Way Out by G. Harry Stine writing as Lee Correy, 1966; A Criminal Act by **Harry Harrison**, 1967; Open Warfare by James E. Gunn, 1954; A Gun for Dinosaur by L. Sprague de Camp, 1956; Man in a Quandary by L. J. Stecher, Jr., 1958; The Santa Claus Problem by J. W. Schutz, 1979; Why Johnny Can't Speed by Alan Dean Foster, 1971; For the Sake of Grace by Suzette Haden Elgin, 1969; In the Jaws of Danger by Piers Anthony, 1967; In the Abyss by **H. G. Wells**, 1896; The Troublemaker by Christopher Anvil, 1960; Top Secret by **Eric Frank Russell**, 1956; A Pail of Air by **Fritz Leiber**, 1951; The Snowball Effect by Katherine MacLean, 1952; Life Hutch by **Harlan Ellison**, 1956; The Mother of Necessity by Chad Oliver, 1955; The Silk and the Song by Charles L. Fontenay, 1956; The Last Monster by **Poul Anderson**, 1951; The Odor of Thought by Robert Sheckley, 1953; Game Preserve by Rog Phillips, 1957; A Museum Piece by Roger Zelazny, 1963; Creature of the Snows by William Sambrot, 1960; The Long Way Home by Fred Sagerhagen, 1961; Transstar by Raymond E. Banks, 1961; All Cats Are Gray by **Andre Norton** writing as Andrew North, 1953; The Draw by Jerome Bixby, 1954; The Man from Earth by **Gordon R. Dickson**, 1964; Gantlet by Richard E. Peck, 1972; The Cabbage Patch by Theodore R. Cogswell, 1952; A Touch of Grapefruit by Richard Matheson, 1959; Only Love Have I by Robert F. Young, 1955; No Harm Done by Jack Sharkey, 1961; Down to the Worlds of Men by Alexei Panshin, 1963; The Great Secret by George H. Smith, 1959; Skirmish on a Summer Morning by Bob Shaw, 1976; Custer's Last Jump by Steven Utley and Howard Waldrop, 1976; The Underdweller by William F. Nolan, 1957; Dream Damsel by Evan Hunter, 1954; and Too Soon to Die by Tom Godwin, 1957.

50. Isaac Asimov Presents the Best Fantasy of the 19th Century. With Martin H. Greenberg and Charles G. Waugh. Published by Beaufort Books, New York City, 1982. Hardcover. Herein: Introduction: When Fantasy Became Fantasy by Asimov; The Man Who Could Work Miracles by **H. G. Wells**, 1898; Lot No. 249 by Arthur Conan Doyle, 1892; The Canterville Ghost by Oscar Wilde, 1887; Dr. Heidegger's Experiment by Nathaniel Hawthorne, 1837; The Bottle Imp by Robert Louis Stevenson, 1891; The Legend of Sleepy Hollow by Washington Irving, 1819; Black Heart and White Heart by H. Rider Haggard, 1896; The Christmas Shadrach by Frank R. Stockton, 1891; How Much Land Does a Man Need by Leo Tolstoi, 1886; Hands Off by Edward Everett Hale writing anonymously, 1881; The Snow Queen by Hans Christian Andersen, 1844; A Christmas Carol in Prose: Being a Ghost Story of Christmas by Charles Dickens, 1843; The Overcoat by Nikolai Gogol, 1842; and Federigo by Prosper Merimee, 1829.

51. Isaac Asimov Presents the Great SF Stories 8: 1946. With Martin H. Greenberg. Published by DAW Books, New York City, 1982. Softcover. DAW Collector's Book 507. This contains: Introduction by Greenberg; A Logic Named Joe by Murray Leinster writing as Will F. Jenkins, 1946; Memorial, 1946; Mewhu's Jet, 1946, by **Theodore Sturgeon**; Loophole, 1946; Rescue Party, 1946; and Technical Error, 1946, by **Arthur C. Clarke**; The Nightmare by Chan Davis, 1946; Placet is a Crazy Place by Fredric Brown, 1946; Conqueror's Isle by Nelson S. Bond, 1946; Lorelei of the Red Mist by **Ray Bradbury** and Leigh Brackett, 1946; The Million Year Picnic by **Ray Bradbury**, 1946; The Last Objective by Paul A. Carter, 1946; Meihem in Ce Klasrum by Dolton Edwards, 1946; Vintage Season by **C. L. Moore** and Henry Kuttner writing as Lawrence O'Donnell, 1946; Absalom by Henry Kuttner, 1946; and Evidence by **Isaac Asimov**, 1946.

52. Isaac Asimov Presents the Great SF Stories 9: 1947. With Martin H. Greenberg. Published by DAW Books, New York City, 1982. Softcover. DAW Collector's Book 519. Herein: Introduction by Greenberg; Child's Play by William Tenn, 1947; E For Effort by T. L. Sherred, 1947; Hobbyist by **Eric Frank Russell**, 1947; Exit the Professor by Henry Kuttner and **C. L. Moore** writing as Lewis Padgett, 1947; Tiny and the Monster by **Theodore Sturgeon**, 1947; The Fires Within by **Arthur C. Clarke**, 1947; The Figure by Edward Grendon, 1947; Letter to Ellen by Chan Davis, 1947; Time and Time Again by H. Beam Piper, 1947; Tomorrow's Children by **Poul Anderson**, 1947; With Folded Hands by **Jack Williamson**, 1947; Zero Hour by **Ray Bradbury**, 1947; and Little Lost Robot by **Isaac Asimov**, 1947.

53. Show Business Is Murder. With Carol-Lynn Rossel Waugh and Martin H. Greenberg. Published by Avon Books, New York City, 1983. Softcover.

Isaac Asimov

54. Hallucination Orbit: Psychology in Science Fiction. With Martin H. Greenberg and Charles G. Waugh. Farrar Straus and Giroux, New York City, 1983. Hardcover. Herein: Introduction by Asimov; It's a Good Life by Jerome Bixby, 1953; The Sound Machine by Roald Dahl, 1949; Hallucination Orbit by J. T. McIntosh, 1952; The Winner by Donald E. Westlake, 1970; A Rose by Other Name by Christopher Anvil, 1960; The Man Who Never Forgot by **Robert Silverberg**, 1958;
Runaround by **Isaac Asimov**, 1942; Absalom by Henry Kuttner, 1946; Wings Out of Shadow by Fred Saberhagen, 1974; In Case of Fire by Randall Garrett, 1960; What Friends Are For by John Brunner, 1974; and The Drivers by Edward W. Ludwig, 1956.

55. Caught in the Organ Draft: Biology in Science Fiction. With Martin H. Greenberg and Charles G. Waugh. Farrar Straus and Giroux, New York City, 1983. Hardcover. This contains: Introduction by Asimov; Nine Lives by **Ursula K. Le Guin**, 1969; Alien Earth by Edmond Hamilton, 1949; Tomorrow's Children by **Poul Anderson** and F. N. Waldrop, 1947; Sea Change by Thomas N. Scortia; Grandpa by James H. Schmitz, 1955; Keep Out by Fredric Brown, 1954; Caught in the Organ Draft by **Robert Silverberg**, 1972; The Exterminator by A. Hyatt Verrill, 1931; A Sound of Thunder by **Ray Bradbury**, 1952; Mary and Joe by Naomi Mitchison, 1962; and Student Body by F. L. Wallace, 1953.

56. The Science Fiction Weight-Loss Book. With George R. R. Martin and Martin H. Greenberg. Published by Crown Publishers, New York City, 1983. Hardcover. This contains: Fat!, an essay by Asimov; Quitters, Inc. by Stephen King, 1978; The Malted Milk Monster by William Tenn, 1959; Fat Farm by Orson Scott Card, 1980; The Food Farm by Kit Reed, 1967; The Man Who Ate the World by **Frederik Pohl**, 1956; The iron Chancellor by **Robert Silverberg**, 1958; Sylvester's Revenge by Vance Aandahl, 1975; Camels and Dromedaries, Clem by R. A. Lafferty, 1967; Abercrombie Station by **Jack Vance**, 1952; Gladys's Gregory by John Anthony West, 1963; The Artist of Hunger by Scott Russell Sanders, 1983; Shipping Clerk by William Morrison, 1952; The Champ by T. Coraghessan Boyle, 1978; and The Stretch by Sam Merwin Jr., 1956.

57. Isaac Asimov Presents the Best Supernatural Stories of the 19th Century. With Martin H. Greenberg and Charles G. Waugh. Published by Beaufort Books, New York City, 1983. Hardcover. Herein: The Lure of Horror, an essay by Asimov; The Adventure of the German Student by Washington Irving, 1824; El Verdugo by Honore de Balzac, 1830; The Story of the Greek Slave by Frederick Marryat writing as Captain Frederick Marryat, 1831; The Iron Shroud by William Mudford, 1830; Schalken the Painter, by Joseph Sheridan Le Fanu, 1839; The Tell-Tale Heart by Edgar Allan Poe, 1843; The Doom of the Griffiths by Elizabeth Gaskell, 1856; Circumstance by Harriet Prescott Spofford, 1860; Torture by Hope by Villiers de l'Isle-Adam, 1883; The Diamond Necklace by Guy de Maupassant, 1884; The Strange Ride of Morrowbie Jukes by Rudyard Kipling, 1885; Markheim by Robert Louis Stevenson, 1886; Sleepyhead by Anton Chekhov, 1888; His Unconquerable Enemy by W. C. Morrow, 1929; The Gravedigger's Daughter by Leopold von Sacher-Masoch, 1889; An Occurrence at Owl Creek Bridge by Ambrose Bierce, 1890; Vengeance by Lorimer Stoddard, 1892; Desiree's Baby by Kate Chopin, 1893; The Squaw by Bram Stoker, 1893; A Dreadful Night by Edwin L. Arnold, 1894; The Dead Valley by Ralph Adams Cram; Pollock and the Porroh Man by **H. G. Wells**, 1895; The Story of the Brazilian Cat by Arthur Conan Doyle, 1898; The Dead Smile by F. Marion Crawford, 1899; and A Game of Chess by Robert Barr, 1900.

58. Starships: Stories Beyond the Boundaries of the Universe. With Martin H. Greenberg and Charles G. Waugh. Published by Fawcett Crest, New York City, 1983. Softcover. Herein: The Longest Voyage, an essay by Asimov; The Burning of the Brain by Cordwainer Smith, 1958; Home the Hard Way by Richard McKenna, 1967; Potential by Robert Sheckley, 1953; Bill for Delivery by Christopher Anvil, 1964; Story of a Curse by Doris Pitkin Buck, 1965; The Oceans Are Wide by Frank M. Robinson, 1954; Far Centaurus by **A. E. van Vogt**, 1944; The Ship Who Sang by **Anne McCaffrey**, 1961; Avoidance Situation by James V. McConnell, 1956; Chance Encounter by A. Bertram Chandler, 1959; Allamagoosa by **Eric Frank Russell**, 1955; Founding Father by **Isaac Asimov**, 1965; and Wings Out of Shadow by Fred Saberhagen, 1974.

59. Isaac Asimov Presents the Great SF Stories 10: 1948. With Martin H. Greenberg. Published by DAW Books, New York City, 1983. Softcover. DAW Collector's Book 543. This contains: Introduction by Greenberg; Don't Look Now by Henry Kuttner, 1948; Redhead by John D. MacDonald, 1948; Knock by Fredric Brown, 1948; He Walked Around the Horses by H. Beam Piper, 1948; The Strange Case of John Kingman by Murray Leinster, 1948; That Only a Mother by Judith Merril, 1948; The Monster, 1948; and Dormant, 1948, by **A. E. Van Vogt**; Dreams are Sacred by Peter Phillips, 1948; Mars is Heaven by **Ray Bradbury**, 1948; Thang by Martin Gardner, 1948; Brooklyn Project by William Tenn, 1948; Period Piece by J. J. Coupling, 1948; In Hiding by Wilmar H. Shiras, 1948; and Late Night Final by **Eric Frank Russell**, 1948.

60. Thirteen Horrors of Halloween. With Carol-Lynn Rossel Waugh and Martin H. Greenberg. Published by Avon Books, New York City, 1983. Softcover. This anthology contains: Introduction: The Forces of Evil, an essay by **Isaac Asimov**, 1983; Halloween by **Isaac Asimov**, 1975; Unholy Hybrid by William Bankier, 1963; Trick-or-Treat by Anthony Boucher, 1945; The October Game by **Ray Bradbury**, 1948; Halloween Girl by Robert Grant, 1982; Day of the Vampire by Edward D. Hoch, 1972; Night of the Goblin by Talmage Powell, 1981; The Adventure of the Dead Cat by Ellery Queen, 1946; Pumpkin Head by Al Sarrantonio, 1982; The Circle by Lewis Shiner, 1982; All Souls by Edith Wharton, 1937; Yesterday's Witch by Gahan Wilson, 1973; and Victim of the Year by Robert F. Young, 1962.

61. Creations: The Quest for Origins in Story and Science. With George Zebrowski and Martin H. Greenberg. Published by Crown Publishers, New York City, 1983. Hardcover. Herein: Introduction by Asimov; The Ugly Little Boy by **Isaac Asimov**,

1958; Mine Own Ways by Richard McKenna, 1960; Exposures by Gregory Benford, 1981; The Seesaw by **A. E. van Vogt**, 1941; Seeds of the Dusk by Raymond Z. Gallun, 1938; Heathen God by George Zebrowski, 1971; Transfusion by Chad Oliver, 1959; Non-Isotropic by **Brian W. Aldiss**, 1978; First Person Singular by **Eric Frank Russell**, 1950; The Living Galaxy by Laurence Manning, 1934; The Doctor by Theodore L. Thomas, 1967; The Creator by Clifford D. Simak, 1935; A Letter from God by Ian Watson, 1981; Genesis 1:20-25 and Genesis 2:1-25 - excerpt - New English Bible; Genesis 1:20-25 - excerpt - New English Bible; Project Genesis by Stanislaw Lem, 1981; Genesis 1:1-19 - excerpt - New English Bible; The Song of Creation, a poem by Hindu Rg-Veda; The Grisly Folk, an essay by **H. G. Wells**, 1921; The Cosmic Connection, an essay by Carl Sagan, 1973; The Threat of Creationism, an essay by **Isaac Asimov**, 1981; The Crucial Asymmetry, an essay by **Isaac Asimov**, 1981; and Kindergarten by James E. Gunn, 1970.

62. Wizards - Isaac Asimov's Magical Worlds of Fantasy 1. With Martin H. Greenberg and Charles G. Waugh. Published by Signet Books - New American Library, New York City, 1983. Softcover. Herein: Introduction by Asimov; Mazirian The Magician by **Jack Vance**, 1950; Please Stand By by Ron Goulart, 1962; What Good is a Glass Dagger? by Larry Niven, 1972; The Eye of Tandyla by L. Sprague de Camp, 1951; The White Horse Child by Greg Bear, 1979; Semley's Necklace by **Ursula K. Le Guin**, 1964; And The Monsters Walk by John Jakes, 1952; The Seeker in the Fortress by Manly Wade Wellman, 1979; The Wall Around the World by Theodore Cogswell, 1953; and The People of the Black Circle by Robert E. Howard, 1934.

63. Those Amazing Electronic Thinking Machines!: An Anthology of Robot and Computer Stories. With Martin H. Greenberg and Charles G. Waugh. Published by Franklin Watts, New York City, 1983. Hardcover. This contains: Introduction by Asimov; Sally by **Isaac Asimov**, 1953; Full Circle by H. B. Hickey, 1952; To Avenge Man by Lester del Rey, 1964; Prototaph by Keith Laumer, 1966; Dial "F" for Frankenstein by **Arthur C. Clarke**, 1965; The Other Side by Walter Kubilius, 1951; Computers Don't Argue by **Gordon R. Dickson**, 1965; Placement Test by Keith Laumer, 1964; and Answer by Fredric Brown, 1954.

64. Computer Crimes and Capers. With Martin H. Greenberg and Charles G. Waugh. Published by Academy Chicago Publishers, Chicago, Illinois, 1983. Hardcover. Herein: Introduction: Crime Up to Date by Asimov; DARL I LUV U by Joe Gores, 1963; An End of Spinach by Stan Dryer, 1981; Computers Don't Argue by **Gordon R. Dickson**, 1965; Goldbrick by Edward Wellen, 1978; Computer Cops by Edward D. Hoch, 1969; Sam Hall by **Poul Anderson**, 1953; Spanner in the Works by J. T. McIntosh; While-You-Wait by Edward Wellen, 1979; Getting Across by **Robert Silverberg**, 1973; and All the Troubles of the World by **Isaac Asimov**, 1958.

65. Intergalactic Empires - Isaac Asimov's Wonderful Worlds of Science Fiction 1. With Martin H. Greenberg and Charles G. Waugh. Published by Signet Books - New American Library, New York City, 1983. Softcover. Herein: Introduction by Asimov; Diabologic by **Eric Frank Russell**, 1955; Chalice of Death by **Robert Silverberg**, 1957; Orphan of the Void by Lloyd Biggle Jr., 1960; Down to the Worlds of Men by Alexei Panshin, 1963; Ministry of Disturbance by H. Beam Piper, 1958; A Planet Named Shayol by Cordwainer Smith, 1961; Fighting Philosopher by E. B. Cole, 1954; Honorable Enemies by **Poul Anderson**, 1951; and Blind Alley by **Isaac Asimov**, 1945.

66. Machines That Think: The Best Science Fiction Stories about Robots and Computers. With Patricia S. Warrick and Martin H. Greenberg. Published by Holt Rinehart and Winston, New York City, 1984. Hardcover. This contains: Introduction: Robots, Computers an Fear by **Isaac Asimov**, 1984; Moxon's Master by Ambrose Bierce, 1910; The Lost Machine by John Wyndham, 1932; Rex by Harl Vincent, 1934; Robbie by **Isaac Asimov**, 1940; Farewell to the Master by Harry Bates, 1940; Robot's Return by Robert Moore Williams, 1938; Through Dreamers Die by Lester del Rey, 1944; Fulfillment by **A. E. van Vogt**, 1951; Runaround by **Isaac Asimov**, 1942; I Have No Mouth and I Must Scream by **Harlan Ellison**, 1967; The Evitable Conflict by **Isaac Asimov**, 1950; A Logic Named Joe by Murray Leinster writing as Will F. Jenkins, 1946; Sam Hall by **Poul Anderson**, 1953; I Made You by Walter M. Miller, Jr., 1954; Triggerman by J. F. Bone, 1958; War with the Robots by **Harry Harrison**, 1962; Evidence by **Isaac Asimov**, 1946; 2066: Election Day by Michael Shaara, 1956; If There Were No Benny Cemoli by **Philip K. Dick**, 1963; The Monkey Wrench by **Gordon R. Dickson**, 1951; Dial F for Frankenstein by **Arthur C. Clarke**, 1964; The Macauley Circuit by **Robert Silverberg**, 1956; Judas by John Brunner, 1967; Answer by Fredric Brown, 1954; The Electric Ant by **Philip K. Dick**, 1969; The Bicentennial Man by **Isaac Asimov**, 1976; Long Shot by Vernor Vinge, 1972; Alien Stones by **Gene Wolfe**, 1972; and Starcrossed by George Zebrowski, 1973.

67. One Hundred Great Fantasy Short-Short Stories. With Terry Carr and Martin H. Greenberg. Published by Doubleday & Company, Garden City, New York, 1984. Hardcover. Herein: Angelica; The Tower Bird; and The Lady and the Merman by Jane Yolen; The Other; and Perchance to Dream by Katherine MacLean; Paranoid Fantasy #1 by Lawrence Watt-Evans; A Prophecy of Monsters by Clark Ashton Smith; A Dozen of Everything by Marion Zimmer Bradley; Displaced Person by **Eric Frank Russell**; Ex Oblivione by H. P. Lovecraft; The Human Angle by William Tenn; The Man Who Sold Rope to the Gnoles by Margaret St. Clair; The Toe by Phyllis Ann Karr; Tommy's Christmas by John R. Little; Vernon's Dragon by John Gregory Betancourt; Wisher Takes All by William F. Temple; The World Where Wishes Worked by Stephen Goldin; The Devil Finds Work; and Your Soul Comes C.O.D. by Mack Reynolds; Miranda Escobedo by James Sallis; Mr. Wilde's Second Chance by Joanna Russ; Naturally; and Voodoo by Fredric Brown; Once Upon a Unicorn by F. M. Busby; Night Visions by Jack Dann; $1.98 by Arthur Porges; Opening a Vein by Bill Pronzini and Barry N. Malzberg; The Other Train Phenomenon

Isaac Asimov

by Richard Bowker; Personality Problem by Joe R. Lansdale; Pharaoh's Revenge by C. Bruce Hunter; Pick-up for Olympus by Edgar Pangborn; Prayer War by Jonathan V. Post; The Prophecy by Bill Pronzini; The Recording by **Gene Wolfe**; Red Carpet Treatment by Robert Lipsyte; The Sacrifice by Gardner Dozois; Some Days Are Like That by Bruce J. Balfour; Santa's Tenth Reindeer by Gordon Van Gelder; The Second Short Shortest Fantasy Ever Published by Barry N. Malzberg; The Importance of Being Important by Calvin W. Demmon; Interview with a Gentleman Farmer by Bruce Boston; Judgment Day; and Mortimer Snodgrass Turtle by Jack C. Haldeman II; Just One More; The Maiden's Sacrifice; Who Rides with Santa Anna; and The Last Unicorns by Edward D. Hoch; Letters from Camp by Al Sarrantonio; Love Filter by Gregg Chamberlain; Echoes by Lawrence C. Connolly; Feeding Time by James Gunn; Final Version by John Morressy; Five Minutes Early by Robert Sheckley; Garage Sale by Janet Fox; Getting Back to Before by Raylyn Moore; Give Her Hell; Malice Aforethought; The Rag Thing; and The Haters by **Donald A. Wollheim**; God's Nose; and The Handler by **Damon Knight**; The Good Husband; and Weather Prediction by Evelyn E. Smith; The House by Andre Maurois; How Georges Duchamps Discovered a Plot to Take Over the World by Alexei Panshin; The Abraham Lincoln Murder Case; Mouse Kitty; The Other One; The Third Wish; and Freedom by Rick Norwood; The Anatomy Lesson by Scott Sanders; And I Alone Escaped to Tell Thee; and But Not the Herald by Roger Zelazny; Apocryphal Fragment; and Chalk Talk by Edward Wellen; At the Bureau; The Painters Are Coming Today; The Poor; Sleep; and The Giveaway by Steve Rasnic Tem; Aunt Agatha by Doris Pitkin Buck; The Boulevard of Broken Dreams; and L is for Loup Garou by **Harlan Ellison**; Chained by Barry N. Malzberg; Climacteric; and The Last Wizard by Avram Davidson; The Contest by Robert J. Sawyer; Controlled Experiment by Rick Conley; The Curse of Hooligan's Bar by Charles E. Fritch; The Dark Ones by Richard Christian Matheson; Dead Call by William F. Nolan; Deadline by Mel Gilden; Deal with the D.E.V.I.L. by Theodore R. Cogswell; Devlin's Dream by George Clayton Johnson; Temporarily at Liberty by Lawrence Goldman; Farewell Party; and The Thing That Stared by Richard Wilson; Thinking the Unthinkable by Will Creveling; Those Three Wishes by Judith Gorog, 1982; and Thus I Refute by Terry Carr, 1972.

68. Bug Awful. With Martin H. Greenberg and Charles G. Waugh. Raintree Reading Series III. Published by Raintree Publishers, Milwaukee, Wisconsin, 1984. Hardcover. Herein: Introduction by Asimov; Mimic by **Donald A. Wollheim**, 1942; Meddler by **Philip K. Dick**, 1954; and The Useless Bugbreeders by James Stamers, 1961.

69. Children of the Future. With Martin H. Greenberg and Charles G. Waugh. Raintree Reading Series III. Published by Raintree Publishers, Milwaukee, Wisconsin, 1984. Hardcover. Introduction by Asimov; All Summer in a Day by **Ray Bradbury**, 1954; Teething Ring by James Causey, 1953; An End of Spinach by Stan Dryer, 1981; and The Boy Who Predicted Earthquakes by Margaret St. Clair, 1950.

70. The Immortals. With Martin H. Greenberg and Charles G. Waugh. Raintree Reading Series III. Published by Raintree Publishers, Milwaukee, Wisconsin, 1984. Hardcover. This contains: Introduction by Asimov; And Thou Beside Me by Mack Reynolds, 1954; Invariant by John Pierce, 1944; Hail and Farewell by **Ray Bradbury**, 1953; and The Eternal Man by D. D. Sharp, 1929.

71. Time Warps. With Martin H. Greenberg and Charles G. Waugh. Raintree Reading Series III. Published by Raintree Publishers, Milwaukee, Wisconsin, 1984. Hardcover. Herein: Introduction by Asimov; Experiment, 1954; Nightmare in Time, 1961, by Fredric Brown; For the Love of Barbara Allen by Robert E. Howard, 1966; The Biography Project by H. L. Gold, 1951; Time for Survival by George O. Smith, 1960; and Over the River and Through the Woods by Clifford D. Simak, 1965.

72. Isaac Asimov Presents the Great SF Stories 11: 1949. With Martin H. Greenberg. Published by DAW Books, New York City, 1984. Softcover. DAW Collector's Book 571. Herein: Introduction by Greenberg; The Witches of Karres by James H. Schmitz, 1949; Flaw by John D. MacDonald, 1949; Manna by Peter Phillips, 1949; Private Eye by Henry Kuttner and **C. L. Moore** writing as Lewis Padgett, 1949; Cold War by Henry Kuttner, 1949; Alien Earth by Edmond Hamilton, 1949; History Lesson by **Arthur C. Clarke**, 1949; Eternity Lost by Clifford D. Simak, 1949; Private - Keep Out by Philip MacDonald, 1949; The Hurkle is a Happy Beast by **Theodore Sturgeon**, 1949; Kaleidoscope by **Ray Bradbury**, 1949; Defense Mechanism by Katherine MacLean, 1949; and The Red Queen's Race by **Isaac Asimov**, 1949.

73. Witches - Isaac Asimov's Magical Worlds of Fantasy 2. With Martin H. Greenberg and Charles G. Waugh. Published by Signet Books - New American Library, New York City, 1984. Softcover. This contains: Introduction by Asimov; The Witches of Karres by James H. Schmitz, 1949; The Ipswich Phial by Randall Garrett, 1976; Black Heart and White Heart by H. Rider Haggard, 1896; My Mother Was a Witch by William Tenn, 1966; A Message from Charity by William M. Lee, 1967; The Witch by **A. E. van Vogt**, 1943; Spree by Barry N. Malzberg, 1984; Devil's Henchman by Murray Leinster, 1952; Malice in Wonderland by Rufus King, 1957; Wizard's World by **Andre Norton**, 1967; Operation Salamander by **Poul Anderson**, 1957; Sweets to the Sweet by Robert Bloch, 1947; Poor Little Saturday by Madeleine L'Engle, 1956; and Squeakie's First Case by Margaret Manners, 1943.

74. Murder on the Menu. With Carol-Lynn Rossel Waugh and Martin H. Greenberg. Published by Avon Books, New York City, 1984. Softcover. Herein: Introduction by Asimov; The Chicken Soup Kid by Edward D. Hoch writing as R. L. Stevens, 1984; The Case of the Shaggy Caps by Ruth Rendell, 1977; Poison a la Carte by Rex Stout, 1960; Garden of Evil by Carol Cail, 1973; The Specialty of the House by Stanley Ellin, 1948; Lamb to the Slaughter by Roald Dahl, 1953; When No Man Pursueth by **Isaac Asimov** 1974; The Two Bottles of Relish by Lord Dunsany, 1932; The Theft of the Used Tea Bag by Edward D. Hoch, 1982; The Refugees by T. S. Stribling, 1929; Recipe for a Happy Marriage by Nedra Tyre, 1971; The Norwegian Apple Mystery by James Holding, 1961; Gideon and the Chestnut Vendor by John Creasey writing as J. J. Marric, 1971; The Same Old Grind by Bill Pronzini, 1978; and Dogsbody by Francis M. Nevins Jr.

75. Young Mutants. With Martin H. Greenberg and Charles G. Waugh. Published by Harper and Row, New York City, 1984. Hardcover. This contains: Introduction by Asimov; Hail and Farewell by **Ray Bradbury**, 1953; Keep Out by Fredric Brown, 1954; What Friends Are For by John Brunner, 1974; The Wonder Horse by George Bryam, 1957; He That Hath Wings by Edmond Hamilton, 1938; Second Sight by Alan E. Nourse, 1956; I Can't Help Saying Goodbye by Ann Mackenzie, 1978; The Listening Child by Margaret St. Clair writing as Idris Seabright, 1950; The Children's Room by Raymond F. Jones, 1942; The Lost Language by David H. Keller, 1934; Prone by Mack Reynolds, 1954; and Come On, Wagon! by Zenna Henderson, 1951.

76. Isaac Asimov Presents the Best Science Fiction Firsts. With Martin H. Greenberg and Charles G. Waugh. Published by Beaufort Books, New York City, 1984. Hardcover. Herein: Introduction: To Be the First by Asimov; Minus Planet by John D. Clark, 1937; Yesterday House by **Fritz Leiber**, 1952; Neutron Star by Larry Niven, 1966; The Conversation of Eiros and Charmion by Edgar Allan Poe, 1839; The Faithful by Lester del Rey, 1938; The Voyage That Lasted 600 Years by Don Wilcox, 1940; A Logic Named Joe by Murray Leinster writing as Will F. Jenkins; What Was It? by Fitz-James O'Brien, 1859; The Diamond Lens by Fitz-James O'Brien, 1858; The Test by Richard Matheson, 1954; Reason by **Isaac Asimov**; and The Land Ironclads by **H. G. Wells**, 1903.

77. The Science Fictional Olympics - Isaac Asimov's Wonderful Worlds of Science Fiction 2. With Martin H. Greenberg and Charles G. Waugh. Published by Signet Books - New American Library, New York City, 1984. Softcover. Herein: Introduction: Competition by Asimov; For the Sake of Grace by Suzette Haden Elgin, 1968; The Kokod Warriors by **Jack Vance,** 1952; Run to Starlight by George R. R. Martin, 1974; A Day for Dying by Charles Nuetzel, 1969; Why Johnny Can't Speed by Alan Dean Foster, 1971; A Glint of Gold by Nicholas V. Yermakov who became Simon Hawke, 1980; The Mickey Mouse Olympics by Tom Sullivan, 1979; Dream Fighter by Bob Shaw, 1977; Getting Through University by Piers Anthony, 1968; The National Pastime by Norman Spinrad, 1973; The People Trap by Robert Sheckley; Nothing in the Rules by L. Sprague de Camp, 1939; The Olympians by Mike Resnick, 1982; The Wind from the Sun by **Arthur C. Clarke**, 1964; Prose Bowl by Bill Pronzini and Barry N. Malzberg, 1979; From Downtown at the Buzzer by George Alec Effinger, 1977; and The Survivor by Walter F. Moudy, 1965.

78. Fantastic Reading: Stories and Activities for Grade 5 - 8. With Martin H. Greenberg and David C. Yeager. Published by Scott Foresman & Co., Glenview, Illinois, 1984. Softcover.

79. Election Day 2084: Science Fiction Stories on the Politics of the Future. With Martin H. Greenberg. Published by Prometheus Books, New York City, 1984. Hardcover. Herein: Introduction by Asimov; Franchise by **Isaac Asimov**, 1955; Death and the Senator by **Arthur C. Clarke**, 1961; Committee of the Whole by **Frank Herbert**, 1965; Political Machine by John Jakes, 1961; The Children of Night by **Frederik Pohl**, 1964; 2066: Election Day by Michael Shaara, 1956; On the Campaign Trail by Barry N. Malzberg, 1975; Hail to the Chief by Randall Garrett, 1962; A Rose by Other Name by Christopher Anvil, 1960; Beyond Doubt by **Robert A. Heinlein** and Elma Wentz, 1941; Frank Merriwell in the White House by Ward Moore, 1973; Hail to the Chief by Sam Sackett, 1954; Polity and Custom of the Camiroi by R. A. Lafferty, 1967; May the Best Man Win by Stanley Schmidt, 1971; The Delegate from Guapanga by Wyman Guin, 1964; The Chameleon by Larry Eisenberg, 1970; and Evidence by **Isaac Asimov**, 1946.

80. Isaac Asimov Presents the Great SF Stories 12: 1950. With Martin H. Greenberg. Published by DAW Books, New York City, 1984. Softcover. DAW Collector's Book 594. This contains: Not With a Bang, 1950; and To Serve Man, 1950, by **Damon Knight**; Spectator Sport by John D. MacDonald, 1950; There Will Come Soft Rains by **Ray Bradbury**, 1950; Dear Devil by **Eric Frank Russell**, 1950; Scanners Live in Vain by Cordwainer Smith, 1950; Born of Man and Woman by Richard Matheson, 1950; The Little Black Bag, 1950; The Silly Season, 1950; and The Mindworm, 1950, by C. M. Kornbluth; Enchanted Village, 1950; and Process, 1950, by **A. E. van Vogt**; Oddy and Id by **Alfred Bester**, 1950; The Sack by William Morrison, 1950; Coming Attraction by **Fritz Leiber**, 1950; A Subway Named Mobius by A. J. Deutsch, 1950; The New Reality by Charles L. Harness, 1950; and Misbegotten Missionary by **Isaac Asimov**, 1950.

81. Young Extraterrestrials. With Martin H. Greenberg and Charles G. Waugh. Published by Harper and Row, New York City, 1984. Hardcover. Herein: Introduction by Asimov; Doorstep by Keith Laumer, 1961; Who's on First? by Lloyd Biggle Jr., 1958; In the Jaws of Danger by Piers Anthony, 1967; The Witness by **Eric Frank Russell**, 1951; The Mississippi Saucer by Frank Belknap Long, 1951; Primary Education of the Camiroi by R. A. Lafferty, 1966; Tween by J. F. Bone, 1978; Zoo by Edward D. Hoch, 1958; Subcommittee by Zenna Henderson, 1962; Keyhole by Murray Leinster, 1951; and Kindergarten by James E. Gunn, 1970.

82. Sherlock Holmes Through Time and Space. With Martin H. Greenberg and Charles G. Waugh. Published by Bluejay Books, Gordonsville, Virginia, 1984. Hardcover. This anthology contains: Sherlock Holmes, an essay by **Isaac Asimov**; The Adventure of the Devil's Foot by Arthur Conan Doyle, 1910; The Problem of the Sore Bridge - Among Others by Philip Jose Farmer, 1975; The Adventure of the Global Traveler by Anne Lear, 1978; The Great Dormitory Mystery by Sharon N. Farber, 1976; The Adventure of the Misplaced Hound by **Poul Anderson** and **Gordon R. Dickson**, 1953; The Thing Waiting Outside by Barbara Williamson, 1977;

Isaac Asimov

A Father's Tale by Sterling E. Lanier, 1974; The Adventure of the Extraterrestrial by Mack Reynolds, 1965; A Scarletin Study by Philip Jose Farmer, 1975; Voiceover by Edward Wellen, 1984; Adventure of the Metal Murderer by Fred Saberhagen, 1980; Slaves of Silver by **Gene Wolfe**, 1971; God of the Naked Unicorn by Richard A. Lupoff, 1976; Death in the Christmas Hour by James Powell, 1983; and The Ultimate Crime by **Isaac Asimov**, 1976.

83. Supermen - Isaac Asimov's Wonderful Worlds of Science Fiction 3. With Martin H. Greenberg and Charles G. Waugh. Published by Signet Books - New American Library, New York City, 1984. Softcover. Herein: Introduction by Asimov; Angel, Dark Angel by Roger Zelazny, 1967; Worlds to Kill by **Harlan Ellison**, 1968; In the Bone by **Gordon R. Dickson**, 1966; What Rough Beast? by **Damon Knight**, 1959; Death by Ecstasy by Larry Niven, 1969; Un-Man by **Poul Anderson**, 1953; Muse by Dean R. Koontz, 1969; Resurrection by **A. E. van Vogt**, 1948; Pseudopath by Philip E. High, 1959; After the Myths Went Home by **Robert Silverberg**, 1969; Before the Talent Dies by Henry Slesar, 1957; and Brood World Barbarian by Perry A. Chapdelaine, 1969.

84. Baker's Dozen: 13 Short Fantasy Novels. With Martin H. Greenberg and Charles G. Waugh. Published by Crown Publishers, New York City, 1984. Hardcover. Herein: Introduction: Larger Than Life by Asimov; Red Nails by Robert E. Howard, 1936; Storm in a Bottle by John Jakes, 1977; Spider Silk by **Andre Norton**, 1976; Guyal of Sfere by **Jack Vance**, 1950; Tower of Ice by Roger Zelazny, 1981; Unicorn Tapestry by Suzy McKee Charnas, 1980; Black Heart and White Heart by H. Rider Haggard, 1896; Ill Met in Lankhmar by **Fritz Leiber**, 1970; The Lands Beyond the World by **Michael Moorcock**, 1977; A Man and His God by Janet Morris, 1981; Where is the Bird of Fire? by Thomas Burnett Swann, 1962; Sleep Well of Night by Avram Davidson, 1978; and The Gate of the Flying Knives by **Poul Anderson**, 1979.

85. Cosmic Knights - Isaac Asimov's Magical Worlds of Fantasy 3. With Martin H. Greenberg and Charles G. Waugh. Published by Signet Books - New American Library, New York City, 1985. Softcover. This contains: Introduction: In Days of Old by Asimov; Crusader Damosel by Vera Chapman, 1978; Divers Hands by Darrell Schweitzer, 1979; The Reluctant Dragon by Kenneth Grahame, 1898; The Immortal Game by **Poul Anderson**, 1954; The Stainless Steel Knight by John T. Phillifent, 1941; Diplomat At Arms by Keith Laumer, 1960; Dream Damsel by Evan Hunter, 1954; The Last Defender of Camelot by Roger Zelazny, 1979; A Knyght Ther Was by Robert F. Young, 1963; and Divide and Rule by L. Sprague de Camp, 1939.

86. The Hugo Winners - Volume IV. Published by Doubleday & Company, Garden City, New York, 1985. Hardcover. This contains: Introduction: What Again? by Asimov; Home is the Hangman by Roger Zelazny, 1975; The Borderland of Sol by Larry Niven, 1975; Catch That Zeppelin! by **Fritz Leiber**, 1975; By Any Other Name by Spider Robinson, 1976; Houston, Houston, Do You Read? by James Tiptree, Jr., 1976; The Bicentennial Man by **Isaac Asimov**, 1976; Tricentennial by Joe Haldeman, 1976; Stardance by Spider Robinson and Jeanne Robinson, 1977; Eyes of Amber by Joan D. Vinge, 1977; Jeffty Is Five by **Harlan Ellison**, 1977; The Persistence of Vision by John Varley, 1978; Hunter's Moon by **Poul Anderson**, 1978; and Cassandra by C. J. Cherryh, 1978.

87. Young Monsters. With Martin H. Greenberg and Charles G. Waugh. Published by Harper and Row, New York City, 1985. Hardcover. Herein: Introduction by Asimov; Homecoming by **Ray Bradbury**, 1946; Good-by, Miss Patterson by Phyllis MacLennan, 1972; Disturb Not My Slumbering Fair by Chelsea Quinn Yarbro, 1978; The Wheelbarrow Boy by Richard Parker, 1950; The Cabbage Patch by Theodore R. Cogswell, 1952; The Thing Waiting Outside by Barbara Williamson, 1977; Red as Blood by Tanith Lee, 1979; Gabriel-Ernest by Saki, 1909; Fritzchen by Charles Beaumont, 1953; The Young One by Jerome Bixby, 1954; Optical Illusion by Mack Reynolds, 1953; Idiot's Crusade by Clifford D. Simak, 1954; One for the Road by Stephen King, 1977; and Angelica by Jane Yolen, 1979.

88. Spells - Isaac Asimov's Magical Worlds of Fantasy 4. With Martin H. Greenberg and Charles G. Waugh. Published by Signet Books - New American Library, New York City, 1985. Softcover. Herein: Introduction by Asimov; The Candidate by Henry Slesar, 1961; The Christmas Shadrach by Frank R. Stockton, 1891; The Miracle Workers by **Jack Vance**, 1958; I Know What You Need by Stephen King, 1976; Toads of Grimmerdale by **Andre Norton**, 1973; The Snow Women by **Fritz Leiber**, 1970; Invisible Boy by **Ray Bradbury**, 1945; The Hero Who Returned by Gerald W. Page, 1979; Satan and Sam Shay by Robert Arthur, 1942; Lot No. 249 by Sir Arthur Conan Doyle, 1892; The Witch is Dead by Edward D. Hoch, 1956; and A Literary Death by Martin Harry Greenberg, 1985.

89. Great Science Fiction Stories by the World's Great Scientists. With Martin H. Greenberg and Charles G. Waugh. Published by Donald I. Fine, New York City, 1985. Hardcover. This contains: Introduction by Asimov; White Creatures by Gregory Benford, 1975; The Singing Diamond by Robert L. Forward, 1979; Publish and Perish by Paul J. Nahin, 1978; Skystalk by Charles Sheffield, 1979; The Universal Library by Kurd Lasswitz, 1901; Long Shot by Vernor Vinge, 1972; Blackmail by Fred Hoyle, 1967; Jeannette's Hands by R. S. Richardson writing as Philip Latham, 1973; The Warm Space by David Brin, 1985; The Wind from the Sun by **Arthur C. Clarke**, 1964; Industrial Accident by G. Harry Stine writing as Lee Correy, 1980; Choice by John R. Pierce, 1971; The Winnowing by **Isaac Asimov**, 1976; Dr. Snow Maiden by Larry Eisenberg, 1975; On the Fourth Planet by J. F. Bone, 1963; Learning Theory by James V. McConnell, 1957; Love is the Plan the Plan is Death by James Tiptree Jr., 1973; Transfusion by Chad Oliver, 1959; In the Beginning by Morton Klass, 1954; Modulation in All Things by Suzette Haden Elgin, 1980; and The Bones of Charlemagne by Mario A. Pei, 1958.

90. Isaac Asimov Presents the Great SF Stories 13: 1951. With Martin H. Greenberg. Published by DAW Books, New York City, 1985. Softcover. DAW

Collector's Book 636. This contains: Null P by William Tenn, 1951; The Sentinel by **Arthur C. Clarke**, 1951; The Fire Balloons by **Ray Bradbury**, 1951; The Marching Morons by C. M. Kornbluth, 1951; The Weapon by Fredric Brown, 1951; Angel's Egg by Edgar Pangborn, 1951; Breeds There a Man by **Isaac Asimov**, 1951; Pictures Don't Lie by Katherine MacLean, 1951; Superiority by **Arthur C. Clarke**, 1951; I'm Scared by Jack Finney, 1951; The Quest for St. Aquin by Anthony Boucher, 1951; Tiger by the Tail by Alan E. Nourse, 1951; With These Hands by C. M. Kornbluth, 1951; A Pail of Air by **Fritz Leiber**, 1951; and Dune Roller by Julian May, 1951.

91. Amazing Stories: Sixty Years of the Best Science Fiction. With Martin H. Greenberg. Published by TSR Inc., Lake Geneva, Wisconsin, 1985. Softcover. Herein: Amazing Stories and I by **Isaac Asimov**; The Revolt of the Pedestrians by David H. Keller, 1928; The Gostak and the Doshes by Miles J. Breuer, 1930; Pilgrimage by Nelson S. Bond, 1939; I, Robot by Otto Binder writing as Eando Binder, 1939; The Strange Flight of Richard Clayton by Robert Bloch, 1939; The Perfect Woman by Robert Sheckley, 1953; Memento Homo by Walter M. Miller, Jr., 1954; What Is This Thing Called Love? by **Isaac Asimov**, 1961; Requiem by Edmond Hamilton, 1962; Hang Head, Vandal! by Mark Clifton, 1962; Drunkboat by Cordwainer Smith, 1963; The Days of Perky Pat by **Philip K. Dick**, 1963; Semley's Necklace by **Ursula K. Le Guin**, 1964; Calling Dr. Clockwork by Ron Goulart, 1965; There's No Vinism Like Chauvinism by John Jakes, 1965; The Oogenesis of Bird City by Philip Jose Farmer, 1970; The Man Who Walked Home by James Tiptree, Jr., 1972; Manikins by John Varley, 1976; and In the Islands by Pat Murphy, 1983.

92. Young Ghosts. With Martin H. Greenberg and Charles G. Waugh. Published by Harper and Row, New York City, 1985. Hardcover. Herein: Introduction: Ghosts by Asimov; Lost Hearts by M. R. James, 1895; On the Brighton Road by Richard Middleton, 1912; Poor Little Saturday by Madeleine L'Engle, 1956; The Lake by **Ray Bradbury**, 1944; A Pair of Hands by Arthur Quiller-Couch, 1898; Old Haunts by Richard Matheson, 1957; An Uncommon Sort of Spectre by Edward Page Mitchell, 1879; The House of the Nightmare by Edward Lucas White, 1906; The Shadowy Third by Ellen Glasgow, 1916; The Twilight Road by H. F. Brinsmead, 1967; The Voice of El Dorado by Howard Goldsmith, 1974; and The Changing of the Guard, an essay by Anne Serling-Sutton, 1985.

93. Baker's Dozen: Thirteen Short Science Fiction Novels. With Martin H. Greenberg and Charles G. Waugh. Published by Crown Publishers, New York City, 1985. Hardcover. This contains: : Introduction: Novellas by Asimov; Profession by **Isaac Asimov**, 1957; Who Goes There? by **John W. Campbell** writing as Don A. Stuart, 1938; For I Am a Jealous People! by Lester del Rey, 1954; The Mortal and the Monster by **Gordon R. Dickson**, 1976; Time Safari by David Drake, 1981; In the Western Tradition by Phyllis Eisenstein, 1981; The Alley Man by Philip Jose Farmer, 1959; The Sellers of the Dream by John Jakes, 1963; The Moon Goddess and the Son by Donald Kingsbury, 1979; Enemy Mine by Barry B. Longyear, 1979; Flash Crowd by Larry Niven, 1973; In the Problem Pit by **Frederik Pohl**, 1973; and The Desert of Stolen Dreams by **Robert Silverberg**, 1981.

94. Giants - Isaac Asimov's Magical Worlds of Fantasy 5. With Martin H. Greenberg and Charles G. Waugh. Published by Signet Books - New American Library, New York City, 1985. Softcover. Herein: Introduction by Asimov; The Colossus of Ylourgne by Clark Ashton Smith, 1934; The Thirty and One by David H. Keller, 1938; The Riddle of Ragnarok by **Theodore Sturgeon**, 1955; Straggler From Atlantis by Manly Wade Wellman, 1977; He Who Shrank by Henry Hasse, 1936; From the Dark Waters by David Drake, 1976; Small Lords by **Frederik Pohl**, 1957; The Mad Planet by Murray Leinster, 1920; The Law Twister Shorty by **Gordon R. Dickson**; In The Lower Passage by Harle Owen Cummins, 1902; Cabin Boy by **Damon Knight**, 1951; and Dreamworld by **Isaac Asimov**, 1955.

95. The Mammoth Book of Short Fantasy Novels. With Martin H. Greenberg and Charles G. Waugh. Published by Robinson Publishing, London, 1986. Hardcover. Herein: Herein: Introduction: by Asimov; Red Nails by Robert E. Howard, 1936; Storm in a Bottle by John Jakes, 1977; Spider Silk by **Andre Norton**, 1976; Guyal of Sfere by **Jack Vance**, 1950; Tower of Ice by Roger Zelazny, 1981; Unicorn Tapestry by Suzy McKee Charnas, 1980; Black Heart and White Heart by H. Rider Haggard, 1896; Ill Met in Lankhmar by **Fritz Leiber**, 1970; The Lands Beyond the World by **Michael Moorcock**, 1977; A Man and His God by Janet Morris, 1981; Where is the Bird of Fire? by Thomas Burnett Swann, 1962; Sleep Well of Night by Avram Davidson, 1978; and The Gate of the Flying Knives by **Poul Anderson**, 1979.

96. Isaac Asimov Presents the Great SF Stories 14: 1952. With Martin H. Greenberg. Published by DAW Books, New York City, 1986. Softcover. DAW Collector's Book 660. This contains: Introduction by Greenberg; The Pedestrian by **Ray Bradbury**, 1952; The Moon is Green by **Fritz Leiber**, 1952; Lost Memory by Peter Phillips, 1952; What Have I Done by Mark Clifton, 1952; Fast Falls the Eventide by **Eric Frank Russell**, 1952; The Business as Usual by Mack Reynolds, 1952; A Sound of Thunder by **Ray Bradbury**, 1952; Hobson's Choice **by Alfred Bester**, 1952; Yesterday House by **Fritz Leiber**, 1952; The Snowball Effect by Katherine MacLean, 1952; Delay in Transit by F. L. Wallace, 1952; Game for Blondes by John D. MacDonald, 1952; The Altar at Midnight by Cyril Kornbluth, 1952; Command Performance by Walter M. Miller Jr. , 1952; The Martian Way by **Isaac Asimov**, 1952; The Impacted Man by Robert Sheckley, 1952; What's It Like Out There by Edmond Hamilton, 1952; Sail On Sail On by Philip Jose Farmer, 1952; and Cost of Living by Robert Sheckley, 1952.

97. Comets - Isaac Asimov's Wonderful Worlds of Science Fiction 4. With Martin H. Greenberg and Charles G. Waugh. Published by Signet Books - New American Library, New York City, 1986. Softcover. Herein: Introduction by Asimov; Into the Sun by Robert Duncan Milne, 1882; Captain Stormfield's Visit to Heaven (extract) by Mark Twain, 1907; The

Isaac Asimov

Comet Doom by Edmond Hamilton, 1927; Sunspot by **Hal Clement**, 1960; Inside the Comet by **Arthur C. Clarke**, 1960; Raindrop by **Hal Clement**, 1965; Comet Wine by Ray Russell, 1967; The Red Euphoric Bands by R. S. Richardson writing as Philip Latham, 1967; Throwback by Sydney J. Bounds, 1969; Kindergarten by James E. Gunn, 1970; West Wind Falling by Gregory Benford and Gordon Eklund, 1971; The Comet, the Cairn and the Capsule by Duncan Lunan, 1972; Some Joys Under the Star by **Frederik Pohl**, 1973; The Death of Princes by **Fritz Leiber**, 1976; The Funhouse Effect by John Varley, 1976; The Family Man by Theodore L. Thomas, 1978; Double Planet by John Gribbin, 1984; and Pride by **Poul Anderson**, 1985.

98. Young Star Travelers. With Martin H. Greenberg and Charles G. Waugh. Published by Harper and Row, New York City, 1986. Hardcover. This contains: Introduction: Wilderness by Asimov; If I Forget Thee, Oh Earth by **Arthur C. Clarke**, 1951; Berserker's Prey by Fred Saberhagen, 1967; Call Me Proteus by Edward Wellen, 1973; Teddi by **Andre Norton**, 1973; The Gambling Hell and the Sinful Girl by Katherine MacLean; Invasion Report by Theodore R Cogswell, 1954; A Start in Life by Arthur Sellings, 1954; Big Sword by Pauline Ashwell, 1958; and The Gift by **Ray Bradbury**, 1952.

99. The Hugo Winners - Volume V. Published by Doubleday & Company, Garden City, New York, 1986. Hardcover. Herein: Introduction: My Magazine by Asimov; 1980: 38th Convention, Boston, an essay by Barry B. Longyear, 1986; Enemy Mine by Barry B. Longyear, 1979; Sandkings by George R. R. Martin, 1979; The Way of Cross and Dragon by George R. R. Martin, 1979; 1981: 39th Convention, Denver an essay by **Gordon R. Dickson**, 1986; Lost Dorsai by **Gordon R. Dickson**, 1980; The Cloak and the Staff by **Gordon R. Dickson**, 1980; Grotto of the Dancing Deer by Clifford D. Simak, 1980; 1982: 40th Convention, Chicago, an essay by **Poul Anderson**, 1986; The Saturn Game by **Poul Anderson**, 1981; Unicorn Variation by Roger Zelazny, 1981; and The Pusher by John Varley, 1981.

100. Mythical Beasties - Isaac Asimov's Magical Worlds of Fantasy 6. With Martin H. Greenberg and Charles G. Waugh. Published by Signet Books - New American Library, New York City, 1986. Softcover. Herein: Centaur Fielder for the Yankees by Edward D. Hoch, 1986; The Kragen by **Jack Vance**, 1964; The Gorgon by Tanith Lee, 1982; The Griffin and the Minor Canon by Frank R. Stockton, 1885; The Ice Dragon by George R. R. Martin, 1980; Prince Prigio by Andrew Lang, 1889; Letters from Laura by Mildred Clingerman, 1954; The Triumph of Pegasus by F. A. Javor, 1965; Caution! Inflammable! by Thomas N. Scortia, 1955; The Pyramid Project by Robert F. Young, 1964; The Silken-Swift by **Theodore Sturgeon**, 1953; Mood Wendigo by Thomas A. Easton, 1980; and The Little Mermaid by Hans Christian Andersen, 1837.

101. Tin Stars - Isaac Asimov's Wonderful Worlds of Science Fiction 5. With Martin H. Greenberg and Charles G. Waugh. Published by Signet Books - New American Library, New York City, 1986. Softcover. This contains: Introduction by Asimov; Into the Shop by Ron Goulart, 1964; Cloak of Anarchy by Larry Niven, 1972; The King's Legions by Christopher Anvil, 1967; Finger of Fate, 1980; and Voiceover, 1984, by Edward Wellen; Arm of the Law, 1958; and The Powers of Observation, 1968, by **Harry Harrison**; The Fastest Draw by Larry Eisenberg, 1963; Brillo by **Harlan Ellison** and Ben Bova, 1970; Faithfully Yours by Lou Tabakow, 1955; Safe Harbor by Donald Wismer, 1986; Examination Day by Henry Slesar, 1958; The Cruel Equations by Robert Sheckley, 1971; Animal Lover by Stephen R. Donaldson, 1978; and Mirror Image by **Isaac Asimov**, 1972.

102. Magical Wishes - Isaac Asimov's Magical Worlds of Fantasy 7. With Martin H. Greenberg and Charles G. Waugh. Published by Signet Books - New American Library, New York City, 1986. Softcover. Herein: Introduction: Wishing Will Make It So by Asimov; The Monkey's Paw by W. W. Jacobs, 1902; Behind the News by Jack Finney, 1952; The Flight of the Umbrella by Marvin Kaye, 1977; Tween by J. F. Bone, 1978; The Boy Who Brought Love by Edward D. Hoch, 1974; The Vacation by **Ray Bradbury**, 1963; The Anything Box by Zenna Henderson, 1956; A Born Charmer by Edward P. Hughes, 1981; Millennium by Fredric Brown, 1955; Dreams are Sacred by Peter Phillips, 1948; The Same to You Doubled by Robert Sheckley, 1970; Gifts by **Gordon R. Dickson**, 1958; I Wish I May, I Wish I Might by Bill Pronzini, 1973; Three Day Magic by Charlotte Armstrong, 1948; The Bottle Imp by Robert Louis Stevenson, 1891; and What If by **Isaac Asimov**, 1952.

103. Isaac Asimov Presents the Great SF Stories 15: 1953. With Martin H. Greenberg. Published by DAW Books, New York City, 1986. Softcover. DAW Collector's Book 694. Herein: Introduction by Greenberg; Imposter by **Philip K. Dick**, 1953; Crucifixus Etiam by Walter M. Miller Jr., 1953; The Liberation of Earth by William Tenn, 1953; Lot by Ward Moore, 1953; The Nine Billion Names of God by **Arthur C. Clarke**, 1953; It's a Good Life by Jerome Bixby, 1953; Hall of Mirrors by Fredric Brown, 1953; The Model of a Judge by William Morrison, 1953; The Wall Around the World by Theodore R. Cogswell, 1953; Time Is the Traitor by **Alfred Bester**, 1953; Common Time by **James Blish**, 1953; A Bad Day for Sales, 1953; and The Big Holiday, 1953, by **Fritz Leiber**; The World Well Lost, 1953; and Saucer of Loneliness, 1953, by **Theodore Sturgeon**; Four in One by **Damon Knight**, 1953; and Warm by Robert Sheckley, 1953.

104. The Twelve Frights of Christmas. With Martin H. Greenberg and Charles G. Waugh. Published by Avon Books, New York City, 1986. Softcover. This contains: Introduction: The New Beginning by Asimov; The Chimney by Ramsey Campbell, 1977; Markheim by Robert Louis Stevenson, 1886; The Night Before Christmas by Robert Bloch, 1980; The Festival by H. P. Lovecraft, 1923; The Old Nurse's Story by Elizabeth Gaskell, 1852; Glamr by Sabine Baring-Gould, 1904; Pollock and the Porroh Man by **H. G. Wells**, 1895; The Weird Woman, published anonymously in 1871; The Hellhound Project by Ron Goulart, 1973; Wolverden Tower by Grant Allen, 1896; Planet of Fakers by J. T. McIntosh, 1966; Life Sentence by James V. McConnell; and The Star by **Arthur C. Clarke**, 1955.

105. Isaac Asimov Presents the Great SF Stories 16: 1954. With Martin H. Greenberg. Published by DAW Books, New York City, 1987. Softcover. DAW Collector's Book 709. Herein: Introduction by Greenberg; Down Among the Dead Men by William Tenn, 1954; Letters From Laura by Mildred Clingerman, 1954; Transformer by Chad Oliver, 1954; The Father-Thing by **Philip K. Dick**, 1954; Balaam by Anthony Boucher, 1954; Answer by Fredric Brown, 1954; The Hunting Lodge by Randall Garrett, 1954; The Lysenko Maze by **Donald A. Wollheim**, 1954; Fondly Fahrenheit by **Alfred Bester**, 1954; The Cold Equations by Tom Godwin, 1954; The Music Master of Babylon by Edgar Pangborn, 1954; The End of Summer by Algis Budrys, 1954; The Deep Range by **Arthur C. Clarke**, 1954; Man of Parts by H. L. Gold, 1954; The Test by Richard Matheson, 1954; Anachron by **Damon Knight**, 1954; and Black Charlie by **Gordon R. Dickson**, 1954.

106. Young Witches and Warlocks. With Martin H. Greenberg and Charles G. Waugh. Published by Harper and Row, New York City, 1987. Hardcover. This contains: Introduction: How Exciting! by Asimov; The April Witch by **Ray Bradbury**, 1952; Witch Girl by Elizabeth Coatsworth, 1953; The Wonderful Day by Robert Arthur, 1940; With Four Lean Hounds by Pat Murphy, 1984; Mistress Sary by William Tenn, 1947; Teragram by Evelyn E. Smith, 1955; Stevie and the Dark by Zenna Henderson, 1952; A Message from Charity by William M. Lee, 1967; The Entrance Exam by Mary Carey, 1976; and The Boy Who Drew Cats by Lafcadio Hearn, 1898.

107. Devils - Isaac Asimov's Magical Worlds of Fantasy 8. With Martin H. Greenberg and Charles G. Waugh. Published by Signet Books - New American Library, New York City, 1987. Softcover. Herein: Introduction: The Devil by Asimov; The Howling Man by Charles Beaumont, 1959; I'm Dangerous Tonight by Cornell Woolrich, 1937; The Devil in Exile by Brian Cleeve, 1968; The Cage by Ray Russell, 1959; The Tale of Ivan the Fool by Leo Tolstoy, 1886; Rustle of Wings by Fredric Brown, 1953; The Shepherds by Ruth Sawyer, 1941; He Stepped on the Devil's Tail by Winston Marks, 1955; That Hell Bound Train by Robert Bloch, 1958; Added Inducement by Robert F. Young, 1957; The Devil and Daniel Webster by Stephen Vincent Benet, 1936; Colt .24 by Rick Hautala, 1987; The Making of Revelation, Part 1 by Philip Jose Farmer, 1980; Trace by Jerome Bixby, 1961; Guardian Angel by **Arthur C. Clarke**, 1950; The Devil Was Sick by Bruce Elliot, 1951; Deal with the D.E.V.I.L. by Theodore R. Cogswell, 1981; and Dazed by **Theodore Sturgeon**, 1971.

108. Hound Dunnit. With Martin H. Greenberg and Carol-Lynn Rossel Waugh. Published by Carroll & Graf, New York City, 1987. Hardcover. Herein: The Sleeping Dog by Isaac Asimov; The Enemy by Charlotte Armstrong; The Dog who Hated Jazz by William Bankier; Silver Blaze by Arthur Conan Doyle; The Dark Road Home by Paul W. Fairman; The Emergency Exit Affair by Michael Gilbert; How Come My Dog Don't Bark? by Ron Goulart; Dispatching Bootsie by Joyce Harrington; Captain Leopold Goes to the Dogs by Ed Hoch; Lincoln's Doctor's Son's by Warner Law; The Dogsbody Case by Francis M. Nevins Jr.; Puzzle for Poppy by Q. Patrick; Chambrun Gets the Message by Hugh Pentecost; Raffles on the Trail of the Hound by Barry Perowne; Coyote and Quartermoon by Bill Pronzini and Jeffrey Wallman; Sellin' Some Wood by John Rudin; and, A Dog in the Daytime by Rex Stout.

109. Space Shuttles - Isaac Asimov's Wonderful Worlds of Science Fiction 7. With Martin H. Greenberg and Charles G. Waugh. Published by Signet Books - New American Library, New York City, 1987. Softcover. Please note that Book 6 in this series, Neanderthals, was actually edited by **Robert Silverberg**, not by Asimov. Herein: Introduction by Asimov; Hitchhiker by Sheila Finch, 1987; Truck Driver by Robert Chilson, 1972; Hermes to the Ages by Frederick D. Gottfried, 1980; Pushbutton War by Joseph P. Martino, 1960; The Getaway Special by Jerry Oltion, 1985; Between a Rock and a High Place by Timothy Zahn, 1982; To Grab Power by Hayden Howard, 1971; Coming of Age in Henson's Tube by William Jon Watkins, 1977; Deborah's Children by Grant D. Callin, 1983; The Book of Baraboo by Barry B. Longyear, 1980; The Speckled Gantry by Joseph Green and Patrice Milton, 1979; The Nanny by Thomas Wylde, 1983; Dead Ringer by Edward Wellen, 1987; and The Last Shuttle by **Isaac Asimov**, 1981.

110. Atlantis - Isaac Asimov's Magical Worlds of Fantasy 9. With Martin H. Greenberg and Charles G. Waugh. Published by Signet Books - New American Library, New York City, 1988. Softcover. Herein: Introduction: The Lost City by Asimov; The Shadow Kingdom by Robert E. Howard, 1929; The Double Shadow by Clark Ashton Smith, 1933; The Brigadier in Check and Mate by Sterling Lanier, 1986; Dragon Moon by Henry Kuttner, 1941; Treaty in Tartessos by Karen Anderson, 1963; The Vengeance of Ulios by Edmond Hamilton, 1935; Scar-Tissue by Henry S. Whitehead, 1946; The Dweller in the Temple by Manly Wade Wellman, 1977; Gone Fishing by J. A. Pollard, 1988; The Lamp by L. Sprague de Camp, 1975; and The New Atlantis by **Ursula K. Le Guin**, 1975.

111. Isaac Asimov Presents the Great SF Stories 17: 1955. With Martin H. Greenberg. Published by DAW Books, New York City, 1988. Softcover. DAW Collector's Book 733. This contains: Introduction by Greenberg; The Tunnel Under the World by **Frederik Pohl**, 1955; The Darfstellar by Walter M. Miller Jr., 1955; The Cave of Night by James E. Gunn, 1955; Grandpa by James H. Schmitz, 1955; Who by **Theodore Sturgeon**, 1955; The Short Ones by Raymond E. Banks, 1955; Captive Market by **Philip K. Dick**, 1955; Allamagoosa by **Eric Frank Russell**, 1955; The Vanishing American by Charles Beaumont, 1955; The Game of Rat and Dungeon by Cordwainer Smith, 1955; The Star by **Arthur C. Clarke**, 1955; Nobody Bothers Gus by Algis Budrys, 1955; Delenda Est by **Poul Anderson**, 1955; and Dreaming is a Private Thing by **Isaac Asimov**, 1955.

112. Encounters. With Martin H. Greenberg and Charles G. Waugh. Published by Headline Books, London, 1988. Softcover. Introduction by Asimov; Contact! by David Drake, 1974; Capsule by Rosalind

Isaac Asimov

M. Greenberg writing as Rosalind Stanley, 1982; Cabin Boy by **Damon Knight**, 1951; First Love by Lloyd Biggle, Jr., 1959; All the Way Back by Michael Shaara, 1952; A Death in the House by Clifford D. Simak, 1959; Firewater by William Tenn, 1952; Hiding Place by **Poul Anderson**, 1961; Final Contact by J. A. Pollard, 1988; Proof by **Hal Clement**, 1942; Scientific Method by Chad Oliver, 1953; First Contact by Murray Leinster, 1945; Not Final! by **Isaac Asimov**, 1941; Angel's Egg by Edgar Pangborn, 1951; The Victim from Space by Robert Sheckley, 1957; and Invasion of Privacy by Bob Shaw, 1970.

113. The Death of the Clever Criminal: Isaac Asimov Presents the Best Crime Stories of the 19th Century. With Martin H. Greenberg and Charles G. Waugh. Published by Dembner Books, New York City, 1988. Hardcover. Herein: The Man That Corrupted Hadleyburg by Mark Twain; His Defense by Harry Stillwell Edwards; The Nameless Man by Rodriguez Ottolengui; The Affair of the Avalanche Bicycle and Tyre Co. Ltd. by Arthur Morrison; The Episode of the Mexican Seer by Grant Allen; The Sheriff of Gullmore by Melville Davisson Post; The Chemistry of Anarchy by Robert Barr; Cheating the Gallows by Israel Zangwill; The Red Headed League by Sir Arthur Conan Doyle; Gallegher by Richard Harding Davis; The Three Strangers by Thomas Hardy; Murder Under the Microscope by William Russell; A Terribly Strange Bed by Wilkie Collins; The Purloined Letter by Edgar Allan Poe; and Mr. Higginbotham's Catastrophe by Nathaniel Hawthorne.

114. The Mammoth Book of Classic Science Fiction: Short Novels of the 1930s. With Charles G. Waugh. Published by Carroll & Graf, New York City, 1988. Hardcover. Herein: Introduction: Science Fiction Finds Its Voice by Asimov; The Shadow Out of Time by H. P. Lovecraft, 1936; A Matter of Form by Horace L. Gold, 1938; Jane Brown's Body by Cornell Woolrich, 1938; Who Goes There? by **John W. Campbell** writing as Don A. Stuart, 1938; Sidewise in Time by Murray Leinster, 1934; Alas, All Thinking! by Harry Bates, 1935; Seeker of Tomorrow by Leslie J. Johnson and **Eric Frank Russell**, 1937; Dawn of Flame by Stanley G. Weinbaum, 1936; Divide and Rule by L. Sprague de Camp, 1939; and Wolves of Darkness by **Jack Williamson**, 1932.

115. Monsters - Isaac Asimov's Wonderful Worlds of Science Fiction 8. With Martin H. Greenberg and Charles G. Waugh. Published by Signet Books - New American Library, New York City, 1988. Softcover. Herein: Introduction by Asimov; The Men in the Walls by William Tenn, 1963; The Doors of His Face the Lamps of His Mouth by Roger Zelazny, 1965; Passengers by **Robert Silverberg**, 1968; The Botticelli Horror by Lloyd Biggle Jr., 1960; The Shapes by J. H. Rosny aine, 1968; The Clone by Theodore L. Thomas, 1959; Student Body by F. L. Wallace, 1953; Black Destroyer by **A. E. van Vogt**, 1939; Mother by Philip Jose Farmer, 1953; Exploration Team by Murray Leinster, 1956; and All the Way Back by Michael Shaara, 1952.

116. Isaac Asimov Presents the Great SF Stories 18: 1956. With Martin H. Greenberg. Published by DAW Books, New York City, 1988. Softcover. DAW Collector's Book 754. Herein: Introduction by Greenberg; 2066: Election Day by Michael Shaara, 1956; The Doorstop by Reginald Bretnor, 1956; Horrer Howce by Margaret St. Clair, 1956; A Work of Art by **James Blish**, 1956; Brightside Crossing by Alan E. Nourse, 1956; Clerical Error by Mark Clifton, 1956; Silent Brother by Algis Budrys, 1956; The Country of the Kind by **Damon Knight**, 1956; Exploration Team by Murray Leinster, 1956; Rite of Passage by Henry Kuttner and **C. L. Moore**, 1956; The Man Who Came Early by **Poul Anderson**, 1956; Compounded Interest by Mack Reynolds, 1956; And Now the News by **Theodore Sturgeon**, 1956; and The Last Question by **Isaac Asimov**, 1956.

117. Ghosts - Isaac Asimov's Magical Worlds of Fantasy 10. With Martin H. Greenberg and Charles G. Waugh. Published by Signet Books - New American Library, New York City, 1988. Softcover. Herein: Introduction by Asimov; King of Thieves by **Jack Vance**, 1949; The Lady's Maid's Bell by Edith Wharton, 1902; Daemon by **C. L. Moore**, 1946; A Passion for History by Stephen Minot, 1976; Elle Est Trois (La Mort) by Tanith Lee, 1983; A Terrible Vengeance by Charlotte Riddell writing as Mrs. J. H. Riddell, 1889; The Invasion of the Church of the Holy Ghost by Russell Kirk, 1983; The Toll-House by W. W. Jacobs, 1907; The Fire When it Comes by Parke Godwin, 1981; Come Dance with Me on My Pony's Grave by Charles L. Grant, 1973; The Wind in the Rose Bush by Mary Wilkins Freeman, 1902; Ringing the Changes by Robert Aickman, 1955; Touring by Gardner Dozois, Jack Dann and Michael Swanwick, 1981; and Author! Author! by **Isaac Asimov**, 1964.

118. The Sport of Crime. With Carol-Lynn Rossel Waugh and Martin H. Greenberg. Published by Lynx Books, New York City, 1988. Softcover.

119. Isaac Asimov Presents the Great SF Stories 19: 1957. With Martin H. Greenberg. Published by DAW Books, New York City, 1989. Softcover. DAW Collector's Book 772. This contains: Introduction by Greenberg; Game Preserve by Rog Phillips, 1957; Soldier by **Harlan Ellison**, 1957; The Last Man Left in the Bar, 1957; and The Education of Tigress McCardle, 1957, by C. M. Kornbluth; Omnilingual by H. Beam Piper, 1957; The Mile Long Spaceship by **Kate Wilhelm**, 1957; Call Me Joe by **Poul Anderson**, 1957; You Know Willie by Theodore R. Cogswell, 1957; Hunting Machine by Carol Emshwiller, 1957; World of a Thousand Colors by **Robert Silverberg**, 1957; Let's be Frank by **Brian W. Aldiss**, 1957; The Cage by A. Bertram Chandler, 1957; The Tunesmith by Lloyd Biggle Jr., 1957; and A Loint of Paw, 1957; and Strikebreaker, 1957, by **Isaac Asimov**.

120. Isaac Asimov Presents Tales of the Occult. With Martin H. Greenberg and Charles G. Waugh. Published by Prometheus Books, New York City, 1989. Hardcover. Introduction by Asimov; Under the Knife by **H. G. Wells**, 1896; Children of the Zodiac by Rudyard Kipling 1891; The Girl Who Found Things by Henry Slesar, 1973; The Emigrant Banshee by Gertrude Henderson, 1901; Young Goodman Brown by Nathaniel Hawthorne, 1835; Through a Glass, Darkly by Helen McCloy, 1948; Dumb Supper by Kris Neville, 1950; The Tell-Tale Heart by Edgar Allan Poe, 1843; The House and the Brain by Edward

Bulwer-Lytton, 1859; The Dead Man's Hand by Manly Wade Wellman, 1944; The Scythe by **Ray Bradbury**, 1943; The Great Keinplatz Experiment by Arthur Conan Doyle, 1885; Do You Know Dave Wenzel? by **Fritz Leiber**, 1974; August Heat by W. F. Harvey, 1910; Speak to Me of Death by Cornell Woolrich, 1937; The Woman Who Thought She Could Read by Avram Davidson, 1959; Tryst in Time by **C. L. Moore**, 1936; The Blood Seedling by John Hay, 1905; The Tracer of Lost Persons and the Seal of Solomon Cypher by Robert W. Chambers, 1906; Miss Esperson by August Derleth, 1954; Peeping Tom by Judith Merril; and The Moving Finger by Edith Wharton, 1901.

121. The Purr-fect Crime. With Carol-Lynn Rossel Waugh and Martin H. Greenberg. Published by Lynx Books, New York City, 1989. Softcover.

122. Robots - Isaac Asimov's Wonderful Worlds of Science Fiction 9. With Martin H. Greenberg and Charles G. Waugh. Published by Signet Books - New American Library, New York City, 1989. Softcover. Herein: Introduction by Asimov; Second Variety by **Philip K. Dick**, 1953; Though Dreamers Die by Lester del Rey, 1944; The Tunnel Under the World by **Frederik Pohl**, 1955; Brother Robot by Henry Slesar, 1958; The Lifeboat Mutiny by Robert Sheckley, 1955; The Warm Space by David Brin, 1985; How-2 by Clifford D. Simak, 1954; Too Robot to Marry by George H. Smith, 1959; The Education of Tigress McCardle by C. M. Kornbluth, 1957; Breakfast of Champions by Thomas Easton, 1980; Sun Up by A. A. Jackson and Howard Waldrop, 1976; The Problem Was Lubrication by David R. Bunch, 1961; First to Serve by Algis Budrys, 1954; Two-Handed Engine by Henry Kuttner and **C. L. Moore**, 1955; Soldier Boy by Michael Shaara, 1953; Farewell to the Master by Harry Bates, 1940; and Sally by **Isaac Asimov**, 1953.

123. Visions of Fantasy: Tales from the Masters. With Martin H. Greenberg. Published by Doubleday & Company, Garden City, New York, 1989. Hardcover. Herein: Introduction by Asimov; Voices in the Wind by Elizabeth S. Helfman, 1987; Things That Go Quack in the Night by Lewis Shiner and Edith Shiner, 1983; The Smallest Dragonboy by **Anne McCaffrey**, 1973; The Seventh Mandarin by Jane Yolen, 1970; A Dozen of Everything by Marion Zimmer Bradley, 1959; Poor Little Saturday by Madeleine L'Engle, 1956; A Message from Charity by William Lee, 1967; The Voices of El Dorado by Howard Goldsmith, 1974; The Box by Bruce Coville, 1986; Letters from Camp by Al Sarrantonio, 1982; The Lake by **Ray Bradbury**, 1944; and The Fable of the Three Princes by **Isaac Asimov**, 1987.

124. Curses - Isaac Asimov's Magical Worlds of Fantasy 11. With Martin H. Greenberg and Charles G. Waugh. Published by Signet Books - New American Library, New York City, 1989. Softcover. This contains: Introduction: Malevolence by Asimov; The Doom of the Griffiths by Elizabeth Gaskell, 1858; The Little Black Train by Manly Wade Wellman, 1954; A Hunger in the Blood by Talmage Powell, 1989; The Curse by **Arthur C. Clarke**, 1946; Julia Cahill's Curse by George Moore, 1903; The Red Swimmer by Robert Bloch, 1939; You Know Willie by Theodore R. Cogswell, 1957; Trouble With Water by H. L. Gold, 1939; Mad Monkton by Wilkie Collins, 1855; Long Chromachy of the Crows by Seumas MacManus, 1905; The Curse of the Catafalgues by F. Antsy, 1882; A Seance in Summer by Mario Martin Jr., 1974; Transformations by Christopher Fahy, 1989; In Dark New England Days by Sarah Orne Jewett, 1890; The Messenger by Robert W. Chambers, 1897; Or the Grasses Grow by Avram Davidson, 1958; and The Dollar by Morgan Robertson, 1905.

125. The New Hugo Winners. With Martin H. Greenberg. Published by Wynwood Press, New York City, 1989. Hardcover. Herein: Speech Sounds by Octavia E Butler, 1983; Press Enter by John Varley, 1984; Fire Watch by **Connie Willis**, 1982; The Crystal Spheres by David Brin, 1984; Souls by Joanna Russ, 1982; Blood Music by Greg Bear, 1983; Cascade Point by Timothy Zahn, 1983; and Melancholy Elephants by Spider Robinson, 1982.

126. The Mammoth Book of Golden Age Science Fiction: Short Novels of the 1940s. With Martin H. Greenberg and Charles G. Waugh. Published by Carroll and Graf, New York City, 1989. Hardcover. Herein: Introduction: The Age of Campbell by Asimov; Time Wants a Skeleton by Ross Rocklynne, 1941; The Weapons Shop by **A. E. van Vogt**, 1942; Nerves by Lester del Rey, 1942; Daymare by Fredric Brown, 1942; Killdozer! by **Theodore Sturgeon**, 1944; No Woman Born by **C. L. Moore**, 1944; The Big and the Little by **Isaac Asimov**, 1944; Giant Killer by A. Bertram Chandler, 1945; E for Effort by T. L. Sherred, 1947; and With Folded Hands by **Jack Williamson**, 1947.

127. Senior Sleuths: A Large Print Anthology of Mysteries and Puzzlers. With Martin H. Greenberg and Carol-Lynn Rossel Waugh.
Published by G. K. Hall & Co., Thorndike, Maine, 1989. Hardcover.

128. Cosmic Critiques: How and Why Ten Science Fiction Stories Work. With Martin H. Greenberg. Published by Writer's Digest Books, Cincinnati, Ohio, 1989. Softcover. Herein: Introduction by Asimov; Neutron Star by Larry Niven, 1966; Rock On by Pat Cadigan, 1984; Transstar by Raymond E. Banks, 1960; Billenium by J. G. Ballard, 1961; Grandpa by James H. Schmitz, 1955; The Last Question by Isaac Asimov, 1956; In the Circle of Nowhere by Irving E. Cox, Jr., 1954; The Silk and the Song by Charles L. Fontenay, 1956; Dial F for Frankenstein by **Arthur C Clarke**, 1965; and Carcinoma Angels by Norman Spinrad, 1967.

129. Isaac Asimov Presents the Great SF Stories 20: 1958. With Martin H. Greenberg. Published by DAW Books, New York City, 1990. Softcover. DAW Collector's Book 808. Herein: Introduction by Greenberg; Unhuman Sacrifice by Katherine MacLean, 1958; The Immortals by James E. Gunn, 1958; The Yellow Pill by Rog Phillips, 1958; The Burning of the Brain by Cordwainer Smith, 1958; The Big Front Yard by Clifford D. Simak, 1958; Two Dooms by C. M. Kornbluth, 1958; Or All The Seas With Oysters by Avram Davidson, 1958; The Prize of Peril by Robert Sheckley, 1958; The Iron Chancellor by **Robert Silverberg**, 1958; Poor Little Warrior by **Brian W. Aldiss**, 1958; The Last of the Deliverers by **Poul Anderson**, 1958; and The Feeling of Power by **Isaac Asimov**, 1958.

Isaac Asimov

130. Isaac Asimov Presents the Great SF Stories 21: 1959. With Martin H. Greenberg. Published by DAW Books, New York City, 1990. Softcover. DAW Collector's Book 823. Herein: Introduction by Greenberg; The Wind People by Marion Zimmer Bradley, 1959; Make a Prison by Lawrence Block, 1959; The Malted Milk Monster by William Tenn, 1959; Adrift on the Policy Level by Chandler Davis; What Now Little Man by Mark Clifton, 1959; Multum in Parvo by Jack Sharkey, 1959; The Pi Man by **Alfred Bester**, 1959; No, No Not Rogov by Cordwainer Smith, 1959; What Rough Beast by **Damon Knight**, 1959; The Alley Man by Philip Jose Farmer, 1959; Day at the Beach by Carol Emshwiller, 1959; The World of Heart's Desire by Robert Sheckley, 1959; The Man Who Lost the Sea by **Theodore Sturgeon**, 1959; and A Death in the House by Clifford D. Simak, 1959.

131. Invasions - Isaac Asimov's Wonderful Worlds of Science Fiction 10. With Martin H. Greenberg and Charles G. Waugh. Published by ROC - Penguin Books, New York City, 1990. Softcover. This contains: Introduction by Asimov; The Liberation of Earth by William Tenn, 1953; Asylum by **A. E. van Vogt**, 1942; Exposure by **Eric Frank Russell**, 1950; Invasion of Privacy by Bob Shaw, 1970; What Have I Done? by Mark Clifton, 1952; Imposter by **Philip K. Dick**, 1953; The Soul-Empty Ones by Walter M. Miller Jr., 1951; The Cloud Men by Owen Oliver, 1990; The Stone Man by Fred Saberhagen, 1967; For I Am A Jealous People by Lester del Rey, 1954; Don't Look Now by Henry Kuttner, 1948; The Certificate by Avram Davidson, 1959; The Alien Rulers by Piers Anthony, 1968; Squeeze Box by Philip E. High, 1959; and Living Space by **Isaac Asimov**, 1956.

132. The Mammoth Book of Vintage Science Fiction: Short Novels of the 1950s. With Martin H. Greenberg and Charles G. Waugh. Published by Carroll and Graf, New York City, 1990. Hardcover. Herein: The Age of the Troika, an essay by Asimov; Flight to Forever by **Poul Anderson**, 1950; The Martian Way by **Isaac Asimov**, 1952; Second Game by Katherine MacLean and Charles V. De Vet, 1958; Dark Benediction by Walter M. Miller, Jr., 1951; The Midas Plague by **Frederik Pohl**, 1954; The Oceans Are Wide by Frank M. Robinson, 1954; And Then There Were None by **Eric Frank Russell**, 1951; Baby Is Three by **Theodore Sturgeon**, 1952; Firewater by William Tenn, 1952; and The Alley Man by Philip Jose Farmer, 1959.

133. Isaac Asimov Presents the Great SF Stories 22: 1960. With Martin H. Greenberg. Published by DAW Books, New York City, 1991. Softcover. DAW Collector's Book 842. Herein: Introduction by Greenberg; The Voices of Time by J. G. Ballard, 1960; The Handler by **Damon Knight**, 1960; Mind Partner by Christopher Anvil, 1960; Chief by Henry Slesar, 1960; I Remember Babylon by **Arthur C. Clarke**, 1960; The Lady Who Sailed the Soul by Cordwainer Smith, 1960; Make Mine Homogenized by Rick Raphael, 1960; Mine Own Ways by Richard McKenna, 1960; The Fellow Who Married The Maxill Girl by Ward Moore, 1960; The Day the Icicle Works Closed by **Frederik Pohl**, 1960; and Mariana by **Fritz Leiber**, 1960.

134. Isaac Asimov Presents the Great SF Stories 23: 1961. With Martin H. Greenberg. Published by DAW Books, New York City, 1991. Softcover. DAW Collector's Book 856. This contains: Introduction by Greenberg; The Highest Treason by Randall Garrett, 1961; The Moon Moth by **Jack Vance**, 1961; Hothouse by **Brian W. Aldiss**, 1961; Hiding Place by **Poul Anderson**, 1961; A Prize for Edie by J. F. Bone, 1961; The Ship Who Sang by **Anne McCaffrey**, 1961; Death and the Senator by **Arthur C. Clarke**, 1961; The Quaker Cannon by **Frederik Pohl** and C. M. Kornbluth, 1961; A Planet Named Shayol by Cordwainer Smith, 1961; Rainbird by R. A. Lafferty, 1961; Wall of Crystal, Eye of Night by Algis Budrys, 1961; Remember the Alamo by R. R. Fehrenbach, 1961; and What is this Thing Called Love by **Isaac Asimov**, 1961.

135. Faeries - Isaac Asimov's Magical Worlds of Fantasy 12. With Martin H. Greenberg and Charles G. Waugh. Published by ROC - Penguin Books, New York City, 1991. Softcover. Herein: Fairyland, an essay by Asimov; The Long Night of Waiting by **Andre Norton**, 1974; The King of the Elves by **Philip K. Dick**; How the Fairies Came to Ireland by Herminie Templeton, 1902; The Manor of Roses by Thomas Burnett Swann, 1966; The Fairy Prince by H. C. Bailey, 1911; The Ugly Unicorn by Jessica Amanda Salmonson, 1991; The Brownie of the Black Haggs by James Hogg, 1828; The Dream of Akinosuke by Lafcadio Hearn, 1904; Elfinland by Johann Ludwig Tieck, 1823; Darby O'Gill and the Good People by Herminie Templeton, 1901; No-Man's-Land by John Buchan, 1899; The Prism by Mary E. Wilkins Freeman writing as Mary E. Wilkins, 1901; The Kith of the Elf-Folk by Lord Dunsany, 1908; The Secret Place by Richard McKenna, 1966; Flying Pan by Robert F. Young, 1956; My Father the Cat by Henry Slesar, 1957; The Queen of Air and Darkness by **Poul Anderson**, 1971; and Kid Stuff by **Isaac Asimov**, 1953.

136. The Mammoth Book of New World Science Fiction: Short Novels of the 1960s. With Martin H. Greenberg and Charles G. Waugh. Published by Carroll and Graf, New York City, 1991. Hardcover. This contains: The Eve of RUMOKO by Roger Zelazny, 1969; The Night of the Trolls by Keith Laumer, 1963; Mercenary by Mack Reynolds, 1962; Soldier, Ask Not by **Gordon R. Dickson**, 1964; Weyr Search by **Anne McCaffrey**, 1967; Code Three by Rick Raphael, 1963; How It Was When the Past Went Away by **Robert Silverberg**, 1969; The Highest Treason by Randall Garrett, 1961; Hawk Among the Sparrows by Dean McLaughlin, 1968; and The Suicide Express by Philip Jose Farmer, 1966.

137. The New Hugo Winners - Volume II. Published by Baen Publishing, Riverdale, New York, 1991. Introduction by Asimov; 24 Views of Mr. Fuji, by Hokusai by Roger Zelazny, 1985; Paladin of the Lost Hour by **Harlan Ellison**, 1985; Fermi and Frost by **Frederik Pohl**, 1985; Gilgamesh in the Outback by **Robert Silverberg**, 1986; Permafrost by Roger Zelazny, 1986; Tangents by Greg Bear, 1986; Eye for Eye by Orson Scott Card, 1987; Buffalo Gals, Won't You Come Out Tonight by **Ursula K. Le Guin**, 1987; and Why I Left Harry's All-Night Hamburgers by Lawrence Watt-Evans, 1987.

138. Isaac Asimov Presents the Great SF Stories 24: 1962. With Martin H. Greenberg. Published by DAW Books, New York City, 1992. Softcover. DAW Collector's Book 871. Herein: Introduction by Greenberg; The Insane Ones by J. G. Ballard, 1962; Christmas Treason by James White, 1962; Seven Day Terror by R. A. Lafferty, 1962; Kings Who Die by **Poul Anderson**, 1962; The Man Who Made Friends With Electricity by **Fritz Leiber**, 1962; Hang Head, Vandal by Mark Clifton, 1962; The Weather Man by Theodore L. Thomas, 1962; Earthlings Go Home by Mack Reynolds, 1962; The Streets of Ashkelon by **Harry Harrison**, 1962; When You Care, When You Love by **Theodore Sturgeon**, 1962; The Ballad of Lost C'Mell by Cordwainer Smith, 1962; Gadget vs. Trend by Christopher Anvil, 1962; and Roofs of Silver by **Gordon R. Dickson**, 1962.

139. Isaac Asimov Presents the Great SF Stories 25: 1963. With Martin H. Greenberg. Published by DAW Books, New York City, 1992. Softcover. DAW Collector's Book 885. This contains: Introduction by Greenberg; If There Were No Benny Cemoli by **Philip K. Dick**, 1963; Bernie the Faust by William Tenn, 1963; A Rose for Ecclesiastes by Roger Zelazny, 1963; Fortress Ship by Fred Saberhagen, 1963; Not in the Literature by Christopher Anvil, 1963; The Totally Rich by John Brunner, 1963; New Folks' Home by Clifford D. Simak, 1963; The Faces Outside by Bruce McAllister, 1963; Hot Planet by **Hal Clement**, 1963; Turn Off the Sky by Ray Nelson, 1963; They Don't Make Life Like They Used To by **Alfred Bester**, 1963; The Pain Peddlers by **Robert Silverberg**, 1963; and No Truce With Kings by **Poul Anderson**, 1963.

140. The Mammoth Book of Fantastic Science Fiction: Short Novels of the 1970s. Published by Carroll and Graf, New York City, 1992. Hardcover. Herein: Born with the Dead by **Robert Silverberg**, 1974; The Moon Goddess and the Son by Donald Kingsbury, 1979; Tin Soldier by Joan D. Vinge, 1974; In the Problem Pit by **Frederik Pohl**, 1973; Riding the Torch by Norman Spinrad, 1974; Mouthpiece by Edward Wellen, 1974; ARM by Larry Niven, 1975; The Persistence of Vision by John Varley, 1978; The Queen of Air and Darkness by **Poul Anderson**, 1971; and The Monster and the Maiden by **Gordon R Dickson**, 1976.

141. The Mammoth Book of Modern Science Fiction: Short Novels of the 1980s. With Martin H. Greenberg and Charles G. Waugh. Published by Carroll and Graf, New York City, 1993. Hardcover. This contains: Slow Music by James Tiptree Jr., 1980; Le Croix (The Cross) by Barry N. Malzberg, 1980; Scorched Supper on New Niger by Suzy McKee Charnas, 1980; The Saturn Game by **Poul Anderson**, 1981; Hardfought by Greg Bear, 1983; Swarmer Skimmer by Gregory Benford, 1981; Sailing to Byzantium by **Robert Silverberg**, 1985; Trinity by Nancy Kress, 1984; The Blind Geometer by Kim Stanley Robinson, 1986; and Surfacing by Walter Jon Williams, 1988.

***

NON-FICTION

1. Biochemistry and Human Metabolism. With Burnham S. Walker and William C. Boyd. Published by Williams and Wilkins, Baltimore, Maryland, 1952. Hardcover.

2. The Chemicals of Life: Enzymes, Vitamins and Hormones. Published by Abelard-Schuman, New York City, 1954. Hardcover.

3. Races and People. With William C. Boyd. Published by Abelard-Schuman, New York City, 1955. Hardcover.

4. Chemistry and Human Health. With Burnham S. Walker and M. K. Nicholas. Published by McGraw Hill, New York City, 1956. Hardcover.

5. Inside the Atom. Published by Abelard-Schuman, New York City, 1956. Hardcover.

6. Building Blocks of the Universe. Published by Abelard-Schuman, New York City, 1957. Hardcover.

7. Only a Trillion - Essays. Published by Abelard-Schuman, New York City, 1957. Hardcover.

8. The World of Carbon. Published by Abelard-Schuman, New York City, 1958. Hardcover.

9. The World of Nitrogen. Published by Abelard-Schuman, New York City, 1958. Hardcover.

10. Words of Science and the History Behind Them. Published by Houghton Mifflin, Boston, 1959. Hardcover.

11. Realm of Numbers. Published by Houghton Mifflin, Boston, 1959. Hardcover.

12. The Clock We Live On. Published by Abelard-Schuman, New York City, 1959. Hardcover.

13. Inside the Atom - Second Edition, Revised. Published by Abelard-Schuman, New York City, 1960. Hardcover.

14. The Living River. Published by Abelard-Schuman, New York City, 1960. Hardcover.

15. The Wellsprings of Life. Published by Abelard-Schuman, New York City, 1960. Hardcover.

16. Breakthroughs in Science. Published by Houghton Mifflin, Boston, 1960. Hardcover.

17. Realm of Measure. Published by Houghton Mifflin, Boston, 1960. Hardcover.

18. The Intelligent Man's Guide to Science. Published by Basic Books, New York City, 1960. Hardcover.

19. The Kingdom of the Sun. Published by Abelard-Schuman, New York City, 1960. Hardcover.

20. The Double Planet. Published by Abelard-Schuman, New York City, 1960. Hardcover.

21. Satellites in Outer Space. Published by Random House, New York City, 1960. Hardcover.

22. Realm of Algebra. Published by Houghton

Mifflin, Boston, 1961. Hardcover.

23. Words from the Myths. Published by Houghton Mifflin, Boston, 1961. Hardcover.

24. Words on the Map. Published by Houghton Mifflin, Boston, 1962. Hardcover.

25. Words in Genesis. Published by Houghton Mifflin, Boston, 1962. Hardcover.

26. Life and Energy. Published by Doubleday & Company, Garden City, New York, 1962. Hardcover.

27. The Search for the Elements. Published by Basic Books, New York City, 1962. Hardcover.

28. Fact and Fancy - Essays. Published by Doubleday & Company, Garden City, New York, 1962. Hardcover.

29. Words from the Exodus. Published by Houghton Mifflin, Boston, 1963. Hardcover.

30. View from a Height - Essays. Published by Doubleday & Company, Garden City, New York, 1963. Hardcover.

31. The Genetic Code. Published by Orion Press, New York City, 1963. Hardcover.

32. The Human Body: Its Structure and Operation. Published by Houghton Mifflin, Boston, 1963. Hardcover.

33. The Kite That Won the Revolution. Published by Houghton Mifflin, Boston, 1963. Hardcover.

34. Adding a Dimension - Essays. Published by Doubleday & Company, Garden City, New York, 1964. Hardcover.

35. The Human Brain: Its Capacities and Functions. Published by Houghton Mifflin, Boston, 1964. Hardcover.

36. Asimov's Biographical Encyclopedia of Science and Technology. Published by Doubleday & Company, Garden City, New York, 1964. Hardcover.

37. Quick and Easy Math. Published by Houghton Mifflin, Boston, 1964. Hardcover.

38. Planets for Man. With Stephen H. Dole. Published by Random House, New York City, 1964. Hardcover.

39. The Greeks: A Great Adventure. Published by Houghton Mifflin, Boston, 1965. Hardcover.

40. Of Time and Space and Other Things - Essays. Published by Doubleday & Company, Garden City, New York, 1965. Hardcover.

41. A Short History of Biology. Published by Natural History Press - Doubleday & Company, Garden City, New York, 1965. Hardcover.

42. A Short History of Chemistry. Published by Doubleday & Company, Garden City, New York, 1965. Hardcover.

43. An Easy Introduction to the Slide Rule. Published by Houghton Mifflin, Boston, 1965. Hardcover.

44. The New Intelligent Man's Guide to Science. Published by Basic Books, New York City, 1965. Hardcover.

45. The Roman Republic. Published by Houghton Mifflin, Boston, 1966. Hardcover.

46. From Earth to Heaven - Essays. Published by Doubleday & Company, Garden City, New York, 1966. Hardcover.

47. Inside the Atom - Third Edition, Revised. Published by Abelard-Schuman, New York City, 1966. Hardcover.

48. The Neutrino: Ghost Particle of the Atom. Published by Doubleday & Company, Garden City, New York, 1966. Hardcover.

49. The Noble Gases. Published by Basic Books, New York City, 1966. Hardcover.

50. The Universe: From Flat Earth to Quasar. Published by Walker and Company, New York City, 1966. Hardcover.

51. The Genetic Effects of Radiation. With Theodosius Dobzhansky. Published by The U.S. Atomic Energy Commission, Division of Technical Information, Oak Ridge, Tennessee, 1966. From the Understanding the Atom Series. Staple-bound pamphlet.

52. Understanding Physics - Volume I. Published by Walker and Company, New York City, 1966. Hardcover.

53. Understanding Physics - Volume II. Published by Walker and Company, New York City, 1966. Hardcover.

54. Understanding Physics - Volume III. Published by Walker and Company, New York City, 1966. Hardcover.

55. The Roman Empire. Published by Houghton Mifflin, Boston, 1967. Hardcover.

56. The Egyptians. Published by Houghton Mifflin, Boston, 1967. Hardcover.

57. Is Anyone There? - Essays. Published by Doubleday & Company, Garden City, New York, 1967. Hardcover.

58. The Moon. Published by Follet Publishing Company, United States, 1967. Hardcover.

59. Environments Out There. Published by Abelard-Schuman, New York City, 1967. Hardcover.

60. To the Ends of the Universe. Published by Walker and Company, New York City, 1967. Hardcover.

61. Mars. Published by Follet Publishing Company, United States, 1967. Hardcover.

62. The Near East: 10,000 Years of History. Published by Houghton Mifflin, Boston, 1968. Hardcover.

63. The Dark Ages. Published by Houghton Mifflin, Boston, 1968. Hardcover.

64. Words from History. Published by Houghton Mifflin, Boston, 1968. Hardcover.

65. Science, Numbers and I - Essays. Published by Doubleday & Company, Garden City, New York, 1968. Hardcover.

66. Stars. Published by Follet Publishing Company, United States, 1968. Hardcover.

67. Galaxies. Published by Follet Publishing Company, United States, 1968. Hardcover.

68. Asimov's Guide to The Bible - Volume I. Published by Doubleday & Company, Garden City, New York, 1968. Hardcover.

69. Asimov's Guide to The Bible - Volume II. Published by Doubleday & Company, Garden City, New York, 1969. Hardcover.

70. The Shaping of England. Published by Houghton Mifflin, Boston, 1969. Hardcover.

71. Photosynthesis. Published by Basic Books, New York City, 1969. Hardcover.

72. Twentieth Century Discovery. Published by Doubleday & Company, Garden City, New York, 1969. Hardcover.

73. Great Ideas of Science. Published by Houghton Mifflin, Boston, 1969. Hardcover.

74. Opus 100. Published by Houghton Mifflin, Boston, 1969. Hardcover.

75. Constantinople: The Forgotten Empire. Published by Houghton Mifflin, Boston, 1970. Hardcover.

76. Asimov's Guide to Shakespeare - Volume I. Published by Doubleday & Company, Garden City, New York, 1970. Hardcover.

77. Asimov's Guide to Shakespeare - Volume II. Published by Doubleday & Company, Garden City, New York, 1970. Hardcover.

78. The Solar System and Back - Essays. Published by Doubleday & Company, Garden City, New York, 1970. Hardcover.

79. Light. Published by Follet Publishing Company, United States, 1970. Hardcover.

80. ABCs of the Ocean. Published by Walker and Company, New York City, 1970. Hardcover.

81. The Land of Canaan. Published by Houghton Mifflin, Boston, 1971. Hardcover.

82. The Sensuous Dirty Old Man. Published by Walker and Company, New York City, 1971. Hardcover.

83. Isaac Asimov's Treasury of Humor. Published by Houghton Mifflin, Boston, 1971. Hardcover.

84. The Stars in Their Courses - Essays. Published by Doubleday & Company, Garden City, New York, 1971. Hardcover.

85. ABCs of the Earth. Published by Walker and Company, New York City, 1971. Hardcover.

86. What Makes the Sun Shine? Published by Walker and Company, New York City, 1971. Hardcover.

87. The Shaping of France. Published by Houghton Mifflin, Boston, 1972. Hardcover.

88. The Story of Ruth. Published by Doubleday & Company, Garden City, New York, 1972. Hardcover.

89. Asimov's Annotated Don Juan. Published by Doubleday & Company, Garden City, New York, 1972. Hardcover.

90. The Left Hand of the Electron - Essays. Published by Doubleday & Company, Garden City, New York, 1972. Hardcover.

91. Asimov's Biographical Encyclopedia of Science and Technology - New Revised Edition. Published by Doubleday & Company, Garden City, New York, 1972. Hardcover.

92. ABCs of Ecology. Published by Walker and Company, New York City, 1972. Hardcover.

93. Asimov's Guide to Science. Published by Basic Books, New York City, 1972. Hardcover.

94. More Words of Science. Published by Houghton Mifflin, Boston, 1972. Hardcover.

95. Electricity and Man. Published by The U.S. Atomic Energy Commission, Division of Technical Information, Oak Ridge, Tennessee, 1972. Staple-bound pamphlet.

96. Worlds Within Worlds. Published by The U.S. Atomic Energy Commission, Division of Technical Information, Oak Ridge, Tennessee, 1972. Staple-bound pamphlet.

97. Ginn Science Program - Intermediate Level A. Published by Ginn and Company, United States, 1972. Hardcover.

98. Ginn Science Program - Intermediate Level B. Published by Ginn and Company, United States, 1972. Hardcover.

99. Ginn Science Program - Intermediate Level C. Published by Ginn and Company, United States, 1972. Hardcover.

100. Ginn Science Program - Advanced Level A. Published by Ginn and Company, United States, 1973. Hardcover.

101. Ginn Science Program - Advanced Level B. Published by Ginn and Company, United States, 1973. Hardcover.

102. The Shaping of North America: From Earliest Times to 1763. Published by Houghton Mifflin, Boston, 1973. Hardcover.

103. How Did We Find Out About Numbers? Published by Walker and Company, New York City, 1973. Hardcover.

104. How Did We Find Out About Electricity?

Isaac Asimov

Published by Walker and Company, New York City, 1973. Hardcover.

105. How Did We Find Out About Dinosaurs? Published by Walker and Company, New York City, 1973. Hardcover.

106. Today and Tomorrow and... - Essays. Published by Doubleday & Company, Garden City, New York, 1973. Hardcover.

107. The Tragedy of the Moon - Essays. Published by Abelard-Schuman, New York City, 1973. Hardcover.

108. Comets and Meteors. Published by Follet Publishing Company, United States, 1973. Hardcover.

109. The Sun. Published by Follet Publishing Company, United States, 1973. Hardcover.

110. Please Explain. Published by Houghton Mifflin, Boston, 1973. Hardcover.

111. Jupiter, the Largest Planet. Published by Lothrop Lee and Shepard, New York City, 1973. Hardcover.

112. How Did We Find Out the Earth Is Round? Published by Walker and Company, New York City, 1973. Hardcover.

113. The Birth of the United States. Published by Houghton Mifflin, Boston, 1974. Hardcover.

114. Asimov's Annotated Paradise Lost. Published by Doubleday & Company, Garden City, New York, 1974. Hardcover.

115. Earth: Out Crowded Spaceship. Published by John Day, New York City, 1974. Hardcover.

116. Asimov on Astronomy - Essays. Published by Doubleday & Company, Garden City, New York, 1974. Hardcover.

117. Asimov on Chemistry - Essays. Published by Doubleday & Company, Garden City, New York, 1974. Hardcover.

118. How Did We Find Out About Germs? Published by Walker and Company, New York City, 1974. Hardcover.

119. How Did We Find Out About Vitamins? Published by Walker and Company, New York City, 1974. Hardcover.

120. Our World in Space. Published by the New York Graphic Society, New York City, 1974. Hardcover.

121. Our Federal Union. Published by Houghton Mifflin, Boston, 1975. Hardcover.

122. Lecherous Limericks. Published by Walker and Company, New York City, 1975. Hardcover.

123. Of Matters Great and Small - Essays. Published by Doubleday & Company, Garden City, New York, 1975. Hardcover.

124. Science Past, Science Future - Essays. Published by Doubleday & Company, Garden City, New York, 1975. Hardcover.

125. The Ends of the Earth: The Polar Regions of the World. Published by Weybright and Talley, New York City, 1975. Hardcover.

126. The Solar System. Published by Follet Publishing Company, United States, 1975. Hardcover.

127. How Did We Find Out About Energy? Published by Walker and Company, New York City, 1975. Hardcover.

128. How Did We Find Out About Comets? Published by Walker and Company, New York City, 1975. Hardcover.

129. Eyes on the Universe: A History of the Telescope. Published by Houghton Mifflin, Boston, 1975. Hardcover.

130. More Lecherous Limericks. Published by Walker and Company, New York City, 1976. Softcover.

131. Alpha Centauri, the Nearest Star. Published by Lothrop Lee and Shepard, New York City, 1976. Hardcover.

132. Asimov on Physics - Essays. Published by Doubleday & Company, Garden City, New York, 1976. Hardcover.

134. The Planet That Wasn't - Essays. Published by Doubleday & Company, Garden City, New York, 1976. Hardcover.

135. How Did We Find Out About Atoms? Published by Walker and Company, New York City, 1976. Hardcover.

136. How Did We Find Out About Nuclear Power? Published by Walker and Company, New York City, 1976. Hardcover.

137. The Golden Door. Published by Houghton Mifflin, Boston, 1977. Hardcover.

138. Familiar Poems Annotated. Published by Doubleday & Company, Garden City, New York, 1977. Hardcover.

139. Asimov's Sherlockian Limericks. Published by Mysterious Press, New York City, 1977. Hardcover.

140. Still More Lecherous Limericks. Published by Walker and Company, New York City, 1977. Softcover.

141. Asimov on Numbers - Essays. Published by Doubleday & Company, Garden City, New York, 1977. Hardcover.

142. The Beginning and the End - Essays. Published by Doubleday & Company, Garden City, New York, 1977. Hardcover.

143. The Collapsing Universe: The Story of Black Holes. Published by Walker and Company, New York City, 1977. Hardcover.

144. How Did We Find Out About Space? Published by Walker and Company, New York City, 1977. Hardcover.

145. Mars, the Red Planet. Published by Lothrop Lee and Shepard, New York City, 1977. Hardcover.

146. Animals of the Bible. Published by Doubleday & Company, Garden City, New York, 1978. Hardcover.

147. Limericks: Too Gross; or Two Dozen Dirty Stanzas. With John Ciardi. Published by W. W. Norton, New York City, 1978. Hardcover.

148. Quasar, Quasar, Burning Bright - Essays. Published by Doubleday & Company, Garden City, New York, 1978. Hardcover.

149. Life and Time - Essays. Published by Doubleday & Company, Garden City, New York, 1978. Hardcover.

150. How Did We Find Out About Black Holes? Published by Walker and Company, New York City, 1978. Hardcover.

151. How Did We Find Out About Earthquakes? Published by Walker and Company, New York City, 1978. Hardcover.

152. The Road to Infinity - Essays. Published by Doubleday & Company, Garden City, New York, 1979. Hardcover.

153. How Did We Find Out About Antarctica? Published by Walker and Company, New York City, 1979. Hardcover.

154. How Did We Find Out About Our Human Roots? Published by Walker and Company, New York City, 1979. Hardcover.

155. Saturn and Beyond. Published by Lothrop Lee and Shepard, New York City, 1979. Hardcover.

156. A Choice of Catastrophes. Published by Simon and Schuster, New York City, 1979. Hardcover.

157. Extraterrestrial Civilizations. Published by Crown Publishers, New York City, 1979. Hardcover.

158. Isaac Asimov's Book of Facts. Published by Grosset and Dunlap, New York City, 1979. Hardcover.

159. Opus 200. Published by Houghton Mifflin, Boston, 1979. Hardcover.

160. In Memory Yet Green. Published by Doubleday & Company, Garden City, New York, 1979. Hardcover.

161. The Annotated Gulliver's Travels. Published by Clarkson N. Potter, New York City, 1980. Hardcover.

162. How Did We Find Out About Oil? Published by Walker and Company, New York City, 1980. Hardcover.

163. In Joy Still Felt. Published by Doubleday & Company, Garden City, New York, 1980. Hardcover.

164. In the Beginning. Published by Crown Publishers - Stonesong Press, New York City, 1981. Hardcover.

165. Asimov's Guide to the Bible: Two Volumes in One: The Old and New Testaments. Published by Wings Books, Avenal, New Jersey, 1981. Hardcover.

166. A Grossery of Limericks. With John Ciardi. Published by W. W. Norton, New York City, 1981. Hardcover.

167. The Sun Shines Bright - Essays. Published by Doubleday & Company, Garden City, New York, 1981. Hardcover.

168. Change!: Seventy-one Glimpses of the Future - Essays. Published by Houghton Mifflin, Boston, 1981. Hardcover.

169. Asimov on Science Fiction - Essays. Published by Doubleday & Company, Garden City, New York, 1981. Hardcover.

170. How Did We Find Out About Volcanoes? Published by Walker and Company, New York City, 1981. Hardcover.

171. How Did We Find Out About Solar Power? Published by Walker and Company, New York City, 1981. Hardcover.

172. Venus, Near Neighbor of the Sun. Published by Lothrop Lee and Shepard, New York City, 1981. Hardcover.

173. Visions of the Universe. Published by The Cosmos Store, Salt Lake City, 1981. Hardcover. Paintings by Kazuaki Iwasaki; preface by Carl Sagan.

174. Exploring the Earth and the Cosmos. Published by Crown Publishers, New York City, 1982. Hardcover.

175. Asimov's Biographical Encyclopedia of Science and Technology - Second Revised Edition. Published by Doubleday & Company, Garden City, New York, 1982. Hardcover.

176. How Did We Find Out About the Universe? Published by Walker and Company, New York City, 1982. Hardcover.

177. How Did We Find Out About Life in the Deep Sea? Published by Walker and Company, New York City, 1982. Hardcover.

178. How Did We Find Out About the Beginning of Life? Published by Walker and Company, New York City, 1982. Hardcover.

179. Isaac Asimov Presents Super Quiz. By Ken Fisher. Published by Dembner Books, New York City, 1982. Softcover.

180. Isaac Asimov Presents Super Quiz II. By Ken Fisher. Published by Dembner Books, New York City, 1983. Softcover.

181. How Did We Find Out About Genes? Published by Walker and Company, New York City, 1983. Hardcover.

182. The Measure of the Universe. Published by Harper and Row, New York City, 1983. Hardcover.

183. Counting the Eons - Essays. Published by Doubleday & Company, Garden City, New York, 1983. Hardcover.

Isaac Asimov

184. The Roving Mind - Essays. Published by Prometheus Books, New York City, 1983. Hardcover.

185. Isaac Asimov's Limericks for Children. Published by Caedmon Children's Books, New York City, 1984. Hardcover.

186. X Stands for Unknown - Essays. Published by Doubleday & Company, Garden City, New York, 1984. Hardcover.

187. Asimov's New Guide to Science. Published by Basic Books, New York City, 1984. Hardcover.

188. How Did We Find Out About Computers? Published by Walker and Company, New York City, 1984. Hardcover.

189. How Did We Find Out About Rockets? Published by Walker and Company, New York City, 1984. Hardcover.

190. Opus 300. Published by Houghton Mifflin, Boston, 1984. Hardcover.

191. Living in the Future. Edited by Isaac Asimov. Published by Harmony House, New York City, 1985. Hardcover.

192. The Subatomic Monster - Essays. Published by Doubleday & Company, Garden City, New York, 1985. Hardcover.

193. Robots, Machines in Man's Image. With Karen Frenkel. Published by Harmony House, New York City, 1985. Hardcover.

194. Asimov's Guide to Halley's Comet. Published by Walker and Company, New York City, 1985. Hardcover.

195. The Exploding Suns: The Secrets of the Supernovas. Published by E. P. Dutton, New York City, 1985. Hardcover.

196. How Did We Find Out About the Atmosphere? Published by Walker and Company, New York City, 1985. Hardcover.

197. How Did We Find Out About DNA? Published by Walker and Company, New York City, 1985. Hardcover.

198. Futuredays: A Nineteenth-Century Vision of the Year 2000. Published by Henry Holt, New York City, 1986. Hardcover.

199. The Dangers of Intelligence and Other Science Essays. Published by Houghton Mifflin, Boston, 1986. Hardcover.

200. How Did We Find Out About the Speed of Light? Published by Walker and Company, New York City, 1986. Hardcover.

201. Isaac Asimov Presents Super Quiz III. By Ken Fisher. Published by Dembner Books, New York City, 1987. Softcover.

202. How to Enjoy Writing: A Book of Aid and Comfort. With Janet Asimov. Published by Walker and Company, New York City, 1987. Hardcover.

203. Far as the Human Eye Could See - Essays. Published by Doubleday & Company, Garden City, New York, 1987. Hardcover.

204. Past, Present and Future - Essays. Published by Prometheus Books, New York City, 1987. Hardcover.

205. How Did We Find Out About Blood? Published by Walker and Company, New York City, 1987. Hardcover.

206. How Did We Find Out About Sunshine? Published by Walker and Company, New York City, 1987. Hardcover.

207. How Did We Find Out About the Brain? Published by Walker and Company, New York City, 1987. Hardcover.

208. Beginnings: The Story of Origins: of Mankind, Life, the Earth, the Universe. Published by Walker and Company, New York City, 1987. Hardcover.

209. Did Comets Kill the Dinosaurs? - Ask Isaac Asimov. Published by Gareth Stevens Publishing, United States, 1987. Hardcover.

210. Isaac Asimov Presents from Harding to Hiroshima. By Barrington Boardman. Published by Dembner Books, New York City, 1988. Softcover.

211. Asimov's Annotated Gilbert and Sullivan. Published by Doubleday & Company, Garden City, New York, 1988. Hardcover.

212. The Relativity of Wrong - Essays. Published by Doubleday & Company, Garden City, New York, 1988. Hardcover.

213. How Did We Find Out About Superconductivity? Published by Walker and Company, New York City, 1988. Hardcover.

214. The Asteroids. Published by Gareth Stevens Publishing, United States, 1988. Hardcover.

215. The Earth's Moon. Published by Gareth Stevens Publishing, United States, 1988. Hardcover.

216. Mars: Our Mysterious Neighbor. Published by Gareth Stevens Publishing, United States, 1988. Hardcover.

217. Our Milky Way and Other Galaxies. Published by Gareth Stevens Publishing, United States, 1988. Hardcover.

218. Quasars, Pulsars, and Black Holes. Published by Gareth Stevens Publishing, United States, 1988. Hardcover.

219. Rockets, Probes, and Satellites. Published by Gareth Stevens Publishing, United States, 1988. Hardcover.

220. Our Solar System. Published by Gareth Stevens Publishing, United States, 1988. Hardcover.

221. The Sun. Published by Gareth Stevens Publishing, United States, 1988. Hardcover.

222. Uranus: The Sideways Planet. Published by Gareth Stevens Publishing, United States, 1988. Hardcover.

223. Saturn: The Ringed Beauty. Published by Gareth Stevens Publishing, United States, 1988. Hardcover.

224. How Was the Universe Born? Published by Gareth Stevens Publishing, United States, 1988. Hardcover.

225. Earth: Our Home Base. Published by Gareth Stevens Publishing, United States, 1988. Hardcover.

226. Ancient Astronomy. Published by Gareth Stevens Publishing, United States, 1988. Hardcover.

227. Unidentified Flying Objects. Published by Gareth Stevens Publishing, United States, 1988. Hardcover.

228. Space Spotter's Guide. Published by Gareth Stevens Publishing, United States, 1988. Hardcover.

229. Isaac Asimov's Book of Science and Nature Quotations. With Jason A. Shulman. Weidenfeld and Nicholson, New York City, 1988. Hardcover.

230. History of Biology - A Chart. Published by Carolina Biological Supplies, 1988.

231. History of Mathematics - A Chart. Published by Carolina Biological Supplies, 1989.

232. Isaac Asimov's Science Fiction and Fantasy Story-a-Month 1989 Calendar. Published by Pomegranate Calendars and Books, 1988.

233. Isaac Asimov Presents Super Quiz IV. By Ken Fisher. Published by Dembner Books, New York City, 1989. Softcover.

234. The Complete Science Fair Handbook. With Anthony D. Fredericks. Published by Scott Foresman, New York City, 1989. Softcover.

235. Asimov's Galaxy: Reflections on Science Fiction - Essays. Published by Doubleday & Company, Garden City, New York, 1989. Hardcover.

236. The Tyrannosaurus Prescription: And One Hundred Other Science Essays. Published by Prometheus Books, New York City, 1989. Hardcover.

237. Asimov on Science: A 30 Year Retrospective 1959 - 1989 - Essays. Published by Doubleday & Company, Garden City, New York, 1989. Hardcover.

238. Is There Life On Other Planets? Published by Gareth Stevens Publishing, United States, 1989. Hardcover.

239. Science Fiction, Science Fact. Published by Gareth Stevens Publishing, United States, 1989. Hardcover.

240. Mercury: The Quick Planet. Published by Gareth Stevens Publishing, United States, 1989. Hardcover.

241. Space Garbage. Published by Gareth Stevens Publishing, United States, 1989. Hardcover.

242. Jupiter: The Spotted Giant. Published by Gareth Stevens Publishing, United States, 1989. Hardcover.

243. The Birth and Death of Stars. Published by Gareth Stevens Publishing, United States, 1989. Hardcover.

244. Asimov's Chronology of Science and Discovery. Published by Harper and Row, New York City, 1989. Hardcover.

245. Think About Space: Where Have We Been and Where Are We Going? Published by Walker and Company, New York City, 1989. Hardcover.

246. How Did We Find Out About Photosynthesis? Published by Walker and Company, New York City, 1989. Hardcover.

247. How Did We Find Out About Microwaves? Published by Walker and Company, New York City, 1989. Hardcover.

Little Library of Dinosaurs. Published by Crown Publishers - Random House, New York City, 1989. Five hardcovers in a slipcase:
248. Volume One: Giant Dinosaurs.
249. Volume Two: Armored Dinosaurs.
250. Volume Three: Small Dinosaurs.
251. Volume Four: Sea Reptiles and Flying Reptiles.
252. Volume Five: Meat-Eating Dinosaurs and Horned Dinosaurs.

253. Colonizing the Planets and the Stars. Published by Gareth Stevens Publishing, United States, 1989. Hardcover.

254. Astronomy Today. Published by Gareth Stevens Publishing, United States, 1989. Hardcover.

255. Pluto: A Double Planet? Published by Gareth Stevens Publishing, United States, 1989. Hardcover.

256. Piloted Space Flights. Published by Gareth Stevens Publishing, United States, 1989. Hardcover.

257. Comets and Meteors. Published by Gareth Stevens Publishing, United States, 1989. Hardcover.

258. Neptune: The Farthest Giant. Published by Gareth Stevens Publishing, United States, 1990. Hardcover.

259. Venus: A Shrouded Mystery. Published by Gareth Stevens Publishing, United States, 1990. Hardcover.

260. The World's Space Programs. Published by Gareth Stevens Publishing, United States, 1990. Hardcover.

261. How Did We Find Out About Neptune? Published by Walker and Company, New York City, 1990. Hardcover.

262. How Did We Find Out About Lasers? Published by Walker and Company, New York City, 1990. Hardcover.

Isaac Asimov

263. Frontiers: New Discoveries About Man and His Planet, Outer Space and the Universe - Essays. Published by E. P. Dutton, New York City, 1990.

264. Out of the Everywhere - Essays. Published by Doubleday & Company, Garden City, New York, 1990. Hardcover.

265. The March of the Millennia: A Key to Looking At History. With Frank White. Published by Walker and Company, New York City, 1991. Hardcover.

266. Asimov's Chronology of the World. Published by Harper Collins, New York City, 1991. Hardcover.

267. Christopher Columbus: Navigator to the New World. Published by Gareth Stevens, United States, 1991. Hardcover.

268. Ferdinand Magellan: Opening the Door to World Exploration. Published by Gareth Stevens, United States, 1991. Hardcover.

269. The Secret of the Universe - Essays. Published by Doubleday & Company, Garden City, New York, 1991. Hardcover.

270. How Did We Find Out About Pluto? Published by Walker and Company, New York City, 1991. Hardcover.

271. Our Angry Earth: A Ticking Time Bomb. With **Frederik Pohl**. Published by Tor Books - Tom Doherty Associates, New York City, 1991. Hardcover.

272. Atom: Journey Across the Subatomic Cosmos. Published by E. P. Dutton, New York City, 1991. Hardcover.

273. What Is a Shooting Star? - Ask Isaac Asimov. Published by Gareth Stevens Publishing, United States, 1991. Hardcover.

274. Why Do Stars Twinkle? - Ask Isaac Asimov. Published by Gareth Stevens Publishing, United States, 1991. Hardcover.

275. Why Does the Moon Change Shape? - Ask Isaac Asimov. Published by Gareth Stevens Publishing, United States, 1991. Hardcover.

276. What Is an Eclipse? - Ask Isaac Asimov. Published by Gareth Stevens Publishing, United States, 1991. Hardcover.

277. Why Do We Have Different Seasons? - Ask Isaac Asimov. Published by Gareth Stevens Publishing, United States, 1991. Hardcover.

278. Is Our Planet Warming Up? - Ask Isaac Asimov. Published by Gareth Stevens Publishing, United States, 1991. Hardcover.

279. Why Is the Air Dirty? - Ask Isaac Asimov. Published by Gareth Stevens Publishing, United States, 1991. Hardcover.

280. Why Are Whales Vanishing? - Ask Isaac Asimov. Published by Gareth Stevens Publishing, United States, 1991. Hardcover.

281. Where Does Garbage Go? - Ask Isaac Asimov. Published by Gareth Stevens Publishing, United States, 1991. Hardcover.

282. What Causes Acid Rain? - Ask Isaac Asimov. Published by Gareth Stevens Publishing, United States, 1991. Hardcover.

283. The Future in Space. Published by Gareth Stevens Publishing, United States, 1991. Hardcover.

284. Isaac Asimov's Guide to Earth and Space. Published by Random House, New York City, 1991. Hardcover.

285. Asimov Laughs Again: More Than 700 Favorite Jokes, Limericks and Anecdotes. Published by Harper Collins, New York City, 1992. Hardcover.

286. Why Are Some Beaches Oily? - Ask Isaac Asimov. Published by Gareth Stevens Publishing, United States, 1992. Hardcover.

287. Why Are Animals Endangered? - Ask Isaac Asimov. Published by Gareth Stevens Publishing, United States, 1992. Hardcover.

288. What's Happening to the Ozone Layer? - Ask Isaac Asimov. Published by Gareth Stevens Publishing, United States, 1992. Hardcover.

289. Why Are the Rain Forests Vanishing? - Ask Isaac Asimov. Published by Gareth Stevens Publishing, United States, 1992. Hardcover.

290. Why Does Litter Cause Problems? - Ask Isaac Asimov. Published by Gareth Stevens Publishing, United States, 1992. Hardcover.

291. Frontiers II: More Recent Discoveries About Life, Earth, Space and the Universe. With Janet Asimov. Published by E. P. Dutton, New York City, 1993. Hardcover.

292. I. Asimov: A Memoir. Published by Doubleday & Company, Garden City, New York, 1994. Hardcover.

293. Yours, Isaac Asimov. Edited by Stan Asimov. Published by Doubleday & Company, Garden City, New York, 1995. Hardcover.

294. It's Been a Good Life. Edited by Janet Jeppson Asimov. Published by Prometheus Books, Amherst, New York, 2002. Hardcover.

***

RELATED

1. The Magazine of Fantasy and Science Fiction - Special Isaac Asimov Issue - October 1966. Published by Mercury Press, Cornwall, Connecticut, 1966. Softcover. Herein: The Key by **Isaac Asimov**; Portrait of the Writer as a Boy - an essay by Isaac Asimov; The Prime of Life - a poem by **Isaac Asimov**; and You Can't Beat Brains - an essay by L. Sprague de Camp; along with the usual features.

2. Asimov Analyzed. By Neil Goble. Published by

Mirage Press, Baltimore, Maryland, 1972. Hardcover.

3. The Science Fiction of Isaac Asimov. By Joseph F. Patrouch. Published by Doubleday & Company, Garden City, New York, 1974. Hardcover.

4. Isaac Asimov. Edited by Martin H. Greenberg and Joseph D. Olander. Published by Taplinger, New York City, 1977. Hardcover.

5. Isaac Asimov: The Foundations of Science Fiction. By James Gunn. Published by Oxford University Press, New York City, 1982. Hardcover.

6. Isaac Asimov: Scientist and Storyteller. By Ellen Erlanger. Published by Lerner Publications, Minneapolis, Minnesota, 1986. Hardcover.

7. Isaac Asimov: Master of Science Fiction. By Karen Judson. Published by Enslow Publishers, Berkeley Heights, New Jersey, 1998. Hardcover.

8. Isaac Asimov: Writer of the Future. By William J. Boerst. Published by Morgan Reynolds Publishing, Greensboro, North Carolina, 1999. Hardcover.

9. Notes for a Memoir: On Isaac Asimov, Life and Writing. By Janet Asimov. Published by Prometheus Books, New York, 2006. Hardcover.

Sir Arthur C. Clarke.

Arthur Charles Clarke was born on December 16th, 1917 in Minehead, Somerset, England. And he died on March 19th, 2008 from complications that arose from post-polio syndrome, with which he had been diagnosed ten years earlier. Clarke had contracted polio in 1959 and had served for years as a Vice Patron of the British Polio Fellowship.

Clarke left school in 1936 and went to work for the government. It wasn't until after World War Two (he had served in the Royal Air Force, finishing up as a Flight Lieutenant) that he was able to afford to attend university, which he did, graduating with a degree in math and physics from King's College in London. Between 1937 and 1945, Clarke had had some of his fiction published in amateur science fiction magazines - fanzines. Clarke was also co-editor of Britain's first fanzine, Novae Terrae with John (Ted) Carnell until it folded because of the war. He sold his first stories to **John W. Campbell** at Astounding Science Fiction in 1946. The stories were Loophole, which appeared in the April issue, and Rescue Party, which appeared in May, 1946. Along with the usual features, April contained: Pattern for Conquest - part 2 of 3 by George O. Smith; Swamper by Jerry Shelton; Black Market by Raymond F. Jones; and Memorial by **Theodore Sturgeon**. May featured: The Nightmare by Chan Davis; The Cure by Henry Kuttner and **C. L. Moore**; A Son Is Born by **A. E. van Vogt**; Alexander the Bait by William Tenn; Placet Is a Crazy Place by Fredric Brown; and Pattern for Conquest - part 3 of 3 by George O. Smith.

In 1948, he wrote a story that would later become his signature work. It was called The Sentinel, penned for a writing competition at the BBC. It didn't win, didn't even earn an honourable mention. But it was published as Sentinel of Eternity in the only issue of 10 Story Fantasy Magazine, Spring 1951. The editor, **Donald A. Wollheim**, did not think Clarke warranted mention on the cover. Along with Clarke's story, the issued contained: Friend to Man by C. M. Kornbluth; Uneasy Lies the Head by Lester del Rey; Artist and Slave Girl by John Wyndham writing as John Beynon; The Poisonous Soul by Franklin Gregory; Gateway on Krishna by L. Sprague de Camp; Haunted Atoms by **A. E. van Vogt**; The Other Side of the Wall by August Derleth; Private World by **Donald A. Wollheim** writing as Martin Pearson; Who Builds Maos Traps? by K. W. Bennett; and The Woodworker by Gene A. Davidson.

The Sentinel, of course, was the inspiration for the novel and the film, 2001: A Space Odyssey. And 2001 changed science fiction filmmaking forever.

In the late 1940s, Clarke worked briefly as an assistant editor for Science Abstracts. But by 1951, when his first two novels were published - Prelude to Space and The Sands of Mars - he was writing full time and had gained credibility as both an author and a futurist.

His idea that geostationary satellites would be perfect as telecommunications relays - a system that became known as Telstar - caught on and was adopted. The geostationary orbit itself became known as the Clarke Orbit. As **Isaac Asimov** pointed out in 1963, **Arthur C. Clarke** didn't build or launch Telstar, but "he saw it in the sky years before anyone else did."

Sir Arthur C. Clarke

In 1956, Clarke moved to Ceylon - now Sri Lanka - where he could pursue his love for scuba diving all year long. And he held dual citizenship - Sri Lanka and Britain - for the rest of his life.

After being diagnosed with post-polio syndrome in 1988, he was confined to a wheelchair for most of the next twenty years. In 1989, for his services to British cultural interests in Sri Lanka, Clarke was given a CBE - Commander of the Order of the British Empire. In 1998, he was awarded a knighthood but, at his own request, the award was delayed. The Sunday Mirror had accused Clarke of paedophilia and he demanded that his name be cleared before he would accept the knighthood. Clarke's sexuality had often been an issue - was he gay, was he straight. And for the most part, he laughed it off. But this was too much. The charge was found to be spurious, the Mirror published an apology, and Clarke received his knighthood on May 26th, 2000.

As Clarke once said, "As our own species is in the process of proving, one cannot have superior science and inferior morals. The combination is unstable and self-destroying."

On his ninetieth birthday, in 2007, knowing he hadn't much time left, Clarke recorded a good-bye video message for his friends and fans. Three months later, with his final book being finished by **Frederik Pohl**, he died.

The first editions of Childhood's End and Reach for Tomorrow tend to be the highest priced of Clarke's collectible books, each in $6,000 range.

Pen names used: Charles Willis; and E. G. O'Brien.

Clarke's Three Laws:
1. When a distinguished but elderly scientist states that something is possible, he is almost certainly right. When he states that something is impossible, he is very probably wrong.
2. The only way of discovering the limits of the possible is to venture a little way past them into the impossible.
3. Any sufficiently advanced technology is indistinguishable from magic.

***

AWARDS

1952. The International Fantasy Award for Non-Fiction for The Exploration of Space.
1956. Hugo Award for Best Short Story, The Star - Infinity Science Fiction, November 1955.
1973. Nebula Award for Best Novella, A Meeting with Medusa.
1974. John W. Campbell Memorial Award for Best Novel, Rendezvous with Rama.
1974. Nebula Award for Best Novel, Rendezvous

with Rama.
1974. Hugo Award for Best Novel, Rendezvous with Rama.
1974. Locus Poll Award for Best SF Novel, Rendezvous with Rama.
1980. Nebula Award for Best Novel, Fountains of Paradise.
1980. Hugo Award for Best Novel, Fountains of Paradise.
1985. Nebula Grand Master Award.
1989. Commander of the Order of the British Empire - CBE. He was awarded this for his services to British cultural interests in Sri Lanka.
1997. Inducted into The Science Fiction Hall of Fame.
2000. Knight Bachelor.
2003. Telluride Tech Festival Award of Technology.
2005. Sri Lankabhimanya. Awarded for his contributions to science and technology and for his commitment to Sri Lanka, his adopted country.

***

FILM AND TELEVISION

1. Captain Video and His Video Rangers. The television show was the first American SF series and it ran from June 27th, 1949 until April 1st, 1955. It is known that Clarke wrote at least one episode between 1952 and 1955 but the details of that seem to be lost.

2. All the Time in the World. A Clarke short story that was used on the television series Tales of Tomorrow, Season 1, Episode 37, originally aired on June 13th, 1952, starring Esther Ralston; Jack Warden; Don Hanmer; Lewis Charles; and Sam Locante.

3. 2001: A Space Odyssey. Based on his story The Sentinel, Clarke wrote the screenplay for the film, which was directed by Stanley Kubrick and released in the States on April 6th, 1968, starring: Keir Dullea; Gary Lockwood; William Sylvester; Daniel Richter; Leonard Rossiter; Margaret Tyzack; Robert Beatty; Sean Sullivan; Douglas Rain - the voice of HAL 9000; Frank Miller; Bill Weston; Ed Bishop; Glenn Beck; Alan Gifford; Ann Gillis; and many others, mostly as semi-apes.

4. The City in the Image of Man: Ideas and Work of Paolo Soleri. This documentary was directed by Merrill Brockway and released in May, 1972. **Arthur C. Clarke** was one of the guests interviewed for the film.

5. The Journey Begins. This was Season 1, Episode 1, of Mysterious World, 1980. **Arthur C. Clarke** was the host.

6. Baddegama. A Sri Lankan film based on the novel The Village in the Jungle, written by Leonard Woolf, the husband of Virginia Woolf. **Arthur C. Clarke** played Woolf in the film, which was directed by Lester James Peries.

7. 2010: The Odyssey Continues. This was a short promotional film directed by Les Mayfield. **Arthur C. Clarke** made an uncredited appearance as himself.

8. 2010: The Year We make Contact. This was based on Clarke's novel, 2010, directed by Peter Hyams and released on December 7th, 1984, starring: Roy Scheider; John Lithgow; Helen Mirren; Bob Balaban; Keir Dullea; Douglas Rain - the voice of HAL 9000; Madolyn Smith Osborne; Dana Elcar; Taliesin Jaffe; James McEachin; Mary Jo Deschanel; Elya Baskin; Saveli Kramarov; Oleg Rudnick; Natasha Shneider; and a number of others, including Candice Bergen as the voice of SAL 9000 and **Arthur C. Clarke** in an uncredited role as a man on a park bench.

9. Arthur C. Clarke's World of Strange Powers. A thirteen-part Yorkshire Television show hosted by **Arthur C. Clarke** in 1985.

10. The Star. A story by Clarke used on The Twilight Zone, Season 1, Episode 13, originally aired on December 20th, 1985. That segment of the show starred Fritz Weaver; Donald Moffat; and Elizabeth Huddie.

11. God, the Universe and Everything Else. This was a British show that featured **Arthur C. Clarke** and Stephen Hawking, with Carl Sagan joining them by satellite, discussing the Big Bang theory, God and just about everything else for almost an hour.

12. Brave New Worlds: The Science Fiction Phenomena. A 1993 documentary directed by Paul Oremland. **Arthur C. Clarke** was one of guests, along with: **Robert Silverberg**; **Brian Aldiss**; **William Gibson**; J. G. Ballard; Kim Stanley Robinson; John Clute; Karen Joy Fowler; Octavia Butler; Paul Verhoeven; and many others.

13. Arthur C. Clarke: Before 2001. This was co-written by Clarke and Robert Lewis Knecht, also directed by Knecht, and released in the States on November 1st, 1993. This was about Clarke's life before the 2001 phenomena.

14. Arthur C. Clarke's Mysterious Universe. A thirteen-part Yorkshire Television show hosted by **Arthur C. Clarke** in 1994.

15. Without Warning. A 1994 film, directed by Robert Iscove, in which **Arthur C. Clarke** appeared as himself.

16. Trapped in Space. This was based on Clarke's short story Breaking Strain, directed by Arthur Allan Seidelman in 1994 and starring: Jack Wagner; Jack Coleman; Craig Wasson; Sigrid Thornton; Kay Lenz; Kevin Colson; and many others.

17. The Colours of Infinity. Written and hosted by Clarke, this was a documentary about the discovery of the infinitely complex geometrics of the Mandelbrot Set, this aired in 1995.

18. This Is Your Life. Season 35, Episode 11, which aired on January 11th, 1995, featured **Arthur C. Clarke**.

19. The Man Who Saw the Future. This was from the UK television series The Works, Season 3, Episode 8, aired on July 13th, 1997 and featuring **Arthur C. Clarke**.

Sir Arthur C. Clarke

20. 2001: HAL's Legacy. A 2001 Documentary directed by David John Kennard and Michael O'Connell. **Arthur C. Clarke** appeared as one of the guests interviewed.

21. 2001: The Making of a Myth. A 2001 documentary directed by Paul Joyce. **Arthur C. Clarke** was one of the guests.

22. Letadlo. A 2001 television show from the Czech Republic. **Arthur C. Clarke** appeared in one of the episodes.

23. Stanley Kubrick: A Life in Pictures. A 2001 documentary directed by Jan Harlan. **Arthur C. Clarke** was one of the guests.

24. The 73rd Annual Academy Awards. From March, 2001, **Arthur C. Clarke**, by satellite from Sri Lanka, was one the presenters.

25. To Mars by A-Bomb: The Secret History of Project Orion. A 2003 documentary written and directed by Christopher Sykes. **Arthur C. Clarke** was one of the guests.

26. Mars, the Next Frontier. Arthur C. Clarke appeared as himself in August 2003 on the UK television series The Sky at Night.

27. 50 Terrible Predictions. A made for television documentary, directed by Mark McMullen and Gareth Williams. **Arthur C. Clarke** was one of the guests.

28. We Love The Sky at Night. A documentary tribute to the 50th anniversary of the UK television show, The Sky at Night. **Arthur C. Clarke** was one of the guests.

29. Vision of a Future Passed: The Prophecy of 2001. A documentary directed by Gary Leva in 2007. **Arthur C. Clarke** was interviewed.

30. Rendezvous with Rama. A film based on Clarke's novel, directed by David Fincher and with a screenplay by Scott Brick. Starring Morgan Freeman, it is slated for release somewhere between 2009 and 2011.

***

RADIO

1. A Walk in the Dark. This 1950 story was used on Mind Webs on October 1st, 1976.

2. The Nine Billion Names of God. This 1953 story was broadcast on Mind Webs on September 9th, 1978.

3. Summertime on Icarus. This 1960 story, also known as The Hottest Piece of Real Estate in the Solar System, was used on Mind Webs on April 14th, 1978.

4. The Sentinel. This 1951 story, which grew up to be 2001: A Space Odyssey, was broadcast on Mind Webs on January 28th, 1979.

5. The Haunted Spacesuit. This 1958 story, also known as Who's There? was used on Mind Webs.

6. Childhood's End. This 1953 novel was used on CBC's The Vanishing Point in 1989.

7. The Nine Billion Names of God. This 1953 story was used on CBC's The Vanishing Point in the 1980s.

8. Rescue Party. This 1946 story was used on Omni Audio Experience during the 1980s.

9. Childhood's End. This 1953 novel was used on BBC Radio and released on CD in 2007.

10. Wall of Darkness. This 1949 story was used on Sci-Fi Radio.

11. A Fall of Moondust. This was used on BBC Radio and released on CD in 2008.

***

NOVELS AND COLLECTIONS

1. Prelude to Space. Published by World Editions, New York City, 1951. Softcover. Galaxy Science Fiction Novel number 3.

2. The Sands of Mars. Published by Sidgwick and Jackson, London, 1951. Hardcover.

3. Islands in the Sky. Published by The John C. Winston Company, Philadelphia and Toronto, 1952. Hardcover.

4. Islands in the Sky. Published by Sidgwick and Jackson, London, 1952. Hardcover. This left out the preface that was in the Winston edition.

5. Prelude to Space. Published by Sidgwick and Jackson, London, 1953. First hardcover edition of the softcover original from 1951, containing some revisions.

6. Against the Fall of Night. Published by Gnome Press, New York City, 1953. Hardcover.

7. Childhood's End. Published by Ballantine Books, New York City, 1953. Simultaneously issued in hardcover and softcover. Ballantine Book 33.

8. Expedition to Earth. Published by Ballantine Books, New York City, 1953. Simultaneously issued in hardcover and softcover. Ballantine Book 52. Herein: Second Dawn, 1951; If I Forget Thee, Oh Earth..., 1951; Breaking Strain, 1949; History Lesson, 1949; Superiority, 1951; Exile of the Eons, 1950; Hide and Seek, 1949; Expedition to Earth, 1953; Loophole, 1946; Inheritance, 1947; and The Sentinel, 1951.

9. Expedition to Earth. Published by Sidgwick and Jackson, London, 1954. Mostly the same as the American edition but the titles of three of the stories were changed: History Lesson became Expedition to Earth; Expedition to Earth became Encounter in the Dawn; and Exile of the Eons became Nemesis. This contains: Second Dawn, 1951; If I Forget Thee, Oh Earth..., 1951; Breaking Strain, 1949; Expedition to Earth, 1949; Superiority, 1951; Nemesis, 1950; Hide and Seek, 1949; Encounter in the Dawn, 1953; Loophole, 1946; Inheritance, 1947; and The Sentinel, 1951.

10. Prelude to Space. Published by Gnome Press, New York City, 1954. Hardcover. Enough changes in the text to make this a new edition.

11. Earthlight. Published by Ballantine Books, New York City, 1955. Simultaneously issued in hardcover and softcover. Ballantine Book 97.

12. The City and the Stars. Published by Harcourt, Brace and Company, New York City, 1956. Hardcover.

13. Reach for Tomorrow. Published by Ballantine Books, New York City, 1956. Simultaneously issued in hardcover and softcover. Ballantine Book 135. Herein: Preface by Clarke; Rescue Party, 1946; A Walk in the Dark, 1950; The Forgotten Enemy, 1948; Technical Error, 1946; The Parasite, 1953; The Fires Within, 1947; The Awakening, 1942; Trouble with the Natives, 1951; The Curse, 1946; Time's Arrow, 1950; Jupiter Five, 1953; and The Possessed, 1953.

14. The Deep Range. Published by Harcourt, Brace and Company, New York City, 1957. Hardcover.

15. Tales from the White Hart. Published by Ballantine Books, New York City, 1957. Softcover. Ballantine Book 186. This contains: Preface by Clarke; Silence, Please!, 1950; Big Game Hunt, 1956; Patent Pending, 1954; Armaments Race, 1954; Critical Mass, 1949; The Ultimate Melody, 1957; The Pacifist, 1956; The Next Tenants, 1957; Moving Spirit, 1957; The Man Who Ploughed the Sea, 1957; The Reluctant Orchid, 1956; Cold War, 1957; What Goes Up, 1956; Sleeping Beauty, 1957; and The Defenestration of Ermintrude Inch, 1957.

16. The Other Side of the Sky. Published by Harcourt, Brace and Company, New York City, 1958. Hardcover. This collection contains: Bibliographical Note by Clarke; The Nine Billion Names of God, 1953; Refugee, 1955; Special Delivery, 1957; Feathered Friend, 1957; Take a Deep Breath, 1957; Freedom of Space, 1957; Passer-By, 1957; The Call of the Stars, 1957; The Wall of Darkness, 1949; Security Check, 1956; No Morning After, 1954; The Starting Line, 1956; Venture to the Moon, 1956; Robin Hood F.R.S., 1956; Green Fingers, 1956; All That Glitters, 1956; Watch This Space, 1956; A Question of Residence, 1956; Publicity Campaign, 1953; All the Time in the World, 1952; Cosmic Casanova, 1958; The Star, 1955; Out of the Sun, 1958; Transience, 1949; and The Songs of Distant Earth, 1958.

17. Across the Sea of Stars. Published by Harcourt, Brace and Company, New York City, 1959. Hardcover. An omnibus collection, gathering Childhood's End, 1953; Earthlight, 1955; and an assortment of short stories: The Sentinel, 1951; Time's Arrow, 1950; Technical Error, 1946; Superiority, 1951; Rescue Party, 1946; History Lesson, 1949; Hide and Seek, 1949; Armaments Race, 1954; Breaking Strain, 1954; If I Forget Thee Oh Earth..., 1951; Inheritance, 1947; Jupiter Five, 1953; The Next Tenants, 1957; The Pacifist, 1956; The Reluctant Orchid, 1956; Silence, Please!, 1950; The Fires Within, 1947; and Encounter in the Dawn, 1953; along with an introduction by Clifton Fadiman.

18. A Fall of Moondust. Published by Harcourt, Brace and World, New York City, 1961. Hardcover.

19. Master of Space. Published by Lancer Books, New York City, 1961. This was Prelude to Space, 1951, with a new title and a new forward by the author. Softcover. Lancer Book 71-610.

20. From the Ocean, From the Stars. Published by Harcourt, Brace and World, New York City, 1962. Hardcover. An omnibus collection, gathering The City and the Stars, 1956; The Deep Range, 1957; and The Other Side of the Sky, 1958: Bibliographical Note by Clarke; The Nine Billion Names of God, 1953; Refugee, 1955; Special Delivery, 1957; Feathered Friend, 1957; Take a Deep Breath, 1957; Freedom of Space, 1957; Passer-By, 1957; The Call of the Stars, 1957; The Wall of Darkness, 1949; Security Check, 1956; No Morning After, 1954; The Starting Line, 1956; Venture to the Moon, 1956; Robin Hood F.R.S., 1956; Green Fingers, 1956; All That Glitters, 1956; Watch This Space, 1956; A Question of Residence, 1956; Publicity Campaign, 1953; All the Time in the World, 1952; Cosmic Casanova, 1958; The Star, 1955; Out of the Sun, 1958; Transience, 1949; and The Songs of Distant Earth, 1958.

21. Tales of Ten Worlds. Published by Harcourt, Brace and Company, New York City, 1962. Hardcover. Herein: I Remember Babylon, 1960; Before Eden, 1961; Death and the Senator, 1961; The Road to the Sea, 1951; Dog Star, 1962; Saturn Rising, 1961; Trouble with Time, 1960; Summertime on Icarus, 1960; Out of the Cradle, Endlessly Orbiting..., 1959; Who's There?, 1958; Hate, 1961; Into the Comet, 1960; An Ape About the House, 1962; Let There Be Light, 1957; and A Slight Case of Sunstroke, 1958.

22. Glide Path. Published by Harcourt, Brace and World, New York City, 1963. Hardcover.

23. Dolphin Island. Published by Holt, Rinehart and Winston, New York City, 1963. Hardcover.

24. Prelude to Mars. Published by Harcourt, Brace and World, New York City, 1965. Hardcover. An omnibus edition that gathers: Prelude to Space, 1951; The Sands of Mars, 1951; and an assortment of short stories from earlier collections: The Forgotten Enemy, 1948; The Parasite, 1953; Critical Mass, 1949; The Awakening, 1942; The Curse, 1946; Exile of the Eons, 1950; The Possessed, 1953; Second Dawn, 1951; Trouble with the Natives, 1951; A Walk in the Dark, 1950; Big Game Hunt, 1956; Moving Spirit, 1957; Cold War, 1957; What Goes Up..., 1956; The Ultimate Melody, 1957; and The Man Who Ploughed the Sea, 1957; along with a Foreword by Clarke.

25. An Arthur C. Clarke Omnibus. Published by Sidgwick and Jackson, London, 1965. Hardcover. This gathered: Childhood's End, 1953; Prelude to Space, 1951; and a selection of short stories: Expedition to Earth, 1953; Superiority, 1951; Loophole, 1946; History Lesson, 1949; Hide and Seek, 1949; Breaking Strain, 1949; Exile of the Eons, 1950; If I Forget Thee, Oh Earth..., 1951; Inheritance, 1947; and Second Dawn, 1951.

26. The Nine Billion Names of God. Published by Harcourt, Brace and World, New York City, 1967. Hardcover. Herein: The Sentinel, 1951; Superiority, 1951; The Star, 1955; Rescue Party, 1946; The Nine

Sir Arthur C. Clarke

Billion Names of God, 1953; I Remember Babylon, 1960; Before Eden, 1961; Death and the Senator, 1961; Hide and Seek, 1949; The Curse, 1946; If I Forget Thee, Oh Earth..., 1951; No Morning After, 1954; Out of the Sun, 1958; Patent Pending, 1954; The Possessed, 1953; The Reluctant Orchid, 1956; Transience, 1949; A Walk in the Dark, 1950; Dog Star, 1962; Trouble with Time, 1960; The Call of the Stars, 1957; The Wall of Darkness, 1949; Summertime on Icarus, 1960; Who's There?, 1958; and Encounter in the Dawn, 1953; along with an introduction by Clarke.

27. The Sands of Mars. With a new foreword by the author. Published by Harcourt, Brace and World, New York City, 1967. Hardcover.

28. 2001: A Space Odyssey. Published by NAL - The New American Library, New York City, 1968. Hardcover.

29. An Arthur C. Clarke Second Omnibus. Published by Sidgwick and Jackson, London, 1968. Hardcover. This gathered: A Fall of Moondust, 1961; Earthlight, 1955; and Sands of Mars, 1951.

30. The Lion of Comarre - with - Against the Fall of Night. Published by Harcourt, Brace and World, New York City, 1968. Hardcover. From 1949 and 1948, respectively.

31. The Space Dreamers. Published by Lancer Books, New York City, 1969. Softcover. Another re-issue of Prelude to Space, 1951. Lancer Book 74-524.

32. Prelude to Space. With a Post-Apollo preface by the author. Published by Harcourt, Brace Jovanovich, New York City, 1970. Hardcover.

33. Expedition to Earth. With a new preface by the author. Published by Harcourt, Brace Jovanovich, New York City, 1970. Hardcover. Herein: Second Dawn, 1951; If I Forget Thee, Oh Earth..., 1951; Breaking Strain, 1949; History Lesson, 1949; Superiority, 1951; Exile of the Eons, 1950; Hide and Seek, 1949; Expedition to Earth, 1953; Loophole, 1946; Inheritance, 1947; and The Sentinel, 1951.

34. Earthlight. With a new preface by the author. Published by Harcourt, Brace Jovanovich, New York City, 1972. Hardcover.

35. Of Time and Stars. Published by Victor Gollancz, London, 1972. A collection of short stories from previous collections with a preface by the author. Herein: Introduction by J. B. Priestley; Foreword by Clarke; The Sentinel, 1951; The Nine Billion Names of God, 1953; The Forgotten Enemy, 1948; Hide and Seek, 1949; All the Time in the World, 1952; If I Forget Thee, Oh Earth..., 1951; No Morning After, 1954; The Reluctant Child, 1956; Security Check, 1956; Trouble with the Natives, 1951; Feathered Friend, 1957; Who's There?, 1958; Into the Comet, 1960; An Ape About the House, 1963; Robin Hood F.R.S., 1956; Green Fingers, 1956; The Fires Within, 1947; and Encounter in the Dawn, 1953.

36. The Wind from the Sun. Published by Harcourt, Brace Jovanovich, New York City, 1972. Hardcover. This contains: Preface by Clarke; The Shining Ones, 1962; Maelstrom II, 1962; Transit of Earth, 1971; The Longest Science Fiction Story Ever Told, 1966; Neutron Tide, 1970; A Meeting with Medusa, 1971; The Food of the Gods, 1964; The Secret, 1963; The Last Command, 1965; Dial "F" for Frankenstein, 1965; Reunion, 1971; Playback, 1966; The Light of Darkness, 1966; Love That Universe, 1961; Crusade, 1968; The Cruel Sky, 1967; and The Wind from the Sun, 1964; along with an essay, Herbert George Morley Roberts Wells, Esq., 1967.

37. The Best of Arthur C. Clarke: 1937 - 1971. Published by Sidgwick and Jackson, London, 1973. Hardcover. This collection contains: The Sentinel, 1951; The Star, 1955; History Lesson, 1949; Death and the Senator, 1961; Hide and Seek, 1949; The Awakening, 1942; A Meeting with Medusa, 1971; Refugee, 1955; Second Dawn, 1951; Summertime on Icarus, 1960; Hate, 1961; Into the Comet, 1960; Venture to the Moon, 1956; The Starting Line, 1956; Robin Hood F.R.S., 1956; Green Fingers, 1956; All That Glitters, 1956; Watch This Space, 1956; A Question of Residence, 1956; Castaway, 1947; Whacky, 1942; Retreat from Earth, 1938; Travel By Wire!, 1937; and Sunjammer, 1964; along with 1933: A Science Fiction Odyssey, an essay, 1973.

38. Rendezvous with Rama. Published by Victor Gollancz, London, 1973. Hardcover.

39. Imperial Earth. Published by Victor Gollancz, London, 1975. Hardcover.

40. Imperial Earth. Published by Harcourt Brace Jovanovich, 1976. Hardcover. This was roughly 10,000 words longer than the British edition.

41. The Best of Arthur C. Clarke: 1937 - 1955. Published by Sphere Books, London, 1976. Softcover. Herein: Introduction: 1933: A Science Fiction Odyssey, 1973; Travel By Wire!, 1937; Retreat from Earth, 1938; The Awakening, 1942; Whacky, 1942; Castaway, 1947; History Lesson, 1949; Second Dawn, 1951; The Sentinel, 1951; The Star, 1955; and Refugee, 1955.

42. The Best of Arthur C. Clarke: 1956 - 1972. Published by Sphere Books, London, 1977. Softcover. This contains: Introduction: 1933: A Science Fiction Odyssey, 1973; Venture to the Moon, 1956; Into the Comet, 1960; Summertime on Icarus, 1960; Death and the Senator, 1961; Hate, 1961; Sunjammer, 1965; and A Meeting with Medusa, 1971.

43. Four Great Novels. Published by Victor Gollancz, London, 1978. Hardcover. This gathered Rendezvous with Rama, 1973; A Fall of Moondust, 1961; The City and the Stars, 1956; and The Deep Range, 1857.

44. The Fountains of Paradise. Published by Victor Gollancz, London, 1979. Hardcover.

45. 2010: Odyssey Two. Published by Del Rey Books, New York City, 1982. Hardcover.

46. The Sentinel. Published by Berkley Books, New York City, 1983. Softcover. This contains: Introduction: Of Sand and Stars by Clarke; The Sentinel, 1951; The Songs of Distant Earth, 1958; Rescue Party, 1946; Breaking Strain, 1949; A

Meeting with Medusa, 1971; Refugee, 1955; The Wind from the Sun, 1964; Guardian Angel, 1950; and Jupiter V, 1953.

47. The Songs of Distant Earth. Published by Del Rey Books, New York City, 1986. Hardcover.

48. Arthur C. Clarke's July 20, 2019: Life in the 21st Century. Published by Macmillan Publishing, London, 1986. Hardcover.

49. 2061: Odyssey Three. Published by Del Rey Books, New York City, 1987. Hardcover.

50. 2001: A Space Odyssey; The City and the Stars; The Deep Range; A Fall of Moondust; Rendezvous with Rama. Published by Octopus Books, New York, 1987. Hardcover.

51. Cradle. With Gentry Lee. Published by Warner Aspect, New York City, 1988. Softcover.

52. A Meeting with Medusa. Published by Tor Books - Tom Doherty Associates, New York City, 1988. Released in softcover as a Tor Double number 1 and bound with Green Mars by Kim Stanley Robinson.

53. Rama II. With Gentry Lee. Published by Victor Gollancz, London, 1989. Hardcover.

54. Tales from Planet Earth. Published by Legend, London, 1989. Hardcover. Herein: Preface by **Isaac Asimov**; Preface Addendum by Clarke; The Road to the Sea, 1951; Hate, 1961; Publicity Campaign, 1953; The Other Tiger, 1953; The Deep Range, 1954; If I Forget Thee, Oh Earth..., 1951; The Cruel Sky, 1967; The Parasite, 1953; The Next Tenants, 1957; Saturn Rising, 1961; The Man Who Ploughed the Sea, 1957; The Wall of Darkness, 1949; Death and the Senator, 1961; Maelstrom II, 1962; Second Dawn, 1951; and On Golden Seas, 1986.

55. Beyond the Fall of Night. With Gregory Benford. Published by Ace Putnam, New York City, 1990. Hardcover.

56. The Ghost from the Grand Banks. Published by Victor Gollancz, London, 1990. Hardcover.

57. The Garden of Rama. With Gentry Lee. Published by Victor Gollancz, London, 1991. Hardcover.

58. Against the Fall of Night - with - Beyond the Fall of Night. With Gregory Benford. Published by Victor Gollancz, London, 1991. Hardcover.

59. More Than One Universe: The Collected Stories of Arthur C. Clarke. Published by Bantam Books, New York City, 1991. Softcover. Herein: I Remember Babylon, 1960; Summertime on Icarus, 1960; Out of the Cradle, Endlessly Orbiting..., 1959; Who's There?, 1958; Hate, 1961; Into the Comet, 1960; An Ape about the House, 1962; Let There Be Light, 1957; Death and the Senator, 1961; Trouble with Time, 1960; Before Eden, 1961; A Slight Case of Sunstroke, 1958; Dog Star, 1962; The Nine Billion Names of God, 1953; Refugee, 1955; Special Delivery, 1957; Feathered Friend, 1957; Take a Deep Breath, 1957; Freedom of Space, 1957; Passer-by, 1957; The Call of the Stars, 1957; Security Check, 1956; No Morning After, 1954; The Starting Line, 1956; Robin Hood F.R.S., 1956; Green Fingers, 1956; All That Glitters, 1956; Watch This Space, 1956; A Question of Residence, 1956; All the Time in the World, 1952; Cosmic Casanova, 1958; The Star, 1955; Out of the Sun, 1958; Transience, 1949; The Songs of Distant Earth, 1958; The Food of the Gods, 1964; Maelstrom II, 1962; The Shining Ones, 1962; The Wind from the Sun, 1964; The Secret, 1963; The Last Command, 1965; Dial F for Frankenstein, 1965; Reunion, 1971; Playback, 1966; The Light of Darkness, 1966; The Longest Science Fiction Story Ever Told, 1966; Herbert George Morley Roberts Wells, Esq., 1967; Love That Universe, 1961; Crusade, 1968; The Neutron Tide, 1970; Transit of Earth, 1971; A Meeting with Medusa, 1971; When the Twerms Came, 1978; Quarantine, 1977; siseneG, 1984; Rescue Party, 1946; **The Curse**, 1946; Hide and Seek, 1949; The Possessed, 1953; Superiority, 1951; A Walk in the Dark, 1950; The Reluctant Orchid, 1956; Encounter in the Dawn, 1953; Patent Pending, 1954; and The Sentinel, 1951.

60. Rama Revealed. With Gentry Lee. Published by Victor Gollancz, London, 1993. Hardcover.

61. The Hammer of God. Published by Victor Gollancz, London, 1990. Hardcover.

62. Richter 10. With Mike McQuay. Published by Victor Gollancz, London, 1996. Hardcover.

63. 3001: The Final Odyssey. Published by Del Rey Books, New York City, 1997. Hardcover.

64. The Trigger. With Michael Kube-McDowell. Published by Harper Collins Voyager, London, 1999. Hardcover.

65. The Light of Other Days. With Stephen Baxter. Published by Tor Books - Tom Doherty Associates, New York City, 2000. Hardcover.

66. The Collected Stories of Arthur C. Clarke. Published by Victor Gollancz, London, 2000. Hardcover. Herein: Travel by Wire, 1937; How We Went to Mars, 1938; Retreat from Earth, 1938; Reverie, 1939; The Awakening, 1942; Whacky, 1942; Loophole, 1946; Rescue Party, 1946; Technical Error, 1946; Castaway, 1947; The Fires Within, 1947; Inheritance, 1947; Nightfall, 1947; History Lesson, 1949; Transience, 1949; The Wall of Darkness, 1949; The Lion of Comarre, 1949; The Forgotten Enemy, 1948; Hide and Seek, 1949; Breaking Strain, 1949; Nemesis, 1954; Guardian Angel, 1950; Time's Arrow, 1950; A Walk in the Dark, 1950; Silence Please, 1950; Trouble with the Natives, 1951; The Road to the Sea, 1951; The Sentinel, 1951; Holiday on the Moon, 1951; Earthlight, 1951; Second Dawn, 1951; Superiority, 1951; If I Forget Thee, Oh Earth..., 1951; All the Time in the World, 1952; The Nine Billion Names of God, 1953; The Possessed, 1953; The Parasite, 1953; Jupiter Five, 1953; Encounter in the Dawn, 1953; The Other Tiger, 1953; Publicity Campaign, 1953; Armaments Race, 1954; The Deep Range, 1954; No Morning After, 1954; Big Game Hunt, 1956; Patent Pending, 1954; Refugee, 1955; The Star, 1955; What Goes Up, 1956; Venture to the Moon, 1956; The Pacifist,

Sir Arthur C. Clarke

1956; The Reluctant Orchid, 1956; Moving Spirit, 1957; The Defenestration of Ermintrude Inch, 1957; The Ultimate Melody, 1957; The Next Tenants, 1957; Cold War, 1957; Sleeping Beauty, 1957; Security Check, 1956; The Man Who Ploughed the Sea, 1957; Critical Mass, 1949; The Other Side of the Sky, 1957; Let There Be Light, 1957; Out of the Sun, 1958; Cosmic Casanova, 1958; The Songs of Distant Earth, 1958; A Slight Case of Sunstroke, 1958; Who's There?, 1958; Out of the Cradle, Endlessly Orbiting..., 1959; I Remember Babylon, 1960; Trouble with Time, 1960; Into the Comet, 1960; Summertime on Icarus, 1960; Saturn Rising, 1961; Death and the Senator, 1961; Before Eden, 1961; Hate, 1961; Love that Universe, 1961; Dog Star, 1962; Maelstrom II, 1962; An Ape About the House, 1962; The Shining Ones, 1962; The Secret, 1963; Dial F for Frankenstein, 1964; The Wind from the Sun, 1964; The Food of the Gods, 1964; The Last Command, 1965; The Light of Darkness, 1966; The Longest Science Fiction Story Ever Told, 1966; Playback, 1966; The Cruel Sky, 1967; Herbert George Morley Roberts Wells, Esq., an essay, 1967; Crusade, 1968; Neutron Tide, 1970; Reunion, 1971; Transit of Earth, 1971; A Meeting with Medusa, 1971; Quarantine, 1977; siseneG, 1984; The Steam Powered Word Processor, 1986; On Golden Seas, 1986; The Hammer of God, 1992; The Wire Continuum, writing with Stephen Baxter, 1998; and Improving the Neighbourhood, 1999.

67. The City and the Stars - with - The Sands of Mars. Published by Warner Aspect, New York City, 2001. Softcover.

68. The Space Trilogy. Published by Victor Gollancz, London, 2001. Softcover. This gathers Islands in the Sky, 1952; The Sands of Mars, 1951; and Earthlight, 1955. It also includes two essays by Clarke: The Space Trilogy, 2001; and The Sands of Mars, 1967. And an essay by Donna Shirley: The Sands of Mars, 2001.

69. The Ghost from the Grand Banks - with - The Deep Range. Published by Warner Aspect, New York City, 2001. Softcover.

70. Time's Eye. With Stephen Baxter. Published by Del Rey Books, New York City, 2003. Hardcover.

71. Sunstorm. With Stephen Baxter. Published by Del Rey Books, New York City, 2005. Hardcover.

72. The Dark Blue Depths: Adventures from Inner to Outer Space. Published by iBooks, United States, 2005. Softcover. This gathers Islands in the Sky, 1952; and Dolphin Island: A Story of the People of the Sea, 1963.

73. Clarke's Universe. Published by iBooks, United States, 2006. Softcover. This gathers A Fall of Moondust, 1961, and The Lion of Comarre, 1968.

74. Firstborn. With Stephen Baxter. Published by Del Rey Books, New York City, 2007. Hardcover.

75. The Last Theorem. With **Frederik Pohl**. Published by Harper Collins Voyager, London, 2008. Hardcover.

***

ANTHOLOGIES

1. Time Probe. Published by Delacorte Press, New York City, 1966. Hardcover. Herein: And He Built a Crooked House by **Robert A. Heinlein**, 1941; The Wabbler by Murray Leinster, 1942; The Weather Man by Theodore L. Thomas, 1962; The Artifact Business by **Robert Silverberg**, 1957; Grandpa by James Schmitz, 1955; Not Final by **Isaac Asimov**, 1941; The Little Black Bag by C. M. Kornbluth, 1950; The Blindness by R. S. Richardson writing as Philip Latham, 1946; Take a Deep Breath by **Arthur C. Clarke**, 1957; The Potters of Firsk by **Jack Vance**, 1950; and The Tissue Culture King by Julian Huxley, 1926.

2. Three for Tomorrow. With **Robert Silverberg**. Published by Meredith Press, New York City, 1969. Hardcover. This includes: Foreword by Clarke; Introduction by Silverberg; We All Die Naked, 1969, **James Blish**; The Eve of RUMOKO by Roger Zelazny, 1969; and How It Was When the Past Went Away by **Robert Silverberg**, 1969.

3. The Science Fiction Hall of Fame - Volume III. With Geo. W. Proctor. Published by Victor Gollancz, London, 1981. Hardcover.

This contains: Repent Harlequin Said the Ticktockman, 1965; and A Boy and His Dog, 1969, by **Harlan Ellison**; The Doors of His Face, The Lamps of His Mouth by Roger Zelazny, 1965; The Saliva Tree by **Brian W. Aldiss**, 1965; He Who Shapes by Roger Zelazny, 1964; The Secret Place by Richard McKenna, 1966; Call Him Lord by **Gordon R. Dickson**, 1966; The Last Castle by **Jack Vance**, 1966; Aye and Gomorrah by **Samuel R. Delany**, 1967; Gonna Roll the Bones by **Fritz Leiber**, 1967; Behold the Man by **Michael Moorcock**, 1966; The Planners by **Kate Wilhelm**, 1968; Dragonrider by **Anne McCaffrey**, 1967; Passengers by **Robert Silverberg**, 1968; and Time Considered as a Helix of Semi-Precious Stones by **Samuel R. Delany**, 1968.

4. Project Solar Sail. With David Brin and Jonathan Vos Post. Published by NAL - The New American Library, New York City, 1990. Softcover. Herein: Foreword: The Winds of Space by Clarke; Introduction: Sailing the Void by **Isaac Asimov**; The Wind from by Sun by **Arthur C. Clarke**, 1964; To Sail Beyond the Sun - A Luminous Collage, a poem by **Ray Bradbury** and Jonathan V. Post, 1990; The Canvas of the Night, an essay by K. Eric Drexler, 1990; Ice Pilot by David Brin, 1990; A Solar Privateer, a poem by Jonathan Eberhart, 1981; Sunjammer by **Poul Anderson**, 1964; A Rebel Technology Comes Alive, an essay by Chauncey Uphoff and Jonathan V. Post, 1990; Argosies of Magic Sails - excerpts from Locksley Hall by Lord Alfred Tennyson; Ion Propulsion: The Solar Sail's Competition for Access to the Solar System, an essay by Bryan Palaszewski, 1990; The Grand Tour by Charles Sheffield, 1987; Lightsail, a poem by Scott E. Green, 1990; Rescue at L-5 by Kevin J. Anderson and Doug Beason, 1990; Lightsails to the Stars, an essay by Robert L. Forward and Joel Davis, 1990; The Fourth Profession by Larry Niven, 1971; Goodnight, Children by Joe Clifford Faust, 1990; Solar Sails in an Interplanetary Economy, an essay by Robert L. Staehle and Louis

Friedman, 1990; and an afterword: Project Solar Sail, by Clarke.

***

NON-FICTION

1. Interplanetary Flight. Published by Temple Press, London, 1950. Hardcover.

2. The Exploration of Space. Published by Harper, New York City, 1951. Hardcover.

3. The Exploration of the Moon. With R. A. Smith. Published by Frederick Muller, London, 1954. Hardcover.

4. The Coast of Coral. Published by Shakespeare's Head Press, New York City, 1956. Hardcover.

5. The Making of a Moon. Published by Harper Brothers, New York City, 1957. Hardcover.

6. The Reefs of Taprobane. Published by Frederick Muller, London, 1957. Hardcover.

7. The Challenge of the Spaceship. Published by Frederick Muller, London, 1960. Hardcover.

8. The Challenge of the Sea. Published by Holt' Rinehart and Winston, New York City, 1960. Hardcover.

9. Profiles of the Future. Published by Victor Gollancz, London, 1962. Hardcover.

10. The Treasure of the Great Reef. Published by Harper and Row, New York City, 1964. Hardcover.

11. Man and Space. With the Editors of Life. Published by Time-Life Books, New York City, 1964. Hardcover.

12. Voice from the Sky. Published by Harper and Row, New York City, 1967. Hardcover.

13. The Coming of the Space Age. Published by Meredith Press, New York City, 1967. Hardcover.

14. The Promise of Space. Published by Hodder and Stoughton, London, 1968. Hardcover.

15. Into Space: A Young Person's Guide to Space Exploration. With **Robert Silverberg**. Published by Harper and Row, New York City, 1971. Hardcover.

16. The Lost Worlds of 2001. Published by Signet Books - New American Library, New York City, 1972. Softcover. Signet Book Y4949.

17. The Lost Worlds of 2001. Published by Sidgwick and Jackson, London, 1972. First hardcover of the paperback original.

18. Report on Planet Three and Other Speculations. Published by Harper and Row, New York City, 1972. Hardcover.

19. Voice Across the Sea. Published by William Luscombe, London, 1974. Hardcover.

20. The View from Serendip. Published by Random House, New York City, 1977. Hardcover.

21. The Odyssey File. With Peter Hyams. Published by Ballantine Books, New York City, 1984. Softcover.

22. 1984: Spring. A Choice of Futures. Published by Granada Publishing, London, 1984. Hardcover.

23. Ascent to Orbit: The Technical Writings of Arthur C. Clarke. Published by John Wiley and Sons, New York City, 1984. Hardcover.

24. Astounding Days: A Science Fictional Autobiography. Published by Victor Gollancz, London, 1989. Hardcover.

25. How the World Was One: Beyond the Global Village. Published by Bantam Books, New York City, 1992. Hardcover.

26. By Space Possessed: Essays on the Exploration of Space. Published by Victor Gollancz, London, 1993. Hardcover.

27. The Snows of Olympus: A Garden on Mars. Published by Victor Gollancz, London, 1994. Hardcover.

28. Arthur C. Clarke & Lord Dunsany: A Correspondence. Published by Anamnesis Press, Tallahassee, Florida, 1998. Limited to 500 softcover copies.

29. Greetings, Carbon-Based Bipeds! Collected Works 1934 - 1988. Published by St. Martin's Press, New York City, 1999.

30. From Narnia to a Space Odyssey: The War of Letters Between Arthur C. Clarke and C. S. Lewis. With C. S. Lewis. Published by iBooks, United States, 2003. Hardcover.

***

RELATED

1. Arthur C. Clarke. By Eric S. Rabkin. Published by Starmont House, West Linn, Oregon, 1979. Softcover. Starmont Reader's Guide number 1.

2. Arthur C. Clarke. Edited by Joseph D. Olander and Martin Harry Greenberg. Published by Taplinger, New York City, 1977. Hardcover.

3. The Space Odysseys of Arthur C. Clarke. By George Edgar Slusser. The Borgo Press, San Bernardino, California, 1978. Softcover.

4. Against the Night, the Stars: The Science Fiction of Arthur C. Clarke. By John Hollow. Published by Harcourt Brace Jovanovich, New York City, 1983. Hardcover.

5. Arthur C. Clarke: The Authorized Biography. By Neil McAleer. Published by Contemporary Books, Chicago, Illinois, 1992. Hardcover.

6. Arthur C. Clarke: A Critical Companion. By Robin Anne Reid. Published by Greenwood Press, Westport, Connecticut, 1997. Hardcover.

Andre Norton.

Alice Mary Norton was born on February 17th, 1912 in Cleveland, Ohio, and she died in Murfreesboro, Tennessee from congestive heart failure on March 17th, 2005.

In 1932, after graduating high school and spending a couple of years at Flora Stone Mather College, which was associated with Western Reserve University, Norton became a librarian in Cleveland. She worked at that for the next eighteen years except for a brief stint as a bookseller. In 1950, she was hired as a reader by Gnome Press and she stayed with Gnome until 1958 when her writing finally found a large enough audience to allow her to write full-time.

Unlike most science fiction writers of the era, Norton did not start out with short stories in the pulp magazines (which is not meant to imply she was not a short story writer - she was, although she always claimed she wasn't very good at it). Nor did she begin with science fiction.

She was a teenager when she started writing and submitting her work to publishers. She wrote her first book while she was in school, but that one did not sell. At the time, writing was a male-dominated business. In 1934, she legally changed her name to Andre Alice Norton and that same year, her second novel but her first one in print, The Prince Commands, being the Sundry Adventures of Michael Karl, Sometime Crown Prince and Pretender to the Throne of Morvania, an historical adventure, was published by Appleton-Century under the name Andre Norton.

It was four years before she published another novel. Ralestone Luck came out in 1938 under the name Andre Alice Norton, another historical novel. She followed those with more historical adventures until 1951 when she wrote Huon of the Horn, as Alice Mary Norton.

Huon started with an historical theme, but it was a true fantasy. It was not her first fantasy - that was a short story called The People of the Crater as by Andrew North, published in Fantasy Book, July 1947, along with: Black Lotus by Robert Bloch; Strange Alliance by Charles McNutt; Micro-Man by Forrest J. Ackerman writing as Weaver Wright; Flight Through Tomorrow by Stanton A. Coblentz; Walls of Acid by Henry Hasse; and The Cataaaaa by **A. E. van Vogt**.

But Huon of the Horn was her first fantasy novel. And she followed it a year later with her first science fiction novel, Star Man's Son, 2250 A.D. It was her SF novels for a mainly teen-age audience that jump-started her career and even though she would occasionally make a foray into other genres, science fiction and fantasy were her primary focus.

A number of Norton's early novels, The Beast Master, The Sioux Spaceman, Star Rangers and others, all tend to sell in the same price range these days, between $800.00 and $1,200.00.

Pen Names used: Andrew North; Allen Weston; Andre Alice Norton; and Alice Mary Norton.

***

AWARDS

1946. Plaque of Honour. Presented by the government of the Netherlands for her historical novel, The Sword Is Drawn.
1951. Boy's Clubs of America Medal. This was presented for her work as editor of Bullard of the Space Patrol by Malcolm Jameson.
1952. American Newspaper Guild Page One Award of Distinguished Books. This was presented for Huon of the Horn.
1963. Invisible Little Man for Life Achievements. This was presented to Norton for sustained excellence in science fiction.
1965. Boy's Clubs of America Certificate of Merit. This was presented for Night of Masks.
1965. Book of the Year Award. Presented by the Child Study Association for Steel Magic.
1975. Phoenix Award. This was presented for overall writing achievement.
1977. Grand Master of Fantasy Award - The Gandalf. This was presented at the World Science Fiction Convention.
1978. Orlando Science Fiction Society Life Achievement Award.
1979. Balrog Fantasy Award for Life Achievements.
1980. Career Achievement Award. This was presented at the Science Fiction Weekend.
1980. Martha Kinney Cooper Ohioana Library Award for Lifetime Achievement.
1981. Inducted into the Ohio Women Hall of Fame.
1983. Fritz Leiber Award.
1983. E. E. Doc Smith Award - The Skylark.
1984. Nebula Grand Master Award.
1984. Jules Verne Award.
1986. Daedalus Award for Life Achievement.
1987. The Second Stage Lensman Award for Lifetime Achievement.
1987. The Howard World Fantasy Convention Award.
1988. The E. E. Evans Big Heart Award.
1991. The Science Fiction Book Club Book of the Year Award, presented for The Elvenbane.
1994. Scientificon First Fandom Hall of Fame Award.
1997. Magic Carpet Con Award.
1997. Inducted into The Science Fiction Hall of Fame.
1998. World Fantasy Convention Lifetime Achievement Award.

***

FILM AND TELEVISION

1. The Beastmaster. This was a 1982 film, directed by Don Coscarelli and starring Marc Singer, Tanya Roberts, Rip Torn, John Amos, and others. It was based on Norton's novel of the same name but her contribution to this was uncredited. Coscarelli and Paul Pepperman shared the writing credits.

2. Beastmaster 2: Through the Portal of Time. For this new Beastmaster film, Norton was given the proper credit for her novel. This one was directed by Sylvio Tabet and starred: Marc Singer; James Avery; Michael Berryman; David Carrera; Carl Ciafalio; Sarah Douglas; and many others.

3. BeastMaster. This was television series that ran from 1999 through 2002, based on the novel by Andre Norton. The series starred Daniel Goddard and Jackson Raine, along with Monika Schnarre and Marjean Holden. Marc Singer, from the original Beastmaster films, was a guest star in seven episodes.

***

NOVELS AND COLLECTIONS

1. The Prince Commands, being the Sundry Adventures of Michael Karl, Sometime Crown Prince and Pretender to the Throne of Morvania. Published by D. Appleton-Century, New York City, 1934. Hardcover.

2. Ralestone Luck. Published by D. Appleton-Century, New York City, 1938. Hardcover.

3. Follow the Drum, being the Ventures and Misadventures of One Johanna Lovell, Sometime Lady of Catkept Manor in Kent County of Lord Baltimore's Proprietary of Maryland, in the Gracious Reign of King Charles the Second. Published by William Penn Publishing, New York City, 1942. Hardcover.

4. The Sword Is Drawn. Published by Houghton Mifflin, Boston, 1944. Hardcover.

5. Rogue Reynard, being a Tale of the Fortunes and Misfortunes and Divers Misdeeds of that Great Villain, Baron Reynard, The Fox, and How He Was Served with King Lion's Justice. Based Upon the Beast Saga. Published by Houghton Mifflin, Boston, 1947. Hardcover.

6. Scarface, being the Story of One Justin Blade, Late of the Pirate Isle of Tortuga, and How Fate Did Justly Deal with Him, to His Great Profit. Plague Ship: A Dane Thorson-Solar Queen Adventure. Published by Harcourt, Brace and Company, New York City, 1948. Hardcover.

7. Sword in Sheath. Published by Harcourt, Brace and Company, New York City, 1949. Hardcover.

8. Huon of the Horn, being a Tale of that Duke of Bordeaux Who Came to Sorrow at the Hand of Charlemagne and Yet Won the Favor of Oberon, the Elf King, to His Lasting Fame and Great Glory. Published by Harcourt Brace and Company, New York City, 1951. Hardcover.

9. Star Man's Son 2250 A.D. Published by Harcourt, Brace and Company, New York City, 1952. Hardcover.

10. Island of the Lost. Published by Staples Press, London, 1953. Hardcover. UK issue of Sword in Sheath, 1949.

11. Star Rangers. Published by Harcourt, Brace and Company, New York City, 1953. Hardcover.

12. At Swords' Points. Published by Harcourt Brace and Company, New York City, 1954. Hardcover.

13. Murder for Sale. As by Allen Weston, with Grace Allen Hogarth. Published by Hammond, Hammond and Company, London, 1954. Hardcover.

14. Daybreak - 2250 A.D. Published by Ace Books, New York City, 1954. Softcover. Ace Book D-69. Bound with Beyond Earth's Gates by Lewis Padgett and **C. L. Moore**. A re-titled reprint of Star Man's Son 2250 A.D., 1952.

15. The Stars Are Ours. Published by The World Publishing Company, Cleveland and New York, 1954. Hardcover.

16. The Last Planet. Published by Ace Books, New York City, 1955. Softcover. Ace Book D-96. Bound with A Man Obsessed by Alan E. Nourse. A re-titled reprint of Star Rangers., 1953.

17. Sargasso of Space. By Andrew North. Published by Gnome Press, New York City, 1955. Hardcover.

18. Star Guard. Published by Harcourt, Brace and Company, New York City, 1955. Hardcover.

19. Yankee Privateer. Published by The World Publishing Company, Cleveland and New York, 1955. Hardcover.

20. The Crossroads of Time. Published by Ace Books, New York City, 1956. Softcover. Ace Book D-164. Bound with Mankind on the Run by **Gordon R. Dickson**.

21. Plague Ship: A Dane Thorson-Solar Queen Adventure. By Andrew North. Published by Gnome Press, New York City, 1956. Hardcover.

22. Stand to Horse. Published by Harcourt, Brace and Company, New York City, 1956. Hardcover.

23. Sea Siege. Published by Harcourt, Brace and Company, New York City, 1957. Hardcover.

24. Star Born. Published by The World Publishing Company, Cleveland and New York, 1957. Hardcover.

25. Star Gate. Published by Harcourt, Brace and Company, New York City, 1958. Hardcover.

26. The Time Traders. Published by The World Publishing Company, Cleveland and New York, 1958. Hardcover.

27. Galactic Derelict. Published by The World Publishing Company, Cleveland and New York, 1959. Hardcover.

28. The Beastmaster. Published by Harcourt Brace and Company, New York City, 1959. Hardcover.

29. Voodoo Planet. By Andrew North. Published by Ace Books, New York City, 1959. Softcover. Ace Book D-345. Bound with the first paperback printing of Plague Ship by Andrew North.

30. Secret of the Lost Race. Published by Ace

Andre Norton

Books, New York City, 1959. Softcover. Ace Book D-381. Bound with One Against Herculum by Jerry Sohl.

31. Shadow Hawk. Published by Harcourt Brace and World, New York City, 1960. Hardcover.

32. Storm Over Warlock. Published by The World Publishing Company, Cleveland and New York, 1960. Hardcover.

33. The Sioux Spaceman. Published by Ace Books, New York City, 1960. Softcover. Ace Book D-437. Bound with And Then the Town Took Off by Richard Wilson.

34. Star Hunter. Published by Ace Books, New York City, 1961. Softcover. Ace Book D-509. Bound with The Beastmaster by Andre Norton.

35. Catseye. Published by Harcourt Brace and World, New York City, 1961. Hardcover.

36. Ride Proud, Rebel. Published by The World Publishing Company, Cleveland and New York, 1961. Hardcover.

37. Eye of the Monster. Published by Ace Books, New York City, 1962. Softcover. Ace Book F-147. Bound with Sea Siege, also by Andre Norton.

38. The Defiant Agents. Published by The World Publishing Company, Cleveland and New York, 1962. Hardcover.

39. Lord of Thunder. Published by Harcourt, Brace and World, New York City, 1962. Hardcover.

40. Rebel Spurs. Published by The World Publishing Company, Cleveland and New York, 1962. Hardcover.

41. Judgment on Janus. Published by Harcourt, Brace and World, New York City, 1963. Hardcover.

42. Star Gate. Published by Ace Books, New York City, 1963. First softcover printing of this 1958 title; includes a new Prologue by Andre Norton.

43. Key Out of Time. Published by The World Publishing Company, Cleveland and New York, 1963. Hardcover.

44. Moon of Three Rings. Published by The Viking Press, New York City, 1963. Hardcover.

45. Witch World. Published by Ace Books, New York City, 1963. Softcover. Ace Book F-197.

46. Night of Masks. Published by Harcourt Brace and World, New York City, 1964. Hardcover.

47. Ordeal in Otherwhere. Published by The World Publishing Company, Cleveland and New York, 1964. Hardcover.

48. Web of the Witch World. Published by Ace Books, New York City, 1964. Softcover. Ace Book F-263.

49. Year of the Unicorn. Published by Ace Books, New York City, 1965. Softcover. Ace Book F-357.

50. Quest Crosstime. Published by The Viking Press, New York City, 1965. Hardcover.

51. Steel Magic. Published by The World Publishing Company, Cleveland and New York, 1965. Hardcover.

52. Three Against the Witch World. Published by Ace Books, New York City, 1965. Softcover. Ace Book F-332.

53. Victory on Janus. Published by Harcourt, Brace and World, New York City, 1966. Hardcover.

54. Octagon Magic. Published by The World Publishing Company, Cleveland and New York, 1967. Hardcover.

55. Gray Magic. Published by Scholastic Book Services, New York City, 1967. Softcover. Scholastic Book SBS TX 919. Re-titled version of Steel Magic, 1965.

56. The X Factor. Published by Harcourt, Brace and World, New York City, 1965. Hardcover.

57. Operation Time Search. Published by Harcourt, Brace and World, New York City, 1967. Hardcover.

58. Warlock of the Witch World. Published by Ace Books, New York City, 1967. Softcover. Ace Book G-630.

59. Dark Piper. Published by Harcourt, Brace and World, New York City, 1968. Hardcover.

60. Fur Magic. Published by The World Publishing Company, Cleveland and New York, 1968. Hardcover.

61. Sorceress of the Witch World. Published by Ace Books, New York City, 1968. Softcover. Ace Book H-84.

62. Star Hunter. Published by Ace Books, New York City, 1968. Softcover. Ace Book G-723. Bound with Voodoo Planet by Andre Norton.

63. Voodoo Planet. Published by Ace Books, New York City, 1968. Softcover. Ace Book G-723. Bound with Star Hunter by Andre Norton. Reissued the 1959 edition of Voodoo Planet but with the Norton name, rather than Andrew North.

64. The Zero Stone. Published by The Viking Press, New York City, 1968. Hardcover.

65. Bertie and May. With Bertha Stemm Norton. Published by The World Publishing Company, New York and Cleveland, 1969. Hardcover.

66. Postmarked the Stars. Published by Harcourt, Brace and World, New York City, 1969. Hardcover.

67. Uncharted Stars. Published by The Viking Press, New York City, 1969. Hardcover.

68. Dread Companion. Published by Harcourt Brace Jovanovich, New York City, 1970. Hardcover.

69. High Sorcery. Published by Ace Books, New York City, 1970. Softcover. Ace Book 33700. Herein: Wizard's World, 1967; Through the Needle's Eye, 1970; By a Hair, 1958; Ully the Piper, 1970; and Toys of Tamisan, 1969.

70. Ice Crown. Published by The Viking Press, New York City, 1970. Hardcover.

73

71. Android at Arms. Published by Harcourt Brace Jovanovich, New York City, 1971. Hardcover.

72. Exiles of the Stars. Published by The Viking Press, New York City, 1971. Hardcover.

73. Breed to Come. Published by The Viking Press, New York City, 1972. Hardcover.

74. The Crystal Gryphon. Published by Atheneum, New York City, 1972. Hardcover.

75. Dragon Magic. Published by Thomas Y. Crowell, New York City, 1972. Hardcover.

76. Spell of the Witch World. Published by DAW Books, New York City, 1972. Softcover. DAW Collector's Book 1. Herein: Dragon Scale Silver, 1972; Dream Smith, 1972; and Amber Out of Quayth, 1972.

77. Garan the Eternal. Published by Fantasy Publishing, Alhambra, California, 1973. Hardcover. Herein: One Spell Wizard, 1973; The People of the Crater, 1947; Legacy from Sorn Fen, 1973; and Garan of Yu-Lac, 1970.

78. Forerunner Foray. Published by The Viking Press, New York City, 1973. Hardcover.

79. Here Abide Monsters. Published by Atheneum, New York City, 1973. Hardcover.

80. Garan the Eternal. Published by DAW Books, New York City, 1973. Softcover. DAW Collector's Book 45. Herein: Garan the Eternal, 1972; One Spell Wizard, 1973; and Legacy from Sorn Fen, 1973.

81. The Many Worlds of Andre Norton. Published by The Chilton Book Company, Radnor, Pennsylvania, 1974. Hardcover. Herein: Introduction by **Donald A. Wollheim**; On Writing Fantasy, an essay by Norton, 1971; Andre Norton: Loss of Faith, an essay by Rick Brooks, 1971; London Bridge, 1973; Mousetrap, 1954; The Long Night of Waiting, 1974; The Toads of Grimmerdale, 1973; All Cats Are Gray, writing as Andrew North, 1953; The Gifts of Asti, 1948; Long Live Lord Kor!, 1970; and a Norton Bibliography by Rick Brooks, 1974.

82. Iron Cage. Published by The Viking Press, New York City, 1974. Hardcover.

83. The Jargoon Pard. Published by Atheneum, New York City, 1974. Hardcover.

84. Lavender-Green Magic. Published by Thomas Y. Crowell, New York City, 1974. Hardcover.

85. Crosstime Agent. Published by Victor Gollancz, London, 1975. Hardcover. Originally published as Quest Crosstime, 1965.

86. Merlin's Mirror. Published by DAW Books, New York City, 1975. Softcover. DAW Collector's Book 152.

87. The Book of Andre Norton. Published by DAW Books, New York City, 1975. Softcover. DAW Collector's Book 165. Herein: Introduction by **Donald A. Wollheim**; On Writing Fantasy, an essay by Norton, 1971; Andre Norton: Loss of Faith, an essay by Rick Brooks, 1971; London Bridge, 1973; Mousetrap, 1954; The Long Night of Waiting, 1974; The Toads of Grimmerdale, 1973; All Cats Are Gray, writing as Andrew North, 1953; The Gifts of Asti, 1948; Long Live Lord Kor!, 1970; and a Norton Bibliography by Rick Brooks, 1974.

88. The Day of the Ness. With Michael Gilbert. Published by Walker and Company, New York City, 1975. Hardcover.

89. Knave of Dreams. Published by The Viking Press, New York City, 1975. Hardcover.

90. No Night Without Stars. Published by Atheneum, New York City, 1975. Hardcover.

91. The White Jade Fox. Published by E. P. Dutton, New York City, 1975. Hardcover.

92. Merlin's Mirror. Published by Sidgwick and Jackson, London, 1976. First hardcover edition of the 1975 paperback original.

93. Perilous Dreams. Published by DAW Books, New York City, 1976. Softcover. DAW Collector's Book 196. This contains: Toys of Tamisan, 1969; Ship of Mist, 1976; Get Out of My Dream, 1976; and Nightmare, 1976.

94. Red Hart Magic. Published by Thomas Y. Crowell, New York City, 1976. Hardcover.

95. The Sioux Spaceman. Published by Robert Hale and Company, London, 1976. First hardcover edition of the 1960 paperback original.

96. Star Ka'at. With Dorothy Madlee. Published by Walker and Company, New York City, 1976. Hardcover.

97. Wraiths of Time. Published by Atheneum, New York City, 1976. Hardcover.

98. The Opal-Eyed Fan. Published by E. P. Dutton, New York City, 1977. Hardcover.

99. Velvet Shadows. Published by Fawcett Publications, Greenwich, Connecticut, 1977. Softcover. Fawcett Crest Book 2-3135-6.

100. Witch World. Published by Gregg Press, Boston, 1977. First hardcover edition of the 1963 paperback original.

101. Web of the Witch World. Published by Gregg Press, Boston, 1977. First hardcover edition of the 1964 paperback original.

102. Year of the Unicorn. Published by Gregg Press, Boston, 1977. First hardcover edition of the 1965 paperback original.

103. Warlock of the Witch World. Published by Gregg Press, Boston, 1977. First hardcover edition of the 1967 paperback original.

104. Sorceress of the Witch World. Published by Gregg Press, Boston, 1977. First hardcover edition of the 1968 paperback original.

105. Spell of the Witch World. Published by Gregg Press, Boston, 1977. First hardcover edition of the 1972 paperback original.

Andre Norton

106. Trey of Swords. Published by Grosset and Dunlap, New York City, 1977. Hardcover.

107. Wolfshead. Published by Robert Hale, London, 1977. Hardcover. Re-titled but first hardcover edition of Secret of the Lost Race, 1959.

108. Secret of the Lost Race. Published by Gregg Press, Boston, 1978. First U.S. hardcover edition of the 1959 paperback original.

109. Yurth Burden. Published by DAW Books, New York City, 1978. Softcover. DAW Collector's Book 304.

110. Zarthor's Bane. Published by Ace Books, New York City, 1978. Softcover.

111. Star Ka'at World. With Dorothy Madlee. Published by Walker and Company, New York City, 1978. Hardcover.

112. Star Ka'ats and the Plant People. With Dorothy Madlee. Published by Walker and Company, New York City, 1979. Hardcover.

113. Seven Spells to Sunday. With Phyllis Miller. Published by Atheneum, New York City, 1979. Hardcover.

114. Snow Shadow. With Enid Cushing. Published by Fawcett Publications, Greenwich, Connecticut, 1979. Softcover.

115. Quag Keep. Published by DAW Books, New York City, 1979. Softcover. DAW Collector's Book 353.

116. Voorloper. Published by Ace Books, New York City, 1980. Softcover.

117. Lore of the Witch World. Published by DAW Books, New York City, 1980. Softcover. DAW Collector's Book 400. This contains: Introduction by C. J. Cherryh; Spider Silk, 1976; Sand Sister, 1979; Falcon Blood, 1979; Legacy from Sorn Fen, 1972; Sword of Unbelief, 1977; The Toads of Grimmerdale, 1973; and Changeling, 1980.

118. Iron Butterflies. Published by Fawcett Publications, Greenwich, Connecticut, 1980. Softcover.

119. Star Hunter - and - Voodoo Planet. Published by Ace Books, New York City, 1980. Softcover.

120. Forerunner. Published by Tor Books - Tom Doherty Associates, New York City, 1981. Hardcover.

121. Star Ka'ats and the Winged Warriors. With Dorothy Madlee. Published by Walker and Company, New York City, 1981. Hardcover.

122. Maid at Arms. With Enid Cushing. Published by Fawcett Publications, Greenwich, Connecticut, 1981. Softcover.

123. Horn Crown. Published by DAW Books, New York City, 1981. Softcover. DAW Collector's Book 440.

124. Gryphon in Glory. Published by Atheneum, New York City, 1981. Hardcover.

125. Ten Mile Treasure. Published by Archway Paperbacks, New York City, 1981. Softcover.

126. Moon Called. Published by Simon and Schuster, New York City, 1982. Hardcover.

127. 'Ware Hawk. Published by Atheneum, New York City, 1983. Hardcover.

128. Caroline. With Enid Cushing. Published by Tor Books - Tom Doherty Associates, New York City, 1983. Softcover.

129. Wheel of Stars. Published by Simon and Schuster, New York City, 1983. Softcover.

130. House of Shadows. With Phyllis Miller. Published by Atheneum, New York City, 1984. Hardcover.

131. Stand and Deliver. Published by Dell Publishing, New York City, 1984. Softcover.

132. Gryphon's Eyrie. With A. C. Crispin. Published by Tor Books - Tom Doherty Associates, New York City, 1984. Hardcover.

133. Were-Wrath. Published by Cheap Street, New Castle, Virginia, 1984. Hardcover limited edition of one hundred and seventy-seven copies, all signed and numbered by the author and the illustrator, Judy King-Rieniets.

134. Forerunner: The Second Venture. Published by Tor Books - Tom Doherty Associates, New York City, 1985. Hardcover.

135. Ride the Green Dragon. Published by Atheneum, New York City, 1985. Hardcover.

136. Swords Series Trilogy. Published by Unicorn Star Press, United States, 1985. This re-issues the Swords trilogy in softcover in a boxed set. The titles are: Sword Is Drawn, 1944; Sword in Sheath, 1949; and At Swords' Point, 1954.

137. Flight in Yiktor. Published by Tor Books - Tom Doherty Associates, New York City, 1986. Hardcover.

138. The Gate of the Cat. Published by Ace Books, New York City, 1987. Hardcover.

139. Serpent's Tooth. Privately printed in 1987. Softcover, limited to 999 copies, all signed by Andre Norton.

140. Witch World: Swords and Spells. Published by The Science Fiction Book Club, Garden City, New York, 1987. Hardcover. An omnibus edition containing: Trey of Swords, 1977; Ware Hawk, 1983; and The Gate of the Cat, 1987.

141. Moon Mirror. Published by Tor Books - Tom Doherty Associates, New York City, 1988. Hardcover. This contains: How Many Miles to Babylon?, 1988; The Toymaker's Snuffbox, 1988; Teddi, 1973; Desirable Lakeside Residence, 1973; The Long Night of Waiting, 1974; Through the Needle's Eye, 1970; One Spell Wizard, 1973; Outside, 1974; and Moon Mirror, 1982.

142. The Magic Books. Published by Roc Books - New American Library, New York City, 1988.

Softcover. Omnibus edition containing: Fur Magic, 1968; Steel Magic, 1965; Octagon Magic, 1967.

143. Wizard's Worlds. Published by Tor Books - Tom Doherty Associates, New York City, 1989. Hardcover. Herein: Sword of Unbelief, 1977; Wizard's World, 1967; Mousetrap, 1954; Falcon Blood, 1979; The Toads of Grimmerdale, 1973; Changeling, 1980; Spider Silk, 1976; Sand Sister, 1979; Toys of Tamisan, 1969; Were-Wrath, 1984; By a Hair, 1958; All Cats Are Gray, writing as Andrew North, 1953; and Swamp Dweller, 1984.

144. Dare to Go A-Hunting. Published by Tor Books - Tom Doherty Associates, New York City, 1989. Hardcover.

145. Imperial Lady: A Fantasy of Han China. With Susan Shwartz. Published by Tor Books - Tom Doherty Associates, New York City, 1989. Hardcover.

146. The Jekyll Legacy. With Robert Bloch. Published by Tor Books - Tom Doherty Associates, New York City, 1990. Hardcover.

147. Black Trillium. With Marion Zimmer Bradley and Julian May. Published by Doubleday & Company, Garden City, New York, 1990. Hardcover.

148. The Elvenbane. With Mercedes Lackey. Published by Tor Books - Tom Doherty Associates, New York City, 1991. Hardcover.

149. Port of Dead Ships. Published by Tor Books - Tom Doherty Associates, New York City, 1991. Hardcover. This was an omnibus edition under the title Storms of Victory. It contained: Port of Dead Ships by Andre Norton and Seakeep by Pauline M. Griffin.

150. The Mark of the Cat. Published by Ace Books, New York City, 1992. Hardcover.

151. Songsmith. With A. C. Crispin. Published by Tor Books - Tom Doherty Associates, New York City, 1992. Hardcover.

152. Sneeze on Sunday. With Grace Allen Hogarth. Published by Tor Books - Tom Doherty Associates, New York City, 1992. Hardcover. Re-titled reprint of Murder for Sale, 1954.

153. Empire of the Eagle. With Susan Shwartz. Published by Tor Books - Tom Doherty Associates, New York City, 1993. Hardcover.

154. Golden Trillium. Published by Bantam Spectra, New York City, 1993. Hardcover.

155. Redline the Stars. With P. M. Griffin. Published by Tor Books - Tom Doherty Associates, New York City, 1993. Hardcover.

156. Firehand. With P. M. Griffin. Published by Tor Books - Tom Doherty Associates, New York City, 1994. Hardcover.

157. The Hands of Lyr. Published by William Morrow, New York City, 1994. Hardcover.

158. Annals of the Witch World. Published by The Science Fiction Book Club, Garden City, New York, 1994. Hardcover. An omnibus edition containing: Witch World, 1963; Web of the Witch World, 1964; and Year of the Unicorn, 1965.

159. Mirror of Destiny. Published by William Morrow, New York City, 1995. Hardcover.

160. The Key to the Keplian. With Lyn McConchie. Published by Warner Books, New York City, 1995. Softcover.

161. Elvenblood. With Mercedes Lackey. Published by Tor Books - Tom Doherty Associates, New York City, 1995. Hardcover.

162. Tiger Burning Bright. With Marion Zimmer Bradley and Mercedes Lackey. Published by William Morrow, New York City, 1995. Hardcover.

163. The Monster's Legacy. Published by Atheneum, New York City, 1996. Hardcover.

164. The Magestone. With Mary H. Schaub. Published by Warner Books, New York City, 1996. Hardcover.

165. The Warding of the Witch World. Published by Warner Books, New York City, 1996. Hardcover.

166. Derelict for Trade. With Sherwood Smith. Published by Tor Books - Tom Doherty Associates, New York City, 1997. Hardcover.

167. A Mind for Trade. With Sherwood Smith. Published by Tor Books - Tom Doherty Associates, New York City, 1997. Hardcover.

168. The Scent of Magic. Published by Eos - Harper Collins Books, New York City, 1998. Hardcover.

169. Ciara's Song. With Lyn McConchie. Published by Warner Books, New York City, 1998. Softcover.

170. Chronicles of the Witch World. Published by The Science Fiction Book Club, Garden City, New York, 1998. Hardcover. An omnibus edition containing: Three Against the Witch World, 1965; Warlock of the Witch World, 1967; and Sorceress of the Witch World, 1968.

171. Wind in the Stone. Published by Eos - Harper Collins Books, New York City, 1999. Hardcover.

172. Echoes in Time. With Sherwood Smith. Published by Tor Books - Tom Doherty Associates, New York City, 1999. Hardcover.

173. The Shadow of Albion. With Rosemary Edghill. Published by Tor Books - Tom Doherty Associates, New York City, 1999. Hardcover.

174. To the King a Daughter: The Book of the Oak. With Sasha Miller. Published by Tor Books - Tom Doherty Associates, New York City, 2000. Hardcover.

175. Time Traders. Published by Baen Books, New York City, 2000. Hardcover. This an omnibus edition containing The Time Traders, 1958; and Galactic Derelict, 1959.

176. Knight or Knave: The Book of the Yew. With Sasha Miller. Published by Tor Books - Tom Doherty Associates, New York City, 2001. Hardcover.

177. Leopard in Exile. With Rosemary Edghill.

Andre Norton

Published by Tor Books - Tom Doherty Associates, New York City, 2001. Hardcover.

178. Star Soldiers. Published by Baen Books, New York City, 2001. Hardcover. Omnibus edition containing Star Guard, 1955, and Star Rangers, 1953.

179. Time Traders II. Published by Baen Books, New York City, 2001. Hardcover. This an omnibus edition containing The Defiant Agents, 1962; and Key Out of Time, 1963.

180. The Gates to the Witch World. Published by Tor Books - Tom Doherty Associates, New York City, 2001. Hardcover. A re-issue of Annals of the Witch World, 1994. An omnibus edition containing: Witch World, 1963; Web of the Witch World, 1964; and Year of the Unicorn, 1965.

181. Elvenborn. With Mercedes Lackey. Published by Tor Books - Tom Doherty Associates, New York City, 2002. Hardcover.

182. A Crown Disowned: the Book of the Ash and the Rowan. With Sasha Miller. Published by Tor Books - Tom Doherty Associates, New York City, 2002. Hardcover.

183. Beast Master's Ark. With Lyn McConchie. Published by Tor Books - Tom Doherty Associates, New York City, 2002. Hardcover.

184. Mark of the Cat: Year of the Rat. Published by Meisha Merlin Publishing, Decatur, Georgia, 2002. Hardcover.

185. Atlantis Endgame. With Sherwood Smith. Published by Tor Books - Tom Doherty Associates, New York City, 2002. Hardcover.

186. Janus. Published by Baen Books, New York City, 2002. Hardcover. Omnibus edition containing Judgment on Janus, 1963, and Victory on Janus, 1966.

187. Time Traders III. Published by Baen Books, New York City, 2002. Hardcover. This an omnibus edition containing Echoes in Time, 1999; and Atlantis Endgame, 2002.

188. Warlock. Published by Baen Books, New York City, 2002. Hardcover. This an omnibus edition containing Storm Over Warlock, 1960; Ordeal in Otherwhere, 1964; and Forerunner Foray, 1973.

189. Darkness and Dawn. Published by Baen Books, New York City, 2003. Hardcover. Omnibus edition containing Daybreak 2250 AD, 1954, and No Night Without Stars, 1975.

190. Solar Queen. Published by Baen Books, New York City, 2003. Hardcover. This an omnibus edition containing Sargasso of Space, 1955; and Plague Ship, 1956.

191. Gods and Androids. Published by Baen Books, New York City, 2004. Hardcover. Omnibus edition containing Android at Arms, 1971; and Wraiths of Time, 1976.

192. Beast Master's Circus. With Lyn McConchie. Published by Tor Books - Tom Doherty Associates, New York City, 2004. Hardcover.

193. Beast Master Team. With Lyn McConchie. Published by The Science Fiction Book Club, Garden City, New York, 2004. Hardcover. Omnibus edition containing Beast Master's Ark, 2002, and Beast Master's Circus, 2004.

194. Lost Lands of the Witch World. Published by Tor Books - Tom Doherty Associates, New York City, 2004. Hardcover. A re-issue of Chronicles of the Witch World, 1998. An omnibus edition containing: Three Against the Witch World, 1965; Warlock of the Witch World, 1967; and Sorceress of the Witch World, 1968.

195. Dragon Blade: The Book of the Rowan. With Sasha Miller. Published by Tor Books - Tom Doherty Associates, New York City, 2005. Hardcover.

196. Return to Quag Keep. With Jean Rabe. Published by Tor Books - Tom Doherty Associates, New York City, 2005. Hardcover.

197. Quag Keep - and - Return to Quag Keep. With Jean Rabe. Published by The Science Fiction Book Club, Garden City, New York, 2005. Hardcover.

198. The Dukes Ballad. With Lyn McConchie. Published by Tor Books - Tom Doherty Associates, New York City, 2005. Hardcover.

199. Silver May Tarnish. With Lyn McConchie. Published by Tor Books - Tom Doherty Associates, New York City, 2005. Hardcover.

200. Dark Companion. Published by Baen Books, New York City, 2005. Hardcover. Omnibus edition containing: Dark Piper, 1968; and Dread Companion, 1970.

201. Three Hands for Scorpio. Published by Tor Books - Tom Doherty Associates, New York City, 2005. Hardcover.

202. Beast Master's Planet. Published by Tor Books - Tom Doherty Associates, New York City, 2005. Hardcover. Omnibus edition containing: The Beast Master, 1959; and Lord of Thunder, 1962.

203. Masks of the Outcasts. Published by Baen Books, New York City, 2005. Hardcover. Omnibus edition containing: Catseye, 1961; and Night of Masks, 1964.

204. A Taste of Magic. With Jean Rabe. Published by Tor Books - Tom Doherty Associates, New York City, 2006. Hardcover.

205. Moonsinger. Published by Baen Books, New York City, 2006. Hardcover. Omnibus edition containing: Exiles of the Stars, 1971; and Moon of Three Rings, 1966.

206. Beast Master's Quest. With Lyn McConchie. Published by Tor Books - Tom Doherty Associates, New York City, 2006. Hardcover.

207. From the Sea to the Stars. Published by Baen Books, New York City, 2007. Hardcover. Omnibus edition containing: Sea Siege, 1957; and Star Gate, 1958.

208. Star Flight. Published by Baen Books, New York City, 2007. Hardcover. Omnibus edition containing: The Stars Are Ours, 1954; and Star Born, 1957.

209. Knight of the Red Beard. With Sasha Miller. Published by Tor Books - Tom Doherty Associates, New York City, 2008. Hardcover.

210. Dragon Mage: A Sequel to Dragon Magic. With Jean Rabe. Published by Tor Books - Tom Doherty Associates, New York City, 2008. Hardcover.

211. Crosstime. Published by Baen Books, New York City, 2008. Hardcover. Omnibus edition containing: Crossroads of Time, 1956; and Quest Crosstime, 1965.

212. Search for the Star Stones. Published by Baen Books, New York City, 2008. Hardcover. Omnibus edition containing: The Zero Stone, 1968; and Uncharted Stars, 1969.

213. The Game of Stars and Comets. Published by Baen Books, New York City, 2009. Hardcover. Omnibus edition containing: The Eye of the Monster, 1962; The Sioux Spaceman, 1960; Voorloper, 1980; and The X Factor, 1965.

214. Elvenbred. With Mercedes Lackey. Incomplete as of this writing but listed as a work in progress on Ms Lackey's website: http://www.mercedeslackey.com

***

ANTHOLOGIES

1. Space Service. Published by The World Publishing Company, Cleveland and New York, 1953. Hardcover. Herein: Preface by Norton; The Specter General by Theodore R. Cogswell, 1952; Star-Linked by H. B. Fyfe, 1952; The Share of Glory by C. M. Kornbluth, 1952; Implode and Peddle by H. B. Fyfe, 1951; For the Public by Bernard I. Kahn, 1946; Expedition Polychrome by Joseph A. Winter, 1949; Return of a Legend by Raymond Z. Gallun, 1952; Chore for a Spaceman by Walt Sheldon, 1950; and The Steel Brother by **Gordon R. Dickson,** 1952.

2. Space Pioneers. Published by The World Publishing Company, Cleveland and New York, 1954. Hardcover. This contains: Preface by Norton; Moonwalk by H. B. Fyfe, 1952; The Farthest Horizon by Raymond F. Jones, 1952; The End of the Line by James H. Schmitz, 1951; A Pail of Air by **Fritz Leiber,** 1951; The Illusionaries by **Eric Frank Russell,** 1951; Asteroid of Fear by Raymond Z. Gallun, 1951; Trail Blazer by Raymond Z. Gallun, 1951; Page and Player by Jerome Bixby, 1952; and Thou Good and Faithful by John Brunner writing as K. Houston Brunner, 1953.

3. Space Police. Published by The World Publishing Company, Cleveland and New York, 1956. Hardcover. Herein: Foreword by Norton; Agent of Vega by James H. Schmitz, 1949; Pax Galactica by Ralph Williams, 1952; Police Operation by H. Beam Piper, 1948; The Sub-Standard Sardines by **Jack Vance,** 1949; Tough Old Man by L. Ron Hubbard, 1950; Of Those Who Came by Francis G. Rayer writing as George Longdon, 1952; The Closed Door by Kendell Foster Crossen, 1953; Bait by Roy L. Clough; and Beep by **James Blish,** 1956.

4. Gates of Tomorrow. With Ernestine Donaldy. Published by Atheneum, New York City, 1973. Hardcover. This anthology contains: Introduction by Norton and Ernestine Donaldy; Shape by Robert Sheckley, 1953; Rust by Joseph E. Kelleam, 1939; Living Fossil by L. Sprague de Camp, 1939; The Plague by Keith Laumer, 1970; Command by Bernard I. Kahn, 1947; Expedition Polychrome by Joseph A. Winter, 1949; Ultimatum by Keith Laumer, 1965; The Sheriff of Canyon Gulch by **Poul Anderson** and **Gordon R. Dickson,** 1951; **The Naming of Names** by Ray Bradbury, 1949; The Flame Midget by Frank Belknap Long; and Untouched by Human Hands by Robert Sheckley, 1953.

5. Small Shadows Creep. Published by E. P. Dutton, New York City, 1974. Hardcover. Herein: Saloozy by Margery Lawrence, 1959; Herodes Redivivus by A. B. L. Munby, 1949; The First Sheaf by H. Russell Wakefield, 1939; How Fear Departed from the Long Gallery by E. F Benson, 1911; The Old Nurse's Story by Elizabeth Gaskell writing as Mrs. Gaskell, 1852; Lost Hearts by M. J. James, 1895; A Little Ghost by Hugh Walpole, 1922; Playmates by A. M. Burrage, 1927; and Faithful Jenny Dove by Eleanor Farjeon, 1925.

6. Baleful Beasts and Eerie Creatures. Published by Rand McNally and Company, New York City, 1976. Hardcover.

7. Magic in Ithkar. Edited with Robert Adams. Published by Tor Books - Tom Doherty Associates, New York City, 1985. Softcover. All new stories written for this anthology. Herein: Prologue by Robert Adams; The Prince Out of the Past by Nancy Springer; Swamp Dweller by Andre Norton; Cold Spell by Elisabeth Waters; Homecoming by Susan Shwartz; Dragon's Horn by J. W. Schutz; For Lovers Only by Roger C. Schlobin; Quazia and a Ferret-Fetch by Judith Sampson; Esmene's Eyes by Ardath Mayhar; Well Met in Ithkar by Patricia Mathews; Fletcher Found by Morgan Llywelyn; Jezeri and Her Beast Go to the Fair and Find More Excitement Than They Want by Jo Clayton; To Take a Thief by C. J. Cherryh; and The Goblinry of Ais by Lin Carter.

8. Magic in Ithkar 2. Edited with Robert Adams. Published by Tor Books - Tom Doherty Associates, New York City, 1985. Softcover. All new stories: Prologue by Robert Adams; Flux of Fortune by Mildred Downey Broxon; Geydelle's Protective by Lin Carter; If There Be Magic by Marylois Dunn; Babes on Bawd Way by George Alec Effinger; Sardofa's Horseshoes by Gregory Frost; The Ruby Wand of Asrazel by Joseph Green; Bird of Paradise by Linda Haldeman; Flaming Arrow by R. A. Lafferty; The Shaman Flute by Shariann Lewitt; Shadow Quest by Brad Linaweaver; Kissmeowt and the Healing Friar by A. R. Major; The Cards of Eldrianza by Mary H. Schaub; and The Marbled Horn by Lynn Ward.

9. Magic in Ithkar 3. Edited with Robert Adams. Published by Tor Books - Tom Doherty Associates, New York City, 1986. Softcover. All new stories:

Andre Norton

Prologue by Robert Adams; Covenant by P. M. Griffin; The Silverlord by Morgan Llywelyn; Fiddler Fair by Mercedes Lackey; Hair's Breath by Susan Shwartz; What Little Girls Are Made Of by Tanya Huff; Eyes of the Seer by Caralyn Inks and Georgia Miller; Three Knives in Ithkar by Gareth Bloodwine; Were Sisters by Ann R. Brown; The Magic Carpet by James Clark; The Amiable Assassin by A. C. Crispin; Guardians of the Secret by Monika Conroy and Ginger Curry; The Beggar and His Cat by Gene DeWeese; Flarrin Red Chin by M. Coleman Easton; Sundark in Ithkar by S. Lee Rouland; and The Singing Eggs by Kiel Stuart.

10. Magic in Ithkar 4. Edited with Robert Adams. Published by Tor Books - Tom Doherty Associates, New York City, 1987. Softcover. These stories were written for this anthology. Herein: Prologue by Robert Adams; A Quiet Day at the Fair by Sharon Green; To Trap a Demon by Ardath Mayhar; Day of Strange Fortune by Carol Severence; The Clockwork Woman by Ann R. Brown; First Do No Harm by Mildred Downey Broxon; Honeycomb by Esther M. Friesner; Demon Luck by Craig Shaw Gardner; Mandrake by Caralyn Inks; Trave by Shirley Meier; The Book Healer by Sandra Miesel; The Demon's Gift by Kathleen O'Malley; The Gentle Art of Making Enemies by Claudia Peck; Cat and Muse by Rose Wolf; and The Talisman by Timothy Zahn.

11. Tales of the Witch World. Published by Tor Books - Tom Doherty Associates, New York City, 1987. Hardcover. All new stories: The White Road by Charles de Lint; Heir Apparent by Robert Bloch; Fenneca by Wilanne Schneider Belden; Bloodspell by A. C. Crispin; Cat and the Other by Marylois Dunn; Oath Bound by Pauline Griffin; Of Ancient Swords and Evil Mist by James R. Heidbrink; Nine Words in Winter by Caralyn Inks; Were Hunter by Mercedes Lackey; Neither Rest nor Refuge by Ardath Mayhar; To Rebuild the Eyrie by Sasha Miller; Milk from a Maiden's Breast by Elizabeth Scarborough; Night Hound's Moon by Mary H. Schaub; Isle of Illusion by Carol Severance; Green in High Hallack by Kiel Stuart; The Road of Dreams and Death by Robert E. Vardeman; and Of the Shaping of Ulm's Heir by Andre Norton.

12. Tales of the Witch World II. Published by Tor Books - Tom Doherty Associates, New York City, 1988. Hardcover. All new stories: Heroes by Diana L. Paxson; Rite of Failure by Susan Shwartz; The Hunting of Lord Etsalian's Daughter by Clare Bell; Sea Serpents of Domnudale by Ginger Simpson Curry; Old Toad by Geary Gravel; The Judgment of Neave by S. N. Lewitt; Through the Moon Gate by Jacqueline Lichtenberg; Dream Pirates' Jewel by Brad Linaweaver and Cynthia Linaweaver; La Verdad: The Magic Sword by A. R. Major; Darkness Over Mirhold by Patricia Shaw Mathews; Peacock Eyes by Shirley Meier; The Salt Garden by Sandra Miesel; The Stones of Sharnon by Ann Miller; Futures Yet Unseen by Melinda M. Snodgrass; S'Olcarias's Sons by Lisa Swallow; The Sentinel at the Edge of the World by David Wind; and Tall Dames Go Walking by Rose Wolf.

13. Four from the Witch World. Published by Tor Books - Tom Doherty Associates, New York City, 1989. Hardcover. Herein: The Stillborn Heritage by Elizabeth H. Boyer; Stormbirds by C. J. Cherryh; Rampion Meredith Ann Pierce; and Falcon Law by Judith Tarr.

14. Grand Master's Choice. Edited with Ingrid Zierhut and Robert Bloch. Published by NESFA Press, Boston, 1989. Hardcover. Herein: Introduction by Robert Bloch; The Long Watch by **Robert A. Heinlein**, 1948; With Folded Hands by **Jack Williamson**, 1947; The Autumn Land by Clifford Simak, 1971; A Gun for Dinosaur by L. Sprague de Camp, 1956; Lean Times in Lankhmar by **Fritz Leiber**, 1968; Toads of Grimmerdale by Andre Norton, 1974; Transit of Earth by **Arthur C. Clarke**, 1958; and The Last Question by **Isaac Asimov**, 1956.

15. Catfantastic: Nine Lives and Fifteen Tales. Edited with Martin H. Greenberg. Published by MJF Books, New York City, 1989. Hardcover. New stories: Introduction: Speaking of Cats - A Very Weighty Subject by Norton; The Gate of the Kittens by Wilanne Schneider Belden; The Damcat by Clare Bell; Borrowing Trouble by Elizabeth H. Boyer; Day of Discovery by Blake Cahoon; Wart by Jayge Carr; Yellow Eyes by Marylois Dunn; It Must Be Some Place by Donna Farley; The Dreaming Kind by C. S. Friedmann; Trouble by P. M. Griffin; Skitty by Mercedes Lackey; The Game of Cat and Rabbit by Patricia Shaw Mathews; From the Diary of Hermione by Ardath Mayhar; It's a Bird It's a Plane It's... Supercat by Ann Miller and Karen Elizabeth Rigley; Noble Warrior by Andre Norton; and Bastet's Blessing by Elizabeth Ann Scarborough.

16. Tales of the Witch World III. Published by Tor Books - Tom Doherty Associates, New York City, 1990. Hardcover. All new stories: Introduction by Andre Norton; Voice of Memory by M. E. Allen; Plumduff Potato-Eye by Jayge Carr; The Scent of Magic by Juanita Coulson; The Weavers by Esther M. Friesner; The Root of All Evil by Sharon Green; Knowledge by P. M. Griffin; The Circle of Sleep by Caralyn Inks; Falcon's Chick by Patricia Shaw; Fortune's Children by Patricia A. McKillip; Godron's Daughter by Ann Miller and Karen Elizabeth Rigley; A Question of Magic by Marta Randall; Strait of Storms by K. L. Roberts; Candletrap by Mary H. Schaub; Whispering Cane by Carol Severence; Gunnora's Gift by Elisabeth Waters; Wolfhead by Michael D. Winkle; Were-Flight by Lisa Woodworth; and The Sword Seller by Patricia C. Wrede.

17. Catfantastic II. Edited with Martin H. Greenberg. Published by DAW Books, New York City, 1991. Softcover. DAW Collector's Book 839. New stories: Introduction by Norton and Greenberg; Bomber and Bismarck by Clare Bell; A Puma and a Panther by Wilanne Schneider Belden; The Last Gift by Elizabeth H. Boyer; Papercut Luck by Patricia B. Cirone; Shado by Marylois Dunn; In Bastet's Service by P. M. Griffin; Shadows by Caralyn Inks; The Execution by A. R. Major; Hermione at Moon House by Ardath Mayhar; Quest of Souls by Ann Miller and Karen Rigley; Ede's Earrings by Sasha Miller; Clara's Cat by Elizabeth Moon; Hob's Pot by **Andre Norton**; The Queen Cat's Tale by Elizabeth Ann Scarborough; The Keep Shape Spell by Mary H. Schaub; Of Age and Wisdom by Roger C. Schlobin; Critical Cats by Susan Shwartz; and In Carnation by Nancy Springer.

18. Catfantastic III. Edited with Martin H. Greenberg. Published by DAW Books, New York City, 1994. Softcover. DAW Collector's Book 942. New stories: Introduction by **Andre Norton**; A Woman of Her Word by Lee Barwood; A Tangled Tahitian Tail by Clare Bell; Saxophone Joe and the Woman in Black by Charles de Lint; Teddy Cat by Marylois Dunn; Cat O'Nine Tales by Charles L. Fontenay; Partners by P. M. Griffin; But a Glove by John E. Johnston; Fear in Her Pocket by Caralyn Inks; A Tail of Two Skittys by Mercedes Lackey; Hermoine as Spy by Ardath Mayhar; Moon Scent by Lyn McConchie; Cat's World by Cynthia McQuillin; Snake Eyes by Ann Miller and Karen Rigley; One Too Many Cats by Sasha Miller; Noble Warrior Meets with a Ghost by Andre Norton; Connecticat by Raul Reyes and Elisabeth Waters; The Cat-Quest of Mu Mao the Magnificent by Elizabeth Ann Scarborough; The Cat the Wizards and the Bedpost by Mary H. Schaub; To Skein a Cat by Lawrence Schimel; and Asking Mr. Bigelow by Susan Shwartz.

19. Catfantastic IV. Edited with Martin H. Greenberg. Published by DAW Books, New York City, 1996. Softcover. DAW Collector's Book 1030. New stories: Introduction by **Andre Norton**; Noh Cat Afternoon by Jane M. Lindskold; Born Again by Elizabeth Ann Scarborough; Scat by Mercedes Lackey; The Cat, the Sorcerer and the Magic Mirror by Mary Schaub; One With Jazz by Janet Pack; Deathsong by Lyn McConchie; Totem Cat by A. R. Major; Professor Purr's Guaranteed Allergy Cure by Brad Linaweaver and Dana Fredsti; Tinkerbell by Sharman Horwood; The Last Answer by Wilanne Schneider Belden; The Quincunx Solution by Anne Braude; Circus by Jayge Carr; Tybalt's Tale by India Edghill; The Tale of the Virtual Cat by Heather Gladney, Don Clayton and Alan Rice Osborn; Arrows by Jane Hamilton; Miss Hettie and Harlan by Charles L. Fontenay; The Neighbor by P. M. Griffin and Andre Norton.

20. Catfantastic V. Edited with Martin H. Greenberg. Published by DAW Books, New York City, 1999. Softcover. DAW Collector's Book 1128. New stories: Introduction by **Andre Norton**; The Golden Cats by Robin Wayne Bailey; Grow Old Along With Me by Lee Barwood; Puss by Jayge Carr; Goliath by R. Davis; Dragon, The Book by David Drake; The Courtesan Who Loved Cats by India Edghill; The Maltese Feline by Rosemary Edghill; A Cat's Tale by Paul Goode; Tenth-Life Cat by P. M. Griffin; Kindred Hearts by Caralyn Inks; A Better Mousetrap by Mercedes Lackey; The Big Ice by Sharon Lee; Preliminary Report by Barry B. Longyear; Lullaby by Lyn McConchie; The Very Early Hermione by Ardath Mayhar; Miss Lotte by Sandra Miesel; Kitten Claws by Sasha Miller; Noble Warrior and the Gentleman by Andre Norton; The Cat, the Sorceress, the Buttons and Why by Mary Schaub; Hobson's Choice by Susan Shwartz; Rosemary for Remembrance by Estelle Traylor; Patches' Pride by Laura Underwood; Trixie by Lawrence Watt-Evans; and Pick Cry and Grin Again by Rose Wolf.

21. Fantastic Cat. Edited with Martin H. Greenberg. Published by iBooks, New York City, 2004. Softcover. Re-issue of Catfantastic II, 1991. Herein: Introduction by Norton and Greenberg; Bomber and Bismarck by Clare Bell; A Puma and a Panther by Wilanne Schneider Belden; The Last Gift by Elizabeth H. Boyer; Papercut Luck by Patricia B. Cirone; Shado by Marylois Dunn; In Bastet's Service by P. M. Griffin; Shadows by Caralyn Inks; The Execution by A. R. Major; Hermione at Moon House by Ardath Mayhar; Quest of Souls by Ann Miller and Karen Rigley; Ede's Earrings by Sasha Miller; Clara's Cat by Elizabeth Moon; Hob's Pot by Andre Norton; The Queen Cat's Tale by Elizabeth Ann Scarborough; The Keep Shape Spell by Mary H. Schaub; Of Age and Wisdom by Roger C. Schlobin; Critical Cats by Susan Shwartz; and In Carnation by Nancy Springer.

22. Renaissance Faire. Edited with Jean Rabe. Published by DAW Books, New York City, 2005. Softcover. DAW Collector's Book 1320. New stories: Introduction by Rabe and Norton; Jewels Beyond Price by Elizabeth Ann Scarborough; Diminished Chord by Joe Haldeman; Splinter by Kevin J. Anderson and Rebecca Moesta; Girolamo and Mistress Willendorf by John Maddox Roberts; A Time for Steel by Robert E. Vardeman; One Hot Day by Stephen Gabriel; Wimpin' Wady by Jayge Carr; Brewed Fortune by Michael A. Stackpole; Marriage a la Modred by Esther M. Friesner; A Dance of Seven Vales by Rose Wolf; Moses' Miracles by Roberta Gellis; Grok by Donald J. Bingle; Renaissance Fear by Stephen D. Sullivan; The Land of the Awful Shadow by Brian A. Hopkins; and Faire Likeness by Andre Norton.

***

RELATED

1. The First Editions of Andre Norton. By David G. Turner. Published by David G. Turner - Bookman, Menlo Park, California, 1974. Softcover.

H. G. Wells.

Herbert George Wells was born in Bromley, Kent, on September 21st, 1866 and died in London, probably from diabetic complications although the exact cause was undetermined, on August 13th, 1946. From a relatively poor family, Wells still managed to acquire an education and, after failing as an apprenticed draper, and then as a chemist's assistant, he landed a job as an assistant grammar school teacher. It was while doing that that he won a scholarship and moved on to London to study biology at the Normal School of Science as taught by T. H. Huxley, the grandfather of Aldous Huxley. The science was Darwinian and inspired much of what Wells wrote about later.

As one of the founders of the school magazine, The Science School Journal, Wells began to develop as a socialist, a futurist, an essayist and historian... as a writer. The earliest version of The Time Machine, The Chronic Argonauts, was published here in 1888. It wasn't his first published work, but it was the first to give a hint about where his writing would take him.

When The Time Machine was published in 1895, it was more than just a best-selling book, it was the first modern science fiction novel. As **Isaac Asimov** explained it, **H. G. Wells** managed to invent completely impossible science, the time machine, and make the reader believe it, at least during the time of his reading. And that was the creation of the modern science fiction story: a story that could not exist without the science. But Wells was not content to come up with a scientific approach to time travel, which became an entire sub-genre of SF, he also went on to imagine evolution run amok, an invisible man, an alien invasion, serious space flight... The list goes on.

In spite of all his amazing science fiction, first editions of which tend to sell well over $40,000.00, this was not his main focus. More than anything, Wells wanted social reform. And almost everything he did was coloured by that.

Pen names used: Reginald Bliss; Septimus Browne; Walter Shockenhammer; and Sosthenes Smith.

***

AWARDS

1997. Inducted into The Science Fiction Hall of Fame.

***

FILM AND TELEVISION

1. Le Voyage Dans la Lune. A short film, made in France and released in October 1902 in the States with the actual title A Trip to Mars. It was based on De la Terre a la Lune - From the Earth to the Moon, 1867, by **Jules Verne** and on First Men in the Moon, 1901, by **H. G. Wells**. Directed by Georges Melies, the film starred: Victor Andre; Bleuette Bernon; Jeanne d'Alcy; Henri Delannoy; and others.

2. Il Giustiziere Invisibile. A film made in Italy in 1916 and based on the novel The Invisible Man, 1897. Directed by Mario Roncoroni, this starred: Arnaldo Arnaldi; Valeria Creti; Casco Creti; Armando Fineschi; Antonio Mugnaini; and many others.

3. The First Men in the Moon. A 1919 film based on the Wells novel of the same name from 1901, directed by Bruce Gordon and J. L. V. Leigh and starring: Bruce Gordon; Heather Thatcher; Hector Abbas; Lionel d'Aragon; and Cecil Morton York.

4. Kipps. This was a comedic film released in the UK in 1921, based on the 1905 novel and directed by Harold M. Shaw. It starred: George K. Arthur; Edna Flugrath; Christine Rayner; Teddy Arundell; Norman Thorpe; Arthur Helmore; John East; and many others.

5. Die Insel der Verschollenen. A 1921 German film based on The Island of Dr Moreau, 1896. It was released in the U.S. as The Island of the Lost. Directed by Urban Gad, it starred: Fritz Beckmann; Hans Behrendt; Loo Bell; Alf Blutecher; Lewis Brody; Tronier Funder; Umberto Guarracino; Ludmilla Hell; and many others.

6. The Passionate Friends. Based on the 1913 Wells novel and released in 1922, this film was directed by Maurice Elvey and starred: Milton Rosmer; Fred Raynham; Valia, also known as Mademoiselle Valia; Madge Stuart; Lawford Davidson; Ralph Forster; Teddy Arundell; and others.

7. The Wheels of Chance. This film was based on the 1896 Wells novel and released in 1922, directed by Harold M. Shaw and starring: George K. Arthur; Olwen Roose; Gordon Parker; Bertie Wright; Mabel Archdale; Judd Green; and others.

8. They Forgot to Read the Directions. Written by Rebecca West, this 1924 UK short film starred: Lord Beaverbrook; Rebecca West; and H. G. Wells as Rev. Jeremiah Honeydew.

9. Marriage. Based on the 1912 novel of the same name and released in 1927, this was directed by Roy William Neill and starred: Virginia Valli; Allan Durant; Gladys McConnell; Lawford Davidson; Donald Stuart; Frank Dunn; Edwards Davis; James A. Marcus; and Billie Bennett.

10. H. G. Wells Comedies. This was made in the UK in 1928 and used an assortment of Wells' stories, directed by Ivor Montagu: The Tonic, starring: Elsa Lanchester and Renee De Vaux; Blue Bottles, starring: Elsa Lanchester; Joe Beckett; Dorice Fordred; Marie Wright; Charles Laughton; and Norman Haire; Daydreams, starring: Elsa Lanchester; Harold Warrender; Dorice Fordred; Marie Wright; and Charles Laughton.

11. Island of Lost Souls. Based on The Island of Dr Moreau, 1896, this was released in 1932, directed by Erle C. Kenton and starring: Charles Laughton;

Richard Arlen; Leila Hyams; Bela Lugosi; Kathleen Burke; Arthur Hohl; Stanley Fields; Paul Hurst; Hans Steinke; Tetsu Komai; George Irving; and others. A number of the beasts were uncredited actors and some were even unconfirmed but rumour has it that amongst the beasts were: Buster Crabbe; Rosemary Grimes; Alan Ladd; and Randolph Scott.

12. The Invisible Man. Based on the 1895 novel and released in 1933, this was directed by James Whale and starred: Claude Rains; Gloria Stuart; William Harrigan; Henry Travers; Una O'Connor; Forrester Harvey; Holmes Herbert; E. E. Clive; Merle Tottenham; and others, including Walter Brennan and John Carradine in small, uncredited roles.

13. Things to Come. This was based on the Wells novel, The Shape of Things to Come, 1933, and released in the U.S. in 1936. Wells also wrote the screenplay. The film was directed by William Cameron Menzies and starred: Raymond Massey; Edward Chapman; Ralph Richardson; Margaretta Scott; Cedric Hardwicke; Maurice Braddell; Sophie Stewart; Derrick De Marney; Ann Todd; Pearl Argyle; Kenneth Villiers; Anne McLaren; and many others.

14. The Man Who Could Work Miracles. Based on the 1888 story, this was directed by Lothar Mendes. Wells also developed the story for filming. Released in 1936, it starred: Roland Young; Ralph Richardson; Edward Chapman; Ernest Thesiger; Joan Gardner; Sophie Stewart; Robert Cochran; Lady Tree; Laurence Hanray; George Zucco; Wallace Lupino; Joan Hickson; George Sanders; and others, including Michael Rennie in an uncredited bit part.

15. The Invisible Man Returns. Inspired by the 1897 novel, this was directed by Joe May and released in 1940, starring: Cedric Hardwicke; Vincent Price; Nan Grey; John Sutton; Cecil Kellaway; Alan Napier; Forrester Harvey; and many others.

16. Kipps. Directed by Carol Reed, this filmed version of the 1905 novel was released in 1941, starring: Michael Redgrave; Diana Wynyard; Diana Calderwood; Phyllis Calvert; Arthur Riscoe; Philip Frost; Max Adrian; Helen Haye; Betty Jardine; Hermione Baddeley; and many others.

17. Invisible Agent. Another film inspired by Wells, loosely based on The Invisible Man, 1897, this one had a screenplay by Curt Siodmak and was directed by Edwin L. Marin. Released in 1942, it starred: Ilona Massey; Jon Hall; Peter Lorre; Cedric Hardwicke; J. Edward Bromberg; Albert Bassermann; John Litel; Holmes Herbert; Keye Luke; and many others.

18. The Invisible Man's Revenge. Yet another one inspired by The Invisible Man, 1897, this one was released in 1944, directed by Ford Beebe and starring: Jon Hall; Leon Errol; John Carradine; Alan Curtis; Evelyn Ankers; Gale Sondergaard; Lester Matthews; Halliwell Hobbes; Doris Lloyd; Grey Shadow the dog; and many others.

19. Dead of Night. This 1945 film combined a number of stories, only one of which belonged to Wells. He was responsible for the segment called Golfing Story, directed by Charles Crichton and starring: Basil Radford; Naunton Wayne; and Peggy Bryan.

20. The Inexperienced Ghost. A 1902 short story that was adapted for the television series The Actor's Studio in 1948, season 1, episode 6, starring: Dennis King; Rex O'Malley; and Lou Gilbert.

21. The Time Machine. This 1895 novel was adapted by Robert Barr for UK television, airing on January 24th, 1949. It starred: Mary Donn; Christopher Gill; Eugene Leahy; Russell Napier; Anthony Nicholls; and George Stanford.

22. The Passionate Friends. Filmed in 1949, this was released in the U.S. as One Woman's Story. Based on the 1913 Wells novel, the writing was handled by Eric Ambler, Stanley Haynes and David Lean. The film was directed by David Lean and starred: Ann Todd; Claude Rains; Trevor Howard; Isabel Dean; Betty Ann Davies; Arthur Howard; Guido Lorraine; Marcel Poncin; Natasha Sokolova; Helene Burls; Jean Serret; and others.

23. The History of Mr. Polly. A 1949 film based on the 1910 novel and directed by Anthony Pelissier, starring: John Mills; Betty Ann Davies; Megs Jenkins; Finlay Currie; Diana Churchill; Shelagh Fraser; Edward Chapman; Dandy Nichols; Sally Ann Howes; Juliet Mills; and many others.

24. Abbott and Costello Meet the Invisible Man. Also inspired by 1897 novel, this film was released in 1951, directed by Charles Lamont and starring, of course, Bud Abbott and Lou Costello, along with: Nancy Guild; Arthur Franz; Adele Jergens; Sheldon Leonard; William Frawley; Gavin Muir; and many others.

25. The Crystal Egg. This 1897 story was adapted for the television series Tales of Tomorrow. It aired on October 12th, 1951, season 1, episode 9, directed by Charles S. Dubin and starring: Josephine Brown; Gage Clarke; Sally Gracie; Thomas Mitchell; and Edgar Stehli.

26. The History of Mr Polly. This was adapted from the 1910 novel for BBC Sunday Night Theatre by Robert Christie and aired on August 13th, 1950, season 1, episode 33. It starred: Emrys Jones; Erik Chitty; George Woodbridge; Victor Platt; Barry Steele; Stanley Vilven; Cecil Petty; Mary Mackenzie; Gladys Henson; Elizabeth Maude; Lalage Lewis; and many others.

27. The Wonderful Visit. This was adapted from the 1895 novel for BBC Sunday Night Theatre by Robert Christie and aired on February 3rd, 1952, Season 3, Episode 5. It starred: Margaret Barton; Kathleen Boutall; Margery Brice; Jean Cadell; Wyndham Goldie; Noel Howlett; Barry Jones; Donald Kemp; Sam Kydd; Edie Martin; Elizabeth Maude; Margaret McCourt; Alexis Milne; and others.

28. Love and Mr Lewisham. This was adapted from the 1899 novel for BBC Sunday Night Theatre by Robert Christie and aired on May 4th, 1952, Season 3, Episode 18. It starred: Emrys Jones; Sheila Shand Gibbs; Denis Bedford; Gordon Bell; Frank Birch; Robert Brown; Fanny Carby; Aubrey Dexter; Pauline Jameson; and many others.

29. Ann Veronica. This was adapted from the 1909 novel for BBC Sunday Night Theatre by Ronald Gow

H.G. Wells

and aired on June 22nd, 1952, Season 3, Episode 25. It starred: Margaret Lockwood; Malcolm Black; Claude Bonser; Diana Calderwood; Robert Eddison; Alexis France; Robert Harris; Henry Hewitt; Anthea Holloway; Enid Lindsey; Cicely Paget-Bowman; and many others.

30. The War of the Worlds. Adapted from the 1898 novel, this was directed by Byron Haskin and released in the States on August 26th, 1953, starring: Gene Barry; Ann Robinson; Les Tremayne; Robert Cornthwaite; Sandro Giglio; Cedric Hardwicke; William Phipps; and many others.

31. In the Country of the Blind. A 1904 short story that was adapted for the television series Your Favorite Story, 1954.

32. Gorunmeyen adam Istanbul'da. A 1955 Turkish film based on The Invisible Man, 1897, directed by Lutfi Akad and starring: Turan Seyfioglu; Nese Yulac; Abdurrahman Palay; Atif Kaptan; and many more.

33. The Door in the Wall. Adapted from the 1906 short story, this was made in the UK in 1956, directed by Glenn H. Alvey Jr. and starring: Stephen Murray; Ian Hunter; Leonard Sachs; Ann Blake; Malcolm Knight; Kit Terrington; and others.

34. Ann Veronica. This 1909 novel was directed by Walter Grauman for the television series Matinee Theatre, Season 2, Episode 215. It was shown on July 29th, 1957 and starred: Wendy Hiller; and Patric Knowles.

35. The Invisible Man. From 1897, this was directed by Larry Schwab for the television series Matinee Theatre, Season 2, Episode 223. It was shown on August 8th, 1957 and starred: Geoffrey Toone; Chester Stratton; and Angela Thornton.

36. Ann Veronica. This 1909 novel was directed by Vivian Milroy for the television series Armchair Theatre. It aired October 27th, 1957, Season 2, Episode 6, starring: Margaret Dale; Joan Greenwood; and Robert Urquhart.

37. The History of Mr. Polly. This was a UK television series based on the 1910 novel. It ran for six episodes, starting August 28th, 1959 and finishing on October 2nd, 1959. It starred: Emrys Jones; Mary Mackenzie; Daphne Anderson; Richard Caldicot; Edna Morris; Wilfrid Brambell; Fabia Drake; Gladys Henson; Barbara Lott; Brian Moorehead; Dorothy Robson; and Patrick Troughton.

38. Terror is a Man. A 1959 film, shot in the Philippines and based on The Island of Dr. Moreau, 1896, although Wells did not receive credit for that. It was directed by Gerardo de Leon and starred: Francis Lederer; Greta Thyssen; Richard Derr; Oscar Keesee; Lilia Duran; Peyton Keesee; and Flory Carlos. Working titles and other releases had the names: Blood Creature; Creature from Blood Island; Island of Terror; and The Gory Creatures.

39. Invisible Man. Also known as H. G. Wells' Invisible Man. A British television series inspired by the 1897 novel, it started in 1958 and ran for two seasons, twenty-six episodes in all, starring: Lisa Daniely; Tim Turner; Johnny Scripps; Deborah Watling; Ernest Clark; Robert Raglan; Bruce Seton; Lloyd Lamble; Howard Pays; Derek Sydney; Michael Ripper; and Derren Nesbitt.

40. The Time Machine. A 1960 film based on the 1895 novel, it was directed by George Pal and starred: Rod Taylor; Alan Young; Yvette Mimieux; Sebastian Cabot; Tom Helmore; Whit Bissell; Doris Lloyd; and others.

41. Kipps. A 1960 television mini-series based on the 1905 novel, starting in the UK on October 14th, 1960. It was directed by Stuart Latham and starred: Bryan Murray; Kenneth Cope; Lloyd Pearson; Richard Statman; Sheila Steafel; Dudley Sutton; and Beatrice Varley.

42. The Richest Man in Bogota. This was based on Wells' story In the Country of the Blind, 1904. Directed by Ralph Nelson, it was aired on the U.S. series The DuPont Show of the Week, June 17th, 1961, Season 1, Episode 28. It starred: E. J. Andre; Miriam Colon; Richard Eastman; Eugene Iglesias; and Lee Marvin.

43. One Step from the Pavement. This was based on the Wells' story The Magic Shop, 1903. Directed by Waris Hussein, it was shown on the UK series Suspense, January 14th, 1963, Season 2, Episode 3. It starred: Elsie Arnold; David Garth; Sonia Graham; Gordon Jackson; Philip Needs; Donald Tandy; Molly Urquhart; and Christopher Witty.

44. The Magic Shop. With a teleplay by John Collier, this was based on Wells' 1903 story. Directed by Robert Stevens, it was shown on The Alfred Hitchcock Hour, January 10th, 1964, Season 2, Episode 13. It starred: Leslie Nielsen; Peggy McCay; John Megna; David Opatoshu; Paul Hartman; William Sargent; Audrey Swanson; Rob Reiner; Ted de Corsia; Hugh Sanders; Rolfe Sedan; and Brian Corcoran.

45. Ann Veronica. This was a British television mini-series based on the 1909 novel. It started on May 23rd, 1964, directed by Christopher Barry and starring: Rosemary Nicols; Laurence Hardy; Barrie Ingham; and Gillian Lind.

46. First Men in the Moon. Based on the 1901 novel, this was filmed in the UK and released in 1964. Directed by Nathan Juran, it starred: Edward Judd; Martha Hyer; Lionel Jeffries; Miles Malleson; Norman Bird; Gladys Henson; Hugh McDermott; Betty McDowell; and many others, including Peter Finch in an uncredited bit part.

47. Village of the Giants. This was based on Wells' novel The Food of the Gods and How It Came to Earth, 1904. Filmed in the U.S. and directed by Bert I. Gordon, it was released in October 1965. It starred: Tommy Kirk; Johnny Crawford; Beau Bridges; Ron Howard; Tisha Sterling; Joy Harmon; Robert Random; Tim Rooney; and many others, including the band The Beau Brummels.

48. Days to Come. Based on the Wells' tale A Story of the Days to Come, 1897, this was adapted for the British series Play of the Month. Directed by Alan Bridges, it aired on October 25th, 1966,

Season 2, Episode 2. The show starred: Judi Dench; Dinsdale Landen; Bernard Archard; Michael Gough; John Quentin; Alan Rowe; Michael Brennan; Peggy Sinclair; and many others.

49. Half a Sixpence. A musical based on Kipps, 1905. Filmed in the UK, it was directed by George Sidney and released in 1968, starring: Tommy Steele; Julia Foster; Cyril Ritchard; Penelope Horner; Elaine Taylor; Grover Dale; Hilton Edwards; Julia Sutton; Leslie Meadows; Sheila Falconer; Pamela Brown; James Villiers; Christopher Sandford; Jean Anderson; and many others, including Ray Davies of The Kinks as a dancer.

50. Dan-dan han changugi gyo in. A 1970 South Korean film based on The Food of the Gods and How It Came to Earth, 1904. It starred: Capri; Hyang-a Kim; Beru-Bera Lin; Oh-jang Mun; and Mi Yu.

51. The Island of Doctor Agor. A Tim Burton animated film, in fact, his first film, based on The Island of Dr. Moreau, 1896, and released in 1971. Burton was thirteen years old at the time and made the film on a Super 8 camera.

52. Love and Mr. Lewisham. A UK television miniseries, based on the 1899 novel and starting on August 31st, 1972. Directed by Christopher Barry, it starred: Brian Deacon; Carolyn Courage; Robert James; and Jane Lapotaire.

53. The Twilight People. This 1973 American/Philippines film was based on The Island of Dr. Moreau, 1896, although no credit was given. It was also known as Beasts and Island of the Twilight People. Directed by Eddie Romero, it starred: John Ashley; Pat Woodell; Jan Merlin; Charles Macaulay; Pam Grier; Ken Metcalfe; Tony Gosalvez; Kim Ramos; Mona Morena; Eddie Garcia; and many more.

54. La Merveilleuse Visite. This was based on The Wonderful Visit, 1895. In Italy it was called La Meravigliosa Visita; and the English titled was The Marvelous Visit. The film was a French/Italian production, released in 1974 and directed by Marcel Carne. It starred: Gilles Kohler; Roland Lesaffre; Debra Berger; Lucien Barjon; Mary Marquet; Yves Barsacq; and many others.

55. The Invisible Man. This was an American television series that took only the title and the concept from Wells, 1897; all the rest was their own invention. It was a short-lived show starring: David McCallum; Melinda O. Fee; Jackie Cooper; Henry Darrow; Alex Henteloff; and others.

56. Riding with Death. This was an 1976 American TV movie, based on The Invisible Man, 1897. Directed by Alan J. Levi and Don McDougall, it starred: Ben Murphy; Katherine Crawford; Richard Dysart; William Sylvester; Andrew Prine; John Mitford; and many others.

57. Das Land der Blinden order Von einem der auszog. Made for West German television in 1976, this was based on In the Country of the Blind, 1904. Directed by Pete Ariel, it starred: Rainer Langhans; Fred Stillkrauth; and Jutta Winkelmann.

58. Gemini Man. This was an American TV movie, based on The Invisible Man, 1897. Directed by Alan J. Levi, it was aired on May 10th, 1976, starring: Ben Murphy; Katherine Crawford; Richard Dysart; Dana Elcar; Paul Shenar; Quinn K. Redeker; Gregory Walcott; Cheryl Miller; and many others.

59. The Food of the Gods. Filmed in the U.S. and directed by Bert I. Gordon, this was released in June, 1976. It starred: Marjoe Gortner; Pamela Franklin; Ralph Meeker; Jon Cypher; Ida Lupino; John McLiam; Belinda Belaski; Tom Stovall; Chuck Courtney; and Reg Tunnicliffe.

60. Gemini Man. This was an American television series, based on The Invisible Man, 1897. Directed by Alan J. Levi, Alan Crosland and Michael Caffey, it started on September 23rd, 1976, starring: Ben Murphy; Katherine Crawford; William Sylvester; and Jim Stafford.

61. Empire of the Ants. Based on Wells' story of the same name, 1905, this was filmed in the U.S. in 1977, directed by Bert I. Gordon and starring: Joan Collins; Robert Lansing; John David Carson; Albert Salmi; Jacqueline Scott; Pamela Susan Shoop; Robert Pine; Edward Power; Brooke Palance; and many others.

62. The Island of Dr. Moreau. An American film made in 1977, directed by Don Taylor and starring: Burt Lancaster; Michael York; Nigel Davenport; Barbara Carrera; Richard Basehart; Nick Cravat; Bob Ozman; Fumio Demura; Gary Baxley; John Gillespie; and others.

63. The Time Machine. A U.S. television film from 1978, directed by Henning Schellerup and starring: John Beck; Priscilla Barnes; Andrew Duggan; Rosemary DeCamp; Jack Kruschen; Whit Bissell; John Hansen; R. G. Armstrong; John Doucette; and many others.

64. The Shape of Things to Come. Based on Wells' 1933 novel, this was a Canadian film made in 1979 and directed by George McCowan. It starred: Jack Palance; Carol Lynley; Barry Morse; John Ireland; Nicholas Campbell; Anne-Marie Martin; Greg Swanson; Mike Parr; William Hutt; Ardon Bess; and many others.

65. The History of Mr. Polly. A UK miniseries which started on March 5th, 1980, directed by Lovett Bickford and starring: Andrew Sachs; Glynn Edwards; Holly Aird; Ann Beach; Peter Bourke; Fanny Carby; Anita Carey; Nigel Lambert; Patsy Rowlands; Mildred Shay; and Gay Soper.

66. The Magic Shop. A short film made in the UK in 1982, directed by Ian Emes and starring: Karl Johnson; Ron Cook; and Paul Erangey.

67. Chelovek-nevidimka. A 1984 Russian film, based on The Invisible Man, 1897. Directed by Aleksandr Zakharovk, it starred: Andrei Kharitonov; Romualdas Ramanauskas; Leonid Kuravlyov; Natalya Danilova; Nina Agapova; Viktor Sergachyov; and others.

68. The Invisible Man. A British television series based on the 1897 novel. It started on September

H.G. Wells

10th, 1985. Directed by Brian Lighthill, it starred: Jonathan Adams; Keith Ashton; Jiggy Bhore; Donald Bisset; Anthony Brown; Ruby Buchanan; Deddie Davies; Pip Donaghy; Helen Gold; Nigel Gregory; and many others.

69. War of the Worlds. An American television series based on the 1898 novel. It started on October 7th, 1988. It starred: Jared Martin; Lynda Mason Green; Richard Chaves; Rachel Blanchard; Philip Akin; Denis Forest; Adrian Paul; Catherine Disher; Ilse von Glatz; Julian Richings; Michael Rudder; Richard Comar; and many more, including Jill Hennessy for two episodes.

70. Time Machine. A 1992 film inspired by the 1895 novel and made in India and starring: Aamir Khan; Amrish Puri; Rekha; Naseerudding Shah; Raveena Tandon; and others.

71. Volshebnaya Lavka. A 1992 Russian film, based on The Magic Shop, 1902. Directed by Aleksandr Zakharovk, it starred: Aleksandr Zakharov; Sergei Seleznyov; Yuri Katin-Yartsev; and others.

72. The Island of Dr. Moreau. This version of the 1896 novel was directed by John Frankenheimer and released in 1996. It starred: David Thewlis; Fairuza Balk; Ron Perlman; Marlon Brando; Val Kilmer; Marco Hofschneider; Teuuera Morrison; William Hootkins; Daniel Rigney; Nelson de la Rosa; Peter Elliott; Mark Decascos; and others.

73. Things 3: Old Things - AKA Dead Time Tales. One segment called Crystal Gazing was based on Wells' The Crystal Egg, 1897.

74. The Invisible Man. Another one based on Wells' 1897 idea, this was an American television series that first aired on January 6th, 2002. Directed by Carlton Prickett and Breck Eisner, it starred: Vincent Ventresca; Paul Ben-Victor; Shannon Kenny; Eddie Jones; Michael McCafferty; and many others.

75. The Infinite Worlds of H. G. Wells. A UK/U.S. production, this was filmed in London and directed by Robert Young, the first episode of this three-part mini-series aired on August 5th, 2001. It utilised a number of Wells stories, and also featured Wells a character, played by Tom Ward. Also featured in this were: Katy Carmichael; Eve Best; Nicholas Rowe; Matthew Cottle; Barry Stanton; Raymond Coulthard; Mark Lewis Jones; Stephen Critchlow; Tilly Vosburgh; and many other.

76. The Time Machine. A 2002 U.S. film inspired by the 1895 novel, directed by Simon Wells and starring: Guy Pearce; Samantha Mumba; Mark Addy; Sienna Guillory; Phyllida Law; Alan Young; Omero Mumba; Yancey Arias; Orlando Jones; Jeremy Irons; Laura Kirk; Josh Stamberg; and others.

77. War of the Worlds. The 2005 **Steven Spielberg** version of the 1898 novel, starring: Tom Cruise; Dakota Fanning; Justin Chatwin; Tim Robbins; Rick Gonzalez; Yul Vazquez; Lenny Venito; Lisa Ann Walter; Ann Robinson; Gene Barry; David Alan Basche; and many others.

78. The War of the Worlds. A 2005 U.S. film based on the 1898 novel, directed by Timothy Hines and purporting to be the Classic War of the Worlds. It starred: Anthony Piana; Jack Clay; James Lathrop; Darlene Sellers; John Kaufmann; Jamie Lynn Sease; Susan Goforth; and W. Bernard Bauman.

79. War of the Worlds. Yet another 2005 American version of War of the Worlds, 1898, this one directed by David Michael Latt and starring: C. Thomas Howell; Rhett Giles; Andrew Lauer; Tinarie Van Wyk-Loots; Jake Busey; Dashiell Howell; Peter Green; Kim Little;; Edward DeRuiter; Meredith Lane; and many others.

80. Overlap. Based on The Remarkable Case of Davidson's Eyes, aka The Story of Davidson's Eyes, 1895, this was made in Norway in 2006, directed by Mirko Stopar and starring Arild Boe and Thorbjorn Harr.

81. The History of Mr. Polly. Made in the UK and based on the 1910 novel, it started on television on May 7th, 2007. Directed by Gillies MacKinnon, it starred: Lee Evans; Anne-Marie Duff; Julie Graham; Richard Coyle; Beans El-Balawi; Richard Elfyn; Paul Bown; Catrin Morgan; John Warnaby; and many others.

***

RADIO

1. H. G. Wells Radio Broadcasts. Wells was regularly invited into the BBC studios in London to voice his opinions on virtually everything. One of the earliest surviving broadcasts was from July 13th, 1931. Wells called it Russia in the Melting Pot.

2. The Country of the Blind. Starting in 1933, and going through five other versions, 1945, 1946, 1954, 1959, 1966, the BBC made The Country of the Blind, 1904, one of its favourites.

3. The Man Who Could Work Miracles. Starting in 1934 and running through 1944, 1951, 1956, and 1975, the BBC broadcast five versions of this 1898 story.

4. The Purple Pileus. Starting in 1935 and running through 1937, 1939, 1944 and 1963, 1953, the BBC broadcast five versions of this 1896 story.

5. The War of the Worlds. On October 30th, 1938, Orson Welles read his adaptation of this story to America as a radio drama on Mercury Theatre of the Air, WABC Radio. Welles presented the story as a series of news bulletins, commercial free. Millions of people did not, in fact, flee their homes in mindless panic - that is merely urban legend, fuelled by the newspapers of the time. But there was a form of mass hysteria and many people were, indeed, somewhat frightened that the entire event was true; and a number did actually panic. But most of the people who heard the broadcast were merely confused.

6. The Truth About Pyecraft. Starting in 1946 and running through 1949, 1953, and 1965, the BBC broadcast four versions of this 1903 story.

85

7. Pollock and the Porrah Man. This 1895 story was used on Escape, November 5th, 1947.

8. The Country of the Blind. This 1904 story was used on Escape, November 26th, 1947.

9. Jimmy Goggles the God. This 1898 story was used on Escape, March 7th, 1948.

10. The Time Machine. This 1895 novel was broadcast on Escape, May 9th, 1948.

11. Strange Valley. Adapted from The Country of the Blind, 1904, this was broadcast on Favorite Story, May 18th, 1948.

12. The Magic Shop. This 1903 story was used on Favorite Story, June 29th, 1948.

13. A Dream of Armageddon. This 1901 story was broadcast on Escape, September 5th, 1948.

14. The Man Who Could Work Miracles. This 1898 story was used on Escape, September 9th, 1948.

15. The History of Mr Polly. This 1910 novel was featured on NBC Radio Theater on October 17th, 1948.

16. The Time Machine. This 1895 story was used on Favorite Story, November 30th, 1948.

17. The Invisible Man. This 1897 novel was broadcast by the BBC in 1948.

18. The First Men in the Moon. Starting in 1948, and going through five other versions, 1953, 1954, 1981, 1996, and 1999, the BBC made good use of The First Men in the Moon, 1901.

19. The Country of the Blind. This 1904 story was used on Escape, March 20th, 1949.

20. Tono Bungay. This 1909 novel was featured on NBC Radio Theater on March 5th, 1950.

21. The Time Machine. This 1895 novel was broadcast on Escape, October 22nd, 1950 and October 27th, 1950.

22. The Man Who Could Work Miracles. This 1898 story was used on Escape, December 31st, 1950.

23. The War of the Worlds. Starting in 1950 and running through 1967 and 1987, the BBC broadcast three versions of this 1898 novel.

24. Tono-Bungay. Starting in 1951 and running through 1952, 1966, 1973 and 1993, the BBC broadcast five versions of this 1909 novel.

25. The War of the Worlds. This 1898 novel was featured on Lux Radio Theater on February 8th, 1955.

26. The Country of the Blind. This 1904 story was used on Suspense, October 27th, 1957.

27. The Country of the Blind. A different version of this 1904 story was used on Suspense, December 13th, 1959.

28. The Time Machine. This 1895 novel was broadcast on Escape, October 22nd, 1960.

29. The Crystal Egg. This was used by the CBC (Canadian Broadcasting Corporation) on their program Theater 10:30 during the 1970s.

30. The Sleeper Awakes. This 1899 novel was broadcast by the BBC in 1972.

31. The Time Machine. The BBC broadcast this 1895 novel in 1974.

32. The Man Who Could Work Miracles. This 1898 story was episode 510 on CBS Radio Mystery Theater, August 26th, 1976.

33. Search for Eden. Adapted from the story The Country of the Blind, 1904, this was used on CBS Radio Mystery Theater May 7th, 1979, episode 977.

34. The Truth About Pyecraft. This 1903 story was featured on Vanishing Point, a show that ran on CBC Radio from 1984 until 1986.

35. The Flowering of the Strange Orchid. This 1894 story was broadcast on the BBC in 1986.

36. The Magic Shop. This 1903 story was used on the BBC in 1986.

37. The Island of Dr. Moreau. This 1896 novel was first broadcast on the BBC in 1990.

38. The Invisible Man. This 1897 novel was originally produced by the Atlanta Radio Theater Co. in 1992.

39. The Time Machine. This 1895 novel was originally produced by the Atlanta Radio Theater Co. in 1994.

40. The Island of Doctor Moreau. This 1896 novel was originally produced by the Atlanta Radio Theater Co. in 1995.

41. The Invisible Man. In 1996, Alien Voices used this 1895 novel, featuring Leonard Nimoy and John de Lancie.

42. The Invisible Man. In 1998, Alien Voices used this 1897 novel, featuring Leonard Nimoy and John de Lancie.

43. The First Men in the Moon. In 1999, Alien Voices used this 1901 novel, featuring Leonard Nimoy, William Shatner and John de Lancie.

44. A Dream of Armageddon. This 1901 story was used on 2000X on November 6th, 2000.

45. The Door in the Wall. This 1906 story was used on the BBC in 1991 and again in 2001.

46. The Door in the Wall. Written in 1906, this was read on Mike Hodel's Hour 25 on February 16th, 2001.

47. The Time Machine. Written in 1895, this was broadcast on The Radio Tales on XM Satellite Radio, January 25th, 2003.

48. War of the Worlds. Written in 1898, this was broadcast on The Radio Tales on XM Satellite Radio, February 8th, 2003.

49. Moon Voyager. This was adapted from The

H.G. Wells

First Men in the Moon, 1901 and broadcast on The Radio Tales on XM Satellite Radio, February 15th, 2003.

50. Fifth Dimension. This was adapted from the short story The Plattner Story, 1896. It was broadcast on The Radio Tales on XM Satellite Radio, March 29th, 2003.

51. The Invisible Man. Written in 1897, this was broadcast on The Radio Tales on XM Satellite Radio, May 10th, 2003.

52. Asteroid. This was adapted from the short story The Star, 1897. It was broadcast on The Radio Tales on Sonic Theater, July 5th, 2003.

53. Time Warp. This was adapted from the short story The New Accelerator, 1901. It was broadcast on The Radio Tales on XM Satellite Radio, July 5th, 2003.

54. The Island of Doctor Moreau. Written in 1896, this was broadcast on The Radio Tales on XM Satellite Radio, August 30th, 2003.

55. Otherworld. This was adapted from the short story The Remarkable Case of Davidson's Eyes, 1895. It was broadcast on The Radio Tales on XM Satellite Radio, November 29th, 2003.

56. Watchers. This was adapted from the short story The Crystal Egg, 1897. It was broadcast on The Radio Tales on XM Satellite Radio, November 29th, 2003.

57. The Star. This 1897 story was first used on the BBC on September 7th, 2004.

58. The New Accelerator. This 1901 story was first broadcast on the BBC on March 27th, 2008.

***

NOVELS AND COLLECTIONS

1. The Time Machine. Published by Henry Holt and Company, New York City, 1895. The American edition actually pre-dated the British edition, which was published by William Heinemann, London, also 1895. The Holt edition was hardcover. The Heinemann edition was simultaneously published in hardcover and softcover.

2. The Wonderful Visit. Published by J. M. Dent in London and Macmillan and Co. in New York City, 1895. Hardcover.

3. Select Conversations with an Uncle. Published by John Lane, London and The Merriam Company, New York City, 1895. Hardcover.

4. The Stolen Bacillus and Other Incidents. Published by Methuen and Co., London, 1895. Hardcover. Herein: Aepyornis Island, 1894; The Flowering of the Strange Orchid, 1894; The Lord of the Dynamos, 1894; The Remarkable Case of Davidson's Eyes, 1895; In the Avu Observatory, 1894; The Stolen Bacillus, 1894; The Triumphs of a Taxidermist, 1894; The Temptation of Harringay, 1895; The Diamond Maker, 1894; The Hammerpond Park Burglary, 1894; The Treasure in the Forest, 1894; A Deal in Ostriches, 1894; The Moth, 1895; The Flying Man, 1893; and Through a Window, 1894.

5. The Island of Doctor Moreau. Published by William Heinemann, London, 1896. Also: Stone and Kimball, New York City, 1898. Hardcover.

6. The Red Room. Published by Stone and Kimball, Chicago, 1896. Softcover.

7. The Invisible Man. Published by C. Arthur Pearson, London, 1897. Hardcover. Also: Edward Arnold, New York City, 1897. Hardcover.

8. Thirty Strange Stories. Published by Edward Arnold, New York City, 1897. Hardcover. This collection contains: Aepyornis Island, 1894; In the Abyss, 1896; The Lord of the Dynamos, 1894; The Moth, 1895; The Plattner Story, 1896; Pollock and the Porroh Man, 1895; The Remarkable Case of Davidson's Eyes, 1895; The Story of the Late Mr. Elvesham, 1896; The Argonauts of the Air, 1895; In the Avu Observatory, 1894; The Stolen Bacillus, 1894; The Triumphs of a Taxidermist, 1894; The Apple, 1896; The Red Room, 1896; The Cone, 1895; The Purple Pileus, 1896; The Jilting of Jane, 1894; A Catastrophe, 1895; The Lost Inheritance, 1897; A Slip Under the Microscope, 1896; The Treasure in the Forest, 1894; A Deal in Ostriches, 1894; The Sea-Raiders, 1896; In the Modern Vein: An Unsympathetic Love Story, 1894; The Reconciliation, 1895; Le Mari Terrible, 1897; The Rajah's Treasure, 1896; The Strange Orchid, 1894; and Slip Under the Knife, 1896.

9. The Plattner Story and Others. Published by Methuen and Co., London, 1897. Hardcover. Herein: In the Abyss, 1896; The Plattner Story, 1896; Pollock and the Porroh Man, 1895; The Story of the Late Mr. Elvesham, 1896; The Argonauts of the Air, 1895; The Apple, 1896; The Red Room, 1896; The Cone, 1895; The Purple Pileus, 1896; The Jilting of Jane, 1894; A Catastrophe, 1895; The Lost Inheritance, 1897; A Slip Under the Microscope, 1896; The Sea-Raiders, 1896; In the Modern Vein: An Unsympathetic Love Story, 1894; and Under the Knife, 1896.

10. The War of the Worlds. Published by William Heinemann, London, 1898.

11. The War of the Worlds. Published by Harper and Brothers, New York, 1898. Hardcover. Some differences in the text between the British and the U.S. editions.

12. The Wheels of Chance. Published by J. M. Dent, London, and The Macmillan Co., New York, 1898. Hardcover.

13. A Cure for Love. A Story of Days to Come. Published by E. Scott Co., New York City, 1899. Pamphlet. Softcover.

14. Tales of Space and Time. Published by Harper and Brothers, London and New York, 1899. Hardcover. Herein: The Crystal Egg, 1897; The Man Who Could Work Miracles, 1898; The Star, 1897; A Story of the Days to Comes, 1899; and A Story of the Stone Age, 1897.

87

15. When the Sleeper Wakes. Published by Harper and Brothers, London and New York, 1899.

16. Love and Mr. Lewisham: The Story of a Very Young Couple. Published by Frederick A. Stokes, New York City, 1900. Softcover, a copyright registration issue only, filed in January 1900.

17. Love and Mr. Lewisham: The Story of a Very Young Couple. Published by Frederick A. Stokes, New York City, 1900. Hardcover.

18. Love and Mr. Lewisham: The Story of a Very Young Couple. Published by Harper and Brothers, London, June 1900 and New York, September 1900. Hardcover.

19. The First Men in the Moon. Published by Bowen-Merrill Company, Indianapolis, Minnesota, October 1901. This American edition preceded the UK edition by one month. The UK edition was published by George Newnes, London, November 1901. Hardcover.

20. The Sea Lady. Published by Methuen and Co., London, 1902. Hardcover.

21. Twelve Stories and a Dream. Published by Macmillan and Co., London and New York, 1903. Hardcover. Herein: The Valley of Spiders, 1903; The New Accelerator, 1901; The Stolen Body, 1898; A Dream of Armageddon, 1901; Filmer, 1901; The Magic Shop, 1903; The Truth About Pyecraft, 1903; Mr. Skelmersdale in Fairyland, 1901; Jimmy Goggles the God, 1898; Miss. Winchelsea's Heart, 1898; Mr. Ledbetter's Vacation, 1898; Mr. Brisher's Treasure, 1899; and The Inexperienced Ghost, 1902.

22. The Food of the Gods. Published by Macmillan and Co., London, 1904. Hardcover.

23. Kipps: A Monograph. Published by Charles Scribner's Sons, New York City, 1905. Softcover. Released in March 1905.

24. Kipps: The Story of a Simple Soul. Published by Charles Scribner's Sons, New York City, 1905. Hardcover. Released in October 1905, predating the British edition by roughly a month. The UK edition was published by Macmillan and Co., London, November 1905.

25. A Modern Utopia. Published by Chapman and Hall, London, 1905. Hardcover.

26. In the Days of the Comet. Published by Macmillan and Co., London, 1906. Hardcover.

27. The War in the Air. Published by George Bell and Sons, London, 1908. Hardcover.

28. Ann Veronica. Published by T. Fisher Unwin, London, 1909. Hardcover.

29. Tono-Bungay. Published by Macmillan and Co., London, 1909. Hardcover.

30. The History of Mr. Polly. Published by Thomas Nelson and Sons, London and New York City, 1910. Hardcover.

31. The New Machiavelli. Published by Duffield and Company, New York City, 1910. Hardcover.

32. The Sleeper Awakes. Published by Thomas Nelson and Sons, London and New York City, 1910. Hardcover. Revised version of When the Sleeper Awakes, 1899.

33. The Country of the Blind and Other Stories. Published by Thomas Nelson and Sons, London and New York City, 1911. Hardcover. Herein: The Valley of the Spiders, 1903; Aepyornis Island, 1894; The Country of the Blind, 1904; The Crystal Egg, 1897; The Empire of the Ants, 1905; The Flowering of the Strange Orchid, 1894; The Lord of the Dynamos, 1894; The Man Who Could Work Miracles, 1898; The New Accelerator, 1901; The Plattner Story, 1896; The Remarkable Case of Davidson's Eyes, 1895; The Star, 1897; The Story of the Late Mr. Elvesham, 1896; A Dream of Armageddon, 1901; In the Avu Observatory, 1894; The Magic Shop, 1903; The Stolen Bacillus, 1894; The Truth About Pyecraft, 1903; A Vision of Judgement, 1899; The Door in the Wall, 1906; The Red Room, 1896; The Cone, 1895; The Purple Pileus, 1896; The Jilting of Jane, 1894; A Slip Under the Microscope, 1896; Jimmy Goggles the God, 1898; Miss. Winchelsea's Heart, 1898; The Treasure in the Forest, 1894; The Moth, 1895; The Sea-Raiders, 1896; The Beautiful Suit, 1909; Under the Knife, 1896; and The Obliterated Man, 1911.

34. The Door in the Wall and Other Stories. Published by Mitchell Kennerley, New York and London, 1911. Limited to 600 copies. Hardcover. This contains: The Country of the Blind, 1904; The Lord of the Dynamos, 1894; The Star, 1897; A Dream of Armageddon, 1901; The Door in the Wall, 1906; The Diamond Maker, 1894; The Cone, 1895; and The Moonlight Fable, 1909.

35. Marriage. Published by Macmillan and Co., London, 1912. Hardcover.

36. The Passionate Friends. Published by Methuen and Co., London, 1913. Hardcover.

37. The Wife of Sir Isaac Harman. Published by Macmillan and Co., London, 1914. Hardcover.

38. The World Set Free. Published by Macmillan and Company, London, 1914. Hardcover.

39. Bealby: A Holiday. Published by Methuen and Co., London, 1915. Hardcover.

40. Country of the Blind. This was privately printed for the Christmas of 1915, New York City. Hardcover.

41. Boon, The Mind of the Race, The Wild Asses of the Devil, and The Last Trump. By Reginald Bliss. Published by T. Fisher Unwin, London, 1915. Hardcover.

42. The Research Magnificent. Published by Macmillan and Company, London, 1915. Hardcover.

43. Mr. Britling Sees it Through. Published by Cassell and Company, London and New York, 1916. Hardcover.

44. The Soul of a Bishop. Published by Cassell and Company, London and New York, 1917. Hardcover.

45. Joan and Peter: A Story of an Education.

H.G. Wells

Published by Cassell and Company, London and New York, 1918. Hardcover.

46. The Country of the Blind. Published by Haldeman-Julius Company, Girard, Kansas. Undated but from 1921. Little Blue Book 161. Softcover.

47. The Sleeper Awakes. Published by Wm. Collins, London, 1921. Hardcover. Abridged version of When the Sleeper Awakes, 1899.

48. The World Set Free. With a new preface by Wells. Published by Wm. Collins, London, 1921. Hardcover.

49. The Secret Places of the Heart. Published by Cassell and Company, London and New York, 1922. Hardcover.

50. Tales of the Unexpected. Published by Wm. Collins and Co., London, 1922. Hardcover. Herein: The Crystal Egg, 1897; The Man Who Could Work Miracles, 1898; The Moth, 1895; The New Accelerator, 1901; The Plattner Story, 1896; The Remarkable Case of Davidson's Eyes, 1895; The Stolen Body, 1898; The Story of the Late Mr. Elvesham, 1896; A Dream of Armageddon, 1901; The Door in the Wall, 1906; The Temptation of Harringay, 1895; The Apple, 1896; Mr. Skelmersdale in Fairyland, 1901; The Inexperienced Ghost, 1902; and Under the Knife, 1896.

51. Tales of Life and Adventure. Published by Wm. Collins and Co., London. Undated but circa 1923. Hardcover. Herein: The Lord of the Dynamos, 1894; The Argonauts of the Air, 1895; Filmer, 1901; The Stolen Bacillus, 1894; The Diamond Maker, 1894; The Hammerpond Park Burglary, 1894; The Cone, 1895; The Jilting of Jane, 1894; A Catastrophe, 1895; The Lost Inheritance, 1897; A Slip Under the Microscope, 1896; Jimmy Goggles the God, 1898; Mr. Ledbetter's Vacation, 1898; Miss. Winchelsea's Heart, 1898; Mr. Brisher's Treasure, 1899; The Treasure in the Forest, 1894; A Deal in Ostriches, 1894; In the Modern Vein: An Unsympathetic Love Story, 1894; The Obliterated Man, 1913; The Flying Man, 1893; and Through a Window, 1894.

52. Tales of Wonder. Published by Wm. Collins and Co., London. Undated but circa 1923. Hardcover.

53. Men Like Gods. Published by Cassell and Company, London and New York, 1923. Hardcover.

54. The Dream. Published by Jonathan Cape, London, 1924. Hardcover.

55. Christina Alberta's Father. Published by Jonathan Cape, London, 1925. Hardcover.

56. The World of William Clissold. Published by Ernest Benn, London, 1926. Hardcover.

57. Meanwhile. Published by Ernest Benn, London, 1927. Hardcover.

58. The Short Stories of H. G. Wells. Published by Ernest Benn, London, 1927. Hardcover. Herein: The Empire of the Ants, 1905; A Vision of Judgment, 1927; The Beautiful Suit, 1909; The Door in the Wall, 1906; The Flowering of the Strange Orchid, 1894; In the Avu Observatory, 1894; The Triumphs of a Taxidermist, 1894; A Deal in Ostriches, 1894; Through a Window, 1894; The Temptation of Harringay, 1895; The Flying Man, 1893; The Diamond Maker, 1894; Aepyornis Island, 1894; The Remarkable Case of Davidson's Eyes, 1895; The Lord of the Dynamos, 1894; The Hammond Park Burglary, 1894; The Moth, 1895; The Treasure of the Forest, 1894; The Argonauts of the Air, 1895; The Story of the Late Mr. Elvesham, 1896; In the Abyss, 1896; The Apple, 1896; Under the Knife, 1896; The Sea-Raiders, 1896; Pollock and the Porroh Man, 1895; The Red Room, 1896; The Cone, 1895; The Purple Pileus, 1896; The Jilting of Jane, 1894; In the Modern Vein: An Unsympathetic Love Story, 1894; A Catastrophe, 1895; The Lost Inheritance, 1897; The Sad Story of a Dramatic Critic, 1915; A Slip Under the Microscope, 1896; The Crystal Egg, 1897; The Star, 1897; The Man Who Could Work Miracles, 1898; Filmer, 1901; The Magic Shop, 1903; The Valley of Spiders, 1903; The Truth About Pyecraft, 1903; and Mr. Skelmersdale in Fairyland, 1901.

59. The Works of H. G. Wells. Published by T. Fisher Unwin, London, and Charles Scribner's Sons, New York City, 1927. Twenty-eight hardcover volumes, limited to 1670 sets. 620 sets were distributed in the UK; 1050 were distributed in the States.

60. Mr. Blettsworthy on Rampole Island. Published by Ernest Benn, London, 1928. Hardcover.

61. A Quartet of Comedies. Published by Ernest Benn, London, 1928. Hardcover.

62. The Adventures of Tommy. Published by The Amalgamated Press, London, 1928. Limited softcover edition.

63. The Adventures of Tommy. Published by George G. Harrap and Co., London, 1929. First hardcover edition.

64. The King Who Was a King. Published by Ernest Benn, London, 1929. Hardcover.

65. The Empire of the Ants and Other Stories. Published by Haldeman-Julius Company, Girard, Kansas. Undated but circa 1930s. Little Blue Book 925. Softcover. Herein: The Cone, 1895; The Remarkable Case of Davidson's Eyes, 1895; and The Empire of the Ants, 1905.

66. The Obliterated Man and Other Stories. Published by Haldeman-Julius Company, Girard, Kansas. Undated but circa 1930s. Little Blue Book 926. Softcover.

67. The Stolen Bacillus and Other Stories. Published by Haldeman-Julius Company, Girard, Kansas. Undated but circa 1930s. Little Blue Book 927. Softcover.

68. The Man Who Could Work Miracles. Published by Haldeman-Julius Company, Girard, Kansas. Undated but circa 1930s. Little Blue Book 1661. Softcover.

69. The Valley of Spiders. Published by Haldeman-Julius Company, Girard, Kansas. Undated but circa 1930s. Little Blue Book 1662. Softcover.

70. The Autocracy of Mr. Parham. Published by William Heinemann, London, 1930. Hardcover.

71. The Bulpington of Blup. Published by Hutchinson and Co., London, 1932. Hardcover.

72. Stories of Men and Women in Love. Published by Hutchinson and Co., London, 1933. Hardcover.

73. The Scientific Romances of H. G. Wells. With a new preface by H. G. Wells. Published by Victor Gollancz, London, 1933. Hardcover. Omnibus edition, this gathers: The Time Machine, 1895; The Island of Doctor Moreau, 1896; The Invisible Man, 1897; The War of the Worlds, 1898; The First Men in the Moon, 1901; The Food of the Gods, 1904; In the Days of the Comet, 1906; and Men Like Gods, 1923.

74. The Shape of Things to Come. Published by Hutchinson, London, 1933. Hardcover.

75. Seven Famous Novels by H. G. Wells. Published by Alfred A. Knopf, New York City, 1934. Hardcover. Omnibus edition, this gathers: The Time Machine, 1895; The Island of Doctor Moreau, 1896; The Invisible Man, 1897; The War of the Worlds, 1898; The First Men in the Moon, 1901; The Food of the Gods, 1904; and In the Days of the Comet, 1906.

76. Things to Come - A Film Story. Published by The Cresset Press, London, 1935. Hardcover.

77. The Croquet Player. Published by Chatto and Windus, London, 1936. Hardcover.

78. The Treasure in the Forest. Published by The Press of the Woolly Whale, New York City, 1936. Hardcover. Limited to 130 copies.

79. The Camford Visitation. Published by Methuen and Company, London, 1937. Hardcover.

80. Brynhild. Published by Methuen and Company, London, 1937. Hardcover.

81. Star Begotten. Published by Chatto and Windus, London, 1937. Hardcover.

82. The Famous Short Stories of H. G. Wells. Published by Doubleday & Company, Garden City, New York, 1937. Hardcover.

83. The Favorite Short Stories of H. G. Wells. Published by Doubleday & Company, Garden City, New York, 1937. Hardcover. An abridged version of The Famous Short Stories of H. G. Wells, 1937.

84. Apropos of Dolores. Published by Jonathan Cape, London, 1938. Hardcover.

85. The Brothers. Published by Chatto and Windus, London, 1938. Hardcover.

86. The Country of the Blind. The Golden Cockerel Press, London, 1939. Limited to 280 copies, the first 250 of which were signed by the author. New introduction by Wells. Hardcover.

87. The Holy Terror. Published by Michael Joseph, London, 1939. Hardcover.

88. All Aboard for Ararat. Published by Secker and Warburg, London, 1940. Hardcover.

89. Short Stories... First Series. Published by Thomas Nelson and Sons, London and New York, 1940. Hardcover.

90. Babes in the Darkling Wood. Published by Secker and Warburg, London, 1940. Hardcover.

91. The Final Men. Published by Robert W. Lowndes, United States, 1940. Stapled mimeographed pages - the first separate printing of an omitted episode from The Time Machine. The 1895 serialised version contained a chapter about kangaroo rat men and giant insects but that chapter was left out of all future printings of The Time Machine, with once exception: In 1960, Three Prophetic Novels of H. G. Wells was printed: this contained the serialised version of The Time Machine.

92. Two Film Stories: Things to Come; Man Who Could Work Miracles. Published by The Cresset Press, London, 1940. Hardcover.

93. You Can't Be Too Careful. Published by Secker and Warburg, London, 1941. Hardcover.

94. The Man Who Could Work Miracles. Todd Publishing - Pollybooks, London, 1943. Softcover.

95. The Truth About Pyecraft and Other Short Stories. Todd Publishing - Pollybooks, London, 1943. Softcover.

96. The Inexperienced Ghost - and - The New Accelerator. Published by Vallancey Press, London, 1944. Softcover.

97. The Happy Turning: A Dream of Life. Published by William Heinemann, London, 1945. Hardcover.

98. The Time Machine: An Invention and Other Stories. Published by Penguin Books, Middlesex, England, 1946. Softcover.

99. The Country of the Blind and Other Stories. Published by Longmans, Green & Co., London - New York - Toronto, 1947. Softcover.

100. 28 Science Fiction Stories of H. G. Wells. Published by Dover Publications, New York City, 1952. Hardcover. Herein: Star Begotten, 1937; Men Like Gods, 1923; The Valley of Spiders, 1903; Aepyornis Island, 1894; The Country of the Blind, 1904; The Crystal Egg, 1897; The Empire of the Ants, 1905; The Flowering of the Strange Orchid, 1894; In the Abyss, 1896; The Man Who Could Work Miracles, 1898; The New Accelerator, 1901; The Plattner Story, 1896; The Remarkable Case of Davidson's Eyes, 1985; The Star, 1897; The Stolen Body, 1898; The Story of the Late Mr. Elvesham, 1896; The Argonauts of the Air, 1895; A Dream of Armageddon, 1901; Filmer, 1901; In the Avu Observatory, 1894; The Land Ironclads, 1903; The Magic Shop, 1903; The Stolen Bacillus, 1894; A Story of the Days to Come, 1899; The Truth About Pyecraft, 1903; The Sea-Raiders, 1896; and Under the Knife, 1896.

101. The First Men in the Moon. Edited and abridged by Latif Doss. Published by Longmans, Green and Co. - London - New York - Toronto, 1954. Softcover.

H.G. Wells

102. The War of the Worlds - and - The Time Machine. Published by The Globe Book Company, New York City, 1956. Hardcover.

103. The Desert Daisy. Published by Beta Phi Mu, Urbana, Illinois, 1957. Limited edition. Hardcover.

104. Selected Short Stories. Published by Penguin Books, Middlesex, England, 1958. Softcover. Penguin Book 1310. This contains: The Time Machine, 1895; The Land Ironclads, 1903; The Door in the Wall, 1906; The Country of the Blind, 1904; The Stolen Bacillus, 1894; The Diamond Maker, 1894; Aepyornis Island, 1894; The Remarkable Case of Davidson's Eyes, 1895; The Lord of the Dynamos, 1894; The Plattner Story, 1896; The Argonauts of the Air, 1885; In the Abyss, 1896; Under the Knife, 1896; The Sea Raiders, 1896; The Cone, 1895; The Purple Pileus, 1896; The Grisly Folk, 1921; The Man Who Could Work Miracles, 1898; The Truth about Pyecraft, 1903; Jimmy Goggles the God, 1898; and The New Accelerator, 1901.

105. Bealby: A Holiday. Published by Methuen and Co., London, 1958. Hardcover. An abridged edition.

106. Best Stories of H. G. Wells. Published by Ballantine Books, New York City, 1960. Softcover. Ballantine Book S414K. This contains: The Lord of the Dynamos, 1894; The Plattner Story, 1896; The Argonauts of the Air, 1895; The Story of the Late Mr. Elvesham, 1896; The Crystal Egg, 1897; The Star, 1897; The Man Who Could Work Miracles, 1898; The Sea-Raiders, 1896; The Magic Shop, 1903; The Valley of Spiders, 1903; The Truth About Pyecraft, 1903; The Land Ironclads, 1903; Mr. Skelmersdale in Fairyland, 1901; The New Accelerator, 1901; and A Story of the Days to Come, 1899.

107. Three Prophetic Novels of H. G. Wells. Published by Dover Publications, New York City, 1960. Softcover. An omnibus edition that collects: When the Sleeper Wakes, 1899; A Story of the Days to Come, 1897; and The Time Machine, 1895.

108. Three Novels. Published by Heinemann, London, 1963. Hardcover. An omnibus edition that collects: The Time Machine, 1895; The War of the Worlds, 1898; and The Island of Doctor Moreau, 1896.

109. The Time Machine and Other Stories. Published by Scholastic Book Services, New York City, 1963. Softcover. Scholastic Book T530. Herein: A Word to the Reader by Richard J. Hurley; The Time Machine, 1895; The Country of the Blind, 1904; The Empire of the Ants, 1905; and The Man Who Could Work Miracles, 1898.

110. The War of the Worlds, The Time Machine, and Selected Short Stories. Published by Platt and Munk, New York City, 1963. Hardcover. Herein: The War of the Worlds, 1898; The Time Machine, 1895; The Valley of Spiders, 1903; The Crystal Egg, 1897; In the Abyss, 1896; The Story of the Late Mr. Elvesham, 1896; In the Avu Observatory, 1894; The Truth About Pyecraft, 1903; The Red Room, 1896; and H. G. Wells, an essay by Kingsley Amis.

111. The Valley of Spiders: A New Collection of Short Stories. Published by Fontana Books, London, 1964. Paperback. Fontana Book 1035.

112. The Cone: Another Collection of Horror Stories. Published by Collins - Fontana Books, London, 1965. Softcover. Fontana Book 1125.

113. The Inexperienced Ghost and Nine Other Stories. Published by Bantam Books, New York City, 1965. Softcover. Bantam Pathfinder FB81.

114. Best Science Fiction Stories of H. G. Wells. Published by Dover Publications, New York City, 1966. Softcover.

115. The Complete Short Stories of H. G. Wells. Published by Ernest Benn, London, 1966. Hardcover.

116. The Wealth of Mr Waddy. Published by Southern Illinois University Press, 1969. Hardcover.

117. H. G. Wells: Early Writings in Science and Science Fiction. Published by the University of California Press, Berkeley, California, 1975. Hardcover.

118. A Story of the Days to Come. Published by Corgi Books, London, 1976. Softcover.

119. The Man with the Nose and Other Uncollected Stories of H. G. Wells. Published by Athlone Press, United States, 1984. Hardcover.

120. The Red Room and Other Stories. Published by Happy Hour Library, New York City, 1998. Softcover.

121. Selected Stories of H. G. Wells. Edited by Ursula K. Le Guin. Published by Modern Library, New York City, 2004. Softcover.

122. The Collector's Book of Science Fiction. Published by Castle Books, Secaucus, New Jersey, 2005. Hardcover.

123. The Man Who Could Work Miracles: The Supernatural Tales of H. G. Wells. Published by Tartarus Press, London, 2006. Hardcover.

***

NON-FICTION

1. Honours Physiography. With R. A. Gregory. Published in England, 1893. Hardcover.

2. Text-Book of Biology/Zoology. Published in England, 1893. Hardcover.

3. Certain Personal Matters: A Collection of Material, Mainly Autobiographical. Published by Lawrence and Bullen, London, 1897. Hardcover.

4. Anticipations of the Reactions of Mechanical and Scientific Progress upon Human Life and Thought. Published by Chapman and Hall, London, 1901. Hardcover.

5. Mankind in the Making. Published by Chapman and Hall, London, 1903. Hardcover.

6. The Future in America: A Search After Realities. Published by Chapman and Hall, London, 1906. Hardcover.

7. **Socialism and the Family.** Published by A. C. Fifield, London, 1906. Hardcover.

8. **This Misery of Boots.** Published by The Fabian Society, London, 1907. Softcover.

9. **Will Socialism Destroy the Home?** Published by the Independent Labour Party, London, 1907. Softcover.

10. **New Worlds for Old: A Plain Account of Modern Socialism.** Published by Constable, London, 1908. Hardcover.

11. **First and Last Things: A Confession of Faith and Rule of Life.** Published by Constable, London, 1908. Hardcover.

12. **This Misery of Boots.** Published by Ball Publishing, Boston, 1908. First hardcover edition.

13. **Floor Games: A Father's Account of Play and Its Legacy of Healing.** Published by Palmer, London, 1911. Hardcover.

14. **Socialism and the Great State: Essays in Construction.** Published by Harper and Brothers, London and New York, 1912. Hardcover.

15. **Great Thoughts From H. G. Wells.** Published by Dodge Publishing, New York City, 1912. Hardcover.

16. **Little Wars: A Game for Boys from Twelve Years of Age to One Hundred and Fifty and for That More Intelligent Sort of Girls Who Like Boys' Games.** Published by Palmer, London, 1913. Hardcover.

17. **The War That Will End War.** Published by Palmer, London, 1914. Hardcover.

18. **An Englishman Looks at the World.** Published by Cassell, London, 1914. Hardcover.

19. **The Peace of the World.** Published by The Daily Chronicle, London, 1914. Softcover.

20. **What Is Coming: A Forecast of Things After the War.** Published by Cassell, London, 1916. Hardcover.

21. **God the Invisible King.** Published by Cassell, London, 1917. Hardcover.

22. **The Idea of a League of Nations.** With Viscount Edward Grey; Lionel Curtis; William Archer; H. Wickham Steed; A. E. Zimmern; J. A. Spencer; Viscount Bryce; and Gilbert Murray. Published by The Atlantic Monthly Press, Boston, 1919. Hardcover.

23. **The Outline of History.** Published by George Newnes, London, 1920. Hardcover.

24. **Russia in the Shadows.** Published by Hodder and Stoughton, London, 1920. Hardcover.

25. **Frank Swinnerton: Personal Sketches.** With Arnold Bennett and Grant M. Overton. Published by George H. Doran, New York City, 1920. Hardcover.

26. **The Salvaging of Civilization.** Published by Cassell, London, 1921. Hardcover.

27. **A Short History of the World.** Published by Cassell, London, 1922. Hardcover.

28. **Washington and the Hope of Peace.** Published by Wm. Collins, London, 1922. Hardcover.

29. **Washington and the Riddle of Peace.** Published by The Macmillan Company, New York City, 1922. Hardcover. Re-titled version of Washington and the Hope of Peace.

30. **Socialism and the Scientific Motive.** Published by the Co-operative Printing Society, London, 1923. Softcover.

31. **The Story of a Great Schoolmaster: Being a Plain Account of the Life and Ideas of Sanderson of Oundle.** Published by Chatto and Windus, London, 1924. Hardcover.

32. **A Year of Prophesying.** Published by T. Fisher Unwin, London, 1924. Hardcover.

33. **A Short History of Mankind.** Published by the Macmillan Company, New York City, 1925. Hardcover.

34. **Mr. Belloc Objects to the Outline of History.** Published by Watts and Co., London, 1926. Hardcover.

35. **Wells' Social Anticipations.** Published by Vanguard Press, New York City, 1927. Hardcover.

36. **The Way the World Is Going.** Published by Ernest Benn, London, 1928. Hardcover.

37. **The Book of Amy Catherine Wells.** Published by Chatto and Windus, London, 1928. Hardcover.

38. **The Open Conspiracy: Blueprints for a World Revolution.** Published by Victor Gollancz, London, 1928. Hardcover.

39. **The Science of Life: A Summary of Contemporary Knowledge About Life and its Possibilities.** With Julian S. Huxley and G. P. Wells. Published by The Waverley Book Company, London, 1930. Hardcover.

40. **The Work, Wealth and Happiness of Mankind.** Doubleday Doran, Garden City, New York, 1931. Hardcover.

41. **What Are We To Do With Our Lives?** Published by Heinemann, London, 1931. Hardcover. Revised edition of The Open Conspiracy, 1928.

42. **The New Russia.** Published in England, 1931.

43. **After Democracy.** Published by Watts and Co., London, 1932. Hardcover.

44. **An Experiment in Autobiography.** Published by Victor Gollancz, London, 1934. Hardcover.

45. **The New America: The New World.** Published by Cresset Press, London, 1935. Hardcover.

46. **The Anatomy of Frustration.** Published by Cresset Press, London, 1936. Hardcover.

47. **World Brain.** Published by Methuen, London, 1938. Hardcover.

H.G. Wells

48. **The Fate of Homo Sapiens.** Published by Secker and Warburg, London, 1939. Hardcover.

49. **The Fate of Man.** Published by Alliance Book Corporation, New York City, 1939. Hardcover. Re-titled version of The Fate of Homo Sapiens.

50. **The New World Order.** Published by Secker and Warburg, London, 1939. Hardcover.

51. **Travels of a Republican Radical in Search of Hot Water.** Published by Penguin Books, Middlesex, England, 1939. Softcover in a dustjacket. Penguin Book S41.

52. **The Rights of Man, or What Are We Fighting For?** Published by Penguin Books, Middlesex, England, 1940. Softcover in a dustjacket. Penguin Book S50.

53. **The Common Sense of War and Peace: World Revolution or War Unending.** Published by Penguin Books, Middlesex, England, 1940. Softcover in a dustjacket. Penguin Book S64.

54. **The Pocket History of the World.** Published by Pocket Books, New York City, 1941. Softcover. Pocket Book 119.

55. **The Outlook for Homo Sapiens.** Published by Secker and Warburg, London, 1942. Hardcover.

56. **The Conquest of Time.** Published by Watts and Co., London, 1942. Hardcover.

57. **Science and the World Mind.** Published by New Europe Publishing Company, London, 1942. Softcover.

58. **Phoenix: A Summary of the Inescapable Conditions of World Organisation.** Published by Secker and Warburg, London, 1942. Hardcover.

59. **A Thesis on the Quality of Illusion on the Continuity of the Individual Life in the Higher Metazoa, with Particular Reference to the Species Homo Sapiens.** Published by C. A. Watts, London, 1942. A private softcover printing made for the author.

60. **Modern Russia and English Revolutionaries.** With Lev Uspensky. Published in England in 1942.

61. **Crux Ansata: An Indictment of the Roman Catholic Church.** Published by Penguin Books, Middlesex, England, 1943. Softcover. Penguin Book S129.

62. **Crux Ansata: An Indictment of the Roman Catholic Church.** Published by Agora Publishing, New York City, 1944. First hardcover edition.

63. **'42 to '44: A Contemporary Memoir.** Published by Secker and Warburg, London, 1944. Hardcover.

64. **The Happy Turning: A Dream of Life.** Published by Heinemann, London, 1945. Hardcover.

65. **Mind at the End of Its Tether.** Published by Heinemann, London, 1945. Hardcover.

66. **Marxism vs. Liberalism.** Published by New Century Publishers, New York City, 1945. Softcover.

67. **Henry James and H. G. Wells: A Record of Their Friendship, Their Debate on the Art of Fiction, and Their Quarrel.** Edited by Leon Edel and Gordon N. Ray. Published by Rupert Hart-Davis, London, 1958.

68. **Arnold Bennett and H. G. Wells: A Record of a Personal and a Literary Friendship.** Edited by Harris Wilson. Published by Rupert Hart-Davis, London, 1960.

69. **George Gissing and H. G. Wells: Their Friendship and Correspondence.** Edited by Royal A. Gettmann. Published by Rupert Hart-Davis, London, 1960.

70. **H. G. Wells in Love: Postscript to an Experiment in Autobiography.** Published by Faber and Faber, London, 1984. Hardcover.

71. **Bernard Shaw and H. G. Wells: Selected Correspondence of Bernard Shaw - Volume 2.** Published by the University of Toronto Press, Toronto, 1995. Hardcover.

72. **The Correspondence of H. G. Wells - Volume 1: 1880 - 1903.** Published by Pickering and Chatto, London, 1998. Hardcover.

73. **The Correspondence of H. G. Wells - Volume 2: 1904 - 1918.** Published by Pickering and Chatto, London, 1998. Hardcover.

74. **The Correspondence of H. G. Wells - Volume 3: 1919 - 1934.** Published by Pickering and Chatto, London, 1998. Hardcover.

75. **The Correspondence of H. G. Wells - Volume 4: 1935 - 1946.** Published by Pickering and Chatto, London, 1998. Hardcover.

***

RELATED

1. **A Bibliography of the Works of H. G. Wells 1893 - 1925.** By Geoffrey H. Wells. Published by George Routledge, London, 1925. Hardcover.

2. **The Works of H. G. Wells: 1887 - 1925.** By Geoffrey H. Wells. Published by George Routledge, London, 1926. Hardcover. Revised and expanded edition of A Bibliography of the Works of H. G. Wells 1893 - 1925.

3. **The Early H. G. Wells: A Story of the Scientific Romances.** By Bernard Bergonzi. Published by The University of Toronto Press, Toronto, 1961. Hardcover.

4. **H. G. Wells and the World State.** By W. Warren Wagar. Published by Yale University Press, New Haven, Connecticut, 1961. Hardcover.

5. **H. G. Wells: A Comprehensive Bibliography.** Compiled by The H. G. Wells Society, London, 1966. Hardcover.

6. **H. G. Wells: A Comprehensive Bibliography.** Compiled by The H. G. Wells Society, London, 1968. Hardcover. Revised edition.

7. H. G. Wells: His Turbulent Life and Times. By Lovat Dickson. Published by Macmillan, London, 1969. Hardcover.

8. H. G. Wells. By Patrick Parrinder. Published by Oliver and Boyd, Edinburgh, 1970. Published simultaneously in hardcover and softcover.

9. H. G. Wells: The Critical Heritage. By Patrick Parrinder. Published by Routledge Kegan and Paul, London, 1972. Hardcover.

10. H. G. Wells: A Comprehensive Bibliography. Compiled by The H. G. Wells Society, Middlesex, England, 1972. Hardcover. Third edition, with a new index.

11. H. G. Wells: Critic of Progress. By Jack Williamson. Published by Mirage Press, Baltimore, Maryland, 1973. Hardcover.

12. The Time Traveller: The Life of H. G. Wells. By Norman and Jeanne Mackenzie. Published by Weidenfeld and Nicolson, London, 1973. Hardcover.

13. Catalogue of the H. G. Wells Collection in the Bromley Public Libraries. Edited by A. H. Watkins. Published by London Borough of Bromley Public Libraries, 1974. Hardcover.

14. H. G. Wells and Rebecca West. By Gordon N. Ray. Published by Yale University Press, New Haven, Connecticut, 1974. Hardcover.

15. Scientific Romances of H. G. Wells: A Critical Study. By Stephen Gill. Published by Vesta Publications, Cornwall, Ontario, 1975. Softcover.

16. H. G. Wells: A Collection of Critical Essays. By Bernard Bergonzi. Published by Prentice-Hall, New Jersey, 1976. Hardcover.

17. H. G. Wells and Modern Science Fiction. By Darko Suvin and Robert M. Philmus. Published by Associated University Presses, London, 1977. Hardcover.

18. Herbert George Wells: An Annotated Bibliography of His Works. By J. R. Hammond. Published by Garland Publishing, New York and London, 1977. Hardcover.

19. H. G. Wells in the Cinema. By Alan Wykes. Published by Jupiter, London, 1977. Hardcover.

20. H. G. Wells: A Pictorial Biography. By Frank Wells. Published by Jupiter, London, 1977. Hardcover.

21. The H. G. Wells Scrapbook. Edited by Peter Haining. Published by NEL - New English Library, London, 1978. Hardcover.

22. Who's Who in H. G. Wells. By Brian Ash. Elm Tree Books - Hamish Hamilton, London, 1979. Hardcover.

23. H. G. Wells: First Citizen of the Future. By Keith Ferrell. Published by M. Evans, New York City, 1983. Hardcover.

24. H. G. Wells: Aspects of Life. By Anthony West. Published by Random House, New York City, 1984. Hardcover.

25. H. G. Wells. By John Batchelor. Published by Cambridge University Press, 1985. Softcover.

26. H. G. Wells. By Richard Hauer Costa. Published by Twayne Publishers, Boston, 1985. Hardcover.

27. H. G. Wells: Desperately Mortal. By David C. Smith. Published by Yale University Press, New Haven, Connecticut, 1986. Softcover.

28. H. G. Wells. By Michael Draper. Published by Macmillan, London, 1987. Hardcover.

29. H. G. Wells: Life and Works. By Christopher Martin. Published by Wayland, East Sussex, England, 1988. Hardcover.

30. H. G. Wells Under Revision: Proceedings of the International H. G. Wells Symposium - 1986. By Patrick Parrinder and Christopher Rolfe. Published by Susquehanna University Press, Cranbury, New Jersey, 1990. Hardcover.

31. H. G. Wells. By Brian Murray. Published by Continuum, New York City, 1990. Hardcover.

32. The Invisible Man: The Life and Liberties of H. G. Wells. By Michael Coren. Published by Bloomsbury Publishing, London, 1993. Hardcover.

33. H. G.: The History of Mr. Wells. By Michael Foot. Published by Counterpoint, Washington, DC, 1995. Hardcover.

34. An H. G. Wells Chronology. By J. R. Hammond. Published by Palgrave Macmillan, London, 1999. Hardcover.

35. Shadow Lovers: The Last Affairs of H. G. Wells. By Andrea Lynn. Published by Westview Press, Cambridge, Massachusetts, 2001. Hardcover.

36. The Picshuas of H. G. Wells: A Burlesque Diary. By Gene K. Rinkel and Margaret Rinkel. Published by the University of Illinois Press, 2006. Hardcover.

Hal Clement

-1998-

Hal Clement.

Harry Clement Stubbs was born on May 30th, 1922 in Somerville, Massachusetts and died in his sleep, probably from diabetic complications, on October 29th, 2003 in Milton, Massachusetts.

Better known as Hal Clement, his first story was sold to **John W. Campbell**. Proof appeared in the June 1942 issue of Astounding Science Fiction, along with: Bridle and Saddle by **Isaac Asimov**; My Name Is Legion by Lester Del Rey; The Slaver by L. Ron Hubbard; On Pain of Death by Robert Moore Williams; A Nose for News by Roby Wentz; Time Dredge by Robert Arthur; Mudman by Myer Krulfeld; and Heritage by Robert Abernathy.

The following year, Clement graduated Harvard with a Bachelor of Science in Astronomy. After graduation, he joined the 8th Air Force and became both a co-pilot and pilot, flying thirty-five combat missions over Europe. When he retired from the military, it was with the rank of Colonel.

Well known for the hard science in his stories, he never became a full-time writer. He taught science at the Milton Academy in Massachusetts for thirty-eight years. And, using the name George Richard, he painted science fictional and astronomical themes.

It was said that writers read his stories to become better writers.

Signed copies of his earlier books tend to run between $600.00 and $1,200.00. Mission of Gravity, unsigned, runs between $500.00 and $600.00.

***

AWARDS

Starting in 1992, the Hal Clement Award to give to young adults to encourage the writing of science fiction.

1998. Grand Master Award.
1998. Inducted into The Science Fiction Hall of Fame.

***

RADIO

1. MIKE HODEL'S HOUR 25 featured an interview with Hal Clement. The show was broadcast on June 24th, 2003.

***

NOVELS AND COLLECTIONS

1. Needle. Published by Doubleday & Company, Garden City, New York, 1950. Hardcover.

2. Iceworld. Published by Gnome Press, New York City, 1953. Hardcover.

3. Mission of Gravity. Published by Doubleday & Company, Garden City, New York, 1954. Hardcover.

4. The Ranger Boys in Space. Published by L. C. Page, Boston, 1956. Hardcover.

5. Cycle of Fire. Published by Ballantine Books, New York City, 1957. Published simultaneously in hardcover and softcover. The softcover was Ballantine Book 200.

6. From Other Space. Published by Avon Books, New York City, 1957. Softcover. Avon Book T-175. Re-titled re-issue of Needle, 1950.

7. Close to Critical. Published by Ballantine Books, New York City, 1964. Softcover. Ballantine Book U2215.

8. Natives of Space. Published by Ballantine Books, New York City, 1965. Softcover. Ballantine Book U2235. Story collection containing: Assumption Unjustified, 1946; Technical Error, 1944; and Impediment, 1942.

9. Close to Critical. Published by Victor Gollancz, London, 1966. First hardcover edition of the 1964 paperback original.

10. Small Changes. Published by Doubleday & Company, Garden City, New York, 1969. Hardcover. This contains: The Mechanic, 1966; Uncommon Sense, 1945; Raindrop, 1965; The Foundling Stars, 1966; Sunspot, 1960; Dust Rag, 1956; Fireproof, 1949; Halo, 1952; and Trojan Fall, 1944.

11. Space Lash. Published by Dell Books, New York City, 1969. Softcover. Dell Book 8039. Re-titled re-issue of Small Changes, 1969.

12. Star Light. Published by Ballantine Books, New York City, 1971. Softcover. Ballantine Book 02361.

13. Ocean on Top. Published by DAW Books, New York City, 1973. Softcover. DAW Collector's Book 57.

14. Left of Africa. Published by The Aurian Society Press, New Orleans, 1976. Hardcover.

15. Mission of Gravity - with Lecture Demonstration. Published by Gregg Press, Boston, 1978. Hardcover. Lecture Demonstration was originally published in 1973; Mission of Gravity, 1954.

16. The Best of Hal Clement. Edited by Lester del Rey. Published by Del Rey - Ballantine Books, New York City, 1979. Softcover. This contains: Hal Clement: Rationalist - an essay by Lester del

95

Rey; Impediment, 1942; Technical Error, 1944; Uncommon Sense, 1945; Assumption Unjustified, 1946; Answer, 1947; Dust Rag, 1956; Bulge, 1968; Mistaken for Granted, 1974; A Question of Guilt, 1976; Stuck With It, 1976; and Afterword - an essay by Hal Clement.

17. The Nitrogen Fix. Published by Ace Books, New York, 1980. Softcover.

18. Still River. Published by Del Rey - Ballantine Books, New York City, 1987. Hardcover.

19. Intuit. Published by NESFA Press, Framingham, Massachusetts, 1987. Hardcover. This collection contains: Introduction by **Poul Anderson**; Foreword: The Guide Who Needs Steering - an essay by Hal Clement; Uncommon Sense, 1945; The Logical Life, 1974; Stuck With It, 1976; and Status Symbol, 1987.

20. Fossil: Isaac's Universe. Published by DAW Books, New York City, 1993. Softcover. DAW Collector's Book 930.

21. Half Life. Published by Tor Books - Tom Doherty Associates, New York City, 1999. Hardcover.

22. The Essential Hal Clement - Volume 1: Trio for Slide Rule and Typewriter. Published by NESFA Press, Framingham, Massachusetts, 1999. Hardcover. This contains: Introduction by **Poul Anderson**; Needle, 1950; Iceworld, 1953; and Close to Critical, 1964.

23. The Essential Hal Clement - Volume 2: Music of Many Spheres. Published by NESFA Press, Framingham, Massachusetts, 2000. Hardcover. Herein: Introduction by Ben Bova; Cold Front, 1946; Proof, 1942; Raindrop, 1965; Longline, 1976; Planetfall, 1957; Sun Spot, 2000; The Mechanic, 1966; Attitude, 1943; Halo, 1952; Impediment, 1942; Technical Error, 1944; Bulge, 1968; Avenue of Escape, 1942; Status Symbol, 1987; The Logical Life, 1974; Stuck With It, 1976; and Uncommon Sense, 1945.

24. The Essential Hal Clement - Volume 3: Variations on a Theme by Sir Isaac Newton. Published by NESFA Press, Framingham, Massachusetts, 2000. Hardcover. This contains: Introduction by David Langford; Mission of Gravity, 1954; Under, 2000; Lecture Demonstration, 1973; Star Light, 1971; Whirligig World - an essay, 1953; Addendum to Whirligig World - essay, 2000; I Discover Hal Clement - essay by Anthony R. Lewis; and The Perfect Hard SF Novel - essay by Mark L. Olson.

25. Heavy Planet: The Classic Meskin Stories. Published by Orb Books, New York City, 2002. Softcover. Mission of Gravity, 1954; Under, 2000; Introduction to Lecture Demonstration - essay, 2000; Lecture Demonstration, 1973; Star Light, 1971; Whirligig World - essay, 1953; and Addendum to Whirligig World - essay, 2000.

26. Noise. Published by Tor Books - Tom Doherty Associates, New York City, 2003. Hardcover.

***

ANTHOLOGIES

1. First Flights to the Moon. Published by Doubleday & Company, Garden City, New York, 1970. Hardcover. Herein: Foreword: Essay by Hal Clement; Introduction: First Flights to the Moon by **Isaac Asimov**; Extending the Holdings by **Donald A. Wollheim** writing as David Grinnell, 1951; Once Around the Moon by Vic Phillips, 1937; Trends by **Isaac Asimov**, 1939; The Missing Symbol by Paul W. Fairman writing as Ivar Jorgensen, 1952; Ideas Die Hard by **Isaac Asimov**, 1957; Jetsam by A. Bertram Chandler, 1953; Wrong-Way Street by Larry Niven, 1965; Intruders by Edmund Cooper, 1957; Report on the Nature of the Lunar Surface by John Brunner, 1960; Critical Angle by A. Bertram Chandler, 1958; Venture to the Moon by **Arthur C. Clarke**, 1956; Moondust, the Smell of Hay, and Dialectical Materialism by Thomas M. Disch, 1967; Essay Part Two by Hal Clement.

***

RELATED

1. A Hal Clement Checklist. By Chris Drumm. Privately printed, United States, 1981. Softcover.

2. Hal Clement - Starmont Reader's Guide. By Donald M. Hassler. Published by Starmont House, 1982. Softcover.

3. Hal Clement: Scientist with a Mission. Published by Galactic Central Publications, Albuquerque, New Mexico, 1985. Softcover.

4. Hal's Worlds: Stories and Essays in Memory of Hal Clement. Edited by Shane Tourtellotte. Published by Wildside Press, Rockville, Maryland, 2005. Softcover.

5. Hal Clement. By Donald M. Hassler. Published by Borgo Press, San Bernardino, California, 2007. Softcover.

Robert Heinlein

Robert A. Heinlein.

Robert Anson Heinlein was born in Butler, Missouri on July 7th, 1907 and died of emphysema and heart failure on May 8th, 1988 in Carmel, California. In between, after not quite succeeding at anything else, he managed to establish himself as one of the finest writers of serious science fiction... ever. His first published story was Life-Line. It was bought by **John W. Campbell** and used in the August 1939 issue of Astounding Science Fiction, just one month after van Vogt and Asimov made their Astounding debut. It appeared with: The Luck of Ignatz by Lester del Rey; Heavy Planet by Milton A. Rothman writing as Lee Gregor; General Swamp, C.I.C. - part 1 of 2 by L. Ron Hubbard writing as Frederick Engelhardt; Stowaway by Nelson S. Bond; The Blue Giraffe by L. Sprague de Camp; An Ultimatum from Mars by Ray Cummings; and Pleasure Trove by P. Schuyler Miller.

Heinlein was educated by the U.S. Naval Academy and served in the Navy until 1934 when ill-health forced them to let him go. After further studies at the University of California, he went on to try his hand at a number of different things, real estate, silver mining, politics; each one unsuccessfully. It wasn't until Campbell bought Life-Life that Heinlein discovered what he called, "a pleasant way to live without working."

Within three years, he developed into one of Campbell's main stars at Astounding. Not only was his science good, but his writing was literate, readable. Heinlein was a writer, not just a science fiction writer. And his stories were consistently believable.

After World War Two, he, along with **Ray Bradbury**, led the way from the ghetto of the pulp magazines to the slick and glossy world of The Saturday Evening Post and Town and Country, et cetera, general fiction magazines where most of the science fiction guys, indeed, most of the pulp writers at the time, were unwelcome.

Heinlein always maintained that any good story well-written was suitable for the slick magazines... Also in 1947, Heinlein cracked the mainstream hardcover market when Charles Scribner's Sons - Ernest Hemingway's publisher - printed the first of his juveniles, Rocket Ship Galileo. This was a bit like some street-smelly homeless guy showing up for a New Year's bash at the Ritz.

But Heinlein wasn't done there. In 1950, he became only the second SF writer to be involved in a serious science fiction film (the first, of course, was H. G. Wells) when he worked as the technical advisor on the George Pal production of Destination Moon. When the film was done, Heinlein covered it with a story that he published in the September 1950 issue of Short Stories Magazine. He was also one of the first SF writers to get his long, serialised stories published as novels between boards.

His Future History concept, covering a two thousand year period, tied many of his stories into a single universe. For a time, most of what he wrote that was apart from that particular universe became the work of Anson MacDonald or Lyle Monroe or whomever.

Stranger in a Strange Land, 1961, broke the last barriers between the world of science fiction and the world of mainstream fiction. Heinlein said his purpose in writing it was to examine "every major axiom of the western culture," to throw doubt on them, and to offer alternatives that seemed reasonable. People who rarely read science fiction, non-SF readers, if you will, flocked to the book and made it a bestselling paperback.

Donald A. Wollheim once called him a universe maker. **Alfred Bester** said he was the writer who brought science fiction from the gutter to the heights. And **Theodore Sturgeon** said his influence on science fiction was huge as he inspired all sorts of new writers - and many old ones - to write well, inspired them to shoot for some sort of literary quality while they extrapolated their latest scientific gimmick or invention.

First Editions of Stranger in a Strange Land sell for anywhere from $7,500.00 to $9,500.00.

Pen names Used: Anson MacDonald; Caleb Saunders; John Riverside; Simon York; and Lyle Monroe.

Heinlein's rules for writing:
1. You must write.
2. You must finish what you start.
3. You must refrain from re-writing except to editorial order.
4. You must put it on the market.
5. You must keep it on the market until sold.

***

AWARDS

1956. Hugo Award for Double Star as Best Novel.
1960. Hugo Award for Starship Troopers as Best Novel.
1962. Hugo Award for Stranger in a Strange Land as Best Novel.
1967. Hugo Award for The Moon Is a Harsh Mistress as Best Novel.
1973. Locus Poll All-time Favorite Author Award.
1974. Grand Master Award presented by the Science Fiction Writers of America.
1977. Locus Poll All-Time Best Author Award.
1983. Prometheus Hall of Fame Award for The Moon is a Harsh Mistress.
1985. Locus Poll Best Fantasy Novel Award for Job: A Comedy of Justice.
1987. Locus Poll All-Time Best SF Novelist Award.
1987. Prometheus Hall of Fame Award for Stranger in a Strange Land.
1988. Locus Poll All-Time Best Author Award.
1990. Locus Poll Best Non-Fiction Award for Grumbles from the Grave.
1996. Prometheus Hall of Fame Award for Red Planet.

1997. Prometheus Hall of Fame Award for Methuselah's Children.
1998. Locus Poll All-Time Best SF Novelist Award.
1998. Inducted into The Science Fiction Hall of Fame.
1998. Prometheus Hall of Fame Award for Time Enough for Love.
1999. Locus Poll All-Time Best Author Award.
2001. Retro Hugo Award or his novel Farmer in the Sky, 1951.
2001. Retro Hugo Award for his novella, The Man Who Sold the Moon, 1950.
2003. Prometheus Hall of Fame Award for Requiem.

***

FILM AND TELEVISON

1. Destination Moon. A 1950 U.S. film, loosely based on Rocketship Galileo, 1947. Heinlein worked on the film as a technical advisor and also worked on the screenplay. It was produced by George Pal, directed by Irving Pichel and starring: John Archer; Warner Anderson; Tom Powers; Dick Wesson; Erin O'Brien-Moore; and others.

2. Tom Corbett - Space Cadet. A U.S. television series that started on October 1st, 1950. Heinlein did some writing for the series.

3. Ordeal in Space. Published in 1948, this was used on the television series Out There, airing on November 4th, 1951, Season 1, Episode 2. It starred: John Ericson; William A. Lee; Joe Mantell; Robert Paige; Rod Steiger; and Howard Wierum. **Theodore Sturgeon**, writing as Edward Waldo, wrote the teleplay.

4. Misfit. Published in 1939, Heinlein's second published story, this was used on the television series Out There, airing on November 18th, 1951, Season 1, Episode 4. It starred: Arthur Batanides; Ray Danton; Eddie Hyans; Jerry Paris; Wendell K. Phillips; Gene Saks; and John Sylvester.

5. The Green Hills of Earth. Published in 1947, this was used on the television series Out There, airing on December 2nd, 1951, Season 1, Episode 6. It starred: Jay Barney; Harry Cooke; Logan Field; Eddie Hyans; David McKay; Herbert Nelson; John Raitt; and Mary Sinclair.

6. Project Moon Base. Working with Jack Seaman, Heinlein wrote the story and the screenplay for this 1953 film. Directed by Richard Talmadge, the movie starred: Donna Martell; Hayden Rorke; Ross Ford; Larry Johns; Herb Jacobs; Barbara Morrison; Ernestine Barrier; James Craven; and many others.

7. The Brain Eaters. Based on The Puppet Masters, 1951, this was directed by Bruno VeSota and released in September 1958. It starred: Ed Nelson; Alan Frost; Cornelius Keefe; Joanna Lee; Jody Fair; David Hughes; Robert Ball; Greigh Phillips; Orville Sherman; and Leonard Nimoy (misspelled Nemoy); along with many others.

8. Uchu no senshi. An animated film from Japan, based on Starship Troopers, 1959. Made in 1989, the film was directed by Tetsuro Amino and starred: Yasunori Matsumoto; Shuichi Ikeda; Kzuhiko Inoue; Akira Kamiya; Yuji Mitsuya; Shinji Ogawa; and others.

9. Red Planet. Based on the juvenile novel from 1949, this was an animated film made for television in 1994. This starred: Pat Fraley; Benny Grant; Mark Hamill; Haven Hartman; Roddy McDowell; Marcia Mitzman Gaven; Stanley Ralph Ross; Nick Tate; and Jess Harnell.

10. The Puppet Masters. Based on the 1951 novel, this was released in October 1994. It was directed by Stuart Orme and starred: Donald Sutherland; Eric Thal; Julie Warner; Keith David; Will Patton; Richard Belzer; Tom Mason; Yaphet Kotto; Gerry Bamman; Sam Anderson; J. Patrick McCormack; Marshall Bell; and many others.

11. Starship Troopers. Released in November 1997, this was based on the 1959 novel and directed by Paul Verhoeven. It starred: Casper Van Dien; Dina Meyer; Denise Richards; Jake Busey; Neil Patrick Harris; Clancy Brown; Seth Gilliam; Patrick Muldoon; Michael Ironside; Rue McClanahan; Marshall Bell; Eric Bruskotter; Matt Levin; Blake Lindsley; Anthony Ruivivar; Brenda Strong; Dean Norris; and many others, including Robert David Hall as a recruiting sergeant and Amy Smart as a pilot cadet.

12. Roughnecks: The Starship Troopers Chronicles. This was an animated television series based on Heinlein's story. Released in August 1999, this starred: Elizabeth Daily; Bill Fagerbakke; James Horan; Alexander Polinsky; Rino Romano; Rider Strong; David DeLuise; Jamie Hanes; Steve Staley; and many others.

13. Jerry Was a Man. Based on the 1947 short story, this was directed by Michael Tolkin for the television series Masters of Science Fiction. It was released on August 18th, 2007, Season 1, Episode 3. The show starred Stephen Hawking as himself, the host, along with: Malcolm McDowell; Anne Heche; Russell Porter; Jason Diablo; Bill Dow; Sonja Bennett; Richard Ian Cox; Val Cole; and others.

***

RADIO

1. Requiem. Published in 1940, this was used on Beyond Tomorrow in early 1950.

2. The Green Hills of Earth. Published in 1947, this was aired on Dimension X, June 10th, 1950.

3. Destination Moon. Published in 1950, this was aired on Dimension X, June 24th, 1950.

4. The Roads Must Roll. Published in 1940, this was used on Destination X on September 1st, 1950.

5. Universe. This was Part One of what became Orphans of the Sky, 1963. From Astounding Science Fiction, May 1941, it aired on the show Destination X on August 2nd, 1951.

6. Requiem. Published in 1940, this was used on Destination X on September 22nd, 1951.

7. Universe. This was Part One of what became Orphans of the Sky, 1963. From Astounding Science

Fiction, May 1941, it aired on X Minus One on May 15th, 1955.

8. The Green Hills of Earth. Published in 1947, this was aired
on X Minus One, July 7th, 1955.

9. Requiem. Published in 1940, this was used on X Minus One, October 27th, 1955.

10. The Roads Must Roll. Published in 1940, this was used on X Minus One, January 4th, 1956.

11. The Green Hills of Earth. Published in 1947, this was used
On CBS Radio Workshop, a show that ran between 1956 and 1957.

12. Requiem. Published in 1940, this was used on Exploring Tomorrow, the **John W. Campbell** show that ran in 1957 and 1958.

13. By His Bootstraps. Originally published in 1941 as by Anson MacDonald, this was produced in 1982 for 2000X - Tales of the Next Millennia - Hollywood Theater of the Ear. It was directed by Yuri Rasovsky and starred Richard Dreyfuss.

***

NOVELS AND COLLECTIONS

1. Rocket Ship Galileo. Published by Charles Scribner's Sons, New York City, 1947. Hardcover.

2. Beyond This Horizon. Published by Fantasy Press, Reading Pennsylvania, 1948. Hardcover.

3. Space Cadet. Published by Charles Scribner's Sons, New York City, 1948. Hardcover.

4. Red Planet. Published by Charles Scribner's Sons, New York City, 1949. Hardcover.

5. Sixth Column. Published by Gnome Press, New York City, 1949. Hardcover.

6. Farmer in the Sky. Published by Charles Scribner's Sons, New York City, 1950. Hardcover.

7. The Man Who Sold the Moon. Published by Shasta Publishers, Chicago, 1950. Hardcover. This collection contains: Introduction by **John W. Campbell**; Preface by **Robert A. Heinlein**; Let There Be Light, 1951; The Roads Must Roll, 1940; The Man Who Sold the Moon, 1950; Requiem, 1940; Life-Line, 1939; and Blowups Happen, 1940.

8. Waldo and Magic Inc. Published by Doubleday & Company, Garden City, New York, 1950. Herein: Waldo, 1942; Magic Inc., 1940.

9. The Man Who Sold the Moon. Published by Signet Books - The New American Library, New York City, 1951. An abridged edition, Signet Book 847. Herein: Preface: It Does Not Pay a Prophet to Be Too Specific - essay by **Robert A. Heinlein**, 1950; Let There Be Light, 1951; The Roads Must Roll, 1940; The Man Who Sold the Moon, 1950; and Requiem, 1940.

10. The Puppet Masters. Published by Doubleday & Company, Garden City, New York, 1951. Hardcover.

11. Between Planets. Published by Charles Scribner's Sons, New York City, 1951. Hardcover.

12. The Green Hills of Earth. Published by Shasta Publishers, Chicago, 1951. Hardcover. Herein: Delilah and the Space-Rigger, 1949; Space Jockey, 1947; The Long Watch, 1948; Gentlemen, Be Seated, 1948; The Black Pits of Luna, 1948; It's Great to Be Back!, 1947; We Also Walk Dogs, 1941; Ordeal in Space, 1948; The Green Hills of Earth, 1947; and Logic of Empire, 1941.

13. Universe. Published by Dell Publishing, New York City, 1951. Softcover, Dell 10-cent Book 36.

14. The Day After Tomorrow. Published by Signet Books - The New American Library, New York City, 1951. A softcover re-titled re-issue of *Sixth Column*, 1949, Signet Book 882.

15. The Rolling Stones. Published by Charles Scribner's Sons, New York City, 1952. Hardcover.

16. Assignment in Eternity. Published by Fantasy Press, Reading Pennsylvania, 1953. Hardcover. This contains: Gulf, 1949; Elsewhen, 1941; Lost Legacy, 1941; and Jerry Was a Man, 1947.

17. Revolt in 2100. Published by Shasta Publishers, Chicago, 1953. Hardcover.

18. Starman Jones. Published by Charles Scribner's Sons, New York City, 1953. Hardcover.

19. The Star Beast. Published by Charles Scribner's Sons, New York City, 1954. Hardcover.

20. Tunnel in the Sky. Published by Charles Scribner's Sons, New York City, 1955. Hardcover.

21. Double Star. Published by Doubleday & Company, Garden City, New York, 1956. Hardcover.

22. Time for the Stars. Published by Charles Scribner's Sons, New York City, 1956. Hardcover.

23. Citizen of the Galaxy. Published by Charles Scribner's Sons, New York City, 1957. Hardcover.

24. The Door Into Summer. Published by Doubleday & Company, Garden City, New York, 1957. Hardcover.

25. Have Space Suit - Will Travel. Published by Charles Scribner's Sons, New York City, 1958. Hardcover.

26. Methuselah's Children. Published by Gnome Press, Hicksville, New York, 1958. Hardcover.

27. Waldo: Genius in Orbit. Published by Avon Publications, New York City, 1958. A softcover re-titled re-issue of Waldo and Magic Inc, 1950.

28. The Robert Heinlein Omnibus. Published by The Science Fiction Book Club, London, England, 1958. Hardcover. This contains: Preface: It Does Not Pay a Prophet to Be Too Specific - an essay, 1950; The Roads Must Roll, 1940; Requiem, 1940; The Man Who Sold the Moon, 1950; It's Great to Be Back!, 1947; The Green Hills of Earth, 1947; Logic of Empire, 1941; The Black Pits of Luna, 1948; Delilah and the Space-Rigger, 1949; Gentlemen, Be

Seated!, 1948; Let There Be Light, 1940; We Also Walk Dogs, 1941; The Long Watch, 1948; Ordeal in Space, 1948; and Space Jockey, 1947.

29. The Unpleasant Profession of Jonathan Hoag. Published by Gnome Press, Hicksville, New York, 1959. Hardcover. This collection contains: They, 1941; The Elephant Circuit, 1957; Universe, 1941; Our Fair City, 1949; All You Zombies, 1959; And He Built a Crooked House, 1941; and The Unpleasant Profession of Jonathan Hoag, writing as John Riverside, 1942.

30. The Menace from Earth. Published by Gnome Press, Hicksville, New York, 1959. Hardcover. Herein: The Year of the Jackpot, 1952; By His Bootstraps, 1941; Columbus Was a Dope, 1947; The Menace from Earth, 1957; Sky Lift, 1953; Goldfish Bowl, 1942; Project Nightmare, 1953; and Water Is for Washing, 1947.

31. Starship Troopers. Published by G. P. Putnam's Sons, New York City, 1959. Hardcover.

32. Lost Legacy. Published by Digit Books - Brown, Watson Ltd, London, 1960. Softcover. Digit Book D386. This took two stories from Assignment in Eternity, 1953: Jerry Was a Man, 1947; and Lost Legacy, 1941.

33. Stranger in a Strange Land. Published by G. P. Putnam's Sons, New York City, 1961. Hardcover.

34. 6 X H. Published by Pyramid Books, New York City, 1961. A softcover re-titled re-issue of The Unpleasant Profession of Jonathan Hoag, 1959, Pyramid Book G642. Herein: They, 1941; The Elephant Circuit, 1957; Universe, 1941; Our Fair City, 1949; All You Zombies, 1959; And He Built a Crooked House, 1941; and The Unpleasant Profession of Jonathan Hoag, writing as John Riverside, 1942.

35. Glory Road. Published by G. P. Putnam's Sons, New York City, 1963. Hardcover.

36. Podkayne of Mars. Published by G. P. Putnam's Sons, New York City, 1963. Hardcover.

37. Orphans of the Sky. Published by Victor Gollancz, London, 1963. Hardcover.

38. Farnham's Freehold. Published by G. P. Putnam's Sons, New York City, 1964. Hardcover.

39. Three by Heinlein. Published by Doubleday & Company, Garden City New York, 1965. An omnibus edition, this gathered: The Puppet Masters, 1951; Waldo, 1942; and Magic Inc, 1940. Waldo and Magic Inc were both originally written as by Anson MacDonald.

40. The Moon Is a Harsh Mistress. Published by G. P. Putnam's Sons, New York City, 1966. Hardcover.

41. The Worlds of Robert A. Heinlein. Published by Ace Books, New York City, 1966. Softcover. Ace Book F-375. Herein: Pandora's Box - essay by **Robert A. Heinlein**, 1966; Free Men, 1966; Blowups Happen, 1940; Searchlight, 1962; Life-Line, 1939; and Solution Unsatisfactory - as by Anson MacDonald, 1941.

42. A Heinlein Triad. Published by Victor Gollancz, London, 1966. An omnibus edition, this gathered: The Puppet Masters, 1951; Waldo, 1942; and Magic Inc, 1940. Waldo and Magic Inc were both originally written as by Anson MacDonald.

43. A Robert A. Heinlein Omnibus. Published by Sidgwick and Jackson, London, 1966. Hardcover. This collected: Beyond This Horizon, 1948; The Man Who Sold the Moon, 1950; and The Green Hills of Earth, 1951.

44. The Past Through Tomorrow. Published by G. P. Putnam's Sons, New York City, 1967. Hardcover. Herein: Introduction by **Damon Knight**; Life-Line, 1939; The Roads Must Roll, 1940; Blowups Happen, 1940; The Man Who Sold the Moon, 1950; Delilah and the Space-Rigger, 1949; Space Jockey, 1947; Requiem, 1940; The Long Watch, 1948; Gentlemen, Be Seated!, 1948; The Black Pits of Luna, 1948; It's Great to Be Back!, 1947; We Also Walk Dogs, 1941; Searchlight, 1962; Ordeal in Space, 1948; The Green Hills of Earth, 1947; Logic of Empire, 1941; The Menace from Earth, 1957; If This Goes On, 1940; Coventry, 1940; Misfit, 1939; and Methuselah's Children, 1958.

45. Space Family Stone. Published by Victor Gollancz, London, 1969. Hardcover. A re-titled version of The Rolling Stones, 1952.

46. I Will Fear No Evil. Published by G. P. Putnam's Sons, New York City, 1970. Hardcover.

47. The Best of Robert A. Heinlein. Edited by Angus Wells. Published by Sidgwick and Jackson, London, 1973. Hardcover. Herein: Introduction by **Robert A. Heinlein**; And He Build a Crooked House, 1941; All You Zombies, 1959; Life-Line, 1939; The Green Hills of Earth, 1947; The Long Watch, 1948; The Man Who Sold the Moon, 1950; The Roads Must Roll, 1940; The Unpleasant Profession of Jonathan Hoag, 1942; and Bibliography: The Best of Robert Heinlein - uncredited, 1973.

48. Time Enough for Love. Published by G. P. Putnam's Sons, New York City, 1973. Hardcover.

49. The Past Through Tomorrow. Published by New English Library, London, 1977. This was released in two volumes and was abridged to delete Methuselah's Children, 1958.

50. The Best of Robert A. Heinlein 1939 - 1942. Edited by Angus Wells. Published by Sphere Books, London, 1977. Softcover. Herein: Introduction by **Robert A. Heinlein**; And He Build a Crooked House, 1941; Life-Line, 1939; The Roads Must Roll, 1940; The Unpleasant Profession of Jonathan Hoag, 1942; and Bibliography: The Best of Robert Heinlein - uncredited, 1973.

51. The Best of Robert A. Heinlein 1947 - 1959. Edited by Angus Wells. Published by Sphere Books, London, 1977. Softcover. Herein: Introduction by Peter R. Weston; The Green Hills of Earth, 1947; The Long Watch, 1948; The Man Who Sold the Moon, 1950; All You Zombies, 1959; and Bibliography - uncredited, 1977.

52. Destination Moon. Published by Gregg Press,

Robert Heinlein

Boston, 1979. Hardcover. Herein: Introduction by David G. Hartwell; Destination Moon, 1950; Shooting Destination Moon - essay by **Robert A. Heinlein**, 1950; and Facts About Destination Moon - an uncredited essay, 1979.

53. The Number of the Beast. Published by Fawcett Gold Medal Books, New York City, 1980. Softcover.

54. Expanded Universe - The New Worlds of Robert A Heinlein. Published by Ace Books, New York City, 1980. Softcover. This contains: Foreword by **Robert A. Heinlein**; Life-Line, 1939; Successful Operation, writing as Lyle Monroe, 1940; Blowups Happen, 1940; Solution Unsatisfactory, writing as Anson MacDonald, 1941; The Last Days of the United States - essay, 1980; How to Be a Survivor - essay, 1980; Pie from the Sky - essay, 1980; They Do It With Mirrors, writing as Simon York, 1947; Free Men, 1966; No Bands Playing, No Flags Flying, 1973; A Bathroom of Her Own, 1980; On the Slopes of Vesuvius, 1980; Nothing Ever Happens on the Moon, 1949; Pandora's Box - essay, 1966; Where To? - essay, 1952; Cliff and the Calories, 1980; Ray Guns and Rocket Ships - essay, 1952; The Third Millennium Opens - essay, 1956; Who Are the Heirs of Patrick Henry? - essay, 1958; Pravda Means Truth - essay, 1960; Inside Intourist - essay, 1960; Searchlight, 1962; The Pragmatics of Patriotism - essay, 1973; Paul Dirac, Antimatter and You - essay, 1975; Larger Than Life: A Memoir Tribute to Dr. Edward E. Smith - essay, 1980; and The Happy Days Ahead - essay, 1980.

55. Expanded Universe - The New Worlds of Robert A Heinlein. Grosset and Dunlap, New York City, 1980. First hardcover edition.

56. A Heinlein Trio. Published by Nelson Doubleday, Science Fiction Book Club, Garden City, New York, 1980. An omnibus edition, this gathered: The Puppet Masters, 1951; Double Star, 1956; and The Door into Summer, 1957.

57. Friday. Published by Holt, Rinehart and Winston, New York City, 1982. Hardcover.

58. Job: A Comedy of Justice. Published by Del Rey - Ballantine Books, New York City, 1984. Hardcover.

59. The Cat Who Walks Through Walls. Published by G. P. Putnam's Sons, New York City, 1985. Hardcover.

60. To Sail Beyond the Sunset. Published by Ace/Putnam, New York City, 1987. Hardcover.

61. The Fantasies of Robert A Heinlein. Published by Tor Books - Tom Doherty Associates, New York City, 1999. Hardcover. An omnibus edition that collected the stories from: Waldo and Magic Inc, 1950; and The Unpleasant Profession of Jonathan Hoag, 1959.

62. Revolt in 2100 - with - Methuselah's Children. Published by Baen Books, New York City, 1999. Softcover.

63. For Us, The Living: A Comedy of Customs. Published by Scribner's, New York City, 2003. Hardcover. Actually written in 1938, this was left unpublished for sixty-five years.

64. Infinite Possibilities. Published by Nelson Doubleday, Science Fiction Book Club, Garden City, New York, 2003. Hardcover. An omnibus edition, this gathered: Tunnel in the Sky, 1955; Time for the Stars, 1956; and Citizen of the Galaxy, 1957.

65. To the Stars. Published by Nelson Doubleday, Science Fiction Book Club, Garden City, New York, 2004. Hardcover. An omnibus edition, this gathered: Between Planets, 1951; The Rolling Stones, 1952; Starman Jones, 1953; and The Star Beast, 1954.

66. Off the Main Sequence. Published by Nelson Doubleday, Science Fiction Book Club, Garden City, New York, 2005. Hardcover. Herein: Introduction by Greg Bear; Foreword by Michael Cassutt; Editor's Note by Andrew Wheeler; Successful Operation, 1940; Let There Be Light, 1940; And He Built a Crooked House, 1941; Beyond Doubt - written with Elma Wentz, 1941; They, 1941; Solution Unsatisfactory, 1941; Universe, 1941; Elsewhen, 1941; Common Sense, 1941; By His Bootstraps, 1941; Lost Legacy, 1941; My Object All Sublime, 1942; Goldfish Bowl, 1942; Pied Piper, 1942; Free Men, 1966; On the Slopes of Vesuvius, 1980; Columbus Was a Dope, 1947; Jerry Was a Man, 1947; Nothing Ever Happens on the Moon, 1949; Gulf, 1949; Destination Moon, 1950; The Year of the Jackpot, 1952; Project Nightmare, 1953; Sky Lift, 1953; Tenderfoot in Space, 1958; and All You Zombies, 1959.

67. Four Frontiers. Published by Nelson Doubleday, Science Fiction Book Club, Garden City, New York, 2005. Hardcover. An omnibus edition, this gathered: Rocket Ship Galileo, 1947; Space Cadet, 1948; Red Planet, 1949; and Farmer in the Sky, 1950.

68. Outward Bound. Published by Nelson Doubleday, Science Fiction Book Club, Garden City, New York, 2006. Hardcover. An omnibus edition, this gathered: Have Space Suit - Will Travel, 1958; Starship Troopers, 1959; and Podkayne of Mars, 1963.

69. Variable Star. With Spider Robinson. Published by Tor Books - Tom Doherty Associates, New York City, 2006. Hardcover. Working from seven surviving pages from an eight-page outline that Heinlein wrote in 1955, Robinson wrote this with no intention of copying Heinlein's actual writing style.

70. Project Moonbase and Others: The Scripts of Robert A. Heinlein - Volume 1. Published by Subterranean Press, Burton, Michigan, 2008. Hardcover. This contains: Introduction by John Scalzi; Project Moonbase - Screenplay; It's Great to Be Back - Screenplay with Jack Seaman; Space Jockey - Screenplay with Jack Seaman; The Black Pits of Luna - Screenplay with Jack Seaman; The Long Watch - Screenplay with Jack Seaman; Delilah and the Space Rigger - Screenplay with Jack Seaman; Life-Life - Screenplay with Jack Seaman; Requiem - Screenplay with Jack Seaman; And He Built a Crooked House - Screenplay with Jack Seaman; Crooked House - Sets, Scenes and Camera

Angles - an essay by Jack Seaman and **Robert A. Heinlein**; We Also Walk Dogs - Screenplay with Jack Seaman; Home Sweet Home - Story Line with Jack Seaman; and The Tourist - TV Screenplay with Jack Seaman.

71. The Virginia Edition. This is the complete collected works of **Robert A. Heinlein**, published by Virginia Edition Publishing Co. in a limited, leather-bound edition.

***

ANTHOLOGIES

1. Tomorrow the Stars. Published by Doubleday & Company, Garden City, New York, 1952. Hardcover. Heinlein did not, in fact, select the stories for this but he was given the credit. He wrote the foreword; the actual selections were made by **Frederik Pohl** and Judith Merril. This collected: I'm Scared by Jack Finney, 1951; The Silly Season by C. M. Kornbluth, 1950; The Report on the Barnhouse Effect by Kurt Vonnegut Jr., 1950; The Tourist Trade by Bob Tucker, 1950; Rainmaker by John Reese, 1949; Absalom by **Henry Kuttner**, 1946; The Monster by Lester del Rey, 1951; Jay Score by **Eric Frank Russell**, 1941; Betelgeuse Bridge by William Tenn, 1950; Survival Ship by Judith Merril, 1950; Keyhole by Murray Leinster, 1951; Misbegotten Missionary by **Isaac Asimov**, 1950; The Sack by William Morrison, 1950; and Poor Superman by **Fritz Leiber**, 1951.

***

NON-FICTION

1. The Discovery of the Future. This was a speech delivered at the 3rd World Science Fiction convention, when Heinlein was the Guest of Honor. It was published in a limited softcover edition of 200 copies by Novacious Publications, 1941.

2. The Science Fiction Novel. With C. M. Kornbluth, Basil Davenport, **Alfred Bester** and Robert Bloch. Advent Publishers, New York City, 1959. Hardcover. Herein: Introduction by Basil Davenport; Science Fiction: Its Nature, Faults and Virtues by **Robert A. Heinlein**; The Failure of the Science Fiction Novel as Social Criticism by C. M. Kornbluth; Science Fiction and the Renaissance Man by **Alfred Bester**; and Imagination and Modern Science Fiction by Robert Bloch.

3. Grumbles from the Grave. Published by Del Rey - Ballantine Books, New York City, 1989. Hardcover.

4. Requiem: New Collected Works by Robert A. Heinlein and Tributes to the Grand Master. Published by Tor Books - Tom Doherty Associates, New York City, 1992. This actually collects some fiction but is primarily a selection of essays. Herein: Preface by Virginia Heinlein; Editor's Foreword by Yoji Kondo. Part One: Works of **Robert A. Heinlein**: Requiem, 1940; Tenderfoot in Space, 1958; Destination Moon, 1958; Shooting Destination Moon - essay, 1950; The Witch's Daughters - poem, 1946; The Bulletin Board, 1992; Poor Daddy, 1992; Guest of Honor Speech at the Third World Science Fiction Convention, Denver 1941; Guest of Honor Speech at the XIXth World Science Fiction Convention, Seattle 1961; Guest of Honor Speech, Rio de Janeiro Movie Festival, 1969; Guest of Honor Speech at the XXXIVth World Science Fiction Convention, Kansas City, 1976. Part Two: National Air and Space Museum Heinlein Retrospective, October 6, 1988: NASA Medal for Distinguished Public Service for **Robert A. Heinlein** - speech by James C. Fletcher; This I Believe - essay by **Robert A. Heinlein**, read by Virginia Heinlein; Speeches by the following: Tom Clancy; L. Sprague de Camp; Jerry Pournelle; Charles Sheffield; Jon McBride; Catherine Crook de Camp; and Tetsu Yano. Part Three: Tributes to **Robert A. Heinlein**: **Poul Anderson**; Jim Baen; Greg Bear; J. Hartley Brown Jr.; **Arthur C. Clarke**; **Gordon R. Dickson**; Joe Haldeman; Larry Niven; Spider Robinson; **Robert Silverberg**; Harry Turtledove; **Jack Williamson**; and Yoji Kondo with Charles Sheffield.

5. Tramp Royale. Published by Ace Books, New York City, 1992. Hardcover.

6. Take Back Your Government: A Practical Handbook for the Private Citizen Who Wants Democracy to Work. Published by Baen Books, New York City, 1992. Hardcover.

***

RELATED

1. Of Worlds Beyond: A Symposium by Edward E. Smith, Ph.D.; John W. Campbell; L. Sprague de Camp; Robert A. Heinlein; Jack Williamson; A. E. van Vogt; and John Taine. Edited by Lloyd Arthur Eschbach. Published by Advent Publishers, Chicago, 1964. Softcover.

2. Of Worlds Beyond: A Symposium by Edward E. Smith, Ph.D.; John W. Campbell; L. Sprague de Camp; Robert A. Heinlein; Jack Williamson; A. E. van Vogt; and John Taine. Edited by Lloyd Arthur Eschbach. Published by Dennis Dobson, London, 1965. First hardcover edition.

3. Heinlein in Dimension. By Alexei Panshin. Published by Advent Publishers, Chicago, 1968. Softcover.

4. Robert A. Heinlein: A Bibliography. By Mark Owings. Published by Croatan House, Baltimore, Maryland, 1973. Softcover.

5. Stranger in a Strange Land and Other Works: Notes. By Baird Searles. Published by Cliffs Notes Incorporated, Lincoln, Nebraska, 1975.

6. Robert A. Heinlein: Stranger in His Own Land. By George Edgar Slusser. Published by R. Reginald - The Borgo Press, San Bernardino, California, 1976. Softcover.

7. The Classic Years of Robert A. Heinlein. By George Edgar Slusser. Published by R. Reginald - The Borgo Press, San Bernardino, California, 1977. Softcover.

8. Robert A. Heinlein. Edited by Joseph D. Olander and Martin Harry Greenberg. Published by Taplinger Publishing, New York City, 1978. Hardcover.

Robert Heinlein

9. Robert A. Heinlein: America As Science Fiction. By H. Bruce Franklin. Published by Oxford University Press, New York City, 1980. Hardcover.

10. Robert A. Heinlein. By Leon Stover. Published by Twayne Publishers, Boston, 1987. Hardcover.

11. New Destinies: Volume VI - Winter 1988: Robert A. Heinlein Memorial Issue. Edited by Jim Baen. Published by Baen Books, New York City, 1988. Softcover. Herein: In Appreciation: **Robert A. Heinlein** by Jerry Pournelle; The Long Watch by **Robert A. Heinlein**, 1948; Dance Session - a poem by **Robert A. Heinlein**, 1946; Rah Rah R.A.H. by Spider Robinson; Excerpts from The Notebooks of Lazarus Long by **Robert A. Heinlein**, 1978; **Robert A. Heinlein** and the Coming of the Space Age by Rick Cook; More Excerpts from The Notebooks of Lazarus Long by **Robert A. Heinlein**; The Man Who Traveled in Elephants by **Robert A. Heinlein**, 1948 - first published in 1957 as The Elephant Circuit; Farewell to the Master by Yoji Kondo and Charles Sheffield; The Witch's Daughters - a poem by **Robert A. Heinlein**, 1946. Other stories in the issue were: Copyright Violation by Spider Robinson; The Blabber by Vernor Vinge; Counting Up - an essay by Charles Sheffield; Megaphone by Rick Cook; Freeze Frame by John Moore; and King of All by Harry Turtledove.

12. A Guide Through the Worlds of Robert A. Heinlein. By J. Lincoln Thorner and Bill Ware. Published by Gryphon Books, Brooklyn, New York, 1989. Limited to 500 copies. Softcover.

13. Science Fiction Review - Spring 1990: Robert A. Heinlein. A magazine featuring Heinlein's last interview.

14. Robert Heinlein: Stormtrooping Guru: A Working Bibliography. By Phil Stephensen-Payne. Published by Galactic Central Publications, Leeds, England, 1993. Softcover.

15. A Checklist of Robert A. Heinlein. By Christopher P. Stephens. Published by Ultramarine, United States, 1994. Softcover.

16. The Robert Heinlein Interview and Other Heinleiniana. By J. Neil Schulman. Published by Pulpless.Com, United States, 1999. Softcover on demand.

17. Robert A. Heinlein: A Reader's Companion. By James Gifford. Published by Nitrosyncretic Press, Sacramento, California, 2000. Hardcover.

18. The Martian Names Smith: Critical Perspectives on Robert A. Heinlein's Stranger in a Strange Land. By William H. Patterson Jr and Andrew Thornton. Published by Nitrosyncretic Press, Sacramento, California, 2001. Softcover.

19. Author Price Guide 115.3: Robert A. Heinlein. Published by Quill and Brush, 2004. Softcover.

20. Robert Heinlein's Shadow: The Seven Starlings - and - How Aeneas Browning Got Rich. Both stories by Jubal Harshaw. Published by iUniverse.com, 2007.

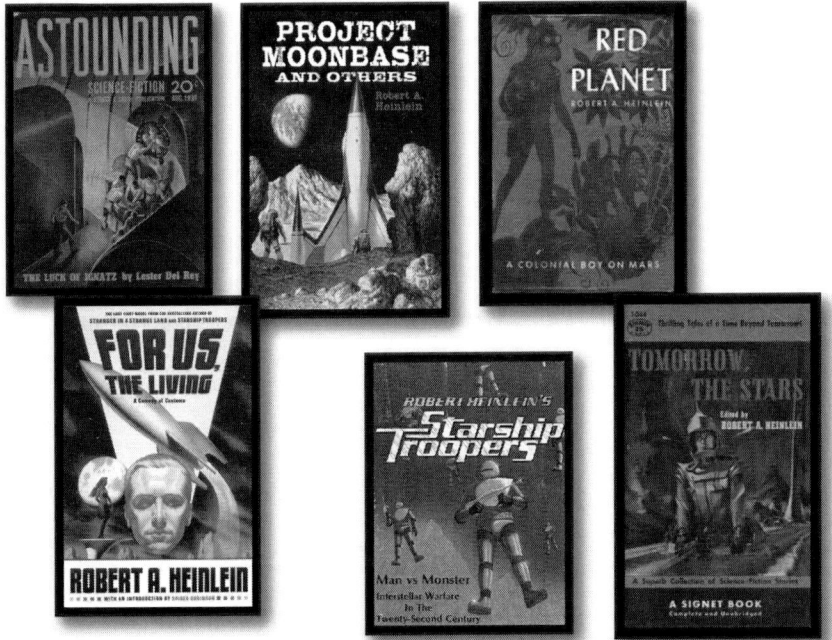

C. L. Moore.

Catherine Lucille Moore was born January 24th, 1911, in Indianapolis, Indiana, and died April 4th, 1987 after years of Alzheimer's disease. She was one of the first women to write science fiction and fantasy, although she hid her gender by using her initials rather than her name. It was quite logical that when a young writer and fan named Henry Kuttner wrote a fan letter to Ms Moore in 1936, he addressed it to *Mr.* C. L. Moore. Obviously, that confusion was soon cleared up.

Catherine sold her first story, Shambleau - about her hero Northwest Smith - to Weird Tales in 1933. It was the lead story in the November issue, along with: The War of the Sexes by Edmond Hamilton; The Premature Burial by Edgar Allan Poe; The Man Who Saw Red by Wilmer Benjamin; The Accursed Isle by Mary Elizabeth Counselman; On Top by Ralph Allen Lang; The Holiness of Azedarac by Clark Ashton Smith; Lord of the Fourth Axis by E. Hoffman Price; and The Vampire Master - part 2 of 4 by Edmond Hamilton writing as Hugh Davidson.

Shambleau was moody, atmospheric... and a smash hit with Weird Tales readers - and authors. Even H. P. Lovecraft had praise for the story. She did fourteen more stories for Weird Tales during the 1930s, including a round-robin tale called The Challenge from Beyond, 1935, with H. P. Lovecraft, A. Merritt, Frank Belknap Long and Robert E. Howard.

Kuttner and Moore eventually met in California at the home of one of Moore's friends. And later, when Henry Kuttner was living in New York City, they began a romance that led to marriage in 1940.

And collaboration.

It was well-known but rarely mentioned that Catherine was the better writer of the two. Kuttner, though, is far more well-known. But they rarely worked individually. They worked on each others' stories, and they worked jointly and used at least seventeen pen names, the dominant two being Lawrence O'Donnell and Lewis Padgett. Catherine rarely used her own name because Henry commanded higher pay rates for his work. It was said that their collaborations were so good, no one could actually distinguish one from the other.

Catherine and Henry collaborated for the rest of Henry's life, which, unfortunately, ended abruptly in 1958 when he died from a heart attack at 43 years old.

Moore continued writing, working in television and also spinning some mysteries, but she abandoned science fiction completely.

Under her own name, Northwest of Earth tends to be her highest priced first edition - somewhere around $850.00. A Gnome There Was, written with Henry as Lewis Padgett, and No Boundaries, with both their names on it, also run around that price.

Pen names used: Lewis Padgett; Lawrence O'Donnell; Edward J. Bellin; Paul Edmonds; Noel Gardner; Will Garth (shared house name); James Hall; Keith Hammond; Hudson Hastings; Peter Horn; Kelvin Kent; Robert O. Kenyon; C. H. Liddell; K. Hugh Maepenn; Scott Morgan; Woodrow Wilson Smith; and Charles Stoddard.

***

AWARDS

1981. World Fantasy Award for Lifetime Achievement.
1998. Inducted into the Science Fiction and Fantasy Hall of Fame.
2004. Along with husband Henry Kuttner, **C. L. Moore** was given the Cordwainer Smith Foundation Rediscovery Award.

***

FILM AND TELEVISION

1. The Dark Angel. Written with Henry Kuttner in 1946, working as Lewis Padgett, this was used on *Tales of Tomorrow*. It was originally shown on September 28th, 1951, Season 1, Episode 8. Directed by Charles S. Dubin, it starred: Sidney Blackmer; Meg Mundy; Donald Briggs; and Mel Ruick.

2. The Twonky. Written in 1942 with Henry Kuttner, working as Lewis Padgett, this was filmed in 1953. Directed by Arch Oboler, it starred: Hans Conried; Janet Warren; Billy Lynn; Edwin Max; Gloria Blondell; Evelyn Beresford; Norman Field; and many others.

3. Tales of Frankenstein. Writing with Henry Kuttner as Catherine Kuttner, this was a TV pilot from a story by Curt Siodmak in 1958. Directed by Curt Siodmak, it starred: Anton Diffring; Helen Westcott; Don Megowan; Ludwig Stossel; Richard Bull; Raymond Greenleaf; Peter Brocco; and Sydney Mason. Unfortunately, the series was never picked up.

4. Price on His Head. Writing with Henry Kuttner, she did this teleplay for the series Sugarfoot in 1958. It was shown on April 29th, 1958, Season 1, Episode 17. Directed by Richard L. Bare, it starred: Will Hutchins; Patrick McVey; Venetia Stevenson; Karl Swenson; Dorothy Green; Virginia Gregg; Williams Phipps; and others.

5. The Ghost. Writing as Catherine Kuttner, she did this teleplay for the series Sugarfoot in 1958. It was shown on October 28th, 1958, Season 2, Episode 4. Directed by Lee Sholem, it starred: Will Hutchins; Bill Erwin; Ed Kemmer; Martin Landau; Michael Pate; and Tommy Rettig.

6. The Mountain. Writing as Catherine Kuttner, she did this teleplay for the series Sugarfoot in 1959. It was shown on March 31st, 1959, Season 2, Episode 15. Directed by Joseph Lejtes, it starred: Will Hutchins; Don Devlin; Don Dubbins; Miranda Jones; and Rosa Rey.

7. The Trial of the Canary Kid. Writing as Catherine Kuttner, she did this teleplay for the series

C.L. Moore

Sugarfoot in 1959. It was shown on September 15th, 1959, Season 3, Episode 1. Directed by Montgomery Pittman, it starred: Will Hutchins; Lonnie Blackman; Frank Albertson; Saundra Edwards; Don 'Red' Barry; Yvonne Schubert; Stuart Randall; William Phipps; and Sean Garrison.

8. What You Need. Written in 1945 with Henry Kuttner, working as Lewis Padgett, this was used on the Twilight Zone and shown on December 25th, 1959, Season 1, Episode 12. Narrated by **Rod Serling** and directed by Alvin Ganzer, it starred: Steve Cochran; Ernest Truex; Read Morgan; Arlene Martel; William Edmonson; Doris Karnes; Fred Kruger; and Norman Sturgis.

9. The Antwerp Caper. Writing as Catherine Kuttner, she did this teleplay for the series 77 Sunset Strip in 1960. It was shown on December 2nd, 1960, Season 3, Episode 12. Directed by George Waggner, the show starred: Efrem Zimbalist Jr; Roger Smith; Louis Quinn; Jacqueline Beer; Karen Steele; John Van Dreelan; John Banner; Penny Santon; Roger Til; and Dale Van Sickel.

10. Family Pride. Writing as Catherine Kuttner, she did this teleplay for the series Maverick in 1961. It was shown on January 8th, 1961, Season 4, Episode 17. Directed by John Ainsworth, the show starred: James Garner; Jack Kelly; Robert Cornthwaite; Stacy Keach; Dorothea Lord; Denver Pyle; Wallace Rooney; Anita Sands; Olan Soule; Karl Swenson; and Roger Moore as Beauregarde Maverick.

11. Masquerade. This was credited only to Henry Kuttner but it was written in 1942 and the chances that he wrote it without any input from Catherine are pretty slim. It was used on Boris Karloff's Thriller, directed by Herschel Daugherty and shown on October 30th, 1961, Season 2, Episode 6. It starred: Boris Karloff as himself; John Carradine; Jack Lambert; Elizabeth Montgomery; Dorothy Neumann; and Tom Poston.

12. The Diplomatic Caper. This was a teleplay for the series 77 Sunset Strip in 1962. It was shown on January 26th, 1962, Season 4, Episode 19. Directed by Sidney Salkow, the show starred: Efrem Zimbalist Jr; Robert Logan; Oscar Beregi Jr; Henry Brandon; Edward Colmans; Carolyn Craig; Amy Douglass; Chad Everett; Anna Lee; and John Van Dreelen.

13. Timescape. This was a film based on Vintage Season, which was published in 1946 as by Lawrence O'Donnell. Released in 1992, it was directed by David Twohy and starred: Jeff Daniels; Ariana Richards; Emilia Crow; Jim Haynie; Marilyn Lightstone; George Murdock; David Wells; Nicholas Guest; Robert Colbert; and many others.

14. The Last Mimzy. Based on Mimsy Were the Borogroves, which was published in 1943 as by Lewis Padgett, this film was released in 2007. Directed by Robert Shaye, it starred: Chris O'Neil; Rhiannon Leigh Wryn; Joely Richardson; Timothy Hutton; Rainn Wilson; Kathryn Hahn; Michael Clarke Duncan; Kirsten Williamson; Irene Snow; Marc Musso; Nicole Munoz; and many others.

***

RADIO

1. Housing Problem. This 1944 story, credited to Henry Kuttner, was used on CBS Radio Workshop on June 16th, 1957.

2. Absalom. This 1946 story, credited to Henry Kuttner, was used on Mind Webs on December 31st, 1976.

3. Shambleau. This 1933 Northwest Smith story was produced for *2000X - Tales of the next Millennia* - Hollywood Theater of the Ear.

4. The Proud Robot. This was used on *2000X - Tales of the next Millennia* - Hollywood Theater of the Ear. It was credited to Lewis Padgett, which, of course, was C. L. Moore and Henry Kuttner working together.

5. The Twonky. This 1942 story, written with Henry Kuttner, was featured on Sci-Fi Radio.

6. Vintage Season. From 1946, written with Henry Kuttner, this was featured on Sci-Fi Radio.

***

NOVELS AND COLLECTIONS

Please note: All of Henry Kuttner's post 1940 work will also be listed here because Catherine worked on just about everything he wrote; and, so far, every bibliographer who ever tried to separate the two has gotten into trouble. As was earlier mentioned, most of the stories only carried Henry's name because he could get more money for his work than his wife could get for hers. No matter what, it's difficult to read one without the other.

1. The Brass Ring. Written with Henry Kuttner and credited to Lewis Padgett. Published by Duell Sloan and Pearce, New York City, 1946. Hardcover.

2. The Day He Died. Written with Henry Kuttner and credited to Lewis Padgett. Published by Duell Sloan and Pearce, New York City, 1947. Hardcover.

3. Murder in Brass. Written with Henry Kuttner and credited to Lewis Padgett. Published by Bantam Books, New York City, 1947. Softcover. Bantam Book 107.

4. Fury. Written with Henry Kuttner but credited only to Kuttner. Published by Grosset and Dunlap, New York City, 1950. Hardcover.

5. A Gnome There Was. Written with Henry Kuttner and credited to Lewis Padgett. Published by Simon and Schuster, New York City, 1950. Hardcover. Herein: A Gnome There Was, 1941; What You Need, 1945; The Twonky, 1942; The Cure, 1946; Exit the Professor, 1947; See You Later, 1949; Mimsy Were the Borogoves, 1943; Jesting Pilot, 1947; This Is the House, 1946; Rain Check, 1946; and Compliments of the Author, 1942.

6. Tomorrow and Tomorrow - and - The Fairy Chessmen. Written with Henry Kuttner and credited to Lewis Padgett. Published by Gnome Press, New York City, 1951. Hardcover.

7. Judgment Night. Published by Gnome Press, New York City, 1952. Hardcover. Herein: Judgment Night, 1952; Heir Apparent, 1950; Paradise Street, 1950; Promised Land, 1950; and The Code, 1945.

8. Mutant. Written with Henry Kuttner and credited to Lewis Padgett. Published by Gnome Press, New York City, 1952. Hardcover.

9. Robots Have No Tails. Written with Henry Kuttner and credited to Lewis Padgett. Published by Gnome Press, New York City, 1952. Hardcover. Herein: The Proud Robot, 1943; Gallegher Plus, 1943; The World Is Mine, 1943; Ex Machina, 1948; and Time Locker, 1943.

10. Man Drowning. Written with Henry Kuttner but credited only to Kuttner. Published by Harper and Brothers, New York City, 1952. Hardcover.

11. Well of the Worlds. Written with Henry Kuttner and credited to Lewis Padgett. Published by Galaxy Publishing, New York City, 1953. Softcover. Galaxy Novel 17.

12. Ahead of Time. Written with Henry Kuttner but credited only to Kuttner. Published by Ballantine Books, New York City, 1953. It was issued simultaneously in hardcover and paperback. Ballantine Book 30. This contains: About Henry Kuttner - essay by Henry Kuttner; Or Else, 1953; Home Is the Hunter, 1953; By These Presents, 1953; De Profundis, 1953; Camouflage, 1945; Year Day, 1953; Ghost, 1943; Shock, 1943; Pile of Trouble, 1948; and Deadlock, 1942.

13. Shambleau and Others. Published by Gnome Press, New York City, 1953. Hardcover. This contains: Black God's Kiss, 1934; Shambleau, 1933; Black God's Shadow, 1934; Black thirst, 1934; The Tree of Life, 1936; Jirel Meets Magic, 1935; and Scarlet Dream, 1934.

14. Northwest of Earth. Published by Gnome Press, New York City, 1954. Hardcover. Herein: Dust of the Gods, 1934; Lost Paradise, 1936; The Dark Land, 1936; Julhi, 1935; Hellsgarde, 1939; The Cold Gray God, 1935; and Yvala, 1936.

15. Beyond Earth's Gates. Written with Henry Kuttner and credited to Lewis Padgett. Published by Ace Books, New York City 1954. Softcover. Ace Book D-69. This was bound with *Daybreak - 2250* by Andre Norton.

16. Line to Tomorrow. Written with Henry Kuttner and credited to Lewis Padgett. Published by Bantam Books, New York City 1954. Softcover. Bantam Book 1251. Herein: Line to Tomorrow, 1945; A Gnome There Was, 1941; What You Need, 1945; Private Eye, 1949; The Twonky, 1942; Compliments of the Author, 1942; and When the Bough Breaks, 1944.

17. The Challenge from Beyond. Published by The Pennsylvania Dutch Cheese Press, 1954. Stapled mimeographed sheets. A round robin tale, written with: Robert E. Howard; H. P. Lovecraft; **A. Merritt**; and Frank Belknap Long.

18. No Boundaries. Written with Henry Kuttner and credited jointly. Published by Ballantine Books, New York City, 1955. Hardcover and softcover released simultaneously. Ballantine Book 122. This contains: About the Authors - an uncredited essay; Vintage Season, 1946; The Devil We Know, 1941; Home There's No Returning, 1955; Exit the Professor, 1947; and Two-Handed Engine, 1955.

19. Chessboard Planet. Written with Henry Kuttner and credited to Lewis Padgett. Published by Galaxy Publishing, New York City, 1956. Softcover. Galaxy Novel 26. Re-titled re-issue of *The Fairy Chessmen*, 1951.

20. The Murder of Eleanor Pope. Written with Henry Kuttner but credited only to Kuttner. Published by Permabooks, Garden City, New York, 1956. Softcover. Permabook M-3046.

21. The Murder of Ann Avery. Written with Henry Kuttner but credited only to Kuttner. Published by Permabooks, Garden City, New York, 1956. Softcover. Permabook 3058.

22. Doomsday Morning. Published by Doubleday & Company, Garden City, New York, 1957. Hardcover.

23. Murder of a Mistress. Written with Henry Kuttner but credited only to Kuttner. Published by Permabooks, New York City, 1957. Softcover. Permabook M4082.

24. Murder of a Wife. Written with Henry Kuttner but credited only to Kuttner. Published by Permabooks, New York City, 1958. Softcover. Permabook M4096.

25. Destination Infinity. Published by Avon Publications, New York City, 1958. Softcover. Avon Book T-275. Re-titled re-issue of *Fury*, 1950.

26. Shambleau. Published by Galaxy Publishing, New York City, 1958. Softcover. Galaxy Novel 31. This contains: Black Thirst, 1934; Shambleau, 1933; and The Tree of Life, 1936.

27. Shambleau. Published by World Distributors, London, 1961. Softcover. Consul Books 1009. Abridged reprint, containing only six of the seven stories from Shambleau and Others, 1953. Jirel Meets Magic, 1935, was the deleted story.

28. Bypass to Otherness. Written with Henry Kuttner but credited only to Kuttner. Published by Ballantine Books, New York City, 1961. Softcover. Ballantine Book 497K. This collection contains: Cold War, 1949; Call Him Demon, 1946; The Dark Angel, 1946; The Piper's Son, 1945; Absalom, 1946; The Little Things, 1946; Nothing but Gingerbread Left, 1943; and Housing Problem, 1944.

29. Return to Otherness. Written with Henry Kuttner but credited only to Kuttner. Published by Ballantine Books, New York City, 1962. Softcover. Ballantine Book F619. Herein: See You Later, 1949; This Is the House, 1946; The Proud Robot, 1943; Gallegher Plus, 1943; The Ego Machine, 1952; Android, 1951; The Sky Is Falling, 1950; and Juke Box, 1947.

30. Tomorrow and Tomorrow. Written with Henry Kuttner and credited to Lewis Padgett. Published by World Distributors, London, 1963. Softcover. Consul

C.L. Moore

Books 1265. A re-issue of one half of *Tomorrow and Tomorrow* - and - *The Fairy Chessmen*, 1951.

31. The Far Reality. Written with Henry Kuttner and credited to Lewis Padgett. Published by World Distributors, London, 1963. Softcover. Consul Books 1266. A re-titled re-issue of one half of *Tomorrow and Tomorrow* - and - *The Fairy Chessmen*, 1951.

32. Valley of Flame. Written with Henry Kuttner and credited only to Kuttner. Published by Ace Books, New York City, 1964. Softcover. Ace Book F-297.

33. Earth's Last Citadel. Written with Henry Kuttner and credited jointly. Published by Ace Books, New York City, 1964. Softcover. Ace Book F-306.

34. The Dark World. Written with Henry Kuttner and credited only to Kuttner. Published by Ace Books, New York City, 1965. Softcover. Ace Book F-327.

35. The Time Axis. Written with Henry Kuttner and credited only to Kuttner. Published by Ace Books, New York City, 1965. Softcover. Ace Book F-356.

36. The Best of Henry Kuttner - Volume 1. Written with Henry Kuttner and credited only to Kuttner. Published by Mayflower Dell Books, London, 1965. Softcover. Mayflower Book 0547. Herein: Or Else, 1953; Year Day, 1953; Shock, 1943; See You Later, 1949; The Proud Robot, 1943; The Ego Machine, 1952; Juke Box, 1947; Cold War, 1949; Call Him Demon, 1946; The Piper's Son, 1945; Absalom, 1946; Housing Problem, 1944; A Gnome There Was, 1941; The Big Night, 1947; and Don't Look Now, 1948.

37. The Best of Henry Kuttner - Volume 2. Written with Henry Kuttner and credited only to Kuttner. Published by Mayflower Dell Books, London, 1966. Softcover. Mayflower Book 0547. This Contains: The Voice of the Lobster, 1950; Masquerade, 1942; The Iron Standard, 1943; Endowment Policy, 1943; When the Bough Breaks, 1944; Line to Tomorrow, 1945; Clash by Night, 1943; A Wild Surmise, 1953; What You Need, 1945; The Twonky, 1942; Mimsy Were the Borogoves, 1943; The Devil We Know, 1941; Exit the Professor, 1947; and Two-Handed Engine, 1955.

38. Jirel of Joiry. Published by Paperback Library, New York City, 1969. Softcover. Paperback Library Book 63-166. Herein: Jirel Meets Magic, 1935; Black God's Kiss, 1934; Black God's Shadow, 1934; The Dark Land, 1936; and Hellsgarde, 1939.

39. The Mask of Circe. Written with Henry Kuttner and credited only to Kuttner. Published by Ace Books, New York City, 1971. Softcover. Ace Book 52075.

40. The Best of C. L. Moore. Published by Nelson Doubleday - The Science Fiction Book Club, Garden City, New York, 1975. Hardcover. Herein: Forty Years of C. L. Moore - an essay by Lester del Rey; Shambleau, 1933; Black Thirst, 1934; The Bright Illusion, 1934; Black God's kiss, 1934; Tryst in Time, 1936; Greater than Gods, 1949; Fruit of Knowledge, 1940; No Woman Born, 1944; Daemon, 1946; Vintage Season, 1946; and Afterword: Footnote to Shambleau and Others - an essay by C. L. Moore.

41. The Best of Henry Kuttner. Published by Nelson Doubleday - The Science Fiction Book Club, Garden City, New York, 1975. Hardcover. One story here, from 1939, The Misguided Halo, was likely written by Kuttner alone. Herein: Henry Kuttner: A Neglected Master by **Ray Bradbury**; Mimsy Were the Borogoves, 1943; Two-Handed Engine, 1955; The Proud Robot, 1943; The Misguided Halo, 1939; The Voice of the Lobster, 1950; Exit the Professor, 1947; The Twonky, 1942; A Gnome There Was, 1941; The Big Night, 1947; Nothing but Gingerbread Left, 1943; The Iron Standard, 1943; Cold War, 1949; Or Else, 1953; Endowment Policy, 1943; Housing Problem, 1944; What You Need, 1945; and Absalom, 1946.

42. Black God's Shadow. Published by Donald M. Grant, West Kingston, Rhode Island, 1977. Hardcover in a slipcase. A re-titled re-issue of the paperback original, *Jirel of Joiry*, 1969. This contains: Black God's Kiss, 1934; Black God's Shadow, 1934; Jirel Meets Magic, 1935; The Dark Land, 1936; and Hellsgarde, 1939.

43. Clash by Night and Other Stories. Written with Henry Kuttner and credited jointly. Published by Hamlyn books, London, 1980. Softcover. This contains: Introduction by Peter Pinto; Clash by Night, 1943; When the Bough Breaks, 1944; Juke box, 1947; The Ego Machine, 1952; and Vintage Season, 1946.

44. Scarlet Dream. Published by Donald M. Grant, West Kingston, Rhode Island, 1981. Hardcover. Herein: Shambleau, 1933; Black Thirst, 1934; the Tree of Life, 1936; Scarlet Dream, 1934; Dust of the Gods, 1934; Lost Paradise, 1936; Julhi, 1935; The Cold Gray God, 1935; Yvala, 1936; and Song in a Minor Key, 1940.

45. Chessboard Planet and Other Stories. Written with Henry Kuttner and credited jointly. Published by Hamlyn books, London, 1983. Softcover. Herein: Introduction by Peter Pinto; Note on Fairy Chess - essay by Peter Pinto; Chessboard Planet, 1946; Camouflage, 1945; Android, 1951; and Or Else, 1953.

46. Kuttner Times Three. Published by Virgil Utter, Modesto, California, 1988. Softcover. One of the stories here, Bamboo Death, 1936, was written by Kuttner on his own, the other two, The Old Army Game, 1941, and The Wolf of Aragon, 1941, appear to have had some help from Catherine.

47. Vintage Season. Published by Tor Books - Tom Doherty Associates, New York City, 1990. Softcover. Tor Double 18. Bound with In Another Country by **Robert Silverberg**.

48. Secret of the Earth Star and Others. Published by Starmont House, Mercer Island, Washington, 1991. Softcover. One of the stories here, I, the Vampire, was written in 1937; the rest likely had some help from Catherine. Herein: Introduction by Sheldon Jaffery; Secret of the Earth Star, 1942; World Without Air, 1940; What Hath Me?, 1946; Dragon Moon, 1941; I the Vampire, 1937; The Elixir of Invisibility, 1940; The Uncanny Power of Edwin Cobalt, 1940; and Under Your Spell, 1943.

49. Black Gods and Scarlet Dreams. Published by Victor Gollancz, London, 2002. Softcover. This combines the two collections: Black God's Kiss, 1934; Black God's Shadow, 1934; Jirel Meets Magic, 1935; The Dark Land, 1936; and Hellsgarde, 1939; Shambleau, 1933; Black Thirst, 1934; the Tree of Life, 1936; Scarlet Dream, 1934; Dust of the Gods, 1934; Lost Paradise, 1936; Julhi, 1935; The Cold Gray God, 1935; Yvala, 1936; and Song in a Minor Key, 1940.

50. Two-Handed Engine. Written with Henry Kuttner and credited jointly. Published by Centipede Press, New York City, 2005. Hardcover. This contains: Shambleau, 1933; The Graveyard Rats, 1936; A Gnome There Was, 1941; The Twonky, 1942; Compliments of the Author, 1942; Mimsy Were the Borogoves, 1943; Shock, 1943; Reader I Hate You, 1943; The World Is Mine, 1943; When the Bough Breaks, 1944; The Cure, 1946; The Code, 1945; Line to Tomorrow, 1945; Clash by Night, 1943; Ghost, 1943; The Proud Robot, 1943; Nothing but Gingerbread Left, 1943; No Woman Born, 1944; Housing Problem, 1944; What You Need, 1945; Absalom, 1946; Call Him Demon, 1946; Daemon, 1946; Vintage Season, 1946; The Dark Angel, 1946; Before I Wake, 1945; Exit the Professor, 1947; The Big Night, 1947; A Wild Surmise, 1953; Don't Look Now, 1948; Private Eye, 1949; By These Presents, 1953; Home Is the Hunter, 1953; Or Else, 1953; Year Day, 1953; A Cross of Centuries, 1958; and Two-Handed Engine, 1955.

51. Black God's Kiss. Published by Planet Stories Library - Paizo Publishing, New York City, 2007. Softcover. Herein: Where No Man Had Gone Before - an essay by Suzy McKee Charnas; Black God's Kiss, 1934; Black God's Shadow, 1934; Jirel Meets Magic, 1935; The Dark Land, 1936; Hellsgarde, 1939; Quest of the Starstone, 1937; and About the Author - uncredited essay.

52. Northwest of Earth: The Complete Northwest Smith. Published by Planet Stories Library - Paizo Publishing, New York City, 2008. Softcover. This contains: Teaching the World to Dream - an essay by C. J. Cherryh; Shambleau, 1933; Black Thirst, 1934; Scarlet Dream, 1934; Dust of Gods, 1934; Julhi, 1935; Nymph of Darkness, 1935 - written with Forrest J. Ackerman, 1935; The Cold Gray God, 1935; Yvala, 1936; Lost Paradise, 1936; The Tree of Life, 1936; Quest of the Starstone, 1937; Werewoman, 1938; Song in a Minor Key, 1940; and About the Author - uncredited essay.

53. Miracle in Three Dimensions and Other Stories - The Long Lost Pulp Classics Volume 1. Published by Isle Press, United Kingdom, 2008. Softcover. This contains: The Bright Illusion, 1934; Greater Glories, 1935; Tryst in Time, 1936; Greater Than Gods, 1939; Miracle in Three Dimensions, 1939; Fruit of Knowledge, 1940; There Shall Be Darkness, 1942; Doorway Into Time, 1943; and Here Lies.

***

RELATED

1. Literary Descendants of C. L. Moore. By Rosemarie Arbur. G. K. Hall, Boston, 1982. Hardcover.

Frederik Pohl.

Frederik George Pohl Jr. was born somewhere in the United States on November 26th, 1919. His family moved around a lot, through Texas, New Mexico, California and on into New York City by 1930, where young Frederik discovered Science Wonder Stories Quarterly and was struck with, as he put it, an "irremediable virus."

Ten years later, working with C. M. Kornbluth as S. D. Gottesman, he sold his first short story, Trouble in Time, to Astonishing Stories. It was used in the December 1940 issue, along with: Half-Breeds on Venus by **Isaac Asimov**; The Door at the Opera by Ray Cummings; Rocket of Metal Men by Manly Wade Wellman; Quicksands of Youthwardness - part 2 of 3 by Malcolm Jameson; Hold That Comet! By F. H. Hauser and H. B. Fyfe; and Age of the Cephalods by John C. Craig.

It was likely just a coincidence that Pohl was the editor of Astonishing Stories at the time, his reign there running from the first issue in February 1940 until September 1941. He was also the editor of Super Science Stories, from its inaugural issue in March 1940, until August 1941. He was only nineteen years old when he started his career as an editor. And he went on to edit Galaxy Science Fiction from December 1961 until May 1969 and If - Worlds of Science Fiction from November 1961 until May 1969, when Galaxy and If were both sold to Universal Publishing. He also edited Worlds of Tomorrow from April 1963 until May 1967; and Star Science Fiction Stories for one issue, January 1958.

In fact, that was Star's only issue. It had started life as an anthology series from Ballantine Books, the first two in 1953 and the third one in 1954. In 1958, with Pohl still editing, Ballantine attempted to re-launch Star as a magazine. That flopped and they went back to the paperback book format, printing three more anthologies in 1958 and 1959, all edited by Fred Pohl.

He also edited the only two issues of International Science Fiction, November 1967 and June 1968 and, through the 1970s, functioned as an editor at Bantam Books. He once said that the joy for him, as an editor, was in finding something that no one else thought worth publishing and "making it go."

Not only did he work as an editor, he also represented **Isaac Asimov**, among others, as a literary agent. In fact, it was Pohl that placed Asimov's first science fiction novel, Pebble in the Sky, 1950, with Doubleday.

Most of this grew out of a fan organization called The Futurians which was founded in 1938. It's membership included Pohl, of course, along with: **Isaac Asimov**; **Donald A. Wollheim**; Richard Wilson; Cyril M. Kornbluth; **James Blish**; Robert W. Lowndes; **Damon Knight**; Virginia Kidd; Larry T. Shaw; Walter Kubilius; and others, including Pohl's first of five wives, Leslie Perri. (The other wives, in order: Dorothy LesTina; Judith Merril; Carol Metcal Ulf; and, currently, Elizabeth Anne Hull.)

During the early 1940s, almost half of the American science fiction and fantasy magazines were being edited by members of The Futurians. Pohl with Astonishing and Super Science; Robert W. Lowndes, with Science Fiction and Future Fiction among others; and **Donald A. Wollheim** first with magazines and then on to Avon Books. But nearly all the members of The Futurians had some serious influence on the world of science fiction as writers, editors, agents and publishers.

Even with his editing and agent duties, Pohl still had time to establish himself as an author of some considerable significance... On his own, and in collaboration with C. M. Kornbluth or **Jack Williamson** or Lester del Rey and, recently, Elizabeth Ann Hull, Thomas T. Thomas and **Arthur C. Clarke**, (who chose Pohl to complete his final novel, The Last Theorem, 2008) he has created a large body of truly excellent work while gathering an assortment of Hugo and Nebula Awards along the way.

Gateway is usually his highest priced first edition. It lists between $1,200.00 and $1,500.00.

Pen names used: S. D. Gottesman; James MacCreigh; Paul Dennis Lavond; Warren F. Howard; Charles Satterfield; Paul Flehr; Edson McCann; and Ernest Mason.

***

AWARDS

1966. Hugo Award for If as Best Professional Magazine.
1967. Hugo Award for If as Best Professional Magazine.
1968. Hugo Award for If as Best Professional Magazine.
1973. Hugo Award for Best Short Story, The Meeting, written with C. M. Kornbluth - The Magazine of Fantasy and Science Fiction, November 1972.
1976. Nebula Award for Best Novel, Man Plus.
1977. Nebula Award for Best Novel, Gateway.
1978. Hugo Award for Best Novel, Gateway.
1978. Locus Poll Award for Best Novel, Gateway.
1979. Locus Poll Award for Best Reference Book, The Way The Future Was.
1980. National Book Award for Jem.
1986. Hugo Award for Best Short Story, Fermi and Frost.
1992. Nebula Grand Master Award.
1998. Inducted into The Science Fiction Hall of Fame.
2009. The J. Lloyd Eaton Lifetime Achievement Award in Science Fiction, the second only recipient of this award.

***

FILM AND TELEVISION

1. Many Happy Returns. Worked as a writer on this Raymond Z. Gallum story, adapting it for the television series Tales of Tomorrow, October 24th, 1952, Season 2, Episode 8. This was directed by Don Medford and starred: Flora Campbell; Edwin Cooper; Gene Raymond; Clifford Sales; and Richard Trask.

2. The Midas Plague. This 1954 short story was adapted for the television series Out of the Unknown in 1965. It was shown on December 20th, 1965, Season 1, Episode 12. Directed by Peter Sasdy, the show starred: Graham Stark; Sam Kydd; Ann Lawson; Geoffrey Alexander; Sydney Arnold; Richard Davies; and others.

3. Tunnel Under the World. This 1955 short story was adapted for the television series Out of the Unknown in 1966. It was shown on December 1st, 1966, Season 2, Episode 8. Directed by Alan Cooke, the show starred: Ronald Hines; Petra Davies; Gay Hamilton; Timothy Bateson; Peter Madden; and others.

4. Tunnel Under the World. This 1955 story was adapted as a film in Italy in 1969, titled Tunnel sotto il mondo, Il. Directed by Luigi Cozzi, it starred: Alberto Moro; Bruno Salviero; Anna Mantovani; Lello Maraniello; Gretel Fehr; and many others.

5. Understanding Sex. This was a 1994 television documentary that featured **Frederik Pohl** as one of the interviewees.

***

RADIO

1. Tunnel Under the World. This 1955 was used on X Minus One on March 14th, 1956. It was broadcast again on September 4th, 1956.

2. The Haunted Corpse. From 1957, this story was used on X Minus One on July 25th, 1957 and again on December 12th, 1957.

3. The Map Makers. This 1955 story was used on X Minus One on September 26th, 1956.

4. The Space Merchants. This 1953 story was used on CBS Radio Workshop in two parts, February 10th, 1957 and February 24th, 1957.

5. Target One. From 1955, this story was used on X Minus One on December 26th, 1957.

6. The Meeting. Written with C. M. Kornbluth, this was used on Mindwebs in 1978.

7. The Shape of Things to Come. Based on The Midas Plague, 1954, this was used on BBC on September 4th, 1991.

8. Tunnel Under the World. This was used on BBC Radio in 2000.

9. Hour 25. Pohl was Mike Hodel's guest on July 13th, 2003.

10. The Art, Science and Combat of Collaboration. This was recorded at a panel discussion between **Frederik Pohl** and **Jack Williamson** at ConFusion, 1977. It was broadcast on-line in March 2007.

***

NOVELS AND COLLECTIONS

1. The Space Merchants. With C. M. Kornbluth. Published by Ballantine Books, New York City, 1953. Released simultaneously in hardcover and softcover. Ballantine Book 21.

2. Search the Sky. With C. M. Kornbluth. Published by Ballantine Books, New York City, 1954. Released simultaneously in hardcover and softcover. Ballantine Book 61.

3. Undersea Quest. With **Jack Williamson**. Published by Gnome Press, New York City, 1954. Hardcover.

4. Gladiator-at-Law. With C. M. Kornbluth. Published by Ballantine Books, New York City, 1955. Released simultaneously in hardcover and softcover. Ballantine Book 107.

5. Preferred Risk. Released as by Edson McCann; written with Lester del Rey. Published by Simon and Schuster, New York City, 1955. Hardcover.

6. A Town Is Drowning. With C. M. Kornbluth. Published by Ballantine Books, New York City, 1955. Released simultaneously in hardcover and softcover. Ballantine Book 123.

7. Undersea Fleet. With **Jack Williamson**. Published by Gnome Press, New York City, 1956. Hardcover.

8. Alternating Currents. Published by Ballantine Books, New York City, 1956. Released simultaneously in hardcover and softcover. Ballantine Book 130. This collection contains: Happy Birthday, Dear Jesus, 1956; The Ghost Maker, 1954; Let the Ants Try, 1949; Pythias, 1955; The Mapmakers, 1955; Rafferty's Reasons, 1955; Target One, 1955; Grandy Devil, 1955; The Tunnel Under the World, 1955; and What to Do Until the Analyst Comes, 1956.

9. Sorority House. Released as by Jordan Park, written with C. M. Kornbluth. Published by Lion Library Editions, New York City, 1956. Softcover. Lion Library LL97.

10. The God of Channel 1. Released as by Donald Stacy. Published by Ballantine Books, New York City, 1956. Released simultaneously in hardcover and softcover. Ballantine Book 137. Pohl's contribution to this was anonymous.

11. Presidential Year. With C. M. Kornbluth. Published by Ballantine Books, New York City, 1956. Released simultaneously in hardcover and softcover. Ballantine Book 144.

12. Turn the Tigers Loose. Released as by Walter Lasly. Published by Ballantine Books, New York City, 1956. Released simultaneously in hardcover and softcover. Ballantine Book 173. Pohl's contribution to this was anonymous.

13. Slave Ship. Published by Ballantine Books, New York City, 1957. Released simultaneously in hardcover and softcover. Ballantine Book 192.

14. Edge of the City. Published by Ballantine Books, New York City, 1957. Softcover. Ballantine Book 199.

Frederick Pohl

15. The Case Against Tomorrow. Published by Ballantine Books, New York City, 1957. Softcover. Ballantine Book 206. Herein: The Midas Plague, 1954; The Census Takers, 1956; The Candle Lighter, 1955; The Celebrated No-Hit Inning, 1956; Wapshot's Demon, 1956; and My Lady Green Sleeves, 1957.

16. Undersea City. With **Jack Williamson**. Published by Gnome Press, Hicksville, New York, 1958. Hardcover.

17. Tomorrow Times Seven. Published by Ballantine Books, New York City, 1959. Softcover. Ballantine Book 325K. This contains: The Haunted Corpse, 1957; The Middle of Nowhere, 1955; The Gentle Venusian, 1958; The Day of the Boomer Dukes 1956; Survival Kit, 1957; The Knights of Arthur, 1958; and To See Another Mountain, 1959.

18. Wolfbane. With C. M. Kornbluth. Published by Ballantine Books, New York City, 1959. Softcover. Ballantine Book 335K.

19. The Man Who Ate the World. Published by Ballantine Books, New York City, 1960. Softcover. Ballantine Book 397K. Herein: The Man Who Ate the World, 1956; The Wizards of Pung's Corners, 1958; The Snowmen, 1959; and The Day the Icicle Works Closed, 1960.

20. Drunkard's Walk. Published by Ballantine Books, New York City, 1960. Softcover. Ballantine Book 439K.

21. Wolfbane. With C. M. Kornbluth. Published by Victor Gollancz, London, 1960. First hardcover edition.

22. Drunkard's Walk. Published by Gnome Press, Hicksville, New York, 1961. First hardcover edition.

23. Turn Left At Thursday. Published by Ballantine Books, New York City, 1961. Softcover. Ballantine Book 476K. This contains: Mars by Moonlight, 1958; The Richest Man in Levittown, 1959; The Seven Deadly Virtues, 1958; The Martian in the Attic, 1960; Third Offense, 1958; The Hated, 1958; and I Plinglot, Who You?, 1959.

24. The Wonder Effect. With C. M. Kornbluth. Published by Ballantine Books, New York City, 1962. Softcover. Ballantine Book F638. This contains: Introduction by **Frederik Pohl**; A Gentle Dying, 1961; Nightmare with Zeppelins, 1958; Best Friend, 1941; The World of Myrion Flowers, 1961; Trouble in Time, 1940; The Engineer, 1956; Mars-Tube, 1941; and The Quaker Cannon, 1961.

25. An Abominable Earthman. Published by Ballantine Books, New York City, 1963. Softcover. Ballantine Book F685. This contains: The Abominable Earthman, 1961; We Never Mention Aunt Nora, 1958; A Life and a Half, 1959; Punch, 1961; The Martian Star Gazers, 1963; Whatever Counts, 1959; and Three Portraits and a Prayer, 1962.

26. The Reefs of Space. With **Jack Williamson**. Published by Ballantine Books, New York City, 1964. Softcover. Ballantine Book U2172.

27. Starchild. With **Jack Williamson**. Published by Ballantine Books, New York City, 1965. Softcover. Ballantine Book U2176.

28. The Reefs of Space. With **Jack Williamson**. Published by Dennis Dobson, London, 1965. First hardcover edition.

29. A Plague of Pythons. Published by Ballantine Books, New York City, 1965. Softcover. Ballantine Book U2174.

30. Starchild. With **Jack Williamson**. Published by Dennis Dobson, London, 1966. First hardcover edition.

31. Digits and Dastards. Published by Ballantine Books, New York City, 1966. Softcover. Ballantine Book U2178. Herein: Introduction by **Frederik Pohl**; The Children of the Night, 1964; The Fiend, 1964; Earth Eighteen, 1966; Father of the Stars, 1964; The Five Hells of Orion, 1963; With Redfern on Capella XII, 1955; How to Count on Your Fingers, 1956; and On Binary Digits and Human Habits - an essay, 1962.

32. Alternating Currents. Published by Penguin Books, Middlesex, England, 1966. Softcover. Penguin Book 2452. This dumped Happy Birthday, Dear Jesus, 1956, and replaced it with The Children of Night, 1964.

33. The Frederik Pohl Omnibus. Published by Victor Gollancz, London, 1966. Hardcover. Herein: The Day the Icicle Works Closed, 1960; The Middle of Nowhere, 1955; The Man Who Ate the World, 1956; The Haunted Corpse, 1957; Survival Kit, 1957; The Knights of Arthur, 1958; Mars by Moonlight, 1958; The Seven Deadly Virtues, 1958; The Wizards of Pung's Corners, 1958; The Snowmen, 1959; The Day of the Boomer Dukes, 1956; The Waging of the Peace, 1959; and I Plinglot, Who You?, 1959.

34. A Plague of Pythons. Published by Victor Gollancz, London, 1966. First hardcover edition.

35. The Wonder Effect. With C. M. Kornbluth. Published by Victor Gollancz, London, 1967. First hardcover edition.

36. Digits and Dastards. Published by Dobson Books, London, 1968. First hardcover edition, with a misspelling of Pohl's name on the title page, Frederick instead of Frederik. Herein: Introduction by **Frederik Pohl**; The Children of the Night, 1964; The Fiend, 1964; Earth Eighteen, 1966; Father of the Stars, 1964; The Five Hells of Orion, 1963; With Redfern on Capella XII, 1955; How to Count on Your Fingers, 1956; and On Binary Digits and Human Habits - an essay, 1962.

37. The Age of Pussyfoot. Published by Trident Press, New York City, 1969. Hardcover.

38. Rogue Star. With **Jack Williamson**. Published by Ballantine Books, New York City, 1969. Softcover. Ballantine Book 01797.

39. Day Million. Published by Ballantine Books, New York City, 1970. Softcover. This contains: Introduction by **Frederik Pohl**; Day Million, 1966; Under Two Moons, 1965; The Day After the Day the Martians Came, 1967; Speed Trap, 1967; It's a

Young World, 1941; The Deadly Mission of Phineas Snodgrass, 1962; The Schematic Man, 1969; Way Up Yonder, 1959; Making Love, 1966; and Small Lords, 1957.

40. Day Million. Published by Victor Gollancz, London, 1971. First hardcover edition. Herein: Introduction by **Frederik Pohl**; Day Million, 1966; Under Two Moons, 1965; The Day After the Day the Martians Came, 1967; Speed Trap, 1967; It's a Young World, 1941; The Deadly Mission of Phineas Snodgrass, 1962; The Schematic Man, 1969; Way Up Yonder, 1959; Making Love, 1966; and Small Lords, 1957.

41. The Gold At the Starbow's End. Published by Ballantine Books, New York City, 1972. Softcover. Ballantine Book 02775. Herein: The Gold at the Starbow's End, 1972; Sad Solarian Screenwriter Sam, 1972; Shaffery Among the Immortals, 1972; and The Merchants of Venus, 1972.

42. Rogue Star. With **Jack Williamson**. Published by Dennis Dobson, London, 1972. First hardcover edition, with a misspelling of Pohl's name on the title page, Frederick instead of Frederik.

43. The Gold At the Starbow's End. Published by Victor Gollancz, London, 1973. First hardcover edition. Herein: The Gold at the Starbow's End, 1972; Sad Solarian Screenwriter Sam, 1972; Shaffery Among the Immortals, 1972; and The Merchants of Venus, 1972.

44. The Best of Frederik Pohl. Edited by Lester del Rey. Published by Nelson Doubleday - The Science Fiction Book Club, Garden City, New York, 1975. Hardcover. This contains: A Variety of Excellence - an essay by Lester del Rey; Tunnel Under the World, 1955; Punch, 1961; Three Portraits and a Prayer, 1962; Day Million, 1966; Happy Birthday, Dear Jesus, 1956; We Never Mention Aunt Nora, 1958; Father of the Stars, 1964; The Day the Martians Came, 1967; Midas Plague, 1954; The Snowmen, 1959; How to Count on Your Fingers, 1956; Grandy Devil, 1955; Speed Trap, 1967; The Richest Man in Levittown, 1959; The Day the Icicle Works Closed, 1960; Hated; The Martian in the Attic, 1960; The Census Takers, 1956; The Children of Night, 1964; and What the Author Has to Say About All This - an essay by **Frederik Pohl**.

45. Farthest Star. With **Jack Williamson**. Published by Ballantine Books, New York City, 1975. Softcover. Ballantine Book 24330.

46. The Early Pohl. Published by Doubleday & Company, Garden City, New York, 1976. Hardcover. Herein: Introduction by **Frederik Pohl**; Elegy to a Dead Planet: Luna as by Elton Andrews, 1937; The Dweller in the Ice, 1941; The King's Eye, 1941; It's a Young World, 1941; Daughters of Eternity, 1942; Earth Farewell, 1943; Conspiracy on Callisto, 1943; Highwayman of the Void, 1944; and Double Cross as by James MacCreigh, 1944.

47. Man Plus. Published by Random House, New York City, 1976. Hardcover.

48. In the Problem Pit. Published by Bantam Books, New York City, 1976. Softcover. Bantam Book T8857. Herein: Introduction: Science Fiction Games - an essay by **Frederik Pohl**; In the Problem Pit, 1973; Let the Ants Try as by James MacCreigh, 1949; To See Another Mountain, 1959; The Deadly Mission of Phineas Snodgrass, 1962; Golden Ages Gone Away - an essay, 1972; Rafferty's Reasons, 1955; I Remember a Winter, 1972; The Schematic Man, 1969; What To do Until the Analyst Comes, 1956; Some Joys Under the Star, 1973; The Man Who Ate the World, 1956; and SF - The Game Playing Literature - a essay by **Frederik Pohl**.

49. Critical Mass. With Cyril M. Kornbluth. Published by Bantam Books, New York City, 1977. Softcover. Bantam Book 19048-0. This contains: Introduction by **Frederik Pohl**; The Quaker Cannon, 1961; Mute Inglorious Tam, 1974; The World of Myrion Flowers, 1961; The Gift of Garigolli, 1974; A Gentle Dying, 1961; A Hint of Henbane, 1961; The Meeting, 1972; The Engineer, 1956; Nightmare with Zeppelins, 1958; Critical Mass, 1962; and Afterword by **Frederik Pohl**.

50. Gateway. Published by St. Martin's Press, New York City, 1977. Hardcover.

51. The Starchild Trilogy. With **Jack Williamson**. Published by Nelson Doubleday - The Science Fiction Book Club, Garden City, New York, 1977. Hardcover. An omnibus edition, this gathered: The Reefs of Space, 1964; Starchild, 1965; and Rogue Star, 1969.

52. The Survival Kit. Published by Panther Books, London, 1979. Softcover. Herein: The Knights of Arthur, 1958; Mars by Moonlight, 1958; The Haunted Corpse, 1957; The Day of the Boomer Dukes, 1956; Survival Kit, 1957; and I Plinglot, Who You?, 1959.

53. Jem. Published by St. Martin's Press, New York City, 1979. Hardcover.

54. Before the Universe. With C. M. Kornbluth. Published by Bantam Books, New York City, 1980. Softcover. This collection contains: Introduction by **Frederik Pohl**; Mars Tube, 1941; Trouble in Time, 1940; Vacant World, 1940; Best Friend, 1941; Before the Universe, 1940; The Extrapolated Dimwit, 1942; and Afterword by **Frederik Pohl**.

55. Beyond the Blue Event Horizon. Published by Del Rey - Ballantine Books, New York City, 1980. Hardcover.

56. This Is My Best. Published by Berkley Books, New York City, 1981. Hardcover.

57. The Cool War. Published by Del Rey - Ballantine Books, New York City, 1981. Hardcover.

58. Syzygy. Published by Bantam Books, New York City, 1982. Softcover.

59. Starburst. Published by Del Rey - Ballantine Books, New York City, 1982. Hardcover.

60. Planets Three. Published by Berkley Books, New York City, 1982. Softcover. This contains: Introduction by **Frederik Pohl**; Figurehead, 1982; Red Moon of Danger, 1951; and Donovan Had a Dream, 1947.

Frederick Pohl

61. BiPohl. Published by Ballantine Books, New York City, 1982. Softcover. An omnibus edition that collected: Drunkard's Walk, 1960; and The Age of Pussyfoot, 1969.

62. Midas World. Published by St. Martin's Press, New York City, 1983. Hardcover. Herein: The Fire Bringer, 1983; The Midas Plague, 1954; The Servant of the People, 1982; The Man Who Ate the World, 1956; The Farmer on the Dole, 1982; The Lord of the Skies, 1983; and The New Neighbors, 1983.

63. Wall Around a Star. With **Jack Williamson**. Published by Del Rey - Ballantine Books, New York City, 1983. Softcover.

64. The Saga of Cuckoo. With **Jack Williamson**. Published by Nelson Doubleday - The Science Fiction Book Club, Garden City, New York, 1983. A omnibus edition that collects: Farthest Star, 1975; and Wall Around a Star, 1983.

65. Heechee Rendezvous. Published by Del Rey - Ballantine Books, New York City, 1984. Hardcover.

66. The Years of the City. Published by Timescape Books, New York City, 1984. Hardcover. This contains: Introduction by **Frederik Pohl**; When New York Hit the Fan, 1984; The Greening of Bed-Stuy, 1984; The Blister, 1984; Second Hand Sky, 1984; and Gwenanada and the Supremes, 1984.

67. Pohlstars. Published by Del Rey - Ballantine Books, New York City, 1984. Softcover. This contains: Introduction by **Frederik Pohl**; The Sad Sweet Queen of the Grazing Isles, 1984; The High Test, 1983; Spending a Day at the Lottery Fair, 1983; Second Coming, 1983; Enjoy, Enjoy, 1974; Growing Up in Edge City, 1975; We Purchased People, 1974; Rem the Rememberer, 1977; The Mother Trip, 1975; A Day in the Life of Able Charlie, 1976; The Way It Was, 1977; Introduction to the Translation: The Wizard Masters of Peng-Shi - essay by F. Gwynplaine MacIntyre; The Wizard Masters of Peng-Shi Angle, 1984; and Notes - essay by F. Gwynplaine MacIntyre..

68. The Merchant's War. Published by St. Martin's Press, New York City, 1984. Hardcover.

69. Black Star Rising. Published by Del Rey - Ballantine Books, New York City, 1985. Hardcover.

70. Venus, Inc. Published by Nelson Doubleday - The Science Fiction Book Club, Garden City, New York, 1985. Hardcover. An omnibus edition that gathered The Space Merchants, 1953, written with C. M. Kornbluth; and The Merchants War, 1984.

71. The Coming of Quantum Cats. Published by Bantam Books, New York City, 1986. Softcover, followed by a hardcover edition three months later, in July.

72. Terror. Published by Berkley Books, New York City, 1986. Softcover.

73. Our Best: The Best of Frederik Pohl and C. M. Kornbluth. Published by Baen Books, New York City, 1987. Softcover. Herein: Introduction by **Frederik Pohl**; Trouble in Time, 1940; Mars Tube, 1941; The Stories of the Sixties - an essay by **Frederik Pohl**, 1987; Critical Mass, 1962; The World of Myrion Flowers, 1961; The Engineer, 1956; A Gentle Dying, 1961; Nightmare with Zeppelins, 1958; The Quaker Cannon, 1961; The 60/40 Stories - an essay by **Frederik Pohl**, 1987; Epilogue to The Space Merchants - an essay by **Frederik Pohl**, 1987; Gravy Planet - excerpt, 1987; The Final Stories - an essay by **Frederik Pohl**, 1987; Mute Inglorious Tam, 1974; The Gift of Garigolli, 1974; and The Meeting, 1972.

74. The Annals of Heechee. Published by Del Rey - Ballantine Books, New York City, 1987. Hardcover.

75. Chernobyl. Published by Bantam Books, New York City, 1987. Hardcover.

76. Land's End. With **Jack Williamson**. Published by Tor Books - Tom Doherty Associates, New York City, 1988. Hardcover.

77. Narabedla Ltd. Published by Del Rey - Ballantine Books, New York City, 1988. Hardcover.

78. The Day the Martians Came. Published in a limited edition by The Easton Press, New York City, November, 1988, followed by the regular trade edition from St. Martin's Press, New York City, December, 1988. Hardcover. This contains: Extract from the Congressional Record, 1988; A Martian Christmas, 1987; From the New York Times: Martians Lack Language but Possess Organized Society, 1988; Sad Screenwriter Sam, 1972; NBC Nightly News: Ferdie Dead, 1988; The View from Mars Hill, 1987; Scientific American: Martian Polar Wanderings, 1988; Saucery, 1986; New Scientist: Mars at the British Ass, 1988; The Beltway Bandit, 1988; The President's News Conference, 1988; Too Much Loosestrife, 1987; Oprah Winfrey, 1988; Iriadeska's Martians, 1986; Notes from the British Interplanetary Society, 1988; The Missioner, 1988; Time Magazine: We Wait with Eagerness and Joy, 1988; Across the River, 1988; The Day After the Day the Martians Came, 1967; and Huddling, 1988.

79. Homegoing. Published by Del Rey - Ballantine Books, New York City, 1989. Hardcover.

80. The Gateway Trip: Tales and Vignettes of the Heechee. Published by Del Rey - Ballantine Books, New York City, 1990. Hardcover. This contains: The Visit, 1990; The Merchants of Venus, 1972; The Gateway Asteroid, 1990; The Starseekers, 1990; The Home Planet, 1990; Other Worlds, 1990; Heechee Treasures, 1990; Looking for Company, 1990; The Age of Gold, 1990; and In the Core, 1990.

81. The World at the End of Time. Published by Del Rey - Ballantine Books, New York City, 1990. Hardcover.

82. The Singers of Time. With **Jack Williamson**. Published by Doubleday Foundation, Garden City, New York, 1991. Hardcover.

83. Outnumbering the Dead. Published by Legend Books, London, 1991. Hardcover.

84. Mining the Oort. Published by Del Rey - Ballantine Books, New York City, 1992. Hardcover.

113

85. The Undersea Trilogy. With **Jack Williamson**. Published by Baen Books, New York City, 1992. Softcover. An omnibus edition that collected: Undersea Quest, 1954; Undersea Fleet, 1956; and Undersea City, 1958.

86. Mars Plus. With Thomas T. Thomas. Published by Baen Books, New York City, 1994. Hardcover.

87. The Voices of Heaven. Published by Tor Books - Tom Doherty Associates, New York City, 1994. Hardcover.

88. The Other End of Time. Published by Tor Books - Tom Doherty Associates, New York City, 1996. Hardcover.

89. The Siege of Eternity. Published by Tor Books - Tom Doherty Associates, New York City, 1997. Hardcover.

90. O Pioneer! Published by Tor Books - Tom Doherty Associates, New York City, 1998. Hardcover.

91. The Far Shore of Time. Published by Tor Books - Tom Doherty Associates, New York City, 1999. Hardcover.

92. The Boy Who Would Live Forever. Published by Tor Books - Tom Doherty Associates, New York City, 2004. Hardcover.

93. Platinum Pohl: The Collected Best Stories. Published by Tor Books - Tom Doherty Associates, New York City, 2005. Hardcover. Herein: Introduction by James Frenkel; The Merchants of Venus, 1972; The Things That Happen, 1985; The High Test, 1983; My Lady Green Sleeves, 1957; The Kindly Isle, 1984; The Middle of Nowhere, 1955; I Remember a Winter, 1972; The Greening of Bed-Stuy, 1984; To See Another Mountain, 1959; The Mapmakers, 1955; Spending a Day at the Lottery Fair, 1983; The Celebrated No-Hit Inning, 1956; Some Joys Under the Star, 1973; Servant of the People, 1983; Waiting for the Olympians, 1988; Criticality, 1984; Shaffery Among the Immortals, 1972; The Day the Icicle Works Closed, 1960; Saucery, 1986; The Gold at the Starbow's End, 1972; Growing Up in Edge City, 1975; The Knights of Arthur, 1958; Creation Myths of the Recently Extinct, 1994; The Meeting - with C. M. Kornbluth, 1972; Let the Ants Try, 1949; Speed Trap, 1967; The Day the Martians Came, 1967; Day Million, 1966; The Mayor of Mare Tranq, 1996; Fermi and Frost, 1985; and Afterword: Fifty Years and Counting - essay by **Frederik Pohl**, 2005.

94. The Last Theorem. With **Arthur C. Clarke**. Published by Harper Voyager - Harper Collins, London, July 2008, followed one month later by the American edition from Del Rey - Ballantine Books, August 2008. Hardcover.

***

ANTHOLOGIES

1. Beyond the End of Time. Published by Permabooks, Garden City, New York, 1952. Softcover. Permabook P145. This contains: The Embassy by **Donald A. Wollheim** and C. M. Kornbluth writing as Martin Pearson, 1942; The Hunted by John D. MacDonald, 1949; Heredity by **Isaac Asimov**, 1941; Rock Diver by **Harry Harrison**, 1951; The Little Black Bag by C. M. Kornbluth, 1950; The Lonely Planet by Murray Leinster, 1949; Operation Peep by John Wyndham, 1951; Let the Ants Try by **Frederik Pohl** writing as James MacCreigh, 1949; There Will Come Soft Rains by **Ray Bradbury**, 1950; Scanners Live in Vain by Cordwainer Smith, 1950; Such Interesting Neighbors by Jack Finney, 1951; Bridge Crossing by Dave Dryfoos, 1951; Letter from the Stars by **A. E. van Vogt**, 1949; Love in the Dark by H. L. Gold, 1951; Obviously Suicide by S. Fowler Wright, 1951; Rescue Party by **Arthur C. Clarke**, 1946; Stepson of Space by Raymund Z. Gallum, 1940; Death is the Penalty by Judith Merril, 1949; and Beyond Doubt by **Robert A. Heinlein** writing as Lyle Monroe and Elma Wentz, 1941.

2. Tomorrow the Stars. Credited to **Robert A. Heinlein** but the actual editing was done by **Frederik Pohl** and Judith Merril. Published by Doubleday & Company, Garden City, New York, 1952. Hardcover. This collected: I'm Scared by Jack Finney, 1951; The Silly Season by C. M. Kornbluth, 1950; The Report on the Barnhouse Effect by Kurt Vonnegut Jr., 1950; The Tourist Trade by Bob Tucker, 1950; Rainmaker by John Reese, 1949; Absalom by **Henry Kuttner**, 1946; The Monster by Lester del Rey, 1951; Jay Score by **Eric Frank Russell**, 1941; Betelgeuse Bridge by William Tenn, 1950; Survival Ship by Judith Merril, 1950; Keyhole by Murray Leinster, 1951; Misbegotten Missionary by **Isaac Asimov**, 1950; The Sack by William Morrison, 1950; and Poor Superman by **Fritz Leiber**, 1951.

3. Shadow of Tomorrow. Published by Permabooks, Garden City, New York, 1953. Softcover. Permabook P236. Herein: The Year of the Jackpot by **Robert A. Heinlein**, 1952; A Bad Day for Sales by **Fritz Leiber**, 1953; C-Chute by **Isaac Asimov**, 1951; Perfect Creature by John Wyndham, 1937; The Marching Morons by C. M. Kornbluth, 1951; Transfer Point by Anthony Boucher, 1950; Watchbird by Robert Sheckley, 1953; To A Ripe Old Age by **Wilson Tucker**, 1952; Orphans of the Void by Michael Shaara, 1952; The Old Order by Lester del Rey, 1951; Genesis by H. Beam Piper, 1951; Halo by **Hal Clement**, 1952; Common Time by **James Blish**, 1953; Love by Richard Wilson, 1952; The Misogynist by James E. Gunn, 1952; The Luckiest Man in Denv by C. M. Kornbluth writing as Simon Eisner, 1952; and Not a Creature was Stirring by Dean Evans, 1951.

4. Star Science Fiction Stories. Published by Ballantine Books, New York City, 1953. Released simultaneously in hardcover and softcover. Ballantine Book 16. These were new stories: The Deserter by William Tenn; The Chronoclasm by John Wyndham; The Journey by Murray Leinster (Will F. Jenkins); A Wild Surmise by Henry Kuttner and **C. L. Moore**; Nobody Here But by **Isaac Asimov**; A Scent of Sarsaparilla by **Ray Bradbury**; The Nine Billion Names of God by **Arthur C. Clarke**; Idealist by Lester del Rey; The Man with English by H. L. Gold; Dominoes by C. M. Kornbluth; The Night He Cried by **Fritz Leiber**; Country Doctor by William Morrison; The Last Weapon by Robert Sheckley; and Contraption by Clifford D. Simak.

Frederick Pohl

5. Star Science Fiction Stories 2. Published by Ballantine Books, New York City, 1954. Released simultaneously in hardcover and softcover. Ballantine Book 55. Herein: Disappearing Act by **Alfred Bester**; The Clinic by **Theodore Sturgeon**; The Congruent People by A. J. Budrys; Critical Factor by **Hal Clement**; It's a Good Life by Jerome Bixby; A Pound of Cure by Lester del Rey; The Purple Fields by Robert Crane; FYI by **James Blish**; Conquest by Anthony Boucher; Hormones by Fletcher Pratt; The Odor of Thought by Robert Sheckley; The Happiest Creature by **Jack Williamson**; The Remorseful by C. M. Kornbluth; and Friend of the Family by Richard Wilson.

6. Star Short Novels. Published by Ballantine Books, New York City, 1954. Released simultaneously in hardcover and softcover. Ballantine Book 89. This contains: Introduction by Frederick Pohl; To Here and the Easel by **Theodore Sturgeon**, 1954; For I Am a Jealous People by Lester Del Rey, 1954; and Little Men by Jessamyn West, 1954.

7. Assignment in Tomorrow. Published by Hanover House, Garden City, New York, 1954. Hardcover. Herein: Introduction by **Frederik Pohl**; 5.271.009 by **Alfred Bester**, 1954; Mother by Philip Jose Farmer, 1953; We Don't Want Any Trouble by James H. Schmitz, 1953; Mr Costello, Hero by **Theodore Sturgeon**, 1953; Hall of Mirrors by Fredric Brown, 1953; The Big Trip Up Yonder by Kurt Vonnegut Jr, 1954; Back to Julie by Richard Wilson, 1954; The Frightened Tree by Algis Budrys, 1953; A Matter of Form by Horace L. Gold, 1938; Helen O'Loy by Lester del Rey, 1938; The Peddler's Nose by **Jack Williamson**, 1951; She Who Laughs by Peter Phillips, 1952; The Adventurer by C. M. Kornbluth, 1953; Angels in the Jets by Jerome Bixby, 1952; Official Record by Fletcher Pratt, 1952; and Subterfuge by **Ray Bradbury**, 1943.

8. Star Science Fiction Stories 3. Published by Ballantine Books, New York City, 1955. Released simultaneously in hardcover and softcover. Ballantine Book 96. This contains: Editor's Note by **Frederik Pohl**; It's Such a Beautiful Day by **Isaac Asimov**; The Strawberry Window by **Ray Bradbury**; The Deep Range by **Arthur C. Clarke**; Alien by Lester del Rey; Foster You're Dead by **Philip K. Dick**; Whatever Happened to Corporal Cuckoo by Gerald Kersh; Dance of the Dead by Richard Matheson; Any More at Home Like You by Chad Oliver; The Devil on Salvation Bluff by **Jack Vance**; and Guinevere for Everybody by **Jack Williamson**.

9. Star Science Fiction Stories 4. Published by Ballantine Books, New York City, 1958. Softcover. Ballantine Book 272K. Herein: A Pinch of Stardust - an essay by **Frederik Pohl**; A Cross of Centuries by Henry Kuttner; The Advent on Channel Twelve by C. M. Kornbluth; Space-Tie for Springers by **Fritz Leiber**; Man Working by Richard Wilson; Helping Hand by Lester del Rey; The Long Echo by Miriam Allen de Ford; Tomorrow's Gift by Edmund Cooper; Idiot Stick by **Damon Knight**; and The Immortals by James E. Gunn.

10. Star Science Fiction Stories 5. Published by Ballantine Books, New York City, 1959. Softcover. Ballantine Book 308K. This contains: Trouble with Treaties by Katherine MacLean and Tom Condit; A Touch of Grapefruit by Richard Matheson; Company Store by **Robert Silverberg**; Adrift on the Policy Level by Chan Davis; Sparkie's Fall by Gavin Hyde; Star Descending by Algis Budrys; Diplomatic Coop by Daniel F. Galouye; The Scene Shifter by Arthur Sellings; and Hair Raising Adventure by Rosel George Brown.

11. Star Science Fiction 6. Published by Ballantine Books, New York City, 1959. Softcover. Ballantine Book 353K. This contains: Danger! Child at Large by C. L. Cottrell; Twin's Wall by Elizabeth Mann Borgese; The Holy Grail by Tom Purdom; Angerhelm by Cordwainer Smith; The Dreamsman by **Gordon R. Dickson**; To Catch an Alien by John J. McGuire; Press Conference by Miriam Allen de Ford; and Invasion from Inner Space by Howard Koch.

12. Star of Stars. Published by Doubleday & Company, Garden City, New York, 1960. Hardcover. Herein: Introduction by **Frederik Pohl**; Whatever Happened to Corporal Cuckoo by Gerald Kersh, 1955; The Advent on Channel Twelve by C. M. Kornbluth, 1958; Disappearing Act by **Alfred Bester**, 1953; Twin's Wail by Elisabeth Mann Borgese, 1959; Country Doctor by William Morrison, 1953; Daybroke by Robert Bloch, 1958; The Deep Range by **Arthur C. Clarke**, 1955; A Cross of Centuries by Henry Kuttner, 1958; The Man with English by H. L. Gold, 1953; Sparkie's Fall by Gavin Hide, 1959; Space Time for Springers by **Fritz Leiber**, 1958; Dance of the Dead by Richard Matheson, 1955; The Happiest Creature by **Jack Williamson**, 1953; and It's a Good Life by Jerome Bixby, 1953.

13. The Expert Dreamers. Published by Doubleday & Company, Garden City, New York, 1962. Hardcover. Herein: Introduction by **Frederik Pohl**; Heavy Planet by Milton A. Rothman writing as Lee Gregor, 1939; Lenny by **Isaac Asimov**, 1958; Chain Reaction by Lyle G. Boyd and William C. Boyd writing as Boyd Ellanby, 1956; A Feast of Demons by William Morrison, 1958; The Test Stand by G. Harry Stine writing as Lee Correy, 1955; To Explain Mrs Thompson by R. S. Richardson writing as Phillip Latham, 1951; Amateur in Chancery by George O. Smith; At the End of the Orbit by **Arthur C. Clarke**, 1961; The Mark Gable Foundation by Leo Szilard, 1961; The Miracle of the Broom Closet by Norbert Wiener writing as W. Norbert, 1952; The Black Cloud - excerpt by Fred Hoyle, 1957; Adrift on the Policy Level by Chandler Davis, 1959; The Invasion by Willy Ley writing as Robert Willey, 1940; The Heart on the Other Side by George Gamow; and On the Feasibility of Coal-Driven Power Stations by O. R. Frisch.

14. Time Waits for Winthrop and Four Other Short Novels from Galaxy. Published by Doubleday & Company, Garden City, New York, 1962. Hardcover. This collects: Natural State by **Damon Knight**, 1954; Galley Slave by **Isaac Asimov**, 1957; to Marry Medusa by **Theodore Sturgeon**, 1958; Accidental Flight by F. L. Wallace, 1952; and Time Waits for Winthrop by William Tenn, 1957.

15. The Seventh Galaxy Reader. Published by Doubleday & Company, Garden City, New York, 1964. Hardcover. This contains: Introduction by **Frederik**

115

Pohl; For Love by Algis Budrys, 1962; Come into My Cellar - Boys! Raise Giant Mushrooms in Your Cellar - by **Ray Bradbury**, 1962; The Tail-Tied Kings by Avram Davidson, 1962; Crime Machine by Robert Bloch, 1961; Return Engagement by Lester del Rey, 1961; Earthmen Bearing Gifts by Fredric Brown, 1960; Rainbird by R. A. Lafferty, 1961; Three Portraits and a Prayer by **Frederik Pohl**, 1962; Something Bright by Zenna Henderson, 1960; On the Gem Planet by Cordwainer Smith, 1963; The Deep Down Dragon by Judith Merril, 1961; The King of the City by Keith Laumer, 1961; The Beat Cluster by **Fritz Leiber**, 1961; An Old Fashioned Bird Christmas by Margaret St Clair, 1961; and The Big Pat Boom by **Damon Knight**, 1963.

16. The Eighth Galaxy Reader. Published by Doubleday & Company, Garden City, New York, 1965. Hardcover. Herein: The Varieties of the Science Fiction Experience - an essay by **Frederik Pohl**, 1965; Comic Inferno by **Brian W. Aldiss**, 1963; The Big Engine by **Fritz Leiber**, 1962; A Day on Death Highway by H. Chandler Elliott, 1963; The End of the Race by Albert Bermel, 1964; The Lonely Man by Theodore L. Thomas, 1963; A Bad Day for Vermin by Keith Laumer, 1964; Dawningsburgh by Wallace West, 1962; And All the Earth a Grave by C. C. MacApp, 1963; Hot Planet by **Hal Clement**, 1963; Final Encounter by **Harry Harrison**, 1964; If There Were No Benny Cemoli by **Philip K. Dick**, 1963; and Critical Mass by **Frederik Pohl** and C. M. Kornbluth, 1962.

17. Star Fourteen. Published by Ronald Whiting and Wheaton, London, 1966. Hardcover. Re-titled re-issue of Star of Stars, 1960.

18. The Ninth Galaxy Reader. Published by Doubleday & Company, Garden City, New York, 1966. Hardcover. This contains: Introduction by **Frederik Pohl**; An Ancient Madness by **Damon Knight**, 1964; The King of the Beasts by Philip Jose Farmer, 1964; The Watchers in the Glade by Richard Wilson, 1964; Jungle Substitute by **Brian W. Aldiss**, 1964; How the Old World Died by **Harry Harrison**, 1964; To Avenge Man by Lester Del Rey, 1964; The Monster and the Maiden by Roger Zelazny, 1964; A Flask of Fine Arcturan by C. C. MacApp, 1965; Wrong Way Street by Larry Niven, 1965; Wasted on the Young by John Brunner, 1965; Slow Tuesday Night by R. A Lafferty, 1965; and The Children of the Night by the **Frederik Pohl**, 1964.

19. The If Reader of Science Fiction. Published by Doubleday & Company, Garden City, New York, 1966. Hardcover. This contains: Introduction by **Frederik Pohl**; When Time Was New by Robert F. Young, 1964; Father of the Stars by **Frederik Pohl**, 1964; The Life Hater by Fred Saberhagen, 1964; Old Testament by Jerome Bixby, 1964; The Silkie by **A. E. van Vogt**, 1964; A Better Mousetrap by John Brunner, 1963; Long Day in Court by Jonathan Brand 1963; Trick or Treaty by Keith Laumer, 1965; and The 64 Square Madhouse by **Fritz Leiber**, 1962.

20. The Tenth Galaxy Reader. Published by Doubleday & Company, Garden City, New York, 1967. Hardcover. Herein: Wall of Crystal Eye of Night by Algis Budrys, 1961; An Elephant for the Prinkip by L. J. Stecher, 1960; The Place Where Chicago Was by Jim Harmon, 1962; Heresies of the Huge God by **Brian W. Aldiss**, 1966; Devil Car by Roger Zelazny, 1965; The Tunnel Under the World by **Frederik Pohl**, 1955; Auto Da Fe by **Damon Knight**, 1961; Door to Anywhere by **Poul Anderson**, 1966; The Primitives by **Frank Herbert**, 1966; If You Were the Only by Richard Wilson, 1953; and Repent Harlequin Said the Ticktockman by Harlan Ellison, 1965.

21. The Second If Reader of Science Fiction. Published by Doubleday & Company, Garden City, New York, 1968. Hardcover. This contains: Introduction by **Frederik Pohl**; In the Arena by **Brian W. Aldiss**, 1963; The Billiard Ball by **Isaac Asimov**, 1967; The Time Tombs by J. G. Ballard, 1963; Die Shadow by Algis Budrys, 1963; The Foundling Stars by **Hal Clement**, 1966; Toys for Debbie by David A. Kyle, 1965; The Forest in the Sky by Keith Laumer, 1967; At the Core by Larry Niven, 1966; Under Two Moons by **Frederik Pohl**, 1965; and Masque of the Red Shift by Fred Saberhagen, 1965.

22. The Eleventh Galaxy Reader. Published by Doubleday & Company, Garden City, New York, 1969. Hardcover. Herein: Introduction by **Frederik Pohl**; When I Was Very Jung by **Brian W. Aldiss**, 1968; The Sharing of the Flesh by **Poul Anderson**, 1968; Sweet Dreams, Melissa by Stephen Goldin, 1968; Jinn by Joseph Green, 1968; One Station of the Way by **Fritz Leiber**, 1968; Find the Face by Ross Rocklynne, 1968; Nightwings by **Robert Silverberg**, 1968; Among the Bad Baboons by Mack Reynolds, 1968; The Time Trawlers by Burt Filer, 1968; and Behind the Sandrat Hoax by Christopher Anvil, 1968.

23. Door to Anywhere. Published by Curtis Books, New York City, 1970. Softcover. Cutis Book 07070. A re-titled re-issue of The Tenth Galaxy Reader, 1967.

24. Final Encounter. Published by Curtis Books, New York City, 1970. Softcover. Cutis Book 07071. A re-titled re-issue of The Eighth Galaxy Reader, 1965.

25. Nightmare Age. Published by Ballantine Books, New York City, 1970. Softcover. Ballantine Book 02044. Herein: Introduction by **Frederik Pohl**; Eco-Catastrophe by Paul R. Ehrlich, 1969; Uncalculated Risk by Christopher Anvil, 1962; The Marching Morons by C. M. Kornbluth, 1951; The Luckiest Man in Denv by C. M. Kornbluth, 1952; A Bad Day for Sales by **Fritz Leiber**, 1953; X Marks the Pedwalk by **Fritz Leiber**, 1963; Station HR972 by Kenneth Bulmer, 1967; Day of Truce by Clifford D. Simak, 1963; Among the Bad Baboons by Mack Reynolds, 1968; New Apples in the Garden by Kris Neville, 1963; The Year of the Jackpot by **Robert A. Heinlein**, 1952; The Census Takers by **Frederik Pohl**, 1956; and The Midas Plague by **Frederik Pohl**, 1954.

26. Best Science Fiction for 1972. Published by Ace Books, New York City, 1972. Softcover. Ace Book 91359. Herein: Introduction by **Frederik Pohl**; Inconstant Moon by Larry Niven, 1971; The Sunset, 2217 AD by Ryu Mitsuse, 1972; Mother in the Sky With Diamonds by James Tiptree, Jr, 1971; Conversational Mode by Grahame Leman, 1972; Sheltering Dream by Doris Piserchia, 1972; At The

Frederick Pohl

Mouse Circus by Harlan Ellison, 1971; Silent in Gehenna by Harlan Ellison, 1971; Too Many People by H. H. Hollis, 1971; The Easy Way Out by John Brunner, 1971; and The Gold at the Starbow's End by **Frederik Pohl**, 1972.

27. Science Fiction: The Great Years. Edited with Carol Pohl. Published by Ace Books, New York City, 1973. Softcover. Ace Book 75430. This contains: Introduction by **Frederik Pohl**; And Then There Were None by **Eric Frank Russell**, 1951; The Liberation of Earth by William Tenn, 1953; Old Faithful by Raymond Z. Gallun, 1934; Placet is a Crazy Place by Fredric Brown, 1946; Wings of the Lightning Land by **Frederik Pohl** writing as James MacCreigh, 1941; The Little Black Bag by C. M. Kornbluth, 1950; and A Matter of Form by Horace L. Gold, 1938.

28. Jupiter. Edited with Carol Pohl. Published by Ballantine Books, New York City, 1973. Softcover. Ballantine Book 23662. This contains: Introduction: Jupiter the Giant by **Isaac Asimov**, 1973; Preface: Jupiter at Last by Frederik and Carol Pohl, 1973; Bridge by **James Blish**, 1952; Victory Unintentional by **Isaac Asimov**, 1942; Desertion by Clifford D. Simak, 1944; The Mad Moon by Stanley G. Weinbaum, 1935; Heavy Planet by Milton A. Rothman writing as Lee Gregor, 1939; The Lotus Engine by Raymond Z. Gallun, 1940; Call Me Joe by **Poul Anderson**, 1957; Habit by Lester del Rey, 1939; and A Meeting with Medusa by **Arthur C. Clarke**, 1971.

29. Science Fiction: The Great Years. Edited with Carol Pohl. Published by Victor Gollancz, London, 1974. First hardcover edition.

30. The Science Fiction Role of Honor. Published by Random House, New York City, 1975. Hardcover. Herein: Introduction by **Frederik Pohl**; Kings Who Die by **Poul Anderson**, 1962; The Last Question by **Isaac Asimov**, 1956; How Beautiful with Banners by **James Blish**, 1966; Daybroke by Robert Bloch, 1958; Who Goes There? by **John W. Campbell**, 1938; Dog Star by **Arthur C. Clarke**, 1962; The Monster by Lester del Rey, 1951; Dust by Lloyd Arthur Eschbach, 1939; The Prophets of Doom - an essay by **Hugo Gernsback**, 1975; The Long Watch by **Robert A. Heinlein**, 1948; Sanity by **Fritz Leiber**, 1944; The Meaning of the Word Impossible - an essay by Willy Ley, 1967; SF: The Spirit of Youth - an essay by **Frank R. Paul**, 1939; From the Skylark of Space - excerpt by **Edward E. Doc Smith**, 1928; The Hurkle Is a Happy Beast by **Theodore Sturgeon**, 1949; and Abdication by **A. E. van Vogt** and E. Mayne Hull, 1943.

31. The Best of C. M. Kornbluth. Published by Nelson Doubleday - The Science Fiction Book Club, Garden City, New York, 1976. Hardcover. Pohl edited this and introduced it with: An Appreciation of C. M. Kornbluth.

32. Science Fiction: The Great Years Volume II. Edited with Carol Pohl. Published by Ace Books, New York City, 1976. Softcover. Ace Book 75431. This contains: Introduction by Carol and **Frederik Pohl**; The Rull by **A. E. van Vogt**, 1948; And Be Merry by Katherine MacLean, 1950; The Sack by William Morrison, 1950; Mewhu's Jet by **Theodore Sturgeon**, 1946; Time is the Traitor by **Alfred Bester**, 1953; Columbus Was a Dope by **Robert A. Heinlein**, 1947; and When Time Went Mad by Dirk Wylie and Frederic Arnold Kummer Jr, 1950.

33. Science Fiction Discoveries. Edited with Carol Pohl. Published by Bantam Books, New York City, 1976. Softcover. Bantam Book 08635-9. Herein: Introduction by Carol and **Frederik Pohl**; Starlady by George R. R. Martin; The Never Ending Western Movie by Robert Sheckley; The Age of Libra by Scott Edelstein; To Mark the Year on Azlaroc by Fred Saberhagen; An Occurrence at the Owl Creek Rest Home by Arthur Jean Cox; The Force That Through the Circuit Drives the Current by Roger Zelazny; Deathrights Deferred by Doris Piserchia; and Error Hurled by Babette Rosmond.

34. Science Fiction of the 40s. With Joseph Olander and Martin H. Greenberg. Published by Avon Books, New York City, 1978. Softcover. This contains: Stepson in Space by Raymond Z. Gallun, 1940; Reason by **Isaac Asimov**, 1941; Magic City by Nelson S. Bond, 1941; Kazam Collects by C. M. Kornbluth, 1941; My Name is Legion by Lester del Rey, 1942; The Wabbler by Murray Leinster, 1942; The Halfling by Leigh Brackett, 1943; Doorway into Time by **C. L. Moore**, 1943; Deadline by Cleve Cartmill, 1944; City by Clifford D. Simak, 1944; Pi in the Sky by Fredric Brown, 1945; The Million Year Picnic by **Ray Bradbury**, 1946; Technical Error by **Arthur C. Clarke**, 1946; Memorial by **Theodore Sturgeon**, 1946; Letter to Ellen by Chandler Davis, 1947; It's Great to be Back! by **Robert A. Heinlein**, 1947; Tiger Ride by **James Blish** and **Damon Knight**, 1948; Don't Look Now by Henry Kuttner, 1948; That Only a Mother by Judith Merril, 1948; Venus and the Seven Sexes by William Tenn, 1949; and Dear Pen Pal by **A. E. van Vogt**, 1949.

35. Nebula Award Winners 14. Published by Harper and Row, New York City, 1980. Hardcover. Herein: Introduction: A Guide to the Perplexed by **Frederik Pohl**; The Persistence of Vision by John Varley, 1978; Stone by Edward Bryant, 1978; A Glow of Candles, a Unicorn's Eye by Charles L. Grant, 1977; Dreamsnake (excerpt) by Vonda N. McIntyre, 1978; Little Green Men from Afar by L. Sprague de Camp -an essay by L. Sprague de Camp, 1976; Cassandra by C. J. Cherryh, 1978; Seven American Nights by **Gene Wolfe**, 1978; Science Fiction: 1938 - an essay by **Isaac Asimov**, 1980; and The Future of Science Fiction - an essay by Norman Spinrad, 1980.

36. Great Science Fiction Series: Stories from the Best of the Science Fiction Series from 1944 to 1980 by All-time Favorite Writers. Edited with Martin H. Greenberg and Joseph Olander. Published by Harper Collins, New York City, 1980. Hardcover. This contains: Introduction by **Frederik Pohl**; The Ship Who Sang by **Anne McCaffrey**, 1961; Hothouse by **Brian W. Aldiss**, 1961; The Game of Rat and Dragon by Cordwainer Smith, 1955; Aesop by Clifford D. Simak, 1947; Burden of Proof by Bob Shaw, 1967; The Lifeboat Mutiny by Robert Sheckley, 1955; A Little Knowledge by **Poul Anderson**, 1971; The Cloud Sculptors of Coral D by J. G. Ballard, 1967; Sign of the Wolf by Fred Saberhagen, 1965; Ballots and Bandits by Keith Laumer, 1970; Bridge by **James Blish**, 1952; Ararat by Zenna Henderson, 1952; Opening Doors by Wilmar H. Shiras, 1949; Surface Tension by **James Blish**, 1956; The Reluctant Orchid by **Arthur C. Clarke**, 1956; No Great Magic by **Fritz Leiber**, 1963; A Relic of Empire by Larry Niven, 1966; The Talking Stone by **Isaac Asimov**, 1955; The Smallest Dragonboy by **Anne McCaffrey**, 1973; The Ancestral Amethyst by L. Sprague de Camp and Fletcher Pratt, 1952; and Through Time and Space with Ferdinand Feghoot by Reginald Bretnor writing as Grendel Briarton, 1978. Also included here are introductions to the various stories and series by: J. A. Lawrence and **James Blish**; L. Sprague de Camp; John J. Pierce; Clifford D. Simak; Wilmar H. Shiras; Robert Sheckley; Bob Shaw; Fred Saberhagen; Larry Niven; **Anne McCaffrey**; **Fritz Leiber**; Keith Laumer; Zenna Henderson; **Arthur C. Clarke**; Grendel Briarton; J. G. Ballard; **Poul Anderson**; **Brian W. Aldiss**; and **Isaac Asimov**.

37. Galaxy: Thirty Years of Innovative Science Fiction. With Martin H. Greenberg and Joseph D. Olander. Published by Playboy Press, Chicago, 1980. Hardcover. This contains: Introduction by **Frederik Pohl**; Horace L. Gold - an essay by **Frederik Pohl**, 1980; Gold on Galaxy - an essay by H. L. Gold, 1980; Coming Attraction by **Fritz Leiber**, 1950; To Serve Man (with memoir) by **Damon Knight**, 1950; Betelgeuse Bridge (with memoir) by William Tenn, 1951; Cost of Living (with memoir) by Robert Sheckley, 1952; The Model of a Judge (with memoir) by William Morrison, 1953; The Holes Around Mars (with memoir) by Jerome Bixby, 1954; Horrer Howce (with memoir) by Margaret St. Clair, 1956; People Soup (with memoir) by Alan Arkin, 1958; Something Bright by Zenna Henderson, 1960; The Lady Who Sailed the Soul by Cordwainer Smith, 1960; The Deep Down Dragon (with memoir) by Judith Merril, 1961; Wall of Crystal, Eye of Night (with memoir) by Algis Budrys, 1961; The Place Where Chicago Was (with memoir) by Jim Harmon, 1962; The Great Nebraska Sea (with memoir) by Allan Danzig; Oh to Be a Blobel (with memoir) by **Philip K. Dick**, 1964; Founding Father (with memoir) by **Isaac Asimov**, 1965; Going Down Smooth (with memoir) by **Robert Silverberg**, 1968; All the Myriad Ways (with memoir) by Larry Niven, 1968; The Last Flight of Dr Ain by James Tiptree Jr, 1969; From the Galaxy Book Shelf - an essay by Algis Budrys, 1969; Slow Sculpture (with memoir) by **Theodore Sturgeon**, 1970; About a Secret Crocodile (with memoir) by R. A. Lafferty, 1970; Cold Friend (with memoir) by Harlan Ellison, 1973; The Day Before the Revolution by **Ursula K. Le Guin**, 1974; The Gift of Garigolli by **Frederik Pohl** and C. M. Kornbluth, 1974; Overdrawn at the Memory Bank (with a note) by John Varley, 1976; Horace Galaxyca - an essay by **Alfred Bester**, 1980; and Index to Galaxy Magazine October 1950 to May 1979.

38. Galaxy Volume 1. With Martin H. Greenberg and Joseph D. Olander. Published by Playboy Paperbacks, Chicago, 1980. Softcover. Ends with The Great Nebraska Sea by Allan Danzig.

39. Galaxy Volume 2. With Martin H. Greenberg and Joseph D. Olander. Published by Playboy Paperbacks, Chicago, 1981. Softcover.

40. Yesterday's Tomorrows. Published by Berkley Books, New York City, 1982. Softcover. Herein: Introduction by **Frederik Pohl**; Into the Darkness by Ross Rocklynne, 1940; Emergency Refueling by **James Blish**, 1940; The Halfling by Leigh Brackett, 1943; Let There Be Light by **Robert A. Heinlein** writing as Lyle Monroe, 1940; Strange Playfellow by **Isaac Asimov**, 1940; Interstellar Way Station by **Wilson Tucker** writing as Bob Tucker, 1941; The Report on the Barnhouse Effect by Kurt Vonnegut Jr, 1950; Eco Catastrophe by Paul R. Ehrlich, 1969; The Nine Billion Names of God by **Arthur C. Clarke**, 1953; The Man with English by H. L. Gold, 1953; Space Time for Springers by **Fritz Leiber**, 1958; The Monster by Lester del Rey, 1951; The Rull by **A. E. van Vogt**, 1948; The Embassy by **Donald A. Wollheim** and C. M. Kornbluth, writing as Martin Pearson, 1942; Guinevere for Everybody by **Jack Williamson**, 1955; Oh to be a Blobel by **Phillip K. Dick**, 1964; The Pain Peddlers by **Robert Silverberg**, 1963; The Ballad of Lost C'Mell by Cordwainer Smith, 1962; A Gentle Dying by **Frederik Pohl** and C. M. Kornbluth, 1961; Slow Tuesday Night by R. A. Lafferty, 1965; Street of Dreams, Feet of Clay by Robert Sheckley, 1967; The Coldest Place by Larry Niven, 1964; The Great Slow Kings by Roger Zelazny, 1963; The Life Hater by Fred Saberhagen, 1964; Old Testament by Jerome Bixby, 1964; The Moon Moth by **Jack Vance**, 1961; The Last Flight of Dr Ain by James Tiptree Jr, 1969; Among the Bad Baboons by Mack Reynolds, 1968; Sweet Dreams Melissa by Stephen Goldin, 1968; A Bad Day for Vermin by Keith Laumer, 1964; At the Mouse Circus by Harlan Ellison, 1971; Dragon Lensman (excerpt) by David A. Kyle - based on the series created by **E. E. Doc Smith**, 1980; Dhalgren (excerpt) by **Samuel R. Delany**, 1974; and The Short Timers (excerpt) by Gustav Hasford, 1979; along with the following essays by Pohl: Afterword; The Paperbacks 1971 - 1978; The Galaxy and If Years 1960 - 1969; The Anthologies; The Pulps 1939 - 1943; and The Fanzines 1933 - 1939.

41. Tales from the Planet Earth. With Elizabeth Anne Hull. Published by St. Martin's Press, New York City, 1986. Hardcover. This contains: Report from the Planet Earth - an essay by **Frederik Pohl**; The Last Word - an essay by Elizabeth Anne Hull; Sitting Around the Pool, Soaking Up the Rays by **Frederik Pohl**, 1984; The Thursday Events by Ye Yonglie, 1986; User Friendly by Spider Robinson, 1986; Life as an Ant by Andre Carneiro, 1986; Fiddling for Waterbuffaloes by S. P. Somtow writing as Somtow Sucharitkul, 1986; S Is for Snake by Lino Aldani, 1986; The Divided Carla by Josef Nesvadba, 1985; The View from the Top of the Tower by **Harry Harrison**, 1986; Don't Knock the Rock by A. Bertram Chandler, 1986; The Owl of Bear Island by Jon Bing, 1986; Contacts of a Fourth Kind by Ljuben Dilov, 1986; Infestation by **Brian W. Aldiss**, 1986; In the Blink of an Eye by Carlos Maria Federici, 1986; Particularly Difficult Territory by Janusz A. Zajdel, 1986; Time Everlasting by Sam Lundwall, 1986; The Middle Kingdom by Tong Enzheng and Elizabeth Anne Hull, 1986; On the Inside Track by Karl-Michael Armer, 1986; The Legend of the Paper Spaceship by Tetsu Yano, 1978; and We Servants of the Stars by **Frederik Pohl**, 1986.

42. Worlds of If: A Retrospective Anthology. With Martin H. Greenberg and Joseph D. Olander. Bluejay Books, Gordonsville, Virginia, 1986. Hardcover. This contains: Introduction by **Frederik**

Frederick Pohl

Pohl; As If It Were in the Beginning - an essay by Larry T. Shaw; The Golden Man by **Philip K. Dick**, 1954; The Battle by Robert Sheckley, 1954; Last Rites by Charles Beaumont, 1955; Game Preserve by Rog Phillips, 1957; The Burning of the Brain by Cordwainer Smith, 1958; The Man Who Tasted Ashes by Algis Budrys, 1959; Kings Who Die by **Poul Anderson**, 1962; Fortress Ship by Fred Saberhagen, 1963; Father of the Stars by **Frederik Pohl**,1964; Trick or Treaty by Keith Laumer, 1965; Nine Hundred Grandmothers by R. A. Lafferty, 1966; Neutron Star by Larry Niven, 1966; The Mortal Mountain by Roger Zelazny, 1967; I Have No Mouth and I Must Scream by Harlan Ellison, 1967; Driftglass by **Samuel R. Delany**, 1967; The Holmes-Ginsbook Device by **Isaac Asimov**, 1968; Down in the Black Gang by Philip Jose Farmer, 1969; The Reality Trip by **Robert Silverberg**, 1970; The Nightblooming Saurian by James Tiptree Jr, 1970; Occam's Scalpel by **Theodore Sturgeon**, 1971; Construction Shack by Clifford D. Simak, 1973; Time Deer by Craig Strete, 1974; and Afterword: Flash Point Middle - an essay by Barry N. Malzberg.

43. Future Quartet: Earth in the Year 2042: A Four-Part Invention. With Ben Bova; Jerry Pournelle; and Charles Sheffield. Avonova Books, New York City, 1994. Hardcover. Herein: Introduction by Charles Sheffield; 2042: A Cautiously Pessimistic View - an essay by Ben Bova, 1991; A Visit to Belinda - an essay by **Frederik Pohl**, 1994; Report on Planet Earth - an essay by Charles Sheffield, 1994; The Price of Civilization by Charles Sheffield, 1992; Democracy in America in the Year 2042 - an essay by Jerry Pournelle, 1994; and Higher Education by Jerry Pournelle and Charles Sheffield, 1994.

44. The SFWA Grandmasters Volume 1. Published by Tor Books - Tom Doherty Associates, New York City, 1999. Hardcover. Introduction by **Frederik Pohl**; **Robert A. Heinlein** - an essay by **Frederik Pohl**. By **Robert A. Heinlein**: The Roads Must Roll, 1940; The Year of the Jackpot, 1952; Jerry Was a Man, 1947; The Farthest Place - excerpt from Tramp Royale, 1992; The Long Watch, 1948. **Jack Williamson** - an essay by **Frederik Pohl**. By **Jack Williamson**: With Folded hands, 1947; Jamboree, 1969; The Manana Literary Society - excerpt from Wonder's Child: My Life In Science Fiction, 1984; The Firefly Tree, 1997. Clifford D. Simak - an essay by **Frederik Pohl**. By Clifford D. Simak: Desertion, 1944; Founding Father, 1957; Grotto of the Dancing Deer, 1980. L. Sprague de Camp - an essay by **Frederik Pohl**. By L. Sprague de Camp: A Gun for Dinosaur, 1956; Little Green Men from Afar, 1976; Living Fossil, 1939. **Fritz Leiber** - an essay by **Frederik Pohl**. By **Fritz Leiber**: Sanity, 1944; The Mer She, 1978; and A Bad Day for Sales, 1953.

45. The SFWA Grandmasters Volume 2. Published by Tor Books - Tom Doherty Associates, New York City, 2000. Hardcover. Herein: Introduction by **Frederik Pohl**. By **Andre Norton**: Mousetrap, 1954; Were-Wrath, 1984; All Cats Are Gray - as by Andrew North, 1953; Serpent's Tooth, 1987. By **Arthur C. Clarke**: Rescue Party, 1946; The Secret, 1963; Reunion, 1971; The Star, 1955; Meeting with Medusa, 1971. By **Isaac Asimov**: The Last Question, 1956; It's Such a Beautiful Day, 1955; Strikebreaker, 1957; The Martian Way, 1952. by **Alfred Bester**: Disappearing Act, 1953; Fondly Fahrenheit, 1954; Comment on Fondly Fahrenheit - an essay, 2000; The Four Hour Fugue, 1974; Hobson's Choice, 1952. By **Ray Bradbury**: The City, 1950; The Million Year Picnic, 1946; All Summer in a Day, 1954; There Will Come Soft Rains, 1950; and The Affluence of Despair - an essay, 2000.

46. The SFWA Grandmasters Volume 3. Published by Tor Books - Tom Doherty Associates, New York City, 2001. Hardcover. This contains: Introduction by **Frederik Pohl**. By Lester del Rey: The Faithful, 1938; The Pipes of Pan, 1940; The Coppersmith, 1939; For I Am a Jealous People!, 1954. By **Frederik Pohl**: Let the Ants Try, 1949; The Tunnel Under the World, 1955; Day Million, 1966; The Gold at the Starbow's End, 1972. By **Damon Knight**: The Handler, 1960; Dio, 1957; Not With a Bang, 1950; I See You, 1976; Masks, 1968. By **A. E. van Vogt**: Black Destroyer, 1939; Far Centaurus, 1944; Vault of the Beast, 1940; Dear Pen Pay, 1949. By **Jack Vance**: Sail 25, 1962; Ullward's Retreat, 1958; and The Miracle Workers, 1958.

***

NON-FICTION

1. Tiberius. As by Ernst Mason. Published by Ballantine Books, New York City, 1960. Softcover. Ballantine Book 361K.

2. Practical Politics 1972. Published by Ballantine Books, New York City, 1971. Softcover. Ballantine Book 02363.

3. The Way the Future Was. Published by Del Rey - Ballantine Books, New York City, 1978. Hardcover.

4. Science Fiction: Studies in Film. With Frederik Pohl IV. Published by Ace Books, New York City, 1981. Softcover.

5. Our Angry Earth. With **Isaac Asimov**. Published by Tor Books - Tom Doherty Associates, New York City, 1991. Hardcover.

6. Chasing Science: Science as Spectator Sport. Published by Tor Books - Tom Doherty Associates, New York City, 2000. Hardcover.

***

RELATED

1. The Magazine of Fantasy and Science Fiction - Special Frederik Pohl Issue - September 1973. Published by Mercury Press, Cornwall, Connecticut, 1973. Softcover. Herein: In the Problem Pit by **Frederik Pohl**; **Frederik Pohl**: Frontiersman - an essay by Lester del Rey; and **Frederik Pohl**: Bibliography by Mark Owings; along with all the usual features.

2. Frederik Pohl: Merchant of Excellence: A Working Bibliography. By Phil Stephensen-Payne and Gordon Benson Jr. Published by Galactic Central Publications, Leeds, United Kingdom, 1989. Softcover.

Ray Bradbury

-1999-

Ray Bradbury.

Raymond Douglas Bradbury was born in Waukegan, Illinois on August 22nd, 1920. By 1934, when he was thirteen, his family settled in Los Angeles, where he finished high school and began a career as a newspaperman... selling papers on the corner of South Norton and Olympic Boulevard. By 1938, he was selling stories to fanzines. Through this, Forrest J. Ackerman invited Ray to join the Clifton's Cafeteria Science Fiction Club, where he met **Robert A. Heinlein**, Emil Petaja, Fredric Brown, Henry Kuttner, Leigh Brackett, and **Jack Williamson**.

In 1939, he started his own fanzine, Futuria Fantasia. It ran for four issues, each with fewer than one hundred printed copies. And two years later, he made his first professional sale. It was written in collaboration with Henry Hasse and it was bought by Alden H. Norton at Super Science Stories. Pendulum was the story and it was printed in the November 1941 issue along with The Biped, Reegan by Alfred Bester; Lost Legion by Monroe Lyle; Monster of the Moon by Ray Cummings; Red Gem of Mercury by Henry Kuttner; and Tumithak of the Towers of Fire by Charles R. Tanner.

Next came The Candle which was sold to Dorothy McIlwraith at Weird Tales and used in the November 1942 issue, along with a stellar line-up that included Nursemaid to Nightmares by Robert Bloch; The Hound by **Fritz Leiber**; The Victory of the Vita-Ray by Stanton A. Coblentz; The Golden Bough by David H. Keller; The Lips of Caya Wu by Frank Owen; Herbert West: Reanimator by H. P. Lovecraft; and The Evil Doll by Hannes Bok, along with a few others.

Ray's third professional sale was to **John W. Campbell** at Astounding Science Fiction. It was Eat, Drink and Be Wary and Campbell used it in the July 1942 issue as part of his Probability Zero series, which was a special category of stories in the 500 to 1,000 word range. Also in that issue was: Brimstone Bill by Malcolm Jameson; The Contraband Cow by L. Sprague de Camp; Secret Unattainable by **A. E. van Vogt**; Space Can by L. Ron Hubbard; Tools by Clifford D. Simak; Penance Cruise by David V. Reed; Collision Orbit by **Jack Williamson** writing as Will Stewart; and the Probability Zero stories: De Gustibus by Randall Hale; The Mysterious Bomb Raid by **Wilson Tucker**; About Quarrels, About the Past by John R. Pierce; The Qwerty of Hrothgar by R. Creighton Buck; and The Floater by Selden G. Thomas.

Having his first book published was still a few years away. But, in retrospect, you could see that it was inevitable. **Ray Bradbury** was a unique writer in a world that hadn't yet learned to fear the unique, the different, a world that hadn't learned to categorize everything and reject what didn't fit.

No one had ever written a story the way Bradbury wrote; no one had ever put the words together in quite that manner. By the late 1940s, with I See You Never, in The New Yorker, 1947, and The Fruit at the Bottom of the Bowl, in Esquire, 1948, among others, Ray had cracked the market for slick magazines.

His first book was Dark Carnival, published by August Derleth at Arkham House. Derleth was the first book publisher to see the value in Bradbury's work. That was in 1947 and it wasn't until 1950 that another publisher, Doubleday, thought he just might have something. Ray wove together a series of stories, called them The Martian Chronicles, and turned Doubleday into a believer. Shortly after the book was published, he met the British critic and writer, Christopher Isherwood, in a bookstore. Ray showed him Chronicles, Isherwood gave it a rave review in the mainstream market, and Ray was on his way.

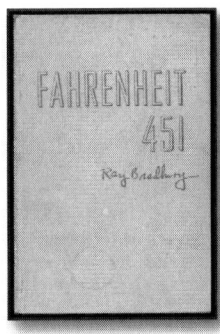

After such a long career and pushing the age of 90, he was asked if there was much left to do. "Bo Derek is a really good friend of mine," said Bradbury. "I'd like to spend more time with her."

Copies of the 1953 Ballantine hardcovers - bound in white asbestos - of Fahrenheit tend to sell for around $17,000.00. The edition was limited to 200 copies, all signed by Bradbury. After that one, Dark Carnival, The Martian Chronicles and the regular trade edition of Fahrenheit 451 all command great prices in decent condition, usually around $6,000.00.

Pen names used: William Elliott; Brett Sterling; Douglas Spaulding; and Leonard Spalding.

***

AWARDS

1977. He was given the World Fantasy Award for Life Time Achievement.
1988. The Damon Knight Memorial Grand Master Award, presented during the Nebula Award ceremonies.
1992. An asteroid was named after him, 9766 Bradbury.
1993. He received an Emmy Award for writing the screenplay to feature-length animated film, The Halloween Tree.
2000. The National Book Foundation presented him with the Distinguished Contribution to American Letters Award.
2002. For his contributions to the film industry, he was given his own star on the Hollywood Walk of Fame.
2003. He received an honorary doctorate from Woodbury University.
2004. He received the National Medal of Arts,

presented by President George W. Bush and Laura Bush.

2005. He received a Retro Hugo for Fahrenheit 451, 1954.

2007. He was awarded a special citation from The Pulitzer Board for his "distinguished, prolific, and deeply influential career as an unmatched author of science fiction and fantasy."

2007. He was awarded the French Commandeur Ordre des Arts et des Lettres medal.

2008. The Science Fiction Poetry Association gave him their Grand Masters award.

2008. The J. Lloyd Eaton Lifetime Achievement Award in Science Fiction, the first recipient of this award.

***

FILM AND TELEVISION

1. The Man. A 1949 story that was adapted for the television series Out There. It was shown on December 23rd, 1951, Season 1, Episode 9. And it starred: Florence Anglin; Philip Bourneuf; Stewart Bradley; Logan Field; Peter Hobbs; John McGovern; and Henry Worth.

2. Summer Night. A 1949 story that was used on the television series Suspense on February 19th, 1952, Season 4, Episode 23. It starred: Parker Fennelly and Carmen Mathews.

3. The Rocket. From 1950, this story was adapted for CBS Television Workshop and aired on March 16th, 1952, Season 1, Episode 10. It starred Martin Ritt and Katherine Squire.

4. Homecoming. This 1946 story was adapted for Tales of Tomorrow and shown on April 10th, 1953, Season 2, Episode 31. It starred Edith Fellows.

5. It Came from Outer Space. This 1953 film was based on Ray's treatment, The Meteor. Directed by Jack Arnold, it starred: Richard Carlson; Barbara Rush; Charles Drake; Joe Sawyer; Russell Johnson; Kathleen Hughes; and many others.

6. The Beast from 20,000 Fathoms. Based on The Fog Horn, 1951, this film was released in 1953. Directed by Eugene Lourie, it starred Paul Hubschmid; Paula Raymond; Cecil Kellaway; Kenneth Tobey; Donald Woods; Lee Van Cleef; Steve Brodie; Ross Elliott; Jack Pennick; and many others, including Merv Griffin as the voice of a radio announcer.

7. Zero Hour. A 1947 story developed for the series Star Tonight. It first aired on April 28th, 1955, Season 1, Episode 13. And it starred: Evan Elliott; Kimetha Laurie; and Judy Sanford.

8. The World Out There. Based on the 1952 story, The Great Wide World Over There, this was used on the television series Windows, July 22nd, 1955.

9. Moby Dick. Working with director John Huston, and based on the novel by Herman Melville, 1851, Bradbury wrote the screenplay for this film, which was released in the States on June 27th, 1956. It starred: Gregory Peck; Richard Basehart; Leo Genn; James Robertson Justice; Harry Andrews; Bernard Miles; Noel Purcell; Edric Connor; Mervyn Johns; Joseph Tomelty; Francis De Wolff; Friedrich von Ledebur; and many others.

10. Shopping for Death. Based on Ray's 1955 story, Touched with Fire, this was used on Alfred Hitchcock Presents, January 29th, 1956, Season 1, Episode 18. Directed by Robert Stevens, it starred: Alfred Hitchcock as the host; Jo Van Fleet, Robert Harris; John Qualen; Michael Ross; Michael Ansara; and many others.

11. And So Died Riabouchinska. Based on the 1953 story, this was used on Alfred Hitchcock Presents, February 12th, 1956, Season 1, Episode 20. Directed by Robert Stevenson, it starred: Alfred Hitchcock as the host; Claude Rains; Charles Bronson; Claire Carleton; Lowell Gilmore; Charles Cantor; Harry Tyler; Iris Adrian; William Haade; and Virginia Gregg.

12. Merry-Go-Round. Based on the 1948 story Black Ferris, this was used in July, 1956 on the television series Sneak Preview.

13. The Marked Bullet. Based on Ray's script The Bullet Trick, this aired on November 20th, 1956, Season 2, Episode 11 of Jane Wyman Presents the Fireside Theatre. It starred: Richard H. Cutting; Fred Johnson; Ed Kemmer; Joseph Wiseman; Howard Wright; and Jane Wyman.

14. A Sound of Different Drummers - or - Sound of a Different Drummer. This was based on Fahrenheit 451, 1953 and aired on Playhouse 90, October 3rd, 1957, Season 2, Episode 4. With a script by Robert Allen Arthur, it starred: Sterling Hayden; John Ireland; Diana Lynn; and David Opatoshu. Unfortunately for the show's producers, they neglected to get Bradbury's permission to use his work - he won the lawsuit.

15. The Wonderful Ice Cream Suit. Based on the 1958 story, this was used on the television series Rendezvous, November 1, 1958, Season 1, Episode 5. Directed by John Newland, it starred: Gerald Hiken; Mike Kellin; James Mitchell; Lou Nova; and Gene Saks.

16. Design for Loving. Based on his story Marionettes Inc., 1949, Ray wrote the teleplay for this, which aired on November 9th, 1958 on Alfred Hitchcock Presents, Season 4, Episode 6. Directed by Robert Stevens, it starred: Alfred Hitchcock as the host; Barbara Baxley; Norman Lloyd; Elliott Reid; and Marian Seldes.

17. The Gift. Based on the comic strip by Milton Caniff, Ray wrote this episode for the Steve Canyon TV series. It aired on December 20th, 1958, Season 1, Episode 13. Directed by Don Taylor, it starred: Dean Fredericks; Sean McClory; Celia Lovsky; William Bryant; Lillian Adams; Barbara Beaird; and Jackson Beck.

18. Special Delivery. Bradbury wrote the story for this episode of Alfred Hitchcock Presents which aired on November 29th, 1959, Season 5, Episode 10. Directed by Norman Lloyd, it starred: Alfred Hitchcock as the host; Michael Burns; Stephen

Ray Bradbury

Dunne; Peter Lazer; Frank Maxwell; James O'Neill; Beatrice Straight; and Cece Whitney. He later turned this into the short story Boys! Raise Giant Mushrooms in Your Cellar!, 1962.

19. Tunnel to Yesterday. He wrote this script for the television series Trouble Shooters. It aired on December 4th, 1959, Season 1, Episode 12. Directed by John Brahm, it starred: Werner Klemperer; Chet Allen; Bob Harris; and Carey Loftin.

20. King of Kings. Uncredited, Ray wrote the narrative parts for this 1961 film, which was directed by Nicholas Ray and starred: Jeffrey Hunter; Siobhan McKenna; Hurd Hatfield; Ron Randell; Viveca Lindfors; Rita Gam; Carmen Sevilla; Brigid Bazlen; Harry Gardino; Rip Torn; Robert Ryan; Edric Connor; Gregoire Aslan; and many others, including Orson Welles as the uncredited narrator.

21. Icarus Montgolfier Wright. This was a short animated film, based on the 1956 story and released in 1962. It was nominated for an Oscar in 1963 in the Best Short Subject, Cartoons category.

22. The Faith of Aaron Menefee. Bradbury wrote the teleplay, based on a story by Stanley Ellin, for this episode of Alfred Hitchcock Presents. It aired on January 30th, 1962, Season 7, Episode 17. Directed by Norman Lloyd, it starred: Alfred Hitchcock as the host; Robert Armstrong; Sidney Blackmer; Gail Bonney; Don Hanmer; Maggie Pierce; Andrew Prine; and Olan Soule.

23. The Jail. This was written for the television series Alcoa Premiere. Directed by Norman Lloyd, it aired on February 6th, 1962, Season 1, Episode 15, starring: Bettye Ackerman; James Barton; John Gavin; Noah Keen; Barry Morse; and Robert Sampson.

24. I Sing the Body Electric. He wrote this for The Twilight Zone and it aired on May 18th, 1962, Season 3, Episode 35. Directed by William F. Claxton and James Sheldon, it starred: **Rod Serling** as the host; Josephine Hutchinson; David White; Vaughn Taylor; Doris Packer; Charles Herbert; Veronica Cartwright; Dana Dillaway; Susan Crane; Paul Nesbitt; and Judee Morton. In 1969, he published this as a short story.

25. Nothing in the Dark. Based on Death and the Maiden, 1960, but uncredited, this was scripted by George Clayton Johnson and directed by Lamont Johnson for The Twilight Zone, January 5th, 1962, Season 3, Episode 16. It starred: **Rod Serling** as the host; Gladys Cooper; Robert Redford; and R. G. Armstrong.

26. Mr. Big. Based on the 1954 story The Dwarf, this was used on the TV series Armchair Theater, September 29th, 1963, Season 4, Episode 85. Directed by Philip Saville, it starred: George Claydon; Clive Colin Bowler; Rosemary Leach; Hilary Martin; Aubrey Morris; Frank Seton; and Peter Vaughan.

27. The Jar. This 1944 story was used on The Alfred Hitchcock Hour, February 14th, 1964, Season 2, Episode 17. Directed by Norman Lloyd, it starred: Alfred Hitchcock as the host; Pat Buttram; Collin Wilcox Paxton; William Marshall; Jane Darwell; Carl Benton Reid; James Bedst; George Lindsey; Jocelyn Brando; Slim Pickens; Alice Backes; Sammy Reese; Marlene De Lamater; and Billy Barty.

28. The Life Work of Juan Diaz. This 1963 story was used on The Alfred Hitchcock Hour, October 26th, 1964, Season 3, Episode 4. Directed by Norman Lloyd, it starred: Alfred Hitchcock as the host; Alejandro Rey; Frank Silvera; Pina Pellicer; Valentin de Vargas; Larry Domasin; Alex Montoya; Hinton Pope; Audrey Swanson; Gale Lindsey; Mark Miranda; Suzanne Barnes; Concepcion Sandoval; Yolanda Alonzo; and Vincent Arias.

29. The Fox and the Forest. A 1950 story, adapted for the television series Out of the Unknown. It aired on November 22nd, 1965, Season 1, Episode 8. Directed by Robin Midgley, it starred: Frederick Bartman; Liane Aukin; Warren Mitchell; Guido Adorni; Jose Berlinka; Serafina Di Leo; Delphine; Robert MacLeod; Marne Maitland; and many others.

30. Fahrenheit 451. Directed by Francois Truffaut, this film was released in the States on November 14th, 1966. It starred: Oskar Werner; Julie Christie; Cyril Cusack; Anton Diffring; Jeremy Spenser; Bee Duffell; Alex Scott; and many others, including Mark Lester as an uncredited schoolboy.

31. The Illustrated Bradbury. This was a 1968 episode on the television series Telescope. Directed by Perry Rosemond, it featured an interview with Ray and trip to the movie set where Rod Steiger was having his illustrations applied for The Illustrated Man, published in 1951 and released as a film in 1969.

32. The Picasso Summer. Based on his story In a Season of Calm Weather, 1957, and using the name Douglas Spaulding, Ray wrote the screenplay for this film which was released in 1969. Directed by Serge Bourguignon and Robert Sallin, it starred: Albert Finney; Yvette Mimieux; Luis Miguel Dominguin; Jim Connell; Georgina Cookson; Bee Duffell; Marty Ingels; Miki Iveria; and many others, including Yul Brynner as an uncredited guest.

33. The Illustrated Man. Directed by Jack Smight from a few of the stories in the 1951 collection, this was released in the States on March 26th, 1969. It starred: Rod Steiger; Claire Bloom; Robert Drivas; Don Dubbins; Jason Evers; Tim Weldon; and Christine Matchett. The stories adapted for the film were: The Veldt, 1950; The Long Rain, 1950; and The Last Night of the World, 1951.

34. The Groon. He wrote this script for the TV series The Curiosity Shop, which aired in 1971, starring: Mel Blanc; Don Herbert; Bob Holt; Chuck Jones; John Levin; Kerry MacLane; Don Messick; Les Tremayne; Pamelyn Ferdin; Jere Fields; June Foray; and Barbara Minkus.

35. The Screaming Woman. Based on the 1951 story, this film was directed for television by Jack Smight and released on January 29th, 1972. It starred: Olivia de Havilland; Ed Nelson; Laraine Stephens; Joseph Cotten; Walter Pidgeon; Charles Robinson; Alexandra Hay; Lonny Chapman; Charles Drake; Russell Wiggins; Gene Andrusco; Joyce Cunningham; and more.

123

36. Distant Early Warning. Uncredited but based on 1948 story Mars Is Heaven, the was used on the television series Wide World Mystery, October 21st, 1975. It starred: Herb Edelman; Mary Frann; Anthony Geary; and Michael Parks.

37. The Murderer. From the 1953 story, this short film was directed by Andrew Silver and shown on television on October 12th, 1976. It starred: Jayne Chamberlin; Paul Guilfoyle; Frederic Kimball; Janet Rodgers; David Wheeler; and Andrea Womack.

38. Science Fiction Film Awards. From 1978, this featured **Ray Bradbury** as one of the guests.

39. The American Comic Strip. Directed by John Musilli, this was released in June 1978 and featured **Ray Bradbury** as one of the interviewees, along with: Ralph Bakshi; Dik Browne; Milton Caniff; Will Eisner; Johnny Romita; and others, including **George Lucas**.
Gnomes. He worked on the screenplay for this 1980 television special. Directed by Jack Zander and Lars Calonius, it starred: Lee Richardson; Arthur Anderson; Rex Everhart; Anne Francine; Hetty Galen; Gordon Halliday; Bob McFadden; Corinne Orr; and Joe Silver.

40. The Martian Chronicles. This was a television mini-series that started on January 27th, 1980. Directed by Michael Anderson and with a screenplay by Richard Matheson, it ran in three parts: The Expeditions; The Settlers; and The Martians; and starred: Rock Hudson; Gayle Hunnicutt; Bernie Casey; Darren McGavin; Christopher Connelly; Nicholas Hammond; Joyce Van Patten; Roddy McDowall; Bernadette Peters; Maria Schell; Fritz Weaver; Linda Lou Allen; Michael Anderson Jr; Robert Beatty; James Faulkner; Barry Morse; and many others.

41. Rich and Famous. This film was directed by George Cukor and released in September 1981. Ray had a bit part as a literary party guest.

42. All Summer in a Day. Directed by Ed Kaplan, this 1954 story was made for television in 1982. It starred: Reesa Mallen; Keith Coogan; Jerry Marchack; Tammy Simpson; Bridget Meade; Edith Fields; Jessie McBride; and others.

43. Robbers, Rooftops and Witches. This was an animated adaptation of three short stories, The Chaparral Prince by O. Henry; Antaeus by Bordon Deal; and The Invisible Boy by **Ray Bradbury**, 1945. Directed by Mark Cullingham, it was shown on CBS Library in 1982, Season 3, Episode 1.

44. The Electric Grandmother. Based on the 1969 story, I Sing the Body Electric, this was directed for television by Noel Black and shown in the States on January 17th, 1982. It starred: Maureen Stapleton; Edward Herrmann; Paul Benedict; Tara Kennedy; Robert MacNaughton; Charles Fields; Madeleine Sherwood; Truman Gaige; Richard Whiting; Dortha Duckworth; and Paula Trueman.

45. Any Friend of Nicholas Nickleby Is a Friend of Mine. This 1966 story was made to the television series American Playhouse. It aired on February 9th, 1982, Season 1, Episode 5. Directed by Ralph Rosenblum, it starred Fred Gwynne as Charles Dickens; Deanna Dunagan as Emily Dickenson; Donna Gibbons; Les Podewell; Jim Pappas; George Womack; Frank Howard; Ralph Rosenblum... and **Ray Bradbury** playing Ralph as a Man.

46. Quest. Based on Frost and Fire, 1946, this short film, which was released in 1983, was directed by Elaine and Saul Bass and starred: John Abbott; David Comfort; Sam Fontana; Noah Hathaway; and Les Tremayne.

47. Something Wicked This Way Comes. This 1962 novel was filmed by Jack Clayton and released on April 29th, 1983 and the States. It starred: Jason Robards; Jonathan Pryce; Diane Ladd; Royal Dano; Vidal Peterson; Shawn Carson; Mary Grace Canfield; Richard Davalos; Jake Dengel; Jack Dodson; Bruce M. Fischer; Ellen Geer; Pam Grier; Brendan Klinger; James Stacy; and many more, including Arthur Hill as the narrator.

48. The Whimsical World of Oz. This 1985 documentary featured **Ray Bradbury** as one of the interviewees, along with: Ray Bolger; Erica Jong; Liza Minnelli; Diana Ross; and others.

49. The Fantasy Film Worlds of George Pal. This was directed by Arnold Leibovit for release in 1985. It featured **Ray Bradbury** as one of the guests, along with: **Chesley Bonestell**; **Ray Harryhausen**; **Gene Roddenberry**; Robert Bloch; Tony Curtis; Barbara Eden; Charlton Heston; Walter Lantz; Janet Leigh; Tony Randall; Rod Taylor; and many others.

50. Time Travel: Fact, Fiction and Fantasy. Directed by Gayle Hollenbaugh and Suzanne McCafferty, this documentary was released in July 1985. **Ray Bradbury** was one of the guests, along with: Michael J. Fox; Ed Krupp; and **Robert Silverberg**.

51. The Burning Man. This 1976 story was directed by J. D. Fiegelson and used as one of the segments in The New Twilight Zone, November 15th, 1985, Season 1, Episode 8. It starred: Piper Laurie; Danny Cooksey; Andre Gower; and Roberts Blossom.

52. The Elevator. This was done by Bradbury for The New Twilight Zone. It was shown on January 31st, 1986, Season 1, Episode 16. Directed by Ralph L. Thomas, it starred: Stephen Geoffreys; Robert Prescott; Douglas Emerson; and Brandon Bluhm.

53. Aliens, Dragons, Monsters, and Me. This was a documentary about **Ray Harryhausen**, directed by Richard Jones and released in 1986. It featured **Ray Bradbury** as one of the guests.

54. The Jar. This 1944 story was directed by Tim Burton for Alfred Hitchcock Presents. It aired on April 6th, 1986, Season 1, Episode 19, starring: Alfred Hitchcock in archival footage as the host; Griffin Dunne; Fiona Lewis; Laraine Newman; Stephen Shellen; Paul Bartel; Werner Pochath; Sunshine Parker; Eileen Barnett; and more.

55. Walking on Air. A story by Bradbury, directed by Ed Kaplan for WonderWorks. It was released on January 17th, 1987 and starred: Lynn Redgrave;

Ray Bradbury

Jordan Marder; Philip Akin; Tom Butler; Danierl Chevrier; David Clement; David Collins; Fran Gebhard; Deborah Grover; Alex Laurier; Bob LeChapelle; and others.

56. Vel'd. This was a 1987 Russian film that adapted The Veldt, 1950; The Garbage Collector, 1953; Hail and Farewell, 1953; The Dragon, 1955; and sections of Dandelion Wine, 1957. Directed by Nazim Tulyakhodzayev, it starred: Yuri Belayayev; Nelli Pshyonnaya; Giorgi Gegechkori; Tamari Skhirtladze; and many others.

57. Trinadtsatyy apostol. This translates from the Russian as The Thirteenth Apostle and was based on The Martian Chronicles, 1950. Directed by Suren Babayan, it was made in 1988 and starred: Juozas Budraitis; Andrei Boltnev; Vladas Bagdonas; Donatas Banionis; and many others.

58. Forrest J. Ackerman's Amazing Worlds of Science Fiction and Fantasy. Directed by Ray Ferry and hosted by Forrest J. Ackerman, this was released in 1991 and featured **Ray Bradbury** as a guest, along with: **Frank Kelly Freas**; **Ray Harryhausen**; **Gene Roddenberry**; **A. E. van Vogt**; John Agar; Rick Baker; Curt Siodmak; and others.

59. Little Nemo: Adventures in Slumberland. Based on the comic strip by Winsor McCary, Ray worked on the concept for this. Released August 21st, 1992 in the States, it was directed by Masami Hata and William Hurtz and starred: Mickey Rooney; Rene Auberjonois; and many others.

The Ray Bradbury Theater. Starting in May 1985, this ran through until October 30th, 1992 and included sixty-five episodes. Ray adapted his own stories for the show, writing all the screenplays.

Season One:

60. Marionettes, Inc. Directed by Paul Lynch, this 1949 story was aired on May 21st, 1985, Season 1, Episode 1. It starred: James Coco; Leslie Nielsen; Jayne Eastwood; Kenneth Walsh; and others.

61. The Playground. From 1953, this story was directed by William Fruet and shown on June 4th, 1985, Season 1, Episode 2. It starred: William Shatner; Steven Andrade; Keith Dutson; Barry Flatman; Mirko Malish; and Kate Trotter.

62. The Crowd. This 1943 story was directed by Ralph L. Thomas and shown on July 2nd, 1985, Season 1, Episode 3. It starred: Nick Mancuso; Victor Ertmanis; David Hughes; and R. H. Thomson.

63. The Town Where No One Got Off. After a long gap, this 1958 story was shown on February 22nd, 1986, Season 1, Episode 4. Directed by Don McBrearty, it starred: Jeff Goldblum; Clare Coulter; Samantha Langevin; Cec Linder; Ed McNamara; Wayne Robson; and Errol Slue.

64. The Screaming Woman. This 1951 story was shown on February 22nd, 1986, Season 1, Episode 5. Directed by Bruce Pittman, it starred: Drew Barrymore; Dick Callahan; Mary Ann Coles; Michael Copeman; Roger Dunn; Fran Gebhard; Janet-Laine Green; Ian Heath; Ken James; Jacqueline McLeod; and Alan Scarfe.

65. Banshee. Written in 1984, this was directed by Douglas Jackson and aired on February 22nd, 1986, Season 1, Episode 6. It starred: Peter O'Toole; Michael Copeman; Jennifer Dale; and Charles Martin Smith.

Season Two:

66. The Fruit at the Bottom of the Bowl. Directed by Gilbert M. Shilton, this 1948 story aired on January 23rd, 1988, Season 2, Episode 1. It starred: Robert Vaughn; Michael Ironside; Sonja Smits; Tom Harvey; Barry Greene; and Wally Dondarenko.

67. Skeleton. Written in 1945, this aired on February 6th, 1988, Season 2, Episode 2. It was directed by Steve DiMarco and starred: Eugene Levy; Diane D'Aquila; Peter Blais; Sean Hewitt; and Thick Wilson.

68. The Emissary. This 1947 story aired February 13th, 1988, Season 2, Episode 3. It was directed by Sturla Gunnarsson and starred: Helen Shaver; Neil Munro; Keram Malicki-Sanchez; Eric Hebert; and Linda Goranson.

69. Gotcha! Directed by Brad Turner, this 1978 story was shown on February 20th, 1988, Season 2, Episode 4. It starred: Saul Rubinek; Sharolyn Sparrow; Kate Lynch; James Kidnie; and Michael Healy.

70. The Man Upstairs. This 1947 story was directed by Alain Bonnot and aired on March 5th, 1988, Season 2, Episode 5. It starred: Feodor Atkine; Bertie Cortez; Kate Hardie; Adam Negley; Henri Poirier; Micheline Presle; and Michel Winogradoff.

71. The Small Assassin. From 1946, this story was shown on April 9th, 1988, Season 2, Episode 6. It starred: Cyril Cusack; Leigh Lawson; Lottie Ward; and Susan Wooldridge.

72. Punishment Without Crime. This 1950 story was directed by Bruce MacDonald and aired on April 16th, 1988, Season 2, Episode 7. It starred: Donald Pleasence; Frank Williams; Will Tacey; Peggy Mount; John McGlynn; William Ivory; Iain Cuthbertson; Bill Croasdale; Lynsey Baxter; and George Anton.

73. On the Orient, North. Written in 1988, this was directed by Frank Cassenti and shown on April 29th, 1988, Season 2, Episode 8. It starred: Ian Bannen; Francois Clavier; Jean Gluck; Tim Holm; Magali Noel; Sylvie Novak; and Herve Pauchon.

74. The Coffin. Directed by Tom Cotter, this 1947 story aired on May 7th, 1988, Season 2, Episode 9. It starred: Denholm Elliott; Dan O'Herlihy; and Clive Swift.

75. Tyrannosaurus Rex. From 1962, this aired on May 14th, 1988, Season 2, Episode 10. It was directed by Gilles Behat and starred: Cris Campion; Daniel Ceccaldi; Jim Dunk; and Julie Reitzman.

76. There Was an Old Woman. This 1944 story was directed by Bruce MacDonald and shown on May 21st, 1988, Season 2, Episode 11. It starred:

Roy Kinnear; Ken Kitson; Louis Emerick; Stephen Boyes; Peter Barton; Fine Time Fontayne; Sylvestra Le Touzel; Ronald Lacey; and Mary Morris.

77. And So Died Riabouchinska. From 1953, this was directed by Denys Granier-Deferre and aired on May 28th, 1988, Season 2, Episode 12. It starred: Alan Bates; and Jean-Pierre Kalfon.

Season Three:

78. The Dwarf. Written in 1954, this was shown on July 7th, 1989, Season 3, Episode 1. Directed by Costa Botes, it starred: David Cameron; Machs Colombani; Miguel Fernandes; and Megan Follows.

79. A Miracle of Rare Device. From 1962, this was directed by Roger Tompkins. Shown on July 14th, 1989, Season 3, Episode 2, it starred: Peter Dennett; Pat Harrington Jr; Desmond Kelly; William Kircher; Stephen Lovatt; Wayne Robson; and Roy Wesney.

80. The Lake. This 1944 story aired on July 21st, 1989, Season 3, Episode 3. It was directed by Pat Robins and starred: Gordon Thomson; Eli Sharplin; Jessica Billingsley; Sylvia Rands; Prue Langbein; Tina Regtien; and Jim Moriarty.

81. The Wind. Written in 1943, this was directed by Graham McLean and shown on July 28th, 1989, Season 3, Episode 4. It starred: Ray Henwood; Ann Pacey; Keith Richardson; and Michael Sarrazin.

82. The Pedestrian. From 1951, this was directed by Alun Bollinger and shown on August 4th, 1989, Season 3, Episode 5. It starred: David Ogden Stiers; Stig Eldred; Matt Murphy; and Grant Tilly.

83. A Sound of Thunder. This 1952 story was directed by Costa Botes and shown on August 11th, 1989, Season 3, Episode 6. It starred: John Bach; Michael Batley; Kiel Martin; John McDavitt; and Michael McLeod.

84. The Wonderful Death of Dudley Stone. Written in 1954, this was directed by David Copeland and shown on August 18th, 1989, Season 3, Episode 7. It starred: John Saxon; Alan Scarfe; and Lewis Rowe.

85. The Haunting of the New. From 1969, this was directed by Roger Tompkins and aired on September 15th, 1989, Season 3, Episode 8. It starred: Susannah York; and Richard Comar.

86. To the Chicago Abyss. Directed by Randy Bradshaw, this 1963 story aired on September 22nd, 1989, Season 3, Episode 9. It starred: Harold Gould; Chad Krowchuk; Arne MacPherson; Bill Meilen; Neil Munro; and Linda Rabinowich.

87. Hail and Farewell. From 1953, this was shown on September 30th, 1989, Season 3, Episode 10. It starred: Chad Cole; Georgie Collins; Christine MacInnis; Mark Parr; Josh Saviano; Frank C. Turner; and Donovan Workun.

88. The Veldt. Directed by Brad Turner, this 1950 story aired on November 10th, 1989, Season 3, Episode 11. It starred: Linda Kelsey; Shana Alexander; Damien Atkins; Del Mehes; Thomas Peacocke; and Malcom Stewart.

89. Boys! Raise Giant Mushrooms in Your Cellar! From 1962, this was directed by Brad Brandes and shown on November 17th, 1989, Season 3, Episode 12. It starred: Charles Martin Smith; Frank C. Turner; Marc Reid; Patricia Phillips; David Mann; and Judy Mahbey.

Season Four:

90. Mars Is Heaven. Directed by John Laing, this 1948 story was shown on July 20th, 1990, Season 4, Episode 1. It starred: Paul Gross; Hal Linden; Helen Moulder; Stephen Papps; and Brian Sergent.

91. The Murderer. Written in 1953, this aired on July 27th, 1990, Season 4, Episode 2. It starred: Cedric Smith; Donna Akersten; Michael Haigh; and Bruce Weitz.

92. Touched with Fire. From 1968, this story was shown on August 3rd, 1990, Season 4, Episode 3. It starred: Eileen Brennan; Barry Morse; Paul Nadas; Michael Noonan; and Joseph Shaw.

93. The Black Ferris. Written in 1948, this story was directed by Roger Tompkins and shown on August 10th, 1990, Season 4, Episode 4. It starred: Jonathan Marks; Zachary Bennett; Cathy Downes; Pat Evison; Stephen Gledhill; Nathaniel Moreau; Duncan Smith; and Frank Whitten.

94. Usher II. This 1950 story this story was directed by Lee Tamahori and shown on August 17th, 1990, Season 4, Episode 5. It starred: Patrick Macnee; Alice Fracer; Desmond Kelly; and Ian Mune.

95. Touch of Petulance. From 1980, this story was directed by John Laing and shown on October 12th, 1990, Season 4, Episode 6. It starred: Eddie Albert; and Jesse Collins.

96. And the Moon Be Still as Bright. This 1948 story was directed by Randy Bradshaw and aired on October 19th, 1990, Season 4, Episode 7. It starred: David Carradine; Kenneth Welsh; James Purcell; Brian Jensen; and Ben Cardinal.

97. The Toynbee Convector. Written in 1984, this story was shown on October 26th, 1990, Season 4, Episode 8. It starred: Michael Hurst; and James Whitmore.

98. Exorcism. From 1957, this story was shown on November 2nd, 1990, Season 4, Episode 9. It starred: Sally Kellerman; Jayne Eastwood; Bartley Bard; and Jordan Singer.

99. The Day It Rained Forever. Written in 1957, this was aired on November 9th, 1990, Season 4, Episode 10. It starred: Vincent Gardenia; Sheila Moore; Gerard Parkes; and Robert Clothier.

100. The Long Years. Originally Dwellers in Silence, 1948, the title was changed for The Martian Chronicles, 1950. Directed by Paul Lynch, this story was shown on November 16th, 1990, Season 4, Episode 11. It starred: Robert Culp; Judith Buchan; Donna Larson; Bruce Mitchell; George Touliatos; and Jason Wolff.

Ray Bradbury

101. Here There Be Tygers. This 1951 story was directed by John Laing and shown on November 30th, 1990, Season 4, Episode 12. It starred: Timothy Bottoms; Peter J. Elliott; George Henare; and Lorae Parry.

Season Five:

102. The Earthmen. From 1948, this story was directed by Graeme Campbell and aired on January 3rd, 1992, Season 5, Episode 1. It starred: Gordon Pinsent; David Birney; Larry Musser; David Neale; Patricia Phillips; Ian Robison; Jim Shepard; and Raul Tome.

103. Zero Hour. Written in 1947, this story was aired on January 10th, 1992, Season 5, Episode 2. It starred: Sally Kirkland; and Katie Murray.

104. The Jar. Directed by Randy Bradshaw, this 1944 story was shown on January 17th, 1992, Season 5, Episode 3. It starred: Jennifer Dale; John Dee; Paul Le Mat; Bill Meilen; Billy Morton; Earl Pastko; and Randal Payne.

105. Colonel Stonesteel and the Desperate Empties. From Colonel Stonesteel's Genuine Home-Made Truly Egyptian Mummy, 1981, this was shown on January 24th, 1992, Season 5, Episode 4. It starred: Shawn Ashmore; Harold Gould; Walter Kaasa; and Wayne Robson.

106. The Concrete Mixer. This 1949 story was shown on January 31st, 1992, Season 5, Episode 5. It starred: Ben Cross; John Gilbert; and Howard Jerome.

107. The Utterly Perfect Murder. Written in 1971, this aired on February 7th, 1992, Season 5, Episode 6. It starred: Robert Clothier; Eric Johnson; Richard Kiley; and David Turri.

108. Let's Play Poison. From 1948, this story was directed by Bruce Pittman and shown on February 14th, 1992, Season 5, Episode 7. It starred: Richard Benjamin; Adam Derges; Warren Graves; and Shane Meier.

109. The Martian. From 1949, this was shown on February 21st, 1992, Season 5, Episode 8. It starred: John Vernon; Janne Mortil; Sheila Moore; Paul Coeur; and Paul Clemens.

Season Six:

110. The Lonely One. This 1949 story was shown on July 10th, 1992, Season 6, Episode 1. It starred: Joanna Cassidy; Sheila McCarthy; Maggie Harper; Kathleen Kelley; Chic Littlewood; Stephen O'Rourke; and Peter Rowley.

111. The Happiness Machine. Directed by Don McBrearty, this 1957 story aired on July 17th, 1992, Season 6, Episode 2. It starred: Kurtis Brown; Ronan Cahill; Claire Chitham; Jill Dyck; Katharine Isabelle; Sally Kirkland; and Brian Taylor.

112. Tomorrow's Child. This 1948 story, also known as The Shape of Things, was directed by Costa Botes and shown on August 14th, 1992, Season 6, Episode 3. It starred: Michael Sarrazin; John Kerr; Carol Kane; Mark Clare; and Peter Bland.

113. The Handler. Directed by Peter Sharp, this 1947 story was shown on August 19th, 1992, Season 6, Episode 4. It starred: Michael J. Pollard; Henry Beckman; Peter Rowley; and John Sumner.

114. The Great Wide World Over There. From 1952, this story was directed by Ian Mune and shown on August 20th, 1992, Season 6, Episode 5. It starred: Tyne Daly; Helen Moulder; David Orth; and Frank Whitten.

115. Fee Fie Foe Fum. Written in 1993, this was directed by John Reid and Shown on August 21st, 1992, Season 6, Episode 6. It starred: Lucy Lawless; Robert Morelli; and Jean Stapleton.

116. The Anthem Sprinters. From 1963, this was shown on August 21st, 1992, Season 6, Episode 7. It starred: Bruce Allpress; Alistair Babbage; Robert Ball; David Baxter; Ken Blackburn; Karl Bradley; Grant Bridger; Len Cariou; Terry Hayman; Maurice Keene; and Ian Watkin.

117. By the Numbers. Directed by Wayne Tourell, this 1984 story aired on September 11th, 1992, Season 6, Episode 8. It starred: Marton Csokas; Nii Hammond; Geordie Johnson; Ciaran Pennington; Ray Sharkey; Bruce Tegart; and Erik Thomson.

118. The Long Rain. From 1950, this story was directed by Lee Tamahori and shown on September 19th, 1992, Season 6, Episode 9. It starred: Marc Singer; Brian Sergent; and Michael Hurst.

119. The Dead Man. Written in 1945, this was directed by Costa Botes and shown on September 26th, 1992, Season 6, Episode 10. It starred: Alistair Douglas; Louise Fletcher; Gilbert Goldie; Peter McCauley; David Telford; and Frank Whitten.

120. Sun and Shadow. This 1953 story aired on October 3rd, 1992, Season 6, Episode 11. It starred: Stuart Margolin; John Bach; Ken Blackburn; James Roberts; and Gregory Sierra.

121. Silent Towns. Written in 1949, this was directed by Lee Tamahori and shown on October 10th, 1992, Season 6, Episode 12. It starred: John Glover; and Monica Parker.

122. Downwind from Gettysburg. From 1969, this was shown on October 17th, 1992, Season 6, Episode 13. It starred: Howard Hesseman; Kelly Johnson; Robert Joy; and Jim Rawdon.

123. Some Live Like Lazarus. Written in 1960, this was directed by Peter Sharp and aired on October 24th, 1992, Season 6, Episode 14. It starred: Yannick Bisson; Kristin Darragh; Deborah Kathrine; Yvonne Lawley; Greer Robson; Janice Rule; Andrew Thurtell; Noel Trevarthen; Catherine Wolf; and Leon Woods.

124. The Tombstone. This 1945 story was the final show in The **Ray Bradbury** Theatre. It was directed by Warrick Attewell and shown on October 30th, 1992, Season 6, Episode 15. It starred: Shelley Duvall; June Bishop; Jocelyn Brodeur; Desmond Kelly; Lyndon Peoples; Paul Royce; John Smythe; and Ron White.

125. The 64th Annual Academy Awards. **Ray Bradbury** was on hand to present the Gordon E. Sawyer Award to **Ray Harryhausen**.

126. The Halloween Tree. Directed by Mario Piluso, this animated film from the 1972 novel was released in 1993. It starred: **Ray Bradbury** as the narrator; Annie Barker; Darleen Carr; Lindsay Crouse; Alex Greenwald; Edan Gross; Andrew Keegan; Kevin Smets; Mark Taylor; and Leonard Nimoy as Mr Moundshroud.

127. In Search of Oz. Directed by Brian Skeet, this documentary was released in June 1994 and featured **Ray Bradbury** as one of the guests, along with: Salman Rushdie; Geoff Ryman; Gore Vidal; Martha Coolidge; and others.

128. Spaceship Earth. Bradbury was a consulting writer on this 1994 short which starred: Judi Dench; and Jeremy Irons as the narrators.

129. 100 Hundred Years of Horror: The Evil Unseeable. A 1996 documentary written by Ted Newsom. It featured **Ray Bradbury** as one of the guests, along with: Christopher Lee as the host and narrator; Turhan Bey; Roger Corman; Beverly Garland; Sheldon Leonard; Richard Matheson; and others.

130. 100 Hundred Years of Horror: Sorcerers. A 1996 documentary written by Ted Newsom. It featured **Ray Bradbury** as one of the guests, along with: Christopher Lee as the host and narrator; Dana Andrews; John Carpenter; Roger Corman; Richard Denning; Beverly Garland; Hugh Hefner; Vincent Price; Richard Matheson; and others.

131. 100 Hundred Years of Horror: Giants and Dinosaurs. A 1996 documentary written by Ted Newsom. It featured **Ray Bradbury** as one of the guests, along with: Christopher Lee as the host and narrator; **Ray Harryhausen**; Richard Denning; Hugh Hefner; Raquel Welch; William Schallert; Donald F. Glut; Richard Matheson; and others.

132. 100 Hundred Years of Horror: Dinosaurs. A 1996 documentary written by Ted Newsom. It featured **Ray Bradbury** as one of the guests, along with: Christopher Lee as the host and narrator; **Ray Harryhausen**; Donald F. Glut; Raquel Welch; and others.

133. 100 Hundred Years of Horror: Aliens. A 1996 documentary written by Ted Newsom. It featured **Ray Bradbury** as one of the guests, along with: Christopher Lee as the host and narrator; John Carpenter; Richard Denning; Beverly Garland; and others.

134. A Century of Science Fiction. This 1996 documentary, written and directed by Ted Newsom, featured **Ray Bradbury** as one of the guests, along with: Yul Brynner; Kevin Costner; Christopher Lee; Arnold Schwarzenegger; and William Shatner.

135. It Came from Outer Space II. Using Ray's idea, Roger Duchowny directed this for release in 1996. It starred: Brian Kerwin; Elizabeth Pena; Jonathan Carrasco; Adrian Sparks; Bill McKinney; Dean Norris; Dawn Zeek; Laren Tewes; Mickey Jones; and many others.

136. Corwin. Written and directed by Les Guthman, for release in June 1996, this was a biography of Norman Corwin, the writer, producer and director from the Golden Age of Radio. **Ray Bradbury** was one of the guests.

137. The Harryhausen Chronicles. This was written and directed by Richard Schickel for release in January 1998. Narrated by Leonard Nimoy, it featured **Ray Bradbury** among the interviewees, along with: Tom Hanks; Dennis Muren; Charles H. Schneer; Henry Selick; **George Lucas**; and **Ray Harryhausen**.

138. In Search of Tarzan with Jonathan Ross. This 1998 British documentary, directed by Luke Jeans, featured interviews with: **Ray Bradbury**; Bo Derek; Ron Ely; Denny Miller; Miles O'Keeffe; Maureen O'Sullivan; Gordon Scott; Eve Brent; and Johnny Weissmuller Jr.

139. Hugh Hefner: American Playboy Revisited. Directed by Kevin Burns and released in 1998, this featured **Ray Bradbury** as one of the guests.

140. The Wonderful Ice Cream Suit. Working from his own short story, 1958, and play, which was published in 1972 in The Wonderful Ice Cream Suit and other Plays for Today, Tomorrow, and Beyond Tomorrow, Ray did the teleplay for this. Directed by Stuart Gordon, it was released in 1998 and starred: Joe Mantegna; Esai Morales; Edward James Olmos; Clifton Collins Jr; Gregory Sierra; Liz Torres; Sid Caesar; Howard Morris; Lisa Vidal; Mike Moroff; Mercedes Ortega; and many others.

141. Universal Horror. This was directed by Kevin Brownlow and released on October 8th, 1998. Narrated by Kenneth Branagh, it featured interviews with an assortment of guests, including **Ray Bradbury**.

142. The Stan Freberg Commercials. This 1999 collection of Freberg's best television commercials featured **Ray Bradbury** playing himself in a segment entitled: Brave New Prune. Hmmmm... That sounds kinda crappy.

143. The Fly Papers: The Buzz on Hollywood's Scariest Insect. A 2000 documentary about the history of all five Fly movies, this featured **Ray Bradbury** as one of the guests, along with: David Cronenberg; Jeff Goldblum; John Goodwin; Hugh Hefner; and others, including Leonard Nimoy as the narrator.

144. Amargosa. This biography of Marta Becket was written and directed by Todd Robinson for release in 2000. **Ray Bradbury** was one of the guests.

145. Lon Chaney: A Thousand Faces. This was directed by Kevin Brownlow and released in October 2000. **Ray Bradbury** was one of the guests, along with: Kenneth Branagh as the narrator; Forrest J. Ackerman; and many, many others.

146. Besuch bei Ray Bradbury. Directed by Eckhart Schmidt, this documentary about Ray was released in 2001.

147. Walt: The Man Behind the Myth. Ray

Ray Bradbury

Bradbury was one of the many guests featured in this documentary about Walt Disney. Directed by Jean-Pierre Isbouts and released on September 16th, 2001, it featured, along with Ray: Dick Van Dyke; Julie Andrews; and many, many others.

148. Poe's Tales of Terror. This was the October 30th, 2001 episode of the television series Great Books and it featured **Ray Bradbury** as one of the guests, along with: Poppy Z. Brite and West Craven.

149. The Tramp and the Dictator. This 2002 documentary, directed by Kevin Brownlow and Michael Kloft, was about Charlie Chaplin's first film with sound, The Great Dictator, 1940. **Ray Bradbury** was one of the guests, though uncredited.

150. Fahrenheit 451, the Novel: A Discussion with Author Ray Bradbury. Directed by Laurent Bouzereau, this short documentary was released in 2003 and featured **Ray Bradbury** as the only guest.

151. The Music of Fahrenheit 451. Directed by Laurent Bouzereau, this short documentary was released in 2003 and featured **Ray Bradbury** as one of the guests.

152. The Making of Fahrenheit 451. Directed by Laurent Bouzereau, this short documentary was released in 2003 and featured **Ray Bradbury** as one of the guests.

153. The Screen Savers. Ray Bradbury was one of the guests on the episode dated September 9th, 2003.

154. Cosmic Thoughts. This short film was written and directed by Mark Young and featured **Ray Bradbury** as one of the guests. It was released in October 2003.

155. Hollywood Legenden - also known as Hollywood Legends. A German-made documentary, directed by Eckhart Schmidt and released in 2004. **Ray Bradbury** was one of the guests, along with: Peter Bogdanovich; Jeff Bridges; Tony Curtis; Angie Dickinson; Tippi Hedren; Samuel L. Jackson; Jerry Lewis; Sidney Poitier; Mickey Rooney; Jane Russell; Omar Sharif; and many, many more.

156. The Optimistic Futurist. Written by Leonard Maltin and directed by Jeff Kurtti, this short was released in May 2004 and featured only **Ray Bradbury**.

157. Hardball with Chris Matthews. Ray Bradbury was a guest on the show that was released June 28th, 2004.

158. Dennis Miller. Ray Bradbury was a guest on the show that was released July 15th, 2004.

159. Ray Harryhausen: The Early Years Collection. This was directed by Harryhausen himself and released in January 2005. **Ray Bradbury** was an interviewee, along with: Forrest J. Ackerman; Tim Burton; James Cameron; Wes Craven; Peter Jackson; John Landis; and many others.

160. A Sound of Thunder. Based on the 1952 story, this was directed by Peter Hyams and released in September 2005. It starred: Armin Rohde; Heike Makatsch; Jemima Rooper; David Oyelowo; Wilfried Hochholdinger; Edward Burns; August Zimer; Ben Kingsley; Catherine McCormack; and many others.

161. A Piece of Wood. This 2005 short was based on the 1952 story and directed by Tony Baez Milan. It starred Larry Dirk and Glen Vaughan.

162. I'm King Kong!: The Exploits of Merian C. Cooper. Directed by Christopher Bird and Kevin Brownlow for release in 2005, this documentary analysed the life of producer, director and writer Merian C. Cooper. **Ray Bradbury** was one of the guests, along with: Alec Baldwin as the narrator and tons of archival footage, including: Cary Grant; John Wayne; Lowell Thomas; John Ford; Theodore Roosevelt; and Cooper himself; along with many others.

163. The Sci-Fi Boys. A documentary about the evolution of science fiction and special effects in movies, this was directed by Paul Davids and released in 2006. **Ray Bradbury** was one of the guests, along with: Peter Jackson; **Ray Harryhausen**; Leonard Maltin; Forrest J. Ackerman; Roger Corman; and many others.

164. The Small Assassin. This 1946 story was directed by Chris Charles for release in 2007. It starred: David Marcotte; Lois Atkins; Robert Breuler; Matthew Erickson; Menachem Reed; Braydon Salata; Ed Gjersten; Debra Rodkin; Jan Rose; Lean Rose Orleans; Noel Olken; Lynette Gaza; and many others; including Kaylee Williams as a hotel guest.

165. Famous Monster: Forrest J. Ackerman. This was directed by Michael MacDonald and released in May 2007. **Ray Bradbury** was one of the featured interviewees, along with: Forrest J. Ackerman; Roger Corman; **Ray Harryhausen**; George Clayton Johnson; David J. Schow; Tim Sullivan; and many others.

166. Who Is Norman Lloyd? Directed by Matthew Sussman and released in 2007, this biography featured **Ray Bradbury** as one of the guests, along with: Cameron Diaz; Karl Malden; Samuel Goldwyn Jr; archival footage of Charlie Chaplin and Alfred Hitchcock; and many others.

167. You must Remember This: The Warner Bros. Story. Narrated by Clint Eastwood and directed by Richard Schickel, this was released in 2008. **Ray Bradbury** was one of the guest interviewees, along with: Carroll Baker; Warren Beatty; George Clooney; Margot Kidder; Jack Nicholson; Arthur Penn; and many others.

168. A Conversation with Ray Bradbury. Directed by Lawrence Bridges, this short film was released in 2008.

169. Chrysalis. Based on the 1946 story, this was directed by Tony Baez Milan for release in either 2008 or 2009. It starred: Elina Madison; Darren Kendrick; John Klemantaski; Corey Landis; Glen Vaughan; Liesel Kopp; Danny Cameron; and Larry Dirk.

170. The Illustrated Man. At the time of this

writing, it had been announced that The Illustrated Man, 1951, was in production. Directed by Zack Snyder, it is scheduled to be released in 2010.

171. Fahrenheit 451. Also at the time of this writing, there had been an announcement that Fahrenheit 451, 1953, was in the process of being developed with a hopeful release in 2010.

***

RADIO

1. Killer, Come Back to Me. Written by Ray, this aired on May 17th, 1946 on the Molle Mystery Theater.

2. The Meadow. Written by Ray, this was used on World Security Workshop, February 1st, 1947. He re-wrote it later into a short story by the same name, published in 1953.

3. The Night. This 1946 story was used by Nelson Olmstead on Stories by Olmstead in 1947.

4. One Timeless Spring. This 1946 story was used by Nelson Olmstead on Stories by Olmstead in 1947.

5. Riabouchinska. Ray wrote the script for this for the show Suspense on CBS radio. It aired on November 13th, 1947. He later turned it into the short story, And So Died Riabouchinska, 1953.

6. Summer Night. Based on Ray's story The Whole Town's Sleeping, which hadn't as yet been published, this was used on CBS's Suspense. It aired on July 15th, 1948. The story remained unpublished until 1950.

7. The Screaming Woman. Based on Ray's story The Screaming Woman, which hadn't as yet been published, this was used on CBS's Suspense. It aired on November 25th, 1948. The story remained unpublished until 1951.

8. The Miracle of Jamie. This 1946 story was used by Nelson Olmstead on Stories by Olmstead in 1948.

9. Powerhouse. This 1948 story was used by Nelson Olmstead on Stories by Olmstead in 1948.

10. The Wind. This 1943 story was used on Radio City Playhouse on October 30th, 1949.

11. To the Future. Based on the 1950 story The Fox and the Forest, this aired on Dimension X on May 27th, 1950.

12. The Crowd. This 1943 story was aired on CBS's Suspense on September 21st, 1950.

13. Mars Is Heaven. This 1948 story aired on CBS's Escape on June 2nd, 1950.

14. There Will Come Soft Rains/Zero Hour. These 1950 and 1947 stories were aired together on Dimension X, June 17th, 1950.

15. Mars Is Heaven. This 1948 story this aired on Dimension X on July 7th, 1950.

16. The Martian Chronicles. Based on the 1950 collection, this aired on Dimension X on August 18th, 1950.

17. And the Moon Be Still As Bright. This 1948 story this aired on Dimension X on September 29th, 1950.

18. Dwellers in Silence. This 1948 story this aired on Dimension X on July 19th, 1951.

19. The Earthmen. This 1948 story aired on CBS's Escape on July 25th, 1951.

20. The Veldt. This 1950 story this aired on Dimension X on August 9th, 1951.

21. Marionettes, Inc. This 1949 story this aired on Dimension X on August 30th, 1951.

22. Kaleidoscope. This 1949 story this aired on Dimension X on September 15th, 1951.

23. The Rocket. This 1950 story was used on NBC's Short Story series on January 4th, 1952.

24. Mars Is Heaven. This 1948 story this aired on Think - ABC Radio Workshop in 1953.

25. The Golden Apples of the Sun. This was a radio anthology series on the BBC in England in 1954. During the course of the show, it featured: The Golden Apples of the Sun, 1953; Hail and Farewell, 1953; The Flying Machine, 1953; The Fruit at the Bottom of the Bowl, 1948; A Sound of Thunder, 1952; The Murderer, 1953; The April Witch, 1952; and The Fog Horn, 1951.

26. The Screaming Woman. This was re-made for CBS's Suspense, starring Sherry Jackson this time - the first version had starred Margaret O'Brien, Oz's wicked witch. The story was in print now, and the show aired on March 1st, 1955.

27. Zero Hour. This 1947 story aired on CBS's Suspense on April 5th, 1955.

28. And the Moon Be Still As Bright. This 1948 story aired on April 22nd, 1955 on X Minus One.

29. Mars Is Heaven. This 1948 story aired on May 8th, 1955 on X Minus One.

30. The Whole Town's Sleeping. This was aired on June 14th, 1955, the second production made for Suspense on CBS Radio. The first version as Summer Night, starred Ida Lupino. This version starred Jeanette Nolan. The story itself was published in 1950.

31. Kaleidoscope. This 1949 story was used on Suspense on CBS Radio on July 12th, 1955.

32. The Veldt. This 1950 story aired on August 4th, 1955 on X Minus One.

33. And the Moon Be Still As Bright. This 1948 story was re-run on September 22nd, 1955 on X Minus One.

34. Dwellers in Silence. This 1948 story was used on X Minus One on November 10th, 1955.

35. Zero Hour. This 1947 story aired on X Minus One on November 23rd, 1955.

36. To the Future. This adaptation of The Fox and the Forest, 1950, was aired on X Minus One on December 14th, 1955.

Ray Bradbury

37. Marionettes, Inc. This 1949 story aired on X Minus One on December 21st, 1955.

38. Season of Disbelief/Hail and Farewell. These 1950 and 1953 stories were adapted for CBS Radio Workshop and were aired on February 17th, 1956.

39. Zero Hour. This second version of the 1947 story aired on CBS's Suspense on May 18th, 1958. This one starred Evelyn Rudie; the first version had starred Evelyn Ashdowne.

40. The Whole Town's Sleeping. This was aired on August 31st, 1958, the third production made for Suspense on CBS Radio. The first version as Summer Night, starred Ida Lupino; the second version starred Jeanette Nolan; and this one starred Agnes Moorehead. The story itself was published in 1950.

41. The Veldt. This 1950 story was used on the BBC Light Programme in 1959.

42. The Fox and the Forest. This 1950 story was used on the BBC Light Programme in 1959.

43. Zero Hour. This third version of the 1947 story aired on CBS's Suspense on January 3rd, 1960. The first version had starred Evelyn Ashdowne; the second one starred Evelyn Rudie; and this final one starred Francie Meyers.

44. There will Come Soft Rains. From 1950, this was used on the BBC Third Programme in 1962.

45. A Sound of Thunder. This 1952 story was used on SF68, a South African series, in 1968.

46. Leviathan 99. This was a play written for radio. Ray sent the script to NBC in 1966 but they rejected it. So he went after the BBC, who accepted it. It ran for ninety minutes and was aired on BBC Radio 3 on May 3rd, 1968.

47. Summer Raptures of Ray Bradbury. This was a ninety minute show that ran on the CBC in Canada in the early 1970s.

48. Fahrenheit 451. Studio 71 at the CBC in Canada did an adaptation of this which aired March 4th, 1971.

49. There will Come Soft Rains. From 1950, this was done on BBC Radio Four in 1971.

50. The Happiness Machine. From 1957, this was used on the CBC in Canada in the 1970s on Theatre 10:30 - Dandelion Wine Part 1.

51. The Time Machine. From 1955, this was used on the CBC in Canada in the 1970s on Theatre 10:30 - Dandelion Wine Part 2.

52. Miss Helen Loomis. From 1957, this excerpt was used on the CBC in Canada in the 1970s on Theatre 10:30 - Dandelion Wine Part 3.

53. Mr. Jonas and Grandpa. From 1957, this excerpt was used on the CBC in Canada in the 1970s on Theatre 10:30 - Dandelion Wine Part 4.

54. The Playground. From 1953, this was used on the CBC in Canada in the 1970s on Vanishing Point.

55. The Fox and the Forest. This 1950 story ran on The Unknown World, Series 3, Episode 4 on the BBC World Service during the mid-1970s.

56. Here There Be Tygers. This 1951 story ran on The Unknown World, Series 5, Episode 5 on the BBC World Service during the mid-1970s.

57. Frost and Fire. This 1946 story aired on CBC Playhouse - Bradbury X 5 - on November 12th, 1973.

58. The Lonely One. This 1949 story aired on CBC Playhouse - Bradbury X 5 - on November 19th, 1973.

59. The Veldt. This 1950 story aired on CBC Playhouse - Bradbury X 5 - on November 26th, 1973.

60. The Day It Rained Forever. From 1957, this aired on CBC Playhouse - Bradbury X 5 - on December 3rd, 1973.

61. I Sing the Body Electric. This 1969 story aired on CBC Playhouse - Bradbury X 5 - on December 10th, 1973.

62. An Imbalance of Species. Based on A Sound of Thunder from 1952, this was used on Future Tense in 1974.

63. Mars is Heaven. This 1948 story was used on Future Tense in 1974.

64. Zero Hour. From 1947, this story was used on Future Tense in 1974.

65. To the Chicago Abyss. This 1963 story aired on Chicago Radio Theater on May 11th, 1975.

66. Kaleidoscope. This 1949 story was adapted for The Mind's Web and used on May 23rd, 1975.

67. The Halloween Tree. From 1972, this novel aired in five episodes on Spider's Web in 1976.

68. The Foghorn. This 1951 story was used on Mindwebs, July 15th, 1977.

69. Kaleidoscope. This 1949 story was used on Mindwebs on September 30th, 1977.

70. The Whole Town's Sleeping. In 1977, Adventure Theater did a series of re-runs on the American Armed Forces Radio and Television Network from the CBS show, Suspense. They used the June 14th, 1955 production of this 1950 story, starring Jeanette Nolan.

71. Zero Hour. As part of Adventure Theater's series of re-runs on the American Armed Forces Radio and Television Network, they did Suspense's first version of this 1947 story, from April 5th, 1955, starring Evelyn Ashdowne. The show aired in 1977.

72. There Will Come Soft Rains. This 1950 story was used on BBC Radio Four in 1977.

73. The Veldt. From 1950, this aired on Mindwebs on January 27th, 1978.

74. Fahrenheit 451. This 1953 novel aired on BBC Radio Four in 1982. The show ran for ninety minutes.

Bradbury 13. This was a radio series that started on National Public Radio in 1984 and ran for thirteen episodes, produced by Mike McDonough. Each one had a voice-over opening by Bradbury:

75. The Ravine. This was Episode 1 and it aired on April 2nd, 1984.

76. Night Call, Collect. Published in 1949, this was Episode 2 and it aired April 9th, 1984.

77. The Veldt. Published in 1950, this was Episode 3 and it aired April 16th, 1984.

78. There Was an Old Woman. Published in 1944, this was Episode 4 and it aired April 23rd, 1984.

79. Kaleidoscope. Published in 1949, this was Episode 5 and it aired April 30th, 1984.

80. Dark They Were and Golden Eyed. Published in 1949, this was Episode 6 and it aired May 7th, 1984.

81. The Screaming Woman. Published in 1951, this was Episode 7 and it aired May 14th, 1984.

82. A Sound of Thunder. Published in 1952, this was Episode 8 and it aired May 21st, 1984.

83. The Man. Published in 1949, this was Episode 9 and it aired May 28th, 1984.

84. The Wind. Published in 1943, this was Episode 10 and it aired June 4th, 1984.

85. The Fox and the Forest. Published in 1950, this was Episode 11 and it aired June 11th, 1984.

86. Here There Be Tygers. Published in 1951, this was Episode 12 and it aired June 18th, 1984.

87. The Happiness Machine. Published in 1957, this was Episode 13 and it aired June 25th, 1984, the final program in the series.

88. October Country. An ABC Radio special from 1984, featuring an interview with Ray and adaptations of a number of stories from the October Country collection, 1955.

89. The Crowd. From 1943, this was used on the program Ghost Story from BBC Radio Four in 1986.

90. A Piece of Wood. This 1952 story was used on Future Imperfect in 1988, a BBC World Service series.

91. Frost and Fire. This 1946 story was used on Sci-Fi Radio. Part One aired on October 29th, 1989; and Part Two was heard on November 5th, 1989.

92. Marionettes, Inc. This 1949 story was used on Audion Theater on September 15th, 1990.

93. Any Friend of Nicholas Nickleby Is a Friend of Mine. This 1966 story was used on California Artists Radio Theater in 1990.

94. Kaleidoscope. From 1949, this was aired on the BBC Radio Four on August 28th, 1991.

95. The Smile. From 1952, this was aired on the BBC Radio Four in 1991.

96. The Next in Line. Published in 1947, this was used on the BBC series Fear on Four, Series 4, Number 2, from December 31st, 1992.

97. The Shoreline at Sunset. This 1959 story was used on BBC Radio Four in 1994.

98. A 75th Birthday Tribute to Ray Bradbury. This was featured on California Artists Radio Theater in 1995 and included extracts from The Martian Chronicles, 1950; The Illustrated Man, 1951; Dandelion Wine, 1957; and Death Is a Lonely Business, 1985; along with The Pedestrian, 1951; and The Beggar on the O'Connell Bridge, 1961.

Tales of the Bizarre. This was a Ray Bradbury anthology that ran in two series on the BBC 4 from December 1995 until December 1997.

Series One:

99. Night Call, Collect. From 1949, this was aired on December 8th, 1995.

100. Have I Got a Chocolate Bar for You. Published in 1973, this was aired on December 15th, 1995.

101. The Jar. This 1944 story was used on December 22nd, 1995.

102. The Fruit at the Bottom of the Bowl. This 1948 story aired on December 29th, 1995.

103. I Sing the Body Electric. From 1969, this was heard on January 5th, 1996.

104. Skeleton. Published in 1945, this was used on January 12th, 1996.

Series Two:

105. The Man Upstairs. From 1947, this played on November 20th, 1997.

106. Jack in the Box. Published in 1947, this was used on November 27th, 1997.

107. The Scythe. This 1943 story aired on December 4th, 1997.

108. The Wind. From 1943, this was used on December 11th, 1997.

109. And So Died Riabouchinska. This 1953 story was heard on December 18th, 1997.

110. The Day It Rained Forever. From 1957, this story was used on December 25th, 1997.

111. An 80th Birthday Tribute to Ray Bradbury. This was put on by California Artists Radio Theater in 2000. It featured extracts from The Martian Chronicles, 1950; and The Machineries of Joy, 1964.

112. Pillar of Fire. This 1948 story was produced by Hollywood Theater of the Ear in 2000.

113. Fahrenheit 451. This 1953 novel aired on BBC Radio Four in 2003. The show ran for sixty minutes.

114. The Pedestrian. This 1951 story was used on BBC Radio Four's series Walking Stories in 2004.

115. Zero Hour. This 1947 story was performed on Radiowest in 2006.

116. Dandelion Wine. This was used on Colonial Radio Theatre on the Air in 2006. Ray wrote the script, based on his stage play.

***

NOVELS AND COLLECTIONS

1. Dark Carnival. Published by Arkham House, Sauk City, Wisconsin, 1947. Hardcover. Herein: The Crowd, 1943; The Emissary, 1947; Interim, 1947; Jack-in-the-Box, 1947; The Jar, 1944; The Lake, 1944; The Man Upstairs, 1947; The Night, 1946; The Scythe, 1943; Skeleton, 1945; The Small Assassin, 1946; There Was an Old Woman, 1944; Uncle Einar, 1947; The Tombstone, 1945; The Next in Line, 1947; The Wind, 1943; The Cistern, 1947; Homecoming, 1946; The Dead Man, 1945; Let's Play Poison, 1946; The Handler, 1947; The Smiling People, 1946; The Coffin, 1947; The Traveller, 1946; The Night Sets, 1947; Reunion, 1944; and The Maiden, 1947.

2. Dark Carnival. Published by Hamish Hamilton, London, 1948. Hardcover. An abridged version, dropping seven of the twenty-seven stories. This contains: The Crowd, 1943; The Emissary, 1947; The Jar, 1944; The Lake, 1944; The Man Upstairs, 1947; The Night, 1946; Skeleton, 1945; The Small Assassin, 1946; There Was an Old Woman, 1944; Uncle Einar, 1947; The Tombstone, 1945; The Next in Line, 1947; The Wind, 1943; The Cistern, 1947; Homecoming, 1946; The Dead Man, 1945; Let's Play Poison, 1946; The Handler, 1947; The Smiling People, 1946; and The Traveller, 1946.

3. The Martian Chronicles. Published by Doubleday & Company, Garden City, New York, 1950. Hardcover. This collection contains: Rocket Summer, 1947; Ylla, 1950; The Summer Night, 1949; The Earth Men, 1948; The Taxpayer, 1950; The Third Expedition, 1948; And the Moon be Still as Bright, 1948; The Settlers, 1950; The Green Morning, 1950; The Locusts, 1950; Night Meeting, 1950; The Shore, 1950; Interim, 1947; The Musicians, 1950; Way in the Middle of the Air, 1950; The Naming of Names, 1949; Usher II, 1950; The Old Ones, 1950; The Martian, 1949; The Luggage Shore, 1950; The Off Season, 1948; The Watchers, 1950; The Silent Towns, 1949; The Long Years, 1948; There Will Come Soft Rains, 1950; and The Million-Year Picnic, 1946.

4. The Silver Locusts. Published by Rupert Hart-Davis, London, 1951. Hardcover. Re-titled British edition of The Martian Chronicles, 1950. This added The Fire Balloons, 1951 and dropped Usher II, 1950. Herein: Rocket Summer, 1947; Ylla, 1950; The Summer Night, 1949; The Earth Men, 1948; The Taxpayer, 1950; The Third Expedition, 1948; And the Moon be Still as Bright, 1948; The Settlers, 1950; The Green Morning, 1950; The Locusts, 1950; Night Meeting, 1950; The Shore, 1950; Interim, 1947; The Musicians, 1950; Way in the Middle of the Air, 1950; The Naming of Names, 1949; The Fire Balloons, 1951; The Old Ones, 1950; The Martian, 1949; The Luggage Shore, 1950; The Off Season, 1948; The Watchers, 1950; The Silent Towns, 1949; The Long Years, 1948; There Will Come Soft Rains, 1950; and The Million-Year Picnic, 1946.

5. The Illustrated Man. Published by Doubleday & Company, Garden City, New York, 1951. Hardcover. This collection contains: Prologue: The Illustrated Man, 1951; The Veldt, 1950; Kaleidoscope, 1949; The Other Foot, 1951; The Highway, 1950; The Man, 1949; The Long Rain, 1950; The Rocket Man, 1951; The Fire Balloons, 1951; The Last Night of the World, 1951; The Exiles, 1949; No Particular Night or Morning, 1951; The Fox and the Forest, 1950; The Visitor, 1948; The Concrete Mixer, 1948; Marionettes Inc, 1949; The City, 1950; Zero Hour, 1947; The Rocket, 1950; and Epilogue, 1951.

6. The Illustrated Man. Published by Rupert Hart-Davis, London, 1952. Hardcover. This dropped four stories that were in the original edition: The Rocket Man, 1951; The Fire Balloons, 1951; The Exiles, 1949; and The Concrete Mixer, 1949. And added two that were not in the original edition: Usher II, 1950; and The Playground, 1952.

7. The Golden Apples of the Sun. Published by Doubleday & Company, Garden City, New York, 1953. Hardcover. Herein: The Fog Horn, 1951; The Pedestrian, 1951; The April Witch, 1951; The Wilderness, 1952; The Fruit at the Bottom of the Bowl, 1948; Invisible Boy, 1945; The Flying Machine, 1953; The Murderer, 1953; The Golden Kite, the Silver Wind, 1953; I See You Never, 1947; Embroidery, 1951; The Big Black and White Game, 1945; A Sound of Thunder, 1952; The Great Wide World Over There, 1952; Powerhouse, 1948; En Le Noche, 1952; Sun and Shadow, 1953; The Meadow, 1953; The Garbage Collector, 1953; The Great Fire, 1949; Hail and Farewell, 1953; and The Golden Apples of the Sun, 1953.

8. The Golden Apples of the Sun. Published by Rupert Hart-Davis, London, 1953. Hardcover. This dropped two stories from the original version: The Great Fire, 1949; and The Big Black and White Game, 1945.

9. Fahrenheit 451. Published by Ballantine Books, New York City, 1953. Softcover. Ballantine Book 41. As well as the title story, this includes two others: And the Rock Cried Out, 1953; and The Playground, 1953.

10. Fahrenheit 451. Published by Ballantine Books, New York City, 1953. First hardcover edition, released subsequent to the softcover. As well as the title story, this includes two others: And the Rock Cried Out, 1953; and The Playground, 1953.

11. Fahrenheit 451. Published by Rupert Hart-Davis, London, 1954. This first British hardcover edition drops the two short stories from the original version.

12. Switch on the Night. Published by Pantheon Books, New York City, 1955. Hardcover.

13. The October Country. Published by Ballantine Books, New York City, 1955. Hardcover. This contains: The Dwarf, 1954; The Next in Line, 1947; The

Watchful Poker Chip of H. Matisse, 1954; Skeleton, 1945; The Jar, 1944; The Lake, 1944; The Emissary, 1947; Touched with Fire, 1955; The Small Assassin, 1946; The Crowd, 1943; Jack-in-the-Box, 1947; The Scythe, 1943; Uncle Einar, 1947; The Wind, 1943; The Man Upstairs, 1947; There Was an Old Woman, 1944; The Cistern, 1947; Homecoming, 1946; and The Wonderful Death of Dudley Stone, 1954.

14. The October Country. Published by Ballantine Books, New York City, 1956. Softcover. Ballantine Book F139. This included a preface by the author that was absent from the hardcover edition.

15. Dandelion Wine. Published by Doubleday & Company, Garden City, New York, 1957. Hardcover. This began as a series of stories that were strung together to make a novel. The stories were: The Happiness Machine, 1957; Good-by Grandma, 1957; The Night, 1946; The Trolley, 1955; Green Wine for Dreaming, 1957; Statues, 1957; Dandelion Wine, 1953; Illumination, 1957; Summer in the Air, 1956; The Last, the Very Last, 1955; Dinner at Dawn, 1954; The Whole Town's Sleeping, 1950; The Swan, 1954; The Window, 1950; The Green Machine, 1951; Season of Disbelief, 1950; The Lawns of Summer, 1952; The Season of Sitting, 1951; Exorcism, 1957; Magic, 1957; and The Tarot Witch, 1957.

16. Sun and Shadow. Published by The Quenian Press, Berkeley, California, 1959. Softcover. This 1953 story was privately printed by Kenneth J. Carpenter for the Roxburghe Club of San Francisco.

17. A Medicine for Melancholy. Published by Doubleday & Company, Garden City, New York, 1959. Hardcover. Herein: In Season of Calm Weather, 1957; The Dragon, 1955; The End of the Beginning, 1956; The Wonderful Ice Cream Suit, 1958; Fever Dream, 1948; The Marriage Mender, 1954; The Town Where No One Got Off, 1958; A Scent of Sarsaparilla, 1953; Icarus Montgolfier Wright, 1956; The Headpiece, 1958; Dark they Were, and Golden-eyed, 1949; The Smile, 1952; The First Night of Lent, 1956; The Time of Going Away, 1956; All Summer in a Day, 1954; The Gift, 1952; The Great Collision of Monday Last, 1958; The Little Mice, 1955; The Shore Line at Sunset, 1959; The Strawberry Window, 1955; The Day it Rained Forever, 1957; and A Medicine for Melancholy, 1959.

18. The Day It Rained Forever. Published by Rupert Hart-Davis, London, 1959. Hardcover. Not only did the British re-title A Medicine for Melancholy, 1959, they also changed it. Four of the original stories were dropped: A Medicine for Melancholy, 1959; The First Night of Lent, 1956; All Summer in a Day, 1954; and The Great Collision of Monday Last, 1958. Five different stories were added: Referent, 1948 - originally as by Brett Sterling; Almost the End of the World, 1957; Here There Be Tygers, 1951; Perchance to Dream, 1948; and And the Rock Cried Out, 1953.

19. The October Country. Published by Ace Books, London, 1961. Softcover. Ace Book H422. This added one story, The Traveller, 1946, and dropped seven from the original version: The Crowd, 1943; The Lake, 1944; The Man Upstairs, 1947; The Small Assassin, 1946; The Next in Line, 1947; The Cistern, 1947; and Jack-in-the-Box, 1947.

20. R Is for Rocket. Published by Doubleday & Company, Garden City, New York, 1962. Hardcover. This contains: Introduction by **Ray Bradbury**; The Rocket Man, 1951; The End of the Beginning, 1956; The Fog Horn, 1951; The Rocket, 1950; The Golden Apples of the Sun, 1953; A Sound of Thunder, 1952; The Long Rain, 1950; The Exiles, 1949; Here There be Tygers, 1951; The Strawberry Window, 1955; The Dragon, 1955; The Gift, 1952; Frost and Fire, 1946; Uncle Einar, 1947; The Time Machine, 1955; The Sound of Summer Running, 1956; and R is for Rocket, 1943.

21. The Small Assassin. Published by NEL - New English Library, London, 1962. Softcover. Re-titled re-issue of Dark Carnival, 1944. This contains: The Crowd, 1943; The Emissary, 1947; The Jar, 1944; The Lake, 1944; The Man Upstairs, 1947; The Night, 1946; Skeleton, 1945; The Small Assassin, 1946; There Was an Old Woman, 1944; Uncle Einar, 1947; The Tombstone, 1945; The Next in Line, 1947; The Wind, 1943; The Cistern, 1947; Homecoming, 1946; The Dead Man, 1945; Let's Play Poison, 1946; The Handler, 1947; The Smiling People, 1946; The Traveller, 1946.

22. Something Wicked This Way Comes. Published by Simon and Schuster, New York City, 1962. Hardcover.

23. The Anthem Sprinters and Other Antics. Published by The Dial Press, New York City, 1963. Released simultaneously in softcover and hardcover. The softcover was Apollo Editions A-75. This contains: A Clear View of an Irish Mist - play, 1963; The Great Collision of Monday Last - play, 1963; The Anthem Sprinters - play, 1963; and The First Night of Lent - play, 1963; along with an afterword: The Queen's Own Evaders by **Ray Bradbury**, 1963.

24. The Machineries of Joy. Published by Simon and Schuster, New York City, 1964. Hardcover. Herein: The One Who Waits, 1949; Tyrannosaurus Rex, 1962; The Vacation, 1964; The Drummer Boy of Shiloh, 1960; Boys! Raise Giant Mushrooms in Your Cellar, 1962; Almost the End of the World, 1957; Perhaps We Are Going Away, 1962; And the Sailor, Home from the Sea, 1960; El Dia de Muerte, 1947; The Illustrated Woman, 1961; Some Live Like Lazarus, 1960; A Miracle of Rare Device, 1962; And So Died Riabouchinsaka, 1953; The Beggar on O'Connell Bridge, 1961; Death and the Maiden, 1960; A Flight of Ravens, 1952; The Best of All Possible Worlds, 1960; The Lifework of Juan Diaz, 1963; To the Chicago Abyss, 1963; The Anthem Sprinters, 1963; and The Machineries of Joy, 1962.

25. The Machineries of Joy. Published by Rupert Hart-Davis, London, 1964. This dropped Almost the End of the World, 1957 and added The Day It Rained Forever, 1957.

26. The Pedestrian. Published by Roy A. Squires, Glendale, California, 1964. Softcover limited edition - 280 copies.

27. The Vintage Bradbury. Published by Vintage Books, New York City, 1965. Hardcover.

Ray Bradbury

This contains: Introduction by Gilbert Highet; The Watchful Poker Chip of H. Matisse, 1954; The Veldt, 1950; Hail and Farewell, 1953; A Medicine for Melancholy, 1959; The Fruit at the Bottom of the Bowl, 1948; Ylla, 1950; The Little Mice, 1955; The Small Assassin, 1946; The Anthem Sprinters, 1963; And the Rock Cried Out, 1953; Invisible Boy, 1945; Night Meeting, 1950; The Fox and the Forest, 1950; Skeleton, 1945; Dandelion Wine, 1953; Illumination, 1957; Statues, 1957; Green Wine for Dreaming, 1957; Kaleidoscope, 1949; Sun and Shadow, 1953; The Illustrated Man, 1950; The Fog Horn, 1951; The Dwarf, 1954; Fever Dream, 1948; The Wonderful Ice Cream Suit, 1958; and There Will Come Soft Rains, 1950.

28. A Device Out of Time. Privately printed in 1965. 35 to 40 copies were printed for the author's personal use.

29. The Autumn People. Published by Ballantine Books, New York City, 1965. Softcover. Ballantine Book U2141. Graphic adaptations, with Albert B. Feldstein. Herein: Foreword by **Ray Bradbury**; There Was an Old Woman; The Screaming Woman; Touch and Go; The Small Assassin; The Handler; The lake; The Coffin; and Let's Play Poison.

30. Tomorrow Midnight. Published by Ballantine Books, New York City, 1966. Softcover. Ballantine Book U2142. Graphic adaptations, with Albert B. Feldstein. This contains: Introduction by **Ray Bradbury**; Punishment Without Crime; I Rocket; King of the Gray Spaces; The One Who Waits; The Long Years; Mars Is Heaven; There Will Come Soft Rains; and Outcast of the Stars.

31. Twice 22. Published by Doubleday & Company, Garden City, New York, 1966. Hardcover. This combined all the stories from The Golden apples of the Sun, 1953, and A Medicine for Melancholy, 1959.

32. The Day It Rained Forever. A Comedy in One Act. Published by Samuel French, New York City, 1966. Softcover.

33. The Pedestrian. A Fantasy in One Act. Published by Samuel French, New York City, 1966. Softcover.

34. S Is for Space. Published by Doubleday & Company, Garden City, New York, 1966. Hardcover. This collection contains: Introduction by **Ray Bradbury**; Chrysalis, 1946; Pillar of Fire, 1948; Zero Hour, 1947; The Man, 1949; Time in Thy Flight, 1953; The Pedestrian, 1951; Hail and Farewell, 1953; Invisible Boy, 1945; Come into My Cellar, 1962; The Million Year Picnic, 1946; The Screaming Woman, 1951; The Smile, 1952; Dark They Were and Golden Eyed, 1949; The Trolley, 1955; The Flying Machine, 1953; and Icarus Montgolfier Wright, 1956.

35. Fahrenheit 451. Published by Simon and Schuster, New York City, 1967. This new edition contains a new introduction by the author. It also includes the two stories from the original: And the Rock Cried Out, 1953; and The Playground, 1953.

36. I Sing the Body Electric. Published by Alfred A. Knopf, New York City, 1969. Hardcover. Herein: The Kilimanjaro Device, 1965; The Terrible Conflagration Up at the Place, 1969; Tomorrow's Child, 1948; The Women, 1948; The Inspired Chicken Motel, 1969; Downwind from Gettysburg, 1969; Yes, We'll Gather at the River, 1969; The Cold Wind and the Warm, 1964; Night Call, Collect, 1949; The Haunting of the New, 1969; The Tombling Day, 1952; Any Friend of Nicholas Nickleby's Is a Friend of Mine, 1966; Heavy Set, 1964; The Man in the Rorschach Shirt, 1966; Henry the Ninth, 1969; The Lost City of Mars, 1967; Christus Apollo - a poem, 1969; and I Sing the Body Electric, 1969.

37. Bloch and Bradbury. With Robert Bloch. Published by Tower Books, New York City, 1969. Softcover. Tower Book 43-246. A collection of four stories by Bradbury and six stories by Robert Bloch. This contains: Bradbury: The Watchers, 1945; Fever Dream, 1948; The Dead Man, 1945; and The Handler, 1947. Bloch: The Shadow from the Steeple, 1950; The Grinning Ghoul, 1936; Mannikins of Horror, 1939; The Druidic Doom, 1936; A Question of Etiquette, 1942; and The Man Who Cried Wolf, 1945.

38. Fever Dream and Other Fantasies. With Robert Bloch. Sphere Books, London, 1970. Softcover. Sphere Book 17140. Re-titled issue of Bloch and Bradbury, 1969.

39. Old Ahab's Friend, and Friend to Noah, Speaks His Piece - Apollo Year Two. Published by Roy A. Squires, Glendale, California, 1971. Softcover.

40. The Halloween Tree. Published by Alfred A. Knopf, New York City, 1972. Hardcover.

41. The Wonderful Ice Cream Suit and Other Plays. Published by Bantam Books, New York City, 1972. Softcover. Bantam Book SP7297. Herein: Introduction with Notes on Staging by **Ray Bradbury**, 1972; The Wonderful Ice Cream Suit - play, 1972; The Veldt - play, 1972; and To the Chicago Abyss - play, 1972.

42. The Wonderful Ice Cream Suit and Other Plays. Published by Hart-Davis MacGibbon, London, 1973. First hardcover edition.

43. When Elephants Last in the Dooryard Bloomed. Published by Alfred A. Knopf, New York City, 1973. Hardcover. Poetry collection.

44. That Son of Richard III. Published by Roy A. Squires, Glendale, California, 1974. Softcover. Limited to 400 copies.

45. Byzantium I Come Not From. Published by Fullerton College, Fullerton, California, 1975. Softcover.

46. Dandelion Wine. Published by Alfred A. Knopf, New York City, 1975. Hardcover. This contains a new introduction by the author.

47. Ray Bradbury. Edited and introduced by Anthony Adams. Published by Harrap, London, 1975. Soft cloth covers. This contains: The Veldt, 1950; Let's Play Poison, 1946; Fever Dream, 1948; Zero Hour, 1947; The Fog Horn, 1951; A Sound of Thunder, 1952; The Wind, 1943; The Scythe, 1943; Marionettes, Inc, 1949; The Other Foot, 1951; The Pedestrian, 1951; The Trolley, 1955; The Smile,

1952; The Gift, 1952; and The Last Night of the World, 1951.

48. Pillar of Fire and Other Plays. Published by Bantam Books, New York City, 1975. Softcover. Bantam Book N2173. Herein: Introduction by **Ray Bradbury**, 1975; Pillar of Fire - play, 1975; Kaleidoscope - play, 1975; and The Fog Horn - play, 1975.

49. Long After Midnight. Published by Alfred A. Knopf, New York City, 1976. Hardcover. The original proof-copy softcovers that were sent out to reviewers contained the story I, Rocket, 1944. Ray was unhappy with this and insisted it be replaced. Subsequent releases contained The Better Part of Wisdom, 1976. Herein: The Blue Bottle, 1950; One Timeless Spring, 1946; The Parrot Who Met Papa, 1972; The Burning Man, 1976; A Piece of Wood, 1952; The Messiah, 1971; G.B.S. - Mark V, 1976; The Utterly Perfect Murder, 1971; Punishment Without Crime, 1950; Getting Through Sunday Somehow, 1962; Drink Entire Against the Madness of Crowds, 1976; Interval in Sunlight, 1954; A Story of Love, 1976; The Wish, 1973; Forever and the Earth, 1950; The Better Part of Wisdom, 1976; Darling Adolf, 1976; The Miracles of Jamie, 1946; The October Game, 1948; The Pumpernickel, 1951; Have I Got a Chocolate Bar for You, 1973; and Long After Midnight, 1963.

50. A Device Out of Time. Published by Dramatic Publishing, United States, 1976. Softcover.

51. That Ghost, That Bride of Time. Excerpts from a Play-in-Progress. Published by Roy A. Squires, Glendale, California, 1976. Softcover. Limited to 400 copies, the first 150 of which were signed by the author.

52. Where Robot Mice and Robot Men Run Round in Robot Towns. Published by Alfred A. Knopf, New York City, 1977. Hardcover. A poetry collection.

53. Twin Hieroglyphs that Swim the River Dust. Published by Lord John Press, Northridge, California, 1978. Hardcover. A poetry collection.

54. The Bike Repairman. Published by Santa Susana Press, Northridge, California, 1978. Softcover.

55. Beyond 1984: A Remembrance of Things Future. Published by Targ Editions, United States, 1979. Hardcover. This contains: Remembrance of Things Future - an essay, 1965; They Have Not Seen the Stars - a poem, 1978; The East Is Up! - a poem, 1979; and Beyond 1984 - an essay, 1979.

56. This Attic Where the Meadow Greens. Published by Lord John Press, Northridge, California, 1979. Hardcover. A poetry collection.

57. The Poet Considers His Resources. Published by Lord John Press, Northridge, California, 1979. Softcover.

58. To Sing Strange Songs. Published by Wheaton & Co., London, 1979. Softcover. This contains: Introduction: Surprise! Surprise! By **Ray Bradbury**; All Summer in a Day, 1954; The April Witch, 1952; Fever Dream, 1948; Icarus Montgolfier Wright, 1956; Uncle Einar, 1947; A Sound of Thunder, 1952; The Fog Horn, 1951; Statues, 1957; Illumination, 1957; Boys! Raise Giant Mushrooms in Your Cellar!, 1962; If Only We Had Taller Been - a poem, 1973; Why Viking Lander, Why the Planet Mars? - a poem, 1976.

59. The Fog Horn and Other Stories. Published by Taiyosha, Tokyo, Japan, 1979. Softcover. Herein: The Pedestrian, 1951; A Sound of Thunder, 1952; The Dwarf, 1954; The Garbage Collector, 1953; The Fog Horn, 1951; and En la Noche, 1952.

60. The Last Circus and the Electrocution. Published by Lord John Press, Northridge, California, 1980. Hardcover. This contains: The Last Circus, 1980; and The Electrocution - written as William Elliott, 1946.

61. The Stories of Ray Bradbury. Published by Alfred A. Knopf, New York City, 1980. Hardcover. Herein: There Will Come Soft Rains, 1950; The Million Year Picnic, 1946; Kaleidoscope, 1949; The Fire Balloons, 1951; The City, 1950; The Crowd, 1943; The Rocket Man, 1951; The Last Night of the World, 1951; No Particular Night or Morning, 1951; Marionettes, Inc, 1949; McGillahee's Brat, 1970; The Wilderness, 1952; All Summer in a Day, 1954; And So Died Riabouchinska, 1953; The April Witch, 1952; The Aqueduct, 1979; The Best of All Possible Worlds, 1960; The Better Part of Wisdom, 1976; The Big Black and White Game, 1945; The Black Ferris, 1948; Calling Mexico, 1950; The Day It Rained Forever, 1957; The Earth Men, 1948; Embroidery, 1951; The Emissary, 1947; Farewell Summer - a poem, 1980; Fever Dream, 1948; The Golden Apples of the Sun, 1953; The Golden Kite, the Silver Wind, 1953; Gotcha!, 1978; The Great Fire, 1949; Hail and Farewell, 1953; The Happiness Machine, 1957; The Haunting of the New, 1969; Have I Got a Chocolate Bar for You!, 1973; The Illustrated Woman, 1961; Interval in Sunlight, 1954; Invisible Boy, 1945; Jack-in-the-Box, 1947; The Jar, 1944; The Lake, 1944; The Man Upstairs, 1947; A Medicine for Melancholy, 1959; The Murderer, 1953; Night Call, Collect, 1949; The Night, 1946; The October Game, 1948; The Off Season, 1948; The One Who Waits, 1949; The Parrot Who Met Papa, 1972; A Piece of Wood, 1952; The Playground, 1953; Powerhouse, 1948; Punishment Without Crime, 1950; A Scent of Sarsaparilla, 1952; The Scythe, 1943; The Silent Towns, 1949; Skeleton, 1945; The Small Assassin, 1946; A Story of Love, 1976; The Strawberry Window, 1955; There Was an Old Woman, 1944; Mars Is Heaven!, 1948; The Tombling Day, 1952; The Two Where No One Got Off, 1958; Uncle Einar, 1947; The Vacation, 1963; The Women, 1948; Yes, We'll Gather at the River, 1969; A Sound of Thunder, 1952; The Next in Line, 1947; Homecoming, 1946; The Screaming Woman, 1951; The Wonderful Ice Cream Suit, 1958; The Fog Horn, 1951; Dark They Were, and Golden-Eyed, 1949; The End of the Beginning, 1956; The Great Wide World Over There, 1952; The Fox and the Forest, 1950; The Anthem Sprinters, 1963; The Veldt, 1950; The Shoreline at Sunset, 1959; The Coffin, 1947; Some Live Like Lazarus, 1960; Boys! Raise Giant Mushrooms in Your Cellar!, 1962; Tyrannosaurus Rex, 1962; Frost and

Ray Bradbury

Fire, 1946; The Long Rain, 1950; I Sing the Body Electric!, 1969; The Inspired Chicken Motel, 1969; Tomorrow's Child, 1948; The Terrible Conflagration Up at the Place, 1969; Touched with Fire, 1955; Long After Midnight, 1963; The Utterly Perfect Murder, 1971; The Blue Bottle, 1950; The Traveller, 1946; The Picasso Summer, 1980; The Leave-Taking, 1957; and Drunk and In Charge of a Bicycle - an essay, 1980.

62. Doing Is Being. Published by WED Imagineering, Los Angeles, California, 1980. Softcover.

63. The Haunted Computer and the Android Pope. Published by Alfred A. Knopf, New York City, 1981. Hardcover. A poetry collection.

64. The Fog Horn and Other Stories. Published by Kinseido, Tokyo, Japan, 1981. Softcover. Herein: Forever and the Earth, 1950; A Story of Love, 1976; The Fog Horn, 1951; and The Miracles of Jamie, 1946.

65. The Ghosts of Forever. Published by Rizzoli, New York City, 1981. Hardcover. Primarily a poetry collection, but it also includes: The God in Science Fiction - an essay, 1977; The Messiah - a short story, 1971; a prologue by Bradbury; and an epilogue by Melvin B. Zisfein.

66. Long After Midnight and Other Stories. Published by Nan'un-do, Japan, 1981. Softcover. Herein: The Man, 1949; The Jar, 1944; The Smile, 1952; and Long After Midnight, 1963.

67. Then Is All Love? It Is, It Is! Published by The Orange County Book Society, California, 1981. Limited edition.

68. The Complete Poems of Ray Bradbury. Published by Del Rey - Ballantine Books, New York City, 1982. Softcover.

69. The Love Affair. Published by Lord John Press, Northridge, California, 1982. Hardcover.

70. The Other Foot. Published by Perfection Form Company, Logan, Iowa, 1982. Softcover.

71. The Veldt. Published by Perfection Form, United States, 1982. Softcover.

72. The Stories of Ray Bradbury. Published by Granada Books, London, 1983. Softcover. Herein: Herein: There Will Come Soft Rains, 1950; The Million Year Picnic, 1946; Kaleidoscope, 1949; The Fire Balloons, 1951; The City, 1950; The Crowd, 1943; The Rocket Man, 1951; The Last Night of the World, 1951; No Particular Night or Morning, 1951; Marionettes, Inc, 1949; McGillahee's Brat, 1970; The Wilderness, 1952; All Summer in a Day, 1954; And So Died Riabouchinska, 1953; The April Witch, 1952; The Aqueduct, 1979; The Best of All Possible Worlds, 1960; The Better Part of Wisdom, 1976; The Big Black and White Game, 1945; The Black Ferris, 1948; Calling Mexico, 1950; The Day It Rained Forever, 1957; The Earth Men, 1948; Embroidery, 1951; The Emissary, 1947; Farewell Summer - a poem, 1980; Fever Dream, 1948; The Golden Apples of the Sun, 1953; The Golden Kite, the Silver Wind, 1953; Gotcha!, 1978; The Great Fire, 1949; Hail and Farewell, 1953; The Happiness Machine, 1957; The Haunting of the New, 1969; Have I Got a Chocolate Bar for You!, 1973; The Illustrated Woman, 1961; Interval in Sunlight, 1954; Invisible Boy, 1945; Jack-in-the-Box, 1947; The Jar, 1944; The Lake, 1944; The Man Upstairs, 1947; A Medicine for Melancholy, 1959; The Murderer, 1953; Night Call, Collect, 1949; The Night, 1946; The October Game, 1948; The Off Season, 1948; The One Who Waits, 1949; The Parrot Who Met Papa, 1972; and A Piece of Wood, 1952.

73. The Stories of Ray Bradbury - Volume 2. Published by Granada, London, 1983. Herein: The Playground, 1953; Powerhouse, 1948; Punishment Without Crime, 1950; A Scent of Sarsaparilla, 1952; The Scythe, 1943; The Silent Towns, 1949; Skeleton, 1945; The Small Assassin, 1946; A Story of Love, 1976; The Strawberry Window, 1955; There Was an Old Woman, 1944; Mars Is Heaven!, 1948; The Tombling Day, 1952; The Two Where No One Got Off, 1958; Uncle Einar, 1947; The Vacation, 1963; The Women, 1948; Yes, We'll Gather at the River, 1969; A Sound of Thunder, 1952; The Next in Line, 1947; Homecoming, 1946; The Screaming Woman, 1951; The Wonderful Ice Cream Suit, 1958; The Fog Horn, 1951; Dark They Were, and Golden-Eyed, 1949; The End of the Beginning, 1956; The Great Wide World Over There, 1952; The Fox and the Forest, 1950; The Anthem Sprinters, 1963; The Veldt, 1950; The Shoreline at Sunset, 1959; The Coffin, 1947; Some Live Like Lazarus, 1960; Boys! Raise Giant Mushrooms in Your Cellar!, 1962; Tyrannosaurus Rex, 1962; Frost and Fire, 1946; The Long Rain, 1950; I Sing the Body Electric!, 1969; The Inspired Chicken Motel, 1969; Tomorrow's Child, 1948; The Terrible Conflagration Up at the Place, 1969; Touched with Fire, 1955; Long After Midnight, 1963; The Utterly Perfect Murder, 1971; The Blue Bottle, 1950; The Traveller, 1946; The Picasso Summer, 1980; The Leave-Taking, 1957; and Drunk and In Charge of a Bicycle - an essay, 1980.

74. Dinosaur Tales. Published by Bantam Books, New York City, 1983. Softcover. This contains: Foreword by **Ray Harryhausen**; Introduction by **Ray Bradbury**; A Sound of Thunder, 1952; Besides a Dinosaur, Whatta Ya Wanna Be When You Grow Up, 1983; Lo the Dear Daft Dinosaurs, 1980; The Fog Horn, 1951; What if I Said the Dinosaur's Not Dead - a poem, 1983; and Tyrannosaurus Rex, 1983.

75. A Memory of Murder. Published by Dell Books, New York City, 1984. Softcover. Herein: Introduction: Hammett? Chandler? Not to Worry by **Ray Bradbury**; The Small Assassin, 1946; A Careful Man Dies, 1946; It Burns Me Up, 1944; Half Pint Homicide, 1944; Four Way Funeral, 1944; The Long Night, 1944; Corpse Carnival, 1945; Hell's Half Hour, 1945; The Long Way Home, 1945; Wake for the Living, 1947; I'm Not So Dumb, 1945; The Trunk Lady, 1944; Yesterday I Lived, 1944; Dead Men Rise Up Never, 1945; and The Candy Skull, 1948.

76. The Novels of Ray Bradbury: Fahrenheit 451; Dandelion Wine; Something Wicked This Way Comes. Published by Harper Collins, New York City, 1984. An omnibus edition that collects the three titles mentions, from 1953, 1957 and 1962 respectively.

77. Forever and the Earth - A Radio Dramatization. Published by Croissant, Athens, Ohio, 1984. Hardcover.

78. The Last Good Kiss. Published by Santa Susana Press, Northridge, California, 1984. Softcover.

79. Death Is a Lonely Business. Published by Alfred A. Knopf, New York City, 1985. Hardcover.

80. Long After Ecclesiastes. Published by Gold Stein Press, United States, 1985. Softcover.

81. Death Has Lost Its Charm for Me. Published by Lord John Press, Northridge, California, 1987. Hardcover. A poetry collection.

82. The April Witch: A Creative Classic. Published by Creative Education, United States, 1987. Softcover.

83. The Fog Horn: A Creative Classic. Published by Creative Education, United States, 1987. Softcover.

84. The Other Foot: A Creative Classic. Published by Creative Education, United States, 1987. Softcover.

85. Fever Dream. Published by St. Martin's Press, New York City, 1987. Hardcover.

86. The Toynbee Convector. Published by Alfred A. Knopf, New York City, 1988. Hardcover. Herein: Trapdoor, 1985; On the Orient North, 1988; One Night in Your Life, 1988; West of October, 1988; The Last Circus, 1980; The Laurel and Hardy Love Affair, 1987; I Suppose You Are Wondering Why We Are Here, 1984; Lafayette Farewell, 1988; Banshee, 1984; Promises, Promises, 1988; The Love Affair, 1982; One for His Lordship and One for the Road, 1985; At Midnight in the Month of June, 1954; Bless Me Father for I Have Sinned, 1984; By the Numbers, 1984; A Touch of Petulance, 1980; Long Division, 1988; Come and Bring Constance, 1988; Junior, 1988; The Tombstone, 1945; The Thing at the Top of the Stairs, 1988; Colonel Stonesteel's Genuine Home-made Truly Egyptian Mummy, 1981; and The Toynbee Convector, 1984.

87. The Dragon. Published by Footsteps Press, Round Top, New York, 1988. Softcover limited edition.

88. Falling Upward. Published by Dramatic Publishing, United States, 1988. Softcover.

89. The Climate of Palettes. Published by Lord John Press, Northridge, California, 1989. Hardcover limited edition.

90. Classic Stories 1: From The Golden Apples of the Sun and R Is for Rocket. Published by Bantam Books, New York City, 1990. Softcover. Herein: The Fog Horn, 1951; The April Witch, 1952; The Wilderness, 1952; The Fruit at the Bottom of the Bowl, 1948; The Flying Machine, 1953; The Murderer, 1953; The Golden Kite, the Silver Wind, 1953; I See You Never, 1947; Embroidery, 1951; The Big Black and White Game, 1945; The Great Wide World Over There, 1952; Powerhouse, 1948; En La Noche, 1952; Sun and Shadow, 1953; The Meadow, 1953; The Garbage Collector, 1953; The Great Fire, 1949; The Golden Apples of the Sun, 1953; Introduction to R Is for Rocket in Classic Stories 1 by **Ray Bradbury**, 1990; R Is for Rocket, 1943; The End of the Beginning, 1956; The Rocket, 1950; The Rocket Man, 1951; A Sound of Thunder, 1952; The Long Rain, 1950; The Exiles, 1949; Here There Be Tygers, 1951; The Strawberry Window, 1955; The Dragon, 1955; Frost and Fire, 1946; Uncle Einar, 1947; The Time Machine, 1955; and The Sound of Summer Running, 1956.

91. Classic Stories 2: From A Medicine for Melancholy and S Is for Space. Published by Bantam Books, New York City, 1990. Softcover. This contains: In a Season of Calm Weather, 1957; A Medicine for Melancholy, 1959; The Wonderful Ice Cream Suit, 1958; Fever Dream, 1948; The Marriage mender, 1954; The Town Where No One Got Off, 1958; A Scent of Sarsaparilla, 1953; The Headpiece, 1958; The First Night of Lent, 1956; The Time of Going Away, 1956; All Summer in a Day, 1954; The Gift, 1952; The Great Collision of Monday Last, 1958; The Little Mice, 1955; The Shoreline at Sunset, 1959; The Day It Rained Forever, 1957; Introduction - S Is for Space by **Ray Bradbury**, 1966; Chrysalis, 1946; Pillar of Fire, 1948; Zero Hour, 1947; The Man, 1949; Time in They Flight, 1953; The Pedestrian, 1951; Hail and Farewell, 1953; Invisible Boy, 1945; Come into My Cellar, 1962; The Million Year Picnic, 1946; The Screaming Woman, 1951; The Smile, 1952; The Trolley, 1955; and Icarus Montgolfier Wright, 1956.

92. A Graveyard for Lunatics. Published by Alfred A. Knopf, New York City, 1990. Hardcover.

93. Ray Bradbury on Stage: A Chrestomathy of His Plays. Published by Donald I. Fine, New York City, 1991. Softcover.

94. The Parrot Who Met Papa. With David Aronovitz. Published by Pretentious Press, United States, 1991. This reproduces Ray's 1972 story with a sequel by Aronovitz.

95. Green Shadows, White Whale. Published by Alfred A. Knopf, New York City, 1992. Hardcover.

96. The Ray Bradbury Chronicles. Volume 1. Published by Bantam Books, New York City, 1992. Softcover. Graphic adaptations of: Dark They Were, and Golden Eyed; The Golden Apples of the Sun; Marionettes, Inc; The Toynbee Convector; The Dragon; and I Rocket.

97. The Ray Bradbury Chronicles. Volume 2. Published by Bantam Books, New York City, 1992. Softcover. Graphic adaptations of: Come into My Cellar; Rocket Summer and the Locusts; Punishment Without Crime; A Piece of Wood; and The Flying Machine.

98. The Ray Bradbury Chronicles. Volume 3. Published by Bantam Books, New York City, 1992. Softcover. Graphic adaptations of: There Will Come Soft Rains; The Veldt; Gotcha!; Homecoming; and The Aqueduct.

Ray Bradbury

99. The Ray Bradbury Chronicles. Volume 4. Published by NBM Publishing, New York City, 1993. Hardcover. Graphic adaptations of: It Burns Me Up!; Touched by Fire; The Black Ferris; A Sound of Thunder; and Tyrannosaurus Rex.

100. The Ray Bradbury Chronicles. Volume 5. Published by NBM Publishing, New York City, 1993. Hardcover. Graphic adaptations of: The Foghorn; Besides a Dinosaur; Whadda Ya Wanna Be When You Grow Up; The City; and Usher II.

101. The Ray Bradbury Chronicles. Volume 6. Published by NBM Publishing, New York City, 1994. Hardcover. Graphic adaptations of: The April Witch; Trapdoor; Picasso Summer; The Illustrated Man; Zero Hour; and The Visitor.

102. The Ray Bradbury Chronicles. Volume 7. Published by NBM Publishing, New York City, 1994. Hardcover. Graphic adaptations of: Skeleton; Home to Say; Off Season; Kaleidoscope; and Uncle Einar.

103. Quicker Than the Eye. Published by Avon Books, New York City, 1996. Hardcover. Herein: Unterderseaboat Doktor, 1994; Zaharoff/Richter Mark V, 1996; Remember Sascha?, 1996; Another Fine Mess, 1995; The Electrocution, 1946; Hopscotch, 1996; The Finnegan, 1996; That Woman on the Lawn, 1996; The Very Gentle Murders, 1994; Dorian in Excelsus, 1995; No News, or What Killed the Dog?, 1996; The Witch Door, 1995; The Ghost in the Machine, 1996; At the End of the Ninth Year, 1995; Bug, 1996; Once More Legato, 1995; Exchange, 1996; Free Dirt, 1996; Last Rites, 1994; The Other Highway, 1996; and Quicker Than the Eye, 1995; along with Make Haste to Live: An Afterword by **Ray Bradbury**.

104. The Illustrated Man - The 45th Anniversary Edition. Published by Gauntlet Press, Springfield, Pennsylvania, 1996. Hardcover limited edition with an introduction by William F. Nolan and an Afterword by Ed Gorman. The dustjacket art was by Bradbury himself.

105. The October Country - The 40th Anniversary Edition. Published by Gauntlet Press, Springfield, Pennsylvania, 1997. Hardcover limited edition with an introduction by Dennis Etchison and an afterword by Robert R. McCammon. Signed by Bradbury, Etchison and McCammon.

106. Driving Blind. Published by Avon Books, New York City, 1997. Hardcover. This contains: Night Train to Babylon, 1997; If MGM Is Killed, Who Gets the Lion?, 1997; Hello, I Must Be Going, 1997; House Divided, 1997; Grand Theft, 1995; Remember Me?, 1997; Fee Fie Foe Fum, 1993; I Wonder What's Become of Sally, 1997; Nothing Changes, 1997; That Old Dog Lying in the Dust, 1974; Someone in the Rain, 1997; Madame et Monsieur Shill, 1997; The Mirror, 1997; End of Summer, 1948; Thunder in the Morning, 1997; The Highest Branch on the Tree, 1997; A Woman Is a Fast-Moving Picnic, 1997; Virgin Resusitas, 1997; Mr Pale, 1997; That Bird That Comes Out of the Clock, 1997; and Driving Blind, 1997; followed by an afterword by **Ray Bradbury**.

107. Dogs Think That Every Day Is Christmas. Published by Gibbs-Smith, Salt Lake City, Utah, 1997. Hardcover.

108. With Cat for Comforter. Published by Gibbs-Smith, Salt Lake City, Utah, 1997. Hardcover.

109. Ahmed and the Oblivion Machine: A Fable. Published by Avon Books, New York City, 1998. Hardcover.

110. Christus Apollo: Cantata Celebrating the Eighth Day of Creation and the Promise of the Ninth. Published by Gold Stein Press, United States, 1998. Softcover.

111. Witness and Celebrate. Published by Lord John Press, Northridge, California, 2000. Hardcover.

112. Something Wicked This Way Comes. Published by Gauntlet Press, Springfield, Pennsylvania, 1999. Hardcover limited edition with a new introduction by the author and afterwords by: Joe Lansdale and Peter Crowther.

113. Ray Bradbury Collected Short Stories. Published by Peterson Publishing, United States, 2001. Hardcover.

114. From the Dust Returned. Published by William Morrow, New York City, 2001. Hardcover.

115. Dark Carnival. Published by Gauntlet Press, Colorado Springs, Colorado, 2001. Hardcover. A limited edition with an afterword by Clive Barker. Both Barker and Bradbury signed the books. Herein: Editor's Notes - an essay by Donn Albright; Dark Carnival Revisited - an essay by **Ray Bradbury**; The Crowd, 1943; The Emissary, 1947; Interim, 1947; Jack-in-the-Box, 1947; The Jar, 1944; The Lake, 1944; The Man Upstairs, 1947; The Night, 1946; The Scythe, 1943; Skeleton, 1945; The Small Assassin, 1946; There Was an Old Woman, 1944; Uncle Einar, 1947; The Tombstone, 1945; The Next in Line, 1947; The Wind, 1943; The Cistern, 1947; Homecoming, 1946; The Dead Man, 1945; Let's Play Poison, 1946; The Handler, 1947; The Smiling People, 1946; The Coffin, 1947; The Traveller, 1946; The Night Sets, 1947; Reunion, 1944; The Maiden, 1947; The Sea Shell, 1944; The Watchers, 1945; Bang! You're Dead, 1944; and The Poems, 1945.

116. Time Intervening. Published by Gauntlet Press, Colorado Springs, Colorado, 2001. Softcover.

117. A Chapbook for Burnt-out Priests, Rabbis and Ministers. Published by Cemetery Dance, Baltimore, Maryland, 2001. Hardcover.

118. One More for the Road. Published by Harper Collins, New York City, 2002. Hardcover. Herein: First Day, 2002; Heart Transplant, 1981; Quid Pro Quo, 2000; After the Ball, 2002; In Memoriam, 2002; Tête-à-Tête, 2002; The Dragon Danced at Midnight, 1967; The Nineteenth, 2002; Beasts, 2002; Autumn Afternoon, 2002; Where All Is Emptiness There Is Room to Move, 2002; One-Woman Show, 2002; The Laurel and Hardy Alpha Centauri Farewell Tour, 2000; Leftovers, 2002; Tangerine, 2002; With Smiles as Wide as Summer, 1961; Time Intervening, 1947; The Enemy in the Wheat, 1994; Fore, 2001; My Son Max, 1993; The F. Scott/Tolstoy/Ahab Accumulator, 2002; Well, What Do You Have to Say for Yourself?,

2002; Diane de Foret, 2002; The Cricket on the Hearth, 2002; and One More for the Road, 2002; followed by an afterword: Metaphors: the Breakfast of Champions - an essay by **Ray Bradbury**.

119. They Have Not Seen the Stars. Published by Stealth Press, United States, 2002. Hardcover. An omnibus edition that gathers five poetry collections: When Elephants Last in the Dooryard Bloomed, 1973; Where Robot Mice and Robot Men Run Round in Robot Towns, 1977; This Attic Where the Meadows Green, 1979; The Haunted Computer and the Android Pope, 1981; and Death Has Lost Its Charm for Me, 1987.

120. I Live by the Invisible. Published by Salmon Publishing, Ireland, 2002. Softcover.

121. Bradbury Stories: 100 of Bradbury's Most Celebrated Tales. Published by Harper Collins, New York City, 2003. Hardcover. Herein: The Whole Town's Sleeping, 1950; The Rocket, 1950; Season of Disbelief, 1950; And the Rock Cried Out, 1953; The Drummer Boy of Shiloh, 1960; The Beggar on O'Connell Bridge, 1961; The Flying Machine, 1953; Heavy Set, 1964; The First Night of Lent, 1956; Lafayette Farewell, 1988; Remember Sascha?, 1996; Junior, 1988; The Woman on the Lawn, 1996; Ylla, 1950; Banshee, 1984; One for His Lordship, and One for the Road!, 1985; The Laurel and Hardy Love Affair, 1987; Unterderseaboat Doktor, 1994; Another Fine Mess, 1995; The Dwarf, 1954; A Wild Night in Galway, 1959; The Wind, 1943; No News, or What Killed the Dog?, 1994; A Little Journey, 1951; Any Friend of Nicholas Nickleby's Is a Friend of Mine, 1966; The Garbage Collector, 1953; The Visitor, 1948; The Man, 1949; Henry the Ninth, 1969; The Messiah, 1971; Bang! You're dead!, 1944; Darling Adolf, 1976; The Beautiful Shave, 1979; Colonel Stonesteel's Genuine Home-Made Truly Egyptian Mummy, 1981; I See You Never, 1947; The Exiles, 1949; At Midnight, in the Month of June, 1954; The Witch Door, 1995; The Watchers, 1945; The Naming of Names, 1949; Hopscotch, 1996; The Illustrated Man, 1950; The Dead Man, 1945; And the Moon Be Still as Bright, 1948; The Burning Man, 1976; G.B.S. - Mark V, 1976; A Blade of Grass, 1949; The Sound of Summer Running, 1956; And the Sailor, Home from the Sea, 1960; The Lonely Ones, 1949; The Finnegan, 1996; On the Orient North, 1988; The Smiling People, 1946; The Fruit at the Bottom of the Bowl, 1948; Bug, 1996; Downwind from Gettysburg, 1969; Time in Thy Flight, 1953; Changeling, 1949; The Dragon, 1955; Let's Play Poison, 1946; The Cold Wind and the Warm, 1964; The Meadow, 1953; The Kilimanjaro Device, 1965; The Man in the Rorschach Shirt, 1966; Bless Me Father, for I Have Sinned, 1984; The Pedestrian, 1951; Trapdoor, 1985; The Swan, 1954; The Sea Shell, 1944; Once More, Legato, 1995; Way in the Middle of the Air, 1950; The Wonderful Death of Dudley Stone, 1954; By the Numbers!, 1984; Usher II, 1950; The Square Pegs, 1948; The Trolley, 1955; The Smile, 1952; The Miracles of Jamie, 1946; A Far-Away Guitar, 1950; The Cistern, 1947; The Machineries of Joy, 1962; Bright Phoenix, 1963; The Wish, 1973; The Lifework of Juan Diaz, 1963; Interim, 1947; Almost the End of the World, 1957; The Great Collision of Monday Last, 1958; The Poems, 1945; The Long Years, 1948; Icarus Montgolfier Wright, 1956; Death and the Maiden, 1960; Zero Hour, 1947; The Toynbee Convector, 1984; Forever and the Earth, 1950; The Handler, 1947; Getting Through Sunday Somehow, 1962; The Pumpernickel, 1951; Last Rites, 1995; The Watchful Poker Chip of H. Matisse, 1954; and All on a Summer's Night, 1950.

122. Let's All Kill Constance. Published by William Morrow, New York City, 2003. Hardcover.

123. Is That You, Herb? Published by Gauntlet Press, Colorado Springs, Colorado, 2003. Softcover.

124. The Best of Ray Bradbury: The Graphic Novel. Published by IBooks, New York City, 2003. Softcover. Graphic adaptations of: A Sound of Thunder; The City; Dark They Were, and Golden-Eyed; The Golden Apples of the Sun; Night Meeting; Picasso Summer; A Piece of Wood; Come into My Cellar; The Visitor; It Burns Me Up!; The April Witch; and The Foghorn.

125. The Cat's Pajamas: Stories. Published by Harper Collins, New York City, 2004. Hardcover. Herein: Introduction: Alive and Kicking and Writing by **Ray Bradbury**; Chrysalis; The Island; Sometime Before Dawn; Hail to the Chief; We'll Just Act Natural; Ole, Orozco! Siqueiros, Si!; The House; The John Wilkes Booth/Warner Brothers; MGM/NBC Funeral Train; A Careful Man Dies; The Cat's Pajamas; Triangle; The Mafioso Cement-Mixing Machine; The Ghosts; Where My Heart, What's My Hurry?; The Transformation; Sixty-six; A Matter of Taste; I Get the Blues When It Rains - a Remembrance; All My Enemies Are Dead; The Completist; and an epilogue.

126. It Came from Outer Space. Published by Gauntlet Press, Colorado Springs, Colorado, 2004. Softcover with cover art by **Ray Bradbury**. Along with interview material, this gathers four different versions of Ray's screen treatment for It Came from Outer Space, 1953.

127. A Sound of Thunder and Other Stories. Published by Perennial, New York City, 2004. Softcover. Herein: Herein: The Fog Horn, 1951; The April Witch, 1952; The Wilderness, 1952; The Fruit at the Bottom of the Bowl, 1948; The Flying Machine, 1953; The Murderer, 1953; The Golden Kite, the Silver Wind, 1953; I See You Never, 1947; Embroidery, 1951; The Big Black and White Game, 1945; The Great Wide World Over There, 1952; Powerhouse, 1948; En La Noche, 1952; Sun and Shadow, 1953; The Meadow, 1953; The Garbage Collector, 1953; The Great Fire, 1949; The Golden Apples of the Sun, 1953; Introduction to R Is for Rocket in Classic Stories 1 by **Ray Bradbury**, 1990; R Is for Rocket, 1943; The End of the Beginning, 1956; The Rocket, 1950; The Rocket Man, 1951; A Sound of Thunder, 1952; The Long Rain, 1950; The Exiles, 1949; Here There Be Tygers, 1951; The Strawberry Window, 1955; The Dragon, 1955; Frost and Fire, 1946; Uncle Einar, 1947; The Time Machine, 1955; and The Sound of Summer Running, 1956.

128. Fragments! Published by Gauntlet Press, Colorado Springs, Colorado, 2005. Softcover.

129. The Halloween Tree. Published by Gauntlet Press, Colorado Springs, Colorado, 2005. Hardcover

Ray Bradbury

limited edition. This restored the text that the original edition deleted as well as including a number of features.

130. Forever and the Earth: Yesterday and Tomorrow Stories. Published by PS Publishing, United Kingdom, 2005. Hardcover. Reprints R Is for Rocket and S Is for Space, and includes eleven more stories that had been intended for S Is for Space but never actually made it: Referent, 1948; The Black Ferris, 1948; Statues, 1957; The Seashell, The Drummer Boy of Shiloh, 1960; The Veldt, 1950; I, Rocket, 1944; Forever and the Earth, 1950; Tomorrow and Tomorrow, 1947; Golden Kite, Silver Wind, 1953; The Day It Rained Forever, 1957.

131. Farewell Summer. Published by William Morrow, New York City, 2006. Hardcover.

132. The Dragon Who Ate His Tail. Published by Gauntlet Press, Colorado Springs, Colorado, 2007. Softcover. Herein: The Dragon Who Ate His Tail; ...To the Future; Screenplay pages from Fox and the Forest; and Sometime Before Dawn.

133. Somewhere a Band Is Playing. Published by Gauntlet Press, Colorado Springs, Colorado, 2007. Hardcover limited edition. Herein: Introduction: And the Band Played On by William F. Nolan; Somewhere a Band Is Playing, 2007; Dandelion Wine - early fragment, 1951; Dandelion Wine - facsimile; Nefertiti, Ohio: early title for Somewhere a Band Is Playing 1960s; The Beautiful One Is Here - a fragment; Follow the Sun - a fragment; Mr Timkins - a fragment; Untitled early fragments; Somewhere a Band Is Playing - the outline for a teleplay; Somewhere a Band Is Playing - facsimile; and Somewhere a Band Is Playing - unfinished screenplay, 1958.

134. Now and Forever: Somewhere a Band Is Playing - and - Leviathan '99. Published by William Morrow, New York City, 2007. Hardcover. Herein: Introduction: Somewhere by **Ray Bradbury**; Somewhere a Band Is Playing, 2007; Radio Dream - introduction to Leviathan '99 by **Ray Bradbury**; and Leviathan '99, 2007.

135. Summer Morning, Summer Night. Published by Subterranean Press, Burton, Michigan, 2008. Hardcover. Herein: End of Summer, 1948; The Great Fire, 1949; All on a Summer's Night, 1950; Miss Bidwell, 2008; The Pumpernickel, 1951; These Things Happen, 2008; At Midnight, in the Month of June, 1954; A Walk in Summer, 2008; Autumn Afternoon, 2002; Arrival and Departure, 2008; The Beautiful Lady, 2008; Love Potion, 2008; Night Meeting, 2008; The Death of So-and-so, 2008; I Got Something You Ain't Got, 2008; The Waders, 2008; The Dog, 2008; The River That Went Out to Sea, 2008; Over, Over, Over, Over, Over, Over, Over!, 2008; The Projector, 1008; The People with Seven Arms, 2008; A Serious Discussion or, Evil in the World, 2008; The Fireflies, 2008; The Circus, 2008; The Cemetery, or The Tombyard; and The Screaming Woman, 1951.

136. Masks. Published by Gauntlet Press, Colorado Springs, Colorado, 2008. Hardcover limited edition.

***

ANTHOLOGIES

1. Timeless Stories for Today and Tomorrow. Published by Bantam Books, New York City, 1952. Softcover. Bantam Book A944. Herein: Putzi by Ludwig Bemelmans, 1935; Heartburn by Hortense Calisher, 1951; A Note for the Milkman, 1950; and None Before Me by Sidney Carroll, 1949; The Enormous Radio by John Cheever, 1947; The Portable Phonograph by Walter van Tilburg Clark, 1941; The Hour After Westerly by Robert M. Coates, 1947; The Glass Eye by John Kier Cross, 1949; The Sound Machine by Roald Dahl, 1949; Mr Death and the Redheaded Woman (The Rider on the Pale Horse) by Helen Eustis, 1950; The Laocoon Complex by J. C. Furnas, 1937; The Demon Lover by Shirley Jackson, 1949; The Cocoon by John B. L. Goodwin, 1946; Miss Winters and the Wind by Christine Noble Govan, 1946; The Eight Mistresses by Jean Hrolda, 1937; I Am Waiting by Christopher Isherwood, 1939; Night Flight by Josephine W. Johnson, 1944; In the Penal Colony by Franz Kafka, 1919; Jeremy in the Wind by Nigel Kneale, 1949; Housing Problem by Henry Kuttner, 1944; Inflexible Logic by Russell Maloney, 1940; The Witnesses by William Sansom, 1944; The Hand by Wessel Hyatt Smitter, 1947; Saint Katy and the Virgin by John Steinbeck, 1938; The Supremacy of Uruguay by E. B. White; and The Pedestrian by **Ray Bradbury**, 1951.

2. The Circus of Dr. Lao and Other Improbable Stories. Published by Bantam Books, New York City, 1956. Softcover. Bantam Book A1519. This contains: Introduction by **Ray Bradbury**; The Circus of Dr Lao by Charles G. Finney, 1935; The Pond by Nigel Kneale, 1949; The Hour of Letdown by E. B. White, 1951; The Wish by Roald Dahl, 1948; The Summer People by Shirley Jackson, 1950; Earth's Holocaust by Nathaniel Hawthorne, 1844; Buzby's Petrified Women by Loren Eiseley, 1948; The Resting Place by Oliver LaFarge, 1954; Threshold by Henry Kuttner, 1940; Greenface by James Schmitz, 1943; The Limits of Walter Horton by John Seymour Sharnik, 1940; and The Man Who Vanished by Robert M. Coates, 1955.

***

NON-FICTION

1. The Essence of Creative Writing: Letters to a Young Aspiring Author. Published by the San Antonio Public Library, San Antonio, Texas, 1962. Softcover.

2. Creative Man Among His Servant Machines. A lecture transcript from 1967.

3. Zen in the Art of Writing - and - The Joy of Writing. Published by Capra Press, Santa Barbara, California, 1973. Softcover.

4. The God in Science Fiction. Published by Santa Susanna Press, Northridge, California - California State University, 1978. Softcover.

5. The Mummies of Guanajuato. Published by Harry N. Abrams, New York City, 1978. Hardcover. Black and white photographs of the mummies by Archie Lieberman, text by **Ray Bradbury**.

6. About Norman Corwin. Published by Santa Susanna Press, Northridge, California - California State University, 1980. Softcover.

7. There Is Life on Mars. Published by Reader's Digest Press, United States, 1981. Hardcover.

8. The Art of Playboy. Published by Alfred Van Der Marck Editions, New York City, 1985. Hardcover.

9. Zen in the Art of Writing. Published by Capra Press, Santa Barbara California, 1990. Softcover.

10. Yestermorrow: Obvious Answers to Impossible Futures. Published by Joshua Odell Editions - Capra Press, Santa Barbara California, 1991.

11. Bradbury on His Life and Work: I Take Joy in What I Do. Privately printed pamphlet, 2001. Softcover.

12. Stars. Published by William Morrow, New York City, 2005. Hardcover.

13. Match to Flame: The Fictional Paths to Fahrenheit 451. Edited by Donn Albright. Introduction by Richard Matheson. Published by Gauntlet Press, Colorado Springs, Colorado, 2007. Hardcover limited edition.

***

RELATED

1. The Case of the Baroque Baby Killer - A Teenage Chum Rattles Some of the Skeletons in the Closet of Ray Bradbury. By Forrest J. Ackerman. Private Printing, California, 1949. Softcover.

2. Ray Bradbury Review. Edited by William F. Nolan. Privately published in San Diego, California, 1952. Softcover.

3. The Magazine of Fantasy and Science Fiction - Special Ray Bradbury Issue - May 1963. Published by Mercury Press, Cornwall, Connecticut, 1963. A special issue of the digest magazine, devoted to **Ray Bradbury**. This contains: Introduction by Avram Davidson; Bradbury: Prose Poet in the Age of Space - an essay by William F. Nolan; Bradbury Film Wins Academy Award Nomination - anonymous essay; Bright Phoenix by **Ray Bradbury**; To the Chicago Abyss by **Ray Bradbury**; and An Index to the Works of **Ray Bradbury** by William F. Nolan; along with the usual features.

4. The Ray Bradbury Companion. By William F. Nolan. Published by Gale Research: A Bruccoli Clark Book, Detroit, Michigan, 1975. Softcover.

5. Xenophile Volume 2, Number 1, Whole Number 13 - May 1975. Ray Bradbury Issue. Edited and published by Nils Hardin, St. Louis, Missouri, 1975. Softcover magazine.

6. The Bradbury Chronicles. By George Edgar Slusser. Published by R. Reginald The Borgo Press, San Bernardino, California, 1977. Softcover.

7. Bradbury's Works. By Audrey Smoak Manning. Published by Cliffs Notes, Lincoln, Nebraska, 1977. Softcover.

8. The Drama of Ray Bradbury. By Ben F. Indick. Published by T. K. Graphics, Baltimore, Maryland, 1977. Softcover.

9. A Ray Bradbury File. By Bill Stevenson. Published by Arnold, Leeds, England, 1977. Softcover.

10. Touchstone: A Tribute to Fritz Leiber and Ray Bradbury. Published by Mysterious Stranger Press, United States, 1978. Softcover.

11. Ray Bradbury - Writers of the 21st Century. By Joseph D. Olander and Martin H. Greenberg. Taplinger Publishing, New York City, 1980. Hardcover.

12. Ray Bradbury. By Wayne L. Johnson. Published by Frederick Ungar, New York City, 1980. Hardcover.

13. The Mental Health Association Tribute to Ray Bradbury. Published by The Mental Health Association, Los Angeles, 1981. Softcover.

14. Ray Bradbury and the Poetics of Reverie. By William F. Touponce. Published by UMI Research, Ann Arbor, Michigan, 1984. Hardcover.

15. Ray Bradbury. By David Mogen. Published by Twayne Publishers, Boston, 1986. Hardcover.

16. Ray Bradbury. By William Golding. Published by St. Martin's Press, New York City, 1986. Hardcover.

17. Ray Bradbury Review. Edited by William F. Nolan. Published by Graham Press, Los Angeles, 1988. Hardcover.

18. Ray Bradbury. Starmont Reader's Guide 31. Edited by William F. Touponce. Published by Starmont House, San Bernardino, California, 1989. Softcover.

19. Kentucky Poetry Review - Ray Bradbury Issue. Edited by Wade Hall, Joy Bale Boone, Gregg Swem and Alice Scott. Published by Bellarmine College, Louisville, Kentucky, 1989. Softcover.

20. Selected from Dark They Were, and Golden-Eyed. Published by Signal Hill Publications, United States, 1991. Softcover. This reproduces the story Dark They Were, and Golden-Eyed, 1949, and adds a number of articles about Bradbury.

21. The Bradbury Chronicles: Stories in Honor of Ray Bradbury. Edited by William F. Nolan and Martin H. Greenberg. Published by ROC - Penguin Books, New York City, 1991. Hardcover.

22. Ray Bradbury: A Critical Companion. By Anne Reid Robin. Published by Greenwood Press, Westport, Connecticut, 2000. Hardcover.

23. Ray Bradbury - Bloom's Modern Critical Views. By Harold Bloom. Published by Chelsea House Publications, Langhorne, Pennsylvania, 2000. Hardcover.

24. Ray Bradbury. An Illustrated Life. By Jerry Weist. Published by William Morrow, New York City, 2002. Hardcover.

Ray Bradbury

25. Conversations with Ray Bradbury. Edited by Steven L. Aggelis. Published by University Press of Mississippi, 2004. Hardcover.

26. Ray Bradbury: Master of Science Fiction and Fantasy. By Wendy Mass. Published by Enslow Publishers, Berkeley Heights, New Jersey, 2004. Hardcover.

27. Ray Bradbury: The Life of Fiction. By William F. Touponce and Jonathan R. Eller with a foreword by William F. Nolan. Published by Kent State University Press, Ashland, Ohio, 2004. Hardcover.

28. Author Price Guide 005.5: Ray Bradbury. Published by Quill and Brush, Dickerson, Maryland, 2004. Softcover.

29. The Bradbury Chronicles: The Life of Ray Bradbury. By Sam Weller. Published by William Morrow, New York City, 2005. Hardcover.

30. Ray Bradbury Uncensored! The Unauthorized Biography. By Gene Beley. Published by iUniverse, United States, 2006. Softcover.

31. Classic Story Tellers: Ray Bradbury. By Michele Griskey. Published by Mitchell Lane Publishing, Hockessin, Delaware, 2006. Hardcover.

32. Dystopian Writing in the Twentieth Century: A Comparative Analysis of Aldous Huxley's Brave New World and Ray Bradbury's Fahrenheit 451. By Dora Kollar. Published by VDM Verlag, Germany, 2008. Softcover.

33. The New Ray Bradbury Review - Number 1, 2008. Edited by William F. Touponce. Published by Kent State University Press, Ashland, Ohio, 2008. Softcover.

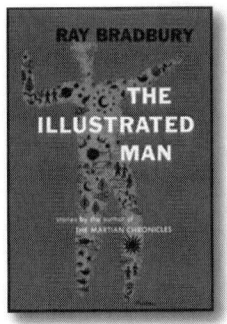 

Abraham Merritt.

Abraham Merritt was born in Beverly, New Jersey on January 20th, 1884 and died of a sudden heart attack in Rock Keys, Florida, August 21st, 1943. His primary career was as a journalist and as the assistant editor of The American Weekly from 1912 until 1937. In 1937, he became the editor and remained in that position until he died.

By 1919, he was making twenty-five grand a year and, when he died, he was making a hundred grand. That was a ton of money for the time and it allowed Merritt to travel to exotic places and to pursue exotic hobbies, to indulge his desire to collect weapons, carvings, occult literature; to indulge his desire to grow plants of a magical nature, peyote, pot, blue datura - a somewhat poisonous hallucinogenic... and wolfsbane, also known as monkshood and leopard's bane and women's bane... A member of the buttercup family, it was said that wolfsbane was the only way to identify a werewolf. If the werewolf stood still long enough for you to hold up the wolfsbane to cast a shadow on it, and if the shadow was yellow, then the test was positive. Merritt kept a supply on hand at his Long Island Estate. You never know.

As an editor, he hired and encouraged two of the best artists of the period, Virgil Finlay and Hannes Bok.

And as a writer, he invented some of the more interesting fantasies of the time and, though the critics have been unkind to him and the fans have largely forgotten him, he still managed to be a major influence on the work of H. P. Lovecraft and Hannes Bok. His first published story, Through the Dragon Glass, was in All-Stories Weekly in 1917; next came The People of the Pit the following year, also in All-Story Weekly. And although he produced a relatively small amount of work, the power of his imagination and the strength of his emotions made him very popular while he was alive and writing.

First editions of his early work tend to sell in the $4,500.00 range.

Pen name used: W. Fenimore for one story, The Pool of the Stone God, 1923.

***

FILM AND TELEVISION

1. **Seven Footprints to Satan.** Published as a novel in 1928, this was filmed in 1929. Directed by Benjamin Christensen, it starred: Thelma Todd; Creighton Hale; Sheldon Lewis; William V. Mong; Sojin; Laska Winters; Ivan Christy; DeWitt Jennings; Nora Cecil; and many others, including Loretta Young in an uncredited part as one of Satan's victims.

2. **The Devil Doll.** Based on the 1933 novel Burn Witch Burn, this film was released in July 1936. It starred: Lionel Barrymore; Maureen O'Sullivan; Frank Lawton; Rafaela Ottiano; Robert Greig; Lucy Beaumont; Henry B. Walthall; Grace Ford; and many others.

***

NOVELS AND COLLECTIONS

1. **The Moon Pool.** Published by G. P. Putnam's Sons, New York City, 1919. Hardcover.

2. **The Ship of Ishtar.** Published by G. P. Putnam's Sons, New York City, 1926. Hardcover.

3. **Seven Footprints to Satan.** Published by Boni and Liveright, New York City, 1928. Hardcover.

4. **The Face in the Abyss.** Published by Horace Liveright, New York City, 1931. Hardcover.

5. **Dwellers in the Mirage.** Published by Liveright, New York City, 1932. Hardcover.

6. **Thru the Dragon Glass.** The ARRA Printers, Jamaica, New York, 1932. Softcover.

7. **Burn Witch Burn!** Published by Liveright, New York City, 1933. Hardcover.

8. **Creep, Shadow.** Published by Doubleday, Doran & Company, Garden City, New York, 1934. Hardcover.

9. **Three Lines of Old French.** Published by The Bizarre Series, Milheim, Pennsylvania, 1937. Softcover. Bizarre Number 1.

10. **Dwellers in the Mirage.** Published by Avon Book Company, New York City, 1944. Softcover. Murder Mystery Monthly 24. Restored the original ending from the serialised magazine version of the story, which was Argosy, January 23rd through February 27th, 1932. When Liveright originally published the novel in 1932, the required a happier ending.

11. **The Fox Woman - with - The Blue Pagoda.** With Hannes Bok. Published by New Collectors' Group, New York City, 1946. The Fox Woman was a story left unfinished by Merritt - Bok completed it. And The Blue Pagoda was Bok's alone.

12. **The Metal Monster.** Published by the Avon Book Company, New York City, 1946. Softcover. Murder Mystery Monthly 41.

13. **The Black Wheel.** Completed by Hannes Bok. This was published by New Collectors' Group, New York City, 1947. Hardcover.

14. **The Drone Man.** Privately printed, 1948. Stapled mimeographed sheets. Printed later in The Fox Woman and Other Stories, 1949.

15. **Rhythm of the Spheres.** Privately printed, 1948. Stapled mimeographed sheets. Re-titled The Last Poet and the Robots and printed in The Fox Woman and Other Stories, 1949.

16. **The People of the Pit.** Privately printed, 1948.

Abraham Merritt

Stapled mimeographed sheets. These stories later appeared in The Fox Woman and Other Stories, 1949.

17. Woman of the Wood. Privately printed, 1948. Stapled mimeographed sheets. Printed later in The Fox Woman and Other Stories, 1949.

18. The Fox Woman and Other Stories. Published by the Avon Publishing Company, New York City, 1949. Softcover. Avon Book 214. This collection contained: Through the Dragon Glass, 1917; The People of the Pit, 1918; Three Lines of Old French, 1919; The Woman of the Wood, 1926; The Drone Man, 1934; The Last Poet and the Robots - an essay, 1934; The Fox Woman - with Hannes Bok, 1948; When Old Gods Wake, 1948; and The White Road, 1949.

19. Seven Footprints to Satan - and - Burn Witch Burn! Published by Liveright Publishing, New York City, 1952. Hardcover omnibus edition.

20. Dwellers in the Mirage - and - The Face in the Abyss. Published by Liveright Publishing, New York City, 1953. Hardcover omnibus edition.

21. The Challenge from Beyond. Published by The Pennsylvania Dutch Cheese Press, 1954. Stapled mimeographed sheets. A round robin tale, written with: **C. L. Moore**; Robert E. Howard; H. P. Lovecraft; and Frank Belknap Long.

22. The Metal Monster. Published by Hyperion Press, New York City, 1974. First hardcover edition.

***

RELATED

1. A. Merritt: A Bibliography of Fantastic Writings. By Walter James Wentz. Published by George A. Bibby, Roseville, California, 1965. Softcover.

2. A. Merritt: Reflections in the Moon Pool. By Sam Moskowitz. Published by Oswald Train, Philadelphia, 1985. Hardcover.

Robert Silverberg.

Robert Silverberg was born in Brooklyn, New York on January 15th, 1935. As with most writers, he was an insatiable reader and the reading inspired him to write and the writing inspired him to submit stories to magazines. And when he was nineteen, it paid off. The first short story he sold was called Gorgon Planet. It was published by Nebula Science Fiction in Glasgow, February 1954. Also in that issue were: Pilot's Hands by William F. Temple; Cold Storage by David S. Gardner; Emancipation by E. C. Tubb; Projectionist by H. J. Campbell; Troubleshooter by Charles Eric Maine; and Divine Right by J. T. McIntosh, which was pretty decent company for your first effort.

His next published story, The Silent Colony, was in the October 1954 issue of Future Science Fiction, edited by Robert A. W. Lowndes. Once again, Silverberg was sharing space with some fine stories by some stellar (pun intended) writers: Conventional Ending by Theodore R. Cogswell; The Crime Therapist by Marion Zimmer Bradley; Dead on Departure by Milton Lesser; Despite All Valor by Algis Budrys; Of Such As These by Irving E. Cox; and Meddler by **Philip K. Dick**.

And his next one, The Martian, was in Imagination Science Fiction, June 1955, the same year his first novel was published. Revolt on Alpha C was published by Thomas Y. Crowell when Silverberg was just twenty years old and still attending Columbia University.

Also in the summer of 1955, with a horseshoe firmly in place, he moved into an apartment building in New York City. It wasn't much of a building. But **Harlan Ellison** lived there. And Randall Garrett lived there. Right next door. Garrett starting introducing Silverberg to editors. And the two of them collaborated... Their first published effort was The Beast with Seven Tails as by Leonard G. Spencer. Editor Howard Browne used it in the August 1956 issue of Amazing Stories. Also in that issue was: Calling Captain Flint, which was Silverberg and Garrett writing as Richard Greer; Vault of the Ages, which was Silverberg writing as **Robert Silverberg**; and Look Homeward Spaceman, which was Silverberg writing as Calvin Knox. Also in that issue were Corn-Fed Genius by Robert Bloch writing as E. K. Jarvis, a house name that Silverberg would employ on occasion; and Death of a Dinosaur by Sam Moskowitz actually writing as Sam Moskowitz.

By the time he graduated in 1956 he had won his first Hugo Award, the youngest writer to ever win one, and his course was set. He was writing, he claimed, about a million words a year under a number of different names. And he pretty much stuck with science fiction through the late fifties.

When the SF market collapsed for a while, he wrote other stuff, everything from history to mysteries to soft porn. He still wrote some science fiction. But in 1960, he published four SF short stories; the previous year he had published forty-four short stories and had used ten different names, including his own. Round about the mid-sixties, **Frederik Pohl** invited Silverberg back to science fiction, telling him he could write whatever he wanted if he would start sending stories to Galaxy and If. So he did. And it was during that period that his writing started to change, to become more literary, more polished. Deeper. More thoughtful. Although he still churned them out at an alarming rate.

By 1975, he felt burned out and announced his retirement from writing. As it turned out, retirement wasn't all that attractive. He was writing again by 1978 - Lord Valentine's Castle marked his return. It was serialised in four parts in The Magazine of Fantasy and Science Fiction starting in November 1979 and finished in February 1980. Two months later, the book was out in hardcover and being nominated for awards. And he was into Stage Three of his career. Stage Three is still going on...

Of his earlier books, his first novel, Revolt on Alpha C, tends to be the most expensive, running around $450.00.

Pen names used: Loren Beauchamp; Lawrence Blaine; Dr. Walter C. Brown used once for The Single Girl, 1961; Robert Burke; David Challon; Walker Chapman; Walter Drummond; Don Elliott; Dan Eliot; Franklin Hamilton; Charles D. Hammer; Paul Hollander; Calvin M. Knox; Marlene Longman; Dan Lynch; Dan Malcolm; Webber Martin; Ray McKensie; Alex Merriman; Clyde Mitchell; Gordon Mitchell; Mildred Nelson; David Osborne; George Osborne; Eric Rodman; Mark Ryan; T. H. Ryders; Lee Sebastian; Winslow Tandy; Hall Thornton; Stan Vincent; Jonas Ward; Richard F. Watson; L. T. Woodward MD; and Ellis Robertson - used for collaborations with Harlan Ellison.

Ziff-Davis house names used: Robert Arnette; T. D. Bethlen; Edgar Black; Alexander Blade; E. K. Jarvis; Warren Kastel; and S. M. Tenneshaw.

Other house names used: Ed Chase; Dirk Clinton; Roy Cook; John Dexter; Ivar Jorgenson; and Ivar Jorgensen.

Names used for collaborations with Randall Garrett: Gordon Aghill; Richard Greer (also a house name); Robert Randall; Leonard G. Spencer; and Gerald Vance.

***

AWARDS

1955. Hugo Award for Most Promising New Author.
1968. Nebula Award for Best Short Story, Passengers - Orbit 4, edited by Damon Knight.
1969. Hugo Award for Best Novella, Nightwings - Galaxy, September 1968.
1970. Nebula Award for Best Novel, A Time of Changes.
1971. Nebula Award for Best Short Story, Good News from the Vatican - Universe 1, edited by Terry Carr.
1974. Nebula Award for Best Novella, Born with the Dead - The Magazine of Fantasy and Science Fiction,

April 1974.
1975. Locus Poll Award for Best Novella, Born with the Dead - The Magazine of Fantasy and Science Fiction, April 1974.
1976. Prix Apollo Award for Nightwings.
1981. Locus Best Fantasy Novel Award for Lord Valentine's Castle.
1985. Nebula Award for Best Novella, Sailing to Byzantium - Asimov's Science Fiction, February 1985.
1987. Hugo Award for Best Novella, Gilgamesh in the Outback - Asimov's Science Fiction, July 1986.
1988. SF Chronicle Best Novella Award for The Secret Sharer - Asimov's Science Fiction, September 1987.
1988. Locus Poll Best Novella Award for The Secret Sharer - Asimov's Science Fiction, September 1987.
1990. Hugo Award for Best Novelette, Enter a Soldier. Later: Enter Another - Asimov's Science Fiction, June 1989.
1993. Locus Poll Best Collection Award for The Collected Stories of Robert Silverberg Volume 2: The Secret Sharers.
1999. Locus Poll Best Anthology Award for Legends.
1999. Inducted into The Science Fiction Hall of Fame.
2000. Locus Poll Best Anthology Award for Far Horizons.
2001. A Retro Hugo Award for the Best Fan Writer, 1953.

***

FILM AND TELEVISION

1. Time Travel: Fact, Fiction and Fantasy. This was a television documentary that was released on July 11th, 1985. Directed by Gayle Hollenbaugh and Suzanne McCafferty, it featured **Robert Silverberg** as one of the guests, along with: Michael J. Fox; Ed Krupp; and **Ray Bradbury**.

2. To See the Invisible Man. This 1963 story was used as segment on The New Twilight Zone, January 31st, 1986, Season 1, Episode 16. Directed by Noel Black, it starred: Cotter Smith; Karlene Crockett; Mary-Robin Redd; Peter Hobbs; Bonnie Campbell-Britton; Jack Gallagher; Kenneth Danziger; and others.

3. Brave New Worlds: The Science Fiction Phenomenon. Directed by Paul Oremland, this 1993 documentary featured **Robert Silverberg** as one of the guests, along with: **Arthur C. Clarke**; **Brian Aldiss**; **William Gibson**; J. G. Ballard; Kim Stanley Robinson; John Clute; Karen Joy Fowler; Octavia Butler; Paul Verhoeven; and many others.

4. Amanda and the Alien. From 1983, this story was filmed for release in August 1995. It was directed by Jon Kroll and starred: Nicole Eggert; John Diehl; Michael Dorn; Stacy Keach; David Millbern; Dan O'Connor; Raymond D. Turner; Alex Meneses; J. Marvin Campbell; Marcia Shapiro; Carol-Ann Plante; Rene Aston; and others, including Silverberg himself as an uncredited talk show guest.

5. Hindsight. Based on the novel Dying Inside, 1972, this short film was released in November 1997. Directed by Patrick Steele, it starred: Jason Sheldon; Jennifer Joplin; Beau Karch; Alex Jones; Judy Jones; John Pieza; Brian Fagan; Daniel Buran; Lisa Roth; Ann Klosterman; and others.

6. The Bicentennial Man. This was based on the **Isaac Asimov** short story, The Bicentennial Man, 1976, and the Asimov and Silverberg novel, The Positronic Man, 1992. Directed by Chris Columbus, it was released in December 1999, starring: Robin Williams; Embeth Davidtz; Sam Neill; Oliver Platt; Kiersten Warren; Wendy Crewson; Hallie Kate Eisenberg; and many others.

***

RADIO

1. Double Dare. This 1956 story was featured on X Minus One, December 19th, 1957.

2. Sound Decision. From 1956 and written with Randall Garrett, this was used by **John W. Campbell** on his show Exploring Tomorrow.

3. The Moon is New. This 1959 story, which was published as by David Osborne, was used by **John W. Campbell** on his show Exploring Tomorrow.

4. The Iron Chancellor. From 1958, this was used on X Minus One, January 27th, 1973.

5. When We Went to See the End of the World. This 1972 story aired on Mind Webs on November 12th, 1976.

6. To See the Invisible Man. From 1963, this was used on Mind Webs on January 28th, 1977.

7. After the Myths Went Home. This 1969 short story was used on Mind Webs on December 23rd, 1977.

8. To the Dark Star. Mind Webs used this 1968 story on July 7th, 1978.

9. Sundance. From 1969, this was used on Sci-Fi Radio.

10. Dying Inside. This 1972 novel was used on the BBC in 2001.

11. A Sleep and a Forgetting. This 1989 story was produced by Hollywood Theater of the Ear and used on 2000 X.

***

NOVELS AND COLLECTIONS

1. Revolt on Alpha C. Published by Thomas Y. Crowell, New York City, 1955. Hardcover.

2. The Thirteenth Immortal. Published by Ace Books, New York City, 1957. Softcover. Bound with This Fortress World by James E. Gunn. Ace Double D-233.

3. Master of Life and Death. Published by Ace Books, New York City, 1957. Softcover. Bound with The Secret Visitors by James White. Ace Double D-237.

4. The Shrouded Planet. With Randall Garrett and writing as Robert Randall. Published by Gnome Press, New York City, 1957. Hardcover.

5. Aliens from Space. Writing as David Osborne. Published by Avalon Books, New York City, 1958. Hardcover.

6. Collision Course. Published by Avalon Books, New York City, 1958. Hardcover.

7. Invisible Barriers. Writing as David Osborne. Published by Avalon Books, New York City, 1958. Hardcover.

8. Invaders from Earth. Published by Ace Books, New York City, 1958. Softcover. Bound with Across Time by David Grinnell, a pen name used by **Donald A. Wollheim**. Ace Double D-286.

9. Lest We Forget Thee, Earth. Writing as Calvin M. Knox. Published by Ace Books, New York City, 1958. Softcover. Bound with People Minus X by Raymond Z. Gallun. Ace Double D-291.

10. Stepsons of Terra. Published by Ace Books, New York City, 1958. Softcover. Bound with A Man Called Destiny by Lan Wright. Ace Double D-311.

11. Starhaven. Writing as Ivar Jorgensen. Published by Avalon Books, New York City, 1958. Hardcover.

12. Love Nest. Writing as Loren Beauchamp. Published by Midwood Books, New York City, 1958. Softcover. Midwood 007.

13. The Dawning Light. With Randall Garrett and writing as Robert Randall. Published by Gnome Press, New York City, 1959. Hardcover.

14. Starman's Quest. Published by Gnome Press, Hicksville, New York, 1959. Hardcover.

15. And When She Was Bad. Writing as Loren Beauchamp. Published by Midwood Books, New York City, 1959. Softcover. Midwood Book F102.

16. Unwilling Sinner. Writing as Loren Beauchamp. Published by Midwood Books, New York City, 1959. Softcover. Re-titled re-issue of And When She Was Bad, 1959. Midwood Book 1439.

17. Connie. Writing as Loren Beauchamp. Published by Midwood Books, New York City, 1959. Midwood Book 18.

18. Another Night, Another Love. Writing as Loren Beauchamp. Published by Midwood Books, New York City, 1959. Midwood Book 29.

19. Suburban Sin Club. Writing as David Challon. Published by Bedside Books, New York City, 1959. Softcover. Bedside Book 803.

20. Twisted Love. Writing as Mark Ryan. Published by Bedside Books, New York City, 1959. Softcover. Bedside Book 807.

21. Campus Love Club. Writing as David Challon. Published by Bedside Books, New York City, 1959. Softcover. Bedside Book 808.

22. Streets of Sin. Writing as Mark Ryan. Published by Bedside Books, New York City, 1959. Softcover. Bedside Book 813.

23. French Sin Port. Writing as David Challon. Published by Bedside Books, New York City, 1959. Softcover. Bedside Book 820.

24. Thirst for Love. Writing as David Challon. Published by Bedside Books, New York City, 1959. Softcover. Bedside Book 821.

25. Gang Girl. Writing as Don Elliott. Published by Corinth Publications - Nightstand Books, United States, 1959. Nightstand Book NB1504.

26. Immoral Wife. Writing as Gordon Mitchell. Published by Midwood Books, New York City, 1959. Softcover. Midwood Book 11.

27. Love Addict. Writing as Don Elliott. Published by Corinth Publications - Nightstand Books, United States, 1959. Nightstand Book NB1501.

28. The Plot Against the Earth. Writing as Calvin M. Knox. Published by Ace Books, New York City, 1959. Softcover. Bound with Recruit for Andromeda by **Milton Lesser**. Ace Double D-358.

29. The Planet Killers. Published by Ace Books, New York City, 1959. Softcover. Bound with We Claim These Stars! by **Poul Anderson**. Ace Double D-407.

30. Lost Race of Mars. Published by John C. Winston, Philadelphia, 1960. Hardcover.

31. Summertime Affair. Writing as Don Elliott. Published by Corinth Publications - Nightstand Books, United States, 1960. Softcover. Nightstand Book NB1508.

32. Party Girl. Writing as Don Elliott. Published by Corinth Publications - Nightstand Books, United States, 1960. Softcover. Nightstand Book NB1509.

33. Naked Holiday. Writing as Don Elliott. Published by Corinth Publications - Nightstand Books, United States, 1960. Softcover. Nightstand Book NB1512.

34. Sin Girls. Writing as Maureen Longman. Published by Corinth Publications - Nightstand Books, United States, 1960. Softcover. Nightstand Book NB1514.

35. Sin on Wheels. Writing as Don Elliott. First version. Published by Corinth Publications - Nightstand Books, United States, 1960. Softcover. Nightstand Book NB1516.

36. The Wild Party. Writing as Ray McKensie. Published by Chariot Books, United States, 1960. Softcover. Chariot Book CB-146.

37. Man Mad. Writing as David Challon. Published by Chariot Books, United States, 1960. Softcover. Chariot Book CB-143.

38. Sex Machine. Writing as Don Elliott. Published by Rapture Books, United States, circa 1960. Softcover. Rapture Book 206.

Robert Silverberg

39. Buchanan on the Prod. Writing as Jonas Ward with William Ard. Published by Gold Medal Books, Greenwich, Connecticut, 1960. Softcover. Gold Medal Book D1938.

40. Passion Trap. Writing as Don Elliott. Published by Corinth Publications - Nightstand Books, United States, 1960. Softcover. Nightstand Book NB1521.

41. Lesbian Love. Writing as Maureen Longman. Published by Corinth Publications - Nightstand Books, United States, 1960. Softcover. Nightstand Book NB1523.

42. Sex Jungle. Writing as Don Elliott. Published by Corinth Publications - Nightstand Books, United States, 1960. Softcover. Nightstand Book NB1524.

43. The Lecher. Writing as Don Elliott. Published by Corinth Publications - Nightstand Books, United States, 1960. Softcover. Nightstand Book NB1528.

44. The Flesh Peddlers. Writing as Don Elliott. Published by Corinth Publications - Nightstand Books, United States, 1960. Softcover. Nightstand Book NB1529.

45. Stripper! Writing as John Dexter. Published by Corinth Publications - Nightstand Books, United States, 1960. Softcover. Nightstand Book NB1530.

46. The Hot Beat. Writing as Stan Vincent. Published by Magnet, United States, 1960. Softcover. Magnet Book 314.

47. Meg. Writing as Loren Beauchamp. Published by Midwood Books, New York City, 1960. Softcover. Midwood Book 30.

48. Mistress of Sin. Writing as Don Elliott. Published by Corinth Publications - Nightstand Books, United States, 1960. Softcover. Nightstand Book NB1537.

49. The Bra Peddlers. Writing as John Dexter. Published by Corinth Publications - Nightstand Books, United States, 1960. Softcover. Nightstand Book NB1568.

50. Suburban Affair. Writing as David Challon. Published by Bedside Books, United States, 1960. Softcover. Bedside Book BB961.

51. The Illicit Affair and Other Stories. Writing as Mark Ryan. Published by Bedside, United States, 1960. Softcover. Bedside Book BB980.

52. Woman Chaser. Writing as Don Elliott. Published by Bedside Books, United States, 1960. Softcover. Bedside Book BB1201.

53. Collision Course. Published by Avalon Books, New York City, 1961. Hardcover.

54. Wild Divorcee. Writing as Don Elliott. Published by Corinth Publications - Nightstand Books, United States, 1961. Softcover. Nightstand Book NB1542.

55. Lust Goddess. Writing as Don Elliott. Published by Corinth Publications - Nightstand Books, United States, 1961. Softcover. Nightstand Book NB1544.

56. Convention Girl. Writing as Don Elliott. Published by Corinth Publications - Nightstand Books, United States, 1961. Softcover. Nightstand Book NB1547.

57. Sin Cruise. Writing as Don Elliott. Published by Corinth Publications - Nightstand Books, United States, 1961. Softcover. Nightstand Book NB1554.

58. Expense Account Sinners. Writing as Don Elliott. Published by Corinth Publications - Nightstand Books, United States, 1961. Softcover. Nightstand Book NB1558.

59. The Sinful Ones. Writing as Don Elliott. Published by Corinth Publications - Nightstand Books, United States, 1961. Softcover. Nightstand Book NB1564.

60. Backstage Sinner. Writing as Don Elliott. Published by Corinth Publications - Nightstand Books, United States, 1961. Softcover. Nightstand Book NB1565.

61. Sin Festival. Writing as John Dexter. Published by Corinth Publications - Nightstand Books, United States, 1961. Softcover. Nightstand Book NB1572.

62. Sin Club. Writing as Don Elliott. Published by Corinth Publications - Nightstand Books, United States, 1961. Softcover. Nightstand Book NB1574.

63. Sex Thieves. Writing as John Dexter. Published by Corinth Publications - Nightstand Books, United States, 1961. Softcover. Nightstand Book NB1576.

64. The Lust Seekers. Writing as Don Elliott. Published by Corinth Publications - Nightstand Books, United States, 1961. Softcover. Nightstand Book NB1577.

65. Lust Queen. Writing as Don Elliott. Published by Freedom Publishing - Midnight Reader, United States, 1961. Softcover. Midnight Reader Book MR401.

66. Sin on Wheels. Writing as Loren Beauchamp. Second version. Published by Midwood Books, New York City, 1961. Softcover. Midwood Book 70.

67. The Fires Within. Writing as Loren Beauchamp. Published by Midwood Books, New York City, 1961. Softcover. Midwood Book 86.

68. Henry's Wife. Writing as Gordon Mitchell. Published by Midwood Books, New York City, 1961. Softcover. Midwood Book 137. Re-titled re-issue of Immoral Wife, 1959.

69. Round the Clock at Volari's. Writing as W. R. Burnett with W. R. Burnett. Published by Gold Medal Books, Greenwich, Connecticut, 1961. Softcover. Gold Medal Book S1145.

70. Frontier Lawyer. Writing as Lawrence L. Blaine. Published by Perma Books, New York City, 1961. Softcover. Perma Book M4210.

71. Recalled to Life. Published by Lancer Books, New York City, 1962. Softcover. Lancer Book 74-810.

72. The Seed of Earth. Published by Ace Books, New York City, 1962. Softcover. Bound with Next Stop the Stars, also by Silverberg. Ace Double F-145.

73. Next Stop the Stars. Published by Ace Books,

New York City, 1962. Softcover. Bound with The Seed of Earth, also by Silverberg. Ace Double F-145. Herein: Slaves of the Star Giants, 1957; The Songs of Summer, 1956; Hopper, 1956; Blaze of Glory, 1957; and Warm Man, 1957.

74. Four-Time Loser. Writing as Dan Lynch with Eleazar Lipsky. Published by Gold Medal Books, Greenwich, Connecticut, 1962. Softcover. Gold Medal Book S1240.

75. The Wife Traders. Writing as Loren Beauchamp. Published by Boudoir Books, United States, 1962. Softcover. Boudoir Book 101.

76. Wayward Widow. Writing as Loren Beauchamp. Published by Midwood Books, New York City, 1962. Softcover. Midwood Book F226.

77. Hotrod Sinners. Writing as Don Elliott. Published by Bedside Books, United States, 1962. Softcover. Bedside Book BB1222.

78. Roadhouse Girl. Writing as Don Elliott. Published by Freedom Publishing - Midnight Reader, United States, 1962. Softcover. Midnight Reader MR412.

79. Three Sinners. Writing as Don Elliott. Published by Freedom Publishing - Midnight Reader, United States, 1962. Softcover. Midnight Reader MR414.

80. Lust Cult. Writing as Don Elliott. Published by Freedom Publishing - Midnight Reader, United States, 1962. Softcover. Midnight Reader MR419.

81. Kept Man. Writing as Don Elliott. Published by Freedom Publishing - Midnight Reader, United States, 1962. Softcover. Midnight Reader MR422.

82. No Lust Tonight. Writing as Don Elliott. Published by Freedom Publishing - Midnight Reader, United States, 1962. Softcover. Midnight Reader MR429.

83. Shame House. Writing as Don Elliott. Published by Freedom Publishing - Midnight Reader, United States, 1962. Softcover. Midnight Reader MR440.

84. The Lust Plotters. Writing as John Dexter. Published by Freedom Publishing - Midnight Reader, United States, 1962. Softcover. Midnight Reader MR441.

85. Lust for Two. Writing as Don Elliott. Published by Freedom Publishing - Midnight Reader, United States, 1962. Softcover. Midnight Reader MR446.

86. Sin Kin. Writing as Don Elliott. Published by Freedom Publishing - Midnight Reader, United States, 1962. Softcover. Midnight Reader MR454.

87. Sexteen. Writing as Don Elliott. Published by Freedom Publishing - Midnight Reader, United States, 1962. Softcover. Midnight Reader MR458.

88. Passion Thieves. Writing as Don Elliott. Published by Freedom Publishing - Midnight Reader, United States, 1962. Softcover. Midnight Reader MR466.

89. Lust Captive. Writing as Don Elliott. Published by Corinth Publications - Nightstand Books, United States, 1962. Softcover. Nightstand Book NB1596.

90. Sex Fury. Writing as Don Elliott. Published by Corinth Publications - Nightstand Books, United States, 1962. Softcover. Nightstand Book NB1605.

91. Sin Bait. Writing as Don Elliott. Published by Corinth Publications - Nightstand Books, United States, 1962. Softcover. Nightstand Book NB1610.

92. Passion Bum. Writing as John Dexter. Published by Corinth Publications - Nightstand Books, United States, 1962. Softcover. Nightstand Book NB1615.

93. Sin Quest. Writing as Don Elliott. Published by Corinth Publications - Nightstand Books, United States, 1962. Softcover. Nightstand Book NB1616.

94. Wild Flesh. Writing as Don Elliott. Published by Corinth Publications - Nightstand Books, United States, 1962. Softcover. Nightstand Book NB1624.

95. Lust Market. Writing as Don Elliott. Published by Corinth Publications - Nightstand Books, United States, 1962. Softcover. Nightstand Book NB1625.

96. Sin Sick. Writing as Don Elliott. Published by Corinth Publications - Nightstand Books, United States, 1962. Softcover. Nightstand Book NB1631.

97. The Orgy Boys. Writing as Don Elliott. Published by Corinth Publications - Nightstand Books, United States, 1962. Softcover. Nightstand Book NB1633.

98. Lust Cat. Writing as Don Elliott. Published by Sundown Books, United States, 1962. Softcover. Sundown Book 589.

99. Strange Delights. Writing as Loren Beauchamp. Published by Midwood Books, New York City, 1962. Softcover. Midwood Book F-145.

100. Sin a la Carte. Writing as Loren Beauchamp. Published by Midwood Books, New York City, 1962. Softcover. Midwood Book 148. Re-titled re-issue of Another Night, Another Love, 1959.

101. Campus Sex Club. Writing as David Challon. Published by Midwood Books, New York City, 1962. Softcover. Midwood Book F206. Re-titled re-issue of Campus Love Club, 1959.

102. The Silent Invaders. Published by Ace Books, New York City, 1963. Softcover. Bound with Battle on Venus by William F. Temple. Ace Double F-195.

103. One of Our Asteroids Is Missing. Writing as Calvin M. Knox. Published by Ace Books, New York City, 1963. Softcover. Bound with The Twisted Men by **A. E. van Vogt**. Ace Double F-253.

104. Dial O-R-G-Y. Writing as Dan Eliot. Published by Ember Books, United States, 1963. Softcover. Ember Book 902.

105. Nympho. Writing as Dan Eliot. Published by Ember Books, United States, 1963. Softcover. Ember Book 905.

106. Flesh Flames. Writing as Dan Eliot. Published by Ember Books, United States, 1963. Softcover. Ember Book 912.

107. Sin Hellion. Writing as Dan Eliot. Published by

Robert Silverberg

Ember Books, United States, 1963. Softcover. Ember Book 913.

108. Sin Made. Writing as Don Elliot. Published by Ember Books, United States, 1963. Softcover. Ember Book 930.

109. Lust Lover. Writing as Dan Eliot. Published by Pillar Books, United States, 1963. Softcover. Pillar Book PB803.

110. Sin Mates. Writing as Dan Eliot. Published by Pillar Books, United States, 1963. Softcover. Pillar Book PB806.

111. Nurse Carolyn. Writing as Loren Beauchamp. Published by Midwood Books, New York, 1963. Softcover. Midwood Book F-292.

112. Sex Bait. Writing as Don Elliott. Published by Corinth Publications - Nightstand Books, United States, 1963. Softcover. Nightstand Book NB1638.

113. Lust Lord. Writing as Don Elliott. Published by Corinth Publications - Nightstand Books, United States, 1963. Softcover. Nightstand Book NB1643.

114. Lust Crew. Writing as Don Elliott. Published by Corinth Publications - Nightstand Books, United States, 1963. Softcover. Nightstand Book NB1648.

115. Sin Servant. Writing as Don Elliott. Published by Corinth Publications - Nightstand Books, United States, 1963. Softcover. Nightstand Book NB1651.

116. Sin Crazed. Writing as Don Elliott. Published by Freedom Publishing - Midnight Reader, United States, 1963. Softcover. Midnight Reader Book MR469.

117. Passion Patsy. Writing as Don Elliott. Published by Freedom Publishing - Midnight Reader, United States, 1963. Softcover. Midnight Reader Book MR475.

118. Sex Bum. Writing as Don Elliott. Published by Freedom Publishing - Midnight Reader, United States, 1963. Softcover. Midnight Reader Book MR489.

119. Sin Doll. Writing as Don Elliott. Published by Corinth Publications - Evening Reader, United States, 1963. Softcover. Evening Reader Book 702.

120. Time of the Great Freeze. Published by Holt, Rinehart and Winston, New York City, 1964. Hardcover.

121. Regan's Planet. Published by Pyramid Books, New York City, 1964. Softcover. Pyramid Book F-986.

122. Godling, Go Home. Published by Belmont Books, New York City, 1964. Softcover. Belmont book L92-591. Herein: Godling, Go Home!, 1957; Why?, 1957; The Silent Colony, 1954; Force of Mortality, 1957; There's No Place Like Space, 1959; Neutral Planet, 1957; The Lonely One, 1956; Solitary, 1957; The Man with Talent, 1956; The Desiccator, 1964; and The World He Left Behind, 1959.

123. Taste of Power. Written with Mildred Nelson. Published by Pyramid Books, New York City, 1964. Softcover. Pyramid Book R-1062.

124. Sin Sold. Writing as Don Elliott. Published by Corinth Publications - Evening Reader, United States, 1964. Softcover. Evening Reader Book 712.

125. Lust League. Writing as Don Elliott. Published by Corinth Publications - Evening Reader, United States, 1964. Softcover. Evening Reader Book 714.

126. Beatnik Wanton. Writing as Don Elliott. Published by Corinth Publications - Evening Reader, United States, 1964. Softcover. Evening Reader Book 717.

127. Passion Partners. Writing as Don Elliott. Published by Corinth Publications - Evening Reader, United States, 1964. Softcover. Evening Reader Book 722.

128. Sin Bin. Writing as Don Elliott. Published by Corinth Publications - Evening Reader, United States, 1964. Softcover. Evening Reader Book 729.

129. Orgy Isle. Writing as Don Elliott. Published by Corinth Publications - Evening Reader, United States, 1964. Softcover. Evening Reader Book 734.

130. Lust Spree. Writing as Don Elliott. Published by Corinth Publications - Evening Reader, United States, 1964. Softcover. Evening Reader Book 742.

131. Flesh Melody. Writing as Don Elliott. Published by Corinth Publications - Evening Reader, United States, 1964. Softcover. Evening Reader Book 752.

132. Switch Trap. Writing as Don Elliott. Published by Corinth Publications - Evening Reader, United States, 1964. Softcover. Evening Reader Book 754.

133. Flesh Bride. Writing as Don Elliott. Published by Corinth Publications - Evening Reader, United States, 1964. Softcover. Evening Reader Book 758.

134. Sin Partners. Writing as Don Elliott. Published by Corinth Publications - Evening Reader, United States, 1964. Softcover. Evening Reader Book 764.

135. Flesh Lesson. Writing as Don Elliott. Published by Corinth Publications - Nightstand Books, United States, 1964. Softcover. Nightstand Book 1759.

136. Gutter Road. Writing as Don Elliott. Published by Sundown Books, United States, 1964. Softcover. Sundown Book 514.

137. Pickup. Writing as Don Elliott. Published by Sundown Books, United States, 1964. Softcover. Sundown Book 519.

138. Flesh Pawns. Writing as Don Elliott. Published by Sundown Books, United States, 1964. Softcover. Sundown Book 525.

139. Passion Trio. Writing as Paul Hollander. Published by Sundown Books, United States, 1964. Softcover.

140. Sin Circuit. Writing as Don Elliott. Published by Ember Books, United States, 1964. Softcover.

141. Flesh Taker. Writing as Don Elliott. Published by Ember Books, United States, 1964. Softcover. Ember Book EB944.

142. Lust Bums. Writing as Don Elliott. Published by Leisure Books, United States, 1964. Softcover. Leisure Book LB611.

143. Passion Pair. Writing as Don Elliott. Published by Leisure Books, United States, 1964. Softcover. Leisure Book LB623.

144. The Flesh Seekers. Writing as Don Elliott. Published by Leisure Books, United States, 1964. Softcover. Leisure Book LB632.

145. Sin Service. Writing as Don Elliott. Published by Leisure Books, United States, 1964. Softcover. Leisure Book LB633.

146. Flesh Prize. Writing as Don Elliott. Published by Leisure Books, United States, 1964. Softcover. Leisure Book LB651.

147. Wanton Web. Writing as Don Elliott. Published by Idle Hour Books, United States, 1964. Softcover. Idle Hour Book 409.

148. Black Market Shame. Writing as Don Elliott. Published by Idle Hour Books, United States, 1964. Softcover. Idle Hour Book 419.

149. Shameless. Writing as Don Elliott. Published by Pillar Books, United States, 1964. Softcover. Pillar Book 824.

150. Orgy Maid. Writing as Don Elliott. Published by Pillar Books, United States, 1964. Softcover. Pillar Book 838.

151. Lust Set. Writing as Don Elliott. Published by Pillar Books, United States, 1964. Softcover. Pillar Book 849.

152. Conquerors from the Darkness. Published by Holt, Rinehart and Winston, New York City, 1965. Hardcover.

153. A Pair From Space. Published by Belmont Books, New York City, 1965. Softcover. Belmont Book 92-612.

154. To Worlds Beyond. Published by Chilton Books, Philadelphia, 1965. Hardcover. This contains: About **Robert Silverberg** by **Isaac Asimov**; Introduction by **Robert Silverberg**; The Old Man, 1957; New Men for Mars, 1957; Collecting Team, 1956; Double Dare, 1956; The Overlord's Thumb, 1958; Ozymandias, 1958; Certainty, 1959; Mind for Business, 1956; and Misfit, 1957.

155. The Mask of Akhnaten. Published by The Macmillan Company, New York City, 1965. Hardcover.

156. The Winning of Mickey Free. Writing as W. R. Burnett with W. R. Burnett. Published by Bantam Books, New York City, 1965. Softcover.

157. Flesh Bigamist. Writing as Don Elliott. Published by Corinth Publications - Evening Reader, United States, 1965. Softcover.

158. Would-Be Sinner. Writing as Don Elliott. Published by Corinth Publications - Evening Reader, United States, 1965. Softcover.

159. Flesh Man. Writing as Don Elliott. Published by Corinth Publications - Evening Reader, United States, 1965. Softcover. Evening Reader Book 776.

160. Lust Doomed. Writing as Don Elliott. Published by Corinth Publications - Evening Reader, United States, 1965. Softcover. Evening Reader Book 1202.

161. Shame Scheme. Writing as Don Elliott. Published by Corinth Publications - Nightstand, United States, 1965. Softcover. Nightstand Book 1729.

162. Of Shame Reborn. Writing as Don Elliott. Published by Corinth Publications - Nightstand, United States, 1965. Softcover. Nightstand Book 1741.

163. Good Girl, Bad Girl. Writing as Don Elliott. Published by Corinth Publications - Nightstand, United States, 1965. Softcover. Nightstand Book 1751.

164. Nudie Packet. Writing as Don Elliott. Published by Idle Hour Books, United States, 1965. Softcover. Idle Hour Book 429.

165. Sin for Solace. Writing as Don Elliott. Published by Idle Hour Books, United States, 1965. Softcover. Idle Hour Book 438.

166. Sin Kill. Writing as Don Elliott. Published by Idle Hour Books, United States, 1965. Softcover. Idle Hour Book 455.

167. Alternate Wife. Writing as Don Elliott. Published by Idle Hour Books, United States, 1965. Softcover. Idle Hour Book 470.

168. Sin Spin. Writing as Don Elliott. Published by Idle Hour Books, United States, 1965. Softcover. Idle Hour Book 475.

169. Passion Peeper. Writing as Don Elliott. Published by Idle Hour Books, United States, 1965. Softcover. Idle Hour Book 482.

170. Teaser. Writing as Don Elliott. Published by Idle Hour Books, United States, 1965. Softcover. Idle Hour Book 493.

171. Lust Finale. Writing as Don Elliott. Published by Sundown Books, United States, 1965. Softcover. Sundown Book 532.

172. Passion Killer. Writing as Don Elliott. Published by Sundown Books, United States, 1965. Softcover. Sundown Book 534.

173. The Young Wantons. Writing as Don Elliott. Published by Sundown Books, United States, 1965. Softcover. Sundown Book 537.

174. The Nite Lusters. Writing as Don Elliott. Published by Sundown Books, United States, 1965. Softcover. Sundown Book 549.

175. Flesh Boarder. Writing as Don Elliott. Published by Sundown Books, United States, 1965. Softcover. Sundown Book 557.

176. Les Floozies. Writing as Loren Beauchamp. Published by Pad Library, United States, 1965.

Softcover. Pad Library Book 504.

177. Orgy Slaves. Writing as Don Elliott. Published by Corinth Publications, United States, 1965. Softcover. Corinth Book 771.

178. Sin Warped. Writing as Don Elliott. Published by Leisure Books, United States, 1965. Softcover. Leisure Book LB657.

179. Flesh Cry. Writing as Don Elliott. Published by Leisure Books, United States, 1965. Softcover. Leisure Book LB677.

180. Escape to Sindom. Writing as Don Elliott. Published by Leisure Books, United States, 1965. Softcover. Leisure Book LB686.

181. Only the Depraved. Writing as Don Elliott. Published by Leisure Books, United States, 1965. Softcover. Leisure Book LB689.

182. The Sin Switch. Writing as Don Elliott. Published by Leisure Books, United States, 1965. Softcover. Leisure Book LB1104.

183. Carnal Carnival. Writing as Don Elliott. Published by Leisure Books, United States, 1965. Softcover. Leisure Book LB1116.

184. The Shame Protector. Writing as Don Elliott. Published by Ember Books, United States, 1965. Softcover. Ember Book 302.

185. The Sins of Seena. Writing as Don Elliott. Published by Ember Books, United States, 1965. Softcover. Ember Book 306.

186. Naked She Died. Writing as Don Elliott. Published by Ember Books, United States, 1965. Softcover. Ember Book 310.

187. Needle in a Timestack. Published by Ballantine Books, New York City, 1966. Softcover. Ballantine Book U2330. Herein: The Pain Peddlers, 1963; Passport to Sirius, 1958; Birds of a Feather, 1958; There Was an Old Woman, 1958; The Shadow of Wings, 1963; Absolutely Inflexible, 1956; His Brother's Weeper, 1959; The Sixth Palace, 1965; To See the Invisible Man, 1963; and The Iron Chancellor, 1958.

188. One Night Stand. Writing as Don Elliott. Published by Ember Books, United States, 1966. Softcover. Ember Book 319.

189. All on Sunday. Writing as Don Elliott. Published by Ember Books, United States, 1966. Softcover. Ember Book 331.

190. Diary of Desire. Writing as Don Elliott. Published by Corinth Publications - Evening Reader, United States, 1966. Softcover.

191. The Gay Girls. Writing as Don Elliott. Published by Corinth Publications, United States, 1966. Softcover.

192. Lust Demon. Writing as Don Elliott. Published by Sundown Books, United States, 1966. Softcover. Sundown Book 578.

193. Initiates. Writing as Don Elliott. Published by Sundown Books, United States, 1966. Softcover. Sundown Book 596.

194. Every Bed Her Own. Writing as Don Elliott. Published by Leisure Books, United States, 1966. Softcover. Leisure Book LB1126.

195. Big Blast. Writing as Don Elliott. Published by Leisure Books, United States, 1966. Softcover. Leisure Book LB1150.

196. Take My Wife. Writing as Don Elliott. Published by Idle Hour Books, United States, 1966. Softcover. Idle Hour Book 481.

197. Cousin Lover. Writing as Don Elliott. Published by Idle Hour Books, United States, 1966. Softcover. Idle Hour Book 489.

198. Pain Lusters. Writing as Don Elliott. Published by Idle Hour Books, United States, 1966. Softcover. Idle Hour Book 492.

199. Campus Traders. Writing as Don Elliott. Published by Idle Hour Books, United States, 1966. Softcover. Idle Hour Book 501.

200. The Virtuous Ones. Writing as Don Elliott. Published by Idle Hour Books, United States, 1966. Softcover. Idle Hour Book 506.

201. The Passion Barons. Writing as Paul Hollander. Published by Corinth Publications - Evening Reader, United States, 1966. Softcover. Re-titled re-issue of Streets of Sin, 1959.

202. The Gate of Worlds. Published by Holt, Rinehart and Winston, New York City, 1967. Hardcover.

203. Planet of Death. Published by Holt, Rinehart and Winston, New York City, 1967. Hardcover.

204. To Open the Sky. Published by Ballantine Books, New York City, 1967. Softcover. Ballantine Book U6093.

205. Thorns. Published by Ballantine Books, New York City, 1967. Softcover. Ballantine Book U6097.

206. Those Who Watch. Published by Signet Books - The New American Library, New York City, 1967. Softcover. Signet Book P3160.

207. The Time Hoppers. Published by Doubleday and Co., Garden City, New York, 1967. Hardcover.

208. The Gate of Worlds. Published by Holt, Rinehart and Winston, New York City, 1967. Hardcover.

209. Diary of a Dyke. Writing as Don Elliott. Published by Pleasure Reader, United States, 1967. Softcover.

210. The Wanton West. Writing as Don Elliott. Published by Late Hour Library, United States, 1967. Softcover.

211. Flesh Fever. Writing as Don Elliott. Published by Late Hour Library, United States, 1967. Softcover. Late Hour Book 713.

212. Flesh Tryst. Writing as Don Elliott. Published

by Ember Books, United States, 1967. Softcover. Ember Book 378.

213. Rogue of the Riviera. Writing as David Challon. Published by Ember Books, United States, 1967. Softcover. Ember Book 362. Re-titled re-issue of French Sin Port, 1959.

214. All the Best Beds. Writing as Loren Beauchamp. Published by Corinth Publications - Nightstand Books, United States, 1967. Softcover. Re-titled re-issue of Meg, 1960.

215. Carnal Counselor. Writing as Don Elliott. Published by Corinth Publications - Nightstand Books, United States, 1967. Softcover. Nightstand Book 1821.

216. Those Who Lust. Writing as Don Elliott. Published by Leisure Books, United States, 1967. Softcover. Leisure Book LB1191.

217. Registered Nympho. Writing as Don Elliott. Published by Companion Books, United States, 1967. Softcover. Companion Book 524. Re-titled re-issue of Nurse Carolyn, 1960.

218. Orgy on Wheels. Writing as Loren Beauchamp. Published by Late Hour Books, United States, 1967. Softcover. Re-titled re-issue of Sin on Wheels - second version, 1961.

219. The Man in the Maze. Published by Avon Books, New York City, 1968. Softcover. Avon Book V2262.

220. The Masks of Time. Published by Ballantine Books, New York City, 1968. Softcover. Ballantine Book U6121.

221. Hawksbill Station. Published by Doubleday & Co., Garden City, New York, 1968. Hardcover.

222. Free Sample. Writing as Loren Beauchamp. Published by Midwood Books, New York City, 1968. Softcover. Midwood Book 34-183. Re-titled re-issue of Wayward Widow, 1962.

223. Thorns. Published by Walker and Company, New York City, 1969. First hardcover edition.

224. The Man in the Maze. Published by Sidgwick and Jackson, London, 1969. First hardcover edition.

225. Across a Billion Years. Published by The Dial Press, New York City, 1969. Hardcover.

226. Downward to the Earth. Published by Nelson Doubleday - Science Fiction Book Club, Garden City, New York, 1969. Hardcover.

227. The Anvil of Time. Published by Sidgwick and Jackson, London, 1969. Re-titled re-issue of Hawksbill Station, 1968. Hardcover.

228. Nightwings. Published by Avon Books, New York City, 1969. Softcover. Avon Book V2303.

229. Three Survived. Published by Holt, Rinehart and Winston, New York City, 1969. Hardcover.

230. To Live Again. Published by Doubleday & Co., Garden City, New York, 1969. Hardcover.

231. Dimension Thirteen. Published by Ballantine Books, New York City, 1969. Softcover. Ballantine Book 01601. This contains: Eve and the Twenty-three Adams, 1958; Warm Man, 1957; By the Seawall, 1967; Dark Companion, 1961; The Four, 1958; Bride Ninety-one, 1967; World of a Thousand Colors, 1957; En Route to Earth, 1957; The King of the Golden River, 1967; Prime Commandment, 1958; Halfway House, 1966; Journey's End, 1958; and Solitary, 1957.

232. Up the Line. Published by Ballantine Books, New York City, 1969. Softcover. Ballantine Book 01680.

233. The Calibrated Alligator and Other Science Fiction Stories. Published by Holt, Rinehart and Winston, 1969. Hardcover. Herein: The Calibrated Alligator, 1960; Blaze of Glory, 1957; The Artifact Business, 1957; Precedent, 1957; Mugwump 4, 1959; Why?, 1957; His Head in the Clouds, 1957; Point of Focus, 1958; and Delivery Guaranteed, 1959.

234. Tower of Glass. Published by Charles Scribner's Sons, New York City, 1970. Hardcover.

235. Nightwings. Published by Walker and Company, New York City, 1970. First hardcover edition.

236. World's Fair 1992. Published by Follett Publishing, New York City, 1970. Hardcover.

237. Voornan 19. Published by Sidgwick and Jackson, London, 1970. A re-titled re-issue of The Masks of Time, 1968. First hardcover edition.

238. Parsecs and Parables. Published by Doubleday & Co., Garden City, New York, 1970. Hardcover. Herein: The Man Who Never Forgot, 1958; Ishmael in Love, 1970; One-Way Journey, 1957; Sunrise on Mercury, 1957; The Outbreeders, 1959; Road to Nightfall, 1958; Going Down Smooth, 1968; Counterpart, 1959; Flies, 1967; and The Fangs of the Trees, 1968.

239. The Cube Root of Uncertainty. Published by The Macmillan Company, New York City, 1970. Hardcover. This contains: Introduction by **Robert Silverberg**; Passengers, 1968; Double Dare, 1956; The Sixth Palace, 1965; Translation Error, 1959; The Shadow of Wings, 1963; Absolutely Inflexible, 1956; The Iron Chancellor, 1958; Mugwump Four, 1959; To the Dark Star, 1968; Neighbor, 1964; Halfway House, 1966; and Sundance, 1969.

240. A Robert Silverberg Omnibus. Published by Sidgwick and Jackson, London, 1970. This gathers: Master of Life and Death, 1957; Invaders from Earth, 58; and The Time-Hoppers, 1967. First hardcover edition of Master of Life and Death and Invaders from Earth.

241. Son of Man. Published by Ballantine Books, New York City, 1971. Softcover. Ballantine Book 02277.

242. Moonferns and Starsongs. Published by Ballantine Books, New York City, 1971. Softcover. Ballantine Book 02278. Herein: A Happy Day

Robert Silverberg

in 2381, 1970; After the Myths Went Home, 1969; Passengers, 1968; To Be Continued, 1956; Nightwings, 1968; We Know Who We Are, 1970; The Pleasure of Their Company, 1970; The Songs of Summer, 1956; A Man of Talent, 1956; Collecting Team, 1956; and Going Down Smooth, 1968.

243. The World Inside. Published by Doubleday & Co., Garden City, New York, 1971. Hardcover.

244. A Time of Changes. Published by Nelson Doubleday - The Science Fiction Book Club, Garden City, New York, 1971. Hardcover.

245. The Book of Skulls. Published by Charles Scribner's Sons, New York City, 1971. Hardcover.

246. Dying Inside. Published by Charles Scribner's Sons, New York City, 1972. Hardcover.

247. The Reality Trip and Other Implausibilities. Published by Ballantine Books, New York City, 1972. Softcover. Ballantine Book 02548. This contains: In Entropy's Jaws, 1971; The Reality Trip, 1970; Black is Beautiful, 1970; Ozymandias, 1958; Caliban, 1971; The Shrines of Earth, 1957; Ringing the Changes, 1970; and Hawksbill Station, 1967.

248. The Second Trip. Published by Nelson Doubleday - The Science Fiction Book Club, Garden City, New York, 1972. Hardcover.

249. Recalled to Life. Published by Doubleday & Company, Garden City, New York, 1972. Revised edition of the 1962 Lancer paperback. Hardcover.

250. Unfamiliar Territory. Published by Charles Scribner's Sons, New York City, 1973. Hardcover. This contains: Caught in the Organ Draft, 1972; {Now + n. Now - n}, 1972; Some Notes on the Pre-Dynastic Epoch, 1973; In the Group, 1973; Caliban, 1971; Many Mansions, 1973; Good News from the Vatican, 1971; Push No More, 1972; The Mutant Season, 1973; When We Went to See the End of the World, 1972; What We Learned from This Morning's Newspaper, 1972; In Entropy's Jaws, 1971; and The Wind and the Rain, 1973.

251. Earth's Other Shadow. Published by Signet Books - The New American Library , New York City, 1973. Softcover. Signet Book Q5538. Herein: Something Wild Is Loose, 1971; To See the Invisible Man, 1963; Ishmael in Love, 1970; How it Was When the Past Went Away, 1969; To the Dark Star, 1968; The Fangs of the Trees, 1968; Hidden Talent, 1957; The Song the Zombie Sang - written with Harlan Ellison, 1970; and Flies, 1967.

252. Valley Beyond Time. Published by Dell Books, New York City, 1973. Softcover. Dell Book 9249. Herein: Introduction by **Robert Silverberg**; Valley Beyond Time, 1957; The Flame and the Hammer, 1957; The Wages of Death, 1958; and Spacerogue, 1958.

253. Carnal Cage. Writing as Don Elliott. Published by Corinth Publications - Nightstand Books, United States, 1973. Softcover. Nightstand Book 3021. Re-titled re-issue of Passion Trap, 1960.

254. Jungle Street. Writing as Don Elliott. Published by Corinth Publications - Nightstand Books, United States, 1973. Softcover. Nightstand Book 3024.

255. The Temptress. Writing as Don Elliott. Published by Corinth Publications - Nightstand Books, United States, 1973. Softcover. Nightstand Book 3028. Re-titled re-issue of Lust Goddess, 1961.

256. The Man Collector. Writing as Don Elliott. Published by Corinth Publications - Nightstand Books, United States, 1973. Softcover. Nightstand Book 3030.

257. Depravity Town. Writing as Don Elliott. Published by Corinth Publications - Nightstand Books, United States, 1973. Softcover. Nightstand Book 3042. Re-titled re-issue of Mistress of Sin, 1960.

258. The Flesh Merchants. Writing as Don Elliott. Published by Corinth Publications - Nightstand Books, United States, 1973. Softcover. Nightstand Book 3043.

259. The Bed and the Beautiful. Writing as Don Elliott. Published by Corinth Publications - Nightstand Books, United States, 1973. Softcover. Nightstand Book 3064.

260. The Instructor. Writing as Don Elliott. Published by Corinth Publications - Nightstand Books, United States, 1973. Softcover. Re-titled re-issue of Sin on Wheels, 1960.

261. Every Night in Rome. Writing as Don Elliott. Published by Greenleaf Books, United States, 1973. Softcover. Greenleaf Book 3063. Re-titled re-issue of The Sinful Ones, 1961.

262. Born with the Dead. Published by Random House, New York City, 1974. Hardcover. Herein: Born with the Dead, 1974; Thomas the Proclaimer, 1972; and Going, 1971.

263. Sundance and Other Science Fiction Stories. Published by Thomas Nelson, Nashville, Tennessee, 1974. Hardcover. This contains: Neighbor, 1964; Passport to Sirius, 1958; Caught in the Organ Draft, 1972; Neutral Planet, 1957; The Pain Peddlers, 1963; The Overlord's Thumb, 1958; The Outbreeders, 1959; Something Wild is Loose, 1971; and Sundance, 1969.

264. The Lady From Soho. Writing as Don Elliott. Published by Corinth Publications - Nightstand Books, United States, 1974. Softcover. Re-titled re-issue of Sin Club, 1961.

265. Till Love Do Us Part. Writing as Don Elliott. Published by Corinth Publications - Nightstand Books, United States, 1974. Softcover. Nightstand Book 4011.

266. The Decadent. Writing as Don Elliott. Published by Corinth Publications - Nightstand Books, United States, 1974. Softcover. Nightstand Book 4021.

267. The Game Susan Played. Writing as Don Elliott. Published by Corinth Publications - Nightstand Books, United States, 1974. Softcover. Nightstand Book 4042.

268. A Change for the Bedder. Writing as Don Elliott. Published by Corinth Publications - Nightstand Books, United States, 1974. Softcover. Nightstand Book 4046.

269. None but the Wicked. Writing as Don Elliott. Published by Corinth Publications - Nightstand Books, United States, 1974. Softcover. Re-titled reissue of Lust Cult, 1962.

270. The Stochastic Man. Published by Harper and Row, New York City, 1975. Hardcover.

271. The Feast of St. Dionysus. Published by Charles Scribner's Sons, New York City, 1975. Hardcover. This contains: Schwartz Between the Galaxies, 1974; Trips, 1974; In the House of Double Minds, 1974; This is the Road, 1973; and The Feast of St. Dionysus, 1973.

272. The Silent Invaders. Published by Dennis Dobson, London, 1975. First hardcover edition.

273. Sunrise on Mercury. Published by Thomas Nelson, Nashville, Tennessee, 1975. Hardcover. This contains: Sunrise on Mercury - writing as Calvin Knox, 1957; Hi Diddle Diddle! - writing as Calvin Knox, 1959; Birds of a Feather, 1958; There Was an Old Woman, 1958; Alaree, 1958; The Macauley Circuit, 1956; Company Store, 1959; and After the Myths Went Home, 1969.

274. Shadrach in the Furnace. Published by Bobbs-Merrill, New York City, 1976. Hardcover.

275. Capricorn Games. Published by Random House, New York City, 1976. Hardcover. Herein: Capricorn Games, 1974; The Science Fiction Hall of Fame, 1973; Ms. Found in an Abandoned Time Machine, 1973; Breckenridge and the Continuum, 1973; Ship-Sister, Star-Sister, 1973; A Sea of Faces, 1974; The Dybbuk of Mazel Tov IV, 1974; and Getting Across, 1973.

276. The Shores of Tomorrow. Published by Thomas Nelson, Nashville, Tennessee, 1976. Hardcover. This contains: Sound Decision - writing with Randall Garrett, 1956; The Day the Founder Died, 1974; Quick Freeze, 1957; Stress Pattern, 1960; The Silent Colony, 1954; The Isolationists, 1958; Deadlock - writing with Barbara Silverberg, 1959; and The Final Challenge, 1956.

277. The Best of Robert Silverberg. Published by Pocket Books, New York City, 1976. Softcover. Pocket Book 80282. This collection contains: Thinking about Silverberg by Barry N. Malzberg; Introduction by **Robert Silverberg**; Road to Nightfall, 1958; Warm Man, 1957; To See the Invisible Man, 1963; The Sixth Palace, 1965; Flies, 1967; Hawksbill Station, 1967; Passengers, 1968; Nightwings, 1968; Sundance, 1969; and Good News from the Vatican, 1971.

278. The Best of Robert Silverberg. Published by Sidgwick and Jackson, London, 1977. First hardcover edition.

279. Invaders from Earth. Published by Sidgwick and Jackson, London, 1977. First stand-alone hardcover edition.

280. Master of Life and Death. Published by Sidgwick and Jackson, London, 1977. First stand-alone hardcover edition.

281. Earth's Other Shadow. Published by Milligan, London, 1977. First hardcover edition.

282. To Open the Sky. Published by Gregg Press, Boston, 1977. First hardcover edition.

283. The Best of Robert Silverberg - Volume I. Published by Gregg Press, Boston, 1978. Hardcover. Herein: Thinking about Silverberg by Barry N. Malzberg; Introduction by **Robert Silverberg**; Road to Nightfall, 1958; Warm Man, 1957; To See the Invisible Man, 1963; The Sixth Palace, 1965; Flies, 1967; Hawksbill Station, 1967; Passengers, 1968; Nightwings, 1968; Sundance, 1969; and Good News from the Vatican, 1971.

284. The Best of Robert Silverberg - Volume II. Published by Gregg Press, Boston, 1978. Hardcover. This contains: Introduction by Thomas D. Clareson; When We Went to See the End of the World, 1972; Entropy's Jaws, 1971; Born with the Dead, 1974; Breckenridge and the Continuum, 1973; Caliban, 1971; Capricorn Games, 1974; The Dybbuk of Mazel Tov IV, 1974; A Happy Day in 2381, 1970; and Trips, 1974.

285. The Songs of Summer. Published by Victor Gollancz, London, 1979. Hardcover. Herein: Double Dare, 1956; Halfway House, 1966; By the Seawall, 1967; Bride Ninety-one, 1967; To Be Continued, 1956; The Songs of Summer, 1956; A Man of Talent, 1956; The Pleasure of Their Company, 1970; The King of the Golden River, 1967; Dark Companion, 1961; and We Know Who We Are, 1970.

286. Conquerors from the Darkness - with - Master of Life and Death. Published by Ace Books, New York City, 1979. Softcover.

287. Invaders from Earth - with - To Worlds Beyond. Published by Ace Books, New York City, 1980. Softcover.

288. Lord Valentine's Castle. Published by Harper and Row, New York City, 1980. Hardcover.

289. A Robert Silverberg Omnibus. Published by Harper and Row, New York City, 1981. Hardcover. This gathers: Downward to the Earth, 1970; Nightwings, 1969; and The Man in the Maze, 1969.

290. Majipoor Chronicles. Published by Arbor House, New York City, 1982. Hardcover. Herein: Prologue by **Robert Silverberg**; Thesme and the Ghayrog, 1982; The Time of the Burning, 1982; In the Fifth Year of the Voyage, 1981; Calintane Explains, 1982; The Desert of Stolen Oceans, 1981; The Soul-Painter and the Shapeshifter, 1981; Crime and Punishment, 1982; Among the Dream-Speakers, 1982; A Thief in Ni-Moya, 1981; Voriax and Valentine, 1982; and Epilogue by **Robert Silverberg**.

291. World of a Thousand Colors. Published by Arbor House, New York City, 1982. This contains: Introduction by **Robert Silverberg**; Something Wild is Loose, 1971; The Pain Peddlers, 1963; Going Down Smooth, 1968; World of a Thousand Colors,

Robert Silverberg

1957; Outbreeders - writing as Calvin M. Knox, 1959; Neighbor, 1964; The Man Who Never Forgot, 1958; Prime Commandment, 1958; One Way Journey, 1957; To the Dark Star, 1958; The Four,1958; Passport to Sirius, 1958; Counterpart, 1959; Neutral Planet, 1957; Solitary, 1957; Journey's End, 1958; The Fangs of the Trees, 1968; En Route to Earth, 1957; and How it Was When the Past Went Away, 1969.

292. Valentine Pontifex. Published by Arbor House, New York City, 1983. Hardcover.

293. Lord of Darkness. Published by Arbor House, New York City, 1983. Hardcover.

294. Sunrise on Mercury. Published by Victor Gollancz, London, 1983. Hardcover. This contains: World of a Thousand Colors, 1957; Going Down Smooth, 1968; After the Myths Went Home, 1969; Precedent, 1957; The Man Who Never Forgot, 1958; Sunrise on Mercury - writing as Calvin M. Knox, 1957; The Artifact Business, 1957; Why?, 1957; The Day the Founder Died, 1974; The Silent Colony, 1954; Alaree, 1958; There Was an Old Woman, 1958; and The Four, 1958.

295. Gilgamesh the King. Published by Arbor House, New York City, 1984. Hardcover.

296. The Conglomeroid Cocktail Party. Published by Arbor House, New York City, 1984. Hardcover. Herein: Introduction by **Robert Silverberg**; The Far Side of the Bell-Shaped Curve, 1982; The Pope of the Chimps, 1982; The Changeling, 1982; The Man Who Floated in Time, 1982; The Palace at Midnight, 1981; A Thousand Paces Along the Via Dolorosa, 1981; Our Lady of the Sauropods, 1980; Gianni, 1982; The Trouble with Sempoanga, 1982; How They pass the Time in Pelpel, 1981; Waiting for the Earthquake, 1981; Not Our Brother, 1982; The Regulars, 1981; Jennifer's Lover, 1982; and Needle in a Timestack, 1983.

297. Tom O'Bedlam. Published by Donald I. Fine, New York City, 1985. Hardcover.

298. The Silent Invaders - Collection. Published by Tor Books - Tom Doherty Associates, New York City, 1985. Hardcover. Herein: The Silent Invaders, 1963; and Valley Beyond Time, 1957.

299. Star of Gypsies. Published by Donald I. Fine, New York City, 1986. Hardcover.

300. Beyond the Safe Zone. Published by Donald I. Fine, New York City, 1986. Hardcover.

301. Project Pendulum. Published by Walker and Company, New York City, 1987. Hardcover.

302. Born with the Dead. Published by Tor Books - Tom Doherty Associates, New York City, 1988. Softcover. Tor Double 3. Bound with The Saliva Tree by **Brian W. Aldiss.**

303. At Winter's End. Published by Warner Books, New York City, 1988. Hardcover.

304. The Queen of Springtime. Published by Victor Gollancz, London, 1989. Hardcover.

305. The Mutant Season. With Karen Haber. Published by Doubleday Foundation, Garden City, New York, 1989. Softcover.

306. To the Land of the Living. Published by Victor Gollancz, London, 1989. Hardcover.

307. Sailing to Byzantium. Published by Tor Books - Tom Doherty Associates, New York City, 1989. Softcover. Tor Double 10. Bound with Seven American Nights by **Gene Wolfe**.

308. Nightwings. Published by Tor Books - Tom Doherty Associates, New York City, 1989. Softcover. Tor Double 15. Bound with The Last Castle by **Jack Vance**.

309. In Another Country. Published by Tor Books - Tom Doherty Associates, New York City, 1990. Softcover. Tor Double 18. Bound with Vintage Season by **C. L. Moore**.

310. Hawksbill Station. Published by Tor Books - Tom Doherty Associates, New York City, 1990. Softcover. Tor Double 26. Bound with Press Enter by John Varley.

311. Nightfall. With **Isaac Asimov**. Published by Victor Gollancz, London, 1990. Hardcover.

312. The New Springtime. Published by Warner Books, New York City, 1990. The U.S. version of The Queen of Springtime, 1989.

313. Letters from Atlantis. Published by Atheneum Books, New York City, 1990. Hardcover.

314. Child of Time. With **Isaac Asimov**. Published by Victor Gollancz, London, 1991. Hardcover.

315. The Face of the Waters. Published by Bantam Books, New York City, 1991. Hardcover.

316. Thebes of the Hundred Gates. Published by Axolotl Press, Eugene, Oregon, 1991. Hardcover.

317. The Ugly Little Boy. With **Isaac Asimov**. Published by Doubleday Foundation, Garden City, New York, 1992. The U.S. version of Child of Time, 1991.

318. The Positronic Man. With **Isaac Asimov**. Published by Victor Gollancz, London, 1992. Hardcover.

319. Kingdoms of the Wall. Published by Harper Collins, London, 1992. Hardcover.

320. The Collected Stories of Robert Silverberg. Published by Dell Books, New York City, 1992. Softcover.

321. Secret Sharers: The Collected Stories of Robert Silverberg - Volume One. Published by Bantam Books, New York City, 1992. Softcover. Introduction by **Robert Silverberg**; Homefaring, 1983; Basileus, 1983; Dancers in the Time-Flux, 1983; Gate of Horn, Gate of Ivory, 1984; Amanda and the Alien, 1983; Snake and Ocean, Ocean and Snake, 1972; Tourist Trade, 1984; Multiples, 1983; Against Babylon, 1986; Symbiont, 1985; Sailing to Byzantium, 1985; Sunrise on Pluto, 1985; Hardware,

1987; Hannibal's Elephants, 1988; The Pardoner's Tale, 1987; The Iron Star, 1987; The Secret Sharer, 1987; House of Bones, 1988; The Dead Man's Eyes, 1988; Chip Runner, 1989; To the Promised Land, 1989; The Asenion Solution, 1989; A Sleep and a Forgetting, 1989; and Enter a Soldier, Later, Enter Another, 1989.

322. Pluto in the Morning Light: The Collected Stories of Robert Silverberg - Volume One. Published by Grafton Books, London 1992. Softcover. Herein: Introduction by **Robert Silverberg**; Homefaring, 1983; Basileus, 1983; Dancers in the Time-Flux, 1983; Gate of Horn, Gate of Ivory, 1984; Amanda and the Alien, 1983; Snake and Ocean, Ocean and Snake, 1972; Tourist Trade, 1984; Multiples, 1983; Against Babylon, 1986; Symbiont, 1985; Sailing to Byzantium, 1985; Sunrise on Pluto, 1985; Hardware, 1987; Hannibal's Elephants, 1988; and Blindsight, 1986.

323. The Secret Sharer: The Collected Stories of Robert Silverberg - Volume Two. Published by Grafton Books, London 1992. Softcover. Herein: Introduction by **Robert Silverberg**; The Pardoner's Tale, 1987; The Iron Star, 1987; The Secret Sharer, 1987; House of Bones, 1988; The Dead Man's Eyes, 1988; Chip Runner, 1989; To the Promised Land, 1989; The Asenion Solution, 1989; A Sleep and a Forgetting, 1989; Enter a Soldier, Later, Enter Another, 1989; and We Are for the Dark, 1988.

324. Beyond the Safe Zone: The Collected Stories of Robert Silverberg - Volume Three. Published by Harper Collins, London 1993. Softcover. Herein: Introduction by **Robert Silverberg**; Capricorn games, 1974; The Dybbuk of Mazel Tov IV, 1974; Ishmael in Love, 1970; Trips, 1974; Schwartz Between the Galaxies, 1974; Many Mansions, 1973; Good News from the Vatican, 1971; In the Group, 1973; The Feast of St. Dionysus, 1973; Caught in the Organ Draft, 1972; {Now = n. Now - n.}, 1972; Caliban, 1971; Getting Across, 1973; Breckenridge and the Continuum, 1973; In the House of Double Minds, 1974; The Science Fiction Hall of Fame, 1973; The Wind and the Rain, 1973; A Sea of Faces, 1974; What We Learned from This Morning's Newspaper, 1972; Ship-Sister, Star-Sister, 1973; When We Went to See the End of the World, 1972; Push No More, 1972; Some Notes on the Pre-Dynastic Epoch, 1973; Entropy's Jaws, 1971; Ms. Found in an Abandoned Time Machine, 1973; The Mutant Season, 1973; and This is the Road, 1973.

325. Hot Sky At Midnight. Published by Bantam Books, New York City, 1994. Hardcover.

326. The Mountains of Majipoor. Published by Bantam Books, New York City, 1995. Hardcover.

327. The Road to Nightfall: The Collected Stories of Robert Silverberg - Volume Four. Published by Harper Collins, London 1996. Softcover. This contains: Introduction by **Robert Silverberg**; Road to Nightfall, 1958; Gorgon Planet, 1954; The Silent Colony, 1954; Absolutely Inflexible, 1956; The Macauley Circuit, 1956; The Songs of Summer, 1956; Alaree, 1958; The Artifact Business, 1957; Collecting Team, 1956; A Man of Talent, 1956; One-Way Journey, 1957; Sunrise on Mercury, 1957; World of a Thousand Colors, 1957; Warm Man, 1957; Blaze of Glory, 1957; Why?, 1957; The Outbreeders, 1959; The Man Who Never Forgot, 1958; There Was an Old Woman, 1958; The Iron Chancellor, 1958; and Ozymandias, 1958.

328. Starborne. Published by Bantam Books, New York City, 1996. Hardcover.

329. Ringing the Changes: The Collected Stories of Robert Silverberg - Volume Five. Published by Harper Collins, London 1997. Softcover. Herein: Introduction by **Robert Silverberg**; To See the Invisible Man, 1963; The Pain Peddlers, 1963; Neighbor, 1964; The Sixth Palace, 1965; Flies, 1967; Halfway House, 1966; To the Dark Star, 1968; Passengers, 1968; Bride 91, 1967; Going Down Smooth, 1968; The Fangs of the Trees, 1968; Ishmael in Love, 1970; Ringing the Changes, 1970; Sundance, 1969; How It Was When the Past Went Away, 1969; After the Myths Went Home, 1969; The Pleasure of Their Company, 1970; We Know Who We are, 1970; Something Wild Is Loose, 1971; and The Reality Trip, 1970.

330. Sorcerers of Majipoor. Published by Harper and Row, New York City, 1997. Hardcover.

331. The Alien Years. Published by Harper Prism, New York City, 1998. Hardcover.

332. Valentine of Majipoor. Published by The Science Fiction Book Club, Garden City, New York, 1999. An omnibus edition that gathers: Lord Valentine's Castle, 1980; Majipoor Chronicles, 1982; and Valentine Pontifex, 1983.

333. Lord Prestimion. Published by Harper and Row, New York City, 1999. Hardcover.

334. Sailing to Byzantium. Published by Simon and Schuster, New York City, 2000. Softcover. Herein: Introduction by **Robert Silverberg**; Sailing to Byzantium, 1985; The Secret Sharer, 1987; Thomas the Proclaimer, 1972; and We Are for the Dark, 1988.

335. Lion Time in Timbuctoo: The Collected Stories of Robert Silverberg - Volume Six. Published by Harper Collins, London 2000. Softcover. This contains: Introduction by **Robert Silverberg**; Lion Time in Timbuctoo, 1990; A Tip on a Turtle, 1991; In the Clone Zone, 1991; Hunters in the Forest, 1991; A Long Night's Vigil at the Temple, 1992; It Comes and Goes, 1992; Looking for the Fountain, 1992; The Way to Spook City, 1992; The Red Blaze Is the Morning, 1995; Death Do Us Part, 1996; The Martian Invasion Journals of Henry James, 1996; Crossing into the Empire, 1995; and The Second Shield, 1995.

336. The King of Dreams. Published by Harper Collins, New York City, 2001. Hardcover.

337. Cronos. Published by Pocket Books, New York City, 2001. Softcover. An omnibus edition, this gathers: Letters from Atlantis, 1990; Project Pendulum, 1987; and The Time Hoppers, 1967.

338. The Longest Way Home. Published by Harper Collins, New York City, 2002. Hardcover.

Robert Silverberg

339. Roma Eterna. Published by Harper Collins, New York City, 2003. Hardcover.

340. Other Dimensions. Published by the Science Fiction Book Club, Garden City, New York, 2003. Hardcover. An omnibus edition, this gathers: The Man in the Maze, 1969; Nightwings, 1969; Up the Line, 1969; and Dying Inside, 1972.

341. Seventh Shrine. With Andres Finer. Published by Devil's Due Publishing, United States, 2004. Softcover.

342. Phases of the Moon: Stories of Six Decades. Published by iBooks, New York City, 2004. Softcover. This contains: Road to Nightfall, 1958; The Macauley Circuit, 1956; Sunrise on Mercury, 1957; Warm Man, 1957; To See the Invisible Man, 1963; Flies, 1967; Passengers, 1968; Nightwings, 1968; Sundance, 1969; Good News from the Vatican, 1971; Capricorn Games, 1874; Born with the Dead, 1974; Schwartz Between the Galaxies, 1974; The Far Side of the Bell-Shaped Curve, 1982; The Pope of the Chimps, 1982; Needle in a Timestack, 1983; Sailing to Byzantium, 1985; Enter a Soldier, Later, Enter Another, 1989; Hunters in the Forest, 1991; Death Do Us Part, 1996; Beauty in the Night, 1997; The Millennium Express, 2000; and With Caesar in the Underworld, 2002.

343. In the Beginning: Tales from the Pulp Era. Published by Subterranean Press, Burton, Michigan, 2006. Hardcover. Herein: Yokel with Portfolio, 1955; Long Live the Kejwa, 1956; Guardian of the Crystal Gate, 1956; Choke Chain, 1956; Citadel of Darkness, 1957; Cosmic Kill, 1957; New Year's Eve - 2000 A.D., 1957; The Android Kill, 1957; The Hunters of the Cutwold, 1957; Come into My Brain!, 1958; Castaways of Space, 1958; Exiled from Earth, 1958; Second Start, 1959; Mournful Monster, 1959; Vampires of Outer Space, 1959; and The Insidious Invaders, 1959.

344. To Be Continued: The Collected Stories of Robert Silverberg - Volume One. Published by Subterranean Press, Burton, Michigan, 2006. Hardcover. Herein: Introduction by **Robert Silverberg**; Gorgon Planet, 1954; The Road to Nightfall, 1958; The Silent Colony, 1954; Absolutely Inflexible, 1956; The Macauley Circuit, 1956; The Songs of Summer, 1956; To Be Continued, 1956; Alaree, 1958; The Artifact Business, 1957; Collecting Team, 1956; A Man of Talent, 1956; One-Way Journey, 1957; Sunrise on Mercury, 1957; World of a Thousand Colors, 1957; Warm Man, 1957; Blaze of Glory, 1957; Why?, 1957; The Outbreeders, 1959; The Man Who Never Forgot, 1958; There Was an Old Woman, 1958; The Iron Chancellor, 1958; Ozymandias, 1958; Counterpart, 1959; and Delivery Guaranteed, 1959.

345. To the Dark Star: The Collected Stories of Robert Silverberg - Volume Two. Published by Subterranean Press, Burton, Michigan, 2007. Hardcover. This contains: Introduction by **Robert Silverberg**; {Now + n. Now - n.}, 2007; A Happy Day in 2381, 1970; After the Myths Went Home, 1969; Bride 91, 1967; The Fangs of the Trees, 1968; Flies, 1967; Going Down Smooth, 1968; Halfway House, 1966; Hawksbill Station, 1967; How It Was When the Past Went Away, 1969; Ishmael in Love, 1970; Neighbor, 1964; Passengers, 1968; Ringing the Changes, 1970; Sundance, 1969; The Pain Peddlers, 1963; The Pleasure of Their Company, 1970; The Sixth Palace, 1965; To See the Invisible Man, 1963; To the Dark Star, 1968; and We Know Who We Are, 1970.

346. Something Wild Is Loose: The Collected Stories of Robert Silverberg - Volume Three 1969 - 1972. Published by Subterranean Press, Burton, Michigan, 2008. Hardcover. Herein: Introduction by **Robert Silverberg**; Caliban, 1971; Many Mansions, 1973; Caught in the Organ Draft, 1972; The Mutant Season, 1973; What We Learned from This Morning's Newspaper, 1972; The Feast of St. Dionysus, 1973; Some Notes on the Pre-Dynastic Epoch, 1973; The Wind and the Rain, 1973; Push No More, 1972; When We Went to See the End of the World, 1972; Thomas the Proclaimer, 1972; Good News from the Vatican, 1971; Going, 1971; The Reality Trip, 1970; In Entropy's Jaws, 1971; and Something Wild Is Loose, 1971.

347. Trips 1972 - 1973: The Collected Stories of Robert Silverberg - Volume Four. Published by Subterranean Press, Burton, Michigan, 2009. Hardcover. Herein: Introduction by **Robert Silverberg**; In the Group, 1973; Getting Across, 1973; Ms. Found in an Abandoned Time Machine, 1973; The Science Fiction Hall of Fame, 1973; A Sea of Faces, 1974; The Dybbuk of Mazel Tov IV, 1974; Breckenridge and the Continuum, 1973; Capricorn Games, 1974; Ship-Sister, Star-Sister, 1973; This Is the Road, 1973; Trips, 1974; Born with the Dead, 1974; D. V. Perrot: Teach Yourself Swahili, 2009; Schwartz Between the Galaxies, 1974; and In the House of Double Minds, 1974.

348. 13th Immortal. Published by Cosmos Books, United States, 2009. Softcover.

***

ANTHOLOGIES

1. Earthmen and Strangers. Published by Duell, Sloan and Pearce, New York City, 1966. Hardcover. This anthology contains: Introduction by **Robert Silverberg**; Dear Devil by **Eric Frank Russell**, 1950; The Best Policy by Randell Garrett writing as David Gordon, 1957; Alaree by **Robert Silverberg**, 1958; Life Cycle by **Poul Anderson**, 1957; The Gentle Vultures by **Isaac Asimov**, 1957; Stranger Station by **Damon Knight**, 1956; Lower Than Angels by Algis Budrys, 1956; Blind Lightning by Harlan Ellison, 1956; and Out of the Sun by **Arthur C. Clarke**, 1958.

2. Voyagers in Time. Published by Meredith Press, New York City, 1967. Hardcover. Herein: Introduction by **Robert Silverberg**; The Sands of Time by P. Schuyler Miller, 1937; And It Comes Out Here by Lester Del Rey, 1951; Brooklyn Project by William Tenn, 1948; The Men Who Murdered Mohammed by **Alfred Bester**, 1958; Time Heals by **Poul Anderson**, 1949; Wrong-Way Street by Larry Niven, 1965; Flux by **Michael Moorcock** and Barrington J. Bayley, 1963; Dominoes by C. M.

Kornbluth, 1953; A Bulletin From the Trustees of the Institute for Advanced Research at Marmouth, Mass by Wilma Shore, 1964; Traveler's Rest by David I. Masson, 1965; The Time Machine - excerpt by H. G. Wells, 1895; and Absolutely Inflexible by **Robert Silverberg**, 1956.

3. Men and Machines. Published by Meredith Press, New York City, 1968. Hardcover. This contains: Introduction by **Robert Silverberg**; Counter Foil by George O. Smith, 1964; The Twonky by Henry Kuttner and **C. L. Moore** writing as Lewis Padgett, 1942; A Bad Day for Sales by **Fritz Leiber**, 1953; Without a Thought by Fred Saberhagen, 1963; Solar Plexus by **James Blish**, 1941; But Who Can Replace a Man? by **Brian W. Aldiss**, 1958; Instinct by Lester del Rey, 1952; The Hunting Lodge by Randall Garrett, 1954; With Folded Hands by **Jack Williamson**, 1947; and The Macauley Circuit by **Robert Silverberg**, 1956.

4. Tomorrow's Worlds. Published by Meredith Press, New York City, 1969. Hardcover. Herein: Introduction by **Robert Silverberg**; Sunrise on Mercury by **Robert Silverberg** writing as Calvin M. Knox, 1957; Before Eden by **Arthur C. Clarke**, 1961; Seeds of the Dusk by Raymond Z. Gallun, 1938; The Black Pits of Luna by **Robert A. Heinlein**, 1948; Crucifixus Etiam by Walter M. Miller Jr, 1953; Desertion by Clifford D. Simak, 1944; Pressure by **Harry Harrison**, 1969; The Planet of Doubt by Stanley G. Weinbaum, 1935; One Sunday in Neptune by Alexei Panshin, 1969; and Wait It Out by Larry Niven, 1968.

5. Three for Tomorrow. With **Arthur C. Clarke**. Published by Meredith Press, New York City, 1969. Hardcover. This contains: Introduction by **Robert Silverberg**; Foreword by **Arthur C. Clarke**; How it Was When the Past Went Away by **Robert Silverberg**, 1969; The Eve of RUMOKO by Roger Zelazny, 1969; and We All Die Naked by **James Blish**, 1969.

6. Dark Stars. Published by Ballantine Books, New York City, 1969. Softcover. Ballantine Book 01796. Herein: Introduction by **Robert Silverberg**; Imposter by **Philip K. Dick**, 1953; The Beast that Shouted Love at the Heart of the World by Harlan Ellison, 1968; Psychosmosis by David I. Masson, 1966; Polity and Custom of the Camiroi by R. A. Lafferty, 1967; Coming-of-Age Day by A. K. Jorgensson, 1965; The Cage of Sand by J. G. Ballard, 1962; On the Wall of the Lodge by **James Blish** and Virginia Kidd, 1962; Keepers of the House by Lester del Rey, 1956; Shark Ship by C. M. Kornbluth, 1958; The Totally Rich by John Brunner, 1963; A Deskful of Girls by **Fritz Leiber**; Masks by **Damon Knight**, 1968; Heresies of the Huge God by **Brian W. Aldiss**, 1966; The Streets of Ashkalon by **Harry Harrison**, 1962; Journey's End by **Poul Anderson**, 1957; and Road to Nightfall by **Robert Silverberg**, 1958.

7. The Science Fiction Hall of Fame - Volume One. Published by Doubleday & Company, Garden City, New York, 1970. Hardcover. Herein: Introduction by **Robert Silverberg**; Mimsy Were the Borogoves by Henry Kuttner and **C. L. Moore** writing as Lewis Padgett, 1943; A Martian Odyssey by Stanley G. Weinbaum, 1934; Twilight by **John W. Campbell**, 1934; Helen O'Loy by Lester del Rey, 1938; The Roads Must Roll by **Robert A. Heinlein**, 1940; Microcosmic God by **Theodore Sturgeon**, 1941; Nightfall by **Isaac Asimov**, 1941; The Weapon Shop by **A. E. van Vogt**, 1942; Huddling Place by Clifford D. Simak, 1944; Arena by Fredric Brown, 1944; First Contact by Murray Leinster, 1945; That Only a Mother by Judith Merril, 1948; Scanners Live in Vain by Cordwainer Smith, 1950; Mars is Heaven by **Ray Bradbury**, 1948; The Little Black Bag by C. M. Kornbluth, 1950; Born of Man and Woman by Richard Matheson, 1950; Coming Attraction by **Fritz Leiber**, 1950; The Quest for Saint Aquin by Anthony Boucher, 1951; Surface Tension by **James Blish**, 1956; The Nine Billion Names of God by **Arthur C. Clarke**, 1953; It's a Good Life by Jerome Bixby, 1953; The Cold Equations by Tom Godwin, 1954; Fondly Fahrenheit by **Alfred Bester**, 1954; The Country of the Kind by **Damon Knight**, 1956; Flowers for Algernon by Daniel Keyes, 1959; and A Rose for Ecclesiastes by Roger Zelazny, 1963.

8. Great Short Novels of Science Fiction. Published by Ballantine Books, New York City, 1970. Softcover. Ballantine Book 01960. This contains: Introduction by **Robert Silverberg**; Giant Killer by A. Bertram Chandler, 1945; Two Dooms by C. M. Kornbluth, 1958; Telek by **Jack Vance**, 1952; Second Game by Charles V. DeVet and Katherine MacLean, 1958; Beyond Bedlam by Wyman Guin, 1951; and The Graveyard Heart by Roger Zelazny, 1964.

9. Alpha One. Published by Ballantine Books, New York City, 1970. Softcover. Ballantine Book 02014. This anthology contains: Introduction by **Robert Silverberg**; The Moon Moth by Jack Vance; The Terminal Beach by J. G. Ballard, 1964; Poor Little Warrior! by **Brian W. Aldiss**, 1958; Testament of Andros by **James Blish**, 1953; A Triptych by Barry N. Malzberg writing as K. M. O'Donnell, 1969; For a Breath I Tarry by Roger Zelazny, 1966; Game for Motel Room by **Fritz Leiber**, 1963; Thus We Frustrate Charlemagne by R. A. Lafferty, 1967; The Man Who Came Early by **Poul Anderson**, 1956; The Time of His Life by Larry Eisenberg, 1968; The Doctor by Ted Thomas, 1967; Time Trap by Charles L. Harness, 1948; The Pi Man by **Alfred Bester**, 1959; and The Last Man Left in the Bar by C. M. Kornbluth, 1957.

10. The Ends of Time. Published by Hawthorn Books, New York City, 1970. Hardcover. Herein: Introduction by **Robert Silverberg**; Alpha Ralpha Boulevard by Cordwainer Smith, 1961; Twilight by **John W. Campbell**, 1934; The Awakening by **Arthur C. Clarke**, 1942; Last by **Fritz Leiber**, 1957; When the Last Gods Die by **Fritz Leiber**, 1951; Gyual of Sfere by **Jack Vance**, 1950; Epilogue by **Poul Anderson**, 1962; and At the End of Days by **Robert Silverberg**, 1965.

11. The Mirror of Infinity. Published by Harper and Row, Evanston, New York, 1970. Hardcover. Herein: The Star by **H. G. Wells**, 1897 - foreword by **Jack Williamson**; Twilight by **John W. Campbell**, 1934 - foreword by Algis Budrys; Nightfall by **Isaac**

Robert Silverberg

Asimov, 1941 - foreword by **Harry Harrison**; Private Eye by Henry Kuttner and **C. L. Moore** writing as Lewis Padgett, 1949 - foreword by **James Blish**; The Sentinel (2001) by **Arthur C. Clarke**, 1951 - foreword by Thomas D. Clareson; Specialist by Robert Sheckley, 1953 - foreword by Robert Conquest; Common Time by **James Blish**, 1953 - foreword by **Damon Knight**; The Game of Rat and Dragon by Cordwainer Smith, 1955 - foreword by Kingsley Amis; All You Zombies by **Robert A. Heinlein**, 1959 - foreword by Alexei Panshin; The Subliminal Man by J. G. Ballard, 1963 - foreword by H. Bruce Franklin; I Have No Mouth and I Must Scream by Harlan Ellison, 1967 - foreword by Willis E. McNelly; The Heat Death of the Universe by P. A. Zoline, 1967 - foreword by **Brian W. Aldiss**; and The Library of Babel by Jorge Luis Borges, 1956 - foreword by Ivor Rogers.

12. Worlds of Maybe. Published by Thomas Nelson, Camden, New York, 1970. Hardcover. This contains: Introduction by **Robert Silverberg**; Sail On! Sail On! By Philip Jose Farmer, 1952; Delenda Est by **Poul Anderson**, 1955; Sidewise in Time by Murray Leinster, 1934; All the Myriad Ways by Larry Niven, 1968; Translation Error by **Robert Silverberg**, 1959; Living Space by **Isaac Asimov**, 1956; and Slips Take Over by Miriam Allen de Ford, 1964.

13. Mind to Mind. Published by Thomas Nelson, Camden, New York, 1971. Hardcover. Herein: Introduction by **Robert Silverberg**; The Mindworm by C. M. Kornbluth, 1950; Psyclops by **Brian W. Aldiss**, 1956; Novice by James H. Schmitz, 1962; Liar! by **Isaac Asimov**, 1956; Riya's Foundling by Algis Budrys, 1953; Through Other Eyes by R. A. Lafferty, 1960; The Conspirators by James White, 1954; Journeys End by **Poul Anderson**, 1957; and Something Wild is Loose by **Robert Silverberg**, 1971.

14. The Science Fiction Bestiary. Published by Thomas Nelson, Camden, New York, 1971. Hardcover. This anthology contains: Introduction by **Robert Silverberg**; The Hurkle is a Happy Beast by **Theodore Sturgeon**, 1949; Grandpa by James H. Schmitz, 1955; The Blue Giraffe by L. Sprague de Camp, 1939; The Preserving Machine by **Philip K. Dick**, 1953; A Martian Odyssey by Stanley G. Weinbaum, 1934; The Sheriff of Canyon Gulch by **Poul Anderson** and **Gordon R. Dickson**, 1951; Drop Dead by Clifford D. Simak, 1956; The Gnurrs Come From the Voodvork Out by R. Bretnor, 1950; and Collecting Team by **Robert Silverberg**, 1956.

15. To the Stars. Published by Hawthorn Books, New York City, 1971. Hardcover. Herein: Introduction by **Robert Silverberg**; The Keys to December by Roger Zelazny, 1966; Common Time by **James Blish**, 1953; Four in One by **Damon Knight**, 1953; Planetoid Idiot by Phyllis Gotlieb, 1967; The End of the Line by James H. Schmitz, 1951; A Walk in the Dark by **Arthur C. Clarke**, 1950; and Ozymandias by **Robert Silverberg** writing as Ivar Jorgenson, 1958.

16. Four Futures. Anonymous editor. Published by Hawthorn Books, New York City, 1971. Hardcover. Herein: Foreword: Four Themes for Four Futures by **Isaac Asimov**; How Can We Sink When We Can Fly? by Alexei Panshin, 1971; Going by **Robert Silverberg**, 1971; Brave Newer World by **Harry Harrison**, 1971; and Ishmael into the Barrens by R. A. Lafferty, 1971.

17. New Dimensions I. Published by Doubleday & Company, Garden City, New York, 1971. Hardcover. All new stories, written for this anthology. Herein: Introduction by **Robert Silverberg**; The Power of Time by Josephine Saxton; The Giberel by Doris Pitkin Buck; Vaster Than Empires and More Slow by **Ursula K. Le Guin**; At the Mouse Circus by Harlan Ellison; The Sliced-Crosswise Only-on-Tuesday World by Philip Jose Farmer; The Trouble with the Past by Phyllis Eisenstein and Alex Eisenstein; Emancipation: A Romance of the Times to Come by Thomas M. Disch; A Special Kind of Morning by Gardner R. Dozois; The Great A by Robert C. Malstrom; A Plague of Cars by Leonard Tushnet; Sky by R. A. Lafferty; Love Song of Herself by Ed Bryant; The Wicked Flee by **Harry Harrison**; and Conquest by Barry N. Malzberg.

18. Alpha Two. Published by Ballantine Books, New York City, 1971. Softcover. Ballantine Book 02419. Herein: Introduction by **Robert Silverberg**; The Men Return by **Jack Vance**, 1957; The Voices of Time by J. G. Ballard, 1960; The Shaker Revival by Gerald Jones, 1970; Call Me Joe by **Poul Anderson**, 1957; Wall of Crystal Eye of Night by Algis Budrys, 1961; Faith of Our Fathers by **Philip K. Dick**, 1967; A Man of the Renaissance by Wyman Guin, 1964; Goodbye Amanda Jean by Wilma Shore, 1970; The Burning of the Brain by Cordwainer Smith, 1958; and That Share of Glory by C. M. Kornbluth, 1952.

19. Alpha Three. Published by Ballantine Books, New York City, 1972. Softcover. Ballantine Book 02883. This contains: Introduction by **Robert Silverberg**; The Gift of Gab by **Jack Vance**, 1955; Beyond Lies the Wub by **Philip K. Dick**, 1952; Under Old Earth by Cordwainer Smith, 1966; Total Environment by **Brian W. Aldiss**, 1968; The Shadow of Space by Philip Jose Farmer, 1967; Rescue Party by **Arthur C. Clarke**, 1946; Nine Hundred Grandmothers by R. A. Lafferty, 1966; Day Million by **Frederik Pohl**, 1966; Come to Venus Melancholy by Thomas M. Disch, 1965; and Aristotle and the Gun by L. Sprague de Camp, 1958.

20. New Dimensions II. Published by Doubleday & Company, Garden City, New York, 1972. Hardcover. New stories for this anthology, this contains: Introduction by **Robert Silverberg**; Nobody's Home by Joanna Russ; Filomena and Greg and Rikki-Tikki and Barlow and The Alien by James Tiptree Jr.; Out from Ganymede; and The Men Inside by Barry N. Malzberg; No. 2 Plain Tank by Edward Bryant; Eurema's Dam by R. A. Lafferty; King Harvest by Gardner R. Dozois; Take a Match by **Isaac Asimov**; f(x)=(11/15/67) by George Alec Effinger; White Summer in Memphis by Gordon Eklund; and Lazarus II Miriam Allen de Ford.

21. Invaders from Space. Published by Hawthorn Books, New York City, 1972. Hardcover. Herein: Introduction by **Robert Silverberg**; The Liberation of Earth by William Tenn, 1953; The Silly Season by C. M. Kornbluth, 1950; Roog by **Philip K. Dick**,

1953; Nightwings by **Robert Silverberg**, 1968; Nobody Saw the Ship by Murray Leinster, 1950; Storm Warning by **Donald A. Wollheim**, 1942; Catch That Martian by **Damon Knight**, 1952; Resurrection by **A. E. van Vogt**, 1948; Pictures Don't Lie by Katherine MacLean, 1951; and Heresies of the Huge God by **Brian W. Aldiss**, 1966.

22. Beyond Control. Published by Thomas Nelson, Nashville, Tennessee, 1972. Hardcover. This contains: Introduction by **Robert Silverberg**; Child's Play by William Tenn, 1947; Autofac by **Philip K. Dick**, 1955; Adam and No Eve by **Alfred Bester**, 1941; City of Yesterday by Terry Carr, 1967; The Box by **James Blish**, 1949; The Dead Past by **Isaac Asimov**, 1956; and The Iron Chancellor by **Robert Silverberg**, 1958.

23. The Day the Sun Stood Still. Published by Thomas Nelson, Nashville, Tennessee, 1972. Hardcover.

24. New Dimensions 3. Published by Nelson Doubleday - Science Fiction Book Club, Garden City, New York, 1973. Hardcover. All new stories for this anthology, herein: Introduction by **Robert Silverberg**; The Ones Who Walk Away from Omelas by **Ursula K. Le Guin**; Down There by **Damon Knight**; How Shall We Conquer by W. Macfarlane; They Live on Levels by Terry Carr; The Girl Who Was Plugged In by James Tiptree Jr.; Days of Grass Days of Straw by R. A. Lafferty; Notes Leading Down to the Conquest by Barry N. Malzberg; At the Bran Foundry by George Alec Effinger; Tell Me All About Yourself by F. M. Busby; Three Comedians by Gordon Eklund; and The Last Day of July by Garner R. Dozois.

25. Chains of the Sea. Published by Thomas Nelson, Nashville, Tennessee, 1973. Hardcover. This contains: Introduction by **Robert Silverberg**; Chains of the Sea by Gardner Dozois, 1973; And Us Too, I Guess by Geo. Alec Effinger, 1973; and The Shrine of Sebastian, 1973.

26. Deep Space. Published by Thomas Nelson, Nashville, Tennessee, 1973. Hardcover. This contains: Introduction by **Robert Silverberg**; Blood's a Rover by Chad Oliver, 1952; Noise by **Jack Vance**, 1952; Life Hutch by Harlan Ellison, 1956; Ticket to Anywhere by **Damon Knight**, 1952; Lulungomeena by **Gordon R. Dickson**, 1954; The Dance of the Changer and the Three by Terry Carr, 1968; Far Centaurus by **A. E. Van Vogt**, 1944; and The Sixth Palace by **Robert Silverberg**, 1965.

27. No Mind of Man. Published by Hawthorn Books, New York City, 1973. Hardcover. Herein: Introduction by **Robert Silverberg**; This Is the Road by **Robert Silverberg**, 1973; The Partridge Project by Richard A. Lupoff, 1973; and The Winds at Starmont by Terry Carr, 1973.

28. Three Trips in Time and Space. Published by Hawthorn Books, New York City, 1973. Hardcover. This contains: Foreword and Introduction by **Robert Silverberg**; Rumfuddle by **Jack Vance**, 1973; Flash Crowd by Larry Niven, 1973; and You'll Take the High Road by John Brunner, 1973.

29. Other Dimensions. Published by Hawthorn Books, New York City, 1973. Hardcover. Herein: Introduction by **Robert Silverberg**; Disappearing Act by **Alfred Bester**, 1953; Mugwump Four by **Robert Silverberg**, 1959; The Destiny of Milton Gomrath by Alexei Panshin, 1967; Narrow Valley by R. A. Lafferty, 1966; The Captured Cross-Section by Miles J. Breuer, 1929; The Worlds of If by Stanley G. Weinbaum, 1935; And He Built a Crooked House by **Robert A. Heinlein**, 1941; The Wall of Darkness by **Arthur C. Clarke**, 1949; and Stanley Toothbrush by Terry Carr writing as Carl Brandon, 1962.

30. Alpha Four. Published by Ballantine Books, New York City, 1973. Softcover. Ballantine Book 23564. Herein: Introduction by **Robert Silverberg**; Casablanca by Thomas M. Disch, 1967; Dio by **Damon Knight**, 1957; Eastward Ho! By William Tenn, 1958; Judas Danced by **Brian W. Aldiss**, 1958; Angel's Egg by Edgar Pangborn, 1951; In His Image by Terry Carr, 1973; All Pieces of a River Shore by R. A. Lafferty, 1970; We All Die Naked by **James Blish**, 1969; Carcinoma Angels by Norman Spinrad, 1967; Mother by Philip Jose Farmer, 1953; and 5,271,009 by **Alfred Bester**, 1954.

31. Alpha Five. Published by Ballantine Books, New York City, 1974. Softcover. Ballantine Book 24140. This anthology contains: Introduction by **Robert Silverberg**; We Can Remember It For You Wholesale by **Philip K. Dick**, 1966; The Star Pit by **Samuel R. Delany**, 1967; Baby, You Were Great! by **Kate Wilhelm**, 1967; Live From Berchtesgaden by George Alec Effinger, 1972; As Never Was by P. Schuyler Miller, 1944; Yesterday House by **Fritz Leiber**, 1952; A Man Must Die by John Clute, 1966; The Skills of Xanadu by **Theodore Sturgeon**, 1956; and A Special Kind of Morning by Gardner R. Dozois.

32. Windows into Tomorrow. Published by Hawthorn Books, New York City, 1974. Hardcover. Herein: Introduction by **Robert Silverberg**; The Year of the Jackpot by **Robert A. Heinlein**, 1952; Billennium by J. G. Ballard, 1961; A Pail of Air by **Fritz Leiber**, 1951; The Electric Ant by **Philip K. Dick**, 1969; The Last of the Romany by Norman Spinrad, 1963; Battlefield by Harlan Ellison, 1958; All the Last Wars at Once by George Alec Effinger, 1971; Dodkin's Job by **Jack Vance**, 1959; and The Pain Peddlers by **Robert Silverberg**, 1963.

33. New Dimensions IV. Published by Signet Books - New American Library, New York City, 1974. Softcover. Signet Book Y6113. All new for this anthology, this contains: After the Dreamtime by Richard A. Lupoff; The Bible After Apocalypse by Laurence M. Janifer; Outer Concentric; and The Examination by Felix C. Gotschalk; The Colors of Fear by Terry Carr; Ariel by Roger Elwood; State of the Art by Barry N. Malzberg; Among the Metal-and-People People by David R. Bunch; Animal Fair by R. A. Lafferty; and Strangers by Gardner R. Dozois.

34. Infinite Jests. Published by the Chilton Book Company, Radnor, Pennsylvania, 1974. Hardcover. This contains: Introduction by **Robert Silverberg**; Venus and the Seven Sexes by William Tenn, 1949; Babel II by **Damon Knight**, 1953; Useful Phrases for the Tourist by Joanna Russ, 1972; Conversational Mode by Grahame Leman, 1972; Heresies of the

Robert Silverberg

Huge God by **Brian W. Aldiss**, 1966; {Now + n, Now - n} by **Robert Silverberg**, 1972; Slow Tuesday Night by R. A. Lafferty, 1965; Help! I am Dr Morris Goldpepper by Avram Davidson, 1957; Oh to Be a Blobel by **Philip K. Dick**, 1964; Hobson's Choice by **Alfred Bester**, 1952; and I Plinglot, Who You? by **Frederik Pohl**, 1959.

35. Mutants. Published by Thomas Nelson, Nashville, Tennessee, 1974. Hardcover. This contains: Introduction by **Robert Silverberg**; The Mute Question by Forrest J. Ackerman, 1950; Liquid Life by Ralph Milne Farley, 1936; Ozymandias by Terry Carr, 1972; Watershed by **James Blish**, 1955; Ginny Wrapped in the Sun by R. A. Lafferty, 1967; Hothouse by **Brian W. Aldiss**; The Conqueror by Mark Clifton, 1952; Let the Ants Try by **Frederik Pohl** writing as James MacCreigh, 1949; It's a Good Life by Jerome Bixby, 1953; Tomorrow's Children by **Poul Anderson** and F. N. Waldrop, 1947; and The Man Who Never Forgot by **Robert Silverberg**, 1958.

36. Threads of Time. Published by Thomas Nelson, Nashville, Tennessee, 1974. Hardcover. This contains: Introduction by **Robert Silverberg**; Threads of Time by Gregory Benford, 1974; The Marathon Photograph by Clifford D. Simak, 1974; and Riding the Torch by Norman Spinrad, 1974.

37. New Dimensions 5. Published by Harper and Row, New York City, 1975. Hardcover. This contains: Find the Lady by Nicholas Fisk, 1975; A Solfy Drink, a Saffel Fragrance by Dorothy Gilbert, 1975; A Scarab in the City of Time by Marta Randall, 1975; Theodora and Theodora by Robert Thurston, 1975; A Day in the South Quad by Felix C. Gotschalk, 1975; Rogue Tomato by Michael Bishop, 1975; The Mothers' March on Ecstasy by George Alec Effinger, 1975; The Local Allosaurus - a poem by Steven Utley; Achievements by David Wise, 1975; The Dybbuk Dolls by Jack Dann, 1975; The Mirror at Sunset by Gil Lamont, 1975; Report to Headquarters by Barry N. Malzberg, 1975; Museum Piece by Drew Mendelson, 1975; White Creatures by Gregory Benford, 1974; The Contributors to Plenum Four by Michael Bishop, 1975; and Sail the Tide of Mourning by Richard A Lupoff, 1975.

38. Epoch. With Roger Elwood. Published by Berkley Books, New York City, 1975. Softcover. Proof copies of this carried Demon with a Glass Hand by Harlan Ellison but the story was removed from the final version. Herein: Introduction by **Robert Silverberg** and Roger Elwood; ARM by Larry Niven, 1975; Angel of Truth by Gordon Eklund, 1975; Mazes by **Ursula K. Le Guin**, 1975; For All Poor Folks at Picketwire by R.A. Lafferty, 1975; Growing Up in Edge City by **Frederik Pohl**, 1975; Durance by Ward Moore, 1975; The Ghost of a Model T by Clifford D. Simak, 1975; Planet Story by **Kate Wilhelm**, 1975; Graduation Day by Wallace Macfarlane, 1975; Timetipping by Jack Dann, 1975; Encounter with a Carnivore by Joseph Green, 1975; Lady Sunshine and the Magoon of Beatus by Alexei Panshin and Cory Panshin, 1975; For a Single Yesterday by George R. R. Martin, 1975; Bloodstream by Lou Fisher, 1975; Existence by Joanna Russ, 1975; Interface by A. A. Attanasio, 1975; Blooded on Arachne by Michael Bishop, 1975; Leviticus: In the Ark by Barry N. Malzberg, 1975; Cambridge, 1:58 A.M. by Gregory Benford, 1975; Run from the Fire by **Harry Harrison**, 1975; Waiting for the Universe to Begin by **Brian W. Aldiss**, 1975; But Without Orifices by **Brian W. Aldiss**, 1975; Aimez-Vous Holman Hunt? by **Brian W. Aldiss**, 1975; Uneasy Chrysalids, Out Memories by John Shirley, 1975; and The Dogtown Tourist Agency by **Jack Vance**, 1975.

39. Explorers of Space. Published by Thomas Nelson, Nashville, Tennessee, 1975. Hardcover. Herein: Introduction by **Robert Silverberg**; What's It Like Out There? by Edmond Hamilton, 1952; Vaster Than Empires and More Slow by **Ursula K. Le Guin**, 1971; Kyrie by **Poul Anderson**, 1968; Jupiter Five by **Arthur C. Clarke**, 1953; Exploration Team by Murray Leinster, 1956; Each an Explorer by **Isaac Asimov**, 1956; Collecting Team by **Robert Silverberg**, 1956; and Beachhead by Clifford D. Simak, 1951.

40. Strange Gifts. Published by Thomas Nelson, Nashville, Tennessee, 1975. Hardcover. This contains: Introduction by **Robert Silverberg**; The Man with English by Horace L. Gold, 1953; The Golden Man by **Philip K. Dick**, 1954; Bettyann by Kris Neville, 1951; Oddly and Id by **Alfred Bester**, 1950; Danger - Human! By **Gordon R. Dickson**, 1957; To Be Continued by **Robert Silverberg**, 1956; All the People by R. A. Lafferty, 1961; and Humpty Dumpty Had a Great Fall by Frank Belknap Long, 1948.

41. The New Atlantis and Other Novellas of Science Fiction. Published by Hawthorn Books, New York City, 1975. Hardcover. This contains: Introduction by **Robert Silverberg**; Silhouette by **Gene Wolfe**, 1975; A Momentary Taste of Being by James Tiptree Jr, 1975; and The New Atlantis by **Ursula K. Le Guin**, 1975.

42. New Dimensions 6. Published by Harper and Row, New York City, 1976. Hardcover. This contains: Target Berlin by George Alec Effinger; The Psychologist Who Wouldn't Do Awful Things to Rats by James Tiptree Jr; Is Your Child Using Drugs by Rachel Pollack; Charisma Leak by Felix C. Gotschalk; Secret Rider by Marta Randall; On the Air by Barry N. Malzberg; Dinosaurs by Tom Reamy; Mask by Donnan Call Jeffers Jr; Water by David Marshak; Osiris on Crutches by Philip Jose Farmer writing as Philip Jose Farmer and Leo Queequeg Tincrowdor; Chase Our Blues Away by George Alec Effinger; and The Alternates by James P. Girard.

43. Alpha Six. Published by Berkley Books, New York City, 1976. Softcover. Berkley Book D3048. This anthology contains: Introduction by **Robert Silverberg**; The Lost Continent by Norman Spinrad, 1970; Light of Other Days by Bob Shaw, 1966; The Secret of the Old Custard by John Sladek, 1966; Down Among the Dead Men by William Tenn, 1954; With These Hands by C. M. Kornbluth, 1951; Short in the Chest by Margaret St Clair writing as Idris Seabright, 1954; Brown Robert by Terry Carr, 1962; The Food Farm by Kit Reed, 1967; An Honorable Death by **Gordon R. Dickson**, 1961; Man of Parts by Horace L. Gold, 1954; and Painwise by James Tiptree Jr, 1972.

163

44. The Aliens. Published by Thomas Nelson, Nashville, Tennessee, 1976. Hardcover. Herein: Introduction by **Robert Silverberg**; Arena by Fredric Brown, 1944; An Eye for a What? by **Damon Knight**, 1957; Sundance by **Robert Silverberg**, 1969; Firewater by William Tenn, 1952; Look, You Think You've Got Troubles by Carol Carr, 1969; Countercharm by James White, 1960; and Hop-Friend by Terry Carr, 1962.

45. The Crystal Ship. Published by Thomas Nelson, Nashville, Tennessee, 1976. Hardcover. This contains: Introduction by **Robert Silverberg**; Megan's World by Marta Randall, 1976; Screwtop by Vonda McIntrye, 1976; and The Crystal Ship by Joan D. Vinge, 1976.

46. New Dimensions 7. Published by Harper and Row, New York City, 1977. Hardcover. All new stories for this anthology, this contains: The Retro Man by Gordon Eklund; The State of the Art on Alyssum by Marta Randall; Black as the Pit from Pole to Pole by Steven Utley and Howard Waldrop; You Are Here by Phyllis and Alex Eisenstein; Twinkle, Twinkle, Little Bat by J. A. Lawrence; The Almost Empty Rooms by John Shirley; In the Stocks by Barry N. Malzberg; Home Sweet Geriatric Dome by Felix C. Gotschalk; Knowing Her by Gregory Benford; The Blood's Horizon by A. A. Attanasio; Several Ways and the Sun by Henry-Luc Planchat; The Princess in the Tower 250,000 Miles High by **Fritz Leiber**.

47. Earth is the Strangest Planet. Published by Thomas Nelson, Nashville, Tennessee, 1977. Hardcover. Herein: Introduction by **Robert Silverberg**; When We Went to See the End of the World by **Robert Silverberg**, 1972; The Night That All Time Broke Out by **Brian W. Aldiss**, 1967; Or All the Seas With Oysters by Avram Davidson, 1958; Davey Jones Ambassador by Raymond Z. Gallun, 1935; The chrysalis by P. Schuyler Miller, 1936; Narrow Valley by R. A. Lafferty, 1966; The Empire of the Ants by **H. G. Wells**, 1905; And Lo! The Bird by Nelson Bond, 1950; Rock Diver by **Harry Harrison**, 1951; and The Rotifers by Robert Abernathy, 1953.

48. Galactic Dreamers. Published by Random House, New York City, 1977. Hardcover. Herein: Introduction by **Robert Silverberg**; The Dead Lady of Clown Town by Cordwainer Smith, 1964; Common Time by **James Blish**, 1953; The Waiting Grounds by J. G. Ballard, 1959; Night by **John W. Campbell**, 1935; Incentive by **Brian W. Aldiss**, 1958; The New Prime by **Jack Vance**, 1951; and Breckenridge and the Continuum by **Robert Silverberg**, 1973.

49. The Infinite Web. Published by The Dial Press, New York City, 1977. Hardcover. Herein: Introduction by **Robert Silverberg**; The Deep Range by **Arthur C. Clarke**, 1955; On the Last Afternoon by James Tiptree Jr, 1972; Of Mist and Grass and Sand by Vonda N. McIntyre, 1973; Grandpa by James H. Schmitz, 1955; There Is a Tide by **Brian W. Aldiss**, 1956; The World Between by **Jack Vance**, 1953; The Wind and the Rain by **Robert Silverberg**, 1973; and Incased in Ancient Rind by R. A. Lafferty, 1971.

50. Alpha Seven. Published by Berkley Books, New York City, 1977. Softcover. Herein: Introduction by **Robert Silverberg**; Rejoice, Rejoice, We Have No Choice by Terry Carr, 1974; Orphans of the Void by Michael Shaara, 1952; World War Two by George Alec Effinger, 1973; Dune Roller by Julian May, 1951; Shape by Robert Sheckley, 1953; Transfer Point by Anthony Boucher, 1950; A Galaxy Called Rome by Barry N. Malzberg, 1975; The Luckiest Man in Denv by C. M. Kornbluth, 1952; For Love by Algis Budrys, 1962; and The Night of Hoggy Darn by Richard McKenna writing as R. M. McKenna, 1958.

51. Alpha Eight. Published by Berkley Books, New York City, 1977. Softcover. This contains: Introduction by **Robert Silverberg**; A Dusk of Idols by **James Blish**, 1961; The Human Operators by Harlan Ellison and **A. E. van Vogt**, 1971; Think Only This of Me by Michael Kurland, 1973; The Short Ones by Raymond E. Banks, 1955; Warm by Robert Sheckley, 1953; When the Change-Winds Blow by **Fritz Leiber**, 1964; One Face by Larry Niven, 1965; The Man Who Lost the Stars by **Theodore Sturgeon**, 1959; The Happiest Creature by **Jack Williamson**, 1953; Klysterman's Silent Violin by Michael Rogers, 1972; and The New Reality by Charles L. harness, 1950.

52. Triax. Published by Pinnacle Books, Los Angeles, 1977. Softcover. This contains: Introduction by **Robert Silverberg**; Molly Zero by Keith Roberts, 1977; If I forget Thee by James Gunn, 1977; and Freitzke's Turn by **Jack Vance**, 1977.

53. Trips in time. Published by Thomas Nelson, Nashville, Tennessee, 1977. Hardcover. Herein: Introduction by **Robert Silverberg**; An Infinite Summer by Christopher Priest, 1976; The King's Wishes by Robert Sheckley, 1953; Manna by Peter Phillips, 1949; The Long Remembering by **Poul Anderson**, 1957; Try and Change the Past by **Fritz Leiber**, 1958; Divine Madness by Roger Zelazny, 1966; Mugwump 4 by **Robert Silverberg**, 1959; Secret Rider by Marta Randall, 1976; and The Seesaw by **A. E. van Vogt**, 1941.

54. Alpha Nine. Published by Berkley Books, New York City, 1978. Softcover. This anthology contains: Introduction by **Robert Silverberg**; Dumb Waiter by Walter M. Miller Jr, 1952; The Monsters by Robert Sheckley, 1953; The Sliced-Crosswise Only-on-Tuesday World by Philip Jose Farmer, 1971; The Funeral by **Kate Wilhelm**, 1972; The Book by Michael Shaara, 1953; Dusty Zebra by Clifford D. Simak, 1954; Goodlife by Fred Saberhagen, 1963; and Nobody's Home by Joanna Russ, 1972.

55. Lost Worlds, Unknown Horizons. Published by Thomas Nelson, Nashville, Tennessee, 1978. Hardcover. Herein: Introduction by **Robert Silverberg**; The Doom That Came to Sarnath by H. P. Lovecraft, 1920; The Country of the Blind by **H. G. Wells**, 1904; A Tale of the Ragged Mountains by Edgar Allan Poe, 1844; The Third Level by Jack Finney, 1950; The Sunken Land by **Fritz Leiber**, 1942; Trips by **Robert Silverberg**, 1974; Phantas by Oliver Onions, 1910; The City of the Singing Flame by Clark Ashton Smith, 1931; and The Balloon Tree by Edward Page Mitchell, 1883.

56. New Dimensions 8. Published by Harper and Row, New York City, 1978. Hardcover. Written for this anthology, this contains: Introduction by **Robert**

Robert Silverberg

Huge God by **Brian W. Aldiss**, 1966; {Now + n, Now - n} by **Robert Silverberg**, 1972; Slow Tuesday Night by R. A. Lafferty, 1965; Help! I am Dr Morris Goldpepper by Avram Davidson, 1957; Oh to Be a Blobel by **Philip K. Dick**, 1964; Hobson's Choice by **Alfred Bester**, 1952; and I Plinglot, Who You? by **Frederik Pohl**, 1959.

35. Mutants. Published by Thomas Nelson, Nashville, Tennessee, 1974. Hardcover. This contains: Introduction by **Robert Silverberg**; The Mute Question by Forrest J. Ackerman, 1950; Liquid Life by Ralph Milne Farley, 1936; Ozymandias by Terry Carr, 1972; Watershed by **James Blish**, 1955; Ginny Wrapped in the Sun by R. A. Lafferty, 1967; Hothouse by **Brian W. Aldiss**; The Conqueror by Mark Clifton, 1952; Let the Ants Try by **Frederik Pohl** writing as James MacCreigh, 1949; It's a Good Life by Jerome Bixby, 1953; Tomorrow's Children by **Poul Anderson** and F. N. Waldrop, 1947; and The Man Who Never Forgot by **Robert Silverberg**, 1958.

36. Threads of Time. Published by Thomas Nelson, Nashville, Tennessee, 1974. Hardcover. This contains: Introduction by **Robert Silverberg**; Threads of Time by Gregory Benford, 1974; The Marathon Photograph by Clifford D. Simak, 1974; and Riding the Torch by Norman Spinrad, 1974.

37. New Dimensions 5. Published by Harper and Row, New York City, 1975. Hardcover. This contains: Find the Lady by Nicholas Fisk, 1975; A Solfy Drink, a Saffel Fragrance by Dorothy Gilbert, 1975; A Scarab in the City of Time by Marta Randall, 1975; Theodora and Theodora by Robert Thurston, 1975; A Day in the South Quad by Felix C. Gotschalk, 1975; Rogue Tomato by Michael Bishop, 1975; The Mothers' March on Ecstasy by George Alec Effinger, 1975; The Local Allosaurus - a poem by Steven Utley; Achievements by David Wise, 1975; The Dybbuk Dolls by Jack Dann, 1975; The Mirror at Sunset by Gil Lamont, 1975; Report to Headquarters by Barry N. Malzberg, 1975; Museum Piece by Drew Mendelson, 1975; White Creatures by Gregory Benford, 1974; The Contributors to Plenum Four by Michael Bishop, 1975; and Sail the Tide of Mourning by Richard A Lupoff, 1975.

38. Epoch. With Roger Elwood. Published by Berkley Books, New York City, 1975. Softcover. Proof copies of this carried Demon with a Glass Hand by Harlan Ellison but the story was removed from the final version. Herein: Introduction by **Robert Silverberg** and Roger Elwood; ARM by Larry Niven, 1975; Angel of Truth by Gordon Eklund, 1975; Mazes by **Ursula K. Le Guin**, 1975; For All Poor Folks at Picketwire by R.A. Lafferty, 1975; Growing Up in Edge City by **Frederik Pohl**, 1975; Durance by Ward Moore, 1975; The Ghost of a Model T by Clifford D. Simak, 1975; Planet Story by **Kate Wilhelm**, 1975; Graduation Day by Wallace Macfarlane, 1975; Timetipping by Jack Dann, 1975; Encounter with a Carnivore by Joseph Green, 1975; Lady Sunshine and the Magoon of Beatus by Alexei Panshin and Cory Panshin, 1975; For a Single Yesterday by George R. R. Martin, 1975; Bloodstream by Lou Fisher, 1975; Existence by Joanna Russ, 1975; Interface by A. A. Attanasio, 1975; Blooded on Arachne by Michael Bishop, 1975; Leviticus: In the Ark by Barry N. Malzberg, 1975; Cambridge, 1:58 A.M. by Gregory Benford, 1975; Run from the Fire by **Harry Harrison**, 1975; Waiting for the Universe to Begin by **Brian W. Aldiss**, 1975; But Without Orifices by **Brian W. Aldiss**, 1975; Aimez-Vous Holman Hunt? By **Brian W. Aldiss**, 1975; Uneasy Chrysalids, Out Memories by John Shirley, 1975; and The Dogtown Tourist Agency by **Jack Vance**, 1975.

39. Explorers of Space. Published by Thomas Nelson, Nashville, Tennessee, 1975. Hardcover. Herein: Introduction by **Robert Silverberg**; What's It Like Out There? by Edmond Hamilton, 1952; Vaster Than Empires and More Slow by **Ursula K. Le Guin**, 1971; Kyrie by **Poul Anderson**, 1968; Jupiter Five by **Arthur C. Clarke**, 1953; Exploration Team by Murray Leinster, 1956; Each an Explorer by **Isaac Asimov**, 1956; Collecting Team by **Robert Silverberg**, 1956; and Beachhead by Clifford D. Simak, 1951.

40. Strange Gifts. Published by Thomas Nelson, Nashville, Tennessee, 1975. Hardcover. This contains: Introduction by **Robert Silverberg**; The Man with English by Horace L. Gold, 1953; The Golden Man by **Philip K. Dick**, 1954; Bettyann by Kris Neville, 1951; Oddly and Id by **Alfred Bester**, 1950; Danger - Human! By **Gordon R. Dickson**, 1957; To Be Continued by **Robert Silverberg**, 1956; All the People by R. A. Lafferty, 1961; and Humpty Dumpty Had a Great Fall by Frank Belknap Long, 1948.

41. The New Atlantis and Other Novellas of Science Fiction. Published by Hawthorn Books, New York City, 1975. Hardcover. This contains: Introduction by **Robert Silverberg**; Silhouette by **Gene Wolfe**, 1975; A Momentary Taste of Being by James Tiptree Jr, 1975; and The New Atlantis by **Ursula K. Le Guin**, 1975.

42. New Dimensions 6. Published by Harper and Row, New York City, 1976. Hardcover. This contains: Target Berlin by George Alec Effinger; The Psychologist Who Wouldn't Do Awful Things to Rats by James Tiptree Jr; Is Your Child Using Drugs by Rachel Pollack; Charisma Leak by Felix C. Gotschalk; Secret Rider by Marta Randall; On the Air by Barry N. Malzberg; Dinosaurs by Tom Reamy; Mask by Donnan Call Jeffers Jr; Water by David Marshak; Osiris on Crutches by Philip Jose Farmer writing as Philip Jose Farmer and Leo Queequeg Tincrowdor; Chase Our Blues Away by George Alec Effinger; and The Alternates by James P. Girard.

43. Alpha Six. Published by Berkley Books, New York City, 1976. Softcover. Berkley Book D3048. This anthology contains: Introduction by **Robert Silverberg**; The Lost Continent by Norman Spinrad, 1970; Light of Other Days by Bob Shaw, 1966; The Secret of the Old Custard by John Sladek, 1966; Down Among the Dead Men by William Tenn, 1954; With These Hands by C. M. Kornbluth, 1951; Short in the Chest by Margaret St Clair writing as Idris Seabright, 1954; Brown Robert by Terry Carr, 1962; The Food Farm by Kit Reed, 1967; An Honorable Death by **Gordon R. Dickson**, 1961; Man of Parts by Horace L. Gold, 1954; and Painwise by James Tiptree Jr, 1972.

163

44. The Aliens. Published by Thomas Nelson, Nashville, Tennessee, 1976. Hardcover. Herein: Introduction by **Robert Silverberg**; Arena by Fredric Brown, 1944; An Eye for a What? by **Damon Knight**, 1957; Sundance by **Robert Silverberg**, 1969; Firewater by William Tenn, 1952; Look, You Think You've Got Troubles by Carol Carr, 1969; Countercharm by James White, 1960; and Hop-Friend by Terry Carr, 1962.

45. The Crystal Ship. Published by Thomas Nelson, Nashville, Tennessee, 1976. Hardcover. This contains: Introduction by **Robert Silverberg**; Megan's World by Marta Randall, 1976; Screwtop by Vonda McIntrye, 1976; and The Crystal Ship by Joan D. Vinge, 1976.

46. New Dimensions 7. Published by Harper and Row, New York City, 1977. Hardcover. All new stories for this anthology, this contains: The Retro Man by Gordon Eklund; The State of the Art on Alyssum by Marta Randall; Black as the Pit from Pole to Pole by Steven Utley and Howard Waldrop; You Are Here by Phyllis and Alex Eisenstein; Twinkle, Twinkle, Little Bat by J. A. Lawrence; The Almost Empty Rooms by John Shirley; In the Stocks by Barry N. Malzberg; Home Sweet Geriatric Dome by Felix C. Gotschalk; Knowing Her by Gregory Benford; The Blood's Horizon by A. A. Attanasio; Several Ways and the Sun by Henry-Luc Planchat; The Princess in the Tower 250,000 Miles High by **Fritz Leiber**.

47. Earth is the Strangest Planet. Published by Thomas Nelson, Nashville, Tennessee, 1977. Hardcover. Herein: Introduction by **Robert Silverberg**; When We Went to See the End of the World by **Robert Silverberg**, 1972; The Night That All Time Broke Out by **Brian W. Aldiss**, 1967; Or All the Seas With Oysters by Avram Davidson, 1958; Davey Jones Ambassador by Raymond Z. Gallun, 1935; The chrysalis by P. Schuyler Miller, 1936; Narrow Valley by R. A. Lafferty, 1966; The Empire of the Ants by **H. G. Wells**, 1905; And Lo! The Bird by Nelson Bond, 1950; Rock Diver by **Harry Harrison**, 1951; and The Rotifers by Robert Abernathy, 1953.

48. Galactic Dreamers. Published by Random House, New York City, 1977. Hardcover. Herein: Introduction by **Robert Silverberg**; The Dead Lady of Clown Town by Cordwainer Smith, 1964; Common Time by **James Blish**, 1953; The Waiting Grounds by J. G. Ballard, 1959; Night by **John W. Campbell**, 1935; Incentive by **Brian W. Aldiss**, 1958; The New Prime by **Jack Vance**, 1951; and Breckenridge and the Continuum by **Robert Silverberg**, 1973.

49. The Infinite Web. Published by The Dial Press, New York City, 1977. Hardcover. Herein: Introduction by **Robert Silverberg**; The Deep Range by **Arthur C. Clarke**, 1955; On the Last Afternoon by James Tiptree Jr, 1972; Of Mist and Grass and Sand by Vonda N. McIntyre, 1973; Grandpa by James H. Schmitz, 1955; There Is a Tide by **Brian W. Aldiss**, 1956; The World Between by **Jack Vance**, 1953; The Wind and the Rain by **Robert Silverberg**, 1973; and Incased in Ancient Rind by R. A. Lafferty, 1971.

50. Alpha Seven. Published by Berkley Books, New York City, 1977. Softcover. Herein: Introduction by **Robert Silverberg**; Rejoice, Rejoice, We Have No Choice by Terry Carr, 1974; Orphans of the Void by Michael Shaara, 1952; World War Two by George Alec Effinger, 1973; Dune Roller by Julian May, 1951; Shape by Robert Sheckley, 1953; Transfer Point by Anthony Boucher, 1950; A Galaxy Called Rome by Barry N. Malzberg, 1975; The Luckiest Man in Denv by C. M. Kornbluth, 1952; For Love by Algis Budrys, 1962; and The Night of Hoggy Darn by Richard McKenna writing as R. M. McKenna, 1958.

51. Alpha Eight. Published by Berkley Books, New York City, 1977. Softcover. This contains: Introduction by **Robert Silverberg**; A Dusk of Idols by **James Blish**, 1961; The Human Operators by Harlan Ellison and **A. E. van Vogt**, 1971; Think Only This of Me by Michael Kurland, 1973; The Short Ones by Raymond E. Banks, 1955; Warm by Robert Sheckley, 1953; When the Change-Winds Blow by **Fritz Leiber**, 1964; One Face by Larry Niven, 1965; The Man Who Lost the Stars by **Theodore Sturgeon**, 1959; The Happiest Creature by **Jack Williamson**, 1953; Klysterman's Silent Violin by Michael Rogers, 1972; and The New Reality by Charles L. harness, 1950.

52. Triax. Published by Pinnacle Books, Los Angeles, 1977. Softcover. This contains: Introduction by **Robert Silverberg**; Molly Zero by Keith Roberts, 1977; If I forget Thee by James Gunn, 1977; and Freitzke's Turn by **Jack Vance**, 1977.

53. Trips in time. Published by Thomas Nelson, Nashville, Tennessee, 1977. Hardcover. Herein: Introduction by **Robert Silverberg**; An Infinite Summer by Christopher Priest, 1976; The King's Wishes by Robert Sheckley, 1953; Manna by Peter Phillips, 1949; The Long Remembering by **Poul Anderson**, 1957; Try and Change the Past by **Fritz Leiber**, 1958; Divine Madness by Roger Zelazny, 1966; Mugwump 4 by **Robert Silverberg**, 1959; Secret Rider by Marta Randall, 1976; and The Seesaw by **A. E. van Vogt**, 1941.

54. Alpha Nine. Published by Berkley Books, New York City, 1978. Softcover. This anthology contains: Introduction by **Robert Silverberg**; Dumb Waiter by Walter M. Miller Jr, 1952; The Monsters by Robert Sheckley, 1953; The Sliced-Crosswise Only-on-Tuesday World by Philip Jose Farmer, 1971; The Funeral by **Kate Wilhelm**, 1972; The Book by Michael Shaara, 1953; Dusty Zebra by Clifford D. Simak, 1954; Goodlife by Fred Saberhagen, 1963; and Nobody's Home by Joanna Russ, 1972.

55. Lost Worlds, Unknown Horizons. Published by Thomas Nelson, Nashville, Tennessee, 1978. Hardcover. Herein: Introduction by **Robert Silverberg**; The Doom That Came to Sarnath by H. P. Lovecraft, 1920; The Country of the Blind by **H. G. Wells**, 1904; A Tale of the Ragged Mountains by Edgar Allan Poe, 1844; The Third Level by Jack Finney, 1950; The Sunken Land by **Fritz Leiber**, 1942; Trips by **Robert Silverberg**, 1974; Phantas by Oliver Onions, 1910; The City of the Singing Flame by Clark Ashton Smith, 1931; and The Balloon Tree by Edward Page Mitchell, 1883.

56. New Dimensions 8. Published by Harper and Row, New York City, 1978. Hardcover. Written for this anthology, this contains: Introduction by **Robert**

Robert Silverberg

Silverberg; A Quiet Revolution for Death by Jack Dann; Yes Sir That's My by Daniel P. Dern; Whores by Christopher Priest; Sun 1 by Gregor Hartmann; This is My Beloved by J. A. Lawrence; Metal by Robert R. Olsen; I Graver by Peter Dillingham; Lifeboat by Jeff Hecht; Blind Man Singing by Drew Mendelson; Three Dream Woman by Craig Strete and Michael Bishop; Mandala by Greg Bear; and When the Morning Stars Sing Together by Donnan Call Jeffers Jr.

57. Car Sinister. With Martin H. Greenberg and Joseph D. Olander. Published by Avon Books, New York City, 1979. Softcover. This anthology contains: Introduction by Martin H. Greenberg, Joseph D. Olander and **Robert Silverberg**; Devil Car by Roger Zelazny, 1965; Auto da Fe by Roger Zelazny, 1967; Vampires Ltd by Josef Nesvadba, 1964; A Plague of Cars by Leonard Tushnet, 1971; Waves of Ecology by Leonard Tushnet, 1974; Traffic Problem by William Earls, 1970; Station HR972 by Kenneth Bulmer, 1967; A Day on Death Highway by H. Chandler Elliott, 1963; The Greatest Car in the World by **Harry Harrison**, 1966; The Roads, the Roads, the Beautiful Roads by Avram Davidson, 1969; The Exit to San Breta by George R. R. Martin, 1972; Car Sinister by **Gene Wolfe**, 1970; The Mary Celeste Move by **Frank Herbert**, 1964; Interurban Queen by R. A. Lafferty, 1970; X Marks the Pedwalk by **Fritz Leiber**, 1963; Wheels by Robert Thurston, 1971; Sedan Deville by Barry N. Malzberg, 1974; Romance in a Twenty-first Century Used Car Lot by Robert F. Young, 1960; East Wind, West Wind by Frank M. Robinson, 1972; and Along the Scenic Route by Harlan Ellison, 1969.

58. Dawn of Time. With Martin H. Greenberg and Joseph D. Olander. Published by Elsevier/Nelson Books, New York City, 1979. Hardcover. Herein: Introduction by **Robert Silverberg**, Martin H. Greenberg and Joseph D. Olander; A Gun for Dinosaur by L. Sprague de Camp, 1956; The Sands of Time by P. Schuyler Miller, 1937; Paleontology: An Experimental Science by Robert Olsen, 1974; The Doctor by Ted Thomas, 1967; The Link by Cleve Cartmill, 1942; The Day Is Done by Lester del Rey, 1939; The Gnarly Man by L. Sprague de Camp, 1939; Brave New World by J. Francis McComas, 1954; and The Peat Bog by **Poul Anderson**, 1975.

59. The Edge of Space. Published by Elsevier/Nelson Books, New York City, 1979. Hardcover. This contains: Introduction by **Robert Silverberg**; In the Blood by Glenn Chang, 1979; Acts of Love by Mark J. McGarry, 1979; and The King's Dogs by Phyllis Gotlieb, 1979.

60. The Androids Are Coming. Published by Elsevier/Nelson Books, New York City, 1979. Hardcover. Herein: Introduction by **Robert Silverberg**; The Captain's Dog by E. C. Tubb, 1958; Good Night, Mr James by Clifford D. Simak, 1951; Evidence by **Isaac Asimov**, 1946; Made in U.S.A. by J. T. McIntosh, 1953; The Electric Ant by **Philip K. Dick**, 1969; The Golem by Avram Davidson, 1955; and Fondly Fahrenheit by **Alfred Bester**, 1954.

61. New Dimensions 9. Published by Harper and Row, New York City, 1979. Hardcover. The stories herein were written for this anthology: Introduction by **Robert Silverberg**; The Pathways of Desire by Ursula K. Le Guin; The Rancher Goes to Tinker Town by Timothy Robert Sullivan; Calibrations and Exercises by Gregory Benford; Binding Energy by Peter S. Alterman; The Attendant by Bruce Taylor; Square Pony Express by Felix C. Gotschalk; Crossing the Wastelands by Jeff Hecht; Three Poems by Peter Dillingham; The Sands of Libya Are Barren by Donnan Call Jeffers Jr; A Passionate State of Mind by Tony Sarowitz; and Last by Michael Conner.

62. The Best of New Dimensions. Published by Pocket Books, New York City, 1979. Softcover.

Herein: Introduction by **Robert Silverberg**; A Special Kind of Morning by Gardner R. Dozois, 1971; The Sliced-Crosswise Only-on-Tuesday World by Philip Jose Farmer, 1971; At the Mouse Circus by Harlan Ellison, 1971; Nobody's Home by Joanna Russ, 1972; Eurema's Dam by R. A. Lafferty, 1972; $f(x) = (11/15/67)$ x = her, $f(x) = 0$ by George Alec Effinger, 1972; The Ones Who Walk Away From Omelas by **Ursula K. Le Guin**, 1973; They Live on Levels by Terry Carr, 1973; Tell Me All About Yourself by F. M. Busby, 1973; The Examination by Felix C. Gotschalk, 1974; Find the Lady by Nicholas Fisk, 1975; A Scarab in the City of Time by Marta Randall, 1975; The Psychologist Who Wouldn't Do Awful Things to Rats by James Tiptree Jr, 1976; On the Air by Barry Malzberg, 1976; A Quiet Revolution for Death by Jack Dann, 1978; When the Morning Stars Sing Together by Donnan Call Jeffers Jr, 1978; Calibrations and Exercises by Gregory Benford, 1979; and Yes, Sir, That's My by Daniel P. Dern, 1978.

63. The Arbor House Treasury of Great Science Fiction Short Novels. With Martin H. Greenberg. Published by Arbor House, New York City, 1980. Hardcover. This contains: Introduction by Martin H. Greenberg and **Robert Silverberg**; Beyond Bedlam by Wyman Guin, 1951; By His Bootstraps by **Robert A. Heinlein**, 1941; Second Game by Katherine MacLean and Charles V. De Vet, 1958; Giant Killer by A. Bertram Chandler, 1945; A Case of Conscience by **James Blish**, 1953; Dio by **Damon Knight**, 1957; Houston, Houston, Do You Read? by James Tiptree Jr, 1976; On the Storm Planet by Cordwainer Smith, 1965; Equinoctial by John Varley, 1977; The Golden Helix by **Theodore Sturgeon**, 1954; The Dead Past by **Isaac Asimov**, 1956; The Road to the Sea by **Arthur C. Clarke**, 1951; The Star Pit by **Samuel R. Delany**, 1967; and Born With the Dead by **Robert Silverberg**, 1974.

64. The Arbor House Treasury of Modern Science Fiction. With Martin H. Greenberg. Published by Arbor House, New York City, 1980. Hardcover. This contains: Introduction by **Robert Silverberg** and Martin H. Greenberg; Winter's King by **Ursula K. Le Guin**, 1969; When It Changed by Joanna Russ, 1972; Wall of Crystal, Eye of Night by Algis Budrys, 1961; Stranger Station by **Damon Knight**, 1956; Shape by Robert Sheckley, 1953; Rescue Party by **Arthur C. Clarke**, 1946; The Queen of Air and Darkness by **Poul Anderson**, 1971; The Man Who Never Grew Young by **Fritz Leiber**, 1947; Light of Other Days by Bob Shaw, 1966; The Keys to December by Roger Zelazny, 1966; Kaleidoscope by **Ray Bradbury**, 1949; I'm Scared by Jack Finney,

1951; Hunting Machine by Carol Emshwiller, 1957; Day Million by **Frederik Pohl**, 1966; Common Time by **James Blish**, 1953; The Bicentennial Man by **Isaac Asimov**, 1976; Alpha Ralpha Boulevard by Cordwainer Smith, 1961; Child's Play by William Tenn, 1947; Unready to Wear by Kurt Vonnegut, Jr, 1953; Or All the Seas with Oysters by Avram Davidson, 1958; The Women Men Don't See by James Tiptree, Jr, 1973; A Galaxy Called Rome by Barry N. Malzberg, 1975; In the Bowl by John Varley, 1975; Of Mist, and Grass, and Sand by Vonda N. McIntyre, 1973; The Human Operators by Harlan Ellison and **A. E. van Vogt**, 1971; Sundance by **Robert Silverberg**, 1969; The Time of His Life by Larry Eisenberg, 1968; Neutron Star by Larry Niven, 1966; The Shadow of Space by Philip Jose Farmer, 1967; The Marching Morons by C. M. Kornbluth, 1951; Grandpa by James H. Schmitz, 1955; The Gift of Gab by **Jack Vance**, 1955; Imposter by **Philip K. Dick**, 1953; Hobson's Choice by **Alfred Bester**, 1952; Private Eye by Henry Kuttner and **C. L. Moore** writing as Lewis Padgett, 1949; Angel's Egg by Edgar Pangborn, 1951; When You Care, When You Love by **Theodore Sturgeon**, 1962; Poor Little Warrior! by **Brian W. Aldiss**, 1956; and All You Zombies by **Robert A. Heinlein**, 1959.

65. New Dimensions 10. Published by Harper and Row, New York City, 1980. Hardcover. Stories written for this anthology, this contains: Holy by Orson Scott Card; Animals by John Kessel; Amadeus by Carter Scholz; Growing Up On Vlin by Sydelle Shamah; Deletions by Joseph V. Francavilla; The Breath Amidst the Stones by Bruce Taylor; A Chrysalis Unbroken by Peter Santiago C.; Mare Somniorum by Stephen W. Potts; Circus by Marta Randall; and A Presidential Tape by Felix C. Gotschalk.

66. New Dimensions 11. With Marta Randall. Published by Pocket Books, New York City, 1980. Softcover. Herein, stories written for this anthology: Foreword: A Time of Changes by **Robert Silverberg**; Unicorn Tapestry by Suzy McKee Charnas; The Haunting by Mary C. Pangborn; The Eros Passage by Scott Sanders; A Sunday Visit with Great Grandfather by Craig Strete; Criers and Killers by Pat Cadigan; The Four by Gary Woolard; Comstock by Alan Ryan; Kid Photon by Steven Bryan Bieler; and The Feast of Saint Janis by Michael Swanwick.

67. New Dimensions 12. With Marta Randall. Published by Pocket Books, New York City, 1981. Softcover. The stories herein were written for this anthology: Foreword: The Second Decade by Marta Randall; Walden Three by Michael Swanwick; Cadenza by Gregory Benford; Drode's Equations by Richard Grant; The Woman in the Phone Booth by Elizabeth A. Lynn; Elfleda by Vonda N. McIntyre; Pain and Glory by Gordon Eklund; Parables of Art by Jack Dann and Barry N. Malzberg; Delta D and She by Michael Ward; A Manner of Speaking by Tony Sarowitz; The Satyrs and Dryads Cotillion by Juleen Brantingham; The Last Concert of Pierre Valdemar by Carter Scholz; and The Celebrants by Peter Santiago.

68. The Science Fictional Dinosaur. With Martin H. Greenberg and Charles G. Waugh. Published by Avon Books, New York City, 1982. Softcover. This anthology contains: Introduction by **Robert Silverberg**, Martin H. Greenberg and Charles G. Waugh; The Wings of a Bat by Paul Ash, 1966; The Ever Branching Tree by **Harry Harrison**, 1970; When Time Was New by Robert F. Young, 1964; Poor Little Warrior! by **Brian W. Aldiss**, 1958; Day of the Hunters by **Isaac Asimov**, 1950; A Statue for Father by **Isaac Asimov**, 1958; Hermes to the Ages by Frederick D. Gottfried, 1980; Wildcat by **Poul Anderson**, 1958; and Our Lady of the Sauropods by **Robert Silverberg**, 1980, along with the following by the three editors: Geologic Time Scale; Selected Mesozoic Reptiles; Glossy; and Further Reading.

69. The Fantasy Hall of Fame. With Martin H. Greenberg. Published by Arbor House, New York City, 1983. Hardcover. This contains: Introduction by **Robert Silverberg**; The Masque of the Red Death by Edgar Allan Poe, 1842; An Inhabitant of Carcosa by Ambrose Bierce, 1886; The Sword of Welleran by Lord Dunsany, 1908; The Women of the Wood **by A. Merritt**, 1926; The Weird of Avoosl Wuthoqquan by Clark Ashton Smith, 1932; The Valley of the Worm by Robert E. Howard, 1934; Black God's Kiss by **C. L. Moore**, 1934; The Silver Key by H. P. Lovecraft, 1929; Nothing in the Rules by L. Sprague de Camp, 1939; A Gnome There Was by Henry Kuttner and **C. L. Moore** writing as Lewis Padgett, 1941; Snulbug by Anthony Boucher, 1941; The Words of Guru by C. M. Kornbluth, 1941; Homecoming by **Ray Bradbury**, 1946; Mazirian the Magician by **Jack Vance**, 1950; O Ugly Bird! by Manly Wade Wellman, 1951; The Silken Swift by **Theodore Sturgeon**, 1953; The Golem by Avram Davidson, 1955; That Hell Bound Train by Robert Bloch, 1958; Kings in Darkness by **Michael Moorcock**, 1962; Pretty Maggie Moneyeyes by Harlan Ellison, 1967; Gonna Roll the Bones by **Fritz Leiber**, 1967; and The Ones Who Walk Away from Omelas by **Ursula K. Le Guin**, 1973.

70. The Arbor House Treasury of Science Fiction Masterpieces. With Martin H. Greenberg. Published by Arbor House, New York City, 1983. Hardcover. Herein: Introduction by **Robert Silverberg** and Martin H. Greenberg; Mellonta Tauta by Edgar Allan Poe, 1849; In the Year 2889 by **Jules Verne**, 1889; Sold to Satan by Mark Twain, 1923; The New Accelerator by **H. G. Wells**, 1901; Finis by Frank Lillie Pollack, 1906; As Easy as A.B.C. by Rudyard Kipling, 1912; Dark Lot of One Saul by M. P. Shiel, 1975; R.U.R. by Karel Capek, 1921; The Tissue Culture King by Julian Huxley, 1926; The Metal Man by **Jack Williamson**, 1928; The Gostak and the Doshes by Miles J. Breuer, 1930; Alas All Thinking by Harry Bates, 1935; The Mad Moon by Stanley G. Weinbaum, 1935; As Never Was by P. Schuyler Miller, 1944; Desertion by Clifford D. Simak, 1944; The Strange Case of John Kingman by Murray Leinster, 1948; Dreams are Sacred by Peter Phillips, 1948; Misbegotten Missionary by **Isaac Asimov**, 1950; Dune Roller by Julian May, 1951; Warm by Robert Sheckley, 1953; A Bad Day for Sales by **Fritz Leiber**, 1953; Man of Parts by H. L. Gold, 1954; The Man Who Came Early by **Poul Anderson**, 1956; The Burning of the Brain by Cordwainer Smith, 1958; The Men Who Murdered Mohammed by **Alfred Bester**, 1958; The Man Who Lost the

Robert Silverberg

Sea by **Theodore Sturgeon**, 1959; Goodlife by Fred Saberhagen, 1963; Travels by Carter Scholz, 1980; The Sliced-Crosswise Only-on-Tuesday World by Philip Jose Farmer, 1971; Gehenna by Barry N. Malzberg, 1971; A Meeting with Medusa by **Arthur C. Clarke**, 1971; Painwise by James Tiptree Jr, 1972; Nobody's Home by Joanna Russ, 1972; Think Only This of Me by Michael Kurland, 1973; Capricorn Games by **Robert Silverberg**, 1974; Doing Lennon by Gregory Benford, 1975; and The Author of Acacia Seeds and Other Extracts from the Journal of the Association of Therolinguistics by **Ursula K. Le Guin**, 1974.

71. Nebula Award Stories 18. Published by Arbor House, New York City, 1983. Hardcover. This contains: Introduction by **Robert Silverberg**; Souls by Joanna Russ, 1982; No Enemy but Time - excerpt by Michael Bishop, 1982; Burning Chrome by **William Gibson**, 1982; A Letter From the Clearys by **Connie Willis**, 1982; Fire Watch by **Connie Willis**, 1982; Corridors by Barry N. Malzberg, 1982; Another Orphan by John Kessel, 1982; Swarm by Bruce Sterling, 1982; and The Pope of the Chimps by **Robert Silverberg**, 1982.

72. The Time Travellers: A Science Fiction Quartet. With Martin H. Greenberg. Published by Donald I. Fine - Primus Books, New York City, 1985. Softcover. Herein: Introduction by **Robert Silverberg**; The Ugly Little Boy by **Isaac Asimov**, 1958; Sidewise in Time by Murray Leinster, 1934; Consider Her Ways by John Wyndham, 1956; and Vintage Season by Henry Kuttner and **C. L. Moore** writing as Lawrence O'Donnell, 1946.

73. Neanderthals: Isaac Asimov's Wonderful Worlds of Science Fiction. With Martin H. Greenberg and Charles G. Waugh. Published by Signet Books - The New American Library , New York City, 1987. Softcover. This contains: Introduction: Neanderthal Man by **Isaac Asimov**; Genesis by H. Beam Piper, 1951; The Ugly Little Boy by **Isaac Asimov**, 1958; The Long Remembering by **Poul Anderson**, 1957; The Apotheosis of Ki by Miriam Allen de Ford, 1956; Man O' Dreams by Will McMorrow, 1987; The Treasure of Odirex by Charles Sheffield, 1978; The Ogre by Avram Davidson, 1959; Alas, Poor Yorick by Thomas A. Easton, 1981; The Gnarly Man by L. Sprague de Camp, 1939; The Hairy Parents by A. Bertram Chandler, 1975; The Alley Man by Philip Jose Farmer, 1959; and Afterword: The Valley of Neander by **Robert Silverberg**.

74. Great Science Fiction of the 20th Century. With Martin H. Greenberg. Published by Avenel Books, New York City, 1987. Hardcover. Re-titled re-issue of The Arbor House Treasury of Modern Science Fiction, 1980.

75. Robert Silverberg's Worlds of Wonder. Published by Warner Books, New York City, 1987. Hardcover. This contains: Foreword by **Robert Silverberg**; Introduction: The Making of a Science Fiction Writer by **Robert Silverberg**; The New Prime by **Jack Vance**, 1951; Colony by **Philip K. Dick**, 1953; Home Is the Hunter by Henry Kuttner and **C. L. Moore**, 1953; No Woman Born by **C. L. Moore**, 1944; Four in One by **Damon Knight**, 1953; Fondly Fahrenheit by **Alfred Bester**, 1954; The Monsters by Robert Sheckley, 1953; Common Time by **James Blish**, 1953; Scanners Live in Vain by Cordwainer Smith, 1950; Hothouse by **Brian W. Aldiss**, 1961; The Little Black Bag by C. M. Kornbluth, 1950; Light of Other Days by Bob Shaw, 1966; and Day Million: A boy, a Girl, a Love Story by **Frederik Pohl**, 1966. Also, each story is accompanied by an essay by **Robert Silverberg**.

76. The Mammoth Book of Fantasy All-Time Greats. With Martin H. Greenberg. Published by Robinson Publishing, London, 1988. Hardcover. Re-titled re-issue of The Fantasy Hall of Fame, 1983.

77. Great Tales of Science Fiction. With Martin H. Greenberg. Published by Galahad Books, New York City, 1988. Softcover. Re-titled re-issue of The Arbor House Treasury of Science Fiction Masterpieces, 1983.

78. Worlds Imagined. With Martin H. Greenberg. Published by Avenel Books, New York City, 1989. Hardcover. Herein: Introduction by **Robert Silverberg** and Martin H. Greenberg; Beyond Bedlam by Wyman Guin, 1951; By His Bootstraps by **Robert A. Heinlein**, 1941; Second Game by Katherine MacLean and Charles V. De Vet, 1958; Giant Killer by A. Bertram Chandler, 1945; A Case of Conscience by **James Blish**, 1953; Dio by **Damon Knight**, 1957; Houston, Houston Do You Read by James Tiptree Jr, 1976; On the Storm Planet by Cordwainer Smith, 1965; Equinoctial by John Varley, 1977; The Golden Helix by **Theodore Sturgeon**, 1954; The Dead Past by **Isaac Asimov**, 1956; The Road to the Sea by **Arthur C. Clarke**, 1951; The Star Pit by **Samuel R. Delany**, 1967; and Born With the Dead by **Robert Silverberg**, 1974.

79. Time Gate. With Bill Fawcett. Published by Baen Books, New York City, 1989. Softcover. This contains: The Resurrection Machine by Robert Sheckley, 1989; Statesmen by **Poul Anderson**, 1989; The Rose and the Scalpel by Gregory Benford, 1989; How I Spent my Summer Vacation by Pat Murphy, 1989; and Enter a Soldier, Later: Enter Another by **Robert Silverberg**, 1989.

80. Time Gate 2: Dangerous Interfaces. Published by Baen Books, New York City, 1990. Softcover. Herein: The Simulated Golem by Christopher Stasheff, 1990; The Murderer by Matthew J. Costello, 1990; Pedigreed Stallion by **Anne McCaffrey**, 1990; Simbody to Love by Karen Haber, 1990; Simul City by Robert Sheckley, 1990; and The Eagle and the Cross by Gregory Benford, 1990.

81. Universe 1. With Karen Haber. Published by Doubleday Foundation, Garden City, New York, 1990. Softcover. All stories herein were written for this anthology: Introduction by **Robert Silverberg**; The Translator by Kim Stanley Robinson; The Shores of Bohemia by Bruce Sterling; River of the Dying by Augustine Funnell; The City of Ultimate Freedom by Geoffrey Landis; The Shobies' Story by **Ursula K. Le Guin**; One Night In Television City by Paul Di Filippo; Playback by Barry N. Malzberg; Moon Blood by M. J. Engh; And of the Earth a Womb by John M. Landsberg; Alimentary Tract by Scott Baker;

The Songs the Anemone Sing by Grania Davis; Alien Used Cars by Richard R. Smith; O Time Your Pyramids by Gregor Hartmann; The Propagation of Light in a Vacuum by James Patrick Kelly; Whalesong by Stoney Compton; The Book of St. Farrin by Jamil Nasir; Bumpie by Francis Valery; Love is a Drug by Leah Alpert; 1099 A. G. F. by K. Hernandez-Brun; and Daniel's Labyrinth by Damian Kilby.

82. The Ultimate Dinosaur. With Byron Preiss. Published by Bantam Books, New York City, 1991. Hardcover. Most of the stories were written for this anthology. This contains: Kingdom of the Titans - an essay by **Robert Silverberg**; Dinosaurs for Adults - an essay by Peter Dodson; The Dawn of the Age of Dinosaurs - an essay by Sankar Chatterjee; Crocamander Quest by L. Sprague de Camp; The First Dinosaurs - an essay by Catherine A. Forster; The Feynman Saltation by Charles Sheffield; The Dinosaur Radiations - an essay by Teresa Maryanska; Siren Song at Midnight by Dave Wolverton; The Jurassic Period: A Time of Great Change - an essay by David D. Gillette; Rhea's Time by Paul Preuss; The Age of Giants - an essay by Anthony R. Fiorillo; Shakers of the Earth by Gregory Benford; Dinosaur Predators - an essay by Halszka Osmolska; Hunters in the Forest by **Robert Silverberg**, 1991; The Cretaceous Dinosaurs - an essay by Don Lessem; In the Late Cretaceous by Connie Willis, 1991; Major League Triceratops by Barry N. Malzberg and Joyce Malzberg; Migrating Dinosaurs - an essay by Philip J. Currie; Herding with the Hadrosaurs by Michael Bishop; The Behavior of Predatory Dinosaurs - an essay by Ralph Molnar; Besides a Dinosaur, Whatta Ya Wanna Be When You Grow Up? by **Ray Bradbury**, 1983; Monsters of the Sea and Air - an essay by Kenneth Carpenter; Unnatural Enemy by **Poul Anderson**; Becoming a Modern World - an essay by William B. Gallagher; Dawn of the Endless Night by **Harry Harrison**; Myths, Theories, and Facts of Dinosaur Extinction - an essay by J. David Archibald; The Bone Wars: Cope, Marsh and American Vertebrate Paleontology 1865 - 1900 - an essay by Ronald Rainger; and The Green Buffalo by Harry Turtledove, 1991.

83. Beyond the Gate of Worlds. Published by Tor Books - Tom Doherty Associates, New York City, 1991. Softcover. This contains: Introduction by **Robert Silverberg**; Lion time in Timbuctoo by **Robert Silverberg**, 1990; At the Sign of the Rose by John Brunner, 1991, with an afterword by the author; and An Exaltation of Spiders by Chelsea Quinn Yarbro, 1991.

84. The Horror Hall of Fame. With Martin H. Greenberg. Published by Carroll and Graf, New York City, 1991. Hardcover. This anthology contains: Pigeons from Hell by Robert E. Howard, 1938; The Graveyard Rats by Henry Kuttner, 1936; Casting the Runes by M. R. James, 1911; The White People by Arthur Machen, 1904; The Reach by Stephen King, 1981; Green Tea by Joseph Sheridan Le Fanu, 1869; The Yellow Sign by Robert W. Chambers, 1895; The Monkey's Paw by W. W. Jacobs, 1902; The Damned Thing by Ambrose Bierce, 1893; The Willows by Algernon Blackwood, 1907; It by **Theodore Sturgeon**, 1940; Smoke Ghost by **Fritz Leiber**; Yours Truly, Jack the Ripper by Robert Bloch, 1943; The Small Assassin by **Ray Bradbury**, 1946; The Whimper of Whipped Dogs by Harlan Ellison, 1973; Calling Card by Ramsey Campbell, 1982; Coin of the Realm by Charles L. Grant, 1981; and The Fall of the House of Usher by Edgar Allan Poe, 1839.

85. Murasaki. With Martin H. Greenberg. Published by Bantam Books, New York City, 1992. Hardcover. Written for this volume: The Treasures of Chujo; and Muraski's Worlds - an essay by **Frederik Pohl**; World Vast, World Various by Gregory Benford; Genji by David Brin; A Plague of Conscience by Greg Bear; Language; and Design for Two Worlds - an essay by **Poul Anderson**; and Birthing Pool by Nancy Kress.

86. Universe 2. With Karen Haber. Published by Bantam Books, New York City, 1992. Hardcover. Written for this anthology, this contains: Introduction by **Robert Silverberg**; Another Way than Death by **Brian W. Aldiss**; Automatic Death by Cary James; Burning Bush by Carolyn Gilman; Be the Mirror of My Youth by Kathe Koja; Forty at the Kiosk by Nicholas A. DiChario; From the Bridge by Alex Jeffers; Job Security by Joe Haldeman; Life on the Artificial Heart by Mark W. Tidemann; Lost in Transmission by Tony Daniel; Memories of Muriel by Paula May; Metal Teeth by Lou Fisher; Most Politely, Most Politely by Barry N. Malzberg; Program's Progress by Jonathan Lathem; Souls in the Great Machine by Sean McMullen; That Particular Green of Obsequies by **Brian W. Aldiss**; The Ancestral Home of Thought, by **Brian W. Aldiss**; The Cool Equations by Deborah Wessell; The fire, the Fire by Alex Jeffers; The Passing of the eclipse by Donna Farley; The Shining Place by Jamil Nasir; The Sum of all Potentials by John M. Landsberg; Triad by Lisa Mason; Waiting for the Rain by Dirk Strasser; and Waterworld by John K. Gibbons.

87. Universe 3. With Karen Haber. Published by Bantam Books, New York City, 1994. Softcover.

Written for this anthology, herein: This contains: The Cure by Joe Haldeman; Composition with Barbarian and Animal by Alex Jeffers; Transcript of Yanda by Terry Boren; Dirtyside Down by Wil McCarthy; Let Me Count the Ways by Larry Tritten; Moths to the Blue Flame by E. Michael Blake; Black Memes by Jamil Nasir; Neezies by Mary A. Turzillo; The Enemies of Nickel City by Nicolas A. DiChario; The Only Thing You Learn by Barry N. Malzberg; The Pigeonhole Principle by David Ira Cleary; Going West Phillip C. Jennings; MacGregor by Paul Di Filippo; The Apples of Venus by Mark Rich; The Madonna of Futurity by **Brian W. Aldiss**.

88. A Century of Fantasy: 1980 - 1989. Published by MJF Books, New York City, 1996. Hardcover. This contains: Introduction by **Robert Silverberg**; The George Business by Roger Zelazny, 1980; Lindsay and the Red City Blues by Joe Haldeman, 1980; A Pattern of Silver Strings by Charles de Lint, 1981; The Quickening by Michael Bishop, 1981; Remembering Melody by George R. R. Martin, 1981; The Unicorn Masque by Ellen Kushner, 1981; Instant With Loud Voices by Alan Dean Foster, 1982; Not Our Brother by **Robert Silverberg**, 1982; Beyond the Dead Reef by James Tiptree, Jr, 1983; Wong's Lost and Found Emporium by William F. Wu, 1986; Laugh Track by Harlan Ellison, 1984; Dead Run by Greg Bear, 1985; The Boy Who Plaited Manes by Nancy

Robert Silverberg

Springer, 1986; Buffalo Gals, Won't You Come Out Tonight by **Ursula K. Le Guin**, 1987; The Dowry of the Rag Picker's Daughter by **Andre Norton**, 1988; The Edge of the World by Michael Swanwick, 1989; Lost Boys by Orson Scott Card, 1989; and The Wishing Game by Larry Niven, 1989.

89. A Century of Science Fiction: 1950 - 1959. Published by MJF Books, New York City, 1997. Hardcover.

90. Legends: Short Novels by the Masters of Modern Fantasy. Published by St. Martin's Press, New York City, 1998. Hardcover. All new for this, herein: Introduction by **Robert Silverberg**; Discworld: The Sea and Little Fishes by Terry Pratchett; Memory Sorrow and Thorn: The Burning Man by Tad Williams; Earthsea: Dragonfly by **Ursula K. Le Guin**; The Wheel of Time: New Spring by Robert Jordan; The Dark Tower: The Little Sisters of Eluria by Stephen King; Tales of Alvin Maker: Grinning Man by Orson Scott Card; The Riftwar Saga: The Wood Boy by Raymond E. Feist; The Sword of Truth: Debt of Bones by Terry Goodkind; A Song of Ice and Fire: The Hedge Knight by George R. R. Martin; Pern: Runner of Pern by **Anne McCaffrey**; and Majipoor: The Seventh Shrine by **Robert Silverberg**.

91. The Fantasy Hall of Fame. Published by Harper Prism, New York City, 1998. Softcover. Unlike The Fantasy Hall of Fame anthology that Silverberg put together with Martin H. Greenberg in 1983, the stories in this one were chosen by the members of The Science Fiction and Fantasy Writers of America. This anthology contains: Introduction by **Robert Silverberg**; Come Lady Death by Peter S. Beagle, 1963; Faith of Our Fathers by **Philip K. Dick**, 1967; The Demoness by Tanith Lee, 1976; Buffalo Gals, Won't You Come Out Tonight by **Ursula K. Le Guin**, 1987; The Man Who Sold Rope to the Gnoles by Margaret St. Clair writing as Idris Seabright, 1951; The Lottery by Shirley Jackson, 1948; The Compleat Werewolf by Anthony Boucher, 1942; The Drowned Giant by J. G. Ballard, 1964; Narrow Valley by R. A. Lafferty, 1966; The Ghost of a Model T by Clifford D. Simak, 1975; Jeffty is Five by Harlan Ellison, 1977; The Detective of Dreams by **Gene Wolfe**, 1980; Unicorn Variations by Roger Zelazny, 1981; The Jaguar Hunter by Lucius Shepard, 1985; Bears Discover Fire by Terry Bisson, 1990; Tower of Babylon by Ted Chiang, 1990; Trouble with Water by H. L. Gold, 1939; Nothing in the Rules by L. Sprague de Camp, 1939; Fruit of Knowledge by **C. L. Moore**, 1940; The Small Assassin by **Ray Bradbury**, 1946; Our Fair City by **Robert A. Heinlein**, 1949; There Shall Be No Darkness by **James Blish**, 1950; The Loom of Darkness by **Jack Vance**, 1950; The Silken Swift by **Theodore Sturgeon**, 1953; The Golem by Avram Davidson; Operation Afreet by **Poul Anderson**, 1956; That Hell Bound Train by Robert Bloch, 1958; The Bazaar of the Bizarre by **Fritz Leiber**, 1963; Tlon Uqbar Orbis Tertius by Jorge Luis Borges, 1961; and Basileus by **Robert Silverberg**, 1983.

92. Far Horizons. Published by Avon Books, New York City, 1999. Hardcover. This contains original stories related to other works by each author: Introduction by **Robert Silverberg**; Old Music and the Slave Women (The Ekumen) by **Ursula K. Le Guin**; A Separate War (The Forever War) by Joe Haldeman; Investment Counselor (The Ender Series) by Orson Scott Card; Temptation (The Uplift Universe) by David Brin; Getting to Know the Dragon (Roma Eterna) by **Robert Silverberg**; Orphans of the Helix (The Hyperion Cantos) by Dan Simmons; Sleeping Dogs (The Sleepless) by Nancy Kress; The Boy Who Would Live Forever (Tales of the Heechee) by **Frederick Pohl**; The Ship That Returned (The Ship Who Sang) by **Anne McCaffrey**; and The Way of All Ghosts (The Way) by Greg Bear.

93. Legends: Volume I. Published by Tor Books, New York, 1999. Softcover. Herein: Introduction by **Robert Silverberg**; The Dark Tower: The Little Sisters of Eluria by Stephen King; Majipoor: The Seventh Shrine by **Robert Silverberg**; Tales of Alvin Maker: Grinning Man by Orson Scott Card; and The Riftwar Saga: The Wood Boy by Raymond E. Feist.

94: Legends: Volume II. Published by Tor Books, New York, 1999. Softcover. Herein: Introduction by **Robert Silverberg**; The Sword of Truth: Debt of Bones by Terry Goodkind; A Song of Ice and Fire: The Hedge Knight by George R. R. Martin; and Pern: Runner of Pern by **Anne McCaffrey**.

95. Legend: Volume III. Published by Tor Books, New York, 2000. Softcover. Herein: Introduction by **Robert Silverberg**; The Wheel of Time: New Spring by Robert Jordan; Discworld: The Sea and Little Fishes by Terry Pratchett; Memory Sorrow and Thorn: The Burning Man by Tad Williams; and Earthsea: Dragonfly by **Ursula K. Le Guin**.

96. Robert Silverberg Presents the Great SF Stories: 1964. With Martin H. Greenberg. Published by NESFRA Press, Framingham, Massachusetts, 2001. Hardcover. Herein: Foreword by **Robert Silverberg**; Introduction by **Robert Silverberg**; Outward Bound by Norman Spinrad, 1964; The Kragen by **Jack Vance**, 1964; The Master Key by **Poul Anderson**, 1964; The Crime and the Glory of Commander Suzdel by Cordwainer Smith, 1964; The Graveyard Heart by Roger Zelazny, 1964; Purple Priestess of the Mad Moon by Leigh Brackett, 1964; The Last Lonely Man by John Brunner, 1964; Soldier, Ask Not by **Gordon R. Dickson**, 1964; A Man of the Renaissance by Wyman Guin, 1964; The Dowry of Angyar by **Ursula K. Le Guin**, 1964; When the Change-Winds Blow by **Fritz Leiber**, 1964; The Fiend by **Frederik Pohl**, 1964; The Life Hater by Fred Saberhagen, 1964; Neighbor by **Robert Silverberg**, 1964; and Four Brands of Impossible by Norman Kagan, 1964.

97. Science Fiction: 101. Published by iBooks, New York City, 2001. Softcover. Re-titled re-issue of **Robert Silverberg**'s Worlds of Wonder, 1987.

98. Nebula Awards Showcase 2001. Published by Harcourt/Harvest Books, New York City, 2001. Hardcover.

99. Science Fiction: The Best of 2001. With Karen Haber. Published by iBooks, New York City, 2002. Softcover. Herein: Introduction by **Robert**

Silverberg and Karen Haber; Undone by James Patrick Kelly; Know How, Can Do by Michael Blumlein; From Here You Can See the Sunquists by Richard Wadholm; Keepers of Earth by Robin Wayne Bailey; Anomalies by Gregory Benford; One of Her Paths by Ian Watson; The Dog Said Bow-Wow by Michael Swanwick; And No Such Things Grow Here by Nancy Kress; Sun Cloud by Stephen Baxter; Into Greenwood by Jim Grimsley; and On K2 with Kanakaredes by Dan Simmons.

100. Fantasy: The Best of 2001. With Karen Haber. Published by Pocket Books, New York City, 2002.

101. Science Fiction: The Best of 2002. With Karen Haber. Published by iBooks, New York City, 2003. Softcover. Herein: Introduction by **Robert Silverberg** and Karen Haber; Tourist by Charles Stross; The Long Chase by Geoffrey A. Landis; Coelacanths by Robert Reed; Liking What You See: A Documentary by Ted Chiang; The Black Abacus by Yoon Ha Lee; The Discharge by Christopher Priest; Aboard the Beatitude by **Brian W. Aldiss**; Droplet by Benjamin Rosenbaum; The War of the Worldviews by James Morrow; Breathmoss by Ian R. MacLeod; and Angles by Orson Scott Card.

102. Fantasy: The Best of 2002. With Karen Haber. Published by iBooks, New York City, 2003. Softcover.

103. Legends II. Published by Harper Collins, London, 2003. Hardcover. Introduction by **Robert Silverberg**; Realm of the Enderlings - an essay by Megan Lindholm writing as Robin Hobb; Homecoming by Megan Lindholm writing as Robin Hobb; A Song of Ice and Fire - an essay by George R. R. Martin; The Sworn Sword by George R. R. Martin; Alvin Maker - an essay by **Robert Silverberg**; The Yazoo Queen by Orson Scott Card; Outlander - an essay by Diana Gabaldon; Lord John and the Succubus by Diana Gabaldon; Majipoor - an essay by **Robert Silverberg**; The Book of Changes by **Robert Silverberg**; Otherland - an essay by Tad Williams; The Happiest Dead Boy in the World by Tad Williams; Pern - an essay by **Anne McCaffrey**; Beyond Between by **Anne McCaffrey**; The Riftwar - an essay by Raymond E. Feist; The Messenger by Raymond E. Feist; The Symphony of Ages - an essay by Elizabeth Haydon; Threshold by Elizabeth Haydon; American Gods - an essay by Neil Gaiman; The Monarch of the Glen by Neil Gaiman; Shannara - an essay by Terry Brooks; and Indomitable by Terry Brooks.

104. Between Worlds. Published by the Science Fiction Book Club, Garden City, New York, 2004. Hardcover. Herein: Introduction: Distant Realms of Space and Time by **Robert Silverberg**; Between Worlds by Stephen Baxter, 2004; The Wreck of the Godspeed by James Patrick Kelly, 2004; Shiva in Shadow by Nancy Kress, 2004; The Colonel Returns to the Stars by **Robert Silverberg**, 2005; Keepsakes by Mike Resnick, 2004; and Investments by Walter Jon Williams, 2004.

105. Legends II: Shadows, Gods and Demons. Published by Del Rey - Ballantine Books, New York, 2004. Softcover. Herein: Shannara: Indomitable by Terry Brooks; A Song of Ice and Fire: The Sworn Sword by George R. R. Martin; The Tales of Alvin Maker: The Yazoo Queen by Orson Scott Card; Outlander: Lord John and the Succubus by Diana Gabaldon; and The Symphony of Ages: Threshold by Elizabeth Haydon.

106. Legends II: Dragon, Sword and King. Published by Del Rey - Ballantine Books, New York, 2004. Softcover. Herein: Realm of the Enderlings: Homecoming by Megan Lindholm writing as Robin Hobb; Majipoor: The Book of Changes by **Robert Silverberg**; Otherland: Happiest Dead Boy in the World by Tad Williams; Pern: Beyond Between by **Anne McCaffrey**; The Riftwar: The Messenger by Raymond E. Feist; and American Gods: The Monarch of the Glen by Neil Gaiman.

***

NON-FICTION

1. Company Girl. Writing as Mark Ryan. Published by Bedside Books, New York City, 1959. Softcover. Bedside Book 957.

2. Treasures Beneath the Sea. Published by Whitman Books, Racine, Wisconsin, 1960. Hardcover.

3. First American into Space. Published by Monarch Books, Connecticut, 1961. Softcover. Monarch Book SP1.

4. Sex Fiend. Writing as L. T. Woodward. Published by Monarch Books, Connecticut, 1961. Softcover. Monarch Book MB511.

5. The Single Girl. Writing as Walter C. Brown. Published by Monarch Books, Connecticut, 1961. Softcover. Monarch Book MB515.

6. Sex and Hypnosis. Writing as L. T. Woodward. Published by Monarch Books, Connecticut, 1961. Softcover. Monarch Book MB516.

7. Sir Winston Churchill. Writing as Edgar Black. Published by Monarch Books, Connecticut, 1961. Softcover. Monarch Book K56.

8. 1001 Answers to Vital Sex Questions. Writing as L. T. Woodward. Published by Parliament Books, United States, 1962. Softcover.

9. 90% of What You Know About Sex Is Wrong. Writing as L. T. Woodward. Published by Parliament Books, United States, 1962. Softcover.

10. The Deceivers. Writing as L. T. Woodward. Published by Beacon Books, United States, 1962. Softcover. Beacon Book B529F.

11. Lost Cities and Vanished Civilizations. Published by the Chilton Book Company, Philadelphia, 1962. Hardcover.

12. Philosopher of Evil: The Life and Works of the Marquis de Sade. Writing as Walter Drummond. Published by Regency Books, New York City, 1962. Softcover.

13. Sex in Our Schools. Writing as L. T. Woodward. Published by Monarch Books, Connecticut, 1962.

Robert Silverberg

Softcover. Monarch Book MB521.

14. Virgin Wives. Writing as L. T. Woodward. Published by Monarch Books, Connecticut, 1962. Softcover. Monarch Book MB530.

15. Empires in the Dust: Ancient Civilizations Brought to Light. Published by the Chilton Book Company, Philadelphia, 1963. Hardcover.

16. Sunken History: The Story of Underwater Archaeology. Published by the Chilton Book Company, Philadelphia, 1963. Hardcover.

17. The Fabulous Rockefellers. Published by Monarch Books, Connecticut, 1963. Softcover. Monarch Book K68.

18. Fifteen Battles That Change the World. Published by G. P. Putnam's Sons, New York City, 1963. Hardcover.

19. The History of Surgery. Writing as L. T. Woodward. Published by Monarch Books, Connecticut, 1963. Softcover. Monarch Book M510.

20. You and Your Sex Life. Writing as L. T. Woodward. Published by Monarch Books, Connecticut, 1963. Softcover. Monarch Book MB538.

21. Sex and the Armed Forces. Writing as L. T. Woodward. Published by Monarch Books, Connecticut, 1963. Softcover. Monarch Book MB541.

22. Twilight Women. Writing as L. T. Woodward. Published by Lancer Books, New York City, 1963. Softcover. Lancer Book 74-821.

23. Home of the Red Man: Indian North America before Columbus. Published by the New York Graphic Society, New York City, 1963. Hardcover.

24. How to Spend Money. Writing as Walter Drummond. Published by Regency Books, New York City, 1963. Softcover.

25. 1066. Writing as Franklin Hamilton. Published by The Dial Press, New York City, 1964. Hardcover.

26. Great Adventures in Archaeology. Published by The Dial Press, New York City, 1964. Hardcover.

27. Akhnaten: The Rebel Pharaoh. Published by the Chilton Book Company, Philadelphia, 1964. Hardcover.

28. The Great Doctors. Published by G. P. Putnam's Sons, New York City, 1964. Hardcover.

29. The Loneliest Continent. Writing as Walker Chapman. Published by the New York Graphic Society, New York City, 1964. Hardcover.

30. Man Before Adam: The Story of Man in Search of Origins. Published by Macrae Smith, New York City, 1964. Hardcover.

31. The Man Who Found Nineveh. Published by Holt, Rinehart and Winston, New York City, 1964. Hardcover.

32. Masochism. Writing as L. T. Woodward. Published by Monarch Books, Connecticut, 1964.

Softcover. Monarch Book MB547.

33. Sex and the Divorced Woman. Writing as L. T. Woodward. Published by Lancer Books, New York City, 1964. Softcover. Lancer Book 73-424.

34. Sadism. Writing as L. T. Woodward. Published by Lancer Books, New York City, 1964. Softcover. Lancer Book 74-835.

35. The Golden Dream: Seekers of El Dorado. Writing as Walker Chapman. Published by Bobbs-Merrill, New York City, 1965. Hardcover.

36. Antarctic Conquest: The Great Explorers in Their Own Words. Published by Bobbs-Merrill, New York City, 1965. Hardcover.

37. The Crusades. Writing as Franklin Hamilton. Published by The Dial Press, New York City, 1965. Hardcover.

38. The Great Wall of China. Published by The Chilton Book Company, Philadelphia, 1965. Hardcover.

39. I Am a Nymphomaniac. Writing as L. T. Woodward. Published by Belmont Books, New York City, 1965. Softcover. Belmont Book B75-212.

40. The Labors of Hercules. Writing as Paul Hollander. Published by G. P. Putnam's Sons, New York City, 1965. Hardcover.

41. Men Who Mastered the Atom. Published by G. P. Putnam's Sons, New York City, 1965. Hardcover.

42. Niels Bohr: The Man Who Mapped the Atom. Published by Macrae Smith, New York City, 1965. Hardcover.

43. The Old Ones: Indians of the American Southwest. Published by The New York Graphic Society, New York City, 1965. Hardcover.

44. Scientists and Scoundrels: A Book of Hoaxes. Published by Thomas Y. Crowell, New York City, 1965. Hardcover.

45. The World of Coral. Published by Duell, Sloan and Pearce, New York City, 1965. Hardcover.

46. Bridges. Published by Macrae Smith, New York City, 1966. Hardcover.

47. Forgotten by Time: A Book of Living Fossils. Published by Thomas Y. Crowell, New York City, 1966. Hardcover.

48. Frontiers in Archeology. Published by The Chilton Book Company, Philadelphia, 1966. Hardcover.

49. The Hopefuls: Ten Presidential Campaigns. Published by Doubleday & Company, Garden City, New York, 1966. Hardcover.

50. Kublai Khan: Lord of Xanadu. Writing as Walker Chapman. Published by Bobbs-Merrill, New York City, 1966. Hardcover.

51. Leaders of labor. Writing as Roy Cook. Published by Lippincott, New York City, 1966. Hardcover.

52. The Long Rampart: The Story of the Great Wall of China. Published by The Chilton Book Company, Philadelphia, 1966. Hardcover.

53. Rivers: A Book to Being On. Writing as Lee Sebastian. Published by Holt, Rinehart and Winston, New York City, 1966. Hardcover.

54. The Rock of Darius: The Story of Henry Rawlinson. Published by Holt, Rinehart and Winston, New York City, 1966. Hardcover.

55. The Dawn of Medicine. Published by G. P. Putnam's Sons, New York City, 1966. Hardcover.

56. The Adventures of Nat Palmer: Antarctic Explorer and Clipper Ship Pioneer. Published by McGraw-Hill, New York City, 1967. Hardcover.

57. The Auk, the Dodo, and the Oryx: Vanished and Vanishing Creatures. Published by Thomas Y. Crowell, New York City, 1967. Hardcover.

58. Challenge for a Throne: The Wars of the Roses. Writing as Franklin Hamilton. Published by The Dial Press, New York City, 1967. Hardcover.

59. Light for the World: Edison and the Power of Electricity. Published by Van Nostrand, New York City, 1967. Hardcover.

60. Men Against Time: Salvage Archeology in the United States. Published by The Macmillan Company, New York City, 1967. Hardcover.

61. The Morning of Mankind: Prehistoric Man in Europe. Published by The New York Graphic Society, New York City, 1967. Hardcover.

62. The Search for Eldorado. Writing as Walker Chapman. Published by Bobbs-Merrill, New York City, 1967. Hardcover.

63. Sophisticated Sex Techniques in Marriage. Writing as L. T. Woodward. Published by Lancer Books, New York City, 1967. Softcover. Lancer Book 75-019.

64. The World of the Rain Forest. Published by Meredith Press, New York City, 1967. Hardcover.

65. Four Men Who Changed the Universe. Published by G. P. Putnam's Sons, New York City, 1968. Hardcover.

66. Ghost Towns of the American West. Published by Thomas Y. Crowell, New York City, 1968. Hardcover.

67. Mound Builders of Ancient America: The Archeology of a Myth. Published by The New York Graphic Society, New York City, 1968. Hardcover.

68. Sam Houston. Writing as Paul Hollander. Published by G. P. Putnam's Sons, New York City, 1968. Hardcover.

69. The South Pole: A Book to Begin On. Writing as Lee Sebastian. Published by Holt, Rinehart and Winston, New York City, 1968. Hardcover.

70. The Stolen Election: Tilden vs. Hayes, 1876. Writing as Lloyd Robinson. Published by Doubleday & Company, Garden City, New York, 1968. Hardcover.

71. Stormy Voyager: The Story of Charles Wilkes. Published by Lippincott, New York City, 1968. Hardcover.

72. The World of the Ocean Depths. Published by Meredith Press, New York City, 1968. Hardcover.

73. Bruce of the Blue Nile. Published by Holt, Rinehart and Winston, New York City, 1969. Hardcover.

74. The Challenge of Climate: Man and His Environment. Published by Meredith Press, New York City, 1969. Hardcover.

75. Vanishing Giants: The Story of the Sequoias. Published by Simon and Schuster, New York City, 1969. Hardcover.

76. Wonders of Ancient Chinese Science. Published by Hawthorne Books, New York City, 1969. Hardcover.

77. The World of Space. Published by Meredith Press, New York City, 1969. Hardcover.

78. If I Forget Thee, O Jerusalem: The Dramatic Story of How American Jews and the United States Helped Create Israel. Published by William Morrow, New York City, 1970. Hardcover.

79. Mammoths, Mastodons and Man. Published by McGraw-Hill, New York City, 1970. Hardcover.

80. The Pueblo Revolt. Published by Weybright and Talley, New York City, 1970. Hardcover.

81. The Seven Wonders of the Ancient World. Published by The Macmillan Company, New York City, 1970. Hardcover.

82. Before the Sphinx: Early Egypt. Published by Nelson-Hall, New York City, 1971. Hardcover.

83. Clocks for the Ages: How Scientists Date the Past. Published by The Macmillan Company, New York City, 1971. Hardcover.

84. Into Space: A Young Person's Guide to Space Exploration. With **Arthur C. Clark**. Published by Harper and Row, New York City, 1971. Hardcover.

85. To the Western Shore: Growth of the United States. Published by Doubleday & Company, Garden City, New York, 1971. Hardcover.

86. John Muir: Prophet Among the Glaciers. Published by G. P. Putnam's Sons, New York City, 1972. Hardcover.

87. The Longest Voyage: Circumnavigation in the Age of Discovery. Published by Bobbs-Merrill, New York City, 1972. Hardcover.

88. The Realm of Prester John. Published by Doubleday & Company, Garden City, New York, 1972. Hardcover.

89. The World Within the Ocean Wave. Published by Weybright and Talley, New York City, 1972. Hardcover.

90. The World Within the Tide Pool. Published

Robert Silverberg

by Weybright and Talley, New York City, 1972. Hardcover.

91. Fifteen Nights of Love. Writing as Don Elliott. Published by Corinth Publications - Nightstand Books, United States, 1973. Nightstand Book 3052.

92. Drug Themes in Science Fiction. Published by National Institute on Drug Abuse, Rockville, Maryland, 1974. Softcover. Research Issues Series 9.

93. The Mound Builders. Published by The New York Graphic Society, New York City, 1974. Hardcover.

94. Reflections and Refractions: Thoughts on Science Fiction, Science and Other Matters. Published by Underwood Books, Grass Valley, California, 1997. Hardcover.

***

RELATED

1. The Magazine of Fantasy and Science Fiction - Special Robert Silverberg Issue - April 1974. Published by Mercury Press, Cornwall, Connecticut, 1974. Softcover. Herein: Born with the Dead by **Robert Silverberg**; **Robert Silverberg**: The Compleat Writer - an essay by Thomas D. Clareson; and **Robert Silverberg**: Bibliography by Donald H. Tuck; along with the usual features.

2. Robert Silverberg: A Primary and Secondary Bibliography. By Thomas D. Clareson. Published by Starmont, Mercer Island, Washington, 1983. Softcover.

3. Robert Silverberg. By Joseph Olander. Published by Taplinger Publishing, New York City, 1987. Hardcover.

4. Robert Silverberg's Many Trapdoors: Critical Essays on His Science Fiction. By Charles L. Elkins and Martin H. Greenberg. Greenwood Press, Westport, Connecticut, 1993. Hardcover.

5. The Road to Castle Mount: The Science Fiction of Robert Silverberg. By Edgar L. Chapman. Greenwood Press, Westport, Connecticut, 1999. Hardcover.

Jules Verne.

Jules Gabriel Verne was born in Nantes, France on February 8th, 1828 and he died in Amiens, France, from complications brought on by diabetes, on March 24th, 1905. In between, he managed to become the first ever science fiction writer. Not the first to ever write science fiction, but the first, as Asimov put it, to specialize in SF.

There is a long list of people who have been called the father of science fiction, **H. G. Wells**, **Hugo Gernsback**, **John W. Campbell**, and so on. But perhaps Verne is the one who deserves it. Wells may have invented modern science fiction, but Verne clearly inspired him and, consequently, just about everyone who came later.

He had dabbled a bit in writing while he was at law school in Paris but when his father found out he was writing, he cancelled Verne's allowance, forcing him to drop out of school. He became a stockbroker and, desperate to get out of it, he heeded some advice given by his friend Alexandre Dumas. Dumas told him he should write.

Encouraged by his new wife, Honorine de Viane Morel, he began to do that in earnest, and set about seeking a publisher. He met Pierre-Jules Hetzel, an important 19th century French publisher, who read Verne's story about exploring Africa by balloon. Other publishers had rejected it, saying it was too scientific. Hetzel helped Verne re-write the story, then published it in 1863 as Cinq semaines en ballon - Five Weeks in a Balloon.

Thereafter, until his death in 1887, Hetzel tried to publish two Verne novels a year. After 1887, Verne's work wrapped itself in a darker cloak. His previous optimism had been inspired, indeed, insisted upon, by Hetzel. And with Hetzel's passing, and his son taking over the business, there was no one to control Verne's darker nature.

One novel written by Verne in 1863, Paris in the 20th Century, was so dark that Hetzel suggested Verne wait a decade or two before publishing it. Verne did put it away. And forgot about it. It was discovered by his great-grandson in 1989 and was printed five years later in 1995, a new **Jules Verne** novel set in a world incredibly like the one in which it was published, a world of tall glass buildings and super-fast trains and worldwide communications networks and cars that ran on gasoline. And Hetzel was right: the book was a bit of a downer as the hero meets his tragic end. It was as if Verne could see that world coming and knew it would not be a happy place... Hmmmm....

On February 21st and 22nd, 1899, Christie, Manson and Woods, a London auction house had some books by **Jules Verne** up for sale. It was a uniform grouping, bound in half-Moroccan leather, ten volumes from 1875. The titles were: Veridiana; Michael Strogoff; From the Earth to the Moon; Dr Ox's Experiment; The Floating City; Twenty Thousand Leagues Under the Sea; The English at the North Pole; Five Weeks in a Balloon; The Fur Country; and Around the World in Eighty Days. The books sold for 2 pounds, 18 shillings, which, at the time, was around $20.00, perhaps a bit more.

As this is being written, a quick search on the internet shows the 1863 first edition of Cinq Semaines en Ballon - Five Weeks in a Balloon - to be listed at $450,000.00; and The Archipelago of Fire, 1886, the first English edition, $250,000.00. Verne's work appears to have gone up a bit...

***

FILM AND TELEVISION

1. Le Voyage dans la lune. Based on De la Terre a la Lune - From the Earth to the Moon, 1867, and First Men in the Moon, 1901, by **H. G. Wells**, this was directed by Georges Meilies and released in 1902. It starred: Victor Andre; Bluette Bernon; Jeanne d'Alcy; Henri Delannoy; and others, all uncredited. Known in the U.S. as A Trip to Mars.

2. Le Voyage a travers l'impossible. Based on Verne's play of the same name. Directed by George Meilies, it was released in 1904.

3. 20000 lieues sous les mers. Based on Vingt Mille Lieues les mers - 20,000 Leagues Under the Sea, 1869, this was directed by George Meilies and released in 1907.

4. Michael Strogoff. Based on the 1876 novel, this was directed by J. Searle Dawley and released in 1910, starring: Charles Ogle; Mary Fuller; Marc McDermott; Harold M. Shaw; and others.

5. Voyage au centre de la terre. Based on the 1864 novel, Voyage au centre de la Terre - Journey to the Center of the Earth, this was directed by Segundo de Chomon and released in 1910.

6. La Conquete du pole. Based on Voyages et aventures du Captaine Hatteras - The Adventures of Captain Hatteras, 1866, this was directed by Georges Melies in 1910 and starred: Georges Melies; and Fernande Albany.

7. Les Enfants du capitaine Grant. Based on the 1868 novel of the same name, which, in English was In Search of the Castaways, this was directed by Victorin-Hippolyte Jasset; Henry Roussel; and Joseph Faivre for release in 1913. Verne's son Michel worked on the screenplay. The film starred: Josette Andriot; Denise Maural; Michel Gilbert; Pierre Delmonde; and others.

8. 'Round the World in 80 Days. Based on the 1873 novel, Le Tour du Monde en quatre-vingts jours - Around the World in Eighty Days, this was released in 1914.

9. Michael Strogoff. Based on the 1876 novel, this was directed by Lloyd B. Carleton and released in 1914. It starred: Jacob P. Adler; Daniel Makarenko; Eleanor Barry; Betty Brice; Ormi Hawley; Peter Lang; George S. Trimble; and Lloyd B. Carleton.

10. 20,000 Leagues Under the Sea. Based on

Jules Verne

the 1869 novel Vingt Mille Lieues les mers - 20,000 Leagues Under the Sea, this was directed by Stuart Paton in 1916. It starred: Lois Alexander; Curtis Benton; Wallace Clarke; Howard Crampton; Jane Gail; Joseph W. Girard; Dan Hanlon; and others, including Allen Holubar as Captain Nemo and William Welsh as Charles Denver.

11. Mathias Sandorf. This 1885 novel was directed by Henri Fescourt for release in 1921. It starred: Romuald Joube; Yvette Andreyor; Jean Toulout; Paul Vermoyal; Gaston Modot; Armand Tallier; Armand Dutertre; Henri Maillard; Gabrielle Ristori; Mario Nasthasio; and others.

12. Michel Strogoff. Based on the 1876 novel, this was directed by Viktor Tourjansky and released in 1926, starring: Ivan Mozzhukhin; Nathalie Kovanko; Acho Chakatouny; Jeanne Brindeau; Tuia de Izarduy; Eugene Gaidaroff; Micolas Kougoucheff; and others.

13. The Mysterious Island. Based on L'île mysterieuse - The Mysterious Island, 1874, this was released in 1929. Directed by Lucien Hubbard; Benjamin Christensen; and Maurice Tourneur, it starred: Lionel Barrymore; Jacqueline Gadsden; Lloyd Hughes; Mantagu Love; Harry Gribbon; Snitz Edwards; Gibson Gowland; Dolores Brinkman; and others.

14. Michel Strogoff. Based on the 1876 novel, this was directed by Jacques de Baroncelli and Richard Eichberg and released in 1935, starring: Anton Walbrook; Colette Darfeuil; Armand Bernard; Charles Vanel; Yvette Lebon; Marcelle Worms; Fernand Charpin; Victor Vina; Camille Bert; Rene Stern; and others.

15. Deti kapitanan Granta. Based on the 1868 novel, Les Enfants du capitaine Grant - In Search of the Castaways, this was directed by Vladimir Vajnshtok and David Gutman in 1936. It starred: Nikolai Cherkasov; Yakov Segel; Olga Bazarova; David Gutman; Mariya Strelkova; Mikhail Romanov; Nikolai Vitovtov; Ivan Chuvelyov; and many others.

16. Der Kurier des Zaren. Based on Michel Strogoff - Michael Strogoff, 1876, this was directed by Richard Eichberg and released in 1936 starring: Anton Walbrook; Lucie Hoflich; Maria Andergast; Alexander Golling; Hilde Hildebrand; Kurt Vespermann; Theo Lingen; Olga Schaub; Hans Zesch-Ballot; and others.

17. The Soldier and the Lady. Based on Michel Strogoff - Michael Strogoff, 1876, this was directed by Richard Eichberg and released in 1937 starring: Anton Walbrook; Elizabeth Allan; Akim Tamiroff; Margot Grahame; Fay Bainter; Eric Blore; Edward Brophy; Paul Guilfoyle; William Stack; Paul Harvey; Michael Visaroff; and others, including Ward Bond in an uncredited part as a Tartar Chief and Richard Loo in an uncredited part as a Tartar.

18. Tainstvennyy ostrov. Based on L'île mysterieuse - The Mysterious Island, 1874, this was made in Russia in 1941, directed by B. M. Chelintsev and Eduard Pentslin and starring: A. Krasnopolsky; Pavel Kiyansky; A. Andriyenko-Zemskov; I. Kozlov; R. Ross; Yuri Grammatikati; Andrei Sova; and others, including Nikolai Komissarov as Captain Nemo.

19. Miguel Strogoff. Based on Michel Strogoff - Michael Strogoff, 1876, this was directed in Mexico by Miguel M. Delgado in 1944. It starred: Julian Soler; Lupita Tovar; Julio Villarreal; Anita Blanch; Andres Soler; Luis G. Barreiro; Victoria Argota; Salvador Quiroz; Manuel Donde; and others.

20. Pyatnadtsatiletniy kapitan. Made in Russia in 1946, this was based on Un capitaine de quinze ans - Dick Sand, A Captain at Fifteen, 1878. Directed by Vasili Zhuravlyov, it starred: Vsevolod Larionov; Yelena Izmailova; Mikhail Astangov; Weyland Rodd; Azharik Messerer; Koretti Arletits; Aleksandr Khvylya; Viktor Kulakov; Osip Abdulov; Sergein Tsenin; and others.

21. Mysterious Island. Based on L'île mysterieuse - The Mysterious Island, 1874, this was directed by Spencer Gordon Bennet and released in August 1951, starring: Richard Crane; Marshall Reed; Karen Randle; Ralph Hodges; Gene Roth; Hugh Prosser; Terry Frost; Rusty Wescoatt; Bernie Hamilton; William Fawcett; George Robotham; and others, including Leonard Penn as Captain Nemo.

22. Twenty Thousand Leagues Under the Sea: Part One: The Chase - and - Part Two: Escape. Based on the 1869 novel Vingt Mille Lieues les mers - 20,000 Leagues Under the Sea, this was made for the television program Tales of Tomorrow, Season 1, Episode 17 and 18, shown on January 25th and February 1st, 152. Directed by Don Medford, it starred: Roger De Koven as the narrator; Eddie Hyans; Brian Keith; Bethel Leslie; Leslie Nielsen; and Thomas Mitchell as Captain Nemo.

23. 20,000 Leagues Under the Sea. Based on the 1869 novel Vingt Mille Lieues les mers - 20,000 Leagues Under the Sea, this was made by Disney for released in December 1954. Directed by Richard Fleischer, it starred: Kirk Douglas; James Mason; Paul Lukas; Peter Lorre; Robert J. Wilke; Ted de Corsia; Carleton Young; J. M. Kerrigan; Percy Helton; Ted Cooper; and many others.

24. Miguel Strogof. Based on Michel Strogoff - Michael Strogoff, 1876, this was directed in Brazil by Luiz Gallon in 1955. It starred: Percy Aires; David Neto; Jose Parisi; Geny Prado; and Turibio Ruiz.

25. Around the World in Eighty Days. Based on Le Tour du Monde en quatre-vingts jours - Around the World in Eighty Days, 1873, this was directed by Michael Anderson for release in 1956. It starred: David Niven; John Gielgud; Noel Coward; Robert Morley; Trevor Howard; Charles Boyer; Evelyn Keyes; Jose Greco; Luis Miguel Dominguin; Gilbert Roland; Cesar Romero; Alan Mowbray; Robert Newton; Cedric Hardwicke; Ronald Colman; Peter Lorre; George Raft; Shirley MacLaine; Red Skelton; Marlene Dietrich; John Carradine; Frank Sinatra; Buster Keaton; Joe E. Brown; Andy Devine; Victor McLaglen; John Mills; Glynis Johns; Hermione Gingold; Edward R. Murrow; Cantinflas; Finlay Currie; Ronald Squire; Basil Sydney; Harcourt Williams; Martine Carol; Fernandel; and many others, including Patrick Cargill in an uncredited bit part and Marion Ross as an uncredited extra.

26. Michel Strogoff. From the 1876 novel, this was directed by Carmine Gallone in 1956. It starred: Curt Jurgens; Genevieve Page; Jacques Dacqmine; Sylva Koscina; Gerard Buhr; Louis Arbessier; Fernand Fabre; Michel Etcheverry; and others.

27. De Reis om de wereld in 80 dagen. This was a 1957 television series from Belgium, based on Le Tour du Monde en quatre-vingts jours - Around the World in Eighty Days, 1873. Directed by Lode Verstraete, it starred: Senne Rouffaer; Cyriel Van Gent; and others.

28. Vynalez zkazy. Based on Face au drapeau - Facing the Flag, 1896, this was directed by Karel Zeman in Czechoslovakia, 1958. It starred: Lubor Tukos; Arnost Navratil; Miroslav Holub; Frantisek Slegr; and others.

29. From the Earth to the Moon. Based on De la terre a la lune - From the Earth to the Moon, 1865, and on Autour de la lune - Around the Moon, 1870, this was directed by Byron Haskin and released in 1958. It starred: Joseph Cotten; George Sanders; Debra Paget; Don Dubbins; Patric Knowles; Henry Daniell; Melville Cooper; Ludwig Stossel; Morris Ankrum; and Carl Esmond as **Jules Verne**.

30. 800 leguas por el amazonas o. Directed in Mexico in 1959 by Emilio Gomez Muriel, this was based on La Jangada - Eight Hundred Leagues on the Amazon, 1881. It starred: Carlos Lopez Moctezuma; Rafael Bertrand; Elvira Quintana; Raul Farell; Maria Duval; Beatriz Aguirre; Federico Curiel; Enrique Aguilar; and many others.

31. Journey to the Center of the Earth. From Voyage au centre de la Terre - Journey to the Centre of the Earth, 1764, this was directed by Henry Levin and released in 1960. It starred: James Mason; Arlene Dahl; Pat Boone; Diane Baker; Thayer David; Peter Ronson; Robert Adler; Alan Napier; and others, including Gertrude the Duck.

32. Fogg Bound. Based on Le Tour du Monde en quatre-vingts jours - Around the World in Eighty Days, 1873, this was adapted for the television series Have Gun - Will Travel, December 3rd, 1960, Season 4, Episode 12. Directed by Andrew V. McLaglen, the show starred Richard Boone in his regular role as Paladin along with: Arlene McQuade; Jon Silo; Peter Whitney; and Patric Knowles as Phileas Fogg.

33. The Terrible Clockman. This was based on the short story Maitre Zacharius - Master Zacharius, 1854. Directed by Allen Reisner, it was used on the television series Shirley Temple's Storybook, January 29th, 1961, Season 2, Episode 18. It starred: Shirley Temple; Eric Portman; Sam Jaffe; John Wengraf; Jacques Aubuchon; David Frankham; Betty Garde; and others, including John Astin as a coachman and Jon Peters as an ironmonger.

34. Master of the World. Based on Maitre du monde - Master of the World, 1904, and Robur-le-Conquerant - Robur the Conqueror, 1886, this was written by Richard Matheson and directed by William Witney for release in May 1961. It starred: Vincent Price; Charles Bronson; Henry Hull; Mary Webster; David Frankham; Richard Harrison; Wally Campo; and others.

35. Mysterious Island. From L'ile mysterieuse - The Mysterious Island, 1875, this was directed by Cy Endfield from a screenplay by John Prebble and Daniel B. Ullman. Released in December 1961, it starred special effects by **Ray Harryhausen**, along with: Michael Craig; Joan Greenwood; Michael Callan; Gary Merrill; Beth Rogan; and others, including Herbert Lom as Captain Nemo.

36. Valley of the Dragons. Also known as Prehistoric Valley, this was directed by Edward Bernds in 1961 from Hector Servadac - Off on a Comet, 1877. It starred: Cesare Danova; Sean McClory; Joan Staley; Danielle De Metz; Gregg Martell; Gil Perkins; I. Stanford Jolley; Mike Lane; and others.

37. Triomphe de Michel Strogoff. Based on Michel Strogoff - Michael Strogoff, 1876, this was directed by Viktor Tourjansky in 1961. It starred: Curt Jurgens; Jacques Bezard; Capucine; Daniel Emilfork; Raymond Gerome; Valery Inkijinoff; Georges Lycan; and others.

38. Five Weeks in a Balloon. From Cinq Semaines en ballon - Five Weeks in a Balloon, 1863, this was directed by Irwin Allen for release in 1962. It starred: Barbara Eden; Red Buttons; Fabian; Cedric Hardwicke; Peter Lorre; Richard Haydn; Barbara Luna; Billy Gilbert; Herbert Marshall; and others.

39. In Search of the Castaways. From Les Enfants du capitaine Grant - In Search of the Castaways, 1868, this was directed by Robert Stevenson for release in December 1962. It starred: Hayley Mills; Maurice Chevalier; George Sanders; Wilfrid Hyde-White; Michael Anderson Jr; Antonio Cifariello; Wilfrid Brambell; Jack Gwillum; and many others.

40. Dos anos de vacaciones. Based on Deux Ans de vacances - Two Years' Vacation, 1888, this was directed in Mexico, 1962, by Emilio Gomez Muriel. It starred: Pablo Alonso; Pablito Calvo; Alejandro Ciangherotti; Jose Ignacio Corrales; Luis Induni; and others.

41. Mathias Sandorf. From the 1885 novel, this was directed by Georges Lampin for release in 1963. It starred: Louis Jourdan; Enaud Mary; Francisco Rabal; Serena Bergano; Antoine Balpetre; Valeria Fabrizi; and many others.

42. The Three Stooges Go Around the World in a Daze. Inspired by Le Tour du Monde en quatre-vingts jours - Around the World in Eighty Days, 1873, this was directed by Norman Maurer and released in August 1963. It starred: Moe Howard; Larry Fine; and Joe DeRita as The Three Stooges: Moe, Larry, and Curly-Joe. Joining them were: Jay Sheffield as Phileas Fogg III; Joan Freeman; Walter Burke; Peter Forster; Maurice Dallimore; Richard Devon; and many more.

43. Les indes noires. Adapted from Les Indes noires - The Child of the Cavern, 1877, this was used on the television show Le Theatre de la jeunesse, December 25th, 1964. Directed by Marcel Bluwal, it starred: Alain Mottet; Georges Poujouly; Andre Valmy; Jean-Pierre Moulin; Genevieve Fontanel; Paloma Matta; Yvette Etievant; and others.

Jules Verne

44. Les Tribulations d'un chinois en Chine. From Les Tribulations d'un chinois en Chine - Tribulations of a Chinaman in China, 1879, this was released in 1965. Directed by Philippe de Broca, it starred: Jean-Paul Belmondo; Ursula Andress; Maria Pacome; Valerie Lagrange; Valery Inkijinoff; Joe Said; Mario David; and more.

45. Cinci saptamini in balon. From Cinq Semaines en ballon - Five Weeks in a Balloon, 1863, this was an animated short directed in Romania by Olimp Varasteanu in 1966.

46. Las Indias Negras. Adapted from Les Indes noires - The Child of the Cavern, 1877, this was used on the television show Novela on July 25th, 1966. The episode starred: Juan Diego; Nicolas Duenas; Jose Maria Escuer; Manuel Peiro; Luisa Sala; and others.

47. Ukradena vzducholod. Based on Deux Ans de vacances - Two Years' Vacation, 1888, this was directed in Czechoslovakia by Karel Zeman in 1967. It starred: Hanus Bor; Jan Cizek; Jan Malat; Michal Pospisil; Josef Stranik; Jitka Zelenohorska; Jana Sedlmajerova; Vera Macku; Eva Kubesova; Marie Brozova; and others.

48. Rocket to the Moon. Inspired by the work of **Jules Verne**, this was directed by Don Sharp and released in June 1967, starring: Burl Ives as Phileas T. Barnum; Troy Donahue; Gert Frobe; Terry-Thomas; Hermione Gingold; Daliah Lavi; Lionel Jeffries; Dennis Price; Edward de Souza; and many others, including Judy Cornwell as Electra.

49. Journey to the Center of the Earth. Inspired by Voyage au centre de la Terre - Journey to the Centre of the Earth, 1764, this was an animated American television series that ran from 1967 to 1969. It starred: Ted Knight; Pat Harrington Jr; and Jane Webb.

50. Le secret de Wilhelm Storitz. Adapted from Le Secret de Wilhelm Storitz - The Secret of William Storitz, 1910, this was used on the television show Le Theatre de la jeunesse in October 1967. Directed by Eric Le Hung, it starred: Jean-Claude Drouot; Pascale Audret; Bernard Verley; Monique Melinand; Robert Vattier; Pierre Leproux; and others.

51. De la tierra a la luna. Based on De la terre a la lune - From the Earth to the Moon, 1865, this was made for Mexican television in 1969. Directed by Jose Sole, it starred: Guillermo Orea; Rafael Llamas; Luis Gimeno; Carlos Ancira; and others.

52. The Southern Star. Based on L'Etoile du sud - The Vanished Diamond, 1884, this was released in 1969. Directed by Sidney Hayers, it starred: George Segal; Ursula Andress; Orson Welles; Ian Hendry; Johnny Sekka; Michel Constantin; Georges Geret; Sylvain Levignac; Charles Lamb; Guy Delorme; and Harry Andrews.

53. Captain Nemo and the Underwater City. Inspired by the work of **Jules Verne**, this was directed by James Hill for release in 1969. It starred: Chuck Connors; Nanette Newman; Luciana Paluzzi; John Turner; Bill Fraser; Kenneth Connor; Allan Cuthbertson; Ian Ramsey; and others, including Robert Ryan as Captain Nemo.

54. Nemo. Based on the 1869 novel Vingt Mille Lieues les mers - 20,000 Leagues Under the Sea, this was made in France for release in 1970. Directed by Jean Bacque, it starred: Michel Le Royer as Nemo, along with: Lucien Barjon; Agnes Desroches; Bernard Cara; Gilberte Rivet; Pierre Mirat; Andre Thorent; Fernand Guiot; Gerard Buhr; and others.

55. Na komete. From Hector Servadac - Off on a Comet, 1877, this was made in Czechoslovakia and released in 1970. Directed by Karel Zeman, it starred: Emil Horvath; Magda Vasaryova; Frantisek Filipovsky; Cestmir Randa; Joseph Hlinomaz; and others.

56. Strogoff. From Michel Strogoff - Michael Strogoff, 1876, this was directed by Eriprando Visconti for release in Italy in 1970. It starred: John Phillip Law; Mimsy Farmer; Hiram Keller; Delia Boccardo; Kurt Meisel; Elisabeth Bergner; Donato Castellaneta; Claudio Gora; and others.

57. The Light at the Edge of the World. Based on Le Phare du bout du monde - The Lighthouse at the End of the World, 1905, this was directed by Kevin Billington for release in 1971. It starred: Kirk Douglas; Yul Brynner; Samantha Eggar; Jean-Claude Drouot; Fernando Rey; Renato Salvatori; and many others.

58. The Brady Kids on Mysterious Island. Inspired by L'ile mysterieuse - The Mysterious Island, 1875, this animated film was made for the television show The ABC Saturday Superstar Movie, September 1972. Directed by Hal Sutherland, it starred: Christopher Knight; Mike Lookinland; Maureen McCormick; Susan Olsen; Eve Plumb; Larry Storch; Jane Webb; and Barry Williams.

59. Around the World in Eighty Days. Based on the 1873 novel, this animated television series was on the air in 1972 and 1973. Directed by Leif Gram, it starred: Alistair Duncan; Ross Higgins; Max Osbiston; Janet Waldo; and Owen Weingott.

60. 20,000 Leagues Under the Sea. From Vingt mille lieues sous les mers - Twenty Thousand Leagues Under the Sea, 1870, this animated feature was directed by Jules Bass and Arthur Rankin Jr and released in 1973.

61. La Isla misteriosa. Based on L'ile mysterieuse - The Mysterious Island, 1875, this was made in Spain and released in 1973. Directed by Juan Antonio Bardem and Henri Colpi, it starred Omar Sharif as Captain Nemo, along with: Ambroise Bia; Jess Hahn; Philippe Nicaud; Gerard Tichy; Gabriele Tinti; and others.

62. Maitre Zaccharius. Based on the 1854 short story, Maitre Zacharius - Master Zacharius, this was made for television in France in 1973. Directed by Pierre Bureau, it starred: Pierre Vial; Jean-Pierre Sentier; Madeleine Barbulee; Jacques Roussillon; Francois Tilly; Jany Gastaldi; and others.

63. Deux ans de vacances. From Deux Ans de vacances - Two Years' Vacation, 1888, this was directed by Gilles Grangier as a TV mini-series in 1974. It starred: Franz Seidenschwan; Marc Di Napoli; Werner Pochath; Rainer Basedow;

Dominique Planchot; Didier Gaudron; Cristian Sofron; Constantin Nedelcu; Horia Pavel; and many others.

64. Un Capitan de quince anos. Based on Un capitaine de quinze ans - Dick Sand, A Captain at Fifteen, 1978, this was a French/Spanish production, directed by Jesus Franco and released in 1974, starring: Jose Manuel Marcos; Edmund Purdom; Marc Cassot; Doris Thomas; Howard Vernon; Armand Mestral; William Berger; Fernando Bilbao; and many others.

65. Kapitan Nemo. Based on Vingt mille lieues sous les mers - Twenty Thousand Leagues Under the Sea, 1870, and La Maison a vapeur - The Steam House, 1880, this was made in Russia for release in 1975. Directed by Vasili Levin and Edgar Smirnov, it starred: Vladimir Basov; N. Bazanova; Viktor Demertash; Nikolai Dupak; Vladislav Dvorzhetsky; Elvira Khomyuk; and many others.

66. Mysterious Island. Based on L'ile mysterieuse - The Mysterious Island, 1875, this animated film was released in November 1975, starring: Alistair Duncan; Tim Elliott; Ron Haddrick; Mark Kelly; and John Llewellyn.

67. Michel Strogoff. From the 1876 novel, this was made into a TV mini-series for release in France in December 1975. Directed by Jean-Pierre Decourt, it starred: Raimund Harmstorf; Lorenza Guerrieri; Valerio Popesco; Rada Rassimov; Jozsef Madaras; Vernon Dobtcheff; Pierre Vernier; and many others.

68. Viaje al centro de la Tierra. Released in 1978, this was a Spanish production of Voyage au centre de la Terre - Journey to the Centre of the Earth, 1864. Directed by Juan Piquer Simon, it starred: Kenneth More; Pep Munne; Ivonne Sentis; Frank Brana; Jack Taylor; Ana Del Arco; Jose Maria Caffarel; Lone Fleming; and many others.

69. 5 Weeks in a Balloon. From Cinq Semaines en ballon - Five Weeks in a Balloon, 1863, this animated short was released in 1977, starring: Brooker Bradshaw; Cathleen Cordell; Johnny Haymer; Loren Lester; Laurie main; John Stephenson; and Gene Whittington.

70. Wielka podroz Bolka i Lolka. Also known as Around the World with Bolek and Lolek, this was loosely based on Le Tour de Monde en quatre-vingts jours - Around the World in Eighty Days, 1873. From Poland, it was released in 1973 and was directed by Stanislaw Dulz and Wladyslaw Nehrebecki, starring: Ewa Zlotowska; Danuta Mancewicz; Jan Kociniak; Wieslaw Michnikowski; and many others.

71. A Journey to the Center of the Earth. From Voyage au centre de la Terre - Journey to the Centre of the Earth, 1864, this 1977 animated short was directed by Richard Slapczynski and starred: Ron Haddrick; Alistair Duncan; Bevan Wilson; Lynette Curran; and Barbara Frawley.

72. The Return of Captain Nemo. Based on the work of **Jules Verne** but with no credit given, this was directed by Alex March and Paul Stader for television release in March 1978, with Robert Bloch as one of the writers. It starred Jose Ferrer as Captain Nemo, along with: Burgess Meredith; Mel Ferrer; Horst Buchholz; Tom Hallick; Burr DeBenning; Lynda Day George; Warren Stevens; and others.

73. Mathias Sandorf. Based on the 1885 novel, this was a French/Hungarian production, released as a television mini-series in 1979. Directed by Jean-Pierre Decourt, it starred: Istvan Bujtor; Claud Giraud; Giuseppe Pambieri; Jacques Breuer; Marie-Christine Demarest; Ivan Desny; Jutta Speidel; Patrick Massieu; and many others.

74. Le Tour de monde en 80 jours. Based on Le Tour de Monde en quatre-vingts jours - Around the World in Eighty Days, 1873, this was released in France in December 1979. Directed by Andre Flederick, it starred: Daniel Ceccaldi; Roger Pierre; Jean-Pierre Darras; Arielle Semenoff; Paul Le Person; Jacques Dynam; Jean-Pierre Delage; and others.

75. Castle in the Carpathians. Based on Le Chateau des Carpathes - Carpathian Castle, 1892, this was made in Romania and released in 1981. Directed by Stere Gulea, it starred: Maria Banica; Ion Caramitru; Cornel Ciupercescu; Octavian Cotescu; Andras Csiky; Marcel Lures; and others.

76. Tajemstvi hradu v Karpatech. Based on Le Chateau des Carpathes - Carpathian Castle, 1892, this was made in Czechoslovakia for release in 1981. It was directed by Oldrich Lipsky and starred: Michal Docolomansky; Evelyna Steimarova; Vlastimil Brodsky; Milos Kopecky; and many others.

77. La Vuelta al mundo de Willy Fog. Inspired by Le Tour de Monde en quatre-vingts jours - Around the World in Eighty Days, 1873, this animated short was a joint Spanish/Japanese production, directed by Luis Ballester Bustos and Fumio Kurokawa and released in 1983.

78. Misterio en la isla de los monstruos. Based on L'Ecole des Robinsons - Godfrey Morgan, 1882, this Spanish/American production was released in 1981. Directed by Juan Piquer Simon, it starred: Terence Stamp; Peter Cushing; Ian Sera; David Hatton; Gasphar Ipua; Blanca Estrada; Ana Obregon; Frank Brana; Paul Naschy; Gerard Tichy; and others .

79. Mysterious Planet. Inspired by the work of **Jules Verne**, this was directed by Brett Piper and released in 1982. It starred: Paula Taupier; Boydd Piper; Michael Quigley; Bruce E. Nadeau Jr; and others.

80. Zacharius. Based on the short story Maitre Zacharius - Master Zacharius, 1954, this was made for television in France in 1984. Directed by Claude Grinberg, it starred: Charles Denner; Emmanuelle Beart; and Pierre-Loup Rajot.

81. 20,000 Leagues Under the Sea. From Vingt mille lieues sous les mers - Twenty Thousand Leagues Under the Sea, 1870, this animated feature was made in Australia in 1985. It starred: Tom Burlinson; Colin Borgonon; Liz Home; Alistair Duncan; and Gilbert Christian.

82. V poiskakh kapitana Granta. Based on Les Enfants du capitaine Grant - In Search of the

Jules Verne

Castaways, 1868, this 1985 Russian television mini-series was directed by Stanislav Govorukhin and starred: Vladimir Smirnov; Lembit Ulfsak; Marina Vlady; Tamara Akulova; Oleg Shtefanko; Rusian Kurashov; Galina Strutinskaya; and others.

83. Le Voyage dans la lune. This 1986 Swiss television production was loosely based on De la terre a la lune - From the Earth to the Moon, 1865. It was directed by Jean Bovon and starred: Joseph Evans; Marie McLaughlin; Monique Barscha; Michel Trempont; Ricardo Cassinelli; and others.

84. Kapitan Piligrima. Based on Un capitaine de quinze ans - Dick Sand, A Captain at Fifteen, 1978, this 1986 Russian production was directed by Andrei Prachenko and starred: Vyacheslav Khodchenko; Nodar Mgaloblishvili; Albert Filozov; Tatyana Parkina; Lev Durov; Leonid Yarmolnik; and many others.

85. Around the World in 80 Days. Based on Le Tour de Monde en quatre-vingts jours - Around the World in Eighty Days, 1873, this animated feature was made in Australia in 1988. It starred: Colin Borgonon; Wallas Eaton; Ross Higgins; Scott Higgins; and Juliette Jordan.

86. Around the World in 80 Days. From Le Tour de Monde en quatre-vingts jours - Around the World in Eighty Days, 1873, this was directed by Buzz Kulik and released in April 1989. It starred: Pierce Brosnan; Eric Idle; Julia Nickson-Soul; Peter Ustinov; Jack Klugman; Roddy McDowall; Darren McGavin; Robert Morley; Stephen Nichols; Lee Remick; Jill St. John; Robert Wagner; Arielle Dombasle; Gabriele Ferzetti; Henry Gibson; John Hillerman; Rick Jason; Christopher Lee; Patrick Macnee; John Mills; Pernell Roberts; James Sikking; Simon Ward; and many, many others.

87. Around the World in 80 Days. Inspired by Le Tour de Monde en quatre-vingts jours - Around the World in Eighty Days, 1873, this seven-part documentary was made for television in 1989. It starred Michael Palin in attempt to follow the path of Verne's Phileas Fogg.

88. Fushigi no umi no Nadia. Inspired by Vingt mille lieues sous les mers - Twenty Thousand Leagues Under the Sea, 1870, this animated Japanese television series ran for thirty-nine episodes, starting on April 13th, 1990. It starred: Noriko Hidaka; Carl Domaski; Judson L. Jones; Craig Kanne; Talbot McKitt; Nathan Parsons; Guy Roberts; Douglas Taylor; James Arnold Taylor; Clay Towery; and many others, including some guy named Nanker Phelge - originally, that was a pseudonym used by The Rolling Stones in group compositions in the early days.

89. Tajomstvo alchymistu Storitza. Based on Le Secret de Wilhelm Storitz - The Secret of William Storitz, 1910, this was made in Czechoslovakia and released in 1991. Directed by Pawel Trzaska, it starred: Vladimir Kratina; Marian Labuda; Milan Lasica; Julius Satinsky; Bozidara Turzonovova; and others.

90. Eight Hundred Leagues Down the Amazon. From La Jangada - Eight Hundred Leagues on the Amazon, 1881, this was directed by Luis Llosa and starred: Daphne Zuniga; Tom Erica; Barry Bostwick; Adam Baldwin; E. E. Bell; Daniel Camino; Rafael De Lucchi; and many others.

91. Willy Fog 2. Inspired by Le Tour de Monde en quatre-vingts jours - Around the World in Eighty Days, 1873, this 1993 animated short was a Spanish production, starring: Claudio Rodriguez; Angel Egido; Luis Reina; Gloria Camara; Daniel Dicenta; and others.

92. Journey to the Center of the Earth. Inspired by Voyage au centre de la Terre - Journey to the Centre of the Earth, 1864, this was made for television and released in February 1993. Directed by William Dear, it starred: David Dundara; Farrah Forke; Kim Miyori; John Neville; Jeffrey Nordling; Tim Russ; Carel Struycken; Fabiana Udenio; Justina Vail; F. Murray Abraham; and others.

93. Mysterious Island. Inspired by the work of **Jules Verne**, this 1995 television series starred: Alan Scarfe; C. David Johnson; Colette Stevenson; Stephan Lovatt; Gordon Michael Woolvett; Andy Marshall; Ross Duncan; Matthew Chamberlain; Anthony Scott; and John Bach as Captain Nemo.

94. Journey to the Center of the Earth. Inspired by Voyage au centre de la Terre - Journey to the Centre of the Earth, 1864, this animated short was made in Canada in 1996. Directed by Laura Shepherd, it starred: Clara Blye; Don Francks; Jennifer Martini; James Rankin; Ron Rubin; Colette Stevenson; and Stuart Stone.

95. The Children of Captain Grant. Based on Les Enfants du capitaine Grant - In Search of the Castaways, 1868, this was released in 1996. Directed by Donovan Scott, it starred: Cassie Branham; Chris Browning; Adam Gregor; Ralph Rieckermann; and Donovan Scott.

96. Michel Strogoff. Based on the 1876 novel, this was directed by Bruno-Rene Huchez and released as an animated television mini-series in France in 1997.

97. 20,000 Leagues Under the Sea. Based on Vingt mille lieues sous les mers - Twenty Thousand Leagues Under the Sea, 1870, this was televised on March 23, 1997. Directed by Michael Anderson, it starred Ben Cross as Captain Nemo along with: Richard Crenna; Julie Cox; Paul Gross; Michael Jayston; Jeff Harding; David Henry; James Vaughan; Susannah Fellows; Joshua Brody; and Phillip Van Dyke.

98. 20,000 Leagues Under the Sea. Based on Vingt mille lieues sous les mers - Twenty Thousand Leagues Under the Sea, 1870, this was televised on May 11th, 1997. Directed by Ron Hardy, it starred Michael Caine as Captain Nemo, along with: Patrick Dempsey; Mia Sara; Bryan Brown; Adewale Akinnouoye-Agbaje; John Bach; Nicholas Hammond; Peter McCauley; Kerry Armstrong; and many others.

99. Around the World in 80 Days. Inspired by Le Tour de Monde en quatre-vingts jours - Around the World in Eighty Days, 1873, this 1999 Canadian animated short starred: Simon Callow; Philip Jackson; Joe Mills; and John Sessions.

100. Michele Strogoff - il corriere dello zar. Inspired by Michel Strogoff - Michael Strogoff, 1876, this Italian/German production was released in December 1999. Directed by Fabrizio Costa, it starred: Paolo Seganti; Lea Bosco; Hardy Kruger Jr; Esther Schweins; Heio von Stetten; Daniel Ceccaldi; Giovanni Lombardo Radice; and many others.

101. Les Voyages extraordinaires de Jules Verne - Le tour du monde en 80 jours. Inspired by Le Tour de Monde en quatre-vingts jours - Around the World in Eighty Days, 1873, this animated short film was made in France for release in 2000. Directed by Henri Heidsieck, it starred Alex Taylor as Phileas Fogg.

102. The Secret Adventures of Jules Verne. Inspired by the work of **Jules Verne**, this Canadian television series ran for twenty-two episodes, starting on June 18th, 2000. Using an assortment of directors, it starred: Francesca Hunt; Michel Courtemanche; Chris Demetral; and Michael Praed; along with an assortment of guest stars, including: Pattie Allan; Rene Auberjonois; David Warner; John Rhys-Davies; Michael Moriarty; and many others.

103. Les Voyages extraordinaires de Jules Verne - La Jangada. Inspired by La Jangada - Eight Hundred Leagues on the Amazon, 1881, this animated short film was directed by Jean-Pierre Jacquet and released in France in 2000.

104. Les Voyages extraordinaires de Jules Verne - Les Voyage au centre de la terre. Inspired by Voyage au centre de la Terre - Journey to the Centre of the Earth, 1864, this animated short film was made in France for release in 2001. Directed by Zoltan Szilagyi Varga, it starred: Pierre Richard; Enrico Salamone; Carole Baillien; and Nicole Valberg.

105. Les Voyages extraordinaires de Jules Verne - Cesar Cascabel. Inspired by Cesar Cascabel, 1890, this animated short film was made in France for release in 2001.

106. Les Voyages extraordinaires de Jules Verne - L'ile mysterieuse. Inspired by L'ile mysterieuse - The Mysterious Island, 1874, this animated short film was made in France for release in 2001. Directed by Claude Allix, it starred: Richard Bohringer and Tom Novembre.

107. Les Voyages extraordinaires de Jules Verne - L'Etoile du sud. Inspired by L'Etoile du sud - The Vanished Diamond, 1884, this animated short film was made in France for release in 2001. Directed by Armando Fereira, it starred: Richard Bohringer; and Tom Novembre.

108. The League of Extraordinary Gentlemen. From 2003, this was inspired only in part by **Jules Verne**. Neseeruddin Shad played Captain Nemo. Other characters involved in this were: Sean Connery as Allan Quatermain from H. Rider Haggard; Peta Wilson as Mina Harker from Bram Stoker's Dracula; Tony Curran as H. G. Wells' Invisible Man; Stuart Townsend as Oscar Wilde's Dorian Gray; Shane West as Mark Twain's Tom Sawyer; Jason Flemyng as Dr Henry Jekyll and Mr. Edward Hyde, from Robert Louis Stevenson... and so on.

109. 20,000 Leagues Under the Sea. Based on Vingt mille lieues sous les mers - Twenty Thousand Leagues Under the Sea, 1870, this animated short was directed by Scott Heming and released in December 2004.

110. Le Docteur Ox. In English, Doctor Ox. From 1874, this short story was filmed in France for release in 2004. Directed by Philippe Beziat, it starred: Jacques Gomez; Laurent Bourdeaux; Jean-Christopher Hurtaud; Sylvia Kevorkian; Sarah Jouffroy; and many others.

111. Around the World in 80 Days. Based on Le Tour de Monde en quatre-vingts jours - Around the World in Eighty Days, 1873, this was released in the States on June 16th, 2004. Directed by Frank Coraci, it starred: Jackie Chan; Steve Coogan; Robert Fyfe; Jim Broadbent; Ian McNeice; David Ryall; Roger Hammond; Adam Godley; Karen Mok; Howard Cooper; and many, many others, including: Arnold Schwarzenegger as Prince Hapi; Rob Schneider as a San Francisco hobo; Luke Wilson as Orville Wright; Owen Wilson as Wilbur Wright; John Cleese as a grizzled sergeant; and Kathy Bates as Queen Victoria.

112. Les Adventures extraordinaires de Michel Strogoff. Based on the 1876 novel, this animated short was released in France in 2004. Directed by Alexandre Huchez and Bruno-Rene Huchez, it starred: Anthony Delon; Claire Keim; Mike Marshall; and Michel Elias.

113. Mysterious Island. Based on L'ile mysterieuse - The Mysterious Island, 1874, this was made for television and show on September 17th, 2005. Directed by Russell Mulcahy, this starred Patrick Stewart as Captain Nemo, along with: Kyle MacLachlan; Danielle Calvert; Gabrielle Anwar; Jason Durr; Omar Gooding; Vinnie Jones; and many others.

114. 80 Jours. Also known as 80 Days. Inspired by Le Tour de Monde en quatre-vingts jours - Around the World in Eighty Days, 1873, this animated feature was released in France in October 2005. It starred: John Bell; Marcus Vowell; Andy Hoyle; Miriam Millikin; Andy Turvey; and others.

115. 30,000 Leagues Under the Sea. Inspired by Vingt mille lieues sous les mers - Twenty Thousand Leagues Under the Sea, 1870, this was released in the States in September 2007. Directed by Gabriel Bologna, it starred: Lorenzo Lamas; Natalie Stone; Kim Little Declan Joyce, and many others, including Sean Lawlor as Captain Nemo.

116. Journey to the Center of the Earth. Also known as Journey to Middle Earth. Inspired by Voyage au centre de la Terre - Journey to the Centre of the Earth, 1864, this was made for release in 2008. Directed by David Jones and Scott Wheeler, it starred: Greg Evigan; Jennifer Dorogi; Dedee Pfeiffer; Vanessa Lee Evigan; Caroline Attwood; Amelia Jackson-Gray; Sara Tomko; Vanessa Mitchell; Michael Tower; and others.

117. Journey to the Center of the Earth. Also known as Journey to Middle Earth. Inspired by

Jules Verne

Voyage au centre de la Terre - Journey to the Centre of the Earth, 1864, this was made in 3D for release in 2008. Directed by Eric Brevig, it starred: Brendan Fraser; Josh Hutcherson; Anita Briem; Seth Meyers; Jean Michel Pare; Jane Wheeler; Frank Fontaine; Giancarlo Caltabiano; Kaniehtiio Horn; and Garth Gilker.

***

RADIO

1. Around the World in Eighty Days. From Le Tour du Monde en quatre-vingts jours - Around the World in Eighty Days, 1873. This was used on Mercury Theater, October 23rd, 1938.

2. 20,000 Leagues Under the Sea. From Vingt mille lieues sous les mers - Twenty Thousand Leagues Under the Sea, 1870. Three different versions of this were used on the BBC: 1945; 1955; and 1972.

3. Journey to the Center of the Earth. From Voyage au centre de la Terre - Journey to the Centre of the Earth, 1864. Five different versions of this were used on the BBC: 1946; 1955; 1962; 1968; and 1994.

4. 20,000 Leagues Under the Sea. From Vingt mille lieues sous les mers - Twenty Thousand Leagues Under the Sea, 1870. This was used on Favorite Story on December 20th, 1947.

5. 20,000 Leagues Under the Sea. From Vingt mille lieues sous les mers - Twenty Thousand Leagues Under the Sea, 1870. This was used on Family Theater on August 23rd, 1950 and again on April 22nd, 1953.

6. 20,000 Leagues Under the Sea. From Vingt mille lieues sous les mers - Twenty Thousand Leagues Under the Sea, 1870. This was used on CBS/General Mills Radio Adventure Theater on March 19th, 1977.

7. Journey to the Center of the Earth. From Voyage au centre de la Terre - Journey to the Centre of the Earth, 1864. This was used on CBS/General Mills Radio Adventure Theater on April 24th, 1977.

8. The Mysterious Island. From L'île mysterieuse - The Mysterious Island, 1875. This was used on CBS Radio Mystery Theater on July 19th, 1977. and again on December 8th, 1977.

9. Around the World in Eighty Days. From Le Tour du Monde en quatre-vingts jours - Around the World in Eighty Days, 1873. This was broadcast on the BBC in 1991.

10. Dr. Ox's Experiment. From the short story Une fantaisie du docteur Ox - Dr. Ox's Experiment, 1872. This was used on the BBC in 1998.

11. Journey to the Center of the Earth. From Voyage au centre de la Terre - Journey to the Centre of the Earth, 1864. This was performed for Alien Voices.

***

NOVELS AND COLLECTIONS

1. Cinq Semaines en ballon - Five Weeks in a Balloon. Published in France in 1863 by Pierre-Jules Hetzel. The first English translation was in 1869 by William Lackland. The first U.S. edition was published by D. Appleton & Company, New York City, 1869 while the first UK edition came out in 1870, published by Chapman and Hall, London. Hardcover.

2. Voyages et aventures du capitaine Hatteras - The Voyage and Adventures of Captain Hatteras. Published in France in 1863 originally as two stories, The English at the North Pole and The Desert of Ice. But the two stories were joined and re-printed by Pierre-Jules Hetzel in 1866. The first English translations were published in the original two volumes in 1875 by George Routledge and Sons, London. Hardcover. The first time the two were joined as The Voyages and Adventures of Captain Hatteras was by James R. Osgood, Boston, 1875. Hardcover.

3. Voyage au centre de la Terre - Journey to the Centre of the Earth. Published in France in 1864 by Pierre-Jules Hetzel. The first English translation was published in 1872 by Griffith and Farran, London, but it was abridged and somewhat altered. The first proper edition was in 1874, New York City, by Scribner Armstrong and Co. Hardcover.

4. De la terre a la lune - From the Earth to the Moon. Published in France in 1865 by Pierre-Jules Hetzel. The first English translation was in 1867 and the book was published, with the sequel, Autour de la lune - Around the Moon, 1870, in 1873 by Sampson Low, Marston and Co., London with the full, unwieldy title of: From the Earth to the Moon Direct in 97 Hours 20 Minutes and a Trip Around It. The following year, Scribner Armstrong and Co, New York City, published the first American edition under the same title. Hardcover.

5. Les Enfants du capitaine Grant - The Children of Captain Grant. Also known as In Search of the Castaways. Published in France in 1868 by Pierre-Jules Hetzel. The first English translation was in 1873 and it was published by J. B. Lippincott and Co. of Philadelphia as In Search of the Castaways. Hardcover.

6. Vingt mille lieues sous les mers - Twenty Thousand Leagues Under the Sea. Published in France in 1870 by Pierre-Jules Hetzel. The first English translation was by Mercier Lewis in 1872, published by Sampson Low, Marston, Low and Searle, London, 1873. And it was released the same year in Boston by James R. Osgood. Hardcover.

7. Around the Moon. Published in France in 1870 by Pierre-Jules Hetzel. The first English translation was published with From the Earth to the Moon as From the Earth to the Moon Direct in 97 Hours 20 Minutes and a Trip Around It by Sampson Low, Marston and Co., London, 1873. Hardcover.

8. Une ville flottante - A Floating City. Published in France in 1871 by Pierre-Jules Hetzel. The first English translation was published by Sampson Low, Marston, Low and Searle, London, 1874, in a double

181

volume with Les Forceurs de blocus - The Blockade Runners, a short story also from 1871. Hardcover.

9. Aventures de trois Russes et de trois Anglais - The Adventures of Three Englishmen and Three Russians in South Africa. Published in France in 1872 by Pierre-Jules Hetzel. The first English translation, as Meridiana: The Adventures of Three Englishmen and Three Russians in South Africa was published by Sampson Low, Marston, Low and Searle, London, 1873. Hardcover.

10. Le Pays des fourrures - The Fur Country or Seventy Degrees North Latitude. Published in France in 1872 by Pierre-Jules Hetzel. The first English translation was by N. D'Anvers - Mrs. Arthur Bell - Nancy Bell. It was published in 1873 by Sampson Low, Marston, Low and Searle, London. Hardcover.

11. Le Tour du Monde en quatre-vingts jours - Around the World in Eighty Days. Published in France in 1873 by Pierre-Jules Hetzel. The first English translation was published by Sampson Low, Marston, Low and Searle, London, 1873. Hardcover.

12. Le Docteur Ox - Doctor Ox's Experiment and Other Stories. A story collection published in France in 1874 by Pierre-Jules Hetzel. The first English translation was published by Sampson Low, Marston, Low and Searle, London, 1874. Hardcover. Herein: Dr Ox's Experiments, 1974; A Drama in the Air, 1851; Master Zacharius, 1852; A Winter Amid the Ice, 1855; and The 40th Ascension of Mount Blanc - an essay by Paul Verne, 1874.

13. L'ile mysterieuse - The Mysterious Island. Published in France in 1874 by Pierre-Jules Hetzel. The first English translation was published by Sampson Low, Marston, Low and Searle, London, 1875. They printed it in three volumes: The Mysterious Island: Dropped from the Clouds; The Mysterious Island: Abandoned; and The Mysterious Island: The Secret of the Island. In the States, also 1875, Scribner Armstrong and Co of New York also published it in three volumes: Mysterious Island: Wrecked in the Air; The Mysterious Island: Abandoned; and The Mysterious Island: The Secret of the Island. The third volume was actually released in 1876. Hardcover.

14. Le Chancellor - The Survivors of the Chancellor. Published in France in 1875 by Pierre-Jules Hetzel. The first English translation was published by Sampson Low, Marston, Low and Searle, London, 1875 as The Survivors of the Chancellor; Diary of J. R. Kazallon, Passenger. In the States, published by James R. Osgood, Boston, 1875, it was called The Wreck of the Chancellor. Hardcover.

15. Michel Strogoff - Michael Strogoff. Published in France in 1876 by Pierre-Jules Hetzel. The first English translation was published by Sampson Low, Marston, Searle and Rivington, London, 1877 as Michael Strogoff, The Courier of the Czar. Hardcover.

16. Hector Servadac - Off on a Comet. Published in France in 1877 by Pierre-Jules Hetzel. The first English translation was published by George Munro, New York City, 1877 as Hector Servadac. The first UK edition, in 1878, was published by Sampson Low, Marston, Searle and Rivington, London, as Hector Servadac; or the Career of a Comet. It wasn't until around 1895 that it became commonly known as Off on a Comet when it was printed by David McKay of Philadelphia. Hardcover.

17. Les Indes noires - The Child of the Cavern. Published in France in 1877 by Pierre-Jules Hetzel. The first English translation was published by Sampson Low, Marston, Searle and Rivington, London, 1877 as The Child of the Cavern; or Strange Doings Underground. In the States, as published by George Munro, New York City, in 1877, it was known as The Black Indies. Hardcover.

18. Un capitaine de quinze ans - Dick Sand; A Captain at Fifteen. Published in France in 1878 by Pierre-Jules Hetzel. The first English translation was published by George Munro, New York City, 1878, as Dick Sand; or A Captain at Fifteen. The first UK printing was by Sampson Low, Marston, Searle and Rivington, London, 1879 as Dick Sands, The Boy Captain. Hardcover.

19. Les Cinq Cents Millions de la Begum - The Begum's Fortune. Published in France in 1879 by Pierre-Jules Hetzel. The first English translation was published by George Munro, New York City, 1879 as 500 Millions of the Begum. The first UK edition was Sampson Low, Marston, Searle and Co., London, 1880 as The Begum's Fortune, which is the title that more or less stuck. Hardcover.

20. Les Tribulations d'un chinois en Chine - Tribulations of a Chinaman in China. Published in France in 1879 by Pierre-Jules Hetzel. The first English translation was published by Sampson Low, Marston, Searle and Rivington, London, 1880. Hardcover.

21. La Maison a vapeur - The Steam House. Published in France in 1880 by Pierre-Jules Hetzel. The first English translation was published by Charles Scribner's Sons, New York City, 1881, in two volumes: The Steam House: Demon of Cawnpore; and The Steam House: Tigers and Traitors. Hardcover.

22. La Jangada - Eight Hundred Leagues on the Amazon. Published in France in 1881 by Pierre-Jules Hetzel. The first English translation was published by Sampson Low, Marston, Searle and Rivington, London, 1881 and 1882 in two volumes: Part One: Eight Hundred Leagues on the Amazon; and Part Two: The Cryptogram. In the States, it was published by George Munro, New York City, 1882, as The Jangada; or 800 Leagues Over the Amazon.

23. L'Ecole des Robinsons - Godfrey Morgan. Published in France in 1882 by Pierre-Jules Hetzel. The first English translation was published by Sampson Low, Marston, Searle and Rivington, London, 1883, as Godfrey Morgan: A Californian Mystery.

24. Le Rayon vert - The Green Ray. Published in France in 1882 by Pierre-Jules Hetzel. The first English translation was published by Sampson Low, Marston, Searle and Rivington, London, 1883.

25. Keraban-le-tetu - Keraban the Inflexible.

Jules Verne

Published in France in 1883 by Pierre-Jules Hetzel. The first English translation was published by Sampson Low, Marston, Searle and Rivington, London, 1884.

26. L'Etoile du sun - The Vanished Diamond. Published in France in 1884 by Pierre-Jules Hetzel. The first English translation was published by Sampson Low, Marston, Searle and Rivington, London, 1885, as The Vanished Diamond, a Tale of South Africa. The first American edition came out the same year from George Munro, New York City, as The Southern Star, or The Diamond Land.

27. L'Archipel en feu - The Archipelago on Fire. Published in France in 1884 by Pierre-Jules Hetzel. The first English translation was published by Sampson Low, Marston and Rivington, London, 1885.

28. Mathias Sandorf. Published in France in 1885 by Pierre-Jules Hetzel. The first English translation was published by Sampson Low, Marston, Searle and Rivington, London, 1886.

29. Un billet de loterie - The Lottery Ticket. Published in France in 1886 by Pierre-Jules Hetzel. The first English translation was published by Sampson Low, Marston, Searle and Rivington, London, 1886.

30. Robur-le-Conquerant - Robur the Conqueror. Published in France in 1886 by Pierre-Jules Hetzel. The first English translation was published by Sampson Low, Marston, Searle and Rivington, London, 1887, as Clipper of the Clouds. The first U.S. edition was published by M. A. Donohue & Company, Chicago, circa 1900, as A Trip Around the World in a Flying Machine.

31. Nord contre Sud - North Against South. Published in France in 1887 by Pierre-Jules Hetzel. The first English translation was published by Sampson Low, Marston, Searle and Rivington, London, 1888.

32. Le Chemin de France - The Flight to France. Published in France in 1887 by Pierre-Jules Hetzel. The first English translation was published by National Publishing Company of Toronto, Toronto, October 1888. The first UK edition was published by Sampson Low, Marston, Searle and Rivington, London, November 1888. And the first U.S. edition was published by Frank F. Lovell and Company, New York City, 1890 as The Flight to France; or The Memories of a Dragoon; A Tale of the Day of Dumouriez.

33. Deux Ans de vacances - Two Years' Vacation. Published in France in 1888 by Pierre-Jules Hetzel. The first English translation was published by Sampson Low, Marston, Searle and Rivington, London, 1889 as Adrift in the Pacific. The first American edition was from Associated Booksellers, Westport, Connecticut in 1964 as Two Year Vacation: Part One: Adrift in the Pacific; and Part Two: Second Year Ashore.

34. Famille-sans-nom - Family Without a Name. Published in France in 1889 by Pierre-Jules Hetzel. The first English translation was published by John W. Lowell, New York City, 1889, in softcover. The first hardcover edition was published by The Musson Book Company, Toronto, 1890. And the first UK edition was published by Sampson Low, Marston, Searle and Rivington, London, 1891.

35. Sans dessus dessous - The Purchase of the North Pole. Published in France in 1889 by Pierre-Jules Hetzel. The first U.S. edition was published by L. S. Ogilvie and Company, New York City, 1890, as Topsy Turvy. The first UK edition was published by Sampson Low, Marston, Searle and Rivington, London, 1891 as The Purchase of the North Pole.

36. Cesar Cascabel - Caesar Cascabel. Published in France in 1890 by Pierre-Jules Hetzel. The first U.S. edition was published by Cassel Publishing, New York City, 1890. The first UK edition was published by Sampson Low, Marston, Searle and Rivington, London, 1891.

37. Mistress Branican. Published in France in 1891 by Pierre-Jules Hetzel. The first U.S. edition was published by Cassel Publishing, New York City, 1891. The first UK edition was published by Sampson Low, Marston, Searle and Rivington, London, 1892.

38. Le Chateau des Carpathes - Carpathian Castle. Published in France in 1892 by Pierre-Jules Hetzel. The first English translation was published by Sampson Low, Marston, Searle and Rivington, London, 1893 as The Castle of the Carpathians. The first American edition was from The Merriam Co, New York City, 1894.

39. Claudius Bombarnac. Published in France in 1892 by Pierre-Jules Hetzel. The first English translation was published by Sampson Low, Marston, Searle and Rivington, London, 1894 as Claudius Bombarnac. The first American edition was from Lovell, Coryell and Co, New York City, 1894, as The Special Correspondent; or The Adventures of Claudius Bombarnac.

40. P'tit-Bonhomme - Foundling Mick. Published in France in 1893 by Pierre-Jules Hetzel. The first English translation was published by Sampson Low, Marston and Co, London, 1895 as Foundling Mick. Apparently, an American edition doesn't exist.

41. Mirifiques Aventures de Maitre Antifer - Captain Antifer. Published in France in 1894 by Pierre-Jules Hetzel. The first English translation was published by Sampson Low, Marston and Co, London, 1895 as Captain Antifer. The first American edition was from R. F. Fenno and Company, New York City, 1895.

42. L'ile a helice - Propeller Island. Published in France in 1895 by Pierre-Jules Hetzel. The first English translation was published by Sampson Low, Marston and Co, London, 1896 as Floating Island; or The Pearl of the Pacific. The first American edition was from Hurst and Company, New York City, 1897. It wasn't until the 1961 edition from ARCO Publishers in London that this became known as Propeller Island.

43. Face au drapeau - Facing the Flag. Published in France in 1896 by Pierre-Jules Hetzel. The first English translation was published by Sampson Low, Marston and Co, London, 1897 as For the Flag. The first American edition was from F. Tennyson Neely Publisher, New York City, 1897, as Facing the Flag.

44. Clovis Dardentor. Published in France in 1896 by Pierre-Jules Hetzel. The first English translation was published by Sampson Low, Marston and Co, London, 1897. Apparently, it was never published in the States.

45. Le Sphinx des glaces - An Antarctic Mystery. Published in France in 1897 by Pierre-Jules Hetzel. The first English translation was published by Sampson Low, Marston and Co, London, 1898 as An Antarctic Mystery. The first American edition was from J. B. Lippincott, Philadelphia, 1898.

46. Le Superbe Orenoque - The Mighty Orinoco. Published in France in 1898 by Pierre-Jules Hetzel. The first English translation was published in softcover by University Press of New England, United States, 2002. The first translated hardcover was from Wesleyan University Press, Middletown, Connecticut, 2003.

47. Le Testament d'un excentrique - The Will of an Eccentric. Published in France in 1899 by Pierre-Jules Hetzel. The first English translation was published by Sampson Low, Marston and Co, London, 1900. To date, there isn't an American edition.

48. Seconde Patrie - Second Fatherland. Published in France in 1900 by Pierre-Jules Hetzel. The first English translation was published by Sampson Low, Marston and Co, London, 1923 in two volumes, as Part One: Their Island Home, the Later Adventures of the Swiss Family Robinson; and Part Two: The Castaways of the Flag, the Final Adventures of the Swiss Family Robinson. The first American edition was from G. Howard Watt, New York City, 1924, with the same titles.

49. Le Village aerien - The Village in the Treetops. Published in France in 1901 by Pierre-Jules Hetzel. The first English translation was published by ARCO, London, 1964 as The Village in the Treetops. The first American edition was from Associated Booksellers, Westport, Connecticut, 1964.

50. Les Histoires de Jean-Marie Cabidoulin - The Yarns of Jean-Marie Cabidoulin. Published in France in 1901 by Pierre-Jules Hetzel. The first English translation was published by ARCO, London, 1967 as The Sea Serpent. Apparently, no American edition exists.

51. Les Freres Kip - The Kip Brothers. Published in France in 1902 by Pierre-Jules Hetzel. The first English translation was published by Wesleyan University Press, Middletown, Connecticut, 2007.

52. Bourses de voyage - Traveling Scholarships. Published in France in 1903 by Pierre-Jules Hetzel. No English translation exists as of December 2008.

53. Un drame en Livonie - A Drama in Livonia. Published in France in 1904 by Pierre-Jules Hetzel. The first English translation was published by ARCO, London, 1967 as Drama in Livonia. The first American edition was from Associated Booksellers, Westport, Connecticut, 1967.

54. Maitre du monde - Master of the World. Published in France in 1904 by Pierre-Jules Hetzel. The first English translation was published by Sampson Low, Marston and Co, London, 1914 as The Master of the World. The first American edition was from J. B. Lippincott, Philadelphia, 1914.

55. L'Invasion de la mer - Invasion of the Sea. Published in France in 1905 by Pierre-Jules Hetzel. Apparently, there was a poorly translated version of this, as Captain Hardizan, serialized in The American Weekly, a Sunday newspaper supplement, in August 1905. But the first book in English was published by Wesleyan University Press, Middletown, Connecticut, 2001.

56. Le Phare du bout du monde - The Lighthouse at the End of the World. With Michel Verne (although it is now believed that Verne's son Michel wrote this on his own). Published in France in 1905 by Pierre-Jules Hetzel. The first English translation was published by Sampson Low, Marston and Co, London, 1923 as The Lighthouse at the End of the World. The first American edition was from G. Howard Watt, New York City, 1924.

57. Le Volcan d'or - The Golden Volcano. With Michel Verne (although it is now believed that Verne's son Michel wrote this on his own). Published in France in 1906 by Pierre-Jules Hetzel. The first English translation was published by ARCO, London, 1962, in two volumes as Golden Volcano Part One: The Claim on Forty Mile Creek and Golden Volcano Part Two: Flood and Flame. The first American edition was from Associated Booksellers, Westport, Connecticut, 1962, using the same titles.

58. L'Agence Thompson - The Thompson Travel Agency. With Michel Verne (although it almost a certainty that Verne's son Michel wrote this on his own). Published in France in 1907 by Pierre-Jules Hetzel. The first English translation was published by ARCO, London, 1965, in two volumes as The Thompson Travel Agency Part One: Package Holiday and The Thompson Travel Agency Part Two: End of the Journey. The first American edition was from Associated Booksellers, Westport, Connecticut, 1965, using the same titles.

59. La Chasse au meteore - The Chase of the Golden Meteor. With Michel Verne. Published in France in 1908 by Pierre-Jules Hetzel. The first English translation was published by Grant Richards, London, 1909 as The Chase of the Golden Meteor. The first American edition was from Associated Booksellers, Westport, Connecticut, 1965, as The Hunt for the Meteor.

60. Le Pilote du Danube - The Danube Pilot. With Michel Verne. Published in France in 1908 by Pierre-Jules Hetzel. The first English translation was published by ARCO, London, 1967 as The Danube Pilot. The first American edition was from Associated Booksellers, Westport, Connecticut, 1967, using the same title.

61. Les Naufrages du Jonathan - The Survivors of the Jonathan. With Michel Verne (although Verne's son Michel wrote most of this on his own).

Jules Verne

Published in France in 1909 by Pierre-Jules Hetzel. The first English translation was published by ARCO, London, 1962, in two volumes as The Survivors of the Jonathan Part One: The Masterless Man and The Survivors of the Jonathan Part Two: The Unwilling Dictator. The first American edition was from Associated Booksellers, Westport, Connecticut, 1962, using the same titles.

62. Le Secret de Wilhelm Storitz - The Secret of William Storitz. With Michel Verne (although Verne's son Michel wrote most of this on his own). Published in France in 1910 by Pierre-Jules Hetzel. The first English translation was published by ARCO, London, 1963 as The Secret of Wilhelm Storitz. The first American edition was from Associated Booksellers, Westport, Connecticut, 1963, using the same title.

63. Hier et Demain - Yesterday and Tomorrow. A story collection published in France in 1910 by Pierre-Jules Hetzel. The first English translation was published by ARCO, London, 1965 as Yesterday and Tomorrow. The first American edition was from Associated Booksellers, Westport, Connecticut, 1965, using the same title. Herein: Gil Bralter, 1887; The Eternal Adam - with Michel Verne, 1910; Mr Ray Sharp and Miss Me Flat, 1893; In the Twenty-Ninth Century: The Diary of an American Journalist in 2889, 1910; Fritt-Flacc, 1884; Ten Hours Hunting, 1910; An Ideal City, 1910; The Fate of Jean Morenas - with Michel Verne, 1910.

64. La Famille Raton - Adventures of the Rat Family. Published in France in 1910 by Pierre-Jules Hetzel. The first English translation was published by Oxford University Press, New York City, 1993.

65. L'Etonnante Aventure de la mission Barsac - The Barsac Mission. With Michel Verne (although Verne's son Michel wrote most of this on his own). Published in France in 1919 by Pierre-Jules Hetzel. The first English translation was published by ARCO, London, 1960, in two volumes as The Barsac Mission Part One: Into the Niger Bend and The Barsac Mission Part Two: The City in the Sahara. The first American edition was from Associated Booksellers, Westport, Connecticut, 1960, using the same titles.

66. Novels. Published by Victor Gollancz, London, 1929. Hardcover. An omnibus edition, this gathered: Hector Servadac, 1877; Twenty Thousand Leagues Under the Sea, 1869; Around the World in Eighty Days, 1873; Propeller Island, 1895; and The Blockade Runners, 1865.

67. The Omnibus. Published by J. P. Lippincott, New York City, 1931. Hardcover. An omnibus edition, this gathered: Journey to the Centre of the Earth, 1864; Twenty Thousand Leagues Under the Sea, 1869; Around the World in Eighty Days, 1873; and The Blockade Runners, 1865.

68. Jules Verne - Master of Science Fiction. Published by Sidgwick and Jackson, London, 1956. Hardcover. Herein: Introduction by I. O. Evans; The Begum's Fortune - excerpt, 1879; Twenty Thousand Leagues Under the Sea - excerpt, 1869; From the Earth to the Moon - excerpt, 1865; A Journey to the Centre of the Earth - excerpt, 1864; Five Weeks in a Balloon - excerpt, 1863; An Antarctic Mystery - excerpt, 1897; For the Flag - excerpt, 1896; The Floating Island - excerpt, 1895; The Clipper of the Clouds - excerpt, 1886; The Steam House - excerpt, 1880; Hector Servadac - excerpt, 1877; The Child of the Cavern - excerpt, 1877; and Round the Moon - excerpt, 1869.

69. Mysterious Island. Introduction by **Ray Bradbury**. Published by Heritage Press, United States, 1959. Hardcover.

70. To the Sun - with - Off on a Comet. Published by Dover Publications, New York City, 1960. Softcover.

71. From the Earth to the Moon - with - All Around the Moon. Published by Dover Publications, New York City, 1960. Softcover.

72. The Mystery of Arthur Gordon Pym. With Edgar Allan Poe. This bound Verne's The Sphinx of the Ice Fields, 1897, as the sequel to Poe's The Narrative of Arthur Gordon Pym of Nantucket, 1838. Published by Associated Booksellers, Westport, Connecticut, 1961. Hardcover.

73. Around the World in Eighty Days. Introduction by **Ray Bradbury**. Published by Heritage Press, United States, 1962. Hardcover.

74. 20,000 Leagues Under the Sea. Introduction by **Ray Bradbury.** Published by Bantam Books, New York City, 1962. Softcover.

75. 20,000 Leagues Under the Sea - with - Around the Moon. Introduction by **Isaac Asimov**. Published by Platt and Munk, New York City, 1965. Hardcover.

76. From the Earth to the Moon. Introduction by **Ray Bradbury**. Easton Press, Norwalk, Connecticut, 1970. Leather-bound.

77. Jules Verne. Published by Octopus Books, London, 1978. Hardcover. An omnibus edition, this gathered: From the Earth to the Moon, 1865; Twenty Thousand Leagues Under the Sea, 1869; and Around the World in Eighty Days, 1873.

78. The Best of Jules Verne. Published by Castle Books, New Jersey, 1978. Herein: Journey to the Centre of the Earth, 1964; Around the World in Eighty Days, 1873; The Clipper of the Clouds, 1886; **Jules Verne** at Home - an essay by Marie Belloc Lowndes, 1895; and The World of **Jules Verne** - an essay by Alan K. Russell, 1978.

79. Works of Jules Verne. Published by Avenel Books, New York City, 1983. Hardcover. An omnibus edition, this gathered: Journey to the Centre of the Earth, 1864; Twenty Thousand Leagues Under the Sea, 1869; Around the World in Eighty Days, 1873; A Drama in the Air, 1851; Doctor Ox's Experiment, 1872; and Master Zacharius, 1852.

80. Voyages a reculons en Angleterre et en Ecosse - Backwards to Britain. First published in Paris by Le cherche midi editeur, 1989. The first English translation of this was published by Chambers, Edinburgh, Scotland 1992, as Backwards to Britain.

81. L'Oncle Robinson - Uncle Robinson. Published in France in 1991 by Le cherche midi editeur, Paris. To date, December 2008, no English edition exists.

82. Un Pretre en 1839 - A Priest in 1839. First published in Paris by Le cherche midi editeur, 1992. To date, December 2008, the book has not been translated into English.

83. En Magellanie - Magellania. This was the original novel that Vern's son Michel re-wrote into Les Naufrages du Jonathan - The Survivors of the Jonathan, 1909. This was first published, in it's original form, in Paris by Societe **Jules Verne**, 1997, as En Magellanie, and in the States in 2002 as Magellania by Welcome Rain Publishers, New York City.

84. Paris au XXe siecle - Paris in the Twentieth Century. Published in France in 1994 by Hachette, le cherche midi editeur, Paris. The first English translation was published by Random House, New York City, 1996, as Paris in the Twentieth Century.

85. The Floating City - with - The Blockade Runners. Published by Pulp Fictions, London, 1999. Softcover.

***

NON-FICTION

1. Histoire des grands voyages et des grands voyageurs: Decouverte de la Terre - and - Les Voyageurs du xix Siecle - The Exploration of the World - and - The Great Explorers of the Nineteenth Century. Published in France in 1870 by Pierre-Jules Hetzel. The first English translation was published by Sampson Low, Marston, Searle and Rivington, London, 1879 as The Exploration of the World. The second volume was published by the same published in 1881 as The Great Explorers of the Nineteenth Century. The first U.S. editions were published by Charles Scribner's Sons, New York City, 1879 and 1881, as The Exploration of the World: Famous Travels and Travellers and The Exploration of the World: The Great Explorers of the Nineteenth Century.

***

RELATED

1. Jules Verne: A Biography. By Kenneth Allott. Published by The Cresset Press, London, 1940. Hardcover.

2. Jules Verne: The Biography of Imagination. By George H. Waltz, Jr. Published by Henry Holt and Company, New York City, 1943. Hardcover.

3. Prize Science Fiction: The Jules Verne Award Stories. Edited by Donald A. Wollheim. Published by The McBride Company, New York City, 1953. Hardcover.

4. Jules Verne. By Marguerite Allotee de La Fuye. Published by Staples Press, London, 1955. Hardcover.

5. Around the World in Eighty Days: A Play in Three Acts Based upon the Jules Verne Novel of the Same Name. By Rodney Dawes. Published by The Dramatic Publishing Company, Chicago, 1957. Softcover.

6. Jules Verne: His Life. By Catherine O. Peare. Published by Dennis Dobson, London, 1961. Hardcover.

7. Jules Verne and His Work. By I. O. Evans. Published by ARCO, London, 1965. Hardcover.

8. Jules Verne. By Beril Becker. Published by G. P. Putnam's Sons, New York City, 1966. Hardcover.

9. Jules Verne: The Man Who Invented the Future. By Franz Born. Published by Prentice Hall, Englewood Cliffs, New Jersey, 1964. Hardcover.

10. Jules Verne: Portrait of a Prophet. By Russell Freedman. Published by Holiday House, New York City, 1965. Hardcover.

11. The Political and Social Ideas of Jules Verne. By Jean Chesneaux. Published by Thames and Hudson, London, 1972. First translated edition.

12. Jules Verne: A Biography. By Jean-Jules Verne. Published by Macdonald and Janes, London, 1976. First translated edition.

13. Jules Verne: Inventor of Science Fiction. By Peter Costello. Published by Charles Scribner's Sons, New York City, 1978. Hardcover.

14. The Jules Verne Companion. By Peter Haining. Published by Souvenir Press, London, 1978. Softcover.

15. Jules Verne: A Primary and Secondary Bibliography. By Edward J. Gallagher; Judith A. Mistichelli; and John A. Van Eerde. Published by G. K. Hall, Boston, 1980. Hardcover.

16. The Other Log of Phileas Fogg. By Philip Jose Farmer. Published by Tor Books - Tom Doherty Associates, New York City, 1982. Softcover.

17. Who Said There No Man on the Moon?: A Story of Jules Verne. By Robert M. Quackenbush. Published by Prentice Hall, Englewood Cliffs, New Jersey, 1985. Hardcover.

18. Jules Verne Rediscovered: Didacticism and the Scientific Novel. By Arthur B. Evans. Published by Greenwood Publishing, Westport, Connecticut, 1988. Hardcover.

19. Verne's Journey to the Centre of Self - Space and Time in the Voyages Extraordinaires. By William Butcher. Published by Macmillan, London, 1990. Hardcover.

20. The Mask of the Prophet: The Extraordinary Fictions of Jules Verne. By Andrew Martin. Published by Oxford University Press - Clarendon Press, Oxford, 1990. Hardcover.

21. Jules Verne: The Man Who Invented Tomorrow. By Peggy Teeters. Published by Walker and Company, New York City, 1992. Hardcover.

Jules Verne

22. Beyond Jules Verne - Circling the World in a Record-Breaking 74 Days. By Robin Knox-Johnston. Published by Hodder and Stoughton, London, 1995. Hardcover.

23. Jules Verne: An Exploratory Biography. By Herbert R. Lottman. Published by St. Martin's Press, New York City, 1997. Hardcover.

24. Predicting the Future: From Jules Verne to Bill Gates. By John Malone. Published by M. Evans and Co, New York City, 1997. Hardcover.

25. Remarkable Journeys: The Story of Jules Verne. By William Schoell. Published by Morgan Reynolds Publishing, Greensboro, North Carolina, 2002. Softcover.

26. Voyage into the Deep: The Sage of Jules Verne and Captain Nemo. By Francoise Riviere. Published by Harry N. Abrams, New York City, 2004. Hardcover.

27. Jules Verne: The Definitive Biography. By William Butcher. Thunder's Mouth Press, United States, 2006. Hardcover.

28. Around the World in 65 Days - with George Griffith: The Story of the Real Phileas Fogg. By Robert Godwin. Published by Apogee Books, Burlington, Ontario, 2008. Softcover.

-2000-

Poul Anderson.

Poul William Anderson was born on November 25th, 1926 in Bristol, Pennsylvania and died of cancer on July 31st, 2001 in Orinda, California.

Writing was only meant to be a hobby. Something he did on the side. Something fun. But irrelevant. He was to be an astrophysicist. And he went to university in order to do that. But when he graduated in 1948, the country was in a bit of a recession and there were no jobs available. Since he had sold a few stories while he was in school, and obviously had a knack for it, he decided to try supporting himself with writing while he looked for a real job. The real job never showed up.

He later admitted to himself that he never would have made it as a first-rate scientist. Mathematically, he wasn't creative enough. And being a second-rate scientist, "did not seem very attractive."

His first appearance in Astounding Science Fiction, indeed, his first professionally published story, was in the September 1944 issue. He was eighteen years old, still attending the University of Minnesota (where he met **Gordon R. Dickson**) and the story was an addition to Campbell's Probability Zero series: A Matter of Relativity; also in that issue were: Business of Killing by **Fritz Leiber**; A Can of Paint by **A. E. van Vogt**; Census by Clifford D. Simak; Culture by Jerry Shelton; Hobo God by Malcolm Jameson; Icicle Built for Groo by John H. Pomeroy; The Case of the Invincible Pirate by Edward Shulman; The Thirty-First of June by Frank Holby; and Renaissance - part 3 of 4 by Raymond F. Jones.

He had to wait awhile for his next appearance. It didn't happen until July 1947. The story was called Logic and it is generally considered Anderson's first published story, although, obviously, it was not. Sharing that issue were: Edward Grendon with The Figure; Lawrence O'Donnell (**C. L. Moore** and Henry Kuttner) - Fury - part 3 of 3; and **Jack Williamson** - With Folded Hands. His next story in Astounding was in the December 1948 issue. It was called Genius, it was featured on the cover, and, with that one, he became a regular contributor. Also on hand were: Late Night Final by **Eric Frank Russell**; Bureau of Slick Tricks by H. B. Fyfe; and The Players of A - part 3 of 4 by **A. E. van Vogt**.

His first novel came in 1952, Vault of the Ages. And there was no going back. He developed into one of the most prolific authors in the field. And one of the very few truly prolific authors who remained consistently good.

Probably, his most expensive book for collectors is Twilight World, around $1,500.00, although, Tau Zero can also command a hefty price.

Pen names used: A. A. Craig; Michael Karageorge; and Winston P. Sanders.

***

AWARDS

1961. Hugo Award for the best short fiction, The Longest Voyage - Analog, December 1960.
1964. Hugo Award for the best short fiction, No Truce with Kings - The Magazine of Fantasy and Science Fiction, June 1963.
1969. Hugo Award for best novelette, The Sharing of Flesh - Galaxy Magazine, December 1968.
1971. Nebula Award for best novelette, The Queen of Air and Darkness - The Magazine of Fantasy and Science Fiction, April 1971.
1972. Hugo Award for best novella, The Queen of Air and Darkness - The Magazine of Fantasy and Science Fiction, April 1971.
1972. Nebula Award for best novelette, Goat Song - The Magazine of Fantasy and Science Fiction, February 1972.
1973. Hugo Award for best novelette, Goat Song - The Magazine of Fantasy and Science Fiction, February 1972.
1974. August Derleth Fantasy Award for best novel, Hrolf Kraaki's Saga.
1975. Mythopoeic Fantasy Award for A Midsummer Tempest.
1978. Gandalf Award for Grand Master.
1979. Hugo Award for best novelette, Hunter's Moon - Analog, November 1978.
1981. Nebula Award for best novella, The Saturn Game - Analog, February 1981.
1982. Skylark - Edward E. Smith Memorial Award for Imaginative Fiction.
1985. Prometheus Hall of Fame Award for Trader to the Stars.
1995. Prometheus Award for The Stars Are Also Fire.
1995. Prometheus Hall of Fame Award for The Star Fox.
1997. Nebula Grand Master award.
1998. Pegasus Award for Best Adaptation, shared with Anne Passovoy, for the song Mary O'Meara.
2000. Inducted into The Science Fiction Hall of Fame.
2001. The John W. Campbell Memorial Award for Genesis.
2001. Prometheus Award for Lifetime Achievement.

***

FILM AND TELEVISION

1. The High Crusade. This 1960 novel was filmed in Germany for released in 1994. Directed by Klaus Knoesel and Holger Neuhauser, it starred: John Rhys-Davies; Rick Overton; Michael Des Barres; Catherine Punch; Patrick Brymer; Debbie Lee Carrington; Rinaldo Talamonti; and many more.

***

Poul Anderson

RADIO

1. Inside Earth. From 1951, this was used on Tales of Tomorrow, which ran from August 1951 until June 1953.

2. The Light. Published in 1957, this was featured on X Minus One on October 24th, 1957.

3. Planet of Geniuses. **John W. Campbell** featured this on Exploring Tomorrow, April 16th, 1958.

4. Time Heals. This 1949 story was used on Exploring Tomorrow on May 14th, 1958.

5. My Objective, All Sublime. From 1961, this was used on Mind Webs on January 21st, 1979.

6. Mike Hodel's Hour 25. Poul Anderson was a guest on September 8th, 2000.

7. Kyrie. This 1968 story was read on Mike Hodel's Hour 25 on February 16th, 2001.

8. Call Me Joe. This 1957 story was read on Mike Hodel's Hour 25 on March 16th, 2001.

7. Call Me Joe. From 1957, this story was used on Sci-Fi Radio.

8. The Martian Crown Jewels. Published in 1957, this was used on Seeing Ear Theater.

***

NOVELS AND COLLECTIONS

1. Vault of the Ages. Published by The John C. Winston Company, Philadelphia, 1952. Hardcover.

2. Brain Wave. Published by Ballantine Books, New York City, 1954. Softcover. Ballantine Book 80.

3. The Broken Sword. Published by Abelard-Schuman, New York City, 1954. Hardcover.

4. Brain Wave. Published by William Heinemann, London, 1955. First hardcover edition.

5. No World of Their Own. Published by Ace Books, New York City, 1955. Softcover. Ace Double D-110. Bound with 1,000 Year Plan by **Isaac Asimov**.

6. Star Ways. Published by Avalon Books, New York City, 1956. Hardcover.

7. Planet of No Return. Published by Ace Books, New York City, 1957. Softcover. Ace Double D-199. Bound with Star Guard by **Andre Norton**.

8. Earthman's Burden. With **Gordon R. Dickson**. Published by Gnome Press, New York City, 1957. Hardcover. Herein: The Sherriff of Canyon Gulch, 1951; Interlude, 1957; Don Jones, 1957; Interlude II, 1957; In Hoka Signo Vinces, 1953; Interlude III, 1957; The Adventure of the Misplaced Hound, 1953; Interlude IV, 1957; Yo Ho Hoka!, 1955; Interlude V, 1957; The Tiddlywink Warriors, 1955; Mysterious Message, 1957; and Postlude, 1957.

9. The Snows of Ganymede. Published by Ace Books, New York City, 1958. Softcover. Ace Double D-303. Bound with War of the Wing Men by **Poul Anderson**.

10. War of the Wing Men. Published by Ace Books, New York City, 1958. Softcover. Ace Double D-303. Bound with The Snows of Ganymede by **Poul Anderson**.

11. The War of Two Worlds. Published by Ace Books, New York City, 1959. Softcover. Ace Double D-335. Bound with Threshold of Eternity by John Brunner.

12. We Claim These Stars. Published by Ace Books, New York City, 1959. Softcover. Ace Double D-407. Bound with The Planet Killers by **Robert Silverberg**.

13. Perish by the Sword. Published by The Macmillan Company, New York City, 1959. Hardcover.

14. Virgin Planet. Published by Avalon Books, New York City, 1959. Hardcover.

15. The Enemy Stars. Published by J. P. Lippincott, New York City, 1959. Hardcover.

16. The High Crusade. Published by Doubleday & Company, Garden City, New York, 1960. Hardcover.

17. The Golden Slave. Published by Avon Books, New York City, 1960. Softcover. Avon Book T-388.

18. Rogue Sword. Published by Avon Books, New York City, 1960. Softcover. Avon Book T-472.

19. Guardians of Time. Published by Ballantine Books, New York City, 1960. Softcover. Ballantine Book 422K. Herein: Time Patrol, 1955; Brave to Be a King, 1959; The Only Game in Town, 1960; and Delenda Est, 1955.

20. Murder in Black Letter. Published by The Macmillan Company, New York City, 1960. Hardcover.

21. Guardians of Time. Published by Victor Gollancz, London, 1961. First hardcover edition.

22. Earthman, Go Home. Published by Ace Books, New York City, 1961. Softcover. Ace Double D-479. Bound with To the Tombaugh Station by **Wilson Tucker**.

23. Mayday Orbit. Published by Ace Books, New York City, 1961. Softcover. Ace Double F-104. Bound with No Man's World by Kenneth Bulmer.

24. Three Hearts and Three Lions. Published by Doubleday & Company, Garden City, New York, 1961. Hardcover.

25. Orbit Unlimited. Published by Pyramid Books, New York City, 1961. Softcover. Pyramid Book G615.

26. Strangers from Earth. Published by Ballantine Books, New York City, 1961. Softcover. Ballantine Book 483K. This contains: Earthman, Beware!, 1951; Quixote and the Windmill, 1950; Gypsy, 1950; For the Duration, 1957; Duel on Syrtis, 1951; The Star Beast, 1950; The Disintegrating Sky, 1953; and Among Thieves, 1957.

27. Twilight World. Published by Dodd, Mead and

Company, New York City, 1961. Hardcover. This contains: Tomorrow's Children, 1947; Chain of Logic, 1947; and Children of Fortune, 1961.

28. After Doomsday. Published by Ballantine Books, New York City, 1962. Softcover. Ballantine Book 579.

29. Murder Bound. Published by The Macmillan Company, New York City, 1962. Hardcover.

30. The Makeshift Rocket. Published by Ace Books, New York City, 1962. Softcover. Ace Double F-139. Bound with Un-Man and Other Novellas by **Poul Anderson**.

31. Un-Man and Other Novellas. Published by Ace Books, New York City, 1962. Softcover. Ace Double F-139. Bound with The Makeshift Rocket by **Poul Anderson**. Herein: Un-Man, 1953; Margin of Profit, 1956; and The Live Coward, 1956.

32. Shield. Published by Berkley Publishing, New York City, 1963. Softcover. Berkley Book F743.

33. Let the Spacemen Beware! Published by Ace Books, New York City, 1963. Softcover. Ace Double F-209. Bound with The Wizard of Starship Poseidon by Kenneth Bulmer.

34. After Doomsday. Published by Victor Gollancz, London, 1963. First hardcover edition.

35. Three Worlds to Conquer. Published by Pyramid Books, New York City, 1964. Softcover. Pyramid Book R-994.

36. Time and Stars. Published by Doubleday & Company, Garden City, New York, 1964. Hardcover. Herein: No Truce with Kings, 1963; The Critique of Impure Reason, 1962; Escape from Orbit, 1962; Eve Times Four, 1960; Turning Point, 1963; and Epilogue, 1962.

37. Time and Stars. Published by Victor Gollancz, London, 1964. Left out one of the stories, Eve Times Four, 1960.

38. Trader to the Stars. Published by Doubleday & Company, Garden City, New York, 1964. Hardcover. Herein: Hiding Place, 1961; Territory, 1963; and The Master Key, 1964.

39. Agent of the Terran Empire. Published by Chilton Books, Philadelphia, 1965. Hardcover. Herein: Tiger by the Tail, 1951; Warriors from Nowhere, 1954; Honorable Enemies, 1951; and Hunters of the Sky Cave, 1965.

40. The Corridors of Time. Published by Doubleday & Company, Garden City, New York, 1965. Hardcover.

41. The Star Fox. Published by Doubleday & Company, Garden City, New York, 1965. Hardcover.

42. Shield. Published by Dennis Dobson, London, 1965. First hardcover edition.

43. Flandry of Terra. Published by Chilton Books, New York City, 1965. Hardcover. This contains: A Message in Secret, 1959; A Plague of Masters, 1961; and The Game of Glory, 1958.

44. Ensign Flandry. Published by Chilton Books, New York City, 1966. Hardcover.

45. The Trouble Twisters. Published by Doubleday & Company, Garden City, New York, 1966. Hardcover. Herein: A Sun Invisible, 1966; The Three-Cornered Wheel, 1963; and The Trouble Twisters, 1965.

46. Planet of No Return. Published by Dennis Dobson, London, 1966. First hardcover edition.

47. The Fox, the Dog, and the Griffin: A Folk Tale Adapted from the Danish of C. Molbech. Published by Doubleday & Company, Garden City, New York, 1966. Hardcover.

48. World Without Stars. Published by Ace Books, New York City, 1966. Softcover. Ace Book F-425.

49. The Horn of Time. Published by Signet Books - The New American Library, New York City, 1968. Softcover. Signet Book P3349. Herein: The Horn of Time the Hunter, 1963; A Man to My Wounding, 1959; The High Ones, 1958; The Man Who Came Early, 1956; Marius, 1957; and Progress, 1962.

50. Satan's World. Published by Doubleday & Company, Garden City, New York, 1969. Hardcover.

51. Seven Conquests. Published by The Macmillan Company - Collier-Macmillan, London, 1969. Hardcover. This contains: Foreword by **Poul Anderson**; Kings Who Die, 1962; Wildcat, 1958; Cold Victory, 1957; Inside Straight, 1955; Details, 1956; License, 1957; and Strange Bedfellows, 1964.

52. Beyond the Beyond. Published by Signet Books - The New American Library, New York City, 1969. Softcover. Signet Book T3947. Herein: Memory, 1957; Brake, 1957; Day of Burning, 1967; The Sensitive Man, 1954; The Moonrakers, 1966; and Starfog, 1967.

53. Beyond the Beyond. Published by Signet Books and The Science Fiction Book Club, Garden City, New York, 1969. First hardcover edition.

54. Let the Spacemen Beware! Published by Dennis Dobson, London, 1969. First hardcover edition.

55. The Makeshift Rocket. Published by Dennis Dobson, London, 1969. First hardcover edition.

56. The Rebel Worlds. Published by Signet Books - The New American Library, New York City, 1969. Softcover. Signet Book T4041.

57. Tau Zero. Published by Doubleday & Company, Garden City, New York, 1970. Hardcover.

58. Beyond the Beyond. Published by Victor Gollancz, London, 1970. First non-book club hardcover edition.

59. Tales of the Flying Mountains. Published by The Macmillan Company, New York City, 1970. Hardcover. Herein: Prologue by **Poul Anderson**; Say It with Flowers - writing as Winston P. Sanders, 1965; Sunjammer - writing as Winston P. Sanders, 1964; Nothing Succeeds Like Failure, 1970; The Rogue, 1970; Ramble with a Gamblin' Man, 1970; Que Donn'rez Vous?, 1970; Recruiting Nation, 1970;

Poul Anderson

and Epilogue, 1962. Also included are a series of Interludes.

60. A Circus of Hells. Published by Signet Books - The New American Library, New York City, 1970. Softcover. Signet Book T4250.

61. The War of Two Worlds. Published by Dennis Dobson, London, 1970. First hardcover edition.

62. The Broken Sword. Published by Ballantine Books, New York City, 1971. Softcover revised edition. Ballantine Book 02107.

63. The Dancer from Atlantis. Published by Nelson Doubleday - The Science Fiction Book Club, Garden City, New York, 1971. Hardcover.

64. Operation Chaos. Published by Doubleday & Company, Garden City, New York, 1971. Hardcover.

65. The Byworlder. Published by Signet Books - The New American Library, New York City, 1971. Softcover. Signet Book T4780.

66. There Will Be Time. Published by Nelson Doubleday - The Science Fiction Book Club, Garden City, New York, 1972. Hardcover.

67. The Byworlder. Published by Victor Gollancz, London, 1972. First hardcover edition.

68. Hrolf Kraaki's Saga. Published by Ballantine Books, New York City, 1973. Softcover. Ballantine Book 23562.

69. The People of the Wind. Published by Signet Books - The New American Library, New York City, 1973. Softcover. Signet Book Q5479.

70. The Queen of Air and Darkness and Other Stories. Published by Signet Books - The New American Library, New York City, 1973. Softcover. Signet Book Q5713. Herein: Foreword by **Poul Anderson**; The Queen of Air and Darkness, 1971; Home, 1966; The Alien Enemy, 1968; The Faun, 1968; In the Shadow, 1967; and Time Lag, 1961.

71. The Day of Their Return. Published by Nelson Doubleday - The Science Fiction Book Club, Garden City, New York, 1974. Hardcover.

72. Fire Time. Published by Doubleday & Company, Garden City, New York, 1974. Hardcover.

73. A Midsummer Tempest. Published by Doubleday & Company, Garden City, New York, 1974. Hardcover.

74. Orbit Unlimited. Published by Sidgwick and Jackson, London, 1974. First hardcover edition.

75. Inheritors of Earth. With Gordon Eklund. Published by The Chilton Book Company, Radnor, Pennsylvania, 1974. Hardcover.

76. The Many Worlds of Poul Anderson. Edited by Roger Elwood. Published by The Chilton Book Company, Radnor, Pennsylvania, 1974. Hardcover. Herein: Foreword by Roger Elwood; The Longest Voyage, 1960; The Queen of Air and Darkness, 1971; Tomorrow's Children, 1947; Day of Burning, 1967; Journeys End, 1957; Epilogue, 1962; The Sheriff of Canyon Gulch - with **Gordon R. Dickson**, 1951; Challenge and Response - an essay by Sandra Miesel; and Her Strong Enchantments Failing - an essay by Patrick McGuire, 1974.

77. The Worlds of Poul Anderson. Published by Ace Books, New York City, 1974. Softcover. Ace Book 91055. An omnibus edition, this gathers: Planet of No Return, 1957; The War of Two Worlds, 1959; and World Without Stars, 1966.

78. Homeward and Beyond. Published by Doubleday & Company, Garden City, New York, 1975. Hardcover. Herein: Introduction by **Poul Anderson**; Goat Song, 1972; The Long Remembering, 1957; Peek! I See You!, 1968; The Pirate, 1968; The Visitor, 1974; Wings of Victory, 1972; Murphy's Hall - written with Karen Anderson, 1971; The Peat Bog, 1975; and Wolfram, 1975.

79. A Knight of Ghosts and Shadows. Published by Nelson Doubleday - The Science Fiction Book Club, Garden City, New York, 1975. Hardcover.

80. The Book of Poul Anderson. Published by DAW Books, New York City, 1975. Softcover. DAW Collector's Book 153. This contains: Foreword by Roger Elwood; The Longest Voyage, 1960; The Queen of Air and Darkness, 1971; Tomorrow's Children, 1947; Day of Burning, 1967; Journeys End, 1957; Epilogue, 1962; The Sheriff of Canyon Gulch - with **Gordon R. Dickson**, 1951; A World Named Cleopatra - an essay by **Poul Anderson**, 1974; Challenge and Response - an essay by Sandra Miesel; and Her Strong Enchantments Failing - an essay by Patrick McGuire, 1974.

81. The Long Way Home. Published by Panther Books, London, 1975. Softcover. A re-titled re-issue of No World of Their Own, 1955, with changes in the text.

82. Star Prince Charlie. With **Gordon R. Dickson**. Published by G. P. Putnam's Sons, New York City, 1975. Hardcover.

83. World Without Stars. Published by Dennis Dobson, London, 1975. First hardcover edition.

84. The Best of Poul Anderson. Published by Pocket Books, New York City, 1976. Softcover. Pocket Book 80671. This contains: Foreword: Recollecting Anderson by Barry N. Malzberg; Introduction by **Poul Anderson**; The Longest Voyage, 1960; The Barbarian, 1956; The Last of the Deliverers, 1958; My Object All Sublime, 1961; Sam Hall, 1953; Kyrie, 1968; The Fatal Fulfillment, 1970; Hiding Place, 1961; and The Sky People, 1959.

85. Homebrew. Published by NESFA Press, Cambridge, Massachusetts, 1976. Hardcover limited edition. Herein: Foreword by **Poul Anderson**; House Rule, 1976; and A Philosophical Dialogue, 1971; along with the following essays: Science Fiction and Freedom, 1969; Notes Toward a Definition of Science Fiction, 1971; The Archetypical Holmes, 1968; A Blessedness of Saints, 1962; Uncleavish Truethinking, 1960; Lost Secrets Revealed, 1972; Herrings, 1959; Two Songs, 1976; and poems: Ballade of an Artificial Satellite, 1958; The First Love,

1960; Upon the Occasion of Being Asked to Argue That Love and Marriage Are Incompatible, 1973; and Limericks, 1976.

86. We Claim These Stars. Published by Dennis Dobson, London, 1976. First hardcover edition.

87. The Winter of the World. Published by Nelson Doubleday - The Science Fiction Book Club, Garden City, New York, 1976. Hardcover.

88. War of the Wing-Men. Published by Gregg Press, Boston, 1976. First hardcover edition.

89. Mirkheim. Published by Berkley Books, New York City, 1977. Softcover.

90. Star Prince Charlie. With **Gordon R. Dickson**. Published by Berkley Books, New York City, 1977. Softcover. First revised edition.

91. The People of the Wind. Published by Gregg Press, Boston, 1977. First hardcover edition.

92. Two Worlds. Published by Gregg Press, Boston, 1978. Hardcover. An omnibus edition, this gathers: Question and Answer - also known as Planet of No Return, 1954; and World Without Stars, 1967.

93. The Earth Book of Stormgate. Published by Berkley/Putnam, New York City, 1978. Hardcover. This contains: The Man Who Counts, 1958; The Problem of Pain, 1973; Wings of Victory, 1972; A Little Knowledge, 1971; Margin of Profit, 1956; Day of Burning, 1967; Esau, 1978; Lodestar, 1973; The Season of Forgiveness, 1973; and Wingless, 1978.

94. The Avatar. Published by Berkley/Putnam, New York City, 1978. Hardcover.

95. The Night Face and Other Stories. Published by Gregg Press, Boston, 1978. Hardcover. Herein: Introduction by **Poul Anderson**; Starfog, 1967; The Sharing of Flesh, 1968; A Tragedy of Errors, 1968; and The Night Face, 1978.

96. The Peregrine. Published by Ace Books, New York City, 1978. Softcover. A re-titled re-issue of Star Ways, 1956.

97. A Stone in Heaven. Published by Ace Books, New York City, 1979. Softcover.

98. The Demon of Scattery. With Mildred Downey Broxon. Published by Ace Books, New York City, 1979. Softcover.

99. The Merman's Children. Published by Berkley/Putnam, New York City, 1979. Hardcover.

100. Conan the Rebel. Published by Bantam Books, New York City, 1980. Softcover.

101. The Devil's Game. Published by Pocket Books, New York City, 1980. Softcover.

102. The Earth Book of Stormgate One. Published by the New English Library - NAL Books, London, 1980. Softcover. Herein: The Earth Book of Stormgate, 1980; Wings of Victory, 1972; The Problem of Pain, 1973; How to be Ethnic in One Easy Lesson, 1973; Margin of Profit, 1956; Esau, 1978; and The Season of Forgiveness, 1973.

103. The Earth Book of Stormgate Two. Published by the New English Library - NAL Books, London, 1980. Softcover.

104. The Golden Horn - The Last Viking. Published by Zebra Books, New York City, 1980. Softcover.

105. The Road of the Sea Horse - The Last Viking. Published by Zebra Books, New York City, 1980. Softcover.

106. The Sign of the Raven - The Last Viking. Published by Zebra Books, New York City, 1980. Softcover.

107. The Earth Book of Stormgate Three. Published by the New English Library - NAL Books, London, 1981. Softcover. Herein: A Little Knowledge, 1971; Day of Burning, 1967; Lodestar, 1973; Wingless, 1978; and Rescue on Avalon, 1973.

108. Explorations. Published by Tor Books - Tom Doherty Associates, New York City, 1981. Softcover. This contains: Introduction by **Poul Anderson**; The Saturn Game, 1981; The Bitter Bread, 1975; The Ways of Love, 1979; The Voortrekkers, 1974; Epilogue, 1962; and Starfog, 1967.

109. Winners. Published by Pinnacle Books, New York City, 1981. Softcover. Herein: No Truce with Kings, 1963; The Longest Voyage, 1960; The Sharing of Flesh, 1968; The Queen of Air and Darkness, 1971; and Goat Song, 1972.

110. Fantasy. Published by Tor Books - Tom Doherty Associates, New York City, 1981. Softcover. This contains: House Rule, 1976; The Tale of Hauk, 1972; A Logical Conclusion, 1960; The Valor of Cappen Varra, 1957; The Gate of the Flying Knives, 1979; The Barbarian, 1956; Interloper, 1951; Pact - writing as Winston P. Sanders, 1959; Superstition, 1956; The Visitor, 1974; and Bullwinch's Mythology, 1981; along with the following essays: Of PIGS and MEN, 1972; On Thud and Blunder, 1978; and Fantasy in the Age of Science, 1981; and Afterword: An Invitation to Elfland by Sandra Miesel, 1981.

111. The Dark Between the Stars. Published by Berkley Books, New York City, 1981. Softcover. Herein: Foreword by **Poul Anderson**; The Sharing of Flesh, 1969; Fortune Hunter, 1972; Eutopia, 1967; The Pugilist, 1973; Night Piece, 1961; The Voortrekkers, 1974; Gibraltar Falls, 1875; Windmill, 1973; and Call Me Joe, 1957.

112. The Psychotechnic League. Published by Pinnacle Books, New York City, 1981. Softcover. Herein: Foreword by Sandra Miesel; Author's Note by **Poul Anderson**; Marius, 1957; Un-Man, 1953; The Sensitive Man, 1954; The Big Rain, 1954; and Afterword by Sandra Miesel.

113. The Guardians of Time. Published by Tor Books - Tom Doherty Associates, New York City, 1982. Softcover. Revised edition of the 1960 collection.

114. The Rebel Worlds - with - A Knight of Ghosts and Shadows. Published by Signet Books - The New American Library, New York City, 1982. Softcover.

Poul Anderson

115. The Gods Laughed. Published by Tor Books - Tom Doherty Associates, New York City, 1982. Softcover. Herein: The Martyr, 1960; Night Piece, 1961; When Half-Gods Go, 1953; Peek! I See You!, 1968; Details, 1956; Captive of the Centaurianess, 1952; The Soldier from the Stars, 1955; The Word to Space, 1960; and A Little Knowledge, 1971.

116. Starship. Published by Tor Books - Tom Doherty Associates, New York City, 1982. Softcover. Herein: Foreword by Sandra Miesel; Gypsy, 1950; Star Ship, 1950; Virgin Planet, 1957; Teucan, 1954; The Pirate, 1968; and The Chapter Ends, 1954; along with A Chronology of the Psychotechnic Series - and essay by Sandra Miesel.

117. Cold Victory. Published by Tor Books - Tom Doherty Associates, New York City, 1982. Softcover. Herein: Foreword by Sandra Miesel; Quixote and the Windmill, 1950; The Troublemakers, 1953; Holmgang, 1955; Cold Victory, 1957; What Shall It Profit?, 1956; and Brake, 1957.

118. New America. Published by Tor Books - Tom Doherty Associates, New York City, 1982. Softcover. This contains: My Own, My Native Land, 1974; Passing the Love of Women, 1974; A Fair Exchange, 1974; To Promote the General Welfare, 1975; The Queen of Air and Darkness, 1971; Home, 1966; and Our Many Roads to the Stars - an essay, 1975.

119. Maurai and Kith. Published by Tor Books - Tom Doherty Associates, New York City, 1982. Softcover. This contains: The Sky People, 1959; Progress, 1962; Windmill, 1973; Ghetto, 1954; and The Horn of Time the Hunter, 1963.

120. The People of the Wind - with - The Day of Their Return. Published by Signet Books - New American Library, New York City, 1982. Softcover.

121. There Will Be Time- with - The Dancer from Atlantis. Published by Signet Books - New American Library, New York City, 1982. Softcover.

122. The Winter of the World - with - The Queen of Air and Darkness and Other Stories. Published by Signet Books - New American Library, New York City, 1982. Softcover.

123. Time Patrolman. Published by Tor Books - Tom Doherty Associates, New York City, 1983. Softcover. Herein: Ivory and Apes and Peacocks, 1983; and The Sorrow of Odin the Goth, 1983.

124. The Long Night. Published by Tor Books - Tom Doherty Associates, New York City, 1983. Softcover. Herein: Prologue by Sandra Miesel; The Star Plunderer, 1952; Outpost of Empire, 1967; A Tragedy of Errors, 1968; The Sharing of Flesh, 1968; and Starfog, 1967; along with A Chronology of Technic Civilization - an essay by Sandra Miesel, 1983

125. Conflict. Published by Tor Books - Tom Doherty Associates, New York City, 1983. Softcover. This contains: Time Lag, 1961; High Treason, 1966; The Alien Enemy, 1968; The Pugilist, 1973; I Tell You, It's True, 1972; Kings Who Die, 1962; A Man to My Wounding, 1968; Among Thieves, 1957; Details, 1956; and The Turning Point, 1983.

126. Orion Shall Rise. Published by Phantasia Press, West Bloomfield, Michigan, 1983. Hardcover.

127. Hoka! With **Gordon R. Dickson**. Published by Simon and Schuster, New York City, 1983. Softcover. Herein: Prologue by **Poul Anderson** and **Gordon R. Dickson**; Joy in Mudville, 1955; Undiplomatic Immunity, 1957; Full Pack - Hokas Wild, 1957; The Napoleon Crime, 1983; and Afterword - Hokas! By Sandra Miesel writing as S*ndr* M**s*.

128. Annals of the Time Patrol. Published by Nelson Doubleday - The Science Fiction Book Club, Garden City, New York, 1984. Hardcover. Omnibus edition, this gathers: The Guardians of Time, 1981; and Time Patrolman, 1983.

129. The Unicorn Trade. With Karen Anderson. Published by Tor Books - Tom Doherty Associates, New York City, 1984. Softcover. Herein: The Unicorn Trade - a poem by Karen Anderson, 1971; Fairy Gold by **Poul Anderson**, 1984; Ballade of an Artificial Satellite - a poem by **Poul Anderson**, 1958; The Innocent Arrival, 1958; Dead Phone, 1964; The Kitten, 1976; Single Jeopardy, 1958; A Feast for the Gods, 1971; Extract From the English Edition of a Guide Michelin, 1973; Treaty in Tartessos by Karen Anderson, 1963; A Philosophical Dialogue by **Poul Anderson**, 1971; Landscape with Sphinxes by Karen Anderson, 1962; The Blessedness of Saints - an essay by **Poul Anderson**, 1962; The Piebald Hippogriff by Karen Anderson, 1962; and The Coasts of Faerie by Karen Anderson, 1982; along with a collection of poems by Karen Anderson; Professor James - a poem by Poul and Karen Anderson, 1965; and Planh on the Death of Willy Ley: June 23, 1969 - a poem by **Poul Anderson**, Karen Anderson and Tim Courtney.

130. Past Times. Published by Tor Books - Tom Doherty Associates, New York City, 1984. Softcover. Herein: Wildcat, 1958; Welcome, 1960; The Nest, 1953; Eutopia, 1967; The Little Monster, 1973; The Light, 1957; The Discovery of the Past, 1984; and Flight to Forever, 1950.

131. The Game of Empire. Published by Baen Books, New York City, 1985. Softcover.

132. Dialogue with Darkness. Published by Tor Books - Tom Doherty Associates, New York City, 1985. Softcover. This contains: A Chapter of Revelation, 1972; Sister Planet, 1959; The Life of Your Time - writing as Michael Karageorge, 1965; Time Heals, 1949; SOS, 1970; Conversation in Arcady, 1963; Dialogue, 1976; and The Communicators, 1970.

133. New America: Grassy Knoll. Published by Tor Books - Tom Doherty Associates, New York City, 1985. Softcover.

134. Roma Mater. With Karen Anderson. Published by Baen Books, New York City, 1986. Softcover.

135. Gallicenae. With Karen Anderson. Published by Baen Books, New York City, 1987. Softcover.

136. Dahut. With Karen Anderson. Published by Baen Books, New York City, 1987. Softcover.

137. The Dog and the Wolf. With Karen Anderson.

Published by Baen Books, New York City, 1988. Softcover.

138. The King of Ys. With Karen Anderson. Published by Nelson Doubleday - The Science Fiction Book Club, Garden City, New York, 1988. Hardcover.

139. The King of Ys Volume One. With Karen Anderson. Published by Nelson Doubleday - The Science Fiction Book Club, Garden City, New York, 1988. Hardcover. An omnibus edition, this gathers: Roma Mater, 1986; and Gallicenae, 1987; along with background material.

140. The King of Ys Volume Two. With Karen Anderson. Published by Nelson Doubleday - The Science Fiction Book Club, Garden City, New York, 1988. Hardcover. An omnibus edition, this gathers: Dahut, 1987; and The Dog and the Wolf, 1988; along with background material.

141. The Year of the Ransom. Published by Walker and Company, New York City, 1988. Hardcover.

142. Space Folk. Published by Baen Books, New York City, 1989. Softcover. Herein: Cradle Song - a poem, 1989; Pride, 1985; Vulcan's Forge, 1983; Escape the Morning, 1966; Quest, 1983; Wherever You Are - writing as Winston P. Sanders, 1959; Elementary Mistake - writing as Winston P. Sanders, 1967; Symmetry, 1989; Hunter's Moon, 1978; Deathwomb, 1983; Horse Trader, 1953; Murphy's Hall - with Karen Anderson, 1971; and Commentary - an essay, 1989.

143. The Boat of a Million Years. Published by Tor Books - Tom Doherty Associates, New York City, 1989. Hardcover.

144. No Truce with Kings. Published by Tor Books - Tom Doherty Associates, New York City, 1989. Softcover. Tor Double Book 5. Bound with Ship of Shadows, 1963, by **Fritz Leiber**.

145. Saturn Game. Published by Tor Books - Tom Doherty Associates, New York City, 1989. Softcover. Tor Double Book 14. Bound with Iceborn by Gregory Benford and Paul A. Carter.

146. The Longest Voyage. Published by Tor Books - Tom Doherty Associates, New York City, 1991. Softcover. Tor Double Book 30. Bound with Slow Lightning by Steven Popkes.

147. Inconstant Star. Published by Baen Books, New York City, 1991. Softcover. Herein: Iron, 1988; and Inconstant Star, 1990.

148. Alight in the Void. Published by Tor Books - Tom Doherty Associates, New York City, 1991. Softcover. Herein: Introduction by **Poul Anderson**; Flight to Forever, 1950; Terminal Quest, 1951; The Star Beast, 1950; Earthman, Beware!, 1951; Son of the Sword, 1952; and Ballade of an Artificial Satellite - a poem, 1958.

149. Kinship with the Stars. Published by Tor Books - Tom Doherty Associates, New York City, 1991. Softcover. This contains: Foreword by **Poul Anderson**; A Bicycle Built for Brew, 1958; Inside Straight, 1955; The Critique of Impure Reason, 1962; Backwardness, 1958; Duel on Syrtis, 1951; Escape from Orbit, 1962; Enough Rope, 1953; The Live Coward, 1956; and Uncleftish Beholding - an essay, 1989.

150. The Armies of Elfland. Published by Tor Books - Tom Doherty Associates, New York City, 1991. Softcover. Herein: Foreword by **Poul Anderson**; The Queen of Air and Darkness, 1971; House Rule, 1976; The Tale of Hauk, 1977; Fairy Gold, 1984; The Valor of Cappen Varra, 1957; The Gate of the Flying Knives, 1979; The Barbarian, 1956; and A Feast for the Gods - written with Karen Anderson, 1971.

151. The Shield of Time. Published by Tor Books - Tom Doherty Associates, New York City, 1991. Hardcover. This contains: The Stranger That is Within Thy Gates, 1991; Women and Horses and Power and War, 1991; Before the Gods That Made the Gods, 1991; Beringia, 1991; Riddle Me This, 1991; and Amazement of the World, 1991.

152. The Time Patrol. Published by Tor Books - Tom Doherty Associates, New York City, 1991. Hardcover. Herein: Time Patrol, 1955; Brave to Be a King, 1959; Gibraltar Falls, 1975; The Only Game in Town, 1960; Delenda Est, 1955; Ivory and Apes and Peacocks, 1983; The Sorrow of Odin the Goth, 1983; Star of the Sea, 1991; and The Year of the Ransom, 1988.

153. Flandry. Published by Baen Books, New York City, 1993. Softcover. An omnibus edition, this gathers: A Circus of Hells, 1970; and The Rebel Worlds, 1969.

154. Harvest of Stars. Published by Tor Books - Tom Doherty Associates, New York City, 1993. Hardcover.

155. The Stars Are Also Fire. Published by Tor Books - Tom Doherty Associates, New York City, 1995. Hardcover.

156. Harvest the Fire. Published by Tor Books - Tom Doherty Associates, New York City, 1995. Hardcover.

157. All One Universe. Published by Tor Books - Tom Doherty Associates, New York City, 1996. Hardcover. Herein: Introduction by **Poul Anderson**; In Memoriam, 1992; Strangers, 1988; The Visitor, 1974; Fortune Hunter, 1972; Wolfram, 1975; The Forest, 1985; The Voortrekkers, 1974; Rokuro, 1991; The House of Sorrows, 1989; Losers' Night, 1996; and Requiem for a Universe, 1987; along with the following essays: Uncleftish Beholding, 1989; Science Fiction and History, 1989; Neptune Diary, 1990; John Campbell, 1996; Rudyard Kipling, 1996; Johannes V. Jensen, 1981; and Wellsprings of Dream, 1996.

158. The Fleet of Stars. Published by Tor Books - Tom Doherty Associates, New York City, 1997. Hardcover.

159. War of the Gods. Published by Tor Books - Tom Doherty Associates, New York City, 1997. Hardcover.

160. Hoka! Hoka! Hoka! With **Gordon R. Dickson**. Published by Baen Books, New York City, 1998. Softcover. Herein: Prologue by **Poul**

Poul Anderson

Anderson and **Gordon R. Dickson**; The Sherriff of Canyon Gulch, 1951; Don Jones, 1957; In Hoka Signo Vinces, 1953; The Adventure of the Misplaced Hound, 1953; Yo Ho Hoka!, 1955; The Tiddlywink Warriors, 1955; Joy in Mudville, 1955; Undiplomatic Immunity, 1957; and Mysterious Message, 1957; along with a series of Interludes.

161. Starfarers. Published by Tor Books - Tom Doherty Associates, New York City, 1998. Hardcover.

162. Operation Luna. Published by Tor Books - Tom Doherty Associates, New York City, 1999. Hardcover.

163. Operation Otherworld. Published by Nelson Doubleday - The Science Fiction Book Club, Garden City, New York, 1999. An omnibus edition, this gathers: Operation Chaos, 1971; and Operation Luna, 1999.

164. Genesis. Published by Tor Books - Tom Doherty Associates, New York City, 2000. Hardcover.

165. Virgin Planet - with - Star Ways. Published by Baen Books, New York City, 2000. Softcover.

166. Hokas Pokas! With **Gordon R. Dickson**. Published by Baen Books, New York City, 2000. Softcover. This contains: Full Pack - Hokas Wild, 1957; The Napoleon Crime, 1983; and Star Prince Charlie, 1975.

167. The Imperial Stars. Published by Nelson Doubleday - The Science Fiction Book Club, Garden City, New York, 2000. An omnibus edition, this gathers: Ensign Flandry, 1966; The Rebel Worlds, 1969; and A Circus of Hells, 1970.

168. Mother of Kings. Published by Tor Books - Tom Doherty Associates, New York City, 2001. Hardcover.

169. The Sound and the Furry: The Complete Hoka Stories. With **Gordon R. Dickson**. Published by Nelson Doubleday - The Science Fiction Book Club, Garden City, New York, 2001. Hardcover. An omnibus edition that gathers: Hoka! Hoka! Hoka!, 1998; and Hokas Pokas, 2000.

170. Going for Infinity. Published by Tor Books - Tom Doherty Associates, New York City, 2002. Hardcover. Herein: Introduction by **Poul Anderson**; The Saturn Game, 1981; Gypsy, 1950; Sam Hall, 1953; Death and the Knight, 1995; Journeys End, 1957; The Horn of Time the Hunter, 1963; The Master Key, 1964; The Problem of Pain, 1973; Quest, 1983; Windmill, 1973; Three Hearts and Three Lions, 1961; Epilogue, 1962; Dead Phone - written with Karen Anderson, 1964; Goat Song, 1972; Kyrie, 1968; A Midsummer Tempest, 1974; The Shrine for Lost Children, 1999; and The Queen of Air and Darkness, 1971.

171. For Love and Glory. Published by Tor Books - Tom Doherty Associates, New York City, 2003. Hardcover.

172. Three Hearts and Three Lions - with - The Broken Sword. Published by Victor Gollancz, London, 2003. Hardcover.

173. To Outlive Eternity and Other Stories. Published by Baen Books, New York City, 2007. Softcover. Herein: To Outlive Eternity, 1967; No Truce with Kings, 1963; Progress, 1962; Un-Man, 1953; The Big Rain, 1954; After Doomsday, 1961; and Epilogue, 1962.

174. The Van Rijn Method: The Technic Civilization Saga 1. Published by Baen Books, New York City, 2008. Hardcover. Herein: Planets and Profits: Introducing Nicholas Van Rijn and the Polesotechnic League by Hank Davis; The Saturn Game, 1981; Wings of Victory, 1972; The Problem of Pain, 1973; Margin of Profit - revised version, 1978; How to Be Ethnic in One Easy Lesson, 1973; The Three-Cornered Wheel, 1963; A Sun Invisible, 1966; The Season of Forgiveness, 1973; The Man Who Counts, 1958; Esau, 1978; Hiding Place, 1961; and A Chronology of Technic Civilization - an essay by Sandra Miesel, 2008.

175. David Falkayn: Star Trader. Published by Baen Books, New York City, 2009. Hardcover. Herein: Introduction: High Profits and High Adventure by Hank Davis; A Historical Reflection, 1966; Territory, 1963; Plus Ca Change Plus C'est La Meme Chose, 1966; The Trouble Twisters, 1965; Day of Burning, 1967; The Master Key, 1964; Satan's World, 1969; A Little Knowledge, 1971; Lodestar, 1973; and Afterword by **Poul Anderson**; along with Chronology of Technic Civilization - an essay by Sandra Miesel, 2008.

176. The Rise of the Terran Empire. Published by Baen Books, New York City, 2009. Softcover. Herein: Introduction by Hank Davis; Mirkheim, 1977; Wingless, 1977; Rescue on Avalon, 1973; The Star Plunderer, 1952; Sargasso of Lost Starships, 1951; and The People of the Wind, 1973; along with Chronology of Technic Civilization - an essay by Sandra Miesel, 2008.

***

ANTHOLOGIES

1. West by One and by One: An Anthology of Irregular Writings by The Scowrers and Molly Maguires of San Francisco and The Trained Cormorants of Los Angeles County. Edited anonymously. Privately printed in San Francisco, 1965.

2. Nebula Award Stories Four. Published by Doubleday & Company, Garden City, New York, 1969. Hardcover. Herein: Introduction by **Poul Anderson**; The Science Fiction Novel in 1968 - an essay by Willis E. McNelly; Mother to the World by Richard Wilson, 1968; The Dance of the Changer and the Three by Terry Carr, 1968; The Planners by **Kate Wilhelm**, 1968; Sword Game by H. H. Hollis, 1968; The Listeners by James E. Gunn, 1968; and Dragonrider by **Anne McCaffrey**, 1967; along with the following memorial essays: Anthony Boucher by J. Francis McComas; Rosel George Brown by Daniel F. Galouye; Bernard I. Kahn by **John W. Campbell**; Groff Conklin by **Isaac Asimov**; Anna Kavan by **Brian W. Aldiss**; Gerald Kersh by Harlan Ellison; Frank Owen by Emil Petaja; Edison Marshall by

Alva Rogers; Mervyn Peake by **Michael Moorcock**; Stuart Palmer by Karen Anderson; Arthur Sellings by Ted Carnell; A. A. Wyn by **Donald A. Wollheim**; and Harl Vincent by Forrest J. Ackerman.

3. A World Named Cleopatra. With Roger Elwood. Published by Pyramid Books, New York City, 1977. Softcover. Herein: Introduction: A World Named Cleopatra by **Poul Anderson**, 1974; A Serpent in Eden by **Poul Anderson**, 1973; Faber Master by Michael Orgill, 1977; Among the Mountains by Jack Dann, 1977; and Wayside World by George Zebrowski, 1977.

4. Mercenaries of Tomorrow. With Martin H. Greenberg and Charles G. Waugh. Published by Critic's Choice, New York City, 1985. Softcover. This contains: Introduction by **Poul Anderson**; The Soldier from the Stars by **Poul Anderson**, 1955; Brothers by **Gordon R. Dickson**, 1973; But Loyal to His Own by David Drake, 1975; That Share of Glory by C. M. Kornbluth, 1952; Priest of the Baraboo by Barry B. Longyear, 1979; Blacksword by Andrew J. Offutt, 1959; The Quest by Kit Read, 1960; Mercenary by Mack Reynolds, 1962; Recruiting Station by **A. E. van Vogt**, 1942; and Straw by **Gene Wolfe**, 1975.

5. Time Wars. With Martin H. Greenberg and Charles G. Waugh. Published by Tor Books - Tom Doherty Associates, New York City, 1986. Softcover. Herein: Introduction by **Poul Anderson**; Frost and Thunder by Randall Garrett, 1979; Gunpowder God by H. Beam Piper, 1964; Amphiskios by John D. MacDonald, 1949; Delenda Est by **Poul Anderson**, 1955; Dragonrider by **Anne McCaffrey**, 1967; The Timesweepers by Keith Laumer, 1969; Run from the Fire by **Harry Harrison**, 1975; and Skirmish on a Summer Morning by Bob Shaw, 1976.

6. Terrorists of Tomorrow. With Martin H. Greenberg and Charles G. Waugh. Published by Critic's Choice, New York City, 1986. Softcover. This contains: Introduction by **Poul Anderson**; The Oracle by Robert Bloch, 1971; Pacifist by Mack Reynolds, 1964; A Time of the Fourth Horseman by Chelsea Quinn Yarbro, 1972; Truck Driver by Robert Chilson, 1972; Satan's Shrine by Daniel F. Galouye, 1954; The Missing Man by Katherine MacLean, 1971; The Movement by Gregory Benford, 1970; The Wind from a Burning Woman by Greg Bear, 1978; How It Was When the Past Went Away by **Robert Silverberg**, 1969; Sam Hall by **Poul Anderson**, 1953; Waterclap by **Isaac Asimov**, 1970; and Very Proper Charlies by Dean Ing, 1978.

7. Space Wars. With Martin H. Greenberg and Charles G. Waugh. Published by Tor Books - Tom Doherty Associates, New York City, 1988. Softcover. Herein: Introduction by **Poul Anderson**; Jackal's Meal by **Gordon R. Dickson**, 1969; Hero by Joe Haldeman, 1972; Shadow on the Stars by Algis Budrys, 1954; The Crime and the Glory of Commander Suzdel by Cordwainer Smith, 1964; Hide and Seek by **Arthur C. Clarke**, 1949; Or Battle's Sound by **Harry Harrison**, 1968; The Highest Treason by Randall Garrett, 1961; No Truce with Kings by **Poul Anderson**, 1963; The Alien Rulers by Piers Anthony, 1968; and Too Soon to Die by Tom Godwin, 1957.

8. The Night Fantastic. With Karen Anderson. Published by DAW Books, New York City, New York City, 1991. Softcover. DAW Collector's Book 848. This contains: Introduction by Poul and Karen Anderson; The Pathways of Desire by **Ursula K. Le Guin**, 1979; Dream Done Green by Alan Dean Foster, 1974; Midnight by the Morphy Watch by **Fritz Leiber**, 1974; All on a Golden Afternoon by Robert Bloch, 1956; The Helmet by Barry N. Malzberg, 1973; Dreams Are Sacred by Peter Phillips, 1948; Dreaming is a Private Thing by **Isaac Asimov**, 1955; The Monarch of Dreams by Thomas Wentworth Higginson, 1886; The Circle of Zero by Stanley G. Weinbaum, 1936; The Soft Predicament by **Brian W. Aldiss**, 1969; Heartstop by George Alec Effinger, 1974; The Detective of Dreams by **Gene Wolfe**, 1980; Jade Blue by Edward Bryant, 1971; Something Wild is Loose by **Robert Silverberg**, 1971; and The Visitor by **Poul Anderson**, 1974.

***

NON-FICTION

1. Is There Life on Other Worlds? Published by Crowell-Collier, New York City, 1963. Hardcover.

2. Thermonuclear Warfare. Published by Monarch Books, Derby, Connecticut, 1963. Softcover. Monarch Book MS15.

3. How to Build a Planet. With Stephen L. Gillett. Published by Pulphouse Publishing, Eugene, Oregon, 1991. Softcover.

***

RELATED

1. A Checklist of Poul Anderson. By Roger G. Peyton. Privately printed in Birmingham, England, 1965. Softcover.

2. The Magazine of Fantasy and Science Fiction - Special Poul Anderson Issue - April 1971. Published by Mercury Press, Cornwall Connecticut, 1971. Softcover. This contains: The Queen of Air and Darkness by **Poul Anderson**; Profile: **Poul Anderson** by **Gordon R. Dickson**; **Poul Anderson**: The Enduring Explosion - an essay by **James Blish**; and a **Poul Anderson** bibliography; along with all the usual features.

3. The Collector's Poul Anderson: Complete Bibliographic Data for the Completist and Future History Guide. By David Allen Stever and Andrew Adams Whyte. Published by Paratime Press, Boston, 1976. Softcover.

4. Against Time's Arrow: The High Crusade of Poul Anderson. By Sandra Miesel. Published by R. Reginald The Borgo Press, San Bernardino, California, 1978. Softcover.

5. Poul Anderson: Myth-Master and Wonder-Weaver: An Interim Bibliography 1947 - 1982. By George Benson. Published by Galactic Central, United States, 1982. Softcover.

Gordon R. Dickson.

Gordon Rupert Dickson was born in Edmonton, Alberta on November 1st, 1923 and died in Minneapolis, Minnesota from complications brought on by asthma on January 31st, 2001.

When he was 13, in 1936, his father died and his mother took him to the States. During World War Two, he was in the army. And when he graduated from the University of Minnesota, where he had met **Poul Anderson**, it was with a BA in Creative Writing.

Still, it wasn't until 1950 that he published his first story. A collaboration with **Poul Anderson** called Trespass!, it appeared in the Spring 1950 issue of Fantastic Story Quarterly, edited by Sam Merwin Jr. This was primarily a pulp reprint magazine and Trespass! was one of the few original pieces that Merwin used (the only other original was by himself), putting it in the issue with: The Hidden World by Edmond Hamilton, 1929; The Molten Bullet by Anthony Rud, 1937; Red Shards on Ceres by Raymond Z. Gallun, 1937; The Star Slaver by Sam Merwin writing as Carter Sprague; The Ideal by Stanley G. Weinbaum, 1935; Death at the Observatory by John Russell Fearn, 1938; A Visit to Venus by Festus Pragnell, 1934; Cosmic Stage by Robert Arthur, 1939; and Children of the Ray by J. Harvey Haggard, 1934.

In May 1951, he published another story with **Poul Anderson**, the first piece in their Hoka series, Heroes Are Made, also known as The Sheriff of Canyon Gulch, in Other Worlds Science Stories, edited by Raymond A. Palmer. But just prior to that he had cracked Astounding Science Fiction with The Friendly Man, February 1951, along with: I Tell You Three Times by Raymond F. Jones; Historical Note by Murray Leinster; Assignment in the Unknown by Frank Quattrocchi; Franchise by Kris Neville; Hideaway by F. L. Wallace; and Fair Prey by J. D. Lucey.

He followed that up with The Error of Their Ways, July 1951, and The Monkey Wrench in August 1951.

John W. Campbell approved.

Dickson was on his way.

Written with Poul Anderson, Earthman's Burden tends to be his highest priced book for collectors. It goes for around $400.00.

Pen names used: Gordon Dickson; and G. Dickson.

***

AWARDS

1965. Hugo Award for the best short fiction, Soldier, Ask Not - Galaxy Magazine, October 1964.
1966. Nebula Award for the best novelette, Call Him Lord - Analog, May 1966.
1975. The Skylark, Edward E. Smith Memorial Award for Imaginative Fiction.
1977. August Derleth Fantasy Award for best novel, The Dragon and the George.
1981. Hugo Award for best novelette, The Cloak and the Staff - Analog, August 1980.
1981. Hugo Award for best novella, Lost Dorsai - Destinies, February/March 1980.

***

FILM AND TELEVISION.

1. The Flight of Dragons. This film was based on The Dragon and the George, 1976, along with Peter Dickinson's novel, The Flight of Dragons. An animated feature, released in the U.S. in 1986, it was directed by Jules Bass and Arthur Rankin Jr. and starred: Victor Buono; James Gregory; James Earl Jones; Harry Morgan; John Ritter; Larry Storch; Don Messick; Bob McFadden; Ed Peck; Jack Lester; Alexandra Stoddart; and Nellie Bellflower.

***

RADIO

1. Lulungameena. This 1954 story was used on X Minus One on May 29th, 1956.

2. Telepathic. Based on Speak No More, this was used by **John W. Campbell** on his show, Exploring Tomorrow on May 7th, 1958.

***

NOVELS AND COLLECTIONS

1. Alien from Arcturus. Published by Ace Books, New York City, 1956. Softcover. Ace Double D-139. Bound with Atom Curtain by Nick Boddie Williams.

2. Mankind on the Run. Published by Ace Books, New York City, 1956. Softcover. Ace Double D-164. Bound with The Crossroads of Time by **Andre Norton**.

3. Earthman's Burden. With **Poul Anderson**. Published by Gnome Press, New York City, 1957. Hardcover. Herein: The Sherriff of Canyon Gulch, 1951; Interlude, 1957; Don Jones, 1957; Interlude II, 1957; In Hoka Signo Vinces, 1953; Interlude III, 1957; The Adventure of the Misplaced Hound, 1953; Interlude IV, 1957; Yo Ho Hoka!, 1955; Interlude V, 1957; The Tiddlywink Warriors, 1955; Mysterious Message, 1957; and Postlude, 1957.

4. The Genetic General. Published by Ace Books, New York City, 1960. Softcover. Ace Double D-449. Bound with Time to Teleport by **Gordon R. Dickson**.

5. Time to Teleport. Published by Ace Books, New York City, 1960. Softcover. Ace Double D-449. Bound with The Genetic General by **Gordon R. Dickson**.

6. Secret Under the Sea. Published by Holt Rinehart and Winston, New York City, 1960. Hardcover.

7. Delusion World. Published by Ace Books, New York City, 1961. Softcover. Ace Double F-119. Bound with Spacial Delivery by **Gordon R. Dickson**.

8. Spacial Delivery. Published by Ace Books, New York City, 1961. Softcover. Ace Double F-119. Bound with Delusion World by **Gordon R. Dickson**.

9. Naked to the Stars. Published by Pyramid Books, New York City, 1961. Softcover. Pyramid Book F-682.

10. Necromancer. Published by Doubleday & Company, Garden City, New York, 1962. Hardcover.

11. Secret Under Antarctica. Published by Holt, Rinehart and Winston, New York City, 1963. Hardcover.

12. No Room for Man. Published by Macfadden Books, New York City, 1963. Softcover. Re-titled re-issue of Necromancer, 1962.

13. Secret Under the Caribbean. Published by Holt, Rinehart and Winston, New York City, 1964. Hardcover.

14. Space Winners. Published by Holt, Rinehart and Winston, New York City, 1965. Hardcover.

15. The Alien Way. Published by Bantam Books, New York City, 1965. Softcover. Bantam Book F2941.

16. Mission to Universe. Published by Berkley Books, New York City, 1965. Softcover. Berkley Book F1147.

17. The Space Swimmers. Published by Berkley Books, New York City, 1967. Softcover. Berkley Book X1371.

18. Soldier, Ask Not. Published by Dell Books, New York City, 1967. Softcover. Dell Book 8090.

19. Planet Run. With Keith Laumer. Published by Doubleday & Company, Garden City, New York, 1967. Hardcover.

20. The Space Swimmers. Published by Sidgwick and Jackson, London, 1968. First hardcover edition.

21. None but Man. Published by Doubleday & Company, Garden City, New York, 1969. Hardcover.

22. Spacepaw. Writing as Gordon Dickson. Published by E. P. Dutton, New York City, 1969. Hardcover.

23. Wolfling. Published by Dell Books, New York City, 1969. Softcover. Dell Book 9633.

24. Danger - Human. Published by Doubleday & Company, Garden City, New York, 1970. Hardcover. Herein: Call Him Lord, 1966; Lulungomeena, 1954; Black Charlie, 1954; Flat Tiger, 1956; Dolphin's Way, 1964; The Quarry, 1958; Danger - Human!, 1957; An Honorable Death, 1961; And Then There Was Peace, 1962; Zeepsday, 1956; James, 1955; The Steel Brother, 1952; and The Man from Earth, 1964.

25. Hour of the Horde. Published by E. P. Dutton, New York City, 1970. Hardcover.

26. Mutants. Published by The Macmillan Company, New York City, 1970. Hardcover. Herein: Introduction by **Gordon R. Dickson**; Warrior, 1965; Of the People, 1955; Danger - Human!, 1957; Rehabilitated, 1961; Listen, 1952; Roofs of Silver, 1962; By New Hearth Fires, 1959; Idiot Solvant, 1962; The Immortal, 1965; Miss Prinks, 1954; and Home from the Shore, 1963.

27. Sleepwalker's World. Published by J. B. Lippincott, New York City, 1971. Hardcover.

28. The Tactics of Mistake. Published by Doubleday & Company, Garden City, New York, 1971. Hardcover.

29. The Pritcher Mass. Published by Doubleday & Company, Garden City, New York, 1972. Hardcover.

30. The Outposter. Published by J. B. Lippincott, New York City, 1972. Hardcover.

31. Alien Art. Published by E. P. Dutton, New York City, 1973. Hardcover.

32. The R-Master. Published by J. B. Lippincott, New York City, 1973. Hardcover.

33. The Star Road. Published by Doubleday & Company, Garden City, New York, 1973. Hardcover. This contains: Whatever Gods There Be, 1961; Hilifter, 1963; Building on the Line, 1968; The Christmas Present, 1958; 3-Part Puzzle, 1962; On Messenger Mountain, 1964; The Catch, 1959; Jackal's Meal, 1969; and The Mousetrap, 1952.

34. The Book of Gordon R. Dickson. Published by DAW Books, New York City, 1973. Softcover. DAW Collector's Book 55. UQ1055. Herein: Call Him Lord, 1966; Lulungomeena, 1954; Black Charlie, 1954; Flat Tiger, 1956; Dolphin's Way, 1964; The Quarry, 1958; Danger - Human!, 1957; An Honorable Death, 1961; And Then There Was Peace, 1962; Zeepsday, 1956; James, 1955; The Steel Brother, 1952; and The Man from Earth, 1964.

35. Ancient, My Enemy. Published by Doubleday & Company, Garden City, New York, 1974. Hardcover. This contains: Ancient, My Enemy, 1969; The Odd Ones, 1955; The Monkey Wrench, 1951; Tiger Green, 1965; The Friendly Man, 1951; Love Me True, 1961; Our First Death, 1955; In the Bone, 1966; and The Bleak and Barren Land, 1953.

36. Gremlins, Go Home. With Ben Bova. Published by St. Martin's Press, New York City, 1974. Hardcover.

37. Star Prince Charlie. With **Poul Anderson**. Published by G. P. Putnam's Sons, New York City, 1975. Hardcover.

38. Three to Dorsai! Published by Nelson Doubleday - The Science Fiction Book Club, Garden City, New York, 1975. Hardcover. An omnibus editions, this gathers: Necromancer, 1962; Tactics of Mistake, 1971; and Dorsai!, 1975.

39. The Dragon and the George. Published by Nelson Doubleday - The Science Fiction Book Club, Garden City, New York, 1976. Hardcover.

40. Dorsai! Published by DAW Books, New York City, 1976. Softcover. DAW Collector's Book 181. UW1218. This started life as The Genetic General, 1960. Revised and expanded edition.

Gordon R. Dickson

41. The Lifeship. With **Harry Harrison**. Harper and Row, New York City, 1976. Hardcover.

42. Mission to Universe. Published by Ballantine Books, New York City, 1977. Softcover. Ballantine Book 25703. Revised and expanded edition of the 1965 paperback original.

43. Star Prince Charlie. With **Poul Anderson**. Published by Berkley Books, New York City, 1977. Berkley Book 03078. Revised edition.

44. Timestorm. Published by St. Martin's Press, New York City, 1977. Hardcover.

45. Home from the Shore. Published by Ace Books, New York City, 1978. Softcover.

46. Pro. Published by Ace Books, New York City, 1978. Softcover.

47. The Far Call. Published by The Dial Press, New York City, 1978. Hardcover.

48. Gordon R. Dickson's SF Best. Published by Dell Books, New York City, 1978. Softcover. This contains: Introduction - The Quiet Giant by Spider Robinson; Foreword by James R. Frenkel; Hilifter, 1963; Brother Charlie, 1958; Act of Creation, 1957; Idiot Solvant, 1962; Call Him Lord, 1966; Tiger Green, 1965; Of the People, 1955; Dolphin's Way, 1964; and In the Bone, 1966.

49. The Spirit of Dorsai. Published by Ace Books, New York City, 1979. Softcover. This contains: Prologue by **Gordon R. Dickson**; Amanda Morgan, 1979; Interlude, 1979; Brothers, 1973; and Epilogue, 1979.

50. Masters of Everon. Published by Nelson Doubleday - Science Fiction Book Club, Garden City, New York, 1979. Hardcover.

51. Lost Dorsai. Published by Ace Books, New York City, 1980. Softcover. Herein: Lost Dorsai, 1980; Warrior, 1965; The Final Encyclopedia: An Excerpt, 1980; and The Plume and the Sword - an essay by Sandra Meisel.

52. In Iron Years. Published by Doubleday & Company, Garden City, New York, 1980. Hardcover. Herein: In Iron Years, 1974; Homecoming, 1959; A Taste of Tenure, 1961; The Hours Are Good, 1960; Gifts, 1958; Zeepsday, 1956; and Things Which Are Caesar's, 1972.

53. Love Not Human. Published by Ace Books, New York City, 1981. Softcover. This contains: Black Charlie, 1954; Moon, June, Spoon, Croon, 1955; The Summer Visitors, 1960; Listen, 1952; Graveyard, 1953; Fido, 1957; The Breaking of Jerry McCloud, 1953; Love Me True, 1961; The Christmas Present, 1958; It Hardly Seems Fair, 1960; and The Monster and the Maiden, 1976.

54. Alien Art - with - Arcturus Landing. Published by Ace Books, New York City, 1981. Softcover.

55. Time to Teleport - with - Delusion World. Published by Ace Books, New York City, 1982. Softcover.

56. Planet Run. With Keith Laumer. Published by Tor Books - Tom Doherty Associates, New York City, 1982. Softcover. This reprints the 1967 collaborative novel and includes the novella Once There Was a Giant, 1968, by Laumer and the short story, Call Him Lord, 1966, by Dickson.

57. Hoka! With **Poul Anderson**. Published by Simon and Schuster, New York City, 1983. Softcover. Herein: Prologue by **Poul Anderson** and **Gordon R. Dickson**; Joy in Mudville, 1955; Undiplomatic Immunity, 1957; Full Pack - Hokas Wild, 1957; The Napoleon Crime, 1983; and Afterword - Hokas! By Sandra Miesel writing as S*ndr* M**s*.

58. The Man from Earth. Published by Tor Books - Tom Doherty Associates, New York City, 1983. Softcover. Herein: Ancient, My Enemy, 1969; Call Him Lord, 1966; Danger - Human!, 1957; In the Bone, 1966; Love Me True, 1961; The Bleak and Barren Land, 1953; The Man from Earth, 1964; The Odd Ones, 1955; The Steel Brother, 1952; and Tiger Green, 1965.

59. The Final Encyclopedia. Published by Tor Books - Tom Doherty Associates, New York City, 1984. Hardcover.

60. The Last Master. Published by Tor Books - Tom Doherty Associates, New York City, 1984. Softcover. A re-titled re-issue of The R-Master, 1973.

61. Jamie the Red. With Roland J. Green. Published by Ace Books, New York City, 1984. Softcover.

62. Survival. Published by Baen Books, New York City, 1984. Softcover. Herein: Preface by Sandra Miesel; The Question, 1958; Our First Death, 1955; No Shield from the Dead, 1953; The Underground, 1955; After the Funeral, 1959; The General and the Axe, 1957; Button, Button, 1960; Rescue, 1954; Friend for Life, 1957; Carry Me Home, 1954; Jean Dupres, 1970; and Breakthrough Gang, 1965.

63. Dickson! Published by NESFA Publishing, Boston, 1984. Hardcover. Introduction by **Poul Anderson**; Out of the Darkness, 1961; The Man in the Mailbag, 1959; The Hard Way, 1963; Perfectly Adjusted, 1955; Steel Brother, 1952; A Conversation with **Gordon R. Dickson** - interview by Sandra Miesel, 1978; and The Child Cycle Status Report - an essay by **Gordon R. Dickson**, 1979.

64. Steel Brother. Published by Tor Books - Tom Doherty Associates, New York City, 1985. Softcover. A re-titled re-issue of Dickson! 1984.

65. Beyond the Dar Al-Harb. Published by Tor Books - Tom Doherty Associates, New York City, 1985. Softcover. This contains: Beyond the Dar al-Harb, 1985; On Messenger Mountain, 1964; and Things Which Are Caesar's, 1972.

66. Invaders! Published by Baen Books, New York City, 1985. Softcover. Herein: Introduction by Sandra Miesel; The Error of Their Ways, 1951; Itco's Strong Right Arm, 1954; Fellow of the Bees, 1954; Ricochet on Miza, 1952; The Law-Twister Shorty, 1971; An Ounce of Emotion, 1965; Roofs of Silver, 1962; The Invaders, 1952; and Rogue Bolo - an excerpt by Keith Laumer, 1985.

67. Forward! Published by Baen Books, New York City, 1985. Softcover. Herein: Introduction by Sandra Miesel; Building on the Line, 1968; Babes in the Wood, 1985; Napoleon's Skullcap, 1962; Rescue Mission, 1957; Robots are Nice?, 1985; The Dreamsman, 1959; The R of A, 1959; One on Trial, 1960; The Queer Critter, 1954; Twig, 1974; The Game of Five, 1960; The Guided Tour - a poem, 1985; and Cloud Warrior - an excerpt by Patrick Tilley, 1985.

68. Secrets of the Deep. Published by Critic's Choice, New York City, 1985. Softcover. An omnibus edition, this gathers: Secret Under the Sea, 1960; Secret Under Antarctica, 1963; and Secret Under The Caribbean, 1964.

69. Mindspan. Published by Baen Books, New York City, 1986. Softcover. Herein: Miss Prinks, 1954; Fleegl of Fleegl, 1958; Show Me the Way to Go Home, 1952; Rex and Mr Rejilla, 1958; Who Dares a Bulbur Eat?, 1962; The Faithful Wilf, 1963; A Wobble in Wockii Futures, 1965; Sleight of Wit, 1961; Operation P-Button, 1970; Soupstone, 1965; Catch a Tartar, 1965; A Matter of Technique, 1958; and Ballad of the Shoshonu - a poem, 1961.

70. The Last Dream. Published by Baen Books, New York City, 1986. Softcover. Herein: Introduction by Sandra Miesel; St Dragon and the George, 1957; The Present State of Igneos Research, 1975; Ye Prentice and Ye Dragon - a poem, 1975; A Case History, 1954; The Girl Who Played Wolf, 1958; Salmanazar, 1962; With Butter and Mustard, 1957; The Amulet, 1959; The Haunted Village, 1961; The Three, 1953; Walker Between the Planes, 1970; and The Last Dream, 1960.

71. The Man the Worlds Rejected. Published by Tor Books - Tom Doherty Associates, New York City, 1986. Softcover. Herein: The Man the Worlds Rejected, 1953; Jackal's Meal, 1969; Minotaur, 1961; Turnabout, 1955; Strictly Confidential, 1956; In Iron Years, 1974; The Monster and the Maiden, 1976; and A Matter of Perspective - and essay by **Gordon R. Dickson** and **Frank Kelly Freas**, 1971.

72. The Dorsai Companion. Published by Ace Books, New York City, 1986. Softcover. Herein: Introduction: See a Thousand Years by **Gordon R. Dickson**; Amanda Morgan, 1979; Warrior, 1965; Lost Dorsai, 1980; and Brothers, 1973; along with the following essays by Sandra Miesel: Stars of the Childe Cycle, 1986; Worlds of the Childe Cycle, 1986; The Morgans, 1986; The Graemes, 1986; Chronology of the Childe Cycle, 1986; and When Your Contract Takes You to the Dorsai World, 1986.

73. The Forever Man. Published by Ace Books, New York City, 1986. Hardcover.

74. The Stranger. Published by Tor Books - Tom Doherty Associates, New York City, 1987. Softcover. This contains: God Bless Them, 1982; James, 1955; E Gubling Dow, 1959; The Stranger, 1952; The Friendly Man, 1951; MX Knows Best, 1957; The Quarry, 1958; 3-Part Puzzle, 1962; IT: Out of Darkest Jungle, 1964; Tempus Non Fugit, 1957; Cloak and Stagger, 1957; And Then There Was Peace, 1962; and The Catch, 1959.

75. Way of the Pilgrim. Published by Ace Books, New York City, 1987. Softcover.

76. In the Bone: The Best Science Fiction of Gordon R. Dickson. Published by Ace Books, New York City, 1987. Softcover. Herein: Twig, 1974; God Bless Then, 1982; Hilifter, 1963; Brother Charlie, 1958; Act of Creation, 1957; Idiot Solvant, 1962; Call Him Lord, 1966; Tiger Green, 1965; Of the People, 1955; Dolphin's Way, 1964; and In the Bone, 1966.

77. Survival. Published by Pocket Books, New York City, 1987. Softcover.

78. The Multiple Men. Published by Tor Books - Tom Doherty Associates, New York City, 1987. Softcover.

79. The Stranger. Published by Tor Books - Tom Doherty Associates, New York City, 1987. Softcover.

80. Guided Tour. Published by Tor Books - Tom Doherty Associates, New York City, 1988. Softcover. Herein: Guided Tour - a poem, 1959; The Monkey Wrench, 1951; The Star-Fool, 1951; Hilifter, 1963; Counter-Irritant, 1953; The Last Voyage, 1958; An Ounce of Emotion, 1965; Rehabilitated, 1961; Lulungomeena, 1954; Time Grabber, 1952; I've Been Trying to Tell You, 1959; Flat Tiger, 1956; The Rebels, 1954; and The Mousetrap, 1952.

81. The Chantry Guild. Published by Ace Books, New York City, 1988. Hardcover.

82. Beginnings. Published by Baen Books, New York City, 1988. Softcover. Herein: Foreword by **Gordon R. Dickson**; The Brown Man - a poem, 1984; Danger - Human!, 1957; Cloak and Stagger, 1957; 3-Part Puzzle, 1962; The Seats of Hell, 1960; Listen, 1952; Soldier, Ask Not, 1964; Strictly Confidential, 1956; Powerway Emergency!, 1988; Idiot Solvant, 1962; and On Messenger Mountain, 1964; finishing with an untitled poem, 1984.

83. Ends. Published by Baen Books, New York City, 1988. Softcover. This contains: Foreword by **Gordon R. Dickson**; A Outrance - a poem, 1984; Computers Don't Argue, 1965; By New Hearth Fires, 1959; Ancient, My Enemy, 1969; Turnabout, 1955; An Honorable Death, 1961; Lost Dorsai, 1980; Last Voyage, 1958; Call Him Lord, 1966; And Then There Was Peace, 1962; Whatever Gods There Be, 1961; Minotaur, 1961; Enter a Pilgrim, 1974; and Armageddon - a poem, 1984.

84. The Earth Lords. Published by Ace Books, New York City, 1989. Softcover.

85. None but Man. Published by Baen Books, New York City, 1989. Softcover. This re-prints None but Man from 1969 and includes the short story Hilifter, 1963.

86. The Dragon Knight. Published by Tor Books - Tom Doherty Associates, New York City, 1990. Hardcover.

87. Wolf and Iron. Published by Tor Books - Tom Doherty Associates, New York City, 1990. Hardcover.

88. Naked to the Stars - with - The Alien Way.

Gordon R. Dickson

Published by Tor Books - Tom Doherty Associates, New York City, 1990. Softcover. Tor Double 31.

89. Young Bleys. Published by Tor Books - Tom Doherty Associates, New York City, 1991. Hardcover.

90. The Dragon on the Border. Published by Nelson Doubleday - The Science Fiction Book Club, Garden City, New York, 1992. Hardcover.

91. The Dragon at War. Published by Ace Books, New York City, 1992. Hardcover.

92. Lost Dorsai: The New Dorsai Companion. Published by Tor Books - Tom Doherty Associates, New York City, 1993. Softcover. Herein: Lost Dorsai, 1980; Warrior, 1965; and A Childe Cycle Concordance - excerpt by David W. Wixon.

93. The Dragon, the Earl and the Troll. Published by Ace Books, New York City, 1994. Hardcover.

94. Other. Published by Tor Books - Tom Doherty Associates, New York City, 1994. Hardcover.

95. The Magnificent Wilf. Published by Baen Books, New York City, 1995. Hardcover.

96. The Dragon and the Djinn. Published by Ace Books, New York City, 1996. Hardcover.

97. The Dragon and the Gnarly King. Published by Tor Books - Tom Doherty Associates, New York City, 1997. Hardcover.

98. The Dragon in Lyonesse. Published by Tor Books - Tom Doherty Associates, New York City, 1998. Hardcover.

99. Hoka! Hoka! Hoka! With **Poul Anderson**. Published by Baen Books, New York City, 1998. Softcover. Herein: Prologue by **Poul Anderson** and **Gordon R. Dickson**; The Sherriff of Canyon Gulch, 1951; Don Jones, 1957; In Hoka Signo Vinces, 1953; The Adventure of the Misplaced Hound, 1953; Yo Ho Hoka!, 1955; The Tiddlywink Warriors, 1955; Joy in Mudville, 1955; Undiplomatic Immunity, 1957; and Mysterious Message, 1957; along with a series of Interludes.

100. The Dragon and the Fair Maid of Kent. Published by Tor Books - Tom Doherty Associates, New York City, 2000. Hardcover.

101. Hokas Pokas! With **Poul Anderson**. Published by Baen Books, New York City, 2000. Softcover. This contains: Full Pack - Hokas Wild, 1957; The Napoleon Crime, 1983; and Star Prince Charlie, 1975.

102. The Right to Bear Arms. Published by Baen Books, New York City, 2000. Softcover. An omnibus edition, this gathers: Spacial Delivery, 1961; Spacepaw, 1969; and the novelette, The Law-Twister Shorty, 1971.

103. The Sound and the Furry: The Complete Hoka Stories. With **Poul Anderson**. Published by Nelson Doubleday - The Science Fiction Book Club, Garden City, New York, 2001. Hardcover. An omnibus edition that gathers: Hoka! Hoka! Hoka!, 1998; and Hokas Pokas, 2000.

104. Hour of the Gremlins. With Ben Bova. Published by Baen Books, New York City, 2002. Softcover. An omnibus edition, this gathers: Gremlins Go Home, 1974 - with Ben Bova; Hour of the Horde, 1970; and Wolfling, 1969.

105. Dorsai Spirit. Published by Tor Books - Tom Doherty Associates, New York City, 2002. Hardcover. An omnibus edition, this gathers: Dorsai!/The Genetic General, 1959/1976; and The Spirit of Dorsai, 1979.

106. Four to Dorsai. Published by Nelson Doubleday - The Science Fiction Book Club, Garden City, New York, 2002. Hardcover. An omnibus edition, this gathers: Necromancer, 1962; Tactics of Mistake, 1970; Dorsai!/The Genetic General, 1959/1976; and Soldier, Ask Not, 1967.

107. The Human Edge. Published by Baen Books, New York City, 2003. Softcover. This contains: Introduction: The Dickson Edge by Hank Davis; Danger - Human!, 1957; Sleight of Wit, 1961; In the Bone, 1966; 3-Part Puzzle, 1962; An Ounce of Emotion, 1965; Brother Charlie, 1958; The Gave of Five, 1960; Tiger Green, 1965; The Hard Way, 1963; Jackal's Meal, 1969; On Messenger Mountain, 1964; and The Catch, 1959.

108. Antagonist. With David W. Wixon. Published by Tor Books - Tom Doherty Associates, New York City, 2007. Hardcover.

***

ANTHOLOGIES

1. Rod Serling's Triple W: Witches, Warlocks and Werewolves. Edited anonymously. Published by Bantam Books, New York City, 1963. Softcover. Bantam Book J2623. Herein: Introduction by **Rod Serling**; Hatchery of Dreams by **Fritz Leiber**, 1961; Blind Alley by Malcolm Jameson, 1943; The Final Ingredient by Jack Sharkey, 1960; Wolves Don't Cry by Bruce Elliott, 1954; The Chestnut Beads by Jane Roberts, 1957; The Black Retriever by Charles G. Finney, 1958; The Amulet by **Gordon R Dickson**, 1959; The Mark of the Beast by Rudyard Kipling, 1890; And Not Quite Human by Joe L. Hensley, 1953; Young Goodman Brown by Nathaniel Hawthorne, 1835; The Story of Sidi Nonman - anonymous; and Witch Trials and the Law - an essay by Charles Mackay, 1841.

2. Rod Serling's Devils and Demons. Edited anonymously. Published by Bantam Books, New York City, 1963. Softcover. Bantam Book H3324. This contains: Introduction by **Rod Serling**; Stars, Won't You Hide Me? by Ben Bova, 1966; Pollock and the Porroh Man by **H. G. Wells**, 1895; The Montavarde Camera by Avram Davidson, 1959; Death Cannot Wither by Judith Merril, 1959; A Time to Keep by **Kate Wilhelm**, 1962; Adapted by Carol Emshwiller, 1961; The Four-fifteen Express by Amelia B. Edwards, 1866; The Story of the Goblins Who Stole a Sexton by Charles Dickens, 1836; The Bottle Imp by Robert Louis Stevenson, 1891; Brother Coelestin by Emil Frida, 1963; The Bisara of Pooree by Rudyard Kipling, 1887; The Blue Sphere by Theodore Dreiser,

1914; and The Coach by Violent Hunt, 1914.

3. Combat SF. Published by Doubleday & Company, Garden City, New York, 1975. Hardcover. Herein: Introduction by **Gordon R. Dickson**; Hide and Seek by **Arthur C. Clarke**, 1949; The Last Command by Keith Laumer, 1967; Men of Good Will by Ben Bova and Myron R. Lewis, 1964; The Pair by Joe L. Hensley, 1958; Situation Thirty by Frank M. Robinson, 1951; The Butcher's Bill by David Drake, 1974; Single Combat by Joseph Green, 1964; The Man Who Came Early by **Poul Anderson**, 1956; Patron of the Arts by Fred Saberhagen, 1965; Time Piece by Joe Haldeman, 1970; Ricochet on Miza **by Gordon R. Dickson**, 1952; The Scavengers by James White, 1953; No War, or Battle's Sound by **Harry Harrison**, 1968; The HORARS of War by **Gene Wolfe**, 1970; and Fireproof by **Hal Clement**, 1949.

4. Nebula Winners Twelve. Published by Harper and Row, New York City, 1978. Hardcover. Herein: Introduction by **Gordon R. Dickson**; Houston, Houston, Do You Read? By James Tiptree, Jr, 1976; Breath's a Ware That Will Not Keep by Thomas F. Monteleone, 1975; The Bicentennial Man by **Isaac Asimov**, 1976; A Crowd of Shadows by Charles L. Grant, 1976; Tricentennial by Joe Haldeman, 1976; In the Bowl by John Varley, 1975; SF in the Marketplace - an essay by Algis Budrys, 1978; and The Academic Viewpoint - an essay by James E. Gunn, 1978.

5. The Harriers: Of War and Honor. Published by Baen Books, New York City, 1991. Softcover. Herein: Of War and Codes and Honor by **Gordon R. Dickson** and Chelsea Quinn Yarbro, 1991; Into the Hot and Moist by Steve Perry, 1991; and Tonight We Improvise by S. N. Lewitt, 1991.

6. Blood and War: The Harriers Book Two. Published by Baen Books, New York City, 1993. Softcover. This contains: The Noble Savages by David Drake, 1993; Down Among the Dead Men by **Gordon R. Dickson** and Chelsea Quinn Yarbro, 1993; and Mission of Mercy by Christopher Stasheff, 1993.

Eric Frank Russell

Eric Frank Russell.

Eric Frank Russell was born on January 6th, 1905, in Sandhurst, England, and died on February 28th, 1978. In 1934, while he was living near Liverpool, he met another science fiction fan, Leslie J. Johnson, and, together, they encouraged each other to write.

Russell took to it and began sending stories off to America. His first published story, The Saga of Pelican West, was in Astounding Stories, February 1937, then edited by F. Orlin Tremaine, where he shared space with: At the Perihelion by Willy Ley writing as Robert Willey; Beyond Which Limits by Nat Schachner; The Blue Spot - part 2 of 2 by **Jack Williamson**; The Comet by K. Raymond; Cosmic Fever by Amelia Reynolds Long; Fractional Ego by Clifton B. Kruse; The Stellar Exodus by Oliver Saari; and The Reign of the Long Tusks by Stanton A. Coblentz.

Next came The Great Radio Peril in Astounding's April 1937 issue, with: Water for Mars by Ross Rocklynne; The Endless Chain by A. Macfadyen; The Eye of Madness by Ray Rooney; Minus Planet by John D. Clark; Down the Dimensions by Nelson S. Bond; Sands of Time by P. Schuyler Miller; and Winter on the Planet by Nelson Tremaine writing as Warner Van Lorne.

The third one was The Prr-r-eet, in the UK magazine, Tales of Wonder, Issue 1, Summer 1937, where it was featured with: Superhuman by John Russell Fearn writing as Geoffrey Armstrong; Seeds from Space by John Russell Fearn; Revolt on Venus by W. P. Cockcroft; Man of the Future by Festus Pragnell; Monsters on the Moon by Festus Pragnell writing as Francis Parnell; Invaders from the Atom by Maurice G. Hugi; and The Perfect Creature by John Wyndham writing as John Beynon.

Russell and Johnson, working together, wrote Seeker of Tomorrow and mailed it off. The story showed up in the July 1937 issue of Astounding, along with: Dawn-world Echoes by Raymond Z. Gallun; Einleil by R. R. Winterbotham; Frontier of the Unknown by Norman Knight; The Great Ones by Leslie Stone; Quicksilver Unlimited by Harry Walton; Sterile Planet by Nat Schachner; and Zero as a Limit by Robert Moore.

When **John W. Campbell** took over Astounding Stories, and re-named it Astounding Science Fiction, Russell was one of the writers he kept from the old guard.

Russell was hooked. Even during World War Two, while he served with the Royal Air Force, he continued to write and publish stories, including his first novel, Sinister Barrier, which was featured in the first issue of Campbell's Unknown, March 1939.

After the war, writing was all he wanted to do. And it became a full time job.

His most valuable books tend to be Dark Tides, Three to Conquer and Dreadful Sanctuary with all three running between $350.00 and $450.00.

Pen names used: Duncan H. Munro; Maurice G. Hugi; Niall Wilde; Webster Craig; E. F. Russell; Naille Wilde; and Maurice A. Hugi.

***

AWARDS

1955. Hugo Award for the best short story, Allamagoosa - Astounding, May 1955.
1985. Prometheus Hall of Fame Award for Best Classic Libertarian SF Novel, The Great Explosion, which had been published in 1962.
2000. Inducted into The Science Fiction Hall of Fame.

***

NOVELS AND COLLECTIONS

1. Sinister Barrier. Published by Fantasy Press, Reading, Pennsylvania, 1948. Hardcover.

2. Dreadful Sanctuary. Published by Fantasy Press, Reading, Pennsylvania, 1951. Hardcover.

3. Sentinels from Space. Published by Bouregy and Curl, New York City, 1953. Hardcover.

4. Sentinels from Space. Published by Ace Books, New York City, 1954. Softcover. Ace Double D-44. Bound with The Ultimate Invader and Other Science Fiction by **Donald A. Wollheim**.

5. Deep Space. Published by Fantasy Press, Reading, Pennsylvania, 1954. Hardcover. A story collection containing: Homo Saps, 1941; Last Blast, 1952; The Undecided, 1949; A Little Oil, 1952; First Person Singular, 1950; Second Genesis, 1951; The Timid Tiger, 1947; The Witness, 1951; and Rainbow's End, 1951.

6. Men, Martians and Machines. Published by Dennis Dobson, London, 1955. Hardcover. A story collection containing: Jay Score, 1941; Mechanistria, 1942; Symbiotica, 1943; and Mesmerica, 1955.

7. Deep Space. Published by Bantam Books, New York City, 1955. Softcover. Bantam Book 1362. This dropped one of the stories from the original edition, First Person Singular, 1950, and kept: Homo Saps, 1941; Last Blast, 1952; The Undecided, 1949; A Little Oil, 1952; Second Genesis, 1951; The Timid Tiger, 1947; The Witness, 1951; and Rainbow's End, 1951.

8. Three to Conquer. Published by Avalon Books, New York City, 1956. Hardcover.

9. Three to Conquer. Published by Ace Books, New York City, 1957. Softcover. Ace Double D-215. Bound with Doomsday Eve by Robert Moore Williams.

10. Wasp. Published by Avalon Books, New York City, 1957. Hardcover.

11. Wasp. Published by Dennis Dobson, London, 1958. First revised edition.

12. The Space Willies. Published by Ace Books, New York City, 1958. Softcover. Ace Double D-315. Bound with Russell's Six Worlds Yonder, a story collection containing: The Waitabits, 1955; Tieline, originally as by Duncan H. Munro, 1955; Top Secret, 1956; Nothing New, 1955; Into Your Tent I'll Creep, 1957; and Diabologic, 1955.

13. Six Worlds Yonder. Published by Ace Books, New York City, 1958. Softcover. Ace Double D-315. Bound with The Space Willies by **Eric Frank Russell**. Six Worlds Yonder, a story collection containing: The Waitabits, 1955; Tieline, 1955, originally as by Duncan H. Munro; Top Secret, 1956; Nothing New, 1955; Into Your Tent I'll Creep, 1957; and Diabologic, 1955.

14. Next of Kin. Published by Dennis Dobson, London, 1959. Hardcover. A revised edition of The Space Willies, 1958.

15. Far Stars. Published by Dennis Dobson, London, 1961. Hardcover. A story collection containing: Legwork, 1956; Diabologic, 1955; Allamagoosa, 1955; The Waitabits, 1955; The Timeless Ones, 1952; and P.S., 1953.

16. The Great Explosion. Published by Dennis Dobson, London, 1962. Hardcover.

17. Dark Tides. Published by Dennis Dobson, London, 1962. Hardcover. A story collection containing: This One's On Me, 1953; The Rhythm of the Rats, 1950; Sole Solution, 1956; The Sin of Hyacinth Peuch, 1952; Bitter End, 1953; Me and My Shadow, 1940; The Ponderer, 1948; Wisel, 1962; I Hear You Calling, 1954; I'm a Stranger Here Myself, 1952; A Matter of Instinct, 1962; and With a Blunt Instrument, 1941; along with an introduction by the author.

18. The Rabble Rousers. Published by Regency Books, New York City, 1963. Softcover. Regency Book RB 317.

19. Dreadful Sanctuary. Published by Lancer Books, New York City, 1963. Softcover. Lancer Book 74-819. First revised edition.

20. With a Strange Device. Published by Dennis Dobson, London, 1964. Hardcover.

21. The Mind Warpers. Published by Lancer Books, New York City, 1965. Softcover. Lancer Book 72-942. A re-issue of With a Strange Device, 1964.

22. Somewhere a Voice. Published by Dennis Dobson, London, 1965. Hardcover. A story collection containing: Dear Devil, 1950; Seat of Oblivion, 1941; U-Turn, 1950, originally as by Duncan H. Munro; Tieline, 1955, originally as by Duncan H. Munro; I Am Nothing, 1952; Displaced Person, 1948; and Somewhere a Voice, 1953.

23. Dreadful Sanctuary. Published by Four Square Books, London, 1967. Softcover. Four Square Book 1719. Newly revised edition.

24. Dreadful Sanctuary. Published by Dennis Dobson, London, 1972. Hardcover. First hardcover edition of the Four Square Revised Edition.

25. Like Nothing on Earth. Published by Dennis Dobson, London, 1975. Hardcover. A story collection containing: Hobbyist, 1947; Exposure, 1950; Into Your Tent I'll Creep, 1957; Nothing New, 1955; Ultima Thule, 1951; and The Mechanical Mice, 1941.

26. The Best of Eric Frank Russell. Published by Del Rey - Ballantine Books, New York City, 1978. Softcover. A story collection containing: The Symbiote of Hooton, an introduction by Alan Dean Foster; and: Mana, 1937; Jay Score, 1941; Homo Saps, 1941; Metamorphosite, 1946; Hobbyist, 1947; Late Night Final, 1948; Dear Devil, 1950; Fast Falls the Eventide, 1952; I Am Nothing, 1952; Weak Spot, 1954; Allamagoosa, 1955; Into Your Tent I'll Creep, 1957; and Study in Still Life, 1959.

27. Design for Great-Day. With Alan Dean Foster. Published by Tor Books - Tom Doherty Associates, New York City, 1995. Hardcover.

28. Major Ingredients: The Selected Short Stories of Eric Frank Russell. Published by NESFA Press, Framingham, Massachusetts, 2000. Hardcover. A story collection containing: Editor's Introduction by Rick Katze; **Eric Frank Russell** by Jack L. Chalker; and: Allamagoosa, 1955; And Then There Were None, 1951; The Army Comes to Venus, 1959; Basic Right, 1958; Dear Devil, 1950; Diabologic, 1955; Fast Falls the Eventide, 1952; Hobbyist, 1947; I Am Nothing, 1952; Into Your Tent I'll Creep, 1957; Jay Score, 1941; Last Blast, 1952; Late Night Final, 1948; A Little Oil, 1952; Meeting on Kangshan, 1965; Metamorphosite, 1946; Minor Ingredient, 1956; Now Inhale, 1959; Nuisance Value, 1957; Panic Button, 1959; Plus X, 1959; A Study in Still Life, 1959; Tieline, 1955; The Timid Tiger, 1947; Top Secret, 1956; The Ultimate Invader, 1954; The Undecided, 1949; U-Turn, 1950; The Waitabits, 1955; and The Man Who (Almost) Never Was, an essay by Mike Resnick.

29. Entities: The Selected Novels of Eric Frank Russell. Published by NESFA Press, Framingham, Massachusetts, 2001. Hardcover. An omnibus edition, containing: Introductions to each novel by Jack L. Chalker; Sinister Barrier, 1948; Call Him Dead - also known as Three to Conquer, 1956; Next of Kin, 1959; Sentinels in Space, 1953; Wasp, 1957; Mana, 1937; Mechanical Mice, 1941; and Leg Work, 1956.

***

NON-FICTION

1. Great World Mysteries. Published by Dennis Dobson, London, 1957. Hardcover.

Theodore Sturgeon

Theodore Sturgeon.

Edward Hamilton Waldo was born on February 26th, 1918 in Staten Island, New York, and died of lung fibrosis in Eugene, Oregon on May 8th, 1985. After his parents divorced, his mother married a gent named Sturgeon and at the age of eight, Edward Hamilton Waldo became, legally, Theodore Hamilton Sturgeon, who sold his first short story, Heavy Insurance, when he was twenty years old.

It was a non-science fiction piece and it was published by McClure's Syndicate in 1938. During the rest of 1938 and through 1939, he went on to publish more non-SF stuff, and then, in the September 1939 issue of Astounding Science Fiction, tucked in amongst: Atmospherics by Victor Valding; Forces Must Balance by Manly Wade Wellman; General Swamp C.I.C. by Frederick Engelhardt; The Last Hope by Don Evans; and Masson's Secret, by Raymond Z. Gallun, came a story called Ether Breather by **Theodore Sturgeon**, his first published foray into science fiction.

That was followed up by Derm Fool which appeared in Campbell's other magazine, Unknown, in March 1940, along with stories by H. W. Guernsey; Robert Arthur; E. A. Grosser; J. Allan Dunn; Malcolm Jameson; and **Jack Williamson**. He was still writing non-SF in almost equal amounts, but by 1941, with Shottle Bop and The Ultimate Egoist, as by E. Hunter Waldo, in the February issue of Unknown, he began to specialize in the fantasy/science fiction/horror stuff that got him inducted into The Science Fiction Hall of Fame in 2000.

At the beginning of his career, he worked at a number of things besides writing. He was a sailor in the merchant marine, drove a bulldozer, managed a hotel, ran a gas station, did a stint in the Army during World War Two, then went on to write advertising copy and to operate as a literary agent. He was also a guitar-playing songwriter who somehow managed to go through five wives, two of them common-law, three of them legally married, and produce seven children.

Signed copies of Without Sorcery, 1948, usually run around $2,500.00 - $3,500.00. Caviar is his next best book, running around $900.00.

Pen names used: Frederick R. Ewing; Billy Watson; Edward Waldo; E. Hunter Waldo; E. Waldo Hunter; Ted Sturgeon; and Ellery Queen.

Sturgeon's Law: Ninety percent of SF is crud, but then, ninety percent of everything is crud.

***

AWARDS

1954. The International Fantasy Award for fiction, More Than Human.
1970. Nebula Award for the best novelette, Slow Sculpture - Galaxy Magazine, February 1970.
1971. Hugo Award for the best short story, Slow Sculpture - Galaxy Magazine, February 1970.
1985. World Fantasy Award for Life Achievement.
2000. Inducted into The Science Fiction Hall of Fame.

***

FILM AND TELEVISION

1. Ordeal in Space. He wrote the teleplay from the **Robert A. Heinlein** story, Ordeal in Space, 1948. It appeared on the TV series Out There on November 4th, 1951, Season 1, Episode 2. It starred: John Ericson; William A. Lee; Joe Mantell; Robert Paige; Rod Steiger; and Howard Wierum.

2. Mewhu's Jet. From his own 1946 story, Sturgeon wrote the teleplay for this. It was used on the television series, Out There, December 9th, 1951, Season 1, Episode 7. It starred: Dennis Alexander; Janie Alexander; John Boruff; Eileen Heckart; Mort Marshall; and Richard McMurray.

3. Verdict from Space. Sturgeon did the story and the teleplay for this Tales of Tomorrow, August 3rd, 1951, Season 1, Episode 1. Directed by Leonard Valenta; it starred: Lon McCallister; Martin Brandt; William Lally; Bernard Lenrow; and Watson White.

4. Enemy Unknown. This was used on Tales of Tomorrow, November 23rd, 1951, Season 1, Episode 12. It starred: Walter Able; Edith Fellows; and Lon McCallister.

5. The Miraculous Serum. Sturgeon wrote the teleplay from this Don Medford Story. It was used on Tales of Tomorrow, June 20th, 1952, Season 1, Episode 38, starring: Lola Albright; Richard Derr; Louis Hector; and Peggy Allison.

6. No Answer. This was used on the Schlitz Playhouse of Stars, December 19th, 1958, Season 8, Episode 7. Directed by Arthur Hiller, it starred: Donald Cook; Barry Kelley; and Keenan Wynn.

7. The Betrayed. He wrote this for The Invaders. It was aired on March 28th, 1967, Season 1, Episode 11. Directed by John Meredyth Lucas, it starred: Roy Thinnes; Laura Devon; Nancy Wickwire; Norman Fell; Ed Begley; Bill Fletcher; Victor Brandt; Ivan Bonar; Joel Fluellen; and others.

8. Shore Leave. This was shown on December 29th, 1966, Season 1, Episode 15 of **Gene Roddenberry's** Star Trek. Directed by Robert Sparr, it starred: William Shatner; Leonard Nimoy; DeForest Kelley; George Takei; Nichelle Nichols; and James Doohan; along with Bruce Mars; Emily Banks; Oliver McGowan; Perry Lopez; Barbara Baldavin; Marcia Brown; Sebastian Tom; and Shirley Bonne.

9. Amok Time. This aired on September 15th, 1967, Season 2, Episode 1 of **Gene Roddenberry's** Star Trek. Directed by Joseph Pevney, it starred: William Shatner; Leonard Nimoy; DeForest Kelley; George Takei; Nichelle Nichols; Walter Koenig; Majel Barrett; and James Doohan; along with Celia Lovsky; Arlene

Martel; Lawrence Montaigne; and Byron Morrow.

10. Killdozer! This 1946 story was filmed for television and shown on February 2nd, 1974. Directed by Jerry London, it starred: Clint Walker; Carl Betz; Neville Brand; James Wainwright; James A. Watson Jr.; and Robert Urich.

11. The Pylon Express. This was from Season 2, Episode 8 of Land of the Lost. Directed by Gordon Wiles, it aired on October 25th, 1975, starring: Spencer Milligan; Wesley Eure; Kathy Coleman; and Philip Paley.

12. A Matter of Minutes. Starring: Adam Arkin; Karen Austin; Adolph Caesar; Marianne Muellerleile; Joanna Johnson; and Alan David Gelman, this was the third segment of The New Twilight Zone, January 24th, 1986, Season 1, Episode 15.

13. A Saucer of Loneliness. This 1953 story aired on The New Twilight Zone, September 27th, 1986, Season 2, Episode 2. Directed by John Hancock, it starred: Shelley Duvall; Richard Libertini; Nan Martin; Edith Diaz; Andrew Masset; Mari Gorman; Myrna White; and others.

14. The Other Celia. From 1957, this story was filmed by the CBC in 2005. Directed by Jon Knautz, it starred: Alan Blenkinsopp; Mike Clark; Jan Crane; Megan Dunlop; Randolph Johnston; Donna Kinch; Sarah Nilson; Nicole White; and Patrick White.

***

RADIO

1. The Sky was Full of Ships. From 1947, this story was used on Beyond Tomorrow as Incident at Switchpath in 1950.

2. The Stars are the Styx. This 1950 story was used on Tales of Tomorrow in 1952 or 1953.

3. Mr. Costello, Hero. This 1953 story was used on X Minus One, July 3rd, 1956.

4. The Stars are the Styx. This 1950 story was used on X Minus One on July 25th, 1956.

5. A Saucer of Loneliness. This 1953 story was used on X Minus One on January 9th, 1957. And it ran again on September 5th, 1957.

6. A Saucer of Loneliness. This 1953 story was used on Future Tense on September 21st, 1973.

7. The Sky was Full of Ships. From 1947, this story was used on Mind Webs on July 28th, 1978.

8. Hurricane Trio. From 1955, this was used on 2000 X.

***

NOVELS AND COLLECTIONS

1. It. Published by The Prime Press, Philadelphia, 1948. Softcover. A promotional item, using just one of the stories from Sturgeon's forthcoming collection, Without Sorcery, there were less than 200 copies printed for The Torcon in 1948.

2. Without Sorcery. Published by The Prime Press, Philadelphia, 1948. Hardcover. A story collection with an introduction by **Ray Bradbury** and a preface by Sturgeon himself, along with: The Ultimate Egoist, 1941, writing as E. Hunter Waldo; It, 1940; Poker Face, 1941; Shottle Bop, 1941; Artnan Process, 1941; Memorial, 1946; Ether Breather, 1939; Butyl and the Breather, 1940; Brat, 1941; Two Percent Inspiration, 1941; Cargo, 1940; Maturity, 1947; and Microcosmic God, 1941.

3. The Dreaming Jewels. Published by Greenberg Publisher, New York City, 1950. Hardcover.

4. More Than Human. Published by Farrar, Straus and Young, New York City, 1953. Hardcover.

5. E Pluribus Unicorn. Published by Abelard Press, New York City, 1953. Hardcover. A story collection: The Silken Swift, 1953; The Professor's Teddy Bear, 1948; Bianca's Hands, 1947; A Saucer of Loneliness, 1953; The World Well Lost, 1953; It Wasn't Syzygy, 1948; The Music, 1953; Scars, 1949; Fluffy, 1947; The Sex Opposite, 1952; Die, Maestro, Die, 1949; Cellmate, 1947; and A Way of Thinking, 1953; along with an essay on Sturgeon by Groff Conklin.

6. Caviar. Published by Ballantine Books, New York City, 1955. Softcover. Ballantine Book 119. A story collection: Bright Segment, 1955; Microcosmic God, 1941; Ghost of a Chance - also known as The Green-Eyed Monster, 1955; Prodigy, 1949; Medusa, 1942; Blabbermouth, 1945; Shadow, Shadow on the Wall, 1951; and Twink, 1955.

7. A Way Home. Published by Funk and Wagnalls, New York City, 1955. Hardcover. A story collection: Introduction by Groff Conklin; Thunder and Roses, 1947; Mewhu's Jet, 1946; And My Fear Is Great, 1953; The Hurkle is a Happy Beast, 1949; Bulkhead, 1955; Hurricane Trio, 1955; Minority Report, 1949; Unite and Conquer, 1948; Special Aptitude, 1951; Tiny and the Monster, 1947; and A Way Home, 1953.

8. A Way Home. Published by Pyramid Books, New York City, 1956. Softcover. Pyramid Book G184. This dropped two stories from the original: And My Fear Is Great, 1953; and Minority Report, 1949; while keeping: Introduction by Groff Conklin; Thunder and Roses, 1947; Mewhu's Jet, 1946; The Hurkle is a Happy Beast, 1949; Bulkhead, 1955; Hurricane Trio, 1955; Unite and Conquer, 1948; Special Aptitude, 1951; Tiny and the Monster, 1947; and A Way Home, 1953.

9. The King and Four Queens. Published by Dell Books, New York City, 1956. Softcover. Dell Book A128. A novelization of the film starring Clark Gable.

10. I, Libertine. Writing as Frederick R. Ewing with Jean Shepherd. Published by Ballantine Books, New York City, 1956. Issued in hardcover and softcover simultaneously. Ballantine Book 165.

11. Thunder and Roses. Published by Michael Joseph, London, 1957. hardcover. A story collection that took it's stories from A Way Home, 1955: Introduction by Groff Conklin; Thunder and Roses, 1947; Mewhu's Jet, 1946; And My Fear Is Great, 1953; The Hurkle is a Happy Beast, 1949; Bulkhead,

Theodore Sturgeon

1955; Tiny and the Monster, 1947; and A Way Home, 1953.

12. The Synthetic Man. Published by Pyramid Books, New York City, 1957. Softcover. Pyramid Book G247. A re-issue of The Dreaming Jewels, 1950.

13. A Touch of Strange. Published by Doubleday & Company, New York City, 1958. Hardcover. A story collection containing: The Pod in the Barrier, 1957; A Crime for Llewellyn, 1957; The Touch of Your Hand, 1953; Affair with a Green Monkey, 1957; Mr. Costello Hero, 1953; The Girl Had Guts, 1957; The Other Celia, 1957; It Opens the Sky, 1957; and A Touch of Strange, 1958.

14. The Cosmic Rape. Published by Dell Books, New York City, 1958. Softcover. Dell Book B120.

15. A Touch of Strange. Published by Berkley Books, New York City, 1959. Softcover. Berkley Book G280. This dropped two stories from the original edition: The Pod in the Barrier, 1957; and Mr. Costello Hero, 1953; while keeping: A Crime for Llewellyn, 1957; The Touch of Your Hand, 1953; Affair with a Green Monkey, 1957; The Girl Had Guts, 1957; The Other Celia, 1957; It Opens the Sky, 1957; and A Touch of Strange, 1958.

16. Aliens 4. Published by Avon Books, New York City, 1959. Softcover. Avon Book T-304. A story collection containing: Killdozer, 1944 - revised version; Cactus Dance, 1954; The Comedians Children, 1958; and The (Widget) The (Wadget) and Boff, 1955.

17. Beyond. Published by Avon Books, New York City, 1960. Softcover. Avon Book T-439. A story collection containing: Need, 1960; Abreaction, 1948; Nightmare Island, 1941; Largo, 1947; The Bones, 1943 - written with James H. Beard; and Like Young, 1960.

18. Venus Plus X. Published by Pyramid Books, New York City, 1960. Softcover. Pyramid Book G544.

19. Voyage to the Bottom of the Sea. Published by Pyramid Books, New York City, 1961. Softcover. Pyramid Book G622.

20. Some of Your Blood. Published by Ballantine Books, New York City, 1961. Softcover. Ballantine Book 458K.

21. Not Without Sorcery. Published by Ballantine Books, New York City, 1961. Softcover. Ballantine Book 506K. A story collection with eight of the stories from Without Sorcery, 1948: It, 1940; Poker Face, 1941; Artnan Process, 1941; Ether Breather, 1939; Butyl and the Breather, 1940; Brat, 1941; Two Percent Inspiration, 1941; and Cargo, 1940

22. The Player on the Other Side. Writing as Ellery Queen. Published by Random House, New York City, 1963. Hardcover.

23. Sturgeon in Orbit. Published by Pyramid Books, New York City, 1964. Softcover. Pyramid Book F-974. A story collection: Introduction by **Theodore Sturgeon**, 1964; Extrapolation, 1954; The Wages of Synergy, 1953; Make Room for Me, 1951; The Heart, 1955; and The Incubi of Parallel X, 1951.

24. And My Fear is Great - with - Baby is Three. Published by Galaxy Publishing, New York City, 1965. Softcover. Galaxy Megabook No. 3. These were originally published in 1953 and 1952.

25. Two Complete Novels. Published by Galaxy Publishing, New York City, 1965. Softcover. Galaxy Megabook. Alternate title for And My Fear is Great with Baby is Three.

26. The Joyous Invasions. Published by Victor Gollancz, London, 1965. Hardcover. A story collection: The (Widget), the (Wadget), and Boff, 1955; The Comedian's Children, 1958; and To Marry Medusa, 1958.

27. Starshine. Published by Pyramid Books, New York City, 1966. Softcover. Pyramid Book X-1543. A story collection containing: Derm Fool, 1940; The Haunt, 1941; Artnan Process, 1941; The World Well Lost, 1953; The Pod and the Barrier, 1957; and How to Kill Aunty, 1961.

28. The Rare Breed. Published by Gold Medal Books - Fawcett Publications, Greenwich, Connecticut, 1966. Softcover. Gold Medal Book d1626. A novelization from the film starring James Stewart and Maureen O'Hara.

29. Starshine. Published by Victor Gollancz, London, 1968. First hardcover edition. A story collection: Derm Fool, 1940; The Haunt, 1941; Artnan Process, 1941; The World Well Lost, 1953; The Pod and the Barrier, 1957; and How to Kill Aunty, 1961.

30. Venus Plus X. Published by Victor Gollancz, London, 1969. First hardcover edition.

31. Sturgeon is Alive and Well. Published by G. P. Putnam's Sons, New York City, 1971. Hardcover. A story collection: Foreword by **Theodore Sturgeon**; To Here and the Easel, 1954; Slow Sculpture, 1970; It's You, 1970; Take Care of Joey, 1971; Crate, 1970; The Girl Who Knew What They Meant, 1970; Jorry's Gap, 1968; It was Nothing - Really, 1969; Brownshoes - also known as The Man Who Learned Loving, 1969; Uncle Fremmis, 1970; The Patterns of Dorne, 1970; and Suicide, 1970.

32. The Worlds of Theodore Sturgeon. Published by Ace Books, New York City, 1972. Softcover. Ace Book 91060. A story collection containing: From Plynck to Planck, 1962, an essay by **Theodore Sturgeon**; The Skills of Xanadu, 1956; There is No Defense, 1948; The Perfect Host, 1948; The Graveyard Reader, 1958; The Other Man, 1956; The Sky Was Full of Ships, 1947; Shottle Bop, 1941; Maturity, 1947; and Memorial, 1946.

33. Sturgeon's West. Published by Doubleday & Company, Garden City, New York, 1973. Hardcover. A story collection: Cactus Dance, 1954; Scars, 1949; The Sheriff of Chayute, 1973; Ride In, Ride Out, with Don Ward, 1973; The Man Who Figured Everything, with Don Ward, 1960; The Waiting Thing Inside, with Don Ward, 1956; Well Spiced, 1948; and Ted Sturgeon's Western Adventure, an essay by Don Ward.

34. To Here and the Easel. Published by Victor Gollancz, London, 1973. Hardcover. A story collection: To Here and the Easel, 1954; Shottle Bop, 1941; The Perfect Host, 1948; There Is No Defense, 1948; The Graveyard Reader, 1958; and The Skills of Xanadu, 1956.

35. Case and the Dreamer. Published by Nelson Doubleday - The Science Fiction Book Club, Garden City, New York, 1974. Hardcover. A story collection containing: If All Men Were Brothers, Would You Let One Marry Your Sister?, 1967; Case and the Dreamer, 1973; and When You Care, When You Love, 1962.

36. Case and the Dreamer and Other Stories. Published by Signet Books - New American Library, New York City, 1974. Softcover. Signet Book Q6074. First printing with that particular title, a story collection containing: If All Men Were Brothers, Would You Let One Marry Your Sister?, 1967; Case and the Dreamer, 1973; and When You Care, When You Love, 1962.

37. The Cosmic Rape - and - To Marry Medusa. Published by Gregg Press, Boston, 1977. Hardcover.

38. Amok Time. This was written for Star Trek and was used on September 15th, 1967, Season 2, Episode 1. In 1978, it was released by Bantam Books, New York City, as a Star Trek Fotonovel, number 12 in the series. Softcover.

39. Visions and Ventures. Published by Dell Books, New York City, 1978. Softcover. A story collection: The Hag Seleen, written with James H. Beard, 1942; The Martian and the Moron, 1949; The Nail and the Oracle, 1965; Won't You Walk..., 1956; Talent, 1953; One Foot and the Grave, 1949; The Touch of Your Hand, 1953; and The Traveling Crag, 1951.

40. The Golden Helix. Published by Nelson Doubleday - The Science Fiction Book Club, Garden City, New York, 1979. Hardcover. A story collection: Introduction by **Theodore Sturgeon**; The Golden Helix, 1954; The Man Who Lost the Sea, 1959; And Now the New..., 1956; The Clinic, 1953; And My Fear Is Great, 1953; The Ultimate Egoist, writing as E. Hunter Waldo, 1941; The Skills of Xanadu, 1956; The Dark Room, 1953; and Yesterday Was Monday, 1941; along with I Say... Ernest..., 1973, an essay by **Theodore Sturgeon**.

41. The Stars Are the Styx. Published by Dell Books, New York City, 1979. Softcover. A story collection: Introduction by **Theodore Sturgeon**; Tandy's Story, 1961; Rule of Three, 1951; The Education of Drusilla Strange, 1954; Granny Won't Knit, 1954; When You're Smiling, 1955; The Claustrophile, 1956; The Other Man, 1956; The Stars Are the Styx, 1950; Occam's Scalpel, 1971; and Dazed, 1971.

42. Maturity: Three Stories by Theodore Sturgeon, including bibliography. Published by Rune Press for Minicon 15, 1979. Hardcover. Sturgeon was the guest of honour. The stories were: Maturity, 1947; The Graveyard Reader, 1958; and Bulkhead, 1955.

43. Alien Cargo. Published by Bluejay Books, Gordonsville, Virginia, 1984. Hardcover. A story collection: Introduction by **Theodore Sturgeon**; It, 1940; Cargo, 1940; Poker Face, 1941; Microcosmic God, 1941; Two Percent Inspiration, 1941; Brat, 1941; Medusa, 1942; The Martian and the Moron, 1949; Shadow, Shadow on the Wall, 1951; The Travelling Crag, 1951; The Touch of Your Hand, 1953; Twink, 1955; Bright Segment, 1955; and Won't You Walk..., 1956.

44. Godbody. Published by Donald I. Fine, New York City, 1986. Hardcover.

45. A Touch of Sturgeon. Published by Simon and Schuster, London, 1987. Hardcover. A story collection containing: Introduction by David Pringle; Killdozer!, 1944; The Sex Opposite, 1952; Mr. Costello, Hero, 1953; The Golden Helix, 1954; When You're Smiling, 1955; And Now the News..., 1956; The Other Celia, 1957; and Slow Sculpture, 1970.

46. To Marry Medusa. Published by Baen Books, New York City, 1987. Softcover. This contains: The Cosmic Rape, 1958; and Killdozer, 1944.

47. The (Widget), the (Wadget) and Boff. Published by Tor Books - Tom Doherty Associates, New York City, 1989. Hardcover. Tor Double Book 9. Bound with The Ugly Little Boy, 1958, also known as Lastborn by **Isaac Asimov**.

48. The Dreaming Jewels - with - The Cosmic Rape - with - Venus Plus X. Published by the Book of the Month Club, New York City, 1990. Hardcover.

49. The Ultimate Egoist: The Complete Short Stories of Theodore Sturgeon - Volume 1. Published by North Atlantic Books, New York City, 1994. Hardcover. This contains: About **Theodore Sturgeon** by **Ray Bradbury**; About **Theodore Sturgeon** by **Arthur C. Clarke**; About **Theodore Sturgeon** by **Gene Wolfe**; Heavy Insurance, 1938; The Heart, 1955; Cellmate, 1947; Fluffy, 1947; Alter Ego, 1994; Mailed through a Porthole, 1994; A Noose of Light, 1994; Strangers on a Train, 1938; Accidentally on Porpoise, 1994; The Right Line, 1994; Golden Day, 1939; Permit Me My Gesture, 1939; Watch My Smoke, 1939; The Other Cheek, 1939; Extraordinary Seaman, 1939; One Sick Kid, 1939; His Good Angel, 1939; Some People Forget, 1939; A God in a Garden, 1939; Fit for a King, 1939; Ex-Bachelor Extract, 1939; East Is East, 1939; Three People, 1939; Eyes of Blue, 1939; Ether Breather, 1939; Her Choice, 1939; Cajun Providence, 1939; Strike Three, 1939; Contact!, 1994; The Call, 1939; Helix the Cat, 1973; To Shorten Sail, 1939; Thanksgiving Again, 1939; Bianca's Hands, 1947; Derm Fool, 1940; He Shuttles, 1940; Turkish Delight, 1939; Niobe, 1994; Mahout, 1940; The Long Arm, 1940; The Man on the Steps, 1940; Punctuational Advice, 1940; Place of Honor, 1940; The Ultimate Egoist, 1941; It, 1940; and Butyl and the Breather, 1940; along with Story Notes by Paul Williams and a poem by Sturgeon called Look About You, 1940.

50. Microcosmic God: The Complete Short Stories of Theodore Sturgeon - Volume 2. Published by North Atlantic Books, New York City, 1995. Hardcover. This contains: Foreword by

Theodore Sturgeon

Samuel R. Delany; Cargo, 1940; Shottle Bop, 1941; Yesterday Was Monday, 1941; Brat, 1941; The Anonymous, 1941; Two Sidecars, 1941; Microcosmic God, 1941; The Haunt, 1941; Completely Automatic, 1941; Poker Face, 1941; Nightmare Island, writing as E. Waldo Hunter, 1941; The Purple Light, writing a E. Waldo Hunter, 1941; Artnan Process, 1941; Biddiver, 1941; The Golden Egg, 1941; Two Percent Inspiration, 1941; and The Jumper, 1942; along with Story Notes by Paul Williams; and an unfinished early draft of Microcosmic God, 1940.

51. Killdozer!: The Complete Short Stories of Theodore Sturgeon - Volume 3. Published by North Atlantic Books, New York City, 1996. Hardcover. This contains: Foreword by **Robert Silverberg**; Blabbermouth, 1945; Medusa, 1942; Ghost of a Chance - also known as The Green-eyed Monster, 1955; The Bones - written with James H. Beard, 1943; The Hag Seleen - written with James H. Beard, 1942; Killdozer! - the revised version, 1959; Abreaction, 1948; Poor Yorick!, 1996; Crossfire, 1996; Noon Gun, 1996; Bulldozer is a Noun, 1996; August Sixth, 1945, 1945; The Chromium Helmet, 1946; Memorial, 1946; and Mewhu's Jet, 1946; along with Story Notes by Paul Williams; and a **Robert A. Heinlein** essay, Killdozer!, as an afterword.

52. Thunder and Roses: The Complete Short Stories of Theodore Sturgeon - Volume 4. Published by North Atlantic Books, New York City, 1997. Hardcover. This contains: Foreword by James Gunn; Tiny and the Monster, 1947; The Sky Was Full of Ships, 1947; Largo, 1947; Thunder and Roses, 1947; It Wasn't Syzygy, 1948; The Blue Letter, 1997; Wham Bop!, 1947; Well Spiced, 1948; Hurricane Trio, 1955; That Low, 1948; Memory, 1948; There Is No Defense, 1948; The Professor's Teddy Bear, 1948; and A Way Home, 1953; along with Story Notes by Paul Williams; and the original second half of Maturity, 1947.

53. The Perfect Host: The Complete Short Stories of Theodore Sturgeon - Volume 5. Published by North Atlantic Books, New York City, 1998. Hardcover. This contains: Foreword by Larry McCaffery; Quietly, 1998; The Music, 1953; Unite and Conquer, 1948; The Love of Heaven, 1948; Till Death Do Us Join, 1948; The Perfect Host, 1948; The Martian and the Moron, 1949; Die, Maestro, Die!, 1949; The Dark Goddess, 1998; Scars, 1949; Messenger, 1949; Minority Report, 1949; Prodigy, 1949; Farewell to Eden, 1949; One Foot and the Grave, 1949; What Dead Men Tell, 1949; and The Hurkle is a Happy Beast, 1949; followed by an essay by **Theodore Sturgeon**.

54. Baby Is Three: The Complete Short Stories of Theodore Sturgeon - Volume 6. Published by North Atlantic Books, New York City, 1999. Hardcover. This contains: Foreword by David Crosby; Shadow, Shadow on the Wall, 1951; The Stars Are the Styx, 1950; Rule of Three, 1951; Make Room for Me, 1951; Special Aptitude, 1951; The Traveling Crag, 1951; Excalibur and the Atom, 1951; The Incubi of Parallel X, 1951; Never Underestimate, 1952; The Sex Opposite, 1952; and Baby Is Three, 1952; along with Story Notes by Paul Williams; and two essays by Sturgeon: Author, Author, 1950; and Men Behind Fantastic Adventures: **Theodore Sturgeon**, 1951.

55. A Saucer of Loneliness: The Complete Short Stories of Theodore Sturgeon - Volume 7. Published by North Atlantic Books, New York City, 2000. Hardcover. This contains: Foreword by Kurt Vonnegut, Jr.; A Saucer of Loneliness, 1953; The Touch of Your Hand, 1953; The World Well Lost, 1953; And My Fear Is Great, 1953; The Wages of Synergy, 1953; The Dark Room, 1953; Talent, 1953; A Way of Thinking, 1953; The Silken-Swift, 1953; The Clinic, 1953; Mr. Costello, Hero, 1953; and The Education of Drusilla Strange, 1954; along with Story Notes by Paul Williams.

56. Selected Stories. Published by Vintage Books, New York City, 2000. Softcover. A story collection: Thunder and Roses, 1947; The Golden Helix, 1954; Mr. Costello, Hero, 1953; Bianca's Hands, 1947; The Skills of Xanadu, 1956; Killdozer! - revised version, 1959; Bright Segment, 1955; The Sex Opposite, 1952; The (Widget), the (Wadget), and Boff, 1955; It, 1940; A Way of Thinking, 1953; and Slow Sculpture, 1970.

57. Bright Segment: The Complete Short Stories of Theodore Sturgeon - Volume 8. Published by North Atlantic Books, New York City, 2002. Hardcover. This contains: Foreword, an essay by William Tenn; Cactus Dance, 1954; The Golden Helix, 1954; Extrapolation, 1954; Granny Won't Knit, 1954; To Here and the Easel, 1954; When You're Smiling, 1955; Bulkhead, 1955; The Riddle of Ragnarok, 1955; Twink, 1955; Bright Segment, 1955; So Near the Darkness, 1955; Clockwise, 1946; and Smoke! - also known as Watch My Smoke, 1947; along with Story Notes by Paul Williams.

58. And Now the News...: The Complete Short Stories of Theodore Sturgeon - Volume 9. Published by North Atlantic Books, New York City, 2003. Hardcover. This contains: Foreword by David G. Hartwell; Won't You Walk..., 1956; New York Vignette, 1999; The Half-Way Tree Murder, 1956; The Skills of Xanadu, 1956; The Claustrophile, 1956; Dead Dames Don't Dial, 1956; Fear Is a Business, 1956; The Other Man, 1956; The Waiting Thing Inside - written with Don Ward, 1956; The Deadly Innocent - written with Don Ward, 1956; And Now the News..., 1956; The Girl Had Guts, 1957; The Other Celia, 1957; Affair with a Green Monkey, 1957; and The Pod in the Barrier, 1957; along with Story Notes by Paul Williams.

59. The Man Who Lost the Sea: The Complete Short Stories of Theodore Sturgeon - Volume 10. Published by North Atlantic Books, New York City, 2005. Hardcover. This contains: Foreword by Jonathan Lethem; A Crime for Llewellyn, 1957; It Opens the Sky, 1957; A Touch of Strange, 1958; The Comedian's Children, 1958; The Graveyard Reader, 1958; The Man Who Told Lies, 1959; The Man Who Lost the Sea, 1959; The Man Who Figured Everything - written with Don Ward, 1960; Like Young, 1960; Night Ride, 1960; Need, 1960; How to Kill Aunty, 1961; and Tandy's Story, 1961; along with Story Notes by Paul Williams.

60. The Nail and the Oracle: The Complete Short Stories of Theodore Sturgeon - Volume 11. Published by North Atlantic Books, New York City, 2007. Hardcover. This contains: Foreword by

Harlan Ellison; Ride In, Ride Out - written with Don Ward, 1973; Assault and Little Sister, 1961; When You Care, When You Love, 1962; Holdup a la Carte, 1964; How to Forget Baseball, 1964; The Nail and the Oracle, 1965; If All Men Were Brothers, Would You Let One Marry Your Sister?, 1967; Runesmith - written with **Harlan Ellison**, 1970; Jorry's Gap, 1968; Brownshoes - also known as The Man Who Learned Loving, 1969; It Was Nothing - Really!, 1969; and Take Care of Joey, 1971; along with Story Notes by Paul Williams.

***

ANTHOLOGIES

1. NEW SOVIET SCIENCE FICTION. Published by Macmillan, New York City, 1979. Hardcover. This contains: The Violet; The Duel; Plot for a Novel; and Escape by Ilya Varshavsky; Share It with Me by Kirill Bulychev; Personality Probe by Dmitri Bilenkin; Theocrates' Blue Window by Gennady Gor; Cheap Sale; and Beware of the Ahs by Vladen Bakhnov; Formula for Immortality by Anatoly Dneprov; Success Algorithm by Vladimir Svachenko; The Pale Neptune Equatin by Mikhail Emtsev and Eremei Parnov; and The Friar of Chikola; and A Provincial's Wing by Vadim Shefner.

***

NON-FICTION

1. Argyll: A Memoir. Published by The Sturgeon Project, United States, 1993. Softcover.

***

RELATED

1. The Magazine of Fantasy and Science Fiction - Special Theodore Sturgeon Issue - September 1962. This special issue featured: When You Care, When You Love by **Theodore Sturgeon**; Theodore Sturgeon's Macrocosm - an essay by **James Blish**; **Theodore Sturgeon** - an essay by Judith Merril; and Fantasy and Science Fiction by **Theodore Sturgeon** - a bibliography by Sam Moskowitz; along with all the usual features.

2. Theodore Sturgeon: A Primary and Secondary Bibliography. By Lahna F. Diskin. Published by G. K. Hall, Boston, 1980. Hardcover.

3, Theodore Sturgeon: Starmont Reader's Guide. By Lahna F. Diskin. Published by Starmont House, Mercer Island, Washington, 1981. Softcover.

4. Theodore Sturgeon. By Lucy Menger. Published by Frederick Unger Publishing, New York City, 1981. Hardcover.

Alfred Bester

-2001-

Alfred Bester.

Alfred Bester was born on December 18th, 1913 in New York City and left this world in Doylestown, Pennsylvania on September 30th, 1987.

He attended the University of Pennsylvania, where he studied humanities and psychology; and he lived in Europe for just over a year during the 1950s. The rest of his time was spent in New York City, until he moved to Pennsylvania with his wife in the early 1980s.

After university, while working for a public relations firm, Bester tried his hand at writing. His first published story was in the April, 1939 issue of Thrilling Wonder Stories, then edited by Mort Weisinger. The story was The Broken Axiom - it won an amateur story contest and part of the prize was publication. Also in that issue was Henry Kuttner's Beyond Annihilation; Experiment by Roscoe Clark; The Jules Verne Express by Eando Binder; Madness from Mars by Clifford D. Simak; Men Must Die by Ward Hawkins; White Barrier by Frank Belknap Long; and Zeoh-X by Ray Cummings.

His next published story was No Help Wanted, in the December, 1939 issue of Thrilling Wonder Stories. And in May, 1942, he cracked Astounding Science Fiction by selling The Push of a Finger to **John W. Campbell**. It appeared with: Asylum by **A. E. van Vogt**; Beyond This Horizon - Part Two - by **Robert A. Heinlein** writing as Anson MacDonald; Forever is Not So Long by Anton Reeds; and Foundation by **Isaac Asimov**. Not bad company for a fledgling author.

But shortly after that, when Mort Weisinger left Thrilling Wonder Stories to get into comic books, Bester went along with him, working for DC and writing scripts for Superman and Green Lantern, as well as working on Lee Falk's comic strips, Mandrake the Magician and The Phantom.

His final published short story during the 1940s was Hell Is Forever, also sold to Campbell, for Unknown Worlds, August, 1942.

After the comic books, he moved on to writing for radio, working on Nick Carter, Master Detective and Charlie Chan, The Shadow, Nero Wolfe and others. It was eight years before he published another short story, The Devil's Invention, also known as Oddy and Id, in the August 1950 issue of Astounding Science Fiction.

Shortly after that, he published some of his most renowned work, The Demolished Man, 1952/53; and The Star My Destination, 1956.

His career was a bit spotty. He stopped writing science fiction in the late fifties to go into television. He returned again to SF during the mid-sixties for a short time before going on to edit Holiday Magazine. That lasted until 1971, when he returned to science fiction yet again. There was another break from 1975 until 1979, and then the final return, when he published a pair of novels.

The lack of quantity in his work is more than made up for by the quality. The style, the innovation... the sheer brilliance...

He once described himself as an "unregenerate optimist." He went on to say that he would never retire, he wanted to die with his head on the typewriter.

In 1987, he fell and broke his hip. He died from complications shortly after learning that he was to receive a 1987 Grand Master Nebula Award in 1988 from the Science Fiction Writers of America.

His highest valued books tend to be Tiger! Tiger! - the British hardcover of The Stars My Destination - and The Demolished Man. These are normally priced between $1,200.00 and $2,000.00.

Pen name used: Sunny Powell.

***

AWARDS

1953. Hugo Award for the best novel, The Demolished Man.
1987. Nebula Grand Master Award.
2001. Inducted into The Science Fiction Hall of Fame.

***

FILM AND TELEVISION

1. Murder and the Android. Based on his 1954 story Fondly Fahrenheit, this was written for the series NBC Sunday Showcase and aired on October 18th, 1959, Season 1, Episode 5. Directed by Alex Marsh, it starred: Martin Ashe; Kevin McCarthy; Suzanne Pleshette; Robert Blackburn; Floyd Ennis; Sono Osato; and Telly Savalas; with Rip Torn as the Android.

2. Turn the Key Deftly. For the series Sunday Showcase, this aired on March 6th, 1960, Season 1, Episode 25. It was directed by George Schaefer and starred: Julie Harris; Maximilian Schell; Francis Lederer; Barbara Bulgakov; Humphrey Davis; Louis Edmonds; and Shaike Ophir.

3. Mr Lucifer. This was written for the show Alcoa Premiere and aired on November 1st, 1962, Season 2, Episode 5. Directed by Alan Crosland Jr, it starred: Elizabeth Montgomery; Milton Frome; Fred Aletter; Joyce Fulifant; Gaylord Cavallaro; George Petrie; and Hal Smith; with Fred Astaire as Mr Lucifer.

***

NOVELS AND COLLECTIONS

1. The Demolished Man. Published by Shasta Publishers, Chicago, 1953. Hardcover.

2. Who He? Published by The Dial Press, New York City, 1953. Hardcover.

3. Tiger! Tiger! Published by Sidgwick and Jackson, London, 1956. Hardcover.

4. The Rat Race. Published by Berkley Books, New York City, 1956. Berkley Book G-19. Softcover.

5. The Stars My Destination. Published by Signet Books - The New American Library, New York City, 1957. Signet Book S1389. Revised version of Tiger! Tiger!, 1956.

6. Starburst. Published by Signet Books - The New American Library, New York City, 1958. Signet Book S1524. Softcover. This contains: Disappearing Act, 1953; Adam and No Eve, 1941; Star Light, Star Bright, 1953; The Roller Coaster, 1953; Oddy and Id, 1950; The Starcomber, 1954; Travel Diary, 1958; Fondly Fahrenheit, 1954; Hobson's Choice, 1952; The Die-Hard, 1958; and Of Time and Third Avenue, 1951.

7. The Dark Side of Earth. Published by Signet Books - The New American Library, New York City, 1964. Signet Book D2474. Softcover. Herein: Time is the Traitor, 1953; The Men Who Murdered Mohammed, 1958; Out of This World, 1964; The Pi Man, 1959; The Flowered Thundermug, 1964; Will You Wait?, 1959; and They Don't Make Life Like They Used To, 1963.

8. An Alfred Bester Omnibus. Published by Sidgwick and Jackson, London, 1967. Hardcover. This gathers: The Demolished Man; Tiger! Tiger!; and The Dark Side of Earth.

9. The Computer Connection. Published by Berkley/Putnam Books, New York City, 1975. Hardcover.

10. Extro. Published by Eyre Methuen, London, 1975. Re-titled version of The Computer Connection, 1975.

11. The Stars My Destination. Published by Gregg Press, Boston, 1975. First hardcover edition.

12. The Light Fantastic. Published by Berkley/Putnam, New York City, 1976. Hardcover. Herein: Disappearing Act, 1953; Ms. Found in a Champagne Bottle, 1968; 5,271,008, 1954; The Men Who Murdered Mohammed, 1958; Hell Is Forever, 1942; Fondly Fahrenheit, 1954; and The Four-Hour Fugue, 1974; along with the essay Comment on Fondly Fahrenheit, 1976.

13. Star Light, Star Bright. Published by Berkley/Putnam, New York City, 1976. Hardcover. Herein: **Alfred Bester** by **Isaac Asimov**, 1973; Adam and No Eve, 1941; Time is the Traitor, 1953; Oddy and Id, 1950; Hobson's Choice, 1952; Star Light, Star Bright, 1953; They Don't Make Life Like They Used To, 1963; Of Time and Third Avenue, 1951; The Pi Man, 1959; Something Up There Likes Me, 1973; and My Affair with Science Fiction - an essay by **Alfred Bester**, 1974.

14. Star Light: The Great Short Fiction of Alfred Bester. Published by Nelson Doubleday, Garden City, New York, 1976. Hardcover. Book Club Code G47. This gathered the stories from The Light Fantastic, 1976; and Star Light, Star Bright, 1976: **Alfred Bester** by **Isaac Asimov**, 1973; Disappearing Act, 1953; Ms. Found in a Champagne Bottle, 1968; 5,271,008, 1954; The Men Who Murdered Mohammed, 1958; Hell Is Forever, 1942; Fondly Fahrenheit, 1954; The Four-Hour Fugue, 1974; Adam and No Eve, 1941; Time is the Traitor, 1953; Oddy and Id, 1950; Hobson's Choice, 1952; Star Light, Star Bright, 1953; They Don't Make Life Like They Used To, 1963; Of Time and Third Avenue, 1951; The Pi Man, 1959; and Something Up There Likes Me, 1973; along with: My Affair with Science Fiction - an essay by **Alfred Bester**, 1974; and the essay Comment on Fondly Fahrenheit, 1976.

15. Golem 100. Published by Simon and Schuster, New York City, 1980. Hardcover.

16. The Deceivers. Published by Simon and Schuster, New York City, 1981. Hardcover.

17. Tender Loving Rage. Published by Tafford Publishing, United States, 1991. Hardcover.

18. Virtual Unrealities: The Short Fiction of Alfred Bester. Published by Vintage Books, New York City, 1997. Softcover. Herein: Introduction by **Robert Silverberg**; Disappearing Act, 1953; Oddy and Id, 1950; Star Light, Star Bright, 1953; 5,271,009, 1954; Fondly Fahrenheit, 1954; Hobson's Choice, 1952; Of Time and Third Avenue, 1951; Time is the Traitor, 1953; The Men Who Murdered Mohammed, 1958; The Pi Man, 1959; They Don't Make Life Like They Used To, 1963; Will You Wait?, 1959; The Flowered Thundermug, 1964; Adam and No Eve, 1941; And 3 1/2 to Go, an unfinished story, 1997; Galatea Galante, 1979; and The Devil Without Glasses, 1997.

19. Psycho Shop. With Roger Zelazny. Published by Vintage Books, New York City, 1998. Softcover. Zelazny completed an unfinished manuscript.

20. Redemolished. Published by iBooks, New York City, 2000. Softcover. Herein: Introduction by Richard Raucci; In Memoriam: **Alfred Bester** - 1913 - 1987 by **Isaac Asimov** and Gregory Benford; The Probable Man, 1941; Hell is Forever, 1942; The Push of a Finger, 1942; The Roller Coaster, 1953; The Lost Child, 2000; I'll Never Celebrate New Year's Again, 2000; Out of This World, 1964; The Animal Fair, 1972; Something Up There Likes Me, 1973; The Four-Hour Fugue, 1974; The Demolished Man: The Deleted Prologue, 2000; and the following articles and essays: Gourmet Dining in Outer Space, 1960; Place of the Month: The Moon, 2000; The Sun, 2000; Science Fiction and the Renaissance Man, 1959; A Diatribe Against Science Fiction, 2000; The Perfect Composite Science Fiction Author, 2000; My Affair with Science Fiction, 1974; John Huston's Unsentimental Journey - an interview with John Huston, 1959; Rex Stout - an interview, 1967; Conversation with Woody Allen - an interview, 1969; **Isaac Asimov** - an interview, 1973; **Robert A.**

Heinlein - an interview, 1973; and Writing and The Demolished Man, 2000.

***

NON-FICTION

1. The Science Fiction Novel. With **Robert A. Heinlein**, C. M. Kornbluth, Basil Davenport, and Robert Bloch. Advent Publishers, New York City, 1959. Hardcover. Herein: Introduction by Basil Davenport; Science Fiction: Its Nature, Faults and Virtues by **Robert A. Heinlein**; The Failure of the Science Fiction Novel as Social Criticism by C. M. Kornbluth; Science Fiction and the Renaissance Man by **Alfred Bester**; and Imagination and Modern Science Fiction by Robert Bloch.

2. The Life and Death of a Satellite. Published by Little, Brown, Boston, 1966. Hardcover.

3. Experiment Perilous. With Marion Zimmer Bradley and Norman Spinrad. Algol Press, New York City, 1976. Softcover. Herein: Experiment Perilous: The Art and Science of Anguish in Science Fiction - an essay by Marion Zimmer Bradley, 1976; The Bug Jack Barron Papers - an essay by Norman Spinrad, 1976; and Writing and the Demolished Man - an essay by **Alfred Bester**, 1976.

***

RELATED

1. Alfred Bester. By Carolyn Wendell. Starmont House, Mercer Island, Washington, 1982. Softcover.

2. The SFWA Grand Masters: Volume 2: Andre Norton, Arthur C. Clarke, Isaac Asimov, Alfred Bester, and Ray Bradbury. Published by Tor Books, New York City, 2001. Hardcover.

Ursula K. Le Guin.

Ursula Kroeber Le Guin was born in Berkeley, California on October 19th, 1929, the daughter of Alfred L. Kroeber, anthropologist, and Theodora Kroeber, writer. She attended both Radcliffe College and Columbia University, graduating with a masters degree in 1952. After finishing with Columbia, she went to Paris for further studies. It was there she met and married Charles Le Guin.

Ursula was eleven years old when she submitted her first short story to **John W. Campbell** at Astounding Science Fiction. He rejected it. Her first published genre story was twenty-two years later. It was April in Paris, bought by Cele Goldsmith for Fantastic Stories of Imagination, September, 1962, along with: Junior Partner by Ron Goulart; New Worlds by Erle Stanley Gardner; Open with Care by Boyd Correll; and Plane Jane by Robert F. Young.

Le Guin never did sell anything to Campbell.

By 1969, when The Left Hand of Darkness won a Nebula award for best novel, it was clear that Le Guin was well on her way to becoming one of the most respected writers in the field.

At the end of 2009, she quit the Author's Guild to protest the Guild's approval of Google's book-digitization scheme. In her resignation letter, she wrote "You decided to deal with the devil. There are principles involved, above all the whole concept of copyright; and these you have seen fit to abandon to a corporation, on their terms, without a struggle."

Always a fighter.

The Left Hand of Darkness and A Wizard of Earthsea tend to be her highest priced books for collectors, averaging around $2,500.00.

***

AWARDS

1968. Boston Globe Horn Book Award for The Left Hand of Darkness.
1969. Nebula Best Novel award for The Left Hand of Darkness.
1970. Hugo Best Novel Award for The Left Hand of Darkness.
1972. Newbery Silver Medal for The Tombs of Atuan.
1972. National Book Award for Children's Books for The Farthest Shore.
1973. Hugo Best Novella Award for The Word for World is Forest - Again, Dangerous Visions, Book 1.
1973. Locus Award for The Lathe of Heaven.
1974. Hugo Best Short Story Award for The Ones Who Walk Away from Omelas - New Dimensions III.
1975. Nebula Best Novel Award for The Dispossessed.
1975. Nebula Best Short Story Award for The Day Before the Revolution - Galaxy, August 1974.
1975. Jupiter Award for The Day Before the Revolution - Galaxy, August 1974.
1975. Hugo Best Novel Award for The Dispossessed.
1976. Jupiter Award for The Diary of the Rose.
1979. Lewis Carroll Shelf Award for A Wizard of Earthsea.
1979. Gandalf Award, Grandmaster of Fantasy.
1982. Rhysling Award for the best long poem, The Well of Bain.
1986. The Ditmar Award for Best International Long Fiction for The Compass Rose.
1986. The Janet Heidinger Kafka Fiction Prize for Always Coming Home.
1988. Hugo Best Novelette Award for Buffalo Gals, Won't You Come Out Tonight - The Magazine of Fantasy and Science Fiction, November 1987.
1988. World Fantasy Best Novella Award for Buffalo Gals, Won't You Come Out Tonight - The Magazine of Fantasy and Science Fiction, November 1987.
1990. Nebula Best Novel Award for Tehanu: The Last Book of Earthsea.
1991. Pushcart Prize for Bill Weisler.
1991. Howard Vursell Award from the American Academy and Institute of Arts and Letters.
1992. H. L. Davis Fiction Award for Searoad: Chronicles of Klatsand.
1993. Prometheus Hall of Fame Award for The Dispossessed as the Best Classic Libertarian SF Novel.
1994. The James Tiptree Jr Award for the best Gender-bending SF story for The Matter of Seggri - Crank!, Spring 1994.
1995. Hubbub Annual Poetry Award for Semen.
1995. Asimov's Readers Award for Forgiveness Day - Asimov's Science Fiction, November 1994.
1995. World Fantasy Life Achievement Award.
1995. Retroactive James Tiptree Jr Award for The Left Hand of Darkness.
1995. Nebula Best Novelette Award for Solitude - The Magazine of Fantasy and Science Fiction, December 1994.
1995. Theodore Sturgeon Memorial Short Story Award for Forgiveness Day - Asimov's Science Fiction, November 1994.
1996. The James Tiptree Jr Award for the best Gender-bending SF story for Mountain Ways - Asimov's Science Fiction, August 1996.
1996. Locus Readers Award for Four Ways to Forgiveness.
1998. Bumbershoot Arts Award.
2000. Robert Kirsch Lifetime Achievement Award.
2001. Lifetime Achievement Award from the Pacific Northwest Booksellers Association.
2001. Endeavour Award for Most Distinguished Novel or Collection for The Telling.
2001. Locus Readers Award for The Telling.
2001. Locus Readers Award for The Birthday of the World - The Magazine of Fantasy and Science Fiction, June 2000.
2001. Inducted into The Science Fiction Hall of Fame.
2002. Nebula Grand Master Award from the Science Fiction Writers of America.
2002. Endeavour Award for Most Distinguished Novel or Collection for Tales from Earthsea.
2002. Willamette Writers Lifetime Achievement Award.
2002. PEN - Malamud Award for Short Fiction.

Ursula K. Le Guin

2002. World Fantasy Best Novel Award for The Other Wind.
2002. Locus Readers Award for The Finder - Tales from Earthsea.
2002. Locus Readers Award for The Bones of the Earth - Tales from Earthsea.
2003. Asimov Reader's Award for The Wild Girls - Asimov's, March 2002.
2003. Locus Readers Award for The Wild Girls - Asimov's, March 2002.
2004. Margaret A. Edwards Award for Lifetime Achievement.
2006. Maxine Cushing Gray Fellowship for Writers for a Distinguished Body of Work.
2008. Nebula Best Novel Award for Powers.
2009. Locus Best Fantasy Novel Award for Lavinia.

***

TELEVISION AND FILM

1. The Goddess Calabra. This was written for The Starlost and aired on October 6th, 1973, Season 1, Episode 3. Directed by Harvey Hart, the show starred: Keir Dullea; Gay Rowan; Robin Ward; John Colicos; Barry Morse; and others.

2. The Starlost: The Beginning. A 1980 made-for-TV movie that adapted Le Guin's The Goddess Calabra.

3. The Lathe of Heaven. This film used Le Guin's 1971 novel. Directed by Fred Barzyk and David R. Loxton, it was released in 1980, starring: Bruce Davison; Peyton E. Park; Niki Flacks; Kevin Conway; Vandi Clark; Bernadette Whitehead; and others.

4. The Lathe of Heaven. A 2002 re-make, directed by Philip Haas and starring: James Caan; Lukas Haas; Lisa Bonet; David Strathairn; Sheila McCarthy; and others.

5. Earthsea. This was adapted from A Wizard of Earthsea, 1968, and The Tombs of Atuan, 1970. Directed by Robert Lieberman and released in 2004, it starred: Shawn Ashmore; Kristin Kreuk; Isabella Rossellini; Sebastian Roche; Chris Gauthier; Alan Scarfe; and many others, including Danny Glover as Ogion and Peter Kent as the dragon's voice.

6. Gedo senki - Tales from Earthsea. An animated Japanese adaptation, released in 2006. It was directed by Goro Miyazaki and featured the voices of: Junichi Okada; Aio Teshima; Bunta Sugawara; Yuko Tanaka; Teruyuki Kagawa; and many others.

***

NOVELS AND COLLECTIONS

1. Rocannon's World. Published by Ace Books, New York City, 1966. Softcover. Ace Double G-574. Together with The Kar-Chee Reign by Avram Davidson.

2. Planet of Exile. Published by Ace Books, New York City, 1966. Softcover. Ace Double G-597. Bound with Mankind Under the Leash by Thomas M. Disch.

3. City of Illusions. Published by Ace Books, New York City, 1967. Softcover. Ace Book G-626.

4. A Wizard of Earthsea. Published by Parnassus Press, Berkeley, California, 1968. Hardcover.

5. The Left Hand of Darkness. Published by Ace Books, New York City, 1969. Softcover. Ace Science Fiction Special 47800.

6. The Left Hand of Darkness. Published by Walker and Company, New York City, 1969. First hardcover edition.

7. City of Illusions. Published by Victor Gollancz, London, 1971. First hardcover edition.

8. The Lathe of Heaven. Published by Charles Scribner's Sons, New York City, 1971. Hardcover.

9. The Tombs of Atuan. Published by Atheneum, New York City, 1971. Hardcover.

10. The Farthest Shore. Published by Atheneum, New York City, 1972. Hardcover.

11. The Farthest Shore. Published by Victor Gollancz, London, 1973. Hardcover. A revised edition.

12. The Dispossessed. Published by Harper and Row, New York City, 1974. Hardcover.

13. The Wind's Twelve Quarters. Published by Harper and Row, New York City, 1975. Hardcover. Herein: Foreword by **Ursula K. Le Guin**; Semley's Necklace, 1964; April in Paris, 1962; The Masters, 1963; Darkness Box, 1963; The Word of Unbinding, 1964; The Rule of Names, 1964; Winter's King, 1969; The Good Trip, 1970; Nine Lives, 1969; Things, 1970; A Trip to the Head, 1970; Vaster Than Empires and More Slow, 1971; The Stars Below, 1974; The Field of Vision, 1973; Direction of the Road, 1975; The Ones Who Walk Away from Omelas, 1973; and The Day Before the Revolution, 1974.

14. Wild Angels. Published by Capra Press, Santa Barbara, California, 1975. Released simultaneously in hardcover and softcover. A poetry collection.

15. Rocannon's World. Published by Garland Publishing, New York and London, 1975. First hardcover edition.

16. Planet of Exile. Published by Garland Publishing, New York and London, 1975. First hardcover edition.

17. The Left Hand of Darkness. Published by Ace Books, New York City, 1976. Softcover. Ace Book 47805. This has a new introduction by Le Guin.

18. Very Far Away from Anywhere Else. Published by Atheneum, New York City, 1976. Hardcover.

19. The Water is Wide. Published by Pendragon Press, Portland, Oregon, 1976. Released in both hardcover and softcover, a limited edition of 1,000, in which the first two hundred were signed and numbered by the author.

20. The World for World is Forest. Berkley Books, New York City, 1976. Softcover.

21. Orsinian Tales. Published by Harper and Row,

215

New York City, 1976. Hardcover. This contains: The Fountains, 1976; The Barrow, 1976; Ile Forest, 1976; Conversations at Night, 1976; The Road East, 1976; Brothers and Sisters, 1976; A Week in the Country, 1976; An die Musik, 1961; The House, 1976; The Lady of Moge, 1976; and Imaginary Countries, 1973.

22. Rocannon's World. Published by Harper and Row, New York City, 1977. Hardcover. New introduction and some revisions by Le Guin.

23. Earthsea. Published by Victor Gollancz, London, 1977. Hardcover. An omnibus edition, this gathers: A Wizard of Earthsea, 1968; The Tombs of Atuan, 1971; and The Farthest Shore, 1972.

24. The Word for World is Forest. Published by Victor Gollancz, London, 1977. Includes an introduction by the author. First hardcover edition.

25. A Very Long Way from Anywhere Else. Published by Peacock Books, Middlesex, England, 1978. Softcover. A re-titled version of Very Far Away from Anywhere Else, 1976.

26. Three Hainish Novels. Published by Nelson Doubleday, Garden City, New York, 1978. Book Club Code T19. Hardcover. An omnibus edition, this contains: Rocannon's World, 1966; Planet of Exile, 1966; and City of Illusions, 1967.

27. Malafrena. Published by G. P. Putnam's Sons, New York City, 1979. Hardcover.

28. The Beginning Place. Published by Harper and Row, New York City, 1980. Hardcover.

29. Hard Winds and Other Poems. Published by Harper Colophon, New York City, 1981. Softcover. A poetry collection.

30. The Eye of the Heron. Published by Victor Gollancz, London, 1982. Hardcover. The U.S. first was released the following year by Harper and Row.

31. The Compass Rose. Published by Underwood Miller - Pendragon Press, San Francisco, 1982. Hardcover. Herein: Preface by **Ursula K. Le Guin**; The Author of the Acacia Seeds and Other Extracts from the Journal of the Association of Therolinguistics, 1974; The New Atlantis, 1975; Schrodinger's Cat, 1974; Two Delays on the Northern Line, 1979; SQ, 1978; Small Change, 1981; The Diary of the Rose, 1976; The White Donkey, 1980; The Phoenix, 1982; Intracom, 1974; The Eye Altering, 1974; Mazes, 1975; The Pathways of Desire; Gwilan's Harp, 1977; Malheur Country, 1979; The Water is Wide; The Wife's Story, 1982; Sur, 1982; Some Approaches to the Problem of the Shortage of Time, 1979; and The First Report of the Shipwrecked Foreigner to the Kadanh of Derb, 1978.

32. Solomon Leviathan's Nine Hundred and Thirty-First Trip Around the World. Published by Philomel Books, New York City, 1983. Hardcover.

33. King Dog - Dostoevsky. Published by Capra Press, Santa Barbara, California, 1985. Softcover. This contains: King Dog - a Screenplay, 1985; and A Movie for the Mind's Eye - an essay by **Ursula K. Le Guin**; along with Dostoevsky by Raymond Carver and Tess Gallagher, 1985; and Dostoevsky: A Screenplay by Raymond Carver, 1985.

34. Always Coming Home. Published by Harper and Row, New York City, 1985. Hardcover.

35. Five Complete Novels. Published by Avenel Books, New York City, 1985. Hardcover. An omnibus edition, this collects: Rocannon's World, 1966; Planet of Exile, 1966; City of Illusions, 1967; The Left Hand of Darkness, 1969; and The Word for World is Forest, 1972.

36. A Visit from Dr Katz. Published by Atheneum, New York City, 1988. Hardcover.

37. Catwings. Published by Franklin Watts/Orchard, New York City, 1988. Hardcover.

38. Wild Oats and Fireweed. Published by Perennial Library - Harper and Row, New York City, 1988. Hardcover. A poetry collection.

39. Catwings Return. Published by Franklin Watts/Orchard, New York City, 1989. Hardcover.

40. Fire and Stone. Published by Atheneum, New York City, 1989. Hardcover.

41. Way of the Water's Going: Images of the Northern California Coastal Range. Published by Harper and Row, New York City, 1989. Hardcover. A collection of black and white photographs with excepts from Always Coming Home, 1985.

42. The New Atlantis - with - The Blind Geometer. Tor Books, New York City, 1989. Tor Double 13. The New Atlantis by **Ursula K. Le Guin**, 1975; The Blind Geometer, 1986, and The Return from the Rainbow Bridge, 1987, by Kim Stanley Robinson.

43. Tehanu: The Last Book of Earthsea. Published by Atheneum, New York City, 1990. Hardcover.

44. Buffalo Gals and Other Animal Presences. Published by Roc - Penguin Books, New York City, 1990. Softcover. This collection contains: Introduction by **Ursula K. Le Guin**; Buffalo Gals, Won't You Come Out Tonight, 1987; The Wife's Story, 1982; Mazes, 1975; The Direction of the Road, 1973; Vaster than Empires and More Slow, 1971; The White Donkey, 1980; Horse Camp, 1986; Schrodinger's Cat, 1974; The Author of the Acacia Seeds and Other Extracts from the Journal of the Association of Therolinguistics, 1974; May's Lion, 1983; The Eighth Elegy from The Duino Elegies of R. M. Rilke, 1990; She Unnames Them, 1985; Four Cat Poems: Tabby Lorenzo; Black Leonard in Negative Space; A Conversation with Silence; For Leonard, Darko and Burton Watson, 1990; Three Rock Poems: The Basalt; Flints; Mt. St. Helen's/Omphalos, 1990; Five Vegetable Poems: Torrey Pines Reserve; Lewis and Clark and After; West Texas; Xmas Over; The Crown of Laurel, 1990; and Seven Bird and Beast Poems: What is Going on in the Oaks; For Ted; Found Poem; Totem; Winter Downs; The Man Eater; and Sleeping Out, 1990.

45. The Lathe of Heaven - The Dispossessed - The Wind's Twelve Quarters. Published by the

Book of the Month Club, New York City, 1991. An omnibus edition, this gathered the three titles from, respectively, 1971, 1974 and 1975.

46. Searoad: Chronicles of Klatsand. Published by Harper Collins, New York City, 1991. Hardcover. Herein: Foam Women, Rain Women, 1991; The Ship Ahoy, 1987; Hand, Cup, Shell, 1989; Geezers, 1991; In and Out, 1989; Bill Weisler, 1990; True Love, 1991; Sleepwalkers, 1991; Quoits, 1991; Crosswords, 1990; Texts, 1990; and Hernes, 1991.

47. The Eye of the Heron - and - The Word for World is Forest. Published by Victor Gollancz, London, 1991. Softcover. An omnibus edition, this collects: The Word for World is Forest, 1972; and The Eye of the Heron, 1978; along with an introduction by the author.

48. Fish Soup. Published by Atheneum, New York City, 1992. Hardcover.

49. A Ride on the Red Mare's Back. Published by Orchard Books, New York City, 1992. Hardcover.

50. The Earthsea Quartet. Published by Puffin Books, Middlesex, England, 1993. Softcover. This omnibus edition gathers: A Wizard of Earthsea, 1968; The Tombs of Atuan, 1971; The Farthest Shore, 1972; and Tehanu: The Last Book of Earthsea, 1990.

51. Blue Moon Over Thurman Street. Published by New Sage Press, Troutdale, Oregon, 1993. A collection of poetry and fragments, gathered with black and white photographs by Roger Dorband.

52. Wonderful Alexander and the Catwings. Published by Orchard Books, New York City, 1994. Hardcover.

53. Going Out with Peacocks and Other Poems. Published by Harper Perennial, New York City, 1994. Softcover. A poetry collection.

54. A Fisherman of the Inland Sea. Published by Harper Prism, New York, 1994. Hardcover. Herein: Introduction: On Not Reading Science Fiction by **Ursula K. Le Guin**; The First Contact with the Gorgonids, 1992; Newton's Sleep, 1991; The Ascent of the North Face, 1983; The Rock That Changed Things, 1992; The Kerastion, 1990; The Shobies' Story, 1990; Dancing to Ganam, 1993; and Another Story, or A Fisherman of the Inland Sea, 1994.

55. Four Ways to Forgiveness. Published by Harper Prism, New York City, 1995. Hardcover. This contains: Betrayals, 1995; Forgiveness Day, 1994; A Man of the People, 1995; A Woman's Liberation, 1995; O Yeowe - a poem, 1995; and Notes of Werel and Yeowe, 1995.

56. Unlocking the Air and Other Stories. Published by Harper Collins, New York City, 1996. Hardcover. This contains: Half Past Four, 1987; The Professor's Houses, 1982; Ruby on the 67, 1996; Limberlost, 1989; The Creatures of My Mind, 1990; Standing Ground, 1992; The Spoons in the Basement, 1982; Sunday in Summer in Seatown, 1995; In the Drought, 1994; Ether, OR, 1995; A Child Bride, 1988; Climbing to the Moon, 1992; Daddy's Big Girl, 1987; Findings, 1992; Olders, 1995; The Wise Woman, 1996; The Poacher, 1993; and Unlocking the Air, 1990.

57. Worlds of Exile and Illusion. Published by Orb Books, London, 1996. Softcover. A re-titled re-issue of The Hainish Novels, 1978.

58. Jane on Her Own. Published by Orchard Books, New York City, 1999. Hardcover.

59. Sixty Odd: New Poems. Published by Shambhala Publications, Boston, 1999. Softcover. A poetry collection with a preface by Le Guin.

60. Tales of the Catwings. Published by Puffin Books, Middlesex, England, 1999. Softcover. An omnibus edition, this collects: Catwings, 1988; and Catwings Return, 1989.

61. More Tales of the Catwings. Published by Puffin Books, Middlesex, England, 2000. Softcover. An omnibus edition, this collects: Wonderful Alexander and the Catwings, 1994; and Jane on Her Own, 1999.

62. The Telling. Published by Harcourt Brace, New York City, 2000. Hardcover.

63. The Other Wind. Published by Harcourt Brace, New York City, 2001. Hardcover.

64. Tales from Earthsea. Published by Harcourt Brace, New York City, 2001. Hardcover. Herein: Foreword by **Ursula K. Le Guin**; The Finder, 2001; Darkrose and Diamond, 1999; The Bones of the Earth, 2001; On the High Marsh, 2001; Dragonfly, 1998; and A Description of Earthsea, 2001.

65. Tales from Earthsea - and - The Other Wind. Published by the Science Fiction Book Club, Garden City, New York, 2001. Hardcover. An omnibus edition, this gathers: Tales from Earthsea, 2001; and The Other Wind, 2001.

66. Tom Mouse. Published by Roaring Brook Press, Brookfield, Connecticut, 2002. Hardcover.

67. The Birthday of the World and Other Stories. Published by Harper Collins, New York City, 2002. Hardcover. Herein: Foreword by **Ursula K. Le Guin**; Coming of Age in Karhide by Sov Thade Tage em Ereb. Of Rer, in Karhide, on Gethen, 1995; A Matter of Seggri, 1994; Unchosen Love, 1994; Mountain Ways, 1996; Solitude, 1994; Old Music and the Slave Woman, 1999; The Birthday of the World, 2000; and Paradises Lost, 2002.

68. Changing Planes. Published by Harcourt Brace, New York City, 2003. Hardcover. Herein: Author's Note; Sita Dulip's Method, 2003; Porridge on Islac, 2003; The Silence of the Asonu, 2003; Feeling at Home with the Hennebet, 2003; The Ire of the Veksi, 2003; Seasons of the Ansarac, 2002; Social Dreaming of the Frin, 2002; the Royals of Hegn, 2003; Woeful Tales from Mahigul, 2003; Great Joy, 2003; Wake Island, 2003; The Nna Mmoy Language, 2003; The Building, 2001; The Fliers of Gy, 2000; The Island of the Immortals, 1998; and Confusions of Uni, 2003.

69. Gifts. Published by Harcourt Brace, New York City, 2004. Hardcover.

70. Voices. Published by Harcourt Brace, New York City, 2006. Hardcover.

71. Powers. Published by Harcourt Brace, New York City, 2007. Hardcover.

72. Lavinia. Published by Harcourt Brace, New York City, 2008. Hardcover.

***

ANTHOLOGIES

1. Nebula Award Stories 11. Published by Victor Gollancz, London, 1976. Hardcover. The U.S. edition was released the following year by Harper and Row. Herein: Introduction by **Ursula K. Le Guin**; Catch That Zeppelin by **Fritz Leiber**, 1975; End Game by Joe Haldeman, 1975; 1975: The Year in Science Fiction or Let's Hear It for the Decline and Fall of the Science Fiction Empire - an essay by Peter Nicholls, 1976; Home is the Hangman by Roger Zelazny, 1975; Child of All Ages by P. J. Plauger, 1975; Potential and Actuality in Science Fiction - an essay by Vonda N. McIntyre, 1976; Shatterday by Harlan Ellison, 1975; San Diego Lightfoot Sue by Tom Reamy, 1975; and Time Deer by Craig Strete, 1974.

2. Edges. With Virginia Kidd. Published by Pocket Books, New York City, 1980. Softcover. Herein: Introduction by **Ursula K. Le Guin**; The Ballad of Bowsprit Bear's Stead by Damien Broderick, 1980; Omens by Carol Emshwiller, 1980; Touch the Earth by Scott Sanders, 1980; The Other Magus by Avram Davidson, 1980; Peek-a-Boom by Sonya Dorman, 1980; Suzanne Delage by **Gene Wolfe**, 1980; The Finger by Naomi Mitchison, 1980; Barranca, King of the Tree Streets by Lowry Pei, 1980; Thomas in Yahvestan by George P. Elliot, 1980t; The Vengeance of Hera by Thomas M. Disch, 1980; Falling by Raylyn Moore, 1980; Father Returns from the Mountain by Luis Urrea, 1980; and The Oracle by M. J. Engh, 1980.

3. Interfaces. With Virginia Kidd. Published by Ace Books, New York City, 1980. Softcover. This contains: Introduction by **Ursula K. Le Guin** and Virginia Kidd; The Reason for the Visit by John Crowley, 1980; Set Piece by Jill Paton Walsh, 1980; Everything Blowing Up: An Adventure of Una Persson, 1980, Heroine of Time and Space by Hilary Bailey, 1980; Shadows Moving by Vonda N. McIntyre, 1980; The Gods in Winter by Sonya Dorman, 1980; The New Zombies by Avram Davidson and Grania Davis, 1980; Earth and Stone by Robert Holdstock, 1980; A Short History of the Bicycle: 401 B.C. to 2677 A.D. by Michael Bishop, 1980; Two Poems by Laurence Josephs, 1980; The Pastseer by Phillippa C. Maddern, 1980; Hunger and the Computer by Gary Weimberg, 1980; Household Gods by Daphne Castell, 1980; Bender Fenugreek Slatterman and Mupp by D. G. Compton, 1980; Precession by Edward Bryant, 1980; A Criminal Proceeding by **Gene Wolfe**, 1980; For Whom are Those Serpents Whistling Overhead by Jean Femling, 1980; The Summer Sweet the Winter Mild by Michael G. Coney, 1980; and Slow Music by James Tiptree Jr, 1980.

4. THE NORTON BOOK OF SCIENCE FICTION - North American Science Fiction 1960 - 1990. With Brian Attebery. Published by W. W. Norton, New York City, 1993. Hardcover. This anthology contains: Introduction by **Ursula K. Le Guin**; The Handler by **Damon Knight**, 1960; Alpha Ralpha Boulevard by Cordwainer Smith, 1961; Tandy's Story by **Theodore Sturgeon**, 1961; 2064 or Thereabouts by David R. Bunch, 1964; Balanced Ecology by James H. Schmitz, 1965; The House the Blakeneys Built by Avram Davidson, 1965; On the River and Through the Woods by Clifford D. Simak, 1965; How Beautiful with Banners by **James Blish**, 1966; Nine Hundred Grandmothers by R. A. Lafferty, 1966; When I Was Miss Dow by Sonya Dorman Hess, 1966; Comes Now the Power by Roger Zelazny, 1966; Day Million by Frederik Pohl, 1966; The Winter Flies by **Fritz Leiber**, 1967; High Weir by **Samuel R. Delany**, 1968; Kyrie by **Poul Anderson**, 1968; For the Sake of Grace by Suzette Haden Elgin, 1969; As Simple As That by Zenna Henderson, 1971; Good News from the Vatican by **Robert Silverberg**, 1971; Gather Blue Roses by Pamela Sargent, 1971; The Women Men Don't See by James Tiptree, Jr, 1973; Feather Tigers by **Gene Wolfe**, 1973; The Mountains of Sunset, the Mountains of Dawn by Vonda N. McIntyre, 1974; The Private War of Private Jacob by Joe Haldeman, 1974; The Warlord of Saturn's Moons by Eleanor Arnason, 1974; Making It All the Way into the Future on Gaxton Falls of the Red Planet by Barry N. Malzberg, 1974; The New Atlantis by **Ursula K. Le Guin**, 1975; A Few Things I Know About Whileaway by Joanna Russ, 1974; Strange Wine by Harlan Ellison, 1976; Lillipop and the Tar Baby by John Varley, 1977; Night Rise by Katherine MacLean, 1978; Frozen Journey by **Philip K. Dick**, 1980; Precession by Edward Bryant, 1980; Elbow Room by Marion Zimmer Bradley, 1980; Tauf Aleph by Phyllis Gotlieb, 1980; Exposures by Gregory Benford, 1981; The Gernsback Continuum by **William Gibson**, 1981; The Start of the End of the World by Carol Emshwiller, 1981; Schrodinger's Plague by Greg Bear, 1982; ...the World as We Know't by Howard Waldrop, 1982; The Byrds by Michael G. Coney, 1983; Speech Sounds by Octavia Butler, 1983; Distant Signals by Andrew Weiner, 1984; The Lucky Strike by Kim Stanley Robinson, 1984; The Life of Anybody by Robert Sheckley, 1984; Interlocking Pieces by Molly Gloss, 1984; The War at Home by Lewis Shiner, 1985; The Lake Was Full of Artificial Things by Karen Joy Fowler, 1985; Snow by John Crowley, 1985; After the Days of Dead-Eye 'Dee by Pat Cadigan, 1985; The Bob Dylan Tambourine Software and Satori Sapport Services Consortium Ltd. by Michael Bishop, 1985; His Vegetable Wife by Pat Murphy, 1986; The Brains of Rats by Michael Blumlein, 1986; Out of All Them Bright Stars by Nancy Kress, 1986; Rat by James Patrick Kelly, 1986; America by Orson Scott Card, 1987; Schwarzschild Radius by **Connie Willis**, 1987; Stable Strategies for Middle Management by Eileen Gunn, 1988; Kirinyaga by Mike Resnick, 1988; A Midwinter's Tale by Michael Swanwick, 1988; Learning About Machine Sex by Candas Jane Dorsey, 1988; We See Things Differently by Bruce Sterling, 1989; Half-Life by Paul Preuss, 1989; Homelanding by Margaret Atwood, 1989; And the Angels Sing by **Kate Wilhelm**, 1990; Aunt Parnetta's Electric

Ursula K. Le Guin

Blisters by Diane Glancy, 1990; Midnight News by Lisa Goldstein, 1990; and Invaders by John Kessel, 1990.

***

NON-FICTION

1. From Elfland to Poughkeepsie. With Vonda N. McIntyre. Published by Pendragon Press, Portland, Oregon, 1973. A limited edition released simultaneously in hardcover and softcover with twenty-six lettered copies signed by **Ursula K. Le Guin** and Vonda N. McIntyre and the first one hundred numbered copies signed by Le Guin.

2. Dreams Must Explain Themselves. Published by Algol Press, New York City, 1975. Softcover.

3. The Altered I: Ursula K. Le Guin's Science Fiction Writing Workshop. With Lee Harding. Published by Berkley Windhover, New York City, 1978. Softcover.

4. The Language of the Night - Essays on Fantasy and Science Fiction. Published by G. P. Putnam's Sons, New York City, 1979. Hardcover. This contains: Introductions by Susan Wood; A Citizen of Mondath, 1982; On Fantasy and Science Fiction, 1982; Why Are Americans Afraid of Dragons?, 1982; Dreams Must Explain Themselves, 1973; National Book Award Acceptance Speech, 1973; The Child and the Shadow, 1982; Myth and Archetype in Science Fiction, 1982; From Elfland to Poughkeepsie, 1973; American SF and the Other, 1976; Science Fiction and Mrs. Brown, 1977; Do It Yourself Cosmology, 1982; The Book is What is Real, 1982; Introduction to Rocannon's World, 1982; Introduction to Planet of Exile, 1982; Introduction to City of Illusions, 1982; Introduction to The Word for World is Forest, 1982; Introduction to The Left Hand of Darkness, 1982; Is Gender Necessary?, 1976; The Staring Eye, 1982; The Modest One, 1982; Introduction to Star Songs of an Old Primate, 1982; Telling the Truth, 1982; Introduction to The Altered I, 1982; Talking About Writing, 1982; Escape Routes, 1974; Pushing at the Limits, 1982; The Stalin in the Soul, 1973; The Stone Ax and the Muskoxen, 1982; and a bibliography by Lloyd W. Currey.

5. Dancing at the Edge of the World: Thoughts on Words, Women, Places. Published by Grove Press, New York City, 1989. Hardcover. Herein: Introductory Note by **Ursula K. Le Guin**; The Space Crone, 1976; Is Gender Necessary? Redux, 1986; Moral and Ethical Implications of Family Planning, 1978; It Was a Dark and Stormy Night, 1979; Working on The Lathe, 1979; Some Thoughts on Narrative, 1989; World Making, 1981; Hunger, 1981; Places Names, 1981; The Princess, 1982; A Non-Euclidean View of California as a Cold Place to Be, 1982; Facing It, 1989; Reciprocity of Prose and Poetry, 1983; A Left Handed Commencement Address, 1983; Along the Platte, 1983; Whose Lathe?, 1984; The Woman Without Answers, 1984; The Second Report of the Shipwrecked Foreigner to the Kadanh of Derb, 1984; Room 9, Car 1430, 1985; Theodora, 1985; Science Fiction and the Future, 1985; The Only Good Author?, 1985; Bryn Mawr Commencement Address, 1986; Woman/Wilderness, 1986; The Carrier Bag Theory of Fiction, 1986; Heroes, 1986; Prospects for Women in Writing, 1986; Text, Silence, Performance, 1986; Who is Responsible?, 1987; Conflict, 1987; Where Do You Get Your Ideas From?, 1987; Over the Hills and a Great Way Off, 1988; and The Fisherwoman's Daughter, 1988; followed by a series of book reviews.

6. Steering the Craft. Published by Eight Mountain Press, Portland, Oregon, 1998. Softcover.

7. The Wave in the Mind: Talks and Essays on the Writer, the Reader, and the Imagination. Published by Shambhala Publications, Boston, 2004. Softcover. These are all dated 2004. Herein: Introduction by **Ursula K. Le Guin**; Being Taken for Granite; Indians Uncles; My Libraries; My Island; On the Frontier; All Happy Families; Things Not Actually Present; Reading Young, Reading Old; Thinking About Cordwainer Smith; Stress-Rhythm in Poetry and Prose; Rhythmic Pattern in the Lord of the Rings; The Wilderness Within: The Sleeping Beauty and The Poacher and a PS about Sylvia Townsend Warner; Off the Page: Loud Cows: A Talk and a Poem about Reading Aloud; Fact and/or/plus Fiction; Award and Gender; On Genetic Determinism; About Feet; Dogs, Cats, and Dancers: Thoughts about Beauty; Collectors, Rhymesters, and Drummers; Telling is Listening; The Operating Instructions; A War Without End; A Matter of Trust; The Writer and the Character; Unquestioned Assumptions; Prides: An Essay on Writing Workshops; Alone in the Desert of Words; Heading for the Waterhole; The Question I Get Asked Most Often; Old Body Not Writing; and The Writer on, and at, Her Work.

8. Cheek by Jowl. Published by Aqueduct Press, Gilsum, New Hampshire, 2009. Softcover.

***

RELATED

1. The Farthest Shores of Ursula K. Le Guin. By George Edgar Slusser. Published by R. Reginald - The Borgo Press, San Bernardino, California, 1976. Softcover.

2. Ursula K. Le Guin: Voyager to Inner Lands and to Outer Space. Edited by Joe De Bolt. Published by Kennikat Press, Port Washington, New York and London, 1979. Hardcover.

3. Ursula K. Le Guin. Edited by Joseph D. Olander and Martin H. Greenberg. Published by Taplinger Publishing, New York City, 1979. Hardcover.

4. Ursula K. Le Guin. By Barbara J. Bucknall. Published by Frederick Unger, New York City, 1981. Hardcover.

5. Ursula K. Le Guin: A Primary and Secondary Bibliography. By Elizabeth C. Cogell. Published by G. K. Hall, Boston, Massachusetts, 1983. Hardcover.

6. Approaches to the Fiction of Ursula K. Le Guin. By James W. Bittner. Published by UMI Research Press, Ann Arbor, Michigan, 1984. Hardcover.

7. Ursula K. Le Guin. By Charlotte Spivack.

Published by Twayne Publishers, Boston, 1984. Softcover.

8. Understanding Ursula K. Le Guin. By Elizabeth Cummins. Published by the University of South Carolina Press, 1992. Softcover.

9. Presenting Ursula K. Le Guin. By Suzanne Elizabeth Reid. Published by Twayne Publishers, Boston, 1997. Hardcover.

10. Communities of the Heart: The Rhetoric of Myth in the Fiction of Ursula K. Le Guin. By Warren Rochelle. Published by The University of Liverpool Press, 2000. Hardcover.

11. Ursula K. Le Guin. By Harold Bloom. Published by Chelsea House, United States, 2000. Hardcover.

12. Ursula K. Le Guin. By Heinz Tschachler. Published by Boise State University, Boise, Idaho, 2001. Softcover.

13. Ursula K. Le Guin to Helen Oxenbury - Favorite Children's Authors and Illustrators Volume 4. By E. Russell Primm. Tradition Books, United States, 2002. Hardcover.

14. Ursula K. Le Guin Beyond Genre: Fiction for Children and Adults. By Mike Cadden. Published by Taylor and Francis (Routledge), United Kingdom, 2004. Hardcover.

15. The New Utopian Politics of Ursula K. Le Guin's The Dispossessed. By Laurence Davis and Peter Stillman. Published by Lexington Books, New Britain, Connecticut, 2005.

16. Ursula K. Le Guin: A Critical Companion. By Graham J. Murphy and Susan M. Bernardo. Published by Greenwood Press, 2006. Hardcover.

17. Political Theory, Science Fiction, and Utopian Literature: Ursula K. Le Guin and the Dispossessed. By Tony Burns. Published by Lexington Books, New Britain, Connecticut, 2008. Hardcover.

18. Conversations with Ursula K. Le Guin. Edited by Carl Freedman. Published by the University Press of Mississippi, 2008. Hardcover.

19. One Earth, One People: The Mythopoeic Fantasy Series of Ursula K. Le Guin. By Marek Oziewicz. Published by McFarland and Company, Jefferson, North Carolina. Softcover.

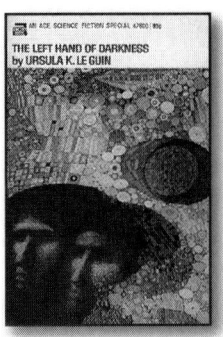

Fritz Leiber

Fritz Leiber.

Fritz Reuter Leiber Jr. was born on in Chicago on December 24th, 1910 and died on September 5th, 1992 of an organic brain disease. He collapsed on the way home from a Science Fiction Convention in London, Ontario and died two weeks later. While he was at the convention, he was in such rough shape that his hand needed to be guided while he was signing autographs.

His parents were reasonably well-known theatre actors and it seemed he would become one as well. He toyed with it before and after university - he graduated with honours from the University of Chicago in 1932, then went on to study theology and even became a preacher. In 1936, he married Jonquil Stephens.

By 1939, he was writing as **Fritz Leiber Jr.** His first sale was to **John W. Campbell**, for Unknown in 1939. It was Unknown's first year in business and Leiber had sold his first Fafhrd and the Gray Mouser story, Two Sought Adventure. It appeared along with: Don't Dream by **Donald A. Wollheim**; Forsaking All Others by Lester del Rey; The Ghoul by L. Ron Hubbard; and The Misguided Halo by Henry Kuttner.

The next sale was to Dorothy McIlwraith at Weird Tales for the May, 1940 issue. The story was The Automatic Pistol and it shared the pulp space with: The City from the Sea by Edmond Hamilton; The Ghost Writer by Robert Bloch; Khosru's Garden by E. Hoffman Price; Wind in the Moonlight by Gretchen Ruediger; A Million Years in the Future by Thomas P. Kelley; Black Was the Night by Laurence Bour Jr; The Red Gibbet by F. B. Ghensi; and The Soul of Ra-Moses by John Murray Reynolds; along with some poetry and true adventure tales.

But he had established Fafhrd and the Gray Mouser with Campbell and they became a regular feature in Unknown. His first "science fiction" sale, They Never Come Back, was to Robert A. W. Lowndes for his first issue as editor at Future Fiction - August 1941. Also in that issue were: The Barbarians by William Morrison; A Million Years and a Day by Lawrence Woods; The Shadowless World by Oliver Saari; The Stone Men of Ignota by Victor Rousseau; The Time Maker by R. Winterbotham; and The Topaz Gate by **James Blish**. Blish himself was new to writing at the time and had, to date, less than ten magazine sales.

When his wife died in 1969, Leiber spent a few years consorting with alcohol, busting out of that new relationship to get on with his writing. It has been said that he was quite poor, which was quite probably true - for instance, when **Donald A. Wollheim** published Leiber's novel The Big Time at Ace Books, Leiber received a royalty of one penny for each copy sold. But it is certain that he did not die poor. TSR had bought the rights to Fafhrd and the Gray

Mouser for their gaming world...

He always claimed that, even though he liked science fiction, he had trouble writing it. His best work was always his horror and his heroic fantasy...

The Wanderer and Night's Black Agents tend to be his highest priced books for collectors, usually selling between $500.00 and $600.00.

***

AWARDS

1958. Hugo Best Novel Award for The Big Time.
1965. Hugo Best Novel Award for The Wanderer.
1967. Nebula Best Novelette Award for Gonna Roll the Bones - Dangerous Visions..
1968. Hugo Best Novelette Award for Gonna Roll the Bones - Dangerous Visions.
1970. Hugo Best Novella Award for Ship of Shadows - The Magazine of Fantasy and Science Fiction, July 1969.
1970. Nebula Best Novella Award for Ill Met in Lankhmar - The Magazine of Fantasy and Science Fiction, April 1970.
1971. Hugo Best Novella Award for Ill Met in Lankhmar - The Magazine of Fantasy and Science Fiction, April 1970.
1975. Gandalf Award as Grandmaster of Fantasy.
1975. Locus Poll Best Single Author Collection Award for The Best of Fritz Leiber.
1975. Nebula Best Short Story Award for Catch That Zeppelin! - The Magazine of Fantasy and Science Fiction, March 1975.
1976. British Fantasy Award for Best Short Story Collection for The Second Book of Fritz Leiber.
1976. World Fantasy Award for Life Achievement.
1976. World Fantasy Best Short Fiction Award for Belsen Express - The Second Book of Fritz Leiber.
1978. World Fantasy Best Novel Award for Our Lady of Darkness.
1980. Nebula Grand Master award.
1980. British Fantasy Best Short Fiction Award for The Button Molder - Whispers 13/14, October 1979.
1981. Balrog Special Award.
1985. Locus Poll Best Collection Award for The Ghost Light.
1987. Bram Stoker Award for Lifetime Achievement.
2001. Inducted into The Science Fiction Hall of Fame.

***

FILM AND TELEVISION

1. Camille. Directed by George Cukor, **Fritz Leiber Jr.** had an uncredited bit part as Valentin in this 1936 film, which starred: Greta Garbo; Robert Taylor; and Lionel Barrymore.

2. The Great Garrick. Fritz Leiber Jr. had an uncredited bit part as Fortinbras in this 1937 film which was directed by James Whale and starred: Olivia de Havilland; Brian Aherne; and Edward Everett Horton.

3. Weird Woman. Based on Leiber's 1943 novel, Conjure Wife, this was directed by Reginald Le Borg and released in March, 1944, starring: Lon Chaney Jr.; Anne Gwynne; Evelyn Ankers; Ralph Morgan; and others.

4. The Web. Based on a story by Harry Kurnitz, this was directed by Michael Gordon and released in May 1947, starring: Ella Raines, Edmond O'Brien; William Bendix; Vincent Price; and many others, including **Fritz Leiber** as Leopold Kroner.

5. The Accomplice. Based on Leiber's 1943 novel, Conjure Wife, this was adapted for the television series Moment of Fear, airing on August 26th, 1960, Season 1, Episode 7. It starred: Robert Dowdell; Geoffrey Home; Will Kuluva; Nehemiah Persoff; and Lilia Skala.

6. Night of the Eagle. This was based on Conjure Wife, 1943, and released in the U.S. as Burn, Witch, Burn! In April, 1962. Directed by Sidney Hayers and with a screenplay by Charles Beaumont, Richard Matheson and George Baxt, it starred: Peter Wyngarde; Janet Blair; Margaret Johnston; Anthony Nicholls; Colin Gordon; and others.

7. Equinox. Based on a story by Mark Thomas McGee and directed by Jack Woods, this film was released in October 1970, starring: Edward Connell; Barbara Hewitt; Frank Bonner; Robin Christopher; and others, including **Fritz Leiber** as Dr Arthur Waterman.

8. The Dead Man. Based on Leiber's 1950 short story, this was used on Rod Serling's Night Gallery and aired on December 16th, 1970, Season 1, Episode 1. Directed by Douglas Heyes, it starred: **Rod Serling** as the host; Carl Betz; Jeff Corey; Louise Sorel; Michael Blodgett; and Glenn Dixon.

9. The Girl with the Hungry Eyes. From 1949, this story was used on Rod Serling's Night Gallery, airing on October 1st, 1972, Season 3, Episode 2. Directed by John Badham, it starred: **Rod Serling** as the host; James Farentino; John Astin; Joanna Pettet; Kip Niven; and Bruce Powers.

10. The Bermuda Triangle. Based on the book by Charles Berlitz, this was directed by Richard Friedenberg and released in 1979, starring: Brad Crandall; Donald Albee; Lin Berlitz; Larry Bisman; John Bohan; and many others, including **Fritz Leiber** as Chavez.

11. Witches' Brew. Also known as Which Witch is Which?, this was a remake of the 1944 Lon Chaney Jr. film, Weird Woman. It was also, of course, based on Conjure Wife, 1943. Directed by Richard Shorr and Herbert L. Strock, it was released in 1980 and starred: Teri Garr; Richard Benjamin; Lana Turner; James Winkler; Kathryn Leigh Scott; and many others.

12. The Girl with the Hungry Eyes. Based on Leiber's 1949 story, this was directed by Jon Jacobs and released in 1985, starring: Christina Fulton; Isaac Turner; Leon Herbert; Susan Rhodes; Leroy Jones; and many others, including Jed Curtis as the uncredited voice of The Monster.

13. Conjure Wife. Directed by Billy Ray, this 1943 story is scheduled for yet another remake, ostensibly for release in 2010.

***

RADIO

1. A Pail of Air. This 1951 story was done for X Minus One and first aired on March 28th, 1956.

2. Appointment in Tomorrow. Also from 1951, this story aired on X Minus One on November 7th, 1956.

Please note: The above stories were released on Audio CD by Wildside Audio Library in 2007.

3. The Moon is Green. This 1952 story aired on X Minus One on January 2nd, 1957.

***

NOVELS AND COLLECTIONS

1. Night's Black Agents. Published by Arkham House, Sauk City, Wisconsin, 1947. Hardcover. Herein: Foreword by **Fritz Leiber**; Smoke Ghost, 1941; The Automatic Pistol, 1940; The Inheritance, 1942; The Hill and the Hole, 1942; The Dreams of Albert Moreland, 1945; The Hound, 1942; Diary in the Snow, 1947; The Man Who Never Grew Young, 1947; The Sunken Land, 1942; and Adept's Gambit, 1947.

2. Gather, Darkness. Published by Pellegrini and Cudahy, New York City, 1950. Hardcover.

3. Conjure Wife. Published by Twayne Publishers, New York City, 1953. Hardcover. The first actual publication of this was in Unknown Worlds, April 1943.

4. The Green Millennium. Published by Abelard Press, New York City, 1953. Hardcover.

5. The Sinful Ones. Published by Universal, New York City, 1953. Softcover. Universal Giant 5. Together with Bulls, Blood and Passion by David Williams.

6. Destiny Times Three. Published by Galaxy Publishing, New York City, 1957. Softcover. Galaxy Novel 28.

7. Two Sought Adventure. Published by Gnome Press, New York City, 1957. Hardcover. Herein: Two Sought Adventure, 1939; Thieves' House, 1943; The Bleak Shore, 1940; The Howling Tower, 1941; The Sunken Land, 1942; The Seven Black Priests, 1953; and Dark Vengeance, 1951.

8. The Big Time. Published by Ace Books, New York City, 1961. Ace Double D-491. Softcover. Bound with The Mind Spider and Other Stories by **Fritz Leiber**.

9. The Mind Spider and Other Stories. Published by Ace Books, New York City, 1961. Ace Double D-491. Softcover. Bound with The Big Time by **Fritz Leiber**. The Mind Spider contains: Foreword by **Fritz Leiber**; The Haunted Future, 1959; Damnation Morning, 1959; The Oldest Soldier, 1960; Try and Change the Past, 1958; The Number of the Beast, 1958; and The Mind Spider, 1959.

Fritz Leiber

10. Tales from Night's Black Agents. Published by Ballantine Books, New York City, 1961. Ballantine Book 508K. Herein: The Sunken Land, 1942; The Man Who Never Grew Young, 1947; Smoke Ghost, 1941; The Automatic Pistol, 1940; The Inheritance, 1942; The Hill and the Hole, 1942; The Dreams of Albert Moreland, 1945; The Hound, 1942; and Diary in the Snow, 1947.

11. The Silver Eggheads. Published by Ballantine Books, New York City, 1962. Ballantine Book 561. Softcover.

12. Shadows with Eyes. Published by Ballantine Books, New York City, 1962. Ballantine Book 577. Softcover. Herein: A Bit of the Dark World, 1962; The Dead Man, 1950; The Power of the Puppets, 1942; Schizo Jimmie, 1960; The Man Who Made Friends with Electricity, 1962; and A Deskful of Girls, 1958.

13. A Pail of Air. Published by Ballantine Books, New York City, 1964. Ballantine Book U2216. Softcover. Herein: The Beat Cluster, 1961; The Foxholes of Mars, 1952; Pipe Dream, 1959; Time Fighter, 1957; The 64-Square Madhouse, 1962; Bread Overhead, 1958; The Last Letter, 1958; Rump-Titty-Titty-Tum-Tah-Tee, 1958; Coming Attraction, 1950; Nice Girl with Five Husbands, 1951; and A Pail of Air, 1951.

14. Ships to the Stars. Published by Ace Books, New York City, 1964. Ace Double F-285. Softcover. Together with The Million Year Hunt by Kenneth Bulmer. Ships to the Stars contains: Dr Kometevsky's Day, 1952; The Big Trek, 1957; The Enchanted Forest, 1950; Deadly Moon, 1960; The Snowbank Orbit, 1962; and The Ship Sails at Midnight, 1950.

15. The Wanderer. Published by Ballantine Books, New York City, 1964. Ballantine Book U6010. Softcover.

16. The Night of the Wolf. Published by Ballantine Books, New York City, 1966. Ballantine Book U2254. Softcover. Herein: The Lone Wolf, 1962; The Wolf Pair, 1960; Crazy Wolf, 1944; and The Wolf Pack, 1950.

17. Tarzan and the Valley of Gold. Published by Ballantine Books, New York City, 1966. Softcover. Ballantine Book U6125.

18. The Wanderer. Published by Dennis Dobson, London, 1967. First hardcover edition.

19. The Secret Songs. Published by Rupert Hart-Davis, London, 1968. Hardcover. Herein: Introduction by **Fritz Leiber**; Winter Flies, 1967; The Man Who Made Friends with Electricity, 1962; Rump-Titty-Titty-Tum-Tah-Tee, 1958; Mariana, 1960; Coming Attraction, 1950; The Moon is Green, 1952; A Pail of Air, 1951; Smoke Ghost, 1941; The Girl with the Hungry Eyes, 1949; No Great Magic, 1963; and The Secret Songs, 1962.

20. The Swords of Lankhmar. Published by Ace Books, New York City, 1968. Ace Book H-38. Softcover.

21. Swords Against Wizardry. Published by Ace Books, New York City, 1968. Ace Book H-73. Softcover. Herein: In the Witch's Tent, 1968; Stardock, 1965; The Two Best Thieves in Lankhmar, 1968; and The Lords of Quarmall, 1964.

22. Swords in the Mist. Published by Ace Books, New York City, 1968. Ace Book H-90. Softcover. Herein: The Cloud of Hate, 1963; Lean Times in Lankhmar, 1959; Their Mistress, the Sea, 1968; When the Sea King's Away, 1960; The Wrong Branch, 1968; and Adept's Gambit, 1947.

23. The Swords of Lankhmar. Published by Rupert Hart-Davis, London, 1969. First hardcover edition.

24. A Specter is Haunting Texas. Published by Walker and Company, New York City, 1969. Hardcover.

25. Night Monsters. Published by Ace Books, New York City, 1969. Ace Double 30300. Bound with The Green Millennium by **Fritz Leiber**. Night Monsters contains: The Black Gondolier, 1964; Midnight in the Mirror World, 1964; I'm Looking for Jeff, 1952; and The Casket Demon, 1963.

26. The Green Millennium. Published by Ace Books, New York City, 1969. Ace Double 30300. Bound with Night Monsters by **Fritz Leiber**.

27. Swords Against Death. Published by Ace Books, New York City, 1970. Ace Book 79150. Softcover. This contains: The Circle Curse, 1970; The Jewels in the Forest, 1939; Thieves' House, 1943; The Bleak Shore, 1940; The Howling Tower, 1941; The Sunken Land, 1942; The Seven Black Priests, 1953; Claws from the Night, 1951; The Price of Pain Ease, 1970; and Bazaar of the Bizarre, 1963.

28. Swords and Deviltry. Published by Ace Books, New York City, 1970. Ace Book 79170. Softcover. Herein: Induction, 1957; The Snow Women, 1970; The Unholy Grail, 1962; and Ill Met in Lankhmar, 1970.

29. You're All Alone. Published by Ace Books, New York City, 1972. Ace Book 95146. Softcover. This collection contains: Four Ghosts in Hamlet, 1965; The Creature from Cleveland Depths, 1962; and You're All Alone - a revised version of The Sinful Ones, 1953.

30. Night Monsters. Published by Victor Gollancz, London, 1974. Hardcover. This dropped The Casket Demon, 1963, and added some extra stories: The Black Gondolier, 1964; Midnight in the Mirror World, 1964; I'm Looking for Jeff, 1952; The Creature from the Cleveland Depths, 1962; The Oldest Soldier, 1960; The Girl with the Hungry Eyes, 1949; and A Bit of the Dark World, 1962.

31. The Best of Fritz Leiber. Published by Sphere Books, London, 1974. Softcover. This contains: Gonna Roll the Bones, 1967; Sanity, 1944; Wanted - An Enemy, 1945; The Man Who Never Grew Young, 1947; The Ship Sails at Midnight, 1950; The Enchanted Forest, 1050; Coming Attraction, 1950; Poor Superman, 1951; A Pail of Air, 1951; The Foxholes of Mars, 1952; The Big Trek, 1957; The Big Holiday, 1953; The Night He Cried, 1953; Space Time for Springers, 1958; Try and Change the Past, 1958; A Deskful of Girls, 1958; Rump-Titty-Titty-Tum-Tah-Tee, 1958; Little Old Miss Macbeth, 1958;

Mariana, 1960; The Man Who Made Friends With Electricity, 1962; The Good New Days, 1965; and America the Beautiful, 1970; along with an afterword by **Fritz Leiber** and a bibliography by Gerald Bishop.

32. The Best of Fritz Leiber. Published by Nelson Doubleday, Garden City, New York, 1974. The first hardcover edition, though with a slight difference from the British paperback. This has an introduction by **Poul Anderson** and does not have the Bishop bibliography.

33. The Best of Fritz Leiber. Published by Sidgwick and Jackson, London, 1974. The first hardcover edition of the British version.

34. The Book of Fritz Leiber. Published by DAW Books, New York City, 1974. DAW Collector's Book 87 - UQ1091. Softcover. Herein: Foreword by **Fritz Leiber**. The Spider, 1963; Monsters and Monster Lovers, 1965; A Hitch in Space, 1963; Hottest and Coldest Molecules, 1952; Kindergarten, 1963; Those Wild Alien Worlds - an essay, 1974; Crazy Annaoj, 1968; Debunking the I Machine, 1949; When the Last Gods Die, 1951; King Lear - an essay, 1934; Yesterday House, 1952; After Such Knowledge, 1974; Knight to Move, 1965; Weird World of the Knight - an essay, 1960; To Arkham and the Stars, 1966; The Whisperer Re-examined - an essay, 1964; Beauty and the Beasts, 1974; Masters of Mace and Magic, an essay, 1974; and Cat's Cradle, 1974.

35. The Second Book of Fritz Leiber. Published by DAW Books, New York City, 1975. DAW Collector's Book 164 - UY1195. Softcover. Herein: Foreword by **Fritz Leiber**; The Lion and the Lamb, 1950; Trapped in the Sea of Stars, 1975; The Mighty Tides - an essay, 1961; Fafhrd and Me - an essay, 1963; Belsen Express, 1975; Scream Wolf, 1961; The Mechanical Bride, 1954; Through Hyperspace with Brown Jenkin, 1963; and A Defense of Werewolves, 1948.

36. The Mind Spider and Other Stories. Published by Ace Books, New York City, 1976. Ace Book 53330. Softcover. This added a new foreword by **Fritz Leiber** and dropped Try and Change the Past, replacing it with Midnight in the Mirror World. Foreword by **Fritz Leiber**; The Haunted Future, 1959; Damnation Morning, 1959; The Oldest Soldier, 1960; Midnight in the Mirror World, 1964; The Number of the Beast, 1958; and The Mind Spider, 1959.

37. The Big Time. Published by Gregg Press, Boston, 1976. First hardcover edition.

38. The Worlds of Fritz Leiber. Published by Ace Books, New York City, 1976. Ace Book 91640. Softcover. Herein: Introduction by **Fritz Leiber**; Hatchery of Dreams, 1961; The Goggles of Dr Dragonet, 1961; Far Reach to Cygnus, 1965; Night Passage, 1975; Nice Girl with Five Husbands, 1951; When the Change Winds Blow 1964; 237 Talking Statues, Etc., 1963; Improper Authorities, 1959; Our Saucer Vacation, 1959; Pipe Dream, 1959; What's He Doing in There?, 1957; Friends and Enemies, 1957; The Last Letter, 1958; Endfray of the Ofay, 1969; Cyclops, 1965; Mysterious Doings in the Metropolitan Museum, 1974; The Bait, 1973; The Lotus Eaters, 1972; Waif, 1974; Myths My Great Granddaughter Taught Me, 1963; Catch That Zeppelin!, 1975; and Last, 1957.

39. Our Lady of Darkness. Published by Berkley/Putnam, New York City, 1977. Hardcover.

40. Rime Isle. Published by Whispers Press, Chapel Hill, North Carolina, 1977. Hardcover. This contains: The Frost Monstreme, 1976; and Rime Isle, 1977.

41. Swords and Ice Magic. Published by Ace Books, New York City, 1977. Softcover. Ace Book 79166-2. Herein: The Sadness of the Executioner, 1973; Beauty and the Beasts, 1974; Trapped in Shadowland, 1973; The Bait, 1973; Under the Thumbs of the Gods, 1975; Trapped in the Sea of Stars, 1975; The Frost Monstreme, 1976; and Rime Isle, 1977.

42. Swords Against Wizardry. Published by Gregg Press, Boston, 1977. First hardcover edition. Herein: In the Witch's Tent, 1968; Stardock, 1965; The Two Best Thieves in Lankhmar, 1968; and The Lords of Quarmall, 1964.

43. Swords in the Mist. Published by Gregg Press, Boston, 1977. First hardcover edition. Herein: The Cloud of Hate, 1963; Lean Times in Lankhmar, 1959; Their Mistress, the Sea, 1968; When the Sea King's Away, 1960; The Wrong Branch, 1968; and Adept's Gambit, 1947.

44. Swords Against Death. Published by Gregg Press, Boston, 1977. First hardcover edition. This contains: The Circle Curse, 1970; The Jewels in the Forest, 1939; Thieves' House, 1943; The Bleak Shore, 1940; The Howling Tower, 1941; The Sunken Land, 1942; The Seven Black Priests, 1953; Claws from the Night, 1951; The Price of Pain Ease, 1970; and Bazaar of the Bizarre, 1963.

45. Swords and Deviltry. Published by Gregg Press, Boston, 1977. First hardcover edition. Herein: Induction, 1957; The Snow Women, 1970; The Unholy Grail, 1962; and Ill Met in Lankhmar, 1970.

46. Swords and Ice Magic. Published by Gregg Press, Boston, 1977. First hardcover edition. Herein: The Sadness of the Executioner, 1973; Beauty and the Beasts, 1974; Trapped in Shadowland, 1973; The Bait, 1973; Under the Thumbs of the Gods, 1975; Trapped in the Sea of Stars, 1975; The Frost Monstreme, 1976; and Rime Isle, 1977.

47. The Worlds of Fritz Leiber. Published by Gregg Press, Boston, 1977. First hardcover edition. This ads an introduction by the author's son, Justin Leiber.

48. Heroes and Horrors. Published by Whispers Press, Chapel Hill, North Carolina, 1978. Hardcover. Herein: Preface by Stuart David Schiff; **Fritz Leiber**: An Appreciation by John Jakes; Sea Magic, 1977; The Mer She, 1978; A Bit of the Dark World, 1962; Belsen Express, 1975; Midnight in the Mirror World, 1964; Richmond, Late September 1849, 1969; Midnight by the Morphy Watch, 1974; The Terror from the Depths, 1976; and Dark Wings, 1978.

49. Bazaar of the Bizarre. Published by Donald M. Grant, New Providence, Rhode Island, 1978. Hardcover limited edition with a dropped-in signature

Fritz Leiber

sheet signed by **Fritz Leiber** and by the illustrator, Stephan Peregrine. Herein: Introduction to **Fritz Leiber**; Bazaar of the Bizarre, 1963; The Cloud of Hate, 1963; and Lean Times in Lankhmar, 1959.

50. The Change War. Published by Gregg Press, Boston, 1978. Hardcover. Herein: Introduction by John Silbersack; No Great Magic, 1963; The Oldest Soldier, 1960; Knight to Move, 1965; Damnation Morning, 1959; Try and Change the Past, 1958; A Deskful of Girls, 1958; The Number of the Beast, 1958; The Haunted Future, 1959; The Mind Spider, 1959; and Black Corridor, 1967.

51. Ship of Shadows. Published by Victor Gollancz, London, 1979. Hardcover. This contains: The Big Time, 1958; Ill Met in Lankhmar, 1970; Gonna Roll the Bones, 1967; Belsen Express, 1975; Catch That Zeppelin!, 1975; and Ship of Shadows, 1969.

52. The Book of Fritz Leiber - Volume I and II. Published by Gregg Press, Boston, 1977. First hardcover edition. An omnibus, this gathers: The Book of Fritz Leiber, 1974; and The Second Book of Fritz Leiber, 1975; Introduction by T. Collins.

53. Ervool. Published by Cheap Street, Roanoke, Virginia, 1980. Softcover. Produced in a limited edition for the 6th World Fantasy Convention in Baltimore, Maryland, October 1980.

54. Riches and Powers. Published by Cheap Street, Roanoke, Virginia, 1980. Limited edition softcover.

55. Changewar. Published by Ace Books, New York City, 1983. Softcover. Herein: Try and Change the Past, 1958; The Oldest Soldier, 1960; Damnation Morning, 1959; When the Change-Winds Blow, 1964; Knight to Move, 1965; A Deskful of Girls, 1958; and No Great Magic, 1963.

56. Quicks Around the Zodiac - a Farce. Afterword by **Gene Wolfe**. Published by Cheap Street, New Castle, Virginia, 1983. Signed limited edition hardcover.

57. In the Beginning. Published by Cheap Street, New Castle, Virginia, 1983. Signed limited edition hardcover.

58. The Ghostlight. Published by Berkley Books, New York City, 1984. A signed and numbered limited hardcover edition. Herein: Coming Attraction, 1950; A Deskful of Girls, 1958; Space-Time for Springers, 1958; Four Ghosts in Hamlet, 1965; Gonna Roll the Bones, 1967; Bazaar of the Bizarre, 1963; Midnight by the Morphy Watch, 1974; Black Glass, 1978; Not Much Disorder and Not So Early Sex: An Autobiographic Essay, 1984; and The Ghost Light, 1984.

59. The Knight and Knave of Swords. Published by William Morrow, New York City, 1988. Hardcover. This contains: Sea Magic, 1977; The Mer She, 1978; The Curse of the Smalls and the Stars, 1983; and The Mouser Goes Below, 1988.

60. The Three of Swords. Published by Nelson Doubleday, Garden City, New York, 1989 for the Science Fiction Book Club. Hardcover. An omnibus edition, this gathers: Swords and Deviltry, 1970; Swords Against Death, 1970; and Swords in the Mist, 1968.

61. Ship of Shadows. Published by Tor Books, New York City, 199.8 Tor Double 5. Softcover. Bound with No Truce with Kings by **Poul Anderson**.

62. Swords' Masters. Published by Guild America Books, New York City, 1990. Book Club edition. Hardcover. An omnibus, this collects: Swords Against Wizardry, 1968; The Swords of Lankhmar, 1968; and Swords and Ice Magic, 1977.

63. Ill Met in Lankhmar. Published by Tor Books, New York City, 1990. Tor Double 19. Softcover. Bound with The Fair in Emain Macha by Charles de Lint.

64. The Leiber Chronicles: Fifty Years of Fritz Leiber. Published by Dark Harvest, Arlington Hts., Illinois, 1990. Hardcover. Herein: Two Sought Adventure, 1939; The Automatic Pistol, 1940; Smoke Ghost, 1941; The Hound, 1942; Sanity, 1944; Wanted - An Enemy, 1945; Alice and the Allergy, 1946; The Girl with the Hungry Eyes, 1949; The Man Who Never Grew Young, 1947; Coming Attraction, 1950; A Pail of Air, 1951; Poor Superman, 1951; Yesterday House, 1952; The Moon is Green, 1952; A Bad Day for Sales, 1953; The Night He Cried, 1953; What's He Doing in There?, 1957; Try and Change the Past, 1958; Rump-Titty-Titty-Tum-Tah-Tee, 1958; The Haunted Future, 1959; Mariana, 1960; The Beat Cluster, 1961; The 64-Square Madhouse, 1962; The Man Who Made Friends with Electricity, 1962; Bazaar of the Bizarre, 1963; 237 Talking Statues, Etc., 1963; When the Change-Winds Blow, 1964; Four Ghosts in Hamlet, 1965; Gonna Roll the Bones, 1967; The Inner Circles, 1967; Ship of Shadows, 1969; Endfray of the Ofay, 1969; America the Beautiful, 1970; Ill Met in Lankhmar, 1970; The Bait, 1973; Midnight by the Morphy Watch, 1974; Belsen Express, 1975; Catch That Zeppelin!, 1975; The Glove, 1975; The Death of Princes, 1976; A Rite of Spring, 1977; The Button Molder, 1979; Horrible Imaginings, 1982; and The Curse of the Smalls and the Stars, 1983.

65. Conjure Wife - with - Out Lady of Darkness. Published by Tor Books, New York City, 1991. Tor Double 36. Softcover. This combines: Conjure Wife; 1952; and Out Lady of Darkness, 1977.

66. Gummitch and Friends. Published by Donald M. Grant, Hampton Falls, New Hampshire, 1992. Hardcover. Herein: Introduction by **Fritz Leiber**; Space-Time for Springers, 1958; Kreativity for Kats, 1959; Cat's Cradle, 1974; The Cat Hotel, 1983; Thrice the Brinded Cat, 1992; The Lotus Eaters, 1972; Cat Three, 1973; The Bump, 1972; The Great San Francisco Glacier, 1981; and Ship of Shadows, 1969; along with a series of poems by Margo Skinner; Sestina of the Cat in the Doorway - a poem by **Poul Anderson**, 1959; and Afterword by Margo Skinner.

67. Kreativity for Kats and Other Feline Fantasies. Published by Wildside Press, Rockville, Maryland, 1992. Softcover. Herein: Kreativity for Kats, 1959; The Cat Hotel, 1983; and Cat Three, 1973.

225

68. Ill Met in Lankhmar. Published by Borealis - White Wolf Publishing, Clarkston, Georgia, 1995. Hardcover. Herein: Introduction by **Michael Moorcock**; Swords and Deviltry, 1970; The Gray Mouser 1 - a poem, 1959; The Gray Mouser 2 - a poem, 1959; and Swords Against death, 1970.

69. Lean Times in Lankhmar. Published by Borealis - White Wolf Publishing, Clarkston, Georgia, 1996. Hardcover. Herein: Introduction by Raymond E. Feist; Swords in the Mist, 1968; Swords Against Wizardry, 1968.

70. Return to Lankhmar. Published by Borealis - White Wolf Publishing, Clarkston, Georgia, 1997. Hardcover. Herein: Introduction by Neil Gaiman; The Swords of Lankhmar, 1968; and Swords and Ice Magic, 1977.

71. The Dealings of Daniel Kesserich. Published by Tor Books, New York City, 1997. Hardcover.

72. Dark Ladies. Published by Orb - Tor Books, New York City, 1999. Softcover. Reissues the Tor Double that featured: Conjure Wife; 1952; and Out Lady of Darkness, 1977.

73. Lankhmar: Tales of Fafhrd and the Gray Mouser. Published by White Wolf Publishing, Clarkston, Georgia, 2000. Hardcover. Herein: Introduction by **Fritz Leiber**; The Snow Women, 1970; The Unholy Grail, 1962; Ill Met in Lankhmar, 1970; The Circle Curse, 1970; and The Jewels in the Forest, 1939.

74. Thieves' House: Tales of Fafhrd and the Gray Mouser - Volume 2. Published by White Wolf Publishing, Clarkston, Georgia, 2001. Hardcover. Herein: Thieves' House, 1943; The Bleak Shore, 1940; The Howling Tower, 1941; The Sunken Land, 1942; The Seven Black Priests, 1953; Claws from the Night, 1951; The Price of Pain Ease, 1970; Bazaar of the Bizarre, 1963; The Cloud of Hate, 1963; and Lean Times in Lankhmar, 1959.

75. The Black Gondolier and Other Stories. Published by Midnight House, Rio Rancho, New Mexico, 2001. Hardcover. This contains: Introduction by John Pelan; The Black Gondolier, 1964; The Dreams of Albert Moreland, 1945; Game for Motel Room, 1963; The Phantom Slayer, 1942; Lie Still, Snow White, 1964; Mr Bauer and the Atoms, 1946; In the X-Ray, 1949; Spider Mansion, 1942; The Secret Songs, 1962; The Man Who Made Friends with Electricity, 1962; The Dead Man, 1950; The Thirteenth Step, 1962; The Repair People, 1980; Black Has Its Charms, 1984; Schizo Jimmie, 1960; The Creature from Cleveland Depths, 1962; The Casket-Demon, 1963; and Dr Adams' Garden of Evil, 1963; followed by an afterword by Steve Savile.

76. Smoke Ghost and Other Apparitions. Published by Midnight House, Rio Rancho, New Mexico, 2002. Hardcover. Herein: Introduction by Ramsey Campbell; Smoke Ghost, 1941; The Power of the Puppets, 1942; Cry Witch!, 1951; The Hill and the Hole, 1942; The Enormous Bedroom, 2002; Black Glass, 1978; I'm Looking for Jeff, 1952; The Eeriest Ruined Dawn World, 1976; Richmond, Late September, 1849, 1969; The House of Mrs Delgato, 1959; The Black Ewe, 1950; Replacement for Wilmer: A Ghost Story, 1990; MS Found in a Maelstrom, 1959; The Winter Flies, 1967; The Button Molder, 1979; Do You Know Dave Wenzel?, 1974; A Visitor from Back East, 1961; Dark Wings, 1976; and Some Notes on the Texts by John Pelan and Steve Savile.

77. Day Dark, Night Bright. Published by Darkside Press, Rio Rancho, New Mexico, 2002. Hardcover. Herein: The Man Who Made Science Fiction Grow Up by John Pelan; Time Fighter, 1957; Night Passage, 1975; Moon Duel, 1965; Later Than You Think, 1950; Mirror, 1965; The 64-Square Madhouse, 1962; All the Weed in the World, 1961; The Mutant's Brother, 1943; The Man Who Was Married to Space and Time, 1979; Thought, 1944; The Crystal Prison, 1966; Bullet with His Name, 1958; Success, 1963; To Make a Roman Holiday, 1943; Bread Overhead, 1958; The Reward, 1959; Taboo, 1944; Business of Killing, 1944; and Day Dark, Night Bright, 1972.

78. Fritz Leiber and H. P. Lovecraft: Writers of the Dark. Edited by Ben J. S. Szumskyi and S. T. Joshi. Published by Wildside Press, Rockville, Maryland, 2004. Softcover. Herein: Introduction by Ben. S. J. Szumskyi; Letters to Fritz and Jonquil Leiber from H. P. Lovecraft; Adept's Gambit, 1947; The Demons of the Upper Air, 2004; The Sunken Land, 1942; Diary in the Snow, 1947; The Dreams of Albert Moreland, 1945; The Dead Man, 1950; A Bit of the Dark World, 1962; To Arkham and the Stars, 1966; The Terror from the Depths, 1976; and the following essays by **Fritz Leiber**: The Works of H. P. Lovecraft: Suggestions for a Critical Appraisal, 1944; Some Random Thoughts About Lovecraft's Writings, 1945; Leiber on Onderdonk, 1945; A Literary Copernicus, 1949; My Correspondence with Lovecraft, 1958; Lovecraft: A Symposium - written with Leland Shapiro and Arthur Jean Cox, 1963; The Whisperer Re-examined, 1964; The Cthulhu Mythos: Wondrous and Terrible, 1975; Lovecraft in My Life, 1976; and an afterword by S. T. Joshi.

79. The Creature from Cleveland Depths and Other Tales. Published by Wildside Press, Rockville, Maryland, 2007. Hardcover. Herein: The Creature from Cleveland Depths, 1962; Bread Overhead, 1958; and No Great Magic, 1963.

***

ANTHOLOGIES

1. The World Fantasy Awards - Volume 2. With Stuart David Schiff. Published by Doubleday & Company, Garden City, New York, 1980. Hardcover. Herein: Introduction: Terror, Mystery, Wonder by **Fritz Leiber**; Preface by Stuart David Schiff; Jerusalem's Lot by Stephen King, 1978; Smoke Ghost by **Fritz Leiber**, 1941; There's a Long, Long Trail A-Winding by Russell Kirk, 1976; The Whimper of Whipped Dogs by Harlan Ellison, 1973; Belsen Express by **Fritz Leiber**, 1975; The Ghastly Priest Doth Reign by Manly Wade Wellman, 1975; The Barrow Troll by David Drake, 1975; The Companion by Ramsey Campbell, 1976; It Only Comes Out at Night by Dennis Etchison, 1976; Two Suns Setting by Karl Edward Wagner, 1976; The October Game by **Ray Bradbury**, 1948; A Visitor from Egypt by Frank

Fritz Leiber

Belknap Long, 1930; The King's Shadow Has No Limits by Avram Davidson, 1975; Best Artist - Frank Frazetta - an essay by Roger Dean; and Special Award - Non-Professional - Carcosa - an essay by Stuart David Schiff.

***

NON-FICTION

1. Journal of the H. P. Lovecraft Society - Number 1: Featuring Fritz Leiber. Published by The H. P. Lovecraft Society, Richmond, California, 1976. Softcover. Features Lovecraft in My Life and The Stage in My Stories by **Fritz Leiber**.

2. Fafhrd and Me: A Collection of Essays. Edited by John Gregory Betancourt; Introduction by Darrell Schweitzer. Published by Wildside Press, Newark, New Jersey, 1990. Softcover. Herein: Introduction by Darrell Schweitzer; Fafhrd and Me, 1963; Monsters and Monster Lovers, 1965; The Anima Archetype in Science Fantasy; Debunking the I-Machine, 1949; Robert E. Howard's Style, 1961; John Carter, Sword of Theosophy, 1959; My Life and Writings, 1983; A Literary Copernicus, 1949; My Correspondence with Lovecraft, 1958; The Whisperer Re-Examined, 1964; and Through Hyperspace with Brown Jenkin, 1963.

***

RELATED

1. The Magazine of Fantasy and Science Fiction - Fritz Leiber Special Issue - July 1969. Published by Mercury Press, Cornwall, Connecticut, 1969. Softcover. Herein: Ship of Shadows by **Fritz Leiber**; **Fritz Leiber** - a profile by Judith Merril; Demons of the Upper Air - a poem by **Fritz Leiber**; and **Fritz Leiber**: A Bibliography by Al Lewis; along with all the usual features.

2. Fritz Leiber: A Bibliography 1934 - 1979. By Chris Morgan. Published by Morgernstern, Birmingham, England, 1979. Softcover.

3. Fritz Leiber. By Jeff Frane. Published by Starmont, Mercer Island, Washington, 1980. Starmont Reader's Guide 8. Softcover.

4. Fritz Leiber. By Tom Staicar. Published by Frederick Ungar, New York City, 1983. Hardcover.

5. Tales of the Unanticipated #6 - Fritz Leiber. Published by The Minnesota Science Fiction Society, 1989. Softcover. Features some work by **Fritz Leiber**, along with an interview and two articles about him: **Fritz Leiber** by Eric M. Heideman and **Fritz Leiber** and His Work by Rodger Gerberding.

6. Fritz Leiber: Sardonic Swordsman: A Working Bibliography. By Phil Stephensen, Payne Benson and Gordon Benson. Published by Galactic Central Publications, Leeds, England, 1990. Softcover.

7. Witches of the Mind: A Critical Study of Fritz Leiber. By Bruce Byfield. Published by Necronomicon Press, West Warwick, Rhode Island, 1991. Softcover.

8. The SFWA Grand Masters - Volume 1: Robert A. Heinlein; Jack Williamson; Clifford D. Simak; L. Sprague de Camp; and Fritz Leiber. Published by Tor Books, New York City, 1999. Hardcover.

9. Fritz Leiber: Critical Essays. Edited by Benjamin Szumsky. Published by McFarland and Company, Jefferson, North Carolina, 2007. Hardcover.

Jack Vance.

John Holbrook Vance was born on August 28th, 1916 in San Francisco, California.

He recently said that life was too short not to get as much into it as you possibly could. And that is how he lives it. From very early on, he worked to support himself, labouring at everything from bell boy to carpenter, from electrician to deck hand on a merchant ship during World War Two after being rejected by the Army for failing the eye test. Legend has it that he memorised the eye chart and bluffed his way into the Merchant Marine.

He attended the University of California in Berkeley and spread his education out over six years, first majoring in mining engineering, on to physics and then into journalism and English.

He travelled widely and worked job after job. And even though he made his first professional magazine sale in 1945, and worked as a screenwriter on the Captain Video television series, it wasn't until the 1970s that he established himself well enough as a writer to write full-time without having to think about finding something to support such a nasty habit.

The first story sold was The World-Thinker - in 1996, it was awarded a Retro Hugo for Best Short Story. Sam Merwin, Jr bought it for Thrilling Wonder Stories and it appeared in the Summer 1945 issue along with: The Deconventionalizers by Edmond Hamilton; Things Pass By by Murray Leinster; Percy the Pirate by Henry Kuttner; The Purple Dusk by Frank Belknap Long writing as Leslie Northern; and The Shadow Dwellers by Frank Belknap Long writing as Frank Belknap Long.

The following year, he sold a couple more stories, including Planet of the Black Dust, again to Sam Merwin, Jr, this time for the Summer 1946 issue of Startling Stories, where it appeared with some familiar faces: The Man Who Saw Everything by Edmond Hamilton; and The Dark World by Henry Kuttner; along with The Vicious Circle by John Russell Fearn writing as Polton Cross; and Extra Earth by Ross Rocklynne.

By 1959, Vance had been nominated for his first Hugo award. It was for The Miracle Workers, which had been published by **John W. Campbell** in Astounding Science Fiction, July 1958.

The Miracle Workers failed to win. But Vance's next nomination did win. The Dragon Masters, from Galaxy Magazine, August 1962, took the Hugo for best short fiction, 1963.

When asked recently if he had always wanted to be a writer, Vance said yes. He explained that it wasn't because he had any sort of great creative instinct but he liked the idea of not having a boss, of not having to be in any particular place at a particular time, day-after-day.

About the actual writing, he said, "After fooling around I finally made it stick."

Some of his mystery writing tends to bring higher prices than his science fiction/fantasy. British hardcovers of The Madman Theory and A Room to Die In, both written as Ellery Queen, go for around $2,000.00. Another mystery, Island of Peril, sells in the $1,300.00 range. But his highest priced science fiction work, aside from some of the Underwood Miller limited editions, is Emphyrio from 1969. It sells for around $800.00.

Pen names used: John Holbrook Vance; Alan Wade; Peter Held; John Van See; and Ellery Queen.

***

AWARDS

1963. Hugo Best Short Fiction Award for The Dragon Masters - Galaxy Magazine, August 1962.
1966. Nebula Best Novella Award for The Last Castle - Galaxy Magazine, April 1966.
1967. Hugo Best Novelette Award for The Last Castle - Galaxy Magazine, April 1966.
1984. World Fantasy Award for Lifetime Achievement.
1990. World Fantasy Best Novel Award for Lyonesse: Madouc.
1996. Nebula Grand Master Award.

***

FILM AND TELEVISION

1. Adventure on Phobos. This was for the television series Captain Video and His Video Rangers. The show aired on May 11th, 1953 and starred: Al Hodge; Don Hastings; Ben Lackland; and Hal Conklin.

2. Black Planet Academy. Also for the television series Captain Video and His Video Rangers. The show aired on May 18th, 1953 and starred: Al Hodge; Don Hastings; Ben Lackland; and Hal Conklin.

3. Man in a Cage. This 1960 novel was adapted for the television series Thriller. Directed by Gerald Mayer, it aired on January 17th, 1961, Season 1, Episode 18. The show starred: Joe Abdullah; Danielle Aubry; Russ Bender; Philip Carey; Lilyan Chauvin; Guy Stockwell; and many others, including Boris Karloff as himself.

4. Bad Ronald. From 1973, this novel was made into a TV movie, airing on October 23rd, 1974. Directed by Buzz Kulik, it starred: Scott Jacoby; Pippa Scott; John Larch; Dabney Coleman; Kim Hunter; and many others.

5. Mechant garcon - Bad Ronald. Again from the 1973 novel, this was released in France on March 11th, 1992. Directed by Charles Gassot, it starred: Catherine Hiegel; Joachim Lombard; Donald Sumpter; Patty Hannock; Geraldine Alexander; Juliette Caton; and many others.

***

RADIO

The Potters of Firsk. From Astounding Science

Fiction, May 1950, this was used on Dimension X and aired on July 28th, 1950.

***

NOVELS AND COLLECTIONS

1. The Dying Earth. Published by Hillman Periodicals, New York City, 1950. Hillman Book HP 41. Softcover. Herein, from 1950: Mazirian the Magician; Turjan of Miir; Tsais; Liane the Wayfarer; Ulan Dhor Ends a Dream; and Guyal of Sfere.

2. Vandals of the Void. Published by John C. Winston, Toronto and Philadelphia, 1953. Hardcover.

3. The Space Pirate. Published by Toby Press, New York City, 1953. Softcover. A shorter version of this was released in 1963 by Ace Books.

4. To Live Forever. Published by Ballantine Books, New York City, 1956. Issued simultaneously in hardcover and softcover. The paperback version is Ballantine Book 167.

5. Big Planet. Published by Avalon Books, New York City, 1957. Hardcover.

6. Isle of Peril. Writing as Alan Wade. Published by Mystery House, New York City, 1957. Hardcover.

7. Take My Face. Writing as Peter Held. Published by Mystery House, New York City, 1957. Hardcover.

8. Big Planet. Published by Ace Books, New York City, 1958. Ace Double D-295. Bound with Slaves of the Klau by **Jack Vance**.

9. Slaves of the Klau. Published by Ace Books, New York City, 1958. Ace Double D-295. Bound with Big Planet by **Jack Vance**.

10. The Languages of Pao. Published by Avalon Books, New York City, 1958. Hardcover.

11. The Man in the Cage. Writing as John Holbrook Vance. Published by Random House, New York City, 1960. Hardcover.

12. The Dragon Masters. Published by Ace Books, New York City, 1963. Ace Double F-185. Softcover. Bound with The Five Gold Bands by **Jack Vance**, 1950.

13. The Five Gold Bands. Published by Ace Books, New York City, 1963. Ace Double F-185. Softcover. Bound with The Dragon Masters by **Jack Vance**.

14. The Houses of Iszm. Published by Ace Books, New York City, 1964. Ace Double F-265. Softcover. Bound with Son of the Tree by **Jack Vance**.

15. Son of the Tree. Published by Ace Books, New York City, 1964. Ace Double F-265. Softcover. Bound with The Houses of Iszm by **Jack Vance**.

16. The Killing Machine. Published by Berkley Books, New York City, 1964. Berkley Book F1003. Softcover.

17. The Four Johns. Writing as Ellery Queen. Published by Pocket Books, New York City, 1964. Pocket Book 6229. Softcover.

18. The Star King. Published by Berkley Books, New York City, 1964. Berkley Book F905. Softcover.

19. Future Tense. Published by Ballantine Books, New York City, 1964. Ballantine Book U2214. Softcover. Herein: Dodkin's Job, 1959; Ullward's Retreat, 1958; Sail 25, 1962; and The Gift of Gab, 1955.

20. Space Opera. Published by Pyramid Books, New York City, 1965. Pyramid Book R-1140. Softcover.

21. Monsters in Orbit. Published by Ace Books, New York City, 1965. Ace Double M-125. Softcover. Together with The World Between and Other Stories by **Jack Vance**.

22. The World Between and Other Stories. Published by Ace Books, New York City, 1965. Ace Double M-125. Softcover. Together with Monsters in Orbit by **Jack Vance**. The World Between contains: The World Between, 1953; The Moon Moth, 1961; Brain of the Galaxy, 1951; The Devil on Salvation Bluff, 1955; and The Men Return, 1957.

23. The Dragon Masters. Published by Dennis Dobson, London, 1965. First hardcover edition.

24. A Room to Die In. Writing as Ellery Queen. Published by Pocket Books, New York City, 1965. Pocket Book 35067. Softcover.

25. The Blue World. Published by Ballantine Books, New York City, 1966. Ballantine Book U2169. Softcover.

26. The Brains of Earth. Published by Ace Books, New York City, 1966. Ace Double M-141. Softcover. Together with The Many Worlds of Magnus Ridolph by **Jack Vance**.

27. The Many Worlds of Magnus Ridolph. Published by Ace Books, New York City, 1966. Ace Double M-141. Softcover. Together with The Brains of Earth by **Jack Vance**. The Many Worlds of Magnus Ridolph contains: The Kokod Warriors, 1952; The Unspeakable McInch, 1948; The Howling Bounders, 1949; The King of Thieves, 1949; The Spa of the Stars, 1950; and Coup de Grace, 1958.

28. The Eyes of the Overworld. Published by Ace Books, New York City, 1966. Ace Book M-149. Softcover.

29. The Fox Valley Murders. Writing as John Holbrook Vance. Published by Bobbs-Merrill, New York City, 1966. Hardcover.

30. The Madman Theory. Writing as Ellery Queen. Published by Pocket Books, New York City, 1966. Pocket Book 50496. Softcover.

31. The Star King. Published by Dennis Dobson, London, 1966. First hardcover edition.

32. The Pleasant Grove Murders. Writing as John Holbrook Vance. Published by Bobbs-Merrill, New York City, 1967. Hardcover.

33. The Last Castle. Published by Ace Books,

New York City, 1967. Ace Double H-21. Softcover. Together with World of the Sleeper by Tony Wayman.

34. The Palace of Love. Published by Berkley Books, New York City, 1967. Berkley Book X1454. Softcover.

35. The Killing Machine. Published by Dennis Dobson, London, 1967. First hardcover edition.

36. The Palace of Love. Published by Dennis Dobson, London, 1968. First hardcover edition.

37. The City of Chasch. Published by Ace Books, New York City, 1968. Ace Book G-688. Softcover.

38. The Deadly Isles. Writing as John Holbrook Vance. Published by Bobbs-Merrill, New York City, 1968. Hardcover.

39. Servants of the Wankh. Published by Ace Books, New York City, 1969. Ace Book 66900. Softcover.

40. The Dirdir. Published by Ace Books, New York City, 1969. Ace Book 66901. Softcover.

41. Eight Fantasms and Magics. Published by The Macmillan Company, New York City, 1969. Herein: Foreword by **Jack Vance**; The Miracle Workers, 1958; When the Five Moons Rise, 1954; Telek, 1952; Noise, 1952; The New Prime, 1951; Cil, 1966; Guyal of Sfere, 1950; and The Men Return, 1957.

42. Emphyrio. Published by Doubleday & Company, Garden City, New York, 1969. Hardcover.

43. The Pnume. Published by Ace Books, New York City, 1970. Ace Book 66902. Softcover.

44. The Anome. Published by Dell Books, New York City, 1973. Dell Book 0441. Softcover.

45. The Dragon Masters/The Last Castle. Published by Ace Books, New York City, 1973. Ace Double 16641. Softcover. Herein: The Dragon Masters, 1962; The Last Castle, 1966.

46. The Brave Free Men. Published by Dell Books, New York City, 1973. Dell Book 1708. Softcover.

47. Bad Ronald. Writing as John Holbrook Vance. Published by Ballantine Books, New York City, 1973. Softcover.

48. Trullion: Alastor 2262. Published by Ballantine Books, New York City, 1973. Softcover.

49. The Worlds of Jack Vance. Published by Ace Books, New York City, 1973. Ace Book 90955. Softcover. Herein: The World Between, 1953; The Moon Moth, 1961; Brain of the Galaxy, 1951; The Devil on Salvation Bluff, 1955; The Men Return, 1957; The Kokod Warriors, 1952; The King of Thieves, 1949; Coup De Grace, 1958; and The Brains of Earth, 1966.

50. The Asutra. Published by Dell Books, New York City, 1974. Dell Book 3157. Softcover.

51. The Gray Prince. Published by Bobbs-Merrill, New York City, 1974. Hardcover.

52. Showboat World. Published by Pyramid Books, New York City, 1975. Pyramid Book V3698. Softcover.

53. The Brains of Earth. Published by Dennis Dobson, London, 1975. First hardcover edition.

54. The City of Chasch. Published by Dennis Dobson, London, 1975. First hardcover edition.

55. Servants of the Wankh. Published by Dennis Dobson, London, 1975. First hardcover edition.

56. The Dirdir. Published by Dennis Dobson, London, 1975. First hardcover edition.

57. The Pnume. Published by Dennis Dobson, London, 1975. First hardcover edition.

58. Marune: Alastor 933. Published by Ballantine Books, New York City, 1975. Ballantine Book 24518. Softcover.

59. The Moon Moth and Other Stories. Published by Dennis Dobson, London, 1976. Hardcover. Previously issued as The World Between, Ace Books, 1965. This contains: The World Between, 1953; The Moon Moth, 1961; Brain of the Galaxy, 1951; The Devil on Salvation Bluff, 1955; and The Men Return, 1957.

60. Maske: Thaery. Published by Berkley Books, New York City, 1976. Softcover.

61. The Best of Jack Vance. Published by Pocket Books, New York City, 1976. Pocket Book 80510. Softcover. Herein: Preface by **Jack Vance**; Introduction: Capturing Vance by Barry N. Malzberg; Sail 25, 1962; Ullward's Retreat, 1958; The Last Castle, 1966; Abercrombie Station, 1952; The Moon Moth, 1961; and Rumfuddle, 1973.

62. Four Men Called John. Writing as Ellery Queen. Published by Victor Gollancz, London, 1976. Hardcover. Re-titled hardcover issue of The Four Johns, 1964.

63. The Dying Earth. Published by Underwood Miller, Columbia, Pennsylvania, 1976. Signed limited edition. First hardcover edition. Herein: Guyal of Sfere, 1950; Liane the Wayfarer, 1950; Mazirian the Magician, 1950; Tsais, 1950; Turjan of Miir, 1950; and Ulan Dhor Ends a Dream, 1950.

64. The Eyes of the Overworld. Published by Gregg Press, Boston, 1977. First hardcover edition.

65. Wyst: Alastor 1716. Published by DAW Books, New York City, 1978. DAW Collector's Book 312. Softcover.

66. Fantasms and Magics. Published by Mayflower Books, London, 1978. Softcover. Herein: Foreword by **Jack Vance**; Guyal of Sfere, 1950; The Men Return, 1957; The Miracle Workers, 1958; The New Prime, 1951; Noise, 1952; and When the Five Moons Rise, 1954.

67. The Face. Published by DAW Books, New York City, 1979. DAW Book Collector's 361. Softcover.

68. The House on Lily Street. Writing as John Holbrook Vance. Published by Underwood Miller,

Jack Vance

Columbia, Pennsylvania, 1979. Limited edition hardcover.

69. The View from Chickweed's Window. Writing as John Holbrook Vance. Published by Underwood Miller, Columbia, Pennsylvania, 1979. Limited edition hardcover.

70. Green Magic - The Fantasy Realms of Jack Vance. Published by Underwood Miller, Columbia, Pennsylvania, 1979. Limited edition hardcover. Herein: Introduction by John Shirley; Foreword by **Poul Anderson**; The Miracle Workers, 1958; The Moon Moth, 1961; The Mitr, 1953; The Men Return, 1957; The Narrow Land, 1967; The Pilgrims, 1966; The Secret, 1966; and Liane the Wayfarer, 1950.

71. Morreion: A Tale of The Dying Earth. Published by Underwood Miller, Columbia, Pennsylvania, 1979. Limited edition hardcover.

72. Nopalgarth: Three Complete Novels. Published by DAW Books, New York City, 1980. DAW Collector's Book 402. Softcover. An omnibus edition, this gathers: Nopalgarth - aka The Brains of Earth, 1966; Son of the Tree, 1951; and The Houses of Iszm, 1954.

73. Galactic Effectuator. Published by Underwood Miller, Columbia, Pennsylvania, 1980. Limited edition hardcover. Herein: The Dogtown Tourist Agency, 1975; and Freitzke's Turn, 1977. First trade edition, a paperback published by Ace Books, New York City, 1981.

74. Slaves of the Klau. Published by Coronet Books, New York City, 1980. Softcover.

75. The Many Worlds of Magnus Ridolph. Published by DAW Books, New York City, 1980. DAW Collector's Book 381. Softcover. An expanded version, this contains: The Kokod Warriors, 1952; The Unspeakable McInch, 1948; The Howling Bounders, 1949; The King of Thieves, 1949; The Spa of the Stars, 1950; Coup de Grace, 1958; The Sub Standard Sardines, 1949; and To B or Not to C or to D, 1950.

76. The Book of Dreams. Published by DAW Books, New York City, 1981. DAW Collector's Book 416. Softcover.

77. Lost Moons. Published by Underwood Miller, Columbia, Pennsylvania, 1982. Limited edition hardcover. Herein: Foreword by **Jack Vance**; Assault on a City, 1974; The Potters of Firsk, 1950; Winner Lose All, 1951; Four Hundred Blackbirds, 1953; Meet Miss Universe, 1955; Seven Exits from Bocz, 1952; The World Thinker, 1945; Sabotage on Sulphur Planet, 1952; and Dream Castle, 1947.

78. The Narrow Land. Published by DAW Books, New York City, 1982. DAW Collector's Book 490. Softcover. Herein: Green Magic, 1963; The Masquerade on Dicantropus, 1951; The Narrow Land, 1967; Where Hesperus Falls, 1956; The World Thinker, 1945; Chateau D'If, 1950; and The Ten Books, 1951.

79. The Durdane Trilogy. Published by Underwood Miller, Columbia, Pennsylvania, 1983. Limited edition hardcover. This gathers: The Faceless Man - aka The Anome, 1973; The Brave Free Men, 1973; and The Asutra, 1974.

80. Cugel's Saga. Published by Timescape Books, New York City, 1983. Hardcover.

81. Lyonesse: Suldrun's Garden. Published by Underwood Miller, Columbia, Pennsylvania, 1983. Limited edition hardcover. The first trade edition was released in trade paperback by Berkley Books, New York City, 1983. The first trade hardcover edition was printed by the Science Fiction Book Club, Garden City, New York, 1986.

82. Rhialto the Marvellous. Published by Brandywyne Books, San Francisco, 1984. Hardcover limited edition. The first trade edition was released by Baen Books and Simon and Schuster, New York City, 1984. Herein: Foreword by **Jack Vance**; The Murthe, 1984; Fader's Waft, 1984; and Morreion, 1973.

83. Lyonesse II: The Green Pearl. Published by Underwood Miller, Columbia, Pennsylvania, 1985. Limited edition hardcover. The first trade edition was released Berkley Books, New York City, 1985.

84/85. Strange Notions - with - The Dark Ocean. Published by Underwood Miller, Columbia, Pennsylvania, 1985. Limited edition hardcover. Two volumes issued in the same slipcase.

86. The Complete Magnus Ridolph. Published by Underwood Miller, Columbia, Pennsylvania, 1985. Limited edition hardcover. This contains: The Kokod Warriors, 1952; The Unspeakable McInch, 1948; The Howling Bounders, 1949; The King of Thieves, 1949; The Spa of the Stars, 1950; Coup de Grace, 1958; The Sub Standard Sardines, 1949; To B or Not to C or to D, 1950; Hard Luck Diggings, 1948; and Sanatoris Short Cut, 1948.

87. Light from a Lone Star. Published by NESFA Press, Framingham, Massachusetts, 1985. Hardcover. Herein: Introduction by Russell Letson; Cat Island, 1985; First Star I See Tonight, 1985; Hard Luck Diggings, 1948; Noise, 1952; The Men Return, 1957; and The Potters of Firsk, 1950; along with A Talk with **Jack Vance** by Tim Underwood.

88. Planet of Adventure. Published by Grafton Books, London, 1985. Softcover. An omnibus edition, this collects: City of the Chasch, 1968; Servants of the Wankh, 1969; The Dirdir, 1969; and The Pnume, 1970.

89. The Augmented Agent. Published by Underwood Miller, Los Angeles, 1987. Limited edition hardcover. Herein: Introduction by Steven Owen Gordersky; Shape-Up, 1953; The Man from Zodiac, 1967; Golden Girl, 1951; The Planet Machine, 1951; Crusade to Maxus, 1951; Three-Legged Joe, 1953; Sjambak, 1953; and The Augmented Agent, 1961. The first trade edition of this is a paperback from Ace Books, New York City, 1988.

90. Araminta Station. Published by Underwood Miller, Los Angeles, 1987. Limited edition hardcover. The first trade edition was released by Tor Books, New York City, 1988.

231

91. Bird Isle. Published by Underwood Miller, Columbia, Pennsylvania, 1988. Limited edition hardcover.

92. Lyonesse: Madouc. Published by Underwood Miller, Columbia, Pennsylvania, 1989. Limited edition hardcover. The first trade edition was released in trade paperback by Ace Books, New York City, 1990. The first trade hardcover edition was printed by the Science Fiction Book Club, Garden City, New York, 1990.

93. The Last Castle - with - Nightwings. With **Robert Silverberg**. Published by Tor Books, New York City, 1989. Tor Double 15. This binds The Last Castle by **Jack Vance**, 1966, with Nightwings by **Robert Silverberg**, 1968.

94. Ecce and Old Earth. Published by Tor Books, New York City, 1991. Hardcover.

95. Throy. Published by Underwood Miller, Los Angeles, 1992. Limited edition hardcover. The first trade edition was released by Tor Books, New York City, 1993.

96. When the Five Moons Rise. Published by Underwood Miller, Los Angeles, 1992. Limited edition hardcover. This contains: Dodkin's Job, 1959; Telek, 1952; Ullward's Retreat, 1958; Ecological Onslaught, 1953; The Devil on Salvation Bluff, 1955; Dust of Far Suns, 1962; The Masquerade on Dicantropus, 1951; Men of the Ten Books, 1951; The New Prime, 1951; Noise, 1952; When the Five Moons Rise, 1954; and Where Hesperus Falls, 1956.

97. Planet of Adventure. Published by Tor Books, New York City, 1993. First hardcover edition. An omnibus edition, this collects: City of the Chasch, 1968; Servants of the Wankh, 1969; The Dirdir, 1969; and The Pnume, 1970.

98. Alastor. Published by Tor Books, New York City, 1995. Hardcover. An omnibus edition, this gathers: Trullion: Alastor 2262, 1973; Marune: Alastor 933, 1975; and Wyst: Alastor 1716, 1978.

99. Night Lamp. Published by Tor Books, New York City, 1996. Hardcover.

100. The Demon Princes - Volume 1: The Star King, The Killing Machine, The Palace of Love. Published by Tor Books, New York City, 1997. An omnibus edition, this gathers: The Star King, 1964; The Killing Machine, 1964; and The Palace of Love, 1967.

101. The Demon Princes - Volume 2: The Book of Dreams, The Face. Published by Tor Books, New York City, 1997. An omnibus edition, this collects: The Book of Dreams, 1981; and The Face, 1979.

102. The Demon Princes. Published by the Science Fiction Book Club, Garden City, New York, 1998. This omnibus gathers: The Star King, 1964; The Killing Machine, 1964; The Palace of Love, 1967; The Face, 1979; and The Book of Dreams, 1981.

103. The Laughing Magician. Published by Underwood Miller, Los Angeles, 1998. Limited edition hardcover. This collects: The Eyes of the Overworld, 1966; and Cugel's Saga, 1983.

104. Ports of Call. Published by Underwood Miller, Los Angeles, 1998. Limited edition hardcover. The first trade edition was published by Tor Books, New York City, 1998. Hardcover.

105. Coup de Grace and Other Stories. Published by the Vance Integral Edition, United States, 2001. Hardcover. This contains: Introduction by Paul Rhodes; Alfred's Ark, 1965; The Moon Moth, 1961; Coup de Grace, 1958; Flutic, 2001; Dodkin's Job, 1959; Green Magic, 1963; and The Murthe, 1984.

106. Golden Girl and Other Stories. Published by the Vance Integral Edition, United States, 2002. Hardcover. Herein: Golden Girl, 1951; Masquerade on Dicantropus, 1951; Abercrombie Station, 1952; Cholwell's Chickens, 1952; The Mitr, 1953; The World Between, 1953; When the Five Moons Rise, 1954; Meet Miss Universe, 1955; and The Insufferable Red-headed Daughter of Commander Tynott, O.T.E., 2002.

107. Lyonesse II: The Green Pearl and Madouc. Published by Victor Gollancz, London, 2003. Softcover.

108. Gadget Stories. Published by the Vance Integral Edition, United States, 2005. Hardcover. Herein: Planet of the Black Dust, 1946; Dead Ahead, 2005; Hard Luck Diggings, 1948; Sanatoris Short Cut, 1948; The Unspeakable McInch, 1948; The Howling Bounders, 1949; The King of Thieves, 1949; The Sub-Standard Sardines, 1949; To B or Not to C or to D, 1950; Spa of the Stars, 1950; The Enchanted Princess, 1954; The Potters of Firsk, 1950; The Visitors, 2005; Plagian Siphon, 1951; Dover Spargill's Ghastly Floater, 1951; Sabotage on Sulfur Planet, 1952; Three-Legged Joe, 1953; Four Hundred Blackbirds, 1953; Sjambak, 1953; Parapsyche, 1959; and Sail 25, 1962.

109. Son of the Tree and Other Stories. Published by the Vance Integral Edition, United States, 2005. Hardcover. This contains: The Man from Zodiac, 1967; The Augmented Agent, 1961; Shape-Up, 1953; Son of the Tree, 1951; Crusade to Maxus, 1951; Chateau D'If, 1949; and Phalid's Fate, 1946.

110. The World-Thinker and Other Stories. Published by the Vance Integral Edition, United States, 2005. Hardcover. Herein: The World-Thinker, 1945; Dream Castle, 1947; Seven Exits from Bocz, 1952; The God and the Temple Robber, 2005; Telek, 1952; Men of the Ten Books, 1951; DP, 2005; Noise, 1952; The Absent Minded Professor, 2005; The Devil on Salvation Bluff, 1955; Where Hesperus Falls, 1956; The Phantom Milkman, 1956; A Practical Man's Guide, 1957; and The House Lords, 1957.

111. The Houses of Iszm and Other Stories. Published by the Vance Integral Edition, United States, 2005. Hardcover. Herein: The Houses of Iszm, 1954; The Gift of Gab, 1955; Nopalgarth, 2005; and The Narrow Land, 1967.

112. Lurulu. Published by Tor Books, New York City, 2004. Hardcover.

113. Ports of Call - with - Lurulu. Published by the Science Fiction Book Club, Garden City, New York, 2004. Hardcover.

Jack Vance

114. The Jack Vance Treasury. Edited by Terry Dowling and Jonathan Strahan. Published by Subterranean Press, Burton, Michigan, 2007. Hardcover. Herein: Preface by **Jack Vance**; **Jack Vance**: An Appreciation by George R. R. Martin; Introduction by Terry Dowling and Jonathan Strahan; The Dragon Masters, 1962; Liane the Wayfarer, 1950; Sail 25, 1962; The Gift of Gab, 1955; The Miracle Workers, 1958; Guyal of Sfere, 1950; Noise, 1952; The Kokod Warriors, 1952; The Overworld, 1965; The Men Return, 1957; The Sorcerer Pharesm, 1966; The New Prime, 1951; The Secret, 1966; The Moon Moth, 1961; The Bagful of Dreams, 1977; The Mitr, 1953; Morreion, 1973; The Last Castle, 1966; and Biographical Sketch and Other Facts - an essay by **Jack Vance**, 2000.

115. The Jack Vance Reader. Published by Subterranean Press, Burton, Michigan, 2007. Hardcover. An omnibus edition, this gathers: The Domains of Koryphon, 1974; Emphyrio, 1969; and The Languages of Pao, 1958.

116. Wild Thyme, Green Magic. Edited by Terry Dowling and Jonathan Strahan. Published by Subterranean Press, Burton, Michigan, 2009. Hardcover. Herein: Introduction by Terry Dowling and Jonathan Strahan; Assault on a City, 1974; Rumfuddle, 1973; The Augmented Agent, 1961; Green Magic, 1963; Ullward's Retreat, 1958; Coup de Grace, 1958; Chateau D'If, 1949; The Potters of Firsk, 1950; The World-Thinker, 1945; Seven Exits fro Bocz; and Wild Thyme and Violets, 2009.

The Vance Integral Edition. This was a project designed to gather together the collected works of **Jack Vance** in a uniform hardcover edition. The project was started in 1999 and completed in 2006 and finished at forty-four volumes, many of which were unique.

***

RELATED

1. Jack Vance: Science Fiction Stylist. By Richard Tiedman. Published by Robert and Juanita Coulson, Wabash, Indiana, 1965. Softcover.

2. Fantasms: A Bibliography of the Literature of Jack Vance. By Daniel J. H. Levack and Tim Underwood. Published by Underwood Miller, Columbia, Pennsylvania, 1978. Hardcover limited edition.

3. Jack Vance. By Tim Underwood and Chuck Miller. Published by Taplinger, New York City, 1980. Hardcover.

4. Demon Prince: The Dissonant Worlds of Jack Vance. By Jack Rawlings. Published by Borgo Press, San Bernardino, California, 1985. Hardcover.

5. Jack Vance: A Fantasmic Imagination: A Working Bibliography. By Phil Stevensen-Payne, Phil Benson and Gordon Benson. Published by Galactic Central Publications, Leeds, England, 1990. Softcover.

6. The Work of Jack Vance: An Annotated Bibliography and Guide. By Jerry Hewett and Daryl F. Mallett. Published by Underwood Books, Grass Valley, California, 1994. Hardcover.

7. Jack Vance: Critical Appreciations and a Bibliography. By A. E. Cunningham. Published by the British Library, London, 2000. Hardcover.

8. The SFWA Grand Masters: Volume 3: Lester del Rey, Frederik Pohl, Damon Knight, A. E. van Vogt and Jack Vance. Published by Tor Books, New York City, 2002. Softcover.

9. An Encyclopedia of Jack Vance: 20th Century Science Fiction Writer - in Two Volumes. By David G. Mead. Published by EMP - Edwin Mellen Press, Lewiston, New York, 2002. Hardcover.

-2002-

James Blish.

James Benjamin Blish was born in East Orange, New Jersey on May 23rd, 1921 and died of lung cancer at Henley-on-Thames, England, on July 30th, 1975.

Blish studied biology at Rutgers and Columbia. After graduating Rutgers with a BA in microbiology, he was drafted for the war and served as a medical technician until 1944. After the war, he went to Columbia for a couple of years, then took a job as science editor for a pharmaceutical company.

He was a member of The Futurians when he sold his first published short story to fellow-Futurian **Frederik Pohl** at Super Science Stories for the March 1940 issue. It was Emergency Refueling and appeared with: Gravity Island by Harl Vincent; Guyon 45X by Dean D. O'Brien; The Lotus Engine by Raymond Z. Gallun; Phantom from Space by John Russell Fearn; Trans-Plutonian Trap by Ross Rocklynne, World Reborn by John Russell Fearn writing as Thornton Ayre; and A Stitch in Time by Frank Belknap Long.

He also appeared in the following issue of Super Science, May 1940, with his story Bequest of an Angel, accompanied by: Arton's Metal by Ray Cummings; Castaway by **Donald A. Wollheim**; Guardian Angel by Raymond Z. Gallun; Hollow of the Moon by Manly Wade Wellman writing as Gabriel Barclay; Juice by L. Sprague de Camp; King Cole of Pluto by C. M. Kornbluth writing as S. D. Gottesman; Let There Be Light by **Robert A. Heinlein** writing as Lyle Monroe; and Living Isotopes by P. Schuyler Miller.

It was round about then he began to think of himself as a Science Fiction writer. And from then on, his work sold constantly, although he was usually employed somewhere, even while he was writing all those lucrative Star Trek stories. Between 1962 and 1968, he worked for the Tobacco Institute, an American trade group founded in 1958 to promote tobacco sales, which is somewhat ironic, considering how Blish died.

In 1968, he moved to England. Explaining the move in an interview with **Brian W. Aldiss**, he said, "I was actually headed for Italy when I stopped off here, and I felt no reason to go any further." He went on to explain that he was not any sort of exile, he simply liked England better than the States. "It has benefited me because it has made it financially possible for me to live on my income from writing, which I could not do in the U.S.A."

The UK edition of A Case of Conscience is his highest priced First Edition, selling for between $1,750.00 and $2,500.00.

Pen names: Arthur Merlyn and William Atheling.

***

AWARDS

1959. Hugo Best Novel Award for A Case of Conscience.
2004. A 1953 Retro-Hugo Award for Best Novelette for Earthman Come Home - Astounding Science Fiction, November 1953.
2004. A 1953 Retro-Hugo Award for Best Novella for A Case of Conscience - If Magazine, September 1953.

***

FILM AND TELEVISION

1. The Box. This was for The Secret Files of Captain Video. Directed by Pat Fay, it first aired on September 5th, 1953, Season 1, Episode 1, starring: Al Hodge; and Werner Klemperer.

2. The Beast Must Die. Based on the story There Shall Be No Darkness, 1950, this was filmed for release in 1974. Directed by Paul Annett, it starred: Calvin Lockhart; Peter Cushing; Marlene Clark; Anton Diffring; Charles Gray; Tom Chadbon; and many others. It was released on video in the U.S. as Black Werewolf.

***

NOVELS AND COLLECTIONS

1. Jack of Eagles. Published by Greenberg, New York City, 1952. Hardcover.

2. The Warriors of Day. Published by Galaxy Publishing, New York City, 1953. Galaxy Science Fiction Novel 16. Softcover.

3. Earthman, Come Home. Published by G. P. Putnam's Sons, New York City, 1955. Hardcover.

4. They Shall Have the Stars. Published by Faber and Faber, London, 1956. Hardcover.

5. Year 2018. Published by Avon Books, New York City, 1957. Avon Book T-193. Softcover. Revised edition of They Shall Have the Stars, 1956. This contains: Foreword: to the American Edition; Year 2018, 1957; At Death's End, 1954; Bridge, 1952; Chronology of Cities in Flight - an essay, 1957.

6. The Seedling Stars. Published by Gnome Press, New York City, 1957. Hardcover. This contains: Seeding Program, 1956; The Thing in the Attic, 1954; Surface Tension, 1956; and Watershed, 1955.

7. The Frozen Year. Published by Ballantine Books, New York City, 1957. Issued first in softcover and one month later in hardcover. The softcover is

James Blish

Ballantine Book 197.

8. Fallen Star. Published by Faber and Faber, London, 1957. Hardcover. A re-titled version of The Frozen Year, 1957.

9. Earthman, Come Home. Published by Avon Books, New York City, 1958. Avon Book T-225. Softcover. An abridged version.

10. Esper. Published by Avon Books, New York City, 1958. Avon Book T-268. Softcover. A re-titled re-issue of Jack of Eagles, 1952.

11. A Case of Conscience. Published by Ballantine Books, New York City, 1958. Ballantine Book 256. Softcover.

12. Vor. Published by Avon Books, New York City, 1958. Avon Book T-238. Softcover.

13. The Triumph of Time. Published by Avon Books, New York City, 1958. Avon Book T-279. Softcover.

14. A Clash of Cymbals. Published by Faber and Faber, London, 1959. Hardcover. Re-titled hardcover edition of The Triumph of Time, 1958.

15. A Case of Conscience. Published by Faber and Faber, London, 1959. First hardcover edition.

16. The Duplicated Man. With Robert Lowndes. Published by Avalon Books, New York City, 1959. Hardcover.

17. Galactic Cluster. Published by Signet Books - The New American Library, New York City, 1959. Signet Book S1719. Softcover. Herein: Tomb Tapper, 1956; King of the Hill, 1955; Common Time, 1953; A Work of Art, 1956; To Pay the Piper, 1956; Nor Iron Bars - a revised version, 1957; Beep, 1954; and This Earth of Hours, 1959.

18. Galactic Cluster. Published by Faber and Faber, London, 1960. Hardcover. With line-up changes, this contains: Common Time, 1953; A Work of Art, 1956; To Pay the Piper, 1956; Beep, 1954; This Earth of Hours, 1959; and Beanstalk, 1952.

19. The Star Dwellers. Published by G. P. Putnam's Sons, New York City, 1961. Hardcover.

20. Titan's Daughter. Published by Berkley Books, New York City, 1961. Berkley Book G507. Softcover.

21. So Close to Home. Published by Ballantine Books, New York City, 1961. Ballantine Book 465K. Softcover. Herein: Struggle in the Womb, 1950; Sponge Dive, 1956; The Box, 1955; First Strike, 1953; The Abattoir Effect, 1961; The Oath, 1960; F.Y.I., 1953; The Masks, 1959; and Testament of Andros, 1953.

22. A Life for the Stars. Published by G. P. Putnam's Sons, New York City, 1962. Hardcover.

23. The Night Shapes. Published by Ballantine Books, New York City, 1962. Ballantine Book F-647. Softcover.

24. Doctor Mirabilis. Published by Faber and Faber, London, 1964. Hardcover.

25. Best Science Fiction Stories of James Blish. Published by Faber and Faber, London, 1965. Hardcover. Herein: A Work of Art, 1956; There Shall Be No Darkness, 1950; Testament of Andros, 1953; Common Time, 1953; Tomb Tapper, 1956; Surface Tension, 1956; and The Oath, 1960.

26. Mission to the Heart Stars. Published by G. P. Putnam's Sons, New York City, 1965. Hardcover. Published on exactly the same day as the UK edition.

27. Mission to the Heart Stars. Published by Faber and Faber, London, 1965. Hardcover. Published on exactly the same day as the American edition.

28. A Torrent of Faces. With Norman L. Knight. Published by Doubleday & Company, New York City, 1967. Hardcover.

29. Welcome to Mars. Published by Faber and Faber, London, 1967. Hardcover.

30. Star Trek. Published by Bantam Books, New York City, 1967. Bantam Book F3459. Softcover. All from 1967, this contains: Charlie's Law; Dagger of the Mind; The Unreal McCoy; Balance of Terror; The Naked Time; Miri; and The Conscience of the King.

31. Star Trek 2. Published by Bantam Books, New York City, 1968. Bantam Book F3439. Softcover. All from 1968, this contains: Arena; A Taste of Armageddon; Tomorrow is Yesterday; Errand of Mercy; Court Martial; Operation - Annihilate!; The City on the Edge of Forever; and Space Seed.

32. The Vanished Jet. Published by Weybright and Talley, New York City, 1968. Hardcover.

33. Black Easter. Published by Doubleday & Company, Garden City, New York, 1968. Hardcover.

34. Doctor Mirabilis. Private printing, 1968. Two hundred and fifty mimeographed copies were released in the U.S. to protect the copyright.

35. Star Trek 3. Published by Bantam Books, New York City, 1969. Bantam Book F4371. Softcover. All from 1969, this contains: Preface: Some Awards for Star Trek and an Open Letter; The Trouble with Tribbles; The Last Gunfight; The Doomsday Machine; Assignment Earth; Mirror, Mirror; Friday's Child; and Amok Time.

36. Cities in Flight. Published by Avon Books, New York City, 1970. Avon Book W187. Softcover. Herein: They Shall Have Stars, 1956; A Life for the Stars, 1962; Earthman, Come Home, 1955; and The Triumph of Time, 1958.

37. Spock Must Die! Published by Bantam Books, New York City, 1970. Bantam Book H5515. Softcover.

38. Star Trek 4. Published by Bantam Books, New York City, 1971. Bantam Book S7009. Softcover. All from 1971, this contains: Preface; A Piece of the Action; All Our Yesterdays; The Enterprise Incident; The Menagerie; Journey to Babel; and The Devil in the Dark.

39. Anywhen. Published by Doubleday & Company, Garden City, New York, 1970. Hardcover. Herein:

Preface by **James Blish**; A Style in Treason, 1970; No Jokes on Mars, 1965; And Some Were Savages, 1960; A Dusk of Idols, 1961; How Beautiful with Banners, 1966; None So Blind, 1962; and The Writing of the Rat, 1956.

40. Anywhen. Published by Faber and Faber, London, 1971. Hardcover. This UK edition has a revised preface and adds a story, Skysign, 1968.

41. Doctor Mirabilis. Published by Dodd, Mead and Company, New York City, 1971. First U.S. hardcover edition - with revisions.

42. The Day After Judgment. Published by Doubleday & Company, Garden City, New York, 1971. Hardcover.

43. And All the Stars a Stage. Published by Doubleday & Company, Garden City, New York, 1971. Hardcover.

44. Star Trek 5. Published by Bantam Books, New York City, 1972. Bantam Book S7300. Softcover. All from 1972, this contains: Preface; Whom Gods Destroy; The Tholian Web; Let That Be Your Last Battlefield; This Side of Paradise; Turnabout Intruder; Requiem for Methuselah; and The Way to Eden.

45. Star Trek 6. Published by Bantam Books, New York City, 1972. Bantam Book S7364. Softcover. From 1972, this contains: Preface; The Savage Curtain; The Lights of Zetar; The Apple; By Any Other Name; The Cloud Minders; and The Mark of Gideon.

46. Star Trek 7. Published by Bantam Books, New York City, 1972. Bantam Book S7480. Softcover. All from 1972, this contains: Who Mourns for Adonais?; The Changeling; The Paradise Syndrome; Metamorphosis; The Deadly Years; and Elaan of Troyius.

47. Star Trek 8. Published by Bantam Books, New York City, 1972. Bantam Book S7550. Softcover. From 1972, this contains: Spock's Brain; The Enemy Within; Catspaw; Where No Man Has Gone Before; Wolf in the Fold; and For the World is Hollow and I Have Touched the Sky.

48. Midsummer Century. Published by Doubleday & Company, Garden City, New York, 1972. Hardcover.

49. Star Trek 9. Published by Bantam Books, New York City, 1973. Bantam Book S7808. Softcover. From 1973, this contains: Preface; Return to Tomorrow; The Ultimate Computer; That Which Survives; Obsession; The Return of the Archons; and The Immunity Syndrome.

50. Cities in Flight. Published by Doubleday & Company, Garden City, New York, 1973. First hardcover edition. Herein: They Shall Have Stars, 1956; A Life for the Stars, 1962; Earthman, Come Home, 1955; and The Triumph of Time, 1958.

51. The Quincunx of Time. Published by Dell Books, New York City, 1973. Dell Book 7244. Softcover.

52. The Testament of Andros. Published by Faber and Faber, London, 1973. Hardcover. Herein: A Preface to Tomorrow - an essay, 1972; Surface Tension, 1956; Testament of Andros, 1953; Common Time, 1953; A Work of Art, 1956; Tomb Tapper, 1956; The Oath, 1960; How Beautiful with Banners, 1966; and We All Die Naked, 1969.

53. Star Trek. Published by White Lion Publishers, London, 1974. First hardcover edition. All from 1967, this contains: Charlie's Law; Dagger of the Mind; The Unreal McCoy; Balance of Terror; The Naked Time; Miri; and The Conscience of the King.

54. Star Trek 10. Published by Bantam Books, New York City, 1974. Bantam Book S8401. Softcover. From 1974, this contains: Preface; The Alternative Factor; The Empath; The Galileo Seven; Is There in Truth No Beauty?; A Private Little War; and The Omega Glory.

55. Midsummer Century. Published by DAW Books, New York City, 1974. DAW Collector's Book 89. Softcover. This includes two stories that were not printed with the original version of the novel: Skysign, 1968; and A Style in Treason, 1970.

56. The Quincunx of Time. Published by Faber and Faber, London, 1975. First hardcover edition.

57. Star Trek 2. Published by White Lion Publishers, London, 1975. First hardcover edition. All from 1968, this contains: Arena; A Taste of Armageddon; Tomorrow is Yesterday; Errand of Mercy; Court Martial; Operation - Annihilate!; The City on the Edge of Forever; and Space Seed.

58. Star Trek 3. Published by White Lion Publishers, London, 1975. First hardcover edition. All from 1969, this contains: Preface: Some Awards for Star Trek and an Open Letter; The Trouble with Tribbles; The Last Gunfight; The Doomsday Machine; Assignment Earth; Mirror, Mirror; Friday's Child; and Amok Time.

59. Star Trek 11. Published by Bantam Books, New York City, 1975. Bantam Book Q8717. Softcover. From 1975, herein: Preface; What Are Little Girls Made Of?; The Squire of Gothos; Wink of an Eye; Bread and Circuses; Day of the Dove; and Plato's Stepchildren.

60. The Star Trek Reader. Published by E. P. Dutton, New York City, 1976. Hardcover. An omnibus edition, this gathers: Star Trek 2; Star Trek 3; and Star Trek 8.

61. Star Trek 4. Published by Severn House, London, 1977. First hardcover edition. All from 1971, this contains: Preface; A Piece of the Action; All Our Yesterdays; The Enterprise Incident; The Menagerie; Journey to Babel; and The Devil in the Dark.

62. Star Trek 5. Published by Severn House, London, 1977. First hardcover edition. All from 1972, this contains: Preface; Whom Gods Destroy; The Tholian Web; Let That Be Your Last Battlefield; This Side of Paradise; Turnabout Intruder; Requiem for Methuselah; and The Way to Eden.

63. Star Trek 12. With Judith A. Lawrence. Published by Bantam Books, New York City, 1977. Bantam Book 11382-8. Softcover. From 1977, herein: Foreword by J. A. Lawrence; Preface by

James Blish

James Blish; Patterns of Force; The Gamesters of Triskelion; And the Children Shall Lead - completed by J. A. Lawrence; The Corbomite Maneuver; and Shore Leave - completed by J. A. Lawrence, Mrs. James Blish.

64. The Star Trek Reader II. Published by E. P. Dutton, New York City, 1977. Hardcover. An omnibus edition, this gathers: Star Trek 1; Star Trek 4; and Star Trek 9.

65. The Star Trek Reader III. Published by E. P. Dutton, New York City, 1977. Hardcover. An omnibus edition, this gathers: Star Trek 5; Star Trek 6; and Star Trek 7.

66. The Testament of Andros. Published by Arrow Books, London, 1977. Softcover. Revised edition.

67. The Best of James Blish. Published by Del Rey - Ballantine Books, New York City, 1979. Softcover. Herein: Introduction by Robert A. W. Lowndes; Citadel of Thought, 1941; The Box, 1949; There Shall Be No Darkness, 1950; Surface Tension, 1956; Testament of Andros, 1953; Common Time, 1953; Beep, 1954; A Work of Art, 1956; This Earth of Hours, 1959; The Oath, 1960; How Beautiful with Banners, 1966; A Style in Treason, 1970; and Porbapossible Prolegomena to Idearal History - an essay by **James Blish** writing as William Atheling, Jr.

68. Black Easter/The Day After Judgment. Published by Gregg Press, Boston, 1980. Hardcover. This combines: Black Easter, 1968; and the Day After Judgment, 1971.

69. Get Out of My Sky. Published by Panther Books, London, 1980. Softcover. Herein: Get Out of My Sky, 1960; and There Shall Be No Darkness, 1950.

70. The Seedling Stars - with - Galactic Cluster. Published by Signet Books - The New American Library, New York City, 1983. Softcover. An omnibus edition, gathering the stories from both collections: The Seedling Stars, 1956; and Galactic Cluster, 1959.

71. The Devil's Day. Published by Baen Books, New York City, 1990. Softcover. This gathers: Black Easter, 1968; and the Day After Judgment, 1971.

72. After Such Knowledge. Published by Legend Books, London, 1991. Softcover. An omnibus edition, this gathers: Dr Mirabilis, 1964; Black Easter, 1968; The Day After Judgement, 1971; and A Case of Conscience, 1958.

73. Star Trek: The Classic Episodes - Volume 1. With J. A. Lawrence. Published by Bantam Spectra, New York City, 1991. Softcover. Herein: Introduction by D. C. Fontana; The Collected Prefaces from the Original Star Trek Books; Foreword by J. A. Lawrence; Where No Man Has Gone Before, 1972; The Corbomite Maneuver, 1977; The Enemy Within, 1972; The Unreal McCoy, 1967; The Naked Time, 1967; Charlie's Law, 1967; Balance of Terror, 1967; What Are Little Girls Made Of?, 1975; Dagger of the Mind, 1967; Miri, 1967; The Conscience of the King, 1967; The Galileo Seven, 1974; Court Martial, 1968; The Menagerie, 1971; Shore Leave, 1977; The Squire of Gothos, 1975; Arena, 1968; The Alternative Factor, 1974; Tomorrow is Yesterday, 1968; The Return of the Archons, 1973; A Taste of Armageddon, 1968; Space Seed, 1968; This Side of Paradise, 1973; The Devil in the Dark, 1971; Errand of Mercy, 1968; The City on the Edge of Forever, 1968; and Operation - Annihilate!, 1968.

74. Star Trek: The Classic Episodes - Volume 2. Published by Bantam Books, New York City, 1991. Softcover. Herein: The Transcendental Vision - an essay by David Gerrold, 1991; Catspaw, 1972; Metamorphosis, 1972; Friday's Child, 1969; Who Mourns for Adonais?, 1972; Amok Time, 1969; The Doomsday Machine, 1969; Wolf in the Fold, 1972; The Changeling, 1972; The Apple, 1972; Mirror, Mirror, 1969; The Deadly Years, 1972; The Trouble with Tribbles, 1969; Bread and Circuses, 1975; Journey to Babel, 1971; A Private Little War, 1974; The Gamesters of Triskelion, 1977; Obsession, 1973; The Immunity Syndrome, 1973; A Piece of the Action, 1971; By Any Other Name, 1972; Return to Tomorrow, 1973; Patterns of Force, 1977; The Ultimate Computer, 1973; The Omega Glory, 1974; and Assignment - Earth, 1969.

75. Star Trek: The Classic Episodes - Volume 3. With J. A. Lawrence. Published by Bantam Books, New York City, 1991. Softcover. Herein: Star Trek in the Real World - an essay by Norman Spinrad; The Last Gunfight, 1969; Elaan of Troyius, 1972; The Paradise Syndrome, 1972; The Enterprise Incident, 1971; And the Children Shall Lead - with J. A. Lawrence, 1977; Spock's Brain, 1972; Is There in Truth No Beauty?, 1974; The Empath, 1974; The Tholian Web, 1972; For the World is Hollow and I Have Touched the Sky, 1972; Day of the Dove, 1975; Plato's Stepchildren, 1975; Wink of an Eye, 1975; That Which Survives, 1973; Let That Be Your Last Battlefield, 1972; Whom Gods Destroy, 1972; The Mark of Gideon, 1972; The Lights of Zetar, 1972; The Cloud Minders, 1972; The Way to Eden, 1972; Requiem for Methuselah, 1972; The Savage Curtain, 1972; All Our Yesterdays, 1971; and Turnabout Intruder, 1972.

76. A Work of Art and Other Stories. Published by Severn House, London, 1993. Hardcover. This contains: Introduction by Francis Lyall; Common Time, 1953; Testament of Andros, 1953; The Art of the Sneeze - an essay, 1982; Statistician's Day, 1970; Who's in Charge Here?, 1962; How Beautiful with Banners, 1966; This Earth of Hours, 1959; There Shall Be No Darkness, 1950; and A Work of Art, 1956.

77. With All of Love: Selected Poems. Published by Anamnesis Press, Tallahassee, Florida, 1995. Hardcover. Limited to 150 copies.

78. A Dusk of Idols and Other Stories. Published by Severn House, London, 1996. Hardcover. Herein: Introduction by Francis Lyall; To Pay the Piper, 1956; Beep, 1954; The Box, 1949; The Writing of the Rat, 1956; A Matter of Energy, 1955; King of the Hill, 1955; Mistake Inside, 1948; and A Dusk of Idols, 1961.

79. Faust Aleph-Null. Published by Buccaneer Books, UK, 1999. Hardcover. Re-titled version of Black Easter, 1968.

237

80. In This World or Another. Published by Five Star, Waterville, Maine, 2003. Hardcover. Preface by **James Blish**; Citadel of Thought, 1941; Get Out of My Sky, 1960; Nor Iron Bars, 1957; A Work of Art, 1956; The Oath, 1960; A Dusk of Idols, 1961; How Beautiful with Banners, 1966; Testament of Andros, 1953; Common Time, 1953; Surface Tension, 1956; and Scenario: The Edifice - a poem, 1976.

81. Works of Art. Published by NESFA Press, Framingham, Massachusetts, 2008. Hardcover. Herein: **James Blish** and the Beginning of Interpretation - an essay by Gregory Feeley; Work of Art, 1956; Surface Tension, 1956; The Bridge, 1952; Tomb Tapper, 1956; The Box, 1949; The Oath, 1960; Beep, 1954; F.Y.I., 1953; Common Time, 1953; There Shall Be No Darkness, 1950; A Dusk of Idols, 1961; Earthman, Come Home, 1955; How Beautiful with Banners, 1966; This Earth of Hours, 1959; Testament of Andros, 1953; A Style in Treason, 1970; A Case of Conscience, 1953; Making Waves, 2008; and two poems.

***

ANTHOLOGIES

1. New Dreams This Morning. Published by Ballantine Books, New York City, 1966. Ballantine Book U2331. Softcover. Herein: Preface by **James Blish**; Dreaming is a Private Thing by **Isaac Asimov**, 1955; A Work of Art by **James Blish**, 1956; The Dark Night of the Soul by **James Blish**, 1956; Portrait of the Artist by **Harry Harrison**, 1964; The Country of the Kind by **Damon Knight**, 1956; With These Hands by C. M. Kornbluth, 1951; A Master of Babylon by Edgar Pangborn, 1966; and A Man of Talent by **Robert Silverberg**, 1966.

2. Nebula Award Stories 5. Published by Doubleday & Company, Garden City, New York, 1970. Hardcover. Herein: Introduction by **James Blish**; Time Considered as a Helix of Semi-Precious Stones by **Samuel R. Delany**, 1968; Passengers by **Robert Silverberg**, 1968; Nine Lives by **Ursula K. Le Guin**, 1968; A Boy and His Dog by Harlan Ellison; The Man Who Learned Loving by **Theodore Sturgeon**, 1969; Not Long Before the End by Larry Niven, 1969; Short SF in 1968 - an essay by Alexei Panshin; and The SF Novel in 1969 - an essay by Darko Suvin.

3. Thirteen O'Clock and Other Zero Hours. By C. M. Kornbluth. Edited and with a preface by **James Blish**. Published by Dell Books, New York City, 1970. Dell Book 8731. Softcover.

4. Thirteen O'Clock and Other Zero Hours. By C. M. Kornbluth. Edited and with a preface by **James Blish**. Published by Robert Hale & Company, London, 1972. First hardcover edition.

***

NON-FICTION

1. The Issue at Hand. Writing as William Atheling Jr. Published by Advent Publishers, Chicago, 1964. Hardcover.

2. More Issues at Hand. Writing as William Atheling Jr. Published by Advent Publishers, Chicago, 1970. Hardcover.

***

RELATED

1. The Magazine of Fantasy and Science Fiction - Special James Blish Issue - April 1972. Published by Mercury Press, New York City, 1972. Softcover. Along with Midsummer Century by **James Blish** and the usual magazine features, this has **James Blish**: A Profile by Robert A. W. Lowndes; and **James Blish**: Bibliography by Mark Owings.

2. James Blish: A Biography 1940 - 1976. By Judith A. Blish. Published by Judith A. Blish, Harpsden, Henley-on-Thames, England, 1976. Softcover.

3. A Clash of Symbols: The Triumph of James Blish. By Brian M. Stableford. Published by Borgo Press, San Bernardino, California, 1979. Hardcover.

4. Imprisoned in a Tesseract: The Life and Work of James Blish. By David Ketterer. Published by Kent State University Press, Ohio, 1987. Hardcover.

5. James Blish: Author Mirabilis: A Working Bibliography. By Phil Stephensen-Payne. Published by Galactic Central Publications, Leeds, England, 1996. Softcover.

Samuel R. Delany.

Samuel Ray Delany Jr. was born on April 1st, 1942 in New York City. Raised in Harlem by a reasonably well-off family, he had his first novel published when he was just twenty years old, the second year into his marriage to the poet, Marilyn Hacker and the same year his father died.

His wife was an editorial assistant at Ace Books; she arranged for an editor to read Delany's first novel, The Jewels of Aptor. And they published it in December, 1962, bound as an Ace Double with Second Ending by James White. Whether intentionally or unintentionally, he became one of the leaders of the New Wave movement that shook up the science fiction world during the 60s.

As a young, gay black man married to a white Jewish woman, he certainly had the opportunity to develop his own particular point of view. He once explained in an interview that he had been able to experience different cultures "in a way that still influences what I do and what I write."

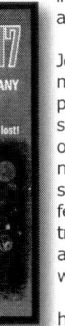

Obviously, The Jewels of Aptor was merely a starting point. During the next six years, he came out with seven more novels, along with some short fiction and a few essays, all the while travelling, exploring, and experimenting... with life itself.

Over the years, he accepted an assortment of academic positions and continued to write books that inspired others to write books about his books...

His most valuable titles tend to be the British hardcover firsts of Babel 17 and The Einstein Intersection, going for between $1,200.00 and $2,000.00.

Pen Name: K. Leslie Steiner.

***

AWARDS

1966. Nebula Best Novel Award for Babel-17.
1967. Nebula Best Novel Award for The Einstein Intersection.
1967. Nebula Best Short Story Award for Aye, and Gomorrah - Dangerous Visions, edited by Harlan Ellison.
1969. Nebula Best Novelette Award for Time Considered as a Helix of Semi-Precious Stones - New Worlds, December 1968.
1970. Hugo Best Short Story Award for Time Considered as a Helix of Semi-Precious Stones - New Worlds, December 1968.
1989. Hugo Best Related Non-fiction Book Award for The Motion of Light in Water: Sex and Science Fiction Writing in the East Village 1957 -1965.
1995. Babel-17 received the James Tiptree Jr Classics Award.

1995. Triton received the James Tiptree Jr Classics Award.

***

FILM AND TELEVISION

1. New York Underground. This was made for the television series Great Writers, Great Cities. Directed by Fred Barney Taylor, this aired on September 15th, 2001 and featured an interview with **Samuel R. Delany**; The Blue Man Group; Fran Liebowitz; and others.

2. Jules Verne and Walt Disney: Explorers of the Imagination. Written and directed by David J. Skal, this documentary was released in May 2003 and featured interviews with: **Samuel R. Delany**; Forrest J. Ackerman; Rudy Behlmer; Gregory Benford; Bob Burns; Vincent De Fate; and George A. Slusser.

3. The Polymath, or The Life and Opinions of Samuel R. Delany, Gentleman. Directed by Fred Barney Taylor, this 2007 documentary Delany's life.

4. Wrangler: Anatomy of an Icon. Directed by Jeffrey Schwarz in 2008, this documentary explored the life - and death - of porn star Jack Wrangler. **Samuel R. Delany** was among the many interviewees.

***

NOVELS AND COLLECTIONS

1. The Jewels of Aptor. Published by Ace Books, New York City, 1962. Ace Double F-173. Softcover. Together with Second Ending by James White.

2. Captives of the Flame. Published by Ace Books, New York City, 1963. Ace Double F-199. Softcover. Partnered with The Psionic Menace by John Brunner writing as Keith Woodcott.

3. The Towers of Toron. Published by Ace Books, New York City, 1963. Ace Double F-261. Softcover. Bound with The Lunar Eye by Robert Moore Williams.

4. City of a Thousand Suns. Published by Ace Books, New York City, 1965. Ace Book F-322. Softcover.

5. The Ballad of Beta-2. Published by Ace Books, New York City, 1965. Ace Double M-121. Softcover. Together with Alpha Yes, Terra No! by Emil Petaja.

6. Babel-17. Published by Ace Books, New York City, 1966. Ace Book F-388. Softcover.

7. Empire Star. Published by Ace Books, New York City, 1966. Ace Double M-139. Softcover. Bound with The Tree Lord of Imeten by Tom Purdon.

8. The Einstein Intersection. Published by Ace Books, New York City, 1967. Ace Book F-427. Softcover.

9. Babel-17. Published by Victor Gollancz, London, 1967. First hardcover edition.

10. The Jewels of Aptor. Published by Ace Books,

New York City, 1968. Ace Book G-706. Softcover. Revised edition.

11. The Jewels of Aptor. Published by Victor Gollancz, London, 1968. First hardcover edition.

12. The Einstein Intersection. Published by Victor Gollancz, London, 1968. First hardcover edition.

13. Out of the Dead City. Published by Sphere Books, London, 1968. Sphere Book 28835. Softcover. Revised re-titled version of Captives of the Flame, 1963.

14. The Towers of Toron. Published by Sphere Books, London, 1968. Sphere Book 28843. Softcover. Revised edition.

15. Nova. Published by Doubleday & Company, Garden City, New York, 1968. Hardcover.

16. Nova. Published by Science Fiction Book Club, Garden City, New York, 1969. Hardcover. Revised edition.

17. City of a Thousand Suns. Published by Sphere Books, London, 1969. Sphere Book 28851. Softcover. Revised edition.

18. Babel-17. Published by Sphere Books, London, 1969. Sphere Book 28887. Softcover. Revised edition.

19. The Fall of Towers. Published by Ace Books, New York City, 1970. Ace Book 22640. Softcover. An omnibus edition, this gathers: Notes on Revision; and Prologue by **Samuel R. Delany**; Out of the Dead City - aka Captives of the Flame, 1966; The Towers of Toron, 1964; and City of a Thousand Suns, 1965; along with an epilogue and an afterword by Delany.

20. The Ballad of Beta-2. Published by Ace Books, New York City, 1971. Ace Book 4722. Softcover. With corrections.

21. The Jewels of Aptor. Published by Sphere Books, London, 1971. Sphere Book 28894. Softcover. More revisions.

22. Driftglass. Published by Nelson Doubleday, Science Fiction Book Club, Garden City, New York, 1971. Book Club Code 24M. Herein: The Star Pit, 1967; Dog in a Fisherman's Net, 1971; Corona, 1967; Aye, and Gomorrah, 1967; Driftglass, 1967; We, in Some Strange Power's Employ, Move on a Rigorous Line, 1968; Cage of Brass, 1968; High Weir, 1968; Time Considered as a Helix of Semi-Precious Stones, 1968; and Night and the Loves of Joe Dicostanzo, 1970.

23. The Tides of Lust. Published by Lancer Books, New York City, 1973. Lancer Book 71344. Softcover.

24. Dhalgren. Published by Bantam Books, New York, 1975. Bantam Book Y8554. Softcover.

25. The Ballad of Beta-2 - with - Empire Star. Published by Ace Books, New York City, 1975. Ace Double 20571. Softcover. An omnibus edition: The Ballad of Beta-2, 1965; and Empire Star, 1966.

26. The Jewels of Aptor. Published by Gregg Press, Boston, 1976. First hardcover edition of the newly revised edition.

27. Babel-17. Published by Gregg Press, Boston, 1976. First hardcover edition of the revised edition.

28. Triton. Published by Bantam Books, New York City, 1976. Bantam Book Y2567. Softcover.

29. The Ballad of Beta-2. Published by Gregg Press, Boston, 1977. First hardcover edition.

30. Empire Star. Published by Gregg Press, Boston, 1977. First hardcover edition.

31. The Fall of Towers. Published by Gregg Press, Boston, 1977. First hardcover edition.

32. Dhalgren. Published by Gregg Press, Boston, 1977. First hardcover edition. Also, revised edition.

33. Empire. With Howard V. Chaykin. Published by Berkley Windhover, New York City, 1978. Softcover.

34. Tales of Neveryon. Published by Bantam Books, New York City, 1979. Softcover. Herein: The Tale of Gorgik, 1979; The Tale of Old Venn, 1979; The Tale of Small Sarg, 1979; The Tale of Potters and Dragons, 1979; and The Tale of Dragons and Dreamers, 1979; followed by Appendix: Some Informal Remarks Toward the Modular Calculus - Part Three.

35. Distant Stars. Published by Bantam Books, New York City, 1981. Softcover. Herein: Of Doubts and Dreams - an essay, 1981; Prismatica, 1977; Corona, 1967; Empire Star, 1966; Time Considered as a Helix of Semi-Precious Stones, 1968; Omegahelm, 1981; Ruins, 1968; and We, in Some Strange Power's Employ, Move on a Rigorous Line, 1968.

36. Neveryona. Published by Bantam Books, New York City, 1983. Softcover.

37. Stars in My Pocket Like Grains of Sand. Published by Bantam Books, New York City, 1984. Hardcover.

38. Flight from Neveryon. Published by Bantam Books, New York City, 1985. Softcover. Herein: The Tale of Fog and Granite, 1985; and The Mummer's Tale, 1985; along with: Appendix A: Some Informal Remarks Toward the Modular Calculus - Part Five; and Appendix B: Closures and Openings - an essay, 1985.

39. The Complete Nebula Award Winning Fiction. Published by Bantam Spectra, New York City, 1986. Softcover. Herein: The Einstein Intersection, 1967; Babel-17, 1966; Aye and Gomorrah, 1967; and Time Considered as a Helix of Semi-Precious Stones, 1968; along with Foreword to an Afterword; and Afterword: A Fictional Architecture that Manages Only with Great Difficulty Not Once to Mention Harlan Ellison.

40. The Bridge of Lost Desire. Published by Arbor House, New York City, 1987. Hardcover. Herein: The Game of Time and Pain, 1987; The Tale of Rumor and Desire, 1987; The Tale of Gorgik, 1979; and

Samuel R. Delany

Appendix: Return... A Preface, writing as K. Leslie Steiner.

41. Return to Neveryon. Published by Grafton Books, London, 1989. Re-titled UK issue of The Bridge of Lost Desire, 1987. This drops Appendix: Return... A Preface, writing as K. Leslie Steiner; and includes Buffon's Needle, an essay by Robert Wentworth and **Samuel R. Delany**, 1987; and Closures and Openings - an essay by **Samuel R. Delany**, 1985.

42. The Star Pit - with - Tango Charlie and Foxtrot Romeo. With John Varley. Published by Tor Books, New York City, 1989. Tor Double 4. Softcover.

43. We, in Some Strange Power's Employ, Move on a Rigorous Line - with - Home is the Hangman. With Roger Zelazny. Published by Tor Books, New York City, 1990. Tor Double 21. Softcover.

44. They Fly at Ciron. Published by Incunabula, Nutley, New Jersey, 1993. Hardcover limited edition. The first trade edition was published by Tor Books, New York City, 1995. Herein: They Fly at Ciron, 1993; Ruins, 1968; and Return to Ciron, 1993.

45. Driftglass/Starshards. Published by Grafton Books, London, 1993. Softcover. This combines the stories from Driftglass, 1971; and Distant Stars, 1981.

46. The Mad Man. Published by Richard Kasak Books, UK, 1994. Softcover.

47. Atlantis: Three Tales. Published by Wesleyan University Press, Middletown, Connecticut, 1995. Hardcover. Herein: Atlantis Model 1924, 1995; Eric Gwen and D. H. Lawrence's Esthetic of Unrectified Feeling, 1995; and Citre et Trans, 1991.

48. Hogg. Published by Fiction Collective Two - Black Ice Books, United States, 1995. Hardcover.

49. Bread & Wine: An Erotic Tale of New York. Published by Powerhouse Books, New York City, 1999. Softcover.

50. Babel 17 - with - Empire Star. Published by Vintage Books, New York City, 2001. Softcover.

51. Aye, and Gomorrah: and Other Stories. Published by Vintage Books, New York City, 2003. Softcover. Herein: The Star Pit, 1967; Corona, 1967; Aye, and Gomorrah, 1967; We, in Some Strange Power's Employ, Move on Rigorous Line, 1968; Cage of Brass, 1968; High Weir, 1968; Time Considered as a Helix of Semi-Precious Stones, 1968; Omegahelm, 1981; Among the Blobs, 1988; Tapestry, 2003; Prismatica, 1977; Ruins, 1968; Dog in a Fisherman's Net, 1971; and Night and the Loves of Joe Dicostanzo, 1970; along with Of Doubts and Dreams - an essay, 1981.

52. Dark Reflections. Published by Carroll and Graf, New York City, 2007. Softcover.

***

ANTHOLOGIES

1. Quark 1. With Marilyn Hacker. Published by Paperback Library, New York City, 1970. Paperback Library Book 66-480. Softcover. All new work, this contains: Editorial by **Samuel R. Delany** and Marilyn Hacker; The Cliff Climbers by R. A. Lafferty; The Sound of Muzak by Gardner R. Dozois; A Trip to the Head by **Ursula K. Le Guin**; Let Us Quickly Hasten to the Gate of Ivory by Thomas M. Disch; Inalienable Rite by Gregory Benford; Orion by George Stanley; The View from this Window by Joanna Russ; Gone Are the Lupo by H. B. Hickey; Fire Storm by Christopher Priest; Getting to Know You by Link; Dogman of Islington by Hilary Bailey; Shades by Sandy Boucher; Twelve Ancillary Animations for the Quark/Cover Called Appomattox by Russell FitzGerald; Carthing by **A. E. van Vogt**; Daughter of Roses by Helen Adam; Adrift on the Freeway by Ed Bryant; My Father's Guest by Joan Bernott; Critical Methods: Speculative Fiction by **Samuel R. Delany**; Ramona Come Softly by Gordon Eklund; and Six Drawings by Stephen Gilden.

2. Quark 2. With Marilyn Hacker. Published by Paperback Library, New York City, 1971. Paperback Library Book 66-530. Softcover. All new work, this contains: Introduction by **Samuel R. Delany** and Marilyn Hacker; The Interstate by John Sladek; A Possible Episode in the Picaresque Adventures of Mr J. H. B. Monstrosee by Carol Emshwiller; Trojak by Marek Obtulowicz; Gold Black and Silver by **Fritz Leiber**; Mensuration by James Sallis; Six Drawings by Roger Penney; The Voice of the Sonar in My Vermiform Appendix by Philip Jose Farmer; The Way Home by Joan Bernott; Among the Dead by Ed Bryant; The Last Supper by Russell FitzGerald; The Village by Leland Stoney; Arpad by Alexei Panshin; Bitching It by Sonya Dorman; Five Drawings by Nemi Frost; Et in Arcadia Ego by Thomas M. Disch; Landscape for Insurrection by Marilyn Hacker; The People of Prashad by James Keilty; The Inception of the Epoch of Mrs Bedoneby Asyoudid by John Brunner; and The Electric Neon Mermaid by Laurence Yep.

3. Quark 3. With Marilyn Hacker. Published by Paperback Library, New York City, 1971. Paperback Library Book 66-593. Softcover. All new work, this contains: Foreword by **Samuel R. Delany** and Marilyn Hacker; Continuous Landscape by Donald Simpson; Encased in Ancient Rind by R. A. Lafferty; Home Again Home Again by Gordon Eklund; Dog in a Fisherman's Net by **Samuel R. Delany**; Six Drawings by Robert La Vigne; The Zanzibar Cat by Joanna Russ; Field by James Sallis; Vanishing Point by Sonya Dorman; Where Have You Been Billy Boy Billy Boy by **Kate Wilhelm**; Brave Salt by Richard Hill; Nature Boy by Josephine Saxon; Balls: A Meditation at the Graveside by Virginia Kidd; Ring of Pain by M. John Harrison; To the Child Whose Birth Will Change the Way the Universe Works by George Stanley; A Sexual Song by Tom Veitch; Twenty-four Letters from Underneath the Earth by Hilary Bailey; Six More Drawings by Robert La Vigne; and The Coded Sun Game by Brian Vickers.

4. Quark 4. With Marilyn Hacker. Published by Paperback Library, New York City, 1971. Paperback

241

Library Book 66-658. Softcover. All new work, this contains: Foreword: On Speculative Fiction by **Samuel R. Delany** and Marilyn Hacker; Basileikon: Summer by Avram Davidson; Voortrekker by **Michael Moorcock**; Brass and Gold by Philip Jose Farmer; Norman vs. America by Charles Platt; The True Reason for the Dreadful Death of Mr Rex Arundel by Helen Adam; Acid Soap Opera by Gail Madonia; Bodies by Thomas M. Disch; Nightsong by Marilyn Hacker; Cages by Vonda N. McIntyre; A Man of Letters by Marek Obtulowicz; The Fourth Profession by Larry Niven; and Twelve Drawings by Olivier Olivier.

5. Nebula Winners 13. Published by Harper and Row, New York City, 1980. Hardcover. Herein: Introduction by **Samuel R. Delany**; Jeffty is Five by Harlan Ellison, 1977; Air Raid by John Varley writing as Herb Boehm, 1977; The Screwfly Solution by Alice B. Sheldon - James Tiptree, Jr writing as Raccoona Sheldon, 1977; Particle Theory by Edward Bryant, 1977; Stardance by Spider and Jeanne Robinson, 1977; and Aztecs by Vonda N. McIntyre, 1977.

***

NON-FICTION

1. The Jewel-Hinged Jaw: Notes on the Language of Science Fiction. Published by Dragon Press, Elizabethtown, New York, 1977. Hardcover limited edition.

2. The American Shore: Meditations on a Tale of Science Fiction by Thomas M. Disch - Angouleme. Published by Dragon Press, Elizabethtown, New York, 1978. Hardcover.

3. Heavenly Breakfast. Published by Bantam Books, New York City, 1979. Softcover.

4. Starboard Wine. Published by Dragon Press, Elizabethtown, New York, 1984. Hardcover.

5. The Motion of Light in Water: Sex and Science Fiction Writing in the East Village 1957 - 1965. Published by Arbor House, New York City, 1988. Hardcover.

6. Wagner/Artaud: A Play of 19th and 20th Century Critical Fictions. Published by Ansatz Press, New York City, 1988. Softcover.

7. The Straights of Messina. Published by Serconia Press, New York City, 1989. Hardcover.

8. Silent Interviews: On Language, Race, Sex, Science Fiction, and Some Comics. Published by Wesleyan University Press, Middletown, Connecticut, 1994. Hardcover.

9. Longer Views. Published by the University Press of New England, 1996. Softcover.

10. Shorter Views: Queer Thoughts and the Politics of the Paraliterary. Published by Wesleyan University Press, Middletown, Connecticut, 1999. Hardcover.

11. Times Square Red, Times Square Blue. Published by the New York University Press, 1999. Hardcover.

12. 1984: Selected Letters. Published by Voyant Publishing, Rutherford, New Jersey, 2000. Hardcover.

13. About Writing: Seven Essays, Four Letters, and Five Interviews. Published by Wesleyan University Press, Middletown, Connecticut, 2007. Hardcover.

***

RELATED

1. The Delany Intersection: Samuel R. Delany Considered as a Writer of Semi-Precious Words. By George Edgar Slusser. Published by R. Reginald - The Borgo Press, San Bernardino, California, 1977. Softcover.

2. Worlds Out of Words: The SF Novels of Samuel R. Delany. By Douglas Barbour. Published by Brian's Head, Somerset, UK, 1979. Hardcover.

3. Samuel R. Delany: A Primary and Secondary Bibliography 1962 - 1979. By Michael W. Peplow and Robert S. Bravard. Published by G. K. Hall, Boston, 1981. Hardcover.

4. Samuel R. Delany. By Jane Weedman. Published by Borgo Press, Mercer Island, Washington, 1982.

5. Samuel R. Delany. By Seth McEvoy. Published by Frederick Unger, New York City, 1984.

6. The Black American Literature Forum. Edited by Joe Weixlmann and Terra Haute. The 1984 Special Science Fiction Issue featured an assortment of critical and bibliographical articles regarding Delany.

7. Conscientious Sorcerers: The Black Postmodernist Fiction of LeRoi Jones/ Amiri Baraka, Ishmael Reed and Samuel R. Delany - Contribution in Afro-American and African Studies. By Robert Elliot Fox. Published by Greenwood Press, United States, 1987. Hardcover.

8. Checklist of Samuel R. Delany. By Christopher P. Stevens. Published by Ultramarine Publishing, United States, 1991. Softcover.

9. Ash of Stars: On the Writing of Samuel R. Delany. By James Sallis. Published by the University Press of Mississippi, 1996. Hardcover.

10. The Review of Contemporary Fiction - Volume 16, number 3, Fall 1996. An Edmund White - Samuel R. Delany issue. Edited by James Sallis. Dalkey Archive Press, softcover.

11. A Sense of Wonder: Samuel R. Delany, Race, Identity and Difference. By Jeffrey Allen Tucker. Published by Wesleyan University Press, Middletown, Connecticut, 2004. Hardcover.

Michael Moorcock.

Michael John Moorcock was born on December 19th, 1939 in London. By 1955, at fifteen - some accounts say sixteen - he was the editor of the Tarzan Adventures magazine, something akin to a comic book.

His approach was, apparently, too radical for their tastes, and he moved on to edit the Sexton Blake Library, which actually started in 1915. The digest series that Moorcock edited ended in 1963 and the Blake series moved on to a regular paperback format.

By that time, Moorcock was at the helm of New Worlds Magazine, although not before he published his first novel-length story, A Caribbean Crisis, Sexton Blake Library Number 501, Fleetway Publications, 1962. It was written under the name Desmond Reid, a well-used house name. His actual first published work was Johnny Lonesome Comes to Town, which appeared in The Searchlight Book for Boys, 1956. This was followed by Sojan the Swordsman, in Tarzan Adventures, August 31st, 1957. Considering his age, the early work was quite remarkable.

But it didn't prepare the world for what was coming. In the fantasy field, he published The Dreaming City in the June 1961 issue of Science Fantasy, edited by John Carnell. It appeared with: Blood Offering by John Kippax; The Veil of Isis by John T. Phillifent writing as John Rackham; and Valley of the Rainbirds by W. T. Webb; and Studies in Science Fiction 12: Stanley G. Weinbaum - an essay by Sam Moskowitz.

The Dreaming City was the first Elric story and Elric, within the confines of Sword and Sorcery or Heroic Fantasy, was a revolutionary character, an anti-hero, tortured by his own personal demons.

Elric was well on the way to being firmly established when Moorcock became the editor of New Worlds, another revolutionary event. His first issue was May/June 1964, which featured the first instalment of Equinox by J. G. Ballard; along with: Never Let Go of My Hand by **Brian W. Aldiss**; The Last Lonely Man by John Brunner; The Star Virus by Barrington J. Bayley; and Myth-maker of the 20th Century - an essay by J. G. Ballard.

New Worlds had been a traditional SF magazine from its inception in 1946.

That changed.

Drastically.

With the help of a few friends, Moorcock and New Worlds led the New Wave in Britain. He said, "I was able to promote a kind of fiction I liked..." When he published Bug Jack Barron by Norman Spinrad, New Worlds was receiving government funding. British politicians were so outraged by Spinrad's novel, they tried to put New Worlds out of business, tried to halt the flow of funds. Obviously, they failed.

Moorcock edited New Worlds until March 1971, then took it up again in 1976 and ran with it until 1996. Meanwhile, he went through a couple of marriages, flirted with the music scene - in particular with the band Hawkwind, also with **Michael Moorcock** and The Deep Fix.

And all the while, he developed his own writing, the work becoming richer, more literary. He once explained that he was doing things other people had not been able to do, that he had an assortment of techniques that other writers would love to have, abilities that he developed through hard work. In an interview, he said, "What I'm aiming toward ultimately is to produce something like a Dickens novel..." Or War and Peace.

The Stealer of Souls and Other Stories, published in hardcover by Neville Spearman, London, 1963, is Moorcock's most valuable collectible book. It normally sells for between $850.00 and $950.00.

Pen names: Desmond Reid; Edward P. Bradbury; George Collyn; James Colvin; J. R. Taylor; Michael Barrington; Roger Harris; William Barclay; Bill Barclay; and Mike Moorcock.

***

AWARDS

1957. Hugo Best British Professional Magazine Award for New Worlds.
1967. Nebula Best Novella Award for Behold the Man - New Worlds 166.
1972. British Fantasy - August Derleth Fantasy Best Novel Award for The Knight of Swords.
1973. British Fantasy - August Derleth Fantasy Best Novel Award for The King of Swords.
1974. British Fantasy Best Short Story Award for The Jade Man's Eyes - Flashing Swords 2, edited by Lin Carter.
1975. British Fantasy - August Derleth Fantasy Best Novel Award for The Sword and the Stallion.
1976. British Fantasy - August Derleth Fantasy Best Novel Award for The Hollow Lands.
1977. Guardian Fiction Award for The Condition of Muzak.
1979. The John W. Campbell Memorial Award for Gloriana.
1979. The World Fantasy Best Novel Award for Gloriana.
1993. The British Fantasy Committee Award.
2000. World Fantasy Lifetime Achievement Award.
2002. Inducted into The Science Fiction Hall of Fame.
2004. Prix Utopiales Grandmaster Lifetime Achievement Award.
2004. Bram Stoker Lifetime Achievement Award.
2008. SFWA Grand Master Award.

***

FILM AND TELEVISION

1. The Final Programme. Also known as The Last Days of Man on Earth, this 1968 novel was released as a film in 1974. Directed by Robert Fuest, it starred: Jon Finch as Jerry Cornelius; along with Jenny Runacre; Hugh Griffith; Patrick Magee; Sterling Hayden; Harry Andrews; and others.

2. The Land That Time Forgot. Moorcock, working with James Cawthorn, did the screenplay for the filming of this 1924 **Edgar Rice Burroughs** novel. The film was released in 1975, directed by Kevin Connor and starring: Doug McClure; John McEnery; Susan Penhaligon; Keith Barron and others, including Colin Farrell as Whiteley and Steve James as First Sto-Lu.

3. Heavy Metal. For this 1981 film, directed by Gerald Potterton, **Michael Moorcock**, working with Eric Bloom, wrote one of the songs for the soundtrack, Veteran of the Psychic Wars, performed by Blue Oyster Cult.

4. Hawkwind: The Chronicle of the Black Sword. This was Hawkwind's stage production from 1985 at the Hammersmith Odeon Theatre in London. It was based on Moorcock's work and he did the narration. Tony Crerar starred as Elric. Working with Dave Brock, the singing guitar-playing keyboardist with Hawkwind, **Michael Moorcock** also wrote some of the songs: Choose Your Masques; Horn of Destiny; and Arrival in Utopia. One more song, Coded Languages, was written by Moorcock with Harvey Bainbridge, another singing keyboardist with the band.

5. Asylum. Directed for television in 2000 by Christopher Petit and Iain Sinclair, this featured **Michael Moorcock**, along with Ed Dorn; James Sallis; Marina Warner; and others.

6. Conan: The Rise of a Fantasy Legend. This 2005 documentary featured interviews with **Michael Moorcock**, along with Roy Thomas; Don Herron; James Earl Jones; Michael Scott Myers; Edward Waterman; and many others.

7. Hawkwind: Do Not Panic. Directed by Simon Chu, this 2007 documentary featured **Michael Moorcock** along with many others. It also featured Sonic Attack, written by Moorcock and performed by Hawkwind.

8. Elric. In 2007, directors Chris and Paul Weitz announced they were making Elric films for Universal Pictures. No release date has been set.

***

NOVELS AND COLLECTIONS

1. The Caribbean Crisis. Writing as Desmond Reid - with James Cawthorn. Published by Fleetway Publications, London, 1962. Sexton Blake Library 501. Softcover.

2. The Sundered Worlds. Published by Compact Books, London, 1965. Compact Book F266. Softcover.

3. Warriors of Mars. Writing as Edward P. Bradbury. Published by Compact Books, London, 1965. Compact Book F275. Softcover.

4. Blades of Mars. Writing as Edward P. Bradbury. Published by Compact Books, London, 1965. Compact Book F279. Softcover.

5. The Fireclown. Published by Compact Books, London, 1965. Compact Book F281. Softcover.

6. The Barbarians of Mars. Writing as Edward P. Bradbury. Published by Compact Books, London, 1965. Compact Book F291. Softcover.

7. Stormbringer. Published by Herbert Jenkins, London, 1965. Hardcover. Abridged.

8. The LSD Dossier. Anonymously re-writing Robert Harris. Published by Compact Books, London, 1966. Compact Book F 303. Softcover.

9. The Deep Fix. Writing as James Colvin. Published by Compact Books, London, 1966. Compact Book F305. Softcover. Herein: The Deep Fix, 1964; Peace on Earth - with Barrington J. Bayley, 1959; The Lovebeast, 1966; The Pleasure Garden of Felipe Sagittarius, 1965; The Real Life of Mr Newman, 1966; and Wolf, 1966.

10. Somewhere in the Night. Writing as Bill Barclay. Published by Compact Books, London, 1966. Compact Book F309. Softcover.

11. The Twilight Man. Published by Compact Books, London, 1966. Compact Book F313. Softcover.

12. Printer's Devil. Writing as Bill Barclay. Published by Compact Books, London, 1966. Compact Book F322. Softcover.

13. The Wrecks of Time. Published by Ace Books, New York City, 1967. Ace Double H-36. Bound with Tramontane by Emil Petaja.

14. The Jewel in the Skull. Published by Lancer Books, New York City, 1967. Lancer Book 73-688. Softcover.

15. Sorcerer's Amulet. Published by Lancer Books, New York City, 1968. Lancer Book 73-707. Softcover.

16. The Final Programme. Published by Avon Books, New York City, 1968. Avon Book S351. Softcover.

17. The Sword of the Dawn. Published by Lancer Books, New York City, 1968. Lancer Book 73-761. Softcover.

18. The Mad God's Amulet. Published by Mayflower Books, London, 1969. Mayflower Book 113850. Softcover.

19. The Secret of the Secret of the Runestaff. Published by Lancer Books, New York City, 1969. Lancer Book 73-824. Softcover.

20. The Runestaff. Published by Mayflower Books, London, 1969. Mayflower Book 114997. Softcover. A re-titled version of The Secret of the Runestaff, 1969.

21. The Winds of Limbo. Published by Paperback Library, New York City, 1969. Paperback Library Book 63-149. Softcover. Re-titled re-issue of The Fire Clown, 1965.

22. The Final Programme. Published by Allison and Busby, London, 1969. First hardcover edition.

Michael Moorcock

23. Behold the Man. Published by Allison and Busby, London, 1969. Hardcover.

24. The Ice Schooner. Published by Sphere Books, London, 1969. Sphere Book 62162. Softcover.

25. The Time Dweller. Published by Rupert Hart-Davis, London, 1969. Hardcover. Herein: The Deep Fix, 1964; The Mountain, 1965; The Pleasure Garden of Felipe Sagittarius, 1965; The Time Dweller, 1964; Escape from Evening, 1965; The Golden Barge - writing as William Barclay, 1965; Wolf, 1966; Consuming Passion, 1966; and The Ruins - writing as James Colvin, 1966.

26. The Black Corridor. Published by Mayflower Books, London, 1969. Mayflower Book 583 11640. Softcover.

27. The Black Corridor. Published by Ace Books, New York City, 1969. Ace Science Fiction Special 06530. Softcover. Revised edition.

28. The Black Corridor. Published by the Science Fiction Book Club, Garden City, New York, 1970. Book Club Code 16L. First hardcover edition.

29. The Eternal Champion. Published by Dell Books, New York City, 1970. Dell Book 2383. Softcover.

30. The Blood Red Game. Sphere Books, London, 1970. Sphere Book 62146. Re-titled re-issue of The Sundered Worlds, 1965.

31. The Shores of Death. Sphere Books, London, 1970. Sphere Book 62154. Re-titled re-issue of The Twilight Man, 1966.

32. The Chinese Agent. Published by Macmillan, New York City, 1970. Hardcover. Seriously revised version of Somewhere in the Night, 1966.

33. The City of the Beast. Published by Lancer Books, New York City, 1970. Lancer Book 74668. Originally published as Warriors of Mars by Edward P. Bradbury, this re-titled version credits **Michael Moorcock**.

34. The Lord of the Spiders. Published by Lancer Books, New York City, 1970. Lancer Book 74736. Originally published as Blades of Mars by Edward P. Bradbury, this re-titled version credits **Michael Moorcock**.

35. The Masters of the Pit. Published by Lancer Books, New York City, 1970. Lancer Book 75199. Originally published as Barbarians of Mars by Edward P. Bradbury, this re-titled version credits **Michael Moorcock**.

36. Phoenix in Obsidian. Published by Mayflower Books, London, 1970. Softcover.

37. The Singing Citadel. Published by Mayflower Books, London, 1970. Softcover. Herein: To Rescue Tanelorn, 1962; Master of Chaos, 1964; The Singing Citadel, 1967; and The Greater Conqueror, 1963.

38. The Knight of Swords. Published by Mayflower Books, London, 1971. Softcover.

39. The Queen of Swords. Published by Berkley Books, New York City, 1971. Berkley Book S1999. Softcover.

40. The King of Swords. Published by Berkley Books, New York City, 1971. Berkley Book S2070. Softcover.

41. The Sleeping Sorceress. Published by New English Library, London, 1971. Hardcover.

42. A Cure for Cancer. Published by Allison and Busby, London, 1971. Hardcover.

43. The Warlord of the Air. Published by Ace Books, New York City, 1971. Ace Book 87060. Softcover.

44. The Warlord of the Air. Published by New English Library, London, 1971. First hardcover edition. Edited text.

45. The Rituals of Infinity. Published by Arrow Books, London, 1971. Arrow Book 488. Softcover. Revised edition of The Wrecks of Times, 1967.

46. The English Assassin. Published by Allison and Busby, London, 1972. Hardcover.

47. An Alien Heat. Published by MacGibbon and Kee, London, 1972. Hardcover.

48. Breakfast in Ruins. Published by New English Library, London, 1972. Hardcover.

49. Elric of Melnibone. Published by Hutchinson, London, 1972. Hardcover.

50. The Vanishing Tower. Published by Lancer Books, New York City, 1972. Lancer Book 75375. Softcover. Unauthorized re-titled re-issue of The Sleeping Sorceress, 1971.

51. The Dreaming City. Published by Lancer Books, New York City, 1972. Lancer Book 75376. Softcover. An unauthorized version of Elric of Melnibone with revisions.

52. Elric: The Return to Melnibone. Published by the Unicorn Bookshop, Brighton, UK, 1973. Softcover.

53. The Jade Man's Eyes. Published by the Unicorn Bookshop, Brighton, UK, 1973. Softcover.

54. The Jewel in the Skull. Published by White Lion Publishers, London, 1973. First hardcover edition.

55. The Mad God's Amulet. Published by White Lion Publishers, London, 1973. First hardcover edition.

56. The Sword of the Dawn. Published by White Lion Publishers, London, 1973. First hardcover edition.

57. Count Brass. Published by Mayflower Books, London, 1973. Softcover.

58. The Champion of Garathorm. Published by Mayflower Books, London, 1973. Softcover.

59. The Bull and the Spear. Published by Allison and Busby, London, 1973. Hardcover.

60. The Oak and the Ram. Published by Allison and Busby, London, 1973. Hardcover.

61. The Silver Warriors. Published by Dell Books, New York City, 1973. Dell Book 7994. Re-titled version of Phoenix in Obsidian, 1970.

62. The Runestaff. Published by White Lion Publishers, London, 1974. First hardcover edition.

63. The Sword and the Stallion. Published by Berkley Books, New York City, 1974. Softcover.

64. The Sword and the Stallion. Published by Allison and Busby, London, 1974. First hardcover edition.

65. The Hollow Lands. Published by Harper and Row, New York City, 1974. Hardcover.

66. The Land Leviathan. Published by Quartet Books, London, 1974. Hardcover. A softcover edition was published simultaneously.

67. The Quest for Tanelorn. Published by Mayflower Books, London, 1975. Softcover.

68. The Distant Suns. Written with James Cawthorn, writing as Philip James. Published by Unicorn Bookshop, Cardiff, Wales, 1975. Softcover.

69. The Adventures of Una Persson and Catherine Cornelius in the Twentieth Century. Published by Quartet Books, London, 1976. Hardcover.

70. Moorcock's Book of Martyrs. Published by Quartet Books, London, 1976. Softcover. Herein: Introduction by **Michael Moorcock**; Behold the Man, 1966; Flux - with Barrington J. Bayley; The Greater Conqueror, 1963; Good-Bye, Miranda, 1964; A Dead Singer, 1974; Islands, 1963; and Waiting for the End of Time, 1970.

71. The End of All Songs. Published by Harper and Row, New York City, 1976. Hardcover with a misspelling of Moorcock's name on the spine - Moorock.

72. Legends from the End of Time. Published by Harper and Row, New York City, 1976. Hardcover. Herein: Pales Roses, 1974; White Stars, 1975; and Ancient Shadows, 1975.

73. The Sailor on the Seas of Fate. Published by Quartet Books, London, 1976. Hardcover.

74. The Lives and Times of Jerry Cornelius. Published by Allison and Busby, London, 1976. Hardcover. Herein: The Peking Junction, 1969; The Delhi Division, 1968; The Tank Trapeze, 1969; The Nature of the Catastrophe, 1970; The Swastika Set-up, 1972; The Sunset Perspective, 1970; Sea Wolves, 1970; Voortrekker, 1971; Dead Singers, 1971; The Longford Cup, 1976; and The Entropy Circuit, 1974.

75. The Time of the Hawklords. Written by Michael Butterworth and based on an idea by **Michael Moorcock**. Published by Aidan Ellis, Henley-on-Thames, UK, 1976. Softcover.

76. The Bane of the Black Sword. Published by DAW Books, New York City, 1977. DAW Collector's Book 254 - UY1316. Softcover. A revised version of portions of Stealer of Souls, 1963. Herein: To Rescue Tanelorn, 1962; The Stealer of Souls, 1962; Kings in Darkness, 1962; and The Flame Bringers, 1962.

77. The Jewel in the Skull. Published by DAW Books, New York City, 1977. DAW Collector's Book 225 - UY1276. Softcover. Revised edition.

78. The Weird of the White Wolf. Published by DAW Books, New York City, 1977. DAW Collector's Book 233 - UY1286. Softcover. Herein: The Dream of Aubec, 1964; The Dreaming City, 1961; While the Gods Laugh, 1961; and The Singing Citadel, 1967.

79. The Mad God's Amulet. Published by DAW Books, New York City, 1977. DAW Collector's Book 238 - UY1289. Softcover. Revised edition.

80. The Vanishing Tower. Published by DAW Books, New York City, 1977. DAW Collector's Book 245 - UY1304. Softcover. Re-titled version of The Sleeping Sorceress, 1971.

81. The Sword of the Dawn. Published by DAW Books, New York City, 1977. DAW Collector's Book 249 - UY1310. Softcover. Revised edition.

82. The Runestaff. Published by DAW Books, New York City, 1977. DAW Collector's Book 257 - UY1324. Softcover. Revised edition.

83. Stormbringer. Published by DAW Books, New York City, 1977. DAW Collector's Book 264 - UY1335. Softcover. Unabridged.

84. The Condition of Muzak. Published by Allison and Busby, London, 1977. Hardcover.

85. The Knight of Swords. Published by Allison and Busby, London, 1977. First hardcover edition.

86. The Swords Trilogy. Published by Berkley Books, New York City, 1977. Softcover. An omnibus edition, this contains: The Knight of Swords, 1971; The Queen of Swords, 1971; and The King of Swords, 1971.

87. The Cornelius Chronicles. Published by Avon Books, New York City, 1977. Avon Book 31468. Softcover. An omnibus edition, this gathers: The Repossession of Jerry Cornelius - an introduction by John Clute; The Final Programme, 1968; A Cure for Cancer, 1971; The English Assassin, 1972; and The Condition of Muzak, 1977. All four titles have some revisions.

88. The Ice Schooner. Published by Harper and Row, New York City, 1977. First hardcover edition. Includes revisions.

89. Sojan. Published by Savoy, Manchester, UK, 1977. Softcover. Herein: The Stone Thing: A Tale of Strange Parts, 1974; The Dying Castles, 1970; Sojan the Swordsman, 1957; Sojan, Swordsman of Zylor!, 1957; Sojan and the Sea of Demons, 1958; Sojan and the Plain of Mystery, 1958; Sojan and the Sons of the Snake-God, 1958; Sojan and the Devil Hunters of Norj, 1958; Klan the Spoiler - writing as J. R. Taylor, 1958; Rens Karto of Bersnol, 1958; The Secret Life of Elric of Melnibone - an essay, 1964;

Michael Moorcock

New Worlds - Jerry Cornelius - an essay, 1972; and In a Lighter Vein: A Note on the Jerry Cornelius Tetralogy - an essay, 1977.

90. The Transformation of Miss Mavis Ming. Published by W. H. Allen, London, 1977. Hardcover.

91. Queens of Deliria. By Michael Butterworth, based on an idea by **Michael Moorcock**. Published by Star Books, London, 1977. Softcover.

92. A Messiah at the End of Time, or The Transformation of Miss Mavis Ming. Published by DAW Books, New York City, 1978. DAW Collector's Book 277. Softcover. Re-titled re-issue of The Transformation of Miss Mavis Ming, 1977.

93. The Chronicles of Corum. Published by Berkley Books, New York City, 1978. Softcover. An omnibus edition, this gathers: The Bull and the Spear, 1973; The Oak and the Ram, 1973; and The Sword and the Stallion, 1974.

94. Gloriana, or the Unfulfilled Queen. Published by Fontana/Collins, London, 1978. Softcover.

95. The History of the Runestaff. Published by Rupert Hart-Davis, London, 1979. Hardcover. An omnibus edition, this gathers: The Jewel in the Skull, 1967; The Mad God's Amulet, 1968; The Sword of the Dawn, 1968; and The Runestaff, 1969.

96. The Golden Barge: A Fable. Published by Savoy Books, Manchester, UK, 1979. Softcover. Herein: Introduction by M. John Harrison; Introduction by **Michael Moorcock**.

97. The Real Life Mr Newman. Published by A. J. Callow, Worcester, UK, 1979. Softcover.

98. The Russian Intelligence. Published by Savoy Books, Manchester, UK, 1980. Softcover.

99. My Experiences in the Third World War. Published by Savoy, Manchester, UK, 1980. Softcover. Herein: Introduction by **Michael Moorcock**; Going to Canada, 1980; Leaving Pasadena, 1980; Crossing into Cambodia, 1979; The Dodgem Division, 1969; The Adventures of Jerry Cornelius: The English Assassin - writing with M. John Harrison, 1980; Peace on Earth - writing with Barrington J. Bayley, 1959; The Lovebeast, 1966; and The Real Life of Mr Newman, 1966.

100. The Great Rock 'n' Roll Swindle. Published by Virgin Books, London, 1981. Softcover.

101. Byzantium Endures. Published by Secker and Warburg, London, 1981. Hardcover.

102. The Entropy Tango. Published by New English Library, London, 1981. Hardcover. Herein: Harlequin's Lament, 1981; The Minstrel Girl, 1977; Revolutions, 1981; The Kassandra Peninsula, 1978; and For One Day Only: Two Mighty Empires Crash, 1981.

103. The Dancers at the End of Time. Published by Book Club Associates, London, 1981. Hardcover. An omnibus, this contains: An Alien Heat, 1972; The Hollow Lands, 1974; and The End of All Songs, 1976.

104. The Steel Tsar. Published by Granada Books, London, 1981. Softcover.

105. The War Hound and the World's Pain. Published by Timescape Books, New York City, 1981. Hardcover.

106. The Nomad of Time. Published by Nelson Doubleday - The Science Fiction Book Club, Garden City, New York, 1982. Hardcover. An omnibus edition, this gathers: The Warlord of the Air, 1971; The Land Leviathan, 1974; and The Steel Tsar, 1981.

107. The Brothel in Rosenstrasse: An Extravagant Tale. Published by New English Library, London, 1982. Hardcover.

108. The Golden Barge: A Fable. Published by New English Library, London, 1983. First hardcover edition.

109. The Laughter of Carthage. Published by Secker and Warburg, London, 1984. Hardcover.

110. The Elric Saga - Part I. Published by Nelson Doubleday - The Science Fiction Book Club, Garden City, New York, 1984. Hardcover. An omnibus, this collects: Elric of Melnibone, 1972; The Sailor on the Seas of Fate, 1976; and The Weird of the White Wolf, 1977.

111. The Elric Saga - Part II. Published by Nelson Doubleday - The Science Fiction Book Club, Garden City, New York, 1984. Hardcover. An omnibus, this contains: The Vanishing Tower, 1970; The Bane of the Black Sword, 1977; and Stormbringer, 1965.

112. The Opium General. Published by Harrap, London, 1984. Hardcover. Herein: The Alchemist's Question, 1984; The Opium General, 1984; Going to Canada, 1980; Leaving Pasadena, 1980; Crossing into Cambodia, 1979; Starship Stormtroopers - an essay, 1984; Nestor Makhno - an Essay, 1984; and Who'll Be Next? - an essay, 1984.

113. Elric at the End of Time. Published by New English Library, London, 1984. Hardcover. Herein: Introduction by **Michael Moorcock**; Elric at the End of Time, 1981; The Last Enchantment, 1978; The Secret Life of Elric of Melnibone - an essay, 1964; Sojan the Swordsman, 1984; New Worlds - Jerry Cornelius - an essay, 1972; and In Lighter Vein, 1977.

114. The Chronicles of Castle Brass. Published by Granada Books, London, 1985. Hardcover. An omnibus edition, this gathers: Count Brass, 1973; The Champion of Garathorm, 1973; and The Quest for Tanelorn, 1975.

115. The City in the Autumn Stars. Published by Grafton Books, London, 1986. Hardcover.

116. The Dragon in the Sword. Published by Ace Books, New York City, 1986. Hardcover.

117. The Cornelius Chronicles - Volume II. Published by Avon Books, New York City, 1986. Softcover. Herein: The Lives and Times of Jerry Cornelius, 1976; and The Entropy Tango, 1981.

118. The Cornelius Chronicles - Volume III.

Published by Avon Books, New York City, 1987. Softcover. Herein: The Adventures of Una Persson and Catherine Cornelius in the Twentieth Century, 1976; and The Alchemist's Question, 1984.

119. The Cornelius Chronicles - Book One. Published by Fontana Books, London, 1988. Softcover. Herein: The Repossession of Jerry Cornelius - an essay by John Clute, 1977; The Final Programme, 1968; and A Cure for Cancer, 1971.

120. The Cornelius Chronicles - Book Two. Published by Fontana Books, London, 1988. Softcover. Herein: The Condition of Muzak, 1977; and The English Assassin, 1972.

121. Mother London. Published by Secker and Warburg, London, 1988. Hardcover.

122. Warrior of Mars. Published by New English Library, London, 1988. Softcover. An omnibus, this gathers: New Introduction to the Kane Series by **Michael Moorcock**; City of the Beast, 1965; Lord of the Spiders, 1965; and Masters of the Pit, 1965.

123. The Fortress of the Pearl. Published by Victor Gollancz, London, 1989. Hardcover.

124. Tales from the End of Time. Published by The Science Fiction Book Club, Garden City, New York, 1989. Hardcover. Herein: Legends from the End of Time, 1975; and A Messiah at the End of Time, 1978.

125. Casablanca. Published by Victor Gollancz, London, 1989. Hardcover. Herein: Introduction by **Michael Moorcock**; Casablanca, 1989; The Frozen Cardinal, 1987; Hanging the Fool, 1989; The Murderer's Song, 1987; Mars, 1988; The Last Call, 1989; and Gold Diggers of 1977, 1989; along with seventeen essays: Scratching a Living; Mervyn Peake; Harlan Ellison; Angus Wilson; Andrea Dworkin; Maeve Gilmore; Taking the Life Out of London; The Smell of Old Vienna; Literally London; People of the Book; London Lost and Found; Building the New Jerusalem; Who's Really Covering Up?, What Feminism Has Done for Me; Caught Up in Reality; Anti-Personnel Capability; and the Case Against Pornography.

126. The Revenge of the Rose: A Tale of the Albino Prince in the Years of His Wandering. Published by Grafton Books, London, 1991. Softcover.

127. The Revenge of the Rose. Published by Ace Books, New York City, 1991. First hardcover edition.

128. Jerusalem Commands. Published by Jonathan Cape, London, 1992. Hardcover.

129. Von Bek. Published by Millennium Books, London, 1992. Hardcover. An omnibus edition: Dear Reader - an essay by **Michael Moorcock**; The Warhound and the World's Pain, 1992; The City in the Autumn Stars, 1986; and The Pleasure Garden of Felipe Sagittarius, 1965

130. The Eternal Champion. Published by Millennium Books, London, 1992. Hardcover. An omnibus edition: Dear Reader - an essay by **Michael Moorcock**; The Eternal Champion, 1970; Phoenix in Obsidian, 1970; and The Dragon in the Sword, 1986.

131. Hawkmoon. Published by Millennium Books, London, 1992. Hardcover. An omnibus edition: Dear Reader - an essay by **Michael Moorcock**; The Jewel in the Skull, 1967; The Mad God's Amulet, 1968; The Sword of the Dawn, 1968; and The Runestaff, 1969.

132. Corum. Published by Millennium Books, London, 1992. Hardcover. An omnibus edition: Dear Reader - an essay by **Michael Moorcock**; The Knight of Swords, 1971; The Queen of Swords, 1971; and The King of Swords, 1971.

133. Sailing to Utopia. Published by Millennium Books, London, 1993. Softcover. An omnibus edition: Dear Reader - an essay by **Michael Moorcock**; The Ice Schooner, 1969; The Black Corridor - with Hilary Bailey, 1969; The Distant Suns - with Jim Cawthorn, 1975; and Flux - with Barrington J. Bayley, 1963.

134. A Nomad of the Time Streams. Published by Millennium Books, London, 1993. Softcover. An omnibus edition: Dear Reader - an essay by **Michael Moorcock**; The Warlord of the Air, 1971; The Land Leviathan, 1974; and The Steel Tsar, 1981.

135. The Dancers at the End of Time. Published by Millennium Books, London, 1993. Softcover. An omnibus edition: Prologue by **Michael Moorcock**; An Alien Heat, 1972; The Hollow Lands, 1974; The End of All Songs, 1976.

136. Elric of Melnibone. Published by Millennium Books, London, 1993. Softcover. An omnibus edition: Dear Reader - an essay by **Michael Moorcock**; Elric of Melnibone, 1972; The Fortress of the Pearl, 1989; The Sailor on the Seas of Fate, 1976; The Dreaming City, 1961; While the Gods Laugh, 1961; and The Singing Citadel, 1967.

137. The New Nature of Catastrophe. With Langdon Jones. Published by Millennium Books, London, 1993. Softcover. Part anthology, part story collection, this contains: Introductions by **Michael Moorcock**; The Peking Junction by **Michael Moorcock**, 1969; The Delhi Division by **Michael Moorcock**, 1968; The Tank Trapeze by **Michael Moorcock**, 1969; The Ash Circus by M. John Harrison, 1969; The Firmament Theorem by **Brian W. Aldiss**, 1969; The Last Hurrah of the Golden Horde by Norman Spinrad, 1969; The Dedgem Decision by **Michael Moorcock**, 1993; The Nash Circuit by M. John Harrison, 1969; Lines of White on a Sullen Sea by Maxim Jakubowski, 1969; The Anxiety in the Eyes of a Cricket by James Sallis, 1993; The End of the Cycle - a poem by Langdon Jones, 1969; Sea Wolves by **Michael Moorcock**, 1970; Voortrekker by **Michael Moorcock**, 1971; The Flesh Circle by M. John Harrison, 1971; A Prayer to Men by Alex Krislov, 1971; Dead Singers by **Michael Moorcock**, 1971; The Swastika Set-up by **Michael Moorcock**, 1972; The Longford Cup by **Michael Moorcock**, 1976; The Entropy Circuit by **Michael Moorcock**, 1974; Interlude: Miss Brunner and Jerry by Giles Gordon, 1993; The Repossession of Jerry Cornelius - an essay by John Clute, 1977; Niki Hoeky by Charles Partington, 1979; Everything Blowing Up by Hilary Bailey, 1993; The Murderer's

Michael Moorcock

Song by **Michael Moorcock**, 1987; The Gangrene Collection, 1993; The Roumanian Question, 1993; Bruised Time by Simon Ings, 1992; Epilogue: Jerry and Miss Brunner at the Beginning by Langdon Jones, 1993; and Jerry Cornelius: A Reader's Guide by John Davey.

138. The Prince with the Silver Hand. Published by Millennium Books, London, 1993. Softcover. An omnibus edition: Dear Reader - an essay by **Michael Moorcock**; The Bull and the Spear, 1973; The Oak and the Ram, 1973; and The Sword and the Stallion, 1974.

139. Tales from the End of Time. Published by Millennium Books, London, 1993. Softcover. This contains: Pale Roses, 1974; White Stars, 1975; Ancient Shadows, 1975; Constant Fire - an excerpt, 1978; and Elric at the End of Time, 1981.

140. Stormbringer. Published by Millennium Books, London, 1993. Softcover. This contains: Dear Reader - an essay by **Michael Moorcock**; The Sleeping Sorceress, 1970; The Revenge of the Rose 1991; The Stealer of Souls, 1962; Kings in Darkness, 1962; The Caravan of Forgotten Dreams, 1962; and Stormbringer, 1965.

141. Earl Aubec. Published by Millennium Books, London, 1993. Softcover. Herein: Dear Reader - an essay by **Michael Moorcock**; Early Aubec, 1993; Jesting with Chaos, 1993; The Greater Conqueror, 1963; Going Home, 1962; Hanging the Fool, 1989; Consuming Passion, 1966; Wolf, 1966; Environment Problem, 1973; The Opium General, 1984; A Dead Singer, 1974; The Lovebeast, 1966; The Golden Barge, 1965; The Deep Fix, 1964; The Real Life of Mr Newman, 1966; Goodbye, Miranda, 1964; Islands, 1963; Casablanca, 1989; Going to Canada, 1980; Leaving Pasadena, 1980; Crossing into Cambodia, 1979; Mars, 1988; The Frozen Cardinal, 1987; Peace on Earth - with Barrington J. Bayley, 1959; The Mountain, 1965; The Time Dweller, 1964; Escape from Evening, 1965; Waiting for the End of time, 1970; The Stone Thing, 1975; The Last Call, 1989; My Life, 1993; The Museum of the Future, 1993; and To Rescue Tanelorn, 1962.

142. Count Brass. Published by Millennium Books, London, 1993. Softcover. An omnibus edition, this gathers: The Champion of Garathorm, 1973; The Quest for Tanelorn, 1975; and Count Brass, 1973.

143. A Cornelius Calendar. Phoenix House, London, 1993. Hardcover. Herein: Adventures of Una Persson and Catherine Cornelius in the Twentieth Century, 1976; Gold Diggers of 1977, 1993; and The Alchemist's Question, 1984.

144. Count Brass. Published by Millennium, London, 1993. Hardcover. A re-issue of The Chronicles of Castle Brass.

145. Behold the Man and Other Stories. Published by Phoenix House, London, 1994. Hardcover. An omnibus edition, this collects: Behold the Man, 1969; Constant Fire, 1977; and Breakfast in the Ruins, 1972.

146. The Eternal Champion - The Tale of the Eternal Champion. White Wolf Publishing, Stone Mountain, Georgia, 1994. Hardcover. Herein: Introduction by **Michael Moorcock**; The Eternal Champion, 1970; The Sundered Worlds, 1965; Phoenix in Obsidian, 1970; and To Rescue Tanelorn, 1962.

147. Blood: A Southern Fantasy. Published by Millennium Books, London, 1995. Hardcover.

148. The Birds of the Moon. Published by Jayde Design, London, 1995. Softcover.

149. Fabulous Harbours. Published by Millennium Books, London, 1995. Hardcover. Herein: Introduction by **Michael Moorcock**; The White Pirate, 1994; Some Fragments Found in the Effects of Sam Oakenhurst, 1995; The Black Blade's Summoning, 1994; Lunching with the Antichrist, 1995; The Affair of the Seven Virgins, 1995; The Girl Who Killed Sylvia Blade, 1995; Crimson Eyes, 1995; No Ordinary Christian, 1994; The Enigma Windows, 1995; and Epilogue: The Birds of the Moon, 1995.

150. Lunching with the Antichrist: A Family History: 1925 - 2015. Published by Mark V. Ziesing, United States, 1995. Hardcover. Herein: Introduction by **Michael Moorcock**; A Winter Admiral, 1994; Wheel of Fortune, 1995; Dead Singers, 1971; Lunching with the Antichrist, 1995; The Opium General, 1984; The Cairene Purse, 1990; and Crossing into Cambodia, 1979.

151. Von Bek - The Tale of the Eternal Champion. White Wolf Publishing, Clarkston, Georgia, 1995. Hardcover. Herein: Introduction by **Michael Moorcock**; The War Hound and the World's Pain; The City in the Autumn Stars, 1986; The Dragon in the Sword, 1986; and The Pleasure Garden of Filipe Sagittarius.

152. Hawkmoon - The Tale of the Eternal Champion. White Wolf Publishing, Clarkston, Georgia, 1995. Hardcover. Herein: Introduction by **Michael Moorcock**; The Jewel in the Skull, 1967; The Mad God's Amulet, 1968; The Sword of the Dawn, 1968; and The Runestaff, 1969.

153. A Nomad of the Time Streams - The Tale of the Eternal Champion. White Wolf Publishing, Clarkston, Georgia, 1995. Hardcover. Herein: Introduction by **Michael Moorcock**; The Warlord of the Air, 1971; The Land Leviathan, 1974; The Steel Tsar, 1981.

154. Elric: Song of the Black Sword - The Tale of the Eternal Champion. White Wolf Publishing, Clarkston, Georgia, 1995. Hardcover. Herein: Introduction by **Michael Moorcock**; Elric of Melnibone, 1972; The Fortress of the Pearl, 1989; The Sailor on the Seas of Fate, 1976; The Dreaming City, 1961; While the Gods Laugh, 1961; and The Singing Citadel, 1967.

155. The Roads Between Worlds - The Tale of the Eternal Champion. White Wolf Publishing, Clarkston, Georgia, 1996. Hardcover. Herein: Introduction by **Michael Moorcock**; The Wrecks of Time, 1967; The Winds of Limbo, 1969; and The Shores of Death, 1970.

**156. The Roads Between Worlds - The Tale

of the Eternal Champion. White Wolf Publishing, Clarkston, Georgia, 1996. Hardcover. Herein: Introduction by **Michael Moorcock**;

157. The War Amongst the Angels. Published by Millennium Books, London, 1996. Hardcover.

158. Corum: The Coming of Chaos - The Tale of the Eternal Champion. White Wolf Publishing, Clarkston, Georgia, 1997. Hardcover. Herein: Introduction by **Michael Moorcock**; The Knight of the Swords, 1971; The Queen of the Swords, 1971; and The King of the Swords, 1971.

159. Sailing to Utopia - The Tale of the Eternal Champion. White Wolf Publishing, Clarkston, Georgia, 1997. Hardcover. Herein: Introduction by **Michael Moorcock**; The Ice Schooner, 1969; The Black Corridor - with Hilary Bailey, 1969; The Distant Suns - with Jim Cawthorn, 1975; and Flux - with Barrington J. Bayley, 1963.

160. Tales from the Texas Woods. Published by Mojo Press, Austin, Texas, 1997. Hardcover. Herein: Introduction by **Michael Moorcock**; The Ghost Warriors, 1997; About My Multiverse - an essay, 1997; The Further Adventures of Sherlock Holmes, 1995; How Tom Mix Saved My Live - an essay, 1994; A Catalogue of Memories - an essay, 1997; Sword of Irony; An Introduction to Fritz Leiber's Grey Mouser Stories - an essay, 1995; The Sun of It Parts - an essay, 1994; Review: The Arabian Nights: A Companion by Robert Irwin - a book review, 1994; My Comic Life - an essay, 1997; Johnny Lonesome Comes to Town: A Tale of the Far West, 1956; Bryan Talbot's The Adventures of Luther Arkwright - an essay, 1997; Review: From the Teeth of Angels by Jonathan Carroll - a book review, 1994; and Sir Milk-and-Blood: An Incident in the Life of the Eternal Champion, 1996.

161. Kane of Old Mars - The Tale of the Eternal Champion. White Wolf Publishing, Clarkston, Georgia, 1998. Hardcover. Herein: Introduction by **Michael Moorcock**; City of the Beast, 1965; Lord of the Spiders, 1965; and Masters of the Pit, 1965.

162. The Dancers at the End of Time - The Tale of the Eternal Champion. White Wolf Publishing, Clarkston, Georgia, 1998. Hardcover. Herein: Introduction by **Michael Moorcock**; An Alien Heat, 1972; The Hollow Lands, 1974; and The End of Al Songs, 1976.

163. Elric: The Stealer of Souls - The Tale of the Eternal Champion. White Wolf Publishing, Clarkston, Georgia, 1998. Hardcover. Herein: Introduction by **Michael Moorcock**; The Sleeping Sorceress, 1970; The Revenge of the Rose, 1991; The Stealer of Souls, 1962; Kings in Darkness, 1962; The Caravan of Forgotten Dreams, 1962; Stormbringer, 1965; and Elric: A Reader's Guide by John Davey, 1998.

164. Corum: The Prince with the Silver Hand - The Tale of the Eternal Champion. White Wolf Publishing, Clarkston, Georgia, 1999. Hardcover. Herein: Introduction by **Michael Moorcock**; The Bull and the Spear, 1973; The Oak and the Ram, 1973; and The Sword and the Stallion, 1974.

165. Legends from the End of Time - The Tale of the Eternal Champion. White Wolf Publishing, Clarkston, Georgia, 1999. Hardcover. Herein: Introduction by **Michael Moorcock**; Pale Roses, 1974; White Stars, 1975; Ancient Shadows, 1975; Constant Fire, 1977; and Elric at the End of Time, 1981.

166. Earl Aubec and Other Stories - The Tale of the Eternal Champion. White Wolf Publishing, Clarkston, Georgia, 1999. Hardcover. This drops To Rescue Tanelorn, 1962, from the Millennium edition, 1993 and adds Sir Milk-and-Blood, 1996.

167. Count Brass - The Tale of the Eternal Champion. White Wolf Publishing, Clarkston, Georgia, 2000. Hardcover. Herein: Introduction by **Michael Moorcock**; Count Brass, 1973; The Champion of Garathorm, 1973; and The Quest for Tanelorn, 1975.

168. Silverheart. With Storm Constantine. Published by Earthlight, London, 2000. Hardcover.

169. King of the City. Published by Scribner's, London, 2000. Hardcover.

170. The Dreamthief's Daughter - A Tale of the Albino. Published by Earthlight, London, 2001. Hardcover.

171. London Bone. Published by Scribner's, London, 2001. Softcover. This contains: A Winter Admiral, 1994; London Blood, 2000; Doves in the Circle, 1997; The Clapham Antichrist, 1993; London Bone, 1997; The Cairene Purse, 1990; Furniture, 2000; Through the Shaving Mirror, or How We Abolished the Future, 2000; and Afterword: Lost London Writers - an essay, 2000.

172. Firing the Cathedral. Published by PS Publishing, UK, 2002. Hardcover. Signed limited edition. Introduction by Alan Moore.

173. The Elric Saga - Volume III. Published by the Science Fiction Book Club, Garden City, New York, 2002. Hardcover. Herein: The Fortress of the Pearl, 1989; and The Revenge of the Rose, 1991.

174. The Skrayling Tree - A Tale of the Albino. Published by Warner Aspect, New York City, 2003. Hardcover.

175. The White Wolf's Son - The Albino in the Middle March. Published by Warner Aspect, New York City, 2005. Hardcover.

176. The Elric Saga - Volume IV. Published by the Science Fiction Book Club, Garden City, New York, 2005. Hardcover. Herein: The Dreamthief's Daughter, 2001; The Skrayling Tree, 2003; and The White Wolf's Son, 2005.

177. Jerry Cornell's Comic Capers. Published by Immanion Press, UK, 2005. Herein: The Chinese Agent, 1970; and The Russian Intelligence, 1980.

178. Gloriana, or The Unfulfill'd Queen. Published by the Science Fiction Book Club, Garden City, New York, 2005. First hardcover edition.

179. The Vengeance of Rome. Published by

Michael Moorcock

Jonathan Cape, London, 2006. Hardcover.

180. The Metatemporal Detective. Published by Pyr Books, Amherst, New York, 2007. Hardcover. Herein: The Affair of the Seven Virgins, 1995; Crimson Eyes, 1995; The Ghost Warriors, 2007; The Girl Who Killed Sylvia Blade, 1995; The Case of the Nazi Canary, 2003; Sir Milk-and-Blood, 1996; The Mystery of the Texas Twister, 2007; London Flesh, 2007; The Pleasure Garden of Felipe Sagittarius, 1965; The Affair of Le Bassin Les Hivers, 2007; and The Flaneur des Arcades de l'Opera, 2007.

181. Elric: Stealer of Souls - Chronicles of the Last Emperor of Melnibone - Volume 1. Published by Del Rey - Ballantine Books, New York City, 2008. Softcover.

182. Elric: To Rescue Tanelorn - Chronicles of the Last Emperor of Melnibone - Volume 2. Published by Del Rey - Ballantine Books, New York City, 2008. Softcover.

183. Elric: The Sleeping Sorceress - Chronicles of the Last Emperor of Melnibone - Volume 3. Published by Del Rey - Ballantine Books, New York City, 2008. Softcover.

184. Elric: Duke Elric - Chronicles of the Last Emperor of Melnibone - Volume 4. Published by Del Rey - Ballantine Books, New York City, 2009. Softcover.

185. The Best of Michael Moorcock. Published by Tachyon Publications, San Francisco, 2009. Softcover. Herein: Introduction by John Davey; A Portrait in Ivory, 2009; The Visible Men, 2009; A Dead Singer, 1974; Lunching with the Antichrist, 1995; The Opium General, 1984; Behold the Man, 1966; A Winter Admiral, 1994; London Bone, 1997; Colour, 1991; My Experiences in the Third World War, 1980; Going to Canada, 1980; Leaving Pasadena, 1980; Crossing into Cambodia, 1979; Doves in a Circle, 1997; The Deep Fix, 1964; The Birds of the Moon, 2009; The Cairene Purse, 1990; and A Slow Saturday Night at the Surrealist Sporting Club, 2001; followed by an Afterword by Ann and Jeff VanderMeer.

***

ANTHOLOGIES

1. The Best of New Worlds. Published by Compact Books, London, 1965. Compact Book H287. Softcover. Herein: The Terminal Beach by J. G. Ballard, 1964; The Last Lonely Man by John Brunner, 1964; All the King's Men by Barrington J. Bayley, 1965; The Time Dweller by **Michael Moorcock**, 1964; I See You by **Harry Harrison**, 1959; The Fall of Frenchy Steiner by Hilary Bailey, 1964; The Pit My Parish by **Brian W. Aldiss**, 1958; Tableau by James White, 1958; The Mountain by **Michael Moorcock** writing as James Colvin, 1965; New Experience by E. C. Tubb, 1964; I Remember, Anita by Langdon Jones, 1964; The Railways Up on Cannis by Colin Kapp, 1959; The Traps of Time by John Baxter, 1964; The Outstretched Hand by Arthur Sellings, 1959; and Another Word for Man, 1958.

2. SF Reprise 1. Published by Compact Books, London, 1966. Compact Book H323. Softcover. Herein: The Shores of Death - Part 1 and 2 - by **Michael Moorcock**, 1966; Private Shape by Sydney J. Bounds, 1964; Integrity by Barrington J. Bayley writing as P. F. Woods, 1964; I Remember, Anita by Langdon Jones, 1964; Andromeda by Clifford C. Reed, 1964; New Experience by E. C. Tubb, 1964; Mix-Up by **Michael Moorcock** writing as George Collyn, 1964; Gamma Positive by Ernest Hill, 1964; Some Will Be Saved by Colin R. Fry, 1964; The Patch by Barrington J. Bayley writing as Peter Woods; and Emissary by John Hamilton, 1964.

3. SF Reprise 2. Published by Compact Books, London, 1966. Compact Book H324. Softcover. Herein: The Power of Y - Part 1 and 2 - by Arthur Sellings, 1966; The Sailor in the Western Stars by Bob Parkinson, 1965; Tunnel of Love by Joseph Green, 1965; There's a Starman in Ward 7 by David Rome, 1965; Election Campaign by Thom Keyes, 1965; More Than a Man by John Baxter, 1965; When the Skies Fall by John Hamilton, 1965; The Singular Quest of Martin Borg by **Michael Moorcock** writing as George Collyn; The Mountain by **Michael Moorcock** writing as James Colvin; and Box by Richard Wilson.

4. SF Reprise 3. Published by Compact Books, London, 1966. Compact Book H325. Softcover. Herein: The Blue Monkeys by Thomas Burnett Swann, 1964; Escapism by Keith Roberts, 1964; Anita by Keith Roberts, 1964; One of Those Days by Charles Platt, 1964; The Island by Roger Jones, 1965; Not Me. Not Amos Cabot! by **Harry Harrison**, 1964; As Easy as A. B. C. by Rudyard Kipling, 1912; Period of Gestation by Thom Keyes, 1964; The Typewriter by Keith Roberts writing as Alistair Bevan, 1965; Only the Best by Patricia Hocknell, 1965; Flight of Fancy by Keith Roberts, 1965; Petros by Philip Wordley, 1965; Harvest by Johnny Byrne, 1965; The Empathy Machine by Langdon Jones, 1965; Present from the Past by Douglas Davis, 1965; Joik by Ernest Hill, 1964; The Madman by Keith Roberts writing as Alistair Bevan, 1964; The Charm by Keith Roberts, 1964; Room with a Skew by John T. Phillifent writing as John Rackham, 1964; Love Feast by Johnny Byrne, 1964; Symbiote by George Rigg, 1964; Dummy Run by Colin Hume, 1964; and E. J. Carnell - A Quick Look - an essay by **Harry Harrison**, 1964.

5. SF Reprise 4. Published by Compact Books, London, 1966. Compact Book H326. Softcover. Herein: Man in His Time by **Brian W. Aldiss**, 1965; Susan by Keith Roberts writing as Alistair Bevan, 1965; Hunt a Wild Dream by D. R. Heywood, 1965; Over and Out by George Hay, 1965; The Excursion by Brian N. Ball, 1965; The Chicken Switch by Elleston Trevor, 1965; The War at Foxhanger by Keith Roberts, 1965; A Cave in the Hills by R. W. Mackelworth, 1965; The Jennifer by Keith Roberts, 1965; Bring Back a Life by John T. Phillifent writing as John Rackham, 1965; Moriarty by Philip Wordley, 1965; Song of the Syren by Robert Wells, 1965; and The Outcast by **Harry Harrison**, 1965.

6. SF Reprise 5. Published by Compact Books, London, 1966. Compact Book H329. Softcover. Herein: The Life Buyer by E. C. Tubb, 1965; Time Trap by Charles L. Harness, 1948; Prisoner of the

Coral Deep by J. G. Ballard, 1964; Apartness by Vernor Vinge, 1965; Nobody Axed You by John Brunner, 1965; The Small Betraying Detail by **Brian W. Aldiss**, 1965; The Ship of Disaster by Barrington J. Bayley, 1965; The Last Man Home by R. W. Mackelworth, 1965; Convolutions by **Michael Moorcock** writing as George Collyn; Alfred's Ark by **Jack Vance**, 1965; Reactionary by Barrington J. Bayley writing as P. F. Woods; The Flowers of the Valley by Keith Roberts; What Next? By Edward Mackin, 1965; Third Party by Dan Morgan, 1965; Death of an Earthman by George Locke writing as Gordon Walters, 1965; In One Sad Day by **Michael Moorcock** writing as George Collyn, 1965; and The Changing Shape of Charlie Snuff by R. W. Mackelworth, 1965.

7. Best S.F. Stories from New Worlds. Published by Panther Books, London, 1967. Panther Book 2243. Softcover. Herein: Introduction by **Michael Moorcock**; The Small Betraying Detail by **Brian W. Aldiss**, 1965; The Keys to December by Roger Zelazny, 1966; The Assassination Weapon by J. G. Ballard, 1966; Nobody Axed You by John Brunner, 1965; A Two Timer by David Masson, 1966; The Music Makers by Langdon Jones, 1965; and The Squirrel Cage by Thomas M. Disch, 1966.

8. The Traps of Time. Published by Rapp and Whiting, London, 1968. Hardcover. Herein: Introduction by **Michael Moorcock**; Man in His Time by **Brian W. Aldiss**, 1965; Time Trap by Charles L. Harness, 1948; The Great Clock by Langdon Jones, 1966; Mr F is Mr F by J. G. Ballard, 1961; Traveller's Rest by David I. Masson, 1965; The Garden of Forking Paths by Jorge Luis Borges, 1948; Unification Day by **Michael Moorcock** writing as George Collyn, 1966; Now is Forever by Thomas M. Disch, 1964; Divine Madness by Roger Zelazny, 1966; and How to Construct a Time Machine by Alfred Jarry, 1965.

9. Best S.F. Stories from New Worlds 2. Published by Panther Books, London, 1968. Panther Book 23690. Softcover. Herein: Introduction by **Michael Moorcock**; Another Little Boy by **Brian W. Aldiss**, 1966; The Poets of Millgrove, Iowa by John T. Sladek, 1966; The Transfinite Choice by David I. Masson, 1966; You: Coma: Marilyn Monroe by J. G. Ballard, 1966; Three Short Stories: The Contest; The Empty Room; and The Descent of the West End by Thomas M. Disch, 1967; The Singular Quest of Martin Borg by **Michael Moorcock** writing as George Collyn, 1965; The Countenance by Barrington J. Bayley writing as P. F. Woods, 1964; The Pleasure Garden of Felipe Sagittarius by **Michael Moorcock** writing as James Colvin, 1965; Sisohpromatem by Kit Reed, 1967; and For a Breath I Tarry by Roger Zelazny, 1966.

10. Best S.F. Stories from New Worlds 3. Published by Panther Books, London, 1968. Panther Book 24956. Softcover. Herein: Introduction by **Michael Moorcock**; In Passage of the Sun by **Michael Moorcock** writing as George Collyn, 1966; Multi-Value Motorway by **Brian W. Aldiss**, 1967; The Great Clock by Langdon Jones, 1966; The Post-Mortem People by Peter Tate, 1966; The Disaster Story by Charles Platt, 1966; The Heat Death of the Universe by Pamela Zoline, 1967; Coranda by Keith Roberts, 1967; The Soft World Sequence - a poem by George MacBeth, 1967; Kazoo by James Sallis, 1967; Integrity by Barrington J. Bayley writing as P. F. Woods, 1965; and The Mountain by **Michael Moorcock** writing as James Colvin, 1965.

11. Best S.F. Stories from New Worlds 4. Published by Panther Books, London, 1969. Panther Book 027947. Softcover. Herein: Introduction by **Michael Moorcock**; The Ship of Disaster by Barrington J. Bayley, 1965; The Square Root of Brain by **Fritz Leiber**, 1968; In Seclusion by Harvey Jacobs, 1966; Transient by Landgon Jones, 1965; The Head Rape - a poem by D. M. Thomas, 1968; The Source by **Brian W. Aldiss**, 1965; Period of Gestation by Thom Keyes, 1964; Dr Gelabius by Hilary Bailey, 1968; The Valve Transcript by Joel Zoss, 1968; Linda and Daniel and Spike by Thomas M. Disch, 1967; and Masterson and the Clerks by John T. Sladek, 1967.

12. Best S.F. Stories from New Worlds 5. Published by Panther Books, London, 1969. Softcover. Herein: Introduction by **Michael Moorcock**; The Last Hurrah of the Golden Horde by Norman Spinrad, 1969; Notes Toward a Mental Breakdown by J. G. Ballard, 1967; The Last Inn on the Road by Roger Zelazny and Danny Plachta, 1967; The Spectrum by D. M. Thomas; The Tennyson Effect by Graham M. Hall, 1966; The Serpent of Kundalini by **Brian W. Aldiss**, 1968; Mars Pastorale by Peter Tate, 1967; Biographical Note on Ludwig van Beethoven II by Langdon Jones, 1968; A Landscape of Shallows by Christopher Finch, 1968; Scream by Giles Gordon, 1968; and The Rodent Laboratory by Charles Platt, 1966.

13. The Inner Landscape. Published by Allison and Busby, London, 1969. Hardcover. Edited anonymously. Herein: Boy in Darkness by Mervyn Peake, 1956; Danger: Religion! By **Brian W. Aldiss**, 1962; and The Voices of Time by J. G. Ballard, 1960.

14. Best S.F. Stories from New Worlds 6. Published by Panther Books, London, 1970. Softcover. Herein: Introduction by **Michael Moorcock**; The Killing Ground by J. G. Ballard, 1969; Gravity by Harvey Jacobs, 1969; The Eye of the Lens by Langdon Jones, 1968; A Man Must Die by John Clute, 1966; Mr Black's Poems of Innocence by D. M. Thomas, 1969; In Reason's Ear by Hilary Bailey, 1965; The Ersatz Wine by Christopher Priest, 1966; Lib by Carol Emshwiller, 1968; Baa Baa Blocksheep by M. John Harrison, 1968; The Luger is a 9mm Automatic Handgun with a Parabellum Action by J. J. Mundis, 1969; and The Delhi Division by **Michael Moorcock**, 1968.

15. The Nature of the Catastrophe. With Langdon Jones. Published by Hutchinson, London, 1971. Hardcover. Herein: Introduction by **Michael Moorcock** writing as James Colvin; The Nature of the Catastrophe by **Michael Moorcock**, 1970; The Firmament Theorem by **Brian W. Aldiss**, 1969; The Nash Circuit by M. John Harrison, 1969; Jeremiad by James Sallis, 1969; Sea Wolves by **Michael Moorcock**, 1970; The End of the Cycle - a poem by Langdon Jones, 1969; The Ash Circus by M. John Harrison, 1969; The Tank Trapeze by **Michael Moorcock**, 1969; The Last Hurrah of the Golden

Michael Moorcock

Horde by Norman Spinrad, 1969; The Adventures of Jerry Cornelius: The English Assassin - an essay by Mal Dean and Richard Glyn Jones; The Delhi Division by **Michael Moorcock**, 1968; Marrow by James Sallis, 1971; The Flesh Circle by M. John Harrison, 1971; A Prayer to Men by Alex Krislov, 1971; Lines of White on a Sullen Sea by Maxim Jakubowski, 1969; The Sunset Perspective by **Michael Moorcock**, 1970; and Chronology - an essay by **Michael Moorcock** and Langdon Jones, 1971.

16. Best S.F. Stories from New Worlds 7. Published by Panther Books, London, 1971. Softcover. Herein: Introduction by **Michael Moorcock**; The Ash Circus by M. John Harrison, 1969; All the King's Men by B. J. Bayley, 1965; Mix-up by **Michael Moorcock** writing as George Collyn, 1964; Time Considered as a Helix of Semi-precious Stones by **Samuel R. Delany**, 1968; Lone Zone by Charles Platt, 1965; Two Poems: Flower Gathering and Transplant by Langdon Jones, 1969; The Apocalypse Machine by Leo Zorin, 1968; The Beach Murders by J. G. Ballard, 1969; The Wall by Josephine Saxton, 1965; and The Tank Trapeze by **Michael Moorcock**, 1969.

17. New Worlds - The Science Fiction Quarterly 1. Published by Sphere Books, London, 1971. Sphere Book 62081. Softcover. Most of the work here was done in the year of publication; exceptions are noted. This contains: Introduction by **Michael Moorcock**; Angouleme by Thomas M. Disch; Prisoners of Paradise by David Redd, 1966; Journey Across a Crater by J. G. Ballard, 1970; The Lamia and Lord Cromis by M. John Harrison; Pemberly's Start Afresh Calliope by John T. Sladek; The God House by Keith Roberts; The Day We Embarked for Cythera by **Brian W. Aldiss**; The Short Happy Wife of Mansard Eliot by John T. Sladek; A Place and a Time to Die by J. G. Ballard, 1969; Exit from City 5 by Barrington Bayley; and A Literature for Comfort - an essay by M. John Harrison.

18. New Worlds - The Science Fiction Quarterly 2. Published by Sphere Books, London, 1971. Sphere Book 62103. Softcover. Most of the work here was done in the year of publication; exceptions are noted. This contains: Introduction: Keeping Perspective by **Michael Moorcock**; Monkey and Pru and Sal by Keith Roberts; No Direction Home by Norman Spinrad; The Meek by William Woodrow; The Causeway; and By Tennyson Out of Disney by W. John Harrison; Visions of Hell - an essay by J. G. Ballard, 1966; Four-Color Problem by B. J. Bayley; Fifth Person Singular by Peter Tate, 1966; Listen Love by George Zebrowski and Jack Dann; Feathers from the Wings of an Angel by Thomas M. Disch; Monitor Found in Orbit by Michael G. Coney; Pandora's Bust by Richard A. Pollack; The Key of the Door by Arthur Sellings, 1967; and By Tennyson Out of Disney by M. John Harrison.

19. New Worlds - The Science Fiction Quarterly 3. Published by Sphere Books, London, 1972. Sphere Book 62111. Softcover. Most of the work here was done in the year of publication; exceptions are noted. This contains: Introduction by **Michael Moorcock**; The Machine in Shaft Ten by Joyce Churchill; I Lose Medea by Alistair Bevan; As For Our Fatal Continuity by **Brian W. Aldiss**; Julio by Pamela Sargent; The Wonderful World of Griswald Tractors by Thomas M. Disch, 1971; And Dug the Dog a Tomb by Laurence James; The Grain Kings by Keith Roberts; Windows by Jack Dann; A Cleansing of the System by Charles Platt; The Purloined Butter by John T. Sladek; The Head and the Hand by Christopher Priest; The History Machine by George Zebrowski; A Chronicle of Blackton by Hilary Bailey; and The Black Glak by M. John Harrison.

20. New Worlds - The Science Fiction Quarterly 4. Published by Sphere Books, London, 1972. Sphere Book 62200. Softcover. All of the work here was done in the year of publication. Herein: The Problem of Sympathy by M. John Harrison; The Exploration of Space by B. J. Bayley; Simon by William Woodrow; The First of Two Raped Prospects by Marek Obtulowicz; 334 by Thomas M. Disch; Man in Transit by Barrington J. Bayley writing as Alan Aumbry; The Locked Room by John T. Sladek; Weihnachtabend by Keith Roberts; and Attack-Escape - an interview with **Alfred Bester** by Charles Platt.

21. New Worlds - The Science Fiction Quarterly 5. Published by Sphere Books, London, 1973. Sphere Book 62006. Softcover. All of the work here was done in the year of publication. This contains: Introduction by **Michael Moorcock**; The Crack by Emma Tennant; Some Rooms by Merle Kessler; Name (Please Print); Bill Gets Hep to God; and Flatland by John Sladek; Sonoran Poems by D. M. Thomas; The Mammoth Hunters by David Redd; The Future on a Chipped Plate by **Brian W. Aldiss**; The Cake Chronicle by Michael Ahern; Me and My Antronoscope by Barrington Bayley; Family Literature; Motivation Chart by Charles Platt; There Are No Banisters by Jack M. Dann; Walking Backwards by Phillip Lopate; The Disinheriting Party; and Shucksma by John Clute; Smack Run by Marta Bergstresser; Ode to a Time Flower by Robert Calvert; The Only Man on Earth by Laurence James; To the Stars and Beyond on the Fabulous Anti-Syntax Drive by M. John Harrison; The Trustie Tree by Keith Roberts; and The Assassination of the Mayor by Thomas M. Disch.

22. New Worlds - The Science Fiction Quarterly 6. With Charles Platt. Published by Sphere Books, London, 1973. Softcover. All of the work here was done in the year of publication. This contains: Introduction by **Michael Moorcock**; Coming from Behind by M. John Harrison; An Office Meeting by Giles Gordon; Count D'Unadix by Marek Obtulowicz; Behind the Walls by Laura Tokunaga; Among Other Things by Robert Meadley; My Eight Days in the Automotive Industry by Charles Arnold; The Coldness by Charles Platt; The Story of the Three Cities by Ronald Cross and Anthony Cross; Tubs of Slaw by Rachel Pollack; Tulpa by Jack Dann; An Overload by Barrington Bayley; Scholia, Seasoned with Crabs, Blish Is by John Clute; Night Marriage by D. M. Thomas; Accepting for Winkelmeyer by Harvey Jacobs; The Beautiful One by Keith Roberts; Gorgias by Peder Carlsson; Bella Goes to the Dark Tower by Hilary Bailey; An Unpleasant End by Scott Edelstein; A Clear Day in the Motor City by Eleanor Aranson; There is No More Away by Steve Cline; Origins of the Universe by Gwyneth Cravens; Stance of Splendour by George Zebrowski; Thy Blood like

Milk by Ian Watson; Aurora in Zenith by Gordon Abbott; Disintegration by Michael Butterworth; Filling Us Up by M. John Harrison; and Introduction to New Readers by Charles Platt.

23. Best S.F. Stories from New Worlds 8. Published by Panther Books, London, 1974. Softcover. Herein: Introduction by **Michael Moorcock**; A Boy and His Dog by Harlan Ellison, 1969; The Fall of Frenchy Steiner by Hilary Bailey, 1964; The Bait Principle by M. John Harrison, 1970; Salvador Dali: The Innocent as Paranoid - an essay by J. G. Ballard, 1969; The Last Lonely Men by John Brunner, 1964; The Radius Riders by Barrington J. Bayley, 1962; The Big Sound by Barrington J. Bayley, 1964; The Ship that Sailed the Ocean of Space by Barrington J. Bayley, 1962; Double Time by Barrington J. Bayley, 1962; and The Erogenous Zone by Graham Charnock, 1969.

24. Before Armageddon. Published by W. H. Allen, London, 1975. Hardcover. Herein: Introduction by **Michael Moorcock**; The Battle of Dorking by G. T. Chesney, 1871; Dr Trifulgas by **Jules Verne**, 1884; The Raid of Le Vengeur by George Griffith, 1901; The Great War in England in 1897 by William Le Queux, 1893; Life in Our New Century by W. J. Wintle, 1901; and The Three Drugs by E. Nesbit, 1908.

25. England Invaded. Published by W. H. Allen, London, 1977. Hardcover. This contains: Introduction by **Michael Moorcock**; When William Came by H. H. Munro writing as Saki, 1913; The Monster of Lake LaMetrie by Wardon Allan Curtis, 1899; The Abduction of Alexandra Seine by Fred C. Smale, 1900; When the New Zealander Comes by Blyde Muddersnook, 1911; The Uses of Advertisement - an Aeroplane Adventure by Tristram Crutchley, 1909; and Is the End of the World Near? By john Munro, 1899.

26. New Worlds: An Anthology. Published by Fontana Flamingo, London, 1983. Softcover. Herein: The Assassination Weapon by J. G. Ballard, 1966; Alphabets of Unreason - an essay by J. G. Ballard, 1969; Angouleme by Thomas M. Disch, 1971; A Landscape of Shallows by Christopher Finch, 1968; Scholia, Seasoned with Crabs, Blish Is - an essay by John Clute, 1973; Running Down by M. John Harrison, 1975; Sweet Analaytics - an essay by M. John Harrison, 1975; Gravity by Harvey Jacobs, 1969; Concentrate 3 by Michael Butterworth, 1970; Dr Gelabius by Hilary Bailey, 1968; The Four Colour Problem by Barrington Bayley, 1971; The Eye of the Lens by Langdon Jones, 1968; The Heat Death of the Universe by Pamela Zoline, 1967; The Valve Transcript by Joel Zoss, 1968; Scream by Giles Gordon, 1968; Masterson and the Clerks by John T. Sladek, 1967; Space Hopping with Captain God - an essay by John T. Sladek, 1969; Multi-Value Motorway by **Brian W. Aldiss**, 1967; Traveller's Rest by David I. Masson, 1965; The Disaster Story by Charles Platt, 1966; Conversations at Ma Maia Metron by Robert Meadley, 1971; No Direction Home by Norman Spinrad, 1971; Mr Black's Poems of Innocence by D. M. Thomas, 1969; The Soft World Sequence by George MacBeth, 1967; A Literature of Acceptance - an essay by **Michael Moorcock** writing as James Colvin, 1067; The Languages of Science - an essay by David Harvey, 1967; The Circle of the White Horse - an essay by Francis Arnold, 1952; and **The Tank Trapeze** by **Michael Moorcock**, 1969.

27. Michael Moorcock's Elric: Tales of the White Wolf. Created by **Michael Moorcock** and edited by Edward E. Kramer and Richard Gilliam. Published by White Wolf Publishing, Stone Mountain, Georgia, 1994. Hardcover. All new work for this anthology. Herein: Introduction by **Michael Moorcock**; Go Ask Elric by Tad Williams; The White Child by Jody Lynn Nye; Celebration of Celene by Gary Gygax; The Dragon's Heart by Nancy A. Collins; The Gothic Touch by Karl Edward Wagner; Beyond the Balance by Nancy Holder; One Life Furnished with Early Moorcock by Neil Gaiman; Now Cracks a Noble Heart by David M. Honigsberg; A Devil Unknown by Roland J. Green and Frieda A. Murray; Kingsfire by Richard Lee Byers; The Gate of Dreaming by Brad Strickland; The Littlest Stormbringer by Brad Linaweaver and William Alan Ritch; Providence by Kevin T. Stein; The Guardian at the Gate by Scott Ciencin; The Song of Shaarilla by James S. Dorr; Too Few Years of Solitude by Stewart von Allman; White Wolf's Awakening by Paul W. Cashman; A Woman's Power by Doug Murray; The Soul of an Old Machine by Thomas E. Fuller; Temptations of Iron by Colin Greenland; The Other Sword by Robert Weinberg; Arioch's Gift by Charles Partingon; The Trembler on the Axis by Peter Crowther and James Lovegrove; and The White Wolf's Song by **Michael Moorcock**.

28. Michael Moorcock's Pawn of Chaos - Tales of the Eternal Champion. Created by **Michael Moorcock** and edited by Edward E. Kramer. Published by White Wolf, Clarkston, Georgia, 1996. Softcover. All new work for this anthology. Herein: Introduction by **Michael Moorcock**; The War Skull of Hel by C. Dean Anderson; Sign of the Silver Hand by Nancy A. Collins; Evening Odds by Gary Gygax; Acorns by Richard Lee Byers; The Captive Soul by Bill Crider; Trail-Ways by James S. Dorr; In the Machinery of Dreams by Thomas E. Fuller; Even the Night by Don Webb; Isle of Lost Souls by Robert E. Vardeman; Raider from the Ghost World by Brian Herbert; and Marie Landis; The Last Short Story Writer at the End of Time by Brad Linaweaver; Angle of War by James Lovegrove; Editor by Dafydd ab Hugh; Dragging the Line by Mike Lee; Awakening - A Symphony by Alexandra Elizabeth Honigsberg; To Speak With Men and Angels by Roland Green and Frieda Murray; Giants in the Earth by Caitlin R. Kiernan; The Festive Season by David Ferring; Halfway House by Peter Crowther; Fiery Spirits by Colin Greenland; and In the Cornelius Arms by John Shirley.

29. New Worlds: An Anthology. Published by Thunder's Mouth Press, United States, 2004. Softcover. Slight revised from the 1983 edition.

***

NON-FICTION

1. Epic Pooh. Published by the British Fantasy Society, Essex, UK, 1978. Softcover.

2. The Retreat from Liberty: The Erosion of Democracy in Today's Britain. Published by Bee in Bonnet - Zomba Books, London, 1983. Softcover.

Michael Moorcock

3. Letters from Hollywood. Published by Harrap, London, 1986. Hardcover.

4. Wizardry and Wild Romance: A Study of Epic Fantasy. Published by Victor Gollancz, London, 1987. Hardcover.

5. Fantasy: The 100 Best Books. With James Cawthorn. Published by Xanadu, London, 1988. Hardcover.

6. Michael Moorcock - Bibliography and General Information. Private printing, UK, 1990. Softcover.

7. Into the Media Web - Collected Short Non-Fiction 1956 - 2006. Edited by John Davey. Not in print at the time of this writing. To be published by Savoy Books, Manchester, UK, 2009.

***

RELATED

1. Michael Moorcock: A Bibliography. By Andrew Harper and George McAulay. Published by T-K Graphics, Baltimore, Maryland, 1976.

2. The Chronicles of Moorcock. By A. J. Callow. Published by A. J. Callow, Worcester, UK, 1978. Softcover.

3. The Tanelorn Archives: A Primary and Secondary Bibliography of the Works of Michael Moorcock 1949 - 1979. By Richard Bilyeu. Published by Pandora's Books, Manitoba, Canada, 1981. Softcover.

4. Michael Moorcock - Death is No Obstacle. By Colin Greenland; introduction by Angela Carter. Published by Savoy Books - Griffin Music, UK, 1992. Hardcover.

5. Michael Moorcock: A Reader's Guide. By John Davey. Published by Nomads of the Time Stream, UK, 1994. Softcover.

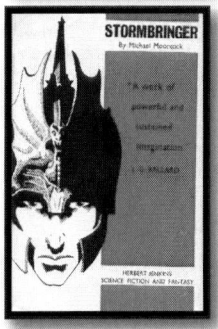

Donald A. Wollheim.

Donald Allen Wollheim was born in New York City on October 1st, 1914 and died in his sleep of a heart attack on November 2nd, 1990, not far from where he was born.

One of the first super-fans, Wollheim edited and published an assortment of fan-zines and he was one of the original members of The Futurians. He was also involved with Hugo Gernsback's Science Fiction League, which was founded to promote science fiction, the first fan club.

And he organized the first ever Science Fiction convention. It took place in Philadelphia on October 22nd, 1936, just a couple of years after his first professional story was published in the January 1934 issue of Hugo Gernsback's Wonder Stories.

The story was The Man from Ariel and it shared space with Gernsback's essay Wonders of Micro-Life; along with a couple of serials, The Exile of the Skies by Richard Vaughan and Evolution Satellite by J. Harvey Haggard; and, of course, a number of stories: Garfield's Invention by Leo am Bruhl; Moon Plague by Raymond Z. Gallun; The Secret of the Microcosm by F. Golub; and Today's Yesterday by Russell Blaiklock writing as Rice Ray.

When Gernsback neglected to pay him for the story, Wollheim gathered up a few others writers and took the old gent to court. Gernsback settled out of court for $75.00 and then promptly kicked Wollheim out of the Science Fiction League, calling him a disruptive influence.

Wollheim also sold his next story to Gernsback. He sent it in as Millard Verne Gordon. It was called The Space Lens and Gernsback used it in the September 1935 issue of Wonder Stories, along with: Wonders of Transplanted Organs - an essay by Gernsback; The Green Man of Graypec - part 3 of 3 by Festus Pragnell; World of the Mist - part 1 of 2 by Laurence Manning; One Hundred Generations by Philip Jacques Bartel; and The Ideal by Stanley G. Weinbaum.

Gernsback neglected to pay him for that one, too.

He didn't sell another story until 1940 when he placed The Castaway with **Frederik Pohl** at Super Science Stories, May 1940. Also in that issue were: Let There Be Light by **Robert A. Heinlein** writing as Lyle Monroe; King Cole of Pluto by C. M. Kornbluth writing as S. D. Gottesman; Living Isotopes by P. Schuyler Miller; Arton's Metal by **James Blish**; Guardian Angel by Raymond Z. Gallun; Hollow of the Moon by Manly Wade Wellman; and The Ersatz World - an essay by Willy Ley.

He got paid for that one without having to sue anyone.

After that, his sales were quite regular.

But it was as an editor that he shone. **Robert Silverberg** claimed Wollheim might be considered the most significant figure in science fiction publishing. When he edited The Pocket Book of Science Fiction in 1943, it was the first science fiction anthology to be aimed at a mass market; it was also the first book to have "science fiction" in the title. Two years later, he edited the first hardcover anthology from a mainstream publisher, The Viking Portable Novels of Science, 1945.

He went to work at Avon Books as an editor in 1947 and stayed there until 1951, developing their science fiction and fantasy catalogues. And he left there to go to Ace Books where he became their science fiction editor, working for Ace from 1952 until 1971 when Ace was sold to a gang of people who didn't have a clue how to run a publishing company.

Frustrated, Wollheim left and founded his own publishing company, DAW Books. They were the first paperback specialist publishing company to offer only fantasy and science fiction. April 1972 saw them publish their first four titles: 1. Spell of the Witch World by **Andre Norton**; 2. The Mind Behind the Eye by Joseph Green; 3. The Probability Man by Brian N. Ball; and 4. The Book of van Vogt by **A. E. van Vogt**.

By the time he died in 1990, his impact as an editor and a publisher was clear to just about everyone.

His most consistently valuable book is The Secret of the Ninth Planet, published in 1959 by the John C. Winston Company. It averages around $450.00.

Pen names used: David Grinnell; Martin Pearson; Millard Verne Gordon; W. Malcolm White; Lawrence Woods; Millard V. Gordon; Martin barrow; and Allen Warland.

***

AWARDS

1975. Special Hugo Award for The Fan Who Has Done Everything.
1980. Special Professional World Fantasy Award for DAW Books.
1986. World Fantasy Special Convention Award.

***

FILM AND TELEVISION

1. Mimic. This 1942 story was filmed for release in 1997. Directed by Guillermo del Toro, it starred: Mira Sorvino; Jeremy Northam; Josh Brolin; Alexander Goodwin; and many others.

2. Mimic 2. Again based on Wollheim's 1942 story, this version was directed by Jean de Seqonzac in 2001. It starred: Alix Koromzay; Bruno Campos; Will Estes; Gaven E. Lucas; Edward Albert; and many others.

3. Mimic: Sentinel. Also known as Mimic 3. Wollheim's story was filmed yet again, this time for release in 2003 and directed by J. T. Petty. It starred: Lance Henriksen; Karl Geary; Alexis Dziena; Keith Robinson; Rebecca Mader; and more, including Amanda Plummer as Simone Montrose.

***

Donald A. Wollheim

RADIO

1. The Embassy. This 1942 story was used on Dimension X, June 6th, 1950.

2. The Embassy. Used again on X Minus One, airing on July 25th, 1955.

***

NOVELS AND COLLECTIONS

1. The Secret of Saturn's Rings. Published by The John C. Winston Company, Philadelphia, 1954. Hardcover.

2. The Secret of the Martian Moons. Published by The John C. Winston Company, Philadelphia, 1955. Hardcover.

3. One Against the Moon. Published by The World Publishing Company, Cleveland and New York, 1956. Hardcover.

4. Across Time. Writing as David Grinnell. Published by Avalon Books, New York City, 1957. Hardcover.

5. Across Time. Writing as David Grinnell. Published by Ace Books, New York City, 1958. Ace Double D-286. Bound with Invaders from Earth by **Robert Silverberg**.

6. Edge of Time. Writing as David Grinnell. Published by Avalon Books, New York City, 1958. Hardcover.

7. Edge of Time. Writing as David Grinnell. Published by Ace Books, New York City, 1959. Ace Double D-362. Softcover. Bound with The 100th Millennium by John Brunner.

8. The Secret of the Ninth Planet. Published by The John C. Winston Company, Philadelphia, 1959. Hardcover.

9. The Martian Missile. Writing as David Grinnell. Published by Avalon Books, New York City, 1959. Hardcover.

10. The Martian Missile. Writing as David Grinnell. Published by Ace Books, New York City, 1960. Ace Double D-465. Softcover. Bound with The Atlantic Abomination by John Brunner.

11. Destiny's Orbit. Writing as David Grinnell. Published by Avalon Books, New York City, 1961. Hardcover.

12. Mike Mars, Astronaut. Doubleday & Company, Garden City, New York, 1961. Hardcover.

13. Mike Mars Flies the X-15. Doubleday & Company, Garden City, New York, 1961. Hardcover.

14. Mike Mars at Cape Canaveral. Doubleday & Company, Garden City, New York, 1961. Hardcover.

15. Mike Mars in Orbit. Doubleday & Company, Garden City, New York, 1961. Hardcover.

16. Destiny's Orbit. Writing as David Grinnell. Published by Ace Books, New York City, 1962. Ace Double F-161. Softcover. Bound with Times Without Number by John Brunner.

17. Mike Mars Flies the Dyna-Soar. Doubleday & Company, Garden City, New York, 1962. Hardcover.

18. Mike Mars, South Pole Spaceman. Doubleday & Company, Garden City, New York, 1962. Hardcover.

19. Mike Mars and the Mystery Satellite. Doubleday & Company, Garden City, New York, 1963. Hardcover.

20. Mike Mars Around the Moon. Doubleday & Company, Garden City, New York, 1964. Hardcover.

21. Destination: Saturn. Writing as David Grinnell and working with Lin Carter. Published by Avalon Books, New York City, 1967. Hardcover.

22. Destination: Saturn. Writing as David Grinnell and working with Lin Carter. Published by Ace Books, New York City, 1968. Ace Double H-85. Softcover. Bound with Invader on My Back by Philip E. High.

23. Two Dozen Dragon Eggs. Published by Powell Publications, Reseda, California, 1969. Powell Book PP181. Softcover. Herein: Introduction by **Donald A. Wollheim**; The Eggs and I - an essay by Forrest J. Ackerman; Mimic, 1942; Extending the Holdings, 1951; Storm Warning, 1942; The Poetess and the 21 Gray-Haired Cadavers, 1969; Malice Aforethought, 1952; Santa Rides a Saucer, 1969; Ganymede House, 1953; Road to Rome, 1953; The Rag Thing, 1951; The Feminine Fraction, 1964; Ein Blick in Die Zukunft, 1969; top Secret, 1948; How Many Miles to Babylon?, 1963; Shoo, Fly, 1953; The Lysenko Maze, 1953; Landragon, 1969; Give Her Hell, 1969; Disguise, 1953; The Garrison, 1965; Doorslammer, 1963; The Egg from Alpha Centauri, 1969; Last Stand of a space Grenadier, 1954; An Advance Post in the War Between the Sexes, 1969; and Web Sixty-four, 1969.

24. To Venus! To Venus! Writing as David Grinnell. Published by Ace Books, New York City, 1970. Ace Double 8610. Bound with The Jester at Scar by E. C. Tubb.

25. The Man from Ariel. Published by NESFA, Cambridge, Massachusetts, 1982. Hardcover. Herein: Introduction by **Donald A. Wollheim**; The Horror Out of Lovecraft, 1969; The Rules of the Game, 1973; Miss McWhortle's Weird, 1970; Colt Cash Cache, 1952; The Hook, 1963; Ishkabab, 1982; Who's There, 1982; The Lost Poe, 1982; The Man from Ariel, 1934; and Still Life, 1945.

26. Up there and Other Strange Directions. Published by NESFA, Cambridge, Massachusetts, 1988. Hardcover. Herein: Introduction by **Donald A. Wollheim**; The Colossus of Maia - writing with Robert A. W. Lowndes as Lawrence Woods, 1941; The Planet Called Aquella, 1942; The Mask of Demeter - writing with C. M. Kornbluth, 1953; Blueprint, 1941; The Hidden Conflict - writing as Martin Pearson, 1942; The World on the Edge of the Universe, 1941; The Hat, 1988; Castaway, 1940; The Outpost at Altark, 1940; Interplane Express - writing with C. M. Kornbluth, 1988; Cosmophobia, 1941; Bones, 1941; The Man from the Future, 1941;

The World in Balance, 1942; The World in Balance, 1942; The Booklings, 1943; and Up There - writing as Martin Pearson, 1942.

***

ANTHOLOGIES

1. The Pocket Book of Science Fiction. Published by Pocket Books, New York City, 1943. Pocket Book 214. Softcover. Herein: Introduction by **Donald A. Wollheim**; The Last Man by Wallace G. West, 1929; Green Thoughts by John Collier, 1931; By the Waters of Babylon by Stephen Vincent Benet, 1937; Moxon's Monster by Ambrose Bierce, 1909; In the Abyss by **H. G. Wells**, 1896; The Green Splotches by T. S. Stribling, 1920; A Martian Odyssey by Stanley G. Weinbaum, 1934; Twilight by **John W. Campbell** writing as Don A. Stuart; Microcosmic God by **Theodore Sturgeon**, 1941; and And He Built a Crooked House by **Robert A. Heinlein**, 1941.

2. The Portable Novels of Science. Published by Viking Press, New York City, 1945. Hardcover. Herein: Introduction by **Donald A. Wollheim**; The First Men in the Moon by **H. G. Wells**, 1901; Before the Dawn by Eric Temple Bell writing as John Taine; The Shadow Out of Time by H. P. Lovecraft, 1936; and Odd John by Olaf Stapledon, 1935.

3. Avon Western Reader 3. Published by the Avon Publishing Company, New York City, 1947. Softcover.

4. Avon Western Reader 4. Published by the Avon Publishing Company, New York City, 1947. Softcover.

5. Avon Fantasy Reader 1. Published by the Avon Book Company, New York City, 1947. Softcover. Herein: The Voice in the Night by William Hope Hodgson, 1907; The Woman of the Wood by **A. Merritt**, 1926; The Vaults of Yoh Vombis by Clark Ashton Smith, 1932; The Central Figure by H. Russell Wakefield, 1929; The Three Infernal Jokes by Lord Dunsany, 1915; The Power Planet by Murray Leinster, 1931; The Shuttered House by August Derleth, 1937; Climax for a Ghost Story by I. A. Ireland, 1919; Justice by The Gibsons, 1947; The Truth About Pyecraft by **H. G. Wells**, 1903; and Nostalgia - a poem by H. P. Lovecraft, 1930.

6. Avon Fantasy Reader 2. Published by the Avon Book Company, New York City, 1947. Softcover. Herein: Stenographer's Hands by David H. Keller, 1928; The Strange Case of Lemuel Jenkins by Philip M. Fisher, 1919; The Day of the Dragon by Guy Endore, 1934; The Mirrors of Tuzun Thune - King Kull by Robert E. Howard, 1929; The Yellow Sign by Robert W. Chambers, 1895; Automata by S. Fowler Wright, 1929; and The City of the Living Dead by Laurence Manning and Fletcher Pratt, 1930.

7. Avon Fantasy Reader 3. Published by the Avon Book Company, New York City, 1947. Softcover. Herein: Mimic by **Donald A. Wollheim** writing as Martin Pearson; The Silver Key by H. P. Lovecraft, 1929; Evening Primrose by John Collier, 1940; Black Thirst by **C. L. Moore**, 1934; Homecoming by **Ray Bradbury**, 1946; Bishop's Gambit by August Derleth writing as Stephen Grendon, 1947; Rhythm of the Spheres by **A. Merritt**, 1934; The Queer Story of Brownlow's Newspaper by **H. G. Wells**, 1932; and The Phantom Wooer - a poem by Thomas Lovell Beddoes, 1850.

8. Avon Fantasy Reader 4. Published by the Avon Book Company, New York City, 1947. Softcover. Herein: The Arrhenius Horror by P. Schuyler Miller, 1931; The Hollow Man by Thomas Burke, 1933; Conquerors' Isle by Nelson Bond, 1947; The Hoard of the Gibbelins by Lord Dunsany, 1911; The Derelict by William Hope Hodgson, 1912; The Man Upstairs by **Ray Bradbury**, 1947; The Planet of the Dead by Clark Ashton Smith, 1932; A Warning to the Curious by M. R. James, 1925; and Defense by **A. E. van Vogt**, 1947.

9. Avon Fantasy Reader 5. Published by the Avon Book Company, New York City, 1947. Softcover. Herein: Scarlet Dream by C. L. Moore, 1934; Sambo by William Fryer Harvey, 1910; Fane of the Black Pharaoh by Robert Bloch, 1937; The Random Quantity by Carl Jacobi, 1947; The Gold Dress by Stephen Vincent Benet, 1942; The Miracle of the Lily by Clare Winger Harris, 1928; In the Court of the Dragon by Robert W. Chambers, 1895; A Study in Amber by Frank Owen, 1947; and The Words of Guru by C. M. Kornbluth, 1941.

10. Avon Detective Mysteries 3. Edited anonymously. Published by Avon Book Company, New York City, 1947. Softcover.

11. Avon Fantasy Reader 6. Published by the Avon Book Company, New York City, 1948. Softcover. Herein: The Crawling Horror by Thorp McClusky, 1936; Beyond the Wall of Sleep by H. P. Lovecraft, 1919; The Metal Man by **Jack Williamson**, 1928; The Thing in the Cellar by David H. Keller, 1932; The Drone by **A. Merritt**, 1934; From the Dark Waters by Joseph E. Kelleam, 1948; The Star Stealers by Edmond Hamilton, 1929; The Philosophy of Relative Existences by Frank R. Stockton, 1893; and The Trap by Henry S. Whitehead, 1932.

12. Avon Fantasy Reader 7. Published by Avon Publishing, New York City, 1948. Softcover. This contains: Shambleau by **C. L. Moore**, 1933; The Curse of a Thousand Kisses by Sax Rohmer, 1918; The Dreams of Albert Moreland by **Fritz Leiber**, 1945; The Slugly Beast by Lord Dunsany, 1934; The Cairn on the Headland by Robert E. Howard, 1933; Aquella by **Donald A. Wollheim** writing as Martin Pearson, 1942; The Empire of the Necromancers by Clark Ashton Smith, 1932; When Old Gods Wake **by A. Merritt**, 1948; The Were Snake by Frank Belknap Long, 1925; and The Gun by Frank Gruber, 1942.

13. Avon Fantasy Reader 8. Published by Avon Publishing, New York City, 1948. Softcover. Herein: Zero Hour by **Ray Bradbury**, 1947; The Temple by H. P. Lovecraft, 1920; The Machine Man of Ardathia by Francis Flagg, 1927; Queen of the Black Coast by Robert E. Howard, 1934; The Cat Woman by Mary Elizabeth Counselman, 1933; The Other Wing by Algernon Blackwood, 1915; The Canal by Everil Worrell, 1927; An Inhabitant of Carcosa by Ambrose Bierce, 1886; The Man with a Thousand Legs by Frank Belknap Long, 1927; and The Goblins Wills

Get You by John B. Michel writing as Hugh Raymond.

14. Avon Fantasy Reader 9. Published by Avon Publishing, New York City, 1949. Softcover. This contains: The Flower Woman by Clark Ashton Smith, 1935; The Night Wire by H. F. Arnold, 1926; Through the Vibrations by P. Schuyler Miller, 1931; The Man Who Never Grew Young by **Fritz Leiber**, 1947; The Man from the Moon by Otis Adelbert Kline, 1930; The Unspeakable Betrothal by Robert Bloch, 1949; The Stone Ship by William Hope Hodgson, 1914; Child's Play by Alice Mary Schnirring, 1942; The Madness of Andelsprutz by Lord Dunsany, 1908; and The Painted Mirror by Donald Wandrei, 1937.

15. Avon Fantasy Reader 10. Published by Avon Publishing, New York City, 1949. Softcover. This contains: A Witch Shall Be Born by Robert E. Howard, 1934; The Statement of Randolph Carter by H. P. Lovecraft, 1920; Vengeance in Her Bones by Malcolm Jameson, 1942; The Mentanicals by Francis Flagg, 1934; The Gostak and the Doshes by Miles J. Breuer, 1930; Bimini by Bassett Morgan, 1929; Omega by Amelia Reynolds Long, 1932; and Storm Warning by **Donald A. Wollheim** writing as Millard Verne Gordon, 1942.

16. Avon Fantasy Reader 11. Published by Avon Novels, New York City, 1949. Softcover. Herein: Glamour by Seabury Quinn, 1939; The Golden Hour of Kwoh Fan by Frank Owen, 1930; Uncommon Castaway by Nelson Bond, 1949; Mogglesby by T. S. Stribling, 1930; Asleep in Armageddon by **Ray Bradbury**, 1948; The Inheritors by John Michel and Robert Lowndes, 1942; and The Dancer in the Crystal by Francis Flagg, 1929.

17. Avon Bedside Companion: A Treasury of Tales for the Sophisticated. Edited anonymously. Published by Avon Book Company, New York City, 1949. Avon Book 109. Softcover. Herein: The Devil George and Rosie by John Collier; Dusk before Fireworks by Dorothy Parker; Civilized by John O'Hara; The Shadow in the Rose Garden by D. H. Lawrence; It Never Happened by Emily Hahn; Dusky Ruth by A. E. Coppard; Sam Small's Better Half by Eric Knight; Thanks to the Arabs Maybe by Howard Rodman; Regret by Guy de Maupassant; The Kimono by Ira V. Morris; The Strange Adventure of Madame Esquollier by Pierre Louys; Thereby Hangs a Tale by Thomas Grant Springer; The Works by Nathan Asch; Lover's Gifts by Paul Eldridge; and The Baltic Night by Paul Morand.

18. Avon Book of New Stories of the Great Wild West. Edited anonymously. Published by Avon Book Company, New York City, 1949. Avon Book 194. Softcover.

19. The Girl with the Hungry Eyes. Edited anonymously. Published by the Avon Publishing Company, New York City, 1949. Avon Book 184. Softcover. Herein: The Girl with the Hungry Eyes by **Fritz Leiber**, 1949; Mrs Manifold by August Derleth writing as Stephen Grendon, 1949; Venus and the Seven Sexes by William Tenn, 1949; Come into My Parlor by Manly Wade Wellman, 1949; Maturity Night by Frank Belknap Long, 1949; and Daydream by P. Schuyler Miller, 1949.

20. Avon Fantasy Reader 12. Published by Avon Novels, New York City, 1950. Softcover. Herein: The Blonde Goddess of Bal Sagoth by Robert E. Howard, 1931; The Chain of Aforgomon by Clark Ashton Smith, 1935; In the Valley of the Sorceress by Sax Rohmer, 1916; The Kelpie by Manly Wade Wellman, 1936; The Captured Cross Section by Miles J. Breuer, 1929; The Wonderful Window by Lord Dunsany, 1911; Tiger Dust by Bassett Morgan, 1932; An Episode of Cathedral History by M. R. James, 1914; and The Day Has Come by Walter Kublius, 1942.

21. Avon Fantasy Reader 13. Published by Avon Novels, New York City, 1950. Softcover. Herein: The Lost Street by Clifford D. Simak and Carl Jacobi, 1941; Original Sin by S. Fowler Wright, 1946; The Forgotten Planet by Sewell Peaslee Wright, 1930; The Thing That Walked on the Wind by August Derleth, 1933; Raiders of the Universes by Donald Wandrei, 1932; The Love-Slave and the Scientists by Frank Belknap Long, 1935; The Curious Case of Norton Hoorne by Ray Cummings, 1920; The Cave by Beatrice Grimshaw, 1932; The Power and the Glory by Charles W. Diffin, 1930; The House of Shadows by Mary Elizabeth Counselman, 1932; and The Ship of Silence by Albert Richard Wetjen, 1932.

22. Avon Fantasy Reader 14. Published by Avon Novels, New York City, 1950. Softcover. Herein: Temptress of the Tower of Torture by Robert E. Howard, 1930; Ylla by **Ray Bradbury**, 1950; The Three Eyed Man by Ray Cummings, 1921; The Cave of the Invisible by James Francis Dwyer, 1937; Guard in the Dark by Allison V. Harding, 1944; The Still Small Voice by Clive G. B. Jackson, 1950; The Curse of Yig by Zealia Brown Bishop and H. P. Lovecraft, 1928; The Yeast Men by David H. Keller, 1927; The Headless Miller of Kobold's Keep by Irvin Ashkenazy writing as G. Garnet, 1937; and The Shadows by Henry S. Whitehead, 1927.

23. Flight into Space. Published by Frederick Fell, New York City, 1950. Hardcover. This contains: Parasite Planet by Stanley G. Weinbaum, 1935; Red Storm on Jupiter by Frank Belknap Long, 1936; A Baby on Neptune by Miles J. Breuer and Clare Winger Harris, 1929; The Death of the Moon by A. M. Phillips; The Rape of the Solar System by Leslie F. Stone, 1934; Planet Passage by **Donald A. Wollheim**, 1942; Hermit of Saturn's Ring by Neil R. Jones, 1940; Ajax of Ajax by **Donald A. Wollheim** writing as Martin Pearson, 1942; The Seekers by Robert Moore Williams, 1948; Peril of the Blue World by Robert Abernathy, 1942; The Mercurian by Frank Belknap Long, 1941; and Sunward by Stanton A. Coblentz, 1940.

24. Giant Mystery Reader. Published by the Avon Publishing Company, New York City, 1951. Avon Book G-1004. Softcover.

25. Avon Fantasy Reader 15. Published by Avon Novels, New York City, 1951. Softcover. This contains: Ubbo Sathla by Clark Ashton Smith, 1933; Mommy by Mary Elizabeth Counselman, 1939; A Man, a Maid and Saturn's Temptation by Stanley G. Weinbaum, 1935; Gray Ghouls by Bassett Morgan, 1927; Ship-in-a-Bottle by P. Schuyler Miller, 1944; Venus by Maurice Baring, 1909; The Einstein See-

Saw by Miles J. Breuer, 1932; The Great Gizmo by Gilbert Wright, 1945; Kazam Collects by C. M. Kornbluth, 1941; In Amundsen's Tent by John Martin Leahy, 1928; and Up There by **Donald A. Wollheim**, 1942.

26. Avon Fantasy Reader 16. Published by Avon Novels, New York City, 1951. Softcover. Herein: The Black Kiss by Henry Kuttner and Robert Bloch, 1937; Mr Strenberry's Tale by J. B. Priestley, 1930; The Man Who Lived Backward by Gelett Burgess, 1945; Something from Above by Donald Wandrei, 1930; The Wax Doll by Greye La Spina, 1919; The Forest of Lost Men by Beatrice Grimshaw, 1934; The Place of Pain by M. P. Shiel, 1914; The River by L. Major Reynolds, 1951; The Water Ghost of Harrowby Hall by John Kendrick Bangs, 1891; The Hounds of Tindalos by Frank Belknap Long, 1929; and The Picture by Francis Flagg, 1931.

27. Avon Fantasy Reader 17. Published by Avon Novels, New York City, 1951. Softcover. This contains: The Sapphire Siren by Nictzin Dyalhis, 1934; Jack-in-the-Box by **Ray Bradbury**, 1947; The Noticeable Conduct of Professor Chadd by G. K. Chesterton, 1904; The Pink Caterpillar by Anthony Boucher, 1945; The Phantom Dictator by Wallace West, 1935; Through the Gates of the Silver Key by H. P. Lovecraft and E. Hoffmann Price, 1934; The Bookshop by Nelson Bond, 1941; One-Man God by Frank Owen, 1951; and The Mystery of the Sargasso by William Hope Hodgson, 1907.

28. Avon Science Fiction Reader 1. Published by Avon Novels, New York City, 1951. Softcover. Herein: Love Was Treason in That Future War - an essay by **Donald A. Wollheim**; The War of the Sexes by Edmond Hamilton, 1933; Green Glory by Frank Belknap Long, 1935; The Immeasurable Horror by Clark Ashton Smith, 1931; The Morrison Monument by Murray Leinster, 1935; The Incubator Man by Wallace West, 1928; The Dark Side of Antri by Sewell Peaslee Wright, 1931; Blind Flight by **Donald A. Wollheim**, 1942; Rhythm of the Spheres by **A. Merritt**, 1934; Madness of the Dust by R. F. Starzl, 1930; and The Cosmic Express by **Jack Williamson**, 1930.

29. Avon Science Fiction Reader 2. Published by Avon Novels, New York City, 1951. Softcover. Herein: The Schemes of This Fatal Beauty Challenged the Very Stars Themselves - an essay by **Donald A. Wollheim**; Priestess of the Flame by Sewell Peaslee Wright, 1932; The Whisperers by Donald Wandrei, 1935; When Half-Worlds Meet by John Michel, 1941; The Superperfect Bride by Bob Olsen, 1929; Vulthoom by Clark Ashton Smith, 1935; The Man Who Discovered Nothing by Ray Cummings, 1920; Highway by Robert W. Lowndes, 1942; When the Flame Flowers Blossomed by Leslie F. Stone, 1935; The Book of Worlds by Miles J. Breuer, 1929; and The Rebuff by Lord Dunsany, 1945.

30. The Avon All-American Fiction Reader. Edited anonymously. Published by Avon Books, New York City, 1951. Avon Book 1002. Softcover. Herein: The Root of His Evil by James M. Cain; I'll Never Go There Anymore by Jerome Weidman; Ten Indians by Ernest Hemingway; Patsy Gilbride by James T. Farrell; The Eighty-Yard Run by Irwin Shaw; Famous by Stephen Vincent Benet; A Bottle of Milk for Mother by Nelson Algren; Over the River and Through the Wood by John O'Hara; The Old People by William Faulkner; If God Can Be Amused by Lloyd C. Douglas; Winter Voyage, 1916 by H. L. Mencken; An Old Sweetheart of Mine by James Whitcomb Riley; The Face Upon the Floor by H. Antoine D'Arcy; Come Home, Father! - Anonymous; The Shooting of Dan McGrew by Robert W. Service; Casey at the Bat by Ernest Lawrence Thayer; Frankie and Johnny - Anonymous; and The Lure of the Tropics - Anonymous.

31. Every Boy's Book of Science Fiction. Published by Frederick Fell, New York City, 1951. Hardcover. This contains: Introduction by **Donald A. Wollheim**; Dr Lu-Mie by Clifton B. Kruse, 1934; The Four-Dimensional Roller-Press by Bob Olsen, 1927; King of the Gray Spaces by **Ray Bradbury**, 1943; The Infra-Medians by Sewell Peaslee Wright, 1931; A Conquest of Two Worlds by Edmond Hamilton, 1932; In the Scarlet Star by **Jack Williamson**, 1933; The Asteroid of Gold by Clifford D. Simak, 1932; The Living Machine by David H. Keller, 1935; The White Army by Daniel Dressler, 1929; and The Gravity Professor by Ray Cummings, 1921.

32. Hollywood Bedside Reader. Edited anonymously. Published by the Avon Publishing Company, New York City, 1951. Avon Book 338. Softcover.

33. Avon Fantasy Reader 18. Published by Avon Novels, New York City, 1952. Softcover. Herein: The Witch from Hell's Kitchen by Robert E. Howard, 1951; The Devil in Hollywood by Dale Clark, 1936; The Watcher in the Green Room by Hugh B. Cave, 1933; A Victim of Higher Space by Algernon Blackwood, 1914; Out of the Eons by Hazel Heald and H. P. Lovecraft, 1935; Just What Happened by Gelett Burgess, 1944; The Phantom Ship of Dirk Van Tromp by James Francis Dwyer, 1915; Amina by Edward Lucas White, 1907; and The Haunted Jarvee by William Hope Hodgson, 1929.

34. Avon Science Fiction Reader 3. Published by Avon Novels, New York City, 1952. Softcover. Herein: Flesh or the Machine - Which? - an essay by **Donald A. Wollheim**; The Robot Empire by Frank Belknap Long, 1934; P. N. 40 by S. Fowler Wright, 1929; The Master Ants by Francis Flagg, 1928; In the Walls of Eryx by Kenneth Sterling and H. P. Lovecraft, 1939; The Black Stone Statue by Mary Elizabeth Counselman, 1937; The Planet of Dread by R. F. Starzl, 1930; The Alien Vibration by Hannes Bok, 1942; and The Ultimate Paradox by Thorp McClusky, 1945.

35. Let's Go Naked. Published by Pyramid Books, New York City, 1952. Pyramid Book 62. Softcover.

36. Prize Science Fiction. Published by McBride, New York City, 1953. Hardcover. Herein: Introduction by **Donald A. Wollheim**; Listen by **Gordon R. Dickson**, 1952; Demotion by Robert Donald Locke, 1952; The Big Hunger by Walter M. Miller, Jr, 1952; Star, Bright by Mark Clifton, 1952; The Altar at Midnight by C. M. Kornbluth, 1952; All the Time in the World by **Arthur C. Clarke**, 1952; The Timeless

Donald A. Wollheim

Ones by **Eric Frank Russell**, 1952; The Last Days of Shandakor by Leigh Brackett, 1952; McIlvaine's Star by August Derleth, 1952; The Peacemaker by Alfred Coppel, 1953; The Beautiful People by Charles Beaumont, 1952; and Mask of Demeter by **Donald A. Wollheim** and C. M. Kornbluth writing as Martin Pearson and Cecil Corwin, 1953.

37. Prize Stories of Space and Time. Published by Weidenfeld and Nicholson, London, 1953. Hardcover. Re-titled version of Prize Science Fiction, 1953.

38. The Ultimate Invader and Other Science Fiction. Published by Ace Books, New York City, 1954. Ace Double D-44. Softcover. Together with Sentinels of Space by **Eric Frank Russell**. The Ultimate Invader contains: The Ultimate Invader by **Eric Frank Russell**, 1954; Alien Envoy by Malcolm Jameson, 1944; Malignant Marauder by Murray Leinster, 1954; and The Temporal Transgressor by Frank Belknap Long, 1954.

39. Adventures in the Far Future. Published by Ace Books, New York City, 1954. Ace Double D-73. Softcover. Together with Tales of Outer Space by **Donald A. Wollheim**. Adventures in the Far Future contains: The Wind Between the Worlds by Lester del Rey, 1951; Stardust by Chad Oliver, 1952; Overdrive by Murray Leinster, 1953; The Chapter Ends by **Poul Anderson**; and The Millionth Year by **Donald A. Wollheim** writing as Martin Pearson, 1943.

40. Tales of Outer Space. Published by Ace Books, New York City, 1954. Ace Double D-73. Softcover. Together with Adventures in the Far Future by **Donald A. Wollheim**. Tales of Outer Space contains: Doorway in the Sky by Ralph Williams, 1954; Here Lie We by Fox B. Holden, 1953; Operation Mercury by Clifford D. Simak, 1941; Lord of a Thousand Suns by **Poul Anderson**, 1951; and Behind the Black Nebula by L. Ron Hubbard, 1942.

41. Terror in the Modern Vein. Published by Hanover House, Garden City, New York, 1955. Hardcover. Herein: Introduction by **Donald A. Wollheim**; They by **Robert A. Heinlein**, 1941; Mimic by **Donald A. Wollheim** writing as Martin Pearson, 1942; The Crowd by **Ray Bradbury**, 1943; He by H. P. Lovecraft, 1926; Shipshape Home by Richard Matheson, 1952; Fishing Season by Robert Sheckley, 1953; The Girl with the Hungry Eyes by **Fritz Leiber**, 1949; The Dream Makers by Robert Bloch, 1953; The Silence by Bernard McLaughlin, 1941; The Strange Case of Lemuel Jenkins by Philip M. Fisher, 1919; Fritzchen by Charles Beaumont, 1953; The Inheritors by Robert A. W. Lowndes and John B. Michel, 1942; The Republic of the Southern Cross by Valery Brussov, 1918; The Burrow by Franz Kafka, 1946; The Rag Thing by **Donald A. Wollheim** writing as David Grinnell, 1951; and The Croquet Player - an excerpt by **H. G. Wells**, 1936.

42. Adventures on Other Planets. Published by Ace Books, New York City, 1955. Ace Book S-133. Softcover. Herein: The Obligation by Roger Dee, 1952; The Sound of Bugles by Robert Moore Williams, 1949; Ogre by Clifford D. Simak, 1944; Assignment on Pasik by Murray Leinster writing as William Fitzgerald, 1949; and The Rull by **A. E. van Vogt**, 1948.

43. The End of the World. Published by Ace Books, New York City, 1956. Ace Book S-183. Softcover. This contains: Imposter by **Philip K. Dick**, 1953; The Year of the Jackpot by **Robert A. Heinlein**, 1952; Last Night of Summer by Alfred Coppel, 1954; Rescue Party by **Arthur C. Clarke**, 1946; Omega by Amelia Reynolds Long, 1932; and In the World's Dusk by Edmond Hamilton, 1936.

44. The Earth in Peril. Published by Ace Books, New York City, 1957. Ace Double D-205. Softcover. Bound with Who Speaks of Conquest? By Ian Wright. The Earth in Peril contains: Things Pass By by Murray Leinster, 1945; Letter from the Stars by **A. E. van Vogt**, 1949; The Silly Season by C. M. Kornbluth, 1950; The Plant Revolt by Edmund Hamilton, 1930; Mary Anonymous by Bryce Walton, 1954; and The Star by H. G. Wells, 1897.

45. Men on the Moon. Published by Ace Books, New York City, 1958. Ace Double D-277. Softcover. Bound with City on the Moon by Murray Leinster. Men on the Moon contains: Introduction by **Donald A. Wollheim**; Operation Pumice by Raymond Z. Gallun, 1949; Jetsam by A. Bertram Chandler, 1953; The Reluctant Heroes by Frank M. Robinson, 1951; Moonwalk by H. B. Fyfe, 1952; and Keyhole by Murray Leinster, 1951.

46. The Hidden Planet: Science Fiction Adventures on Venus. Published by Ace Books, New York City, 1959. Ace Book D-354. Softcover. Herein: Introduction by **Donald A. Wollheim**; Field Expedient by Chad Oliver, 1955; Terror Out of Space by Leigh Brackett, 1944; The Luck of Ignatz by Lester del Rey, 1939; Venus Mission by J. T. McIntosh, 1951; and The Lotus Eaters by Stanley G. Weinbaum, 1935.

47. The Macabre Reader. Published by Ace Books, New York City, 1959. Ace Book D-353. Softcover. Herein: The Crawling Horror by Thorp McClusky, 1936; The Opener of the Way by Robert Bloch, 1936; In Amundsen's Tent by John Martin Leahy, 1928; The Thing on the Doorstep by H. P. Lovecraft, 1937; The Hollow Man by Thomas Burke, 1933; It Will Grow on You by Donald Wandrei, 1942; The Hunters from Beyond by Clark Ashton Smith, 1932; The Curse of Yig by Zealia Brown Bishop and H. P. Lovecraft, 1927; The Cairn on the Headland by Robert E. Howard, 1933; The Trap by Henry S. Whitehead, 1932; The Phantom Wooer - a poem by Thomas Lovell Beddoes, 1850; and The Dweller - a poem by H. P. Lovecraft, 1930.

48. More Macabre. Published by Ace Books, New York City, 1961. Ace Book D-508. Softcover. This contains: Mother by Protest by Richard Matheson, 1953; The Wheel by H. Warner Munn, 1933; The Yellow Wall Paper by Charlotte Perkins Gilman, 1892; The Cookie Lady by **Philip K. Dick**, 1953; The Spider by Hanns Heinz Ewers, 1915; The Curse Kiss by Theodore Roscoe, 1930; Fungus Isle by Philip M. Fisher, 1923; and The Copper Bowl by George Fielding Eliot, 1928.

49. More Terror in a Modern Vein. Published by Digit Books, London, 1961. Digit Book R508. Softcover. Herein: Mimic by **Donald A. Wollheim**

writing as Martin Pearson, 1942; Shipshape Home by Richard Matheson, 1952; The Dream Makers by Robert Bloch, 1953; The Silence by Bernard McLaughlin, 1941; The Inheritors by Robert A. W. Lowndes and John B. Michel; The Republic of the southern Cross by Valery Brussov, 1918; and Gone Away by A. E. Coppard, 1935.

50. More Adventures on Other Planets. Published by Ace Books, New York City, 1963. Ace Book F-178. Softcover. This contains: Introduction by **Donald A. Wollheim**; Child of the Sun by Leigh Brackett, 1942; Sunrise on Mercury by **Robert Silverberg**, 1957; By the Name of Man by John Brunner, 1956; The Red Death of Mars by Robert Moore Williams, 1940; The Planet of Doubt by Stanley G. Weinbaum, 1935; and Tiger by the Tail by **Poul Anderson**, 1951.

51. Swordsmen in the Sky. Published by Ace Books, New York City, 1964. Ace Book F-311. Softcover. This contains: People of the Crater by **Andre Norton**, 1947; A Vision of Venus by Otis Adelbert Kline, 1933; The Moon That Vanished by Leigh Brackett, 1948; Kaldar, World of Antares by Edmond Hamilton, 1933; and Swordsman of Lost Terra by **Poul Anderson**, 1951.

52. World's Best Science Fiction 1965. With Terry Carr. Published by Ace Books, New York City, 1965. Ace Book G-551. Softcover. All stories from 1964. Herein: Introduction by **Donald A. Wollheim** and Terry Carr; Greenplace by Tom Purdom; Men of Good Will by Ben Bova and Myron R. Lewis; Bill For Delivery by Christopher Anvil; Four Brands of Impossible by Norman Kagan; A Niche in Time by William F. Temple; Sea Wrack by Edward Jesby; For Every Action by C. C. MacApp; Vampires Ltd. by Josef Nesvadba; The Last Lonely Man by John Brunner; The Star Party by Robert Lory; The Weather in the Underworld by Colin Free; Oh To Be a Blobel by **Philip K. Dick**; The Unremembered by Edward Mackin; What Happened to Sergeant Masuro? By Harry Mulisch; Now is Forever by Thomas M. Disch; The Competitors by Jack B. Lawson; and When the Change-Winds Blow by **Fritz Leiber**.

53. World's Best Science Fiction 1966. With Terry Carr. Published by Ace Books, New York City, 1966. Ace Book H-15. Softcover. All stories from 1965. Herein: Introduction by **Donald A. Wollheim** and Terry Carr; Sunjammer by **Arthur C. Clarke**; Calling Dr Clockwork by Ron Goulart; Becalmed in Hell by Larry Niven; Apartness by Vernor Vinge; Over the River and Through the Woods by Clifford D. Simak; Planet of Forgetting by James H. Schmitz; Repent Harlequin said the Ticktockman by Harlan Ellison; The Decision Makers by Joseph Green; Traveler's Rest by David I. Masson; Uncollected Works by Lin Carter; Vanishing Point by Jonathan Brand; In Our Block by R. A. Lafferty; Masque of the Red Shift by Fred Saberhagen; The Captive Djinn by Christopher Anvil; and The Good New Days by **Fritz Leiber**.

54. World's Best Science Fiction 1967. With Terry Carr. Published by Ace Books, New York City, 1967. Ace Book A-10. Softcover. All stories from 1966. Herein: Introduction by **Donald A. Wollheim** and Terry Carr; We Can Remember it for You Wholesale by **Philip K. Dick**; Light of Other Days by Bob Shaw; The Keys to December by Roger Zelazny; Nine Hundred Grandmothers by R. A. Lafferty; Bircher by A. A. Walde; Behold the Man by **Michael Moorcock**; Bumberboom by Avram Davidson; Day Million by **Frederik Pohl**; The Wings of a Bat by Paul Ash; The Man from When by Dannie Plachta; Amen and Out by **Brian W. Aldiss**; and For a Breath I Tarry by Roger Zelazny.

55. Operation Phantasy: The Best from the Phantagraph. Published by The Phantagraph Press, Rego Park, New York, 1967. This contains: Introduction by **Donald A. Wollheim**; The Booklings by **Donald A. Wollheim**, 1943; Stuff by Dirk Wylie, 1940; Ex Oblivione by H. P. Lovecraft, 1921; The Objective Approach by C. M. Kornbluth, 1967; and Poetry: The Memnons of the Night by Clark Ashton Smith, 1922; Harbor Whistles by H. P. Lovecraft, 1936; Chant of the Black Magicians by C. M. Kornbluth, 1944; Quarry by Robert A. W. Lowndes, 1967; Innocence by Graham Conway, 1942; Song at Midnight by Robert E. Howard, 1940; Only Deserted by August Derleth, 1937; The Unconquerable Fire by John B. Michel, 1942; Old Trinity Churchyard - 5 A.M. Spring by **A. Merritt**, 1941; Jump-Out-of-Bed by F. Stanislaus Prosody, 1941; Fateful Hour by Robert A. W. Lowndes, 1937; Segment by C. M. Kornbluth, 1942; Versiflage by **Frederik Pohl**, 1940; Contrast by **James Blish**, 1937; The Sunken towers by Henry Kuttner, 1936; and Essays: All Out by **Donald A. Wollheim**, 1967; Howard Phillips Lovecraft by **Donald A. Wollheim**, 1967; How I Get My Inspiration by Robert Bloch, 1935; and Weird Music by Duane W. Rimel and Emil Petaja, 1936.

56. World's Best Science Fiction 1968. With Terry Carr. Published by Ace Books, New York City, 1968. Ace Book A-15. Softcover. All stories from 1967. Herein: Introduction by **Donald A. Wollheim** and Terry Carr; See Me Not by Richard Wilson; Driftglass by **Samuel R. Delany**; Ambassador to Verdammt Colin Kapp; The Man Who Never Was by R. A. Lafferty; Thus We Frustrate Charlemagne by R. A. Lafferty; Hawksbill Station by **Robert Silverberg**; The Number You Have Reached by Thomas M. Disch; The Man Who Loved the Faioli by Roger Zelazny; Population Implosion by Andrew J. Offutt; I Have No Mouth and I Must Scream by Harlan Ellison; The Sword Swallower by Ron Goulart; Coranda by Keith Roberts; Handicap by Larry Niven; Full Sun by **Brian W. Aldiss**; It's Smart To Have an English Address by D. G. Compton; and The Billiard Ball by **Isaac Asimov**.

57. World's Best Science Fiction 1968. With Terry Carr. Published by Victor Gollancz, London, 1969. First hardcover edition.

58. World's Best Science Fiction 1969. With Terry Carr. Published by Ace Books, New York City, 1969. Ace Book 91352. Softcover. All stories from 1968. Herein: Introduction by **Donald A. Wollheim** and Terry Carr; Street of Dreams Feet of Clay by Robert Sheckley; Backtracked by Burt Filer; Kyrie by **Poul Anderson**; Going Down Smooth by **Robert Silverberg**; The Worm that Flies by **Brian W.**

Donald A. Wollheim

Aldiss; Masks by **Damon Knight**; Time Considered as a Helix of Semi Precious Stones by **Samuel R. Delany**; Hemeac by E. G. Von Wald; The Cloudbuilders by Colin Kapp; This Grand Carcass by R. A. Lafferty; A Visit to Cleveland General by Sydney J. Van Scyoc; The Selchey Kids by Laurence Yep; Welcome to the Monkey House by Kurt Vonnegut; The Dance of the Changer and the Three by Terry Carr; Sword Game by H. H. Hollis; Total Environment by **Brian W. Aldiss**; The Square Root of Brain by **Fritz Leiber**; Starsong by Fred Saberhagen; and Fear Hound by Katherine MacLean.

59. World's Best Science Fiction 1969. With Terry Carr. Published by the Science Fiction Book Club, Garden City, New York, 1969. Book Club Code 28K. First hardcover edition.

60. The Avon Fantasy Reader. Published by Avon Books, New York City, 1969. Avon Book S384. Softcover. Herein: The Witch from Hell's Kitchen by Robert E. Howard, 1951; Black Thirst by **C. L. Moore**, 1934; A Victim of Higher Space by Algernon Blackwood, 1917; The Sapphire Siren by Nictzin Dyalhis, 1934; A Voice in the Night by William Hope Hodgson; The Crawling Horror by Thorp McClusky, 1936; and The Kelpie by Manly Wade Wellman, 1936.

61. The 2nd Avon Fantasy Reader. Published by Avon Books, New York City, 1969. Avon Book S385. Softcover. This contains: Foreword by George Ernsberger; The Blonde Goddess of Bal-Sagoth by Robert E. Howard, 1931; Shambleau by **C. L. Moore**, 1933; The Curse of Yig by Zealia Brown Reed and H. P. Lovecraft, 1928; Ubbo-Sathla by Clark Ashton Smith, 1933; The Painted Mirror by Donald Wandrei, 1937; Amina by Edward Lucas White, 1907; The Black Kiss by Robert Bloch, 1937; The City of the Living Dead by Laurence Manning and Fletcher Pratt, 1930; and The Curse of a Thousand Kisses by Sax Rohmer, 1918.

62. A Quintet of Sixes. Published by Ace Books, New York City, 1969. Ace Book 70000. Softcover. Herein: The Trailsman by Allan Vaughn Elston; Gun Search by Giles A. Lutz; Born to the Brand by D. B. Newton; The Gunsmoke King Calls Quits by Thomas Thompson; and They Hanged Wild Bill Murphy by Wayne D. Overholser.

63. World's Best Science Fiction 1970. With Terry Carr. Published by Ace Books, New York City, 1970. Ace Book 91357. Softcover. All stories from 1969. Herein: Introduction by **Donald A. Wollheim** and Terry Carr; A Man Spekith by Richard Wilson; After the Myths Went Home by **Robert Silverberg**; Death by Ecstasy by Larry Niven; One Sunday in Neptune by Alexei Panshin; For the Sake of Grace by Suzette Haden Elgin; Your Haploid Heart by James Tiptree, Jr; Therapy 2000 by Keith Roberts; Sixth Sense by Michael G. Coney; A Boy and His Dog by Harlan Ellison; And So Say All of Us by Bruce McAllister; Ship of Shadows by **Fritz Leiber**; Nine Lives by **Ursula K. Le Guin**; and The Big Flash by Norman Spinrad.

64. World's Best Science Fiction 1970. With Terry Carr. Published by the Science Fiction Book Club, Garden City, New York, 1970. Book Club Code 31L. First hardcover edition.

65. Ace Science Fiction Reader. Published by Ace Books, New York City, 1971. Ace Book 00275. Softcover. Herein: The Trouble with Tycho by Clifford Simak, 1960; Empire Star by **Samuel R. Delany**, 1966; and The Last Castle by **Jack Vance**, 1966.

66. Fortress of the Six Moons - Perry Rhodan 7. Edited with Forrest J Ackerman. Published by Ace Books, New York City, 1971. Ace Book 441 65976. Softcover. Herein: Perry Rhodan and His Electric Time Machine - essay by Forry Rhodan - Forrest J. Ackerman; Fortress of the Six Moons by K. H Scheer; Scientfilm World - an essay by Forrest J. Ackerman; and The Perryscope - an essay by Forry Rhodan - Forrest J. Ackerman.

67. World's Best Science Fiction 1971. With Terry Carr. Published by Ace Books, New York City, 1971. Ace Book 91358. Softcover. All stories from 1970. Herein: Introduction by **Donald A. Wollheim** and Terry Carr; Slow Sculpture by **Theodore Sturgeon**; Bird in the Hand by Larry Niven; Ishmael in Love by **Robert Silverberg**; Invasion of Privacy by Bob Shaw; Waterclap by **Isaac Asimov**; Continued on Next Rock by R. A. Lafferty; The Thing in the Stone by Clifford D. Simak; Nobody Lives on Burton Street by Gregory Benford; Whatever Became of the McGowans by Michael G. Coney; The Last Time Around by Arthur Sellings; Greyspun's Gift by Neal Barrett Jr.; The Shaker Revival by Gerald Jonas; Dear Aunt Annie by Gordon Eklund; Confessions by Ron Goulart; and Gone are the Lupo by H. B. Hickey.

68. World's Best Science Fiction 1971. With Terry Carr. Published by the Science Fiction Book Club, Garden City, New York, 1971. First hardcover edition.

69. The 1972 Annual World's Best SF. With Arthur W. Saha. Published by DAW Books, New York City, 1972. DAW Collector's Book 5. UQ1005. Softcover. All stories from 1971. This contains: Introduction by **Donald A. Wollheim**; The Fourth Profession by Larry Niven; Gleepsite by Joanna Russ; The Bear with the Knot on His Tail by Stephen Tall; The Sharks of Pentreath by Michael G. Coney; A Little Knowledge by **Poul Anderson**; Real-Time World by Christopher Priest; All Pieces of a River Shore by R. A. Lafferty; With Friends Like These by Alan Dean Foster; Aunt Jennie's Tonic by Leonard Tushnet; Timestorm by Eddy C. Bertin; Transit of Earth by **Arthur C. Clarke**; Gehenna by Barry Malzberg writing as K. M. O'Donnell; One Life Furnished in Early Poverty by Harlan Ellison; and Occam's Scalpel by **Theodore Sturgeon**.

70. The 1972 Annual World's Best SF. With Arthur W. Saha. Published by the Science Fiction Book Club, Garden City, New York, 1972. First hardcover edition.

71. Trilogy of the Future. Published by Sidgwick and Jackson, London, 1972. Hardcover. Re-titled version of The Ace Science Fiction Reader, 1971.

72. The 1973 Annual World's Best SF. With Arthur W. Saha. Published by DAW Books, New York City, 1973. DAW Collector's Book 53. UQ1053.

263

Softcover. All stories from 1972. This contains: Introduction by **Donald A. Wollheim**; Goat Song by **Poul Anderson**; The Man Who Walked Home by James Tiptree, Jr; Oh Valindai by Michael G. Coney; The Gold at the Starbow's End by **Frederik Pohl**; To Walk a City Street by Clifford D. Simak; Rorqual Maru by T. J. Bass; Changing Woman by W. Macfarlane; Willie's Blues by Robert J. Tilley; Long Shot by Vernor Vinge; and Thus Love Betrays Us by Phyllis MacLennon.

73. The 1973 Annual World's Best SF. With Arthur W. Saha. Published by the Science Fiction Book Club, Garden City, New York, 1973. First hardcover edition.

74. The 1974 Annual World's Best SF. With Arthur W. Saha. Published by DAW Books, New York City, 1974. DAW Collector's Book 101. YU1109. Softcover. All stories from 1973. Herein: Introduction by **Donald A. Wollheim**; A Suppliant in Space by Robert Sheckley; Parthen by R. A. Lafferty; Doomship by **Frederik Pohl** and **Jack Williamson**; Weed of Time by Norman Spinrad; A Modest Genius by Vadim Shefner; The Deathbird by Harlan Ellison; Evane by E. C. Tubb; Moby, Too by Gordon Eklund; Death an Designation Among the Asadi by Michael Bishop; and Construction Shack by Clifford D. Simak.

75. The 1974 Annual World's Best SF. With Arthur W. Saha. Published by the Science Fiction Book Club, Garden City, New York, 1974. First hardcover edition.

76. The World's Best SF Short Stories 1. With Arthur W. Saha. Published by The Elmfield Press, UK, 1975. Hardcover. Re-titled version of The 1974 Annual World's Best SF.

77. The 1975 Annual World's Best SF. With Arthur W. Saha. Published by DAW Books, New York City, 1975. DAW Collector's Book 148. UW1170. Softcover. All stories from 1974. Herein: Introduction by **Donald A. Wollheim**; A Song for Lya by George R. R. Martin; Deathsong by Sydney J. Van Scyoc; A Full Member of the Club by Bob Shaw; The Sun's Tears by Brian M. Stableford; The Gift of Garigolli by **Frederik Pohl** and C. M. Kornbluth; The Four Hour Fugue by **Alfred Bester**; Twig by **Gordon R. Dickson**; Cathadonian Odyssey by Michael Bishop; The Bleeding Man by Craig Strete; and Stranger in Paradise by **Isaac Asimov**.

78. The 1975 Annual World's Best SF. With Arthur W. Saha. Published by the Science Fiction Book Club, Garden City, New York, 1975. First hardcover edition.

79. The World's Best SF Short Stories 2. With Arthur W. Saha. Published by The Elmfield Press, UK, 1976. Hardcover. Re-titled version of The 1975 Annual World's Best SF.

80. The 1976 Annual World's Best SF. With Arthur W. Saha. Published by DAW Books, New York City, 1976. DAW Collector's Book 192. UW1232. Softcover. All stories from 1975. Herein: Introduction by **Donald A. Wollheim**; Catch That Zeppelin by **Fritz Leiber**; The Peddler's Apprentice by Joan D. Vinge and Vernor Vinge; The Bees of Knowledge by Barrington J. Bayley; The Storms of Windhaven by Lisa Tuttle and George R. R. Martin; The Engineer and The Executioner by Brian M. Stableford; Allegiances by Michael Bishop; Child of All Ages by P. J. Plauger; Helbent 4 by Stephen Robinett; The Protocols of the Elders of Britain by John Brunner; and The Custodians by Richard Cowper.

81. The 1976 Annual World's Best SF. With Arthur W. Saha. Published by the Science Fiction Book Club, Garden City, New York, 1976. First hardcover edition.

82. The Best from the Rest of the World: European Science Fiction. Published by Doubleday & Company, Garden City, New York, 1976. Hardcover. Herein: Introduction by **Donald A. Wollheim**; Party Line by Gerard Klein, 1973; Pairpuppets by Manuel Van Loggem, 1974; The Scythe by Sandro Sandrelli, 1963; A Whiter Shade of Pale by Jon Bing, 1976; Paradise 3000 by Herbert W. Franke, 1976; My Eyes, They Burn by Eddy C. Bertin, 1972; A Problem in Bionics by Pierre Barbet, 1974; The King and the Dollmaker by Wolfgang Jeschke, 1970; Codemus by Tor Age Bringsvaerd, 1968; Rainy Day Revolution No. 39 by Luidi Cozzi, 1965; Nobody Here But Us Shadows by Sam J. Lundwall, 1975; Round and Round and Round Again by Domingo Santos, 1970; Planet for Sale by Niels E. Nielson, 1964; and Ysolde by Nathalie-Charles Henneberg,1961.

83. The DAW Science Fiction Reader. Published by DAW Books, New York City, 1976. DAW Collector's Book 200 - UW1242. Softcover. Herein: Introduction by **Donald A. Wollheim**; Fur Magic by **Andre Norton**, 1968; Warrior by **Gordon R. Dickson**, 1965; The Truce by Tanith Lee, 1976; The Martian El Dorado of Parker Wintley by Lin Carter, 1976; The Day of the Butterflies by Marion Zimmer Bradley, 1976; Captain Fagan Died Alone by Brian M. Stableford, 1976; and Wizard of Scorpio by Kenneth Bulmer writing as Alan Burt Akers.

84. The 1977 Annual World's Best SF. With Arthur W. Saha. Published by DAW Books, New York City, 1977. DAW Collector's Book 240. UE1297. Softcover. All stories from 1976. Herein: Introduction by **Donald A. Wollheim**; Appearance of Life by **Brian W. Aldiss**; Overdrawn at the Memory Bank by John Varley; Those Good Old Days of Liquid Fuel by Michael G. Coney; The Hertford Manuscript by Richard Cowper; Natural Advantage by Lester del Rey; The Bicentennial Man by **Isaac Asimov**; The Cabinet of Oliver Naylor by Barrington J. Bayley; My Boat by Joanna Russ; Houston, Houston, Do You Read by James Tiptree, Jr.; and I See You by **Damon Knight**.

85. The 1977 Annual World's Best SF. With Arthur W. Saha. Published by the Science Fiction Book Club, Garden City, New York, 1977. First hardcover edition.

86. The 1978 Annual World's Best SF. With Arthur W. Saha. Published by DAW Books, New York City, 1978. DAW Collector's Book 288. UJ1376. Softcover. All stories from 1977. Herein: Introduction by **Donald A. Wollheim**; In the Hall of the Martian Kings by John Varley; A Time to Live by Joe Haldeman; The House of Compassionate Sharers by

Donald A. Wollheim

Michael Bishop; Particle Theory by Edward Bryant; The Taste of the Dish and the Savor of the Day by John Brunner; Jeffty is Five by Harlan Ellison; The Screwfly Solution by James Tiptree, Jr writing as Raccoona Sheldon; Eyes of Amber by Joan D. Vinge; Child of the Sun by James E. Gunn; and Brother by Clifford D. Simak.

87. The 1978 Annual World's Best SF. With Arthur W. Saha. Published by the Science Fiction Book Club, Garden City, New York, 1978. First hardcover edition.

88. The World's Best SF 3. With Arthur W. Saha. Published by Dennis Dobson, London, 1979. Hardcover. Re-titled version of The 1976 Annual World's Best SF.

89. The World's Best SF 4. With Arthur W. Saha. Published by Dennis Dobson, London, 1979. Hardcover. Re-titled version of The 1977 Annual World's Best SF.

90. The 1979 Annual World's Best SF. With Arthur W. Saha. Published by DAW Books, New York City, 1979. DAW Collector's Book 337. UE1459. Softcover. All stories from 1978. Herein: Introduction by **Donald A. Wollheim**; Cassandra by C. J. Cherryh; Dance Band on the Titanic by Jack L. Chalker; Come to the Party by **Frank Herbert** and F. M. Busby; Creator by David Lake; In Alien Flesh by Gregory Benford; SQ by **Ursula K. Le Guin**; The Persistence of Vision by John Varley; We Who Stole the Dream by James Tiptree, Jr; Scattershot by Greg Bear; and Carruthers' Last Stand by Don Henderson.

91. The World's Best SF 5. With Arthur W. Saha. Published by Dennis Dobson, London, 1980. Hardcover. Re-titled version of The 1978 Annual World's Best SF.

92. The 1980 Annual World's Best SF. With Arthur W. Saha. Published by DAW Books, New York City, 1980. DAW Collector's Book 384. UE1535. Softcover. All stories from 1979. This contains: Introduction by **Donald A. Wollheim**; Daisy In The Sun by **Connie Willis**; The Thaw by Tanith Lee; The Extraordinary Voyages of Amelie Bertrand by Joanna Russ; The Way of Cross and Dragon by George R. R. Martin; The Thirteenth Utopia by Somtow Sucharitkul; Options by John Varley; Unaccompanied Sonata by Orson Scott Card; The Story Writer by Richard Wilson; The Locusts by Larry Niven and Steve Barnes; Out There Where The Big Ships Go by Richard Cowper; and Can These Bones Live by Ted Reynolds.

93. The 1980 Annual World's Best SF. With Arthur W. Saha. Published by the Science Fiction Book Club, Garden City, New York, 1980. First hardcover edition.

94. The 1981 Annual World's Best SF. With Arthur W. Saha. Published by DAW Books, New York City, 1981. DAW Collector's Book 432. Softcover. All stories from 1980. Herein: Introduction by **Donald A. Wollheim**; Variation On A Theme From Beethoven by Sharon Webb; Beatnik Bayou by John Varley; Elbow Room by Marion Zimmer Bradley; The Ugly Chickens by Howard Waldrop; Prime Time by Norman Spinrad; Nightflyers by George R. R. Martin; A Spaceship Built of Stone by Lisa Tuttle; Window by Bob Leman; The Summer Sweet, The Winter Wild by Michael G. Coney; and Achronos by Lee Killough.

95. The 1981 Annual World's Best SF. With Arthur W. Saha. Published by the Science Fiction Book Club, Garden City, New York, 1981. First hardcover edition.

96. The 1982 Annual World's Best SF. With Arthur W. Saha. Published by DAW Books, New York City, 1982. DAW Collector's Book 480. Softcover. All stories from 1981. Herein: Introduction by **Donald A. Wollheim**; Blind Spot by Jayge Carr; Highliner by C. J. Cherryh; The Pusher by John Varley; Polyphemus by Michael Shea; Absent Thee From Felicity by Somtow Sucharitkul; Out of the Everywhere by James Tiptree Jr.; Slac by Michael P. Kube-McDowell; The Cyphertone by S. C. Sykes; Through All Your Houses Wandering by Ted Reynolds; and The Last Day of Christmas by David J. Lake.

97. The 1982 Annual World's Best SF. With Arthur W. Saha. Published by the Science Fiction Book Club, Garden City, New York, 1982. First hardcover edition.

98. The 1983 Annual World's Best SF. With Arthur W. Saha. Published by DAW Books, New York City, 1983. DAW Collector's Book 528. Softcover. All stories from 1982. Herein: Introduction by **Donald A. Wollheim**; The Scourge by James White; A Letter From the Clearys by **Connie Willis**; Farmer on the Dole by **Frederik Pohl**; Playing the Game by Gardner Dozois and Jack Dann; Pawn's Gambit by Timothy Zahn; The Comedian by Timothy Robert Sullivan; Written in Water by Tanith Lee; Souls by Joanna Russ; Swarm by Bruce Sterling; and Peg-Man by Rudy Rucker.

99. The 1983 Annual World's Best SF. With Arthur W. Saha. Published by the Science Fiction Book Club, Garden City, New York, 1983. First hardcover edition.

100. The 1984 Annual World's Best SF. With Arthur W. Saha. Published by DAW Books, New York City, 1984. DAW Collector's Book 581. Softcover. All stories from 1983. Herein: Introduction by **Donald A. Wollheim**; Blood Music by Greg Bear; Potential by **Isaac Asimov**; Knight of Shallows by Rand B. Lee; Spending a Day at the Lottery Fair by **Frederik Pohl**; In the Face of My Enemy by Joseph H. Delaney; The Nanny by Thomas Wylde; The Leaves of October by Don Sakers; As Time Goes By by Tanith Lee; The Harvest of Wolves by Mary Gentle; and Homefaring by **Robert Silverberg**.

101. The 1984 Annual World's Best SF. With Arthur W. Saha. Published by the Science Fiction Book Club, Garden City, New York, 1984. First hardcover edition.

102. The 1985 Annual World's Best SF. With Arthur W. Saha. Published by DAW Books, New York City, 1985. DAW Collector's Book 630. Softcover. All stories from 1984. Herein: Introduction by **Donald A. Wollheim**; The Picture Man by John Dalmas; Cash Crop by **Connie Willis**; We Remember

Babylon by Ian Watson; What Makes Us Human by Stephen R. Donaldson; Salvador by Lucius Shepard; Press Enter by John Varley; The Aliens Who Knew I Mean Everything by George Alec Effinger; Bloodchild by Octavia E. Butler; The Coming of the Goonga by Gary W. Shockley; and Medra by Tanith Lee.

103. The 1985 Annual World's Best SF. With Arthur W. Saha. Published by the Science Fiction Book Club, Garden City, New York, 1985. First hardcover edition.

104. The 1986 Annual World's Best SF. With Arthur W. Saha. Published by DAW Books, New York City, 1986. DAW Collector's Book 675. Softcover. All stories from 1985. Herein: Introduction by **Donald A. Wollheim**; Earthgate by J. Brian Clarke; On the Dream Channel Panel by Ian Watson; The Gods of Mars by Gardner Dozois; Jack Dann; and Michael Swanwick; The Jaguar Hunter by Lucius Shepard; Sailing to Byzantium by **Robert Silverberg**; Webrider by Jayge Carr; With Virgil Oddum at the East Pole by Harlan Ellison; The Curse of Kings by **Connie Willis**; Fermi and Frost by **Frederik Pohl**; and Pots by C. J. Cherryh.

105. The 1986 Annual World's Best SF. With Arthur W. Saha. Published by the Science Fiction Book Club, Garden City, New York, 1986. First hardcover edition.

106. The 1987 Annual World's Best SF. With Arthur W. Saha. Published by DAW Books, New York City, 1987. DAW Collector's Book 711. Softcover. All stories from 1986. Herein: Introduction by **Donald A. Wollheim**; Permafrosta by Roger Zelazny; Timerider by Doris Egan; Pretty Boy Crossover by Pat Cadigan; R & R by Lucius Shepard; Lo, How an Oak E'er Blooming by Suzette Haden Elgin; Dream in a Bottle by Derry Meredith and D. E. Smirl; Into Gold by Tanith Lee; The Lions Are Asleep This Night by Howard Waldrop; Against Babylon by **Robert Silverberg**; and Strangers on Paradise by **Damon Knight**.

107. The 1987 Annual World's Best SF. With Arthur W. Saha. Published by the Science Fiction Book Club, Garden City, New York, 1987. First hardcover edition.

108. The 1988 Annual World's Best SF. With Arthur W. Saha. Published by DAW Books, New York City, 1988. DAW Collector's Book 747. Softcover. All stories from 1987. Herein: Introduction by **Donald A. Wollheim**; The Pardoner's Tale by **Robert Silverberg**; Rachel In Love by Pat Murphy;

America by Orson Scott Card; Crying in the Rain by Tanith Lee; The Sun Spider by Lucius Shepard; Angel by Pat Cadigan; Forever Yours, Anna by **Kate Wilhelm**; Second Going by James Tiptree, Jr; Dinosaurs by Walter Jon Williams; and All Fall Down by Don Sakers.

109. The 1988 Annual World's Best SF. With Arthur W. Saha. Published by the Science Fiction Book Club, Garden City, New York, 1988. First hardcover edition.

110. The 1989 Annual World's Best SF. With Arthur W. Saha. Published by DAW Books, New York City, 1989. DAW Collector's Book 783. Softcover. All stories from 1988. Herein: Introduction by **Isaac Asimov**; Skin Deep by Kristine Kathryn Rusch; A Madonna of the Machine by Tanith Lee; Ain't Nothin' But a Hound Dog by B. W. Clough; Adrift Among the Ghosts by Jack Chalker; Ripples in the Dirac Sea by Geoffrey A. Landis; The Giving Plague by David Brin; Peaches For Mad Molly by Steven Gould; Shaman by John Shirley; Schrodinger's Kitten by George Alec Effinger; The Flies of Memory by Ian Watson; and Waiting for the Olympians by **Frederik Pohl**.

111. The 1989 Annual World's Best SF. With Arthur W. Saha. Published by the Science Fiction Book Club, Garden City, New York, 1989. First hardcover edition.

112. The 1990 Annual World's Best SF. With Arthur W. Saha. Published by DAW Books, New York City, 1990. DAW Collector's Book 820. Softcover. All stories from 1989. Herein: Introduction by **Donald A. Wollheim**; Death Ship by Barrington J. Bayley; In Translation by Lisa Tuttle; Not Without Honor by Judith Moffett; Dogwalker by Orson Scott Card; Surrender by Lucius Shepard; War Fever by J. G. Ballard; Abe Lincoln in McDonald's by James Morrow; Alphas by Gregory Benford; The Magic Bullet by Brian Stableford; North of the Abyss by **Brian W. Aldiss**; and Chiprunner by **Robert Silverberg**; and A Sleep and A Forgetting by **Robert Silverberg**.

113. The 1990 Annual World's Best SF. With Arthur W. Saha. Published by the Science Fiction Book Club, Garden City, New York, 1990. First hardcover edition.

***

NON-FICTION

1. The Universe Makers. Published by Harper and Row, New York City, 1971. Hardcover.

Edgar Rice Burroughs

-2003-

Edgar Rice Burroughs.

Edgar Rice Burroughs was born in Chicago on September 1st, 1875 and died of a heart attack on March 19th, 1950. Along the way, he created some of the most famous works in the history of fantasy and science fiction.

After screwing up at just about everything he tried, he decided to take a shot at writing some fiction. He had read some pulp magazines and figured that he could certainly do better. With that as the competition, he should at least be able to make more money writing than selling pencil sharpeners, which was what he was doing while he wrote his first story.

He said, "I had gone thoroughly through some of the all-fiction magazines, and made up my mind that if people were paid for writing rot such as I read, I could write stories just as rotten. I knew absolutely that I could write stories just as entertaining and probably a lot more so than any I chanced to read in those magazines."

His first story was serialized in six parts in The All-Story Magazine, starting in February 1912 and finished in July 1912. It was called Under the Moons of Mars and he was paid $400.00 for it, which was somewhat more than the pencil sharpeners were bringing in. This new venture was pretty easy.

As legend has it, Burroughs had tried to publish his first effort under the name Normal Bean but the publisher assumed the name was a typo and called him Norman Bean. The story, of course, is better known as A Princess of Mars, which was what it was called when McClurg published it in hardcover in 1917. A decent copy in the Frank Schoonover dustjacket can usually be found at around $1200.00.

Nobody wanted his next story, The Outlaw of Torn.

He almost gave up writing. But he liked it so he tried again.

His next published story was also used in All-Story Magazine, in October, 1912. They paid him $700.00 for it, which was damned good money when the average wage was about $20.00 a week.

The story was Tarzan of the Apes. And Burroughs became first, a sensation, next, an institution. Tarzan of the Apes was actually his first story to be published in book form. A decent first-state copy in a dustjacket can go for around $35,000.00. The second Tarzan novel, The Return of Tarzan, in a dustjacket, has sold for up to $450,000.00. The jacket was by N. C. Wyeth and very few copies still exist...

***

FILM AND TELEVISION

1. Tarzan of the Apes. Directed by Scott Sidney, this 1914 novel was filmed for release in 1918, starring: Elmo Lincoln as Tarzan, Enid Markey as Jane Porter, and Gordon Griffith as the young Tarzan; along with True Boardman; Kathleen Kirkham; George B. French; Thomas Jefferson; and others.

2. The Romance of Tarzan. Again based on Tarzan of the Apes, 1914, this was released late in 1918, this was directed by Wilfred Lucas and starred: Elmo Lincoln as Tarzan, Enid Markey as Jane Porter, and Gordon Griffith as the young Tarzan; along with True Boardman; Kathleen Kirkham; George B. French; Thomas Jefferson; and others.

3. The Oakdale Affair. From 1918, this story was filmed for release in 1919. Directed by Oscar Apfel, it starred: Evelyn Greeley; Eric Mayne; Maude Turner Gordon; Charles Mackay; Mona Kingsley; and many others.

4. The Revenge of Tarzan. Based on The Return of Tarzan, 1915, this was directed by Harry Revier and George M. Merrick and released in 1920. It starred: Gene Pollar as Tarzan and Karla Schramm as Jane; along with Estelle Taylor; Armand Cortes; Franklin B. Coates; George Romain; and Walter Miller.

5. The Son of Tarzan. Based on the 1917 novel, this was released in 1920. Directed by Arthur J. Flaven and Harry Revier, it starred: Kamuela C. Searle as Korak and Gordon Griffith as the young Korak; with P. Dempsey Tabler as Tarzan/Lord Greystoke and Karla Schramm as Jane. Also on hand were Manilla Martan; Mae Giraci; Eugene Burr; Frank Morrell; and Ray Thompson.

6. The Adventures of Tarzan. Released in 1921, this was directed by Robert F. Hill and Scott Sidney. Elmo Lincoln was back as Tarzan, along with Louise Lorraine as Jane; and Scott Pembroke; Frank Whitson; George Monberg; Lillian Worth; Charles Gay; and many others.

7. Tarzan and the Golden Lion. Based on the 1923 novel, this was released in March 1927. Directed by J. P. McGowan, it starred: James Pierce as Tarzan; along with Frederick Peters; Edna Murphy; Harold Goodwin; Dorothy Dunbar; D'Arcy Corrigan; and Robert Bolder. Also on hand was Boris Karloff as Owaza, in one of his earliest roles.

8. Tarzan the Mighty. Supposedly based on Jungle Tales of Tarzan from 1919, this was directed by Jack Nelson and Ray Taylor and released in 1928 with Frank Merrill as Tarzan; along with Al Ferguson; Natalie Kingston; bobby Nelson; and Lorimer Johnston.

9. Tarzan the Tiger. From Tarzan and the Jewels of Opar, 1918, this was directed by Henry MacRae and released in 1929. It starred: Frank Merrill as Tarzan and Natalie Kingston as Jane; along with:

Al Ferguson; Sheldon Lewis; Paul Panzer; Clive Morgan; and Mademoiselle Kithnou and Queen La of Opar.

10. Tarzan the Ape Man. Directed by W. S. Van Dyke for release in 1932, this first talking Tarzan was played by Johnny Weissmuller with Maureen O'Sullivan as his Jane. Also on hand were: C. Aubrey Smith; Doris Lloyd; Forrester Harvey; Ivory Williams; and Neil Hamilton.

11. Tarzan the Fearless. From 1933, this was directed by Robert F. Hill and starred Buster Crabbe as Tarzan, along with: Julie Bishop; E. Alyn Warren; Edward Woods; Philo McCullough; Matthew Betz; Franck Lacktten; and others.

12. Tarzan and His Mate. Directed by Cedric Gibbons, Jack Conway and James C. McKay, this was released in 1934 with Johnny Weissmuller back as Tarzan and Maureen O'Sullivan back as Jane. Also along were: Neil Hamilton; Paul Cavanagh; Forrester Harvey; Nathan Curry; Doris Lloyd; and others.

13. The New Adventures of Tarzan. From 1935, this was produced by Burroughs himself and directed by Edward A. Kull and Wilbur McGaugh. It featured Bruce Bennet - using the name Herman Brix - as Tarzan; along with: Ula Holt; Ashton Dearholt; Frank Baker; Lewis Sargent; and others.

14. The Lion Man. Loosely based on a Burroughs' story, this was directed by John P. McCarthy and released in 1936. It starred: Jon Hall; Kathleen Burke; Ted Adams; Jimmy Aubrey; Richard Carlyle; Finis Barton; Eric Snowden; Bobby Fairy; Henry Hale; and Lal Chand Mehra.

15. Tarzan Escapes. From 1936, this was directed by Richard Thorpe and brought back Johnny Weissmuller as Tarzan and Maureen O'Sullivan as Jane; along with: John Buckler; Benita Hume; William Henry; Herbert Mundin; E. E. Clive; Darby Jones; and others.

16. Tarzan's Revenge. Directed by D. Ross Lederman for 1938, this starred Glenn Morris as Tarzan; along with: Eleanor Holm; George Barbier; C. Henry Gordon; Joe Sawyer; George Meeker; and others, including Hedda Hopper as Penny Reed.

17. Tarzan and the Green Goddess. This produced by **Edgar Rice Burroughs** and directed by Edward A. Kull and Wilbur McGaugh, with was released in 1938. It featured Bruce Bennet/Herman Brix as Tarzan; along with: Ula Holt; Frank Baker; Ashton Dearholt; Lewis Sargent; Jack Mower; and others.

18. Tarzan Finds a Son. From 1939, this was directed by Richard Thorpe, reunited with Johnny Weissmuller as Tarzan and Maureen O'Sullivan as Jane. Joining them was Johnny Sheffield as Boy; along with Ian Hunter; Henry Stephenson; Frieda Inescort; Henry Wilcoxon; Laraine Day; and others.

19. Jungle Girl. Based on the 1932 novel, this was directed by John English and William Witney for release in 1941. It starred: Frances Gifford; Tom Neal; Trevor Bardette; Gerald Mohr; Eddie Acuff; Frank Lackteen; Tommy Cook; and many others, including Jay Silverheels in an uncredited roll as a Lion Man Guard.

20. Tarzan's Secret Treasure. Released in 1941, this was directed by Richard Thorpe and starred: Johnny Weissmuller as Tarzan, Maureen O'Sullivan as Jane and Johnny Sheffield as Boy; along with: Reginald Owen; Tom Conway; Philip Dorn; Cordell Hickman; and others, including Barry Fitzgerald as O'Doul.

21. Tarzan's New York Adventure. From 1941, this was directed by Richard Thorpe and starred: Johnny Weissmuller as Tarzan, Maureen O'Sullivan as Jane and Johnny Sheffield as Boy; along with: Virginia Grey; Charles Bickford; Paul Kelly; Cy Kendall; Russell Hicks; and others, including Chill Wills as Manchester Montford.

22. Tarzan Triumphs. Released in 1943, this was directed by Wilhelm Thiele and starred: Johnny Weissmuller as Tarzan and Johnny Sheffield as Boy; along with: Shanley Ridges; Sig Ruman; Philip Van Zandt; Rex Williams; and others, including Frances Gifford as Zandra.

23. Tarzan's Desert Mystery. From 1944, this was directed by Wilhelm Thiele and starred: Johnny Weissmuller as Tarzan and Johnny Sheffield as Boy; along with: Otto Kruger; Joe Sawyer; Lloyd Corrigan; Robert Lowrey; Philip Van Zandt; and others, including Nancy Kelly as Connie Bryce.

24. Tarzan and the Amazons. Directed by Kurt Neumann for release in 1945, this one starred: Johnny Weissmuller as Tarzan, Johnny Sheffield as Boy, and Brenda Joyce as the new Jane; along with: Henry Stephenson; Maria Ouspenskaya; Barton MacLane; Donald Douglas; Steven Geray; J. M. Kerrigan; and Shirley O'Hara.

25. Tarzan and the Leopard Woman. Released in 1946, this was directed by Kurt Neumann and starred: Johnny Weissmuller as Tarzan, Johnny Sheffield as Boy, and Brenda Joyce as Jane; along with: Acquanetta; Edgar Barrier; Dennis Hoey; Tommy Cook; and Anthony Caruso; along with a huge uncredited cast.

26. Tarzan and the Huntress. Released in 1947, this was directed by Robert Florey and starred: Johnny Weissmuller as Tarzan and Brenda Joyce as Jane; along with: Patricia Morison; Barton MacLane; John Warburton; Charles Trowbridge; Ted Hecht; Wallace Scott; and others.

27. Tarzan and the Mermaids. Released in 1948, this was directed by Kurt Neumann and starred: Johnny Weissmuller as Tarzan, Johnny Sheffield as Boy, and Brenda Joyce as Jane; along with: George Zucco; Andrea Palma; Fernando Wagner; Edward Ashley; and others.

28. Tarzan's Magic Fountain. From 1949, this was directed by Lee Sholem, featured a screenplay by Curt Siodmak, and introduced Lex Barker as Tarzan while keeping Brenda Joyce as Jane. Also on hand were: Albert Dekker; Evelyn Ankers; Charles Drake; Alan Napier; Ted Hecht; and Henry Brandon; along with Elmo Lincoln in an uncredited role as a fisherman.

Edgar Rice Burroughs

29. Tarzan and the Slave Girl. Directed by Lee Sholem, this was released in 1950 starring: Lex Barker as Tarzan and Vanessa Brown as Jane; with: Robert Alda; Hurd Hatfield; Arthur Shields; Anthony Caruso; Denise Darcel; and many others.

30. Tarzan's Peril. From 1951, this was directed by Byron Haskin and starred Lex Barker as Tarzan with Virginia Huston as Jane; and: George Macready; Douglas Fowley; Glenn Anders; Alan Napier; Edward Ashley; and others, including Dorothy Dandrige as Melmendi, Queen of the Ashuba.

31. Tarzan Istanbul'da. Also known as Tarzan in Istanbul, this was made in Turkey and released in 1952. Directed by Orhan Atadeniz, it starred Tamer Balci as Tarzan along with: Hayri Esen; Necla Aygul; Aziz Basmaci; Cemil Demirel; and many others.

32. Tarzan's Savage Fury. Directed by Cy Endfield, this was released in 1952, starring: Lex Barker as Tarzan and Dorothy Hart as Jane, with: Patric Knowles; Charles Korvin; and Tommy Carlton.

33. Tarzan and the She Devil. From 1953, this was directed by Kurt Neumann and starred Lex Barker as Tarzan with Joyce Mackenzie as Jane; with: Monique van Vooren; Tom Conway; Michael Granger; Henry Brandon; and many others, including Raymond Burr as Vargo.

34. Tarzan's Hidden Jungle. Directed by Harold D. Schuster and released in 1955, this introduced Gordon Scott as Tarzan. Joining him were: Peter van Eyck; Charles E. Fredericks; Richard Reeves; and others, including Vera Miles as Jill Hardy and Jack Elam as Burger.

35. Tarzan and the Lost Safari. From 1957, this was directed by H. Bruce Humberstone and starred Gordon Scott as Tarzan, along with: Robert Beatty; Yolande Donlan; Betta St John; George Coulouris; Peter Arne; Orlando Martins; and others, including Wilfred Hyde-White as Doodles Fletcher.

36. Tarzan and the Trappers. Released in 1958, this was directed by Charles F. Haas and Sandy Howard and featured Gordon Scott as Tarzan, Eve Brent as Jane and Rickie Sorensen as Boy; along with: Leslie Bradley; Maurice Marsac; Bruce Lester; William Keene; Paul Thompson; and others, including "Scatman" Sherman Crothers as Tyana.

37. Tarzan's Fight for Life. Also from 1958, this was directed by H. Bruce Humberstone and starred Gordon Scott as Tarzan, Eve Brent as Jane and Rickie Sorensen as Boy; along with: Jil Jarmyn; James Edward; Carl Benton Reid; Harry Lauter; and Woody Strode as Ramo.

38. Tarzan's Greatest Adventure. Directed by John Guillermin, this was released in 1959 starring Gordon Scott as Tarzan, with: Sara Shane; Niall MacGinnis; Al Mulock; Scilla Gabel; and others, including Anthony Quayle as Slade; and Sean Connery as O'Bannion.

39. Tarzan, the Ape Man. Also from 1959, this was directed by Joseph M. Newman and starred Denny Miller as Tarzan and Joanna Barnes as Jane; along with: Cesare Danova; Robert Douglas; and others.

40. Tarzan the Magnificent. Directed by Robert Day and released in 1961, this featured Gordon Scott as Tarzan; along with: Jock Mahoney, the next Tarzan, as Coy Banton; Betta St John; Lionel Jeffries; Alexandra Stewart; Earl Cameron; and many others, including John Carradine as Abel Banton.

41. Tarzan Goes to India. From 1962, this was directed by John Guillermin and introduced Jock Mahoney as Tarzan; along with: Leo Gordon; Mark Dana; Feroz Khan; Simi Garewal; Aaron Joseph; and many others.

42. Tansan vs. Tarsan. Made in the Philippines in 1963, this was directed by Carols Vander Tolosa and starred Dolphy as Tansan and Vic Vargas as Tarsan; with: Sarah Calvin; Herminia Carranza; Willie Dado; and many others.

43. Tarzan's Three Challenges. Released in 1963, this was directed by Robert Day and starred Jock Mahoney as Tarzan; along with: Woody Strode; Earl Cameron; Jimmy Jamal; Anthony Chinn; Robert Hu; and many others.

44. Per una manciata d'oro. Made in Italy and directed by Carlo Veo, this starred Mario Novelli as Tarzak, along with: Brad Euston; Luigi Batzella; Aldo Bonamano; and many others.

45. Tarzan and the Valley of Gold. Directed by Robert Day and released in 1966, this starred Mike Henry as Tarzan. Joining him were: David Opatoshu; Manuel Padilla Jr; Nancy Kovack; Don Megowan; John Kelly; and many others.

46. Tarzan. The television season first aired on September 8th, 1966. Directed by Alex Nicol, it starred Ron Ely as Tarzan and ran for thirty-six episodes between 1966 and 1968. Some of the guest stars along the way included: Woody Strode; Jock Mahoney; Maurice Evans; Julie Harris; Lloyd Haynes; Strother Martin; Ethel Merman; Nichelle Nichols; James Earl Jones; John Anderson; Sam Jaffe; and many, many others.

47. Tarzan and the Great River. Directed by Robert Day and released in 1967, this starred Mike Henry as Tarzan. With him were: Manuel Padilla Jr; Jan Murray; Diana Millay; Rafer Johnson; and others.

48. Tarzan and the Jungle Boy. From 1968, this was directed by Robert Gordon and starred Mike Henry as Tarzan, along with: Rafer Johnson; Aliza Gur; Steve Bond; Ron Gans; Edward Johnson; and others.

49. The Land That Time Forgot. From the 1924 novel, this was directed by Kevin Connor and released in 1975. It starred: Doug McClure; John McEnery; Susan Penhaligon; Keith Barron; Anthony Ainley; and others, including Colin Farrell as Whiteley.

50. Tarzan, Lord of the Jungle. Animated for television in 1976, this featured Robert Ridgely as the voice of Tarzan.

51. At the Earth's Core. From the 1922 novel, this was directed by Kevin Connor and released in 1976. It starred: Doug McClure; Caroline Munro; Cy Grant; Godfrey James; Sean Lynch; and others, including Peter Cushing as Dr Abner Perry.

52. The People That Time Forgot. From the 1918 story, this was directed by Kevin Connor and released in 1977. It starred: Doug McClure; Patrick Wayne; Sarah Douglas; Dana Gillespie; Thorley Walters; Shane Rimmer; and many others.

53. Tarzan, the Ape Man. This 1981 film was directed by John Derek and used Miles O'Keeffe as Tarzan and Bo Derek as Jane, along with: Richard Harris; John Phillip Law; Akushula Selayah; Steve Strong; Wilfrid Hyde-White; and others.

54. Greystoke: The Legend of Tarzan, Lord of the Apes. Directed by Hugh Hudson, this was released in 1984. It starred Christopher Lambert as Tarzan and Andie MacDowell as Jane, along with: Ralph Richardson; Ian Holm; James Fox; Cheryl Campbell; Ian Charleson; Nigel Davenport; and many, many others.

55. Tarzan. This television series started December 23rd, 1991 and ran for forty-two episodes starring Wolf Larson as Tarzan and Lydie Denier as Jane.

56. Tarzan: The Epic Adventures. A television series that was on for one season, starting August 28th, 1996 and finishing May 25th, 1997. It starred Joe Lara as Tarzan, along with: Aaron Seville; Lydie Denier; Andrew Divoff; Dennis Christopher; and Ralph Wilcox.

57. Investigating Tarzan. This 1997 documentary was written and directed by Alain D'Aix and featured interviews with: Danton Burroughs; Peter Elliott; Tracy Griffin; Denny Miller; Tanya Roberts; Gordon Scott; Johnny Weissmuller, Jr; and France Zobda.

58. Tarzan and the Lost City. Released in 1998, this was directed by Carl Schenkel and starred Casper Van Dien as Tarzan and Jane March as Jane. Also along were: Steve Waddington; Winston Ntshona; Rapulana Seiphemo; Ian Roberts; Sean Taylor; Gys De Villiers; and many others.

59. Tarzan. This 1999 animated feature from Disney was directed by Chris Buck and Kevin Lima and features the voices of Tony Goldwyn and Minnie Driver as the voices of Tarzan and Jane. Also involved were: Glenn Close; Brian Blessed; Nigel Hawthorne; Lance Henriksen; Wayne Knight; Alex D. Linz; Rosie O'Donnell; and many, many others.

60. The Legend of Tarzan. Also produced by Disney and also directed by Chris Buck, this animated television series launched on September 3rd, 2002 and ran for thirty-two episodes into 2003. Michael T. Weiss was the voice of Tarzan and Olivia d'Abo played Jane. Also featured were: Jim Cummings; April Winchell; Nicolette Sheridan; and many others, including Rene Auberjonois for eleven episodes and Craig Ferguson for four.

61. Tarzan. This television series ran for eight episodes in 2003, starring Travis Fimmel as Tarzan and Sarah Wayne Callies as Jane; along with: Miguel A. Nunez, Jr; Mitch Pileggi; and others, including Lucy Lawless as Kathleen Clayton for seven episodes.

62. The Land That Time Forgot. This remake of the 1975 film was directed by C. Thomas Howell for release in 2009. It starred: C. Thomas Howell; Timothy Bottoms; Lindsey McKeon; Darren Dalton; Stephen Blackehart; Christopher Showerman; and many others.

63. John Carter of Mars. In production at the time of this writing and slated for release in 2012. Directed by Andrew Stanton, it stars: Taylor Kitsch as John Carter and Lynn Collins as Dejah Thoris.

***

RADIO

1. Tarzan. The show debuted on radio on September 10th, 1932. It ran in fifteen minute episodes and aired nightly until 1936 with James Pierce as Tarzan.

2. Tarzan and the Diamond of Asher. This was a thirteen-week serial produced by **Edgar Rice Burroughs**.

3. Tarzan. Another Tarzan radio show started up in 1951, one episode a week, and ran into 1953 with Lamont Johnson as Tarzan.

***

NOVELS AND COLLECTIONS

1. Tarzan of the Apes. Published by A. C. McClurg, Chicago, 1914. Hardcover.

2. The Return of Tarzan. Published by A. C. McClurg, Chicago, 1915. Hardcover.

3. The Beasts of Tarzan. Published by A. C. McClurg, Chicago, 1916. Hardcover.

4. The Son of Tarzan. Published by A. C. McClurg, Chicago, 1917. Hardcover.

5. A Princess of Mars. Published by A. C. McClurg, Chicago, 1917. Hardcover.

6. The Gods of Mars. Published by A. C. McClurg, Chicago, 1918. Hardcover.

7. Tarzan and the Jewels of Opar. Published by A. C. McClurg, Chicago, 1918. Hardcover.

8. Jungle Tales of Tarzan. Published by A. C. McClurg, Chicago, 1919. Hardcover.

9. The Warlord of Mars. Published by A. C. McClurg, Chicago, 1919. Hardcover.

10. Tarzan the Untamed. Published by A. C. McClurg, Chicago, 1920. Hardcover.

11. Thuvia, Maid of Mars. Published by A. C. McClurg, Chicago, 1920. Hardcover.

12. Tarzan and the Terrible. Published by A. C. McClurg, Chicago, 1921. Hardcover.

13. The Mucker. Published by A. C. McClurg, Chicago, 1921. Hardcover.

14. The Mucker. Published by Methuen, London, 1921. Hardcover. This was part one of the U.S. edition of The Mucker, 1921.

15. At the Earth's Core. Published by A. C. McClurg, Chicago, 1922. Hardcover.

Edgar Rice Burroughs

16. The Chessmen of Mars. Published by A. C. McClurg, Chicago, 1922. Hardcover.

17. The Man Without a Soul. Published by Methuen, London, 1922. Hardcover. This was part two of the U.S. edition of The Mucker, 1921.

18. Tarzan and the Golden Lion. Published by A. C. McClurg, Chicago, 1923. Hardcover.

19. Pellucidar. Published by A. C. McClurg, Chicago, 1923. Hardcover.

20. The Girl from Hollywood. Published by The Macaulay Company, New York City, 1923. Hardcover.

21. Tarzan and the Ant Men. Published by A. C. McClurg, Chicago, 1924. Hardcover.

22. The Land That Time Forgot. Published by A. C. McClurg, Chicago, 1924. Hardcover. This contained all three parts of the serialized story from Blue Book which started running in August 1918. All three were later printed by Ace in separate volumes.

23. Tarzan and the Ant Men. Published by Methuen, London, 1925. Hardcover. This edition used the magazine version from Argosy in 1924.

24. The Bandit from Hell's Bend. Published by A. C. McClurg, Chicago, 1925. Hardcover.

25. The Eternal Lover. Published by A. C. McClurg, Chicago, 1925. Hardcover.

26. The Cave Girl. Published by A. C. McClurg, Chicago, 1925. Hardcover.

27. The Mad King. Published by A. C. McClurg, Chicago, 1926. Hardcover.

28. The Moon Maid. Published by A. C. McClurg, Chicago, 1926. Hardcover.

29. The War Chief. Published by A. C. McClurg, Chicago, 1927. Hardcover.

30. The Tarzan Twins. Published by The P. F. Volland Company, New York, 1927. Hardcover.

31. The Outlaw of Torn. Published by A. C. McClurg, Chicago, 1927. Hardcover.

32. The Mastermind of Mars. Published by A. C. McClurg, Chicago, 1928. Hardcover.

33. Tarzan, Lord of the Jungle. Published by A. C. McClurg, Chicago, 1928. Hardcover.

34. The Monster Men. Published by A. C. McClurg, Chicago, 1929. Hardcover.

35. Tarzan and the Lost Empire. Published by Metropolitan Books, New York City, 1929. Hardcover.

36. Tarzan at the Earth's Core. Published by Metropolitan Books, New York City, 1930. Hardcover.

37. Tanar of Pellucidar. Published by Metropolitan Books, New York City, 1930. Hardcover.

38. A Fighting Man of Mars. Published by Metropolitan Books, New York City, 1931. Hardcover.

39. Tarzan the Invincible. Published by Edgar Rice Burroughs Inc., Tarzana, California, 1931. Hardcover.

40. Jungle Girl. Published by Edgar Rice Burroughs Inc., Tarzana, California, 1932. Hardcover.

41. Tarzan Triumphant. Published by Edgar Rice Burroughs Inc., Tarzana, California, 1932. Hardcover.

42. Tarzan and the City of Gold. Published by Edgar Rice Burroughs Inc., Tarzana, California, 1933. Hardcover.

43. Apache Devil. Published by Edgar Rice Burroughs Inc., Tarzana, California, 1933. Hardcover.

44. Pirates of Venus. Published by Edgar Rice Burroughs Inc., Tarzana, California, 1934. Hardcover.

45. Tarzan and the Lion Man. Published by Edgar Rice Burroughs Inc., Tarzana, California, 1934. Hardcover.

46. Tarzan and the Leopard Men. Published by Edgar Rice Burroughs Inc., Tarzana, California, 1935. Hardcover.

47. Lost on Venus. Published by Edgar Rice Burroughs Inc., Tarzana, California, 1935. Hardcover.

48. Tarzan's Quest. Published by Edgar Rice Burroughs Inc., Tarzana, California, 1936. Hardcover.

49. Swords of Mars. Published by Edgar Rice Burroughs Inc., Tarzana, California, 1936. Hardcover.

50. Tarzan and the Tarzan Twins with Jad-Bal-Ja the Golden Lion. Published by Whitman Publishing, Racine, Wisconsin, 1936. Hardcover.

51. Back to the Stone Age. Published by Edgar Rice Burroughs Inc., Tarzana, California, 1937. Hardcover.

52. The Oakdale Affair - with - The Rider. Published by Edgar Rice Burroughs Inc., Tarzana, California, 1937. Hardcover.

53. Tarzan and the Forbidden City. Published by Edgar Rice Burroughs Inc., Tarzana, California, 1938. Hardcover.

54. The Lad and the Lion. Published by Edgar Rice Burroughs Inc., Tarzana, California, 1938. Hardcover.

55. Tarzan the Magnificent. Published by Edgar Rice Burroughs Inc., Tarzana, California, 1939. Hardcover.

56. Carson of Venus. Published by Edgar Rice Burroughs Inc., Tarzana, California, 1939. Hardcover.

57. Synthetic Men of Mars. Published by Edgar Rice Burroughs Inc., Tarzana, California, 1940. Hardcover.

58. The Deputy Sheriff of Comanche County. Published by Edgar Rice Burroughs Inc., Tarzana, California, 1940. Hardcover.

59. John Carter of Mars. Published by the Whitman Publishing Company, Racine, Wisconsin, 1940. Hardcover.

60. Land of Terror. Published by Edgar Rice

Burroughs Inc., Tarzana, California, 1944. Hardcover.

61. Escape on Venus. Published by Edgar Rice Burroughs Inc., Tarzana, California, 1946. Hardcover.

62. Tarzan and the Foreign Legion. Published by Edgar Rice Burroughs Inc., Tarzana, California, 1947. Hardcover.

63. Llana of Gathol. Published by Edgar Rice Burroughs Inc., Tarzana, California, 1948. Hardcover.

64. Beyond Thirty. Published without authorization by Lloyd A. Eshbach, 1955. Softcover. Limited to 300 copies.

65. The Man-Eater. Published without authorization by Lloyd A. Eshbach, 1955. Softcover. Limited to 300 copies.

66. Beyond Thirty - and - The Man-Eater. Published by Science Fiction and Fantasy Publications, South Ozone Park, New York, 1957. Hardcover. This collects: The Man-Eater, 1915; and Beyond 30, 1916.

67. The Girl from Farris's. Published by The Wilma Company, Tacoma, Washington, 1959. Limited to 250 copies, 150 hardcover, 20 black leatherette, and 80 softcover.

68. The Moon Maid. Published by Published by Ace Books, New York City, 1962. Ace Book F-157=7. Softcover. Slightly different than the hardcover edition.

69. The Moon Men. Published by Published by Ace Books, New York City, 1962. Ace Book F-159. Softcover. Includes The Argosy version of The Moon Men, 1925; and The Red Hawk, also from Argosy in 1925.

70. The Moon Men. Published by Canaveral Press, New York City, 1962. Re-titled version of The Moon Maid, 1926.

71. Three Martian Novels. Published by Dover Publications, New York City, 1962. Softcover. This collects: Thuvia, Maid of Mars, 1916; The Chessmen of Mars, 1922; and The Mastermind of Mars, 1928.

72. Three Science Fiction Novels: At the Earth's Core, Pellucidar and Tanar of Pellucidar. Published by Dover Publications, New York City, 1963. Softcover. Collects the three titles listed: At the Earth's Core, 1922; Pellucidar, 1923; and Tanar of Pellucidar, 1930.

73. The Pirates of Venus - and - Lost on Venus. Published by Dover Publications, New York City, 1963. Softcover. From 1934 and 1935.

74. Savage Pellucidar. Published by Canaveral Press, New York City, 1963. Hardcover. This collection contains: Savage Pellucidar, 1963; Men of the Bronze Age, 1942; Tiger Girl, 1943; and The Return to Pellucidar, 1942.

75. The Land That Time Forgot. Published by Published by Ace Books, New York City, 1963. Ace Book F-213. Softcover. Part One of the original version.

76. The People That Time Forgot. Published by Published by Ace Books, New York City, 1963. Ace Book F-220. Softcover. The second part of The Land That Time Forgot.

77. The Land of Hidden Men. Published by Ace Books, New York City, 1963. Ace Book F-232. Softcover. Re-titled re-issue of Jungle Girl, 1932.

78. Out of Time's Abyss. Published by Published by Ace Books, New York City, 1963. Ace Book F-233. Softcover. The third part of The Land That Time Forgot.

79. The Eternal Savage. Published by Ace Books, New York City, 1963. Ace Book F-234. Softcover. Re-titled re-issue of The Eternal Lover, 1925.

80. The Lost Continent. Published by Ace Books, New York City, 1963. Ace Book F-235. Softcover. Re-titled version of Beyond Thirty, 1916.

81. Tarzan and the Tarzan Twins. Published by Canaveral Press, New York City, 1963. Hardcover. This collects: Tarzan and the Tarzan Twins, 1936; and Tarzan and the Tarzan Twins with Jad-Bal-Ja the Golden Lion, 1936.

82. The Land That Time Forgot - and - The Moon Maid. Published by Dover Publications, New York City, 1963. Softcover. Herein: The Land That Time Forgot, 1918; The People That Time Forgot, 1918; Out of Time's Abyss, 1918; The Moon Maid, 1923; The Red Hawk, 1925; and The Moon Men, 1925.

83. A Princess of Mars - and - A Fighting Man of Mars. Published by Dover Publications, New York City, 1964. Softcover. From 1912 and 1931.

84. Tales of Three Planets. Published by Canaveral Press, New York City, 1964. Hardcover. Herein: Introduction by Richard A. Lupoff; The Resurrection of Jimber Jaw, 1937; Beyond the Farthest Star, 1942; Tangor Returns, 1964; and The Wizard of Venus, 1964.

85. Beyond the Farthest Star. Published by Ace Books, New York City, 1964. Ace Book F-282. Softcover. Herein: Introduction by **Donald A. Wollheim**; Beyond the Farthest Star, 1942; and Tangor Returns, 1964.

86. John Carter of Mars. Published by Canaveral Press, New York City, 1964. Hardcover. Revised and expanded edition.

87. Tarzan and the Madman. Published by Canaveral Press, New York City, 1965. Hardcover.

88. Tarzan and the Castaways. Published by Canaveral Press, New York City, 1965. Hardcover. Herein: Tarzan and the Jungle Murders, 1940; Tarzan and the Champion, 1940; and Tarzan and the Castaways, 1941.

89. The Efficiency Expert. Published by House of Greystoke, Kansas City, Missouri, 1966. Softcover.

90. I Am a Barbarian. Published by Edgar Rice Burroughs Inc., Tarzana, California, 1967. Hardcover.

Edgar Rice Burroughs

91. The Wizard of Venus. Published by Ace Books, New York City, 1970. Ace Book 90190. Softcover. Herein: Foreword by **Edgar Rice Burroughs**, 1941; The Wizard of Venus, 1964; About Pirate Blood - an essay by **Donald A. Wollheim**, 1970; and Pirate Blood, 1970.

92. A Princess of Mars. Published by Nelson Doubleday - The Science Fiction Book Club, Garden City, New York, 1970. Hardcover. Adds a foreword by **Edgar Rice Burroughs**.

93. The Gods of Mars - and - The Warlord of Mars. Published by Nelson Doubleday - The Science Fiction Book Club, Garden City, New York, 1971. Hardcover. From 1918 and 1913.

94. Thuvia, Maid of Mars - and - The Chessmen of Mars. Published by Nelson Doubleday - The Science Fiction Book Club, Garden City, New York, 1973. Hardcover. From 1916 and 1922.

95. The Master Mind of Mars - and - A Fighting Man of Mars. Published by Nelson Doubleday - The Science Fiction Book Club, Garden City, New York, 1974. Hardcover. From 1928 and 1931.

96. The Man-Eater. Published by Fantasy House, North Hollywood, California, 1974. Fantasy Reader 5. Softcover. Abridged.

97. The Mucker. Published by Ace Books, New York City, 1974. Ace Book 54460. Softcover. Part One of the original book.

98. The Oakdale Affair. Published by Ace Books, New York City, 1974. Ace Book 60563. Softcover.

99. The Return of the Mucker. Published by Ace Books, New York City, 1974. Ace Book 71815. Softcover. Part Two of the original book.

100. The Rider. Published by Ace Books, New York City, 1974. Ace Book 72280. Softcover.

101. Swords of Mars - and - Synthetic Men of Mars. Published by Nelson Doubleday - The Science Fiction Book Club, Garden City, New York, 1975. Hardcover. From 1936 and 1940.

102. Llana of Gathol - and - John Carter of Mars. Published by Nelson Doubleday - The Science Fiction Book Club, Garden City, New York, 1977. Hardcover. From 1948 and 1954.

103. The Burroughs Bestiary: An Encyclopedia of Monsters and Imaginary Beings Created by Edgar Rice Burroughs. By Eric Howley and David Day. Published by New English Library, London, 1978. Softcover.

104. Edgar Rice Burroughs: Science Fiction Classics. Published by Castle Books, New York City, 1982. Hardcover. Herein: Pellucidar, 1915; Thuvia, Maid of Mars, 1916; Tanar of Pellucidar, 1930; The Chessmen of Mars, 1922; and The Master Mind of Mars, 1928.

105. Tarzan of the Apes: Four Volumes in One. Published by Avenel Books, New York City, 1988. Hardcover. An omnibus, this gathers: Introduction by Stefan R. Dziemianowicz; Tarzan of the Apes, 1912; The Son of Tarzan, 1915; Tarzan at the Earth's Core, 1929; and Tarzan Triumphant, 1932.

106. Tarzan of the Apes: Three Complete Novels. Published by Gramercy Books, New York City, 1988. Hardcover. An omnibus, this gathers: Introduction by Stefan Dziemianowicz; Tarzan of the Apes, 1912; The Son of Tarzan, 1915; and Tarzan at the Earth's Core, 1929.

107. Tarzan: The Lost Adventure. With Joe R. Lansdale. Published by Dark Horse, Milwaukee, Oregon, 1995. Hardcover.

108. Tarzan of the Apes - with - The Return of Tarzan. Published by Book of the Month Club - Quality Paperback Book Club, New York City, 1995. From 1912 and 1913.

109. At the Earth's Core - and - A Princess of Mars. Published by The Easton Press, United States, 1996. Leatherbound. Herein: Introduction by L. Sprague de Camp; At the Earth's Core, 1922; and A Princess of Mars, 1912.

110. The Beasts of Tarzan - with - The Son of Tarzan. Published by Del Rey - Ballantine Books, New York City, 1996. Softcover. From 1914 and 1915.

111. Tarzan and the Jewels of Opar - with - Jungle Tales of Tarzan. Published by Del Rey - Ballantine Books, New York City, 1997. Softcover. From 1916 and 1919.

112. Tarzan the Untamed - with - Tarzan the Terrible. Published by Del Rey - Ballantine Books, New York City, 1997. Softcover. From 1919 and 1921.

113. Tarzan and the Golden Lion - with - Tarzan and the Ant Men. Published by Del Rey - Ballantine Books, New York City, 1997. Softcover. From 1922 and 1924.

114. Tarzan, Lord of the Jungle - with - Tarzan and the Lost Empire. Published by Del Rey - Ballantine Books, New York City, 1997. Softcover. From 1927 and 1928.

115. Tarzan at the Earth's Core - with - Tarzan the Invincible. Published by Del Rey - Ballantine Books, New York City, 1997. Softcover. From 1929 and 1931.

116. Tarzan and the City of Gold - with - Tarzan Triumphant. Published by Del Rey - Ballantine Books, New York City, 1997. Softcover. From 1932 and 1932.

117. Mindoka, 937th Earl of One Mile Series: An Historical Fairy Tale. Published by Dark Horse, Milwaukee, Oregon, 1998. Hardcover.

118. You Lucky Girl: A Love Story in Three Acts. Published by Donald M. Grant, Hampton Falls, New Hampshire, 1999. Hardcover.

119. Marcia on the Doorstep. Published by Donald M. Grant, Hampton Falls, New Hampshire, 1999. Hardcover.

120. Under the Moons of Mars. Published by Bison Books, United States, 2003. Softcover. Herein: Introduction by James P. Hogan; A Princess of Mars, 1912; The Gods of Mars, 1918; and The Warlord of Mars, 1913.

121. The Martian Tales Trilogy. Published by Barnes and Noble, New York City, 2004. Hardcover. Herein: Introduction by Aaron Parrett; A Princess of Mars, 1912; The Gods of Mars, 1918; and The Warlord of Mars, 1913.

122. Men of Mars. Published by the Science Fiction Book Club, Garden City, New York, 2006. Hardcover. An omnibus, this gathers: A Fighting Man of Mars, 1931; Swords of Mars, 1936; and Synthetic Men of Mars, 1940.

123. A Treasury of Edgar Rice Burroughs. Published by Wilder Publications, United States, 2007. Softcover. An omnibus edition, this gathers: At the Earth's Core, 1914; Pellucidar, 1915; The Outlaw of Torn, 1914; The Efficiency Expert, 1921; The Monster Men, 1929; The Oakdale Affair, 1937; The Land That Time Forgot, 1918; The People That Time Forgot, 1918; and The Lost Continent, 1963.

***

RELATED

1. A Golden Anniversary Bibliography of Edgar Rice Burroughs. By Henry Hardy Heins. Private printing, Albany, New York, 1962. Softcover. Limited to 148 copies.

2. The Literature of Burroughsiana. By John Harwood. Published by Camille Cazedessus, Baton Rouge, Louisiana, 1963. Softcover.

3. The Reader's Guide to Barsoom and Amtor. Edited by Richard A. Lupoff. Published by Richard Lupoff, New York City, 1963. Softcover, limited to 200 signed and numbered copies.

4. A Golden Anniversary Bibliography of Edgar Rice Burroughs. By Henry Hardy Heins. Published by Donald M. Grant, West Kingston, Rhode Island, 1965. Hardcover. Revised edition.

5. Edgar Rice Burroughs: Master of Adventure. By Richard A. Lupoff. Published by Canaveral Press, New York City, 1965. Hardcover.

6. The Big Swingers. By Robert W. Fenton. Published by Prentice Hall, New Jersey, 1967. Hardcover.

7. Edgar Rice Burroughs: Master of Adventure. By Richard A. Lupoff. Published by Ace Books, New York City, 1968. Ace Book N-6. Revised edition.

8. Burroughs Science Fiction. By Robert R. Kudlay and Joan Leiby. Published by State University College of Arts and Science, Genesco, New York, 1973. Softcover.

9. Edgar Rice Burroughs: The Man Who Created Tarzan. By Edwin Porges, Brigham Young University Press, Provo, Utah, 1975. Hardcover.

10. Barsoom: Edgar Rice Burroughs and the Martian Vision. By Richard A. Lupoff. Published by The Mirage Press, Baltimore, Maryland, 1976. Hardcover.

11. A Guide to Barsoom. By John Flint Roy. Published by Ballantine Books, New York City, 1976. Ballantine Book 24722. Softcover.

12. Edgar Rice Burroughs: 1875 - 1950. Edited by George McWhorter. Published by the Library Review, University of Louisville, 1980. Softcover.

13. Edgar Rice Burroughs. By Erling B. Holstsmark. Published by Twayne, Boston, 1986. Hardcover.

14. Burroughs Dictionary: An Alphabetical List of Proper Names, Words, Phrases and Concepts Contained in Burroughs. Edited by George McWhorter. Published by the University Press of America, Lanham, Maryland, 1987. Softcover.

15. Price and Reference Guide to Books Written by Edgar Rice Burroughs. By James A. Bergen. Published by The Golden Lion, Beaverton, Oregon, 1991. Softcover.

16. The Burroughs Cyclopedia: Characters, Places, Fauna, Flora, Technologies, Languages, Ideas and Terminologies Found in the Works of Edgar Rice Burroughs. By Clark A. Brady. Published by McFarland and Company, Jefferson, North Carolina, 1996. Hardcover.

17. Edgar Rice Burroughs: The Exhaustive Scholar's and Collector's Descriptive Bibliography of American Periodical, Hardcover, Paperback, and Reprint Editions. By Robert B. Zeuschner. Published by McFarland and Company, Jefferson, North Carolina, 1996. Hardcover.

18. Tarzan Forever: The Life of Edgar Rice Burroughs, Creator of Tarzan. By John Taliaferro. Published by Scribner's, New York City, 1999. Hardcover.

19. Edgar Rice Burroughs Bibliography: Artist and Humorist. By Edward Gilbert. Published by Burroughs Bibliophiles, United States, 1999. Softcover.

20. Collecting Edgar Rice Burroughs. By Glenn Erardi. Published by Schiffer Publishing, Atglen, Pennsylvania, 2000. Softcover.

21. Edgar Rice Burroughs: Creator of Tarzan. By William J. Boerst. Published by Morgan Reynolds, Greensboro, North Carolina, 2000. Hardcover.

22. The Tarzan Novels of Edgar Rice Burroughs: An Illustrated Reader's Guide. By David A. Ullery. Published by McFarland and Company, Jefferson, North Carolina, 2001. Softcover.

23. Them Was the Days!: Edgar Rice Burroughs and the History of the Michigan Military Academy. By Brian J. Bohnett. Published by Mad Kings Publishing, Holt, Michigan, 2001. Softcover.

24. Edgar Rice Burroughs and Tarzan: A Biography of the Author and His Creation.

Edgar Rice Burroughs

By Robert W. Fenton. Published by McFarland and Company, Jefferson, North Carolina, 2003. Hardcover.

25. Edgar Rice Burroughs Collectors Treasury: Tarzan Big Little Books. By Brian J. Bohnett. Published by Mad Kings Publishing, Holt, Michigan, 2003. Softcover.

26. Edgar Rice Burroughs and the Silent Screen. By Jerry L. Schneider. Published by Booksurge, United States, 2003. Softcover.

27. Brother Men: The Correspondence of Edgar Rice Burroughs and Herbert T. Weston. Edited by Matt Cohen. Published by Duke University Press, 2005. Hardcover.

28. Edgar Rice Burroughs' Fantastic Worlds. By James Van Hise. Published by James Van Hise, Yucca Valley, California, 2005. Softcover.

29. The Edgar Rice Burroughs Newsbeat Omnibus. By James Van Hise. Published by James Van Hise, Yucca Valley, California, 2005. Softcover.

30. Master of Adventure: The Worlds of Edgar Rice Burroughs. By Richard A. Lupoff; foreword by **Michael Moorcock**; preface by Henry Hardy Heins. Revised. Published by Bison Books, United States, 2005. Softcover.

31. Collected Works of Edgar Rice Burroughs. Published by BiblioLife, United States, 2008. Softcover.

32. Edgar Rice Burroughs Tells All. By Jerry L. Schneider. Self-published at Lulu.com, 2008. Softcover.

33. The Ancestry of Edgar Rice Burroughs. By Jerry L. Schneider. Self-published at Lulu.com, 2008. Softcover.

34. Tarzan Collected, Mars Reflected: A Sales Catalogue of the Edgar Rice Burroughs Collection formed by the Late Hamilton M. Johnson of New Orleans. By Joseph Cohen. Published by Joseph Cohen, New Orleans, 2009. Softcover. Limited to 105 copies.

***

Damon Knight.

Damon Francis Knight was born in Baker City, Oregon on September 19th, 1922 and died on April 15th, 2002.

His first published story was Resilience. It was purchased by **Donald A. Wollheim** for Stirring Science Stories, February 1941, where it shared space with: Dead Center by C. M. Kornbluth writing as S. D. Gottesman; Lunar Gun by John L. Chapman; Golden Nemesis by David A. Kyle; Citadel of Thought by **James Blish**; Strange Return by **Donald A. Wollheim** writing as Lawrence Woods; Thirteen O'Clock by C. M. Kornbluth writing as Cecil Corwin; Bones by **Donald A. Wollheim**; Old Trinity Churchyard - 5 A.M. Spring - a poem by A. Merritt; The Key to Cornwall by David H. Keller; Out of the Jar by Charles R. Tanner; The Devotee of Evil by Clark Ashton Smith; The Abyss by Robert A. W. Lowndes; and Always Comes Evening - a poem by Robert E. Howard, 1941.

Quite a line-up to share with your first effort. Apparently, though, Wollheim made an editorial mistake that screwed up the story's ending which wasn't rectified until considerably later, when the story was reprinted.

His next story went to Robert A. W. Lowndes at Future Fantasy and Science Fiction for the October 1942 issue. It was called Devil's Pawn and was featured along with: The Extrapolated Dimwit by C. M. Kornbluth, Robert A. W. Lowndes and **Frederik Pohl** writing as S. D. Gottesman; The Powerful Ones by John B. Michel writing as Hugh Raymond; Planet Passage by **Donald A. Wollheim** writing as Martin Pearson; Storm Warning by **Donald A. Wollheim** writing as Millard Verne Gordon; Beauty by Wayne Woodard writing as Hannes Bok; The Inheritors by Robert A. W. Lowndes and John B. Michel; The Case of the Baby Dinosaur by Walter Kubilius writing as J. S. Klimaris; Wide-Open Ship by Richard Wilson; The Collector by Robert A. W. Lowndes writing as Mallory Kent; and When the Earth Shook by Walter Kubilius.

When Knight sold his first story, he was a member of The Futurians, along with **Donald A. Wollheim**, Robert A. W. Lowndes, **Frederik Pohl**, **James Blish**, and others, most of whom tended to support each others' writing endeavours.

Through the 1940s, Knight established himself as an SF critic, working at that for the better part of a decade while also writing a few short stories. He did more writing during the 1950s, and then moved on to work as an editor, starting with Chilton Books in the mid-sixties.

He remained an influential editor throughout most of his career, as well as a reasonably successful writer. It tended to be a balancing act. He once said that for a writer married with kids who isn't bringing in enough money, he "feels a terrific impulse to do something else to make money."

Far Out: Thirteen Science Fiction Stories is his consistently highest priced book on the secondary market, usually running around $150.00.

Pen Name: Stuart Fleming.

***

AWARDS

1956. Special Hugo Award as Best Book Reviewer.
1994. Nebula Grand Master Award.
2001. Retro Hugo Award for Best Short Story, 1951. The story was To Serve Man from Galaxy Science Fiction, November 1950.
2003. Inducted into The Science Fiction Hall of Fame.

***

FILM AND TELEVISION

1. The Invisible Saboteur. This was for an episode of Captain Video and His Video Rangers. It aired on January 4th, 1954 and starred: Al Hodge; Don Hastings; Ben Lackland; Hal Conklin; and others.

2. To Serve Man. Directed by Richard L. Bare, this 1950 story was adapted for The Twilight Zone. It aired on March 2nd, 1962, Season 3, Episode 24, starring: Lloyd Bochner; Susan Cummings; Richard Kiel; Hardie Albright; Theodore Marcuse; and, of course, **Rod Serling** as the narrator.

***

NOVELS AND COLLECTIONS

1. Hell's Pavement. Published by Lion Books, New York City, 1955. Lion Book LL 13. Softcover.

2. Masters of Evolution. Published by Ace Books, New York City, Ace Double D-375. Together with Fire in the Heavens by George O. Smith.

3. The People Maker. Published by Zenith Books, Rockville Center, New York, 1959. Zenith book ZB-14. Softcover.

4. A for Anything. Published by Four Square Books, London, 1961. Four Square book 382. Softcover. An enlarged version of The People maker, 1959.

5. Far Out. Published by Simon an Schuster, New York City, 1961. Hardcover. Herein: Introduction by Anthony Boucher; To Serve Man, 1950; Idiot Stick, 1958; Thing of Beauty, 1958; The Enemy, 1958; Not with a Bang, 1950; Babel II, 1953; Anachron, 1954; Special Delivery, 1954; You're Another, 1955; Time Enough, 1960; Extempore, 1956; Cabin Boy, 1951; and The Last Word, 1967.

6. The Sun Saboteurs. Published by Ace Books, New York City, 1961. Ace Double F-108. Softcover. Together with The Light of Lilith by G. McDonald Wallis.

7. Analogue Men. Published by Berkley Books, New York City, 1962. Berkley Book F647. Softcover. A re-titled version of Hell's Pavement, 1955.

Damon Knight

8. In Deep. Published by Berkley Books, New York City, 1963. Berkley Book F760. Softcover. This contains: Four in One, 1953; An Eye for a What?, 1957; The Handler, 1960; Stranger Station, 1956; Ask Me Anything, 1951; The Country of the Kind, 1956; Ticket to Anywhere, 1952; and Beachcomber, 1952.

9. Beyond the Barrier. Published by Doubleday & Company, Garden City, New York, 1964. Hardcover.

10. In Deep. Published by Victor Gollancz, London, 1964. First hardcover edition, this drops The Handler, 1960, and keeps: Four in One, 1953; An Eye for a What?, 1957; Stranger Station, 1956; Ask Me Anything, 1951; The Country of the Kind, 1956; Ticket to Anywhere, 1952; and Beachcomber, 1952.

11. Off Center. Published by Ace Books, New York City, 1965. Ace Double M-113. Softcover. Bound with The Rithian Terror by **Damon Knight**. Off Center contains: What Rough Beast, 1959; The Second-Class Citizen, 1963; God's Nose, 1964; and Catch That Martian, 1952.

12. The Rithian Terror. Published by Ace Books, New York City, 1965. Ace Double M-113. Softcover. Together with Off Center by **Damon Knight**.

13. Mind Switch. Published by Berkley Books, New York City, 1965. Berkley Book F1160. Softcover.

14. The Other Foot. Published by Ronald Whiting and Wheaton, London, 1966. Hardcover. Re-titled re-issue of Mind Switch, 1965.

15. Turning On. Published by Doubleday & Company, Garden City, New York, 1966. Hardcover. Herein: Don't Live in the Past, 1951; Backward, O Time, 1956; The Big Pat Boom, 1963; Eripmav, 1958; A Likely Story, 1956; Man in the Jar, 1957; Mary, 1964; Semper Fi, 1964; Auto-da-Fe, 1961; To the Pure, 1966; The Night of Lies, 1958; Maid to Measure, 1964; and Collector's Item, 1963.

16. Turning On. Published by Victor Gollancz, London, 1967. Hardcover. This adds The Handler, 1960, to the Doubleday edition, 1966.

17. Three Novels. Published by Doubleday & Company, Garden City, New York, 1967. Hardcover. Herein: Rule Golden, 1954; The Dying Man, 1957; and Natural State,1954.

18. Off Centre. Published by Victor Gollancz, London, 1969. First hardcover edition. Includes three more stories: Dulcie and Decorum; Masks; and To Be Continued.

19. World Without Children - and - The Earth Quarter. Published by Lancer Books, New York City, 1970. Lancer Book 74-601. Softcover. From 1951 and 1961.

20. Two Novels. Published by Victor Gollancz, London, 1974. Hardcover. This includes: The Earth Quarter - originally The Sun Saboteurs, 1961; and Double Meaning, 1953.

21. Natural State and Other Stories. Published by Pan Books, London, 1975. Softcover. Herein: Rule Golden, 1954; The Dying Man, 1957; and Natural State,1954. Re-titled re-issue of Three Novels, 1967.

22. The Best of Damon Knight. Published by Nelson Doubleday - The Science Fiction Book Club, Garden City, New York, 1976. Hardcover. Herein: Preface: Dark of the Knight by Barry N. Malzberg; Introduction by **Damon Knight**; Not with a Bang, 1950; To Serve Man, 1950; Cabin Boy, 1951; The Analogues, 1952; Babel II, 1953; Special Delivery, 1954; Thing of Beauty, 1958; Anachron, 1954; Extempore, 1956; Backward, O Time, 1956; The Last Word, 1957; Man in the Jar, 1957; The Enemy, 1958; Erpimav, 1958; A Likely Story, 1956; Time Enough, 1960; Mary, 1964; The Handler, 1960; The Big Pat Boom, 1963; Semper Fi, 1964; Masks, 1968; and Down There, 1973.

23. Rule Golden and Other Stories. Published by Avon Books, New York City, 1979. Softcover. This contains: Introduction by **Damon Knight**; Rule Golden, 1954; Natural State, 1954; Double Meaning, 1953; The Earth Quarter, 1970; and The Dying Man, 1957.

24. The World and Thorinn. Published by Berkley Putnam, New York City, 1980. Hardcover. This contains: The Garden of Ease, 1968; The Star Below, 1968; and The World and Thorinn, 1968.

25. Better Than One. With **Kate Wilhelm**. Published by NESFA Press for Noreascon II, Boston, 1980. Hardcover. Herein: Introductions by **Kate Wilhelm** and **Damon Knight**; Baby, You Were Great by **Kate Wilhelm**, 1965; and Semper Fi by **Damon Knight**, 1964; along with some poetry from each.

26. The Man in the Tree. Published by Berkley Books, New York City, 1984. Softcover.

27. The Man in the Tree. Published by Victor Gollancz, London, 1985. First hardcover edition.

28. CV. Published by Tor Books, New York City, 1985. Hardcover.

29. The Observers. Published by Tor Books, New York City, 1988. Hardcover.

30. A Reasonable World. Published by Tor Books, New York City, 1991. Hardcover.

31. One Side Laughing: Stories Unlike Other Stories. Published by St Martin's Press, New York City, 1991. Hardcover.

32. Rule Golden - and - Double Meaning. Published by Tor Books, New York City, 1991. Tor Double 34. Herein: Beauty, Stupidity, Injustice and Science Fiction - an introduction by **Damon Knight**; Rule Golden, 1954; and Double Meaning, 1953.

33. God's Nose - Author's Choice Monthly 21. Published by Pulphouse Publishing, Eugene, Oregon, 1991. Softcover. This contains: Introduction by **Damon Knight**; God's Nose, 1964; Catch That Martian, 1952; Four in One, 1953; You're Another, 1955; The Country of the Kind, 1956; and Shall the Dust Praise Thee?, 1967.

34. Faking the Reader Out - - Author's Choice Monthly 27. Published by Pulphouse Publishing,

Eugene, Oregon, 1991. Softcover.

35. Why Do Birds. Published by Tor Books, New York City, 1992. Hardcover.

36. Humpty Dumpty: An Oval. Published by Tor Books, New York City, 1997. Hardcover.

37. Late Knight Edition. Published by NESFA Press, Cambridge, Massachusetts, 1997. Hardcover. Herein: Introduction by **Kate Wilhelm**; What Is Science Fiction? - an essay, 1991; The Third Little Green Man, 1948; Definition, 1953; I See You, 1976; Tarcan of the Hoboes, 1982; La Ronde, 1983; The Cage, 1997; Good-Bye, Henry J. Kostkos, Good-Bye - an essay, 1997; and Who Is **Damon Knight**?, 1997.

***

ANTHOLOGIES

1. A Century of Science Fiction. Published by Simon and Schuster, New York City, 1962. Hardcover. This contains: Introduction by **Damon Knight**; Cease Fire by **Frank Herbert**, 1958; Sky Lift by **Robert A. Heinlein**, 1953; The Ideal - an excerpt by Stanley G. Weinbaum, 1935; The Wind People by Marion Zimmer Bradley, 1959; Unhuman Sacrifice by Katherine MacLean, 1958; What Was It? A Mystery by Fitz-James O'Brien, 1859; The First Days of May by Claude Veillot, 1961; Another World by J. H. Rosny Aine, 1895; Odd John - an excerpt by Olaf Stapledon, 1965; Twenty Thousand Leagues Under the Sea - an excerpt by **Jules Verne**, 1869; From the London Times of 1904 by Mark Twain, 1898; You Are With It by Will Stanton, 1961; The Crystal Egg by **H. G. Wells**, 1897; Call Me Joe by **Poul Anderson**, 1957; Angel's Egg by Edgar Pangborn, 1951; Day of Succession by Theodore L. Thomas, 1959; The Star by **Arthur C. Clarke**, 1955; What's It Like Out There? by Edmond Hamilton, 1952; The Business, as Usual by Mack Reynolds, 1952; Worlds of the Imperium - an excerpt by Keith Laumer, 1961; Sail On! Sail On! by Philip Jose Farmer, 1952; Of Time and Third Avenue by **Alfred Bester**, 1951; But Who Can Replace a Man by **Brian W. Aldiss**, 1958; Moxon's Master by Ambrose Bierce, 1909; and Reason by **Isaac Asimov**, 1941.

2. First Flight. Published by Lancer Books, New York City, 1963. Lancer Book 72-672. Softcover. Herein: Introduction by **Damon Knight**; That Only a Mother by Judith Merril, 1948; Loophole by **Arthur C. Clarke**, 1946; Life-Line by **Robert A. Heinlein**, 1939; Ether Breather by **Theodore Sturgeon**, 1939; Black Destroyer by **A. E. van Vogt**, 1939; Tomorrow's Children by **Poul Anderson** and F. N. Waldrop, 1947; The Isolinguals by L. Sprague de Camp, 1937; The Faithful by Lester del Rey, 1938; T by **Brian W. Aldiss**, 1956; and Walk to the World by Algis Budrys, 1952.

3. A Century of Great Short Science Fiction Novels. Published by Delacorte Press, New York City, 1964. Hardcover. Herein: Hunter, Come Home by Richard McKenna, 1963; E for Effort by T. L. Sherred, 1947; Gulf by **Robert A. Heinlein**, 1949; The Absolute at Large by Karel Capek, 1927; The Invisible Man by **H. G. Wells**, 1897; and Strange Case of Dr Jekyll and Mr Hyde by Robert Louis Stevenson, 1886.

4. Tomorrow X 4. Published by Fawcett Books, Greenwich, Connecticut, 1964. Gold Medal book D1428. Softcover. Herein: The Roads Must Roll by **Robert A. Heinlein**, 1940; The Night of Hoggy Darn by R. M. McKenna, 1958; The Sources of the Nile by Avram Davidson, 1961; and No Woman Born by **C. L. Moore**, 1944.

5. Beyond Tomorrow. Published by Harper and Row, New York City, 1965. Hardcover. This contains: Introduction by **Damon Knight**; Brightside Crossing by Alan E. Nourse, 1956; The Deep Range by **Arthur C. Clarke**, 1955; Coventry by **Robert A. Heinlein**, 1940; The Mile-Long Spaceship by **Kate Wilhelm**, 1957; The Seesaw by **A. E. van Vogt**, 1941; Nightfall by **Isaac Asimov**, 1941; The Million-Year Picnic by **Ray Bradbury**, 1946; Desertion by Clifford D. Simak, 1944; Twilight by **John W. Campbell** writing as Don A. Stuart, 1934; and Happy Ending by Henry Kuttner, 1948.

6. Thirteen French Science Fiction Stories. Published by Bantam Books, New York City, 1965. Bantam Book F2817. Softcover. This contains: Introduction by **Damon Knight**; Juliette by Claude F. Cheinisse, 1961; The Blind Pilot by Charles Henneberg, 1960; Moon Fishers by Charles Henneberg, 1962; The Non-Humans by Charles Henneberg, 1960; Olivia by Henri Damonti, 1965; The Notary and the Conspiracy by Henri Damonti, 1962; The Vana by Alain Doremieux, 1961; The Devil's Goddaughter by Suzanne Malaval, 1962; After Three Hundred Years by Pierre Mille, 1965; The Monster by Gerard Klein, 1965; A Little More Caviar? by Claude Veillot, 1965; The Chain of Love by Catherine Cliff, 1965; and The Dead Fish by Boris Vian, 1955.

7. The Dark Side. Published by Doubleday & Company, Garden City, New York, 1965. Hardcover. Herein: Introduction by **Damon Knight**; Nellthu by Anthony Boucher, 1955; Casey Agonistes by Richard McKenna, 1958; Eye for Iniquity by T. L. Sherred, 1953; C/O Mr. Makepeace by Peter Phillips, 1954; Mistake Inside by **James Blish**, 1948; They by **Robert A. Heinlein**, 1941; The Black Ferris by **Ray Bradbury**, 1948; Trouble With Water by H. L. Gold, 1939; The Golem by Avram Davidson, 1955; The Story of the Late Mr. Elvesham by **H. G. Wells**, 1896; It by **Theodore Sturgeon**, 1940; and The Man Who Never Grew Young by **Fritz Leiber**, 1947.

8. Cities of Wonder. Published by Doubleday & Company, Garden City, New York, 1965. Hardcover. Herein: Introduction by **Damon Knight**; Single Combat by Robert Abernathy, 1955; Dumb Waiter by Walter M. Miller, Jr, 1952; Billenium by J. G. Ballard, 1961; The Machine Stops by E. M. Forster, 1909; It's Great to Be Back! by **Robert A. Heinlein**, 1947; Jesting Pilot by Henry Kuttner and **C. L. Moore** writing as Lewis Padgett, 1947; Okie by **James Blish**, 1950; The Luckiest Man in Denv by C. M. Kornbluth, 1952; By the Waters of Babylon by Stephen Vincent Benet, 1937; The Under-Privileged by **Brian W. Aldiss**, 1963; and Forgetfulness by **John W. Campbell** writing as Don A. Stuart, 1937.

Damon Knight

9. The Shape of Things. Published by Popular Library, New York City, 1965. Popular Library Book SP352. Softcover. Herein: Introduction by **Damon Knight**; Don't Look Now by Henry Kuttner, 1948; The Box by **James Blish**, 1949; The New Reality by Charles L. Harness, 1950; The Eternal Now by Murray Leinster, 1944; The Sky Was Full of Ships by **Theodore Sturgeon**, 1947; The Only Thing We Learn by C. M. Kornbluth, 1949; The Hibited Man by L. Sprague de Camp, 1949; Dormant by **A. E. van Vogt**, 1948; The Ambassadors by Anthony Boucher, 1952; A Child is Crying by John D. MacDonald, 1948; and The Shape of Things by **Ray Bradbury**, 1948.

10. Nebula Award Stories 1965. Published by Doubleday & Company, Garden City, New York, 1966. Hardcover. Herein: Introduction by **Damon Knight**; The Doors of His Face the Lamps of His Mouth by Roger Zelazny, 1965; He Who Shapes by Roger Zelazny, 1965; Balanced Ecology by James H. Schmitz, 1965; Repent Harlequin Said the Ticktockman by Harlan Ellison, 1965; Computers Don't Argue by **Gordon R. Dickson**, 1965; Becalmed in Hell by Larry Niven, 1965; The Saliva Tree by **Brian W. Aldiss**, 1965; and The Drowned Giant by J. G. Ballard, 1964.

11. Orbit 1. Published by G. P. Putnam's Sons, New York City, 1966. Hardcover. All from the year of publication, this contains: Introduction by **Damon Knight**; Staras Flonderans by **Kate Wilhelm**; The Secret Place by Richard McKenna; How Beautiful with Banners by **James Blish**; The Disinherited by **Poul Anderson**; The Loolies are Here by Allison Rice; Kangaroo Court by Virginia Kidd; Splice of Life by Sonya Dorman; 5 Eggs by Thomas M. Disch; and The Deep by Keith Roberts.

12. Orbit 2. Published by G. P. Putnam's Sons, New York City, 1967. Hardcover. All from the year of publication, this contains: Introduction by **Damon Knight**; The Doctor by Ted Thomas; Baby, You Were Great! by **Kate Wilhelm**; Fiddler's Green by Richard McKenna; Trip Trap by **Gene Wolfe**; The Dimple in Draco by Philip Latham; I Gave Her Sack and Sherry, by Joanna Russ; The Adventuress by Joanna Russ; The Hole in the Corner by R. A. Lafferty; The Food Farm by Kit Reed; and Full Sun by **Brian W. Aldiss**.

13. Worlds to Come. Published by Harper and Row, New York City, 1967. Hardcover. Herein: Introduction by **Damon Knight**; The Sentinel by **Arthur C. Clarke**, 1941; Moonwalk by H. B. Fyfe, 1952; Mars Is Heaven by **Ray Bradbury**, 1948; The Edge of the Sea by Algis Budrys, 1958; The Martian Way by **Isaac Asimov**, 1952; The Big Contest by John D. MacDonald, 1950; Ordeal in Space by **Robert A. Heinlein**, 1948; That Share of Glory by C. M. Kornbluth, 1952; and Sunken Universe by **James Blish**, 1942.

14. Science Fiction Inventions. Published by Lancer Books, New York City, 1967. Lancer Book 73-691. Softcover. Herein: Introduction by **Damon Knight**; No, No, Not Rogov! by Cordwainer Smith, 1959; Hunting Machine by Carol Emshwiller, 1957; Employment by L. Sprague de Camp, 1939; Committee of the Whole by **Frank Herbert**, 1965; Private Eye by Henry Kuttner and **C. L. Moore** writing as Lewis Padgett, 1949; The Snowball Effect by Katherine MacLean, 1952; The Chromium Helmet by **Theodore Sturgeon**, 1946; Invariant by John R. Pierce, 1944; Dreaming Is a Private Thing by **Isaac Asimov**, 1955; and Rock Diver by **Harry Harrison**, 1951.

15. Orbit 3. Published by G. P. Putnam's Sons, New York City, 1968. Hardcover. All from the year of publication, this contains: Introduction by **Damon Knight**; Mother to the World by Richard Wilson; Bramble Bush by Richard McKenna; The Barbarian by Joanna Russ; The Changeling by **Gene Wolfe**; Why They Mobbed the White House by Doris Pitkin Buck; The Planners by **Kate Wilhelm**; Don't Wash the Carats by Philip Jose Farmer; Letter to a Young Poet by James Sallis; and Here is Thy Sting by John Jakes.

16. Orbit 4. Published by G. P. Putnam's Sons, New York City, 1968. Hardcover. All from the year of publication, this contains: Introduction by **Damon Knight**; Windsong by **Kate Wilhelm**; Probable Cause by Charles L. Harness; Shattered Like a Glass Goblin by Harlan Ellison; This Corruptible by Joan Matheson writing as Jacob Transue; Animal by Carol Emshwiller; One at a Time by R. A. Lafferty; Passengers by **Robert Silverberg**; Grimm's Story by Vernor Vinge; and A Few Last Words by James Sallis.

17. The Metal Smile. Published by Belmont Books, New York City, 1968. Belmont Book B60-082. Softcover. This contains: The New Father Christmas by **Brian W. Aldiss**, 1958; Answer by Fredric Brown, 1954; Fool's Mate by Robert Sheckley, 1953; Quixote and the Windmill by **Poul Anderson**, 1950; Two Handed Engine by Henry Kuttner and **C. L. Moore**, 1955; First to Serve by Algis Budrys; I Made You by Walter M. Miller, Jr, 1954; The Monkey Wrench by **Gordon R. Dickson**, 1951; Imposter by **Philip K. Dick**, 1953; Someday by **Isaac Asimov**, 1956; Short in the Chest by Margaret St Clair writing as Idris Seabright, 1954; and Nightmare Number Three - a poem by Stephen Vincent Benet, 1935.

18. Toward Infinity. Published by Simon and Schuster, New York City, 1968. Hardcover. This contains: Introduction by **Damon Knight**; The Man Who Lost the Sea by **Theodore Sturgeon**, 1959; March Hare Mission by Ford McCormack, 1951; The Earth Men by **Ray Bradbury**, 1948; Who Goes There (aka The Thing) by **John W. Campbell** writing as Don A. Stuart, 1938; In Hiding by Wilmar H. Shiras, 1948; Not Final by **Isaac Asimov**, 1941; And Be Merry by Katherine Maclean, 1950; The Witches of Karres by James H. Schmitz, 1949; and Resurrection by **A. E. van Vogt**, 1948.

19. One Hundred Years of Science Fiction. Published by Simon and Schuster, New York City, 1968. Hardcover. This contains: Introduction by **Damon Knight**; The Voices of Time by J. G. Ballard, 1960; Sanity by **Fritz Leiber**, 1944; The Nine Billion Names of God by **Arthur C. Clarke**, 1953; The Mindworm by C. M. Kornbluth, 1950; The Man Who Came Early by **Poul Anderson**, 1956; Black Charlie by **Gordon R. Dickson**, 1954; The Other Celia by **Theodore Sturgeon**, 1957; The Quest for Saint Aquin by Anthony Boucher, 1951; A Subway Named Mobius by A. J. Deutsch, 1950; The Shapes by J. H.

Rosny aine, 1968; The Man Who Could Work Miracles by **H. G. Wells**, 1898; The Other Now by Murray Leinster, 1951; The Equalizer by Norman Spinrad, 1964; New Apples in the Garden by Kris Neville, 1963; Business As Usual, During Alterations by Ralph Williams, 1958; Nobody Bothers Gus by Algis Budrys writing as Paul Javier, 1955; Whatever Happened to Corporal Cuckoo? By Gerald Kersh, 1955; Mr Murphy of New York by Thomas McMorrow, 1930; With the Night Mail by Rudyard Kipling, 1905; Splice of Life by Sonya Dorman, 1966; and The Ingenious Planet by Ambrose Bierce, 1891.

20. Orbit 5. Published by G. P. Putnam's Sons, New York City, 1969. Hardcover. All from the year of publication, this contains: Somerset Dreams by **Kate Wilhelm**; The Roads, the Roads, the Beautiful Roads by Avram Davidson; Look You Think You've Got Troubles by Carol Carr; Winter's King by **Ursula K. Le Guin**; The Time Machine by Langdon Jones; Configuration of the North Shore by R. A. Lafferty; Paul's Treehouse by **Gene Wolfe**; The Price by C. Davis Belcher; The Rose Bowl Pluto Hypothesis by Philip Latham; Winston by Kit Reed; The History Makers by James Sallis; and The Big Flash by Norman Spinrad.

21. Now Begins Tomorrow. Published by Lancer Books, New York City, 1969. Lancer Book 74-585. Softcover. Re-titled re-issue of First Flight, 1963.

22. Orbit 6. Published by G. P. Putnam's Sons, New York City, 1970. Hardcover. All from the year of publication, this contains: The Second Inquisition by Joanna Russ; Remembrance to Come by **Gene Wolfe**; How the Whip Came Back by **Gene Wolfe**; Goslin Day by Avram Davidson; Maybe Jean Baptiste Pierre Antoine de Monet Chevalier de Lamarck Was a Little Bit Right by Robin Scott; The Chosen by **Kate Wilhelm**; Entire and Perfect Chrysolite by R. A. Lafferty; Sunburst by Roderick Thorp; The Creation of Bennie Good by James Sallis; The End by **Ursula K. Le Guin**; A Cold Dark Night with Snow by **Kate Wilhelm**; Fame by Jean Cox; Debut by Carol Emshwiller; Where No Sun Shines by Gardner R. Dozois; and The Asian Shore by Thomas M. Disch.

23. Orbit 7. Published by G. P. Putnam's Sons, New York City, 1970. Hardcover. All from the year of publication, this contains: April Fool's Day Forever by **Kate Wilhelm**; Eyebem by **Gene Wolfe**; Continued on Next Rock by R. A. Lafferty; To Sport with Amaryllis by Richard Hill; In the Queue by Keith Laumer; The Living End by Sonya Dorman; A Dream at Noonday by Gardner R. Dozois; Woman Waiting by Carol Emshwiller; Jim and Mary G by James Sallis; Old Foot Forgot by R. A. Lafferty; The Island of Doctor Death and Other Stories by **Gene Wolfe**; and The Pressure of Time by Thomas M. Disch.

24. Orbit 8. Published by G. P. Putnam's Sons, New York City, 1970. Hardcover. All from the year of publication, this contains: Horse of Air by Gardner R. Dozois; One Life Furnished in Early Poverty by Harlan Ellison; Rite of Spring by Avram Davidson; The Bystander by Thom Lee Wharton; All Pieces of a River Shore by R. A. Lafferty; Sonya Crane Wessleman and Kittee by **Gene Wolfe**; Tablets of Stone by Liz Hufford; Starscape with Frieze of Dreams by Robert F. Young; The Book by Robert E. Margoff and Andrew J. Offutt; Inside by Carol Carr; Right Off the Map by Pip Winn; The Weather on the Sun by Ted Thomas; The Chinese Boxes by Graham Charnock; A Method Bit in B by **Gene Wolfe**; Interurban Queen by R. A. Lafferty; and The Encounter by **Kate Wilhelm**.

25. Dimension X. Published by Simon and Schuster, New York City, 1970. Hardcover. Herein: The Ugly Little Boy by **Isaac Asimov**, 1958; The Man Who Sold the Moon by **Robert A. Heinlein**, 1950; The Saliva Tree by **Brian W. Aldiss**, 1965; Fiddler's Green by Richard McKenna, 1967; and The Marching Morons by C. M. Kornbluth, 1951.

26. Orbit 9. Published by G. P. Putnam's Sons, New York City, 1971. Hardcover. All from the year of publication, this contains: Heads Africa Tails America by Josephine Saxton; What We Have Here is Too Much Communication by Leon E. Stover; Dominant Species by Kris Neville; The Toy Theater by **Gene Wolfe**; Stop Me Before I Tell More by Robert Thurston; Gleepsite by Joanna Russ; Binaries by James Sallis; Only the Words Are Different by James Sallis; Lost in the Marigolds by Lee Hoffman and Robert E. Toomey Jr.; Across the Bar by Kit Reed; The Science Fair by Vernor Binge; The Last Leaf by W. Macfarlane; When All the Lands Pour Out Again by R. A. Lafferty; and The Infinity Box by **Kate Wilhelm**.

27. First Contact. Published by Pinnacle Books, New York City, 1971. Pinnacle Book P062N. Softcover. Herein: Introduction by **Damon Knight**; Doomsday Deferred by Murray Leinster writing under his real name, Will F. Jenkins, 1949; The Hurkle is a Happy Beast by **Theodore Sturgeon**, 1949; Not Final by **Isaac Asimov**, 1941; The Blind Pilot by Charles Henneberg, 1960; The Silly Season by C. M. Kornbluth, 1950; Goldfish Bowl by **Robert A. Heinlein** writing as Anson MacDonald, 1942; In Value Deceived by H. B. Fyfe, 1950; The Waveries by Fredric Brown, 1945; In the Abyss by **H. G. Wells**, 1896; and First Contact by Murray Leinster, 1945.

28. A Pocketful of Stars. Published by Doubleday & Company, Garden City, New York, 1971. Hardcover. Herein: Introduction by **Damon Knight**; Windsong by **Kate Wilhelm**, 1968; The Intruder by Theodore L. Thomas, 1961; An Honorable Death by **Gordon R. Dickson**, 1961; The Burning by Theodore R Cogswell, 1960; Harry the Tailor by Sonya Dorman, 1961; Fifteen Miles by Ben Bova, 1967; I Have No Mouth, and I Must Scream by Harlan Ellison, 1967; The Winter Flies by **Fritz Leiber**, 1967; Sun by Burk K. Filer, 1971; The HORARS of War by **Gene Wolfe**, 1970; Hop-Friend by Terry Carr, 1962; A Few Last words by James Sallis, 1968; This Night, at My Fire by Joanna Russ, 1966; Look, You Think You've Got Troubles by Carol Carr, 1969; Unclear Call for Lee by Richard McKenna, 1971; The Last Command by Keith Laumer, 1967; Pelt by Carol Emshwiller, 1958; Masks by **Damon Knight**, 1968; and The Sources of the Nile by Avram Davidson, 1961.

29. Orbit 10. Published by G. P. Putnam's Sons, New York City, 1972. Hardcover. All from the year of publication, this contains: The Fifth Head of Cerberus by **Gene Wolfe**; Jody After the War by Edward Bryant; Al by Carol Emshwiller; Now I'm Watching Roger by Alexei Panshin; Whirl Cage by Jack M. Dann; A Kingdom by the Sea by Gardner

Damon Knight

R. Dozois; Christlings by Albert Teichner; Live From Berchtesgaden by George Alec Effinger; Dorg by R. A. Lafferty; Gantlet by Richard E. Peck; and The Fusion Bomb by **Kate Wilhelm**.

30. Orbit 11. Published by G. P. Putnam's Sons, New York City, 1972. Hardcover. All from the year of publication, this contains: On The Road to Honeyville by **Kate Wilhelm**; Alien Stones by **Gene Wolfe**; Spectra by Vonda N. McIntyre; I Remember a Winter by **Frederik Pohl**; Doucement, S'il Vous Plait by James Sallis; The Summer of the Irish Sea by Charles L. Grant; Good-Bye Shelley Shirley Charlotte Charlene by Robert Thurston; Father's in the Basement by Philip Jose Farmer; Down by the Old Maelstrom by Edward Wellen; Things Go Better by George Alec Effinger; Dissolve by Gary K. Wolf; Dune's Edge by Edward Bryant; The Drum Lollipop by Jack Dann; Machines of Loving Grace by Gardner R. Dozois; They Cope by Dave Skal; Counterpoint by Joe W. Haldeman; Old Soul by Steve Herbst; New York Times by Charles Platt; The Chrystallization of the Myth by John Barfoot; and To Plant a Seed by Hank Davis.

31. Perchance to Dream. Published by Doubleday & Company, Garden City, New York, 1972. Hardcover. Herein: Introduction by **Damon Knight**; The Circular Ruins by Jorge Luis Borges, 1962; A Friend to Alexander by James Thurber, 1942; The Secret Songs by **Fritz Leiber**, 1962; Under the Knife by **H. G. Wells**, 1896; Interpretation of a Dream by John Collier, 1951; Mr Arcularis by Conrad Aiken, 1922; Lord Mountdrago by W. Somerset Maugham, 1939; The Brushwood Boy by Rudyard Kipling, 1895; The Dream of a Ridiculous Man by Fyodor Dostoevsky, 1877; An Occurrence at Owl Creek Bridge by Ambrose Bierce, 1890; Dream's End by Henry Kuttner, 1947; and The End of the Party by Graham Greene, 1932.

32. A Science Fiction Argosy. Published by Simon and Schuster, New York City, 1972. Hardcover. Herein: Introduction by **Damon Knight**; Green Thoughts by John Collier, 1931; The Red Queen's Race by **Isaac Asimov**, 1949; The Cure by Henry Kuttner and **C. L. Moore** writing as Lewis Padgett, 1946; Consider Her Ways by John Wyndham, 1956; An Ornament to His Profession by Charles L. Harness, 1966; The Third Level by Jack Finney, 1950; One Ordinary Day, with Peanuts by Shirley Jackson, 1955; Bernie the Faust by William Tenn, 1963; Light of Other Days by Bob Shaw, 1966; The Game of Rat and Dragon by Cordwainer Smith, 1955; Becalmed in Hell by Larry Niven, 1965; Apology to Inky by Robert M. Green, 1966; The Demolished Man by **Alfred Bester**, 1952; Day Million by **Frederik Pohl**, 1966; Manna by Peter Phillips, 1949; Can You Feel Anything When I Do This? by Robert Sheckley, 1969; Somerset Dreams by **Kate Wilhelm**, 1969; He Walked Around the Horses by H. Beam Piper, 1948; Rump-Titty-Titty-Tum-TAH-Tee by **Fritz Leiber**, 1958; Sea Wrack by Edward Jesby, 1964; Man in His Time by **Brian W. Aldiss**, 1965; Four Brands of Impossible by Norman Kagan, 1964; Built Up Logically by Howard Schoenfeld, 1949; Judgment Day by L. Sprague de Camp, 1955; Journeys End by **Poul Anderson**, 1957; and More Than Human by **Theodore Sturgeon**, 1953.

33. The Golden Road. Published by Simon and Schuster, New York City, 1973. Hardcover. Herein: Introduction by **Damon Knight**; Are You Too Late or Was I Too Early? by John Collier, 1951; Entire and Perfect Chrysolite by R. A. Lafferty, 1970; Jenny with Wings by **Kate Wilhelm**, 1963; The Truth About Pyecraft by **H. G. Wells**, 1903; The Words of Guru by C. M. Kornbluth, 1941; Postpaid to Paradise by Robert Arthur, 1940; The White People by Arthur Machen, 1904; Extract from Captain Stormfield's Visit to Heaven - an excerpt by Mark Twain, 1908; Will You Wait? by **Alfred Bester**, 1959; The King of the Cats by Stephen Vincent Benet, 1929; The World of Unbinding by **Ursula K. Le Guin**, 1964; Magic, Inc by **Robert A. Heinlein**, 1940; Anything Box by Zenna Henderson, 1956; Artist Unknown by Heywood Broun, 1941; The Silence by Bernard McLaughlin, 1941; The Dream Quest of Unknown Kadath by H. P. Lovecraft, 1943; The Weeblies by Algis Budrys, 1953; Phantas by Oliver Onions, 1910; and Not Long Before the End by Larry Niven, 1969.

34. Tomorrow and Tomorrow. Published by Simon and Schuster, New York City, 1973. Hardcover. Herein: Foreword by **Damon Knight**; The Man Who Always Knew by Algis Budrys, 1956; Rogue Ship by **A. E. van Vogt**, 1950; A Sign in Space by Italo Calvino, 1968; The Liberation of Earth by William Tenn, 1953; The Sound Sweep by J. G. Ballard, 1959; And Now the News by **Theodore Sturgeon**, 1956; Hobson's Choice by **Alfred Bester**, 1952; Gomez by C. M. Kornbluth, 1954; The Portable Phonograph by Walter van Tilburg Clark, 1941; and Self Portrait by Bernard Wolfe, 1951.

35. Orbit 12. Published by G. P. Putnam's Sons, New York City, 1973. Hardcover. All from the year of publication, this contains: Shark by Edward Bryant; Direction of the Road by **Ursula K. Le Guin**; The Windows in Dante's Hell by Michael Bishop; Serpent Burning on an Altar by **Brian W. Aldiss**; Woman in Sunlight with Mandolin by **Brian W. Aldiss**; The Young Soldier's Horoscope by **Brian W. Aldiss**; Castle Scene with Penitents by **Brian W. Aldiss**; The Red Canary by **Kate Wilhelm**; What's the Matter with Herbie by Mel Gilden; Pinup by Edward Bryant; The Genius Freaks by Vonda N. McIntyre; Burger Creature by Steve Chapman; Half the Kingdom by Doris Piserchia; and Continuing Westward by **Gene Wolfe**.

36. Orbit 13. Published by Berkley Putnam, New York City, 1974. Hardcover. All from the year of publication, this contains: The Scream by **Kate Wilhelm**; Young Love by Grania Davis; And Name My Name by R. A. Lafferty; Going West by Edward Bryant; My Friend Zarathustra by James Sallis; Therapy by Gary K. Wolf; Gardening Notes From All Over by W. Macfarlane; Idio by Doris Piserchia; Fantasy's Profession by Albert Teichner; Spring Came to Blue Ridge Early This Year by Charles Arnold; Creation of a Future World in The Tracer by Steve Herbst; Coils by John Barfoot; and Time Bind by Sonya Dorman.

37. Orbit 14. Published by Harper and Row, New York City, 1974. Hardcover. All from the year of publication, this contains: They Say - an essay by **Damon Knight**; Tin Soldier by Joan D. Vinge; Reasonable People by Joanna Russ; Royal Licorice by R. A. Lafferty; The Stars Below by **Ursula K. Le Guin**; A Brother to Dragons a Companion to Owls by **Kate Wilhelm**; The Bridge Builder by Gary K. Wolf; The Winning of the Great American Greening Revolution by Murray Yaco; and Forlesen by **Gene Wolfe**; along with an assortment of book reviews.

38. Orbit 15. Published by Harper and Row, New York City, 1974. Hardcover. All from the year of publication, this contains: They Say - an essay by **Damon Knight**; Flaming Ducks and Giant Bread by R. A. Lafferty; Pale Hands by Doris Piserchia; Where Late the Sweet Birds Sang by **Kate Wilhelm**; Melting by **Gene Wolfe**; In the Lilliputian Asylum by Michael Bishop; Ernie by Lowell Kent Smith; Live? Out Computers Will Do That for Us by **Brian W. Aldiss**; Ace 167 by Eleanor Arnason; and Biting Down Hard on Truth by George Alec Effinger.

39. A Shocking Thing. Published by Pocket Books, New York City, 1974. Pocket Book 77775. Softcover. This anthology contains: Man from the South by Roald Dahl, 1948; The Snail Watcher by Patricia Highsmith, 1964; Bianca's Hands by **Theodore Sturgeon**, 1947; Poor Little Warrior by **Brian W. Aldiss**, 1958; The Hounds by **Kate Wilhelm**, 1974; The Clone by Theodore L. Thomas, 1959; The Touch of Nutmeg Makes It by John Collier, 1941; Casey Agonistes by Richard McKenna, 1958; The Abyss by Leonid Andreyev, 1943; A Case History by John Anthony West, 1973; Fondly Fahrenheit by **Alfred Bester**, 1954; The Year of the Jackpot by **Robert A. Heinlein**, 1952; Lukundoo by Edward Lucas White, 1925; The Cabbage Patch by Theodore R. Cogswell, 1952; Oil of Dog by Ambrose Bierce, 1890; The Time of the Big Sleep by Jean Pierre Andrevon, 1974; and The Right Man for the Right Job by J. C. Thompson, 1962.

40. Happy Endings. Published by Bobbs Merrill, New York City, 1974. Hardcover. Herein: Introduction by **Damon Knight**; Father's in the Basement by Philip Jose Farmer, 1972; The Idol of the Flies by Jane Rice, 1942; The Damnedest Thing by Garson Kanin, 1956; Winter by Kit Reed, 1969; De Mortuis by John Collier, 1942; The Way Up to Heaven by Roald Dahl, 1954; A Letter by Isaac Babel, 1929; Ashes to Ashes by Nunnally Johnson, 1934; The red-Headed Murderess by Robert Branson, 1958; Undertaker Song by Damon Runyon, 1934; Tobermory by H. H. Monroe writing as Saki, 1909; Miss Thompson by W. Somerset Maugham, 1921; The Greatest Man in the World by James Thurber, 1931; and The Purist - a poem by Ogden Nash, 1935.

41. Dimension X. Published by Coronet Books, London, 1974. Softcover. This dropped all but two of the stories from the original edition of Dimension X, 1970, keeping only: The Man Who Sold the Moon by **Robert A. Heinlein**, 1950; and The Marching Morons by C. M. Kornbluth, 1951.

42. Elsewhere X 3. Published by Coronet Books, London, 1974. Softcover. This prints the rest of the stories from Dimension X, 1970: Herein: The Ugly Little Boy by **Isaac Asimov**, 1958; The Saliva Tree by **Brian W. Aldiss**, 1965; and Fiddler's Green by Richard McKenna, 1967.

43. Orbit 16. Published by Harper and Row, New York City, 1975. Hardcover. All from the year of publication, this contains: They Say - an essay by **Damon Knight**; The Skinny People of Leptophlebo Street by R. A Lafferty; Euclid Alone by William F. Orr; The House by the Sea by Eleanor Arnason; Binary Justice by Richard Birely; Ambience by David J. Skal; In Donovan's Time by Charles L. Grant; Sandial by Moshe Feder; Heartland by Gustav Hasford; Prison of Clay, Prison of Steel by Henry-Luc Planchat; Jack and Betty by Robert Thurston; Phoenix House by Jesse Miller; A Brilliant Curiosity by Doris Piserchia; and Mother and Child by Joan D. Vinge.

44. Orbit 17. Published by Harper and Row, New York City, 1975. Hardcover. All from the year of publication, this contains: Introduction by **Damon Knight**; The Anthropologist by Kathleen M. Sidney; The Man with the Golden Reticulates by Felix C. Gotschalk; The Steel Sonnets by Jeff Duntemann; Toto I Have a Feeling We're Not in Kansas Anymore by Jeff Millar; Autopsy in Transit by Steve Chapman; House by John Barfoot; Fun Palace by Raylyn Moore; When We Were Good by Dave Skal; Which in the Wood Decays by Seth McEvoy; Great Day in the Morning by R. A. Lafferty; The Maze by Stuart Dybek; Quite Late One Spring Night by John M. Curlovich; and Under the Hollywood Sign by Tom Reamy.

45. Best Stories from Orbit, Volumes 1 - 10. Published by Berkley Putnam, New York City, 1975. Hardcover. Herein: The Secret Place by Richard McKenna, 1966; The Loolies Are Here by Allison Rice, 1966; The Doctor by Ted Thomas, 1967; Baby, You Were Great by **Kate Wilhelm**, 1967; The Hole on the Corner by R. A. Lafferty, 1967; I Gave Her Sack and Sherry by Joanna Russ, 1967; Mother to the World by Richard Wilson, 1968; Don't Wash the Carats by Philip Jose Farmer, 1968; The Planners by **Kate Wilhelm**, 1968; The Changeling by **Gene Wolfe**, 1968; Passengers by **Robert Silverberg**, 1968; Shattered Like a Glass Goblin by Harlan Ellison, 1968; The Time Machine by Langdon Jones, 1969; Look, You Think You've Got Troubles by Carol Carr, 1969; The Big Flash by Norman Spinrad, 1969; Jim and Mary G by James Sallis, 1970; The End by **Ursula K. Le Guin**, 1970; Continued on Next Rock by R. A. Lafferty, 1970; The Island of Doctor Death and Other Stories by **Gene Wolfe**, 1970; Horse of Air by Gardner R. Dozois, 1970; One Life, Furnished in Early Poverty by Harlan Ellison, 1970; Rite of Spring by Avram Davidson, 1970; The Bystander by Thom Lee Wharton, 1970; The Encounter by **Kate Wilhelm**, 1970; Gleepsite by Joanna Russ, 1971; Binaries by James Sallis, 1971; Al by Carol Emshwiller, 1972; and Live from Berchtesgaden by George Alec Effinger, 1972.

46. Science Fiction of the Thirties. Published by Bobbs Merrill, New York City, 1975. Hardcover. Herein: Foreword by **Damon Knight**; The Fifth-Dimension Catapult by Murray Leinster, 1931; The Battery of Hate by **John W. Campbell**, 1933; The Lost Language by David H. Keller, 1934; The Mad Moon by Stanley G. Weinbaum, 1935; Seeker of Tomorrow by **Eric Frank Russell** and Leslie T. Johnson, 1937; Pithecanthropus Rejectus by Manly Wade Wellman, 1938; The Day is Done by Lester

Damon Knight

del Rey, 1939; Out Around Rigel by Robert H. Wilson, 1931; Into the Meteorite Orbit by Frank K. Kelly, 1933; The Wall by Howard Wandrei writing as Howard W. Graham, 1934; The Other by Howard Wandrei writing as Howard W. Graham, 1934; The Last Men by Frank Belknap Long, 1934; Davey Jones' Ambassador by Raymond Z. Gallun, 1935; Alas All Thinking by Harry Bates; The Time Decelerator by A. Macfaydyen, 1936; The Council of Drones by W. K. Sonnemann, 1936; Hyperpelosity by L. Sprague de Camp, 1938; and The Merman by L. Sprague de Camp, 1938; along with some essays by **Damon Knight**: The End; The Middle Period; and The Early Years, all from 1975.

47. Orbit 18. Published by Harper and Row, New York City, 1976. Hardcover. All from the year of publication, this contains: Introduction by **Damon Knight**; Ladies and Gentlemen, This Is Your Crisis by **Kate Wilhelm**; The Hand with One Hundred Fingers by R. A. Lafferty; Meathouse Man by George R. R. Martin; Rules of Moopsball - an essay by Gary Cohn; Who Was the First Oscar to Win a Negro? by Craig Strete, 1976; In Pierson's Orchestra by Kim Stanley Robinson; Mary Margaret Road-Grader by Howard Waldrop; The Family winter of 1986 by Felix C. Gotschalk; The Teacher by Kathleen M. Sidney; Coming Back to Dixieland by Kim Stanley Robinson; A Modular Story by Raylyn Moore; The M & M Seen as a Low-Yield Thermonuclear Device by John Varley; and The Eye of the Last Apollo by Carter Scholz.

48. Orbit 19. Published by Harper and Row, New York City, 1977. Hardcover. All from the year of publication, this contains: Introduction by **Damon Knight**; Lollipop and the Tar Baby by John Varley; State of Grace by **Kate Wilhelm**; Many Mansions by **Gene Wolfe**; The Veil Over the River by Felix C. Gotschalk; Fall of Pebble Stones by R. A. Lafferty; Tomus by Stephen Robinett; Under Jupiter by Michael W. McClintock; To the Dark Tower Came by **Gene Wolfe**; Vamp by Michael Conner; Beings of Game P-U by Phillip Teich; Night Shift by Kevin O'Donnell; Going Down by Eleanor Aranson; and The Disguise by Kim Stanley Robinson.

49. Westerns of the 40s: Classics from the Great Pulps. Published by Bobbs Merrill, New York City, 1977. Hardcover. Herein: Gun Devil of Red God Desert by Tom Roan, 1943; Boss of Buckskin Empire by Cliff Farrell, 1943; Good-by Mimbres Kid by Frank Bonham, 1944; Bearhide's Moonshine War by Roy M. O'Mara, 1944; Teetotal and the Six-gun Spirits by Murray Leinster, 1947; Flatwheel Draws the Line by Tom W. Blackburn, 1944; The Line Camp Terror by Walt Coburn, 1943; Hell Trail Pilgrim by Murray Leinster, 1947; The Parson of Owlhoot Junction by Charles W. Tyler, 1943; Trail City's Hotlead Crusaders by Clifford D. Simak, 1944; Crazy Springs, Write-in Vote by Roy M. O'Mara, 1944; Col. Colt Buys a Border Herd by Bennett Foster, 1947; The Corpse Rides at Dawn by John D. MacDonald, 1948; The Long Arm of the Law by James Shaffer, 1946; By the Guns Forgot by Murray Leinster, 1947; and Deadman's Derringers by Tom W. Blackburn, 1947.

50. Orbit 20. Published by Harper and Row, New York City, 1978. Hardcover. All from the year of publication, this contains: Introduction by **Damon Knight**; Moongate by **Kate Wilhelm**; The Novella Race by Pamela Sargent; Bright Coins in a Never Ending Stream by R. A. Lafferty; The Synergy Sculpture by Terrence L. Brown; The Birds Are Free by Ronald Anthony Cross; A Right Handed Wrist by Steve Chapman; The Made Us Not To Be and They Are Not by Philippa C. Maddern; and Seven American Nights by **Gene Wolfe**.

51. Orbit 21. Published by Harper and Row, New York City, 1980. Hardcover. All from the year of publication, this contains: Introduction by **Damon Knight**; Love Death and Katie by Richard Kearns; The Greening by Eileen Roy; Abominable by Carol Emshwiller; Underwood and the Slaughterhouse by Raymond G. Embrak; Hope by Lelia Rose Foreman; The Mother of the Beast by Gordon Eklund; Robert Fraser: The Xenologist as Hero by Sydelle Shamah; Persephone by Rhondi Vilott; The Smell of the Noose the Foar of the Blood by John Barfoot; And the TV Changed Colors When She Spoke by Lyn Schumaker; The Only Tune that He Could Play by R. A. Lafferty; Survivors by Rita-Elizabeth Harper; and On the North Pole of Pluto by Kim Stanley Robinson.

52. First Voyages. With Martin H. Greenberg and Joseph D. Olander. Published by Avon Books, New York City, 1981. Softcover. Herein: Come On, Wagon by Zenna Henderson, 1951; Beyond Lies the Wub by **Philip K. Dick**, 1952; Prima Belladonna by J. G. Ballard, 1956; April in Paris by **Ursula K. Le Guin**, 1962; Life-Line by **Robert A. Heinlein**, 1939; That Only A Mother by Judith Merril, 1948; Defense Mechanism by Katherine MacLean, 1949; The Isolinguals by L. Sprague de Camp, 1937; The Faithful by Lester del Rey, 1938; Black Destroyer by **A. E. van Vogt**, 1939; Ether Breather by **Theodore Sturgeon**, 1939; Proof by Hal Clement, 1942; Loophole by **Arthur C. Clarke**, 1946; Tomorrow's Children by **Poul Anderson** and F. N. Waldrop, 1947; Scanners Live in Vain by Cordwainer Smith, 1950; Time Trap by Charles L. Harness, 1948; Angel's Egg by Edgar Pangborn, 1951; Walk to the World by Algis Budrys, 1952; My Boy Friend's Name is Jello by Avram Davidson, 1952; and T by **Brian W. Aldiss**, 1956.

53. The Clarion Awards. Published by Doubleday & Company, Garden City, New York, 1984. Hardcover. All from 1984, this anthology contains: Introduction by **Damon Knight**; The Etheric Transmitter (First Prize) by Lucius Shepard; Beast and Beauty by Kristi Olesen; Lost Lives by Nina Kiriki Hoffman; Flawless Execution by Dean Wesley Smith; Geometry by Jan Herschel; One Last Hunting Pack by Patricia Linehan; The Coming of the Goonga (Second Prize) by Gary W. Shockley; Fugue by William Knuttel; Up Above the World So High by Mario Milosevic; Snows of Yesteryear by Barbara Rausch; The Cottage in Winter by McNevin Hayes; Loaded Dice by Rena Leith; Vines by Lois Wickstrom; and Pursuit of Excellence (Third Prize) by Rena Yount.

***

NON-FICTION

1. In Search of Wonder. Published by Advent Publishers, New York City, 1956. Hardcover.

2. Turning Points: Essays on the Art of Science Fiction. Published by Harper and Row, New York City, 1977. Hardcover. Science Fiction: Its Nature Faults and Virtues by **Robert A. Heinlein**, 1959; Social Science Fiction by **Isaac Asimov**, 1953; What Is Science Fiction by **Damon Knight**, 1977; Pilgrim Fathers: Lucien and All That by **Brian W. Aldiss**, 1973; Science Fiction Before Gernsback by H. Bruce Franklin; The Situation Today by Kingsley Amis, 1960; On Science Fiction by C. S. Lewis, 1955; Alien Monsters by Joanna Russ, 1968; Cathedrals in Space by **James Blish** writing as William Atheling, 1964; Contact by Pierre Versins, 1972; No Copying Allowed by **John W. Campbell**, 1948; Scientists in SF: A Debate with: Milton A. Rothman, **John W. Campbell**, James V. McConnell, and Philip R. Geffe, 1966; On the Writing of Speculative Fiction by **Robert A. Heinlein**, 1947; How to Build a Planet by **Poul Anderson**, 1966; How to Collaborate Without Getting Your Head Shaved by Keith Laumer, 1967; Writing and Selling Science Fiction by **Damon Knight**, 1977; Chemical Persuasion by Aldous Huxley, 1958; Pandora's Box by **Robert A. Heinlein**, 1966; Gourmet Dining in Outer Space by **Alfred Bester**, 1960; Why So Much Syzygy by **Theodore Sturgeon**, 1953; There's Nothing Like a Good Foundation by **Isaac Asimov**, 1967; Son of Dr Strangelove by **Arthur C. Clarke**, 1972; and Journey with a Little Man by Richard McKenna, 1967.

3. The Futurians. Published by John Day, New York City, 1977. Hardcover.

4. Creating Short Fiction. Published by Writer's Digest Books, Cincinnati, Ohio, 1981. Hardcover.

5. Monad: Essays on Science Fiction 1. Published by Pulphouse Publishing, Eugene, Oregon, 1990. Hardcover.

6. Monad: Essays on Science Fiction 2. Published by Pulphouse Publishing, Eugene, Oregon, 1992. Softcover.

***

RELATED

1. The Magazine of Fantasy and Science Fiction - Volume 51, number 5 - November 1976. Published by Mercury Press, Cornwall, Connecticut, 1976. Softcover. The special **Damon Knight** issue. Herein: I See You by **Damon Knight**; **Damon Knight**: Bibliography by Vincent Miranda; **Damon Knight**: An Appreciation by **Theodore Sturgeon**; and **Damon Knight**: Word-wise Puzzle by John Grabowski; along with the usual features and stories.

2. The SFWA Grand Masters: Volume 3: Lester del Rey, Frederik Pohl, Damon Knight, A. E. van Vogt and Jack Vance. Published by Tor Books - Tom Doherty Associates, New York City, 2001. Hardcover.

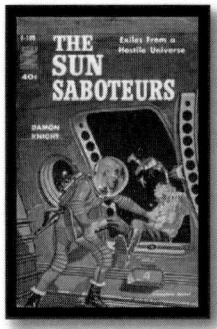

Wilson Tucker.

Arthur Wilson 'Bob' Tucker was born on November 23rd, 1914 and died on October 6th, 2006 in a hospital in St Petersburg, Florida. He lived a sort segmented life, writing for fanzines as Bob Tucker, writing professionally as **Wilson Tucker**, and all the while, again as Bob Tucker, working a job as a full-time movie projectionist - he kept that job from 1933 until 1972.

He started writing as a fan in 1932. And his first professional sale came in 1941. The story was Interstellar Way-Station, bought by **Frederik Pohl** for the May 1941 issue of Super Science Novels. The story accompanied: Best Friend by **Frederik Pohl** and C. M. Kornbluth writing as S. D. Gottesman; The Rannie by Willard Hawkins; The Brothers by Michael D. Shea; Smugglers of the Moon by P. Schuyler Miller; and Mission Unknown! by Henry Hasse.

Next came Gentlemen - The Queen! to Robert A. W. Lowndes for Science Fiction Quarterly, Fall 1942. Under the name Bob Tucker, it was printed along with: The Hidden Conflict by **Donald A. Wollheim** writing as Martin Pearson; The Half-Man by Basil Wells; Glory Road by John B. Michel writing as Hugh Raymond; and Highway by Robert A. W. Lowndes writing as Wilfred Owen Morley.

By 1952, he settled on Wilson for his professional work and Bob for the rest of his life.

The Year of the Quiet Sun, published by Robert Hale in London, 1971, as the first hardcover edition of this title, tends to be his highest priced collectible book, going for around $850.00.

***

AWARDS

1970. Hugo Award for Best Fan Writer.
1976. The John W. Campbell Memorial Award for The Year of the Quiet Sun.
1995. Nebula Award for Special Author Emeritus.

***

NOVELS AND COLLECTIONS

1. The Chinese Doll. Published by Rinehart & Company, New York City, 1946. Hardcover.

2. To Keep or Kill. Published by Rinehart & Company, New York City, 1947. Hardcover.

3. Prison Planet - Space Trails: Summer 1947. Published by Pegasus Publications, Buffalo, New York, 1947. Softcover.

4. The Dove. Published by Rinehart & Company, New York City, 1948. Hardcover.

5. The Stalking Man. Published by Rinehart & Company, New York City, 1949. Hardcover.

6. The City in the Sea. Published by Rinehart & Company, New York City, 1951. Hardcover.

7. Red Herring. Published by Rinehart & Company, New York City, 1951. Hardcover.

8. The Long Loud Silence. Published by Rinehart & Company, New York City, 1952. Hardcover.

9. The Time Masters. Published by Rinehart & Company, New York City, 1953. Hardcover.

10. The Time Masters - and - Wild Talent. Published by Stuart Hoffman, United States, 1953. Hardcover.

11. Wild Talent. Published by Rinehart & Company, New York City, 1954. Hardcover.

12. The Science Fiction Subtreasury. Published by Rinehart & Company, New York City, 1954. Hardcover. Herein: Introduction by **Wilson Tucker**; Exit, 1943; The Street Walker, 1954; Home Is Where the Wreck Is, 1954; My Brother's Wife, 1951; The Job Is Ended, 1950; The Wayfaring Strangers, 1952; Able to Zebra, 1953; The Mountaineer, 1953; and Gentlemen - The Queen!, 1942.

13. Man from Tomorrow. Published by Bantam Books, New York City, 1955. Bantam Book 1343. Softcover. Re-titled re-issue of Wild Talent, 1954.

14. Time: X. Published by Bantam Books, New York City, 1955. Bantam Book 1400. Softcover. Re-titled re-issue of The Science Fiction Subtreasury, 1954.

15. Time Bomb. Published by Rinehart & Company, New York City, 1955. Hardcover.

16. The Man in My Grave. Published by Rinehart & Company, New York City, 1956. Hardcover.

17. The Hired Target. Published by Ace Books, New York City, 1957. Ace Double D-241. Softcover. Bound with One Deadly Dawn by Harry Whittington.

18. Tomorrow Plus X. Published by Avon Books, New York City, 1957. Avon Book T168. Softcover. Re-titled re-issue of Time Bomb, 1955.

19. The Lincoln Hunters. Published by Rinehart & Company, New York City, 1958. Hardcover.

20. To the Tombaugh Station. Published by Ace Books, New York City, 1960. Ace Double D-479. Softcover. Bound with Earthman, Go Home! by **Poul Anderson**.

21. Last Stop. Published by Doubleday & Company, Garden City, New York, 1963. Hardcover.

22. A Procession of the Damned. Published by Doubleday & Company, Garden City, New York, 1965. Hardcover.

23. The Warlock. Published by Doubleday & Company, Garden City, New York, 1967. Hardcover.

24. The Long Loud Silence. Published by Lancer Books, New York City, 1970. Lancer Book 74-600. Softcover. Revised edition.

25. The Year of the Quiet Sun. Published by Ace Books, New York City, 1970. Ace Science Fiction Special 94200. Softcover.

26. This Witch. Published by Doubleday & Company, Garden City, New York, 1971. Hardcover.

27. The Year of the Quiet Sun. Published by Robert Hale & Company, London, 1971. First hardcover edition.

28. Ice and Iron. Published by Doubleday & Company, Garden City, New York, 1974. Hardcover.

29. Ice and Iron. Published by Ballantine Books, New York City, 1975. Ballantine Book 24660. Softcover. Revised edition.

30. Resurrection Days. Published by Timescape - Pocket Books, New York City, 1981. Softcover.

31. The Best of Wilson Tucker. Published by Timescape - Pocket Books, New York City, 1982. Softcover. Herein: To the Tombaugh Station, 1960; To a Ripe Old Age, 1952; King of the Planet, 1959; Exit, 1943; The Tourist Trade, 1951; My Brother's Wife, 1951; The Job Is Ended, 1950; Able to Zebra, 1953; and Time Exposures, 1971.

***

RELATED

1. Wilson 'Bob' Tucker: Wild Talent: A Working Bibliography. By Phil Stephensen-Payne and Gordon Benson, Jr. Published by Galactic Central Publications, Leeds, 1994. Softcover.

Kate Wilhelm

Kate Wilhelm.

Kate Wilhelm was born in Toledo, Ohio on June 8th, 1928. With her husband, **Damon Knight**, she taught at the Clarion SF and Fantasy Writers' Workshop.

Her first professional sale was The Pint-Size Genie to Paul W. Fairman at Fantastic for the October 1956 issue where it appeared with: The Passionate Pitchman by Milton Lesser writing as Stephen Wilder; The Man Who Knew Everything by Randall Garrett; An Eye for the Ladies by Milton Lesser writing as Darius John Granger; Peter Merton's Private Mint by Harlan Ellison writing as Lee Archer; and The Girl from Bodies, Inc by **Robert Silverberg** and Randall Garrett writing as Leonard G. Spencer.

The next was The Mile-Long Spaceship to **John W. Campbell** for the April 1957 issue of Astounding Science Fiction. She shared the pages with: Call Me Joe by **Poul Anderson**; Torch by Christopher Anvil; Chain Reaction by Algis Budrys writing as John A. Sentry; The Unblind Workings of Chance - an essay by **Isaac Asimov**; The Lost Vegan by E. J. McKenzie; and The Dawning Light - part two of three of a serial by **Robert Silverberg** and Randall Garrett writing as Robert Randall.

She once said she didn't like any of her public work. She could always see where it went wrong, where it failed to accomplish what she had hoped. "I think they've all failed in one way or another, " she said, "and I don't like any of them."

Her highest priced book for collectors tends to be Where Late the Sweet Birds Sang, published by Harper and Row in 1976. This usually goes for around $450.00

***

AWARDS

1968. Nebula Best Short Story Award for The Planners from Orbit 3 as edited by Damon Knight, 1968.
1975. Locus Poll Best Novella Award for Where Late the Sweet Birds Sang - Orbit 15.
1977. Hugo Best Novel Award for Where Late the Sweet Birds Sang.
1977. Locus Poll Best Novel Award for Where Late the Sweet Birds Sang.
1981. Prix Apollo for Juniper Time.
1986. Nebula Best Novelette Award for The Girl Who Fell into the Sky - Isaac Asimov's Science Fiction Magazine, October 1986.
1988. Nebula Best Short Story Award for Forever Yours, Anna - Omni, July 1987.
1995. A James Tiptree, Jr Classics Award for The Clewiston Test, 1976.
2003. Induction into The Science Fiction Hall of Fame.

***

FILM AND TELEVISION

1. Andover and the Android. This 1963 short story was adapted for Out of the Unknown, airing on November 29th, 1965, Season 1, Episode 9. Directed by Alan Cooke, it starred: Tom Criddle; Annette Robertson; Peter Bathurst; and others.

2. The Lookalike. This 1988 story was adapted for television, being shown on December 12th, 1990. It was directed by Gary Nelson and starred: Melissa Gilbert; Diane Ladd; Frances Lee McCain; and Jason Scott Lee; along with many others.

3. Naming the Flowers. From the 1992 story, this was filmed for release in 2010.

***

NOVELS AND COLLECTIONS

1. More Bitter Than Death. Published by Simon and Schuster, New York City, 1963.

2. The Mile-Long Spaceship. Published by Berkley Books, New York City, 1963. Berkley Book F862. Softcover. Herein: The Mile-Long Spaceship, 1957; Fear Is a Cold Black, 1963; Jenny with Wings, 1963; A Is for Automation, 1959; Gift from the Stars, 1958; No Light in the Window, 1963; One for the Road, 1959; Andover and the Android, 1963; The Man Without a Planet, 1962; The Apostolic Travelers, 1963; and The Last Days of the Captain, 1962.

3. Andover and the Android. Published by Dennis Dobson, London, 1966. First hardcover edition. A re-titled re-issue of The Mile-Long Spaceship, 1963.

4. The Clone. With Theodore L. Thomas. Published by Berkley Books, New York City, 1965. Berkley Book F1169. Softcover.

5. The Nevermore Affair. Published by Doubleday & Company, Garden City, New York, 1966. Hardcover.

6. The Killer Thing. Published by Doubleday & Company, Garden City, New York, 1967. Hardcover.

7. The Killing Thing. Published by Herbert Jenkins, London, 1967. Hardcover. Slightly different title and some revisions.

8. The Clone. With Theodore L. Thomas. Published by Robert Hale, London, 1968. First hardcover edition.

9. The Downstairs Room and Other Speculative Fiction. Published by Doubleday & Company, Garden City, New York, 1968. Hardcover. Herein: Introduction by **Kate Wilhelm**; Unbirthday Party, 1968; Baby, You Were Great!, 1967; When the Moon Was Red, 1960; Sirloin and White Wine, 1968; Perchance to Dream, 1968; How Many Miles to Babylon?, 1968; The Downstairs Room, 1968; Countdown, 1968; The Plausible Improbable, 1968; The Feel of Desperation, 1964; A Time to Keep, 1962; The Most Beautiful Woman in the World, 1968; The Planners, 1968; and Windsong, 1968.

10. Let the Fire Fall. Published by Doubleday & Company, Garden City, New York, 1969. Hardcover.

11. Year of the Cloud. Writing with Theodore L. Thomas. Published by Doubleday & Company, Garden City, New York, 1970. Hardcover.

12. Abyss. Published by Doubleday & Company, Garden City, New York, 1971. Hardcover. Herein: The Plastic Abyss, 1971; and Stranger in the House, 1968.

13. Margaret and I. Published by Little Brown, Boston, 1971. Hardcover.

14. Let the Fire Fall. Published by Panther Books, London, 1972. Softcover. Revised edition.

15. City of Cain. Published by Little Brown, Boston, 1974. Hardcover.

16. The Infinity Box. Published by Harper and Row, New York City, 1975. Hardcover. Herein: The Time Piece, 1975; The Red Canary, 1973; Man of Letters, 1975; April Fools' Day Forever, 1970; Where Have You Been, Billy Boy, Billy Boy, 1971; The Fusion Bomb, 1972; The Village, 1973; The Funeral, 1972; and The Infinity Box, 1971.

17. The Clewiston Test. Published by Farrar Straus Giroux, New York City, 1976. Hardcover.

18. Fault Lines. Published by Harper and Row, New York City, 1977. Hardcover.

19. Where Late the Sweet Birds Sang. Published by Harper and Row, New York City, 1977. Hardcover.

20. Somerset Dreams and Other Fictions. Published by Harper and Row, New York City, 1978. Hardcover. Herein: Introduction by R. Glenn Wright; The Encounter, 1970; Planet Story, 1975; Mrs Bagley Goes to Mars, 1978; Symbiosis, 1972; Ladies and Gentlemen, This is Your Crisis, 1976; The Hounds, 1974; State of Grace, 1977; and Somerset Dreams, 1969.

21. Juniper Time. Published by Harper and Row, New York City, 1979. Hardcover.

22. Better Than One. With **Damon Knight**. Published by NESFA Press for Noreascon II, Boston, 1980. Hardcover. Herein: Introductions by **Kate Wilhelm** and **Damon Knight**; Baby, You Were Great by **Kate Wilhelm**, 1965; and Semper Fi by **Damon Knight**, 1964; along with some poetry from each.

23. A Sense of Shadow. Published by Houghton Mifflin, Boston, 1981. Hardcover.

24. Listen, Listen. Published by Houghton Mifflin, Boston, 1981. Hardcover. Herein: The Winter Beach, 1981; Julian, 1978; With Thimbles, with Forks, and Hope, 1981; Moongate, 1978; and The Uncertain Edge of Reality - an essay, 1980.

25. Oh, Susannah!. Published by Houghton Mifflin, Boston, 1982. Hardcover.

26. Welcome, Chaos. Published by Houghton Mifflin, Boston, 1983. Hardcover.

27. Huysman's Pets. Published by Bluejay Books, New York City, 1986. Hardcover.

28. The Hamlet Trap. Published by St Martin's Press, New York City, 1987. Hardcover.

29. The Dark Door. Published by St Martin's Press, New York City, 1988. Hardcover.

30. Crazy Time. Published by St Martin's Press, New York City, 1988. Hardcover.

31. Smart House. Published by St Martin's Press, New York City, 1989. Hardcover.

32. Children of the Wind. Published by St Martin's Press, New York City, 1989. Hardcover. Herein: The Gorgon Field, 1985; A Brother to Dragons, a Companion to Owls, 1974; The Blue Ladies, 1983; The Girl Who Fell into the Sky, 1986; and Children of the Wind, 1989.

33. The Infinity Box - with - He Who Shapes. With Roger Zelazny. Tor Books - Tom Doherty Associates, New York City, 1989. Tor Double 12. Softcover.

34. Sweet, Sweet Poison. Published by St Martin's Press, New York City, 1990. Hardcover.

35. Cambio Bay. Published by St Martin's Press, New York City, 1990. Hardcover.

36. State of Grace - Author's Choice Monthly 16. Published by Pulphouse Publishing, Eugene, Oregon, 1991. Herein: The Book of Yin, 1983; Jenny with Wings, 1963; The Downstairs Room, 1968; State of Grace, 1977; Isosceles, 1988; and The Death of Mrs Stringfellow, 1980.

37. Death Qualified: A Mystery of Chaos. Published by St Martin's Press, New York City, 1991. Hardcover.

38. Seven Kinds of Death. Published by St Martin's Press, New York City, 1992. Hardcover.

39. And the Angels Sing. Published by St Martin's Press, New York City, 1992. Hardcover. Herein: Foreword by Karen Joy Fowler; The Look Alike, 1988; O Homo, O Femina, O Tempora, 1985; The Chosen, 1970; On the Road to Honeyville, 1972; The Great Doors of Silence, 1986; The Loiterer, 1986; The Scream, 1974; Strangeness, Charm and Spin, 1984; The Dragon Seed, 1985; Forever Yours, Anna, 1987; and And the Angels Sing, 1990.

40. Justice for Some. Published by St Martin's Press, New York City, 1993. Hardcover.

41. The Best Defense. Published by St Martin's Press, New York City, 1994. Hardcover.

42. A Flush of Shadows. Published by St Martin's Press, New York City, 1995. Hardcover. Herein: Introduction by Robin Scott Wilson; With Thimbles, with Forks, and Hope, 1981; Sister Angel, 1983; All for One, 1995; The Gorgon Field, 1985; and Torch Song, 1995.

43. Malice Prepense. Published by St Martin's Press, New York City, 1996. Hardcover.

44. The Good Children. Published by St Martin's Press, New York City, 1998. Hardcover.

45. Defense for the Devil. Published by St Martin's Press, New York City, 1999. Hardcover.

46. The Casebook of Constance and Charlie - Volume 1. Published by St Martin's Minotaur, New York City, 1999. Hardcover. Herein: The Hamlet Trap, 1987; Smart House, 1989; and Seven Kinds of Death, 1992.

47. The Casebook of Constance and Charlie - Volume 2. Published by St Martin's Minotaur, New York City, 2000. Hardcover. Herein: The Dark Door, 1988; Sweet, Sweet Poison, 1990; Torch Song, 1995; Christ's Tears, 1996; and An Imperfect Gift, 1999.

48. No Defense. Published by St Martin's Press, New York City, 2000. Hardcover.

49. The Deepest Water. Published by St Martin's Minotaur, New York City, 2000. Hardcover.

50. Desperate Measures. Published by St Martin's Minotaur, New York City, 2001. Hardcover.

51. The Deepest Water. Published by St Martin's Minotaur, New York City, 2002. Hardcover.

52. Clear and Convincing Proof. Published by Mira Books, New York City, 2003. Hardcover.

53. The Unbidden Truth. Published by Mira Books, New York City, 2004. Hardcover.

54. The Price of Silence. Published by Mira Books, New York City, 2005. Hardcover.

55. Sleight of Hand. Published by Mira Books, New York City, 2006. Hardcover.

56. A Wrongful Death. Published by Mira Books, New York City, 2008. Hardcover.

57. Cold Case. Published by Mira Books, New York City, 2008. Hardcover.

***

ANTHOLOGIES.

1. Nebula Award Stories 9. Published by Harper and Row, New York City, 1975. Hardcover. All fiction from 1973: Introduction by **Kate Wilhelm**, 1974; The Death of Doctor Island by **Gene Wolfe**; Shark by Edward Bryant; With Morning Comes Mistfall by George R. R. Martin; Of Mist and Grass and Sand by Vonda N. McIntyre; The Deathbird by Harlan Ellison; A Thing of Beauty by Norman Spinrad; Love is the Plan, the Plan is Death by James Tiptree Jr.; The Childhood of the Human Hero by Carol Emshwiller; along with some essays: 1973 The Year in Science Fiction by **Damon Knight**, 1974; The Future of Science: Prometheus, Apollo, Athena by Ben Bova, 1974.

2. Clarion SF. Published by Berkley Books, New York City, 1977. Softcover. All from 1977, this contains: Introduction by **Kate Wilhelm**; Landscape with Aliens by Larry W. Martin; A Matter of Honor by Pat Hodgell; Closed Circuit by Carter Scholz; The Leader of the Club by Marc Scott Zicree; The Bellman's Wonder Ring by **Gene Wolfe**; The Enemy You Killed My Friend by Richard S. Bready; Stormfall by Bill Johnson; Can Anything Be Taught by Vonda N. McIntyre; The Thing Itself by Kim Stanley Robinson; Poppin' Fresh by Michael West; With Crooked Hands by Robert Crais; Brian In the Dreaming Seat by Alan Brennert; Something That Works by **Damon Knight**; No Specific Time Mentioned by Lois Metzger; Two People Within The Design by Vic Webb; and The Traders by Kathleen M. Sidney.

***

NON-FICTION

1. The Hills Are Dancing. With Richard Wilhelm. Published by Corroboree Press, Minneapolis, Minnesota, 1986. Hardcover.

2. Storyteller: Writing Lessons and More from 27 Years of the Clarion Writers' Workshop. Published by Small Beer Press, United States, 2005. Softcover.

***

RELATED

1. The Works of Kate Wilhelm. Published by Houghton Mifflin, Boston, for Worldcon, 1983. Softcover.

2. The Magazine of Fantasy and Science Fiction - Special Kate Wilhelm Issue - September 2001. Published by Spilogale Inc, United States, 2001. Softcover. Herein: Yesterday's Tomorrows by **Kate Wilhelm**; **Kate Wilhelm**: An Appreciation by Gordon Van Gelder; and **Kate Wilhelm**: Bibliography by William Contento; along with the usual features.

-2004-

Brian W. Aldiss

Brian Wilson Aldiss, OBE, was born on August 18th, 1925 in Norfolk, England. His father operated a department store and, at six years old, he sent Brian off to boarding school.

In 1943, he went to war in Burma with the Royal Signals Regiment. And when he left the service in 1948, he worked in a bookshop in Oxford.

While he was working there, he wrote a series of stories about bookselling for The Bookseller magazine. These were so well received that an editor at Faber and Faber asked Aldiss to gather the stories together for a book. In 1955, The Brightfount Diaries, his first novel, was published, and a career was launched.

His first science fiction story, Criminal Record, was published by John Carnell in Science Fantasy Magazine, Volume 3, Number 9, in 1954. It appeared with Haven by Peter Hawkins; Family Secret by Richard deMille writing as Arthur Coster; Last Man on Mars by W. P. Cockcroft; Six of One by A. Bertram Chandler; This Precious Stone by H. J. Murdoch; and Occupational Hazard by E. C. Tubb; along with Something New Wanted - an essay by J. T. McIntosh.

Next came Pogsmith in Authentic Science Fiction Monthly, May 1955, where it landed with Parry's Paradox by Lyn Venable; Down to Earth by John Kippax; Otherwise by John Ashcroft; Kwakiutl by Dan Morgan; The Big Hop - part 1 of 2 by J. T McIntosh; and Repair Job by E. C. Tubb writing as Julian Carey.

And in 1958 he was voted the Most Promising New Author at the World Science Fiction Convention - that was the year he published his first science fiction novel, Non-Stop. He followed that up by getting elected President of the British Science Fiction Association in 1960. A year after being inducted into the SF Hall of Fame, he was awarded an OBE by Queen Elizabeth for his contributions to literature. And in 2008 he was awarded an honorary doctorate by the University of Liverpool, also for his contributions to literature.

Aldiss once said, "Science Fiction should tell you things you don't want to know."

Too true.

His most consistently valuable book for collectors tends to be Non-Stop, Faber and Faber, 1958. This runs around $850.00 to $1,000.00.

Pen names used: Brian Aldiss; and Jael Cracken.

***

AWARDS

1958. Most Promising New Author - World Science Fiction Convention.
1962. Hugo Best Short Fiction Award for Hothouse in The Long Afternoon of Earth.
1965. Nebula Best Novella Award for The Saliva Tree from The Magazine of Fantasy and Science Fiction, September 1965.
1969. Ditmar Award for Best Contemporary Writer of Science Fiction.
1971. British Science Fiction Best Novel Award for The Moment of Eclipse.
1973. British Science Fiction Special Award for Billion Year Spree.
1982. British Science Fiction Best Novel Award for Helliconia Spring.
1983. The John W. Campbell Memorial Award for Helliconia Spring.
1985. British Science Fiction Best Novel Award for Helliconia Winter.
2004. Inducted into The Science Fiction Hall of Fame.
2005. OBE.
2007. British Science Fiction Fiftieth Anniversary Award for Non-Stop as the best novel of 1958.

***

FILM AND TELEVISION

1. Frankenstein Unbound. This 1973 novel was directed by Roger Corman for release in 1990. The screenplay was also by Roger Corman and the film starred: John Hurt as Dr Joe Buchanan; Raul Julia as Dr Victor Frankenstein; Nick Brimble as the Monster; Bridget Fonda as Mary Wollstonecraft Godwin; Catherine Rabett as Elizabeth Levenza; Jason Patric as Lord Byron; and Michael Hutchence as Percy Bysshe Shelley.

2. Brave New Worlds: The Science Fiction Phenomenon. This 1993 documentary was directed by Paul Oremland. **Brian Aldiss** was one of the many guests, along with **Robert Silverberg**; **Sir Arthur C. Clarke**; **William Gibson**; J. G. Ballard; John Clute; Kim Stanley Robinson; Octavia Butler; Karen Joy Fowler; and others.

3. The War of the Worlds: Great Books. A 1994 documentary, directed by Dale Minor. **Brian Aldiss** appeared as himself, a science fiction writer. Also included, either in person or on archival film footage, were: Leonard Nimoy; Howard Koch; Orson Welles; William Shatner; Albert Einstein; and many others.

4. Drug Taking and the Arts. Another 1994 documentary, this one directed by Storm Thorgerson. **Brian Aldiss** appeared as himself.

5. On the Edge of Blade Runner. Directed by Andrew Abbott and released in 2000. **Brian Aldiss** appeared as himself, along with **Philip K. Dick** (2005 Hall of Fame); Joanna Cassidy; Daryl Hannah; Rutger Hauer; **Ridley Scott** (2007 Hall of Fame);

Brian W. Aldiss

and many others.

6. Stanley Kubrick: A Life in Pictures. A 2001 documentary directed by Jan Harlan and narrated by Tom Cruise. **Brian Aldiss** appeared as himself, along with **Sir Arthur C. Clarke** (1997 Hall of Fame); Keir Dullea; Woody Allen; Nicole Kidman; and others.

7. Artificial Intelligence: AI. This 1969 short story, Supertoys Last All Summer Long, was directed by **Steven Spielberg** (2005 Hall of Fame) for release in 2001. It starred: Haley Joel Osment; Frances O'Connor; Sam Robards; Jake Thomas; William Hurt; and Ken Leung; with Ashley Scott as Gigolo Jane and Jude Law as Gigolo Joe.

8. Brothers of the Head. From the 1977 novel of the same name, this was directed by Keith Fulton and Louis Pepe for release in 2005
and starring: Jonathan Pryce; Harry Treadaway; Luke Treadaway; Elizabeth Rider; John Simm; Sean Harris; James Greene as **Brian Aldiss**; and Ken Russell as himself.

9. Sacrificial Sheep: The Novel vs. The Film. A 2007 documentary, directed by Charles de Lauzirika. **Brian Aldiss** appeared as himself, along with Tim Powers; **Ridley Scott** (2007 Hall of Fame); **Philip K. Dick** (2005 Hall of Fame); and many others.

10. The Electric Dreamer: Remembering Philip K. Dick. Another 2007 documentary directed by Charles de Lauzirika. **Brian Aldiss** appeared as himself, along with many others.

***

NOVELS AND COLLECTIONS

1. The Brightfount Diaries. Published by Faber and Faber, London, 1955. Hardcover.

2. Space, Time and Nathaniel. Published by Faber and Faber, London, 1957. Hardcover. Herein: Psyclops, 1956; Not for an Age, 1955; Outside, 1955; Criminal Record, 1954; T, 1956; Our Kind of Knowledge, 1955; Conviction, 1956; The Shubshub Race, 1957; Supercity, 1957; Pogsmith, 1955; Panel Game, 1955; Dumb Show, 1956; There Is a Tide, 1956; and The Failed men, 1956.

3. Equator. Published by Digit Books, London, 1958. Digit Book R695. Softcover. Bound with Segregation, 1958.

4. Non-Stop. Published by Faber and Faber, London, 1958. Hardcover.

5. The Canopy of Time. Published by Faber and Faber, London, 1959. Hardcover. Herein: Judas Danced, 1958; All the World's Tears, 1957; Blighted Profile, 1958; Gene-Hive, 1958; Incentive, 1958; O Ishrail!, 1957; Secret of a Mighty City, 1958; They Shall Inherit, 1958; Visiting Amoeba, 1957; Who Can Replace a Man?, 1958; and Three's a Cloud, 1959.

6. No Time Like Tomorrow. Published by Signet Books - New American Library, New York City, 1959. Signet Book S163. Softcover. Herein: T, 1956; Not for an Age, 1955; Poor Little Warrior!, 1958; The Failed Men, 1956; Carrion Country, 1958; Judas Danced, 1958; Psyclops, 1956; Outside, 1955; Gesture of Farewell, 1957; The New Father Christmas, 1958; Blighted Profile, 1958; and Our Kind of Knowledge, 1955.

7. Starship. Published by Criterion Books, New York City, 1959. Hardcover. Revised edition of Non-Stop, 1958.

8. Vanguard from Alpha. Published by Ace Books, New York City, 1959. Ace Double D-369. Softcover. Together with The Changeling Worlds by Kenneth Bulmer.

9. Bow Down to Nul. Published by Ace Books, New York City, 1960. Ace Double D-433. Softcover. Together with The Dark Destroyers by Manly Wade Wellman.

10. Galaxies Like Grains of Sand. Published by Signet Books - New American Library, New York City, 1960. Signet Book S1815. Softcover. Herein: Out of Reach, 1957; The War Millennia, 1960; The Sterile Millennia, 1960; All the World's Tears, 1957; The Robot Millennia, 1960; Who Can Replace a Man?, 1958; The Dark Millennia, 1960; O Ishrail!, 1957; The Star Millennia, 1960; Incentive, 1958; The Mutant Millennia, 1960; Gene-Hive, 1958; The Megalopolis Millennia, 1960; Secret of a Mighty City, 1958; The Ultimate Millennia, 1960; and Visiting Amoeba, 1957.

11. The Primal Urge. Published by Ballantine Books, New York City, 1961. Ballantine Book F555. Softcover.

12. The Interpreter. Published by Digit Books, London, 1961. Digit Book R506. Softcover. Re-titled re-issue of Bow Down to Nul, 1960.

13. The Male Response. Published by Galaxy Publishing, New York City, 1961. Beacon Book 305. Softcover.

14. The Long Afternoon of Earth. Published by Signet Books - New American Library, New York City, 1962. Signet Book D2018. Softcover.

15. Hothouse. Published by Faber and Faber, London, 1962. Hardcover. Expanded version of The Long Afternoon of Earth, 1962.

16. The Airs of Earth. Published by Faber and Faber, London, 1963. Hardcover. Herein: Introduction by **Brian W. Aldiss**; A Kind of Artistry, 1962; How to Be a Soldier, 1963; Basis for Negotiation, 1962; Shards, 1962; O Moon of My Delight!, 1961; The International Smile, 1963; The Game of God, 1957; and Old Hundredth, 1960.

17. The Male Response. Published by Dennis Dobson, London, 1963. First hardcover edition.

18. Starswarm. Published by Signet Books - New American Library, New York City, 1964. Signet Book D2411. Softcover. Herein: Sector Vermilion, 1964; A Kind of Artistry, 1962; Sector Gray, 1965; Hearts and Engines, 1964; Sector Violet, 1964; The Underprivileged, 1963; Sector Diamond, 1964; The Game of God, 1964; Sector Green, 1964; Shards, 1962; Sector Yellow, 1964; Legends of Smith's

Burst, 1959; Sector Azure, 1964; O Moon of My Delight, 1964; The Rift, 1964; and Old Hundredth, 1960.

19. The Dark Light Years. Published by Faber and Faber, London, 1964. Hardcover.

20. Greybeard. Published by Harcourt, Brace & World, New York City, 1964.

21. Earthworks. Published by Faber and Faber, London, 1965. Hardcover.

22. Best Science Fiction Stories of Brian W. Aldiss. Published by Faber and Faber, London, 1965. Hardcover. Herein: Introduction by **Brian W. Aldiss**; Who Can Replace a Man?, 1958; Not for an Age, 1955; Psyclops, 1956; Outside, 1955; Dumb Show, 1956; The New Father Christmas, 1958; Ahead, 1956; Poor Little Warrior!, 1958; Man on Bridge, 1964; The Impossible Star, 1963; Basis for Negotiation, 1962; Old Hundredth, 1960; A Kind of Artistry, 1962; and Man in His Time, 1965.

23. The Saliva Tree and Other Strange Growths. Published by Faber and Faber, London, 1966. Hardcover. Herein: Danger: Religion!, 1962; The Source, 1965; The Lonely Habit, 1966; A Pleasure Shared, 1962; One Role with Relish, 1966; Legends of Smith's Burst, 1959; The Day of the Doomed King, 1965; Paternal Care, 1966; The Girl and the Robot with Flowers, 1965; and The Saliva Tree, 1965.

24. Who Can Replace a Man? Published by Harcourt, Brace & World, New York City, 1966. Re-titled re-issue of Best Science Fiction Stories of **Brian W. Aldiss**, 1965.

25. An Age. Published by Faber and Faber, London, 1967. Hardcover.

26. Cryptozoic. Published by Doubleday & Company, Garden City, New York, 1968. Hardcover. A re-titled re-issue of An Age, 1967.

27. Report on Probability A. Published by Faber and Faber, London, 1968. Hardcover.

28. Barefoot in the Head. Published by Faber and Faber, London, 1969. Hardcover.

29. Intangibles, Inc. and Other Stories. Published by Faber and Faber, London, 1969. Hardcover. Herein: Neanderthal Planet, 1960; Randy's Syndrome, 1967; Send Her Victorious, 1968; Since the Assassination, 1969; and Intangibles Inc., 1959.

30. A Brian Aldiss Omnibus. Published by Sidgwick and Jackson, London, 1969. Hardcover. This gathers: The Primal Urge, 1961; Man in His Time, 1965; The Impossible Star, 1963; The Saliva Tree, 1965; Basis for Negotiation, 1962; and The Interpreter - aka Bown Down to Nul, 1961.

31. The Hand-Reared Boy. Published by Weidenfeld and Nicolson, London, 1970. Hardcover.

32. Neanderthal Planet. Published by Avon Books, New York City, 1970. Avon Book V2372. Softcover. A re-titled re-issue of Intangibles, Inc., 1969.

33. Neanderthal Planet. Published by The Science Fiction Book Club, Garden City, New York, 1970. First hardcover edition under the new title.

34. The Moment of Eclipse. Published by Faber and Faber, London, 1970. Hardcover. Herein: Poem at a Lunar Eclipse by Thomas Hardy; The Moment of Eclipse, 1969; The Day We Embarked for Cythera, 1970; Orgy of the Living and the Dying, 1970; Super-Toys Last All Summer Long, 1969; The Village Swindler, 1968; Down the Up Escalation, 1967; The Uncomfortable Pause Between Life and Art, 1969; Confluence, 1967; Heresies of the Hugh God, 1966; The Circulation of the Blood, 1966; And the Stagnation of the Heart, 1968; The Worm That Flies, 1968; Working in the Spaceship Yards, 1969; and Swastika!, 1970.

35. A Soldier Erect. Published by Weidenfeld and Nicolson, London, 1971. Hardcover.

36. Brian Aldiss Omnibus 2. Published by Sidgwick and Jackson, London, 1971. Hardcover. Herein: Non-Stop, 1958; The Male Response, 1961; Not for an Age, 1955; Outside, 1955; Criminal Record, 1954; T, 1956; Out Kind of Knowledge, 1955; Conviction, 1956; The Shubshub Race, 1957; Supercity, 1957; Pogsmith, 1955; Panel Game, 1955; Dumb Show, 1956; There Is a Tide, 1956; The Failed Men, 1956; and Space, Time and Nathaniel, 1957.

37. Best Science Fiction Stories of Brian W. Aldiss. Published by Faber and Faber, London, 1971. Hardcover. Revised edition. Herein: Introduction by **Brian W. Aldiss**; Who Can Replace a Man?, 1958; Not for an Age, 1955; Outside, 1955; Poor Little Warrior!, 1958; Man on Bridge, 1964; The Impossible Star, 1963; Old Hundredth, 1960; Man in His Time, 1965; Shards, 1962; Girl and Robot with Flowers, 1965; The Moment of Eclipse, 1969; Swastika!, 1970; Sober Noises of Morning in a Marginal Land, 1971; Judas Danced, 1958; Still Trajectories, 1967; and Another Little Boy, 1966.

38. The Book of Brian Aldiss. Published by DAW Books, New York City, 1972. Daw Collector's Book 29. UQ1029. Softcover. Herein: Introduction by **Brian W. Aldiss**; Comic Inferno, 1963; the Underprivileged, 1963; Cardiac Arrest, 1970; In the Arena, 1963; All the World's Tears, 1957; Amen and Out, 1966; The Soft predicament, 1969; As for Our Fatal Continuity, 1972; and Send Her Victorious, 1968.

39. The Comic Inferno. Published by New English Library, London, 1973. NEL Book 016366. Softcover. A re-titled re-issue of The Book of Brian Aldiss, 1972.

40. Frankenstein Unbound. Published by Jonathan Cape, London, 1974. Hardcover.

41. The Eighty-Minute Hour: A Space Opera. Published by Doubleday & Company, Garden City, New York, 1974. Hardcover.

42. The Eighty-Minute Hour: A Space Opera. Published by Jonathan Cape, London, 1974. Hardcover. Revised edition.

43. Excommunication. Published by Post Card Partnership, London, 1975. Postcard format, using a single short, short story.

Brian W. Aldiss

44. The Malacia Tapestry. Published by Jonathan Cape, London, 1976. Hardcover.

45. Brothers of the Head. Published by Pierrot Publishing, London, 1977. Hardcover.

46. Galaxies Like Grains of Sand. Published by Gregg Press, Boston, 1977. First hardcover edition.

47. Last Orders. Published by Jonathan Cape, London, 1977. Hardcover. Herein: Last Orders, 1976; Creatures of Apogee, 1977; Within the Black Circle, 1975; Killing Off the Big Animals, 1975; What Are You Doing? Why Are You Doing It?, 1975; Enigma 2: Diagrams for Three Stories - an essay, 1974; The Girl in the Tau-Dream, 1974; The Immobility Crew, 1974; A Cultural Side-Effect, 1974; Live? Our Computers Will Do That for Us, 1974; The Monsters of Ingratitude IV, 1974; Waiting for the Universe to Begin, 1975; But Without Orifices, 1975; Aimez-Vous Holman Hunt?, 1975; Backwater, 1977; The Eternal Theme of Exile, 1973; All Those Enduring Old Charms, 1973; Nobody Spoke or Waved Goodbye, 1973; The Expensive Delicate Ship, 1973; Carefully Observed Women by **Brian W. Aldiss**, 1975; The Daffodil Returns the Smile, 1975; The Year of the Quiet Computer, 1975; Appearance of Life, 1976; Wired for Sound, 1974; and Journey to the Heartland, 1976.

48. Enemies of the System. Published by Jonathan Cape, London, 1978. Hardcover.

49. Rude Awakening. Published by Random House, New York City, 1978. Hardcover.

50. New Arrivals, Old Encounters. Published by Jonathan Cape, London, 1979. Hardcover. Herein: New Arrivals, Old Encounters, 1977; The Small Stones of Tu Fu, 1978; Three Ways, 1978; Amen and Out, 1966; A Spot of Konfrontation, 1973; The Soft Predicament, 1969; Non-Isotropic, 1978; One Blink of the Moon, 1979; Space for Reflection, 1976; Song of the Silence, 1979; Indifference, 1978; and The Impossible Puppet Show, 1974.

51. Brothers of the Head and Where the Lines Converge. Published by Panther Books, London, 1979. Softcover. Herein: Brothers of the Head, 1979; and Where the Lines Converge, 1979; along with an assortment of poetry.

52. Life in the West. Published by Weidenfeld and Nicolson, London, 1980. Hardcover.

53. Moreau's Other Island. Published by Jonathan Cape, London, 1980. Hardcover.

54. An Island Called Moreau. Published by Simon and Schuster, New York City, 1981. Re-titled from Moreau's Other Island, 1980.

55. Foreign Bodies. Published by Chopmen, Singapore, 1981, to celebrate the appearance of Aldiss at the Singapore Book Fair. A hardcover and a softcover edition were issued simultaneously. Herein: A Romance of the Equator, 1980; Boat Animals, 1981; Foreign Bodies, 1981; Frontiers, 1981; The Skeleton, 1981; and Just Back from Java, 1981.

56. Farewell to a Child. Published by Priapus Press, Hertfordshire, UK, 1982. Softcover pamphlet. Limited edition collection of poetry.

57. Helliconia Spring. Published by Jonathan Cape, London, 1982. Hardcover.

58. Helliconia Summer. Published by Jonathan Cape, London, 1983. Hardcover.

59. Bestsellers Volume 3, Number 9 - Best of Aldiss. Published by Viaduct, UK, 1983. Softcover. This contains: Introduction by **Brian W. Aldiss**; Oh. For a Closer Brush with God, 1979; Appearance of Life, 1976; The Small Stones of Tu Fu, 1978; The Game with the Big Heavy Ball, 1977; A Romance of the Equator, 1980; The Fall of Species B, 1980; In the Halls of the Hereafter, 1980; The Ancestral Home of Thought, 1980; The Blue Background, 1983; A Private Whale, 1982; Consolations of Age, 1983; and The Girl Who Sang, 1982.

60. Seasons in Flight. Published by Jonathan Cape, London, 1984. Hardcover. Herein: The Gods in Flight, 1984; A Romance of the Equator, 1980; The Blue Background, 1983; The Girl Who Sang, 1982; Igur and the Mountain, 1983; The O in Jose, 1966; The Other Side of the Lake, 1984; The Plain, the Endless Plain, 1984; and Incident in a Far Country, 1984.

61. Helliconia Winter. Published by Jonathan Cape, London, 1985. Hardcover.

62. The Horatio Stubbs Saga. Published by Granada Books, London, 1985. Softcover. An omnibus edition, this contains: Hand Reared Boy, 1970; Soldier Erect, 1971; and Rude Awakening, 1978.

63. The Year Before Yesterday. Published by Franklin Watts, New York City, 1987. Hardcover.

64. Ruins. Published by Hutchinson, London, 1987. Hardcover.

65. Cracken at Critical. Published by Kerosina Books, London, 1987. Hardcover. Re-titled re-issue of The Year Before Yesterday, 1987.

66. The Magic of the Past. Published by Kerosina Books, London, 1987. Hardcover. Herein: Introduction by **Brian W. Aldiss**; North Scarning, 1986; and The Magic of the Past, 1987.

67. The Saliva Tree. Published by Tor Books - Tom Doherty Associates, New York City, 1988. Softcover. Tor Double 3. Bound with Born with the Dead by **Robert Silverberg**.

68. Forgotten Life. Published by Victor Gollancz, London, 1988. Hardcover.

69. Best Science Fiction Stories of Brian W. Aldiss. Published by Victor Gollancz, London, 1988. Hardcover. Revised edition. Herein: Ahead, 1956; Outside, 1955; All the World's Tears, 1957; Poor Little Warrior!, 1958; Who Can Replace a Man?, 1958; Man on Bridge, 1964; The Girl and the Robot with Flowers, 1965; The Saliva Tree, 1965; Man in His time, 1965; Heresies of the Huge God, 1966; Confluence, 1967; Working in the Spaceship Yards, 1969; Super-Toys Last All Summer Long, 1969; Sober Noises of Morning in a Marginal Land, 1971; The Dark Soul of the Night, 1976; Appearance of

Life, 1976; Last Orders, 1976; Door Slams in Fourth World, 1982; The Gods in Flight, 1984; My Country 'Tis Not Only of Thee, 1987; Infestation, 1986; and The Difficulties Involved in Photographing Nix Olympica, 1986.

70. A Romance of the Equator. Published by Victor Gollancz, London, 1989. Hardcover. This contains: Introduction by **Brian W. Aldiss**; Old Hundredth, 1960; Day of the Doomed King, 1965; The Source, 1965; The Village Swindler, 1968; The Worm that Flies, 1968; The Moment of Eclipse, 1969; So Far from Prague, 1969; The Day We Embarked for Cythera, 1974; Castle Scene with Penitents, 1973; The Game with the Big Heavy Ball, 1977; Creatures of Apogee, 1977; The Small Stones of Tu Fu, 1978; Just Back from Java, 1981; A Romance of the Equator, 1980; Journey to the Goat Star, 1989; The Girl Who Sang, 1982; Consolations of Age, 1983; The Blue Background, 1983; The Plain, the Endless Plain, 1984; You Never Asked My Name, 1985; Lies!, 1989; North Scarning, 1986; The Big Question, 1989; The Ascent of Humbelstein, 1989; How an Inner Door Opened to My Heart, 1988; and Bill Carter Takes Over, 1979.

71. Dracula Unbound. Published by Harper Collins, New York City, 1991. Hardcover.

72. Kindred Blood in Kensington Gore - Philip K. Dick in the Afterlife: An Imaginary Conversation. Published by Avernus Creative Media, London, 1992. Pamphlet.

73. Remembrance Day. Published by Harper Collins, London, 1993. Hardcover.

74. A Tupolev Too Far and Other Stories. Published by Harper Collins, London, 1993. Hardcover. Herein: A Tupolev Too Far, 1989; Ratbird, 1992; FOAM, 1991; Summertime Was Nearly Over, 1991; Better Morphosis, 1990; Three Degrees Over, 1989; A Life of Matter and Death, 1990; A Day in the Life of a Galactic Empire, 1989; Confluence, 1967; Confluence Revisited, 1988; North of the Abyss, 1989; and Alphabet of Ameliorating Hope, 1993.

75. Somewhere East of Life. Published by Harper Collins Flamingo, London, 1994. Hardcover.

76. The Secret of This Book. Published by Harper Collins, London, 1995. Hardcover. Herein: Common Clay, 1992; The Mistakes, Miseries and Misfortunes of Mankind, 1994; How the Gates Opened and Closed, 1995; Headless, 1994; Travelling Towards Humbris, 1995; If Hamlet's Uncle Had Been a Nicer Guy, 1995; Else the Isle with Calibans, 1993; A Swedish Birthday Present, 1995; His Seventieth Heaven, 1995; Rose in the Evening, 1995; On the Inland Sea, 1995; A Dream of Antigone, 1994; The God Who Slept with Women, 1994; Evans in His Moment of Glory, 1995; Horse Meat, 1992; An Unwritten Love Note, 1995; Making My father Read Revered Writings, 1995; Sitting with Sick Wasps, 1995; Becoming the Full Butterfly, 1995; Traveller, Traveller, Seek Your Wife in the Forests of This Life, 1987; Another Way Than Death, 1992; That Particular Green of Obsequies, 1992; and The Ancestral Home of Thought, 1992.

77. Helliconia. Published by Harper Collins Voyager, London, 1996. An omnibus edition, this contains: Introduction by **Brian W. Aldiss**; Helliconia Spring, 1982; Helliconia Summer, 1983; Helliconia Winter, 1985; and Appendices.

78. Common Clay: 20-Odd Stories. Published by St Martin's Press, New York City, 1996. Hardcover. Re-titled from The Secret of This Book, 1995.

79. White Mars, or, The Mind Set Free: A 21st Century Utopia. Writing with Roger Penrose. Published by Little Brown, London, 1999. Hardcover.

80. Super-Toys Last All Summer Long and Other Stories of Future Time. Published by Orbit Books, London, 2001. Softcover. Herein: Foreword: Attempting to Please by **Brian W. Aldiss**; Supertoys Last All Summer Long, 1969; Supertoys When Winter Comes, 2001; Supertoys in Other Seasons, 2001; Apogee Again, 1999; III, 2001; The Old Mythology, 2001; Headless, 1994; Beef, 1995; Nothing in Life Is Ever Enough, 1999; A Matter of Mathematics, 2001; The Pause Button, 1997; Three Types of Solitude, 2001; Steppenpferd, 2000; Cognitive Ability and the Light Bulb, 2000; Dark Society, 1996; Galaxy Zee, 2001; Marvells of Utopia, 2001; Becoming the Full Butterfly, 1995; and A Whiter Mars: A Socratic Dialogue of Times to Come, 1995.

81. Super-State. Published by Orbit Books, London, 2002. Hardcover.

82. The Cretan Teat. Published by House of Stratus, London, 2002. Hardcover.

83. Affairs at Hampden Ferrers. Published by Little Brown, London, 2004. Hardcover.

84. Sanity and the Lady. Published by PS Publishing, London, 2005. Hardcover.

85. Cultural Breaks. Published by Tachyon Publications, United States, 2005. Hardcover. Herein: Foreword: The Crocodile's Apprentice by Andy Duncan; Tarzan of the Alps, 2004; Tralee of Man Young, 2005; The Eye Opener, 1993; Aboard the Beatitude, 2002; the Man and A Man with His Mule, 2002; Dusk Flight, 2005; Commander Calex Killed, Fire and Fury at the Edge of the World, Scones Perfect, 2003; The Hibernators, 2003; The National Heritage, 2005; How the Gates Opened and Closed, 1995; Total Environment, 1968; and A Chinese Perspective, 1978.

86. Jocasta. Published by Rose Press International, United States, 2006. Softcover.

87. HARM. Published by Del Rey - Ballantine Books, New York City, 2007. Hardcover.

***

ANTHOLOGIES

1. Penguin Science Fiction. Published by Penguin Books, Middlesex, England, 1961. Penguin Book 1638. Softcover. This contains: Introduction by **Brian W. Aldiss**; Command Performance by Walter M. Miller, Jr, 1952; Sole Solution by **Eric Frank Russell**, 1956; The Snowball Effect by Katherine Maclean, 1952; Track 12 by J. G. Ballard, 1958; Lot by Ward

Brian W. Aldiss

Moore, 1953; The Short-Short Story of Mankind by John Steinbeck, 1958; Skirmish by Clifford Simak, 1950; Grandpa by James H. Schmitz, 1955; The Half Pair by A. Bertram Chandler, 1957; Nightfall by **Isaac Asimov**, 1941; The End of Summer by Algis Budrys, 1954; and Poor Little Warrior! by **Brian W. Aldiss**, 1958.

2. Best Fantasy Stories. Published by Faber and Faber, London, 1962. Hardcover. Herein: Introduction by **Brian W. Aldiss**; Intangibles, Inc. by **Brian W. Aldiss**; In a Season of Calm Weather by **Ray Bradbury**, 1957; You Can't Have Them All by Charles Beaumont, 1956; The Story-Teller by H. H. Monroe writing as Saki, 1914; Cousin Len's Wonderful Adjective Cellar by Jack Finney, 1948; Mummy to the Rescue, 1950; Incident on a Lake by John Collier, 1941; Baron Bagge by Alex Lernet-Holenia, 1956; Perchance to Dream by Michael Joyce, 1930; and The Jet-Propelled Couch - an essay by Robert Lindner, 1954.

3. More Penguin Science Fiction. Published by Penguin Books, Middlesex, England, 1963. Penguin Book 1963. Softcover. Herein: Introduction by **Brian W. Aldiss**; The Monkey Wrench by **Gordon R. Dickson**, 1951; The First Men by Howard Fast, 1960; Counterfeit by Alan E. Nourse, 1952; The Greater Thing by Tom Godwin, 1954; Build Up Logically by Howard Schoenfeld, 1949; The Liberation of Earth by William Tenn, 1953; An Alien Agony by **Harry Harrison**, 1962; The Tunnel Under the World by **Frederik Pohl**, 1955; The Store of the Worlds by Robert Sheckley, 1959; Jokester by **Isaac Asimov**, 1956; Pyramid by Robert Abernathy, 1954; and The Forgotten Enemy by **Arthur C. Clarke**, 1948.

4. Yet More Penguin Science Fiction. Published by Penguin Books, Middlesex, England, 1964. Penguin Book 2189. Softcover. Herein: Introduction by **Brian W. Aldiss**; The Wall Around the World by Theodore Cogswell, 1953; Before Eden by **Arthur C. Clarke**, 1961; Protected Species by H. B. Fyfe, 1951; The Rescuer by Arthur Porges, 1962; I Made You by Walter M. Miller, Jr, 1954; The Country of the Kind by **Damon Knight**, 1956; MS Found in a Chinese Fortune Cookie by C. M. Kornbluth, 1957; The Cage by A. Bertram Chandler, 1957; Eastward Ho! by William Tenn, 1958; The Windows of Heaven by John Brunner, 1956; Common Time by **James Blish**, 1953; and Fulfilment by **A. E. van Vogt**, 1951.

5. Nebula Award Stories Two. With **Harry Harrison**. Published by Doubleday & Company, Garden City, New York, 1967. Hardcover. Herein: Introduction by **Brian W. Aldiss** and **Harry Harrison**; We Can Remember It For You Wholesale by **Philip K. Dick**, 1966; The Secret Place by Richard McKenna, 1966; Light of Other Days by Bob Shaw, 1967; Who Needs Insurance by Robin S. Scott, 1966; Among the Hairy Earthmen by R. A. Lafferty, 1966; The Last Castle by **Jack Vance**, 1966; Day Million by **Frederik Pohl**, 1966; When I Was Miss Dow by Sonya Dorman, 1966; Call Him Lord by **Gordon R. Dickson**, 1966; In the Imagicon by George Henry Smith, 1966; and Man in His Time by **Brian W. Aldiss**, 1965.

6. Best SF: 1967. With **Harry Harrison**. Published by Berkley Books, New York City, 1968. Berkley Book S1529. Softcover. Herein: Introduction by **Harry Harrison**; Credo - an essay by **James Blish**, 1968; Hawksbill Station by **Robert Silverberg**, 1967; 1937 A.D. by John T. Sladek, 1967; Fifteen Miles by Ben Bova, 1967; The Vine by Kit Reed, 1967; Interview with a Lemming by James Thurber, 1941; The Left Hand Way by A. Bertram Chandler, 1967; The Wreck of the Ship John B by Frank M. Robinson, 1967; The Forest of Zil by Kris Neville, 1967; The Assassination of John Fitzgerald Kennedy Considered as a Downhill Motor Race by J. G. Ballard, 1966; Answering Service by **Fritz Leiber**, 1967; The Last Command by Keith Laumer, 1967; Mirror of Ice by Gary Wright, 1967; Pretty Maggie Moneyeyes by Harlan Ellison, 1967; and Afterword - Knights of the Paper Spaceship by **Brian W. Aldiss**.

7. The Year's Best Science Fiction No. 1. With **Harry Harrison**. Published by Sphere Books, London, 1968. Sphere Book 43311. Softcover. Herein: Introduction by **Harry Harrison**; Credo - an essay by **James Blish**, 1968; Hawksbill Station by **Robert Silverberg**, 1967; 1937 A.D. by John T. Sladek, 1967; Fifteen Miles by Ben Bova, 1967; The Vine by Kit Reed, 1967; Interview with a Lemming by James Thurber, 1941; The Left Hand Way by A. Bertram Chandler, 1967; The Wreck of the Ship John B by Frank M. Robinson, 1967; The Forest of Zil by Kris Neville, 1967; The Assassination of John Fitzgerald Kennedy Considered as a Downhill Motor Race by J. G. Ballard, 1966; Answering Service by **Fritz Leiber**,1967; The Last Command by Keith Laumer, 1967; Mirror of Ice by Gary Wright, 1967; Pretty Maggie Moneyeyes by Harlan Ellison, 1967; and Afterword - Knights of the Paper Spaceship by **Brian W. Aldiss**.

8. All About Venus. With **Harry Harrison**. Published by Dell Books, New York City, 1968. Dell Book 0085. Softcover. Herein: Foreword by **Brian W. Aldiss**; Clouded Judgements - an essay by **Brian W. Aldiss**, 1968; Destinies of the Stars - an essay by Svante Arrhenius, 1971; Last and First Men - an excerpt by Olaf Stapledon, 1930; Pirates of Venus - an excerpt by **Edgar Rice Burroughs**, 1932; Perelandra - an excerpt by C. S. Lewis, 1943; Exploring the Planets - an essay by V. A. Firsoff, 1964; The Big Rain by **Poul Anderson**, 1954; Big sister - an essay by **Brian W. Aldiss**, 1968; Intelligent Life in the Universe - an essay by Carl Sagan, 1966; Escape to Venus by S. Makepeace Lott, 1956; The Open Question - an essay by **Brian W. Aldiss**, 1968; Sister Planet by **Poul Anderson**, 1959; Before Eden by **Arthur C. Clarke**, 1961; Some Mysteries of Venus Resolved - an essay by Sir Bernard Lovell, 1967; Dream of Distance - Anonymous essay, 1967; and Venus Mystery for Scientists - an essay by John Davy, 1967.

9. Farewell, Fantastic Venus! With **Harry Harrison**. Published by Macdonald, London, 1968. Hardcover. Herein: Foreword by **Brian W. Aldiss**; Before Eden by **Arthur C. Clarke**, 1961; The Big Rain by **Poul Anderson**, 1954; Sister Planet by **Poul Anderson**, 1959; Escape to Venus - an excerpt by S. Makepeace Lott, 1956; Perelandra - an excerpt by C. S. Lewis, 1943; Pirates of Venus - an excerpt by **Edgar Rice Burroughs**, 1932; Intelligent Life in the

Universe - an excerpt by Carl Sagan, 1966; A City on Venus by Henry Gade, 1941; Alchemy by John de Courcy and Dorothy de Courcy, 1950; A Honeymoon in Space - an excerpt by George Griffith, 1900; A Trip to Venus - an excerpt by John Munro, 1897; Last and First Men - an excerpt by Olaf Stapledon, 1930; along with an assortment of essays: Scientist Says Icecaps on Venus Would Make Life Possible by Evert Clark, 1968; Venus Mystery for Scientists by John Davy, 1967; Dream of Distance - anonymous, 1967; Some Mysteries of Venus Resolved by Sir Bernard Lovell, 1967; The Open Question by **Brian W. Aldiss**, 1968; Big Sister by **Brian W. Aldiss**, 1968; Exploring the Planets by V. A. Firsoff, 1996; Venus Is Hell! by **Brian W. Aldiss**, 1968; Unveiling the Mystery Planet by Willy Ley, 1955; The Man from Venus by Frank R. Paul, 1949; Swamp and Sand by **Brian W. Aldiss**, 1968; The Destinies of the Stars by Svante Arrhenius, 1917; Never-Fading Flowers by **Brian W. Aldiss**, 1968; The Story of the Heavens by Sir Robert Ball, 1882; and Clouded Judgements by **Brian W. Aldiss**, 1968.

10. The Year's Best Science Fiction No. 2. With **Harry Harrison**. Published by Sphere Books, London, 1969. Sphere Book 43354. Softcover. Herein: Introduction by **Harry Harrison**; Budget Planet by Robert Sheckley, 1968; Appointment on Prila by Bob Shaw, 1968; Lost Ground by David I. Masson, 1966; The Rime of the Ancient SF Author or Conventions and Recollections - a poem by J. R. Pierce, 1968; The Annex by John D. MacDonald, 1968; Segregationist by **Isaac Asimov**, 1968; Final War by Barry N. Malzberg writing as K. M. O'Donnell, 1968; 2001: A Space Odyssey - Some Selected Reviews from 1968 by Lester del Rey; **Samuel R. Delaney**; Ed Emshwiller; and Leon E. Stover; Golden Acres by Kit Reed, 1967; Criminal in Utopia by Mack Reynolds, 1968; One Station on the Way by **Fritz Leiber**, 1968; Sweet Dreams, Melissa by Stephen Goldin, 1968; To the Dark Star by **Robert Silverberg**, 1968; Like Young by **Theodore Sturgeon**, 1960; and Afterword - The House that Jules Built by **Brian W. Aldiss**.

11. Best SF: 1968. With **Harry Harrison**. Published by G. P. Putnam's Sons, New York, 1969. Hardcover. Herein: Introduction by **Harry Harrison**; Budget Planet by Robert Sheckley, 1968; Appointment on Prila by Bob Shaw, 1968; Lost Ground by David I. Masson, 1966; The Rime of the Ancient SF Author or Conventions and Recollections - a poem by J. R. Pierce, 1968; The Annex by John D. MacDonald, 1968; Segregationist by **Isaac Asimov**, 1968; Final War by Barry N. Malzberg writing as K. M. O'Donnell, 1968; 2001: A Space Odyssey - Some Selected Reviews from 1968 by Lester del Rey; **Samuel R. Delaney**; Ed Emshwiller; and Leon E. Stover; Golden Acres by Kit Reed, 1967; Criminal in Utopia by Mack Reynolds, 1968; One Station on the Way by **Fritz Leiber**, 1968; Sweet Dreams, Melissa by Stephen Goldin, 1968; To the Dark Star by **Robert Silverberg**, 1968; The Serpent of Kundalini by **Brian W. Aldiss**, 1968; and Afterword - The House that Jules Built by **Brian W. Aldiss**.

12. The Year's Best Science Fiction No. 3. With **Harry Harrison**. Published by Sphere Books, London, 1970. Sphere Book 43419. Softcover. Herein: Introduction by **Harry Harrison**; The Muse by Anthony Burgess, 1968; Working in the Spaceship Yards by **Brian W. Aldiss**, 1969; The Schematic Man by **Frederik Pohl**, 1969; The Snows are Melted, the Snows are Gone by James Tiptree, Jr, 1969; Hospital of Transplanted Hearts by D. M. Thomas, 1969; Eco-Catastrophe by Paul Ehrlich, 1969; The Castle on the Crag by P. G. Wyal, 1969; Nine Lives by **Ursula K. Le Guin**, 1969; Progression of the Species by **Brian W. Aldiss**, 1967; Report Back - a poem by John Cotton, 1969; The Killing Ground by J. G. Ballard, 1969; The Dannold Cheque by Ken W. Purdy, 1969; Womb to Tomb by Joseph Wesley, 1969; Like Father by Jon Hartridge, 1969; The Electric Ant by **Philip K. Dick**, 1969; The Man Inside by Bruce McAllister, 1969; Now Hear the Word of the Lord by Algis Budrys, 1969; and Afterword - An Awful Lot of Copy by **Brian W. Aldiss**.

13. Best SF: 1969. With **Harry Harrison**. Published by G. P. Putnam's Sons, New York City, 1970. Hardcover. Herein: Introduction by **Harry Harrison**; The Muse by Anthony Burgess, 1968; Working in the Spaceship Yards by **Brian W. Aldiss**, 1969; The Schematic Man by **Frederik Pohl**, 1969; The Snows are Melted, the Snows are Gone by James Tiptree, Jr, 1969; Hospital of Transplanted Hearts by D. M. Thomas, 1969; Eco-Catastrophe by Paul Ehrlich, 1969; The Castle on the Crag by P. G. Wyal, 1969; Nine Lives by **Ursula K. Le Guin**, 1969; Progression of the Species by **Brian W. Aldiss**, 1967; Report Back - a poem by John Cotton, 1969; The Killing Ground by J. G. Ballard, 1969; The Dannold Cheque by Ken W. Purdy, 1969; Womb to Tomb by Joseph Wesley, 1969; Like Father by Jon Hartridge, 1969; The Electric Ant by **Philip K. Dick**, 1969; The Man Inside by Bruce McAllister, 1969; Now Hear the Word of the Lord by Algis Budrys, 1969; and Afterword - An Awful Lot of Copy by **Brian W. Aldiss**.

14. The Year's Best Science Fiction No. 4. With **Harry Harrison**. Published by Sphere Books, London, 1971. Sphere Book 43435. Softcover. Herein: Introduction by **Harry Harrison**; Gone Fishin' by Robin Scott Wilson, 1970; Black is Beautiful by **Robert Silverberg**, 1970; The Lost Face by Josef Nesvadba, 1964; Mary and Joe by Naomi Mitchison, 1962; The Asian Shore by Thomas M. Disch, 1970; Gorman by Jerry Farber, 1969; Oil-Mad Bug-Eyed Monsters by Hayden Howard, 1970; A Pedestrian Accident by Robert Coover, 1969; Traffic Problem by William Earls, 1970; Erem by Gleb Anfilov, 1963; Car Sinister by **Gene Wolfe**, 1970; Franz Kafka by Jorge Luis Borges by Alvin Greenberg, 1970; Pacem Est by Kris Neville and Barry N. Malzberg writing as K. M. O'Donnell; 1970; The Ugupu Bird by Slawomir Mrozk, 1968; and The Afterword: The Day Equality Broke Out by **Brian W. Aldiss**.

15. Best SF: 1970. With **Harry Harrison**. Published by G. P. Putnam's Sons, New York City, 1971. Hardcover. Herein: Introduction by **Harry Harrison**; Gone Fishin' by Robin Scott Wilson, 1970; Black is Beautiful by **Robert Silverberg**, 1970; The Lost Face by Josef Nesvadba, 1964; Mary and Joe by Naomi Mitchison, 1962; The Asian Shore by Thomas M. Disch, 1970; Gorman by Jerry Farber, 1969; Oil-Mad Bug-Eyed Monsters by Hayden Howard, 1970; A Pedestrian Accident by Robert Coover, 1969;

Traffic Problem by William Earls, 1970; Erem by Gleb Anfilov, 1963; Car Sinister by **Gene Wolfe**, 1970; Franz Kafka by Jorge Luis Borges by Alvin Greenberg, 1970; Pacem Est by Kris Neville and Barry N. Malzberg writing as K. M. O'Donnell; 1970; The Ugupu Bird by Slawomir Mrozk, 1968; and The Afterworld: The Day Equality Broke Out by **Brian W. Aldiss**.

16. Best SF: 1971. With **Harry Harrison**. Published by G. P. Putnam's Sons, New York City, 1972. Herein: Introduction by **Harry Harrison**; Doctor Zombie and His Little Furry Friends by Robert Sheckley, 1971; Conquest by Barry N. Malzberg, 1971 Gehenna by Barry N. Malzberg writing as K. M. O'Donnell, 1971; A Meeting with Medusa by **Arthur C. Clarke**, 1971; The Genius by Donald Barthelme, 1971; Angouleme by Thomas M. Disch, 1971; If Hair Were Revived in 2016 by Arnold M. Auerbach, 1971; Statistician's Day by **James Blish**, 1970; The Science Fiction Horror Movie Pocket Computer - an essay by Gahan Wilson, 1971; The Hunter at His Ease by **Brian W. Aldiss**, 1970; The Cohen Dog Exclusion Act by Steven Schrader - 1971; Gauntlet by Richard E. Peck, 1972; Three Poems: Report by Kingsley Amis, 1971; Fisherman by Lawrence Sail, 1971; The Ideal Police State by Charles Baxter, 1971; The Pagan Rabbi by Cynthia Ozick, 1966; An Uneven Evening by Steve Herbst, 1971; Ornithanthropus by B. Alan Burhoe, 1971; No Direction Home by Norman Spinrad, 1971; and Afterword: A Day in the Life-Style of... by **Brian W. Aldiss**.

17. The Year's Best Science Fiction No. 5. With **Harry Harrison**. Published by Sphere Books, London, 1972. Sphere Book 43443. Softcover. Herein: Introduction by **Harry Harrison**; Doctor Zombie and His Little Furry Friends by Robert Sheckley, 1971; Conquest by Barry N. Malzberg, 1971 Gehenna by Barry N. Malzberg writing as K. M. O'Donnell, 1971; A Meeting with Medusa by **Arthur C. Clarke**, 1971; The Genius by Donald Barthelme, 1971; Angouleme by Thomas M. Disch, 1971; If Hair Were Revived in 2016 by Arnold M. Auerbach, 1971; Statistician's Day by **James Blish**, 1970; The Science Fiction Horror Movie Pocket Computer - an essay by Gahan Wilson, 1971; The Hunter at His Ease by **Brian W. Aldiss**, 1970; The Cohen Dog Exclusion Act by Steven Schrader - 1971; Gauntlet by Richard E. Peck, 1972; Three Poems: Report by Kingsley Amis, 1971; Fisherman by Lawrence Sail, 1971; The Ideal Police State by Charles Baxter, 1971; The Pagan Rabbi by Cynthia Ozick, 1966; An Uneven Evening by Steve Herbst, 1971; Ornithanthropus by B. Alan Burhoe, 1971; No Direction Home by Norman Spinrad, 1971; and Afterword: A Day in the Life-Style of... by **Brian W. Aldiss**.

18. The Astounding - Analog Reader, Volume 1. With **Harry Harrison**. Published by Doubleday & Company, Garden City, New York, 1972. Hardcover. Herein: Introduction by **Harry Harrison** and **Brian W. Aldiss**; Forgetfulness by **John W. Campbell** writing as Don A Stuart, 1937; Seeds of the Dusk by Raymond Z. Gallun, 1938; Farewell to the Master by Harry Bates, 1940; Trouble on Tantalus by P. Schuyler Miller, 1941; Time Wants a Skeleton by Ross Rocklynne, 1941; Nightfall by **Isaac Asimov**, 1941; By His Bootstraps by **Robert A. Heinlein** writing as Anson MacDonald, 1941; and The Push of a Finger by **Alfred Bester**, 1942; Clash by Night by Henry Kuttner and **C. L. Moore** writing as Lawrence O'Donnell, 1943; The Storm by **A. E. van Vogt**, 1943; City by Clifford D. Simak, 1944; First Contact by Murray Leinster, 1945; Giant Killer by A. Bertram Chandler, 1945; Vintage Season by Henry Kuttner and **C. L. Moore** writing as Lawrence O'Donnell, 1946; and Placet Is a Crazy Place by Fredric Brown, 1946.

19. The Astounding - Analog Reader, Volume 2. With **Harry Harrison**. Published by Doubleday & Company, Garden City, New York, 1973. Hardcover. Herein: Introduction by **Harry Harrison** and **Brian W. Aldiss**; Thunder and Roses by **Theodore Sturgeon**, 1947; Dreams Are Sacred by Peter Phillips, 1948; Computers Don't Argue by **Gordon R. Dickson**, 1965; Child's Play by William Tenn, 1947; The Little Black Bag by C. M. Kornbluth, 1950; Rescue Operation by **Harry Harrison**, 1964; The Rescuer by Arthur Porges, 1962; The Weather Man by Theodore L. Thomas, 1962; The Yellow Pill by Rog Phillips, 1958; Call Me Joe by **Poul Anderson**, 1957; The Waitabits by **Eric Frank Russell**, 1955; Grandpa by James H. Schmitz, 1954; Pyramid by Robert Abernathy, 1954; The Cold Equations by Tom Godwin, 1954; Imposter by **Philip K. Dick**, 1953; Potential by Robert Sheckley, 1953; Bridge by **James Blish**, 1952; What Have I Done? By Mark Clifton, 1952; Noise Level by Raymond F. Jones, 1952; Hide and Seek by **Arthur C. Clarke**, 1949; and After a Few Words by Randall Garrett writing as Seaton McKettrig.

20. The Astounding - Analog Reader, Volume 1. With **Harry Harrison**. Published by Sphere Books, London, 1973. Softcover. Herein: Introduction by **Harry Harrison** and **Brian W. Aldiss**; Forgetfulness by **John W. Campbell** writing as Don A Stuart, 1937; Seeds of the Dusk by Raymond Z. Gallun, 1938; Farewell to the Master by Harry Bates, 1940; Trouble on Tantalus by P. Schuyler Miller, 1941; Time Wants a Skeleton by Ross Rocklynne, 1941; Nightfall by **Isaac Asimov**, 1941; By His Bootstraps by **Robert A. Heinlein** writing as Anson MacDonald, 1941; and The Push of a Finger by **Alfred Bester**, 1942.

21. The Astounding - Analog Reader, Volume 2. With **Harry Harrison**. Published by Sphere Books, London, 1973. Softcover. Herein: Clash by Night by Henry Kuttner and **C. L. Moore** writing as Lawrence O'Donnell, 1943; The Storm by **A. E. van Vogt**, 1943; City by Clifford D. Simak, 1944; First Contact by Murray Leinster, 1945; Giant Killer by A. Bertram Chandler, 1945; Vintage Season by Henry Kuttner and **C. L. Moore** writing as Lawrence O'Donnell, 1946; and Placet Is a Crazy Place by Fredric Brown, 1946.

22. The Penguin Science Fiction Omnibus. Published by Penguin Books, Middlesex, England, 1973. Penguin book 3145. Softcover. An omnibus edition, this collects all the stories for Penguin Science Fiction, 1961; More Penguin Science Fiction, 1963; and Yet More Penguin Science Fiction, 1964.

23. Best SF: 1972. With **Harry Harrison**. Published by G. P. Putnam's Sons, New York City,

1973. Herein: Introduction by **Harry Harrison**; In the Matter of the Assassin Merefirs by Ken W. Purdy, 1972; The Old Folks by James E. Gunn, 1972; From Sea to Shining Sea by Jonathan Ela, 1972; Weihnachtabend by Keith Roberts, 1972; The Years by Robert F. Young, 1972; Darkness by Andre Carneiro, 1965; Cymbal Player - a poem by Lawrence Sail, 1972; Report From the Planet Proteus - a poem by Lawrence Sail, 1972; Columbus on St. Domenica - a poem by John Cotton, 1972; After Death - a poem by Patricia Beer, 1972; Faex Delenda Est - a poem by Theodore R. Cogswell, 1972; Words of Warning by Alex Hamilton, 1972; Out Wit by Howard L. Myers, 1972; An Imaginary Journey to the Moon by Victor Sabah, 1972; The Head and the Hand by Christopher Priest, 1972; Hero by Joe W. Haldeman, 1972; As For Our Fatal Continuity by **Brian W. Aldiss**, 1972; and Afterword: The Year of the Big Spring Clean by **Brian W. Aldiss**.

24. The Year's Best Science Fiction No. 6. With **Harry Harrison**. Published by Sphere Books, London, 1973. Softcover. Herein: Introduction by **Harry Harrison**; In the Matter of the Assassin Merefirs by Ken W. Purdy, 1972; The Old Folks by James E. Gunn, 1972; From Sea to Shining Sea by Jonathan Ela, 1972; Weihnachtabend by Keith Roberts, 1972; The Years by Robert F. Young, 1972; Darkness by Andre Carneiro, 1965; Cymbal Player - a poem by Lawrence Sail, 1972; Report From the Planet Proteus - a poem by Lawrence Sail, 1972; Columbus on St. Domenica - a poem by John Cotton, 1972; After Death - a poem by Patricia Beer, 1972; Faex Delenda Est - a poem by Theodore R. Cogswell, 1972; Words of Warning by Alex Hamilton, 1972; Out Wit by Howard L. Myers, 1972; An Imaginary Journey to the Moon by Victor Sabah, 1972; The Head and the Hand by Christopher Priest, 1972; Hero by Joe W. Haldeman, 1972; As For Our Fatal Continuity by **Brian W. Aldiss**, 1972; and Afterword: The Year of the Big Spring Clean by **Brian W. Aldiss**.

25. Best SF: 73. With **Harry Harrison**. Published by Berkley Books, New York City, 1974. Softcover. Herein: Introduction by **Harry Harrison**; A Curse - a poem by W. H. Auden, 1972; Auto-Apotheosis - a poem by Anthony Haden-Guest, 1972; Captain Nemo's Last Adventure by Josef Nesvadba, 1964; Early Bird by Theodore R. Cogswell and Theodore L. Thomas, 1973; Escape by Ilya Varshavsky, 1973; La Befana by **Gene Wolfe**, 1983; Mason's Life by Kingsley Amis, 1972; Parthen by R. A. Lafferty, 1973; Roller Ball Murder by William Harrison, 1973; Serpent Burning on an Altar by **Brian W. Aldiss**, 1973; Sister Francetta and Pig Baby by Kenneth Bernard, 1973; Sport - a poem by Steven Utley, 1973; Ten Years Ago by Max Beerbohm, 1972; The Birds by Thomas M. Disch, 1973; The Man Who Collected the First of September 1973 by Tor Age Bringsvaerd, 1973; The Wind and the Rain by **Robert Silverberg**, 1973; Two poems by William Jon Watkins, 1973; We Are Very Happy Here by Joe Haldeman, 1973; Welcome to the Standard Nightmare by Robert Sheckley, 1973; The Window in Dante's Hell by Michael Bishop, 1973; and Afterword: The Wizard and the Plumber by **Brian W. Aldiss**.

26. Best SF: 73. With **Harry Harrison**. Published by G. P. Putnam's Sons, New York City, 1974. First hardcover edition.

27. The Year's Best Science Fiction No. 7. With **Harry Harrison**. Published by Sphere Books, London, 1974. Softcover. Abridged edition. Herein: Introduction by **Harry Harrison**; Mason's Life by Kingsley Amis, 1972; Roller Ball Murder by William Harrison, 1973; Welcome to the Standard Nightmare by Robert Sheckley, 1973; We Are Very Happy Here by Joe W. Haldeman, 1973; The Birds by Thomas M. Disch, 1973; The Wind and the Rain by **Robert Silverberg**, 1973; Ten Years Ago by Max Beerbohm, 1972; Parthen by R. A. Lafferty, 1973; The Man Who Collected the First of September 1973 by Tor Age Bringsvaerd, 1973; Captain Nemo's Last Adventure by Josef Nesvadba, 1964; La Befana by **Gene Wolfe**, 1983; and Serpent Burning on an Altar by **Brian W. Aldiss**, 1973.

28. Space Odysseys. Published by Futura Books, London, 1974. Softcover. Herein: Introductions by **Brian W. Aldiss**; The Sentinel by **Arthur C. Clarke**, 1951; Galactic Patrol - an excerpt by **Edward E. Smith**, 1974; The Lake of Gone Forever by Leigh Brackett, 1949; Reason by **Isaac Asimov**, 1941; Time is the Traitor by **Alfred Bester**, 1953; The Unfinished by Frank Belknap Long, 1951; And I Awoke and Found Me Here on the Cold Hill's Side by James Tiptree, Jr, 1972; Empress of Mars by Ross Rocklynne, 1939; I'm Going to Get You by F. M. Busby, 1974; Strange Exodus by Robert Abernathy, 1950; Star Ship by **Poul Anderson**, 1950; To Each His Star by Bryce Walton, 1952; The Big Hunger by Walter M. Miller, Jr, 1952; Night Watch by James Inglis, 1965; and The Impossible Planet by **Philip K. Dick**, 1953.

29. Space Opera. Published by Futura Books, London, 1974. Softcover. Herein: Introduction by **Brian W. Aldiss**; Answer by Fredric Brown, 1954; Zirn Left Unguarded, the Jenghik Palace in Flames, Jon Westerley Dead by Robert Sheckley, 1972; Honeymoon in Space - excerpt by George Griffiths, 1900; Tonight the Sky Will Fall by Daniel Galouye, 1952; The Star of Life - an excerpt by Edmond Hamilton, 1947; After Ixmal by Jeff Sutton, 1962; Sea Change by Thomas N. Scortia, 1956; Colony by **Philip K. Dick**, 1953; The Sword of Rhiannon - an excerpt by Leigh Brackett, 1949; All Summer in a Day by Ray Bradbury, 1954; The Mitr by **Jack Vance**, 1953; The Storm by **A. E. van Vogt**, 1943; The Paradox Men by Charles Harness, 1949; Time Fuze by Randall Garrett, 1954; and The Last Question by **Isaac Asimov**, 1956.

30. Best SF: 1974. With **Harry Harrison**. Published by Bobbs Merrill, New York City, 1975. Hardcover. This contains: Introduction by **Harry Harrison**; The Scream by **Kate Wilhelm**, 1974; Time Deer by Craig Strete, 1974; After King Kong Fell by Philip Jose Farmer, 1973; The Women Men Don't See by James Tiptree, Jr, 1973; The Four-Hour Fugue by **Alfred Bester**, 1974; A Typical Day by Doris Piserchia, 1974; Programmed Love Story by Ian Watson, 1974; Songs of War by Kit Reed, 1974; The Executioner's Beautiful Daughter by Angela Carter, 1974; When Petals Fall by Sydney J. Van Scyoc, 1973; Paleontology: An Experimental

Brian W. Aldiss

Science by Robert R. Olsen, 1974; Lost and Found by Thomas Baum, 1974; Owing to Circumstances Beyond Our Control, 1984 Has Been Unavoidably Detained by Alan Coren, 1974; The Rise of Airstrip One by Clive James, 1974; Listen with Big Brother by **Brian W. Aldiss**, 1974; Science Fiction Story - a poem by Duane Ackerson, 1973; Eyes of a Woman - from a Portrait by Picasso - a poem by Lisa Conesa, 1975; After Weightlessness - a poem by Lawrence Sail, 1974; and Afterword: The Galaxy Begins at Home by **Brian W. Aldiss**.

31. The Year's Best Science Fiction No. 8. With **Harry Harrison**. Published by Sphere Books, London, 1975. Softcover. Abridged edition. Herein: Introduction by **Harry Harrison**; The Scream by **Kate Wilhelm**, 1974; Time Deer by Craig Strete, 1974; After King Kong Fell by Philip Jose Farmer, 1973; The Women Men Don't See by James Tiptree, Jr, 1973; The Four-Hour Fugue by **Alfred Bester**, 1974; A Typical Day by Doris Piserchia, 1974; Programmed Love Story by Ian Watson, 1974; Songs of War by Kit Reed, 1974; The Executioner's Beautiful Daughter by Angela Carter, 1974; When Petals Fall by Sydney J. Van Scyoc, 1973; Paleontology: An Experimental Science by Robert R. Olsen, 1974; Lost and Found by Thomas Baum, 1974; Owing to Circumstances Beyond Our Control, 1984 Has Been Unavoidably Detained by Alan Coren, 1974; The Rise of Airstrip One by Clive James, 1974; Listen with Big Brother by **Brian W. Aldiss**, 1974; Science Fiction Story - a poem by Duane Ackerson, 1973; After Weightlessness - a poem by Lawrence Sail, 1974; and Afterword: The Galaxy Begins at Home by **Brian W. Aldiss**.

32. Evil Earths. Published by Weidenfeld and Nicolson, London, 1975. Hardcover. Herein: Introduction by **Brian W. Aldiss**; What Is Wrong? What Is Right? Anyway, We're Here - an essay by **Brian W. Aldiss**, 1975; The Last Word by Charles Beaumont and Chad Oliver, 1955; Film of Death by J. Scott Campbell, 1948; The Wound by Howard Fast, 1970; Three Green Blades of Grass - an essay by **Brian W. Aldiss**, 1975; The Golden Men by **Philip K. Dick**, 1954; Guest Expert by Allen K. Lang, 1951; The Valley by Richard Stockham, 1954; Dark They Were and Golem-Eyed - an essay by **Brian W. Aldiss**, 1975; Down Among the Dead Men by William Tenn, 1954; Among the Hairy Earthmen by R. A. Lafferty, 1966; Later Than You Think by **Fritz Leiber**, 1950; Yesterday, Tomorrow and the Desert - an essay by **Brian W. Aldiss**; The Time Trap by Henry Kuttner, 1938; Towards the Fall of Night - an essay by **Brian W. Aldiss**; The Men Return by **Jack Vance**, 1957; Heresies of the Huge God by **Brian W. Aldiss**; If I Forget Thee Oh Earth by **Arthur C. Clarke**, 1951; and Night by **John W. Campbell**, 1935.

33. Decade the 1940s. With **Harry Harrison**. Published by Macmillan, London, 1975. Hardcover. Herein: Introduction by **Brian W. Aldiss; Hobbyist by Eric Frank Russell**, 1947; The Xi Effect by Robert Shirley Richardson writing as Philip Latham, 1950; Huddling Place by Clifford D. Simak, 1944; The Last Objective by Paul Carter, 1946; Fireproof by **Hal Clement**, 1949; Arena by Fredric Brow, 1944n; Co-operate or Else by **A. E. van Vogt**, 1942; and Reason by **Isaac Asimov**, 1941.

34. The Year's Best Science Fiction No. 9. With **Harry Harrison**. Published by Weidenfeld and Nicolson, London, 1976. Hardcover. Herein: Introduction by **Harry Harrison**; A Scraping at the Bones by Algis Budrys, 1975; Changelings by Lisa Tuttle, 1975; The Santa Claus Compromise by Thomas M. Disch, 1974; A Galaxy Called Rome by Barry N. Malzberg, 1975; A Twelvemonth - a poem by Peter Redgrove, 1975; The Custodians by Richard Cowper, 1975; The Linguist by Stephen Robinett, 1975; Settling the World by M. John Harrison, 1975; The Chaste Planet by John Updike, 1975; End Game by Joe Haldeman, 1975; The Lop Eared Cat that Devoured Philadelphia - a poem by Louis Phillips, 1975; A Dead Singer by **Michael Moorcock**, 1974; and Afterword: Science Fiction on The Titanic by **Brian W. Aldiss**.

35. Best SF: 75 - The Ninth Annual. With **Harry Harrison**. Published by Bobbs Merrill, New York City, 1976. Hardcover. Herein: Introduction by **Harry Harrison**; A Scraping at the Bones by Algis Budrys, 1975; Changelings by Lisa Tuttle, 1975; The Santa Claus Compromise by Thomas M. Disch, 1974; A Galaxy Called Rome by Barry N. Malzberg, 1975; A Twelvemonth - a poem by Peter Redgrove, 1975; The Custodians by Richard Cowper, 1975; The Linguist by Stephen Robinett, 1975; Settling the World by M. John Harrison, 1975; The Chaste Planet by John Updike, 1975; End Game by Joe Haldeman, 1975; The Lop Eared Cat that Devoured Philadelphia - a poem by Louis Phillips, 1975; A Dead Singer by **Michael Moorcock**, 1974; and Afterword: Science Fiction on The Titanic by **Brian W. Aldiss**.

36. Galactic Empires - Volume 1. Published by Weidenfeld and Nicolson, London, 1976. Hardcover. Herein: Introduction by **Brian W. Aldiss**; Foundation by **Isaac Asimov**, 1942; Age of Retirement by Hal Lynch, 1954; Immigrant by Clifford D. Simak, 1964; All the Way Back by Michael Shaara, 1952; Protected Species by H. B. Fyfe, 1951; The Possessed by **Arthur C. Clarke**, 1953; The Crime and the Glory of Commander Suzdal by Cordwainer Smith, 1964; Been a Long, Long Time by R. A. Lafferty, 1970; The Star Plunderer by **Poul Anderson**, 1952; We're Civilized by Mark Clifton and Alex Apostolides, 1953; Brightness Falls from the Air by Margaret St Clair writing as Idris Seabright, 1951; The Rebel of Valkyr by Alfred Coppel, 1950; Planting Time by Pete Adams and Charles Nightingale, 1975; and Resident Physician by James White, 1961; along with a series of 1976 essays by Aldiss: The Health Service in the Skies; Horses in the Starship Hold; Wider Still and Wider; and A Sense of Perspective.

37. Galactic Empires - Volume 2. Published by Weidenfeld and Nicolson, London, 1976. Hardcover. Herein: Introduction by **Brian W. Aldiss**; Escape to Chaos by John D. MacDonald, 1951; Concealment by **A. E. van Vogt**, 1943; To Civilize by Algis Budrys, 1954; Beep by **James Blish**, 1954; Down the River by Mack Reynolds, 1950; The Bounty Hunter by Avram Davidson, 1958; Not Yet the End by Fredric Brown, 1941; Tonight the Stars Revolt! by Gardner F. Fox, 1952; Final Encounter by **Harry Harrison**, 1964; Lord of a Thousand Suns by **Poul**

Anderson; Big Ancestor by Floyd L. Wallace, 1954; and The Interlopers by Roger Dee, 1954; along with a series of 1976 essays by Aldiss: You Can't Impose Civilization by Force; The Other end of the Stick; All Things Are Cyclic; and Big Ancestors and Descendants.

38. Decade the 1950s. With **Harry Harrison**. Published by Macmillan, London, 1976. Hardcover. Herein: Introduction by **Harry Harrison**; Grandpa by James H. Schmitz, 1955; The Snowball Effect by Katherine Maclean, 1952; The Edge of the Sea by Algis Budrys, 1958; Scanners Live in Vain by Cordwainer Smith, 1950; The Last Day by Richard Matheson, 1953; The Large Ant by Howard Fast, 1960; Sail On, Sail On by Philip Jose Farmer, 1952; The Holes Around Mars by Jerome Bixby, 1954; Two Handed Engine by Henry Kuttner and **C. L. Moore** writing as Henry Kuttner, 1955; The Star by **Arthur C. Clarke**, 1955; Early Model by Robert Sheckley, 1956; and The Pedestrian by **Ray Bradbury**, 1951.

39. Decade the 1960s. With **Harry Harrison**. Published by Macmillan, London, 1977. Hardcover. Herein: Introduction by **Brian W. Aldiss** and **Harry Harrison**; The Assassination of John Fitzgerald Kennedy Considered as a Motor Race by J. G. Ballard, 1966; Gravity by Harvey Jacobs, 1969; Harrison Bergeron by Kurt Vonnegut, Jr, 1961; Descending by Thomas M. Disch, 1964; Devil Car by Roger Zelazny, 1965; The Nature of the Catastrophe by **Michael Moorcock**, 1970; The Electric Ant by **Philip K. Dick**, 1969; The Last Hurrah of the Golden Horde by Norman Spinrad, 1969; Hemingway in Space by Kingsley Amis, 1960; Computers Don't Argue by **Gordon R. Dickson**, 1965; The Food Goes in the Top by Will Worthington, 1961; Subversive by Mack Reynolds, 1962; Manscarer by Keith Roberts, 1966; Hybrid by Keith Laumer, 1961; The Heat Death of the Universe by Pamela Zoline, 1967; Day Million by **Frederik Pohl**, 1966; Hawksbill Station by **Robert Silverberg**, 1967; and The Village Swindler by **Brian W. Aldiss**, 1968.

40. Galactic Empires. Published by Legend, London, 1988. Softcover. Herein: Introduction by **Brian W. Aldiss**; Foundation by **Isaac Asimov**, 1942; Age of Retirement by Hal Lynch, 1954; Immigrant by Clifford D. Simak, 1964; All the Way Back by Michael Shaara, 1952; Protected Species by H. B. Fyfe, 1951; The Possessed by **Arthur C. Clarke**, 1953; The Crime and the Glory of Commander Suzdal by Cordwainer Smith, 1964; Been a Long, Long Time by R. A. Lafferty, 1970; The Star Plunderer by **Poul Anderson**, 1952; We're Civilized by Mark Clifton and Alex Apostolides, 1953; Brightness Falls from the Air by Margaret St Clair writing as Idris Seabright, 1951; The Rebel of Valkyr by Alfred Coppel, 1950; Planting Time by Pete Adams and Charles Nightingale, 1975; and Resident Physician by James White, 1961; Escape to Chaos by John D. MacDonald, 1951; Concealment by **A. E. van Vogt**, 1943; To Civilize by Algis Budrys, 1954; Beep by **James Blish**, 1954; Down the River by Mack Reynolds, 1950; The Bounty Hunter by Avram Davidson, 1958; Not Yet the End by Fredric Brown, 1941; Tonight the Stars Revolt! by Gardner F. Fox, 1952; Final Encounter by **Harry Harrison**, 1964; Lord of a Thousand Suns by **Poul Anderson**; Big Ancestor by Floyd L. Wallace, 1954; and The Interlopers by Roger Dee, 1954; along with a series of 1976 essays by Aldiss: The Health Service in the Skies; Horses in the Starship Hold; Wider Still and Wider; A Sense of Perspective; You Can't Impose Civilization by Force; The Other end of the Stick; All Things Are Cyclic; and Big Ancestors and Descendants.

41. Perilous Planets. Published by Weidenfeld and Nicolson, London, 1978. Hardcover. Herein: Introduction by **Brian W. Aldiss**; Schwartz Between the Galaxies by **Robert Silverberg**, 1974; Brightside Crossing by Alan E. Nourse, 1956; Four in One by **Damon Knight**, 1953; The Sack by William Morrison, 1950; The age of Invention by Norman Spinrad, 1966; Grenville's Planet by Michael Shaara, 1952; When the People Fell by Cordwainer Smith, 1959; Mouth of Hell by David I. Masson, 1966; The Snowmen by **Frederik Pohl**, 1959; Goddess in Granite by Robert F. Young, 1957; The Monsters by Robert Sheckley, 1953; The Titan by P. Schuyler Miller, 1934; The Monster by **A. E. van Vogt**, 1948; The Art of James Carlyle by Cherry Wilder, 1974; The Seekers by E. C. Tubb, 1965; Beachhead by Clifford D. Simak, 1951; On the River by Robert F. Young, 1965; How Are They All on Deneb IV? - an essay by C. C. Shackleton; and Afterword by **Brian W. Aldiss**.

42. The Penguin World Omnibus of Science Fiction. With Sam Lundwall. Published by Penguin Books, Middlesex, England, 1986. Softcover. This contains: Foreword by Krsto A. Mazuranic; Introduction by **Brian W. Aldiss**; The Half-wit of Xeenemuende by Josef Nesvadba, 1986; Alter Ego by Hugo Correa, 1967; A Perfect Marriage by Andre Carneiro, 1986; The Legend of the Paper Spaceship by Tetsu Yano, 1978; Small World by Bob Shaw, 1978; The Whore of Babylon by Leon Zeldis, 1986; Cost of Living by Robert Sheckley, 1952; Night Broadcast by Ion Hobana, 1986; A Perfect Christmas Evening by Konrad R. Fialkowski, 1986; A Meeting in Georgestown by Jon Bing, 1986; Victims of Time by H. Sridhar Rao, 1969; Myxomatosis Foret by Bertil Martensson, 1986; BCO Equipment by Karl-Michael Armer, 1986; Six Matches by Arkady Strugatsky and Boris Strugatsky, 1961; The Ring by Goran Hudec, 1986; Oh, Lenore! Came the Echo by Carols Maria Federici, 1986; Forward, Mankind! By Ljuben Dilov, 1986; The Mirror Image of the Earth by Zheng Wenguang, 1986; Rising Sun by Peter Lengyel, 1986; The Lens by Annemarie van Ewyck, 1985; Progenitor by Philippe Curval, 1986; The Cage by A. Bertram Chandler, 1957; and An Imaginary Journey to the Moon by Victor Sabah, 1972.

***

NON-FICTION

1. Cities and Stones: A Travellers' Jugoslavia. Published by Faber and Faber, London, 1966. Hardcover.

2. The Shape of Further Things: Speculations on Change. Published by Faber and Faber, London, 1970. Hardcover.

**3. Billion Year Spree: The History of Science

Brian W. Aldiss

Fiction. Published by Weidenfeld and Nicolson, London, 1973. Hardcover.

4. **Science Fiction Art.** Published by New English Library, London, 1975. Softcover.

5. **SF Horizons. With Harry Harrison**. Published by Arno Press, United States, 1975. Hardcover.

6. **Hell's Cartographers: Some Personal Histories of Science Fiction Writers.** With **Harry Harrison**. Published by Weidenfeld and Nicolson, London, 1973. Hardcover. Herein: Sounding Brass Tinkling Cymbal by **Robert Silverberg**; My Affair with Science Fiction by **Alfred Bester**; Knight Piece by **Damon Knight**; Ragged Claws by **Frederik Pohl**; Magic and Bare Boards by **Brian W. Aldiss**; and The Beginning of the Affair by **Harry Harrison**.

7. **This World and Nearer Ones.** Published by Kent State University Press, Ohio, 1981. Softcover.

8. **Science Fiction Quiz.** Published by Weidenfeld and Nicolson, London, 1983. Hardcover.

9. **The Pale Shadow of Science.** Published by Serconia Press, New York City, 1985. Hardcover.

10. **And the Lurid Glare of the Comet.** Published by Serconia Press, New York City, 1985. Hardcover.

11. **Trillion Year Spree: The History of Science Fiction.** With David Wingrove. Published by Victor Gollancz, London, 1986. Hardcover.

12. **Science Fiction Blues: The Show that Brian Aldiss Took on the Road: A Selection of His Best Stories, Poetry and Speculations - An Evening of Wonders.** Published by Avernus, London, 1988. Hardcover.

13. **Bury My Heart at W. H. Smith's.** Hodder and Stoughton, London, 1990. Hardcover.

14. **Science Fiction as Science Fiction.** Published by Bran's Head, UK, 1990. Softcover.

15. **Bodily Functions: Stories, Poems and a Letter on the Subject of Bowel Movement, Addressed to Sam J. Lundwall on the Occasion of His Birthday, February 24th, 1991.** Published by Avernus, London, 1991. Hardcover.

16. **The Detached Retina: Aspects of SF and Fantasy.** Published by the Liverpool University Press, UK, 1995. Hardcover.

17. **The Twinkling of an Eye: My Life as an Englishman.** Published by Little Brown, London, 1998. Hardcover.

***

RELATED

1. **Item Eighty-Three: Brian W. Aldiss, a Bibliography 1954 - 1972.** By Margaret Manson. Published by Dryden Press, Birmingham, UK, 1972. Softcover.

2. **Aldiss Unbound: The Science Fiction of Brian W. Aldiss - The Milford Series of Popular Writers of Today - Volume Nine.** By Richard Mathews. Published by The Borgo Press, San Bernardino, California, 1977. Softcover.

3. **Apertures: A Study of the Writings of Brian W. Aldiss.** Published by Greenwood Press, Westport, Connecticut, 1984. Hardcover.

4. **Brian W. Aldiss: A Man for All Seasons: A Working Bibliography.** By Phil Stephensen-Payne. Published by Galactic Central Publications, Leeds, UK, 1990. Softcover.

5. **A is for Brian: A 65th Birthday Present for Brian W. Aldiss from His Family, Friends, Colleagues and Admirers.** Published by Avernus, London, 1990. Softcover.

6. **Brian W. Aldiss - English Authors Series.** By Tom Henighan. Published by Twayne Publishers, Boston, 1999. Hardcover.

7. **Brian Aldiss.** By Michael R. Collings. Published by Borgo Press, San Bernardino, California, 2008. Hardcover.

Harry Harrison.

Harry Maxwell Harrison was born in Stamford, Connecticut on March 12th, 1925. He got his start in the science fiction business as an illustrator for EC Comics, after working with Wally Wood on a number of romance comics. When the comic industry came under heavy censorship, he moved on to write for syndicated comic strips, including Rick Random - Space Detective, Merlo the Magician, on to The Saint and, eventually, Flash Gordon, which he wrote from 1958 until 1968. He once explained that he had spent those ten years writing Flash Gordon... "to stay alive."

His first published short story was Rock Diver, which he sold to **Damon Knight** for Worlds Beyond, February 1951. It showed up with: Brain of the Galaxy by **Jack Vance**; The Deadliest Female by Lester del Rey; Like a Bird, Like a Fish by H. B. Hickey; The Old Brown Coat, a 1919 reprint by Lord Dunsany; The Acolytes by **Poul Anderson**; Forgotten Tongue, a 1941 reprint by C. M. Kornbluth writing as Walter C. Davies; Clothes Make the Man by Richard Matheson; The Rocket of 1955, a 1939 reprint by C. M. Kornbluth; and Valley of Doom, a 1939 reprint by Halliday Sutherland.

It was 1953 before he had another professional story sale, the next to Rocket Stories for the September 1953 issue. It was An Artist's Life with Harrison writing as Felix Boyd. Also on hand were: Apprentice to the Lamp by Irving E. Cox; Killer by James E. Gunn; Flower Girl by Chester Cohen; The Robot Moon by Stanley Mullen; Underestimation by Jerome Bixby and Algis Budrys writing as Alger Rome; Technical Difficulty by Kirby Brooks; and Day's Work by Noel Loomis.

By 1956, he considered himself a professional writer.

Sometime later, he considered himself a successful one. Between his novels, stories and edited anthologies - most particularly, the anthologies edited with his friend **Brian W. Aldiss** - he made it.

In a recent interview, Harrison said, "I've always had very good reviews." And he went on to talk about how his sales had been good and how his books had stayed in print, one of the keys to good sales. In another interview, he explained that his only serious ambition in this life had been to stay alive as an artist, rather than have a job. "I loathed jobs."

Considering how much work Harrison and **Brian W. Aldiss** produced together, it is no surprise they were both inducted into The Science Fiction Hall of Fame in the same year, 2004.

First editions of Make Room! Make Room! and The Stainless Steel Rat tend to be valued roughly the same for decent copies, somewhere between $400 and $600.00.

Pen names used: Leslie Charteris; Hank Dempsey; Felix Boyd; and Wade Kaempfert.

***

AWARDS

1974. Locus Poll Best Original Anthology Award for Astounding: The John W. Campbell Memorial Anthology.

***

FILMS AND TELEVISION

1. Soylent Green. Based on the 1966 novel, Make Room! Make Room!, this was filmed for release in 1973. Directed by Richard Fleischer, it starred: Charlton Heston; Leigh Taylor-Young; Chuck Connors; Joseph Cotten; Edward G. Robinson; Stephen Young; Mike Henry; Dick Van Patten; Brock Peters; and many others.

2. The History of the SF Film. Directed by Thys Ockersen and released in 1982, **Harry Harrison** was one of the guests in this documentary, along with: Forrest J. Ackerman; Harlan Ellison; **Ridley Scott**; Richard Fleischer; and others.

3. Dream of Doom. Directed by Walter Hill, this was made for the television series Perversions of Science. It aired on June 7th, 1997, Season 1, Episode 1. The show starred: Keith Carradine; Lolita Davidovich; Adam Arkin; Gretchen Palmer; Peter Jason; Lin Shaye; and Maureen Teefy as the voice of Chrome.

4. Soylent Green. It has been announced that David S. Goyer will produce a remake of Soylent Green for Warner Bros.

***

NOVELS AND COLLECTIONS

1. Deathworld. Published by Bantam Books, New York City, 1960. Bantam Book A2160. Softcover.

2. The Stainless Steel Rat. Published by Pyramid Books, New York City, 1961. Pyramid Book F672. Softcover.

3. Planet of the Damned. Published by Bantam Books, New York City, 1962. Bantam Book J2316. Softcover.

4. War with the Robots. Published by Pyramid Books, New York City, 1962. Pyramid Book F-771. Softcover. Herein: Introduction by **Harry Harrison**; Simulated Trainer, 1958; The Velvet Glove, 1956; Arm of the Law, 1958; The Robot Who Wanted to Know, 1958; I See You, 1959; The Repairman, 1958; Survival Planet, 1961; and War with the Robots, 1962.

5. Deathworld 2. Published by Bantam Books, New York City, 1964. Bantam Book F2838. Softcover.

6. The Ethical Engineer. Published by Victor Gollancz, London, 1964. Re-titled from Deathworld 2, the first hardcover edition.

7. Vendetta for The Saint. Ghostwritten for Leslie

Harry Harrison

Charteris. Published by Doubleday & Company, Garden City, New York, 1964. Hardcover.

8. Two Tales and Eight Tomorrow. Published by Victor Gollancz, London, 1965. Hardcover. Herein: Introduction by **Brian W. Aldiss**; The Streets of Ashkelon, 1962; Portrait of the Artist, 1964; Rescue Operation, 1964; Captain Bedlam, 1957; Final Encounter, 1964; Unto My Manifold Dooms, 1964; The Pliable Animal, 1962; Captain Honario Harpplayer R.N., 1963; According to His Abilities, 1964; and I Always Do What Teddy Says, 1965.

9. Plague from Space. Published by Doubleday & Company, Garden City, New York, 1965. Hardcover.

10. Bill, the Galactic Hero. Published by Doubleday & Company, Garden City, New York, 1965. Hardcover.

11. Make Room! Make Room!. Published by Doubleday & Company, Garden City, New York, 1966. Hardcover.

12. The Technicolor Time Machine. Published by Doubleday & Company, Garden City, New York, 1967. Hardcover.

13. Sense of Obligation. Published by Dennis Dobson, London, 1967. Hardcover. Re-titled from Planet of the Damned, 1962.

14. The Man from P.I.G. Published by Avon Books, New York City, 1968. Avon Camelot Book ZS136. Softcover.

15. Deathworld 3. Published by Dell Books, New York City, 1968. Dell Book 1849. Softcover.

16. Deathworld 3. Published by Faber and Faber, London, 1969. First hardcover edition.

17. Captive Universe. Published by G. P. Putnam's Sons, New York City, 1969. Hardcover.

18. The Stainless Steel Rat. Published by Walker and Company, New York City, 1970. First hardcover edition.

19. The Stainless Steel Rat's Revenge. Published by Walker and Company, New York City, 1970. Hardcover.

20. The Jupiter Legacy. Published by Bantam Books, New York City, 1970. Bantam Book S5445. Softcover. Re-titled from Plague from Space, 1965.

21. Prime Number. Published by Berkley Books, New York City, 1970. Berkley Book S1857. Softcover. This contains: Mute Milton, 1966; The Greatest Car in the World, 1966; The Final Battle, 1970; The Powers of Observation, 1968; The Ghoul Squad, 1969; Toy Shop, 1962; You Men of Violence, 1967; The Finest Hunter in the world, 1970; Down to Earth, 1963; Commando Raid, 1970; Not Me, Not Amos Cabot!, 1964; The Secret of Stonehenge, 1968; Incident in the IND, 1964; If, 1969; Contact Man, 1966; The Pad, 1970; A Civil Service Servant, 1967; A Criminal Act, 1967; and Famous Last Words, 1965.

22. The Daleth Effect. Published by G. P. Putnam's Sons, New York City, 1970. Hardcover.

23. In Our Hands, the Stars. Published by Faber and Faber, London, 1970. Hardcover. Re-titled from The Daleth Effect, 1970.

24. Spaceship Medic. Published by Faber and Faber, London, 1970. Hardcover.

25. One Step from Earth. Published by Macmillan, New York City, 1970. Hardcover. Herein: Introduction: The Matter Transmitter by **Harry Harrison**; Pressure, 1969; No War, or Battle's Sound, 1968; Wife to the Lord, 1970; Waiting Place, 1968; The Life Preservers, 1970; From Fanaticism, or for Reward, 1969; Heavy Duty, 1970; A Tale of the Ending, 1970; and One Step from Earth, 1970.

26. Stonehenge. With Leon E. Stover. Published by Peter Davies, London, 1972. Hardcover.

27. The Stainless Steel Rat Saves the World. Published by G. P. Putnam's Sons, New York City, 1972. Hardcover.

28. Tunnel Through the Deeps. Published by G. P. Putnam's Sons, New York City, 1972. Hardcover.

29. A Transatlantic Tunnel, Hurrah! Published by Faber and Faber, London, 1972. Hardcover. Re-titled from Tunnel Through the Deeps, 1972.

30. Montezuma's Revenge. Published by Doubleday & Company, Garden City, New York, 1972. Hardcover.

31. Star Smashers of the Galaxy Rangers. Published by G. P. Putnam's Sons, New York City, 1970. Hardcover.

32. Queen Victoria's Revenge. Published by Doubleday & Company, Garden City, New York, 1974. Hardcover.

33. The Deathworld Trilogy. Published by Nelson Doubleday - The Science Fiction Book Club, Garden City, New York, 1974. First hardcover of Deathworld, 1960. An omnibus, this collects: Deathworld, 1960; Deathworld 2, 1964; and Deathworld 3, 1968.

34. The Man from P.I.G. and R.O.B.O.T. Published by Faber and Faber, London, 1974. Hardcover. Herein: The Graduates, 1974; The Man from P.I.G., 1967; and The Man from R.O.B.O.T., 1969.

35. The California Iceberg. Published by Faber and Faber, London, 1975. Hardcover.

36. Skyfall. Published by Faber and Faber, London, 1976. Hardcover.

37. The Best of Harry Harrison. Published by Pocket Books, New York City, 1976. Pocket Book 80525. Softcover. Herein: Foreword: **Harry Harrison**: The Man Who Walked Home by Barry N. Malzberg; Introduction by **Harry Harrison**; The Streets of Ashkelon, 1962; Captain Honario Harpplayer R. N., 1963; Rescue Operation, 1964; At Last, the True Story of Frankenstein, 1965; I Always Do What Teddy Says, 1965; Portrait of the Artist, 1964; Not Me, Not Amos Cabot!, 1964; Mute Milton, 1966; A Criminal Act, 1967; Waiting Place, 1968; If, 1968; I Have My Vigil, 1968; From Fanaticism, or For Reward, 1969; By the Falls, 1970; The Ever

Branching Tree, 1970; Brave Newer World, 1971; Roommates, 1971; The Mothballed Spaceship, 1973; An Honest Day's Work, 1973; and Space Rats of the C.C.C., 1974.

38. The Best of Harry Harrison. Published by Sidgwick and Jackson, London, 1976. First hardcover edition but it deletes the Malzberg foreword, leaves out one story, Not Me, Not Amos Cabot!, 1964, and adds two extras: The Wicked Flee, 1971; and We Ate the Whole Thing, 1973.

39. The Lifeship. With **Gordon R. Dickson**. Harper and Row, New York City, 1976. Hardcover.

40. The Adventures of the Stainless Steel Rat. Published by Nelson Doubleday - The Science Fiction Book Club, Garden City, New York, 1977. Hardcover. An omnibus edition, this gathers: The Stainless Steel Rat, 1961; The Stainless Steel Rat's Revenge, 1970; and The Stainless Steel Rat Saves the World, 1972.

41. The Stainless Steel Rat Wants You! Published by Bantam Books, New York City, 1978. Softcover.

42. The Stainless Steel Rat Wants You! Published by Michael Joseph, London, 1978. First hardcover edition.

43. Homeworld. Published by Bantam Books, New York City, 1980. Softcover.

44. Wheelworld. Published by Bantam Books, New York City, 1981. Softcover.

45. Starworld. Published by Bantam Books, New York City, 1981. Softcover.

46. To the Stars. Published by Nelson Doubleday - The Science Fiction Book Club, Garden City, New York, 1981. Hardcover. An omnibus edition, this gathers: Homeworld, 1980; Wheelworld, 1981; and Starworld, 1981.

47. Planet of No Return. Published by Simon and Schuster, New York City, 1981. Softcover.

48. The QE2 Is Missing. Published by Tor Books - Tom Doherty Associates, New York City, 1982. Softcover.

49. Invasion: Earth. Published by Ace Books, New York City, 1983. Softcover.

50. The Stainless Steel Rat for President. Published by Bantam Books, New York City, 1982. Softcover.

51. The Stainless Steel Rat for President. Published by Nelson Doubleday - The Science Fiction Book Club, Garden City, New York, 1982. First hardcover edition.

52. A Rebel in Time. Published by Pinnacle Books, New York City, 1983. Softcover.

53. West of Eden. Published by Bantam Press, New York City, 1984. Hardcover.

54. A Stainless Steel Rat is Born. Published by Bantam Spectra, New York City, 1985. Softcover.

55. A Stainless Steel Rat is Born. Published by Titan Books, London, 1985. First hardcover edition.

56. Winter in Eden. Published by Bantam Spectra, New York City, 1986. Hardcover.

57. The Stainless Steel Rat Gets Drafted. Published by Bantam Books, London, 1987. Hardcover.

58. Return to Eden. Published by Bantam Spectra, New York City, 1988. Hardcover.

59. You Can Be the Stainless Steel Rat. Published by Ace Books, New York City, 1988. Softcover.

60. Bill the Galactic Hero: The Planet of the Robot Slaves. Published by Avon Books, New York City, 1989. Softcover.

61. Bill the Galactic Hero on the Planet of the Robot Slaves. Published by Victor Gollancz, London, 1989. First hardcover edition.

62. Bill the Galactic Hero on the Planet of the Bottled Brains. With Robert Sheckley. Published by Avon Books, New York City, 1990. Softcover.

63. Bill the Galactic Hero on the Planet of the Bottled Brains. With Robert Sheckley. Published by Victor Gollancz, London, 1990. First hardcover edition.

64. Bill the Galactic Hero on the Planet of Tasteless Pleasure. With David Bischoff. Published by Avon Books, New York City, 1991. Softcover.

65. Bill the Galactic Hero on the Planet of Tasteless Pleasure. With David Bischoff. Published by Victor Gollancz, London, 1991. First hardcover edition.

66. Bill the Galactic Hero on the Planet of Zombie Vampires. With Jack C. Haldeman II. Published by Avon Books, New York City, 1991. Softcover.

67. Bill the Galactic Hero on the Planet of Ten Thousand Bars. With David Bischoff. Published by Avon Books, New York City, 1991. Softcover.

68. Bill the Galactic Hero on the Planet of Zombie Vampires. With Jack C. Haldeman II. Published by Victor Gollancz, London, 1992. First hardcover edition.

69. Bill the Galactic Hero on the Planet of the Hippies from Hell. With David Bischoff. Published by Victor Gollancz, London, 1992. First hardcover edition. Re-titled from Bill the Galactic Hero on the Planet of Ten Thousand Bars, 1991.

70. Bill the Galactic Hero: The Final Incoherent Adventure!. With David Harris. Published by AvoNova Books, New York City, 1992. Softcover.

71. The Turing Option. With Marvin Minsky. Published by Warner Books, New York City, 1992. Hardcover.

72. Bill the Galactic Hero: The Final Incoherent Adventure!. With David Harris. Published by Victor Gollancz, London, 1993. First hardcover edition.

Harry Harrison

73. Stainless Steel Visions. Published by Legend Books, London, 1993. Hardcover. This contains: Introduction by **Harry Harrison**; The Streets of Ashkelon, 1962; Toy Shop, 1962; Not Me, Not Amos Cabot!, 1964; The Mothballed Spaceship, 1973; Commando Raid, 1970; The Repairman, 1958; Brave Newer World, 1971; The Secret of Stonehenge, 1968; Rescue Operation, 1964; Portrait of the Artist, 1964; Survival Planet, 1961; Roommates, 1971; and The Golden Years of the Stainless Steel Rat, 1993.

74. The Hammer and the Cross. With Tom Shippey writing as John Holm. Published by Legend Books, London, 1993. Hardcover.

75. The Stainless Steel Rat Sings the Blues. Published by Bantam Books, London, 1994. Hardcover.

76. Galactic Dreams. Published by Tor Books - Tom Doherty Associates, New York City, 1994. Hardcover. Herein: Introduction: A Writer's Life by **Harry Harrison**; Bill the Galactic Hero's Happy Holiday, 1995; I Always Do What Teddy Says, 1965; Space Rats of the CCC, 1974; Down to Earth, 1963; A Criminal Act, 1967; Famous First Words, 1965; The Pad - A Story of the Day After the Day After Tomorrow, 1995; If, 1969; Mute Milton, 1966; Simulated Trainer, 1958; At Last, the True Story of Frankenstein, 1965; and The Robot Who Wanted to Know, 1958.

77. One King's Way. With Tom Shippey writing as John Holm. Published by Legend Books, London, 1995. Hardcover.

78. Warriors of the Way. With Tom Shippey writing as John Holm. Published by Guild America Books, New York City, 1995. An omnibus edition, this collects: The Hammer and the Cross, 1993; and One King's Way, 1995.

79. King and Emperor. With Tom Shippey writing as John Holm. Published by Legend Books, London, 1996. Hardcover.

80. The Stainless Steel Rat Goes to Hell. Published by Tor Books - Tom Doherty Associates, New York City, 1996. Hardcover.

81. Stars and Stripes Forever. Published by Hodder and Stoughton, London, 1998. Hardcover.

82. The Deathworld Omnibus. Published by Orbit/Little Brown, London, 1999. Reprints The Deathworld Trilogy, 1974, and adds a new introduction by **Harry Harrison**.

83. The Stainless Steel Rat Joins the Circus. Published by Tor Books - Tom Doherty Associates, New York City, 1999. Hardcover.

84. Stars and Stripes in Peril. Published by Hodder and Stoughton, London, 2000. Hardcover.

85. 50 in 50. Published by Tor Books - Tom Doherty Associates, New York City, 2001. Hardcover. Herein: Introduction by **Harry Harrison**; The Streets of Ashkelon, 1962; Rescue Operation, 1964; The Repairman, 1958; Pressure, 1969; Welcoming Committee, 1957; Heavy Duty, 1970; A Criminal Act, 1967; Roommates, 1971; The Pliable Animal, 1962; After the Storm, 1985; Down to Earth, 1963; Final Encounter, 1964; Speed of the Cheetah, Roar of the Lion, 1975; The Greatest Car in the World, 1966; Rock Driver, 1951; Toy Shop, 1962; I Always Do What Teddy Says, 1965; From Fanaticism, or For Reward, 1969; I See You, 1959; The Greening of the Green, 1978; The Day After the End of the World, 1980; The Man from P.I.G., 1967; Space Rats of the CCC, 1974; Captain Horatio Harpplayer R.N., 1963; Simulated Trainer, 1958; Survival Planet, 1961; How the Old World Died, 1964; The K-Factor, 1960; Arm of the Law, 1958; The Robot Who Wanted to Know, 1958; I Have My Vigil, 1968; The Velvet Glove, 1956; Not Me, Not Amos Cabot!, 1964; The Gods Themselves Throw Incense, 1966; You Men of Violence, 1967; A Civil Service Servant, 1967; Captain Bedlam, 1957; At Last, the True Story of Frankenstein, 1965; Incident in the IND, 1964; Portrait of the Artist, 1964; Mute Milton, 1966; An Artist's Life, 1953; The Ever-Branching Tree, 1970; By the Falls, 1970; American Dead, 1970; Dawn of the Endless Night, 1992; An Honest Day's Work, 1973; If, 1969; Brave Newer World, 1971; and The Road to the Year 3000, 2001.

86. Stars and Stripes Triumphant. Published by Hodder and Stoughton, London, 2002. Hardcover.

87. A Stainless Steel Trio. Published by Tor Books - Tom Doherty Associates, New York City, 2002. Hardcover. An omnibus, this gathers: Introduction by **Harry Harrison**; A Stainless Steel Rat Is born, 1985; The Stainless Steel Rat Gets Drafted, 1987; and The Stainless Steel Rat Sings the Blues, 1994.

88. The Stainless Steel Rat Omnibus. Published by Victor Gollancz, London, 2008. Softcover. Retitled from The Adventures of the Stainless Steel Rat, 1977.

***

ANTHOLOGIES

1. Nebula Award Stories Two. With **Brian W. Aldiss**. Published by Doubleday & Company, Garden City, New York, 1967. Hardcover. Herein: Introduction by **Brian W. Aldiss** and **Harry Harrison**; We Can Remember It For You Wholesale by **Philip K. Dick**, 1966; The Secret Place by Richard McKenna, 1966; Light of Other Days by Bob Shaw, 1967; Who Needs Insurance by Robin S. Scott, 1966; Among the Hairy Earthmen by R. A. Lafferty, 1966; The Last Castle by **Jack Vance**, 1966; Day Million by **Frederik Pohl**, 1966; When I Was Miss Dow by Sonya Dorman, 1966; Call Him Lord by **Gordon R. Dickson**, 1966; In the Imagicon by George Henry Smith, 1966; and Man in His Time by **Brian W. Aldiss**, 1965.

2. All About Venus. With **Brian W. Aldiss**. Published by Dell Books, New York, 1968. Dell Book 0085. Softcover. Herein: Foreword by **Brian W. Aldiss**; Clouded Judgements - an essay by **Brian W. Aldiss**, 1968; Destinies of the Stars - an essay by Svante Arrhenius, 1971; Last and First Men - an excerpt by Olaf Stapledon, 1930; Pirates of Venus - an excerpt by **Edgar Rice Burroughs**, 1932; Perelandra - an excerpt by C. S. Lewis, 1943; Exploring the Planets - an essay by V. A. Firsoff,

1964; The Big Rain by **Poul Anderson**, 1954; Big sister - an essay by **Brian W. Aldiss**, 1968; Intelligent Life in the Universe - an essay by Carl Sagan, 1966; Escape to Venus by S. Makepeace Lott, 1956; The Open Question - an essay by **Brian W. Aldiss**, 1968; Sister Planet by **Poul Anderson**, 1959; Before Eden by **Arthur C. Clarke**, 1961; Some Mysteries of Venus Resolved - an essay by Sir Bernard Lovell, 1967; Dream of Distance - Anonymous essay, 1967; and Venus Mystery for Scientists - an essay by John Davy, 1967.

3. Apeman, Spaceman. With Leon E. Stover. Published by Doubleday & Company, Garden City, New York, 1968. Hardcover. Herein: Foreword by Carleton S. Coon; Introduction by Leon E. Stover and **Harry Harrison**; Neanderthal - a poem by Marijane Allen, 1956; Goldfish Bowl by **Robert A. Heinlein** writing as Anson MacDonald, 1942; Throwback by L. Sprague de Camp, 1949; Apology for Man's Physique by Earnest A. Hooton, 1968; The Renegade by Lester Del Rey writing as Marion Henry, 1943; Eltonian Pyramid - an essay by Ralph W. Dexter, 1952; The Second-class Citizen by **Damon Knight**, 1963; Culture by Jerry Shelton, 1944; The Man of the Year Million by H. G. Wells, 1893; In the Beginning by Morton Klass, 1954; The Future of the Races of Man - an essay by Carleton S. Coon, 1965; The Evolution Man by Roy Lewis, 1960; The Kon-Tiki Myth - an essay by Robert C. Suggs, 1960; A Medal for Horatius by William C. Hall, 1955; Omnilingual by H. Beam Piper, 1957; For Those Who Follow After by Dean McLaughlin, 1951; A Preliminary Investigation of an Early Man Site in the Delaware River Valley by Charles W. Ward and Timothy J. O'Leary, 1968; Body Ritual Among the Nacirema by Horace M. Miner, 1966; The Wait by Kit Reed, 1958; Everbodyovskyism in Cat City by Lao Shaw, 1968; The Nine Billion Names of God by **Arthur C. Clarke**, 1953; The Captives by Julian Chain, 1953; Men in Space - an essay by Harold D. Lasswell, 1968; Of Course by Chad Oliver, 1954; and an afterword by Leon E. Stover.

4. Backdrop of Stars. Published by Dennis Dobson, London, 1968. Hardcover. Herein: Introduction by **Harry Harrison**; Consumer's Report by Theodore R. Cogswell, 1955; Day Million by **Frederik Pohl**, 1966; End-Game by J. G. Ballard, 1963; Judas Danced by **Brian W. Aldiss**, 1958; Missing Link by **Frank Herbert**, 1959; Myths My Great-Grandfather Taught Me by **Fritz Leiber**, 1963; Proposal by L. Sprague de Camp, 1952; Retaliation by Mack Reynolds, 1965; Sail On! Sail On! By Philip Jose Farmer, 1952; Syndrome Johnny by Katherine MacLean, 1951; The Last of the Deliverers by **Poul Anderson**, 1958; and Tiger Ride by **James Blish** and **Damon Knight**, 1948.

5. SF: Author's Choice. Published by Berkley Books, New York City, 1968. Berkley Book S1567. Softcover. Re-titled from Backdrop of Stars, 1968.

6. Best SF: 1967. With **Brian W. Aldiss**. Published by Berkley Books, New York City, 1968. Berkley Book S1529. Softcover. Herein: Introduction by **Harry Harrison**; Credo - an essay by **James Blish**, 1968; Hawksbill Station by **Robert Silverberg**, 1967; 1937 A.D. by John T. Sladek, 1967; Fifteen Miles by Ben Bova, 1967; The Vine by Kit Reed, 1967; Interview with a Lemming by James Thurber, 1941; The Left Hand Way by A. Bertram Chandler, 1967; The Wreck of the Ship John B by Frank M. Robinson, 1967; The Forest of Zil by Kris Neville, 1967; The Assassination of John Fitzgerald Kennedy Considered as a Downhill Motor Race by J. G. Ballard, 1966; Answering Service by **Fritz Leiber**, 1967; The Last Command by Keith Laumer, 1967; Mirror of Ice by Gary Wright, 1967; Pretty Maggie Moneyeyes by Harlan Ellison, 1967; and Afterword - Knights of the Paper Spaceship by **Brian W. Aldiss**.

7. The Year's Best Science Fiction No. 1. With **Brian W. Aldiss**. Published by Sphere Books, London, 1968. Sphere Book 43311. Softcover. Herein: Introduction by **Harry Harrison**; Credo - an essay by **James Blish**, 1968; Hawksbill Station by **Robert Silverberg**, 1967; 1937 A.D. by John T. Sladek, 1967; Fifteen Miles by Ben Bova, 1967; The Vine by Kit Reed, 1967; Interview with a Lemming by James Thurber, 1941; The Left Hand Way by A. Bertram Chandler, 1967; The Wreck of the Ship John B by Frank M. Robinson, 1967; The Forest of Zil by Kris Neville, 1967; The Assassination of John Fitzgerald Kennedy Considered as a Downhill Motor Race by J. G. Ballard, 1966; Answering Service by **Fritz Leiber**,1967; The Last Command by Keith Laumer, 1967; Mirror of Ice by Gary Wright, 1967; Pretty Maggie Moneyeyes by Harlan Ellison, 1967; and Afterword - Knights of the Paper Spaceship by **Brian W. Aldiss**.

8. Farewell, Fantastic Venus! With **Brian W. Aldiss**. Published by Macdonald, London, 1968. Hardcover. Herein: Foreword by **Brian W. Aldiss**; Before Eden by **Arthur C. Clarke**, 1961; The Big Rain by **Poul Anderson**, 1954; Sister Planet by **Poul Anderson**, 1959; Escape to Venus - an excerpt by S. Makepeace Lott, 1956; Perelandra - an excerpt by C. S. Lewis, 1943; Pirates of Venus - an excerpt by **Edgar Rice Burroughs**, 1932; Intelligent Life in the Universe - an excerpt by Carl Sagan, 1966; A City on Venus by Henry Gade, 1941; Alchemy by John de Courcy and Dorothy de Courcy, 1950; A Honeymoon in Space - an excerpt by George Griffith, 1900; A Trip to Venus - an excerpt by John Munro, 1897; Last and First Men - an excerpt by Olaf Stapledon, 1930; along with an assortment of essays: Scientist Says Icecaps on Venus Would Make Life Possible by Evert Clark, 1968; Venus Mystery for Scientists by John Davy, 1967; Dream of Distance - anonymous, 1967; Some Mysteries of Venus Resolved by Sir Bernard Lovell, 1967; The Open Question by **Brian W. Aldiss**, 1968; Big Sister by **Brian W. Aldiss**, 1968; Exploring the Planets by V. A. Firsoff, 1996; Venus Is Hell! by **Brian W. Aldiss**, 1968; Unveiling the Mystery Planet by Willy Ley, 1955; The Man from Venus by Frank R. Paul, 1949; Swamp and Sand by **Brian W. Aldiss**, 1968; The Destinies of the Stars by Svante Arrhenius, 1917; Never-Fading Flowers by **Brian W. Aldiss**, 1968; The Story of the Heavens by Sir Robert Ball, 1882; and Clouded Judgements by **Brian W. Aldiss**, 1968.

9. Four for the Future. Published by Macdonald Science Fiction, London, 1969. Hardcover. Herein: Introduction by **Harry Harrison**; The Circulation of the Blood by **Brian W. Aldiss**, 1966; And the

Harry Harrison

Stagnation of the Heart by **Brian W. Aldiss**, 1968; A Hero's Life by **James Blish**, 1966; High Treason by **Poul Anderson**, 1966; The Dipteroid Phenomenon by **Poul Anderson**, 1968; The Gods Themselves Throw Incense by **Harry Harrison**, 1966; and The Ghoul Squad by **Harry Harrison**, 1969.

10. Blast Off: SF for Boys. Published by Faber and Faber, London, 1969. Hardcover. Herein: The Wall Around the World by Theodore R. Cogswell, 1953; Keyhole by Murray Leinster, 1951; Heavy Planet by Milton A. Rothman writing as Lee Gregor, 1939; Tricky Tonnage by Malcolm Jameson, 1944; A Pail of Air by **Fritz Leiber**, 1951; Hi Diddle Diddle! by **Robert Silverberg** writing as Calvin M. Knox, 1959; Sunjammer by **Arthur C. Clarke**, 1964; The Howling Bounders by **Jack Vance**, 1949; The Thing Under the Glacier by **Brian W. Aldiss**, 1963; Rock Pilot by **Harry Harrison**, 1965; and Moon Wreck by William F. Temple, 1953.

11. The Year's Best Science Fiction No. 2. With **Brian W. Aldiss**. Published by Sphere Books, London, 1969. Sphere Book 43354. Softcover. Herein: Introduction by **Harry Harrison**; Budget Planet by Robert Sheckley, 1968; Appointment on Prila by Bob Shaw, 1968; Lost Ground by David I. Masson, 1966; The Rime of the Ancient SF Author or Conventions and Recollections - a poem by J. R. Pierce, 1968; The Annex by John D. MacDonald, 1968; Segregationist by **Isaac Asimov**, 1968; Final War by Barry N. Malzberg writing as K. M. O'Donnell, 1968; 2001: A Space Odyssey - Some Selected Reviews from 1968 by Lester del Rey; **Samuel R. Delaney**; Ed Emshwiller; and Leon E. Stover; Golden Acres by Kit Reed, 1967; Criminal in Utopia by Mack Reynolds, 1968; One Station on the Way by **Fritz Leiber**, 1968; Sweet Dreams, Melissa by Stephen Goldin, 1968; To the Dark Star by **Robert Silverberg**, 1968; Like Young by **Theodore Sturgeon**, 1960; and Afterword - The House that Jules Built by **Brian W. Aldiss**.

12. Best SF: 1968. With **Brian W. Aldiss**. Published by G. P. Putnam's Sons, New York, 1969. Hardcover. Herein: Introduction by **Harry Harrison**; Budget Planet by Robert Sheckley, 1968; Appointment on Prila by Bob Shaw, 1968; Lost Ground by David I. Masson, 1966; The Rime of the Ancient SF Author or Conventions and Recollections - a poem by J. R. Pierce, 1968; The Annex by John D. MacDonald, 1968; Segregationist by **Isaac Asimov**, 1968; Final War by Barry N. Malzberg writing as K. M. O'Donnell, 1968; 2001: A Space Odyssey - Some Selected Reviews from 1968 by Lester del Rey; **Samuel R. Delaney**; Ed Emshwiller; and Leon E. Stover; Golden Acres by Kit Reed, 1967; Criminal in Utopia by Mack Reynolds, 1968; One Station on the Way by **Fritz Leiber**, 1968; Sweet Dreams, Melissa by Stephen Goldin, 1968; To the Dark Star by **Robert Silverberg**, 1968; The Serpent of Kundalini by **Brian W. Aldiss**, 1968; and Afterword - The House that Jules Built by **Brian W. Aldiss**.

13. Worlds of Wonder. Published by Doubleday & Company, Garden City, New York, 1969. Hardcover. Herein: Introduction by **Harry Harrison**; Sunjammer by **Arthur C. Clarke**, 1964; We Didn't Do Anything Wrong, Hardly by Roger Kuykendall, 1959; Who Can Replace A Man? by **Brian W. Aldiss**, 1958; Tricky Tonnage by Malcolm Jameson, 1944; Appointment on Prila by Bob Shaw, 1968; Hi Diddle Diddle by **Robert Silverberg**, 1959; A Pail of Air by **Fritz Leiber**, 1951; The Howling Bounders by **Jack Vance**, 1949; Mirror of Ice by Gary Wright, 1967; Heavy Planet by Milton A. Rothman, writing as Lee Gregor, 1939; Keyhole by Murray Leinster, 1951; The Wall Around the World by Theodore R. Cogswell, 1953; Prone by Mack Reynolds, 1954; Escape the Morning by **Poul Anderson**, 1966; Someday by **Isaac Asimov**, 1956; and If by **Harry Harrison**, 1969.

14. The Year 2000. Published by Doubleday & Company, Garden City, New York, 1970. Hardcover. All work was done in 1970: Introduction by **Harry Harrison**; America the Beautiful by **Fritz Leiber**; Prometheus Rebound by Daniel F. Galouye; Far from This Earth by Chad Oliver; After the Accident by Naomi Mitchison; Utopian by Mack Reynolds; Orgy of the Living and the Dying by **Brian W. Aldiss**; Sea Change by Bertram Chandler; Black Is Beautiful by **Robert Silverberg**; Take It or Leave It by David I. Masson; The Lawgiver by Keith Laumer; To Be a Man by J. J. Coupling; Judas Fish by Thomas N. Scortia; and American Dead by **Harry Harrison**.

15. SF: Author's Choice 2. Published by Berkley Books, New York City, 1970. Berkley Book S1837. Softcover. Herein: Introduction by **Harry Harrison**; Proof by **Hal Clement**, 1942; Diplomatic Coop by Daniel F. Galouye, 1959; Fondly Fahrenheit by **Alfred Bester**, 1954; Contact Between Equals by Algis Budrys, 1958; Late by A. Bertram Chandler, 1955; Love in the dark by H. L. Gold, 1951; The Expert Touch by Alan E. Nourse, 1955; A Stick for Harry Eddington by Chad Oliver, 1965; Just Curious by James H. Schmitz, 1968; To See the Invisible Man by **Robert Silverberg**, 1963; Heir Unapparent by **A. E. van Vogt,** 1945; and Auto-Ancestral Fracture by **Brian W. Aldiss**, 1967.

16. Nova 1. Published by Delacorte Press, New York City, 1970. Hardcover. Most of the work was done in the book's publication year: Introduction by **Harry Harrison**; The Big Connection by Robin Scott; A Happy Day in 2381 by **Robert Silverberg**; Terminus Est by Barry N. Malzberg; Hexamnion by Chan Davis; The Higher Things by J. R. Pierce; Swastika by **Brian W. Aldiss**; The HORARS of War by **Gene Wolfe**; Love Story in Three Acts by David Gerrold; Jean Dupres by **Gordon R. Dickson**; In the Pocket by Barry N. Malzberg writing as K. M. O'Donnell; Faces and Hands by James Sallis; The Winner by Donald E. Westlake; and The Whole Truth by Piers Anthony; along with: And This Did Dante Do - a poem by **Ray Bradbury**, 1967; and Mary and Joe by Naomi Mitchison, 1962.

17. The Year's Best Science Fiction No. 3. With **Brian W. Aldiss**. Published by Sphere Books, London, 1970. Sphere Book 43419. Softcover. Herein: Introduction by **Harry Harrison**; The Muse by Anthony Burgess, 1968; Working in the Spaceship Yards by **Brian W. Aldiss**, 1969; The Schematic Man by **Frederik Pohl**, 1969; The Snows are Melted, the Snows are Gone by James Tiptree, Jr, 1969; Hospital of Transplanted Hearts by D. M. Thomas, 1969; Eco-Catastrophe by Paul Ehrlich, 1969; The Castle on the Crag by P. G. Wyal, 1969;

Nine Lives by **Ursula K. Le Guin**, 1969; Progression of the Species by **Brian W. Aldiss**, 1967; Report Back - a poem by John Cotton, 1969; The Killing Ground by J. G. Ballard, 1969; The Dannold Cheque by Ken W. Purdy, 1969; Womb to Tomb by Joseph Wesley, 1969; Like Father by Jon Hartridge, 1969; The Electric Ant by **Philip K. Dick**, 1969; The Man Inside by Bruce McAllister, 1969; Now Hear the Word of the Lord by Algis Budrys, 1969; and Afterword - An Awful Lot of Copy by **Brian W. Aldiss**.

18. Best SF: 1969. With **Brian W. Aldiss**. Published by G. P. Putnam's Sons, New York City, 1970. Hardcover. Herein: Introduction by **Harry Harrison**; The Muse by Anthony Burgess, 1968; Working in the Spaceship Yards by **Brian W. Aldiss**, 1969; The Schematic Man by **Frederik Pohl**, 1969; The Snows are Melted, the Snows are Gone by James Tiptree, Jr, 1969; Hospital of Transplanted Hearts by D. M. Thomas, 1969; Eco-Catastrophe by Paul Ehrlich, 1969; The Castle on the Crag by P. G. Wyal, 1969; Nine Lives by **Ursula K. Le Guin**, 1969; Progression of the Species by **Brian W. Aldiss**, 1967; Report Back - a poem by John Cotton, 1969; The Killing Ground by J. G. Ballard, 1969; The Dannold Cheque by Ken W. Purdy, 1969; Womb to Tomb by Joseph Wesley, 1969; Like Father by Jon Hartridge, 1969; The Electric Ant by **Philip K. Dick**, 1969; The Man Inside by Bruce McAllister, 1969; Now Hear the Word of the Lord by Algis Budrys, 1969; and Afterword - An Awful Lot of Copy by **Brian W. Aldiss**.

19. SF: Author's Choice 3. Published by G. P. Putnam's Sons, New York City, 1971. Herein: Introduction by **Harry Harrison**; Sober Noises of Morning in a Marginal Land by **Brian W. Aldiss**, 1971; The Falcon and the Falconeer by Barry N. Malzberg writing as K. M. O'Donnell, 1969; The Power of Every Root by Avram Davidson, 1967; Bordered in Black by Larry Niven, 1966; By the Falls by **Harry Harrison**, 1970; O Ye of Little Faith by Harlan Ellison, 1968; The Transfinite Choice by David I. Masson, 1966; The Tank Trapeze by **Michael Moorcock**, 1969; The Last Hurrah of the Golden Horde by Norman Spinrad, 1969; Phog by Piers Anthony, 1965; At Central by Kit Reed, 1967; The Deepest Blue in the World by Sonya Dorman, 1964; and The Coming of the Sun by Langdon Jones, 1968.

20. The Year's Best Science Fiction No. 4. With **Brian W. Aldiss**. Published by Sphere Books, London, 1971. Sphere Book 43435. Softcover. Herein: Introduction by **Harry Harrison**; Gone Fishin' by Robin Scott Wilson, 1970; Black is Beautiful by **Robert Silverberg**, 1970; The Lost Face by Josef Nesvadba, 1964; Mary and Joe by Naomi Mitchison, 1962; The Asian Shore by Thomas M. Disch, 1970; Gorman by Jerry Farber, 1969; Oil-Mad Bug-Eyed Monsters by Hayden Howard, 1970; A Pedestrian Accident by Robert Coover, 1969; Traffic Problem by William Earls, 1970; Erem by Gleb Anfilov, 1963; Car Sinister by **Gene Wolfe**, 1970; Franz Kafka by Jorge Luis Borges by Alvin Greenberg, 1970; Pacem Est by Kris Neville and Barry N. Malzberg writing as K. M. O'Donnell; 1970; The Ugupu Bird by Slawomir Mrozk, 1968; and The Afterword: The Day Equality Broke Out by **Brian W. Aldiss**.

21. Best SF: 1970. With **Brian W. Aldiss**. Published by G. P. Putnam's Sons, New York City, 1971. Hardcover. Herein: Introduction by **Harry Harrison**; Gone Fishin' by Robin Scott Wilson, 1970; Black is Beautiful by **Robert Silverberg**, 1970; The Lost Face by Josef Nesvadba, 1964; Mary and Joe by Naomi Mitchison, 1962; The Asian Shore by Thomas M. Disch, 1970; Gorman by Jerry Farber, 1969; Oil-Mad Bug-Eyed Monsters by Hayden Howard, 1970; A Pedestrian Accident by Robert Coover, 1969; Traffic Problem by William Earls, 1970; Erem by Gleb Anfilov, 1963; Car Sinister by **Gene Wolfe**, 1970; Franz Kafka by Jorge Luis Borges by Alvin Greenberg, 1970; Pacem Est by Kris Neville and Barry N. Malzberg writing as K. M. O'Donnell; 1970; The Ugupu Bird by Slawomir Mrozk, 1968; and The Afterword: The Day Equality Broke Out by **Brian W. Aldiss**.

22. The Light Fantastic. Published by Charles Scribner's Sons, New York City, 1971. Hardcover. Herein: Introduction by **James Blish**; The Muse by Anthony Burgess, 1968; The Machine Stops by E. M. Forster, 1909; The Circular Ruins by Jorge Luis Borges, 1962; The Shout by Robert Graves, 1929; The Shoddy Lands by C. S. Lewis, 1956; The Unsafe Deposit Box by Gerald Kersh, 1962; The Mark Gable Foundation by Leo Szilard, 1961; Something Strange by Kingsley Amis, 1960; The End of the Part by Graham Greene, 1932; Sold to Satan by Mark Twain, 1923; The Finest Story in the World by Rudyard Kipling, 1891; The Door by E. B. White, 1939; The Enormous Radio by John Cheever, 1947; and Afterword by **Harry Harrison**.

23. Nova 2. Published by Walker and Company, New York City, 1972. Hardcover. Most of the work was done in 1972: Introduction by **Harry Harrison**; Zirn Left Unguarded, the Jenghik Palace in Flames, Jon Westerly Dead by Robert Sheckley; East Wind, West Wind by Frank M. Robinson; The Sumerian Oath by Philip Jose Farmer; Now + n Now - n by **Robert Silverberg**; Two Odysseys into the Center by Barry N. Malzberg; Darkness by Andre Carneiro, 1965; On the Wheel by **Damon Knight**; Miss Omega Raven by Naomi Mitchison; The Poet in the Hologram in the Middle of Prime Time by Ed Bryant; The Old Folks by James E. Gunn; The Steam-Driven Boy by John Sladek; I Tell You It's True by **Poul Anderson**; And I Have Come Upon This Place By Lost Ways by James Tiptree, Jr; and The Ergot Show by **Brian W. Aldiss**.

24. Best SF: 1971. With **Brian W. Aldiss**. Published by G. P. Putnam's Sons, New York City, 1972. Herein: Introduction by **Harry Harrison**; Doctor Zombie and His Little Furry Friends by Robert Sheckley, 1971; Conquest by Barry N. Malzberg, 1971 Gehenna by Barry N. Malzberg writing as K. M. O'Donnell, 1971; A Meeting with Medusa by **Arthur C. Clarke**, 1971; The Genius by Donald Barthelme, 1971; Angouleme by Thomas M. Disch, 1971; If Hair Were Revived in 2016 by Arnold M. Auerbach, 1971; Statistician's Day by **James Blish**, 1970; The Science Fiction Horror Movie Pocket Computer - an essay by Gahan Wilson, 1971; The Hunter at His Ease by **Brian W. Aldiss**, 1970; The Cohen Dog Exclusion Act by Steven Schrader - 1971; Gauntlet by Richard E. Peck, 1972; Three Poems: Report by Kingsley Amis, 1971; Fisherman by Lawrence Sail, 1971; The Ideal Police State by Charles Baxter, 1971; The Pagan Rabbi by Cynthia Ozick, 1966; An Uneven

Harry Harrison

Evening by Steve Herbst, 1971; Ornithanthropus by B. Alan Burhoe, 1971; No Direction Home by Norman Spinrad, 1971; and Afterword: A Day in the Life-Style of... by **Brian W. Aldiss**.

25. The Year's Best Science Fiction No. 5. With **Brian W. Aldiss**. Published by Sphere Books, London, 1972. Sphere Book 43443. Softcover. Herein: Introduction by **Harry Harrison**; Doctor Zombie and His Little Furry Friends by Robert Sheckley, 1971; Conquest by Barry N. Malzberg, 1971 Gehenna by Barry N. Malzberg writing as K. M. O'Donnell, 1971; A Meeting with Medusa by **Arthur C. Clarke**, 1971; The Genius by Donald Barthelme, 1971; Angouleme by Thomas M. Disch, 1971; If Hair Were Revived in 2016 by Arnold M. Auerbach, 1971; Statistician's Day by **James Blish**, 1970; The Science Fiction Horror Movie Pocket Computer - an essay by Gahan Wilson, 1971; The Hunter at His Ease by **Brian W. Aldiss**, 1970; The Cohen Dog Exclusion Act by Steven Schrader - 1971; Gauntlet by Richard E. Peck, 1972; Three Poems: Report by Kingsley Amis, 1971; Fisherman by Lawrence Sail, 1971; The Ideal Police State by Charles Baxter, 1971; The Pagan Rabbi by Cynthia Ozick, 1966; An Uneven Evening by Steve Herbst, 1971; Ornithanthropus by B. Alan Burhoe, 1971; No Direction Home by Norman Spinrad, 1971; and Afterword: A Day in the Life-Style of... by **Brian W. Aldiss**.

26. The Astounding - Analog Reader, Volume 1. With **Brian W. Aldiss**. Published by Doubleday & Company, Garden City, New York, 1972. Hardcover. Herein: Introduction by **Harry Harrison** and **Brian W. Aldiss**; Forgetfulness by **John W. Campbell** writing as Don A Stuart, 1937; Seeds of the Dusk by Raymond Z. Gallun, 1938; Farewell to the Master by Harry Bates, 1940; Trouble on Tantalus by P. Schuyler Miller, 1941; Time Wants a Skeleton by Ross Rocklynne, 1941; Nightfall by **Isaac Asimov**, 1941; By His Bootstraps by **Robert A. Heinlein** writing as Anson MacDonald, 1941; The Push of a Finger by **Alfred Bester**, 1942; Clash by Night by Henry Kuttner and **C. L. Moore** writing as Lawrence O'Donnell, 1943; The Storm by **A. E. van Vogt**, 1943; City by Clifford D. Simak, 1944; First Contact by Murray Leinster, 1945; Giant Killer by A. Bertram Chandler, 1945; Vintage Season by Henry Kuttner and **C. L. Moore** writing as Lawrence O'Donnell, 1946; and Placet Is a Crazy Place by Fredric Brown, 1946.

27. Nova 3. Published by Walker and Company, New York City, 1973. Hardcover. All the work was done in 1973: Introduction by **Harry Harrison**; Sketches Among the Ruins of My Mind by Philip Jose Farmer; The National Pastime by Norman Spinrad; The Factory by Naomi Mitchison; Welcome to the Standard Nightmare by Robert Sheckley; The Expensive Delicate Ship by **Brian W. Aldiss**; Dreaming and Conversations Two Rules by Which to Live by Barry N. Malzberg; Breakout in Ecol 2 by David R. Bunch; The Cold War ....Continued by Mack Reynolds; The Defensive Bomber by **Harry Harrison** writing as Hank Dempsey; The Ultimate End by Dick Glass; Pity the Poor Outdated Man by Philip Shofner; and The Exhibition by Scott Edelstein.

28. The Astounding - Analog Reader, Volume 2. With **Brian W. Aldiss**. Published by Doubleday & Company, Garden City, New York, 1973. Hardcover. Herein: Introduction by **Harry Harrison** and **Brian W. Aldiss**; Thunder and Roses by **Theodore Sturgeon**, 1947; Dreams Are Sacred by Peter Phillips, 1948; Computers Don't Argue by **Gordon R. Dickson**, 1965; Child's Play by William Tenn, 1947; The Little Black Bag by C. M. Kornbluth, 1950; Rescue Operation by **Harry Harrison**, 1964; The Rescuer by Arthur Porges, 1962; The Weather Man by Theodore L. Thomas, 1962; The Yellow Pill by Rog Phillips, 1958; Call Me Joe by **Poul Anderson**, 1957; The Waitabits by **Eric Frank Russell**, 1955; Grandpa by James H. Schmitz, 1954; Pyramid by Robert Abernathy, 1954; The Cold Equations by Tom Godwin, 1954; Imposter by **Philip K. Dick**, 1953; Potential by Robert Sheckley, 1953; Bridge by **James Blish**, 1952; What Have I Done? By Mark Clifton, 1952; Noise Level by Raymond F. Jones, 1952; Hide and Seek by **Arthur C. Clarke**, 1949; and After a Few Words by Randall Garrett writing as Seaton McKettrig.

29. The Astounding - Analog Reader, Volume 1. With **Brian W. Aldiss**. Published by Sphere Books, London, 1973. Softcover. Herein: Introduction by **Harry Harrison** and **Brian W. Aldiss**; Forgetfulness by **John W. Campbell** writing as Don A Stuart, 1937; Seeds of the Dusk by Raymond Z. Gallun, 1938; Farewell to the Master by Harry Bates, 1940; Trouble on Tantalus by P. Schuyler Miller, 1941; Time Wants a Skeleton by Ross Rocklynne, 1941; Nightfall by **Isaac Asimov**, 1941; By His Bootstraps by **Robert A. Heinlein** writing as Anson MacDonald, 1941; and The Push of a Finger by **Alfred Bester**, 1942.

30. The Astounding - Analog Reader, Volume 2. With **Brian W. Aldiss**. Published by Sphere Books, London, 1973. Softcover. Herein: Clash by Night by Henry Kuttner and **C. L. Moore** writing as Lawrence O'Donnell, 1943; The Storm by **A. E. van Vogt**, 1943; City by Clifford D. Simak, 1944; First Contact by Murray Leinster, 1945; Giant Killer by A. Bertram Chandler, 1945; Vintage Season by Henry Kuttner and **C. L. Moore** writing as Lawrence O'Donnell, 1946; and Placet Is a Crazy Place by Fredric Brown, 1946.

31. Best SF: 1972. With **Brian W. Aldiss**. Published by G. P. Putnam's Sons, New York City, 1973. Herein: Introduction by **Harry Harrison**; In the Matter of the Assassin Merefirs by Ken W. Purdy, 1972; The Old Folks by James E. Gunn, 1972; From Sea to Shining Sea by Jonathan Ela, 1972; Weihnachtabend by Keith Roberts, 1972; The Years by Robert F. Young, 1972; Darkness by Andre Carneiro, 1965; Cymbal Player - a poem by Lawrence Sail, 1972; Report From the Planet Proteus - a poem by Lawrence Sail, 1972; Columbus on St. Domenica - a poem by John Cotton, 1972; After Death - a poem by Patricia Beer, 1972; Faex Delenda Est - a poem by Theodore R. Cogswell, 1972; Words of Warning by Alex Hamilton, 1972; Out Wit by Howard L. Myers, 1972; An Imaginary Journey to the Moon by Victor Sabah, 1972; The Head and the Hand by Christopher Priest, 1972; Hero by Joe W. Haldeman, 1972; As For Our Fatal Continuity by **Brian W. Aldiss**, 1972; and Afterword: The Year of the Big Spring Clean by **Brian W. Aldiss**.

32. The Year's Best Science Fiction No. 6. With **Brian W. Aldiss**. Published by Sphere Books, London, 1973. Softcover. Herein: Introduction by **Harry Harrison**; In the Matter of the Assassin Merefirs by Ken W. Purdy, 1972; The Old Folks by James E. Gunn, 1972; From Sea to Shining Sea by Jonathan Ela, 1972; Weihnachtabend by Keith Roberts, 1972; The Years by Robert F. Young, 1972; Darkness by Andre Carneiro, 1965; Cymbal Player - a poem by Lawrence Sail, 1972; Report From the Planet Proteus - a poem by Lawrence Sail, 1972; Columbus on St. Domenica - a poem by John Cotton, 1972; After Death - a poem by Patricia Beer, 1972; Faex Delenda Est - a poem by Theodore R. Cogswell, 1972; Words of Warning by Alex Hamilton, 1972; Out Wit by Howard L. Myers, 1972; An Imaginary Journey to the Moon by Victor Sabah, 1972; The Head and the Hand by Christopher Priest, 1972; Hero by Joe W. Haldeman, 1972; As For Our Fatal Continuity by **Brian W. Aldiss**, 1972; and Afterword: The Year of the Big Spring Clean by **Brian W. Aldiss**.

33. Astounding: John W. Campbell Memorial Anthology. Published by Random House, New York City, 1973. Hardcover. All the work herein is from 1973: The Father of Science Fiction - an essay by **Isaac Asimov**; Something Up There Likes Me by **Alfred Bester**; Lecture Demonstration by **Hal Clement**; Earlybird by Theodore R. Cogswell and Theodore L. Thomas; Probability Zero: The Population Implosion by Theodore R. Cogswell; The Emperor's Fan by L. Sprague de Camp; Brothers by **Gordon R. Dickson**; Lodestar by **Poul Anderson**; Thiotimoline to the Stars by **Isaac Asimov**; Black Sheep Astray by Mack Reynolds; Epilog by Clifford D. Simak; Interlude by George O. Smith; Helix the Cat by **Theodore Sturgeon**; and The Mothballed Spaceship by **Harry Harrison**.

34. A Science Fiction Reader. With Carol Pugner. Published by Charles Scribner's Sons, New York City, 1973. Hardcover. Herein: Mirror of Ice by Gary Wright, 1967; Sunjammer by **Arthur C. Clarke**, 1964; Escape the Morning by **Poul Anderson**, 1966; If by **Harry Harrison**, 1969; Prone by Mack Reynolds, 1954; The Yellow Pill by Rog Phillips, 1958; Light of Other Days by Bob Shaw, 1966; Who Can Replace a Man? by **Brian W. Aldiss**, 1958; Heavy Planet by Milton A. Rothman writing as Lee Gregor, 1939; Grandpa by James A. Schmitz, 1955; Surface Tension by **James Blish**, 1952; Traffic Problem by William Earls, 1970; Nightfall by **Isaac Asimov**, 1941; and The Cold Equations by Tom Godwin, 1954.

35. SF: Author's Choice 4. Published by G. P. Putnam's Sons, New York City, 1974. Herein: Et in Arcadia Ego by Thomas M. Disch, 1971; Ullward's Retreat by **Jack Vance**, 1958; The Man Who Loved the Faioli by Roger Zelazny, 1967; The Fire and the Sword by Frank M. Robinson, 1951; All of Us Are Dying by George Clayton Johnson, 1956; Old Hundredth by **Brian W. Aldiss**, 1960; Fair by John Brunner writing as Keith Woodcott, 1956; The Forgotten Enemy by **Arthur C. Clarke**, 1948; Warrior by **Gordon R. Dickson**, 1965; But Soft, What Light by Carol Emshwiller, 1966; The Misogynist by James Gunn, 1952; Bad Medicine by Robert Sheckley writing as Finn O'Donnevan, 1956; The Autumn Land by Clifford D. Simak, 1971; A Sense of Beauty by Robert Taylor, 1968; and The Last Flight of Dr Ain by James Tiptree, Jr, 1969.

36. Best SF: 73. With **Brian W. Aldiss**. Published by Berkley Books, New York City, 1974. Softcover. Herein: Introduction by **Harry Harrison**; A Curse - a poem by W. H. Auden, 1972; Auto-Apotheosis - a poem by Anthony Haden-Guest, 1972; Captain Nemo's Last Adventure by Josef Nesvadba, 1964; Early Bird by Theodore R. Cogswell and Theodore L. Thomas, 1973; Escape by Ilya Varshavsky, 1973; La Befana by **Gene Wolfe**, 1983; Mason's Life by Kingsley Amis, 1972; Parthen by R. A. Lafferty, 1973; Roller Ball Murder by William Harrison, 1973; Serpent Burning on an Altar by **Brian W. Aldiss**, 1973; Sister Francetta and Pig Baby by Kenneth Bernard, 1973; Sport - a poem by Steven Utley, 1973; Ten Years Ago by Max Beerbohm, 1972; The Birds by Thomas M. Disch, 1973; The Man Who Collected the First of September 1973 by Tor Age Bringsvaerd, 1973; The Wind and the Rain by **Robert Silverberg**, 1973; Two poems by William Jon Watkins, 1973; We Are Very Happy Here by Joe Haldeman, 1973; Welcome to the Standard Nightmare by Robert Sheckley, 1973; The Window in Dante's Hell by Michael Bishop, 1973; and Afterword: The Wizard and the Plumber by **Brian W. Aldiss**.

37. Best SF: 73. With **Brian W. Aldiss**. Published by G. P. Putnam's Sons, New York City, 1974. First hardcover edition.

38. The Year's Best Science Fiction No. 7. With **Brian W. Aldiss**. Published by Sphere Books, London, 1974. Softcover. Abridged edition. Herein: Introduction by **Harry Harrison**; Mason's Life by Kingsley Amis, 1972; Roller Ball Murder by William Harrison, 1973; Welcome to the Standard Nightmare by Robert Sheckley, 1973; We Are Very Happy Here by Joe W. Haldeman, 1973; The Birds by Thomas M. Disch, 1973; The Wind and the Rain by **Robert Silverberg**, 1973; Ten Years Ago by Max Beerbohm, 1972; Parthen by R. A. Lafferty, 1973; The Man Who Collected the First of September 1973 by Tor Age Bringsvaerd, 1973; Captain Nemo's Last Adventure by Josef Nesvadba, 1964; La Befana by **Gene Wolfe**, 1983; and Serpent Burning on an Altar by **Brian W. Aldiss**, 1973.

39. Science Fiction Novellas. With Willis E. McNelly. Published by Charles Scribner's Sons, New York City, 1975. Hardcover. Herein: Things to Come - an essay by **Harry Harrison** and Willis E. McNelly; Black Destroyer by **A. E. van Vogt**, 1939; East Wind, West Wind by Frank M. Robinson, 1972; Call me Joe by **Poul Anderson**, 1957; Omnilingual by H. Beam Piper, 1957; The Far Look by Theodore L. Thomas, 1956; The Asian Shore by Thomas M. Disch, 1970; and The Streets of Ashkelon by **Harry Harrison**, 1962.

40. Nova 4. Published by Walker and Company, New York City, 1975. Hardcover. All from 1974, this contains: The Monster of Ingratitude iv by **Brian W. Aldiss**; Songs of War by Kit Reed; Protective Temporal Strike by Gerard E. Giannattasio; Making It All the Way into the Future on Gaxton Falls of the

Red Planet by Barry N. Malzberg; Slaves of Time by Robert Sheckley; Singular by Bill Garnett; Too Long at the Fair by Edward Wellen; Not a Petal Falls by Richard Bireley; My Affair with Science Fiction by **Alfred Bester**; Out of the Waters by Naomi Mitchison; Side View of a Circle by Michael Addobati; Beyond the Cleft by Tom Reamy; and Our Lady of the Endless Sky by Jeff Duntemann; along with an afterword by **Harry Harrison**.

41. The Outdated Man. Published by Dell Books, New York City, 1975. Softcover. Re-titled from Nova 3, 1973.

42. Best SF: 1974. With **Brian W. Aldiss**. Published by Bobbs Merrill, New York City, 1975. Hardcover. This contains: Introduction by **Harry Harrison**; The Scream by **Kate Wilhelm**, 1974; Time Deer by Craig Strete, 1974; After King Kong Fell by Philip Jose Farmer, 1973; The Women Men Don't See by James Tiptree, Jr, 1973; The Four-Hour Fugue by **Alfred Bester**, 1974; A Typical Day by Doris Piserchia, 1974; Programmed Love Story by Ian Watson, 1974; Songs of War by Kit Reed, 1974; The Executioner's Beautiful Daughter by Angela Carter, 1974; When Petals Fall by Sydney J. Van Scyoc, 1973; Paleontology: An Experimental Science by Robert R. Olsen, 1974; Lost and Found by Thomas Baum, 1974; Owing to Circumstances Beyond Our Control, 1984 Has Been Unavoidably Detained by Alan Coren, 1974; The Rise of Airstrip One by Clive James, 1974; Listen with Big Brother by **Brian W. Aldiss**, 1974; Science Fiction Story - a poem by Duane Ackerson, 1973; Eyes of a Woman - from a Portrait by Picasso - a poem by Lisa Conesa, 1975; After Weightlessness - a poem by Lawrence Sail, 1974; and Afterword: The Galaxy Begins at Home by **Brian W. Aldiss**.

43. The Year's Best Science Fiction No. 8. With **Brian W. Aldiss**. Published by Sphere Books, London, 1975. Softcover. Abridged edition. Herein: Introduction by **Harry Harrison**; The Scream by **Kate Wilhelm**, 1974; Time Deer by Craig Strete, 1974; After King Kong Fell by Philip Jose Farmer, 1973; The Women Men Don't See by James Tiptree, Jr, 1973; The Four-Hour Fugue by **Alfred Bester**, 1974; A Typical Day by Doris Piserchia, 1974; Programmed Love Story by Ian Watson, 1974; Songs of War by Kit Reed, 1974; The Executioner's Beautiful Daughter by Angela Carter, 1974; When Petals Fall by Sydney J. Van Scyoc, 1973; Paleontology: An Experimental Science by Robert R. Olsen, 1974; Lost and Found by Thomas Baum, 1974; Owing to Circumstances Beyond Our Control, 1984 Has Been Unavoidably Detained by Alan Coren, 1974; The Rise of Airstrip One by Clive James, 1974; Listen with Big Brother by **Brian W. Aldiss**, 1974; Science Fiction Story - a poem by Duane Ackerson, 1973; After Weightlessness - a poem by Lawrence Sail, 1974; and Afterword: The Galaxy Begins at Home by **Brian W. Aldiss**.

44. Decade the 1940s. With **Brian W. Aldiss**. Published by Macmillan, London, 1975. Hardcover. Herein: Introduction by **Brian W. Aldiss; Hobbyist by Eric Frank Russell**, 1947; The Xi Effect by Robert Shirley Richardson writing as Philip Latham, 1950; Huddling Place by Clifford D. Simak, 1944; The Last Objective by Paul Carter, 1946; Fireproof by **Hal Clement**, 1949; Arena by Fredric Brow, 1944n; Co-operate or Else by **A. E. van Vogt**, 1942; and Reason by **Isaac Asimov**, 1941.

45. Nova 1. Published by Robert Hale & Company, London, 1976. Hardcover. Abridged edition.

46. The Year's Best Science Fiction No. 9. With **Brian W. Aldiss**. Published by Weidenfeld and Nicolson, London, 1976. Hardcover. Herein: Introduction by **Harry Harrison**; A Scraping at the Bones by Algis Budrys, 1975; Changelings by Lisa Tuttle, 1975; The Santa Claus Compromise by Thomas M. Disch, 1974; A Galaxy Called Rome by Barry N. Malzberg, 1975; A Twelvemonth - a poem by Peter Redgrove, 1975; The Custodians by Richard Cowper, 1975; The Linguist by Stephen Robinett, 1975; Settling the World by M. John Harrison, 1975; The Chaste Planet by John Updike, 1975; End Game by Joe Haldeman, 1975; The Lop Eared Cat that Devoured Philadelphia - a poem by Louis Phillips, 1975; A Dead Singer by **Michael Moorcock**, 1974; and Afterword: Science Fiction on The Titanic by **Brian W. Aldiss**.

47. Best SF: 75 - The Ninth Annual. With **Brian W. Aldiss**. Published by Bobbs Merrill, New York City, 1976. Hardcover. Herein: Introduction by **Harry Harrison**; A Scraping at the Bones by Algis Budrys, 1975; Changelings by Lisa Tuttle, 1975; The Santa Claus Compromise by Thomas M. Disch, 1974; A Galaxy Called Rome by Barry N. Malzberg, 1975; A Twelvemonth - a poem by Peter Redgrove, 1975; The Custodians by Richard Cowper, 1975; The Linguist by Stephen Robinett, 1975; Settling the World by M. John Harrison, 1975; The Chaste Planet by John Updike, 1975; End Game by Joe Haldeman, 1975; The Lop Eared Cat that Devoured Philadelphia - a poem by Louis Phillips, 1975; A Dead Singer by **Michael Moorcock**, 1974; and Afterword: Science Fiction on The Titanic by **Brian W. Aldiss**.

48. Decade the 1950s. With **Brian W. Aldiss**. Published by Macmillan, London, 1976. Hardcover. Herein: Introduction by **Harry Harrison**; Grandpa by James H. Schmitz, 1955; The Snowball Effect by Katherine Maclean, 1952; The Edge of the Sea by Algis Budrys, 1958; Scanners Live in Vain by Cordwainer Smith, 1950; The Last Day by Richard Matheson, 1953; The Large Ant by Howard Fast, 1960; Sail On, Sail On by Philip Jose Farmer, 1952; The Holes Around Mars by Jerome Bixby, 1954; Two Handed Engine by Henry Kuttner and **C. L. Moore** writing as Henry Kuttner, 1955; The Star by **Arthur C. Clarke**, 1955; Early Model by Robert Sheckley, 1956; and The Pedestrian by **Ray Bradbury**, 1951.

49. Decade the 1960s. With **Brian W. Aldiss**. Published by Macmillan, London, 1977. Hardcover. Herein: Introduction by **Brian W. Aldiss** and **Harry Harrison;** The Assassination of John Fitzgerald Kennedy Considered as a Motor Race by J. G. Ballard, 1966; Gravity by Harvey Jacobs, 1969; Harrison Bergeron by Kurt Vonnegut, Jr, 1961; Descending by Thomas M. Disch, 1964; Devil Car by Roger Zelazny, 1965; The Nature of the Catastrophe by **Michael Moorcock**, 1970; The Electric Ant by **Philip K.**

Dick, 1969; The Last Hurrah of the Golden Horde by Norman Spinrad, 1969; Hemingway in Space by Kingsley Amis, 1960; Computers Don't Argue by **Gordon R. Dickson**, 1965; The Food Goes in the Top by Will Worthington, 1961; Subversive by Mack Reynolds, 1962; Manscarer by Keith Roberts, 1966; Hybrid by Keith Laumer, 1961; The Heat Death of the Universe by Pamela Zoline, 1967; Day Million by **Frederik Pohl**, 1966; Hawksbill Station by **Robert Silverberg**, 1967; and The Village Swindler by **Brian W. Aldiss**, 1968.

50. There Won't Be War. With Bruce McAllister. Published by Tor Books - Tom Doherty Associates, New York City, 1991. Softcover. Most of the work herein was done in the same year as the book's publication, 1991: Introduction by Bruce McAllister; Frustration by **Isaac Asimov**; Known But to God and Wilbur Hines by James Morrow; The Liberation of Earth by William Tenn, 1953; Valkyrie by Jack McDevitt; SEAQ and Destroy by Charles Stross; Iphigenia by Nancy A. Collins; The Lucky Strike by Kim Stanley Robinson, 1984; Brains on the Dump by Nicholas Emmett; Beachhead by Joe Haldeman; There Will Be No More War After This One by Robert Sheckley; We, The People by Jack C. Haldeman II; Wartorn, Lovelorn by Marc Laidlaw; The Peacemakers by Timothy Zahn; The Terminal Beach by J. G. Ballard, 1964; Attack of the Jazz Giants by Gregory Frost; The Long-Awaited Appearance of the Real Black Box by Ratislav Durman; Generation of Noah by William Tenn, 1951; and The Rocky Python Christmas Video Show by **Frederik Pohl**, 1989; along with an afterword by **Harry Harrison**.

***

NON-FICTION

1. Ahead of Time. With Theodore J. Gordon. Published by Doubleday & Company, Garden City, New York, 1972. Hardcover.

2. SF Horizons. With **Brian W. Aldiss**. Published by Arno Press, United States, 1975. Hardcover.

3. Hell's Cartographers: Some Personal Histories of Science Fiction Writers. With **Harry Harrison**. Published by Weidenfeld and Nicolson, London, 1973. Hardcover. Herein: Sounding Brass Tinkling Cymbal by **Robert Silverberg**; My Affair with Science Fiction by **Alfred Bester**; Knight Piece by **Damon Knight**; Ragged Claws by **Frederik Pohl**; Magic and Bare Boards by **Brian W. Aldiss**; and The Beginning of the Affair by **Harry Harrison**.

4. Great Balls of Fire: A History of Sex in Science Fiction Illustrations. Published by Pierrot Publishing, London, 1977. Hardcover and softcover editions issued simultaneously.

5. Mechanismo: An Illustrated Manual of Science Fiction Hardware. Published by Reed Books, United States, 1978. Hardcover.

***

RELATED

1. Harry Harrison: Bibliographia 1951 - 1965. By Francesco Biamonti. Published by Editoriale Libraria, Trieste, Italy, 1965. Softcover.

2. Harry Harrison. By Leon E. Stover. Published by Twayne Publishers, Boston, 1990. Hardcover.

Mary Shelley.

Mary Wollstonecraft Godwin was born on August 30th, 1797 and died from a suspected brain tumour on February 1st, 1851.

In between, she wrote what **Isaac Asimov** called the very first science fiction novel. By that, he meant the first novel ever to use a technological advance to change society. The novel was Frankenstein, or, The Modern Prometheus. It was published in 1818 when Mary was just 21 - she was the first author in history who thought to employ scientific advancement as the main ingredient of her story. And her story was a huge success.

In 1816, Lord Byron was hanging out with his friend Percy Bysshe Shelley, and Shelley's mistress, Mary Godwin, and a few others, including Dr John Polidori. There was a challenge, or at least a proposal, that everyone in the room write something Gothic, some sort of ghost story. Mary was the first one of the group to actually produce something - Polidori came out a year later with The Vampyre.

Shelley's wife killed herself, Mary married Percy, and then launched her literary career with the publication of Frankenstein.

In a January 1818 review for Quarterly Review, Wilson Croker, believing that the book had been written by Percy rather than **Mary Shelley**, wrote that "the dreams of insanity are embodied in the strong and striking language of the insane, and the author, notwithstanding the rationality of his preface, often leaves us in doubt whether he is not as mad as his hero." Walter Scott, in his review, simply said the story was "written in plain and forcible English, without exhibiting the mixture of hyperbolical Germanisms with which tales of wonder are usually told."

Curiously, in an 1899 auction by Sotheby, Wilkinson and Hodge, a copy of the first edition of Frankenstein, or The Modern Prometheus sold for 1 pound, 16 shillings. Around $15.00.

In 2000, it was estimated that the 1818 first edition was worth $50,000.00. And as this is being written, in 2009, the 1823 second edition from G. and W. B. Whittaker in London can be found for sale at $75,000.00, while the first American edition, from Carey, Lean and Blanchard, Philadelphia, 1933, runs around $35,000.

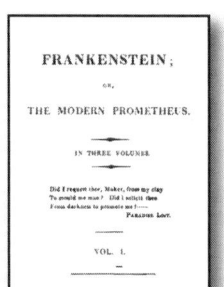

Shelley's other science fiction novel, The Last Man, was published by Henry Colburn, London, 1826. Decent copies sell between $5,000 and $10,000.

***

FILMS AND TELEVISION.

1. Frankenstein. Filmed by Thomas Edison, directed by J. Searle Dawley and released in 1910, this starred: Mary Fuller; Augustus Phillips; and Charles Ogle as The Monster.

2. The Strange Story of Sylvia Gray. This was directed by Charles L. Gaskill and released in 1914, starring: Helen Gardner; Charles Kent; Mary Charleson; Phyllis Grey; and many others, including Charles Dietz as Dr Frankenstein.

3. Life Without Soul. From 1915, this was directed by Joseph W. Smiley and starred: Lucy Cotton; George De Carlton; Pauline Curley; Jack Hopkins; and others, including Percy Standing as The Creation.

4. The Monster of Frankenstein - Il mostro di Frankenstein. Filmed in Italy, this was released in 1921. It was directed by Eugenio Testa and starred: Linda Albertini; Luciano Albertini; and Aldo Mezzanotte; with Umberto Guarracino as The Monster.

5. Frankenstein. Directed by James Whale, this was released in 1931, starring: Colin Clive; Mae Clarke; John Boles; Edward Van Sloan; Frederick Kerr; Dwight Frye; Lionel Belmore; Marilyn Harris; along with many others, including Boris Karloff as The Monster.

6. Bride of Frankenstein. From 1935 and directed by James Whale, this starred: Colin Clive; Valerie Hobson; Ernest Thesiger; Dwight Frye; and many others, including Walter Brennan in an uncredited bit part as a neighbor; John Carradine in an uncredited part as a hunter; Gavin Gordon as Lord Byron; Douglas Walton as Percy Shelley; Elsa Lanchester as **Mary Shelley** and The Bride Monster; and, of course, Boris Karloff as The Monster.

7. Son of Frankenstein. Directed by Rowland V. Lee, this was released in 1939, starring: Basil Rathbone; Bela Lugosi; Lionel Atwill; Josephine Hutchinson; Donnie Dunagan; and many others, including Boris Karloff as The Monster.

8. Abbott and Costello Meet Frankenstein. This was directed by Charles Barton and released in 1948, starring: Bud Abbott; Lou Costello; Lenore Aubert; Jane Randolph; Frank Ferguson; Charles Bradstreet; and many others, including: Vincent Price in an uncredited role as the voice of The Invisible Man; Lon Chaney Jr. as Larry Talbot - The Werewolf; Bela Lugosi as Count Dracula; and Glenn Strange as The Monster.

9. Frankenstein. Directed by Don Medford, this was filmed for the television series Tales of Tomorrow. It aired on January 18th, 1952, Season 1, Episode 16, starring: Peggy Allenby; Raymond Bramley; Michael Mann; Mary Alice Moore; John Newland; and Farrell Pelly, with Lon Chaney Jr as The Monster.

10. The Curse of Frankenstein. Directed by Terence Fisher for Hammer Films, this was released in 1957 and starred: Peter Cushing; Hazel Court; Robert Urquhart; Melvyn Hayes; Valerie Gaunt; and others, including Christopher Lee as The Creature.

11. Frankenstein - 1970. This was directed by Howard W. Koch and released in 1958 and starred: Boris Karloff as Frankenstein and Mike Lane as The Monster, along with: Don Red Barry; Jana Lund;

Tom Duggan; Charlotte Austin; Norbert Schiller; and others.

12. Mr Magoo's Doctor Frankenstein. Animated for The Famous Adventures of Mr Magoo, this was aired on March 13th, 1965, Season 1, Episode 20. It featured the voices of: Mel Blanc; Morey Amsterdam; Dick Beals; Daws Butler; Jack Cassidy; Scatman Crothers; Casey Kasem; Bea Benaderet; and many others.

13. Frankenstein Conquers the World. This was filmed in Japan as Furankenshutain tai chitei kaiju Baragon. It was released in the U.S. in 1966. Directed by Ishiro Honda, it starred: Tadao Takashima; Nick Adams; Kumi Mizuno; Yoshio Tsuchiya; Jun Tazaki; and many others, including Koji Furuhata as The Monster.

14. Frankenstein. This was filmed for the British television series Mystery and Imagination, airing on November 11th, 1968, Season 4, Episode 2. It starred: Sarah Badel; Richard Vernon; Frank Barry; Sam Burston; Michael Francis; Morag Hood; Robert Hunter; Gerald Lawson; and others, including Ian Holm as The Monster.

15. Frankenstein Must Be Destroyed. Still with Hammer Films, this was directed by Terence Fisher for release in 1970. It starred: Peter Cushing as Baron Frankenstein; Veronica Carlson; Freddie Jones; Simon Ward; Thorley Walters; Maxine Audley; George Pravda; and many others.

16. The Horror of Frankenstein. Directed by Jimmy Sangster, this was released in 1971 and starred: Ralph Bates as Victor Frankenstein; Kate O'Mara; Veronica Carlson; Dennis Price; Jon Finch; Bernard Archard; and others, including Dave Prowse as The Monster.

17. Lady Frankenstein - La figlia di Frankenstein. From Italy in 1971, this was directed by Mel Welles and Aureliano Luppi and starred: Joseph Cotten; Rosalba Neri; Paul Muller; Herbert Fux; Renate Kasche; and others, including Paul Whiteman as The Creature.

18. The Curse of Frankenstein. In Canada, this was called The Erotic Adventures of Frankenstein and in the UK, they called it The Erotic Rites of Frankenstein. Directed by Jesus Franco, it was filmed in Spain as La maldicion de Frankenstein and released in 1972. It starred: Alberto Dalbes; Howard Vernon; Beatriz Savon; Anne Libert; Britt Nichols; and others, including Dennis Price as Doctor Frankenstein and Fernando Bilbao as El Monstruo.

19. Dracula vs. Dr Frankenstein. Filmed in Spain as Dracula contra Frankenstein, this was released in 1972. Directed by Jesus Franco, it starred: Dennis Price as Doctor Frankenstein; Howard Vernon as Dracula; and Fernando Bilbao as El Monstruo; along with: Paca Gabaldon; Alberto Dalbes; Britt Nichols; Genevieve Robert; Anne Libert; Luis Barboo; and others.

20. Frankenstein: Part 1. Directed by Glenn Jordan, this was made for the television series Wide World Mystery, January 16th, 1973, Season 1, Episode 2. It starred: Robert Foxworth; Susan Strasberg; Heidi Vaughn; Philip Bourneuf; Robert Gentry; Jon Lormer; William Hansen; and others, with Bo Svenson as The Monster.

21. Frankenstein: The True Story. Directed by Jack Smight and with Christopher Isherwood working on the teleplay, this was released on television in the U. S. on November 30th, 1973. It starred: Michael Sarrazin as The Creature; James Mason as Dr John Polidori; Leonard Whiting as Dr Victor Frankenstein; and David McCallum as Dr Henry Clerval; along with: Jane Seymour; Nicola Pagett; Michael Wilding; Agnes Moorehead; and many others, including Ralph Richardson as Mr Lacey and John Gielgud as a cop.

22. Andy Warhol's Frankenstein. Also known as Flesh for Frankenstein, this American/Italian/French production was directed by Paul Morrissey and Antonio Margheriti and released in 1973. It starred: Udo Kier as Baron Frankenstein, Dalila Di Lazzaro as the Female Monster, Srdjan Zelenovic as the Male Monster; and: Joe Dallesandro; Monique van Vooren; Arno Juerging; Nicoletta Elmi; Marco Liofredi; and others.

23. Allen and Rossi Meet Dracula and Frankenstein. A comedic effort from 1974, starring Marty Allen and Steve Rossi.

24. Frankenstein: Une histoire d'amour. From France in 1974, this was directed by Bob Thenault and starred: Gerard Berner as Frankenstein; along with Karin Petersen; Francoise Lugagne; Gerard Boucaron; Nicolas Silberg; Jean Lepage; Marc Foyolle; and many others.

25. Young Frankenstein. Directed by Mel Brooks, written by Gene Wilder and Mel Brooks, this was released in 1974. It starred: Gene Wilder as Dr Frankenstein; Peter Boyle as The Monster; and Marty Feldman as Igor; along with: Cloris Leachman; Teri Garr; Kenneth Mars; Richard Haydn; Liam Dunn; Danny Goldman; Oscar Beregi; and many others, including Madeline Kahn as Elizabeth, Gene Hackman as a blind man, and Mel Brooks... doing whatever he wanted.

26. Terror of Frankenstein - Victor Frankenstein. Released in 1977, this Swedish/Irish production was directed by Calvin Floyd and starred Leon Vitali as Victor Frankenstein and Per Oscarsson as The Monster. Also along were: Nicholas Clay; Stacy Dorning; Jan Ohlsson; Olof Bergstrom; Mathias Henrikson; and others.

27. Struck by Lightning. This 1979 television series survived only three episodes, September 19th, September 26th and October 3rd. Directed by Joel Zwick, it starred Jack Elam as Frank and Jeffrey Kramer as Ted Stein.

28. Doctor Franken. Released in 1980, this was directed by Marvin J. Chomsky and Jeff Lieberman, starring: Robert Vaughn; David Selby; Teri Garr; Josef Sommer; Cynthia Harris; Takayo Doran; and others.

29. Kyofu densetsu: Kaiki! Furankenshutain. Known in the U.S. as simply Frankenstein, this 1981 animated TV film was directed by Yugo Serikawa and, for the English version, featured the voices of:

Greg Finley; Rebecca Forstadt; Ted Layman; Tony Oliver; and Dan Woren.

30. Frankenstein 90. Directed by Alain Jessua, this French production was released in 1984, starring: Jean Rochefort; Eddy Mitchell; Fiona Gelin; Herma Vos; Ged Marlon; Serge Marquand; Anna Gaylor; and others, including Marc Lavoine as The Creature

31. Frankenstein. Directed by James Ormerod, this was released in 1984, starring: Robert Powell; Carrie Fisher; John Gielgud; Terence Alexander; Michael Cochrane; Graham McGrath; Susan Wooldridge; and David Warner as The Monster.

32. The Bride. Directed by Franc Roddam and released in 1985, this starred: Sting; Jennifer Beals; Anthony Higgins; David Rappaport; Geraldine Page; Alexei Sayle; Phil Daniels; and many others, including Clancy Brown as Viktor.

33. Flesh for Frankenstein. Released in 1987, this porno version was directed by Ron Jeremy and starred: Dana Lynn; Nikki Knights; Ebony Ayes; Tawnee; Ray Victory; Frank James; Billy Dee; Veronica Hall; and others.

34. Frankenstein. Directed by Burt Brinckerhoff, this was made for television in 1987. It starred Chris Sarandon as Frankenstein.

35. Teta - Frankenstein's Aunt. A Czechoslovakian television series, this ran for at least seven episodes in 1987, directed by Juraj Jakubisko and starring: Viveca Lindfors as Hannah von Frankenstein; Martin Hreben; Gerhard Karzel; Barbara De Rossi; and Eddie Constantine; with Flavio Bucci as Talbot the Werewolf; Ferdy Mayne as Count Dracula; and many others.

36. Frankenstein General Hospital. Directed by Deborah Romare, this was released in 1988 and starred: Mark Blankfield as Dr Bob Frankenstein and Irwin Keyes as The Monster, along with: Leslie Jordan; Jonathan Farwell; Kathy Shower; Hamilton Mitchell; Lou Cutell; Katie Caple; Dorothy Patterson; and others, including Ben Stein as Dr Who.

37. O Frankenstein de Moises Neto - Versao Muda. Also known as Frankenstein - Silent Version. From 1989, this Brazilian production was directed by Moises Neto and starred Henrique Amaral; Paula Costa Rego; and Black Escobar as The Monster.

38. Edison's Frankenstein. From 1990, this short fantasy was based on the original 1910 film. It was directed by Robert David and starred: John Golden; Mary Ann Curto; B. J. Cearley; and David Paulson as The Creature.

39. Frankenstein. Also known as Frankenstein: The Real Story, this was directed for television by David Wickes in 1992. It starred: Patrick Bergin; John Mills; Lambert Wilson; Fiona Gillies; Jacinta Mulcahy; Ronald Leigh-Hunt; Timothy Stark and others, including Randy Quaid as The Monster.

40. Frankenstein. Another porno version, also known as Buck Adams' Frankenstein, this was directed by Buck Adams and released in 1994, starring: Buck Adams; Lady Berlin; Asia Carrera; Steve Drake; Felecia; Anna Malle; Brittany O'Connell; Rebecca Wild; and others.

41. Mary Shelley's Frankenstein. Directed by Kenneth Branagh and released in 1994, this starred Robert De Niro as The Creature and Kenneth Branagh as Victor Frankenstein, along with: Tom Hulce; Helena Bonham Carter; Aidan Quinn; Ian Holm; Richard Briers; Robert Hardy; and many, many others, including John Cleese as Professor Waldman.

42. Monster Mash: The Movie. Directed by Joel Cohen and Alec Sokolow, this was filmed in 1995, starring: Ian Bohen; Candace Cameron Bure; Sarah Douglas; John Kassir; Bobby Pickett; Adam Shankman; Mink Stole; Jimmie Walker; and many others, including Anthony Crivello as Dracula and Deron McBee as The Monster.

43. Things 3: Old Things. From 1998 and directed by Ron, this featured three stories: The Mark of the Beast by Rudyard Kipling; The Crystal Egg by **H. G. Wells**; and The Transformation by **Mary Shelley**.

44. Alvin and the Chipmunks Meet Frankenstein. Directed by Kathi Castillo and released in 1999, this featured the voices of: Ross Bagdasarian Jr; Janice Karman; Michael Bell; Jim Meskimen; and others, including Frank Welker as The Monster.

45. La sangre de Frankenstein. Also known as LSD Frankenstein, this was filmed in Argentina and directed by German Magarinos. It starred: Leandro De la Torre; Martin Villagra; Diego Cagide; Mariano Salas; and many others.

46. Frankenstein. Made for television for release in 2004, this was directed by Kevin Connor and starred Alex Newman; Julie Delpy; Nicole Lewis; Monika Hilmerova; Donald Sutherland; William Hurt; and many others, including Luke Goss as The Creature.

47. Frankenstein. Again made for television in 2004, this was based on a concept by Dean R. Koontz and directed by Marcus Nispel. It starred: Parker Posey; Vincent Perez; Thomas Kretschmann; Adam Goldberg; Ivana Milicevic; Michael Madsen; Deborah Duke; and many others.

48. The Last Man. Based on Mary Shelley's other science fiction novel, The Last Man, 1826, this was directed by James Arnett for release in 2008. It starred: Santiago Craig; Teresa Shade; Julio Garcia; Tom Rogers; Courtney Davis; Donavon Baker; Maxine Gillespie; and many others.

49. The Prometheus Project. Directed by Sean Tretta for release in 2009, and crediting Mary Shelley's novel as the source, this starred: Tiffany Shepis; Louis Mandylor; Ed Lauter; Scott Leet; Patti Tindall; David C. Hayes; Noah Todd; Kevin Tye; Joe Ricci; Lillie Richardson; Anthony Pavelich; and others.

***

RADIO

1. Frankenstein. Produced by George Edwards, this was originally broadcast in 13 parts in 1932.

2. Frankenstein. Produced by Antony Ellis, this was first aired in 1955.

3. Mary Shelley's Frankenstein. Produced in 2004 by The Willamette Radio Workshop and broadcast on Hallowe'en.

4. Frankenstein. Released by the BBC in 2008, this radio version starred Michael Maloney as Frankenstein and John Wood as The Creature.

***

Mary Shelley was a prolific author, writing just about everything from travel narratives to short stories, from children's stories to biographies. The bulk of her work was non-fiction so I've decided to limit this to just her major works of fiction.

NOVELS

1. Frankenstein or, The Modern Prometheus. Published by Lackington, Hughes, Harding, Mayor & Jones, London, 1818.

2. Valperga, or, The Life and Adventures of Castruccio, Prince of Lucca. Published by G. and W. B. Whittaker, London, 1823.

3. The Last Man. Published by Henry Colburn, London, 1926.

4. The Fortunes of Perkin Warbeck, a Romance. Published by Henry Colburn and Richard Bentley, London, 1830.

5. Lodore. Published by Richard Bentley, London, 1835.

6. Falkner, a Novel. Published by Saunders and Otley, London, 1837.

7. Mathilda. Published by the University of North Carolina Press, Chapel Hill, North Carolina, 1959. Hardcover.

***

RELATED

1. Mary Wollstonecraft Shelley. By Helen Moore. Published by J. B. Lippincott, Philadelphia, 1886. Hardcover.

2. Mary Wollstonecraft Shelley. By Mrs Julian Marshall. Published by Richard Bentley and Son, London, 1889. Hardcover.

3. The Romance of Mary Wollstonecraft Shelley, John Howard Payne and Washington Irving. By H. H. H. Published by The Bibliophile Society, Boston, 1907. Hardcover.

4. The Elopement of Percy Bysshe Shelly and Mary Wollstonecraft Godwin. By H. Buxton Forman. Privately printed in London, 1911. Hardcover.

5. Mary Shelley. By Richard W. Church. Published by Gerald Howe, London, 1928. Hardcover.

6. Mary Shelley: A Biography. By Rosalie Glynn Grylls. Published by Oxford University Press, London, 1938. Hardcover.

7. Child of Light: A Reassessment of Mary Wollstonecraft Shelley. By Muriel Spark. Published by Tower Bridge, Hadleigh, UK, 1951. Hardcover.

8. Mary Shelley. By Elizabeth Nitchie. Published by Rutgers University Press, New Jersey, 1953. Hardcover.

9. Mary Shelley. By Eileen Bigland. Published by Appleton-Century-Crofts, New York City, 1959. Hardcover.

10. Ariel Like a Harpy: Mary Shelley and Frankenstein. By Christopher Small. Published by Victor Gollancz, London, 1972. Hardcover.

11. Mary Shelley. By William A. Walling. Published by Twayne Publishers, Boston, 1972. Hardcover.

12. Shelley's Mary: A Life of Mary Godwin Shelley. By Margaret Leighton. Published by Farrar, Straus and Giroux, New York City, 1973. Hardcover.

13. The Frankenstein Legend: A Tribute to Mary Shelley and Boris Karloff. By Donald F. Glut. Published by Scarecrow Press, Metuchen, New Jersey, 1973. Hardcover.

14. Daughter of Earth and Water: A Biography of Mary Wollstonecraft Shelley. By Noel Bertram Gerson. Published by William Morrow, New York City, 1973. Hardcover.

15. The Life and Death of Mary Wollstonecraft Shelley. By Claire Tomalin. Published by Weidenfeld and Nicolson, London, 1974. Hardcover.

16. Mary Shelley: An Annotated Bibliography. By W. H. Lyles. Published by Garland Publishing, New York City, 1975. Hardcover.

17. Mary Shelley's Monster: The Story of Frankenstein. By Martin Tropp. Published by Houghton Mifflin, Boston, 1977. Softcover.

18. Moon in Eclipse: A Life of Mary Shelley. By Jane Dunn. Published by Weidenfeld and Nicholson, London, 1978. Hardcover.

19. The Woman Who Created Frankenstein: A Portrait of Mary Shelley. By Janet Harris. Published by Harper and Row, New York City, 1979. Hardcover.

20. Mary Shelley: Romance and Reality. By Emily W. Sunstein. Published by Little Brown, Boston, 1989. Hardcover.

21. Mary Shelley: Her Life, Her Fiction, Her Monsters. By Anne K. Mellor. Published by Routledge, London, 1989. Hardcover.

22. The Other Mary Shelley: Beyond Frankenstein. By Audrey A. Fisch. Published by Oxford University Press, 1993. Hardcover.

23. Spirit Like a Storm: The Story of Mary Shelley. By Calvin Craig Miller. Published by Reynolds, United States, 1996. Hardcover.

24. Mary Shelley: Frankenstein's Creator:

Mary Shelley

The First Science Fiction Writer. By Joan Kane Nichols. Published by Conari Press, United States, 1998. Softcover.

25. Mary Shelley: A Literary Life. By John Williams. Published by Palgrave Macmillan, London, 2000. Hardcover.

26. Mary Shelley: A Biography. By Miranda Seymour. Published by John Murray, London, 2000. Hardcover.

27. Mary Shelley in Her Times. By Betty T. Bennett and Stuart Curran. Published by Johns Hopkins University Press, Baltimore, 2000. Hardcover.

28. Mary Shelley's Literary Lives and Other Writings. By Tilar J. Mazzeo. Published by Pickering and Chatto, London, 2002. In four volumes.

29. Through the Tempests Dark and Wild: A Story of Mary Shelley. By Sharon Darrow. Published by Candlewick Press, Westminster, Maryland, 2003. Hardcover.

30. The Life and Letters of Mary Wollstonecraft Shelley. By A. Marshall Florence. Published by University Press of the Pacific, 2005. Softcover.

31. The Monsters: Mary Shelley and the Curse of Frankenstein. By Dorothy Hoobler and Thomas Hoobler. Published by Little Brown, New York City, 2006. Hardcover.

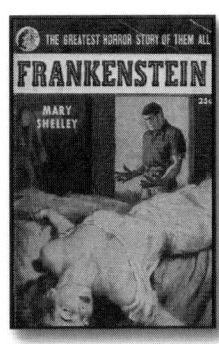

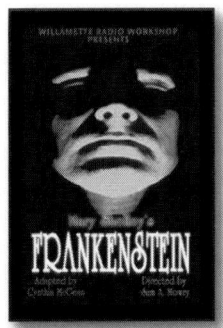

E. E. 'Doc' Smith.

Edward Elmer Smith was born in Sheboygan, Wisconsin on May 2nd, 1890 and died on August 31st, 1965 in Seaside, Oregon. He was educated as a food engineer and specialized in working with doughnuts, but by 1915, he was beginning to develop his writing skills.

Known as the father of the Space Opera, his first published story, written with Lee Hawkins Garby, was The Skylark of Space. **Hugo Gernsback** bought it for Amazing Stories and it ran in three parts between August and October, 1928. Included in the August issue was also the world's introduction to Buck Rogers: Armageddon 2419 by Philip Francis Nowlan. Also featured in the three issues were: August: The Head by Joe Kleier; Hicks Inventions with a Kick: The Perambulating Home by Henry Hugh Simmons; and The Moth by **H. G. Wells**. September: The Ambassador from Mars by Harl Vincent; The Great Steel Panic by Irvin Lester and Fletcher Pratt; The Invisible Bubble by Kirk Meadowcraft; and Unlocking the Past by David H. Keller. And October: The Menace of Mars by Clare Winger Harris; Reprisal by Thomas Richard Jones; To the Moon by Proxy by J. Schlossel; and The Voyage to Kemptonia by E. M. Scott.

Smith received his nickname, Doc, when Gernsback added Ph.D. to his byline. And he continued to write exclusively for the magazines, most particularly Amazing Stories and Astounding Stories, until the specialty publishers started up in the mid-40s. His first story published in book form was also his first story published, The Skylark of Space, 1946. Quite collectible, this usually sells for around $450.00. In fact, most of his early books, the ones from the 1940s, tend to go around the same price, the $300 to $500 range.

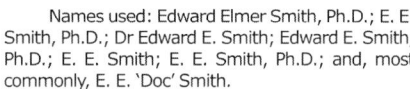

Names used: Edward Elmer Smith, Ph.D.; E. E. Smith, Ph.D.; Dr Edward E. Smith; Edward E. Smith, Ph.D.; E. E. Smith; E. E. Smith, Ph.D.; and, most commonly, E. E. 'Doc' Smith.

***

AWARDS

2004. Inducted into The Science Fiction Hall of Fame.

***

FILM AND TELEVISION

1. SF Shinseiki Lensman. Made in Japan in 1984 but released in the U.S. in 1990, this animated film was directed by Kazuyuki Hirodawa and Yoshiaki Kawajiri. It featured the voices of: Toshio Furukawa; Mami Koyama; Chikao Otsuka; Nachi Nozawa; and many others.

2. Lensman: Kozumosu no daisenso. Also known as Lensman: Great Way of the Cosmos, this animated film was released in Japan in 1987. Directed by Kazuyuki Hirodawa and Yoshiaki Kawajiri. It featured the voices of: Toshio Furukawa; Yasuo Hisamatsu; Reiko Tajima; and Kei-ichi Noda.

3. Lensman: Power of the Lens. Directed by Izo Hashimoto and Tai Kit Mak, this animated film was a re-make of SF Shinseiki Lensman and was made in Japan in 2000, featuring the voices of: Naomi Amamiya; Sonny Chang; Kazuhiko Inoue; Lichun Lee; Mayu Loh; and many others.

4. Lensman. It was announced in 2008 that Universal Pictures and Ron Howard were considering making a Lensman movie.

***

NOVELS AND COLLECTIONS

1. The Skylark of Space. With Mrs Lee Hawkins Garby. Published by The Buffalo Book Co., Providence, Rhode Island, 1946. Hardcover.

2. Spacehounds of IPC. Published by Fantasy Press, Reading, Pennsylvania, 1947. Hardcover.

3. Triplanetary. Published by Fantasy Press, Reading, Pennsylvania, 1948. Hardcover.

4. Skylark Three. Published by Fantasy Press, Reading, Pennsylvania, 1948. Hardcover.

5. Skylark of Valeron. Published by Fantasy Press, Reading, Pennsylvania, 1949. Hardcover.

6. First Lensman. Published by Fantasy Press, Reading, Pennsylvania, 1950. Hardcover.

7. Galactic Patrol. Published by Fantasy Press, Reading, Pennsylvania, 1950. Hardcover.

8. Gray Lensman. Published by Fantasy Press, Reading, Pennsylvania, 1951. Hardcover.

9. Second Stage Lensman. Published by Fantasy Press, Reading, Pennsylvania, 1953. Hardcover.

10. Children of the Lens. Published by Fantasy Press, Reading, Pennsylvania, 1954. Hardcover.

11. The Challenge from Beyond. Published by The Pennsylvania Dutch Cheese Press, 1954. Staple-bound, mimeographed. A round-robin story written with Stanley G. Weinbaum; Donald Wandrei; Harl Vincent; and Murray Leinster.

12. The History of Civilization. Published by Fantasy Press, Reading, Pennsylvania, 1955. Hardcover. A matched set packaged in a slipcase, this featured reprints of: Triplanetary, 1948; First Lensman, 1950; Galactic Patrol, 1950; Gray Lensman, 1951; Second Stage Lensman, 1953; and Children of the Lens, 1954.

13. The Vortex Blaster. Published by Gnome Press, Hicksville, New York, 1960. Hardcover.

E.E. 'Doc' Smith

14. Subspace Explorers. Published by Canaveral Press, New York City, 1965. Hardcover.

15. The Galaxy Primes. Published by Ace Books, New York City, 1965. Ace Book F-326. Softcover.

16. Skylark DuQuesne. Published by Pyramid Books, New York City, 1966. Pyramid Book X-1431. Softcover.

17. Masters of the Vortex. Published by Pyramid Books, New York City, 1968. Pyramid Book X-1851. Softcover. Re-titled from The Vortex Blaster, 1960.

18. The Best of E. E. 'Doc' Smith. Published by Futura Publications, London, 1975. Softcover. Herein: Preface by Philip Harbottle; Foreword by Walter Gillings; to the Far Reaches of Space, 1928; Robot Nemesis, 1934; Pirates of Space, 1934; The Vortex Blaster, 1941; Tedric, 1953; Lord Tedric, 1954; Subspace Survivors, 1960; and The Imperial Stars, 1964; followed by Afterword: The Epic of Space by **E. E. 'Doc' Smith**, 1947; and a Bibliography by Philip Harbottle.

19. Skylark DuQuesne. Published by Garland Publishing, New York City, 1975. First hardcover edition.

20. The Best of E. E. 'Doc' Smith. Published by Weidenfeld and Nicolson, London, 1976. First hardcover edition.

21. Masters of Space. Published by Orbit Books, London, 1976. Softcover.

22. Imperial Stars. With Stephen Goldin. Published by Pyramid Books, New York City, 1976. Pyramid Book V3839. Originally published by **Frederik Pohl** as a novella in the May 1964 issue of If, this was expanded by Stephen Goldin into the novel format. Even though Smith's name appeared on all the subsequent Family D'Alembert novels in the series, they were, in fact, written by Goldin on his own. Doc Smith was dead long before the first book in the series was published but, just as a matter of interest, the titles are listed here. Up to Getaway World, they were published by Pyramid Books, then Berkley Books took over: 2. Strangler's Moon, 1976; 3. The Clockwork Traitor, 1977; 4. Getaway World, 1977; 5. Appointment at Bloodstar, 1978; 6. The Purity Plot; 7. Planet of Treachery, 1982; Eclipsing Binaries, 1983; The Omicron Invasion, 1984; and Revolt of the Galaxy, 1985.

23. Lord Tedric and Alien Realms. Published by Star Books, London, 1980. Softcover. Herein: Lord Tedric by **E. E. 'Doc' Smith** and Gordon Eklund, 1978; and Alien Realms by Gordon Eklund writing as **E. E. 'Doc' Smith**, 1980. Starting in the late 70s, Gordon Eklund did a Lord Tedric series, supposedly working from an outline written by Smith. The American editions credited the books to Smith and Eklund, and the UK editions credited them strictly to **E. E. 'Doc' Smith**. They were: Lord Tedric; Space Pirates; and Black Knight of the Iron Sphere. They were published in softcover by Baronet Books in New York and the first two were done in hardcover by Alan Wingate in London.

24. Subspace Encounter. With Lloyd Arthur Eshbach. Published by Berkley Books, New York City, 1983. Softcover. Introduction by Lloyd Arthur Eshbach, who also completed the story.

25. Chronicles of the Lensmen - Volume 1. Published by The Science Fiction Book Club, Garden City, New York, 1999. Hardcover. An omnibus, this gathers: Foreword by John Clute; Triplanetary, 1948; First Lensman, 1950; Galactic Patrol, 1950.

26. Chronicles of the Lensmen - Volume 2. Published by The Science Fiction Book Club, Garden City, New York, 1999. Hardcover. Herein: Grey Lensman, 1951; Second Stage Lensman, 1953; and Children of the Lens, 1954.

27. Have Trenchcoat - Will Travel and Others. Published by Advent Publishers, Chicago, 2001. Herein: Introduction by Lloyd Arthur Eshbach; Have Trenchcoat - Travel; Motorsickle Cop; Nester of the Caramints; and Full Time Nurse.

***

NON-FICTION

1. What Does This Convention Mean? A Speech Delivered at The 1940 Chicago World's Science Fiction Convention. Published by Al Widner Jr in 1941 for the 1941 World's Science Fiction Convention held in Denver. It was stapled, mimeographed sheets.

2. Of Worlds Beyond: A Symposium by Edward E. Smith, Ph.D.; John W. Campbell; L. Sprague de Camp; Robert A. Heinlein; Jack Williamson; A. E. van Vogt; and John Taine. Edited by Lloyd Arthur Eschbach. Published by Advent Publishers, Chicago, 1964. Softcover.

3. Of Worlds Beyond: A Symposium by Edward E. Smith, Ph.D.; John W. Campbell; L. Sprague de Camp; Robert A. Heinlein; Jack Williamson; A. E. van Vogt; and John Taine. Edited by Lloyd Arthur Eschbach. Published by Dennis Dobson, London, 1965. First hardcover edition.

4. E. E. 'Doc' Smith: Father of Star Wars: Galactic Roamer. An interview with Thomas Sheridan. Published by the Necronomicon Press, West Warwick, Rhode Island, 1977. Limited to 500 softcover copies.

***

RELATED

1. The Universes of E. E. Smith. By Ron Ellik and Bill Evans. Published by Advent Publishers, Chicago, 1966. Hardcover.

2. E. E. 'Doc' Smith. By Joe Sanders. Published by Borgo Press, San Bernardino, California, 1986. Hardcover.

3. Doc - First Galactic Roamer: A Complete Bibliography and Publishing Checklist of Books and Articles By and About E. E. 'Doc' Smith. By Stephen C. Lucchetti. Published by NESFA Press, Framingham, Massachusetts, 2004. Hardcover.

-2005-

Chesley Bonestell.

Chesley Bonestell was born in San Francisco, California on January 1st, 1888 and died in Carmel, California on June 11, 1986. At seventeen, he did his first space painting, Saturn, after seeing it through a telescope. But at school, he studied architecture and then worked for an assortment of architectural firms. After the Great Depression, he went to England where he did some drawing for the Illustrated London News. A few years later, he moved to Hollywood and worked for the film industry.

It wasn't until the mid-1940s that he figured out that he could paint astronomical subjects and actually make a living at it.

He started working for magazines. He lost that very first painting of Saturn to the 1906 San Francisco earthquake. It seemed appropriate that his first venture into the magazines was a series of paintings of Saturn for Life. And that launched a whole new career. He did some work with Willy Ley on The Conquest of Space, 1949, and he stuck with the movies for awhile, getting into science fiction films.

Then he discovered the science fiction magazines.

His first cover was for **John W. Campbell** for Astounding Science Fiction, January 1950. The Xi Effect by Philip Latham was the story featured on the cover; inside were: And Now You Don't - part 3 by **Isaac Asimov**; Gypsy by **Poul Anderson**; Not to be Opened-- by Roger Flint Young; Ole Mother Methuselah by Rene Lafayette; and Undesirable Alien by David McCarthy.

And the next one was for Anthony Boucher at The Magazine of Fantasy and Science Fiction, December 1950, which contained: Take Two Quiggies by Kris Neville; The Better Mousetrap by L. Sprague de Camp and Fletcher Pratt; The Listening Child by Margaret St Clair writing as Idris Seabright; The Wondersmith by Fitz-James O'Brien from 1859; The Angel with Purple Hair by Herb Paul; and Process by **A. E. van Vogt**. Also in that issue was a review of a new book by L. Ron Hubbard. It was called: Dianetics: The Modern Science of Mental Health.

For all its scientific authenticity, the work was magical. The demand for Bonestell's work never abated. Year after year, his work was featured on magazine covers, primarily on The Magazine of Fantasy and Science Fiction, although Campbell used whatever he could get for Astounding and Analog.

He may be long gone but his work is still in demand. In 2005, it was featured on the cover of Little Machines by Paul McAuley from PS Publishing; and also on the August cover of Asimov's Science Fiction.

Some of the early books that he illustrated sell in the $200.00 to $500.00 range, Across the Space Frontier, Mars, et al.

***

AWARDS

1951. International Fantasy Non-Fiction Award for The Conquest of Space.
1968. Special Citation by Midwest Research, Kansas City, Missouri.
1974. Hugo Special Award for Beautiful and Scientifically Accurate Illustrations.
1976. British Interplanetary Society special bronze medal award for lifetime achievement in space exploration.
1976. Dorothea Klumpke-Roberts Award from the Astronomical Society of the Pacific.
1979. Special award from the San Francisco Exploratorium.
1984. G. Bruce Blair Medal from the Western Amateur Astronomers and the Astronomical Association of Northern California.
1986. Asteroid 3129 was named Bonestell by the International Astronomical Union.
1989. Inducted into The International Space Hall of Fame.
1997. Elected to the Society of Illustrators Hall of Fame.
2004. Retro Hugo Award for Best Professional Artist of 1954.
2005. Inducted into The Science Fiction Hall of Fame.

***

FILMS AND TELEVISION

1. Only Angels Have Wings. Uncredited background paintings for this 1939 film. Directed by Howard Hawks, this starred Cary Grant and Jean Arthur.

2. The Hunchback of Notre Dame. Uncredited background paintings in 1939. Directed by William Dieterle, the film starred: Charles Laughton; Cedric Hardwicke; Thomas Mitchell; Maureen O'Hara; Edmond O'Brien; and many others, including Fritz Leiber Sr. as an old nobleman.

3. Swiss Family Robinson. Background paintings in 1940. This was directed by Edward Ludwig and starred: Thomas Mitchell; Edna Best; and Freddie Bartholomew.

4. Citizen Kane. Uncredited background painter for this 1941 film. Directed by Orson Welles and starring Orson Welles, this co-starred: Joseph Cotten; Dorothy Comingore; Agnes Moorehead; and many others.

5. Charley's Aunt. Worked as an uncredited matte

Chesley Bonestell

artist on this 1941 film. Directed by Archie Mayo, the film starred: Jack Benny; Kay Francis; James Ellison; and Anne Baxter.

6. How Green Was My Valley. An uncredited matte artist for this 1941 film, which was directed by John Ford and starred: Walter Pidgeon; Maureen O'Hara; Anna Lee; Donald Crisp; and Roddy McDowall; with Barry Fitzgerald playing Cyfartha.

7. The Magnificent Ambersons. Did background paintings, uncredited, for this 1942 film. This was directed by Orson Welles and starred: Joseph Cotten; Dolores Costello; Anne Baxter; Tim Holt; and Agnes Moorehead.

8. The Adventures of Mark Twain. Again, an uncredited matte artist. Irving Rapper directed this 1944 film, which starred Fredric March and Alexis Smith.

9. The Horn Blows at Midnight. An uncredited matte artist for this 1945 film. It was directed by Raoul Walsh and starred Jack Benny and Alexis Smith, with Robert Blake - Bobby Blake - as Junior Pulplinsky.

10. Rhapsody in Blue. Uncredited matte artist. Directed by Irving Rapper, the film was released in 1945 and starred: Robert Alda; Joan Leslie; Alexis Smith; and Charles Coburn.

11. The Fountainhead. An uncredited matte artist for this 1949 film. Directed by King Vidor, this starred: Gary Cooper; Patricia Neal; and Raymond Massey.

12. Destination Moon. He worked as a technical advisor for this 1950 film which was written by **Robert A. Heinlein**, directed by Irving Pichel, and starred: John Archer; Warner Anderson; Tom Powers; Dick Wesson; Erin O'Brien-Moore; and others.

13. When Worlds Collide. Again, he was a technical advisor. The 1951 film was directed by Rudolph Mate and starred Richard Derr and Barbara Rush.

14. The War of the Worlds. Worked as an uncredited technical advisor on this 1953 film, based on the **H. G. Wells** novel and directed by Byron Haskin. He also produced astronomical paintings - these *were* credited. The movie starred: Gene Barry; Ann Robinson; Les Tremayne; Robert Cornthwaite; and others, with commentary by Cedric Hardwicke.

15. Cat Women on the Moon. This was also known as Rocket to the Moon. Bonestell did the moonscape paintings for this 1953 movie, which was directed by Arthur Hilton and starred Sonny Tufts, Victor Jory, and Marie Windsor.

16. Conquest of Space. Also known as Mars Project. Co-authored the book with Willy Ley in 1949 and supplied the astronomical art for the project. Directed by Byron Haskin, this starred; Walter Brooke; Eric Fleming; Mickey Shaughnessy; Phil Foster; William Hopper; and others.

17. Men into Space. Also known as Space Challenge. He was the creator of the space concepts for thirty-six episodes of this television series during 1959 and 1960.

18. The Fantasy Film Worlds of George Pal. This 1985 documentary was directed by Arnold Leibovit and featured Chesley Bonestell as one of the interviewees, along with: Robert Bloch; Tony Curtis; Barbara Eden; Charlton Heston; Janet Leigh; Tony Randall; Rod Taylor; **Gene Roddenberry**; **Ray Harryhausen**; **Ray Bradbury**; and many others.

***

BOOKS ILLUSTRATED

1. The Conquest of Space. With Willy Ley. Published by Viking Press, New York City, 1949. Hardcover.

2. Across the Space Frontier. Edited by Cornelius Ryan. Published by Viking Press, New York City, 1952. Hardcover.

3. Conquest of the Moon. Edited by Cornelius Ryan, this was by Wernher von Braun; Fred Lawrence Whipple; and Willy Ley. Published by Viking Press, New York City, 1953. Hardcover.

4. The End of the World. By Kenneth Heuer. Published by Rinehart and Company, New York City, 1953.

5. The World We Live In. Edited by Lincoln Barnett and the editors of Life. Published by Time Inc., New York City, 1955. Hardcover.

6. The Exploration of Mars. By Willy Ley and Wernher Von Braun. Published by Viking Press, New York City, 1956. Hardcover.

7. The Next Fifty Billion Years: An Astronomer's Glimpse into the Future. By Kenneth Heuer. Published by Viking Press, New York City, 1957. Hardcover. Revised edition.

8. Man and the Moon. By Robert S. Richardson. Published by World Publishing, Cleveland, 1961. Hardcover.

9. Rocket to the Moon. Written *and* illustrated by **Chesley Bonestell**. Published by the Columbia Record Club, New York, 1961. Hardcover.

10. The Solar System. Written *and* illustrated by **Chesley Bonestell**. Published by the Columbia Record Club, New York, 1961. Hardcover.

11. Mars. By Robert S. Richardson. Published by Harcourt, Brace & World, New York City, 1964. Hardcover.

12. Beyond Jupiter: The Worlds of Tomorrow. By **Arthur C. Clarke**. Published by Little Brown, Boston, 1972. Hardcover.

13. The Golden Era of the Missions, 1769 - 1834: Paintings. By Paul Johnson. Published by Chronicle Books, San Francisco, California, 1974. Softcover.

***

RELATED

1. Worlds Beyond: The Art of Chesley Bonestell. By Ron Miller and Frederick C. Durant III. Published by Starblaze - Donning, Norfolk, Virginia, 1983. Softcover.

2. A Chesley Bonestell Space Art Chronology. By Melvin H. Schuetz. Published by Universal Publishers, UK, 1999. Softcover.

3. The Art of Chesley Bonestell. By Ron Miller and Frederick C. Durant III with a foreword by Melvin H. Schuetz. Published by Paper Tiger, London, 2001. Hardcover.

4. Supplement to A Chesley Bonestell Space Art Chronology. Published by Universal Publishers, UK, 2003. Softcover.

Philip K. Dick

Philip K. Dick.

Philip Kindred Dick was born on December 16th, 1928 in Chicago and died on March 2nd, 1982, in Santa Ana, California, five days after suffering a stroke.

He aspired to write mainstream fiction but only managed to sell one mainstream novel during his lifetime. Luckily, he also loved science fiction.

He once explained that after taking a psychological profile test, he appeared to be paranoid, neurotic, schizophrenic, cyclothymic... and also an incorrigible liar. All because he could see every side of a discussion and could agree to the possible truth in all points of view, or the possible *lack* of truth in all points of view.

He believed that all people lived in their own unique world, that the projection of their individual personalities is what made that world unique. Taking that further, into the realms of science fiction, he did a series of stories in which the world was a projection of each individual's psyche. He said, "My first published story was a perfect example of this."

The story was Beyond Lies the Wub. It appeared in the July 1952 issue of Planet Stories, along with: The Man Who Staked the Stars by Katherine MacLean and Charles Dye; The Wealth of Echindul by Noel Loomis; One Purple Hope! By Henry Hasse; Acid Bath by Vaseleos Garson; Bride of the Dark One by Florence Verbell Brown; Frozen Hell by John Jakes; and Master of the Moondog by Stanley Mullen.

From that moment on, he lived as a professional writer. Times were tough, the money was bad... He once said he didn't have enough cash to pay the library fines for late books. But he kept writing.

And he survived.

His next published story was The Gun and it appeared in the very next issue of Planet Stories, September 1952, along with: Big Pill By Raymond Z Gallun; The Slaves of Venus by James E. Gunn writing as Edwin James; Evil Out of Onzar by Mark Ganes; Zero Data by Charles Saphro; Thompson's Cat by Robert Moore Williams; and The Star Plunderer by **Poul Anderson**.

When he sold his fifth published story, The Defenders, to H. L. Gold at Galaxy Science Fiction for the January 1953 issue, he received the only author-credit on the cover. Also in that issue: The Inhabited by Richard Wilson; Teething Ring by James Causey; Life Sentence by James McConnell; Prott by Margaret St Clair; and Ring Around the Sun - part 2 of 3 by Clifford D. Simak.

He was well on the way to hacking out a career.

One gets the impression that **Philip K. Dick** was a somewhat troubled man who had his own special reality-warp. Somehow, he worked it into readable, thoughtful and unique stories... He said, "They only build as much of the world as they need to, to convince you it's real." Other places don't exist, until you are on your way there.

There are an impressive number of highly-priced highly-collectible books by **Philip K. Dick**. Decent copies range between $3,500.00 and $7,500 and include the first British edition of The World Jones Made, 1968; and The Penultimate Truth, 1967; along with the American first of Solar Lottery; The

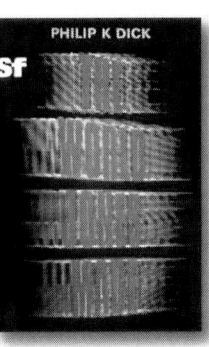

Man in the High Castle; Do Androids Dream of Electric Sheep?; and The Three Stigmata of Palmer Eldritch.

***

AWARDS

1963. Hugo Best Novel Award for The Man in the High Castle.
1966. British Science Fiction Best SF Novel Award for The Three Stigmata of Palmer Eldritch.
1975. The John W. Campbell Memorial Award for Flow My Tears, the Policeman Said.
1978. British Science Fiction Best SF Novel Award for A Scanner Darkly.
2005. Inducted into The Science Fiction Hall of Fame.

***

FILMS AND TELEVISION

1. Imposter. This 1953 short story was used on the television series Out of This World in 1962. Directed by Peter Hammond, it starred: Boris Karloff as the host; Patrick Allen; Keith Anderson; Philip Anthony; Paul Bacon; Angela Browne; and others.

2. Blade Runner. Based on the 1968 novel, Do Androids Dream of Electric Sheep?, this was directed by **Ridley Scott** and starred: Harrison Ford; Rutger Hauer; Sean Young; Edward James Olmos; M. Emmet Walsh; Daryl Hannah; Joanna Cassidy; and many others.

3. Total Recall. From the 1966 short story, We Can Remember It For You Wholesale, this was directed by Paul Verhoeven in 1990 and starred: Arnold Schwarzenegger; Rachel Ticotin; Sharon Stone; Ronny Cox; Michael Ironside; Marshall Bell; and others.

4. Confessions d'un Barjo. Also known as Confessions of a Crap Artist, this was filmed from the only mainstream novel by Dick that was published in his lifetime, 1975. Directed by Jerome Boivin, it was filmed in France in 1992 and released in the U.S. the following year. It starred: Richard Bohringer; Anne Brochet; Hippolyte Girardot; Consuelo De Haviland; Renaud Danner; Nathalie Boutefeu; and many others.

5. Drug Taking and the Arts. This film was made from the works of at least twenty-one different authors, including Jack Kerouac; Ken Kesey; Aldous Huxley; Allen Ginsberg; Arthur Rimbaud; William S. Burroughs; and **Philip K. Dick**. A Scanner Darkly, from 1977, was credited as the source. Directed by Storm Thorgerson in 1994, this featured Bernard Hill as The Presenter; Phil Daniels ad Thomas De Quincey; Daniel Webb as Jean Cocteau; Jon Finch as Gerard de Nerval; and Todd Royco as Andy Warhol;

along with, as themselves: **Brian W. Aldiss**; J. G. Ballard; Ann Charters; Allen Ginsberg; Timothy Leary; and many others.

6. Philip K. Dick: A Day in the Afterlife. Directed by Nicola Roberts for the television series, Arena, this aired on April 9th, 1994. It featured archival footage of **Philip K. Dick**, along with interviews with Elvis Costello; Thomas M. Disch; Terry Gilliam; and Kim Stanley Robinson.

7. Screamers. From the short story Second Variety, 1953, this was directed by Christian Duguay for release in 1995. It starred: Peter Weller; Roy Dupuis; Jennifer Rubin; Andrew Lauer; and many others.

8. Total Recall 2070. A television series inspired by the movie Total Recall from 1990, which was based on the 1966 short story, We Can Remember It For You Wholesale. The series started in January 1999 and ran for twenty-two episodes, until June 1999. It starred: Michael Easton; Judith Krant; and Michael Rawlins.

9. On the Edge of Blade Runner. A television documentary, this was directed by Andrew Abbot and released on July 15th, 2000. It featured archival footage of **Philip K. Dick**, along with interviews with: **Brian W. Aldiss**; Joanna Cassidy; Daryl Hannah; Rutger Hauer; and many others.

10. Imposter. Based on the 1953 short story, this was directed by Gary Fleder in 2001, starring: Gary Sinise; Madeleine Stowe; Vincent D'Onofrio; Tony Shalhoub; Tim Guinee; Gary Dourdan; and many others.

11. Minority Report. Based on the 1956 short story, this was directed by **Stephen Spielberg** for release in 2002. It starred: Tom Cruise; Max von Sydow; Steve Harris; Neal McDonough; Patrick Kilpatrick; Jessica Capshaw; and many others, including Cameron Diaz in an uncredited bit part as a woman on the Metro.

12. Paycheck. From the 1953 short story, this 2003 film was directed by John Woo and starred: Ben Affleck; Aaron Eckhart; Uma Thurman; Paul Giamatti; Colm Feore; and many others.

13. A Scanner Darkly. Based on the 1977 novel, this was directed by Richard Linklater for release in 2006. It starred: Rory Cochrane; Robert Downey, Jr; Mitch Baker; Keanu Reeves; Sean Allen; Winona Ryder; Woody Harrelson; and others.

14. One Summer in Austin: The Story of Filming A Scanner Darkly. Televised in 2006, this was directed by Eric Matthies and featured archival footage of **Philip K. Dick**, along with interviews with: Richard Linklater; Keanu Reeves; Robert Downey, Jr; Woody Harrelson; Winona Ryder; and others.

15. Next. Based on the story The Golden Man, 1954, this was filmed for release in 2007. Directed by Lee Tamahori, it starred: Nicholas Cage; Julianne Moore; Jessica Biel; and others.

16. The Penultimate Truth About Philip K. Dick. Directed by Patricio Vega, this documentary was filmed in Argentina in 2007 and featured archival footage of **Philip K. Dick**.

17. Sacrificial Sheep: The Novel vs. the Film. Directed by Charles de Lauzirika, this short documentary was released in 2007, featuring library footage of **Philip K. Dick**, along with an assortment of interviewees: **Brian W. Aldiss**; Michael Deeley; Tim Powers; **Ridley Scott**; and others.

18. The Electric Dreamer: Remembering Philip K. Dick. From 2007, this documentary was directed by Charles de Lauzirika and featured archival film footage of **Philip K. Dick** along with an assortment of interviews: **Brian W. Aldiss**; James Blaylock; Christopher Dick; Tim Powers; and others.

19. Screamers: The Hunting. Inspired by Second Variety, 1953, this sequel to Screamers was directed by Sheldon Wilson for release in 2009, starring: Gina Holden; Jana Pallaske; Lance Henriksen; Greg Bryk; Christopher Redman; Tim Rozon; and others.

20. Radio Free Albemuth. Based on the 1985 novel, this is planned for release in 2009, directed by John Alan Simon and starring: Jonathan Scarfe; Shea Whigham; Katheryn Winnick; Alanis Morissette; Hanna Hall; and others.

21. The Adjustment Bureau. From the 1954 short story, Adjustment Team, this is being developed for release in 2010, directed by George Nolfi and starring Matt Damon.

22. King of the Elves. Based on the 1953 short story, it has been announced that this will be directed by Aaron Blaise and Robert Walker and ready in 2012, an animated feature.

23. The Owl in Daylight. Based on Owl in Daylight, a biographical piece that was left unfinished when Dick died, this is apparently in very early stages of production. Paul Giamatti plans to play **Philip K. Dick**.

24. Ubik. It has been announced that the 1969 novel is about to be filmed, produced by The Halcyon Company.

25. Flow My Tears, the Policeman Said. Apparently, this 1974 novel is in development for the big screen.

***

NOVELS AND COLLECTIONS

1. Solar Lottery. Published by Ace Books, New York City, 1955. Ace Double D-103. Softcover. Bound with The Big Jump by Leigh Brackett.

2. A Handful of Darkness. Published by Rich and Cowan, London, 1955. Hardcover. Herein: The Indefatigable Frog, 1953; Colony, 1953; Imposter, 1953; The Little Movement, 1952; The Builder, 1953; The Cookie Lady, 1953; Exhibit Piece, 1953; Expendable, 1953; The Impossible Planet, 1953; Planet for Transients, 1953; The Preserving Machine, 1953; Progeny, 1954; Prominent Author, 1954; The Turning Wheel, 1954; and Upon the Dull Earth, 1954.

3. Solar Lottery. Published by Rich and Cowan, London, 1956. Hardcover. Unauthorized changes

Philip K. Dick

were made to the text.

4. The World Jones Made. Published by Ace Books, New York City, 1956. Ace Double D-150. Softcover. Together with Agent of the Unknown by Margaret St Clair.

5. The Man Who Japed. Published by Ace Books, New York City, 1956. Ace Double D-193. Softcover. Bound with The Space-Born by E. C. Tubb.

6. Eye in the Sky. Published by Ace Books, New York City, 1957. Ace Book D-211. Softcover.

7. The Cosmic Puppets. Published by Ace Books, New York City, 1957. Ace Double D-249. Softcover. Together with Sargasso of Space by **Andre Norton** writing as Andrew North.

8. The Variable Man and Other Stories. Published by Ace Books, New York City, 1957. Ace Book D-261. Softcover. Herein: The Variable Man, 1953; Second Variety, 1953; The Minority Report, 1956; Autofac, 1955; and A World of Talent, 1954.

9. Time Out of Joint. Published by J. B. Lippincott, Philadelphia and New York, 1959. Hardcover.

10. Dr Futurity. Published by Ace Books, New York City, 1960. Ace Double D-431. Softcover. Together with Slavers of Space by John Brunner.

11. Vulcan's Hammer. Published by Ace Books, New York City, 1960. Ace Double D-457. Softcover. Together with The Skynappers by John Brunner.

12. The Man in the High Castle. Published by G. P. Putnam's Sons, New York City, 1962. Hardcover.

13. The Game Players of Titan. Published by Ace Books, New York City, 1963. Ace Book F-251. Softcover.

14. The Simulacra. Published by Ace Books, New York City, 1964. Ace Book F-301. Softcover.

15. Clans of the Alphane Moon. Published by Ace Books, New York City, 1964. Ace Book F-309. Softcover.

16. Martian Time-Slip. Published by Ballantine Books, New York City, 1964. Ballantine Book U2191. Softcover.

17. The Penultimate Truth. Published by Belmont Books, New York City, 1964. Belmont Book 92-603. Softcover.

18. Dr Bloodmoney or How We Got Along After the Bomb. Published by Ace Books, New York City, 1965. Ace Book F-337. Softcover.

19. The Three Stigmata of Palmer Eldritch. Published by Doubleday & Company, Garden City, New York, 1965. Hardcover.

20. The Crack in Space. Published by Ace Books, New York City, 1966. Ace Book F-377. Softcover.

21. Now Wait for Last Year. Published by Doubleday & Company, Garden City, New York, 1966. Hardcover.

22. The Unteleported Man. Published by Ace Books, New York City, 1966. Ace Double G-602. Softcover. Together with The Mind Monsters by Howard L. Cory.

23. The Ganymede Takeover. With Ray Nelson. Published by Ace Books, New York City, 1967. Ace Book G-637. Softcover.

24. Counter-Clock World. Published by Berkley Books, New York City, 1967. Berkley Book X1372. Softcover.

25. The Zap Gun. Published by Pyramid Books, New York City, 1967. Pyramid Book R-1569.

26. The Penultimate Truth. Published by Victor Gollancz, London, 1967. First hardcover edition.

27. The World Jones Made. Published by Sidgwick and Jackson, London, 1968. First hardcover edition.

28. Do Androids Dream of Electric Sheep? Published by Doubleday & Company, Garden City, New York, 1968. Hardcover.

29. Galactic Pot-Healer. Published by Berkley Books, New York City, 1969. Berkley Book X1705. Softcover.

30. Ubik. Published by Doubleday & Company, Garden City, New York, 1969. Hardcover.

31. The Preserving Machine. Published by Ace Books, New York City, 1969. Ace Science Fiction Special 67800. Softcover. Herein: The Preserving Machine, 1953; War Game, 1959; Upon the Dull Earth, 1954; Roog, 1953; War Veteran, 1955; Top Stand-By Job, 1963; Beyond Lies the Wub, 1952; We Can Remember It for You Wholesale, 1966; Captive Market, 1955; If There Were No Benny Cemoli, 1963; Retreat Syndrome, 1965; The Crawlers, 1954; Oh, to Be a Blobel!, 1964; What the Dead Men Say, 1964; and Pay for the Printer, 1956.

32. The Preserving Machine. Published by the Science Fiction Book Club, Garden City, New York, 1970. First hardcover edition.

33. Our Friends from Frolix 8. Published by Ace Books, New York City, 1970. Ace Book 64400. Softcover.

34. Galactic Pot-Healer. Published by the Science Fiction Book Club, Garden City, New York, 1970. First hardcover edition.

35. A Maze of Death. Published by Doubleday & Company, Garden City, New York, 1970. Hardcover.

36. A Philip K. Dick Omnibus. Published by Sidgwick and Jackson, London, 1970. Hardcover. Herein: The Crack in Space, 1966; The Unteleported Man, 1964; and Dr Futurity, 1960.

37. Our Friends from Frolix 8. Published by the Science Fiction Book Club, Garden City, New York, 1971. First hardcover edition.

38. The Preserving Machine. Published by Victor Gollancz, London, 1971. This deleted one story from the collection, What the Dead Men Say, 1964.

39. Dr Futurity. Published by Ace Books, New York

325

City, 1972. Ace Double 15697. Softcover. Bound with The Unteleported Man.

40. The Unteleported Man. Published by Ace Books, New York City, 1972. Ace Double 15697. Softcover. Bound with Dr Futurity.

41. We Can Build You. Published by DAW Books, New York City, 1972. DAW Collector's Book 14. UQ1014. Softcover.

42. The Book of Philip K. Dick. Published by DAW Books, New York City, 1973. DAW Collector's Book 44. UQ1044. Softcover. Herein: Nanny, 1955; The Turning Wheel, 1954; The Defenders, 1953; Adjustment Team, 1954; Psi-Man, 1955; The Commuter, 1953; A Present for Pat, 1954; Breakfast at Twilight, 1954; and Shell Game, 1954.

43. The Game Players of Titan. Published by White Lion Publishers, London, 1974. First hardcover edition.

44. Flow My Tears, the Policeman Said. Published by Doubleday & Company, Garden City, New York, 1974. Hardcover.

45. Confessions of a Crap Artist. Published by Entwhistle Books, New York City, 1975. Limited edition hardcover, the first 90 signed by the author, the other 410 unsigned.

46. Deus Irae. Written with Roger Zelazny. Published by Doubleday & Company, Garden City, New York, 1976. Hardcover.

47. Solar Lottery. Published by Gregg Press, Boston, 1976. First hardcover edition with Dick's original text.

48. Martian Time-Slip. Published by New English Library, London, 1976. First hardcover edition.

49. A Scanner Darkly. Published by Doubleday & Company, Garden City, New York, 1977. Hardcover.

50. Counter-Clock World. Published by White Lion Publishers, London, 1977. First hardcover edition.

51. The Simulacra. Published by Eyre Methuen, London, 1977. First hardcover edition.

52. Dr Bloodmoney, or, How We Got Along After the Bomb. Published by Gregg Press, Boston, 1977. First hardcover edition.

53. The Best of Philip K. Dick. Published by Del Rey - Ballantine Books, New York City, 1977. Ballantine Book 25359. Softcover. Herein: Introduction by John Brunner; Second Variety, 1953; If there Were No Benny Cemoli, 1963; Foster, You're Dead, 1955; The Father-Thing, 1954; Faith of Our Fathers, 1967; Beyond Lies the Wub, 1952; Colony, 1953; The Electric Ant, 1969; Autofac, 1955; Imposter, 1953; Breakfast at Twilight, 1954; The Days of Perky Pat, 1963; Expendable, 1953; Human Is, 1955; A Little Something for Us Tempunauts, 1974; Oh. To Be a Blobel!, 1964; Paycheck, 1953; Roog, 1953; and Service Call, 1955; along with Afterthoughts by the Author, 1977.

54. The Turning Wheel and Other Stories. Published by Coronet Books, London, 1977. Softcover. Re-titled from The Book of Philip K. Dick.

55. Clans of the Alphane Moon. Published by Gregg Press, Boston, 1979. First hardcover edition.

56. The Golden Man. Published by Berkley Books, New York City, 1980. Softcover. Herein: Foreword by Mark Hurst; Introduction by **Philip K. Dick**; The Golden Man, 1954; Return Match, 1967; The King of the Elves, 1953; The Mold of Yancy, 1955; Not by Its Cover, 1968; The Little Black Box, 1964; The Unreconstructed M, 1957; The War with the Fnools, 1969; The Last of the Masters, 1954; Meddler, 1954; A Game of Unchance, 1964; Sales Pitch, 1954; Precious Artifact, 1964; Small Town, 1954; and The Pre-Persons, 1974; with an afterword by the author.

57. Valis. Published by Bantam Books, New York City, 1981. Softcover.

58. The Divine Invasion. Published by Timescape Books - Pocket Books, New York City, 1981. Hardcover.

59. The Transmigration of Timothy Archer. Published by Timescape Books - Pocket Books, New York City, 1982. Hardcover.

60. The Man Whose Teeth Were all Exactly Alike. Published by Mark V. Ziesing, Willimantic, Connecticut, 1984. Hardcover.

61. Robots, Androids, and Mechanical Oddities: The Science Fiction of Philip K. Dick. Published by Southern Illinois University Press, 1984. Hardcover. Herein: Second Variety, 1953; War Game, 1959; The Defenders, 1953; The Electric Ant, 1969; Autofac, 1955; Imposter, 1953; The Little Movement, 1952; The Exit Door Leads In, 1979; Frozen Journey, 1980; A Game of Unchance, 1964; The Last of the Masters, 1954; The Preserving Machine, 1953; Sales Pitch, 1954; Service Call, 1955; and To Serve the Master, 1956.

62. Radio Free Albemuth. Published by Arbor House, New York City, 1985. Hardcover.

63. Ubik: The Screenplay. Published by Corroboree Press, Minneapolis, Minnesota, 1985. Hardcover. Introduction by Paul Williams; Foreword by Tim Powers.

64. I Hope I Shall Arrive Soon. Published by Doubleday & Company, Garden City, New York, 1985. Hardcover. This contains: Introduction: How to Build a Universe that Doesn't Fall Apart Two Days Later by **Philip K. Dick**; Chains of Air, Web of Aether, 1980; Explorers We, 1959; Holy Quarrel, 1966; I Hope I Shall Arrive Soon, 1980; Rautavaara's Case, 1980; Strange Memories of Death, 1984; The Alien Mind, 1981; The Exit Door Leads In, 1979; The Short Happy Life of the Brown Oxford, 1954; and What'll We Do with Ragland Park?, 1963.

65. In Milton Lumky Territory. Published by Dragon Press, Pleasantville, New York, 1985. Hardcover.

66. Puttering About in a Small Land. Published by Academy, Chicago, 1985. Hardcover.

67. Humpty Dumpty in Oakland. Published by

Philip K. Dick

Victor Gollancz, London, 1986. Hardcover.

68. Mary and the Giant. Published by Arbor House, New York City, 1987. Hardcover.

69. Valis. Published by Kerosina Books, UK, 1987. First hardcover edition.

70. The Collected Stories of Philip K. Dick, Volume 1: Beyond Lies the Wub. Published by Underwood Miller, Los Angeles, California, 1987. Hardcover. Herein: Preface by **Philip K. Dick**; Foreword by Steven Owen Godersky; Introduction by Roger Zelazny; Beyond Lies the Wub, 1952; The Indefatigable Front, 1953; Colony, 1953; The Defenders, 1953; The Little Movement, 1952; The Builder, 1953; The Crystal Crypt, 1954; Expendable, 1953; The Great C, 1953; The Gun, 1952; The Infinites, 1953; The King of the Elves, 1953; Meddler, 1954; Mr Spaceship, 1953; Nanny, 1955; Out in the Garden, 1953; Paycheck, 1953; Piper in the Woods, 1953; The Preserving Machine, 1953; Prize Ship, 1954; Roog, 1954; The Skull, 1952; The Short Happy Life of the Brown Oxford, 1954; Stability, 1987; and The Variable Man, 1953.

71. The Collected Stories of Philip K. Dick, Volume 2: Second Variety. Published by Underwood Miller, Los Angeles, California, 1987. Hardcover. Herein: Introduction by Norman Spinrad; Second Variety, 1953; Imposter, 1953; Adjustment Team, 1954; Beyond the Door, 1954; Breakfast at Twilight, 1954; The Commuter, 1953; The Cookie Lady, 1953; The Cosmic Poachers, 1953; The Hood Maker, 1955; Human Is, 1955; The Impossible Planet, 1953; James P. Crow, 1954; Jon's word, 1954; Martians Come in Clouds, 1953; Of Withered Apples, 1954; Planet for Transients, 1953; A Present for Pat, 1954; Progeny, 1954; Project: Earth, 1953; Prominent Author, 1954; Small Town, 1954; Some Kinds of Life, 1953; Souvenir, 1954; A Surface Raid, 1955; Survey Team, 1954; The Trouble with Bubbles, 1953; and The World She Wanted, 1953.

72. The Collected Stories of Philip K. Dick, Volume 3: The Father Thing. Published by Underwood Miller, Los Angeles, California, 1987. Hardcover. Herein: Introduction by John Brunner; A World of Talent, 1954; Exhibit Piece, 1954; Fair Game, 1959; Foster, You're Dead, 1955; Misadjustment, 1957; Null-O, 1958; Pay for the Printer, 1956; Psi-Man Heal My Child!, 1955; Sales Pitch, 1954; Shell Game, 1954; Strange Eden, 1954; The Chromium Fence, 1955; The Crawlers, 1954; The Eyes Have It, 1953; The Father-Thing, 1954; The Golden Man, 1954; The Hanging Stranger, 1953; The Last of the Masters, 1954; The Turning Wheel, 1954; To Serve the Master, 1956; Tony and the Beetles, 1953; Upon the Dull Earth, 1954; and War Veteran, 1955.

73. The Collected Stories of Philip K. Dick, Volume 4: The Days of Perky Pat. Published by Underwood Miller, Los Angeles, California, 1987. Hardcover. Herein: Introduction by James Tiptree, Jr; If There Were No Benny Cemoli, 1963; Captive Market, 1955; War Game, 1959; Autofac, 1955; The Days of Perky Pat, 1963; Explorers We, 1959; The Minority Report, 1956; The Mold of Yancy, 1955; novelty Act, 1964; O to Be a Blobel!, 1964; Orpheus with Clay Feet, 1964; Recall Mechanism, 1959; Top Stand-By Job, 1963; The Unreconstructed M, 1957; Waterspider, 1964; What the Dead Men Say, 1964; and What'll We Do with Ragland Park?, 1963.

74. The Collected Stories of Philip K. Dick, Volume 5: The Little Black Box. Published by Underwood Miller, Los Angeles, California, 1987. Hardcover. Herein: Introduction by Thomas M. Disch; We Can Remember It for You Wholesale, 1966; Faith of Our Fathers, 1967; Strange Memories of Death, 1984; The Alien Mind, 1981; The Pre-Persons, 1974; The War with the Fnools, 1969; Return Match, 1967; The Electric Ant, 1969; Holy Quarrel, 1966; Cadbury, the Beaver Who Lacked, 1987; Chains of Air, Web of Aether, 1980; The Day Mr Computer Fell Out of Its Tree, 1987; The Exit Door Leads In, 1979; The Eye of the Sibyl, 1987; A Game of Unchance, 1964; I Hope I Shall Arrive Soon, 1980; The Little Black Box, 1964; A Little Something for Us Tempunauts, 1974; Not by Its Cover, 1968; Precious Artifact, 1964; Rautavaara's Case, 1980; Retreat Syndrome, 1965; The Story to End All Stories for Harlan Ellison's Anthology Dangerous Visions, 1968; A Terran Odyssey, 1987; and Your Appointment Will Be Yesterday, 1966.

75. We Can Build You. Published by Severn House, London, 1988. First hardcover edition.

76. Nick and the Glimmung. Published by Victor Gollancz, London, 1988. Hardcover.

77. The Broken Bubble. Published by Arbor House, New York City, 1988. Hardcover.

78. The Valis Trilogy. Published by the Quality Paperback Book Club, New York City, 1989. Softcover. Herein: Valis, 1981; The Divine Invasion, 1981; and The Transmigration of Timothy Archer, 1982; followed by an afterword by Kim Stanley Robinson.

79. The Valis Trilogy. Published by the Book of the Month Club, New York City, 1990. First hardcover edition.

80. Gather Yourselves Together. Published by WCS Books, Asheville, North Carolina, 1994. Hardcover.

81. Three Early Novels. Published by Millennium/Victor Gollancz, London, 2000. Softcover. An omnibus edition, this gathers: The Man Who Japed, 1956; Dr Futurity, 1960; and Vulcan's Hammer, 1960.

82. Selected Stories of Philip K. Dick. Published by Pantheon Books - Random House, New York City, 2002. Hardcover. Herein: Introduction by Jonathan Lethem; Beyond Lies the Wub, 1952; Roog, 1953; Paycheck, 1953; Second Variety, 1953; Imposter, 1953; The King of the Elves, 1953; Adjustment Team, 1954; Foster, You're Dead, 1955; Upon the Dull Earth, 1954; Autofac, 1955; The Minority Report, 1956; The Days of Perky Pat, 1963; Precious Artifact, 1964; A Game of Unchance, 1964; We Can Remember It for You Wholesale, 1966; Faith of Our Fathers, 1967; The Electric Ant, 1969; A Little Something for Us Tempunauts, 1974; The Exit Door Leads In, 1979; Rautavaara's Case, 1980; and I Hope I Shall Arrive Soon, 1980.

83. Counterfeit Unrealities. Published by the Science Fiction Book Club, Garden City, New York, 2002. Hardcover. This contains: The Three Stigmata of Palmer Eldritch, 1965; Do Androids Dream of Electric Sheep?, 1968; Ubik, 1969; and A Scanner Darkly, 1977.

84. The Short Happy Life of the Brown Oxford and Other Classic Stories. Citadel Press, New York City, 2002. Softcover. Re-titled from The Collected Stories of Philip K. Dick, Volume 1: Beyond Lies the Wub, 1987.

85. Minority Report and Other Classic Stories. Citadel Press, New York City, 2002. Softcover. Re-titled from The Collected Stories of Philip K. Dick, Volume 4: The Days of Perky Pat, 1987.

86. The Eye of the Sibyl. Citadel Press, New York City, 2002. Softcover. Re-titled from The Collected Stories of Philip K. Dick, Volume 5: The Little Black Box, 1987.

87. Minority Report. Published by Gollancz/Orion, London, 2002. Hardcover. Herein: Introduction by Malcolm Edwards; The Minority Report, 1956; Imposter, 1953; Second Variety, 1953; War Game, 1959; What the Dead Men Say, 1964; Oh, to Be a Blobel!, 1964; The Electric Ant, 1969; Faith of Our Fathers, 1967; and We Can Remember It for You Wholesale, 1966.

88. Cantata-140. Published by Victor Gollancz, London, 2003. Softcover.

89. Paycheck. Published by Victor Gollancz, London, 2004. Softcover. Herein: A Little Something for Us Tempunauts, 1974; Autofac, 1955; Breakfast at Twilight, 1954; Jon's World, 1954; Nanny, 1955; Paycheck, 1953; Small Town, 1954; Stand-By, 1963; The Chromium Fence, 1955; The Days of Perky Pat, 1963; The Father-Thing, 1954; and The Pre-Persons, 1974.

90. Five Great Novels. Published by Gollancz/Orion, London, 2004. Softcover. Re-titled from Counterfeit Unrealities, 2002.

91. Vintage PKD. Published by Vintage Books, New York City, 2006. Softcover. This collects excerpts from: The Man in the High Castle; The Three Stigmata of Palmer Eldritch; and Valis; along with some essays and letters and the stories: The Days of Perky Pat, 1963; A Little Something for Us Tempunauts, 1974; and I Hope I Shall Arrive Soon, 1980.

92. Philip K. Dick: Four Novels of the 1960s. Published by the Library of America, United States, 2007. Hardcover. This collects: The Man in the High Castle, 1962; Do Androids Dream of Electric Sheep?, 1968; The Three Stigmata of Palmer Eldritch, 1965; and Ubik, 1969.

93. Voices From the Street. Published by Tor Books - Tom Doherty Associates, New York City, 2007. Hardcover.

94. Human Is?: A Philip K. Dick Reader. Published by Victor Gollancz, London, 2007. Softcover. Herein: Beyond Lies the Wub, 1952; The Defenders, 1953; Roog, 1953; Second Variety, 1953; Imposter, 1953; The Preserving Machine, 1953; The Variable Man, 1953; Paycheck, 1953; Adjustment Team, 1954; The Father-Thing, 1955; Foster, You're Dead, 1955; Human Is, 1955; The Mold of Yancy, 1955; If There Were No Benny Cemoli, 1963; The Days of Perky Pat, 1963; Oh to Be a Blobel!, 1964; We Can Remember It for You Wholesale, 1966; The Electric Ant, 1969; A Little Something for Us Tempunauts, 1974; and The Pre-Persons, 1974.

95. Philip K. Dick: Five Novels of the 1960s and 70s. Published by the Library of America, United States, 2008. Hardcover. Herein: Martian Time-Slip, 1964; Dr Bloodmoney, 1965; Now Wait for Last Year, 1966; Flow My Tears, the Policeman Said, 1974; and A Scanner Darkly, 1977.

96. The Early Work of Philip K. Dick, Volume 1: The Variable Man and Other Stories. Published by Prime Books, United States, 2008. Hardcover.

97. The Early Work of Philip K. Dick, Volume 2: Breakfast at Twilight and Other Stories. Published by United States, New York City, 2008. Hardcover.

***

NON-FICTION

1. The Dark-Haired Girl. Published by Mark V. Ziesing, Willimantic, Connecticut, 1984. Hardcover.

2. Philip K. Dick: In His Own Words. Edited by Gregg Rickman. Published by Valentine Press, Long Beach, California, 1988. Softcover.

3. In Pursuit of Valis. Published by Underwood Miller, Los Angeles, California, 1991. Hardcover.

4. The Selected Letters of Philip K. Dick 1974. Published by Underwood Books, California, 1991. Limited edition hardcover.

5. The Selected Letters of Philip K. Dick 1975 - 76. Published by Underwood Books, California, 1992. Limited edition hardcover.

6. The Selected Letters of Philip K. Dick 1972 - 1973. Published by Underwood Books, California, 1993. Limited edition hardcover.

7. The Selected Letters of Philip K. Dick 1977 - 79. Published by Underwood Books, California, 1993. Limited edition hardcover.

8. The Shifting Realities of Philip K. Dick. By Lawrence Sutin. Published by Pantheon Books, New York City, 1995. Hardcover.

9. The Selected Letters of Philip K. Dick 1938 - 1971. Published by Underwood Books, California, 1996. Limited edition hardcover.

10. The Selected Letters of Philip K. Dick 1980 - 82. Published by Underwood Books, California, 1998. Limited edition hardcover.

11. What If Our World Is Their Heaven? With Gwen Lee and Doris Elaine Sauter. Published by Overlook Press, New York City, 2001. Hardcover.

***

Philip K. Dick

RELATED

1. Human Equation: The Provocative Short Novels of Tomorrow by Alfred Bester, Leigh Brackett, Ray Bradbury, Philip K. Dick and John D. MacDonald: with Authoritative Biographical Prefaces. Edited by William F. Nolan. Published by Sherbourne Press, Los Angeles, California, 1971. Hardcover.

2. Philip K. Dick and the Umbrella of Light. By Angus Taylor. Published by T. K. Graphics, Baltimore, Maryland, 1975. Softcover.

3. Philip K. Dick: Electric Shepherd. Edited by Bruce Gillespie. Published by Norstrilia Press, Melbourne, Australia, 1975. Softcover.

4. Science Fiction Studies: March 1975: The Science Fiction of Philip K. Dick. Edited by R. D. Mullen and Darko Suvin. Published by Indiana State University, 1975. Softcover.

5. PKD: A Philip K. Dick Bibliography. By Steven Owen Godersky and Daniel J. H. Levack. Published by Underwood Miller, San Francisco, California, 1981.

6. Philip K. Dick. By Hazel Pierce. Published by Starmont House, Mercer Island, Washington, 1982. Softcover.

7. Philip K. Dick: Writers of the 21st Century Series. Edited by Martin H. Greenberg and Joseph D. Olander. Published by Taplinger Publishing, New York City, 1983. Hardcover.

8. The Digital Wristwatch of Philip K. Dick. By Richard A. Lupoff with an introduction by Philip Jose Farmer. Published by Canyon Press, San Carlos, California, 1985. Limited to fifty hardcover copies and three hundred softcover.

9. Philip K. Dick: The Last Testament. By Gregg Rickman with a foreword by **Robert Silverberg**. Published by Valentine Press, Long Beach, California, 1985. Softcover.

10. Only Apparently Real: The World of Philip K. Dick. By Paul Williams. Published by Arbor House, New York City, 1986. Hardcover.

11. Philip K. Dick: The Dream Connection. By D. Scott Apel. Published by Permanent Press, San Jose, California, 1987. Hardcover.

12. Wind in Motion: The Fiction of Philip K. Dick. By Patricia S. Warrick. Published by Southern Illinois University Press, 1987. Hardcover.

13. The Secret Ascension: Philip K. Dick is Dead, Alas. By Michael Bishop. Published by Tor Books - Tom Doherty Associates, New York City, 1987. Hardcover.

14. PKD: A Philip K. Dick Bibliography. By Daniel J. H. Levack. Published by the Greenwood Publishing Group, Troy, Missouri, 1988. Hardcover.

15. Philip K. Dick. By Douglas A. MacKey. Published by Twayne Publishers, Boston, 1988. Hardcover.

16. Divine Invasions: A Life of Philip K. Dick. By Lawrence Sutin. Published by Harmony Books, New York City, 1990. Hardcover.

17. Retrofitting Blade Runner: Issued in Ridley Scott's Blade Runner and Philip K. Dick's Do Androids Dream of Electric Sheep?. By Judith Kerman. Published by Popular Press, Bowling Green, Ohio, 1991. Softcover.

18. Welcome to Reality: The Nightmares of Philip K. Dick. Published by Broken Mirrors Press, Michigan, 1991. Hardcover.

19. Kindred Blood in Kensington Gore - Philip K. Dick in the Afterlife: An Imaginary Conversation. By **Brian W. Aldiss**. Published by Avernus Creative Media, London, 1992. Staple-bound pamphlet.

20. On Philip K. Dick: 40 Articles from Science-Fiction Studies. Edited by R. D. Mullen, Istvan Csicsery-Ronay, Arthur Evans, and Veronica Hollinger. Published by SF - TH Inc., Lake Forest, California, 1992. Softcover.

21. Philip K. Dick: Contemporary Critical Interpretations. By Samuel J. Umland. Published by the Greenwood Publishing Group, Troy, Missouri, 1995. Hardcover.

22. Search for Philip K. Dick, 1928 - 1982: A Memoir and Biography of the Science Fiction Writer. By Anne R. Dick. Published by EMP - Edwin Mellen Press, Lewiston, New York, 1995. Hardcover.

23. Philip K. Dick: Exhilaration and Terror of the Postmodern. By Christopher Palmer. Published by Liverpool University Press, 2003. Softcover.

24. Pink Beams of Light from the God in the Gutter: The Science-Fictional Religion of Philip K. Dick. Published by the University Press of America, 2004. Softcover.

25. I Am Alive and You Are Dead: A Journey into the Mind of Philip K. Dick. By Emmanuel Carrere. Published by Bloomsbury, London, 2005. Hardcover.

26. How Much Does Chaos Scare You?: Politics, Religion, and Philosophy in the Fiction of Philip K. Dick. By Aaron Barlow. Published by Lulu Press, 2005. Softcover.

27. Counterfeit Words: Philip K. Dick on Film. By Brian J. Robb. Published by Titan Books, UK, 2006. Softcover.

28. Future Imperfect: Philip K. Dick at the Movies. By Jason Vest. Published by Praeger Publishers, Westport, Connecticut, 2007. Hardcover.

29. Philip K. Dick: Canonical Writer of the Digital Age. By Lejla Kucukalic. Published by the Taylor and Francis Group - Routledge, London, 2008. Hardcover.

30. Blade Runner and the Films of Philip K. Dick. By Jeremy Mark Robinson. Published by Crescent Moon Publishing, UK, 2008. Softcover.

31. The Postmodern Humanism of Philip K. Dick. By Jason Vest. Published by The Scarecrow Press, Lanham, Maryland, 2009. Softcover.

Ray Harryhausen.

Raymond Frederick Harryhausen was born on June 29th, 1920 in Los Angeles, California. Arguably the greatest stop-motion animator in the history of movie-making, he was first inspired by Willis O'Brien and his film, King Kong. O'Brien's film The Lost World was the first time ever for the use of stop-motion special effects. And before Harryhausen came along, King Kong was the greatest example of it.

Ray was taken to Grauman's Chinese Theater in Hollywood by his mother in 1933 to see King Kong. Much later, in an interview, he explained that, before seeing it, he hadn't known anything about the film. Afterwards, he was enthralled. He had seen actors wearing gorilla suits before but, "when I saw Kong I knew he hadn't been done that way." He left the theatre haunted by what he had seen.

Inspired by Willis O'Brien, and by his own interest in science fiction, Harryhausen began to explore and experiment. Eventually, he polished his skills enough to do a demo of fighting dinosaurs and submitted it to Paramount Pictures in 1940. He was hired to work with director George Pal and helped with the animation for Paramount's series Puppetoons. The name came from a combination of the words puppet and cartoon.

This wasn't exactly what Harryhausen had in mind for himself.

But he was in the door.

He worked with George Pal for two years before getting involved in using animation with the Army Motion Picture Unit. After the war, he worked on a series of his own projects based on the Mother Goose Stories. These weren't quite as satisfying as he had hoped. But in 1949, he became the first technician on the film Mighty Joe Young, brought on-board by Willis O'Brien himself.

After that, there was no looking back. His special effects captured the world...

***

AWARDS

1975. Golden Scroll Award for Best Stop Motion Animation for The Golden Voyage of Sinbad, 1974.
1982. Life Career Award from the Academy of Science Fiction, Fantasy & Horror Films.
1991. A Winsor McCay Award from the Annie Awards.
1992. Special Award from the Academy of Science Fiction, Fantasy & Horror Films.
1992. A Gordon E. Sawyer Award from the Academy Awards.
1995. Time-Machine Honorary Award from the Catalonian International Film Festival.
2003. Star on the Walk of Fame.
2003. Annie Award for Outstanding Achievement in an Animated Short Subject for The Story of the Tortoise and the Hare, 2002.
2004. Inspiration Award from the Empire Awards, UK.
2005. Inducted into The Science Fiction Hall of Fame.
2006. A George Pal Memorial Award from the Academy of Science Fiction, Fantasy & Horror Films.
2008. Contribution to Cinematic Imagery Award from the Art Directors Guild.
2008. The Karl Edward Wagner Special Award.

***

FILM AND TELEVISION

1. Tulips Shall Grow. Uncredited chief animator for this animated short, directed by George Pal in 1942.

2. How to Bridge a Gorge. This was an example of three dimensional animation that **Ray Harryhausen** directed to show to Frank Capra, in order to get himself assigned to the Army film unit in 1942. It ran between four and five minutes.

3. The Storybook Review. Also known as The Mother Goose Stories. Producer and director of this eleven-minute animated short from 1946.

4. The Story of Little Red Riding Hood. Producer and director of this nine-minute animated short from 1949, narrated by James Matthews.

5. The Story of Rapunzel. Producer and director of this eleven-minute animated short from 1951, narrated by Del Moore.

6. The Story of Hansel and Gretel. Producer and director of this ten-minute animated short from 1951, narrated by Hugh Douglas.

7. The Story of King Midas. Producer and director of this ten-minute animated short from 1953, narrated by Del Moore.

8. The Beast from 20,000 Fathoms. Based on the 1951 short story by **Ray Bradbury**, The Fog Horn, Harryhausen handled the animation effects. The film was directed by Eugene Lourie and starred: Paul Hubschmid; Paula Raymond; Cecil Kellaway; Kenneth Tobey; and many others, including Lee Van Cleef as Corporal Stone; and Merv Griffin as an uncredited radio announcer.

9. It Came from Beneath the Sea. Technical effects creator for this 1955 film which was directed by Robert Gordon and starred: Kenneth Tobey; Faith Domergue; and Donald Curtis.

10. Earth vs. the Flying Saucers. Harryhausen worked without credit on the special effects for this 1956 film directed by Fred F. Sears and starring: Hugh Marlowe; Joan Taylor; Donald Curtis; and Morris Ankrum.

11. The Animal World. Effects technician on this 1956 documentary film. Directed by Irwin Allen, this featured the voices of John Storm and Theodore von Eltz.

12. 20 Million Miles to Earth. From 1957, Harryhausen handled the visual effects and also had an uncredited role as a man feeding an elephant.

Ray Harryhausen

Directed by Nathan Juran, the film starred: William Hopper; Joan Taylor; Frank Puglia; and John Zaremba.

13. The 27th Day. Directed by William Asher, and working uncredited, he did the flying saucer effects. This 1957 film starred: Gene Barry; Valerie French; George Voskovec; Arnold Moss; and others.

14. The 7th Voyage of Sinbad. From 1958 and directed by Nathan Juran, Harryhausen was an associate producer with his partner Charles H. Schneer. He was also the special visual effects creator and one of the uncredited writers. The film starred: Kerwin Mathews; Kathryn Grant; Richard Eyer; Torin Thatcher; and others.

15. The 3 Worlds of Gulliver. From 1960, directed by Jack Sher, Harryhausen did all the special visual effects. The film starred: Kerwin Mathew; Jo Morrow; June Thorburn; Lee Patterson; and many others.

16. Mysterious Island. Special visual effects creator for this 1961 film, based on the novel by **Jules Verne**, 1875. It was directed by Cy Endfield and starring: Michael Craig; Joan Greenwood; Michael Callan; Gary Merrill; and others, including Herbert Lom as Captain Nemo.

17. Jason and the Argonauts. Associate producer and special visual effects creator for this 1963 film, which was directed by Don Chaffey and starred: Todd Armstrong and Nancy Kovack, with Honor Blackman in a small part as Hera.

18. First Men in the Moon. Based on the 1901 novel by **H. G. Wells** and directed by Nathan Juran, **Ray Harryhausen** produced this 1964 film with his partner Charles H. Schneer. He also handled the special visual effects. The film starred: Edward Judd; Martha Hyer; Lionel Jeffries; and many more, including Peter Finch in an uncredited part as a bailiff's man.

19. One Million Years B.C. Special visual effects for this 1966 film, which was directed by Don Chaffey and starred: Raquel Welch; John Richardson; Percy Herbert; Robert Brown; and others.

20. The Valley of Gwangi. Also known as The Lost Valley, The Valley Time Forgot, and The Valley Where Time Stood Still. **Ray Harryhausen** was the associate producer and handled the visual effects for this 1969 movie. It was directed by Jim O'Connolly and starred: James Franciscus and Gila Golan.

21. The Golden Voyage of Sinbad. In partnership with Charles H. Schneer, Harryhausen produced this 1974 film as well as creating the special visual effects and assisting with the writing. Directed by Gordon Hessler, the movie starred: John Phillip Law; Caroline Munro; Tom Baker; Douglas Wilmer; and others.

22. Sinbad and the Eye of the Tiger. With his partner Charles H. Schneer, Harryhausen produced this, created the special visual effects, and assisted with the story. From 1977, it was directed by Sam Wanamaker and starred: Patrick Wayne; Taryn Power; Margaret Whiting; and Jane Seymour.

23. Clash of the Titans. From 1981, **Ray Harryhausen** created the special visual effects and co-produced this. Directed by Desmond Davis, it starred: Laurence Olivier as Zeus; Claire Bloom as Hera; Maggie Smith as Thetis; Ursula Andress as Aphrodite; Jack Gwillim as Poseidon; Susan Fleetwood as Athena; and many others, including Harry Hamlin as Perseus and Burgess Meredith as Ammon.

24. Spies Like Us. Directed by John Landis, this 1985 film starred: Chevy Chase; Dan Aykroyd; Steve Forrest; Donna Dixon; Bruce Davison; and many, many others, including: Terry Gilliam as Dr Imhaus; Bob Hope as a golfer; Sam Raimi as a security guard; B. B King as an Ace tomato agent; and **Ray Harryhausen** as Dr Marston.

25. The Fantasy Film Worlds of George Pal. Directed by Arnold Leibovit, Harryhausen was one of the guests in this 1985 documentary, along with: Robert Bloch; **Ray Bradbury**; **Chesley Bonestell**; Barbara Eden; and others.

26. Aliens, Dragons, Monsters and Me. Also known as The Fantasy World of **Ray Harryhausen**, this was directed by Richard Jones in 1987 and featured Harryhausen, along with: **Ray Bradbury**; Kerwin Mathews; and Gary Owens.

27. Birth of a Titan. This was an episode of the television series Hollywood the Golden Years: The RKO Story. From 1987, it featured **Ray Harryhausen** as one of the guests.

28. The Puppetoon Movie. Directed by Arnold Leibovit, this 1987 film featured some of Harryhausen's animation.

29. Forrest J. Ackerman's Amazing Worlds of Science Fiction and Fantasy. From 1991 and directed by Ray Ferry, **Ray Harryhausen** was included amongst the guests. Also along were: **Ray Bradbury**; **Frank Kelly Freas**; **Gene Roddenberry**; **A. E. van Vogt**; Curt Siodmak; Forrest J. Ackerman; and others.

30. Dinosaur Movies. Written, directed and hosted by Donald F. Glut in 1993, **Ray Harryhausen** was one of the guests.

31. Stop Motion Animation: One Step at a Time. This was an episode of the 1994 television series, Movie Magic. **Ray Harryhausen** was one of the guests.

32. Hollywood Goes Ape. Written and directed by Donald F. Glut in 1994, **Ray Harryhausen** was one of the guests.

33. Flesh and Blood: The Hammer Heritage of Horror. Directed in 1994 by Ted Newsom, and narrated by Christopher Lee and Peter Cushing, this documentary featured **Ray Harryhausen** as one of the guests.

34. Beverly Hills Cop III. Directed by John Landis and starring Eddie Murphy as Axel Foley, this 1994 film featured **Ray Harryhausen** in a bit part as a drinker in a bar.

35. Jason and the Argonauts: An Interview with Ray Harryhausen. This was directed, and carried out, by John Landis in 1995.

36. 100 Years of Horror: Dinosaurs. From 1996, this featured **Ray Harryhausen** as one of the guests, along with **Ray Bradbury** and others.

37. 100 Years of Horror: Giants and Dinosaurs. From 1996, this featured **Ray Harryhausen** as one of the guests.

38. Mighty Joe Young. In this 1998 re-make of the 1949 film, directed by Ron Underwood, **Ray Harryhausen** had an uncredited bit part as a party guest. The film starred Bill Paxton and Charlize Theron

39. The Harryhausen Chronicles. Written and directed by Richard Schickel in 1998, this was narrated by Leonard Nimoy and featured: **Ray Harryhausen**, of course, along with **Ray Bradbury**; **George Lucas**; Tom Hanks; Charles H. Schneer; and others.

40. Attack of the 50 Foot Monster Mania. This 1999 TV documentary featured Bill Mumy as the narrator, along with Cassandra Peterson as Elvira, and an assortment of guests, including **Ray Harryhausen**.

41. From Star Wars to Star Wars: The Story of Industrial Light & Magic. This made-for-television documentary from 1999 was directed by Jon Kroll and featured Samuel L. Jackson as the host. Among the guests were **Ray Harryhausen**; **George Lucas**; **Steven Spielberg**; James Cameron; Harrison Ford; Jeff Goldblum; Bob Hoskins; Ron Howard; Will Smith; Meryl Streep; and many others.

42. Hollywood Stuntmakers. Directed by Michael Baber in 1999, **Ray Harryhausen** was a guest on two episodes of this television series.

43. Ray Harryhausen: Working with Dinosaurs. Directed for television by Louis Heaton in 1999, Harryhausen was one of the guests.

44. Wallace & Gromit Go Chicken. From the Omnibus television show in 2000, directed by Steve Cole, **Ray Harryhausen** was a guest. The show was narrated by Hugh Laurie and included: Mel Gibson; Terry Gilliam; Leonard Maltin; and many others.

45. Resurrecting Dinosaurs: An Interview with Ray Harryhausen. This was directed by David Gregory in 2002 and featured Jonathan Sothcott as the interviewer.

46. The Story of the Tortoise and the Hare. From 2002, this twelve-minute short was directed by **Ray Harryhausen**. He was also assistant producer and one of the animators. Gary Owens was featured as the voice of the narrator.

47. Elf. Directed by Jon Favreau for 2003, and starring: Will Ferrell; James Caan; Bob Newhart; Edward Asner; Mary Steenburgen; Zooey Deschanel; and others, **Ray Harryhausen** did the voice of a polar bear cub.

48. Breakfast. Ray Harryhausen was one of the interviewees on the November 24th, 2003 television episode.

49. 2nd Annual Spaceys. From 2004, **Ray Harryhausen** was one of the guests at this televised awards show.

50. Comic Book: The Movie. A 2004 film, directed by Mark Hamill and featuring Harryhausen as himself.

51. Starship Troopers 2: Inside the Federation. One of the guests for this 2004 documentary.

52. History Detectives. Directed by Kristian Berg, he was one of the guests on this television series in 2004. The show aired on July 12th, Season 2, Episode 4.

53. The Sky is Falling: Making the War of the Worlds. Harryhausen appeared as himself in this 2005 documentary, as well as supplying some of the images used.

54. Ray Harryhausen: The Early Years Collection. From 2005, this was produced and directed by **Ray Harryhausen**, who also featured himself, along with: Forrest J. Ackerman; **Ray Bradbury**; Tim Burton; James Cameron; Wes Craven; Gordon Hessler; Peter Jackson; John Landis; Leonard Maltin; and many, many more.

55. I'm King Kong!: The Exploits of Mirian C. Cooper. Directed by Christopher Bird and Kevin Brownlow, Harryhausen was one of the interviewees for this 2005 documentary.

56. Hollywood's Prehistoric Superstars. This was an episode from the series Animals Icons. It aired on September 25th, 2005 - Season 1, Episode 9 - and featured **Ray Harryhausen** along with John Landis and **Steven Spielberg**.

57. T-Rex: A Dinosaur in Hollywood. Michael Davies wrote and directed this television documentary. It was shown in 2005 and featured **Ray Harryhausen** as one of the guests.

58. RKO Production 601: The Making of Kong, the Eighth Wonder of the World. One of the guests in this 2005 documentary.

59. Mighty Joe Young: Ray Harryhausen and Mighty Joe Young. From 2005, he was featured in this twelve-minute documentary.

60. Mighty Joe Young: A Conversation with Ray Harryhausen and the Chiodo Brothers. A twenty-three minute special from 2005.

61. Film '72. On of the guests on the television episode from December 5th, 2005.

62. The 100 Greatest Family Films. One of the interviewees from this 2005 documentary. Directed by Mark Murray and Helen Spencer, it was narrated by Bob Hoskins and featured: Richard Attenborough; Scott Baio; Samantha Eggar; Corey Feldman; Jodie Foster; Rupert Grint; John Heard; John Hurt; Dean Jones; Angela Lansbury; Mark Lester; Christopher Lloyd; James MacArthur; Ralph Macchio; Virginia McKenna; Hayley Mills; Olivia Newton-John; Frank Oz; Ivan Reitman; Cliff Richard; Mickey Rooney; Jean Simmons; **Steven Spielberg**; John Travolta; Dick Van Dyke; Jon Voight; and many, many others.

Ray Harryhausen

63. Gumby Dharma. From 2006, **Ray Harryhausen** was one of the guests in this documentary about the Art Clokey, the creator of Gumby.

64. The Sci-Fi Boys. One of the many guests for this 2006 documentary directed by Paul Davis. Also included were: Peter Jackson; Leonard Maltin; Forrest J. Ackerman; John Landis; Roger Corman; **Ray Bradbury**; and many others.

65. Video on Trial. From Episode 2.12, 2006, there was an uncredited bit of archival footage of **Ray Harryhausen**.

66. Ray Harryhausen Presents: The Pit and the Pendulum. From 2006, he was one of the executive producers. The film was directed by Marc Lougee and featured Peter Cugno as the narrator.

67. Blockbuster Visual FX. From the television series Space Top 10 Countdown, Harryhausen was one of the guests on the show that aired November 18th, 2006, Season 1, Episode 10.

68. Famous Monster: Forrest J. Ackerman. Directed by Michael MacDonald in 2007, **Ray Harryhausen** was one of the guests, along with Forrest J. Ackerman, of course, and: **Ray Bradbury**; Roger Corman; John Landis; David J. Schow; Tim Sullivan; George Clayton Johnson; and others, including archival footage of: Lon Chaney; Lon Chaney, Jr; Boris Karloff; Bela Lugosi; Raymond Massy; and Vincent Price.

69. Her Morbid Desires. Directed by Edward L. Plumb, **Ray Harryhausen** had a bit part as himself in this 2008 film, which starred Erica P. Hanson; Molly Murphy; Tippi Hedren; Robert Loggia; Kevin McCarthy; and others, including Ronn Moss as Count Dracula; Cassandra Peterson as Elvira; and George Clayton Johnson as an opium smoking vampire.

70. Masters of Magic: The World of Chandu. One of the guests on this 2008 documentary.

71. Ray Harryhausen Interviews. Himself. This was directed by Scott Essman in 2008.

72. King Kong 75th Anniversary Tribute. Directed by Anthony Helmer in 2008, **Ray Harryhausen** was one of the guests.

73. War Eagles. Currently in production and scheduled for release in 2010, Harryhausen is one of the producers.

***

BOOKS

1. Ray Harryhausen: Film Fantasy Scrapbook. With Tony Dalton. Published by Titan Books, London, 1989. Softcover.

2. Ray Harryhausen: An Animated Life. With Tony Dalton and a foreword by **Ray Bradbury**. Published by Billboard Books, New York City, 2004. Hardcover.

3. The Art of Ray Harryhausen. With Tony Dalton. Published by Billboard Books, New York City, 2006. Hardcover.

4. A Century of Model Animation. With Tony Dalton. Published by Aurum Press, London, 2008. Hardcover.

***

RELATED

1. FXRH: Special Visual Effects Created by Ray Harryhausen. By Ernest D. Farino and Sam Calvin. Published by Talos Publications, Irving, Texas, 1974. Staple-bound softcover.

2. From the Land Beyond Beyond: The Films of Willis O'Brien and Ray Harryhausen. By Jeff Rovin. Published by Berkley Windhover, New York City, 1977. Softcover.

3. The Dinosaur Films of Ray Harryhausen: Features Early 16mm Experiments and Unrealized Projects. By Roy P. Webber. Published by McFarland and Company, Jefferson, North Carolina, 2004. Hardcover.

4. Ray Harryhausen: Master of the Majicks, Volume 2. By Mike Hankin. Published by Archive Editions, United States, 2008. Hardcover.

Steven Spielberg.

Steven Allan Spielberg was born on December 18th, 1946 in Cincinnati, Ohio, although he grew up in New Jersey and Arizona. Working with 8mm film, he started making his first movies as a young teenager. By the time he was 13, he had made a forty-minute film called Escape to Nowhere which won a prize. At 16, in 1963, he made his first full-length movie, a science fiction short that he called Firelight and used as a later-inspiration for Close Encounters of the Third Kind, 1977.

When he moved to California with his father after his parents' divorce, he went to California State University - the University of Southern California School of Theater, Film and Television wouldn't accept him.

His career in moving-making actually started when he got a job at Universal Studios as an unpaid intern. While he was there, he shot a short film called Amblin', 1968. When one of Universal's vice presidents, Sidney Sheinberg, saw it, he got Spielberg into directing and set him to work in television, starting with the segment called Eyes for Rod Serling's Night Gallery, which aired November 8th, 1969.

It wasn't long before Universal gave him his first movie, Duel by Richard Matheson, a 1971 made-for-tv film. That went over well enough that the studio kept Spielberg working regularly until his contract with them expired.

Then he made his first feature film...

Starting in 1971, appearing in a documentary called Directed by John Ford - directed by Peter Bogdanovich - Steven Spielberg made hundreds of appearances on television and in film as himself, either directly or through the use of archival film footage. At last count, there were approximately 295 of these appearances. They won't be listed here.

***

AWARDS

1958. Boy Scout Photography Merit Badge.
1986. Hugo Award for Best Dramatic Presentation for Back to the Future.
1987. The Irving G. Thalberg Memorial Award for is work as a creative producer.
1989. Distinguished Eagle Scout Award for career accomplishments and service to others.
1989. Hugo Award for Best Dramatic Presentation for Who Framed Roger Rabbit?
1993. Academy Award for Best Director for Schindler's List.
1993. Academy Award for Best Picture for Schindler's List.
1994. Honorary Degree from the University of Southern California.
1994. Hugo Award for Best Dramatic Presentation for Jurassic Park.
1998. Academy Award for Best Director for Saving Private Ryan.
1998. Federal Cross of Merit with the Ribbon of the Federal Republic of German in recognition of the film Schindler's List, 1993.
1999. Honorary Degree from Brown University.
1999. Department of Defense Medal for Distinguished Service.
2001. Honorary Knight Commander of the Order of the British Empire - KBE.
2004. Knight of the Legion d'honneur from the president of France.
2005. Inducted into The Science Fiction Hall of Fame.
2006. Gold Hugo Lifetime Achievement Award.
2006. Kennedy Center Honor Award.
2007. Lifetime Achievement Award from the Visual Effects Society.
2008. Legion d'honneur Award.
2008. Arizona State University Hugh Downs Award for Communication Excellence.
2009. Cecil B. DeMille Award.
2009. Honorary degree from Boston University.

***

FILMS AND TELEVISION

1. The Last Gun. A short, eight-minute western shot in 1959.

2. Fighter Squad. Another eight-minute amateur film, made in 1961.

3. Escape to Nowhere. A forty-minute amateur film from 1961.

4. Firelight. Producer, director, writer and film editor, Spielberg made this in 1964. It was one hundred and forty minutes long and used an assortment of actors and production assistants.

5. Slipstream. An unfinished short film from 1967.

6. Amblin'. His last amateur film, a twenty-six minute short shot in Technicolor in 1968.

7. Faces. Worked as an uncredited production assistant on this 1968 film, which was directed by John Cassavetes and starred John Marley and Gena Rowlands.

8. Eyes. Spielberg's professional debut, this was a segment directed for the pilot of Rod Serling's Night Gallery. It aired on November 8th, 1969.

9. The Daredevil Gesture. Directed for the television series Marcus Welby, M.D., this aired on March 17th, 1970, Season 1, Episode 24. The show starred Robert Young and James Brolin.

10. Make Me Laugh. Directed for Rod Serling's Night Gallery, this aired on January 6th, 1971, Season 1, Episode 8. It starred: Godfrey Cambridge; Tom Bosley; and Jackie Vernon.

11. LA 2017. This was directed for TV series The Name of the Game, starring: Gene Barry; Barry Sullivan; Edmond O'Brien; Joan Crawford; and

Steven Spielberg

others. It was shown on January 15th, 1971, Season 3, Episode 16.

12. The Private World of Martin Dalton. Directed for the TV series The Psychiatrist, this aired on February 10th, 1971, Season 1, Episode 2. It starred: Pamelyn Ferdin; Stephen R. Hudis; Jim Hutton; and Roy Thinnes.

13. The Private World of Martin Dalton. Again directed for the TV series The Psychiatrist, this aired on March 10th, 1971, Season 1, Episode 6. This starred: Luther Adler; David Astor; Joan Darling; Clu Gulager; Roy Thinnes; and others.

14. Murder by the Book. An episode of Columbo, Spielberg directed this for the debut show, September 15, 1971. Along with Peter Falk were guest stars Jack Cassidy and Rosemary Forsyth.

15. Eulogy for a Wide Receiver. Directed for Owen Marshall: Counselor at Law. Starring Arthur Hill and Lee Majors, this aired on September 30th, 1971, Season 1, Episode 3.

16. Duel. Directed for television in 1971. Based on a 1971 Richard Matheson story, this was shown in November, starring: Dennis Weaver; Eddie Firestone; Gene Dynarski; Tim Herbert; and many others.

17. Something Evil. A TV movie, Spielberg directed this for release in 1972, starring: Sandy Dennis; Darren McGavin; Ralph Bellamy; Jeff Corey; Johnny Whitaker; and others.

18. Savage. An unsold pilot film, Spielberg directed this in 1973. It starred: Martin Landau; Barbara Bain; Will Geer; Barry Sullivan; Dabney Coleman; Pat Harrington, Jr; and many others.

19. Ace Eli and Rodger of the Skies. Supplied the story for this 1973 film which was directed by John Erman and starred Cliff Robertson, Bernadette Peters and Pamela Franklin.

20. The Sugarland Express. His first feature film, Spielberg assisted with the writing and directed this in 1974. It starred: Goldie Hawn; Ben Johnson; Michael Sacks; William Atherton; Gregory Walcott; and many others.

21. Jaws. Not a bad effort for his second feature film, **Steven Spielberg** directed this for release in 1975, starring: Roy Scheider; Robert Shaw; Richard Dreyfuss; Lorraine Gary; Murray Hamilton; and many others, including the author of the novel, Peter Benchley, in a bit part as a TV interviewer, and himself as the uncredited voice of a life-station worker, as well as a clarinet player in the orchestra.

22. Taxi Driver. Worked as an uncredited supervising editor on this 1976 film which was directed by Martin Scorsese and starred Robert De Niro and Jodie Foster.

23. Close Encounters of the Third Kind. Wrote and directed this for release in 1977, starring: Richard Dreyfuss; Francois Truffaut; Teri Garr; Melinda Dillon; and others.

24. I Wanna Hold Your Hand. The executive producer for this 1978 film, directed by Robert Zemeckis and starring Nancy Allen and Bobby Di Cicco, along with archival film footage of The Beatles.

25. Never Give a Trucker an Even Break. The director of some archival footage that was used for this episode of The Incredible Hulk, which aired on April 29th, 1978, Season 1, Episode 7.

26. 1941. Directed this for 1979, it starred: Dan Aykroyd; Ned Beatty; John Belushi; Lorraine Gary; and many others, including: Christopher Lee; Tim Matheson; Toshiro Mifune; Warren Oates; Robert Stack; Treat Williams; John Candy; Slim Pickens; Dub Taylor; John Landis; and Mickey Rourke; with James Caan and Penny Marshall playing uncredited bit parts.

27. Used Cars. The executive producer, with John Milius, for this 1980 film, directed by Robert Zemeckis and starring Kurt Russell and Jack Warden.

28. The Blues Brothers. Directed by John Landis and starring John Belushi and Dan Aykroyd, **Steven Spielberg** had a bit part in this 1980 film as a Cook County Assessor's Office clerk.

29. Continental Divide. The executive producer for this 1981 film, directed by Michael Apted and starring John Belushi with Blair Brown and Allen Garfield.

30. Raiders of the Lost Ark. Steven Spielberg directed this for **George Lucas** in 1981. The film starred: Harrison Ford; Karen Allen; Paul Freeman; Ronald Lacey; John Rhys-Davies; Denholm Elliott; Alfred Molina; Wolf Kahler; and many others.

31. E.T.: The Extra-Terrestrial. Produced and directed this in 1982. The film starred: Henry Thomas; Dee Wallace; Robert MacNaughton; Drew Barrymore; Peter Coyote; K. C. Martel; Sean Frye; C. Thomas Howell; and a host of others.

32. Poltergeist. Spielberg wrote and produced this. It was released in 1982, directed by Tobe Hooper and starring: Craig T. Nelson; JoBeth Williams; and Heather O'Rourke.

33. Twilight Zone: The Movie. Produced and directed segment 2, Kick the Can, which was written by George Clayton Johnson, Richard Matheson and Melissa Matheson. It starred Scatman Crothers; Bill Quinn; Martin Garner; Selma Diamond; Helen Shaw; Murray Matheson; Peter Brocco; and others.

34. Indiana Jones and the Temple of Doom. Directed this for **George Lucas**. It was released in 1984 starring Harrison Ford and Kate Capshaw.

35. Stokes of Genius. Spielberg directed, without credit, one of the introductory segments for this 1984 project.

36. Gremlins. The executive producer for this 1984 film, directed by Joe Dante and starring: Zack Galligan; Phoebe Cates; Hoyt Axton; Keye Luke; Susan Burgess; Scott Brady; Corey Feldman; Judge Reinhold; and others.

37. Fandango. The uncredited executive producer of this 1985 movie, which was directed by Kevin Reynolds and starred Kevin Costner and Judd Nelson.

38. The Goonies. Writer and executive producer. Directed by Richard Donner, the film was released in 1985 starring: Sean Astin; Josh Brolin; Jeff Cohen; Corey Feldman; Kerri Green; Martha Plimpton; Jonathan Ke Quan; John Matuszak; and many others.

39. Back to the Future. Executive producer of this 1985 film, directed by Robert Zemeckis and starring: Michael J. Fox; Christopher Lloyd; Lea Thompson; Crispin Glover; and others.

40. Steven Spielberg's Amazing Stories. Developer and executive producer quite often the writer of this television series that start in September 1985. The show ran from September 19th, 1985 until April 10th, 1987. There were forty-five episodes.

41. Ghost Train. Director, this was shown on September 29th, 1985, Season 1, Episode 1 of Steven Spielberg's Amazing Stories. This starred: Roberts Blossom; Scott Paulin; Gail Edwards; Lukas Haas; and others.

42. The Mission. Spielberg directed this for November 3rd, Season 1, Episode 5 of Steven Spielberg's Amazing Stories. The show starred: Kevin Costner; Casey Siemaszko; and Kiefer Sutherland.

43. Young Sherlock Holmes. Executive producer of this 1985 movie. It was directed by Barry Levinson and starred Nicholas Rowe as Sherlock Holmes and Alan Cox as John Watson.

44. The Color Purple. Produced and directed this 1985 film, which starred: Danny Glover; Whoopi Goldberg; Margaret Avery; Oprah Winfrey; Willard E. Pugh; and many others, including Rae Dawn Chong as Squeak and Laurence Fishburne as Swain.

45. The Money Pit. Executive producer of this 1985 film, which was directed by Richard Benjamin and starred: Tom Hanks; Shelley Long; Alexander Gudunov; Maureen Stapleton; Joe Mantegna; and many others.

46. An American Tail. Spielberg was an executive producer for this 1986 animated feature, which was directed by Don Bluth and featured the voices of: Erica Yohn; Nehemiah Persoff; Amy Green; Phillip Glasser; Christopher Plummer; John Finnegan; and others, including Madeline Kahn as Gussie Mausheimer and Dom DeLuise as Tiger.

47. Harry and the Hendersons. An uncredited executive producer on this 1987 film. It was directed by William Dear and starred: John Lithgow; Melinda Dillon; and many others, including Kevin Peter Hall as Harry.

48. Innerspace. Executive producer for this 1987 film. Directed by Joe Dante, it starred: Dennis Quaid; Martin Short; Meg Ryan; and many others.

49. Three O'Clock High. An uncredited executive producer on this film. It was directed by Phil Joanou in 1987 and starred Casey Siemaszko and Annie Ryan.

50. Empire of the Sun. Spielberg produced and directed this one in 1987. It starred: Christian Bale; John Malkovich; Miranda Richardson; and others, including Ben Stiller as Dainty.

51. *batteries not included. Worked as the executive producer for this 1987 film. It was directed by Matthew Robbins and starred Hume Cronyn and Jessica Tandy.

52. Who Framed Roger Rabbit. Executive producer for this 1988 film. Directed by Robert Zemeckis, it starred: Bob Hoskins; Christopher Lloyd; Joanna Cassidy; and many others, including the voice of Mel Blanc... and the voice of Kathleen Turner as Jessica Rabbit.

53. The Land Before Time. Steven Spielberg, with **George Lucas**, worked as an executive producer for this 1988 animated feature, which was directed by Don Bluth and featured the voices of: Judith Barsi; Burke Byrnes; Gabriel Damon; and many others, including Helen Shaver as Littlefoot's mother.

54. Indiana Jones and the Last Crusade. Directed this 1989 film for **George Lucas**. It starred: Harrison Ford; Sean Connery; Denholm Elliott; Alison Doody; John Rhys-Davies; River Phoenix; and many others.

55. Always. Produced and directed this 1989 movie, which starred: Richard Dreyfuss; Holly Hunter; Brad Johnson; John Goodman; Audrey Hepburn; and others, including Marg Helgenberger as Rachel.

56. Tummy Trouble. Worked as executive producer on this seven-minute 1989 cartoon, which was directed by Rob Minkoff and featured Charles Fleischer as Roger Rabbit and Kathleen Turner as Jessica Rabbit.

57. Dad. Executive producer on this 1989 film. Directed by Gary David Goldberg, it starred: Jack Lemmon; Ted Danson; Olympia Dukakis; Kathy Baker; Kevin Spacey; Ethan Hawke; J. T. Walsh; and others.

58. Back to the Future Part II. Worked as the executive producer. From 1989, this was directed by Robert Zemeckis and starred: Michael J. Fox; Christopher Lloyd; Lea Thompson; Elisabeth Shue; and others.

59. The Visionary. Shared the directing with Douglas Day Stewart for this 1990 ninety-minute western.

60. Warner Bros. Celebration of Tradition, June 2, 1990. Worked as the executive producer for this 1990 documentary. Directed by Terry Donohue and Gary Halvorson, it featured: Dan Aykroyd; Kim Basinger; John Candy; Chevy Chase; Michael Keaton; and many others.

61. Joe Versus the Volcano. Executive producer. Directed by John Patrick Shanley, this was released in 1990 and starred Tom Hanks and Meg Ryan, along with: Lloyd Bridges; Robert Stack; Abe Vigoda; Amanda Plummer; Ossie Davis; Carol Kane; and many others.

62. Back to the Future Part III. Worked as the executive producer. From 1990, this was directed

Steven Spielberg

by Robert Zemeckis and starred: Michael J. Fox; Christopher Lloyd; Lea Thompson; Elisabeth Shue; Mary Steenburgen; and others.

63. Akira Kurosawa's Dreams. Worked as the executive producer of the international version on this 1990 film. Directed by Akira Kurosawa, it starred: Akira Terao; Mitsuko Baisho; Toshie Negishi; and many others.

64. Gremlins 2: The New Batch. Spielberg was the executive producer for this 1990 sequel. Directed by Joe Dante, it starred: Zach Galligan; Phoebe Cates; Christopher Lee; and others.

65. Roller Coaster Rabbit. Worked as executive producer on this seven-minute 1990 cartoon, which was directed by Rob Minkoff and featured Charles Fleischer as Roger Rabbit and Kathleen Turner as Jessica Rabbit.

66. Steven Spielberg Presents Tiny Toon Adventures. Producer and writer of this animated television series which started on September 14th, 1990 and ran for 102 episodes until February 12th, 1993.

67. Arachnophobia. Worked as the executive producer and the uncredited director of the second unit on this 1990 film. Directed by Frank Marshall, it starred Jeff Daniels, Harley Jane Kozak, and John Goodman.

68. Back to the Future... The Ride. Uncredited creative consultant on this 1991 short. It was directed by Douglas Trumbull and featured William Guest; Christopher Lloyd; Darlene Vogel; and others, including archival footage of The Beatles and Albert Einstein.

69. Hook. Directed this 1991 film, which starred: Robin Williams as Peter Pan; Dustin Hoffman as Captain Hook; Julia Roberts as Tinkerbell; Bob Hoskins as Smee; Maggie Smith as Granny Wendy; and many others, including Phil Collins as Inspector Good.

70. A Brief History of Time. Uncredited executive producer on this 1991 documentary from the book by Stephen Hawking.

71. Cape Fear. Worked, uncredited, as the executive producer on the re-make of this 1962 film. Directed by Martin Scorsese in 1991, this starred: Robert De Niro; Nick Nolte; Jessica Lange; Juliette Lewis; Joe Don Baker; Fred Dalton Thompson; along with many others, including, from the original film, Gregory Peck as Lee Heller and Robert Mitchum as Lieutenant Elgart.

72. An American Tail: Fievel Goes West. Worked as the producer on this 1991 animated feature. Directed by Phil Nibbelink and Simon Wells, it featured the voices of: Phillip Glasser; James Stewart; Erica Yohn; and others.

73. The Plucky Duck Show. Executive producer for this short-lived animated 1992 television series.

74. It's a Wonderful Tiny Toons Christmas Special. Executive producer for this half-hour animated Christmas show. Directed by Art Vitello, it featured Joe Alaskey; Noel Blanc; and others.

75. Roller Coaster Rabbit. Executive producer on this eight-minute 1993 cartoon, which was directed by Barry Cook and featured Charles Fleischer as Roger Rabbit and Kathleen Turner as Jessica Rabbit.

76. Class of '61. Executive producer for this 1993 TV movie. Directed by Gregory Hoblit, it starred: Christien Anholt; Andre Braugher; Dan Gutterman; Josh Lucas; Clive Owen; Laura Linney; and others.

77. Jurassic Park. Directed this 1993 film, which starred: Sam Neill; Laura Dern; Jeff Goldblum; Richard Attenborough; and many others.

78. Show Dog. Executive producer for this episode of the animated tv series, Family Dog, which aired on June 23rd, 1993, Season 1, Episode 1.

79. We're Back! A Dinosaur's Story. Executive producer of this 1993 animated film. Directed by Phil Nibbelink and Simon Wells, it featured the voices of: John Goodman; Rhea Perlman; Jay Leno; and others.

80. Schindler's List. Produced and directed this 1993 film, which starred: Liam Neeson; Ben Kingsley; Ralph Fiennes; Caroline Goodall; and many, many others.

81. SeaQuest DSV. Also known as SeaQuest 2032. He was the executive producer for this television series which ran for forty-four episodes, starting on September 12th, 1993 and finishing on June 9th, 1996.

82. Steven Spielberg Presents Animaniacs. Producer and executive producer for fifteen episodes of this animated television series that first aired on September 13th, 1993 and ran until May 25th, 1998.

83. Yakko's World: An Animaniacs Singalong. Executive producer of this 1994 animated feature.

84. Tiny Toons Spring Break. Executive producer of this 1994 cartoon.

85. I'm Mad. Executive producer of this 1994 five-minute cartoon.

86. The Flintstones. As Steven Spielrock, he was the executive producer of this 1994 feature. Directed by Brian Levant, it starred: John Goodman; Elizabeth Perkins; Rick Moranis; and Rosie O'Donnell.

87. Pinky and the Brain Christmas Special. Executive producer for this 1995 television show. Directed by Rusty Mills, it featured Jeff Bennett; Earl Boen; and others.

88. Casper. Worked as the executive producer. Directed by Brad Silberling, this movie was released in 1995 and starred: Chauncey Leopardi; Spencer Vrooman; Cathy Moriarty; Eric Idle; Ben Stein; Fred Rogers; Bill Pullman; Christina Ricci; and others, including Malachi Pearson as the voice of Casper.

89. Your Studio and You. Played a back-lot tour guide in this Universal Studios seventeen-minute comedy from 1995. Directed by Trey Parker, this featured, along with Spielberg, Sylvester Stallone, Demi Moore, Michael J. Fox; and many, many other.

90. Tiny Toon Adventures: Night Ghoulery. Executive producer for this 1995 television animated special, which was directed by Rich Arons, Michel Gerard, Rusty Mills and Greg Reyna, and featured the voices of: Joe Alaskey; Tress MacNeille; John Kassir; and many others, including Ron Perlman as Mr Scratch.

91. Balto. Executive producer. This 1995 animated feature was directed by Simon Wells and starred the voices of: Kevin Bacon; Bob Hoskins; Bridget Fonda; Jim Cummings; Phil Collins; and many others.

92. Pinky and the Brain. Executive producer on five episodes of this animated television series, which ran from September 9th, 1995 until May 9th, 1998.

93. The Dig. Provided the original idea and additional story elements for this animated special from 1995. Directed by Sean Clark, it featured the voices of: Robert Patrick; Mari Weiss; Steve Blum; and others.

94. Survivors of the Holocaust. The executive producer of this 1996 documentary which was directed by Allan Holzman.

95. Twister. Worked as the executive producer of this 1996 film. It was directed by Jan de Bont and starred: Helen Hunt; Bill Paxton; Cary Elwes; Jami Gertz; Philip Seymour Hoffman; and others.

96. The Best of Roger Rabbit. Executive producer for this 1996 special, which was directed by Barry Cook and Rob Minkoff and featured, of course, Charles Fleischer as Roger Rabbit and Kathleen Turner as Jessica Rabbit.

97. High Incident. One of the executive producers for this television series that first aired on March 4th, 1996 and ran until May 8th, 1997.

98. Island of Dr Mystico. Executive producer for this instalment of the animated show Freakazoid. It aired February 7th, 1997, Season 2, Episode 8. Directed by Rich Arons and Dave Marshall, it featured: Paul Rugg; Edward Asner; Jonathan Harris; David Warner; and others, including Tim Curry as the voice of Dr Mystico.

99. Men in Black. Executive producer. This 1997 film was directed by Barry Sonnenfeld and starred: Tommy Lee Jones; Will Smith; Rip Torn; Linda Fiorentino; Vincent D'Onofrio; and others.

100. The Lost World: Jurassic Park. As well as directing this 1997 film, he also featured himself in an uncredited role as a popcorn-eating man. The film starred: Jeff Goldblum; Julianne Moore; Pet Postlethwaite; Richard Attenborough; Vince Vaughan; Arliss Howard; Vanessa Lee Chester; and many others.

101. The Lost Children of Berlin. Executive producer of this 1997 documentary which was directed by Elizabeth McIntyre and featured Anthony Hopkins as the narrator.

102. Amistad. Produced and directed this 1997 film, which starred: Morgan Freeman; Nigel Hawthorne; Anthony Hopkins; Djimon Hounsou; Matthew McConaughey; and others.

103. Toonsylvania. One of the executive producers of this animated television series that ran during 1998.

104. Deep Impact. The executive producer on this 1998 film, which was directed by Mimi Leder and starred: Robert Duvall; Tea Leoni; Elijah Wood; Vanessa Redgrave; Morgan Freeman and Maximilian Schell.

105. The Mask of Zorro. Executive producer. This 1998 film was directed by Martin Campbell and starred: Anthony Hopkins; Antonio Banderas; and Catherine Zeta-Jones.

106. Saving Private Ryan. Produced and directed this 1998 film, which starred: Tom Hanks; Tom Sizemore; Edward Burns; Barry Pepper; Adam Goldberg; Vin Diesel; Jeremy Davies; Ted Danson; Paul Giamatti; Dennis Farina; and many others, including Matt Damon as Private Ryan.

107. The Last Days. Executive producer on this 1998 documentary which was directed by James Moll.

108. Pinky, Elmyra and the Brain. The executive producer for nine episodes of this animated television series which ran from September 19th, 1998 until April 10th, 1999.

109. The Unfinished Journey. Directed this 1999 documentary that featured: Maya Angelou; Bill Clinton; Ossie Davis; Ruby Dee; Sam Waterston; and Edward James Olmos.

110. The Haunting. Worked uncredited as the executive producer and the director of the second unit on this 1999 film. Directed by Jan de Bont and based on The Haunting of Hill House by Shirley Jackson, it starred: Liam Neeson; Catherine Zeta-Jones; Owen Wilson; Bruce Dern; Virginia Madsen; Lili Taylor; and many others.

111. Wakko's Wish. Uncredited executive producer for this 1999 animated feature, which was directed by Liz Holzman and Rusty Mills and featured the voices of Rob Paulsen and Jess Harnell.

112. Eyes of the Holocaust. Also known as A Holocaust szemei. Executive producer. This documentary was made in Hungary in 2000, directed by Janos Szasz.

113. Men in Black... The Ride. Creative consultant on this 2000 short. It was directed by David C. Cobb, Lyonal Coleman and Linda Hassani and featured Will Smith and Rip Torn.

114. Shooting War. Worked as the editor and executive producer on this 2000 documentary, which was directed by Richard Schickel and featured Tom Hanks as the narrator.

115. What Lies Beneath. Provided the idea, uncredited, for this 2000 film, which was directed by Robert Zemeckis and starred: Harrison Ford and Michelle Pfeiffer.

Steven Spielberg

116. Vanilla Sky. Played an uncredited guest at a party in this 2001 film, which was directed by Cameron Crowe and starred: Tom Cruise; Penelope Cruz; Cameron Diaz; Kurt Russell; Jason Lee; and many others.

117. Semper Fi. Executive producer for this 2001 television film which was directed by Michael W. Watkins and starred: Scott Bairstow; Steven Burton; Alex Burns; and others.

118. Shrek. Uncredited executive producer of this 2001 animated feature. Directed by Andrew Adamson and Vicky Jenson, it starred: Mike Myers; Eddie Murphy; Cameron Diaz; John Lithgow; and many others.

119. Evolution. Uncredited executive producer. This was directed by Ivan Reitman in 2001. It starred: David Duchovny and Julianne Moore.

120. Artificial Intelligence: AI. Produced and directed this 2001 film from the short story by **Brian W. Aldiss**, Supertoys Last All Summer Long, 1969. It starred: Haley Joel Osment; Frances O'Connor; Sam Robards; Jake Thomas; Jude Law; William Hurt; Ken Leung; and many others.

121. Jurassic Park III. Executive producer. The 2001 film was directed by Joe Johnston and starred: Sam Neill; William H. Macy; and Tea Leoni.

122. Currahee. Executive producer of this episode of the television series Band of Brothers. It aired September 9th, 2001, Season 1, Episode 1. Directed by Phil Alden Robinson, this starred: Damian Lewis; Donnie Wahlberg; Ron Livingston; and others.

123. We Stand Alone Together. Executive producer of this 2001 television documentary, directed by Mark Cowan.

124. Austin Powers in Goldmember. Had a small part as the famous director - Austinpussy - in this 2002 Mike Meyers film.

125. Minority Report. Directed this 2002 film from the 1949 short story by **Philip K. Dick**. The film starred: Tom Cruise; Max von Sydow; Steve Harris; and others.

126. Catch Me If You Can. Directed this 2002 movie, which starred: Leonardo DiCaprio; Tom Hanks; Christopher Walken; Martin Sheen; James Brolin; and others.

127. Broken Silence. The executive producer of this 2002 television mini-series.

128. Price for Peace. The executive producer of this 2002 documentary, which was directed by James Moll.

129. Men in Black II. Executive producer. This 2002 movie was directed by Barry Sonnenfeld and starred: Tommy Lee Jones; Will Smith; Rip Torn; Lara Flynn Boyle; and many others.

130. Beyond the Sky. The executive producer for this episode of the 2002 television series, Taken. Directed by Tobe Hooper and starring Julie Benz and Steve Burton, it aired on December 2nd, the first show of the first season.

131. Burma Bridge Busters. The executive producer of this 2003 documentary by James Moll.

132. Voices from the List. Executive producer. This 2004 documentary was directed by Michael Mayhew.

133. A Remarkable Promise. Worked as an advisor on this 2004 short which was directed by James Moll and featured Morgan Freeman as the narrator. It was a biography of John Kerry.

134. The Terminal. Produced and directed this 2004 film, which starred: Tom Hanks and Catherine Zeta-Jones.

135. Dan Finnerty and the Dan Band: I Am Woman. The executive producer of this 2005 TV special.

136. Into the West. Executive producer of this 2005 television mini-series.

137. War of the Worlds. Directed this, using the 1898 H. G. Wells novel as inspiration. It starred: Tom Cruise; Dakota Fanning; Miranda Otto; Tim Robbins; and many, many others.

138. Memoirs of a Geisha. Worked as a producer on this 2005 film, which was directed by Rob Marshall and starred: Suzuaka Ohgo; Togo Igawa; Mako; Samantha Futerman; and others.

139. Munich. Directed this 2005 movie which starred Daniel Craig and Eric Bana.

140. Star Wars: Episode III - Revenge of the Sith. Worked as an assistant director for the action scenes during this 2005 **George Lucas** film, which starred: Ewan McGregor; Natalie Portman; Hayden Christensen; Ian McDiarmid; Samuel L Jackson; Jimmy Smits; Christopher Lee; and many, many more.

141. Scoring War of the Worlds. Worked as a cinematographer on this twelve-minute 2005 documentary, which was written and directed by Laurent Bouzereau.

142. Monster House. Executive producer of this 2006 animated feature which was directed by Gil Kenan and starred the voices of: Ryan Newman; Steve Buscemi; Mitchel Musso; Catherine O'Hara; and many others.

143. Spell Your Name. Executive producer of this 2006 documentary which was directed by Sergey Bukovsky and filmed in the Ukraine.

144. Flags of Our Fathers. One of the producers. Clint Eastwood directed this for release in 2006. It starred: Ryan Phillippe; Jesse Bradford; Adam Beach; John Benjamin Hickey; John Slattery; Barry Pepper; Jamie Bell; and many more.

145. Letters from Iwo Jima. Worked as a producer on this companion piece to Flags of Our Fathers, 2006. Directed by Clint Eastwood for 2006, this starred: Ken Watanabe; Kazunari Ninomiya; Tsuyoshi Ihara; Ryo Kase; Shido Nakamura; Hiroshi Watanabe; and many others.

146. Transformers. Executive producer. This 2007 film was directed by Michael Bay and starred: Shia LaBeouf; Megan Fox; Josh Duhamel; Tyrese Gibson; Rachael Taylor; John Voight; and many others.

147. On the Lot. Executive producer of four episodes of this 2007 television show which ran from May 22nd, 2007 until August 21st, 2007.

148. Eagle Eye. Executive producer of this 2008 film. Directed by D. J. Caruso, it starred: Shia LaBeouf; Michelle Monaghan; Rosario Dawson; and many others, including Billy Bob Thornton as Agent Thomas Morgan.

149. Indiana Jones and the Kingdom of the Crystal Skull. Spielberg directed this from a story by **George Lucas**. It starred: Harrison Ford; Cate Blanchett; Karen Allen; Shia LaBeouf; Ray Winstone; John Hurt; and many others.

150. A Timeless Call. Directed this short 2008 documentary which featured Tom Hanks as the narrator.

151. United States of Tara. Executive producer for twelve episodes of this television series which, so far, has seen twelve instalments, running from January 25th, 2009 until April 5th, 2009.

152. Transformers: Revenge of the Fallen. The executive producer of this 2009 film. Directed by Michael Bay, it starred: Shia LaBeouf; Megan Fox; Josh Duhamel; Tyrese Gibson; et al.

153. The Pacific. Executive producer of this 2009 television mini-series. Directed by Carl Franklin and David Nutter, it starred: Isabel Lucas; Joseph Mazzello; William Sadler; and others.

154. The Adventures of Tintin: The Secret of the Unicorn. Produced and directed of this animated feature which, at the time of writing - July 2009 - is in post-production. It features the voices of: Daniel Craig; Jamie Bell; Simon Pegg; Cary Elwes; and many more.

In the Planning Stages:

155. 2010: The Trial of the Chicago 7. Producer in pre-production.

156. 2010: When Worlds Collide. Producer. Pre-production.

157. 2010: The Talisman. Executive producer for this TV mini-series, from the novel by Stephen King and Peter Straub. Pre-production.

158. 2011: Old Boy. Director in pre-production. Will Smith is apparently on board.

159. 2011: Cowboys and Aliens. Producer in pre-production. Robert Downey Jr is apparently signed to this.

160. 2011: Lincoln. Producer and director in pre-production. Liam Neeson is apparently set to play Lincoln with Sally Field along as his wife.

161. 2011: Interstellar. Producer and director. Just announced.

***

BOOKS

1. Close Encounters of the Third Kind. Published by Delacorte Press, New York City, 1977. Hardcover.

2. Close Encounters of the Third Kind: The Special Edition. Published by Dell Books, New York City, 1980. Softcover.

3. Saving Private Ryan: A Film by Steven Spielberg. Published by Newmarket Press, Scranton, Pennsylvania, 1998.

4. Amistad: Give Us Free: A Celebration of the Film by Steven Spielberg. With Debbie Allen and Maya Angelou. Published by Newmarket Press, 1998.

5. Steven Spielberg's Last Days. With David Cesarani. Published by Weidenfeld and Nicolson, London, 1999. Hardcover.

6. Schindler's List: Images of the Steven Spielberg Film. Published by Newmarket Press, Scranton, Pennsylvania, 2005. Hardcover.

***

RELATED

1. Close Encounters of the third Kind: Diary. By Bob Balaban. Introduction by **Steven Spielberg**. Published by Paradise Books, New York City, 1978. Softcover.

2. Steven Spielberg: Creator of E.T. By Tom Collins. Published by Dillon Press, Minneapolis, Minnesota, 1983. Hardcover.

3. The Steven Spielberg Story. By Tom Crawley. Published by Zomba Books, London, 1983. Softcover.

4. Steven Spielberg Presents Young Sherlock Holmes: The Storybook. By Peter Larangis. Published by Simon and Shuster, New York City, 1985. Hardcover.

5. The Films of Steven Spielberg. By Neil Sinyard. Bison Books, London, 1986. Hardcover.

6. Steven Spielberg. By Donald R. Mott and Cheryl McAllister Saunders. Published by Twayne Publishers, Boston, 1986. Hardcover.

7. An American Tail: A Steven Spielberg Presentation - The Illustrated Story. By Emily Perl Kingsley. Published by Grosset and Dunlap, New York City, 1986. Hardcover.

8. Steven Spielberg. By D. L. Mabery. Published by Lerner Publications, Minneapolis, Minnesota, 1986. Hardcover.

9. Steven Spielberg's Amazing Stories. By Steven Bauer. Published by Ace Books, New York City, 1986. Softcover.

10. Steven Spielberg's Amazing Stories II. By Steven Bauer. Published by Charter Books, New York City, 1986. Softcover.

11. Steven Spielberg's Innerspace. By Nathan

Steven Spielberg

Elliott. Published by Dragon Books, 1987. Softcover.

12. Who Framed Roger Rabbit Movie Storybook - Based on the Motion Picture from Walt Disney and Steven Spielberg. By Justine Korman. Published by Western Publishing, Racine, Wisconsin, 1988. Hardcover.

13. The Picture Life of Steven Spielberg. By Michael Leather. Published by Franklin Watts, New York City, 1988. Hardcover.

14. Steven Spielberg: Amazing Filmmaker. By Jim Hargrove. Published by the Children's Press, Chicago, 1988. Hardcover.

15. Steven Spielberg's E.T.: The Extra-Terrestrial Storybook. By William Kotzwinkle. Published by Berkley Books, New York City, 1988. Softcover.

16. Steven Spielberg Presents Back to the Future Part III - A Robert Zemeckis Film. Published by Antioch Publishing, Yellow Springs, Ohio, 1990. Softcover.

17. Steven Spielberg Presents an American Tail: Fieval Goes West - The Illustrated Story. By Charles Swenson. Published by Grosset and Dunlap, New York City, 1991. Hardcover.

18. The Future of the Movies: Interviews with Martin Scorsese, Stephen Spielberg, and George Lucas. By Roger Ebert and Gene Siskel. Published by Andrew and McMeel, Kansas City, Kansas, 1991. Softcover.

19. Steven Spielberg: The Man, His Movies, and Their Meaning. By Philip M. Taylor. Published by Continuum International Publishing, New York City, 1992. Hardcover.

20. Steven Spielberg Presents We're Back! A Dinosaur's Story. By Justine Korman. Published by Grosset and Dunlap, New York City, 1993. Softcover.

21. Meet Steven Spielberg: He Makes Movie Magic. By Thomas Conklin. Published by Random House, New York City, 1994. Softcover.

22. The Films of Steven Spielberg. By Douglas Brode. Published by Citadel Press, New Jersey, 1995. Hardcover.

23. Steven Spielberg: A Biography. By Elizabeth Ferber. Published by Chelsea House Publications, New York, 1996. Hardcover.

24. Steven Spielberg: Hollywood Filmmaker. By Virginia Meachum. Published by Enslow Publishers, Berkeley Heights, New Jersey, 1996. Hardcover.

25. Steven Spielberg: Father of the Man: His Incredible Life, Tumultuous Times, and Record-Breaking Movies. By Andrew Yule. Published by Little Brown, London, 1996. Hardcover.

26. Steven Spielberg: The Man, the Movies, the Mythology. By Frank Sanello. Published by Taylor Publishing, Dallas, Texas, 1996. Hardcover.

27. Steven Spielberg: The Unauthorized Biography. By John Baxter. Published by Harper Collins, London, 1997. Hardcover.

28. Steven Spielberg: Master Storyteller. By Tom Powers. Published by Lerner Publishing, Minneapolis, Minnesota, 1997. Hardcover.

29. Steven Spielberg: A Biography. By Joseph McBride. Published by Simon and Schuster, New York City, 1997. Hardcover.

30. Amistad: The Official Tie-in to the Major Motion Picture Directed by Steven Spielberg. By Alex Pate. Published by Dreamworks, New York City, 1997. Hardcover.

32. Steven Spielberg: An Unauthorized Biography. By Sean Connolly. Published by Heinemann Library, London, 1998. Hardcover.

33. Magic Man: The Life and Films of Steven Spielberg. By William Schoell. Published by Tudor Publishers, 1998. Hardcover.

34. Saving Private Ryan: A Film by Steven Spielberg: The Men, The Mission, The Movie. By Linda Sunshine and David James. Published by Boxtree, London, 1998. Softcover.

35. People in the News: Steven Spielberg. By Adam Woog. Published by Lucent Books, United States, 1998. Hardcover.

36. Steven Spielberg: Close Up: The Making of His Movies. By George C. Perry. Published by Thunder's Mouth Press, United States, 1998. Hardcover.

37. Steven Spielberg: Master of Movie Magic. By Bertram T. Knight. Published by Crestwood House, New York City, 1998. Hardcover.

38. Steven Spielberg's Saving Private Ryan. By Max Allan Collins. Published by Boxtree, London, 1998. Hardcover.

39. Learning About Creativity from the Life of Steven Spielberg. By Erin M. Hovanec. Published by Rosen Publishing, New York City, 1999. Hardcover.

40. Steven Spielberg: Interviews. By Lester D. Friedman. Published by the University Press of Mississippi, 2000. Softcover.

41. Steven Spielberg: From Reels to Riches. By Ted Gottfried. Published by Franklin Watts, New York City, 2000. Softcover.

42. Steven Spielberg. By James Clarke. Published by Pocket Essentials, UK, 2001. Softcover.

43. Steven Spielberg: Crazy for Movies. By Susan Goldman Rubin. Published by Harry N. Abrams, New York City, 2001. Hardcover.

44. Steven Spielberg: Behind the Camera. By Elizabeth Sirimarco. Published by Chelsea House Publications, New York City, 2002. Hardcover.

45. The Films of Steven Spielberg. By Charles L. P. Silet. Published by The Scarecrow Press, Lanham, Massachusetts, 2002. Hardcover.

46. Steven Spielberg. By Geoffrey M. Horn.

Published by World Almanac Library, UK, 2002. Softcover.

47. Catch Me If You Can: A Steven Spielberg Film. By Jeff Nathanson and Andrew Cooper. Published by Newmarket Press, Scranton, Pennsylvania, 2002. Hardcover.

48. Steven Spielberg: Filmmaker. By James Robert Parish. Published by the Ferguson Publishing Company, 2003. Hardcover.

49. Steven Spielberg: People We Should Know. By Jonathan A. Brown. Published by Weekly Reader Early Learning Library, 2005. Softcover.

50. Steven Spielberg. By Wil Mara. Published by Children's Press, Connecticut, 2005. Softcover.

51. Directed by Steven Spielberg: Poetics of the Contemporary Hollywood Blockbuster. By Warren Buckland. Continuum International, Harrisburg, Pennsylvania, 2006. Hardcover.

52. The Cinema of Steven Spielberg: Empire of Light. By Nigel Morris. Published by Wallflower Press, UK, 2006. Hardcover.

53. Empire of Dreams: The Science Fiction and Fantasy Films of Steven Spielberg. By Andrew M. Gordon. Published by Rowman and Littlefield Publishers, United States, 2007. Softcover.

54. Close Encounters of the Third Kind: The Makin of Steven Spielberg's Classic Film. By Ray Morton. Published by Applause Theatre and Cinema Book Publishers, United States, 2007. Softcover.

55. Steven Spielberg: A Biography. By Kathi Jackson. Published by Greenwood Press, UK, 2007. Hardcover.

56. Steven Spielberg and Philosophy: We're Gonna Need a Bigger Book. By Dean Kowalski. Published by the University Press of Kentucky, 2008. Hardcover.

57. Steven Spielberg: Director of Blockbuster Films. By Laura Bufano Edge. Published by Enslow Publishers, Berkeley Heights, New Jersey, 2008.

Frank Kelly Freas

-2006-

Frank Kelly Freas.

Frank Kelly Freas was born in Hornell, New York, on August 27th, 1922 and died in West Hills, Los Angeles, California on January 2nd, 2005. While he was still in school, the Art Institute of Pittsburgh, he submitted one of his classroom assignments to Dorothy McIlwraith at Weird Tales.

It was his first professional magazine sale, appearing on the November 1950 issue, illustrating the story The Third Shadow by H. Russell Wakefield. Also in that issue were: The Dead Man by **Fritz Leiber**; The Body Snatchers by Seabury Quinn; Something Old by Mary Elizabeth Counselman; The Invisible Reweaver by Margaret St Clair; Grotesquerie by Harold Lawlor; Blue Peter by Murray Sanford; and They Worked the Oracle by H. S. W. Chibbett.

His next sale was also to Weird Tales, showing up a year later in November 1951 and followed a few months later by his first book cover, the dustjacket painting for City by Clifford D. Simak, published by Gnome Press in May 1952.

And he went on to become the most prolific artist in the field, ever. His covers and his interiors graced magazine and books from that slow beginning in 1950 until the final cover printed in his lifetime, Judgment Night by **C. L. Moore**, published by Red Jacket Press, 2004, a reprint of the 1952 Gnome Press dustjacket. His final original appeared on Strange Trades by Paul Di Filippo, Gryphon Press, October 2001, while his final magazine cover was for the June 2001 issue of Analog.

He heard it said that the science fiction magazines had died round about the time he started doing covers. But he remarked that he was too busy doing covers to notice. He considered himself more of an illustrator than an artist. (There's a difference?) He said, "I prefer storytelling pictures and picture-generating stories."

John W. Campbell discovered Kelly Freas in 1953. The October 1953 issue of Astounding carried one of his most famous paintings, the sad robot that illustrated Tom Godwin's story The Gulf Between, the one that was later copied by the band Queen for their album News of the World.

Forever after that first cover for Campbell, Freas was associated with Astounding and, later, Analog. Along the way, he did hundreds of interior line drawings, designed the Skylab I insignia for NASA, and managed to get his artwork on covers for most of the greatest Science Fiction writers of all time: **Poul Anderson**; **Isaac Asimov**; **Arthur C. Clarke**; **Philip K. Dick**; **Gordon R. Dickson**; **Harry Harrison**; **Robert A. Heinlein**; **C. L. Moore**; **Frederik Pohl**; **A. E. van Vogt**; Harlan Ellison; and many, many others.

For about seven years, from 1955 until 1962, he illustrated for Mad Magazine. His image of Alfred E. Newman has become an icon. But he quit when Mad refused to give him a raise. "Alfred E. Newman was making me stale," he said in an interview.

One of the highest priced collectible books

that Freas illustrated is Harlan Ellison's Medea: Harlan's World, the leather-bound, signed limited edition from Phantasia Press in 1985. That runs around $15000.00. And most of his early Gnome Press dustjackets are on books that price out between $500.00 and $1,500.00: Judgment Night by **C. L. Moore**; City by Clifford D. Simak; Against the Fall of Night by **Arthur C. Clarke**, with Clarke's book being the highest.

***

AWARDS

1955. Hugo Award for Best Professional Artist.
1956. Hugo Award for Best Professional Artist.
1958. Hugo Award for Best Professional Artist.
1959. Hugo Award for Best Professional Artist.
1970. Hugo Award for Best Professional Artist.
1972. Hugo Award for Best Professional Artist.
1973. Hugo Award for Best Professional Artist.
1973. Locus Poll Best Magazine Artist.
1973. Locus Poll Best Paperback Cover Artist.
1974. Hugo Award for Best Professional Artist.
1975. Hugo Award for Best Professional Artist.
1975. Locus Poll Best Professional Artist.
1976. Hugo Award for Best Professional Artist.
1977. Frank R. Paul Award.
1979. Inkpot Award.
1981. Skylark Award.
1981. Rova Award.
1982. Lensman Award.
1982. Phoenix Award.
1983. Los Angeles Science Fiction Society Service Award.
1985. Neographics Award.
1987. Daedalos Life Achievement Award.
1989. Best Professional Media Award at the International Fantasy Expo.
1989. Chesley Artistic Achievement Award.
1991. Best Cover Award from the Analog Analytical Laboratory for the Mid-December 1991 issue of Analog.
1991. Inducted into the National Association of Trade and Technical Schools National Hall of Fame.
1993. Chesley Artistic Achievement Award.
2000. Chesley Artistic Achievement Award.
2001. Retro Hugo Award for Best Professional Artist of 1951.
2003. Doctor of Arts from the Art Institute of Pittsburgh.
2006. Inducted into The Science Fiction Hall of Fame.

***

BOOKS

1. Frank Kelly Freas: A Portfolio. Published by Advent Publishers, Chicago, 1957. Staple-bound softcover.

2. Fantastic Science Fiction Art 1926 - 1954: From Frank R. Paul to Frank Kelly Freas. By Lester del Rey. Published by Ballantine Books, New York City, 1975. Softcover.

3. Frank Kelly Freas: The Art of Science Fiction. With an introduction by **Isaac Asimov**. Published by The Donning Company, Norfolk, Virginia, 1977. Hardcover.

4. A Separate Star. With an introduction by **Robert Silverberg**. Published by Greenswamp Publications, Virginia Beach, 1984. Hardcover.

5. Frank Kelly Freas: As He Sees It. With Laura Brodian Freas. Published by Paper Tiger, London, 2000. Hardcover.

Frank Herbert.

Franklin Patrick Herbert, Jr, was born in Tacoma, Washington on October 8th, 1920, and died of a heart attack, while recovering from surgery, on February 11th, 1986 in Madison, Wisconsin.

After graduating high school, he went to work at the Glendale Star in 1939. And except for time served in the Navy, he worked at the newspaper business until 1972, when he retired to become a full-time writer.

And he made a lot of money at it.

Dune, for instance, got him a $7,500 advance in 1964 and within four years, had earned him $20,000. That does not sound like much now. But it was far more than most science fiction novels were earning at the time.

Then came Dune Messiah in 1969 and Children of Dune in 1976. And by then, the entire Great Dune Trilogy was selling well.

There must have been times when he wondered if it would ever happen, if he would ever truly make it. His first two professional sales, Survival of the Cunning to Esquire in March 1945 and Yellow Fire to Alaska Life in 1947, were pulp adventures but not science fiction. His next sale wasn't until 1952 when Samuel Mines bought Looking for Something? for the April issue of Startling Stories where it appeared with: The Glory That Was by L. Sprague de Camp; The Intruder by Oliver Saari; Welcome to Luna by Charles E. Fritch; and The Last Days of Shandakor by Leigh Brackett.

He did not place another story until **John W. Campbell** bought Operation Syndrome for the June 1954 issue of Astounding Science Fiction. It appeared with: Question and Answer - part 1 of 2 by **Poul Anderson**; Lone Bandit by Dennis Wiegand; The Paradoxes by Crispin Kim Bradley; Growth Process by Edward Grendon; Neighbor by Clifford d. Simak; and Wing Shot by Victor Stephan.

After that, he began to sell regularly. And he sold his first novel, The Dragon in the Sea, to Doubleday in 1956, after it was serialised as Under Pressure in Astounding Science Fiction, beginning in November 1955, running through December and into January 1956.

In 1959, he began the research for Dune. Six years later, the writing was finished. Part of it was published by Campbell as Dune World, serialised in 1963 and 1964. The rest of it was serialised in Astounding as The Prophet of Dune in 1965. Campbell understood what he had right away. But Herbert submitted it to twenty book publishers before he landed a contract with Chilton in Philadelphia.

Before **Frank Herbert** came along, Chilton had been known primarily for their car repair manuals. That changed.

Now, that first edition of Dune normally sells for between $10,000.00 and $15,000.00. And Chilton went on to publish James Schmitz, **Poul Anderson**, Sterling E. Lanier, Ben Bova, **Andre Norton**, **Robert Silverberg**, Philip Jose Farmer, and many other well-selling science fiction writers.

He once confessed, "I knew when I was still a child in grade school that I wanted to be... an author."

It would seem he made it.

***

AWARDS

1965. Nebula Best Novel Award for Dune.
1966. Hugo Best Novel Award for Dune.
1975. Locus Poll All-Time Best Novel Award for Dune.
1978. A Prix Apollo for Hellstrom's Hive.
1987. Locus Poll All-Time Best Novel Award for Dune.
1998. Locus Poll All-Time Best Novel before 1990 Award for Dune.
2006. Inducted into The Science Fiction Hall of Fame.

***

FILMS AND TELEVISION

1. Dune. Directed by David Lynch in 1984, this starred: Patrick Stewart; Sting; Dean Stockwell; Max von Sydow; Alicia Witt; Sean Young; Virginia Madsen; and Kyle MacLachlan, et al.

2. The Making of Dune. This was a 1984 documentary that featured **Frank Herbert** as one of the interviewees.

3. Dune. This television mini series was directed by John Harrison for release in December 2000. It was shown in three episodes and starred: William Hurt; Ian McNeice; Matt Keeslar; Julie Cox; Uwe Ochsenknecht; Alec Newman; Saskia Reeves; P. H. Moriarty; and many others.

4. Children of Dune. Directed by Greg Yaitanes, this was made for TV in 2003. It starred: Alec Newman; Edward Atterton; Ian McNeice; Steven Berkoff; P. H. Moriarty; James McAvoy; Rik Young; and others.

5. Dune. It has been announced that Dune will be done yet again, this time directed by Peter Berg for 2010.

***

NOVELS AND COLLECTIONS

1. The Dragon in the Sea. Published by Doubleday & Company, Garden City, New York, 1956. Hardcover.

2. 21st Century Sub. Avon Books, New York City, 1956. Avon Book T-146. Softcover. Re-titled from The Dragon in the Sea, 1956.

3. Dune. Published by Chilton Books, Philadelphia, 1965. Hardcover.

4. Destination: Void. Published by Berkley Books, New York City, 1966. Berkley Book F1249. Softcover.

5. The Eyes of Heisenberg. Published by Berkley

Books, New York City, 1966. Berkley Book F1283. Softcover.

6. The Green Brain. Published by Ace Books, New York City, 1966. Ace Book F379. Softcover.

7. The Saratoga Barrier. Published by Berkley Books, New York City, 1968. Berkley Book S1615. Softcover.

8. The Heaven Makers. Published by Avon Books, New York City, 1968. Avon Book S319. Softcover.

9. Dune Messiah. Published by G. P. Putnam's Sons, New York City, 1969. Hardcover.

10. The Saratoga Barrier. Published by Rapp and Whiting, London, 1970. First hardcover edition.

11. Whipping Star. Published by G. P. Putnam's Sons, New York City, 1970. Hardcover.

12. The Worlds of Frank Herbert. Published by New English Library, London, 1970. Nel Book 2814. Softcover. Herein: The Tactful Saboteur, 1964; Committee of the Whole, 1965; Mating Call, 1961; Escape Felicity, 1966; The GM Effect, 1965; The Featherbedders, 1967; Old Rambling House, 1958; and A-W-F Unlimited, 1961.

13. The Worlds of Frank Herbert. Published by Ace Books, New York City, 1971. Ace Book 90926. Softcover. Add a story to the line-up from New English Library: By the Book 1966.

14. The God Makers. Published by G. P. Putnam's Sons, New York City, 1972. Hardcover.

15. Soul Catcher. Published by G. P. Putnam's Sons, New York City, 1972. Hardcover.

16. Hellstrom's Hive. Published by Nelson Doubleday - The Science Fiction Book Club, Garden City, New York, 1973. Hardcover.

17. The Book of Frank Herbert. Published by DAW Books, New York City, 1973. Daw Collectible book 39. UQ1039. Softcover. Herein: Seed Stock, 1970; The Nothing, 1956; Rat Race, 1955; Gambling Device, 1973; Looking for Something?, 1952; The Gone Dogs, 1954; Passage for Piano, 1973; Encounter in a Lonely Place, 1973; Operation Syndrome, 1954; and Occupation Force, 1955.

18. Under Pressure. Published by Ballantine Books, New York City, 1974. Ballantine Book 23835. Softcover. Re-titled re-issue of The Dragon in the Sea, 1956.

19. The Best of Frank Herbert. Published by Sidgwick and Jackson, London, 1975. Hardcover. Herein: Looking for Something?, 1952; Nightmare Blues, 1954; Dragon in the Sea - extract, 1976; Cease Fire, 1958; Egg and Ashes, 1960; Marie Celeste Move, 1964; Committee of the Whole, 1965; Dune - extract, 1965; By the Book, 1966; The Primitives, 1966; The Heaven Makers - extract, 1967; The Being Machine, 1969; and Seed Stock, 1970.

20. The Eyes of Heisenberg. Published by New English Library, London, 1975. First hardcover edition.

21. Dune Messiah. Published by Berkley Books, New York City, 1975. Berkley book D2952. Softcover. Revised edition.

22. Children of Dune. Published by G. P. Putnam's Sons, New York City, 1976. Hardcover.

23. The Best of Frank Herbert Book (1) One: 1952 - 1964. Published by Sphere Books, London, 1976. Softcover. Herein: Introduction by **Frank Herbert**; Looking for Something?, 1952; Nightmare Blues, 1954; Dragon in the Sea - extract, 1976; Cease Fire, 1958; Egg and Ashes, 1960; and Marie Celeste Move, 1964.

24. The Best of Frank Herbert: Book Two: 1965 - 1970. Published by Sphere Books, London, 1976. Softcover. Herein: Introduction by Angus Wells; Committee of the Whole, 1965; Dune - extract, 1965; By the Book, 1966; The Primitives, 1966; The Heaven Makers - extract, 1967; The Being Machine, 1969; and Seed Stock, 1970.

25. The Dosadi Experiment. Published by G. P. Putnam's Sons, New York City, 1977. Hardcover.

26. The Book of Frank Herbert. Published by Berkley Book, New York City, 1981. Softcover. Herein: Seed Stock, 1970; The Nothing, 1956; Rat Race, 1955; Gambling Device, 1973; Looking for Something?, 1952; The Gone Dogs, 1954; Passage for Piano, 1973; Encounter in a Lonely Place, 1973; Operation Syndrome, 1954; and Occupation Force, 1955; and Listening to the Left Hand - an essay, 1973.

27. The Heaven Makers. Published by Ballantine Books, New York City, 1977. Ballantine Book 25304. Softcover. Revised edition.

28. Destination: Void. Published by Berkley Books, New York City, 1978. Softcover. Revised edition.

29. The Jesus Incident. With Bill Ransom. Published by Berkley Putnam, New York City, 1979. Hardcover.

30. Direct Descent. Published by Ace Books, New York City, 1980. Softcover.

31. The Priests of Psi. Published by Victor Gollancz, London, 1980. Hardcover. Herein: Old Rambling House, 1958; Murder Will In, 1970; Mindfield!, 1962; Try to Remember, 1961; and The Priests of Psi, 1960.

32. The Worlds of Frank Herbert. Published by Gregg Press, Boston, 1980. First hardcover edition.

33. God Emperor of Dune. Published by G. P. Putnam's Sons, New York City, 1981. Hardcover.

34. The White Plague. Published by G. P. Putnam's Sons, New York City, 1982. Hardcover.

35. The Lazarus Effect. With Bill Ransom. Published by G. P. Putnam's Sons, New York City, 1983. Hardcover.

36. Heretics of Dune. Published by G. P. Putnam's Sons, New York City, 1984. Hardcover.

37. Frank Herbert: Four Complete Novels. Published by Avenel Books, New Jersey, 1984.

Frank Herbert

Hardcover. An omnibus edition, this gathers: Whipping Star, 1970; The Dosadi Experiment, 1977; The Saratoga Barrier, 1968; and Soul Catcher, 1972.

38. Chapterhouse: Dune. Published by Victor Gollancz, London, 1985. Hardcover. Preceded the U.S. edition by one month. Printed in March, the Putnam's edition came out in April.

39. Eye. Published by Berkley Books, New York City, 1985. Softcover. Herein: Introduction by **Frank Herbert**; Rat Race, 1955; Dragon in the Sea - excerpt, 1955; Cease Fire, 1958; A Matter of Traces, 1958; Try to Remember, 1961; The Tactful Saboteur, 1964; By the Book, 1966; Seed Stock, 1970; Murder Will In, 1970; Passage for Piano, 1973; Death of a City, 1973; Frogs and Scientists, 1979; and The Road to Dune - an essay with Jim Burns, 1985.

40. Man of Two Worlds. With Brian Herbert. Published by G. P. Putnam's Sons, New York City, 1986. Softcover.

41. The Ascension Factor. With Bill Ransom. Published by Ace Putnam, New York City, 1988. Hardcover.

42. Songs of Muad'Dib: The Poetry of Frank Herbert. Published by Ace Books, New York City, 1992. Softcover. Includes an introduction by Brian Herbert.

43. The Road to Dune. With Brian Herbert and Kevin J. Anderson. Published by Tor Books - Tom Doherty Associates, New York City, 2005. Hardcover. Herein: Foreword by Bill Ransom; Preface and an assortment of essays by Kevin J. Anderson and Brian Herbert, including an introduction, Unpublished Scenes and Chapters from Dune; and the following short fiction from **Frank Herbert**, collected here for the first time: Paul and Reverend Mother Mohiam; Paul and Thufir Hawat; Paul and Gurney Hallack; Paul and Dr Yueh; Paul and Duke Leto Atreides: The Spacing Guild and the Great Convention; Baron Harkonnen and Piter de Vries; From Caladan to Arrakis; Blue-Within-Blue eyes; Jessica and Dr Yueh: The Spice; Paul and Jessica; Escape from the Harkonnens: With Duncan Liet-Kynes at the Desert Base; The Flight from Kyne's Desert Base; Maud'Dib; Original Opening Summary for Dune Messiah; Alia and The Duncan Idaho Ghola; The Human Distrans; Conspiracy's End; Blind Paul in the Desert; and an assortment of short stories by Brian Herbert and Kevin J. Anderson.

44. Missing Link - and - Operation Haystack: Two Classic Stories Starring Lewis Orne. Published by Phoenix Pick, Rockville, Maryland, 2008. Softcover.

***

ANTHOLOGIES

1. Tomorrow, and Tomorrow, and Tomorrow... With Bonnie L. Heintz, Donald A. Joos, and Jane Agorn McGee. Published by Holt Rinehart and Winston, New York City, 1974. Softcover. Herein: Preface by Bonnie L. Heintz, **Frank Herbert**, Donald A. Joos, and Jane Agorn McGee; Science Fiction and You - an essay by **Frank Herbert**, 1974; The Star by **H. G. Wells**, 1897; The Subliminal Man by J. G. Ballard, 1963; The Waveries by Fredric Brown, 1945; Nightfall by **Isaac Asimov**, 1941; The Nothing by **Frank Herbert**, 1956; Bitter End by **Eric Frank Russell**, 1953; The Winner by Donald E. Westlake, 1970; The Lawgiver by Keith Laumer, 1970; Utopian by Mack Reynolds, 1970; Rescue Party by **Arthur C. Clarke**, 1946; For the Sake of Grace by Suzette Haden Elgin, 1969; The Other Foot by **Ray Bradbury**, 1951; Crate by **Theodore Sturgeon**, 1970; The Cloudbuilders by Colin Kapp, 1968; The Shortest Science Fiction Story Ever Told by Forrest J. Ackerman, 1973; Street of Dreams, Feet of Clay by Robert Sheckley, 1967; The Veldt by **Ray Bradbury**, 1950; After the Myths Went Home by **Robert Silverberg**, 1969; Arena by Fredric Brown, 1944; Repent, Harlequin! Said the Ticktockman by Harlan Ellison, 1965; The Hole on the Corner by R. A. Lafferty, 1967; Texas Week by Albert Hernhuter, 1954; HEMEAC by E. G. Von Wald, 1968; This Grand Carcass Yet by R. A. Lafferty, 1968; The Perfect Woman by Robert Sheckley, 1953; Desertion by Clifford D. Simak, 1944; Here There Be Tygers by **Ray Bradbury**, 1951; Crucifixus Etiam by Walter M. Miller, Jr, 1953; Sunrise on Mercury by **Robert Silverberg**, 1957; Omnilingual by H. Beam Piper, 1957; The Sentinel by **Arthur C. Clarke**, 1951; Seeds of the Dusk by Raymond Z. Gallun, 1938; Specialist by Robert Sheckley, 1953; Half-Breed by **Isaac Asimov**, 1940; Bomb Scare by Vernor Vinge, 1970; Keyhole by Murray Leinster, 1951; Sundance by **Robert Silverberg**, 1969; Goldfish Bowl by **Robert A. Heinlein** writing as Anson MacDonald, 1942; Sword Game by H. H. Hollis; The Singing Bell by **Isaac Asimov**, 1955; and Private Eye by Henry Kuttner and **C. L. Moore** writing as Lewis Padgett, 1949.

2. Nebula Winners 15. Published by Harper and Row, New York City, 1981. Hardcover. Herein: Introduction by **Frank Herbert**; Camps by Jack Dann, 1979; Sandkings by George R. R. Martin, 1979; The Straining Your Eyes Through the Viewscreen Blues - an essay by Vonda N. McIntyre, 1981; Enemy Mine by Barry B. Longyear, 1979; giANTS by Edward Bryant, 1979; We Have Met the Mainstream - an essay by Ben Bova, 1981; The Extraordinary Voyages of Amelie Bertrand by Joanna Russ, 1979; and Unaccompanied Sonata by Orson Scott Card, 1979.

***

NON-FICTION

1. New World or No World. Editor. Published by Ace Books, New York City, 1970. Ace Book 57250. Softcover.

2. Threshold: The Blue Angels Experience. Published by Ballantine Books, New York City, 1973. Softcover.

3. Without Me, You're Nothing: The Essential Guide to Home Computers. With Max Barnard. Published by Simon and Schuster, New York City, 1981. Hardcover.

4. Frank Herbert: The Maker of Dune: Insights of a Master of Science Fiction. With Tim O'Reilly.

Published by Berkley Books, New York City, 1987. Softcover.

***

RELATED

1. Herbert's Dune and Other Works: Notes. By L. David Allen. Published by Cliffs Notes, Lincoln, Nebraska, 1975. Softcover.

2. Frank Herbert. By David M. Miller. Published by Starmont, Mercer Island, Washington, 1980. Hardcover.

3. The Dune Storybook. By Joan D. Vinge from the screenplay by David Lynch. Published by G. P. Putnam's Sons, New York City, 1984. Hardcover.

4. The Dune Encyclopedia: The Complete Guide and Companion to Frank Herbert's Masterpiece of the Imagination. By Willis E. McNelly. Published by Berkley Books, New York City, 1983. Softcover.

5. The Dune Encyclopedia: The Complete Guide and Companion to Frank Herbert's Masterpiece of the Imagination. By Willis E. McNelly. Published by the Science Fiction Book Club, Garden City, New York, 1984. First hardcover edition.

6. The Notebooks of Frank Herbert's Dune. Edited by Brian Herbert. Published by Perigee Putnam, New York City, 1988. Softcover.

7. Frank Herbert. By William F. Touponce. Published by Twayne Publishers, Boston, 1988. Hardcover.

8. The Secrets of Frank Herbert's Dune. By James Van Hise. Published by Ibooks, New York City, 2000. Softcover.

9. Dune: Spark Notes. Published by Spark Notes, United States, 2002. Softcover.

10. Dreamer of Dune: The Biography of Frank Herbert. By Brian Herbert. Published by Tor Books - Tom Doherty Associates, New York City, 2003. Hardcover.

11. The Science of Dune: An Unauthorized Exploration into the Real Science Behind Frank Herbert's Fictional Universe. By Kevin Grazier. Published by Benbella Books, Dallas, Texas, 2008. Softcover.

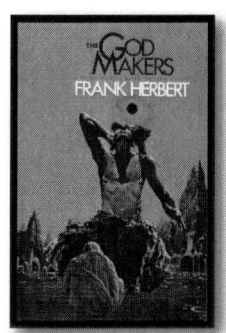

George Lucas

George Lucas.

George Walton Lucas, Jr was born on May 14th, 1944 in Modesto, California. All through high school, movies were just something you watched, probably at the drive-in. He was into cars, the faster the better. He hung out in garages and did as much racing as possible. He had an Autobianchi Bianchina, which was built by Bianchi, Pirelli and Fiat. He had it souped-up for racing. And he wiped out in it on June 12th, 1962.

Instead of going on with racing, he finished high school and went to a community college, then on to junior college where he studied anthropology. He started hanging out in San Francisco jazz clubs, and came across a group of underground film makers. These guys worked in the abstract. And Lucas was captivated. He began to seek out all the avant garde films he could find, studying their work while developing his own camera techniques.

He dropped the anthropology studies, and went to the University of Southern California School of Cinematic Arts. Fascinated with camera work, with the shapes, with chiaroscuro, he began to develop his own approach to pure cinema, to cinema verite. He wanted to be a filmmaker, not particularly a director, a producer, a writer.

While working as a teacher at USC, he made a short film, Electronic Labyrinth: THX 1138 4EB. This won first prize at the 1967/68 National Student Film Festival. For that, Warner Bros. gave him a scholarship that allowed him to work on making any film he wanted. He chose a film that was being done by Francis Ford Coppola, Finian's Rainbow, 1968. He worked as an uncredited production assistant. But meeting Coppola was fortuitous.

The following year, they formed American Zoetrope, with a plan to produce not only their own films, but those of some very distinctive directors as well. Jean-Luc Godard, Akira Kurosawa and many others.

Lucas' first full length film produced by American Zoetrope was based on his student film, Electronic Labyrinth: THX 1138 4EB. It was simply called THX1138.

It was a flop.

But his next one was not.

Basing it on his own love of cars, his own high school days, he called it American Graffiti.

It made him a lot of money and gave him Hollywood power.

His next film gave him the world.

It was made through Fox Studios, which was sort of floundering at the time. Lucas built up their fortunes... and his own as well. To help push through the financing, he didn't take his directors' fee. Instead, he asked for the licensing rights. To Fox, those were meaningless. They were happy to take the deal.

The movie was Star Wars. And the licensing rights, the toys, the collectibles, the games, the books, the comics... Those made Lucas exceedingly wealthy.

He promptly began to lose much of that fortune with a project called Apocalypse Now. He was directing it and doing such a slow and miserable job of it that his partner, Frances Ford Coppola, usurped it. That broke down their partnership.

With money from Star Wars still pouring in, George Lucas set out on his own, formed Lucasfilm and its two subsidiaries, Skywalker Sound and Industrial Light & Magic....

First editions of Star Wars: The Adventures of Luke Skywalker, from 1976, can sell for as much as $2,000.00 for signed copies, $1,000.00 for unsigned copies.

***

AWARDS

1967. First prize at the National Student Film Festival for Electronic Labyrinth: THX 1138 4EB.
1973. A Bronze Leopard from the Locarno International Film Festival for American Graffiti.
1974. Best Screenplay NSFC Award from the National Society of Film Critics Awards for American Graffiti.
1974. Best Screenplay NYFCC Award from the New York Film Critics Circle Awards for American Graffiti.
1977. Special Hugo Award for Star Wars.
1977. Special Nebula Award for Star Wars.
1978. Hugo Award for Best Dramatic Presentation for Star Wars.
1978. Best Director from the Academy of Science Fiction, Fantasy & Horror Films for Star Wars.
1978. Hochi Film Award for Best Foreign Language Film - Star Wars.
1978. ShoWest Award for Director of the Year.
1979. British Fantasy Best Film Award for Star Wars.
1979. Evening Standard British Film Award for Best Film - Star Wars.
1979. Readers' Choice Award at the Kinema Junpo Awards for Best Foreign Language Film Director for Star Wars.
1980. Balrog SF Film Hall of Fame for Star Wars.
1981. Hugo Award for Best Dramatic Presentation for The Empire Strikes Back.
1981. A David di Donatello Award for Best Producer - Foreign Film for Kagemusha, shared with Francis Ford Coppola.
1981. Profession Achievement Balrog Award.
1982. Hugo Award for Best Dramatic Presentation for Raiders of the Lost Ark.
1984. Hugo Award for Best Dramatic Presentation for Return of the Jedi.
1990. Hugo Award for Best Dramatic Presentation for Indiana Jones and the Last Crusade.
1990. Prometheus Hall of Fame Award for Best Classic Libertarian SF Novel for THX 1138.
1992. Irving G. Thalberg Memorial Award from the Academy Awards.
1995. Lifetime Achievement Award from Sci-Fi Universe Magazine.
2000. Jackie Coogan Young Artist Award.
2002. A Britannia Award for Excellence in Film.
2002. Special Award from the National Board of Review.
2003. Vanguard Award.

2003. Razzie Award for the Worst Screenplay - Star Wars: Episode II: Attack of the Clones.
2003. Nicola Tesla Award during the Satellite Awards.
2004. Lifetime Achievement Award from the Visual Effects Society.
2005. Lifetime Achievement Award from the American Film Institute.
2005. Filmmaker's Award from the Motion Picture Sound Editors.
2005. Hollywood Movie of the Year from the Hollywood Film Festival for Star Wars: Episode III: Revenge of the Sith.
2005. Galactic Achievement Award from the ShoWest Convention.
2006. Inducted into The Science Fiction Hall of Fame.
2009. Art Directors Guild award for Contribution to Cinematic Imagery.

***

As with **Steven Spielberg**, **George Lucas** made scores of appearances as himself in television shows and in documentaries. These will not be listed here.

FILMS AND TELEVISION

1. Look at Life. Director, cameraman, editor and writer of this one-minute short from 1965.

2. The Bus. Production assistant on this 1965 Haskell Wexler film.

3. Herbie. Director and writer, cameraman and editor, with Paul Golding, of this 1966 short film.

4. Freiheit. He wrote, directed, handled the camera and did the editing for this three-minute 1966 short.

5. Marcello, I'm Bored. Sound editor on this eight-minute 1966 short, directed by John Milius.

6. 1:42:08: A Man and His Car. Also known as 1:42:08 to Quality, Lucas wrote and directed this 1966 short. He also handled the cinematography and the editing.

7. Grand Prix. Additional camera operator on this 1966 film which was directed by John Frankenheimer and starred: James Garner; Eva Marie Saint; Yves Montand; Toshiro Mifune; and Jessica Walter.

8. The Emperor. He shared the writing with a committee and directed this 1967 short.

9. Electronic Labyrinth: THX 1138 4EB. A fifteen minute short from 1967, Lucas wrote and directed it.

10. Anyone Live in a Pretty How Town. A 1967 short film, he directed it, and shared the writing with Paul Golding, based on a poem by e. e. cummings. He also did the camerawork and the editing.

11. 6-18-67. Did the whole thing again for this 1967 short.

12. Journey to the Pacific. Assistant director on this 1968 short, which was directed by Verna Fields.

13. Why Man Creates. Cameraman on this twenty-nine minute 1968 film which was directed by Elaine Bass and Sam Bass.

14. Filmmaker. Also known as Filmmaker: A Diary by **George Lucas**. Wrote, directed, edited and did the camerawork for this thirty-two minute 1968 short that featured Francis Ford Coppola as the entire cast.

15. Finian's Rainbow. Uncredited production assistant on this 1968 film, directed by Francis Ford Coppola and starring: Fred Astaire; Petula Clark; Tommy Steele; Don Francks; Keenan Wynn; et al.

16. The Rain People. Production associate on this 1969 film. Directed by Francis Ford Coppola, it starred: James Caan; Shirley Knight; Robert Duvall; and many others.

17. The Making of The Rain People. A short documentary made entire by Lucas in 1969.

18. Gimme Shelter. Cameraman on this 1970 Rolling Stones film.

19. Bald: The Making of THX 1138. Director, 1971. This featured, as themselves: Claudette Bessing; Francis Ford Coppola; Robert Duvall; Irene Forrest; Maggie McOmie; David Myers; Matthew Robbins; Johnny Weissmuller, Jr; and **George Lucas**.

20. THX 1138. Wrote, directed and edited the film for 1971 feature, which starred: Robert Duvall and Donald Pleasence.

21. American Graffiti. Director and writer, as well as uncredited editor, of this 1973 film, which starred: Richard Dreyfuss; Ron Howard; Paul Le Mat; Charles Martin Smith; Cindy Williams; Candy Clark; Mackenzie Phillips; Bo Hopkins; Kathleen Quinlan; and Harrison Ford.

22. Star Wars. Director and credited writer, as well as uncredited editor, of this 1977 film, which starred: Mark Hamill; Harrison Ford; Carrie Fisher; Peter Cushing; Alec Guinness; and many others, including: James Earl Jones as the voice of Darth Vader; David Prowse *as* Darth Vader; Peter Mayhew as Chewbacca; Kenny Baker as R2-D2; and Anthony Daniels as C-3PO.

23. More American Graffiti. Executive producer on this 1979 sequel, which was directed by B. W. L. Norton and starred: Candy Clark; Bo Hopkins; Ron Howard; Paul Le Mat; Mackenzie Phillips; Charles Martin Smith; and Cindy Williams; along with the group Country Joe and the Fish; Rosanna Arquette as a girl in a commune; Naomi Judd as girl on a bus; and Harrison Ford in an uncredited part as Officer Bob Falfa.

24. Kagemusha. Executive producer of the international version of this 1980 Akira Kurosawa film, which starred: Tatsuya Nakadai; Tsutomu Yamazaki; Kenichi Hagiwara; et al.

25. The Empire Strikes Back. Executive producer, writer and uncredited editor of this 1980 film. Directed by Irvin Kershner, it starred: Mark Hamill; Harrison Ford; Carrie Fisher; Billy Dee Williams; and Alec Guinness; with Frank Oz as the voice of

George Lucas

Yoda; James Earl Jones as the voice of Darth Vader; David Prowse *as* Darth Vader; Peter Mayhew as Chewbacca; Kenny Baker as R2-D2; and Anthony Daniels as C-3PO.

26. Raiders of the Lost Ark. Executive producer, writer and uncredited editor of this 1980 film, directed by **Steven Spielberg** and starring: Harrison Ford and Karen Allen.

27. Body Heat. Uncredited executive producer of this 1981 film, directed by Lawrence Kasdan and starring: William Hurt; Kathleen Turner; Richard Crenna; Ted Danson; and Mickey Rourke; et al.

28. Return of the Jedi. Writer, executive producer and uncredited editor for this third Star Wars film, 1983. Directed by Richard Marquand, it starred: Mark Hamill; Harrison Ford; Carrie Fisher; Billy Dee Williams; and Alec Guinness; with Frank Oz as the voice of Yoda; James Earl Jones as the voice of Darth Vader; David Prowse *as* Darth Vader; Peter Mayhew as Chewbacca; Kenny Baker as R2-D2; and Anthony Daniels as C-3PO.

29. Twice Upon a Time. Executive producer, 1983. Directed by John Korty and Charles Swenson, this animated film featured the voices of: Lorenzo Music; Marshall Efron; James Cranna; Julie Payne; and many others.

30. Indiana Jones and the Temple of Doom. Executive producer, writer and uncredited editor of this 1984 film, directed by **Steven Spielberg** and starring: Harrison Ford and Kate Capshaw.

31. The Ewok Adventure. Made for television in 1984, Lucas was the writer and the executive producer. John Korty directed and it starred: Burl Ives as the narrator; Eric Walker; Warwick David; Fionnula Flanagan; Debbie Lee Carrington; and others.

32. Ewoks. Creator of the characters and executive producer. This animated TV series ran for two seasons, starting September 7th, 1985 and going until December 13th, 1986. It featured Jim Henshaw and Lesleh Donaldson.

33. Droids. Creator of the characters and executive producer. This animated TV series ran for thirteen episodes, starting September 7th, 1985 and going until November 30th, 1985. It featured the voices of Anthony Daniels; Lesleh Donaldson; Don Francks; and others.

34. Latino. Uncredited editor and uncredited executive producer of this 1985 Haskell Wexler film.

35. Mishima: A Life in Four Chapters. Executive producer, 1985. Directed by Paul Schrader, the film starred: Ken Ogata; Masayuki Shionoya; Hiroshi Mikami; Junya Fukuda; Shigeto Tachihara; and many others.

36. Ewoks: The Battle for Endor. Writer and executive producer. Directed by Jim and Ken Wheat, this was made for television in 1985, starring: Wilford Brimley; Warwick Davis; Aubree Miller; Sian Phillips; and others.

37. Inside the Labyrinth. Executive producer for this 1986 television documentary. Directed by Des Saunders, this featured: Jim Henson; David Bowie; Jennifer Connelly; Brian Froud; Terry Jones; and many others.

38. Labyrinth. Executive producer, 1986. Directed by Jim Henson and featuring the designs of Brian Froud, this starred: David Bowie; Jennifer Connelly; Toby Froud; and many others.

39. Howard the Duck. Executive producer, 1986. This was directed by Willard Huyck and starred: Lea Thompson; Jeffrey Jones; and Tim Robbins; et al.

40. Captain EO. Executive producer for this seventeen-minute 1986 musical which was directed by Francis Ford Coppola and starred: Michael Jackson; Anjelica Huston; and Dick Shawn.

41. The Great Heep. Created the characters featured in this 1986 animated show. Directed by Clive A. Smith, it featured the voices of Anthony Daniels; Long John Baldry; Don Francks; and others.

42. Star Tours. Executive producer of this 1987 promotional film, shown to visitors to the Star Wars universe.

43. Powaqqatsi. Executive producer of this 1988 documentary. Directed by Godfrey Reggio, it featured archival footage of Christie Brinkley; Dan Rather; Cheryl Tiegs; Pope John Paul II; and David Brinkley.

44. Willow. Writer and executive producer of this 1988 film, which was directed by Ron Howard and starred: Val Kilmer; Joanne Whalley; Warwick Davis; Jean Marsh; Patricia Hayes; Billy Barty; David Steinberg; Kevin Pollak; and many others.

45. Tucker: The Man and His Dream. Executive producer, 1988. Directed by Francis Ford Coppola, this starred: Jeff Bridges; Joan Allen; Martin Landau; Mako; Christian Slater; and others.

46. The Land Before Time. Executive producer of this animated feature. Directed by Don Bluth in 1988, this featured the voices of: Gabriel Damon; Burke Byrnes; Judith Barsi; Pat Hingle; Helen Shaver; and others.

47. Raiders of the Lost Ark: The Adaptation. Directed by Eric Zala, this was a remake done by three kids who twelve years old when they started and finished the film six years later.

48. Indiana Jones and the Last Crusade. Executive producer, writer and uncredited editor of this 1989 film, directed by **Steven Spielberg** and starring: Harrison Ford; Sean Connery; Denholm Elliott; and Alison Doody; with River Phoenix as the Young Indy.

49. Wow! Executive producer of this 1990 seven-minute short featuring Ken Fischer.

50. Indiana Jed. One of the writers of this 1992 comedy, directed by Michael Linn and featuring Jed Weyland and Marc Linn.

51. Indiana Jones and Fate of Atlantis. Merely created the characters for this 1992 animated effort, directed by Hal Barwood.

52. The Young Indiana Jones Chronicles. Lucas was the executive producer of this television series which ran for twenty-eight episodes, starting March 4th, 1992 and going to August 21st, 1993. He also took a writing credit for nineteen of the episodes. It starred: Sean Patrick Flanery; George Hall; Ronny Coutteure; and Corey Carrier; et al.

53. The Adventures of Young Indiana Jones: Hollywood Follies. Executive producer, 1994. Made for TV and released on video, this was directed by Michael Schultz and starred Sean Patrick Flanery.

54. Radioland Murders. Writer and executive producer, 1994. Directed by Mel Smith, this starred: Brian Benben; Mary Stuart Masterson; Ned Beatty; George Burns; and Scott Michael Campbell; et al.

55. The Adventures of Young Indiana Jones: Treasure of the Peacock's Eye. Executive producer, 1995. Made for TV and released on video, this was directed by Carl Schultz and starred Sean Patrick Flanery.

56. The Adventures of Young Indiana Jones: Attack of the Hawkmen. Executive producer, 1995. Made for TV and released on video, this was directed by Ben Burtt and starred Sean Patrick Flanery.

57. The Adventures of Young Indiana Jones: Travels with Father. Executive producer, 1996. Made for TV and released on video, this was directed by Michael Schultz and Deepa Mehta and starred Sean Patrick Flanery and Corey Carrier.

58. The Pirates and the Prince. Executive producer. This 1997 animated film was directed by Ken Stephenson and featured the voices of: Donny Burns; Anthony Daniels; Dan Hennessey; et al.

59. The Adventures of Young Indiana Jones: Adventures in the Secret Service. Executive producer, 1999. Made for TV and released on video, this was directed by Vic Armstrong and Simon Wincer and starred Sean Patrick Flanery.

60. The Adventures of Young Indiana Jones: Oganga, the Giver and Taker of Life. Executive producer and writer, 1999. Made for TV and released on video, this was directed by Simon Wincer and starred Sean Patrick Flanery.

61. The Adventures of Young Indiana Jones: Masks of Evil. Executive producer, 1999. Made for TV and released on video, this was directed by Dick Maas and Mike Newell and starred Sean Patrick Flanery.

62. The Adventures of Young Indiana Jones: The Phantom Train of Doom. Executive producer, 1999. Made for TV and released on video, this was directed by Peter MacDonald and starred Sean Patrick Flanery.

63. The Adventures of Young Indiana Jones: Spring Break Adventure. Executive producer, 1999. Made for TV and released on video, this was directed by Joe Johnston and Carl Schultz and starred Sean Patrick Flanery.

64. The Adventures of Young Indiana Jones: The Trenches of Hell. Writer and executive producer, 1999. Made for TV and released on video, this was directed by Simon Wincer and starred Sean Patrick Flanery.

65. The Adventures of Young Indiana Jones: Daredevils of the Desert. Executive producer, 1999. Made for TV and released on video, this was directed by Simon Wincer and starred Sean Patrick Flanery, along with Catherine Zeta-Jones.

66. The Dark Redemption. A thirty-five minute, fan-produced sequel to the Star Wars series. Directed by Peter Mether, this starred: Damian Rice; Jason Chong; and Martin Grelis.

67. Short Chaos 10. From 2000, this included Electronic Labyrinth by **George Lucas**.

68. Star Wars: Episode I: The Phantom Menace. Writer, director, executive producer and uncredited editor, 2002. The film starred: Ewan McGregor; Liam Neeson; Natalie Portman; Jake Lloyd; and Frank Oz as the voice of Yoda.

69. Star Wars: Episode II: Attack of the Clones. Writer, director, executive producer and uncredited editor, 2002. The film starred: Ewan McGregor; Natalie Portman; Hayden Christensen; Christopher Lee; Samuel L. Jackson; Jimmy Smits; and Frank Oz as the voice of Yoda.

70. Star Wars: Clone Wars. Executive producer and credited author of this animated television series. It ran for twenty-five episodes, first airing on November 7th, 2003 and finishing on March 25th, 2005. It featured: Andre Sogliuzzo; Mat Lucas; James Arnold Taylor; and many others.

71. Treasure of the Hidden Planet. Executive producer, 2004. This animated film featured the voices of Anthony Daniels; Jan Austin; Don Francks; Eric Peterson; Graeme Campbell; et al.

72. Star Wars: Episode III: Revenge of the Sith. Writer, director, and executive producer, 2005. The film starred: Ewan McGregor; Natalie Portman; Hayden Christensen; Christopher Lee; Samuel L. Jackson; and Jimmy Smits.

73. Cinema 16: American Short Films. Some his Lucas' early work was featured here in 2006, along with Tim Burton; D. A. Pennebaker; Andy Warhol; and twelve others.

74. The Colbert Report. Uncredited writer and director of the October 11th, 2006 episode of this series, starring Stephen Colbert as the host and **George Lucas** as a guest, using the name George L.

75. The Adventures of Young Indiana Jones: My First Adventure. Writer and executive producer, 2007. Made for TV and released on video, this was directed by Jim O'Brien and Michael Schultz and starred Corey Carrier.

76. The Adventures of Young Indiana Jones:

George Lucas

Passion for Life. Executive producer, 2007. Made for TV and released on video, this was directed by Rene Manzor and Michael Schultz and starred Corey Carrier.

77. The Adventures of Young Indiana Jones: The Perils of Cupid. Writer and executive producer, 2007. Made for TV and released on video, this was directed by Bille August and Mike Newell and starred Corey Carrier.

78. The Adventures of Young Indiana Jones: Journey of Radiance. Executive producer, 2007. Made for TV and released on video, this was directed by Deepa Mehta and Gavin Millar and starred Corey Carrier.

79. The Adventures of Young Indiana Jones: Love's Sweet Song. Executive producer, 2007. Made for TV and released on video, this was directed by Gillies MacKinnon and Carl Schultz and starred Sean Patrick Flanery.

80. The Adventures of Young Indiana Jones: Escapades. Executive producer, 2007. Made for TV and released on video, this was directed by Terry Jones and Robert Young and starred Sean Patrick Flanery.

81. The Adventures of Young Indiana Jones: Demons of Deception. Writer and executive producer, 2007. Made for TV and released on video, this was directed by Rene Manzor and Nicolas Roeg and starred Sean Patrick Flanery.

82. The Adventures of Young Indiana Jones Documentaries. Executive producer, 2007. Made for TV.

83. The Adventures of Young Indiana Jones: Scandal of 1920. Executive producer, 2008. Made for TV and released on video, this was directed by Sydney Macartney and starred Sean Patrick Flanery.

84. The Adventures of Young Indiana Jones: Winds of Change. Executive producer, 2008. Made for TV and released on video, this was directed by David Hare and Michael Shultz and starred Sean Patrick Flanery.

85. Indiana Jones and the Kingdom of the Crystal Skull. The writer and executive producer of this 2008 film. Directed by **Steven Spielberg**, this starred: Harrison Ford; Cate Blanchett; Karen Allen; John Hurt; and many others.

86. Star Wars: The Clone Wars. Executive producer, 2008. Directed by Dave Filoni, this animated film featured the voices of: Matt Lanter; Ashley Eckstein; James Arnold Taylor; Tom Kane; and many others.

87. Robot Chicken: Star Wars Episode II. Simply based on the Lucas characters, this animated film from 2008 was directed by Seth Green and featured: Abraham Benrubi; Bob Bergen; Ahmed Best; Rachael Leigh Cook; Carrie Fisher; Conan O'Brien; Billy Dee Williams; and many others.

88. Star Wars: The Clone Ward. Executive producer and creator of this animated television series. To the date of this writing, July 16th, 2009, there have been twenty-two episodes, starting October 3rd, 2008 and running until March 20th, 2009.

89. Red Tails. Executive producer and writer of this, which is slated for release in 2009. Directed by Anthony Hemingway, the movie stars: Terrence Howard; Bryan Cranston; Cuba Gooding, Jr; Tristan Wilds; Lee Tergesen; and others.

90. Untitled Star Wars. Executive producer of this as yet untitled television series.

***

SELECTED BOOKS

1. Star Wars: From the Adventures of Luke Skywalker. Published by Del Rey - Ballantine Books, New York City, 1977. Softcover.

2. THX 1138. With Ben Bova. Published by Warner Books, New York City, 1978. Softcover.

3. The Empire Strikes Back. With Donald F. Glut, Leigh Brackett and Lawrence Kasdan. Published by Del Rey - Ballantine Books, New York City, 1980. Softcover.

4. Return of the Jedi. With James Kahn and Lawrence Kasdan. Published by Del Rey - Ballantine Books, New York City, 1983. Softcover.

5. The Art of Return of the Jedi. With Lawrence Kasdan. Published by Ballantine Books, New York City, 1983. Hardcover.

6. The Star Wars Saga. With James Khan and Donald F. Glut. Published by Ballantine Books, New York City, 1985. Softcover. Herein: Star Wars - ghost written by Alan Dean Foster, 1976; The Empire Strikes Back by Donald F. Glut, 1980; and Return of the Jedi by James Kahn, 1984.

7. The Star Wars Trilogy. With James Khan and Donald F. Glut. Published by Del Rey - Ballantine Books, New York City, 1993. Softcover. Re-titled from The Star Wars Saga, 1985.

8. Shadow Moon: Chronicles of the Shadow War 1. With Chris Claremont. Published by Bantam Spectra, New York City, 1995. Hardcover.

9. Star Wars: A New Hope. With Tony Roberts. Published by Warner Books, New York City, 1996. Softcover.

10. Star Wars: Episode IV: A New Hope. Published by Del Rey - Ballantine Books, New York City, 1997. Softcover.

11. Shadow Dawn: Chronicles of the Shadow War 2. With Chris Claremont. Published by Bantam Spectra, New York City, 1997. Hardcover.

12. Star Wars: Episode IV: A New Hope - The Illustrated Screenplay. Published by Del Rey - Ballantine Books, New York City, 1998. Softcover.

13. Star Wars: Episode V: The Empire Strikes Back - The Illustrated Screenplay. With Leigh Brackett and Lawrence Kasdan. Published by Del Rey - Ballantine Books, New York City, 1998. Softcover.

14. Star Wars: Episode 6: Return of the Jedi - The Illustrated Screenplay. Published by Del Rey - Ballantine Books, New York City, 1998. Softcover.

15. Star Wars: Episode 4: A New Hope - Script Facsimile. With Lawrence Kasdan. Published by Del Rey - Ballantine Books, New York City, 1998. Softcover.

16. Star Wars: Episode 5: The Empire Strikes Back - Script Facsimile. With Leigh Brackett and Lawrence Kasdan. Published by Del Rey - Ballantine Books, New York City, 1998. Softcover.

17. Star Wars: Episode 6: Return of the Jedi - Script Facsimile. With Lawrence Kasdan. Published by Del Rey - Ballantine Books, New York City, 1998. Softcover.

18. Star Wars: Episode 1: The Phantom Menace - The Illustrated Screenplay. Published by Del Rey - Ballantine Books, New York City, 1999. Softcover.

19. Shadow Star: Chronicles of the Shadow War 3. With Chris Claremont. Published by Bantam Spectra, New York City, 1999. Hardcover.

20. Star Wars: Episode 1: The Phantom Menace - Script Facsimile. Published by Del Rey - Ballantine Books, New York City, 2000. Softcover.

21. The Star Wars Trilogy. With James Khan and Donald F. Glut. Published by Del Rey - Ballantine Books, New York City, 2002. First hardcover edition.

22. The Art of Star Wars: Episode II: Attack of the Clones. With Jonathan Hales. Published by Del Rey - Ballantine Books, New York City, 2002. Hardcover.

23. Star Wars. With Larry Weinberg. Published by Random House Books for Young Readers, New York City, 2004. Hardcover.

***

RELATED

1. Skywalking - The Life and Films of George Lucas. By Dale Pollock. Published by Harmony Books, New York City, 1983. Hardcover.

2. George Lucas. By D. I. Mabery. Published by Lerner Publications, Minneapolis, Minnesota, 1987. Hardcover.

3. The Future of Movies: Interviews with Martin Scorsese, George Lucas, and Steven Spielberg. By Roger Ebert and Gene Siskel. Published by Andrews McMeel Publishing, Kansas City, Missouri, 1991. Softcover.

4. George Lucas: The Creative Impulse: Lucasfilm's First Twenty Years. By Charles Champlin. Published by Harry N. Abrams, New York City, 1992. Hardcover.

5. George Lucas Museum. By Chikako Narita and Tame Kobayashi. Published by Bungeishunju, Japan, 1993. Hardcover.

6. From Star Wars to Indiana Jones: The Best of the Lucasfilm Archives. Published by Chronicles Books, San Francisco, 1994. Hardcover.

7. Star Wars: The National Public Radio Dramatization: Based on Characters and Situations Created by George Lucas. Introduction by Brian Daly. Published by Del Rey - Ballantine Books, New York City, 1994. Softcover.

8. Star Wars: The Empire Strikes Back: The National Public Radio Dramatization: Based on Characters and Situations Created by George Lucas. Introduction by Brian Daly. Published by Del Rey - Ballantine Books, New York City, 1995. Softcover.

9. Monsters and Aliens from George Lucas. By Bob Carrau. Published by Abradale/Abrams, Lebanon, Indiana, 1996. Hardcover.

10. George Lucas: The Making of His Movies. By Chris Salewicz. Published by Orion Books, London, 1998. Softcover.

11. George Lucas: Interviews. Published by the University Press of Mississippi, 1999. Softcover.

12. Mythmaker: The Life and Work of George Lucas. By John Baxter. Published by Avon Books, New York City, 1999. Hardcover.

13. George Lucas Companion: The Complete Guide to Hollywood's Most Influential Filmmaker. By Howard Maxford. Published by B. T. Batsford, London, 1999. Softcover.

14. George Lucas. By James Clarke. Published by Pocket Essentials, New York City, 2002. Softcover.

15. George Lucas. By Jim Smith. Published by Virgin Books, London, 2003. Softcover.

16. Droidmaker: George Lucas and the Digital Revolution. By Michael Ruin. Published by Triad Publishing, Florida, 2005. Hardcover.

17. The Cinema of George Lucas. Published by Harry N. Abrams, New York City, 2005. Hardcover.

Anne McCaffrey.

Anne Inez McCaffrey was born on April 1st, 1926 in Cambridge, Massachusetts. Before settling in as an author, she tried a number of things. She acted, with a performance in the first music circus, which was put on as a summer stock theatre in Lambertville, New Jersey in 1949. And she worked for Liberty Music Store Records in New York. She even tried a marriage, which lasted from 1950 until 1970, at which time she moved to Ireland to write full-time.

Her first published story was in the October 1953 issue of Science-Fiction Plus, a short-lived **Hugo Gernsback** magazine. The story was Freedom of the Race and it appeared along with The Celestial Brake by Thomas Calvert McClary; Operation: Gravity by **Jack Williamson**; Chain Reaction - an essay by Sam Moskowitz; Postscript by **Eric Frank Russell**; Worlds Within Worlds by Roger Dee; and Strange Compulsion by Philip Jose Farmer.

Her next published work in the genre was The Lady in the Tower, bought by Robert P. Mills for The Magazine of Fantasy and Science Fiction, April 1959. Also in that issue were Life's Bottleneck - an essay by **Isaac Asimov**; The Flying Islands by Anton Chekhov, 1883; The Amulet by **Gordon R. Dickson**; Through Time and Space with Ferdinand Feghoot XIII by Reginald Bretnor writing as Grendel Briarton; Unto the Fourth Generation by **Isaac Asimov**; Chemical Persuasion - an essay by Aldous Huxley, 1958; The Martian Crown Jewels by **Poul Anderson**; Nightmare by Jane Roberts; To See Another Mountain by **Frederik Pohl**; and Flowers for Algernon by Daniel Keys.

Again, there was a break for a couple of years. Then came The Ship Who Sang. That also went to Robert Mills for the April 1961 issue of The Magazine of Fantasy and Science Fiction. This time, she had her name on the front cover. Included in the issue were: My Built-in Doubter - an essay by **Isaac Asimov**; Softly While You're Sleeping by Evelyn E. Smith; The Hills of Lodan by Harold Calin; Dead Man's Bottles by Robert Graves, 1950; Through Time and Space with Ferdinand Feghoot XIII by Reginald Bretnor writing as Grendel Briarton; Cosmic Sex and You by Nils Peterson; Daddy's People by Richard Banks; and Nomansland by **Brian W. Aldiss**.

Finally, in 1966 with The Ship Who Mourned and a sequel, The Ship Who Killed, the first one bought by **John W. Campbell** for Analog and the second, by **Frederik Pohl** for Galaxy, she seemed to settle on a career.

She would write. In 1967, with Weyr Search published by Campbell in Analog, she started her Dragonriders of Pern series. And that was that. She became the first female author to win a Hugo Award.

Dragonflight, in the first hardcover edition, tends to be her highest priced book for collectors. Signed copies, of which there are many, run around $2,500.00. And the UK first hardcover edition of Dragonquest sells in the neighbourhood of $1,500.00.

***

AWARDS

1968. Hugo Best Novella Award for Weyr Search - Analog, October 1967.
1968. Nebula Best Novella Award for Dragonrider - Analog, December 1967 and January 1968.
1976. Skylark - The Edward E. Smith Memorial Award for Imaginative Fiction.
1979. Ditmar Award for Best International Long Fiction for The White Dragon.
1979. A Gandalf Award for Best Book-Length Fantasy for The White Dragon.
1980. A Balrog Award for Best Novel for Dragondrums.
1980. A Balrog Award for Professional Achievement.
1986. The Science Fiction Book Club's Book of the Year Award for Killashandra.
1990. The Science Fiction Book Club's Book of the Year Award for The Renegades of Pern.
1991. A HOMer Award for Best SF Novel for All the Weyrs of Pern.
1992. The Science Fiction Book Club's Book of the Year Award for All the Weyrs of Pern.
1993. The Science Fiction Book Club's Book of the Year Award for Damia's Children.
1994. The Science Fiction Book Club's Book of the Year Award for The Dolphins of Pern.
2000. A Karl Edward Wagner Award - a British Fantasy Special Award.
2005. Grand Master Award from the Science Fiction Writers of America, presented at the Nebula Award Ceremonies.
2006. Inducted into The Science Fiction Hall of Fame.

***

NOVELS AND COLLECTIONS

1. Restoree. Published by Ballantine Books, New York City, 1967. Ballantine Book U6108. Softcover.

2. Dragonflight. Published by Ballantine Books, New York City, 1968. Ballantine Book U6124. Softcover.

3. Restoree. Published by Rapp and Whiting, London, 1968. First hardcover edition.

4. Dragonflight. Published by Walker and Company, New York City, 1969. First hardcover edition.

5. The Ship Who Sang. Published by Walker and Company, New York City, 1969. First hardcover edition. This links six stories: The Ship Who Sang, 1961; Dramatic Mission, 1969; The Ship Who Mourned, 1966; The Ship Who Killed, 1966; The Ship Who Dissembled, 1969; and The Partnered Ship, 1969.

6. Decision at Doona. Published by Ballantine Books, New York City, 1969. Ballantine Book 01576. Softcover.

7. **Decision at Doona.** Published by Rapp and Whiting, London, 1970. First hardcover edition.

8. **Dragonquest.** Published by Ballantine Books, New York City, 1971. Ballantine Book 02245. Softcover.

9. **The Mark of Merlin.** Published by Dell Books, New York City, 1971. Dell Book 5466. Softcover.

10. **Ring of Fear.** Published by Dell Books, New York City, 1971. Dell Book 7445. Softcover.

11. **Dragonquest.** Published by Rapp and Whiting, London, 1973. First hardcover edition.

12. **To Ride Pegasus.** Published by Ballantine Books, New York City, 1973. Ballantine Book 23417. Softcover. Herein: To Ride Pegasus, 1973; A Womanly Talent, 1969; Apple, 1969; and A Bridle for Pegasus, 1973.

13. **To Ride Pegasus.** Published by J. M. Dent and Sons, London, 1974. First hardcover edition.

14. **The Kilternan Legacy.** Published by Dell Books, New York City, 1975. Dell Book 7195. Softcover.

15. **A Time When.** Published by NESFA Press, Cambridge, Massachusetts, 1975. Limited hardcover edition, 820 copies signed by **Anne McCaffrey** and the illustrator, Bonnie Dalzell.

16. **Dragonsong.** Published by Atheneum, New York City, 1976. Hardcover.

17. **The Kilternan Legacy.** Published by Millington, London, 1976. First hardcover edition.

18. **Dragonsong.** Published by Atheneum, New York City, 1976. Hardcover.

19. **Dragonsinger.** Published by Atheneum, New York City, 1977. Hardcover.

20. **The Mark of Merlin.** Published by Millington, London, 1977. First hardcover edition.

21. **Dragonsinger.** Published by Atheneum, New York City, 1977. Hardcover.

22. **Get Off the Unicorn.** Published by Ballantine Books, New York City, 1977. Ballantine Book 25666. Softcover. Herein: Introduction by **Anne McCaffrey**; Lady in the Tower, 1959; A Meeting of Minds, 1969; Daughter, 1971; Dull Drums, 1973; Changeling, 1977; Weather on Welladay, 1969; The Thorns of Barevi, 1970; The Horse from a Different Sea, 1977; The Great Canine Chorus, 1970; Finder's Keeper, 1973; A Proper Santa Claus, 1973; The Smallest Dragonboy, 1973; Apple, 1969; and Honeymoon, 1977.

23. **The Dinosaur Planet.** Published by Del Rey - Ballantine Books, New York City, 1978. Softcover.

24. **The White Dragon.** Published by Del Rey - Ballantine Books, New York City, 1978. Hardcover.

25. **The Dragonriders of Pern.** Published by Nelson Doubleday - The Science Fiction Book Club, Garden City, New York, 1978. Hardcover. Herein: Dragonflight, 1968; Dragonquest, 1971; The White Dragon, 1978; and Dragondex - an essay by Wendy Glasser.

26. **Dragondrums.** Published by Atheneum, New York City, 1979. Hardcover.

27. **The Worlds of Anne McCaffrey.** Published by Andre Deutsch, London, 1981. Hardcover. This collects: Decision at Doona, 1969; The Ship Who Sang, 1969; and Restoree, 1967.

28. **The Crystal Singer.** Published by Severn House, London, 1982. Hardcover.

29. **Moreta: Dragonlady of Pern.** Published by Del Rey - Ballantine Books, New York City, 1983. Hardcover.

30. **The Coelura.** Published by Underwood Miller, Los Angeles, California, 1983. Hardcover.

31. **The Harper Hall of Pern.** Published by Nelson Doubleday - The Science Fiction Book Club, Garden City, New York, 1984. Hardcover. This collects: Dragonsong, 1976; Dragonsinger, 1977; and Dragondrums, 1979.

32. **Stitch in Snow.** Published by Brandywine Books, San Francisco, 1984. Hardcover.

33. **Dinosaur Planet Survivors.** Published by Del Rey - Ballantine Books, New York City, 1984. Softcover.

34. **Killashandra.** Published by Del Rey - Ballantine Books, New York City, 1985. Hardcover.

35. **Nerilka's Story.** Published by Del Rey - Ballantine Books, New York City, 1986. Hardcover.

36. **The Year of the Lucy.** Published by Tor Books - Tom Doherty Associates, New York City, 1986. Hardcover.

37. **Nerilka's Story - and - The Coelura.** Published by Bantam Books, London, 1987. Hardcover.

38. **The Lady.** Published by Ballantine Books, New York City, 1987. Hardcover.

39. **Sassinak.** With Elizabeth Moon. Published by Baen Books, New York City, 1987. Softcover.

40. **Dragonsdawn.** Published by Del Rey - Ballantine Books, New York City, 1988. Hardcover.

41. **The Carradyne Touch.** Published by Macdonald, London, 1988. Hardcover. Re-titled from The Lady, 1987.

42. **The Renegades of Pern.** Published by Del Rey - Ballantine Books, New York City, 1989. Hardcover.

43. **The Rowan.** Published by Ace/Putnam, New York City, 1990. Hardcover.

44. **Sassinak.** With Elizabeth Moon. Published by the Science Fiction Book Club, Garden City, New York, 1990. First hardcover edition.

45. **The Death of Sleep** With Jody Lynn Nye. Published by Baen Books, New York City, 1990. Softcover.

46. **The Death of Sleep.** With Jody Lynn Nye. Published by the Science Fiction Book Club, Garden City, New York, 1990. First hardcover edition.

Anne McCaffrey

47. Pegasus in Flight. Published by Del Rey - Ballantine Books, New York City, 1990. Hardcover.

48. All the Weyrs of Pern. Published by Del Rey - Ballantine Books, New York City, 1991. Hardcover.

49. Generation Warriors. With Elizabeth Moon. Published by Baen Books, New York City, 1991. Softcover.

50. Generation Warriors. With Elizabeth Moon. Published by the Science Fiction Book Club, Garden City, New York, 1991. First hardcover edition.

51. Rescue Run. Published by Wildside Press, Newark, New Jersey, 1991. Hardcover.

52. Crisis on Doona. With Jody Lynn Nye. Published by Ace Books, New York City, 1992. Softcover.

53. PartnerShip. With Margaret Ball. Published by Baen Books, New York City, 1992. Softcover.

54. PartnerShip. With Margaret Ball. Published by the Science Fiction Book Club, Garden City, New York, 1992. First hardcover edition.

55. The Ship Who Searched. With Mercedes Lackey. Published by Baen Books, New York City, 1992. Softcover.

56. The Ship Who Searched. With Mercedes Lackey. Published by the Science Fiction Book Club, Garden City, New York, 1992. First hardcover edition.

57. Crisis on Doona. With Jody Lynn Nye. Published by the Science Fiction Book Club, Garden City, New York, 1992. First hardcover edition.

58. Damia. Published by Bantam Books, London, 1992. Hardcover. This was released in March and the American edition came out in July.

59. Crystal Line. Published by Del Rey - Ballantine Books, New York City, 1992. Hardcover.

60. Three Women. Published by Tor Books - Tom Doherty Associates, New York City, 1993. Hardcover. This collects: Ring of Fear, 1971; The Mark of Merlin, 1971; and The Kilternan Legacy, 1975.

61. The City Who Fought. With S. M. Stirling. Published by Baen Books, New York City, 1993. Hardcover.

62. Damia's Children. Published by Ace/Putnam, New York City, 1993. Hardcover.

63. The Chronicles of Pern: First Fall. Published by Del Rey - Ballantine Books, New York City, 1993. Hardcover. Herein: The Survey: P.E.R.N., 1993; The Dolphin's Bell, 1993; The Ford of Red Hanrahan, 1993; The Second Weyr, 1993; and Rescue Run, 1991.

64. The Planet Pirates. With Elizabeth Moon and Jody Lynn Nye. Published by Baen Books, New York City, 1993. Softcover. An omnibus edition, this contains: Sassinak, 1990; The Death of Sleep, 1990; and Generation Warriors, 1991.

65. Powers That Be. With Elizabeth Ann Scarborough. Published by Del Rey - Ballantine Books, New York City, 1993. Hardcover.

66. The Dolphin's Bell. Published by Wildside Press, Newark, New Jersey, 1993. Hardcover.

67. Lyon's Pride. Published by Ace/Putnam, New York City, 1994. Hardcover.

68. Power Lines. With Elizabeth Ann Scarborough. Published by Bantam Books, London, 1994. Hardcover. This came out in June, the U.S. edition was released the following month.

69. The Dolphins of Pern. Published by Del Rey - Ballantine Books, New York City, 1994. Hardcover.

70. The Girl Who Heard Dragons. Published by Tor Books - Tom Doherty Associates, New York City, 1994. Hardcover. Herein: Introduction: So, You're Anne McCaffrey by **Anne McCaffrey**; Cinderella Switch, 1981; The Girl Who Heard Dragons, 1986; Velvet Fields, 1973; Euterpe on a Fling, 1995; Duty Calles, 1988; A Sleeping Humpty Dumpty Beauty, 1990; The Mandalay Cure, 1995; A Flock of Geese, 1985; The Greatest Love, 1977; A Quiet One, 1995; If Madam Likes You..., 1989; Zulei, Grace, Nimshi, and the Damnyankees, 1995; Habit is an Old Horse, 1995; Lady-in-Waiting, 1995; and The Bones Do Lie, 1995.

71. Treaty at Doona. With Jody Lynn Nye. Published by Orbit Books, London, 1994. Hardcover.

72. The Ship Who Won. With Jody Lynn Nye. Published by Baen Books, New York City, 1994. Hardcover.

73. An Exchange of Gifts. Published by Wildside Press, Newark New Jersey, 1995. Hardcover.

74. Freedom's Landing. Published by Ace/Putnam, New York City, 1995. Hardcover.

75. Power Play. With Elizabeth Ann Scarborough. Published by Bantam Books, London, 1995. Hardcover. This came out in April, the U.S. edition was released in July.

76. The Crystal Singer Trilogy. Published by Del Rey - Ballantine Books, New York City, 1996. Hardcover. This collects: The Crystal Singer, 1982; Killashandra, 1984; and Crystal Line, 1992.

77. Red Star Rising. Published by Bantam Books, London, 1996. Hardcover.

78. Black Horses for the King. Published by Harcourt Brace, New York City, 1996. Hardcover.

79. The Dinosaur Planet. Published by Severn House, London, 1996. First hardcover edition.

80. No One Noticed the Cat. Published by Wildside Press, United States, 1996. Hardcover.

81. Dragonseye. Published by Del Rey - Ballantine Books, New York City, 1997. Hardcover. Re-titled from Red Star Rising, 1996.

82. Survivors: Book Two of the Dinosaur Planet Saga. Published by Severn House, London, 1997. First hardcover edition.

83. Freedom's Choice. Published by Ace/Putnam, New York City, 1997. Hardcover.

84. Acorna: The Unicorn Girl. With Margaret Ball. Published by Harper Prism, New York City, 1997. Hardcover.

85. A Diversity of Dragons. With Richard Woods. Published by Harper Prism, New York City, 1997. Hardcover.

86. The Masterharper of Pern. Published by Del Rey - Ballantine Books, New York City, 1998. Hardcover.

87. Freedom's Challenge. Published by Ace/Putnam, New York City, 1998. Hardcover.

88. If Wishes Were Horses. Published by Roc/Penguin, New York City, 1998. Hardcover.

89. Nimisha's Ship. Published by Bantam Books, London, 1998. Hardcover.

90. Acorna's Quest. With Margaret Ball. Published by Harper Prism, New York City, 1998. Hardcover.

91. The Tower and the Hive. Published by Ace/Putnam, New York City, 1999. Hardcover.

92. Acorna's People. With Elizabeth Ann Scarborough. Published by Harper Prism, New York City, 1999. Hardcover.

93. Acorna's World. With Elizabeth Ann Scarborough. Published by Harper Collins, New York City, 2000. Hardcover.

94. Pegasus in Space. Published by Del Rey - Ballantine Books, New York City, 2000. Hardcover.

95. Acorna's Search. With Elizabeth Ann Scarborough. Published by Eos, New York City, 2001. Hardcover.

96. The Skies of Pern. Published by Bantam Books/Transworld, London, 2001. Hardcover. This was released in February - the U.S. edition came out in April.

97. The Dinosaur Planet Omnibus. Published by Orbit/Little Brown, London, 2001. Softcover. Herein: Dinosaur Planet, 1978; and Dinosaur Planet Survivors, 1984.

98. Freedom's Ransom. Published by G. P. Putnam's Sons, New York City, 2002. Hardcover.

99. The Book of Freedoms. Published by the Science Fiction Book Club, Garden City, New York, 2002. An omnibus edition, this gathers: Freedom's Landing, 1995; Freedom's Choice, 1997; and Freedom's Challenge, 1998.

100. A Gift of Dragons. Published by Del Rey - Ballantine Books, New York City, 2002. Hardcover. This contains: The Smallest Dragonboy, 1973; The Girl Who Heard Dragons, 1986; Runner of Pern, 1998; and Ever the Twain, 2002.

101. Brain Ships. With Mercedes Lackey and Margaret Ball. Published by Baen Books, New York City, 2003. Hardcover. This collects: The Ship Who Searched, 1992; and PartnerShip, 1992.

102. On Dragonwings. Published by Del Rey - Ballantine Books, New York City, 2003. Softcover. An omnibus edition, this gathers: Dragonsdawn, 1988; Dragonseye, 1996; and Moreta: Dragonlady of Pern, 1983.

103. The Mystery of Ireta. Published by Del Rey - Ballantine Books, New York City, 2003. Softcover. This collects: Dinosaur Planet, 1978; and Dinosaur Planet Survivors, 1984.

104. The Ship Who Saved the Worlds. With Jody Lynn Nye. Published by Baen Books, New York City, 2003. Hardcover.

105. Acorna's Rebels. With Elizabeth Ann Scarborough. Published by Eos, New York City, 2003. Hardcover.

106. Dragon's Kin. With Todd McCaffrey. Published by Del Rey - Ballantine Books, New York City, 2003. Hardcover.

107. The City and the Ship. With S. M. Stirling. Published by Baen Books, New York City, 2004. Hardcover. Herein: The City Who Fought, 1993; and The Ship Avenged by S. M. Stirling, 1997.

108. Acorna's Triumph. With Elizabeth Ann Scarborough. Published by Eos, New York City, 2004. Hardcover.

109. Doona. Published by Ace Books, New York City, 2004. Softcover. Herein: Crisis on Doona, 1992; and Treaty at Doona, 1994.

110. Moreta's Ride. Published by the Science Fiction Book Club, Garden City, New York, 2005. Hardcover. Herein: Moreta: Dragonlady of Pern, 1983; and Nerilka's Story, 1986.

111. Changelings. With Elizabeth Ann Scarborough. Published by Del Rey - Ballantine Books, New York City, 2005. Hardcover.

112. First Warning - Acorna's Children. With Elizabeth Ann Scarborough. Published by Eos, New York City, 2005. Hardcover.

113. Maelstrom. With Elizabeth Ann Scarborough. Published by Del Rey - Ballantine Books, New York City, 2006. Hardcover.

114. Second Wave - Acorna's Children. With Elizabeth Ann Scarborough. Published by Eos, New York City, 2006. Hardcover.

115. Dragon's Fire. With Todd McCaffrey. Published by Del Rey - Ballantine Books, New York City, 2006. Hardcover.

116. Third Watch - Acorna's Children. With Elizabeth Ann Scarborough. Published by Eos, New York City, 2007. Hardcover.

117. Dragon Harper. With Todd McCaffrey. Published by Del Rey - Ballantine Books, New York City, 2007. Hardcover.

118. Deluge. With Elizabeth Ann Scarborough. Published by Del Rey - Ballantine Books, New York City, 2008. Hardcover.

119. Catalyst: A Tale of the Barque Cats. With Elizabeth Ann Scarborough. To be published by Del Rey - Ballantine Books, New York City, 2010. Hardcover.

***

Anne McCaffrey

ANTHOLOGIES

1. Alchemy and Academe. Published by Doubleday & Company, Garden City, New York, 1970. Hardcover. All from the year the book was published, this anthology contains: Foreword by **Anne McCaffrey**; Morning Glory by **Gene Wolfe**; Ascension - a poem by Virginia Kidd; The Devil You Don't by Keith Laumer; The Triumphant Head by Josephine Saxton; A Mess of Porridge by Sonya Dorman; Big Sam by Avram Davidson; More Light by **James Blish**; The Man Who Could Not See Devils by Joanna Russ; The Institute by Carol Emshwiller; Condillac's Statue by R. A. Lafferty; The Sorcerers by L. Sprague de Camp; The Weed of Time by Norman Spinrad; Night and the Loves of Joe Dicostanzo by **Samuel R. Delany**; Come Up and See Me by Daphne Castell; Shut the Last Door by Joe Hensley; The Key to Out by Betsy Curtis; Ringing the Changes by **Robert Silverberg**; In a Quart of Water by David Telfair; The Dance of the Solids by John Updike; and Mainchance by Peter Tate.

2. Space Opera. With Elizabeth Anne Scarborough. Published by DAW Books, New York City, 1996. DAW Collector's Book 1044. Softcover. All from the year the book was published. Herein: Introduction by **Anne McCaffrey** and Elizabeth Anne Scarborough; Saskia by Charles de Lint; To Drive the Cold Winter Away by Marion Zimmer Bradley; Drift by Stephen Brust; The Last Song of Sirit Byar by Peter S. Beagle; Calling Them Home by Jody Lynn Nye; Our Father's Gold by Elisabeth Waters; A Song of Strange Revenge by Josepha Sherman; Songchild by Robin Wayne Bailey; Thunderbird Road by Leslie Fish; Soulfedge Rock by Suzette Haden Elgin; Ever After by Paula Lalish; The Impossible Place by Alan Dean Foster; Bluesberry Jam by **Gene Wolfe**; Roundelay by Mary C. Pangborn; Space Station Annie by Cynthia McQuillin; Swan Song by Lyn McConchie; Heavenside Song by Warren C. Norwood; A Hole in the Sky by Margaret Ball; Scarborough Fair by Elizabeth Ann Scarborough; and Bird in the Hand by **Anne McCaffrey**.

***

NON-FICTION

1. Cooking Out of This World. Published by Ballantine Books, New York City, 1973. Softcover.

2. People of Pern. With Robin Wood. Published by the Donning Company, Norfolk, Virginia. Hardcover.

3. The Dragonlover's Guide to Pern. With Jody Lynn Nye. Published by Del Rey - Ballantine Books, New York City, 1989. Hardcover.

4. Serve It Forth: Cooking With Anne McCaffrey. With John Gregory Betancourt. Published by Warner Aspect, New York City, 1996. Softcover.

***

RELATED

1. Leigh Brackett, Marion Zimmer Bradley, Anne McCaffrey: A Primary and Secondary Bibliography. Published by G. K. Hall, Boston, 1982. Hardcover.

2. Anne McCaffrey. By Mary T. Brizzi. Published by Starmont House, Mercer Island, Washington, 1986. Hardcover.

3. Dragonharper: A Crossroads Adventure in the World of Anne McCaffrey's Pern. By Jody Lynn Nye. Published by Tor Books - Tom Doherty Associates, New York City, 1987. Softcover.

4. Dragonfire: A Crossroads Adventure in the World of Anne McCaffrey's Pern. By Jody Lynn Nye. Published by Tor Books - Tom Doherty Associates, New York City, 1988. Softcover.

5. The Atlas of Pern: A Complete Guide to Anne McCaffrey's Wonderful World of Dragons and Dragonriders. By Karen Wynn Fonstad. Published by Del Rey - Ballantine Books, New York City, 1989. Hardcover.

6. Anne Inez McCaffrey: Forty Years of Publishing. By Matthew D. Hargreaves. Private Printing, Seattle, Washington, 1992. Limited edition hardcover.

7. Anne McCaffrey: Dragonlady and More: A Working Bibliography. By Phil Stevensen-Payne and Gordon Benson. Published by Galactic Central Publications, Leeds, England, 1992. Softcover.

8. Anne McCaffrey: A Critical Companion. By Robin Roberts. Published by Greenwood Press, Westport, Connecticut, 1996. Hardcover.

9. Anne McCaffrey: Science Fiction Storyteller. By Martha P. Trachtenberg. Published by Enslow Publishers, United States, 2001. Hardcover.

10. Anne McCaffrey: A Life with Dragons. By Robin Roberts and Gloria Wade Gayles. Published by the University of Mississippi Press, 2007. Hardcover.

-2007-

Ed Emshwiller.

Edmund Alexander Emshwiller was born on February 16th, 1925 in Lansing, Michigan and died of cancer on July 27th, 1990 in Valencia, California.

He graduated the University of Michigan in 1947, studied in Paris with his wife, Carol, at Ecole des Beaux Arts during 1949 and 1950. During 1950 and 1951, he was at the Art Students League of New York. Better known to science fiction aficionados as Emsh, which was how he signed most of his covers and interior line drawings, he started illustrating with Galaxy in 1951.

Between 1951 and 1979, he did over seven hundred covers. At the same time, he did abstracts for art galleries, and worked on films, making his first one in 1959, an experimental five-minute piece that showed the creation of an abstract painting, backed by some very loose jazz.

During the mid-sixties, he received a Ford Foundation grant that gave him enough money to work even harder at his multi-media performance art. In some circles, he was better known for his avant-garde movie making than for his painting.

In 1979, he took the position of Dean at the California Institute of Arts School of Film and Video. In 1983, he founded the Computer Animation Lab at CalArts. And he worked at CalArts until he died.

The February 1979 issue of The Magazine of Fantasy and Science Fiction featured the last Emsh cover during his lifetime. The painting illustrated On Wings of Song by Thomas M. Disch. The year after he died, NESFA used some of his art for Stalking the Wild Resnick, a collection of stories by Michael Resnick. In 1998, Gardner Dozois used one of his earlier paintings, the one from Andre Norton's Galactic Derelict, 1959, on The Good Old Stuff: Adventure SF in the Grand Tradition. And there have been a few since, most recently in 2006 on Daughters of Earth, edited by Justine Larbalestier.

But before retiring from the field of science fiction illustration, he produced some of the most memorable covers. And a few of the ones he did for **Andre Norton** are on books that sell to collector's at between $500.00 and $750.00.

***

AWARDS

1953. Hugo Award as Best Cover Artist.
1960. Hugo Award as Best Professional Artist.
1960. Award of Distinction from the Creative Film Foundation for Lifelines.
1961. Hugo Award as Best Professional Artist.
1962. Hugo Award as Best Professional Artist.
1962. Special Award at the Brussels Experimental Film Festival for Thanatopsis.
1963. Festival of Two Worlds Award in Spoleto, Italy for Totem.
1964. Hugo Award as Best Professional Artist.
1966. Special Events Award at the New York Film Festival for Relativity.
1966. London Film Festival for Relativity.
1966. Special Jury Award at the Oberhausen Film Festival for Relativity.
1969. Most Original Film Award at the Mannheim Festival for Image, Flesh and Voice.
2007. Inducted in The Science Fiction Hall of Fame.

***

FILMS AND TELEVISON

1. **Dance Chromatic.** 1959. 7 minutes.
2. **Transformation.** 1959. 5 minutes.
3. **Lifelines.** 1960. 7 minutes.
4. **Variable Studies.** 1960. Incomplete.
5. **Thanatopsis.** 1962. 5 minutes.
6. **The Streets of Greenwood.** 1962. 20 minutes.
7. **Time of the Heathen.** 1962. Cinematography, editing and art direction. 75 minutes.
8. **The American Way.** 1962. Cinematography. 10 minutes.
9. **Totem.** 1963. 16 minutes.
10. **The Existentialist.** 1963. Cinematography. 8 minutes.
11. **Transformations.** 1963. 16 Minutes.
12. **Hallelujah the Hills.** 1963. Actor and cinematography. 88 minutes.
13. **Scrambles.** 1964. 15 minutes.
14. **Body Works.** 1965. Film and performance.
15. **George Dumpson's Place.** 1965. 8 minutes.
16. **Relativity.** 1966. 38 minutes.
17. **Galaxie.** 1966. One of the interviewees. 82 minutes.
18. **Image, Flesh and Voice.** 1969. 77 minutes.
19. **Don't Look Back.** 1967. He worked as a cinematographer on this D. A. Pennebaker film about Bob Dylan. 96 minutes.
20. **Diaries Notes and Sketches.** 1969. One of the interviewees, along with: Timothy Leary; Andy Warhol; Allen Ginsberg; Norman Mailer; John Lennon; Yoko Ono; et al. 180 minutes.
21. **Jr. Trek.** 1969. Cinematography. 8 minutes.
22. **Branches.** 1970. 102 minutes.
23. **Carol.** 1970. 6 minutes.
24. **Film with Three Dancers.** 1970. 20 minutes.
25. **Images.** 1971. 30 minutes.
26. **Choice Chance Woman Dance.** 1971. 44 minutes.
27. **Millhouse.** 1971. Cinematography. 92 minutes.
28. **Scape-mates.** 1972. 28:16 minutes.
29. **Scape-mates.** 1972. 28 minutes.
30. **Thermogenesis.** 1972. 11:55 minutes.
31. **Computer Graphics #1.** 1972. 11:55 minutes.
32. **Thermogenesis - Assembly #2 of Computer**

Ed Emshwiller

Graphics #1. 1972. 12 minutes.
33. Pilobolus and Joan. 1973. 57:40 minutes.
34. Positive Negative Electronic Faces. 1973. 30 minutes.
35. Painters Painting: The New York Art Scene 1940 - 1970. 1973. Uncredited cameraman. 116 minutes.
36. Chrysalis. 1973. 21.5 minutes.
37. Crossings and Meetings. 1974. 27:33 minutes.
38. Family Focus. 1975. 57:33 minutes.
39. Inside Edges. 1975. 16 minutes.
40. Collisions. 1976. 4 minutes.
41. New England Visions past and Present. With William Irwin Thompson. 1976. 29 minutes.
42. Self-Trio. 1976. 8 minutes.
43. Sur Faces. 1977. 58 minutes.
44. Slivers. 1977. Installation. 30 minutes.
45. Dubs. 1978. 24 minutes.
46. Sunstone. 1979. 2:57 minutes.
47. Removes. 1980. 25 minutes.
48. Eclipse. 1980. 30 minutes.
49. The Lathe of Heaven. 1980. Worked on the special effects for this filmed version of the book by **Ursula K. Le Guin**. 105 minutes.
50. Eclipse. 1982. 16 minutes.
51. Passes. 1983. Installation. 25 minutes.
52. Skin Matrix. 1984. 16:57 minutes.
53. Skin Matrix S. 1984. 8:46 minutes.
54. Vertigo. With Roger Ridley. 1986. 19 minutes.
55. Hungers. With Morton Subotnick. 1987. 70 minutes.
57. Hungers. 1988. 28 minutes.
58. Version-Stages. With Roger Reynolds. 1989. 21 minutes.

***

RELATED

1. Intersecting Images: The Cinema of Ed Emshwiller. By Robert A. Haller. Published by Anthology Film Archives, New York City, 1997. Softcover.

2. Emshwiller Infinity X Two: The Art and Life of Ed and Carol Emshwiller. By Luis Ortiz. Published by Nonstop Press, New York City, 2007. Hardcover.

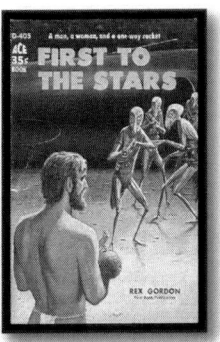

Gene Roddenberry.

Eugene Wesley Roddenberry was born on August 19, 1921 in El Paso, Texas. He died of heart failure in Santa Monica, California on October 24th, 1991. Some of his ashes were taken up to be ditched in space during the STS-52 mission of the Space Shuttle Columbia in 1992.

Five years later, more of his ashes were sent into orbit on a Pegasus XL rocket by Celestis, a company that specializes in sending cremains into space. Another launch is planned for 2012 to send even more of his ashes up, along with those of his wife, Majel Barrett, known to Star Trek fans for her role as Nurse Christine Chapel.

He grew up in Los Angeles, where his father worked for the L.A. Police Department. After high school, he went to Los Angeles City College, then Columbia University, The University of Miami and The University of Southern California without graduating from any of them.

In 1941, he was in the U.S. Army Air Corps and flew somewhere around ninety combat missions in the Pacific, winning both the Distinguished Flying Cross and the Air Medal. After the Army, he was a pilot for Pan American World Airways.

But he wanted to write. He quit flying, signed on as a cop with the L.A. Police Department in 1949, and made a living at that while he tried to break into television.

He quit the cop job in 1956 and went to work full-time as a writer.

Some of his earliest writing was used on Mr District Attorney, which had been a long running radio show. In 1954, it went to television and survived for eight episodes. Roddenberry wrote most of them while was an L.A. cop. Then he was, appropriately, on to Highway Patrol...

***

AWARDS

1967. Hugo Best Dramatic Presentation Award for Star Trek - the Menagerie.
1968. Hugo Special Award for Star Trek.
1977. Executive Achievement Award from the Academy of Science Fiction, Fantasy and Horror Films.
1980. Life Career Award from the Academy of Science Fiction, Fantasy and Horror Films.
1992. George Pal Memorial Award from the Academy of Science Fiction, Fantasy and Horror Films.
2007. Inducted into The Science Fiction Hall of Fame.

***

FILMS AND TELEVISION

1. Mr District Attorney. He wrote six episodes for this series, which starred David Brian and Vicki Vola. They were aired in 1954. The titles were: Patrol Boat; Police Brutality; Court Escape; Police Academy; Defense Plant Gambling; and Wife Killer.

2. Highway Patrol. Wrote five episodes of this in 1955 and 1956. The series starred Broderick Crawford. They were: Human Bomb; Reformed Criminal; Mental Patient; Prospector; and Oil Lease.

3. I Led 3 Lives. He wrote two episodes for this series in 1956. The show starred Patricia Morrow, John Beradino and William Hudson. The episode were: Radioactive; and Discredit Police.

4. Chevron Hall of Stars. One episode for this series in 1956, The Secret Weapon of 117. It starred: Sheila Bromley; John Litel; and Ricardo Montalban.

5. West Point. Also known as The West Point Story. Between October 1956 and July 1957, he wrote nine episodes: The Operator and the Martinet; Man of Action; Double Reverse; Christmas Present; Jet Fight; The Command; The Drowning of the Gun; Pressure; and Dragoon Patrol.

6. Dr Christian. In 1957, Roddenberry wrote two episodes for this series, which starred Macdonald Carey: The Philanthropist; and Bullet Wound.

7. The Kaiser Aluminum Hour. Wrote one episode for this series in 1957, So Short a Season, starring: Seth Edwards; John Litel; Hope Emerson; Albert Salmi; and Susan Oliver.

8. Boots and Saddles. He wrote four of these for 1957 and 1958: The Gatling Gun; Prussian Farmers; The Marquis of Donnybrook; and Rescue of the Stranger. The series starred: John Pickard; Patrick McVey; Gardner McKay; and Dave Willock.

9. Jane Wyman Presents The Fireside Theatre. One episode for this show in 1957, The Perfect Alibi, starring: Vincent Price; Gilman Rankin; and Edwin Reimers.

10. Have Gun - Will Travel. Starting in September 1957 and working until March 1963, Roddenberry wrote twenty-four episodes of this Richard Boone Series: The Great Mojave Chase; The Yuma Treasure; The Hanging Cross; Helen of Abajinian; Ella West; The Hanging of Roy Carter; The Road to Wickenberg; Juliet; The Monster of Moon Ridge; Maggie O'Bannion; Return of Roy Carter; Episode in Laredo; Les Girls; The Posse; The Gold Toad; Tiger; Charley Red Dog; El Paso Stage; Alice; Taylor's Woman; Marshal of Sweetwater; Cage at McNaab; and The Savages.

11. Jefferson Drum. In 1958, he wrote four episodes for this, which starred Jeff Richards: Law and Order; Madame Faro; The Post; and Stagecoach Episode.

12. Harbor Command. He wrote one episode of this, in 1958: The Psychiatrist. The show starred Wendell Corey and Casey Walters.

Gene Roddenberry

13. Hotel de Paree. He wrote one episode of this for 1960, Sundance and the Black Widow, starring Earl Holliman and Jeanette Nolan.

14. The Detectives starring Robert Taylor. He wrote two episodes for this, in 1960: Karate; and Blue Fire.

15. The DuPont Show with June Allyson. Wrote one episode in 1960, Escape, starring Brian Donlevy and Norman Leavitt.

16. Alcoa Theatre. He wrote one episode for this in 1960, 333 Montgomery Street, which starred: Tol Avery; Joanna Barnes; and DeForest Kelly.

17. Wrangler. He wrote a single episode of this in 1960, Incident at the Bar M. The series starred Jason Evers.

18. Whiplash. Roddenberry created four episodes for this series in 1961: Episode in Bathurst; Dutchman's Reef; The Actress; and Sarong. The series starred Peter Graves and Anthony Wickert.

19. Two Faces West. For this series, he wrote one episode in 1961, The Lesson, which starred Charles Bateman and Joyce Meadows.

20. Shannon. Wrote two of these in 1961, The Embezzler's Daughter and The Pickup. The series starred George Nader and Candy Moore.

21. Target: The Corruptors. Wrote one episode, To Wear a Badge, in 1961. It starred: Michael Constantine and Robert Culp, with Robert Vaughn.

22. Dr Kildare. He wrote one episode of this Richard Chamberlain show, A Distant Thunder. It aired in 1962.

23. Naked City. And he wrote one episode for this series, The Rydecker Case for 1962. The show starred Paul Burke.

24. G.E. True. His single episode of this, V-Victor 5, ran in 1962, starring Jack Webb as the host.

25. The Virginian. Wrote one episode for this, Run Away Home, for 1963. It starred: James Drury; Lee J. Cobb; and Doug McClure.

26. The Lieutenant. He worked mainly as the producer on this show, doing 29 shows from September 1963 until April 1964, although he did write three of the episodes: A Very Private Affair; The Alien; and To Kill a Man. The series starred Gary Lockwood and Robert Vaughn.

27. Police Story. This was written and produced by Roddenberry in 1967. It starred Steve Ihnat; Rafer Johnson; and DeForest Kelly.

28. Star Trek. He wrote some of the teleplays, wrote some of the stories, and produced eighty episodes of this between September 8th, 1966 and June 3rd, 1969. Along the way, he managed to use the work of a fairly reasonable number of science fiction writers, including: George Clayton Johnson; Richard Matheson; Robert Bloch; Jerry Sohl; **Theodore Sturgeon**; Fredric Brown; Harlan Ellison; Jerome Bixby; Norman Spinrad; and David Gerrold; et al.

The show starred: William Shatner; Leonard Nimoy; DeForest Kelly; George Takei; Nichelle Nichols; James Doohan; Walter Koenig; Majel Barrett; Eddie Paskey; Bill Blackburn; Frank da Vinci; Roger Holloway; and many, many others.

The episodes were:
Season One:
1966:

1. The Man Trap - September 8th; 2. Charlie X - September 15th; 3. Where No Man Has Gone Before - September 22nd; 4. The Naked Time - September 29th; 5. The Cage - September 30th; 6. The Enemy Within - October 6th; 7. Mudd's Women - October 13th; 8. What Are Little Girls Made Of? - October 20th; 9. Miri - October 27th; 10. Dagger of the Mind - November 3rd; 11. The Corbomite Maneuver, November 10th; 12. The Menagerie: Part One - November 17th; 13. The Menagerie: Part Two - November 24th; 14. The Conscience of the King - December 8th; 15. Balance of Terror - December 15th; 16. Shore Leave - December 19th.

1967:

17. The Galileo Seven - January 5th; 18. The Squire of Gothos - January 12th; 19. Arena - January 19th; 20. Tomorrow Is Yesterday, January 26th; 21. Court Martial - February 2nd; 22. The Return of the Archons - February 9th; 23. Space Seed - February 16th; 24. A Taste of Armageddon - February 23rd; 25. This Side of Paradise - March 2nd; 26. The Devil in the Dark - March 9th; 27. Errand of Mercy - March 23rd; 28. The Alternative Factor - March 30th; 29. The City on the Edge of Forever - April 6th; 30. Operation - Annihilate! - April 13th;

Season Two:

31. Amok Time - September 15th; 32. Who Mourns for Adonais? - September 22nd; 33. The Changeling - September 29th; 34. Mirror, Mirror - October 6th; 35. The Apple - October 13th; 36. The Doomsday machine - October 20th; 37. Catspaw - October 27th; 38. I, Mudd - November 3rd; 39. Metamorphosis - November 10th; 40. Journey to Babel, November 17th; 41. Friday's Child - December 1st; 42. The Deadly Years - December 8th; 43. Obsession - December 15th; 44. Wolf in the Fold, December 22nd; 45. The Trouble with Tribbles - December 29th.

1968:

46. The Gamesters of Triskelion - January 5th; 47. A Piece of the Action - January 12th; 48. The Immunity Syndrome - January 19th; 49. A Private Little War - February 2nd; 50. Return to Tomorrow - February 9th; 51. Patterns of Force - February 16th; 52. By Any Other Name - February 23rd; 53. The Omega Glory - March 1st; 54. The Ultimate Computer - March 8th; 55. Bread and Circuses - March 15th; 56. Assignment: Earth - March 29th;

Season Three:

57. Spock's Brain - September 20th; 58. The Enterprise Incident - September 27th; 59. The Paradise Syndrome - October 4th; 60. And the Children Shall Lead - October 11th; 61. Is There in Truth No Beauty? - October 18th; 62. Spectre of the Gun - October 25th; 63. Day of the Dove - November 1st; 64. For the World Is Hollow and I Have Touched the Sky - November 8th; 65. The Tholian Web - November 15th; 66. Plato's Stepchildren - November 22nd; 67. Wink of an Eye - November 29th; 68. The Empath - December 6th; 69. Elaan of Troyius - December 20th.

1969:
70. Whom the Gods Destroy - January 3rd; 71. Let That Be Your Last Battlefield - January 10th; 72. The Mark of Gideon - January 17th; 73. That Which Survives - January 24th; 74. The Lights of Zetar - January 31st; 75. Requiem for Methuselah - February 14th; 76. The Way to Eden - February 21st; 77. The Cloud Minders - February 28th; 78. The Savage Curtain - March 7th; 79. All Our Yesterdays - March 14th; and 80. Turnabout Intruder - June 3rd.

29. Alias Smith and Jones. He wrote one episode of this in 1971, The Girl in Boxcar #3. The show starred Pete Duel and Ben Murphy.

30. Pretty Maids All in a Row. He produced and did the writing for this 1971 Roger Vadim film which starred: Rock Hudson; Angie Dickinson; Telly Savalas; Roddy McDowall; James Doohan; and many others

31. Genesis II. Produced and wrote this 1973 TV movie, which was directed by John Llewellyn Moxey and starred: Alex Cord; Mariette Hartley; Ted Cassidy; Majel Barrett; et al.

32. Star Trek. The animated series first aired on September 8th, 1973 and ran for twenty-two episodes, until October 12, 1974. Roddenberry was the creator and the executive consultant. The series featured the voices of the original Star Trek cast: William Shatner; Leonard Nimoy; DeForest Kelly; Nichelle Nichols; James Doohan; Majel Barrett; and George Takei.
The episodes were:
1973:
1. Beyond the Farthest Star - September 8th; 2. Yesteryear - September 15th; 3. One of Our Planets Is Missing - September 22nd; 4. The Lorelei Signal - September 29th; 5. More Tribbles, More Troubles - October 6th; 6. The Survivor - October 13th; 7. The Infinite Vulcan - October 20th, 1973; 8. The Magicks of Megas-Tu - October 27th; 9. Once Upon a Planet - November 3rd; 10. Mudd's Passion - November 10th; 11. The Terratin Incident - November 17th; 12. The Time Trap - November 24th; 13. The Ambergris Element - December 1st; 14. The Slaver Weapon - December 15th.
1974:
15. The Eye of the Beholder - January 5th; 16. The Jihad - January 12th; 17. The Pirates of Orion - September 7th; 18. Bem - September 14th; 19. The Practical Joke - September 21st; 20. Albatross - September 28th; 21. How Sharper Than a Serpent's Tooth - October 5th; and 22. The Counter-Clock Incident - October 12th.

33. The Questor Tapes. Wrote and produced this 1974 TV movie, which was directed by Richard A. Colla and starred: Robert Foxworth; Mike Farrell; John Vernon; Lew Ayres; James Shigeta; Dana Wynter; Majel Barrett; and Walter Koenig.

34. Planet Earth. Came up with the story and produced this 1974 movie for television. Directed by Marc Daniels, who did a number of the Star Trek episodes, it starred: John Saxon; Janet Margolin; Ted Cassidy; Diana Muldaur; Majel Barrett; and others.

35. Spectre. Produced and wrote for the screenplay for this 1977 film. Directed by Clive Donner, it starred: Robert Culp; Gig Young; John Hurt; Majel Barrett; and others.

36. Star Trek: The Motion Picture. Working with Alan Dean Foster for the story, Roddenberry produced this for the theatres in 1979. It starred: William Shatner; Leonard Nimoy; DeForest Kelley; James Doohan; George Takei; Nichelle Nichols; Majel Barrett; Walter Koenig; and many, many others.

37. Star Trek: The Wrath of Khan. He acted as a creative consultant on this 1982 film. Directed by Nicholas Meyer, it featured Ricardo Montalban, Kirstie Alley and Paul Winfield, along with the usual cast: William Shatner; Leonard Nimoy; DeForest Kelley; James Doohan; George Takei; Nichelle Nichols; and Walter Koenig.

38. Star Trek III: The Search for Spock. From 1984, Roddenberry was the executive consultant on this and, of course, the creator of the concept. Directed by Leonard Nimoy, it starred: William Shatner; Leonard Nimoy; DeForest Kelley; James Doohan; George Takei; Nichelle Nichols; and Walter Koenig; along with: Christopher Lloyd; John Larroquette; Miguel Ferrer; and many others.

39. Star Trek IV: The Voyage Home. Again directed by Leonard Nimoy and with Roddenberry listed as executive consultant, this 1986 film features all the usual cast: William Shatner; Leonard Nimoy; DeForest Kelley; James Doohan; George Takei; Nichelle Nichols; and Walter Koenig; along with: Jane Wyatt; Catherine Hicks; John Schuck; Mark Lenard; Majel Barrett; et al.

40. Star Trek V: The Final Frontier. Written and directed by William Shatner, Roddenberry was again the executive consultant, 1989. The film starred: William Shatner; Leonard Nimoy; DeForest Kelley; James Doohan; George Takei; Nichelle Nichols; and Walter Koenig; along with: David Warner; Laurence Luckinbill; and others.

41. Star Trek VI: The Undiscovered Country. From 1991, this was written by Leonard Nimoy and was dedicated to the memory of **Gene Roddenberry**. Of course, it starred: William Shatner; Leonard Nimoy; DeForest Kelley; James Doohan; George Takei; Nichelle Nichols; and Walter Koenig. Joining them were: Kim Cattrall; Mark Lenard; Christopher Plummer; David Warner; John Schuck; Michael Dorn; and Christian Slater; with Rene Auberjonois in an uncredited part as Colonel West.

42. Star Trek: The Next Generation. He was the creator of this sequel to Star Trek, and credited as such for all 176 episodes. And he was the executive producer of the first 125 episodes, from 1987 and on into 1992, even after his death in October 1991. The series starred: Patrick Stewart; Jonathan Frakes; LeVar Burton; Marina Sirtis; Brent Spiner; Michael Dorn; Gates McFadden; Majel Barrett; Wil Wheaton; Colm Meaney; Denise Crosby; Whoopi Goldberg; Diana Muldaur; et al.
The following are the episodes for which Roddenberry was listed as the executive producer:
Season One:

Gene Roddenberry

1987:
1. Encounter at Farpoint - September 26th; 2. The Naked Now October 3rd; 3. Code of Honor - October 10th; 4. The Last Outpost - October 17th; 5. Where No One Has Gone Before - October 24th; 6. Lonely Among Us - October 31st; 7. Justice - November 7th; 8. The Battle - November 14th; 9. Hide and Q - November 21st; 10. Haven - November 29th.

1988:
11. The Big Goodbye - January 9th; 12. Datalore - January 16th; 13. Angel One - January 23rd; 14. 11001001 - January 30th; 15. Too Short a Season - February 6th; 16. When the Bough Breaks - February 13th; 17. Home Soil - February 20th; 18. Coming of Age - March 12th; 19. Heart of Glory - March 19th; 20. The Arsenal of Freedom - April 9th; 21. Symbiosis - April 16th; 22. Skin of Evil - April 23rd; 23. We'll Always Have Paris - April 30th; 24. Conspiracy - May 7th; 25. The Neutral Zone - May 14th.

Season Two:
26. The Child - November 19th; 27. Where Silence Has Lease - November 26th; 28. Elementary, Dear Data - December 3rd; 29. The Outrageous Okona - December 10th.

1989:
30. Loud as a Whisper - January 7th; 31. The Schizoid Man - January 21st; 32. Unnatural Selection - January 29th; 33. A Matter of Honor - February 4th; 34. The Measure of a Man - February 11th; 35. The Dauphin - February 18th; 36. Contagion - March 18th; 37. The Royale - March 25th; 38. Time Squared - April 1st; 39. The Icarus Factor - April 22nd; 40. Pen Pals - April 29th; 41. Q Who? - May 6th; 42. Samaritan Snare - May 13th; 43. Up the Long Ladder - May 20th; 44. Manhunt - June 17th; 45. The Emissary - June 24th; 46. Peak Performance - July 8th; 47. Shades of Gray - July 15th.

Season Three:
48. Evolution - September 23rd; 49. The Ensigns of Command - September 30th; 50. The Survivors - October 7th; 51. Who Watches the Watchers - October 14th; 52. The Bonding - October 21st; 53. Booby Trap - October 28th; 54. The Enemy - November 4th; 55. The Price - November 11th; 56. The Vengeance Factor - November 18th; 57. The Defector - December 30th.

1990:
58. The Hunted - January 6th; 59. The High Ground - January 27th; 60. Déjà Q - February 3rd; 61. A Matter of Perspective - February 10th; 62. Yesterday's Enterprise - February 17th; 63. The Offspring - March 10th; 64. Sins of the Father - March 17th; 65. Allegiance - March 24th; 66. Captain's Holiday - March 31st; 67. Tin man - April 21st; 68. Hollow Pursuits - April 28th; 69. The Most Toys - May 5th; 70. Sarek - May 12th; 71. Ménage a Troi - May 26th; 72. Transfigurations - June 2nd; 74. The Best of Both Worlds: Part One - June 16th.

Season Four:
75. The Best of Both Worlds: Part Two - September 22nd; 76. Brothers - October 6th; 77. Suddenly Human - October 13th; 78. Remember Me - October 20th; 79. Legacy - October 27th; 80. Reunion - November 3rd; 81. Future Imperfect - November 10th; 82. Final Mission - November 17th; 83. The Loss - December 29th.

1991:
84. Data's Day - January 5th; 85. The Wounded - January 26th; 86. Devil's Due - February 2nd; 87. Clues - February 9th; 88. First Contact - February 16th; 89. Galaxy's Child - March 9th; 90. Night Terrors - March 16th; 91. Identity Crisis - March 23rd; 92. The Nth Degree - March 30th; 93. Qpid - April 20th; 94. The Drumhead - April 27th; 95. Half a Life - May 4th; 96. The Host - May 11th; 97. The Mind's Eye - May 25th; 98. In Theory - June 1st; 99. Redemption: Part One - June 15th.

Season Five:
100. Redemption: Part Two - September 21st; 101. Darmok - September 28th; 102. Ensign Ro - October 5th; 103. Silicon Avatar - October 12th; 104. Disaster - October 19th; 105. The Game - October 26th; 106. Unification: Part One - November 2nd; 107. Unification: Part Two - November 9th; 108. A Matter of Time - November 16th.

1992:
109. New Ground - January 4th; 110. Hero Worship - January 25th; 111. Violations - February 1; 112. The Masterpiece Society - February 8th; 113. Conundrum - February 15th; 114. Power Play - February 22nd; 115. Ethics - February 29th; 116. The Outcast - March 14th; 117. Cause and Effect - March 21st; 118. The First Duty - March 29th; 119. Cost of Living - April 19th; 120. The Perfect Mate - April 25th; 121. Imaginary Friend - May 2nd; 122. I, Borg - May 9th; 123. The Next Phase - May 16th; 124. The Inner Light - May 30th; and 125. Time's Arrow - Part One - June 13th.

43. Star Trek 25th Anniversary Special. Roddenberry was the executive producer for this. Directed by Donald R. Beck, it was released in 1991 with William Shatner and Leonard Nimoy as the hosts. The guests included: **Gene Roddenberry**; Deforest Kelley; George Takei; Buzz Aldrin; Nichelle Nichols; Ricardo Montalban; Patrick Stewart; Whoopi Goldberg; Jonathan Frakes; and many, many others.

44. Star Trek: Generations. Simply the creator of the concept for this one. The film was directed by David Carson for release in 1994. It starred: Patrick Stewart; Jonathan Frakes; Brent Spiner; LeVar Burton; Michael Dorn; Gates McFadden; Martina Sirtis; William Shatner; James Doohan; Walter Koenig; and Malcolm McDowell; et al.

45. William Shatner's Star Trek Memories. Simply the creator of Star Trek, as in **Gene Roddenberry**'s Star Trek. This was done for television in 1995.

46. Star Trek: First Contact. Simply based on Roddenberry's original idea, this 1996 film was directed by Jonathan Frakes and starred: Patrick Stewart; Jonathan Frakes; Brent Spiner; LeVar Burton; Michael Dorn; Gates McFadden; Martina Sirtis; and others.

47. Star Trek: Insurrection. Again, based on Roddenberry's original idea, this 1998 film was directed by Jonathan Frakes and starred: Patrick Stewart; Jonathan Frakes; Brent Spiner; LeVar Burton; Michael Dorn; Gates McFadden; Martina Sirtis; and others.

48. Star Trek: Deep Space Nine. Based on a concept of Roddenberry's, this television series ran for 173 episodes, beginning on January 3rd, 1993 and finishing on June 2nd, 1999. The stars were: Avery Brooks; Rene Auberjonois; Cirroc Lofton; Alexander Siddig; Colm Meaney; Armin Shimerman; Nana Visitor; Terry Farrell; and Michael Dorn.

49. Star Trek: Voyager. Another Roddenberry concept, this television series survived 171 episodes, from January 16th, 1995 until May 23rd, 2001. The series starred: Kate Mulgrew; Robert Beltran; Roxann Dawson; Robert Duncan McNeill; Ethan Phillips; Robert Picardo; Tim Russ; Garrett Wang; Tarik Ergin; and Jeri Ryan, with Majel Barrett as the voice of the computer.

50. Earth: Final Conflict. Yet another Roddenberry idea, this series ran for 110 episodes, starting October 6th, 1997 and running until May 13th, 2002. It starred: Von Flores; Leni Parker; Anita LaSelva; and others.

51. Star Trek: Nemesis. Again as the creator. This 2002 effort was directed by Stuart Baird and starred: Patrick Stewart; Jonathan Frakes; Brent Spiner; LeVar Burton; Michael Dorn; Marina Sirtis; and Gates McFadden.

52. Gene Roddenberry's Andromeda. Another Roddenberry concept, this produced 110 episodes, starting October 2nd, 2000 and ending on May 13th, 2005. It starred: Kevin Sorbo; Lisa Ryder; Lexa Doig; Gordon Michael Woolvett; and Laura Bertram; et al.

53. Star Trek: Enterprise. Again, a concept. This series went for 98 episodes from September 26th, 2001 until May 13th, 2005. This one starred: Scott Bakula; Jolene Blalock; Dominic Keating; John Billingsley; Anthony Montgomery; Linda Park; Connor Trinneer; and others.

54. Star Trek: Phase II. Originally known as Star Trek: New Voyages, this was put together by fans and stars: James Cawley; Ron Boyd; John M. Kelley; Jeff Mailhotte; and others.

55. Star Trek. For 2009 and directed by J. J. Abrams, this stars: Chris Pine; Zachary Quinto; Leonard Nimoy; Eric Bana; Bruce Greenwood; Karl Urban; Zoe Saldana; Simon Pegg; John Cho; Anton Yelchin; and many others.

***

Published by the Science Fiction Book Club, Garden City, New York, 1980. First hardcover edition.

4. Star Trek. Published by Pocket Books, New York City, 1986. Softcover.

5. The Star Trek Scriptbooks - Book One: The Q Chronicles. Published by Pocket Books, New York City, 1999. Softcover.

***

RELATED

1. Star Trek Speaks: Wit, Wisdom, Humor and Philosophy Directly Culled from the Scripts of the Greatest TV Adventure of All Time. By Susan Sackett, Fred Goldstein and Stan Goldstein. Published by Pocket Books, New York City, 1979. Softcover.

2. The Man Who Created Star Trek: Gene Roddenberry. By James Van Hise. Published by Pioneer Books, Las Vegas, 1992. Softcover.

3. Great Birds of the Galaxy: Gene Roddenberry and the Creators of Trek. By Edward Gross and Mark Altman. Published by Boxtree, London, 1994. Softcover.

4. Star Trek Creator: The Authorized Biography of Gene Roddenberry. By David Alexander with a foreword by **Ray Bradbury**. Published by Roc - Penguin Books, New York City, 1994. Hardcover.

5. Gene Roddenberry: The Last Conversation. By Yvonne Fern with a foreword by **Arthur C. Clarke**. Published by the University of California Press, 1994. Hardcover.

6. Gene Roddenberry: The Myth and the Man Behind Star Trek. By Joel Engel. Published by Hyperion Books, New York City, 1994. Hardcover.

7. Inside Trek: My Secret Life with Star Trek Creator Gene Roddenberry. By Susan Sackett. Published by Hawk Publishing, Tulsa, Oklahoma, 2002. Softcover.

8. Boarding the Enterprise: Transporters, Tribbles and Vulcan Death Grip in Gene Roddenberry's Star Trek. By David Gerrold and Robert J. Sawyer. Published by Benbella Books, Dallas, Texas, 2006. Softcover.

BOOKS

1. The Making of Star Trek. With Stephen E. Whitfield. Published by Ballantine Books, New York City, 1968. Ballantine Book 73004. Softcover.

2. Star Trek: The Motion Picture. Published by Pocket Books, New York City, 1979. Softcover.

3. Star Trek: The Motion Picture.

Ridley Scott.

Sir **Ridley Scott** was born on November 30th, 1937 in South Shields, Tyne and War, England. Always a lover of films, he schooled himself accordingly and graduated the Royal College of Art with a Master of Arts in Graphic Design.

After graduation, he went to work as a set designer-in-training at the BBC. Once he was there, he applied for their director training programme... and was accepted. He worked on some of their more popular television series before striking off on his own in 1968.

He put together his own production company after leaving the BBC, Ridley Scott Associates. Mostly, they made commercials. As he explained it, "I was making far more money in advertising than at the BBC."

In all, his firm produced around 2,500 commercials.

In 1977, he did his first feature film, The Duellists, which won an award at the Cannes Film Festival but was pretty much ignored in the States.

His next film, though, was a huge hit. It was called Alien...

During the making of it, the interference from the studio was so intense that it inspired him to try to take complete control in the future, to produce *and* direct most of his projects. Still, he managed to get the film done in spite of the producers. And Alien re-defined the art of making science fiction movies.

In his pre-Thelma & Louise film-making days, he was often criticized for making long television commercials rather than real movies.

But Alien fans knew better.

***

AWARDS

1977. Best First Work Award at the Cannes Film Festival for The Duellists.
1978. David di Donatello Award for Best Director - Foreign Film for The Duellists.
1980. A Saturn Award for Best Director for Alien from the Academy of Science Fiction, Fantasy and Horror Films.
1983. Hugo Award for Best Dramatic Presentation for Blade Runner.
1991. Golden Spike Award for Thelma & Louise at the Valladolid International Film Festival.
1992. London Critics Circle Film - ALFS Director of the Year Award for Thelma & Louise.
1992. Bodil Award for Best Non-European Film, Thelma & Louise.
2002. Emmy Award for Outstanding Made for Television Movie for The Gathering Storm.
2003. A DVDX Award for Best Audio Commentary for the new DVD, Alien.
2003. Film Excellence Award at the Boston Film Festival.
2003. Knighthood presented by Queen Elizabeth II.
2004. A George Pal Memorial Award from the Academy of Science Fiction, Fantasy and Horror Films.
2007. Inducted into The Science Fiction Hall of Fame.
2008. Audience Sant Jordi Award for Best Foreign Film for American Gangster.

***

As with **Steven Spielberg**, **Ridley Scott** has made a huge number of personal appearances on television and in documentary films; these will not be listed here.

FILMS AND TELEVISION

1. Boy and Bicycle. A twenty-seven minute short film, made in black and white in 1962. His first film, made while he was studying at the Royal College of Art. It starred his brother Tony.

2. Dial M for Murder. Production designer for this BBC Sunday-Night Play. Starring Michael Earl and Diana Fairfax, it aired on August 5th, 1962, Season 3, Episode 44.

3. A Matter of Amnesia. He worked as the production designer on this episode of the series More Faces of Jim, starring: Jimmy Edwards; June Whitefield; and Ronnie Barker. It aired on June 29th, 1963, Season 1, Episode 1.

4. A Matter of Growing Up. Production designer for this installment of More Faces of Jim. It aired on July 5th, 1963, Season 1, Episode 2, starring: Jimmy Edwards; June Whitefield; and Ronnie Barker.

5. A Matter of Spreadeagling. The production designer on this More Faces of Jim episode, 1963. Starring: Jimmy Edwards; June Whitefield; and Ronnie Barker, it aired on July 19th, Season 1, Episode 3.

6. Bold as Brass: Episode 1.1. Production designer for the April 4th, 1964 show, starring: Jimmy Edwards; Beryl Reid; Jill Hyem; and Bill Treacher.

7. Bold as Brass: Episode 1.2. Production designer for the April 18th, 1964 show, starring: Jimmy Edwards; Beryl Reid; Jill Hyem; and Ronnie Barker.

8. Bold as Brass: Episode 1.3. Production designer for the May 2nd, 1964 show, starring: Jimmy Edwards; Beryl Reid; Jill Hyem; and Ronnie Barker.

9. Bold as Brass: Episode 1.4. Production designer for the May 16th, 1964 show, which starred: Jimmy Edwards; Beryl Reid; Jill Hyem; and Ronnie Barker.

10. Bold as Brass: Episode 1.5. Production designer for the May 30th, 1964 show, starring: Jimmy Edwards; Beryl Reid; Jill Hyem; and Ronnie Barker.

11. Bold as Brass: Episode 1.6. Production designer for the June 13th, 1964 show, which starred: Jimmy Edwards; Beryl Reid; Jill Hyem; and Ernest Arnley.

12. Error of Judgement. Directed this episode of Z Cars in 1965. It aired on June 9th, Season 4, Episode 40. This starred: Sara Aimson; Iain Anders; Brian Blessed; Joseph Brady; et al.

13. And No Birds Sang. Production designer for this August 24th, 1965, Season 2, Episode 8 installment of the series R3. It starred: Maurice Hedley; Ken Jones; and Suzy Kendall.

14. Some Lapse of Time. Production designer of this 1965 episode of Out of the Unknown, starring Ronald Lewis and Jane Downs. It aired on December 6th, Season 1, Episode 10.

15. The Hard Word. Directed this for the series Thirty-Minute Theatre. It aired on May 16th, 1966, Season 1, Episode 32. The show starred: Iain Anders; Tony Selby; Jack Woolgar; and Jeremy Young.

16. The League of Uncharitable Ladies. Directed this for the series Adam Adamant Lives! It aired on September 22nd, 1966, Season 1, Episode 13. The stars were: Gerald Harper; Juliet Harmer; Jack May; and others.

17. Death Begins at Seventy. Also directed for Adam Adamant Lives!, this show aired on February 18th, 1967, Season 2, Episode 8, starring: Gerald Harper; Juliet Harmer; Jack May; et al.

18. The Resurrectionists. Directed for the series Adam Adamant Lives! It aired on March 11th, 1967, Season 2, Episode 11. The stars were: Gerald Harper; Juliet Harmer; Jack May; and others.

19. Robert. This was directed for the series Half Hour Story. Starring Robert Langley; Angela Baddeley; Richard Davies; and Freddy Foote, it aired on August 2nd, 1967, Season 1, Episode 12.

20. No Further Questions. Directed for the series The Informer, which starred: Ian Hendry; Neil Hallett; and Jean Marsh. This aired on November 6th, 1967, Season 2, Episode 7.

21. Your Secrets Are Safe with Us, Mr Lambert. Directed for the series The Informer, which starred: Ian Hendry; Neil Hallett; Heather Sears; and Jean Marsh. This aired on November 13th, 1967, Season 2, Episode 8.

22. If He Hollers, Let Him Go. For the series The Troubleshooters, Scott directed this for January 27th, 1969, Season 5, Episode 4. It starred: Basil Clarke; Edward Fox; Lucy Griffiths; and others.

23. One of the Missing. Had an uncredited role as a Unionist Officer in this twenty-six minute, 1971 film which was directed by his brother, Tony Scott and starred Stephen Edwards.

24. The Duellists. As well as directing this, his first feature film, 1977, he was also a camera operator. It was based on the story The Duel, 1908, by Joseph Conrad and starred: Keith Carradine; Harvey Keitel; Albert Finney; Edward Fox; Cristina Raines; Tom Conti; and many others, including Stacy Keach as the narrator.

25. Alien. Directed this 1979 film which starred: Tom Skerritt; Sigourney Weaver; Veronica Cartwright; Harry Dean Stanton; John Hurt; Ian Holm; and Yaphet Kotto; and Bolaji Badejo as the Alien, which was designed by H. R. Giger.

26. Blade Runner. He directed this from the **Philip K. Dick** novel, Do Androids Dream of Electric Sheep?, 1968. He was also the uncredited co-producer. The film was released in 1982, starring: Harrison Ford; Rutger Hauer; Sean Young; Edward James Olmos; M. Emmet Walsh; Daryl Hannah; Joanna Cassidy; and many others.

27. Legend. Based on a story by William Hjortsberg, Scott directed this for release in 1985. The film starred: Tom Cruise; Mia Sara; Tim Curry; Billy Barty; and others.

28. Someone to Watch Over Me. He produced and directed this for released in 1987. It starred: Tom Berenger; Mimi Rogers; Lorraine Bracco; Jerry Orbach; and others.

29. Black Rain. Directed this for 1989, starring: Michael Douglas; Andy Garcia; Ken Takakura; Kate Capshaw; Yusaku Matsuda; Shigeru Koyama; et al.

30. Thelma & Louise. He produced and directed this. From 1991, it starred: Susan Sarandon; Geena Davis; Harvey Keitel; Michael Madsen; and Brad Pitt.

31. 1492: Conquest of Paradise. Producer and director. Released in 1992, this starred: Gerard Depardieu; Armand Assante; Sigourney Weaver; Loren Dean; Angela Molina; Fernando Rey; Frank Langella; and others.

32. Elephant. Directed by Chris Hartwill for television in 1993, Scott was an associate producer on this short film. It starred: Al Gregg; Wayne Michaels; and Lee Sheward.

33. Monkey Trouble. Also known as Pet, Scott was the executive producer. Released in 1994, this was directed by Franco Amurri and starred: Thora Birch; Harvey Keitel; Mimi Rogers; et al.

34. The Browning Version. Working with director Mike Figgis, Scott produced this for 1994. It starred: Albert Finney; Greta Scacchi; Matthew Modine; Julian Sands; Michael Gambon; Ben Silverstone; and many others.

35. White Squall. Produced and directed this 1996 film, which starred: Jeff Bridges; Caroline Goodall; John Savage; Scott Wolf; Jeremy Sisto; and others.

36. The Secret Shih Tan. Produced for the television series The Hunger. It aired on July 27th, 1997, Season 1, Episode 4. The show starred: Jason Scott Lee; Gregoriane Minot Payeur; Robert Ito; and Kenneth Walsh.

37. G. I. Jane. Produced and directed for 1997. The film starred: Demi Moore; Viggo Mortensen; Anne Bancroft; Jason Beghe; John Michael Higgins; Kevin Gage; et al.

38. Clay Pigeons. Producer of this 1998 film, which was directed by David Dobkin and starred: Joaquin Phoenix; Gregory Sporleder; Georgina Cates; Scott

Ridley Scott

Wilson; Vince Vaughn; and others.

39. RKO 281. Executive producer of this 1999 television special, which was directed by Benjamin Ross and starred: Liev Schreiber; James Cromwell; Melanie Griffith; John Malkovich; Brenda Blethyn; Roy Scheider; and others.

40. Where the Money Is. He was the producer on this 2000 film. It was directed by Marek Kanievska and starred: Paul Newman; Linda Fiorentino; Dermot Mulroney; Susan Barnes; and others.

41. Gladiator. As well as directing this, Scott also acted as the uncredited executive producer, and as a camera operator, also uncredited. Released in 2000, the film starred: Russell Crowe; Joaquin Phoenix; Connie Nielsen; Oliver Reed; Richard Harris; Derek Jacobi; Djimon Hounsou; and many, many others.

42. The Last Debate. Executive producer on this 2000 television film. Directed by John Badham, it starred: James Garner; Peter Gallagher; Audra McDonald; Donna Murphy; et al.

43. Hannibal. Produced and directed this 2001 film, which starred: Anthony Hopkins; Julianne Moore; Gary Oldman; Ray Liotta; Francesca Neri; and many others.

44. Black Hawk Down. Producer and director. The 2001 film starred: Josh Hartnett; Ewan McGregor; Tom Sizemore; Eric Bana; William Fichtner; Ewen Bremner; and Sam Shepard.

45. AFP: American Fighter Pilot. One of the executive producers on this reality series, created by Jesse Negron, narrated by Chris Penn and Regina Pope, and showing in 2002.

46. The Gathering Storm. He was the executive producer on this 2002 television film. Directed by Richard Loncraine, it starred: Albert Finney; Vanessa Redgrave; Jim Broadbent; Linus Roache; Lena Headey; Derek Jacobi; Ronnie Barker; Tom Wilkinson; and many others.

47. The Hire: Hostage. Executive producer. Directed by John Woo and released in 2002, this nine-minute short starred: Clive Owen; Maury Chaykin; and Kathryn Morris.

48. The Hire: Beat the Devil. Executive producer on this nine-minute action short. Directed by Tony Scott and released in 2002, it starred: Clive Owen; Gary Oldman; Danny Trejo; and James Brown and Marilyn Manson as themselves.

49. The Hire: Ticker. Executive producer. An eight-minute short, directed by Joe Carnahan in 2002. It starred: Clive Owen; Don Cheadle; and F. Murray Abraham.

50. Cinema 16: British Short Films. Scott's 1962 short, Boy and Bicycle, was featured amongst the films presented here in 2003.

51. Matchstick Men. Produced and directed this for 2003. It starred: Nicolas Cage; Sam Rockwell; Alison Lohman; Bruce Altman; Bruce McGill; Jenny O'Hara; and many others.

52. Kingdom of Heaven. Produced and directed this 2005 film, which starred: Liam Neeson; Orlando Bloom; Eva Green; Jeremy Irons; Edward Norton; et al.

53. In Her Shoes. Producer. This 2005 film was directed by Curtis Hanson and starred: Cameron Diaz; Anson Mount; Toni Collette; and Brooke Smith.

54. All the Invisible Children. Directed the segment titled Jonathan in Italy in 2005. It starred: David Thewlis; Kelly Macdonald; Jordan Clarke; Jack Thompson; Joshua Light; and Jake Ritzema.

55. Numb3rs. The executive producer of this television series, which stars: David Krumholtz; Rob Morrow; and Judd Hirsh. It first aired on January 23, 2005. At the time of this writing, July 2009, the most recent episode, the 103rd, was shown on May 15th, 2009. It is planned that the sixth season will start on Friday, September 25th, 2009.

56. Orpheus. Executive producer. Released for television in 2006, this was directed by Bruce Beresford and starred: Patrick J. Adams; Eion Bailey; Fairuza Balk; Mary Black; and others.

57. Tristan and Isolde. Scott was the executive producer on this 2006 film, which was directed by Kevin Reynolds and starred: James Franco; Sophia Myles; Rufus Sewell; David O'Hara; Mark Strong; Henry Cavill; and many others.

58. A Good Year. He produced and directed this for 2006. It starred: Russell Crowe; Marion Cotillard; Albert Finney; and Freddie Highmore.

59. Law Dogs. Executive producer on this 2007 television special. Directed by Adam Bernstein, it starred: Cassie Benavidez; Ramon Camacho; Rachael Carpani; Lizette Carrion; Josh Cooke; Janeane Garofalo; and others.

60. The Company. Executive producer. This 2007 TV mini-series was directed by Mikael Salomon and starred: Chris O'Donnell; Alfred Molina; Michael Keaton; Alessandro Nivola; Rory Cochrane; Tom Hollander; Natascha McElhone; et al.

61. The Assassination of Jesse James by the Coward Robert Ford. He produced this for 2007. Directed by Andrew Dominik, it starred: Brad Pitt; Mary-Louise Parker; Brooklynn Proulx; Dustin Bollinger; Casey Affleck; Sam Rockwell; and Sam Shepard; et al.

62. American Gangster. Produced and directed this 2007 film, which starred: Denzel Washington; Russell Crowe; Chiwetel Ejiofor; John Brolin; and others.

63. The Andromeda Strain. Executive producer on this television remake of the 1971 movie from Michael Crichton's 1969 novel. Directed by Mikael Salomon, it starred: Benjamin Bratt; Eric McCormack; Christa Miller; Daniel Dae Kim; Viola Davis; and many others.

64. Body of Lies. Produced and directed this for 2008. It starred: Leonardo DiCaprio; Russell Crowe; Mark Strong; et al.

65. Into the Storm. Executive producer for this sequel to The Gathering Storm, 2002. From 2009, this was directed by Thaddeus O'Sullivan and starred: Brendan Gleeson; James D'Arcy; Iain Glen; Janet McTeer; Patrick Malahide; Len Cariou; et al.

66. The Good Wife. Executive producer on this 2009 television series, set to air its pilot on September 22nd, 2009, starring: Julianna Margulies; Christine Baranski; Josh Charles; Matt Czuchry; Archie Panjabi; and others.

67. Welcome to the Rileys. Produced for 2009, this was directed by Jake Scott and starred: Kristen Stewart; James Gandolfini; Melissa Leo; and many others.

68. Cracks. Also produced for 2009, this was directed by Jordan Scott and starred: Evan Green; Juno Temple; Maria Valverde; et al.

69. Robin Hood. Produced and directed and scheduled for release in 2010, this stars: Russell Crowe as Robin Hood and Cate Blanchett as Maid Marian.

70. Sidney Hall. Executive producer. In pre-production, to be directed by Joe Russo, 2010.

71. The A-Team. Producer. In pre-production for 2010, directed by Joe Carnahan and starring Bradley Cooper and Liam Neeson.

72. The Kind One. Producer and director, this has been announced for 2010.

73. The Low Dweller. Producer. This is in pre-production for 2011, directed by Rupert Sanders and supposedly starring Leonard DiCaprio.

74. Emma's War. Producer. This is in production for 2011, directed by Tony Scott.

75. And an untitled prequel to Alien has been announced for 2011.

***

RELATED

1. Blade Runner Sketchbook. By David Scroggy. Published by Blue Dolphin Enterprises, San Diego, California, 1982.

2. Blade Runner Souvenir Magazine. Published by Ira Friedman, New York City, 1982. Softcover.

3. Retrofitting Blade Runner: Issues in Ridley Scott's Blade Runner and Philip K. Dick's Do Androids Dream of Electric Sheep? By Judith B. Kerman. Published by Popular Press of Bowling Green State, Ohio, 1991. Softcover.

4. A Cut Above: 50 Film Directors Talk About Their Craft. By Michael Singer. **Ridley Scott** is one of the directors. Published by Lone Eagle, Los Angeles, 1998. Softcover.

5. Ridley Scott: Close Up: The Making of His Movies. By Paul Sammon. Published by Da Capo Press, New York City, 1999. Softcover.

6. Gladiator: The Making of the Ridley Scott Epic. By David Franzoni, John Logan and William Nicholson, with an introduction by **Ridley Scott**. Published by Newmarket Press, New York City, 2000. Hardcover.

7. The Films of Ridley Scott. By Richard A. Schwartz. Published by Praeger Publishers, Westport, Connecticut, 2001. Hardcover.

8. Black Hawk Down: The Shooting Script. By Ken Nolan, Jerry Bruckheimer and Mark Bowden. Published by Newmarket Press, New York City, 2002. Softcover.

9. Ridley Scott. By James Clarke. Published by Virgin Books, London, 2003. Softcover.

10. Ridley Scott: Interviews. By Laurence F. Knapp and Andrea F. Kulas. Published by the University of Mississippi Press, 2005. Hardcover.

11. Kingdom of Heaven: The Making of the Ridley Scott Epic. By Diana Landau with an introduction by Ridley Scott. Published by Newmarket Press, New York City, 2005. Hardcover.

12. Ridley Scott. By Brian J. Robb. Published by Pocket Essentials, New York City, 2005. Softcover.

13. A Good Year: Portrait of the Film based on the Novel by Peter Mayle. By Marc Klein and Rico Torres, with an introduction by **Ridley Scott**. Published by Newmarket Press, New York City, 2006. Hardcover.

Gene Wolfe.

Gene Rodman Wolfe was born in Brooklyn, New York on May 7th, 1931. After the Korean War, he attended the University of Houston. After graduation, he went to work as an industrial engineer. He also edited the trade journal, Plant Engineering before deciding to take on a full-time career as a writer.

Before the Korean war, he had attended Texas A&M University and it was here that he published his first forays into the genre. The stories were The Grave Secret and The Case of the Vanishing Ghost, both from 1951. When he dropped out of university, he was promptly drafted.

It was 1966 before he began to establish himself. **Frederik Pohl** accepted his story Mountains Like Mice for the May 1966 issue of If, where it appeared with: Silkies in Space by **A. E. van Vogt**; The Hide Hunters by Robert Moore Williams; An APA for Everyone - an essay by Lin Carter; Golden Trabant by R. A. Lafferty; and Earthblood - part 2 of four by Keith Laumer and George Rosel Brown.

His next professional sale was to **Michael Moorcock** for New Worlds Speculative Fiction. It appeared in the August 1967 issue along with: Camp Concentration - part 2 of 4 by Thomas M. Disch; Language Mechanism - an essay by Christopher Finch; Kazoo by James Sallis; Mars Pastorale or, I'm Fertile, Said Felix by Peter Tate; Multi-Value Motorway by **Brian W. Aldiss**; and Concentrate 1 by Michael Butterworth.

It was awhile before he really got going. He recently said he struggled against easy writing. He enjoyed the rewriting, the polishing. "I know where I'm going, but I know too that I mustn't get there too fast."

He published a few more stories during the sixties. Then, in 1970, he was suddenly selling all kinds of short stories and he published his first novel in July, Operation Ares.

Two years later, he won his first Nebula Award.

Wolfe's highest priced collectible books tend to be signed limited editions from specialty publishers such as Ultramarine Publishing or Owlswick or Cheap Street or Ziesing Brothers. These range from around $300.00 to $600.00. Probably the best price for a regular first edition would go to The Shadow of the Torturer. First editions run between $200.00 and $300.00.

***

AWARDS

1973. Nebula Best Novella Award for The Death of Doctor Island - Universe 3, edited by Terry Carr.
1974. Locus Poll Best Novella Award for The Death of Doctor Island - Universe 3, edited by Terry Carr.
1978. Rhysling Long Poem Award for The Computer Iterates the Greater Trumps.
1981. British Science Fiction Best SF Novel Award to The Shadow of the Torturer.
1981. Nebula Best Novel Award for The Claw of the Conciliator.
1981. World Fantasy Best Novel Award for The Shadow of the Torturer.
1982. SF Chronicle Best Novel Award for The Claw of the Conciliator.
1982. Locus Poll Best Fantasy Novel Award for The Claw of the Conciliator.
1983. August Derleth Fantasy Award for Best Novel for The Sword of Lictor.
1982. Locus Poll Best Fantasy Novel Award for The Sword of the Lictor.
1983. SF Chronicle Best Novel Award for The Sword of Lictor.
1984. The John W. Campbell Memorial Award for The Citadel of the Autarch.
1985. Prix Apollo Award for The Citadel of the Autarch.
1987. Locus Poll Best Fantasy Novel Award for Soldier of the Mist.
1988. SF Chronicle Best Novel Award for the Urth of the New Sun.
1989. World Fantasy Best Collection Award for Storeys from the Old Hotel.
1989. A Skylark - the Edward E. Smith Memorial Award for Imaginative Fiction.
1995. Best Collection Award from Deathrealm for Bibliomen.
1996. World Fantasy Lifetime Achievement Award.
2005. Locus Poll Best Novella Award for Golden City Far from Flights: Extreme Visions of Fantasy, edited by Al Sarrantonio.
2007. Inducted into The Science Fiction Hall of Fame.

***

NOVELS AND COLLECTIONS

1. Operation Ares. Published by Berkley Books, New York City, 1970. Berkley Book S1858. Softcover.

2. The Fifth Head of Cerberus. Published by Charles Scribner's Sons, New York City, 1972. Hardcover.

3. Peace. Published by Harper and Row, New York City, 1975. Hardcover.

4. The Devil in a Forest. Published by Follett Publishing, Chicago, 1976. Hardcover.

5. The Shadow of the Torturer. Published by Simon and Schuster, New York City, 1980. Hardcover.

6. The Island of Doctor Death and Other Stories - and Other Stories. Published by Pocket Books, New York City, 1980. Softcover. Herein: The Island of Doctor Death and Other Stories, 1970; Alien Stones, 1972; La Befana, 1973; The Hero as Werewolf, 1975; Three Fingers, 1976; The Death of Dr Island, 1973; Feather Tigers, 1973; Hour of Trust, 1973; Tracking Song, 1975; The Toy Theater, 1971; The Doctor of Death Island, 1978; Cues, 1974; The Eyeflash Miracles, 1976; and Seven American Nights, 1978.

7. Gene Wolfe's Book of Days. Published by Doubleday & Company, Garden City, New York, 1981. Hardcover. Herein: Introduction by **Gene Wolfe**; Against the Lafayette Escadrille, 1972; The Adopted Father, 1980; Car Sinister, 1970; How I Lost the Second World War and Helped Turn Back the German Invasion, 1973; La Befana, 1973; Of Relays and Roses, 1970; An Article About Hunting, 1973; Beautyland, 1973; Forlesen, 1974; The Blue Mouse, 1971; How the Whip Came Back, 1970; Many Mansions, 1977; Melting, 1974; Paul's Treehouse, 1969; St Brandon - Excerpt, 1975; Three Million Square Miles, 1971; The War Beneath the Tree, 1979; and The Changeling, 1968.

8. The Claw of the Conciliator. Published by Timescape Books, New York City, 1981. Hardcover.

9. The Sword of the Lictor. Published by Timescape Books, New York City, 1982. Hardcover.

10. The Citadel of the Autarch. Published by Timescape Books, New York City, 1983. Hardcover.

11. At the Point of Capricorn. Published by Cheap Street, New Castle, Virginia, 1984. Softcover, signed limited edition.

12. The Wolfe Archipelago. Published by the Ziesing Brothers, Willimantic, Connecticut, 1983. Signed limited edition, 200 hardcover copies. Herein: Foreword by **Gene Wolfe**; Death of the Island Doctor, 1983; The Island of Doctor Death and Other Stories, 1970; The Death of Dr Island, 1973; and The Doctor of Death Island, 1978.

13. Free Live Free. Published by the Ziesing Brothers, Willimantic, Connecticut, 1984. Signed limited edition, 750 hardcover copies.

14. Bibliomen: Twenty Characters Waiting for a Book. Published by Cheap Street, New Castle, Virginia, 1984. Hardcover, signed limited edition.

15. Plan[e]t Engineering. Published by NESFA, Cambridge, Massachusetts, 1984. Hardcover. Herein: **Gene Wolfe** by David G. Hartwell; Preface by **Gene Wolfe**; The Books in the Book of the New Sun - an essay by **Gene Wolfe**; In Looking-Glass Castle, 1980; The Rubber Band, 1974; The Marvelous Brass Chessplaying Automaton, 1977; When I Was Ming the Merciless, 1975; The HORARS of War, 1970; A Criminal Proceeding, 1980; The Detective of Dreams, 1980; British Soldier Near Rapier Antiaircraft Missile Battery Scans for the Enemy - a poem, 1984; Last Night in the Garden of Forking Tongues - a poem, 1984; The Computer Iterates the Greater Trumps - a poem, 1977; and The Anatomy of a Robot - an essay, 1983.

16. The Boy Who Hooked the Sun: A Tale from the Book of the Wonders of Urth and Sky. Published by Cheap Street, New Castle, Virginia, 1985. Softcover, signed limited edition.

17. Soldier of the Mist. Published by Tor Books - Tom Doherty Associates, New York City, 1986. Hardcover.

18. Empires of Foliage and Flower: A Tale from the Book of Wonders or Urth and Sky. Published by Cheap Street, New Castle, Virginia, 1987. Hardcover, signed limited edition.

19. The Arimaspian Legacy. Published by Cheap Street, New Castle, Virginia, 1987. Softcover, signed limited edition.

20. The Urth of the New Sun. Published by Tor Books - Tom Doherty Associates, New York City, 1987. Hardcover.

21. There Are Doors. Published by Tor Books - Tom Doherty Associates, New York City, 1988. Hardcover.

22. Storeys from the Old Hotel. Published by Kerosina Books, London, 1988. Hardcover. This contains: Introduction by **Gene Wolfe**; The Green Rabbit from S'Rian, 1985; Beech Hill, 1972; Sightings at Twin Mounds, 1988; Continuing Westward, 1973; Slaves of Silver, 1971; The Rubber Band, 1974; Westwind, 1973; Sonya, Crane Wessleman, and Kittee, 1970; The Packerhaus Method, 1970; Straw, 1975; The Marvelous Brass Chessplaying Automaton, 1977; To the Dark Tower Came, 1977; Parkroads - A Review, 1987; The Flag, 1988; Alphabet, 1988; A Criminal Proceeding, 1980; In Looking-Glass Castle, 1980; Cherry Jubilee, 1982; Redbeard, 1984; A Solar Labyrinth, 1983; Love, Among the Corridors, 1984; Checking Out, 1986; Morning-Glory, 1970; Trip, Trap, 1967; From the Desk of Gilmer C. Merton, 1983; The Recording, 1972; Civis Lapvtvs Sym, 1975; Last Day, 1982; Death of the Island Doctor, 1983; On the Train, 1983; In the Mountains, 1983; At the Volcano's Lip, 1983; In the Old Hotel, 1983; and Choice of the Black Goddess, 1986.

23. For Rosemary. Published by Kerosina Books, London, 1988. Hardcover. Limited to 350 copies. A poetry collection.

24. Seven American Nights. Published by Published by Tor Books - Tom Doherty Associates, New York City, 1989. Tor Double 10. Bound with Sailing to Byzantium by **Robert Silverberg**.

25. Soldier of Arete. Published by Tor Books - Tom Doherty Associates, New York City, 1989. Hardcover.

26. Slow: Children at Play. Published by Cheap Street, New Castle, Virginia, 1989. Softcover, signed limited edition.

27. Endangered Species. Published by Tor Books - Tom Doherty Associates, New York City, 1989. Hardcover. This contains: Introduction by **Gene Wolfe**; A Cabin on the Coast, 1984; The Map, 1984; Kevin Malone, 1980; The Dark of the June, 1974; The Death of Hyle, 1974; From the Notebook of Doctor Stein, 1974; Thag, 1975; The Nebraskan and the Nereid, 1985; In the House of Gingerbread, 1987; The Headless Man, 1972; The Last Thrilling Wonder Story, 1982; House of Ancestors, 1968; Our Neighbour by David Copperfield, 1978; When I Was Ming the Merciless, 1975; The God and His Man, 1980; The Cat, 1983; The War Beneath the Tree, 1979; Eyebem, 1970; THE HORARS of War, 1970; The Detective of Dreams, 1980; Peritonitis, 1973; The Woman Who Loved the Centaur Pholus, 1979; The Woman the Unicorn Loved, 1981; The Peace Spy, 1987; All the Hues of Hell, 1987; Procreation, 1983; Lukora, 1988; Suzanne Delage, 1980; Sweet Forest Maid, 1971; My Book, 1982; The Other Dead Man, 1987; The Most Beautiful Woman on the world, 1987; The Tale of the Rose and the Nightingale (And What Came of It), 1988; and Silhouette, 1975.

Gene Wolfe

28. Pandora by Holly Hollander. Published by Tor Books - Tom Doherty Associates, New York City, 1990. Hardcover.

29. Castleview. Published by Tor Books - Tom Doherty Associates, New York City, 1990. Hardcover.

30. The Old Woman whose Rolling Pin Is the Sun. Published by Cheap Street, New Castle, Virginia, 1991. Softcover, signed limited edition.

31. The Case of the Vanishing Ghost. Published by Cheap Street, New Castle, Virginia, 1991. Softcover, signed limited edition.

32. Castle of Days. Published by Tor Books - Tom Doherty Associates, New York City, 1992. Hardcover. An omnibus edition, this collects the stories from Gene Wolfe's Book of Days, 1981 and the essays from The Castle of the Otter, 1982.

33. Young Wolfe. Published by United Mythologies Press, Toronto, 1992. Hardcover. Herein: Orbital Thoughts - an essay by **Gene Wolfe**; Mountains Like Mice, 1966; The Dead Man, 1965; The Last Casualty of Cambrai, 1992; The Largest Luger, 1992; Volksweapon, 1967; Screen Test, 1967; The Green Wall Said, 1967; The Grave Secret, 1951; and The Case of the Vanishing Ghost, 1951.

34. Nightside of the Long Sun. Published by Tor Books - Tom Doherty Associates, New York City, 1993. Hardcover.

35. Lake of the Long Sun. Published by Tor Books - Tom Doherty Associates, New York City, 1994. Hardcover.

36. Bibliomen. Published by Broken Mirrors Press, Cambridge, Massachusetts, 1995. Softcover. Herein: Foreword by **Gene Wolfe**; John K. (Kinder) Price, 1984; Mary Beatrice Smoot Friarly, SPV, 1984; Captain Roy C. Mirk, B.A., M.A., Ph.D., 1995; Seaman, 1995; The Woman Who Resigned, 1984; Skeeter Smyth, 1984; Rishi, 1984; Paul Rico, 1984; Adam (?) Poor (?), 1984; Anne Parsons, 1984; Lieutenant James Ryan O'Murphy, NYPD, 1984; Xavier McRidy, 1984; John J. Jons, Jr, 1984; Peter O. Henry, 1984; Kopman Goldfleas, 1984; John Glaskin, 1984; Sir Gabriel, 1984; Bernard A. French, 1984; Gertrude S. Spinning Jenny Deplatta, 1984; Hopkins Dalhousie, 1984; Kirk Patterson Arthurs, Ph.D., 1984; and Untitled Letter from the Author to Mr Hiroshi Hayakawa of Hayakawa Publishing Inc., Tokyo, Japan, 1984.

37. Litany of the Long Sun. Published by Guild America Books, New York City, 1994. Book Club edition. Hardcover. An omnibus edition, this collects: Nightside the Long Sun, 1993; and Lake of the Long Sun, 1994.

38. Calde of the Long Sun. Published by Tor Books - Tom Doherty Associates, New York City, 1994. Hardcover.

39. Shadow & Claw. Published by Orb Books, New York City, 1994. Softcover. This collects: The Sword of Lictor, 1982; and The Citadel of the Autarch, 1981.

40. Sword & Citadel. Published by Orb Books, New York City, 1994. Softcover. This collects: The Shadow of the Torturer, 1980; and The Claw of the Conciliator, 1981.

41. Exodus From the Long Sun. Published by Tor Books - Tom Doherty Associates, New York City, 1996. Hardcover.

42. Epiphany of the Long Sun. Published by Guild America Books, New York City, 1997. Book Club edition. Hardcover. An omnibus edition, this collects: Calde the Long Sun, 1994; and Exodus From the Long Sun, 1996.

43. The Book of the New Sun. Published by The Science Fiction Book Club, Garden City, New York, 1998. Hardcover. Herein: The Shadow of the Torturer, 1980; The Claw of the Conciliator, 1981; The Sword of the Lictor, 1982; and The Citadel of the Autarch, 1983.

44. On Blue's Waters. Published by Tor Books - Tom Doherty Associates, New York City, 1999. Hardcover.

45. Strange Travelers. Published by Tor Books - Tom Doherty Associates, New York City, 2000. Hardcover. Herein: Bluesberry Jam, 1996; One-Two-Three for Me, 1996; Counting Cats in Zanzibar, 1996; The Death of Koshchei the Deathless (a tale of old Russia), 1995; No Planets Strike, 1997; Bed & Breakfast, 1996; To the Seventh, 1996; Queen of the night, 1994; And When They Appear, 1993; Flash Company, 1997; The Haunted Boardinghouse, 1990; Useful Phrases, 1993; The Man in the Pepper Mill, 1996; The Ziggurat, 1995; and Ain't You 'Most Done?, 1996.

46. The Book of the New Sun: Volume 1: Shadow and Claw. Published by Millennium/Orion, London, 2000. Softcover. Re-titled version of Shadow & Claw, 1994.

47. The Book of the New Sun: Volume 2: Sword and Citadel. Published by Millennium/Orion, London, 2000. Softcover. Re-titled version of Sword & Citadel, 1994.

48. Innocents Aboard: New Fantasy Stories. Published by Tor Books - Tom Doherty Associates, New York City, 2000. Hardcover. Herein: Introduction by **Gene Wolfe**; The Tree Is My Hat, 1999; The Old Woman Whose Rolling Pin Is the Sun, 1991; The Friendship Light, 1989; Slow Children at Play, 1989; Under Hill, 2002; The Monday Man, 1990; The Waif, 2002; The Legend of Xi Cygnus, 1992; The Sailor Who Sailed After the Sun, 1992; How the Bishop Sailed to Inniskeen, 1989; Houston, 1943, 1988; A Fish Story, 1999; Wolfer, 1997; The Eleventh City, 2000; The Night Chough, 1998; The Wrapper, 1998; A Traveler in Desert Lands, 1999; The Walking Sticks, 1999; Queen, 2001; Pocketsful of Diamonds, 2000; Copperhead, 2001; and The Lost Pilgrim, 2004.

49. In Green's Jungles. Published by Tor Books - Tom Doherty Associates, New York City, 2000. Hardcover.

50. Return to the Whorl. Published by Tor Books - Tom Doherty Associates, New York City, 2001. Hardcover.

51. Book of the Short Sun. Published by The Science Fiction Book Club, Garden City, New York, 2001. Hardcover. Herein: On Blue's Waters, 1999; In Green's Jungles, 2000; and Return to the Whorl, 2001.

52. Latro in the Mist. Published by Orb Books, New

York City, 2003. Softcover. An omnibus, this collects: Soldier of the Mist, 1986; and Soldier of Arete, 1989.

53. Talk of Mandrakes. Published by Sirius Fiction, Albany, California, 2003. Softcover limited edition.

54. The Knight. Published by Tor Books - Tom Doherty Associates, New York City, 2004. Hardcover.

55. The Wizard. Published by Tor Books - Tom Doherty Associates, New York City, 2004. Hardcover.

56. Starwater Strains. Published by Tor Books - Tom Doherty Associates, New York City, 2005. Hardcover. Herein: Introduction by **Gene Wolfe**; Viewpoint, 2001; Rattler - with Brian Hopkins, 2003; In Glory Like Their Star, 2001; Calamity Warps, 2003; Graylord Man's Last Words, 2003; Shields of Mars, 2002; From the Cradle, 2002; Black Shoes, 2003; Has Anybody Seen Junie Moon?, 1999; Pulp Cover, 2004; Of Soil and Climate, 2003; The Dog of the Drops, 2002; Mute, 2002; Petting Zoo, 1997; Castaway, 2003; The Fat Magician, 2000; Hunter Lake, 2003; The Boy Who Hooked the Sun, 1985; Try and Kill It, 1996; Game in the Pope's Head, 1988; Empires of Foliage and Flower, 1987; The Arimaspian Legacy, 1987; The Seraph From Its Sepulcher, 1991; Lord of the Land, 1990; and Golden City Far, 2004.

57. The Knight: Book One of the Wizard Knight. Published by Tor Books - Tom Doherty Associates, New York City, 2005. Softcover. Slight title change from The Knight, 2004.

58. The Wizard: Book Two of the Wizard Knight. Published by Tor Books - Tom Doherty Associates, New York City, 2005. Softcover. Slight title change from The Wizard, 2004.

59. The Wizard Knight. Published by Victor Gollancz, London, 2005. Hardcover. Herein: The Knight, 2004; and The Wizard, 2004.

60. Soldier of Sidon. Published by Tor Books - Tom Doherty Associates, New York City, 2006. Hardcover.

61. Christmas Inn. Published by PS Publishing, Hornsea, UK, 2006. Hardcover limited edition.

62. Strange Birds. Published by DreamHaven Books, Minneapolis, Minnesota, 2006. Limited to 1000 copies. Staple-bound softcover. Herein: On a Vacant Face a Bruise; and Sob in the Silence.

63. Pirate Freedom. Published by Tor Books - Tom Doherty Associates, New York City, 2007. Hardcover.

64. An Evil Guest. Published by Tor Books - Tom Doherty Associates, New York City, 2008. Hardcover.

65. Memorare. Published by Wyrm Publishing, Stirling, New Jersey, 2008. Hardcover, limited edition.

66. The Best of Gene Wolfe: A Definitive Retrospective of His Finest Short Fiction. Published by Tor Books - Tom Doherty Associates, New York City, 2009. Hardcover. Herein: The God and His Man, 1980; On the Train, 1983; From the Desk of Gilmer C. Merton, 1983; Death of the Island Doctor, 1983; Redbeard, 1984; The Boy Who Hooked the Sun, 1985; Parkroads - A Review, 1987; Game in the Pope's Head, 1988; And When They Appear, 1993; Bed & Breakfast, 1996; Petting Zoo, 1997; The Tree Is My Hat, 1997; Has Anybody Seen Junie Moon?, 1999; A Cabin on the Coast, 1984; The Island of Doctor Death and Other Stories, 1970; The Toy Theater, 1971; The Fifth Head of Cerberus, 1972; Beech Hill, 1972; The Recording, 1972; Hour of Trust, 1973; The Death of Dr Island, 1973; La Befana, 1973; Forlesen, 1974; Westwind, 1973; The Hero as Werewolf, 1975; Straw, 1975; The Eyeflash Miracles, 1976; Seven American Nights, 1978; The Detective of Dreams, 1980; and Kevin Malone, 1980.

***

NON-FICTION

1. The Castle of the Otter. Published by the Ziesing Brothers, Willimantic, Connecticut, 1982. Hardcover.

2. Letters Home. Published by the University of Michigan Press, 1991. Softcover.

3. A Wolfe Family Album. Published by United Mythologies Press, Toronto, 1991. Softcover.

***

RELATED

1. Gene Wolfe. By Joan Gordon. Published by Starmont House - Borgo Press, Mercer Island, Washington, 1986. Softcover.

2. Weird Tales - Number 290, Spring 1988: Special Gene Wolfe Issue. Edited by George H. Scithers, Darrell Schweitzer, and John Betancourt. Published by Terminus Publishing, Philadelphia, 1987. Softcover.

3. Gene Wolfe: Urth-Man Extraordinary: A Working Bibliography. By Phil Stephensen-Payne and Gordon Benson. Published by Galactic Central Publishing, Leeds, England, 1991. Softcover.

4. Gene Wolfe's Orbital Thoughts. By Rosemary Wolfe. Published by UM Press, 1992. Softcover.

5. A Checklist of Gene Wolfe. By Christopher P. Stephens. Published by Ultramarine, 1992. Softcover.

6. Attending Daedalus: Gene Wolfe, Artifice and the Reader. By Peter Wright. Published by Liverpool University Press, 2003. Hardcover.

7. Solar Labyrinth: Exploring Gene Wolfe's Book of the New Sun. By Robert Borski. Published by iUniverse, New York City, 2004. Hardcover.

8. The Long and the Short of It: More Essays on the Fiction of Gene Wolfe. By Robert Borski. Published by iUniverse, New York City, 2006. Hardcover.

9. The Magazine of Fantasy and Science Fiction - Special Gene Wolfe Issue - April 2007. Published by Spilogale Inc, United States, 2007. Softcover. Herein: How to Read **Gene Wolfe** - an essay by Neil Gaiman; Memorare by **Gene Wolfe**; The Wolf in the Labyrinth - an essay by Michael Swanwick; and **Gene Wolfe**: The Man and His Work by Michael Andre-Driussi; along with the usual features.

Betty & Ian Ballantine

-2008-

Betty Ballantine.

Betty Ballantine was born in India on September 25th, 1919. She married Ian Ballantine in 1939 and they moved to New York City to begin importing paperback books from England. "We got the agency for bringing Penguins into the US," she explained in an interview.

In 1945, she and her husband, Ian Ballantine, started Bantam Books. And in 1952, they moved on to create Ballantine Books, one of the most influential early science fiction publishers. They were the first to publish original science fiction books and they went for both the paperback and the hardcover formats.

Some of their early hardcover publications were Fahrenheit 451 by **Ray Bradbury**, which sells for $10,000.00+. And Reach for Tomorrow and Childhood's End by **Arthur C. Clarke**, both selling to collectors for around $8,000.00.

In the early 1970s, she and her husband left Ballantine to become freelance editors and consulting publishers.

Talking about her husband, she said his goal was quite simple. He wanted to change the reading habits of America. "That's what we proceeded to do."

***

AWARDS

1975. World Fantasy Special Award.
1984. World Fantasy Special Award.
1995. Literary Market Place Lifetime Achievement Award.
2001. Nebula - SFWA President's Lifetime Achievement Award.
2006. Special Committee Award from LACon IV.
2008. Inducted into The Science Fiction Hall of Fame.

***

BOOKS

1. The Fantastic Art of Frank Frazetta. Edited and with an introduction by Betty Ballantine. Published by Charles Scribner's Sons, New York City, 1975. Hardcover.

2. The Fantastic World of Gervasio Gallardo. Edited and with an introduction by Betty Ballantine. Published by Peacock Press/Bantam Books, New York City, 1976. Softcover.

3. The Fantastic Art of Frank Frazetta: Book Two. Edited and with an introduction by Betty Ballantine. Published by Peacock Press/Bantam Books, New York City, 1977. Softcover.

4. The Fantastic Art of Frank Frazetta: Book Three. Edited and with an introduction by Betty Ballantine. Published by Peacock Press/Bantam Books, New York City, 1978. Softcover.

5. The Fantastic Art of Frank Frazetta: Book Four. Edited and with an introduction by Betty Ballantine. Published by Peacock Press/Bantam Books, New York City, 1980. Softcover.

6. The Fantastic Art of Frank Frazetta: Book Five. Edited and with an introduction by Betty Ballantine. Published by Peacock Press/Bantam Books, New York City, 1985. Softcover.

7. An American Celebration: The Art of Charles Wysocki. Text by Betty Ballantine. Published by Greenwich Press/Workman Publishing, New York City, 1985. Hardcover.

8. The Art of Bev Doolittle. Edited by Betty Ballantine. Published by Greenwich Workshop, Trumbull, Connecticut, 1990. Hardcover.

9. The Frank Frazetta Pillow Book. Edited by Betty Ballantine. Published by Kitchen Sink Press, Northampton, Massachusetts, 1993. Softcover.

10. The Secret Oceans. Published by Bantam Books, New York City, 1994. Hardcover.

11. The Captain's Garden: A Reflective Journey Home Through the Art of Paul Landry. Published by Greenwich Workshop, Trumbull, Connecticut, 1996. Hardcover.

12. The Native Americans: An Illustrated History. Edited by Ian and Betty Ballantine. Published by JG Press/World Publications, North Dighton, Massachusetts, 2001. Softcover.

Ian Ballantine.

Ian Keith Ballantine was born on February 15th, 1916 and died of a heart attack on March 9th, 1995 in Bearsville, New York. Married in 1939 and working with his wife, Betty, he moved to New York City and procured the rights to import Penguin Books.

In 1945, Ian and Betty founded Bantam Books. And in 1952, they moved on to found Ballantine Books, which was the first paperback publisher to print original science fiction.

Ian Ballantine once said his goal was to change the reading habits of America.

And he brought them **Ray Bradbury**, **Arthur C. Clarke**, **Frederik Pohl**, **Theodore Sturgeon**, Henry Kuttner and **C. L. Moore**; **Fritz Leiber**; **James Blish**; J. R. R. Tolkien, the Ballantine Adult Fantasy series as edited by Lin Carter... The list goes on.

A 200-copy limited edition of Fahrenheit 451, by **Ray Bradbury**, wrapped in white asbestos, appeared to be the most valuable book ever published by the Ballantines. It sells for $17,500.00 and higher.

***

AWARDS

1975. World Fantasy Special Award.
1984. World Fantasy Special Award.
1995. Literary Market Place Lifetime Achievement Award.
2008. Inducted into The Science Fiction Hall of Fame.

***

BOOKS

1. The Western Art of James Bama. Edited and with an introduction by Ian Ballantine. Published by Charles Scribner's Sons, New York City, 1975. Hardcover.

2. The Marine Paintings of Carl G. Evers. Edited and with an introduction by Ian Ballantine. Published by Peacock Press/Bantam Books, New York City, 1975. Softcover.

3. The Alaskan Paintings of Fred Machetanz. Edited and with an introduction by Ian Ballantine. Published by Peacock Press/Bantam Books, New York City, 1977. Softcover.

4. Yachting: The Photography of Beken of Cowes. Edited by Ian Ballantine and with an introduction by Richard Ballantine. Published by Peacock Press/Bantam Books, New York City, 1977. Softcover.

5. The Aviation Art of Keith Ferris. Edited and with an introduction by Ian Ballantine. Published by Peacock Press/Bantam Books, New York City, 1978. Softcover.

6. Ballantine Books: The First Decade. With David Aronovitz. Published by Bailiwick Books, 1987. Hardcover.

7. The Native Americans: An Illustrated History. Edited by Ian and Betty Ballantine. Published by JG Press/World Publications, North Dighton, Massachusetts, 2001. Softcover.

William Gibson.

William Ford Gibson was born on March 17th, 1948 in Conway, South Carolina. After high school, he bummed around, travelled throughout the U.S. and into Canada, managed to avoid getting drafted into the Vietnam War, sampled most of the drugs he could find.

From Toronto in the late sixties, he went on to Greece and Turkey with his new girlfriend in 1970. Deciding to get married, they moved to Vancouver to live on his wife's teaching salary while Gibson scouted books and collectibles, selling them wherever he could.

He went back to school and got a bachelor degree in English from the University of British Columbia.

That was when he thought he should try writing.

His first short story was Fragments of a Hologram Rose. It was published by Jonathan Ostrowsky in Unearth in the Summer 1977 issue. Also in that issue were: Red Planet by James P. Blaylock; Side Effect by Richard Bowker; Sunsteps by S. P. Somtow; Walk to the World - an Algis Budrys reprint from 1952; Locksmith and Master of Love by Toby Perkins; and an assortment of reviews and essays, including Writing: First There Was the Title by Harlan Ellison; and Science: Science for Fiction #3 by **Hal Clement**.

It was four years before he sold another story. The Gernsback Continuum was published by Terry Carr in Universe 11, 1981, along with: The Quickening by Michael Bishop; The Snake Who Had Read Chomsky by Josephine Saxton; Shadows on the Cave Wall by Nancy Kress; Venice Drowned by Kim Stanley Robinson; In Reticulum by Carter Scholz; Jean Sandwich, the Sponsor and I by Ian Watson; The Start of the End of the World by Carol Emshwiller; and Mummer Kiss by Michael Swanwick.

His work had a film noir feel to it. And something more. Something new to SF.

Cyberpunk.

The word was coined by Bruce Bethke. And there is little doubt that **William Gibson** was one of the first writers whose work fit that new mood.

When his first novel, Neuromancer, came out in 1984, this whole new science fiction movement, Cyberpunk, was propelled forward at the speed of... Well, never mind. There are too many clichés lining up for that sentence to ever be completed.

The Victor Gollancz UK first hardcover edition of Neuromancer sells to collectors for between $1,800.00 and $2,500.00. The Phantasia Press hardcover from 1986 usually goes for around $600.00. And the Ace softcover edition, the true first, sell for somewhere between $400.00 and $500.00.

***

AWARDS

1984. Nebula Best Novel Award for Neuromancer.
1984. Philip K. Dick Award for Neuromancer.
1985. Best Novel Award from the SF Chronicle.
1985. Ditmar Award for Best International Long Fiction.
1985. Hugo Best Novel Award.
1989. Aurora Award for Best Long-Form Work in English for Mona Lisa Overdrive.
1995. Aurora Award for Best Long-Form Work in English for Virtual Light.
2008. Induction into The Science Fiction Hall of Fame.

***

FILMS AND TELEVISION

1. Cyberpunk. Directed by Marianne Trench, he was a guest, with Timothy Leary, in this 1990 documentary.

2. Brave New Worlds: The Science Fiction Phenomenon. From 1992, he was one of the guests in this 1993 documentary, along with: **Robert Silverberg**; **Arthur C. Clarke**; John Clute; **Brian W. Aldiss**; J. G. Ballard; Kim Stanley Robinson; Karen Joy Fowler; Octavia Butler; and many others.

3. Tomorrow Calling. This twelve-minute short film from 1993 was based on The Gernsback Continuum, 1981. Directed by Tim Leandro, it starred: Colin Salmon; Don Henderson; and Toyah Wilcox.

4. Wild Palms. Had a bit part as himself, along with Oliver Stone, in this 1993 film. Directed by Kathryn Bigelow, Keith Gordon, Peter Hewitt, and Phil Joanou, this starred: James Belushi; Dana Delany; Robert Loggia; Kim Cattrall; Angie Dickinson; Ernie Hudson; Bebe Neuwirth; Nick Mancuso; Robert Morse; David Warner; et al.

5. Johnny Mnemonic. He did the screenplay for this, based on his 1981 short story. Directed by Robert Longo for 1995, the movie starred: Keanu Reeves; Dina Meyer; Ice-T; Takeshi Kitano; Dolph Lundgren; et al.

6. New Rose Hotel. Based on the 1984 short story, this was directed by Abel Ferrara in 1998. It starred; Christopher Walken; Willem Dafoe; Asia Argento; Annabella Sciorra; Gretchen Mol; and others.

7. Kill Switch. He wrote this episode of the television series The X Files, which aired on February 15th, 1998, Season 5, Episode 11. Created by Cris Carter, the show starred David Duchovny and Gillian Anderson.

8. The X-Files Movie Special. From 1998, he was one of the guests. Directed by Thomas C. Grane, the documentary featured: Martin Landau; Gillian Anderson; David Duchovny; Chris Carter; Stephen Kind; Rosie O'Donnell; Melissa Etheridge; and many others.

9. First Person Shooter. This was another X Files by Gibson. It was shown on February 27th, 2000, Season 7, Episode 13 and he had a bit part in the episode.

10. No Maps for These Territories. Directed by Mark Neale in 2000, Gibson was one of the guests.

11. Cyberman. From 2001, this documentary was directed by Peter Lynch. Gibson was one of the guests.

12. The Screen Savers. The episode from February 5th, 2003. A guest on the TV series.

13. Bestseller Samtalen. He was a guest on this Danish television series, February 27th, 2003, Season 9, Episode 2.

14. Filmography. He was a guest on the Keanu Reeves episode of this television series. It aired in 2005.

15. Webnation - Episode 1.14. Directed by Katia Del Col, he was a guest of Amber MacArthur on this television series in 2007.

16. Vat-Grown Sea-Green Nikon Implants. The writer on this one, a fourteen minute short directed by Mad Colonel Corto and released in 2009.

17. Neuromancer. A film from this 1984 novel is supposedly in pre-production and to be directed by Joseph Kahn for release in 2011.

18. Pattern Recognition. It has been announced that this 2003 novel will be filmed for release in 2011.

***

BOOKS AND COLLECTIONS

1. Neuromancer. Published by Ace Books, New York City, 1984. Softcover.

2. Neuromancer. Published by Victor Gollancz, London, 1984. First hardcover edition.

3. Count Zero. Published by Victor Gollancz, London, 1986. Hardcover.

4. Burning Chrome. Published by Arbor House, New York City, 1986. Hardcover. Herein: Preface by Bruce Sterling; Johnny Mnemonic, 1981; The Gernsback Continuum, 1981; Fragments of a Hologram Rose, 1977; The Belonging Kind - written with John Shirley, 1981; Hinterlands, 1981; Red Star Winter Orbit - written with Bruce Sterling, 1983; New Rose Hotel, 1984; The Winter Market, 1985; Dogfight - written with Michael Swanwick, 1985; and

Burning Chrome, 1982.

5. Mona Lisa Overdrive. Published by Victor Gollancz, London, 1988. Hardcover.

6. The Difference Engine. With Bruce Sterling. Published by Victor Gollancz, London, 1993. Hardcover.

7. Virtual Light. Published by Bantam Spectra, New York City and Viking, London, September 1993. Hardcover.

8. Johnny Mnemonic. Published by Ace Books, New York City, 1995. Softcover. Herein: Johnny Mnemonic - short story, 1981; and Johnny Mnemonic - screenplay, 1995.

9. Idoru. Published by G. P. Putnam's Sons, New York City, 1996. Hardcover.

10. All Tomorrow's Parties. Published by G. P. Putnam's Sons, New York City, and Viking, London, October 1999. Hardcover.

11. Pattern Recognition. Published by G. P. Putnam's Sons, New York City, 2003. Hardcover.

12. Spook Country. Published by Putnam, New York City, and Viking Press, London, August 2007. Hardcover.

***

RELATED

1. Cyberpunk and Cyberculture: Science Fiction and the Work of William Gibson. By Dani Cavallaro. Published by Athlone Press, London, 2000. Hardcover.

2. The Cultural Influences of William Gibson, the Father of Cyberpunk Science Fiction: Critical and Interpretive Essays. By Carl B. Yoke and Carol L. Robinson. Published by EMP - Edwin Mellen Press, Lewiston, New York, 2007. Hardcover.

Richard Powers.

Richard Michael Gorman Powers was born in Chicago on February 14th, 1921 and died of an aneurysm on March 9th, 1996 in Madrid, Spain.

As much as that of **Chesley Bonestell** and **Kelly Freas**, his work became the look of science fiction. A very capable illustrator in the traditional style, his paintings soon evolved. Realism was all but abandoned and his own, unique surrealistic vision took over. For the longest time, **Richard Powers** provided the look that everyone came to expect from Ballantine Books.

He went to the Art Institute of Chicago and the University of Illinois School of Fine Art. And after World War Two, during which he was assigned to the Signal Corps film studios painting scenery and props, he went to New York City and briefly studied illustration.

His first assignment as an illustrator was in 1948, a dustjacket for Gulliver's Travels for World Publishing.

This was followed by work for Doubleday & Company, a relationship that lasted for the next twenty years.

One of his earliest dustjackets for Doubleday was on Pebble in the Sky by **Isaac Asimov**, 1950. Decent copies of this sell to collectors for around $600.00.

For Ballantine, he did the dustjacket on Ahead of Time by Henry Kuttner. That one sells for around $300.00. But he also did Reach for Tomorrow and Childhood's End by **Arthur C. Clarke**, Ballantine Books that sell for closer to $10,000.00.

Over the years, his covers graced the books of just about every major science fiction writer. And, most particularly, the authors in The Science Fiction Hall of Fame, including **Edgar Rice Burroughs**. Powers did most of the covers for Ballantine's first Tarzan paperbacks.

One of the last covers published in his lifetime was done in 1992 for The Chalchiuhite Dragon: A Tale of Toltec Times by Kenneth Morris. And in 2001, The Art of Richard Powers, by Frank Jane, was published in hardcover by Collins and Brown, London.

In 2008, the same year as Ian and Betty Ballantine (for whom he created such a distinctive look in the 50s and 60s), he was inducted into The Science Fiction Hall of Fame.

Rod Serling.

Rodman Edward Serling was born on December 25th, 1924 in Syracuse, New York and died at the age of 50 in Rochester, New York on June 28th, 1975. He was in Strong Memorial Hospital in Rochester for heart bypass surgery and had a heart attack on the operating table.

As a paratrooper and demolition expert during World War Two, he was wounded. It was while he was recuperating from his wounds that he started to write. After the war, he went to college in Ohio. And he graduated to work as a radio writer. He was making a living, although nothing much happened for him until he sold a script to the series Stars Over Hollywood in 1950.

He once said in an interview, "I've never planned ahead. I never worry about tomorrow."

And until 1955, he was just another Hollywood writer. He worked mainly for the anthology shows where he would not be bound by the constraints of set characters. He was a good one but still just another writer.

Until he wrote a story called Patterns for Kraft Television Theatre. It was directed by Fielder Cook and starred Hanna Landy, Ed Begley, Richard Kiley and Elizabeth Montgomery. Patterns was presented live on January 12th, 1955 and had the impact of great theatre. In fact, it *was* great theatre. It was so popular, so in demand, that it was performed live again just a few weeks later, on February 9th, 1955. That was the first time in TV history that a show had been re-run because it was so popular. *That* performance was recorded on kinescope, for future viewings. Patterns won Serling his first Emmy award and paved the way for everything else he wanted to do.

Talking about Hollywood, he explained that success was mostly luck. You needed talent, of course, but, "It's always who you know."

After Patterns, everyone wanted to know **Rod Serling**. His next huge television moment was Requiem for a Heavyweight which was shown on CBC Television Playhouse. He received a George Foster Peabody Broadcasting Award for that one. And it was the first time a Peabody had ever been presented to a writer.

By the time he got to The Twilight Zone, that "sixth dimension beyond that which is known to man," his success had given him the power to change television. Just as the Ballantines changed America's reading habits, **Rod Serling** changed what would be expected from good television.

His highest priced book is Twilight Zone Revisited. It was published by Grosset and Dunlap in New York in hardcover and tends to go between $900.00 and $1,500.00

***

AWARDS

From the Second World War: World War II Victory Medal; American Campaign Medal with Arrowhead Device; Good Conduct Medal; Philippine Liberation Medal; Combat Infantryman Badge; Parachutist Badge; Honorable Service Lapel Pin; Purple Heart; and a Bronze Star.
1956. An Emmy Award for Best Original Screenplay - Patterns.
1956. A Christopher Award.
1957. An Emmy Award for Best Original Screenplay - Requiem for a Heavyweight.
1957. George foster Peabody Broadcasting Award for Requiem for a Heavyweight.
1958. An Emmy Award for Best Screenplay Adaption - The Comedian.
1960. An Emmy Award for Outstanding Writing Achievement in Drama - Twilight Zone.
1960. Hugo Best Dramatic Presentation Award for Twilight Zone.
1960. Director's Guild Award.
1960. Producer's Guild Award.
1961. An Emmy Award for Outstanding Writing Achievement in Drama - Twilight Zone.
1961. Hugo Best Dramatic Presentation Award for Twilight Zone.
1961. Unity Award for Outstanding Contributions to Better Race Relations.
1962. Hugo Best Dramatic Presentation Award for Twilight Zone.
1964. An Emmy Award for Best Screenplay Adaption - It's Mental Work.
1969. An Edgar Award for Night Gallery.
1971. Doctorate in Literature - Emerson College.
1971. A Christopher Award.
1972. Doctorate in Literature - Alfred University.
1972. Doctorate in Literature - Ithaca College.
1985. Inducted into the Television Hall of Fame.
1988. A star on the Hollywood Walk of Fame.
2004. Number One in TV Guide's list of twenty-five Greatest Sci-Fi Legends.
2008. Induction into The Science Fiction Hall of Fame.

***

FILMS AND TELEVISION

Rod Serling made numerous personal appearances on television shows and documentaries; and acted as the host on more than one occasion, but most of these will not be mentioned here.

1. Grady Everett for the People. Written for the television series, Stars Over Hollywood. It was shown on September 13th, 1950.

2. Mr Finchley Versus the Bomb. Written for Lux Video Theatre, this was shown on January 7th, 1952, Season 2, Episode 20. It was directed by Fielder Cook and starred Arlene Francis and Henry Hull.

3. The Sergeant. For Armstrong Circle Theatre, this aired on April 29th, 1952, Season 2, Episode 33. Directed by Garry Simpson, it starred Tige Andrews and Robert Brown.

4. Welcome Home, Lefty. Featured on Lux Video

Rod Serling

Theatre on June 23rd, 1952, Season 2, Episode 44. It was directed by Richard Goode and starred David Winters.

5. The Carlson Legend. For Hallmark Hall of Fame, this aired on August 3rd, 1952, Season 1, Episode 32. Directed by Albert McCleery, it starred Tod Andrews.

6. I Lift Up My Lamp. For Hallmark Hall of Fame, this aired on August 17th, 1952, Season 1, Episode 34. Directed by Albert McCleery, it starred Nathaniel Frey, Martin Kosleck and Abby Lewis.

7. You Be the Bad Guy. Written for Lux Video Theatre, this aired on August 18th, 1952, Season 2, Episode 52. It was directed by Richard Goode and starred David Winters and Macdonald Carey.

8. No Gods to Serve. This was written for the TV series The Doctor, starring Dabbs Greer and Robert North. Directed by Don Siegel, it was shown on October 5th, 1952, Season 1, Episode 7.

9. Those Who Wait. For the series The Doctor. It was shown on October 19th, 1952, Season 1, Episode 9.

10. The Face of Autumn. Featured on Lux Video Theatre on November 3rd, 1952, Season 3, Episode 10. It was directed by Richard Goode and starred David Winters, Tony Canzoneri, Bill Erwin and Pat O'Brien.

11. The Hill. Written for Lux Video Theatre, this aired on November 24th, 1952, Season 3, Episode 13. It was directed by Fielder Cook and starred David Winters and Mercedes McCambridge.

12. The Inn of Eagles. For Lux Video Theatre, this aired on January 26th, 1953, Season 3, Episode 22. It was directed by Richard Goode and starred David Winters, Macdonald Carey and Brian Keith.

13. A Time for Heroes. Written for Lux Video Theatre, this aired on March 2nd, 1953, Season 3, Episode 27. It was directed by Fielder Cook and starred David Winters and Dennis O'Keefe.

14. Horace Mann's Miracle. For Hallmark Hall of Fame, this aired on March 3rd, 1953, Season 2, Episode 28. Directed by Albert McCleery, it starred Frank M. Thomas.

15. Next of Kin. For Kraft Television Theatre, this aired on April 8th, 1953, Season 6, Episode 35. It starred Barbara Baxley, Tony Canzoneri and J. Pat O'Malley.

16. The Twilight Rounds. For Kraft Television Theatre, this aired on May 27th, 1953, Season 6, Episode 28. It was directed by Stanley Quinn and starred James Daly.

17. Man Against Pain. Written for Hallmark Hall of Fame, this aired on June 21st, 1953, Season 2, Episode 43. Directed by Albert McCleery, it starred Tod Andrews.

18. Old Macdonald Had a Curve. For Kraft Television Theatre, this aired on August 5th, 1953, Season 6, Episode 44. Directed by Harry Herrmann, it starred Olin Howland and Cameron Prud'Homme.

19. Nightmare at Ground Zero. Written for the television series Suspense, this was directed by Robert Mulligan and starred O. Z. Whitehead, Louise Larabee, Calvin Thomas and Pat Hingle. It was shown on August 18th, 1953, Season 5, Episode 43.

20. The Quiet Village. Written for Medallion Theatre, this starred Robert Preston and Rod Steiger. Directed by Robert Stevens, it aired on August 22nd, 1953, Season 1, Episode 7.

21. The Blue for Joey Menotti. For Kraft Television Theatre, this aired on August 26th, 1953, Season 6, Episode 47. It starred Constance Ford and Dan Morgan.

22. A Long Time Till Dawn. Written for Kraft Television Theatre, this aired on November 11th, 1953, Season 7, Episode 11. Directed by Richard Dunlap, it starred James Dean and Robert Cass.

23. Buffalo Bill Is Dead. For Studio One, this aired on November 23rd, 1953, Season 6, Episode 10. Directed by Franklin J. Schaffner, it starred Anthony Ross, John Cannon and Betty Furness.

24. At Ease. For The Motorola Television Hour, this starred Brian Donlevy, Madge Evans and Pat Harrington. It aired on December 15th, 1953, Season 1, Episode 4.

25. Twenty-Four Men in a Plane. Written for Medallion Theatre, this starred Jackie Cooper and Leslie Nielsen. Directed by Don Medford, it aired on December 19th, 1953, Season 2, Episode 15.

26. The Happy Headline. For Campbell Playhouse, this was directed by Garry Simpson and starred Richard Bishop and James Costigan. It aired on December 25th, 1953, Season 2, Episode 11.

27. They Call Them the Meek. Written for Medallion Theatre, this starred Thomas Gomez and Gene Raymond. Directed by Ralph Nelson, it aired on December 26th, 1953, Season 2, Episode 16.

28. Herman, Come by Bomber. For Studio One, this was shown on February 1st, 1954, Season 6, Episode 20. It was directed by Franklin J. Schaffner and starred Paul Langton, John Cannon and Betty Furness.

29. Walk in the Night. For The Philip Morris Playhouse, this aired on February 18th, 1954, Season 1, Episode 21. It was co-written by Verne Jay and starred Chester Morris.

30. The Muldoon Matter. For The Motorola Television Hour, this starred Patricia Barry, Ed Begley and Christopher Walken. Directed by Don Richardson, it aired on February 23rd, 1954, Season 1, Episode 9.

31. The Strike. For Studio One, this was shown on June 7th, 1954, Season 6, Episode 38. It was directed by Franklin J. Schaffner and starred James Daly, John Cannon and Betty Furness.

32. A Worthy Opponent. Written for Center Stage, this starred Charles Coburn and aired on August 24th, 1954, Season 1, Episode 7.

33. U.F.O. For Studio One, this was shown on September 6th, 1954, Season 6, Episode 51. It was directed by Franklin J. Schaffner and starred Jack Warden, Harry Bellaver, John Cannon and Betty Furness.

34. One for the Angels. From the series Danger, this was directed by Byron Paul and starred Dick Stark. It aired on September 14th, 1954, Season 5, Episode 3.

35. The Summer Memory. For The Ford Television Theatre, this aired on November 18th, 1954, Season 3, Episode 7. Directed by Fred F. Sears, it starred Richard Kiley and Claire Trevor.

36. Knife in the Dark. From the series Danger, this was directed by Stanley Niss and starred Paul Newman, James Gregory and Dick Stark. It aired on December 7th, 1954, Season 5, Episode 14.

37. Save Me from Treason. Done for Armstrong Circle Theatre, this was directed by William Corrigan and starred Ed Begley. It aired on January 4th, 1955, Season 5, Episode 18.

38. Patterns. Written for Kraft Television Theatre, this aired on January 12th, 1955, Season 8, Episode 16. Directed by Fielder Cook, it starred Ed Begley, Richard Kiley, Hanna Landy, and Elizabeth Montgomery.

39. Patterns. Kraft Television Theatre aired this on February 9th, 1955, Season 8, Episode 20. Directed by Fielder Cook, it starred Ed Begley, Richard Kiley, Bea Arthur, and Elizabeth Montgomery.

40. Garrity's Sons. For The Ford Television Theatre, this aired on March 24th, 1954, Season 3, Episode 25. Directed by Jules Bricken, it starred Rory Calhoun, Vince Edwards and James Bell.

41. The Champion. Adapted from a Ring Lardner story and written for Climax!, this was directed by Allen Reisner and starred Geraldine Brooks and Rory Calhoun. It was shown on March 31st, 1955, Season 1, Episode 20.

42. The Rack. For The United States Steel Hour, this aired on April 12th, 1955, Season 2, Episode 16. It was directed by Alex Segal and starred Mitchell Agruss, Wendell Corey, Peggy McCay and Keenan Wynn.

43. The Fateful Pilgrimage. Done for Appointment with Adventure, this aired on April 17th, 1955, Season 1, Episode 3. It starred Theodore Bikel and Olga Fabian.

44. A Man with a Vengeance. Written for General Electric Theater, this starred Luther Adler, Neva Patterson and Barry Sullivan. It was shown on May 15th, 1955, Season 3, Episode 31.

45. Strength of Steel. For Star Tonight, this aired on June 16th, 1955, Season 1, Episode 20. It starred Wyatt Cooper and James Holden.

46. To Wake at Midnight. Written for Climax!, this was directed by John Frankenheimer and starred Wendell Corey, Maria Riva and Akim Tamiroff. It was shown on June 23rd, 1955, Season 1, Episode 29.

47. The Director. For Jane Wyman Presents The Fireside Theatre, this was shown on September 13th, 1955. Directed by Herschel Daugherty, it starred James Barton, Jack Carson and Nancy Gates.

48. Incident in an Alley. For The United States Steel Hour, this aired on November 23rd, 1955, Season 3, Episode 11. It was directed by Sidney Lumet and starred Ed Binns, Larry Gates and Farley Granger.

49. Portrait in Celluloid. For the series Climax!, this was directed by John Frankenheimer and starred Jack Carson and Kim Hunter. It was shown on November 24th, 1955, Season 2, Episode 11.

50. The Man Who Caught the Ball at Coogan's Bluff. For Studio One, this was shown on November 28th, 1955, Season 8, Episode 11. It was directed by Franklin J. Schaffner and starred Gisele MacKenzie, Alan Young, John Cannon and Betty Furness.

51. O'Toole from Moscow. For Matinee Theatre, this aired on December 12th, 1955, Season 1, Episode 30. Directed by Albert McCleery, it starred John Banner, Chuck Connors and Leo Durocher.

52. The Arena. For Studio One, this was shown on April 9th, 1956, Season 8, Episode 30. It was directed by Franklin J. Schaffner and starred Wendell Corey, John Cannon and Betty Furness.

53. Beloved Outcasts. Written for The Catholic Hour, this was shown on April 15th, 1956.

54. Noon on Doomsday. For The United States Steel Hour, this aired on April 25th, 1956, Season 3, Episode 22. It was directed by Daniel Petrie and starred Philip Abbott, Albert Salmi, Jack Warden and Lois Smith.

55. A Man with a Vengeance. Written for General Electric Theater, this was re-done and aired on July 1st, 1956, Season 4, Episode 39. This time, it starred Dennis King and Walter Matthau.

56. Mr Finchley Versus the Bomb. Originally written for Lux Video Theatre, 1952, this was used on The Kaiser Aluminum Hour, September 25th, 1956, Season 1, Episode 6.

57. Forbidden Area. Written for Playhouse 90, this aired on October 4th, 1956, Season 1, Episode 1. Directed by John Frankenheimer, it starred: Charlton Heston; Vincent Price; Diana Lynn; Tab Hunter; Jackie Coogan; Victory Jory; Charles Bickford; et al.

58. Requiem for a Heavyweight. Written for Playhouse 90, this aired on October 11th, 1956, Season 1, Episode 2. It was directed by Ralph Nelson and starred: Jack Palance; Keenan Wynn; Ed Wynn; Kim Hunter; Max Baer; and many others.

59. The Rack. Wrote the teleplay. Directed by Arnold Laven for November 1956, this starred: Paul Newman; Wendell Corey; Walter Pidgeon; Edmond O'Brien; Anne Francis; Lee Marvin; Cloris Leachman; et al.

60. The Comedian. Adapted from a story by Ernest Lehman, this was written for Playhouse 90, and aired on February 14th, 1957, Season 1, Episode 20.

Rod Serling

Directed by John Frankenheimer, it starred: Mickey Rooney; Kim Hunter; Edmond O'Brien; Mel Torme; Constance Ford; et al.

61. Requiem for a Heavyweight. Originally written for Playhouse 90, this was adapted by the BBC London and aired on March 31st, 1957, Season 8, Episode 13 of BBC Sunday-Night Theatre. It was directed by Alvin Rakoff and starred: Sean Connery; Michael Caine; Brenda Duncan; Jacqueline Hill; and many others.

62. The Dark Side of the Earth. Written for Playhouse 90, this aired on September 19th, 1957, Season 2, Episode 2. It was directed by Arthur Penn and starred: Van Heflin; Earl Holliman; Kim Hunter; Dean Jagger; Jerry Paris; and Ian Wolfe.

63. Panic Button. For Playhouse 90, this aired on November 28th, 1957, Season 2, Episode 12. It was directed by Franklin J. Schaffner and starred: Lee J. Cobb; Leif Erickson; Vera Miles; Marian Seldes; and Robert Stack.

64. Saddle the Wind. Did the screenplay for this April 1958 film. Directed by Robert Parrish, it starred: Robert Taylor; Julie London; and John Cassavetes.

65. The Cause. For Matinee Theatre, this was directed by Albert McCleery and starred Richard Crenna, Johnny Crawford, Sidney Blackmer and Lois Smith. It aired on May 12th, 1958, Season 3, Episode 148.

66. Nightmare at Ground Zero. This was adapted from the book by Robert Cahn and John C. Clark for Playhouse 90, May 15th, 1958, Season 2, Episode 34. Directed by Franklin J. Schaffner, it starred: Ainslie Pryor; Carl Benton Reid; Barry Sullivan; and Jack Warden.

67. Bomber's Moon. For Playhouse 90, this aired on May 22nd, 1958, Season 2, Episode 35. It was directed by John Frankenheimer and starred: Martin Balsam; Hazel Court; Robert Cummings; Larry Gates; J. Pat O'Malley; Rip Torn; and Cliff Robertson.

68. A Town Has Turned to Dust. Written for Playhouse 90, this was directed by John Frankenheimer and starred: William Shatner; Rod Steiger; James Gregory; and others. It aired on June 19th, 1958, Season 2, Episode 38.

69. Noon on Doomsday. Written for Armchair Theatre, this was shown on July 6th, 1958, Season 2, Episode 44. It was directed by Philip Saville and starred Marpessa Dawn and Gareth Jones.

70. The Time Element. Written for Westinghouse Desilu Playhouse, this was directed by Allen Reisner and starred: William Bendix; Martin Balsam; Darryl Hickman; et al. It aired on November 10th, 1958, Season 2, Episode 6.

71. The Last Night in August. For Pursuit, this was aired on December 17th, 1958, Season 1, Episode 9. Directed by Paul Stanley, it starred: Jimmy Baird; Whitney Blake; Dennis Hopper; Cameron Mitchell; Franchot Tone; et al.

72. The Velvet Alley. For Playhouse 90, this aired on January 22nd, 1959, Season 3, Episode 16. It was directed by Franklin J. Schaffner and Alex Segal and starred: Art Carney; Leslie Nielsen; Katharine Bard; Jack Klugman; Micky Dolenz as Micky Braddock; and others, including Dyan Cannon as Gloria and Burt Reynolds as The Actor.

73. The Rank and File. Written for Playhouse 90, this aired on May 28th, 1959, Season 3, Episode 34. It was directed by Franklin J. Schaffner and starred: Luther Adler; Whitney Blake; Charles Bronson; Van Heflin; Cameron Prud'Homme; and many others.

74. Come in Razor Red. Written for Armchair Theatre, this was shown on February 14th, 1960, Season 3, Episode 75. It was directed by Alvin Rakoff and starred John Barrie and Richard Harris.

75. In the Presence of Mine Enemies. Written for Playhouse 90, this aired on May 18th, 1960, Season 4, Episode 17. It was directed by Fielder Cook and starred: Robert Redford; Arthur Kennedy; Charles Laughton; Sam Jaffe; George Macready, et al.

76. The Rank and File. Written for Armchair Theatre, this was shown on December 31st, 1961, Season 4, Episode 49. It was directed by Alan Cooke and starred David Bauer and Bruce Boa.

77. The Twilight Zone. Starting on October 2nd, 1959, this ran for 156 episodes, finishing on June 19th, 1964. **Rod Serling** was the host and narrator and usually the executive producer. He also wrote most of the teleplays and many of the stories.

***

Season One:

1. Where Is Everybody. October 2nd, 1959, Season 1, Episode 1. Story by **Rod Serling**. Directed by Robert Stevens. Starring: Earl Holliman; James Gregory; and Paul Langton.

2. One for the Angels. October 9th, 1959, Season 1, Episode 2. Story by **Rod Serling**. Directed by Robert Parrish. Starring: Ed Wynn; Murray Hamilton; and Dana Dillaway.

3. Mr Denton on Doomsday. October 16th, 1959, Season 1, Episode 3. Story by **Rod Serling**. Directed by Allen Reisner. Starring: Dan Duryea; Martin Landau; Jeanne Cooper; and Doug McClure.

4. The Sixteen Millimeter Shrine. October 23rd, 1959, Season 1, Episode 4. Story by **Rod Serling**. Directed by Mitchell Leisen. Starring: Ida Lupino and Martin Balsam.

5. Walking Distance. October 30th, 1959, Season 1, Episode 5. Story by **Rod Serling**. Directed by Robert Stevens. Starring: Gig Young; Frank Overton; Irene Tedrow; and Ronnie Howard.

6. Escape Clause. November 6th, 1959, Season 1, Episode 6. Story by **Rod Serling**. Directed by Mitchell Leisen. Starring: David Wayne and Virginia Christine.

7. The Lonely. November 13th, 1959, Season 1, Episode 7. Story by **Rod Serling**. Directed by Jack Smight. Starring: Jack Warden, John Dehner and Jean Marsh.

8. Time Enough to Last. November 20th, 1959, Season 1, Episode 8. Story by Lynn Venable; teleplay by **Rod Serling**. Directed by John Brahm. Starring: Burgess Meredith; Vaughn Taylor; Jacqueline deWit; and Lela Bliss.

9. Perchance to Dream. November 27th, 1959, Season 1, Episode 9. Story by Charles Beaumont. Directed by Robert Florey. Starring: Richard Conte; John Larch; and Suzanne Lloyd.

10. Judgment Night. December 4th, 1959, Season 1, Episode 10. Story by **Rod Serling**. Directed by John Brahm. Starring: Nehemiah Persoff; Deirdre Owens; James Franciscus; and Patrick Macnee.

11. And When the Sky Was Opened. December 11th, 1959, Season 1, Episode 11. Story by Richard Matheson, teleplay by **Rod Serling**. Directed by Douglas Heyes. Starring: Rod Taylor and Jim Hutton.

12. What You Need. December 25th, 1959, Season 1, Episode 12. Story by Henry Kuttner and **C. L. Moore** writing as Lewis Padgett, teleplay by **Rod Serling**. Directed by Alvin Ganzer. Starring: Steve Cochran and Ernest Truex.

13. The Four of Us Are Dying. January 1st, 1960, Season 1, Episode 13. Story by George Clayton Johnson, teleplay by **Rod Serling**. Directed by John Brahm. Starring: Harry Townes; Phillip Pine; Ross Martin; and Beverly Garland.

14. Third from the Sun. January 8th, 1960, Season 1, Episode 14. Story by Richard Matheson, teleplay by **Rod Serling**. Directed by Richard L. Bare. Starring: Fritz Weaver; Edward Andrews; Denise Alexander; and Lori March.

15. I Shot an Arrow into the Air. January 15th, 1960, Season 1, Episode 15. Story by Madelon Champion, teleplay by **Rod Serling**. Directed by Stuart Rosenberg. Starring: Dewey Martin and Ed Binns.

16. The Hitch-Hiker. January 22nd, 1960, Season 1, Episode 16. Story by Lucille Fletcher, teleplay by **Rod Serling**. Directed by Alvin Ganzer. Starring: Inger Stevens; Leonard Strong; and Adam Williams.

17. The Fever. January 29th, 1960, Season 1, Episode 17. Story by **Rod Serling**. Directed by Robert Florey. Starring: Everett Sloane and Vivi Janiss.

18. The Last Flight. February 5th, 1960, Season 1, Episode 18. Story by Richard Matheson. Directed by William F. Claxton. Starring: Kenneth ;Haigh, Alexander Courby; Simon Scott; and Robert Warwick.

19. The Purple Testament. February 12th, 1960, Season 1, Episode 19. Story by **Rod Serling**. Directed by Richard L. Bare. Starring: Dick York; William Reynolds; William Phipps; and Barney Phillips.

20. Elegy. February 19th, 1960, Season 1, Episode 20. Story by Charles Beaumont. Directed by Douglas Heyes. Starring: Cecil Kellaway; Jeff Morrow; Don Dubbins; and Kevin Hagen.

21. Mirror Image. February 26th, 1960, Season 1, Episode 21. Story by **Rod Serling**. Directed by John Brahm. Starring: Vera Miles and Martin Milner.

22. The Monsters Are Due on Maple Street. March 4th, 1960, Season 1, Episode 22. Story by **Rod Serling**. Directed by Ron Winston. Starring: Claude Akins; Barry Atwater; Jack Weston; et al.

23. A World of Difference. March 11th, 1960, Season 1, Episode 23. Story by Richard Matheson. Directed by Ted Post. Starring: Howard Duff; David White; and Eileen Ryan.

24. Long Live Walter Jameson. March 18th, 1960, Season 1, Episode 24. Story by Charles Beaumont. Directed by Anton Leader. Starring: Kevin McCarthy, Edgar Stehli; Estelle Winwood; and Dodie Heath.

25. People Are Alike All Over. March 25th, 1960, Season 1, Episode 25. Story by Paul W. Fairman, teleplay by **Rod Serling**. Directed by Mitchell Leisen. Starring: Roddy McDowall; Susan Oliver; and Paul Comi.

26. Execution. April 1st, 1960, Season 1, Episode 26. Story by George Clayton Johnson, teleplay by **Rod Serling**. Directed by David Orrick McDearmon. Starring: Albert Salmi and Russell Johnson.

27. The Big Tall Wish. April 8th, 1960, Season 1, Episode 27. Story by **Rod Serling**. Directed by Ron Winston. Starring: Ivan Dixon and Stephen Perry.

28. A Nice Place to Visit. April 15th, 1960, Season 1, Episode 28. Story by Charles Beaumont. Directed by John Brahm. Starring: Larry Blyden and Sebastian Cabot.

29. Nightmare as a Child. April 29th, 1960, Season 1, Episode 29. Story by **Rod Serling**. Directed by Alvin Ganzer. Starring: Janice Rule and Shepperd Strudwick.

30. A Stop at Willoughby. May 6th, 1960, Season 1, Episode 30. Story by **Rod Serling**. Directed by Robert Parrish. Starring: James Daly; Howard Smith; and Patricia Donahue.

31. The Chaser. May 13th, 1960, Season 1, Episode 31. Story by John Collier; teleplay by Robert Presnell, Jr. Directed by Douglas Heyes. Starring: John McIntire; Patricia Barry; and J. Pat O'Malley.

32. A Passage for Trumpet. May 20th, 1960, Season 1, Episode 32. Story by **Rod Serling**. Directed by Don Medford. Starring: Jack Klugman and John Anderson.

33. Mr Bevis. June 3rd, 1960, Season 1, Episode 33. Story by **Rod Serling**. Directed by William Asher. Starring: Orson Bean and Henry Jones.

34. The After Hours. June 10th, 1960, Season 1, Episode 34. Story by **Rod Serling**. Directed by Douglas Heyes. Starring: Anne Francis; James Millhollin; and Elizabeth Allen.

35. The Mighty Casey. June 17th, 1960, Season 1, Episode 35. Story by **Rod Serling**. Directed by Alvin Ganzer and Robert Parrish. Starring: Jack Warden and Robert Sorrells.

Rod Serling

36. A World of His Own. July 1st, 1960, Season 1, Episode 36. Story by Richard Matheson. Directed by Ralph Nelson. Starring: Keenan Wynn; Phyllis Kirk; and Mary LaRoche.

Season Two:

37. King Nine Will Not Return. September 30th, 1960, Season 2, Episode 1. Story by **Rod Serling**. Directed by Buzz Kulik. Starring: Robert Cummings; Gene Lyons; Paul Lambert; and Jenna McMahon.

38. The Man in the Bottle. October 7th, 1960, Season 2, Episode 2. Story by **Rod Serling**. Directed by Don Medford. Starring: Luther Adler and Vivi Janiss.

39. Nervous Man in a Four Dollar Room. October 14th, 1960, Season 2, Episode 3. Story by **Rod Serling**. Directed by Douglas Heyes. Starring: Joe Mantell and William D. Gordon.

40. A Thing About Machines. October 28th, 1960, Season 2, Episode 4. Story by **Rod Serling**. Directed by David Orrick McDearmon. Starring: Richard Haydn and Barbara Stuart.

41. The Howling Man. November 4th, 1960, Season 2, Episode 5. Story by Charles Beaumont. Directed by Douglas Heyes. Starring: John Carradine; H. M. Wynant; and Robin Hughes.

42. Eye of the Beholder. November 11th, 1960, Season 2, Episode 6. Story by **Rod Serling**. Directed by Douglas Heyes. Starring: Maxine Stuart; William D. Gordon; Jennifer Howard; and Donna Douglas.

43. Nick of Time. November 18th, 1960, Season 2, Episode 7. Story by Richard Matheson. Directed by Richard L. Bare. Starring: William Shatner and Patricia Breslin.

44. The Lateness of the Hour. December 2nd, 1960, Season 2, Episode 8. Story by **Rod Serling**. Directed by Jack Smight. Starring: Inger Stevens and John Hoyt.

45. The Trouble with Templeton. December 9th, 1960, Season 2, Episode 9. Story by E. Jack Neuman. Directed by Buzz Kulik. Starring: Brian Aherne; Pippa Scott; Sydney Pollack; et al.

46. A Most Unusual Camera. December 16th, 1960, Season 2, Episode 10. Story by **Rod Serling**. Directed by John Rich. Starring: Fred Clark and Jean Carson.

47. The Night of the Meek. December 23rd, 1960, Season 2, Episode 11. Story by **Rod Serling**. Directed by Jack Smight. Starring: Art Carney and John Fiedler.

48. Dust. January 6th, 1961, Season 2, Episode 12. Story by **Rod Serling**. Directed by Douglas Heyes. Starring: Thomas Gomez; John larch; and Vladimir Sokoloff.

49. Back There. January 13th, 1961, Season 2, Episode 13. Story by **Rod Serling**. Directed by David Orrick McDearmon. Starring: Russell Johnson; Paul Hartman; and John Lasell.

50. The Whole Truth. January 20th, 1961, Season 2, Episode 14. Story by **Rod Serling**. Directed by James Sheldon. Starring: Jack Carson; Loring Smith; and Arte Johnson.

51. The Invaders. January 27th, 1961, Season 2, Episode 15. Story by Richard Matheson. Directed by Douglas Heyes. Starring: Agnes Moorehead.

52. A Penny for Your Thoughts. February 3rd, 1961, Season 2, Episode 16. Story by George Clayton Johnson. Directed by James Sheldon. Starring: Dick York and June Dayton.

53. Twenty-Two. February 10th, 1961, Season 2, Episode 17. Story by Bennett Cerf. Directed by Jack Smight. Starring: Barbara Nichols and Jonathan Harris.

54. The Odyssey of Flight 33. February 24th, 1961, Season 2, Episode 18. Story by **Rod Serling**. Directed by Jus Addiss. Starring: John Anderson; Paul Comi; Sandy Kenyon; Wayne Heffley; Harp McGuire; and Betty Garde.

55. Mr Dingle, the Strong. March 3rd, 1961, Season 2, Episode 19. Story by **Rod Serling**. Directed by John Brahm. Starring: Burgess Meredith and James Westerfield, with Eddie Ryder and Don Rickles.

56. Static. March 10th, 1961, Season 2, Episode 20. Story by Oceo Ritch and Charles Beaumont. Directed by Buzz Kulik. Starring: Dean Jagger and Carmen Mathews.

57. The Prime Mover. March 24th, 1961, Season 2, Episode 21. Story by Charles Beaumont. Directed by Richard L. Bare. Starring: Dane Clark and Buddy Ebsen.

58. Long Distance Call. March 31st, 1961, Season 2, Episode 22. Story by Charles Beaumont and Bill Idelson. Directed by James Sheldon. Starring: Phil Abbott; Patricia Smith; Lili Darvas; and Bill Mumy.

59. A Hundred Yards Over the Run. April 7th, 1961, Season 2, Episode 23. Story by **Rod Serling**. Directed by Buzz Kulik. Starring: Cliff Robertson; John Crawford; and Miranda Jones.

60. The Rip Van Winkle Caper. April 21st, 1961, Season 2, Episode 24. Story by **Rod Serling**. Directed by Jus Addiss. Starring: Simon Oakland and Oscar Beregi.

61. The Silence. April 28th, 1961, Season 2, Episode 25. Story by **Rod Serling**. Directed by Boris Sagal. Starring: Franchot Tone; Liam Sullivan; and Jonathan Harris.

62. Shadow Play. May 5th, 1961, Season 2, Episode 26. Story by Charles Beaumont. Directed by John Brahm. Starring: Dennis Weaver and Harry Townes.

63. The Mind and the Matter. May 12th, 1961, Season 2, Episode 27. Story by **Rod Serling**. Directed by Buzz Kulik. Starring: Shelley Berman; Jack Grinnage; and Chet Stratton.

64. Will the Real Martian Please Stand Up? May 26th, 1961, Season 2, Episode 28. Story by **Rod**

Serling. Directed by Montgomery Pittman. Starring: John Hoyt; Jean Willes; and Jack Elam.

65. The Obsolete Man. June 2nd, 1961, Season 2, Episode 29. Story by **Rod Serling**. Directed by Elliot Silverstein. Starring: Burgess Meredith and Fritz Weaver.

Season Three:

66. Two. September 15th, 1961, Season 3, Episode 1. Story by Montgomery Pittman. Directed by Montgomery Pittman. Starring: Elizabeth Montgomery and Charles Bronson.

67. The Arrival. September 22nd, 1961, Season 3, Episode 2. Story by **Rod Serling**. Directed by Boris Sagal. Starring: Harold J. Stone and Fredd Wayne.

68. The Shelter. September 29th, 1961, Season 3, Episode 3. Story by **Rod Serling**. Directed by Lamont Johnson. Starring: Larry Gates; Jack Albertson; Peggy Stewart; Joseph Bernard; Sandy Kenyon; et al.

69. The Passersby. October 6th, 1961, Season 3, Episode 4. Story by **Rod Serling**. Directed by Elliot Silverstein. Starring James Gregory and Joanne Linville.

70. A Game of Pool. October 13th, 1961, Season 3, Episode 5. Story by George Clayton Johnson. Directed by Buzz Kulik. Starring Jack Klugman and Jonathan Winters.

71. The Mirror. October 20th, 1961, Season 3, Episode 6. Story by **Rod Serling**. Directed by Don Medford. Starring Peter Falk and Will Kuluva.

72. The Grave. October 27th, 1961, Season 3, Episode 7. Story by Montgomery Pittman. Directed by Montgomery Pittman. Starring: Lee Marvin; James Best; Strother Martin; and Lee Van Cleef.

73. It's a Good Life. November 3rd, 1961, Season 3, Episode 8. Story by Jerome Bixby, teleplay by **Rod Serling**. Directed by James Sheldon. Starring: John Larch; Cloris Leachman; Don Keefer; and Billy Mumy.

74. Deaths-Head Revisited. November 10th, 1961, Season 3, Episode 9. Story by **Rod Serling**. Directed by Don Medford. Starring: Joseph Schildkraut and Oscar Beregi Jr.

75. The Midnight Sun. November 17th, 1961, Season 3, Episode 10. Story by **Rod Serling**. Directed by Anton Leder. Starring: Lois Nettleton; Betty Garde; and Tom Reese.

76. Still Valley. November 24th, 1961, Season 3, Episode 11. Story by Manly Wade Wellman, teleplay by **Rod Serling**. Directed by James Sheldon. Starring: Gary Merrill; Vaughn Taylor; and Mark Tapscott.

77. The Jungle. December 1st, 1961, Season 3, Episode 12. Story by Charles Beaumont. Directed by William F. Claxton. Starring: John Dehner; Walter Brooke; and Jay Adler.

78. Once Upon a Time. December 15th, 1961, Season 3, Episode 13. Story by Richard Matheson. Directed by Norman Z. McLeod. Starring: Buster Keaton and Stanley Adams.

79. Five Characters in Search of an Exit. December 22nd, 1961, Season 3, Episode 14. Story by Marvin Petal, teleplay by **Rod Serling**. Directed by Lamont Johnson. Starring: Susan Harrison and William Windom.

80. A Quality of Mercy. December 29th, 1961, Season 3, Episode 15. Story by Sam Rolfe, teleplay by **Rod Serling**. Directed by Buzz Kulik. Starring: Dean Stockwell; Leonard Nimoy; and Albert Salmi.

81. Nothing in the Dark. January 5th, 1962, Season 3, Episode 16. Story by George Clayton Johnson. Directed by Lamont Johnson. Starring: Robert Redford; Gladys Cooper; and R. G. Armstrong.

82. One More Pallbearer. January 12th, 1962, Season 3, Episode 17. Story by **Rod Serling**. Directed by Lamont Johnson. Starring: Joseph Wiseman and Katherine Squire.

83. Dead Man's Shoes. January 19th, 1962, Season 3, Episode 18. Story by Charles Beaumont. Directed by Montgomery Pittman. Starring: Warren Stevens and Richard Devon.

84. The Hunt. January 26th, 1962, Season 3, Episode 19. Story by Earl Hamner, Jr. Directed by Harold D. Schuster. Starring: Arthur Hunnicutt and Jeanette Nolan.

85. Showdown with Rance McGrew. February 2nd, 1962, Season 3, Episode 20. Story by Frederick Louis Fox and **Rod Serling**. Directed by Christian Nyby. Starring: Larry Blyden; Arch Johnson; and Robert Kline.

86. Kick the Can. February 9th, 1962, Season 3, Episode 21. Story by George Clayton Johnson. Directed by Lamont Johnson. Starring: Ernest Truex and Russell Collins.

87. A Piano in the House. February 16th, 1962, Season 3, Episode 22. Story by Earl Hamner, Jr. Directed by David Greene. Starring: Barry Morse and Joan Hackett.

88. The Last Rites of Jeff Myrtlebank. February 23rd, 1962, Season 3, Episode 23. Story by Montgomery Pittman. Directed by Montgomery Pittman. Starring: James Best; Sherry Jackson; Edgar Buchanan; and Dub Taylor.

89. To Serve Man. March 2nd, 1962, Season 3, Episode 24. Story by **Damon Knight**. Directed by Richard L. Bare. Starring: Lloyd Bochner; Susan Cummings; and Richard Kiel.

90. The Fugitive. March 9th, 1962, Season 3, Episode 25. Story by Charles Beaumont. Directed by Richard L. Bare. Starring: Susan Gordon; J. Pat O'Malley; and Nancy Kulp.

91. Little Girl Lost. March 16th, 1962, Season 3, Episode 26. Story by Richard Matheson. Directed by Paul Stewart. Starring: Sarah Marshall and Robert Sampson.

Rod Serling

92. Person or Persons Unknown. March 23rd, 1962, Season 3, Episode 27. Story by Charles Beaumont. Directed by John Brahm. Starring: Richard Long and Frank Silvera.

93. The Little People. March 30th, 1962, Season 3, Episode 28. Story by **Rod Serling**. Directed by William F. Claxton. Starring: Joe Maross; Claude Akins; Michael Ford; and Robert Eaton.

94. Four O'Clock. April 6th, 1962, Season 3, Episode 29. Story by Price Day, teleplay by **Rod Serling**. Directed by Lamont Johnson. Starring: Theodore Bikel; and Phyllis Love.

95. Hocus-Pocus and Frisby. April 13th, 1962, Season 3, Episode 30. Story by Frederick Louis Fox, teleplay by **Rod Serling**. Directed by Lamont Johnson. Starring: Andy Devine and Milton Selzer.

96. The Trade-Ins. April 20th, 1962, Season 3, Episode 31. Story by **Rod Serling**. Directed by Elliot Silverstein. Starring: Joseph Schildkraut; Noah Keen; and Alma Platt.

97. The Gift. April 27th, 1962, Season 3, Episode 32. Story by **Rod Serling**. Directed by Allen H. Miner. Starring: Geoffrey Home; Nico Minardos; Cliff Osmond; and Edmund Vargas.

98. The Dummy. May 4th, 1962, Season 3, Episode 33. Story by lee Polk, teleplay by **Rod Serling**. Directed by Abner Biberman. Starring: Cliff Robertson; and Frank Sutton.

99. Young Man's Fancy. May 11th, 1962, Season 3, Episode 34. Story by Richard Matheson. Directed by John Brahm. Starring: Phyllis Thaxter and Alex Nicol.

100. I Sing the Body Electric. May 18th, 1962, Season 3, Episode 35. Story by **Ray Bradbury**. Directed by William F. Claxton and James Sheldon. Starring: Josephine Hutchinson; David White; Vaughn Taylor; Doris Packer; and Veronica Cartwright.

101. Cavender Is Coming. May 25th, 1962, Season 3, Episode 36. Story by **Rod Serling**. Directed by Christian Nyby. Starring: Jesse White; Carol Burnett; and Donna Douglas.

102. The Changing of the Guard. May 25th, 1962, Season 3, Episode 37. Story by **Rod Serling**. Directed by Robert Ellis Miller. Starring: Donald Pleasence and Liam Sullivan.

Season Four:

103. In His Image. January 3rd, 1963, Season 4, Episode 1. Story by Charles Beaumont. Directed by Perry Lafferty. Starring: George Grizzard and Gail Kobe.

104. The Thirty-Fathom Grave. January 10th, 1963, Season 4, Episode 2. Story by **Rod Serling**. Directed by Perry Lafferty. Starring: Mike Kellin; Simon Oakland; and Bill Bixby.

105. Valley of the Shadow. January 17th, 1963, Season 4, Episode 3. Story by Charles Beaumont. Directed by Perry Lafferty. Starring: David Opatoshu; Ed Nelson; Natalie Trundy; Henry Beckman; and James Doohan.

106. He's Alive. January 24th, 1963, Season 4, Episode 4. Story by **Rod Serling**. Directed by Stuart Rosenberg. Starring: Dennis Hopper and Ludwig Donath.

107. He's Alive. January 31st, 1963, Season 4, Episode 5. Story by Richard Matheson. Directed by Stuart Rosenberg. Starring: Barbara Baxley; Frank Overton; Irene Dailey; and Ann Jillian.

108. Death Ship. February 7th, 1963, Season 4, Episode 6. Story by Richard Matheson. Directed by Don Medford. Starring: Jack Klugman and Ross Martin.

109. Jess-Belle. February 14th, 1963, Season 4, Episode 7. Story by Earl Hamner, Jr. Directed by Buzz Kulik. Starring: Anne Francis and James Best.

110. Miniature. February 21st, 1963, Season 4, Episode 8. Story by Charles Beaumont. Directed by Walter Grauman. Starring: Robert Duvall; Barbara Barrie; and William Windom.

111. Printer's Devil. February 28th, 1963, Season 4, Episode 9. Story by Charles Beaumont. Directed by Ralph Senensky. Starring: Robert Sterling; Pat Crowley; and Burgess Meredith.

112. No Time Like the Past. March 7th, 1963, Season 4, Episode 10. Story by **Rod Serling**. Directed by Jus Addiss. Starring: Dana Andrews; Patricia Breslin; and Robert Cornthwaite.

113. The Parallel. March 14th, 1963, Season 4, Episode 11. Story by **Rod Serling**. Directed by Alan Crosland, Jr. Starring: Steve Forrest; Jacqueline Scott; and Frank Aletter.

114. I Dream of Genie. March 21st, 1963, Season 4, Episode 12. Story by John Furia. Directed by Robert Gist. Starring: Howard Morris; Patricia Barry; and Jack Albertson.

115. The New Exhibit. April 4th, 1963, Season 4, Episode 13. Story by Charles Beaumont. Directed by John Brahm. Starring: Martin Balsam; Will Kuluva; and Margaret Field.

116. Of Late I Think of Cliffordville. April 11th, 1963, Season 4, Episode 14. Story by Malcolm Jameson. Directed by David Lowell Rich. Starring: Albert Salmi; John Anderson; and Julie Newmar.

117. The Incredible World of Horace Ford. April 18th, 1963, Season 4, Episode 15. Story by Reginald Rose. Directed by Abner Biberman. Starring: Pat Hingle; Nan Martin; and Ruth White.

118. On Thursday We Leave for Home. May 2nd, 1963, Season 4, Episode 16. Written by **Rod Serling**. Directed by Buzz Kulik. Starring: James Whitmore; Tim O'Connor; and James Broderick.

119. Passage on the Lady Anne. May 9th, 1963, Season 4, Episode 17. Story by Charles Beaumont. Directed by Lamont Johnson. Starring: Gladys Cooper; Wilfrid Hyde-White; Cecil Kellaway; and Joyce Van Patten.

120. The Bard. May 23rd, 1963, Season 4, Episode 18. Written by **Rod Serling**. Directed by David Butler. Starring: Jack Weston; John McGiver; and Burt Reynolds.

Season Five:

121. In Praise of Pip. September 27th, 1963, Season 5, Episode 1. Written by **Rod Serling**. Directed by Joseph M. Newman. Starring: Jack Klugman; Connie Gilchrist; Bobby Diamond; and Billy Mumy.

122. Steel. October 4th, 1963, Season 5, Episode 2. Written by Richard Matheson. Directed by Don Weis. Starring: Lee Marvin and Joe Mantell.

123. Nightmare at 20,000 Feet. October 11th, 1963, Season 5, Episode 3. Written by Richard Matheson. Directed by Richard Donner. Starring: William Shatner; Christine White; Ed Kemmer; and Asa Maynor.

124. A Kind of Stopwatch. October 18th, 1963, Season 5, Episode 4. Written by Michael D. Rosenthal, teleplay by **Rod Serling**. Directed by John Rich. Starring: Richard Erdman and Herbie Faye.

125. The Last Night of a Jockey. October 25th, 1963, Season 5, Episode 5. Written by **Rod Serling**. Directed by Joseph M. Newman. Starring Mickey Rooney.

126. Living Doll. November 1st, 1963, Season 5, Episode 6. Written by Charles Beaumont. Directed by Richard C. Sarafian. Starring: Telly Savalas; Mary LaRoche; and Tracy Stratford.

127. The Old Man in the Cave. November 8th, 1963, Season 5, Episode 7. Written by Henry Slesar. Directed by Alan Crosland, Jr. Starring: James Coburn; John Anderson; and Josie Lloyd.

128. Uncle Simon. November 15th, 1963, Season 5, Episode 8. Written by **Rod Serling**. Directed by Don Siegel. Starring: Cedric Hardwicke; Constance Ford; and Ian Wolfe.

129. Probe 7, Over and Out. November 29th, 1963, Season 5, Episode 9. Written by **Rod Serling**. Directed by Ted Post. Starring: Richard Basehart and Antoinette Bower.

130. The 7th Is Made Up of Phantoms. December 6th, 1963, Season 5, Episode 10. Written by **Rod Serling**. Directed by Alan Crosland, Jr. Starring: Ron Foster; Warren Oates; Randy Boone; Greg Morris; and Jeff Morris.

131. A Short Drink from a Certain Fountain. December 13th, 1963, Season 5, Episode 11. Written by Lou Holtz, teleplay by **Rod Serling**. Directed by Bernard Girard. Starring: Patrick O'Neal and Ruta Lee.

132. Ninety Years Without Slumbering. December 20th, 1963, Season 5, Episode 12. Written by George Clayton Johnson, teleplay by Richard De Roy. Directed by Roger Kay. Starring: Ed Wynn; Carolyn Kearney; and James T. Callahan.

133. Ring-a-Ding Girl. December 27th, 1963, Season 5, Episode 13. Written by Earl Hamner, Jr. Directed by Alan Crosland, Jr. Starring: Maggie McNamara; Mary Munday; and David Macklin.

134. You Drive. January 3rd, 1964, Season 5, Episode 14. Written by Earl Hamner, Jr. Directed by John Brahm. Starring: Edward Andrews and Helen Westcott.

135. The Long Morrow. January 10th, 1964, Season 5, Episode 15. Written by **Rod Serling**. Directed by Robert Florey. Starring: Robert Lansing and Mariette Hartley.

136. The Self-Improvement of Salvadore Ross. January 17th, 1964, Season 5, Episode 16. Written by Henry Slesar, teleplay by Jerry McNeely. Directed by Don Siegel. Starring: Don Gordon; Gail Kobe; Vaughn Taylor; and J. Pat O'Malley.

137. Number 12 Looks Just Like You. January 24th, 1964, Season 5, Episode 17. Written by Charles Beaumont and John Tomerlin. Directed by Abner Biberman. Starring: Collin Wilcox Paxton; Richard Long; and Pam Austin.

138. Black Leather Jackets. January 31st, 1964, Season 5, Episode 18. Written by Earl Hamner, Jr. Directed by Joseph M. Newman. Starring: Lee Kinsolving; Shelley Fabares; Michael Forest; and Denver Pyle.

139. Night Call. February 7th, 1964, Season 5, Episode 19. Written by Richard Matheson. Directed by Jacques Tourneur. Starring: Gladys Cooper; Nora Marlowe; and Martine Bartlett.

140. From Agnes - with Love. February 14th, 1964, Season 5, Episode 20. Written by Bernard C. Schoenfeld. Directed by Richard Donner. Starring: Wally Cox; Ralph Taeger; and Sue Randall.

141. Spur of the Moment. February 21st, 1964, Season 5, Episode 21. Written by Richard Matheson. Directed by Elliot Silverstein. Starring: Diana Hyland; Marsha Hunt; Philip Ober; Roger Davis; and Robert Hogan.

142. An Occurrence at Owl Creek Bridge. February 28th, 1964, Season 5, Episode 22. Written by Ambrose Bierce and adapted by Robert Enrico. Directed by Robert Enrico.

143. Queen of the Nile. March 6th, 1964, Season 5, Episode 23. Written by Charles Beaumont. Directed by John Brahm. Starring: Ann Blyth; and Lee Philips.

144. What's in the Box. March 13th, 1964, Season 5, Episode 24. Written by Martin Goldsmith. Directed by Richard L. Bare. Starring: Joan Blondell; William Demarest; and Sterling Holloway.

145. The Masks. March 20th, 1964, Season 5, Episode 25. Written by **Rod Serling**. Directed by Ida Lupino. Starring: Robert Keith; Milton Selzer; Virginia Gregg; and Alan Sues.

146. I Am the Night - Color Me Black. March 27th, 1964, Season 5, Episode 26. Written by **Rod Serling**. Directed by Abner Biberman. Starring:

Rod Serling

Michael Constantine; Paul Fix; George Lindsey; and Ivan Dixon.

147. Sounds and Silences. April 3rd, 1964, Season 5, Episode 27. Written by **Rod Serling**. Directed by Richard Donner. Starring: John McGiver; Renee Aubry; and Penny Singleton.

148. Caesar and Me. April 10th, 1964, Season 5, Episode 28. Written by Adele T. Strassfield. Directed by Robert Butler. Starring: Jackie Cooper; Morgan Brittany; and Sarah Selby.

149. The Jeopardy Room. April 17th, 1964, Season 5, Episode 29. Written by **Rod Serling**. Directed by Richard Donner. Starring: Martin Landau; John Van Dreelen; and Robert Kelljan.

150. Stopover in a Quiet Town. April 24th, 1964, Season 5, Episode 30. Written by Earl Hamner, Jr. Directed by Ron Winston. Starring: Barry Nelson and Nancy Malone.

151. The Encounter. May 1st, 1964, Season 5, Episode 31. Written by Martin Goldsmith. Directed by Robert Butler. Starring: Neville Brand and George Takei.

152. Mr Garrity and the Graves. May 8th, 1964, Season 5, Episode 32. Written by Mike Korologos. Directed by Ted Post. Starring: John Dehner; Stanley Adams; and J. Pat O'Malley.

153. The Brain Center at Whipple's. May 15th, 1964, Season 5, Episode 33. Written by **Rod Serling**. Directed by Richard Donner. Starring: Richard Deacon; Paul Newlan; and Ted de Corsia.

154. Come Wander With Me. May 22nd, 1964, Season 5, Episode 34. Written by Anthony Wilson. Directed by Richard Donner. Starring: Gary Crosby and Bonnie Beecher.

155. The Fear. May 29th, 1964, Season 5, Episode 35. Written by **Rod Serling**. Directed by Ted Post. Starring: Peter Mark Richman and Hazel Court.

156. The Bewitchin' Pool. June 19th, 1964, Season 5, Episode 36. Written by Earl Hamner, Jr. Directed by Joseph M. Newman. Starring: Mary Badham; Dee Hartford; Tod Andrews; and Jeffrey Byron.

***

78. Requiem for a Heavyweight. Wrote the story for this November 1962 film, which was directed by Ralph Nelson and starred: Anthony Quinn; Jackie Gleeson; Mickey Rooney; Julie Harris; Stanley Adams; and others, including Jack Dempsey as himself and Cassius Clay as himself.

79. The Yellow Canary. Did the story for this 1963 film which was directed by Buzz Kulik and starred: Pat Boone; Barbara Eden; Steve Forrest; Jack Klugman; et al.

80. A Killing at Sundial. Written for Bob Hope Presents the Chrysler Theatre, this aired on October 4th, 1963, Season 1, Episode 1. It was directed by Alex Segal and starred Angie Dickinson, Stuart Whitman and Melvyn Douglas.

81. It's Mental Work. For Bob Hope Presents the Chrysler Theatre, this aired on December 20th, 1963, Season 1, Episode 10. Directed by Alex March, it starred: Lee J. Cobb; Harry Guardino; and Gena Rowlands.

82. Seven Days in May. Wrote the screenplay for this 1964 film. Directed by John Frankenheimer, it starred: Burt Lancaster; Kirk Douglas; Fredric March; Ava Gardner; Martin Balsam; Andrew Duggan; and many others, including Leonard Nimoy in an uncredited bit part.

83. The Movie Maker. Wrote the story for this 1964 TV film. Directed by Ron Winston, it starred: Dabney Coleman; Robert Culp; James Dunn; Sally Kellerman; and Rod Steiger.

84. A Slow Fade to Black. For Bob Hope Presents the Chrysler Theatre, this was shown on March 27th, 1964, Season 1, Episode 22. It was directed by Ron Winston and starred: Dabney Coleman; Robert Culp; James Dunn; Sharon Farrell; and Sally Kellerman.

85. The Command. Adapted for Bob Hope Presents the Chrysler Theatre from The Strike, 1954, this was shown on May 22nd, 1964, Season 1, Episode 27. It was directed by Fielder Cook and starred: Ed Binns; Andrew Duggan; and Robert Stack.

86. Carol for Another Christmas. Wrote the story for this 1964 television film. Directed by Joseph L. Mankiewicz, it starred: Sterling Hayden; Eva Marie Saint; Ben Gazzara; Barbara Ann Teer; Steve Lawrence; James Shigeta; Pat Hingle; Robert Shaw; Peter Sellers; Britt Ekland; et al.

87. Exit from a Plane in Flight. For Bob Hope Presents the Chrysler Theatre, this was shown on January 22nd, 1965, Season 2, Episode 12. It starred: Sorrell Brooke; Lloyd Bridge; and Hugh O'Brian.

88. The Loner. This television series was created by **Rod Serling** and he wrote many of the scripts. The show ran for 26 episodes, starting on September 18th, 1965 and finishing on March 12th, 1966. It was a western, starring Lloyd Bridges.

89. The Hate Syndrome. This was written for the television series Insight. It aired on May 13th, 1966, starring Jim Begg, Harold J. Stone and Eduard Franz.

90. Assault on a Queen. Based on the novel by Jack Finney, Serling wrote the screenplay for this 1966 film. It was directed by Jack Donohue and starred: Frank Sinatra; Virna Lisi; Anthony Franciosa; Richard Conte;

91. The Doomsday Flight. Wrote this 1966 TV movie. Directed by William A. Graham, it starred: Edward Asner; Van Johnson; Jack Lord; Greg Morris; Edmond O'Brien; John Saxon; Katherine Crawford; and others, including Michael Sarrazin as an unnamed Army corporal.

92. Planet of the Apes. Working with Michael Wilson, he wrote the screenplay for this 1968 film, based on the novel Monkey Planet by Pierre Boulle. It was directed by Franklin J. Schaffner and starred: Charlton Heston; Roddy McDowell; Kim Hunter; Maurice Evans; Linda Harrison; and others.

93. Certain Honorable Men. Serling wrote this 1968 television movie. It was directed by Alex Segal and starred Van Heflin, with Peter Fonda and Will Geer.

94. Night Gallery. Also known as Rod Serling's Wax Museum, this was written for television and shown in November 1969. Directed by Boris Sagal - The Cemetery segment; Barry Shear - Escape Route segment; and **Steven Spielberg** - Eyes segment, this starred: Joan Crawford; Ossie Davis; Richard Kiley; Roddy McDowall; Barry Sullivan; Tom Bosley; George Macready; Sam Jaffe; et al.

95. The New People. This television series was developed by Serling. It first aired on September 22nd, 1969 and ran for seventeen episodes, ending on January 12th, 1970. It starred: Tiffany Bolling; Zooey Hall; Jill Jaress; David Moses; Dennis Olivieri; and Peter Ratray.

96. A Storm in Summer. Also known as The Merchant of Scarsdale, this was written for television in 1970. Directed by Buzz Kulik, it starred: Peter Ustinov; N'Gai Dixon; Marlyn Mason; and others.

97. The Man. Based on the novel by Irving Wallace, he wrote the screenplay for this 1972 movie. Directed by Joseph Sargent, it starred: James Earl Jones; Martin Balsam; Burgess Meredith; Lew Ayres; William Windom; Barbara Rush; Georg Stanford Brown; and many others.

98. Night Gallery. Also known as Rod Serling's Night Gallery, he created and hosted this series, which ran for ninety-five episodes, starting December 16th, 1970 and going until May 27th, 1973. He also wrote a number of the stories and worked out many of the teleplays.

***

1. The Dead Man. December 16th, 1970, Season 1, Episode 1. Story by **Fritz Leiber**, 1950. Directed by Douglas Heyes. This starred: Carl Betz, Jeff Corey and Louise Sorel.

2. The Housekeeper. December 16th, 1970, Season 1, Episode 2. Story by Douglas Heyes. Directed by John Meredyth Lucas. This starred: Larry Hagman; Suzy Parker; and Jeanette Nolan.

3. Room with a View. December 23rd, 1970, Season 1, Episode 3. Story by Hal Dresner. Directed by Jerrold Freedman. This starred: Joseph Wiseman and Diane Keaton.

4. The Little Black Bag. December 23rd, 1970, Season 1, Episode 4. Story by C. M. Kornbluth, 1950. Directed by Jeannot Szwarc. This starred: Burgess Meredith and Chill Wills.

5. The Nature of the Enemy. December 23rd, 1970, Season 1, Episode 5. Story by **Rod Serling**. Directed by Allen Reisner. This starred: Joseph Campanella and Richard Van Vleet.

6. The House. December 30th, 1970, Season 1, Episode 6. Story by Andre Maurois. Directed by John Astin. This starred: Joanna Pettet and Paul Richards.

7. Certain Shadows on the Wall. December 30th, 1970, Season 1, Episode 7. Story by Mary Eleanor Freeman. Directed by Jeff Corey. This starred: Louis Hayward; Grayson Hall; Rachel Roberts; and Agnes Moorehead.

8. Make Me Laugh. January 6th, 1971, Season 1, Episode 8. Story by **Rod Serling**. Directed by **Steven Spielberg**. This starred: Godfrey Cambridge; Tom Bosley; and Jackie Vernon.

9. Clean Kills and Other Trophies. January 6th, 1971, Season 1, Episode 9. Story by **Rod Serling**. Directed by Walter Doniger. This starred: Raymond Massey and Tom Troupe.

10. Pamela's Voice. January 13th, 1971, Season 1, Episode 10. Story by **Rod Serling**. Directed by Richard Benedict. This starred: Phyllis Diller and John Astin.

11. Lone Survivor. January 13th, 1971, Season 1, Episode 11. Story by **Rod Serling**. Directed by Gene Levitt. This starred: John Colicos and Torin Thatcher.

12. The Doll. January 13th, 1971, Season 1, Episode 12. Story by Algernon Blackwood. Directed by Rudi Dorn. This starred: Shani Wallis; John Williams; and Henry Silva.

13. The Last Laurel. January 20th, 1971, Season 1, Episode 13. Story by Davis Grubb - originally The Horsehair Trunk. Directed by Daryl Duke. This starred: Jack Cassidy; Martine Beswick; and Martin E. Brooks.

14. They're Tearing Down Tim Riley's Bar. January 20th, 1971, Season 1, Episode 14. Story by **Rod Serling**. Directed by Don Taylor. This starred: William Windom; Diane Baker; and Bert Convy.

15. The Boy Who Predicted Earthquakes. September 15th, 1971, Season 2, Episode 1. Story by Margaret St Clair. Directed by John Badham. This starred: Michael Constantine; Clint Howard; and Bernie Kopell.

16. Miss Lovecraft Sent Me. September 15th, 1971, Season 2, Episode 2. Story by Jack Laird. Directed by Gene R. Kearney. This starred: Joseph Campanella and Sue Lyon.

17. The Hand of Borgus Weems. September 15th, 1971, Season 2, Episode 3. Story by George Langelaan - originally The Other Hand. Directed by John Meredyth Lucas. This starred: George Maharis; Ray Milland; and Joan Huntington.

18. Phantom of What Opera? September 15th, 1971, Season 2, Episode 4. Story by Gene R. Kearney. Directed by Gene R. Kearney. This starred: Mary Ann Beck and Leslie Nielsen.

19. Death in the Family. September 22nd, 1971, Season 2, Episode 5. Story by Miriam Allen DeFord. Directed by Jeannot Szwarc. This starred: E. G. Marshall and Desi Arnez, Jr.

20. The Merciful. September 22nd, 1971, Season 2, Episode 6. Story by Charles L. Sweeney, Jr. Directed by Jeannot Szwarc. This starred: Imogene Coca and King Donovan.

Rod Serling

21. Class of '99. September 22nd, 1971, Season 2, Episode 7. Story by **Rod Serling**. Directed by Jeannot Szwarc. This starred: Vincent Price; Bandon De Wilde; and Randolph Mantooth.

22. Witches Feast. September 22nd, 1971, Season 2, Episode 8. Directed by Jerrold Freedman. This starred: Agnes Moorehead; Ruth Buzzi; Allison McKay; and Fran Ryan.

23. Since Aunt Ada Came to Stay. September 29th, 1971, Season 2, Episode 9. Story by **A. E. van Vogt**. Directed by William Hale. This starred: James Farentino; Michele Lee; Jeanette Nolan; and Jonathan Harris.

24. With Apologies to Mr Hyde. September 29th, 1971, Season 2, Episode 10. Story by Jack Laird. Directed by Jeannot Szwarc. This starred: Adam West and Jack Laird.

25. The Flip Side of Satan. September 29th, 1971, Season 2, Episode 11. Story by Hal Dresner. Directed by Jerrold Freedman. This starred Arte Johnson.

26. A Fear of Spiders. October 6th, 1971, Season 2, Episode 12. Story by Elizabeth M. Walter. Directed by John Astin. This starred: Kim Stanley; Patrick O'Neal; and Tom Pedi.

27. Junior. October 6th, 1971, Season 2, Episode 13. Story by Gene R. Kearney. Directed by Theodore J. Flicker. This starred: Wally Cox; Barbara Flicker; and Bill Svanoe.

28. Marmalade Wine. October 6th, 1971, Season 2, Episode 14. Story by Joan Aiken. Directed by Jerrold Freedman. This starred: Robert Morse and Rudy Vallee.

29. The Academy. October 6th, 1971, Season 2, Episode 15. Story by David Ely. Directed by Jeff Corey. This starred: Pat Boone; Leif Erickson; and Larry Linville.

30. The Phantom Farmhouse. October 20th, 1971, Season 2, Episode 16. Story by Seabury Quinn. Directed by Jeannot Szwarc. This starred: David McCallum; Linda Marsh; and David Carradine.

31. Silent Snow, Secret Snow. October 20th, 1971, Season 2, Episode 17. Story by Conrad Aiken. Directed by Gene R. Kearney. This starred: Lonny Chapman; Lisabeth Hush; and Orson Welles as the Narrator.

32. A Question of Fear. October 27th, 1971, Season 2, Episode 18. Story by Bryan Lewis. Directed by Jack Laird. This starred: Leslie Nielsen and Fritz Weaver.

33. The Devil Is Not Mocked. October 27th, 1971, Season 2, Episode 19. Story by Manly Wade Wellman. Directed by Gene R. Kearney. This starred: Helmut Dantine and Francis Lederer.

34. Midnight Never Ends. November 3rd, 1971, Season 2, Episode 20. Story by **Rod Serling**. Directed by Jeannot Szwarc. This starred: Robert F. Lyons and Susan Strasberg.

35. Brenda. November 3rd, 1971, Season 2, Episode 21. Story by Margaret St Clair. Directed by Allen Reisner. This starred: Glenn Corbett; Laurie Prange; and Robert Hogan.

36. The Diary. November 10th, 1971, Season 2, Episode 22. Story by **Rod Serling**. Directed by William Hale. This starred: Patty Duke; Virginia mayo; and Lindsay Wagner.

37. A Matter of Semantics. November 10th, 1971, Season 2, Episode 23. Story by Gene R. Kearney. Directed by Jack Laird. This starred: Cesar Romero; E. J. Peaker; and Monie Ellis.

38. Big Surprise. November 10th, 1971, Season 2, Episode 24. Story by Richard Matheson. Directed by Jeannot Szwarc. This starred: John Carradine and Vincent Van Patten.

39. Professor Peabody's Last Lecture. November 10th, 1971, Season 2, Episode 25. Story by Jack Laird. Directed by Jerrold freedman. This starred: Carl Reiner and Louise Lawson; with Johnnie Collins III as Mr (H. P.) Lovecraft; Richard Annis as Mr (Robert) Bloch; and Larry Watson as Mr (August) Derleth.

40. House - with a Ghost. November 17th, 1971, Season 2, Episode 26. Story by August Derleth. Directed by Gene R. Kearney. This starred: Bob Crane and Jo Anne Worley.

41. A Midnight Visit to the Neighborhood Blood Bank. November 17th, 1971, Season 2, Episode 27. Story by Jack Laird. Directed by William Hale. This starred: Victor Buono and Journey Laird.

42. Dr Stringfellow's Rejuvenator. November 17th, 1971, Season 2, Episode 28. Story by **Rod Serling**. Directed by Jerrold Freedman. This starred: Forrest Tucker and Murray Hamilton.

43. Hell's Bells. November 17th, 1971, Season 2, Episode 29. Story by Harry Turner. Directed by Theodore J. Flicker. This starred: John Astin and Theodore J. Flicker.

44. The Dark Boy. November 24th, 1971, Season 2, Episode 30. Story by August Derleth. Directed by John Astin. This starred: Elizabeth Hartman; Gale Sondergaard; and Michael Baseleon.

45. Keep in Touch - We'll Think of Something. November 24th, 1971, Season 2, Episode 31. Story by Gene R. Kearney. Directed by Gene R. Kearney. This starred: Alex Cord and Joanna Pettet.

46. Pickman's Model. December 1st, 1971, Season 2, Episode 32. Story by H. P. Lovecraft. Directed by Jack Laird. This starred: Bradford Dillman and Louise Sorel.

47. The Dear Departed. December 1st, 1971, Season 2, Episode 33. Story by Alice-Mary Schnirring. Directed by Jeff Corey. This starred: Steve Lawrence; Maureen Arthur; and Harvey Lembeck.

48. An Act of Chivalry. December 1st, 1971, Season 2, Episode 34. Story by Jack Laird. Directed by Jack Laird. This starred: Deidre Hall and Ron Stein.

49. Cool Air. December 8th, 1971, Season 2, Episode 35. Story by H. P. Lovecraft. Directed by Jeannot Szwarc. This starred: Barbara Rush and Henry Darrow.

50. Camera Obscura. December 8th, 1971, Season 2, Episode 36. Story by Basil Copper. Directed by John Badham. This starred: Ross Martin and Rene Auberjonois.

51. Quoth the Raven. December 8th, 1971, Season 2, Episode 37. Story by Jack Laird. Directed by John Badham. This starred: Marty Allen as Edgar Allen Poe.

52. The Messiah on Mott Street. December 8th, 1971, Season 2, Episode 38. Story by **Rod Serling**. Directed by Don Taylor. This starred: Edward G. Robinson and Yaphet Kotto.

53. The Painted Mirror. December 8th, 1971, Season 2, Episode 39. Story by Donald Wandrei. Directed by Gene R. Kearney. This starred: Zsa Zsa Gabor; Arthur O'Connell; and Rosemary DeCamp.

54. The Different Ones. December 29th, 1971, Season 2, Episode 40. Story by **Rod Serling**. Directed by John Meredyth Lucas. This starred: Dana Andrews and Monica Lewis.

55. Tell David... December 29th, 1971, Season 2, Episode 41. Story by Penelope Wallace. Directed by Jeff Corey. This starred: Sandra Dee and Jared Martin.

56. Logoda's Heads. December 29th, 1971, Season 2, Episode 42. Story by August Derleth with a teleplay by Robert Bloch. Directed by Jeannot Szwarc. This starred: Patrick Macnee; Brock Peters; Denise Nicholas; and Tim Matheson.

57. Green Fingers. January 5th, 1972, Season 2, Episode 43. Story by R. C. Cook. Directed by John Badham. This starred: Cameron Mitchell and Elsa Lanchester.

58. The Funeral. January 5th, 1972, Season 2, Episode 44. Story by Richard Matheson. Directed by John Meredyth Lucas. This starred: Joe Flynn and Werner Klemperer.

59. The Tune in Dan's Cafe. January 5th, 1972, Season 2, Episode 45. Story by Shamus Frazer. Directed by David Rawlins. This starred: Pernell Roberts and Susan Oliver.

60. Lindemann's Catch. January 12th, 1972, Season 2, Episode 46. Story by **Rod Serling**. Directed by Jeff Corey. This starred: Stuart Whitman and Jack Aranson.

61. A Feast of Blood. January 12th, 1972, Season 2, Episode 47. Story by Dulcie Gray - originally The Fur Brooch. Directed by Jeannot Szwarc. This starred: Sondra Locke; Norman Lloyd; and Hermione Baddeley.

62. The Late Mr Peddington. January 12th, 1972, Season 2, Episode 48. Story by Frank Sisk - originally The Flat Male. Directed by Jeff Corey. This starred: Harry Morgan; Kim Hunter; and Randy Quaid.

63. The Miracle at Camafeo. January 19th, 1972, Season 2, Episode 49. Story by C. B. Gilford. Directed by Ralph Senensky. This starred: Harry Guardino; Julie Adams; and Ray Danton.

64. The Ghost of Sorworth Place. January 19th, 1972, Season 2, Episode 50. Story by Russell Kirk. Directed by Ralph Senensky. This starred: Richard Kiley and Jill Ireland.

65. The Waiting Room. January 26th, 1972, Season 2, Episode 51. Story by **Rod Serling**. Directed by Jeannot Szwarc. This starred: Steve Forrest; Albert Salmi; and Buddy Ebsen.

66. Last Rites for a Dead Druid. January 26th, 1972, Season 2, Episode 52. Story by Alvin Sapinsley. Directed by Jeannot Szwarc. This starred: Bill Bixby; Carol Lynley; and Donna Douglas.

67. Deliveries in the Rear. February 9th, 1972, Season 2, Episode 53. Story by **Rod Serling**. Directed by Jeff Corey. This starred: Cornel Wilde and Rosemary Forsyth.

68. Stop Killing Me. February 9th, 1972, Season 2, Episode 54. Story by Hal Dresner. Directed by Jeannot Szwarc. This starred: Geraldine Page and James Gregory.

69. Dead Weight. February 9th, 1972, Season 2, Episode 55. Story by Jeffry Scott - originally called Out of the Country. Directed by Timothy Galfas. This starred: Jack Albertson and Bobby Darin.

70. I'll Never Leave You - Ever. February 16th, 1972, Season 2, Episode 56. Story by Rene Morris. Directed by Daniel Haller. This starred: Lois Nettleton; John Saxon; Royal Dano; and Peggy Webber.

71. There Aren't Anymore MacBanes. February 16th, 1972, Season 2, Episode 57. Story by Stephen Hall - originally called By One, By Toe and By Three. Directed by John Newland. This starred: Joel Grey; Howard Duff; Darrell Larson; and Mark Hamill.

72. You Can't Get Help Like That Anymore. February 23rd, 1972, Season 2, Episode 58. Story **by Rod Serling**. Directed by Jeff Corey. This starred: Broderick Crawford; Cloris Leachman; Roberta Carol Brahm.

73. The Sins of the Fathers. February 23rd, 1972, Season 2, Episode 59. Story by Christianna Brand. Directed by Jeannot Szwarc. This starred: Geraldine Page; and Richard Thomas.

74. The Caterpillar. March 1st, 1972, Season 2, Episode 60. Story by Oscar Cook - originally Boomerang. Directed by Jeannot Szwarc. This starred: Laurence Harvey and Joanna Pettet.

75. Little Girl Lost. March 1st, 1972, Season 2, Episode 61. Story by E. C. Tubb. Directed by Timothy Galfas. This starred: Ed Nelson and William Windom.

76. Satisfaction Guaranteed. March 1st, 1972, Season 2, Episode 62. Story by Gene R. Kearney. Directed by Jerrold Freedman and Jeannot Szwarc. This starred: Victor Buono.

Rod Serling

77. The Return of the Sorcerer. September 24th, 1972, Season 3, Episode 1. Story by Clark Ashton Smith. Directed by Jeannot Szwarc. This starred: Vincent Price; Tisha Sterling; and Bill Bixby.

78. The Girl with the Hungry Eyes. October 1st, 1972, Season 3, Episode 2. Story by **Fritz Leiber**. Directed by John Badham. This starred: James Farentino; John Astin; and Joanna Pettet.

79. Fright Night. October 15th, 1972, Season 3, Episode 3. Story by Kurt van Elting. Directed by Jeff Corey. This starred: Barbara Anderson; Stuart Whitman and Michael Laird.

80. Rare Objects. October 22nd, 1972, Season 3, Episode 4. Story by **Rod Serling**. Directed by Jeannot Szwarc. This starred: Michel Rooney and Raymond Massey.

81. Spectre in Tap-Shoes. October 29th, 1972, Season 3, Episode 5. Story by Jack Laird. Directed by Jeannot Szwarc. This starred: Dane Clark; Sandra Dee; and Christopher Connelly.

82. The Ring with the Velvet Ropes. November 5th, 1972, Season 3, Episode 6. Story by Edward D. Hoch. Directed by Jeannot Szwarc. This starred: Chuck Connors; Gary Lockwood; and Joan Van Ark.

83. You Can Come Up Now, Mrs Millikan. November 12th, 1972, Season 3, Episode 7. Story by J. Wesley Rosenquest. Directed by John Badham. This starred: Ozzie and Harriet Nelson.

84. Smile Please. November 12th, 1972, Season 3, Episode 8. Story by Jack Laird. Directed by Jack Laird. This starred: Cesare Danova and Lindsay Wagner.

85. The Other Way Out. November 19th, 1972, Season 3, Episode 9. Story by Kurt van Elting. Directed by Gene R. Kearney. This starred: Burl Ives and Ross Martin.

86. Finnegan's Flight. December 3rd, 1972, Season 3, Episode 10. Story by **Rod Serling**. Directed by Gene R. Kearney. This starred: Burgess Meredith; Cameron Mitchell; and Barry Sullivan.

87. She'll Be Company for You. December 24th, 1972, Season 3, Episode 11. Story by Andrea Newman. Directed by Gerald Perry Finnerman. This starred: Leonard Nimoy; Lorraine Gray; and Kathryn Hays.

88. Die Now, Pay Later. January 1st, 1973, Season 3, Episode 12. Story by Mary Linn Roby. Directed by Timothy Galfas. This starred: Will Geer and Slim Pickens.

89. Room for One Less. January 1st, 1973, Season 3, Episode 13. Story by Jack Laird. Directed by Jack Laird. This starred: Lee J. Lambert and James Metropole.

90. Something in the Woodwork. January 14th, 1973, Season 3, Episode 14. Story by R. Chetwynd-Hayes. Directed by Edward M. Abroms. This starred: Leif Erickson and Geraldine Page.

91. Death on a Barge. March 4th, 1973, Season 3, Episode 15. This starred: Lesley Ann Warren and Lou Antonio.

92. Whisper. May 13th, 1973, Season 3, Episode 16. Story by Martin Waddell. Directed by Jeannot Szwarc. This starred: Sally Field and Dean Stockwell.

93. The Doll of Death. May 20th, 1973, Season 3, Episode 17. Story by Vivian Meik. Directed by John Badham. This starred: Barry Atwater; Alejandro Rey; and Susan Strasberg.

94. Hatred Unto Death. May 20th, 1973, Season 3, Episode 18. Story by Milton Geiger. Directed by Gerald Perry Finnerman. This starred: Steve Forrest; Dina Merrill; and Fernando Lamas.

95. How to Cure a Common Vampire. May 27th, 1973, Season 3, Episode 19. Story by Jack Laird. Directed by Jack Laird. This starred: Johnny Brown and Richard Deacon.

96. I Did Not Mean to Slay Thee.

97. The Eyes that Wouldn't Die.

***

99. Time Travellers. This was made for TV in 1976 from a story by **Rod Serling**. Directed by Alexander Singer, it starred: Sam Groom; Tom Hallick; Francine York; and Richard Basehart.

100. The Sad and Lonely Sundays. Written by **Rod Serling** and made for TV in 1976. It was directed by James Goldstone and starred: Jack Albertson; Dori Brenner; and Will Geer.

101. The Salamander. Serling adapted this from a story by Robert Katz. It was directed by Peter Zinner in 1981 and starred: Anthony Quinn; Martin Balsam; Christopher Lee; Cleavon Little; and Sybil Danning.

102. Twilight Zone - The Movie. Serling is given a credit for this but, as he died in 1975, he had nothing to do with the film, other than the creation of the television series The Twilight Zone.

103. The Twilight Zone. The series was fired up again. Serling was merely the creator. It ran for seventy-five episode, starting on September 27th, 1984 and finishing April 15th, 1989.

104. The Enemy Within. This 1994 TV film was based on Serling's screenplay from Seven Days in May, 1964. Directed by Jonathan Darby, it starred: Forest Whitaker; Jason Robards; Dana Delany; and Sam Waterston.

105. Twilight Zone - Rod Serling's Lost Classics. This features two stories by Serling, The Theater, and Where the Dead Are, adapted by Richard Matheson. Directed by Robert Markowitz, it featured James Earl Jones as the host and starred: Amy Irving; Gary Cole; Jack Palance; and Peter McRobbie.

106. End of the Road. Released in 1997, this was from a teleplay by Serling based on a story by Scott Henkel. It was directed by Scott Henkel and starred Nora Rickert and Matthew Sutton.

107. In the Presence of Mine Enemies. Based on a story by Serling, and originally written for

Playhouse 90, May 18th, 1960, Season 4, Episode 17, this was made for television and released in April 1997. It was directed by Joan Micklin Silver and starred: Armin Mueller-Stahl; Charles Dance; Elina Lowensohn; Chad Lowe; et al.

108. A Town Has Turned to Dust. Based on a story by **Rod Serling**, this was directed by Rob Nilsson in 1998. It starred: Stephen Lang; Ron Perlman; Gabriel Olds; Judy Collins; Barbara Jane Reams; and others.

109. A Storm in Summer. Originally written for television in 1970, this was directed by Robert Wise and released in 2000, starring: Peter Falk; Andrew McCarthy; Nastassja Kinski; Ruby Dee; Aaron Meeks; Gillian Barber; et al.

110. For All Time. Originally A Stop at Willoughby from May 6th, 1960, Season 1, Episode 30 of Twilight Zone, this was remade for television, with a new teleplay by Vivienne Radkoff, in 2000. Directed by Steven Schachter, it starred: Mark Harmon; David Lereaney; Mary McDonnell; Catherine Hicks; and others.

111. The Twilight Zone. The series was revived again, running for forty-four shows. Hosted by Forest Whitaker, it started on September 18th, 2002 and finished on May 21st, 2003. **Rod Serling** was credited at the creator of the series.

***

STORY COLLECTIONS

1. Patterns: Four Television Plays. Published by Simon and Schuster, New York City, 1957. This contains: Patterns; The Rack; Old MacDonald Has a Curve; and Requiem for a Heavyweight.

2. Stories from the Twilight Zone. Published by Bantam Books, New York City, 1960. Bantam Book A2046. Softcover. All but one of the stories were from 1960: The Mighty Casey; Walking Distance; The Fever; Where is Everybody; The Monsters are Due on Maple Street; and Escape Clause, 1959.

3. More Stories from the Twilight Zone. Published by Bantam Books, New York City, 1961. Bantam Book A2227. Softcover. All but one of the stories were from 1961: Mr Dingle the Strong; A Thing About Machines; The Big Tall Wish; A Stop at Willoughby; The Odyssey of Flight 83; Dust; and The Lonely, 1959.

4. Requiem for a Heavyweight. Published by Bantam Books, New York City, 1962. Bantam Book J2373. Softcover.

5. New Stories from the Twilight Zone. Published by Bantam Books, New York City, 1962. Bantam Book A2412. Softcover. All from 1962, this contains: The Whole Truth; The Shelter; Showdown with Rance McGrew; The Night of the Meek; The Midnight Sun; and The Rip Van Winkle Caper.

6. From the Twilight Zone. Published by Nelson Doubleday - The Science Fiction Book Club, Garden City, New York, 1962. Hardcover. Herein: The Mighty Casey, 1960; Escape Clause, 1959; Where is Everybody?, 1960; The Monsters are Due on Maple Street, 1960; Mr Dingle, the Strong, 1961; The Big, Tall Wish, 1961; The Odyssey of Flight 83, 1961; The Lonely, 1959; The Whole Truth, 1962; The Shelter, 1962; The Midnight Sun, 1962; and The Rip Van Winkle Caper, 1962.

7. Rod Serling's The Twilight Zone. Published by Grosset and Dunlap, New York City, 1963. Hardcover. Herein, all from 1963: The Thirteenth Story; Dead Man's Chest; The Riddle of the Crypt; Death's Masquerade; The House on the Square; Return from Oblivion; The Avenging Ghost; The Tiger God; The Curse of the Seven Towers; Judgment Night; The Ghost-Town Ghost; Back There; and The Ghost of Ticonderoga.

8. Rod Serling's Twilight Zone Revisited. Published by Grosset and Dunlap, New York City, 1964. Hardcover. All from 1964: Foreword by **Rod Serling**; The Man Who Dropped By; The Mirror Image; The Man in the Bottle; The Ghost of Jolly Roger; Beyond the Rim; The Ghost Train; The Purple Testament; The Ghost of the Dixie Belle; and Two Live Ghosts.

9. Chilling Stories from Rod Serling's The Twilight Zone. Published by Tempo Books - Grosset and Dunlap, New York City, 1965. Tempo Book T89. Softcover. All dated 1963, this contains: Foreword by **Rod Serling**; Dead Man's Chest; The Riddle of the Crypt; Death's Masquerade; The House on the Square; Return from Oblivion; The Avenging Ghost; The Curse of the Seven Towers; Judgment Night; and The Ghost of Ticonderoga.

10. The Season to Be Wary. Published by Little Brown, Boston, 1967. Hardcover. This contains: The Escape Route; Color Scheme; and Eyes.

11. Rod Serling's Night Gallery. Published by Bantam Books, New York City, 1971. Bantam Book S7160. Softcover. Herein, all dated 1971: The Sole Survivor; Make Me Laugh; Pamela's Voice; Does the Name Grimsby Do Anything to You?; Clean Kills and Other Trophies; and They're Tearing Down Tim Riley's Bar.

12. Night Gallery 2. Published by Bantam Books, New York City, 1972. Bantam Book SP7203. Softcover. All but one from 1972: Collector's Items; The Messiah on Mott Street; The Different Ones; Suggestion; and Lindemann's Catch, 1960.

13. Stories from the Twilight Zone. With Horace J. Elias and Carl Pfeufer. Published by Bantam Books, New York City, 1979. Softcover. Illustrated adaptations: The Mighty Casey; Escape Clause; Walking Distance; The Fever; Where Is Everybody?; and The Monsters Are Due on Maple Street.

14. As Timeless As Infinity: The Twilight Zone Scripts of Rod Serling - Volume One. Edited by Tony Albarella. Published by Gauntlet Press, Springfield, Pennsylvania, 2004. Limited edition hardcover.

15. As Timeless As Infinity: The Twilight Zone Scripts of Rod Serling - Volume Two. Edited by Tony Albarella. Published by Gauntlet Press, Springfield, Pennsylvania, 2005. Limited edition hardcover.

Rod Serling

16. As Timeless As Infinity: The Twilight Zone Scripts of Rod Serling - Volume Three. Edited by Tony Albarella. Published by Gauntlet Press, Springfield, Pennsylvania, 2006. Limited edition hardcover.

17. As Timeless As Infinity: The Twilight Zone Scripts of Rod Serling - Volume Four. Edited by Tony Albarella. Published by Gauntlet Press, Springfield, Pennsylvania, 2007. Limited edition hardcover.

***

ANTHOLOGIES

1. Rod Serling's Triple W: Witches, Warlocks and Werewolves. Actually edited anonymously by **Gordon R. Dickson**. Published by Bantam Books, New York City, 1963. Softcover. Bantam Book J2623. Herein: Introduction by **Rod Serling**; Hatchery of Dreams by **Fritz Leiber**, 1961; Blind Alley by Malcolm Jameson, 1943; The Final Ingredient by Jack Sharkey, 1960; Wolves Don't Cry by Bruce Elliott, 1954; The Chestnut Beads by Jane Roberts, 1957; The Black Retriever by Charles G. Finney, 1958; The Amulet by **Gordon R Dickson**, 1959; The Mark of the Beast by Rudyard Kipling, 1890; And Not Quite Human by Joe L. Hensley, 1953; Young Goodman Brown by Nathaniel Hawthorne, 1835; The Story of Sidi Nonman - anonymous; and Witch Trials and the Law - an essay by Charles Mackay, 1841.

2. Rod Serling's Devils and Demons. Edited anonymously by **Gordon R. Dickson**. Published by Bantam Books, New York City, 1963. Softcover. Bantam Book H3324. This contains: Introduction by **Rod Serling**; Stars, Won't You Hide Me? by Ben Bova, 1966; Pollock and the Porroh Man by **H. G. Wells**, 1895; The Montavarde Camera by Avram Davidson, 1959; Death Cannot Wither by Judith Merril, 1959; A Time to Keep by **Kate Wilhelm**, 1962; Adapted by Carol Emshwiller, 1961; The Fourfifteen Express by Amelia B. Edwards, 1866; The Story of the Goblins Who Stole a Sexton by Charles Dickens, 1836; The Bottle Imp by Robert Louis Stevenson, 1891; Brother Coelestin by Emil Frida, 1963; The Bisara of Pooree by Rudyard Kipling, 1887; The Blue Sphere by Theodore Dreiser, 1914; and The Coach by Violent Hunt, 1914.

3. Rod Serling's Other Worlds. Published by Bantam Books, New York City, 1978. Softcover. Herein: Introduction by Richard Matheson; Story Notes by Jack C. Haldeman II; They by **Robert A. Heinlein**, 1941; Fifteen Miles by Ben Bova, 1967; Dolphin's Way by **Gordon R. Dickson**, 1964; The Royal Opera House by Carl Jacobi, 1972; Special Aptitude by **Theodore Sturgeon**, 1951; The Underdweller by William F. Nolan, 1957; I'm in Marsport without Hilda by **Isaac Asimov**, 1957; A Nice Shady Place by Dennis Etchison, 1963; Construction Shack by Clifford D. Simak, 1973; A Little Journey by **Ray Bradbury**, 1951; The Visible Man by Gardner R. Dozois, 1975; Mister Magister by Thomas F. Monteleone, 1978; What Johnny Did on His Summer Vacation by Joe Haldeman and Robert Thurston, 1978; and Little Old Miss Macbeth by **Fritz Leiber**, 1958.

***

RELATED

1. Writing for the Twilight Zone. By George Clayton Johnson. Published by Outre House, Sacramento, California, 1980. Softcover.

2. Rod Serling: The Dreams and Nightmares of Life in the Twilight Zone. By Joel Engel. Published by Contemporary Books, Chicago, 1989. Hardcover.

3. Serling: The Rise and Twilight of Television's Last Angry Man. By Gordon F. Sander. Published by E. P. Dutton, New York City, 1992. Hardcover.

4. Journeys to the Twilight Zone. Edited by Carol Serling. Published by DAW Books, New York City, 1993. DAW Collector's Book 900. Softcover. All but one from the year of this edition: Introduction by Carol Serling; The Field Trip by Elizabeth Ann Scarborough; Goodfood by W. Warren Wagar; Laying Veneer by Alan Dean Foster; I, Monster by Henry Slesar; Good Boy by Jane M. Lindskold; Mists by Kristine Kathryn Rusch and Dean Wesley Smith; Another Kind of Cottage by Hugh B. Cave; On Harper's Road by William F. Nolan; Outside the Windows by Pamela Sargent; The Extra by Jack Dunn; Inside Out by Karen Haber; Soul to Take by Vanessa Crouther; Standing Orders by Barry N. Malzberg; Coming of Age by Susan Cooper; Waifs and Strays by Charles de Lint; and Suggestion by **Rod Serling**, 1972.

5. Return to the Twilight Zone. Edited by Carol Serling and Martin H. Greenberg. Published by DAW Books, New York City, 1994. DAW Collector's Book 969. Softcover. All but one from the year of this edition: Introduction by Carol Serling; The Kaleidoscope by Don D'Ammassa; Afternoon Ghost by Jack Dann and George Zebrowski; Always, in the Dark by Charles L. Grant; Salt by P. D. Cacek; The Duke of Demolition Goes to Hell by John Gregory Betancourt; Messenger by Adam-Troy Castro; Still Waters by Barry B. Longyear; The Cure by Phillip C. Jennings; The Praying Lady by Charles L. Fontenay; Lady in the Cream-Colored Chiffon by Elizabeth Anderson and Margaret Maron; Gordie's Pets by Hugh B. Cave; The Garden by Barbara Delaplace; The Food Court by John MacLay; Maybe Tomorrow by Barry Hoffman; The Midnight El by Robert Weinberg; Big Roots by Pamela Sargent; Night of the Living Bra by K. D. Wentworth; Survival Song - a poem by Ray Russell; and The Sole Survivor by **Rod Serling**, 1971.

6. Adventures in the Twilight Zone. Edited by Carol Serling. Published by DAW Books, New York City, 1995. DAW Collector's Book 999. Softcover. All but one from the year of this edition: Dead and Naked by Pamela Sargent; My Mother and I Go Shopping by Lawrence Watt-Evans; The Repossessed by J. Neil Schulman; Ballad of the Outer Life by Margaret Ball; Desert Passage by Randall Peterson; A Death in the Valley by Robert Sampson; The Sacrifice of Shadows by Billie Sue Mosiman; Darkened Roads by Richard Gilliam; The Knight of Greenwich Village by Don D'Ammassa; Peace on Earth by Wendi Lee and Terry Beatty; A Breeze from A Distant Shore by Peter Crowther; My Wiccan Wiccan Ways by Brad

Linaweaver; Dark Secrets by Edward E. Kramer; Reality by Steve Antczak; Marticora by Brian McNaughton; The Shackles of Buried Sins by Lois Tilton; Sorcerer's Mate by M. E. Beckett; Daddy's Girl by Kimberly Rufer-Back; Something Shiny for Mrs Cauldwell by Fred Olen Ray; Hope As An Element of Cold Dark Matter by Rick Wilber; Mittens and Hotfoot by Walter Vance Awsten; The House at the Edge of the World by Juleen Brantingham; Baby Girl Diamond by Adam-Troy Castro; and featuring Lindemann's Catch by **Rod Serling**, 1960.

7. Trivia from The Twilight Zone. By Bill DeVoe. Published by Bear Manor Media, Albany, Georgia, 2008. Softcover.

8. The Twilight Zone: Unlocking the Door to a Television Classic. By Martin Grams. Published by OTR Publishing, Churchville, Maryland, 2008. Softcover.

Edward L. Ferman

-2009-

Edward L. Ferman.

Edward L. Ferman was born in New York City on March 6th, 1937. In 1964, he took over the editing of his father's magazine, The Magazine of Fantasy and Science Fiction. The masthead lists his father, Joseph, as the editor but, in fact, Edward was doing the job under the old man's supervision.

That first issue by Ferman the son, December 1964, featured: Buffoon by Edward Wellen; The Docs by Richard O. Lewis; The Fatal Eggs by Mikhail Bulgakov; Final Exam by Bryce Walton; The Man with the Speckled Eyes by R. A. Lafferty; On the Orphan's Colony by Kit Reed; and Wilderness Year by Joanna Russ.

Finally, for the January 1966 issue, his name was on the masthead as the editor. He was officially taking over from a long line of fine editors: J. Francis McComas; Anthony Boucher; Cyril M. Kornbluth; William Tenn; Robert P. Mills; and Avram Davidson.

Win or lose, it was his magazine.

That January issue contained: Apology to Inky by Robert M. Green; Beaulieu by Margaret St Clair; L'Arc De Jeanne by Robert F. Young; The Most Wonderful News by Len Guttridge; Representative form Earth by Gregory Benford; Survey of the Third Planet by Keith Roberts; and To the Rescue by Ron Goulart, along with The Proton-Reckoner - an essay by **Isaac Asimov**; and a cartoon by Gahan Wilson.

There were a few other magazines, Venture Science Fiction, which he revived from the 1950s for half-a-dozen issues, and an assortment of non-genre attempts.

But Fantasy and Science Fiction was the one that mattered.

And Ferman stayed at the helm until June 1991, when he turned it over to Kristine Kathryn Rusch. That final issue ran: Royal Gamma - an essay by **Isaac Asimov**; The Dark by Karen Joy Fowler; Wordworld by Carolyn Ives Gilman; Deuce by Henry Slesar; Better Morphosis by **Brian W. Aldiss**; Vacuum Cleaner by Ben Bova; The Day They All Came Back by Avram Davidson; The Day They All Came Back by Avram Davidson; and The Blessed/Damned by Grania Davis.

With his retirement, Ferman went down as one of the most successful magazine editors in the genre. Without ever missing an issue or a deadline, he guided F&SF through major changes in the business, changes that killed other magazines, from huge newsstand sales and low subscription lists to very minor newsstand sales (since the newsstands were vanishing and big chain stores had no interest in small magazines, just money), and a subscriber list of 50,000; from a huge teen-age readership to an almost non-existent teen-age readership as modern teen-agers ceased to be a factor in the science fiction/fantasy field.

And along the way, he published numerous special issues that featured single authors and their bibliographies, not to mention winning Hugo Awards for himself as an editor - and for the authors of a number of stories he published.

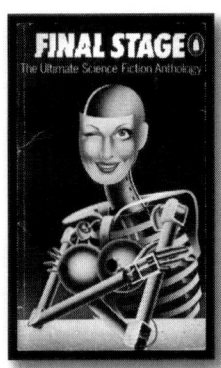

The most highly priced of the collectible issues of The Magazine of Fantasy and Science Fiction were in 1978, the five issue run that serialized The Gunslinger by Stephen King. That goes for around $750.00. Next is likely the special **Isaac Asimov** issue from October 1966 - worth somewhere around $200.00.

***

AWARDS

1969. Hugo Best American Professional Magazine Award for The Magazine of Fantasy and Science Fiction.
1970. Hugo Best American Professional Magazine Award for The Magazine of Fantasy and Science Fiction.
1971. Hugo Best American Professional Magazine Award for The Magazine of Fantasy and Science Fiction.
1972. Hugo Best American Professional Magazine Award for The Magazine of Fantasy and Science Fiction.
1972. Locus Poll Best Magazine Award.
1973. Locus Poll Best Magazine Award.
1974. Locus Poll Best Magazine Award.
1975. Locus Poll Best Magazine Award.
1976. Locus Poll Best Magazine Award.
1977. Locus Poll Best Magazine Award.
1978. Locus Poll Best Magazine Award.
1979. Locus Poll Best Magazine Award.
1979. World Fantasy Special Award for The Magazine of Fantasy and Science Fiction.
1980. Locus Poll Best Magazine Award.
1981. Locus Poll Best Anthology Award for The Magazine of Fantasy and Science Fiction: A 30 Year Retrospective.
1981. Hugo Best Profession Editor Award.
1981. Hugo Special Award for his effort to expand and improve writing quality in the field.
1981. Balrog Profession Publication Award for The Magazine of Fantasy and Science Fiction.
1981. Locus Poll Best Magazine/Fanzine Award.
1982. SF Chronicle Magazine-Editor Award for The Magazine of Fantasy and Science Fiction.
1982. Hugo Best Profession Editor Award.
1982. World Fantasy Special Pro Award for The Magazine of Fantasy and Science Fiction.
1982. Locus Poll Best Magazine/Fanzine Award.
1983. Hugo Best Profession Editor Award.
1983. SF Chronicle Magazine-Editor Award for The Magazine of Fantasy and Science Fiction.
1984. SF Chronicle Magazine-Editor Award for The Magazine of Fantasy and Science Fiction.
1985. Balrog Profession Publication Award for The

Magazine of Fantasy and Science Fiction.
1985. SF Chronicle Magazine-Editor Award for The Magazine of Fantasy and Science Fiction.
1987. Locus Poll Best Magazine/Fanzine Award.
1989. SF Chronicle Magazine-Editor Award for The Magazine of Fantasy and Science Fiction.
1991. SF Chronicle Magazine-Editor Award for The Magazine of Fantasy and Science Fiction.
1998. World Fantasy Lifetime Achievement Award.
2009. Inducted into The Science Fiction Hall of Fame.

***

ANTHOLOGIES.

1. The Best from Fantasy and Science Fiction: 15th Series. Published by Doubleday & Company, Garden City, New York, 1966. Hardcover. All but two poems from 1965: Introduction by Edward L. Ferman; The House the Blakeneys Built by Avram Davidson; Four Ghosts in Hamlet by **Fritz Leiber**; The Doors of His Face, the Lamps of His Mouth by Roger Zelazny; The History of Doctor Frost by Roderic C. Hodgins; Eyes Do More Than See by **Isaac Asimov**; Aunt Millicent at the Races by Len Guttridge; No Different Flesh by Zenna Henderson; Rake by Ron Goulart; The Eight Billion by Richard Wilson; Hog-Belly Honey by R. A. Lafferty; Sea Bright by Hal R. Moore; Something Else by Robert J. Tilley; Keep Them Happy by Robert Rohrer; A Murkle for Jesse by Gary Jennings; Love Letter from Mars - a poem by John Ciardi; From Two Universes - a poem by Doris Pitman Buck, 1964; and Treat - a poem by Walter H. Kerr, 1964.

2. The Best from Fantasy and Science Fiction: 16th Series. Published by Doubleday & Company, Garden City, New York, 1967. Hardcover. Mostly from 1966: Introduction by **Edward L. Ferman**; We Can Remember It for You Wholesale by **Philip K. Dick**; Apology to Inky by Robert M. Green; This Moment of the Story by Roger Zelazny; The Adjusted by Kenneth Bulmer; And Madly Teach by Lloyd Biggle, Jr; Experiment in Autobiography by Ron Goulart; The Age of Invention by Norman Spinrad; Matog by Joan Patricia Basch; The Seven Wonders of the Universe by Mose Mallette; Luana by Gilbert Thomas, 1965; The Key by **Isaac Asimov**; A Few Kindred Spirits by John Christopher, 1965; Three for Carnival by John Shepley; and a series of poems: Mickey Finn - by Doris Pitman Buck; Imaginary Numbers in a Real Garden by Gerald Jones, 1965; Letter to a Tyrant King by Bill Butler; and Memo to Secretary by Pat de Grew.

3. The Best from Fantasy and Science Fiction: 17th Series. Published by Doubleday & Company, Garden City, New York, 1968. Hardcover. Mostly from 1967, this contains: Introduction by **Edward L. Ferman**; Four cartoons by Gahan Wilson; Balgrummo's Hell by Russell Kirk; Cyprian's Room by Monica Sterba; Out of Time, Out of Place by George Collyn; Von Goom's Gambit by Victor Contoski, 1966; Bumberboom by Avram Davidson, 1966; Fill In the Blank by Ron Goulart; Corona by **Samuel R. Delany**; The Inner Circles by **Fritz Leiber;** Problems of Creativeness by Thomas M. Disch; Encounter in the Past by Robert Nathan; The Sea Change by Jean Cox; The Devil and Democracy by Brian Cleeve; and Randy's Syndrome by **Brian W. Aldiss**.

4. Once and Future Tales from the Magazine of Fantasy and Science Fiction. Published by Harris-Wolfe, Jacksonville, Illinois, 1968. Hardcover. Herein: Introduction by Judith Merril; The Manor of Roses by Thomas Burnett Swann, 1966; End of the Line by Chad Oliver, 1965; The Masculinist Revolt by William Tenn, 1965; When You Care, When You Love by **Theodore Sturgeon**, 1962; The Fifteenth Wind of March by Frederick Bland, 1962; Fruiting Body by Rosel George Brown, 1962; The Case of the Homicidal Robots by Murray Leinster, 1961; Open to Me, My Sister by Philip Jose Farmer, 1960; and Journey of Ten Thousand Miles by Will Mohler, 1963.

5. The Best from Fantasy and Science Fiction: 18th Series. Published by Doubleday & Company, Garden City, New York, 1969. Hardcover. Mostly from 1968, this contains: Lunatic Assignment by Sonya Dorman; In His Own Image by Lloyd Biggle, Jr; I Have My Vigil by **Harry Harrison**; The Egg of the Glak by Harvey Jacobs; Final War by Barry N. Malzberg writing as K. M. O'Donnell; Muscadine by Ron Goulart; Beyond the Game by Vance Aandahl; Sea Home by William M. Lee; The People Trap by Robert Sheckley; Sundown by David Redd, 1967; The Cloud Sculptors of Coral D by J. G. Ballard, 1967; That High-up Blue Day That Saw the Black Skytrain Come Spinning by David R. Bunch; Gifts from the Universe by Leonard Tushnet; and Ogre! By Edward Jesby.

6. Twenty Years of Fantasy and Science Fiction. With Robert P. Mills. Published by G. P. Putnam's Sons, New York City, 1970. Hardcover. Herein: F&SF and I - an essay by **Isaac Asimov**; We Can Remember It for You Wholesale by **Philip K. Dick**, 1966; 5,271,009 by **Alfred Bester**, 1954; The Silly Season by C. M. Kornbluth, 1950; 237 Talking Statues by **Fritz Leiber**, 1963; M-1 by Gahan Wilson, 1970; Sweet Helen by Charles W. Runyon, 1969; Feminine Intuition by **Isaac Asimov**, 1969; Prime-Time Teaser by Bruce McAllister, 1968; Becalmed in Hell by Larry Niven, 1965; Something Else by Robert J. Tilley, 1965; A Touch of Strange by **Theodore Sturgeon**, 1958; Free Dirt by Charles Beaumont, 1955; That Hell-Bound Train by Robert Bloch, 1958; Gratitude Guaranteed by Reginald Bretnor and Kris Neville, 1953; The Holiday Man by Richard Matheson, 1957; Private - Keep Out! By Philip MacDonald, 1949; Gladys's Gregory by John Anthony West, 1963; Yes, We Have No Ritchard by Bruce Jay Friedman, 1960; A Final Sceptre, a Lasting Crown by **Ray Bradbury**, 1969; and As Long as You're Here by Will Stanton, 1963.

7. The Best from Fantasy and Science Fiction: 19th Series. Published by Doubleday & Company, Garden City, New York, 1971. Hardcover. Herein: The Man Who Learned Loving by **Theodore Sturgeon**, 1969; Longtooth by Edgar Pangborn, 1970; Dream Patrol by Charles W. Runyon, 1970; The Brief, Swinging Career of Dan and Judy Smythe by Carter Wilson, 1970; Confessions by Ron Goulart, 1970; Gone Fishin' by Robin Scott Wilson, 1970; Starting from Scratch by Robert Sheckley, 1953; Calliope and Gherkin and the Yankee Doodle Thing by Evelyn E. Smith, 1969; Benji's Pencil by Bruce

Edward L. Ferman

McAllister, 1969; Sundance by **Robert Silverberg**, 1969; Litterbug by Tony Morphett, 1969; An Adventure in the Yolla Bolly Middle Eel Wilderness by Vance Aandahl, 1969; Get a Horse! by Larry Niven, 1969; Selectra Six-Ten by Avram Davidson, 1970; and Notes Just Prior to the Fall by Barry N. Malzberg writing as K. M. O'Donnell.

8. The Best from Fantasy and Science Fiction: 20th Series. Published by Doubleday & Company, Garden City, New York, 1973. Hardcover. Herein: Shaffery Among the Immortals by **Frederik Pohl**, 1972; The Deathbird by Harlan Ellison, 1973; The Animal Fair by **Alfred Bester**, 1972; The Problem of Pain by **Poul Anderson**, 1973; Is It the End of the World? By Wilma shore, 1972; Sooner or Later or Never Never by Gary Jennings, 1972; Thus Love Betrays Us by Phyllis MacLennan, 1972; A Different Drummer by Raylyn Moore, 1971; Birdlime by B. L. Keller, 1971; The Bear with the Knot on this Tail by Stephen Tall, 1971; and Born to Exile by Phyllis Eisenstein.

9. The Best from Fantasy and Science Fiction: A Special 25th Anniversary Anthology. Also, The Best from Fantasy and Science Fiction: 21st Series. Published by Doubleday & Company, Garden City, New York, 1974. Hardcover. Herein: Introduction by **Edward L. Ferman**; When You Care, When You Love by **Theodore Sturgeon** with a biography by Judith Merril and a bibliography by Sam Moskowitz, 1962; To the Chicago Abyss by **Ray Bradbury** with a biography and a bibliography by William F. Nolan, 1963; The Key by **Isaac Asimov** with a biography by L. Sprague de Camp and a bibliography, 1966; Ship of Shadows by **Fritz Leiber** with a biography by Judith Merril and a bibliography by Al Lewis, 1969; The Queen of Air and Darkness by **Poul Anderson** with a biography by Gordon R. Dickson and a bibliography, 1971; and Midsummer Century by **James Blish** with a biography by Robert A. W. Lowndes and a bibliography by Mark Owings, 1972.

10. Final Stage. With Barry N. Malzberg. Published by Charterhouse, New York City, 1974. Hardcover. All from the year the book was published, this contains: Introduction by **Edward L. Ferman** and Barry N. Malzberg; We Purchased People by **Frederik Pohl**; The Voortrekkers by **Poul Anderson**; Great Escape Tours Inc. by Kit Reed; Diagrams for Three Enigmatic Stories by **Brian W. Aldiss**; That Thou Art Mindful of Him by **Isaac Asimov**; We Three by Dean R. Koontz; An Old Fashioned Girl by Joanna Russ; Catman by Harlan Ellison; Space Rats of the CCC by **Harry Harrison**; Trips by **Robert Silverberg**; The Wonderful All Purpose Transmogrifier by Barry N. Malzberg; Her Smoke Rose Up Forever by James Tiptree Jr.; and A Little Something for Us Tempunauts by **Philip K. Dick**.

11. Final Stage. With Barry N. Malzberg. Published by Penguin Books, Middlesex, England, 1975. Softcover. Revised edition; the hardcover first edition had been heavily edited, without permission, but the publisher and this restored the original text. This contains: We Purchased People by **Frederik Pohl**; The Voortrekkers by **Poul Anderson**; Great Escape Tours Inc. by Kit Reed; Diagrams for Three Enigmatic Stories by **Brian W. Aldiss**; That Thou Art Mindful of Him by **Isaac Asimov**; We Three by Dean R. Koontz; An Old Fashioned Girl by Joanna Russ; Catman by Harlan Ellison; Space Rats of the CCC by **Harry Harrison**; Trips by **Robert Silverberg**; The Wonderful All Purpose Transmogrifier by Barry N. Malzberg; Her Smoke Rose Up Forever by James Tiptree Jr.; and A Little Something for Us Tempunauts by **Philip K. Dick**.

12. Arena: Sports SF. With Barry N. Malzberg. Published by Doubleday & Company, Garden City, New York, 1976. Hardcover. Herein: Introduction by **Edward L. Ferman**; Whispers in Bedlam by Irwin Shaw, 1973; Mirror of Ice by Gary Wright, 1967; Dodger Fan by Will Stanton, 1957; Closed Sicilian by Barry N. Malzberg, 1973; Arena by Fredric Brown, 1944; Nobody Bothers Gus by Algis Budrys, 1955; Open Warfare by James E. Gunn, 1954; Gladys's Gregory by John Anthony West, 1962; The Night Boxing Ended by Bruce Jay Friedman, 1966; Beyond the Game by Vance Aandahl, 1968; The Hungarian Cinch by Bill Pronzini, 1976; and Afterword: On the Non-transcendence of Sport by Barry N. Malzberg.

13. Graven Images. With Barry N. Malzberg. Published by Nelson Publishers, Nashville, Tennessee, 1977. Hardcover. Herein, all from 1977: Introduction: Science Fiction and the Arts by Barry N. Malzberg; Oh Lovelee Appearance of the Lass from the North Countree by Richard Frede; A Glow of Candles a Unicorn's Eyes by Charles L. Grant; and Choral by Barry N. Malzberg.

14. The Best from Fantasy and Science Fiction: 22nd Series. Published by Doubleday & Company, Garden City, New York, 1977. Hardcover. Herein: Introduction by **Edward L. Ferman**; A Case of the Stubborns by Robert Bloch, 1976; The Hertford Manuscript by Richard Cowper, 1976; This Offer Expires by Liz Hufford, 1976; My Boat by Joanna Russ, 1976; The Women Men Don't See by James Tiptree, Jr, 1973; San Diego Lightfoot Sue by Tom Reamy, 1975; In the Bowl by John Varley, 1975; Sanity Clause by Edward Wellen, 1975; The Ghastly Priest Doth Reign by Manly Wade Wellman, 1975; Dress Rehearsal by Harvey Jacobs, 1974; Mute Inglorious Tam by **Frederik Pohl** and C. M. Kornbluth, 1974; Old Uncle Tom Cobleigh and All by Reginald Bretnor, 1973; Out of Dickinson by Poe, or The Only Begotten Son of Emily and Edgar - a poem by **Ray Bradbury**, 1976; and Thinking About Thinking - an essay by **Isaac Asimov**, 1975; along with an assortment of essays from various essay contests held by the magazine over the years.

15. The Magazine of Fantasy and Science Fiction: A 30 Year Retrospective. Published by Doubleday & Company, Garden City, New York, 1980. Hardcover. Herein: Just Thirty Years - an essay by **Isaac Asimov**, 1979; All You Zombies... by **Robert A. Heinlein**, 1959; A Canticle for Leibowitz by Walter M. Miller, Jr, 1955; And Now the News... by **Theodore Sturgeon**, 1956; Ararat by Zenna Henderson; Born of Man and Woman by Richard Matheson, 1950; Dance Music for a Gone Planet - a poem by Sonya Dorman, 1968; Dreaming Is a Private Thing by **Isaac Asimov**, 1955; Flowers for Algernon by Daniel Keyes, 1959; Fondly Fahrenheit by **Alfred Bester**, 1954; Imaginary Numbers in a Real Garden - a poem by Gerald Jones, 1965; Jeffty Is Five by Harlan Ellison, 1977; Love Letter from

Mars - a poem by John Ciardi, 1965; Me - a poem by Hilbert Schenck, 1959; Not with a Bang by **Damon Knight**, 1950; One Ordinary Day, with Peanuts by Shirley Jackson, 1955; Poor Little Warrior! by **Brian W. Aldiss**, 1958; Problems of Creativeness by Thomas M. Disch, 1967; Selectra Six-Ten by Avram Davidson, 1970; Sundance by **Robert Silverberg**, 1969; The Gnurrs Come from the Voodvork Out by Reginald Bretnor, 1950; The Quest for Saint Aquin by Anthony Boucher, 1951; The Women Men Don't See by James Tiptree, Jr, 1973; Through Time and Space with Ferdinand Feghoot by Reginald Bretnor writing as Grendel Briarton, 1956; and We Can Remember It for You Wholesale by **Philip K. Dic**k, 1966.

16. The Best from Fantasy and Science Fiction: 23rd Series. Published by Doubleday & Company, Garden City, New York, 1980. Hardcover. Herein: Introduction by **Edward L. Ferman**; Stone by Edward Bryant, 1978; The Man Who Had No Idea by Thomas M. Disch, 1978; A House Divided by Lee Killough, 1978; Brother Hart by Jane Yolen, 1978; Project Hi-Rise by Robert F. Young, 1978; Nina by Robert Bloch, 1977; Prismatica by **Samuel R. Delany**, 1977; Zorphwar! By Stan Dryer, 1977; The Detweiler Boy by Tom Reamy, 1977; Upstart by Steven Utley, 1977; In the Hall of the Martian Kings by John Varley, 1977; I See You by **Damon Knight**, 1976; and Clone, Clone of My Own - an essay by **Isaac Asimov**, 1979; along with an assortment of essays from various essay contests held by the magazine over the years.

17. The Magazine of Fantasy and Science Fiction, April 1965. Published by Southern Illinois University Press, 1981. Hardcover. Herein: Each piece is accompanied the author's memories of writing it back in 1965: Arsenal Port by **Poul Anderson**; The History of Doctor Frost by Roderic C. Hodgins; Lord Moon by M. J. Engh writing as Jane Beauclerk; Eyes Do More Than See by **Isaac Asimov**; Aunt Millicent at the Races by Len Guttridge; Bind Date by T. P. Caravan; Keep Them Happy by Robert Roher; The Certainty of Uncertainty - an essay by **Isaac Asimov**; and Imaginary Numbers in a Real Garden - a poem by Gerald Jones.

18. The Best from Fantasy and Science Fiction: 24th Series. Published by Charles Scribner's Sons, New York City, 1982. Hardcover. Herein: Introduction by **Edward L. Ferman**; The Word I Invented - an essay by **Isaac Asimov**, 1980; The Fire When It Comes by Parke Godwin, 1981; The Alien Mind by **Philip K. Dick**, 1981; The Pusher by John Varley, 1981; The Brave Little Toaster by Thomas M. Disch, 1980; Window by Bob Leman, 1980; The Curse of the Mhondoro Nkabele by Eric Norden, 1978; Spidersong by Susan C. Petrey, 1980; The Autopsy by Michael Shea, 1980; Out There Where the Big Ships Go by Richard Cowper, 1979; Wives by Lisa Tuttle, 1979; and A Day at the Fair by Neal Barrett, Jr, 1981; along with a series of entries from numerous competitions held over the years.

19. The Best Fantasy Stories from The Magazine of Fantasy and Science Fiction. Published by Octopus Books, New York City, 1985. Hardcover. Herein: The Man Who Painted the Dragon Griaule by Lucius Shepard, 1984; The Cloud Sculptors of Coral D by J. G. Ballard, 1967; The Fire When It Comes by Parke Godwin, 1981; Another Orphan by John Kessel, 1982; Man Overboard by John Collier, 1960; One Ordinary Day with Peanuts by Shirley Jackson, 1955; Sule Skerry by Jane Yolen, 1982; Ghost of a Crown by Sterling E. Lanier, 1976; Pages from a Young Girl's Journal by Robert Aickman, 1973; Born of Man and Woman by Richard Matheson, 1950; Green Magic by **Jack Vance**, 1963; Black Air by Kim Stanley Robinson, 1983; Far from Home by Walter S. Tevis, 1958; My Dear Emily by Joanna Russ, 1962; The Vanishing American by Charles Beaumont, 1955; The Invasion of the Church of the Holy Ghost by Russell Kirk, 1983; The Accountant by Robert Sheckley, 1954; My Boy Friend's Name is Jello by Avram Davidson, 1954; San Diego Lightfoot Sue by Tom Reamy, 1975; Sooner of Later or Never Never by Gary Jennings, 1972; Jeffty is Five by Harlan Ellison, 1977; The Third Level by Jack Finney, 1950; The Silken Swift by **Theodore Sturgeon**, 1953; The Manor of Roses by Thomas Burnett Swann, 1966; Please Stand By by Ron Goulart, 1962; Downtown by Thomas M. Disch, 1983; Yes We Have No Ritchard by Bruce Jay Friedman, 1960; The Ballad of the Flexible Bullet by Stephen King, 1984; That Hell Bound Train by Robert Bloch, 1958; Will You Wait? by **Alfred Bester**, 1959; La Ronde by **Damon Knight**, 1983; Narrow Valley by R. J. Lafferty, 1966; Not Long Before the End by Larry Niven, 1969; $1.98 by Arthur Porges, 1954; The Tehama by Bob Leman, 1981; Narapoia by Alan Nelson, 1948; Mythago Wood by Robert Holdstock, 1981; Harrison Bergeron by Kurt Vonnegut, 1961; Four Ghosts in Hamlet by **Fritz Leiber**, 1965; and Gorilla Suit by John Shepley, 1956.

20. The Best Horror Stories from The Magazine of Fantasy and Science Fiction. With Anne Jordan. Published by St Martin's Press, New York City, 1988. Hardcover. Herein: Introduction by Anne Jordan; Window by Bob Leman, 1980; Insects in Amber by Tom Reamy, 1977; Free Dirt by Charles Beaumont, 1955; Rising Waters by Patricia Ferrara, 1987; The Night of the Tiger by Stephen King, 1977; Poor Little Warrior! by **Brian W. Aldiss**, 1958; Nina by Robert Bloch, 1977; Werewind by J. Michael Reaves, 1981; Dress of White Silk by Richard Matheson, 1951; Gladys's Gregory by John Anthony West, 1962; By the River, Fontainebleau by Stephen Gallagher, 1986; Pride by Charles L. Grant, 1982; Longtooth by Edgar Pangborn, 1969; Glory by Ron Goulart, 1986; Bug House by Lisa Tuttle, 1980; Hand in Glove by Robert Aickman, 1979; Stillborn by Michael Conner; Balbrummos's Hell by Russell Kirk, 1967; The Old Darkness by Pamela Sargent, 1983; The Night of White Bhairab by Lucius Shepard, 1984; Test by Theodore L. Thomas, 1962; The Little Black Train by Manly Wade Wellman, 1954; and The Autopsy by Michael Shea, 1980.

21. The Best Horror Stories from The Magazine of Fantasy and Science Fiction - Volume 1. With Anne Devereaux Jordan. Published by St Martin's Press, New York City, 1989. Softcover. Herein: Window by Bob Leman, 1980; Insects in Amber by Tom Reamy, 1977; Free Dirt by Charles Beaumont, 1955; Rising Waters by Patricia Ferrara, 1987; The Night of the Tiger by Stephen King, 1977; Poor Little Warrior! by **Brian W. Aldiss**, 1958; Nina by Robert

Edward L. Ferman

Bloch, 1977; Werewind by J. Michael Reaves, 1981; Dress of White Silk by Richard Matheson, 1951; Gladys's Gregory by John Anthony West, 1962; By the River, Fontainebleau by Stephen Gallagher, 1986; Pride by Charles L. Grant, 1982; and Longtooth by Edgar Pangborn, 1969.

22. The Best from Fantasy and Science Fiction: A 40th Anniversary Anthology. Published by St Martin's Press, New York City, 1989. Hardcover. Herein: Preface by **Edward L. Ferman**; Introduction by Harlan Ellison; The God Machine by **Damon Knight**, 1985; Out of All Them Bright Stars by Nancy Kress, 1985; Face Value by Karen Joy Fowler, 1986; Surviving by Judith Moffett, 1986; Uncle Tuggs by Michael Shea, 1986; The Boy Who Plaited Manes by Nancy Springer, 1986; State of the Art by Robert Charles Wilson, 1985; Judgement Call by John Kessel, 1987; In Midst of Life by James Tiptree, Jr, 1987; Cage 37 by Wayne Wightman, 1987; Salvador by Lucius Shepard, 1984; The Cat Hotel by **Fritz Leiber**, 1983; Black Air by Kim Stanley Robinson, 1983; Slow Birds by Ian Watson, 1983; Understanding Human Behavior by Thomas M. Disch, 1982; While You're Up by Avram Davidson, 1988; Eidolons by Harlan Ellison, 1988; The Aliens Who Knew, I Mean, Everything by George Alec Effinger, 1984; Buffalo Gals, Won't You Come Out Tonight by **Ursula K. Le Guin**, 1987; and A Rarebit of Magic by John Morressy, 1983.

23. The Best Horror Stories from The Magazine of Fantasy and Science Fiction - Volume 2. With Anne Devereaux Jordan. Published by St Martin's Press, New York City, 1990. Softcover. Herein: Introduction by Anne Devereaux Jordan; Glory by Ron Goulart, 1986; Bug House by Lisa Tuttle, 1980; Hand in Glove by Robert Aickman, 1979; Stillborn by Michael Conner; Balbrummos's Hell by Russell Kirk, 1967; The Old Darkness by Pamela Sargent, 1983; The Night of White Bhairab by Lucius Shepard, 1984; Test by Theodore L. Thomas, 1962; The Little Black Train by Manly Wade Wellman, 1954; and The Autopsy by Michael Shea, 1980.

24. The Best from Fantasy and Science Fiction: A 45th Anniversary Anthology. With Kristine Kathryn Rusch. Published by St Martin's Press, New York City, 1995. Hardcover. Herein: Introduction by **Edward L. Ferman**; Introduction by Kristine Kathryn Rusch; Susan by Harlan Ellison, 1993; The Last Feast of Harlequin by Thomas Ligotti, 1990; Kirinyaga by Mike Resnick, 1988; Touched by Dale Bailey, 1993; Mom's Little Friends by Ray Vukcevich, 1992; Cast on a Distant Shore by R. Garcia y Robertson, 1989; Graves by Joe Haldeman, 1992; The Dark by Karen Joy Fowler, 1991; Willie by Madeleine E. Robins, 1992; Coffins by Robert Reed, 1992; The Resurrection of Alonso Quijana by Marcos Donnelly, 1992; Steel Dogs by Ray Aldridge, 1989; Abe Lincoln in McDonald's by James Morrow, 1989; On Death and the Deuce by Richard Bowes, 1992; The Honeycrafters by Carolyn Ives Gilman, 1991; Ma Qui by Alan Brennert, 1991; Next by Terry Bisson, 1992; The Friendship Ship by **Gene Wolfe**, 1989; and Guide Dog by Mike Conner, 1991.

25. The Best from Fantasy and Science Fiction: A 50th Anniversary Anthology. With Gordon Van Gelder. Published by Tor Books - Tom Doherty's Associates, New York City, 1999. Hardcover. Herein: Introduction by Gordon Van Gelder; Last Summer at Mars Hill by Elizabeth Hand, 1994; Maneki Neko by Bruce Sterling, 1998; No Planets Strike by **Gene Wolfe**, 1997; Sins of the Mothers by Sharon N. Farber writing as S. N. Dyer, 1997; The Finger by Ray Vukcevich, 1995; Lifeboat on a Burning Sea by Bruce Holland Rogers, 1995; Gone by John Crowley, 1996; First Tuesday by Robert Reed, 1996; The Fool, the Stick, and the Princess by Rachel Pollack, 1998; A Birthday by Esther M. Friesner, 1995; Sensible City by Harlan Ellison, 1994; All the Birds of Hell by Tanith Lee, 1998; We Love Lydia Love by Bradley Denton, 1994; Paul and Me by Michael Blumlein, 1997; Have Gun, Will Edit by Paul Di Filippo, 1996; Forget Luck by **Kate Wilhelm**, 1996; Quinn's Way by Dale Bailey, 1997; Partial People by Terry Bisson, 1993; The Lincoln Train by Maureen F. McHugh, 1995; Solitude by **Ursula K. Le Guin**; and Another Fine Mess by **Ray Bradbury**, 1995.

***

NON-FICTION

1. Oi, Robot. Published by Mercury Press, Cornwall, Connecticut, 1995. Softcover.

Frank R. Paul

Frank R. Paul.

Frank Rudolph Paul was born on April 18th, 1884 in Vienna, Austria and he died in Teaneck, New Jersey, June 29th, 1963. **Hugo Gernsback** discovered him and assigned him to paint the cover for the very first issue of Amazing Stories, April 1926. Along with the cover, he did most of the interior drawings.

The issue contained: A New Sort of Magazine - an essay by **Hugo Gernsback**; Off on a Comet - part 1 of 2 by **Jules Verne**; The New Accelerator by **H. G. Wells**, 1901; The Man from the Atom by G. Peyton Wertenbaker, 1923; The Thing from Outside by George Allan England, 1923; The Man Who Saved the Erath by Austin Hall, 1919; and The Facts in the Case of M. Valdemar by Edgar Allan Poe, 1845.

For the next three years, he painted all the covers for Amazing Stories, defining the look of science fiction. He envisioned the robots and rockets, the aliens and the architecture, and got it down in colour to inspire generations of writers and artists.

In 1939, he was the guest of honour at the first Worldcon ever and, as **Frederik Pohl** has suggested, he was probably the first human being to ever make a living painting spaceships. He gave a memorable speech at that convention, one where he pointed out that every age had visionaries prepared to analyze the wonders of the universe, regardless of whatever insults they received for their efforts.

He believed that, in any age, people were only supposed to think the thoughts approved by the societal authorities at the time. People were not supposed to be rebels, not supposed to dream of the possibilities rather than being nailed down by restrictions. He said science fiction fans were a different breed, science fiction fans could see beyond the restraints of society, science fiction fans could imagine, they could dream.

He was a visionary himself, no doubt about it.

The last cover published in his lifetime was the April 1961 issue of Amazing Stories, edited by Cele Goldsmith. It was more a collage than an actual painting. And the issue featured: I, Rocket by **Ray Bradbury**, 1944; Devolution by Edmond Hamilton, 1936; Armageddon - 2319 - the first Buck Rogers story by Philip Francis Nowlan, 1928; John Carter and the Giant of Mars by **Edgar Rice Burroughs**, 1941; Out of the Sub-Universe by R. F. Starzl, 1928; The Flying Fool by David H. Keller, 1929; a Guest Editorial by **Hugo Gernsback**; and I, Robot by Eando Binder, 1939.

To this day, his covers are still being used. A paperback edition of H. G. Wells' The War of the Worlds, published in 2008, featured a Paul cover... as did Confounding SF, printed in 2008 by **Frederik Pohl** in a effort to secure the 2012 Worldcon for Chicago.

There were no awards of any significance, no huge show of public recognition. But everyone who read science fiction knew his work. And he did what he wanted with his life, incidentally, along the way, changing the way the world was viewed.

The most expensive item with one of his covers tends to be Ralph 124C 41+: A Romance of the Year 2660 by **Hugo Gernsback**, from 1925. Truly good copies in a dustjacket sell for around $12,000.00 to $18,000.00.

Michael Whelan.

Michael Whelan was born in Culver City, California on June 29th, 1950. In the late sixties he went to San Jose State University as a pre-med biology major. After working with just one too many cadavers, he switched his major to art and graduated in 1973 with a Bachelor of Arts in Painting.

In 1974, he was showing his paintings at the World Science Fiction Convention in Washington D.C. And shortly after that, he submitted a series of slides to **Donald A. Wollheim** at DAW Books and Wollheim hired him to do a cover for The Enchantress of World's End by Lin Carter. That was released in 1975, DAW Collector's Book 150. That was followed by The Transition of Titus Crow by Brian Lumley, DAW Collector's Book 151, and The Year's Best Horror Stories: Series III, edited by Richard Davis, DAW Collector's Book 155.

He was well on his way and thirty-five years later, his covers are still in demand. He spends more time working on gallery paintings than covers, but the covers are still appearing...

For collector's, the highest priced books with a Whelan cover tend to be the Stephen King Gunslinger series published by Donald M. Grant. A complete set of first editions can run around $8,000.00, although the signed limited edition of the first one, The Dark Tower, can go for around $5,000.00 all by itself. And a set of signed volumes is worth around $25,000.00.

***

AWARDS

1980. Balrog Best Artist Award.
1980. Hugo Best Professional Artist Award.
1980. Locus Poll Best Artist Award.
1981. Hugo Best Professional Artist Award.
1981. Locus Poll Best Artist Award.
1981. World Fantasy Award for Best Artist.
1982. Hugo Best Professional Artist Award.
1982. World Fantasy Award for Best Artist.
1982. SF Chronicle Best Pro Artist Award.
1982. Locus Poll Best Artist Award.
1983. SF Chronicle Best Pro Artist Award.
1983. World Fantasy Award for Best Artist.
1983. Hugo Best Professional Artist Award.
1983. Locus Poll Best Artist Award.
1984. SF Chronicle Best Pro Artist Award.
1984. Hugo Best Professional Artist Award.
1984. Chesley Award for Best Hardback Cover - The Integral Trees by Larry Niven.
1984. Locus Poll Best Artist Award.
1985. SF Chronicle Best Pro Artist Award.
1985. Hugo Best Professional Artist Award.
1985. Locus Poll Best Artist Award.
1986. SF Chronicle Best Pro Artist Award.
1986. Hugo Best Professional Artist Award.
1986. Chesley Award for Best Paperback Cover - The Cat Who Walks Through Walls by **Robert A. Heinlein**.
1986. Chesley Award for Best Unpublished Colour Work - Sentinels
1986. Locus Poll Best Artist Award.
1987. Locus Poll Best Artist Award.
1987. SF Chronicle Best Pro Artist Award.
1988. Locus Poll Best Artist Award.
1988. Hugo Award for Best Related Non-Fiction Book - Michael Whelan's Works of Wonder.
1988. Hugo Best Professional Artist Award.
1988. SF Chronicle Best Pro Artist Award.
1989. Locus Poll Best Artist Award.
1989. Hugo Best Professional Artist Award.
1990. Chesley Award for Artistic Achievement.
1990. Chesley Award for Best Paperback Cover Illustration - The Madness Season by C. S. Friedman.
1990. Locus Poll Best Artist Award.
1991. Asimov's Reader's Pole - Best Cover Artist.
1991. SF Chronicle Best Pro Artist Award.
1991. Hugo Best Professional Artist Award.
1991. Locus Poll Best Artist Award.
1991. Chesley Award for Best Hardback Cover Illustration - The Summer Queen by Joan D. Vinge.
1991. Chesley Award for the Best Unpublished Monochrome Work - Study for All the Weyrs of Pern by **Anne McCaffrey**.
1992. SF Chronicle Best Pro Artist Award.
1992. Hugo Best Professional Artist Award.
1992. Locus Poll Best Artist Award.
1992. Chesley Award for Best Cover Illustration - Magazine - for Asimov's, November 1992 - **Isaac Asimov** Portrait.
1993. Locus Poll Best Artist Award.
1993. SF Chronicle Best Pro Artist Award.
1994. SF Chronicle Best Pro Artist Award.
1994. Locus Poll Best Artist Award.
1994. Allied Artists of America's Grumbacher Gold Medal for the painting, Climber.
1995. Locus Poll Best Artist Award.
1996. Locus Poll Best Artist Award.
1996. Chesley Award for Best Hardback Cover Illustration - The Golden Key by Melanie Rawn, Jennifer Roberson and Kate Elliot.
1997. Society of Illustrator's Gold Medal for the digital piece, Crux Humanis.
1997. Spectrum Gold Medal.
1997. Locus Poll Best Artist Award.
1998. Locus Poll Best Artist Award.
1999. Locus Poll Best Artist Award.
1999. Chesley Award for Best Hardback Cover Illustration - Otherland: Mountain of Black Glass by Tad Williams.
2000. Hugo Best Professional Artist Award.
2000. Chesley Award for Best Unpublished Color Work.
2000. Spectrum Gold Medal.
2000. Locus Poll Best Artist Award.
2002. Locus Poll Best Artist Award.
2002. Hugo Best Professional Artist Award.
2004. Spectrum Lifetime Achievement Award.
2004. Locus Poll Best Artist Award.
2009. Inducted into The Science Fiction Hall of Fame.

***

BOOKS

1. Wonderworks: Science Fiction and Fantasy Art. Published by Starblaze - Donning, Virginia Beach, Virginia, 1979. Hardcover.

2. Michael Whelan's Works of Wonder. Published by Del Rey - Ballantine Books, New York City, 1987. Hardcover.

3. The Art of Michael Whelan: Scenes/Visions. Published by Bantam Books, New York City, 1993. Hardcover.

4. Something In My Eye. With Cathy and Arnie Fenner. Published by Mark V. Ziesing, Shingletown, California, 1996. Hardcover.

5. A Lovecraft Retrospective: Artists Inspired by H. P. Lovecraft. Published by Centipede Press, United States, 2008. Limited edition leather-bound. Introduction by Harlan Ellison, afterword by Thomas Ligotti. Featuring the work of: Michael Whelan; H. R. Giger; Lee Brown Coye; Virgil Finlay; Gahan Wilson; J. K. Potter; and others.

Connie Willis.

Constance Elaine Trimmer Willis was born on December 31st, 1945 in Denver, Colorado. She once said it made her crazy that science fiction could so easily be dismissed as inconsequential by so many people who knew so little. The first science fiction she ever read was Have Space Suit - Will Travel by **Robert A. Heinlein**, 1958.

After graduating Colorado State College in 1967, a career as a writer seemed reasonable. Writing science fiction seemed even more reasonable.

And the first story she ever had published was Santa Titicaca. It was bought by Ejler Jakobsson for the Winter 1970 issue of Worlds of Fantasy, where it appeared with: What Do You Mean - Fantasy? - an essay by **Theodore Sturgeon**; The Tombs of Atuan by **Ursula K. Le Guin**; Me-Too by Sonya Dorman; Death of a Peculiar Boar by Naomi Mitchison; A Ship Will Come by Robert F. Young; In the Cards by Robert Bloch; Funny Place by Naomi J. Kahn; The Man Doors Said Hello To by James Tiptree, Jr; If a Flower Could Eclipse by Michael Bishop; and Among the Grimoires - an essay by Lester del Rey; along with all the usual features.

Her next published short story was years later, in 1978. It was called Capra Corn and found a home in the March 1978 issue of Charles C. Ryan's Galileo, along with: Loss of Signal by Mark J. McGarry; Do Not Go Gentle by Kevin O'Donnell, Jr; Non-Isotropic by **Brian W. Aldiss**; Evasion by Bill Boggess; and The Masters of Solitude - part 3 of 4 by Marvin Kaye and Parke Godwin.

Her first published novel, Water Witch, written with Cynthia Felice, came out in 1982. And her first in a string of Hugo Awards came two years later for her collection Fire Watch. Since then, she has won ten Hugos and a handful of Nebulas...

And her highest priced book for collectors is Doomsday Book which runs around $2,000.00 and, incidentally, also won a Hugo.

***

AWARDS

1982. Nebula Best Novelette Award for Firewatch - Isaac Asimov's Science Fiction Magazine, February 15, 1982.
1983. Hugo Best Novelette Award for Firewatch - Isaac Asimov's Science Fiction Magazine, February 15, 1982.
1983. SF Chronicle Best Novelette Award for Firewatch - Isaac Asimov's Science Fiction Magazine, February 15, 1982.
1983. Nebula Best Short Story Award for A Letter from the Clearys - Isaac Asimov's Science Fiction Magazine, July 1982.
1987. Asimov's Readers' Poll for best novella, Spice Pogrom.
1988. Nebula Best Novella Award for The Last of the Winnebagos - Isaac Asimov's Science Fiction Magazine, July 1988.
1988. John W. Campbell Memorial Award for Lincoln's Dreams.
1989. Asimov's Readers' Poll for best novella for The Last of the Winnebagos.
1989. Hugo Best Novella Award for The Last of the Winnebagos - Isaac Asimov's Science Fiction Magazine, July 1988.
1989. SF Chronicle Best Novella Award for The Last of the Winnebagos - Isaac Asimov's Science Fiction Magazine, July 1988.
1989. Nebula Best Novelette Award for At the Rialto - Omni Publications, October 1989.
1991. HOMer Short Story Award for In the Late Cretaceous - Isaac Asimov's Science Fiction Magazine, December 1991.
1993. Hugo Best Novel Award for Doomsday Book.
1993. Locus Poll Best Novel Award for Doomsday Book.
1993. Hugo Best Short Story Award for Even the Queen - Isaac Asimov's Science Fiction Magazine, April 1992.
1993. Nebula Best Novel Award for Doomsday Book.
1993. Nebula Best Short Story Award for Even the Queen - Isaac Asimov's Science Fiction Magazine, April 1992.
1993. Locus Poll Best Short Story Award for Even the Queen - Isaac Asimov's Science Fiction Magazine, April 1992.
1993. Asimov's Readers' Poll for best short story, Even the Queen.
1994. Hugo Best Short Story Award for Death on the Nile - Isaac Asimov's Science Fiction Magazine, March 1993.
1994. Locus Poll Best Collection Award for Impossible Things.
1994. Locus Poll Best Short Story Award for Close Encounter - Asimov's Science Fiction, September 1993.
1994. Asimov's Readers' Poll for best short story, Inn.
1994. SF Chronicle Best Short Story Award for Death on the Nile - Isaac Asimov's Science Fiction Magazine, March 1993.
1996. Locus Poll Best Novella Award for Remake.
1997. Locus Poll Best Novella Award for Bellwether.
1997. Hugo Best Short Story Award for The Soul Selects Her Own Society: Invasion and Repulsion: A Chronological Reinterpretation of Two of Emily Dickinson's Poems: A Wellsian Perspective - Isaac Asimov's Science Fiction Magazine, April 1996.
1998. Locus Poll Best Novelette Award for Newsletter - Asimov's Science Fiction, December 1997.
1999. Hugo Best Novel Award for To Say Nothing of the Dog.
1999. Locus Poll Best Novel Award for To Say Nothing of the Dog.
1999. Locus Poll Award for Best SF/Fantasy Author of the 90s.
2000. Hugo Best Novella Award for The Winds of Marble Arch - Isaac Asimov's Science Fiction Magazine, October/November, 1999.
2002. Locus Poll Best SF Novel Award for Passage.
2006. Hugo Best Novella Award for Inside Job - Isaac Asimov's Science Fiction Magazine, January, 2005.
2008. Hugo Best Novella Award for All Seated on the Ground - Isaac Asimov's Science Fiction Magazine, December 2007.
2009. Inducted into The Science Fiction Hall of Fame.

***

TELEVISION

1. Snow Wonder. Based on the short story Just Like the Ones We Used to Know, 2003, this was made for television in 2005. Directed by Peter Werner, it starred: Julie Ann Emery; Jennifer Esposito; Camryn Manheim; Poppy Montgomery; Jason Priestley; Josh Randall; and many others, including Mary Tyler Moore as Aunt Lula.

***

BOOKS AND COLLECTIONS

1. Water Witch. With Cynthia Felice. Published by Ace Books, New York City, 1982. Softcover.

2. Fire Watch. Published by Bluejay Books, New York City, 1985. Hardcover. Herein: Fire Watch, 1982; Service for the Burial of the Dead, 1982; Lost and Found, 1982; All My Darling Daughters, 1985; The Father of the Bride, 1982; A Letter from the Clearys, 1982; And Come from Miles Around, 1979; The Sidon in the Mirror, 1983; Daisy in the Sun, 1979; Mail Order Clone, 1982; Samaritan, 1978; and Blue Moon, 1984.

3. Lincoln's Dreams. Published by Bantam Spectra, New York City, 1987. Hardcover.

4. Light Raid. With Cynthia Felice. Published by Ace Books, New York City, 1989. Hardcover.

5. Distress Call. Published by Roadkill Press, Kent, Connecticut, 1991. Limited to 300 signed softcovers. With On Ghost Stories.

6. Daisy, in the Sun. Published by Pulphouse Publishing, Eugene, Oregon, 1991. Hardcover.

7. Doomsday Book. Published by Bantam Spectra, New York City, 1992. Hardcover.

8. Impossible Things. Published by Bantam Spectra, New York City, 1994. Softcover. Herein: Foreword by Gardner Dozois; The Last of the Winnebagos, 1988; Even the Queen, 1992; Schwarzchild Radius, 1987; Ado, 1988; Spice Pogrom, 1986; Winter's Tale, 1987; Chance, 1986; In the Late Cretaceous, 1991; Time Out, 1989; Jack, 1991; and At the Rialto, 1989.

9. Impossible Things. Published by The Science Fiction Book Club, Garden City, New York, 1994. First hardcover edition.

10. Remake. Published by Mark V. Ziesing, Shingletown, California, 1994. Hardcover.

11. Uncharted Territory. Published by Bantam Spectra, New York City, 1994. Softcover.

12. Bellwether. Published by Bantam Spectra, New York City, 1996. Softcover.

13. Futures Imperfect. Published by Guild America Books, New York City, 1996. Hardcover. Herein: Uncharted Territory, 1994; Remake, 1994; and Bellwether, 1996.

14. Promised Land. With Cynthia Felice. Published by Ace Books, New York City, 1997. Hardcover.

15. To Say Nothing of the Dog. Published by Bantam Spectra, New York City, 1997. Hardcover.

16. Miracle and Other Christmas Stories. Published by Bantam Spectra, New York City, 1999. Hardcover. Herein: Introduction by **Connie Willis**; Miracle, 1991; Inn, 1993; In Coppelius's Toyshop, 1996; The Pony, 1985; Adaptation, 1994; Cat's Paw, 1999; Newsletter, 1997; Epiphany, 1999; A Final Word, 1999; and two essays: Twelve Things to Read, 1999; and Twelve Things to Watch, 1999.

17. Water Witch. Published by G. K. Hall, Boston, 1999. First hardcover edition.

18. Passage. Published by Bantam Spectra, New York City, 2001. Hardcover.

19. A Woman's Liberation: A Choice of Futures By and About Women. With Sheila Williams. Published by Warner Aspect, New York City, 2001. Softcover.

20. The Winds of Marble Arch. Published by Subterranean Press, Burton, Michigan, 2008. Hardcover. Herein: Introduction by **Connie Willis**; The Winds of Marble Arch, 1999; Blued Moon, 1984; Just Like the Ones We Used to Know, 2003; Daisy in the Sun, 1979; A Letter from the Clearys, 1982; Newsletter, 1997; Fire Watch, 1982; Nonstop to Portales, 1996; Ado, 1988; All My Darling Daughters, 1985; In the Late Cretaceous, 1991; The Curse of Kings, 1985; Even the Queen, 1992; Inn, 1993; Samaritan, 1978; Cash Crop, 1984; Jack, 1991; The Last of the Winnebagos, 1988; Service for the Burial of the Dead, 1982; The Soul Selects Her Own Society: Invasion and Repulsion: A Chronological Reinterpretation of Two of Emily Dickinson's Poems: A Wellsian Perspective, 1996; Chance, 1986; At the Rialto, 1989; and Epiphany.

***

ANTHOLOGIES

1. The New Hugo Winners - Volume III. Published by Baen Books, New York City, 1994. Softcover. Herein: Introduction by **Connie Willis**; Kirinyaga by Mike Resnick, 1988; The Manamouki by Mike Resnick, 1990; Schrodinger's Kitten by George Alec Effinger, 1988; Boobs by Suzy McKee Charnas, 1989; Enter a Soldier Later: Enter Another by **Robert Silverberg**, 1989; The Mountains of Mourning by Lois McMaster Bujold, 1989; Bears Discover Fire by Terry Bisson, 1990; The Hemingway Hoax by Joe Haldeman, 1990; and The Last of the Winnebagos by **Connie Willis**, 1988.

2. Nebula Awards 33. Published by Harcourt Brace, New York City, 1999. Hardcover. Herein: The Elizabeth Complex by Karen Joy Fowler, 1996; The Martyr by **Poul Anderson**, 1960; The Dead by Michael Swanwick, 1996; Sister Emily's Lightship by Jane Yolen, 1996; The Flowers of Aulit Prison by Nancy Kress, 1996; Abandon in Place by Jerry Oltion, 1995; The Bookshop by Nelson S. Bond, 1941; Three Hearings on the Existence of Snakes in the Human Bloodstream by James Alan Gardner, 1997; Itsy Bitsy Spider by James Patrick Kelly, 1997; The Crab Lice by Gregory Feeley, 1996; Excerpt from The Moon and the Sun by Vonda N. McIntyre, 1999; and an assortment of essays.

Octavia E. Butler

-2010-

Octavia E. Butler

Octavia Estelle Butler was born in Pasadena, California on June 22nd, 1947 and died from head injuries on February 24th, 2006. The injuries were caused by a fall. Locus Magazine suggested that the fall was caused by a stroke.

Her father died when she was a baby and her mother worked as a maid, raising Butler with the help of her own mother. She was brought up in a strict Baptist household and early on was driven to fantasy and science fiction as an escape from day-to-day life. Also as an escape, she began writing when she was ten years old and, at twelve, wrote her first science fiction. In an interview, she explained, "I was writing my own little stories and when I was 12, I was watching a bad science fiction movie called Devil Girl from Mars and decided I could write a better story than that. And I turned off the TV and proceeded to try, and I've been writing science fiction ever since."

In another interview, she explained she had always felt like an outsider, and "a pessimist, a feminist always, a Black, a quiet egoist, a former Baptist, and an oil-and-water combination of ambition, laziness, insecurity, certainty, and drive."

Her first published short story, Crossover, was used in Clarion – an anthology from Signet Books, 1971, edited by Robin Scott Wilson. And her first novel was Patternmaster, published by Doubleday in 1979. Fine copies of this sell for between $650.00 and $750.00.

***

AWARDS

Creative Arts Award from the YWCA in Los Angeles.
1984. Hugo Award for Best Short Story, presented for Speech Sounds – Isaac Asimov's Science Fiction Magazine, Mid-December 1983.
1984. Nebula Award for Best Novelette, presented for Bloodchild – Isaac Asimov's Science Fiction Magazine, June 1984.
1985. Science Fiction Chronicle Award for best Novelette – Bloodchild, 1984.
1985. Hugo Award for Best Novelette, presented for Bloodchild, 1984.
1995. MacArthur Foundation Genius Grant for "showing exceptional merit and promise for continued and enhanced creative work."
1999. Nebula Award for Best Novel, presented for Parable of the Talents, Seven Stories Press, 1998.
2000. PEN American Center Lifetime Achievement Award.
2010. Inducted into the Science Fiction Hall of Fame.

In 2006, the Octavia E. Butler Memorial Scholarship was set up in her memory to enable writers of color to attend a Clarion writing workshop, a six-week writing workshop at the Clarion State College in Pennsylvania, devoted to science fiction and fantasy. It was created by Robin Scott Wilson in 1968.

***

FILM AND TELEVISION

1. Brave New Worlds: The Science Fiction Phenomenon. Directed by Paul Oremland, the documentary was released in the UK in 1993, starring: **Octavia Butler**; **Arthur C. Clarke**; **Robert Silverberg**; **Brian Aldiss**; J. G. Ballard; Kim Stanley Robinson; John Clute; and many others.

2. The 20th Century: Yesterday's Tomorrows. A 1999 documentary, written by Richard Berge and Kenn Rabin and directed by Barry Levinson. This starred: Octavia Butler; Richard Belzer; Phyllis Diller; Charlton Heston; Walter Mosley; and others.

3. The Charlie Rose Show. Octavia Butler was interviewed by Charlie Rose for an episode that was dated June 1st, 2000.

4. Closer to Truth. Along with David Brin and Michael Crichton, Butler was featured in the first episode from Season 3 – Is Science Fiction Science?

5. Chisholm '72: Unbought and Unbossed. Directed by Shola Lynch, this 2004 documentary featured Butler along with: Shirley Chisholm; Susan Brownmiller; Walter Fauntroy; and many others.

***

NOVELS AND COLLECTIONS

1. Patternmaster. Published by Doubleday & Company, Garden City, New York, 1976. Hardcover.

2. Mind of My Mind. Published by Doubleday & Company, Garden City, New York, 1977. Hardcover.

3. Survivor. Published by Doubleday & Company, Garden City, New York, 1978. Hardcover.

4. Kindred. Published by Doubleday & Company, Garden City, New York, 1979. Hardcover.

5. Wild Seed. Published by Doubleday & Company, Garden City, New York, 1980. Hardcover.

6. Clay's Ark. Published by St. Martin's Press, New York City, 1984. Hardcover.

7. **Dawn.** Published by Warner Books, New York City, 1987. Hardcover.

8. **Adulthood Rites.** Published by Warner Books, New York City, 1988. Hardcover.

9. **Imago.** Published by Warner Books, New York City, 1989. Hardcover.

10. **Xenogenesis.** Published by Guild America Books and the Science Fiction Book Club, New York City, 1989. An omnibus edition, this contained: Dawn, 1987; Adulthood Rites, 1988; and Imago, 1989.

11. **The Evening and the Morning and the Night.** Published by Pulphouse Publishing, Eugene, Oregon, 1991. Simultaneous hardcover and softcover.

12. **Parable of the Sower.** Published by Four Walls Eight Windows, New York City, 1993. Hardcover.

13. **Bloodchild and Other Stories.** Published by Four Walls Eight Windows, New York City, 1995. Hardcover. This story collection contains: Speech Sounds, 1983; Bloodchild, 1984; Crossover, 1971; The Evening and the Morning and the Night, 1987; Near of Kin, 1979; Positive Obsession – an essay, 1989; and Furor Scribendi – an essay, 1993.

14. **Parable of the Talents.** Published by Seven Stories Press, New York City, 1998. Hardcover.

15. **Lilith's Brood.** Published by Warner Aspect, New York City, 2000. A re-titled reprint of Xenogenesis in trade paperback.

16. **Fledgling.** Published by Seven Stories Press, New York City, 2005. Hardcover.

17. **Seed to Harvest.** Published by Warner Books, New York City, 2007. An omnibus edition in trade paperback, this contains: Wild Seed, 1980; Mind of My Mind, 1977; Clay's Ark, 1984; and Patternmaster, 1976.

***

RELATED

1. **Suzy McKee Charnas, Octavia Butler, Joan D. Vinge.** By Marleen S. Barr; Ruth Salvaggio; and Richard Law. Published by Borgo Press, Washington, 1986. A Starmont Reader's Guide. Softcover.

2. **CONVERSATIONS WITH OCTAVIA BUTLER.** Edited by Conseula Francis. Published by the University Press of Mississippi, Jackson, Mississippi, 2010. Trade paperback.

Richard Matheson.

Richard Burton Matheson was born on February 20th, 1926, in Allendale, New Jersey. After high school, he joined the military and fought his way through World War Two with the infantry. In 1949, he graduated university with a journalism degree. And in 1950, he sold his first short story, Born of Man and Woman. Anthony Boucher bought it for the Summer 1950 issue of The Magazine of Fantasy and Science Fiction where it shared space with Friday the Nineteenth by Elisabeth Sanxay Holding; Huge Beast by Cleve Cartmill; The Hat in the Hall by Jack Iams; The War Against the Moon by Andre Maurois; Dumb Supper by Kris Neville writing as Henderson Starke; Ounce of Prevention by Paul A. Carter writing as Philip Carter; The Case of Summerfield by W. H. Rhodes – a reprint from 1871; Divine Right by Betsy Curtis; Professor Pownall's Oversight by H. Russell Wakefield – a reprint from 1928; and Haunt by A. Bertram Chandler. Matheson's story was so well received that Everett F. Bleiler reprinted it in The Best Science Fiction Stories: 1951.

Third from the Sun was his next published work, bought by H. L. Gold for the October 1950 issue of Galaxy Science Fiction. This was printed along with: The Stars Are the Styx by **Theodore Sturgeon**; Later Than You Think by **Fritz Leiber**; Contagion by Katherine MacLean; The Last Martian by Fredric Brown; Darwinian Pool Room by **Isaac Asimov**; and Part One of Time Quarry by Clifford D. Simak.

In 1953, his first books were published and by 1955, when Hollywood approached him about The Shrinking Man, he moved into film and television. In an interview, he explained, "I sold my novel, The Shrinking Man, to Universal and did it on the stipulation that I do the screenplay. I've always liked motion pictures, right from childhood on, so I've always wanted to get into motion pictures..."

One of his more famous episodes of Twilight Zone was Nightmare at 20,000 Feet. About that, he said, "I was on an airplane and I looked out and there was all these fluffy clouds and I thought, gee what if I saw a guy skiing across that like it was snow because it looked like snow. But when I thought it over, that's not very scary, so I turned it into a gremlin out on the wing of the airplane."

"When I write anything – a short story, a novel – I see it in my mind like a movie."

His most expensive books are the first hardcover editions of I Am Legend and The Shrinking Man, each selling for more than $1,500.00, his first story collection, Born of Man and Woman, sells for around $600.00.

He occasionally used the name Logan Swanson.

***

Richard Matheson

AWARDS

1973. Edgar Award for Best Television Feature or Mini Series for The Night Stalker, 1972.
1976. World Fantasy Award for Best Novel, Somewhere in Time, also known as Bid Time Return, 1975.
1984. World Fantasy Award for Life Achievement.
1990. World Fantasy Award for Best Collection, Richard Matheson, Collected Stories, 1988.
1990. Bram Stoker Award for Lifetime Achievement.
1991. Spur Award for Best Western Novel, Journal of the Gun Years, 1991.
1993. World Horror Convention Grand Master Award.
2008. Tahtivaeltaja Award for I Am Legend.
2010. Inducted into the Science Fiction Hall of Fame.

***

FILM AND TELEVISION

1. Young Couples Only. This story was directed for the series Studio 57 by Richard Irving. It aired on September 3rd, 1955, starring Peter Lorre and Barbara Hale.

2. The Incredible Shrinking Man. Based on Matheson's novel The Shrinking Man, this was directed by Jack Arnold and released as a film in April 1957, starring: Grant Williams; Randy Stuart; April Kent; Paul Langton; William Schallert; and others.

3. Act of Faith. This was written with Charles Beaumont for the series Buckskin. It was shown on March 23rd, 1959 – Season 1, Episode 30 – starring: James Griffith; Freeman Lusk; Tyler McVey; and Lyle Talbot.

4. The Beat Generation. Directed by Charles F. Haas, this film was released in July, 1959. It starred: Steve Cochran; Mamie Van Doren; Ray Danton; Fay Spain; Jackie Coogan; James Mitchum; and others, along with Louis Armstrong as himself and Guy Stockwell as an uncredited beatnik.

5. The Healing Woman. Working with Charles Beaumont, he wrote the story for this episode of Wanted: Dead or Alive. Starring Steve McQueen, it aired on September 12th, 1959 – Season 2, Episode 2.

The Twilight Zone. Starting in 1959, Matheson worked on sixteen episodes of The Twilight Zone:

6. And When the Sky Was Opened. Directed by Douglas Heyes, this was from Season 1, Episode 11 – December 11th, 1959. It starred: Rod Taylor; Jim Hutton; Charles Aidman; Maxine Cooper; and others.

7. Third from the Sun. Season 1, Episode 14, this was directed by Richard L. Bare and shown on January 8th, 1960, starring Fritz Weaver and Edward Andrews.

8. The Last Flight. This was directed by William F. Claxton – Season 1, Episode 18 – February 5th, 1960. It starred: Kenneth Haigh; Alexander Courby; Simon Scott; and Robert Warwick.

9. A World of Difference. From March 11th, 1960 – Season 1, Episode 23 – this was directed by Ted Post and starred: Howard Duff; David White; and Eileen Ryan.

10. A World of His Own. Directed by Ralph Nelson, this aired on July 1st, 1960 – Season 1, Episode 36. It starred: Keenan Wynn; Phyllis Kirk; and Mary LaRoche.

11. Nick of Time. This was shown on November 18th, 1960 – Season 2, Episode 7. It was directed by Richard L. Bare and starred William Shatner and Patricia Breslin.

12. The Invaders. Directed by Douglas Heyes, this starred Agnes Moorehead. Season 2, Episode 15, it aired on January 27th, 1961.

13. Once Upon a Time. Season 3, Episode 13, this aired on December 15th, 1961. Directed by Norman Z. McLeod, it starred Buster Keaton and Stanley Adams.

14. Little Lost Girl. Directed by Paul Stewart, this was shown on March 16th, 1962 – Season 3, Episode 26. It starred Sarah Marshall and Robert Sampson.

15. Young Man's Fancy. Starring Phyllis Thaxter and Alex Nicol, this was directed by John Brahm and shown on May 11th, 1962 – Season 3, Episode 34.

16. Mute. Aired on January 31st, 1963 – Season 4, Episode 5 – this was directed by Stuart Rosenberg and starred Barbara Baxley and Frank Overton.

17. Death Ship. This was directed by Don Medford and shown on February 7th, 1963 – Season 4, Episode 6 – starring Jack Klugman and Ross Martin.

18. Steel. Directed by Don Weis, this starred Lee Marvin and Joe Mantell. It aired on October 4th, 1963 – Season 5, Episode 2.

19. Nightmare at 20,000 Feet. Starring William Shatner and Christine White, this was directed by Richard Donner and shown on October 11th, 1963 – Season 5, Episode 3.

20. Night Call. Directed by Jacques Tourneur, this starred Gladys Cooper and Nora Marlowe. It was shown on February 7th, 1964 – Season 5, Episode 19.

21. Spur of the Moment. From February 21st, 1964 – Season 5, Episode 21 – this was directed by Elliot Silverstein and starred Diana Hyland and Marsha Hunt.

22. The Lady on the Wall. Again working with Charles Beaumont, he created this for Have Gun – Will Travel. Directed by Ida Lupino, it was shown on February 20th, 1960 – Season 3, Episode 23. The series starred Richard Boone.

23. Target of Hate. This was written for the series Bourbon Street Beat. It was directed by Leslie H. Martinson – Season 1, Episode 22 – and aired on March 7th, 1960, starring James Coburn and Richard Chamberlain.

24. Home Is the Brave. Matheson did the teleplay for this episode of the series Cheyenne, which starred Clint Walker. Directed by Emory Horger, it aired on March 14th, 1960 – Season 4, Episode 13.

25. House of Usher. Based on the Edgar Allan Poe story, The Fall of the House of Usher, 1839, Matheson did the screenplay for this 1960 Roger Corman film, which starred: Vincent Price; Mark Damon; Myrna Fahey; and Harry Ellerbe.

26. Thirty Minutes. For the series Lawman, starring John Russell, this was directed by Robert Sparr and shown on March 20, 1960 – Season 2, Episode 24.

27. Yawkey. Done for the series Lawman, starring John Russell, Peter Brown and Peggie Castle, this was directed by Stuart Heisler and aired on October 23rd, 1960 – Season 3, Episode 6.

28. Samson the Great. Also for Lawman and also directed by Stuart Heisler, this was shown on November 20th, 1960 – Season 3, Episode 10.

29. Cornered. Directed by Marc Lawrence for the series Lawman, this aired on December 11th, 1960 – Season 3, Episode 13.

30. Master of the World. Based on work by **Jules Verne**, Matheson did the screenplay for this 1961 film. Directed by William Witney, it starred: Vincent Price; Charles Bronson; Henry Hull; Mary Webster; and others.

31. Homecoming. Written for the series Lawman, which starred John Russell, Peter Brown and Peggie Castle, this was directed by Robert B. Sinclair and shown on February 5th, 1961 – Season 3, Episode 21.

32. Pit and the Pendulum. Working from the Edgar Allan Poe story, The Pit and the Pendulum, 1842, Matheson did the screenplay for Roger Corman. Released in August 1961, this starred: Vincent Price; John Kerr; Barbara Steele; Luana Anders; Antony Carbone; and others.

33. The Return of Andrew Bentley. Matheson adapted this from the story of the same title by August Derleth, 1933. Directed by John Newland, it was used in television series Thriller – Season 2, Episode 12. Airing on December 11th, 1961, it starred: Boris Karloff; Antoinette Bower; John Newland; and others.

34. Night of the Eagle. Based on the novel Conjure Wife, 1952, by **Fritz Leiber**, this was alternately titled Burn, Witch, Burn. Directed by Sidney Hayers, it was released in April 1962, starring: Peter Wyngarde; Janet Blair; Margaret Johnson; Anthony Nicholls; and others.

Richard Matheson

35. Forgotten Front. Working as Logan Swanson, he did this teleplay for the series Combat, which starred Vic Morrow, Rick Jason, Shecky Greene and others. Directed by Robert Altman, this was Episode 1, Season 1. It aired on October 2nd, 1962.

36. The Actor. This was written for series Lawman, starring John Russell, Peter Brown and Peggie Castle. Directed by Richard C. Sarafian, it was shown on May 27th, 1962 - Season 4, Episode 37.

37. Tales of Terror. Adapted from short stories by Edgar Allan Poe, Matheson's screenplay was directed by Roger Corman. The film was released in July, 1962, starring: Vincent Price; Peter Lorre; Basil Rathbone; Debra Paget; and others.

38. Ride the Nightmare. Based on Matheson's novel of the same title, this was directed by Bernard Girard for The Alfred Hitchcock Hour. From Season 1, Episode 11, it aired on November 29th, 1962. . It starred: Hugh O'Brian; Gena Rowlands; and John Anderson.

39. The Thirty First of February. Based on the Novel by Julian Symons from 1950, he adapted this for The Alfred Hitchcock Hour. Directed by Alf Kjellin and starring David Wayne, William Conrad, Elizabeth Allen, Bob Crane and others, this aired on January 4th, 1963 – Season 1, Episode 15.

40. The Raven. Based on the poem by Edgar Alan Poe, 1845, this was another screenplay for Roger Corman. Released in January 1963, it starred: Vincent Price; Peter Lorre; Boris Karloff; and others, including Jack Nicholson as Rexford Bedlo.

41. The Comedy of Terrors. This was released in January 22, 1964. Directed by Jacques Tourneur, it starred: Vincent Price; Peter Lorre; Boris Karloff; Basil Rathbone; and many others.

42. The Last Man on Earth. This was based on Matheson's 1954 novel, I Am Legend. Working as Logan Swanson, he did the screenplay. Released in March 1964, it was directed by Ubaldo Ragona and starred Vincent Price, Franca Bettoia and others.

43. Fanatic. Based on the 1961 novel, Nightmare by Anne Blaisdell, this was released in March 1965. Directed by Silvio Narizzano, it starred: Tallulah Bankhead; Stefanie Powers; Peter Vaughan; Donald Sutherland; and others.

44. Time of Flight. This was done for Bob Hope Presents the Chrysler Theatre – Season 4, Episode 2 – airing on September 21st, 1966. It starred: Peter Brocco; Michael Conrad; Lloyd Haynes; Jack Kelly; Jack Klugman; Juliet Mills; and others.

45. The Enemy Within. Directed by Leo Penn, this was Episode 5 in Season 1 of Star Trek. It aired on October 6th, 1966. It probably isn't necessary to mention who the stars of the series were.

46. The Atlantis Affair. This was for The Girl from U.N.C.L.E. starring Stefanie Powers, Noel Harrison and Leo G. Carroll. Directed by E. Darrell Hallenbeck, it aired on November 16th, 1966 – Season 1, Episode 9.

47. The Young Warriors. Based on his own novel, The Beardless Warriors, 1960, Matheson did the screenplay for this. Directed by John Peyser and starring James Drury, Steve Carlson and others, it was released in February 1968.

48. No Such Thing as a Vampire. Directed by Paddy Russell and starring Peter Blythe and Cynthia Etherington, this was used in the series Late Night Horror. Season 1, Episode 1, it aired on April 19th, 1968.

49. The Devil Rides Out. Also known as The Devil's Bride, this was based on the 1935 novel by Dennis Wheatley. Directed by Terence Fisher and starring Christopher Lee, this was released in England in July 1968 and in the States in December that same year.

50. Girl of My Dreams. With the teleplay by Robert Bloch, this was directed by Peter Sasdy for the series Journey to the Unknown. Season 1, Episode 8, it aired on December 26th, 1968, starring Michael Callan and Zena Walker.

51. It's Alive. This was based on the Matheson story, Being, 1954. Directed by Larry Buchanan in 1969, it starred Tommy Kirk, Shirley Bonne, and others.

52. De Sade. Directed by Cy Endfield, with help from Roger Corman and Gordon Hessler, this was released in August 1969, starring Keir Dullea, Senta Berger, and many others.

53. Ride the Nightmare. Based on Matheson's 1959 novel, this was released in France as De la part des copains in December 1970 – but it didn't hit the North American market until June 1974. Directed by Terence Young, it starred Charles Bronson, Liv Ullmann, James Mason and Jill Ireland.

54. The Omega Man. This was the second film based on Matheson's novel, I Am Legend, 1954. Starring Charlton Heston, Anthony Zerbe and Rosalind Cash, it was directed by Boris Sagal and released in August 1971.

55. Big Surprise. This aired on Night Gallery – Season 2, Episode 8 – November 10th, 1971. It was directed by Jeannot Szwarc.

56. Duel. Directed by **Steven Spielberg**, with the screenplay and the story by Matheson, this starred Dennis Weaver and aired on November 13th, 1971.

57. The Funeral. Directed by John Meredyth Lucas for Night Gallery, this aired on January 5th, 1972 – Season 2, Episode 15.

58. The Night Stalker. Based on the novel by Jeffrey Grant Rice, this was directed for television by John Llewellyn Moxey. Starring Darrin McGavin, Carol Lynley, Simon Oakland, Ralph Meeker and Claude Akins, it aired on January 11th, 1972.

Ghost Story. Also known as Circle of Fear. Starting in March 1972, Matheson was the developer of the series, which featured Sebastian Cabot as Winston Essex for the first thirteen episodes. Including the pilot, there were twenty-two episodes:

59. The New House. Directed by John Llewellyn Moxey, this aired on March 17th, 1972. It was the pilot episode and starred David Birney.

60. The Dead We Leave Behind. Episode 1, this was directed by Paul Stanley and aired on September 15th, 1972. This one this starred Jason Robards, Stella Stevens and Jack Kelly.

61. The Concrete Captain. Episode 2. Directed by Richard Donner and show on September 22nd, 1972. This starred Stuart Whitman and Gena Rowlands.

62. At the Cradle Foot. Episode 3. From September 29th, 1972, this was directed by Don McDougall and starred James Franciscus and Elizabeth Ashley.

63. Bad Connection. Episode 4. Directed by Walter Doniger, this aired on October 6th, 1972, starring Karen Black and Michael Tolan.

64. The Summer House. Episode 5. October 13th, 1972. This was directed by Leo Penn and starred Carolyn Jones, Steve Forrest and William Windom.

65. Alter Ego. Episode 6. October 27th, 1972. Directed by David Lowell Rich and starring Helen Hayes and Charles Aidman.

66. Half a Death. Episode 7. November 3rd, 1972. This was directed by Leslie H. Martinson and starred Pamela Franklin, Eleanor Parker and Andrew Duggan.

67. House of Evil. Episode 8. November 10th, 1972. Written by Robert Bloch, this was directed by Daryl Duke and starred Melvyn Douglas, Richard Mulligan and Jodie Foster.

68. Cry of the Cat. Episode 9. November 24th, 1972. Directed by Arnold Laven and starring Doug McClure, Jackie Cooper and Mariette Hartley.

69. Elegy for a Vampire. Episode 10. December 1st, 1972. Directed by Don McDougall, this starred Hal Linden, Marilyn Mason and Mike Farrell.

70. Touch of Madness. Episode 11. December 8th, 1972. This was directed by Robert Day and starred Geraldine Page and Rip Torn.

71. Creatures of the Canyon. Episode 12. December 15th, 1972. Directed by Walter Doniger, this starred Angie Dickinson, John Ireland and Madlyn Rhue.

72. Time of Terror. Episode 13. December 22nd, 1972. This was directed by Robert Day and starred Patricia Neal, Craig Stevens and Alice Ghostley.

73. Death's Head. Episode 14. January 5th, 1973. This was directed by James Neilson and starred Janet Leigh and Rory Calhoun.

74. Dark Vengeance. Episode 15. January 12th, 1973. Directed by Herschel Daugherty, this starred Kim Darby and Martin Sheen.

75. Earth, Air, Fire and Water. Episode 16. January 19th, 1973. Based on a story by Harlan Ellison, this was directed by Alexander Singer and starred Frank Converse, Joan Blackman and Tyne Daly.

76. Doorway to Death. Episode 17. January 26th, 1973. Directed by Daryl Duke, this starred Barry Nelson and Susan Dey.

77. Legion of Demons. Episode 18. February 2, 1973. This was directed by Paul Stanley and starred Shirley Knight and Neva Patterson.

78. Graveyard Shift. Episode 19. February 16th, 1973. Directed by Don McDougall and starring Parry Duke and John Astin.

79. The Ghost of Potter's Field. Episode 20. March 23rd, 1973. Directed by Don McDougall, starring Tab Hunter, Louise Sorel, Gary Conway, Pat Harrington Jr. and Paul Winchell.

80. The Phantom of Herald Square. Episode 21. March 30th, 1973. This was directed by James H. Brown and starred David Soul, Sheila Larkin and Victor Jory.

81. The Night Strangler. Directed by Dan Curtis, this aired on January 16th, 1973, starring: Darrin McGavin; Simon Oakland; Scott Brady; Jo Ann Pflug; Wally Cox; John Carradine; and others.

82. The Legend of Hell House. Based on Matheson's 1971 novel, Hell House, Matheson did the screenplay himself. Released in June 1973, it was directed by John Hough and starred Roddy McDowall and Pamela Franklin.

83. Dying Room Only. Released on September 18th, 1973, this was directed for television by Philip Leacock and starred: Cloris Leachman; Ross Martin; Ned Beatty; Dana Elcar; Louise Latham; Dabney Coleman; and others.

84. Scream of the Wolf. Based on a story by David Case, Matheson did the teleplay. Shown on January 16th, 1974, it was directed by Dan Curtis and starred Peter Graves, Clint Walker, Jo Ann Pflug and many others.

85. Dracula. With Matheson basing his story on Bram Stoker's 1897 novel, this was directed for television by Dan Curtis and aired on February 8th, 1974, starring Jack Palance as Dracula, along with: Simon Ward, Nigel Davenport as Van Helsing, Pamela Brown, Fiona Lewis as Lucy; Penelope Horner as Mina; Murray Brown as Jonathan Harker; and many others.

86. The Morning After. This was based on the

Richard Matheson

1973 novel by Jack B. Weiner and shown on television on February 13th, 1974. It was directed by Richard T. Heffron and starred Dick Van Dyke and Lynn Carlin.

87. Someone Is Bleeding. Based on Matheson's 1953 novel, this was released in France in August 1974 as Les seins de glace. The American release was December 1975. Directed by Georges Lautner, the film starred Alain Delon and Mireille Darc.

88. The Stranger Within. Directed for television by Lee Philips, this aired on October 1st, 1974, starring Barbara Eden, George Grizzard and others.

89. Trilogy of Terror. Working with William F. Nolan, Matheson did the stories and the screenplay for this television film. Directed by Dan Curtis and starring Karen Black, it was shown on March 4th, 1975.

90. Captains and Kings. A television mini-series from September 1976. Matheson played President Garfield.

91. The Strange Possession of Mrs. Oliver. Written for television and directed by Gordon Hessler, this was shown on February 28th, 1977. It starred Karen Black and George Hamilton.

92. Dead of Night. Based on a story by Jack Finney, this was directed for television by Dan Curtis and shown on March 29th, 1977. Anjanette Comer, Joan Hackett and Patrick Macnee were the stars.

93. The Godfather: A Novel for Television. This was a TV mini-series in which Matheson had a bit part as a senator. It was shown in November 1977.

94. The Expeditions. This was for the series The Martian Chronicles, based on Ray Bradbury's 1950 collection of stories. It was Episode 1 and aired on January 27th, 1980, starring Rock Hudson, Roddy McDowall, Darren McGavin, Bernadette Peters, Joyce Van Patten, Fritz Weaver and others.

95. The Settlers. Episode 2 of The Martian Chronicles, from January 28th, 1980.

96. The Martians. Episode 3 of The Martian Chronicles, from January 29th, 1980.

97. Somewhere in Time. Based on his 1975 novel, Bid Time Return, Matheson did the screenplay for this. Directed by Jeannot Szwarc and starring Christopher Reeve, Jane Seymour and Christopher Plummer, this was released in October 1980. Matheson also had a bit part in the film as a somewhat astonished man in 1912.

98. The Incredible Shrinking Woman. Loosely based on Matheson's 1956 novel, The Shrinking Man, this was directed by Joel Schumacher and released in January 1981, starring Lily Tomlin, Charles Grodin, Ned Beatty and Henry Gibson.

99. Twilight Zone: The Movie. Matheson worked on three of the segments for this June 1983 film, which was directed by Joe Dante, John Landis, George Miller and **Steven Spielberg**.

100. Jaws 3-D. Just one of an assortment of writers for this July 1983 film, which was directed by Joe Alves and starred: Dennis Quaid; Bess Armstrong; Simon MacCorkindale; Louis Gossett Jr.; and others.

101. Button, Button. Writing as Logan Swanson, Matheson did this for The Twilight Zone - Season 1, Episode 20 – March 7th, 1986. It was directed by Peter Medak and starred Mare Winningham and Brad Davis.

102. The Doll. Based on the 1982 short story. This was for Steven Spielberg's Amazing Stories – Season 1, Episode 22 – May 4th, 1986. Directed by Phil Joanou, it starred John Lithgow and Anne Helm.

103. One for the Books. Based on the 1955 short story. Steven Spielberg's Amazing Stories – Season 1, Episode 23 – May 11th, 1986. Directed by Lesli Linka Glatter and starring Leo Penn and Joyce Van Patten.

104. Life on Death Row. Creative consultant on Steven Spielberg's Amazing Stories – Season 2, Episode 7 – November 10th, 1986. Directed by Mike Garris, this starred Patrick Swayze and James T. Callahan.

105. Miss Stardust. Based on the 1955 short story. Steven Spielberg's Amazing Stories – Season 2, Episode 21 – April 10th, 1987. The teleplay for this was written by Richard Christian Matheson, based on the story by Richard Matheson. Directed by Tobe Hooper, it starred Libby Aubrey and Jack Carter.

106. Loose Cannons. Matheson worked with his son, Richard Christian, on this February 1990 film. Directed by Bob Clark, it starred Dan Aykroyd and Gene Hackman.

107. The Dreamer of Oz. Matheson worked with David Kirschner on the story for this television film. Directed by Jack Bender and starring John Ritter and Annette O'Toole, this aired on December 10th, 1990.

108. Twilight Zone: Rod Serling's Lost Classics. This was based on writing by **Rod Serling**. Directed for television by Robert Markowitz, it was hosted by James Earl Jones and shown on May 19th, 1994.

109. Rod Serling: Submitted for Your Approval. This was an episode of American Masters and aired on November 29th, 1995. Directed by Susan Lacy, it featured Matheson as himself, along with a host of others.

110. First Anniversary. From Season 2, Episode 7 of The New Outer Limits. Directed by Brad Turner, this aired on February 16th, 1996, starring Matt Frewer, Jayne Heitmeyer and Clint Howard.

111. 100 Years of Horror: Ghosts. A 1996 documentary written by Ted Newsom and featuring Matheson as himself, along with **Ray Bradbury**, Roger Corman, Christopher Lee, and many others.

112. 100 Years of Horror: Boris Karloff. A 1996 documentary written by Ted Newsom and featuring Matheson as himself, along with Roger Corman, Christopher Lee, and many others.

113. 100 Years of Horror: The Evil Unseeable. A 1996 documentary written by Ted Newsom and featuring Matheson as himself, along with Roger Corman, Christopher Lee, and many others, including **Ray Bradbury**.

114. 100 Years of Horror: Sorcerers. A 1996 documentary written by Ted Newsom and featuring Matheson as himself, along with Dana Andrews, Roger Corman, John Carpenter, **Ray Bradbury**, and many others.

115. 100 Years of Horror: Giants and Dinosaurs. A 1996 documentary written by Ted Newsom and featuring Matheson as himself, along with **Ray Bradbury**, **Ray Harryhausen**, Christopher Lee, and many others.

116. 100 Years of Horror: The Aristocrats of Evil. A 1996 documentary written by Ted Newsom and featuring Matheson as himself, along with Roger Corman, Christopher Lee, and many others.

117. Trilogy of Terror II. One segment of this was based on Matheson's 1969 story, Prey. Directed by Dan Curtis, it aired on October 30th, 1996.

118. What Dreams May Come. This was based on Matheson's 1978 novel. Directed by Vincent Ward, it was released in October 1998, starring Robin Williams, Cuba Gooding Jr., Annabella Sciorra and Max von Sydow.

119. Stir of Echoes. Based on Matheson's 1958 novel, A Stir of Echoes, this was directed by David Koepp and released in September 1999. It starred Kevin Bacon and Kathryn Erbe.

120. Back to 'Somewhere in Time'. A documentary by Laurent Bouzereau, released in 2000 and featuring Matheson as himself, along with a host of others, including Christopher Reeve, Jane Seymour, Christopher Plummer and others.

121. Richard Matheson: The Writing of Duel. This 2004 documentary was directed by Laurent Bouzereau and featured only Matheson.

122. Shadows in the Dark: The Val Lewton Legacy. A 2005 documentary, directed by Constantine Nasr and featured Richard Matheson as himself, along with: William Friedkin; Kim Newman; Harlan Ellison; Ramsey Campbell; George A. Romero; John Landis; and a host of others.

123. Twilight Zone: The Definitive Edition Interviews. Released in October 2005, this documentary was directed by Charles Holloway and featured interviews with: Richard Matheson; Bill Mumy; George Clayton Johnson; and many others.

124. Dance of the Dead. From the series Masters of Horror – Season 1, Episode 3 – this was directed by Tobe Hooper and aired on November 11th, 2005. It starred Jonathan Tucker and Jessica Lowndes.

125. Blood Son. A short film based on a Matheson story, this was directed by Michael McGruther and released in 2006, starring Paul Coughlan as Dracula.

126. Trilogy of Terror: Terror Scribe. A 2006 documentary, directed by David Gregory and featuring Matheson.

127. The Box. Based on a story by Matheson, this short film was directed by Kvon Chen and released in 2006. It starred Skylar Countar, Peter E. Lewis, and others.

128. My Ambition. Based on the story Blood Son, this was directed by Keith Dinielli and starred Johnny Simmons. It was released in 2006.

129. The Fearmakers Collection. Released in May 2007, this short documentary was directed by John McCarty and featured Matheson along with: John Carpenter; Roger Corman; John Agar; Donald F. Glut; and many others.

130. I Am Omega. Based on I Am Legend, 1954, this was released in November 2007. Directed by Griff Furst, it starred Mark Dacascos and Jennifer Lee Wiggins.

131. I Am Legend. From HBO First Look, a documentary that aired on December 6th, 2007, featuring Will Smith, Francis Lawrence and others, including Richard Matheson as himself.

132. I Am Legend. Based on the 1954 novel, this was released in December 2007. Directed by Francis Lawrence, it starred Will Smith and Alice Braga.

133. The Box. From the 1970 story Button, Button, this was directed by Richard Kelly and released in November 2009, starring Cameron Diaz, James Marsden and Frank Langella.

134. The Splendid Source. This was used as Episode 19, Season 8 of Family Guy. Directed by Brian Iles, it aired on May 16th, 2010 and featured Seth MacFarlane, Alex Borstein and Seth Green.

135. Charles Beaumont: The Short Life of Twilight Zone's Magic Man. A documentary scheduled to be released in 2010. Directed by Jason Brock, this features Richard Matheson, along with: Roger Corman; Harlan Ellison; George Clayton Johnson; William F. Nolan; Frank M. Robinson; William Shatner; and many others.

136. Real Steel. Set for release in November 2011, this was based on a story by Matheson and directed by Shawn Levy, starring Evangeline Lilly, Hugh Jackman, and Kevin Durand.

137. King of the B's: The Independent Life of Roger Corman. Scheduled for release sometime in the near future, this documentary was directed by Alex Stapleton and features Richard Matheson along with: Roger Corman, of course; Robert De Niro; Jack

Richard Matheson

Nicholson; Martin Scorsese; William Shatner; Ron Howard; David Carradine; Peter Fonda; Bruce Dern; and many others.

***

NOVELS AND COLLECTIONS

1. Someone Is Bleeding. Published by Lion Books, New York City, 1953. Lion Book 137. Paperback original.

2. Fury on Sunday. Published by Lion Books, New York City, 1953. Lion Book 180. Paperback original.

3. Born of Man and Woman. Published by The Chamberlain Press, Philadelphia, Pennsylvania, 1954. Hardcover. Herein: Introduction by Robert Bloch; Disappearing Act, 1953; Born of Man and Woman, 1950; Third from the Sun, 1950; SRL Ad, 1952; Shipshape Home, 1952; Dear Diary, 1954; Dress of White Silk, 1951; F--- - also known as The Foodlegger, 1952; Full Circle, 1953; Mad House, 1953; Return, 1951; Through Channels, 1951; To Fit the Crime, 1952; The Traveller, 1954; The Wedding, 1953; Witch War, 1951; and Lover When You're Near Me, 1952.

4. I Am Legend. Published by Fawcett Gold Medal, New York City, 1954. Gold Medal Book 417. Paperback original.

5. Third from the Sun. Published by Bantam Books, New York City, 1955. Bantam Book 1294. Paperback original. This contains: Born of Man and Woman, 1950; Lover When You're Near Me, 1952; SRL Ad, 1952; Mad House, 1952; F--- - also known as The Foodlegger, 1952; Dear Diary, 1954; To Fit the Crime, 1952; Dress of White Silk, 1951; Disappearing Act, 1953; The Wedding, 1953; Shipshape Home, 1952; The Traveller, 1954; and Third From the Sun, 1950.

6. Born of Man and Woman. Published by Max Reinhardt, London, England, 1956. Hardcover. This is significantly different from the U.S. edition in that it drops four of the stories, and the introduction by Robert Bloch. The stories are: Full Circle, 1953; Disappearing Act, 1953; The Wedding, 1953; and The Traveller, 1954.

7. The Shrinking Man. Published by Fawcett Gold Medal, New York City, 1956. Gold Medal Giant S577. Paperback original.

8. The Shores of Space. Published by Bantam Books, New York City, 1957. Bantam Book A1571. Paperback original. Herein: Being, 1954; Pattern for Survival, 1955; Steel, 1956; The Test, 1954; Clothes Make the Man, 1951; Blood Son – also known as Drink My Red Blood, 1951; Trespass, 1953; When Day Is Dun, 1954; The Curious Child, 1954; The Funeral, 1955; The Last Day, 1953; Little Girl Lost, 1953; and The Doll that Does Everything, 1954.

9. A Stir of Echoes. Published by J. B. Lippincott, Philadelphia and New York City, 1958. Hardcover.

10. Ride the Nightmare. Published by Ballantine Books, New York City, 1959. Ballantine Book 301K. Paperback original.

11. The Beardless Warriors. Published by Little Brown, Boston, Massachusetts, 1960. Hardcover.

12. Shock! Published by Dell Books, New York City, 1961. Dell Book B195. Paperback original. Herein: The Children of Noah, 1957; Lemmings, 1958; The Splendid Source, 1956; Long Distance Call – also known as Sorry, Right Number, 1953; Mantage, 1959; One for the Books, 1955; The Holiday Man, 1957; Dance of the Dead, 1955; Legion of Plotters, 1953; The Edge, 1958; The Creeping Terror – also known as A Touch of Grapefruit, 1959; Death Ship, 1953; and The Distributor, 1958.

13. Shock II. Published by Dell Books, New York City, 1964. Dell Book 7829. Paperback original. This contains: A Flourish of Strumpets, 1956; Brother to the Machine, 1952; No Such Thing As a Vampire, 1959; Descent, 1954; Deadline, 1959; The Man Who Made the World, 1954; Graveyard Shift, 1960; The Likeness of Julie – originally by Logan Swanson, 1962; Lazarus II, 1953; Big Surprise, 1959; Crickets, 1960; Mute, 1962; and From Shadowed Places, 1960.

14. Shock III. Published by Dell Books, New York City, 1966. Dell Book 7830. Paperback original. This contains: Girl of My Dreams, 1963; Tis the Season to be Jelly, 1963; Return, 1951; The Jazz Machine – a poem, 1962; The Disinheritors, 1953; Slaughter House, 1953; Shock Wave – also known as Crescendo, 1963; When the Waker Sleeps – also known as The Waker Dreams, 1950; Witch War, 1951; First Anniversary, 1960; Miss Stardust, 1955; Full Circle, 1953; and Nightmare at 20,000 Feet, 1962.

15. Shock Waves. Published by Dell Books, New York City, 1970. Dell Book 7831. Paperback original. Herein: A Visit to Santa Claus, 1970 – originally titled I'll Make It Look Good as by Logan Swanson, 1957; Finger Prints, 1962; Deus Ex Machina, 1963; The Thing, 1951; The Conqueror, 1954; Dying Room Only, 1953; A Drink of Water, 1967; Advance Notice – also known as Richard Matheson's Letter to the Editor, 1952; Wet Straw, 1953; Therese, 1969; Day of Reckoning, 1960; Prey, 1969; Come Fygures, Come Shadowes, 1970; and The Finishing Touches, 1970.

16. I Am Legend. Published by Walker and Company, New York City, 1970. First hardcover edition.

17. Hell House. Published by The Viking Press, New York City, 1971. Hardcover.

18. The Shrinking Man. Published by David Bruce and Watson, London, England, 1973. First hardcover edition.

19. Bid Time Return. Published by The Viking Press, New York City, 1975. Hardcover.

20. What Dreams May Come. Published by G. P. Putnam's Sons, New York City, 1978. Hardcover.

21. Earthbound. Writing as Logan Swanson. Published by Playboy Paperbacks, New York City, 1982. Paperback original.

22. Somewhere in Time. Published by Ballantine Books, New York City, 1985. Softcover. Simply a re-titled edition of Bid Time Return, 1975.

23. Earthbound. Published by Robinson Publishing, London, England, 1989. First hardcover edition. Issued as by Matheson rather than by Logan Swanson.

24. Through Channels. Published by Footsteps Press, Round Top, New York, 1989. Chapbook. Includes an appreciation by Vincent Price and an afterword by Roger Corman.

25. Richard Matheson: Collected Stories. Published by Dream Press, Los Angeles, California, 1989. Limited edition hardcover. This collection contains: Introduction by the author; From **Ray Bradbury** – an essay; From Robert Bloch – an essay; From William F. Nolan – an essay; From Jack Finney – an essay; From George Clayton Johnson – an essay; From Harlan Ellison – an essay; From Stephen King – an essay; From Dennis Etchison – an essay; From Richard Christian Matheson – an essay; Born of Man and Woman, 1950; Third from the Sun, 1950; When the Waker Sleeps – also known as The Waker Dreams, 1950; Blood Son – originally Drink My Red Blood, 1951; Clothes Make the Man, 1951; Dress of White Silk, 1951; Return, 1951; The Thing, 1951; Through Channels, 1951; Witch War, 1951; Advance Notice – also known as Richard Matheson's Letter to the Editor, 1952; Brother to the Machine, 1952; F-- - also known as The Foodlegger, 1952; Lover When You're Near Me, 1952; Mad House, 1953; Shipshape Home, 1952; SRL Ad, 1952; To Fit the Crime, 1952; Death Ship, 1953; Disappearing Act, 1953; The Disinheritors, 1953; Dying Room Only, 1953; Full Circle, 1953; The Last Day, 1953; Lazarus II, 1953; Legion of Plotters, 1953; Little Girl Lost, 1953; Long Distance Call – also known as Sorry, Right Number, 1953; Slaughter House, 1953; Trespass, 1957; The Wedding, 1953; Wet Straw, 1953; Being, 1954; The Conqueror, 1954; The Curious Child, 1954; Dear Diary, 1954; Descent, 1954; The Doll that Does Everything, 1954; The Man Who Made the World, 1954; The Test, 1954; The Traveller, 1954; When Day is Dun, 1954; Dance of the Dead, 1955; The Funeral, 1955; Miss Stardust, 1955; One for the Books, 1955; Pattern for Survival, 1955; A Flourish of Strumpets, 1956; The Splendid Source, 1956; Steel, 1956; A Visit to Santa Claus, 1970 – originally titled I'll Make It Look Good as by Logan Swanson, 1957; The Children of Noah, 1957; The Holiday Man, 1957; Lemmings, 1958; Old Haunts, 1957; The Distributor, 1958; The Edge, 1958; Big Surprise, 1959; The Creeping Terror – also known as A Touch of Grapefruit, 1959; Deadline, 1959; Mantage, 1959; No Such Thing as a Vampire, 1959; Crickets, 1960; Day of Reckoning, 1960; First Anniversary, 1960; From Shadowed Places, 1960; Nightmare at 20,000 Feet, 1962; Finger Prints, 1962; The Likeness of Julie, 1962; Mute, 1962; Deus Ex Machina, 1963; Girl of My Dreams, 1963; The Jazz Machine – a poem, 1962; Shock Wave – also known as Crescendo, 1963; 'Tis the Season to be Jelly, 1963; Interest, 1965; A Drink of Water, 1967; Therese, 1969; Prey, 1969; Button, Button, 1970; By Appointment Only. 1970; Finishing Touches, 1989; 'Til Death Do Us Part, 1989; The Near Departed, 1987; Buried Talents, 1987; and Duel, 1971.

26. Journal of the Gun Years. Published by M. Evans and Company, New York City, 1991. Hardcover.

27. Somewhere in Time – with – What Dreams May Come. Published by Dream Press, Los Angeles, California, 1992. Hardcover. Omnibus edition containing Somewhere in Time – also known as Bid Time Return, 1975; and What Dreams May Come, 1978.

28. Seven Steps to Midnight. Published by Forge Books – Tom Doherty Associates, New York City, 1993. Hardcover.

29. The Gunfight. Published by M. Evans and Company, New York City, 1993. Hardcover.

30. Shadow on the Sun. Published by M. Evans and Company, New York City, 1994. Hardcover.

31. By the Gun. Published by Berkley Books, New York City, 1994. Paperback original.

32. Now You See It... Published by Tor Books – Tom Doherty Associates, New York City, 1995. Hardcover.

33. I Am Legend. Published by Tor Books – Tom Doherty Associates, New York City, 1995. Softcover. This collection contains: I Am Legend, 1954; Buried Talents, 1987; The Near Departed, 1987; Prey, 1969; Witch War, 1951; Dance of the Dead, 1955; Dress of White Silk, 1951; Mad House, 1953; The Funeral, 1955; From Shadowed Places, 1960; and Person to Person, 1989.

34. The Incredible Shrinking Man. Published by Tor Books – Tom Doherty Associates, New York City, 1995. Softcover. Herein: The Incredible Shrinking Man – also known as The Shrinking Man, 1956; Nightmare at 20,000 Feet, 1962; The Test, 1954; The Holiday Man, 1957; Mantage, 1959; The Distributor, 1958; By Appointment Only, 1970; Button, Button, 1970; Duel, 1971; and Shoo Fly, 1988.

35. I Am Legend. Gauntlet Press, Colorado Springs, Colorado, 1995. Hardcover limited edition. A re-issue but with an introduction by Dan Simmons and George Clayton Johnson and an Afterword by Dennis Etchison.

36. Hell House. Gauntlet Press, Colorado Springs, Colorado, 1996. Hardcover limited edition. A re-issue but with an introduction by Dean Koontz and an Afterword by Richard Christian Matheson.

37. The Memoirs of Wild Bill Hickok. Published

by Jove Books, New York City, 1996. Paperback original.

38. What Dreams May Come. Gauntlet Press, Colorado Springs, Colorado, 1998. Hardcover limited edition. A re-issue but with an introduction by Richard Matheson and an afterword by Douglas E. Winter and the director of the film, Stephen Simon.

39. The Path: A New Look At Reality. Published by Tor Books – Tom Doherty Associates, New York City, 1999. Hardcover.

40. Somewhere in Time. Gauntlet Press, Colorado Springs, Colorado, 1999. Hardcover limited edition. A re-issue but with an introduction by Richard Matheson and a group of photos taking during the movie shoot.

41. Hunger and Thirst. Published by Gauntlet Press, Colorado Springs, Colorado, 2000. Hardcover. Matheson's actual first novel, unpublished until this edition.

42. The Shrinking Man. Gauntlet Press, Colorado Springs, Colorado, 2000. Hardcover limited edition. A re-issue but with an introduction by Richard Matheson and an Afterword by David Morrell.

43. Camp Pleasant. Published by Cemetery Dance Publications, Baltimore, Maryland, 2001. Hardcover.

44. And in Sorrow. Published by Gauntlet Press, Colorado Springs, Colorado, 2001. Chapbook.

45. Purge Among Peanuts. Published by Gauntlet Press, Colorado Springs, Colorado, 2001. Chapbook.

46. Richard Matheson's The Twilight Zone Scripts – Volume 1. Edited by Stanley Wiater. Published by Edge Books - Gauntlet Press, Colorado Springs, Colorado, 2001. Softcover. Herein: Submitted for Your Approval; Letter from **Rod Serling**; Prologue by Stanley Wiater; The Last Flight; A World of Difference; A World of His Own; Nick of Time; The Invaders; Once Upon a Time; Little Girl Lost; and Young Man's Fancy.

47. Richard Matheson's The Twilight Zone Scripts – Volume 2. Edited by Stanley Wiater. Published by Edge Books - Gauntlet Press, Colorado Springs, Colorado, 2002. Softcover. This contains: Prologue by Stanley Wiater; Mute; Death Ship; Steel; Nightmare at 20,000 Feet; Night Call; and Spur of the Moment.

48. A Stir of Echoes. Gauntlet Press, Colorado Springs, Colorado, 2002. Hardcover limited edition. A re-issue but with the screenplay from the film and including an afterword by David Koepp, the director of the film.

49. He Wanted to Live. Published by Gauntlet Press, Colorado Springs, Colorado, 2002. A chapbook.

50. Nightmare at 20,000 Feet: Horror Stories. Published by Tor Books – Tom Doherty Associates, New York City, 2002. Softcover. Herein: Introduction by Stephen King; Nightmare at 20,000 Feet, 1962; Dress of White Silk, 1951; Blood Son – also known as Drink My Red Blood, 1951; Through Channels, 1951; Witch War, 1951; Mad House, 1953; Disappearing Act, 1953; Legion of Plotters, 1953; Long Distance Call – also known as Sorry, Right Number, 1953; Slaughter House, 1953; Wet Straw, 1953; Dance of the Dead, 1955; The Children of Noah, 1957; The Holiday Man, 1957; Old Haunts, 1957; The Distributor, 1958; Crickets, 1960; First Anniversary, 1960; The Likeness of Julie, writing as Logan Swanson, 1962; and Prey, 1969.

51. Off Beat. Published by Subterranean Press, Burton, Michigan, 2002. Hardcover limited edition. Herein: Introduction by William F. Nolan; Relics, 2002; Two O'clock Session, 1991; Always Before Your Voice, 1999; The Prisoner, 2002; And in Sorrow, 2002; Blunder Buss, 1984; And Now I'm Waiting, 1983; Mirror, Mirror, 2002; Phone Call from Across the Street, 2002; Maybe You Remember Him, 2002; All and Only Silence, 2002; and Afterword – Story Notes.

52. Abu and the Seven Marvels. Published by Edge Books – Gauntlet Press, Colorado Springs, Colorado, 2002. Hardcover.

53. Hunted Past Reason. Published by Tor Books – Tom Doherty Associates, New York City, 2002. Hardcover.

54. Come Figures, Come Shadows. Published by Gauntlet Press, Colorado Springs, Colorado, 2003. Hardcover.

55. Pride. Written with Richard Christian Matheson. Published by Gauntlet Press, Colorado Springs, Colorado, 2003. Hardcover.

56. Duel: Terror Stories. Published by Tor Books – Tom Doherty Associates, New York City, 2003. Softcover. Herein: An Appreciation by Ray Bradbury; Third from the Sun, 1950; When the Waker Sleeps – also known as The Waker Dreams, 1950; Born of Man and Woman, 1950; Return, 1951; Brother to the Machine, 1952; F--- - also known as The Foodlegger, 1952; Lover When You're Near Me, 1952; Shipshape Home, 1952; SRL Ad, 1952; Death Ship, 1953; The Last Day, 1953; Little Girl Lost, 1953; Trespass, 1957; Being, 1954; The Test, 1954; One for the Books, 1955; and Steel, 1956.

57. Richard Matheson: Collected Stories – Volume One. Edited by Stanley Wiater. Published by Edge Books – Gauntlet Press, Colorado Springs, Colorado, 2003. Trade paperback. This contains: Editor's Preface; Dream Press Introduction, 1989; Edge Books – Gauntlet Press Introduction, 2003; Born of Man and Woman, 1950; Third from the Sun, 1950; When the Waker Sleeps – also known as The Waker Dreams, 1950; Blood Son – also known as Drink My Red Blood, 1951; Clothes Make the Man, 1951; Dress of White Silk, 1951; Return, 1951; The Thing, 1951; Through Channels, 1951; Witch War, 1951; Advance Notice – also known as Richard Matheson's Letter to the Editor, 1952;

Brother to the Machine, 1952; F-- - also known as The Foodlegger, 1952; Lover When You're Near Me, 1952; Mad House, 1953; Shipshape Home, 1952; SRL Ad, 1952; To Fit the Crime, 1952; Death Ship, 1953; Disappearing Act, 1953; The Disinheritors, 1953; Dying Room Only, 1953; Full Circle, 1953; The Last Day, 1953; Lazarus II, 1953; Legion of Plotters, 1953; Little Girl Lost, 1953; and Long Distance Call, also known as Sorry, Right Number, 1953; along with short essays by **Ray Bradbury**; William F. Nolan; and Robert Bloch.

58. Richard Matheson's Kolchak Scripts. Published by Gauntlet Press, Colorado Springs, Colorado, 2004. Hardcover. Herein: Introduction to The Night Stalker by Mark Dawidziak; The Night Stalker, 1971; Introduction to The Night Strangler by Mark Dawidziak; The Night Stranger, 1972; Introduction to The Night Killers by Mark Dawidziak; The Night Killers by Richard Matheson and William F. Nolan, 2003; The Rest of the Kolchak Story by Mark Dawidziak; Richard Matheson and the TV Movie – an interview with Richard Matheson by Mark Dawidziak; and Richard Matheson and the Vampire Story – an interview with Richard Matheson by Mark Dawidziak.

59. Darker Places. Published by Gauntlet Press, Colorado Springs, Colorado, 2004. Hardcover. All material from 2004, this contains: Introduction by Richard Matheson; Revolution; The Puppy; Little Girl Knocking at My Door; Cassidy's Shoes; The Hill; Intergalactic Report; Introduction to Creature; and Creature: A Screenplay.

60. Unrealized Dreams: Three Scripts by Richard Matheson. Published by Gauntlet Press, Colorado Springs, Colorado, 2004. Hardcover.

61. Duel and the Distributor: Stories and Screenplays. Published by Gauntlet Press, Colorado Springs, Colorado, 2004. Hardcover.

62. Richard Matheson: Collected Stories – Volume Two. Published by Edge Books – Gauntlet Press, Colorado Springs, Colorado, 2005. Trade paperback. Edited by Stanley Wiater. Herein: Editor's Preface; Dream Press Introduction by Richard Matheson, 1989; Gauntlet Press Introduction by Richard Matheson, 2003; Slaughter House, 1953; Trespass, 1957; The Wedding, 1953; Wet Straw, 1953; Being, 1954; The Conqueror, 1954; The Curious Child, 1954; Dear Diary, 1954; Descent, 1954; The Doll That Does Everything, 1954; The Man Who Made the World, 1954; The Test, 1954; The Traveler, 1954; When Day Is Dun, 1954; Dance of the Dead, 1955; The Funeral, 1955; Miss Stardust, 1955; One for the Books, 1955; Pattern for Survival, 1955; A Flourish of Strumpets, 1956; The Splendid Source, 1956; Steel, 1956; A Visit to Santa Claus, 1970 – originally titled I'll Make It Look Good as by Logan Swanson, 1957; The Children of Noah, 1957; The Holiday Man, 1957; Lemmings, 1958; Old Haunts, 1957; The Distributor, 1958; and The Edge, 1958; as well as essays by Jack Finney and George Clayton Johnson.

63. Richard Matheson: Collected Stories – Volume Three. Published by Edge Books – Gauntlet Press, Colorado Springs, Colorado, 2005. Trade paperback. Edited by Stanley Wiater. This contains: Editor's Preface; Dream Press Introduction by Richard Matheson, 1989; Gauntlet Press Introduction by Richard Matheson, 2003; Big Surprise, 1959; The Creeping Terror – also known as A Touch of Grapefruit, 1959; Deadline, 1959; Mantage, 1959; No Such Thing as a Vampire, 1959; Crickets, 1960; Day of Reckoning, 1960; First Anniversary, 1960; From Shadowed Places, 1960; Nightmare at 20,000 Feet, 1962; Finger Prints, 1962; The Likeness of Julie, 1962; Mute, 1962; Deus Ex Machina, 1963; Girl of My Dreams, 1963; The Jazz Machine – a poem, 1962; Shock Wave– also known as Crescendo, 1963; 'Tis the Season to be Jelly, 1963; Interest, 1965; A Drink of Water, 1967; Therese, 1969; Prey, 1969; Button, Button, 1970; By Appointment Only, 1970; Finishing Touches, 1989; 'Til Death Do Us Part, 1989; The Near Departed, 1987; Buried Talents, 1987; and Duel, 1971; as well as essays by Harlan Ellison, Stephen King, Dennis Etchison and Richard Christian Matheson.

64. Woman. Published by Gauntlet Press, Colorado Springs, Colorado, 2005. Hardcover limited edition issued in a wooden slipcase.

65. Noir. Published by Forge Books – Tom Doherty Associates, New York City, 2005. Hardcover. An omnibus edition, this contains: Someone Is Bleeding, 1953; Fury on Sunday, 1953; and Ride the Nightmare, 1959.

66. The Link. Published by Gauntlet Press, Colorado Springs, Colorado, 2006. Hardcover.

67. Bloodlines: Richard Matheson's Dracula, I Am Legend and Other Vampire Stories. Edited by Mark Dawidziak. Published by Gauntlet Press, Colorado Springs, Colorado, 2006. Hardcover. Herein: Preface: Tracing the Bloodlines by Mark Dawidziak; Introduction 1: Richard the Writer, Vlad the Impaler and Dracula the Script by Mark Dawidziak; Dracula – Richard Matheson's complete script for the TV movie; The Dracula Treatment – Richard Matheson's treatment for the script; Gallery A: Pictures from Dracula; Introduction 2: The Unfilmed Legend by Mark Dawidziak; Richard Matheson's I Am Legend script; I Am Legend, the novel, 1954; Gallery B: Pictures from versions of I Am Legend; Introduction 3: The Short Stories by Mark Dawidziak; Blood Son, 1951; The Funeral, 1955; No Such Thing as a Vampire, 1959; and Gallery C: Pictures from The Funeral and No Such Thing as a Vampire.

68. I Am Legend – with – Hell House. Published by the Quality Paperback Book Club, New York City, 2006. Softcover. An omnibus edition containing I Am Legend, 1954; and Hell House, 1971.

69. The Richard Matheson Companion. Edited by Stanley Wiater, Matthew R. Bradley, and Paul Stuve. Published by Gauntlet Press, Colorado Springs, Colorado, 2007. Hardcover.

70. Visions of Death: Richard Matheson's Edgar Allan Poe Scripts. Gauntlet Press, Colorado

Richard Matheson

Springs, Colorado, 2007. Hardcover. Herein: Part One: The Fall of the House of Usher: Introduction by Roger Corman; Preface by Lawrence French; The House Is the Monster – The Making of House of Usher by Lawrence French; House of Usher – The shooting script by Richard Matheson; House of Usher – Complete cast and credits. Part Two: The Pit and the Pendulum: The House of the Dead – The making of The Pit and the Pendulum by Lawrence French; The Pit and the Pendulum – The shooting script by Richard Matheson; The Pit and the Pendulum: Complete cast and credits. Part Three: Richard Matheson interview by Lawrence French; Afterword by Joe Dante.

71. Button, Button: Uncanny Stories. Published by Tor Books – Tom Doherty Associates, New York City, 2008. Softcover. Herein: Introduction by Richard Matheson; Button, Button, 1970; Girl of My Dreams, 1963; Dying Room Only, 1953; A Flourish of Strumpets, 1956; No Such Thing as a Vampire, 1959; Pattern for Survival, 1955; Mute, 1962; The Creeping Terror – also known as A Touch of Grapefruit, 1959; Shock Wave – also known as Crescendo, 1963; Clothes Make the Man, 1951; The Jazz Machine – a poem, 1962; and 'Tis the Season to Be Jelly, 1963.

72. Matheson: Uncollected – Volume One. Gauntlet Press, Colorado Springs, Colorado, 2008. Hardcover. Herein: Introduction to The Enemy Within by George Clayton Johnson; The Enemy Within, a Star Trek script; Colony Seven, an unfinished novel with an outline for the final work; He Wanted to Live; Life Size; Man with a Club; Professor Fritz and the Runaway Train; Purge Among Peanuts; The Prisoner; The Last Blah in the Etc.; Counterfeit Bills; 1984 ½; Pride; and the screenplay for No Such Thing as a Vampire (in the lettered edition only).

73. Visions Deferred: Richard Matheson's Censored I Am Legend Script. Published by Edge Books - Gauntlet Press, Colorado Springs, Colorado, 2009.

74. Legends of the Gun Years. Published by Forge Books – Tom Doherty Associates, New York City, 2010. Softcover. An omnibus edition, this contains Journal of the Gun Years, 1991; and The Memoirs of Wild Bill Hickok, 1996.

75. Richard Matheson's Nightmare at 20,000 Feet. Edited by Tony Albarella. Gauntlet Press, Colorado Springs, Colorado, 2010. Hardcover limited edition.

76. Matheson: Uncollected – Volume Two. Gauntlet Press, Colorado Springs, Colorado, 2010. Hardcover. Scheduled for release in the summer of 2010. Gauntlet Press mentions that this will contain two partially written horror novels, House of the Dead and Red Is the Color of Desire, along with the screenplay from What Dreams May Come and ten short stories.

***

ANTHOLOGIES

1. Twilight Zone: The Original Stories. Edited with Martin H. Greenberg and Charles G. Waugh. Published by Avon Books, New York City, 1985. Softcover. Herein: Preface by Carol Serling; Introduction by **Richard Matheson**; One for the Angels – story by **Rod Serling** with an essay by Anne Serling-Sutton; Perchance to Dream by Charles Beaumont, 1958; Disappearing Act by **Richard Matheson**, 1953; Time Enough at Last by Lyn Venable, 1953; What You Need by Henry Kuttner and **C. L. Moore** writing as Lewis Padgett, 1945; Third from the Sun by **Richard Matheson**, 1950; Elegy by Charles Beaumont, 1953; Brothers Beyond the Void by Paul W. Fairman, 1952; The Howling Man by Charles Beaumont writing as C. B. Lovehill, 1959; It's a Good Life by Jerome Bixby, 1953; The Valley Was Still by Manly Wade Wellman, 1939; The Jungle by Charles Beaumont, 1954; To Serve Man by Damon Knight, 1950; Little Girl Lost by **Richard Matheson**, 1953; Four O'clock by Price Day, 1958; I Sing the Body Electric by **Ray Bradbury**, 1969; The Changing of the Guard – story by **Rod Serling** with an essay by Anne Serling-Sutton; In His Image – also known as The Man Who Made Himself by Charles Beaumont, 1957; Mute by **Richard Matheson**, 1962; Death Ship by **Richard Matheson**, 1953; The Devil You Say? by Charles Beaumont, 1951; Blind Alley by Malcolm Jameson, 1943; Song for a Lady by Charles Beaumont, 1960; Steel by **Richard Matheson**, 1956; Nightmare at 20,000 Feet by **Richard Matheson**, 1962; The Old Man by Henry Slesar, 1962; The Self-Improvement of Salvadore Ross by Henry Slesar, 1961; The Beautiful People by Charles Beaumont, 1952; Long Distance Call – also known as Sorry, Right Number by **Richard Matheson**, 1953; and An Occurrence at Owl Street Bridge by Ambrose Bierce, 1890.

***

NON-FICTION

1. Robert Bloch: Appreciations of the Master. Written with Ricia Mainhardt. Tor Books – Tom Doherty Associates, New York City, 1995. Hardcover.

2. A Primer of Reality. Published by Gauntlet Press, Colorado Springs, Colorado, 2002. Hardcover.

***

RELATED

1. The Beat Generation. By Albert Zugsmith. Published by Bantam Books, New York City, 1959. Bantam Book 1965. Paperback original. Based on the screenplay by Richard Matheson.

2. The Pit and the Pendulum. By Lee Sheridan. Lancer Books, New York City, 1961. Lancer Book 71-303. Based on the screenplay by Richard Matheson.

3. The Raven. By Eunice Sudak. Lancer Books,

New York City, 1963. Lancer Book 70-034. Paperback original. Based on the screenplay by Richard Matheson.

4. The Night Stalker. By Jeff Rice. Published by Pocket Books, New York City, 1973. Pocket Book 78352. Paperback original. Screenplay by Richard Matheson.

5. The Night Strangler. By Jeff Rice and based on the original screenplay by Richard Matheson. Published by Pocket Books, New York City, 1973. Pocket Book 78352. Paperback original.

6. Richard Matheson: He Is Legend – an Illustrated Bio-Bibliography. By Mark Rathbun and Graeme Flanagan. Private Printing, Manuka, Australia, 1984. Softcover.

7. He Is Legend: An Anthology Celebrating Richard Matheson. Edited by Christopher Conlon. Published by Gauntlet Press, Colorado Springs, Colorado, 2009. Hardcover. Herein: Introduction: Matheson the Master by Ramsey Campbell; Throttle by Joe Hill and Stephen King; Recalled by F. Paul Wilson; I Am Legend, Too by Mick Garris; Two Shots from Fly's Photo Gallery by John Shirley; The Diary of Louise Carey by Thomas F. Monteleone; She Screech Like Me by Michael A. Arnzen; Everything of Beauty Taken from You in This Life Remains Forever by Gary A. Braunbeck; The Case of Peggy Ann Lister by John Maclay; Zachry Revisited by William F. Nolan; Comeback by Ed Gorman; An Island Unto Himself by Barry Hoffman; Venturi by Richard Christian Matheson; Quarry by Joe R. Lansdale; Return to Hell House by Nancy A. Collins; Cloud Rider by Whitley Strieber; and an Original Screenplay: Conjure Wife by Richard Matheson and Charles Beaumont.

8. The Twilight and Other Zones: The Dark Worlds of Richard Matheson. Edited by Stanley Wiater, Matthew Bradley and Paul Stuve. Published by Citadel Press, New York City, 2009. Softcover.

Douglas Trumbull.

Douglas Trumbull was born April 8th, 1942 in Los Angeles, California. Some of his earliest work in special effects was done at Graphic Films, where he worked on animated simulations for NASA and the Air Force. He had wanted to go into architecture but, as he said in an interview, "My personal interest at that time was, and had been for many years, science fiction. I'd been reading Arthur C. Clarke and Heinlein and many other science fiction writers, so when I would do illustrations in my own time of subjects that interested me, it would be alien planets and spacecraft and strange worlds in the future... kind of like science fiction book-cover art."

At Graphic Films, he came to the attention of Stanley Kubrick. And when Kubrick was ready to do 2001, he engaged Trumbull. During the making of the film, Trumbull created the Slit Scan machine to create certain light effects.... He explained to Kubrick that, in order to get the required effects, he needed "to build this really weird, never-before-built device that's a camera that's kind of inside-out, where a focal plane shutter is outside the camera rather than inside, and the shutter has to stay open for a minute at a time, and it has to be controlled by a bunch of motors and relays and timers."

And he built it. But working on 2001 spoiled him. He knew how good movies could be. "I became tremendously disillusioned in those years after 2001 (the film)," he said.

Still, he managed to work with **Steven Spielberg**, **Ridley Scott**, and many others.

As with most of the movie makers in this book, we aren't concerned with Trumbull's personal appearances, only with his work.

***

FILMS AND TELEVISION

1. 2001: A Space Odyssey. 1968. Directed by Stanley Kubrick and written by **Arthur C. Clarke**, starring: Keir Dullea; Gary Lockwood; William Sylvester; Daniel Richter; and many others, including Douglas Rain as the voice of HAL 9000. Trumbull was the Special Photographic Effects Supervisor.

2. Candy. 1968. Directed by Christian Marquand, based on the novel by Terry Southern, starring: Marlon Brando; Richard Burton; James Coburn; John Huston; Walter Matthau; Ringo Starr; John Astin; and many others, including Ewa Aulin as Candy. Trumbull provided the visual effects for the opening and closing sequences.

3. The Andromeda Strain. 1971. Directed by Robert Wise and based on the novel by Michael Crichton, starring: Arthur Hill; David Wayne; Kate Reid; Paula Kelly; and many others. Trumbull provided special photographic effects.

4. Silent Running. 1972. Written by Deric Washburn, Michael Cimino and Steven Bochco and starring: Bruce Dern; Cliff Potts; Ron Rifkin; Jesse Vint; and others. Trumbull was the director, the producer, and he provided special photographic effects.

5. The Starlost. 1973 and 1974. Created by Harlan Ellison, who petitioned to have his name removed from the project. Trumbull was the producer and executive producer of all sixteen episodes and he provided visual effects for one episode.

6. Close Encounters of the Third Kind. 1977. Written and directed by Steven Spielberg, starring: Richard Dreyfuss; Teri Garr; Melinda Dillon; and others. Trumbull provided special photographic effects and served as the special photographic effects supervisor.

7. Night of Dreams. 1978. Short film directed by Trumbull.

8. Star Trek: The Motion Picture. 1979. Directed by Robert Wise and written by Alan Dean Foster and Harold Livingston, based on the series created by **Gene Roddenberry** and starring all the Star Trek series regulars. Trumbull was the uncredited Assistant Director, and the Special Photographic Effects Director.

9. Blade Runner. 1982. Based on the novel by **Philip K. Dick** and directed by **Ridley Scott**, starring: Harrison Ford; Rutger Hauer; Sean Young; Edward James Olmos; Daryl Hannah; Joanna Cassidy; and many others. Special photographic effects supervisor.

10. The New Magic. 1983. Written by Stanley Hirson and Tom Sherohman and starring Christopher Lee. Trumbull was the director of this short film.

11. Big Ball. 1983. Written by Stanley Hirson and starring Michael Champion; Marilyn Dodds Frank; Wendy Girard; Darrell Larson; and others. Short film directed by Trumbull.

12. Brainstorm. 1983. Written by Bruce Joel Rubin, Robert Stitzel and Philip Frank Messina. Produced and directed by Trumbull and starring: Christopher Walken; Natalie Wood; Louise Fletcher; Cliff Robertson; Darrell Larson; and many others.

13. The Starlost: Deception. 1984. Directed by Joseph L. Scanlan and Ed Richardson and starring: Keir Dullea; William Osler; Gay Rowan; Robin Ward; and other. Trumbull was the Executive Producer.

14. Tour of the Universe. 1985. Trumbull, with Don Baker, directed this.

15. Let's Go. 1985. Another short film directed by Trumbull.

16. Leonardo's Dream. 1989. Short film written by John Groves, starring Jo Champa and Philippe Leroy and directed by Trumbull.

17. To Dream of Roses. 1990. Short film directed by Keith Melton. Trumbull was the producer.

18. Back to the Future... The Ride. 1991. Uncredited director of this short.

19. In Search of the Obelisk. 1993. Co-directed, and produced, this short with Arish Fyzee, which starred: Michael Corbett; S. A. Griffin; and Marjorie Harris.

20. Theater of Time. 1996. Director of this short film, which starred: Michael Corbett; S. A. Griffin; and Marjorie Harris.

21. Luxor Live. 1996. Director of this short film, which starred: Michael Corbett; S. A. Griffin; and Marjorie Harris.

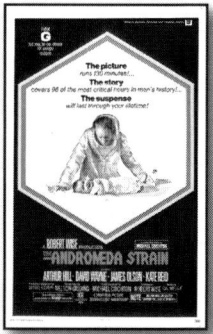

Roger Zelazny.

Roger Joseph Zelazny was born on May 13th, 1937 in Euclid, Ohio and died from kidney failure brought on by colorectal cancer, on June 14th, 1995 in Santa Fe, New Mexico.

After graduating university with Masters Degree in drama in 1962, he worked for the government, first in Cleveland, then in Baltimore, writing in the evening.

During the 1950s a number of his stories were published in fanzines. And he made a professional sale, Mr. Fuller's Revolt, to Literary Cavalcade in 1954. His first published story as a professional author was in August 1962, bought by Cele Goldsmith for Amazing Stories. The story was Passion Play. Also in that issue were: Gateway to Strangeness by **Jack Vance**; **C. L. Moore**: Catherine the Great – an essay by Sam Moskowitz; Through Time and Space with Benedict Breadfruit VI by Randall Garrett writing as Grandall Barretton; Rogue Psi by James H. Schmitz; Dear Nan Glanders by Beta McGavin; and A Trace of Memory – Part 2 by Keith Laumer. Also in August 1962, Goldsmith purchased Zelazny's Horseman for Fantastic Stories, where it was published with: Sword of Flowers by Laurence M. Janifer writing as Larry M. Harris; The Titan by P. Schuyler Miller, 1934; Behind the Door by Jack Sharkey; The Mynah Matter by Larry Eisenberg; And a Tooth by Rosel George Brown; A Devil of a Day by Arthur Porges; Continuity by Albert Teichner; and Victim of the Year by Robert F. Young.

In 1963, he sold his novelette, A Rose for Ecclesiastes, to The Magazine of Fantasy and Science Fiction. The story was so well received that it was nominated for a Hugo Award.

And his first novel, This Immortal, came out in 1966. It was serialized the previous year in Fantasy and Science Fiction under the title ...And Call Me Conrad, and it tied with Dune by **Frank Herbert** for the 1966 Hugo Award for Best Novel. The year before, in 1965, his novelette, The Doors of His Face, the Lamps of His Mouth, won a Nebula Award.

Zelazny continued to win awards throughout the 1960s. And by 1969, with Creatures of Light and Darkness and Damnation Alley, he had had enough of working for the government. Zelazny quit his job to write full time.

In an interview, he said he first wanted to write when he was "about six years old and I read stories and decided I would have done different things with the characters. One day, I realized that, hey, I could do this, so I tried and I've been doing it ever since. I didn't start selling right away.

"The first time I got money for a story, I was fifteen or sixteen years old."

He went on to explain that, as a teenager, he didn't know enough to get into any serious characterization, so he put the writing on hold until he was finished college.

After college, he started to write seriously, beginning with short stories and working his way up to the longer forms. A year after the money he was making from writing equaled what he was earning as a civil servant, he was ready to go without the safety net of a full-time job.

Nine Princes in Amber and Lord of Light tend to be his most valuable books, ranging in price between $4,000.00 and $8,000.00.

Harrison Denmark was a pen name used by Zelazny on occasion.

***

AWARDS

1965. Nebula Best Novelette Award for The Doors of His Face, the Lamps of His Mouth,
1966. Hugo Best Novel Award for ...And Call Me Conrad, The Magazine of Fantasy and Science Fiction, October and November 1965, tied with Dune by **Frank Herbert**.
1968. Hugo Best Novel Award for Lord of Light.
1972. Prix Tour-Apollo Award for Best Novel, Isle of the Dead.
1975. Nebula Best Novella Award for Home Is the Hangman, Analog, November 1975.
1976. Hugo Best Novella Award for Home Is the Hangman, Analog, November 1975.
1976. Seiun Award for Best Foreign Novel for This Immortal.
1980. Balrog Short Fiction Award for The Last Defender of Camelot, Asimov's SF Adventure Magazine, Summer 1979.
1982. Hugo Best Novelette Award for Unicorn Variation, Isaac Asimov's Science Fiction Magazine, April 13, 1981.
1984. Seiun Award for Best Foreign Short Fiction for Unicorn Variation, Isaac Asimov's Science Fiction Magazine, April 13, 1981.
1984. Balrog Best Collection Award for Unicorn Variations.
1986. Hugo Best Novella Award for Twenty-four Views of Mount Fuji by Hokusai, Isaac Asimov's Science Fiction Magazine, July 1985.
1987. Hugo Best Novelette Award for Permafrost, Omni Magazine, April 1986.
2010. Inducted into the Science Fiction Hall of Fame.

***

FILMS AND TELEVISION

1. Damnation Alley. Released in 1977, this was directed by Jack Smight and starred: Jan-Michael Vincent; George Peppard; Dominique Sanda; Paul Winfield; and others.

2. The Last Defender of Camelot. With a teleplay by George R. R. Martin and directed by Jeannot Szwarc, this was used during Season 1 for Episode 24 of The Twilight Zone. It aired on April 11th, 1985, starring Richard Kiley and Jenny Agutter.

3. Chronomaster. Written with Jane Lindskold, this was used as an animated short, directed by Brandon

Chamberlain and Anthony Mollick and starring: Ron Perlman; Brent Spiner; Lolita Davidovich; and others.

***

NOVELS AND COLLECTIONS

1. This Immortal. Published by Ace Books, New York City, 1966. Ace Book F-393. Paperback original.

2. The Dream Master. Published by Ace Books, New York City, 1966. Ace Book F-403. Paperback original.

3. This Immortal. Published by Rupert Hart-Davis, London, England, 1967. First hardcover edition.

4. Lord of Light. Published by Doubleday & Company, Garden City, New York, 1967. Hardcover.

5. Four for Tomorrow. Published by Ace Books, New York City, 1967. Ace Book M-155. Paperback original. This collection contains: Introduction by **Theodore Sturgeon**; The Furies, 1965; The Graveyard Heart, 1964; The Doors of His Face, the Lamps of His Mouth, 1965; and A Rose for Ecclesiastes, 1963.

6. The Dream Master. Published by Rupert Hart-Davis, London, England, 1968. First hardcover edition.

7. Damnation Alley. Published by G. P. Putnam's Sons, New York City, 1969. Hardcover.

8. Creatures of Light and Darkness. Published by Doubleday & Company, Garden City, New York, 1969. Hardcover.

9. A Rose for Ecclesiastes. Published by Rupert Hart-Davis, London, England, 1969. Hardcover. A re-titled re-issue of Four for Tomorrow, 1967.

10. Nine Princes in Amber. Published by Doubleday & Company, Garden City, New York, 1970. Hardcover.

11. The Doors of His Face, the Lamps of His Mouth. Published by Doubleday & Company, Garden City, New York, 1971. Hardcover. Herein: A Rose for Ecclesiastes, 1963; The Keys to December, 1966; Divine Madness, 1966; The Man Who Love the Faioli, 1967; Devil Car, 1965; This Moment of the Storm, 1966; The Doors of His Face, the Lamps of His Mouth, 1965; This Mortal Mountain, 1967; Collector's Fever, 1964; Corrida, 1968; Love is an Imaginary Number, 1966; Lucifer, 1964; The Monster and the Maiden, 1964; A Museum Piece, 1963; and The Great Slow Kings, 1963.

12. Jack of Shadows. Published by Walker and Company, New York City, 1971. Hardcover.

13. The Guns of Avalon. Published by Doubleday & Company, Garden City, New York, 1972. Hardcover.

14. To Die in Italbar. Published by Doubleday & Company, Garden City, New York, 1973. Hardcover.

15. Today We Choose Faces. Published by Signet Books – New American Library, New York City, 1973. Signet Book 451-Q5432. Paperback original.

16. Today We Choose Faces. Published by Millington, London, England, 1974. First hardcover edition.

17. Poems. Published by Discon II and distributed free to the first 1,000 members of the 32nd World Science Fiction Convention, which was held in Washington, D.C. in 1974. Chapbook. Contains 24 poems.

18. Sign of the Unicorn. Published by Doubleday & Company, Garden City, New York, 1975. Hardcover.

19. Four for Tomorrow. Published by Garland Publishing, New York and London, 1975. First hardcover edition. This collection contains: Introduction by **Theodore Sturgeon**; The Furies, 1965; The Graveyard Heart, 1964; The Doors of His Face, the Lamps of His Mouth, 1965; and A Rose for Ecclesiastes, 1963.

20. The Hand of Oberon. Published by Doubleday & Company, Garden City, New York, 1976. Hardcover.

21. Doorways in the Sand. Published by Harper and Row, New York City, 1976. Hardcover.

22. Bridge of Ashes. Published by Signet Books – New American Library, New York City, 1976. Signet Book Y7080. Paperback original.

23. Deus Irae. Written with **Philip K. Dick**. Published by Doubleday & Company, Garden City, New York, 1976. Hardcover.

24. My Name Is Legion. Published by Ballantine Books, New York City, 1976. Paperback original. Herein: The Eve of RUMOKO, 1969; Kjwalll'kje'k'koothailll'kje'k, 1973; and Home is the Hangman, 1975.

25. The Courts of Chaos. Published by Doubleday & Company, Garden City, New York, 1978. Hardcover.

26. The Illustrated Roger Zelazny. Published by Baronet Publishing, New York City, 1978. Limited edition hardcover. Herein: Shadowjack, 1978; A Rose for Ecclesiastes, 1963; The Furies, 1965; Morrow Speaks – an essay by the illustrator, Gray Morrow; Zelazny Speaks – an essay; The Doors of His Face, the Lamps of His Mouth, 1965; and Rock Collector – also known as Collector's Fever, 1964.

27. Roadmarks. Published by Del Rey – Ballantine Books, New York City, 1979. Hardcover.

28. The Bells of Shoredan. Published by Underwood Miller, Lancaster, Pennsylvania and Novato, California, 1979. Chapbook.

29. The Chronicles of Amber: Volume I. Published by Nelson Doubleday and the Science Fiction Book Club, Garden City, New York, 1979.

Hardcover. An omnibus edition, this contains: Nine Princes in Amber, 1970; and The Guns of Avalon, 1972.

30. The Chronicles of Amber: Volume II. Published by Nelson Doubleday and the Science Fiction Book Club, Garden City, New York, 1979. Hardcover. An omnibus edition, this contains: Sign of the Unicorn, 1975; The Hand of Oberon, 1976; and The Courts of Chaos, 1978.

31. Bridge of Ashes. Published by Gregg Press, Boston, Massachusetts, 1979. First hardcover edition.

32. Changeling. Published by Ace Books, New York City, 1980. Softcover.

33. Changeling. Published by the Science Fiction Book Club, Garden City, New York, 1980. First hardcover edition.

34. When Pussywillows Last in the Catyard Bloomed. Published by Norstrilia Press, Carlton, Victoria, Australia, 1980. Hardcover. A collection of poetry.

35. For a Breath I Tarry. Published by Underwood Miller, Lancaster, Pennsylvania and Novato, California, 1980. Issued simultaneously in hardcover and softcover.

36. The Last Defender of Camelot. Published by Pocket Books, New York City, 1980. Paperback original. Herein: Passion Play, 1962; Horseman, 1962; The Stainless Steel Leech – writing as Harrison Denmark, 1963; A Thing of Terrible Beauty– writing as Harrison Denmark, 1963; He Who Shapes, 1965; Comes Now the Power, 1966; Auto Da Fe, 1967; Damnation Alley, 1967; For a Breath I Tarry, 1966; The Engine at Heartspring's Center, 1974; The Game of Blood and Dust, 1975; No Award, 1977; Is There a Demon Lover in the House?, 1977; Stand Pat, Ruby Stone, 1978; Halfjack, 1979; and The Last Defender of Camelot, 1979.

37. The Last Defender of Camelot. Published by Underwood Miller, Lancaster, Pennsylvania and Novato, California, 1981. First hardcover edition, limited.

38. The Last Defender of Camelot. Published by the Science Fiction Book Club, Garden City, New York, 1981. First mass market hardcover edition.

39. To Spin is Miracle Cat. Published by Underwood Miller, Lancaster, Pennsylvania and Novato, California, 1981. Hardcover. Foreword by **Ursula K. Le Guin**. A poetry collection.

40. A Rhapsody in Amber. Published by Cheap Street Press, New Castle, Virginia, 1981. Softcover. Herein: Recital, 1981; Walpurgisnacht, 1981; and a poem, Then, Again, 1981.

41. Today We Choose Faces/Bridge of Ashes. Published by Signet Double Science Fiction, New York City, 1981. An omnibus containing both novels, from 1973 and 1976 respectively.

42. Madwand. Published by Phantasia Press, Huntington Woods, Michigan, 1981. Hardcover limited edition.

43. Madwand. Published by Ace Books, New York City, 1981. First trade edition. Softcover.

44. Madwand. Published by the Science Fiction Book Club, Garden City, New York, 1982. First mass market hardcover.

45. Eye of Cat. Published by Underwood Miller, Lancaster, Pennsylvania and Novato, California, 1982. Hardcover limited edition.

46. Eye of Cat. Published by Timescape Books, New York City, 1982. First mass market hardcover edition.

47. Dilvish, the Damned. Published by Del Rey – Ballantine Books, New York City, 1982. This collection contains: Passage to Dilfar, 1965; Thelinde's Song, 1965; The Bells of Shoredan, 1966; A Knight for Merytha, 1967; The Places of Aache, 1980; A City Divided, 1982; The White Beast, 1979; Tower of Ice, 1981; Devil and the Dancer, 1982; Garden of Blood, 1979; and Dilvish, the Damned, 1982.

48. Coils. Written with Fred Saberhagen. Published by Simon and Schuster, New York City, 1982. Softcover.

49. Coils. Written with Fred Saberhagen. Published by the Science Fiction Book Club, Garden City, New York, 1982. First hardcover edition.

50. Unicorn Variations. Published by Timescape Books, New York City, 1983. Hardcover. Herein: Introduction by the author; Unicorn Variation, 1981; Home is the Hangman, 1975; Angel, Dark Angel, 1967; And I Only Am Escaped to Tell Thee, 1981; But Not the Herald, 1965; Exeunt Omnes, 1980; Fire and/or Ice, 1980; The Force That Through the Circuit Drives the Current, 1976; The George Business, 1980; A Hand Across the Galaxy, 1967; The Horse of Lir, 1981; The Last of the Wild Ones, 1981; My Lady of the Diodes, 1970; The Naked Matador, 1981; The Night Has 999 Eyes, 1964; Recital, 1981; A Very Good Year, 1980; Walpurgisnacht, 1981; Some Science Fiction Parameters: A Biased View – an essay, 1975; and The Parts That Are Only Glimpsed: Three Reflexes – an essay, 1978.

51. Trumps of Doom. Published by Underwood-Miller, Lancaster, Pennsylvania and Novato, California, 1985. Limited edition hardcover.

52. Trumps of Doom. Published by Arbor House, New York City, 1985. First trade hardcover edition.

53. Blood of Amber. Published by Underwood-Miller, Lancaster, Pennsylvania and Novato, California, 1986. Limited edition hardcover.

54. Blood of Amber. Published by Arbor House, New York City, 1986. First trade hardcover edition.

55. Sign of Chaos. Published by Arbor House, New York City, 1987. Hardcover.

56. A Dark Traveling. Published by Walker and Company, New York City, 1987. Hardcover.

57. Roger Zelazny's Visual Guide to Castle Amber. Written with Neil Randall and Todd Cameron Hamilton. Published by Avon Books, New York City, 1988. Softcover.

58. Knight of Shadows. Published by William Morrow, New York City, 1989. Hardcover.

59. Frost and Fire. Published by William Morrow, New York City, 1989. Hardcover. Herein: An Exorcism, of Sorts – an essay, 1989; Constructing a Science Fiction Novel – an essay, 1984; Fantasy and Science Fiction: A Writer's View – an essay, 1985; Permafrost, 1986; 24 Views of Mt. Fuji by Hokusai, 1985; Night Kings, 1986; LOKI 7281, 1984; Dreadsong, 1985; Itself Surprised, 1984; Dayblood, 1985; The Bands of Titan, 1986; Mana from Heaven, 1983; and Quest's End, 1987.

60. Roger Zelazny's Visual Guide to Castle Amber. Written with Neil Randall and Todd Cameron Hamilton. Published by Avon Books and the Science Fiction Book Club, Garden City, New York, 1989. First hardcover edition.

61. He Who Shapes – with – The Infinity Box. Published by Tor Books – Tom Doherty Associates, New York City, 1989. Softcover. Tor Double 12. He Who Shapes, 1965. The Infinity Box by Kate Wilhelm, 1971.

62. The Black Throne. Written with Fred Saberhagen. Published by Baen Books, New York City, 1990. Softcover.

63. The Mask of Loki. Written with Thomas T. Thomas. Published by Baen Books, New York City, 1990. Softcover.

64. Home is the Hangman – with – We, in Some Strange Power's Employ, Move on a Rigorous Line. Published by Tor Books – Tom Doherty Associates, New York City, 1990. Softcover. Tor Double 21. Home is the Hangman, 1975. We, in Some Strange Power's Employ, Move on a Rigorous Line by **Samuel R. Delany**, 1968.

65. The Graveyard Heart – with – Elegy for Angels and Dogs. Published by Tor Books – Tom Doherty Associates, New York City, 1990. Softcover. Tor Double 24. The Graveyard Heart, 1964. Elegy for Angels and Dogs by Walter Jon Williams, 1990.

66. The Black Throne. Written with Fred Saberhagen. Published by the Science Fiction Book Club, Garden City, New York, 1991. First hardcover edition.

67. Wizard World. Published by Baen Books, New York City, 1991. Softcover. An omnibus edition, this contains: Changeling, 1980; and Madwand, 1981.

68. Prince of Chaos. Published by William Morrow, New York City, 1991. Hardcover.

69. Gone to Earth. Published by Pulphouse Publishing, Eugene, Oregon, 1991. Simultaneously released in hardcover and softcover. Herein: Introduction: Themes, Variations and Imitations by Roger Zelazny; Deadboy Donner and the Filstone Cup, 1988; Kalifriki of the Thread, 1989; Devil Car, 1965; and The Last of the Wild Ones, 1981.

70. Bring Me the Head of Prince Charming. Written with Robert Sheckley. Published by Bantam Spectra, New York City, 1991. Hardcover.

71. The Doors of His Face, the Lamps of His Mouth. Published by Pulphouse Publishing, Eugene, Oregon, 1991. Softcover.

72. Flare. Written with Thomas T. Thomas. Published by Baen Books, New York City, 1992. Softcover.

73. If at Faust You Don't Succeed. Written with Robert Sheckley. Published by Bantam Spectra, New York City, 1993. Softcover.

74. A Night in the Lonesome October. Published by Avonova – William Morrow, New York City, 1993. Hardcover.

75. Wilderness. Written with Gerald Hausman. Published by Forge Books – Tom Doherty Associates, New York City, 1994. Hardcover.

76. A Farce to Be Reckoned With. Written with Robert Sheckley. Published by Bantam Spectra, New York City, 1995. Softcover.

77. Hymn to the Sun An Imitation. DNA Publishing, United States, 1996. Softcover. Foreword by Jane M. Lindskold. A poetry collection.

78. Home is the Hangman. Published by the Science Fiction Book Club, Garden City, New York, 1996. Hardcover.

79. Donnerjack. Written with Jane Lindskold. Published by Avon Books, New York City, 1997. Hardcover.

80. Psychoshop. Written with Alfred Bester. Published by Topeka Bindery, United States, 1998. Hardcover.

81. Lord Demon. Written with Jane Lindskold. Published by Avon Eos, New York City, 1999. Hardcover.

82. The Great Book of Amber: The Complete Amber Chronicles 1 – 10. Published by Avon Eos, New York City, 1999. Softcover. An omnibus edition, this contains: Nine Princes in Amber, 1970; The Guns of Avalon, 1972; Sign of the Unicorn, 1975; The Hand of Oberon, 1976; The Courts of Chaos, 1978; Trumps of Doom, 1985; Blood of Amber, 1986; Sign of Chaos, 1987; Knight of Shadows, 1989; and Prince of Chaos, 1991.

Roger Zelazny

83. The First Chronicles of Amber. Published by the Science Fiction Book Club, Garden City, New York, 1999. Hardcover. An omnibus edition, this contains: Nine Princes in Amber, 1970; The Guns of Avalon, 1972; Sign of the Unicorn, 1975; The Hand of Oberon, 1976; and The Courts of Chaos, 1978.

84. Isle of the Dead/Eye of Cat. Published by iBooks Inc., New York City, 2001. Softcover. An omnibus edition, containing both novels, Eye of Cat, 1982; and Isle of the Dead, 1969.

85. The Second Chronicles of Amber. Published by the Science Fiction Book Club, Garden City, New York, 2005. Hardcover. An omnibus edition, this contains: Trumps of Doom, 1985; Blood of Amber, 1986; Sign of Chaos, 1987; Knight of Shadows, 1989; and Prince of Chaos, 1991.

86. To Die in Italbar/A Dark Travelling. Published by iBooks Inc., New York City, 2003. Softcover. An omnibus edition, containing both novels, from 1973 and 1987 respectively.

87. Manna from Heaven. Published by DNA Publications and Wildside Press, United States, 2003. Hardcover. Herein: Introduction by Steven Brust; Godson, 1994; Manna from Heaven, 1983; Corrida, 1968; Prince of the Powers of This World, 1993; The Furies, 1965; The Deadliest Game, 1990; Kalifriki of the Thread, 1989; Come Back to the Killing Ground, Alice, My Love, 1992; Lady of Steel, 1995; Come to Me Not in Winter's White – written with Harlan Ellison, 1969; The New Pleasure, 1964; The House of the Hanged Man, 1966; Epithalamium, 1995; The Last Inn on the Road – written with Dannie Plachta, 1967; Stowaway, 1968; Angel, Dark Angel, 1967; Prologue to the Trumps of Doom, 1985; Blue Horse, Dancing Mountains, 1994; The Salesman's Tale, 1994; Coming to a Cord, 1995; Hall of Mirrors, 1996; and The Shrouding and the Guisel, 1994.

88. The Dead Man's Brother. Published by Hard Case Crime, Dorchester Publishing, New York City, 2009. Paperback original.

89. Threshold: The Collected Stories of Roger Zelazny. Edited by David G. Grubbs, Christopher S. Kovacs and Ann Crimmins. Published by NESFA Press, Framingham, Massachusetts, 2009. Hardcover. Herein: Notes throughout by Christopher S. Kovacs; A Word from the Editors by David G. Grubbs, Christopher S. Kovacs and Ann Crimmins; Out of Nowhere – an essay by **Robert Silverberg**; Before Amber – an essay by Carl B. Yoke; A Rose for Ecclesiastes, 1963; And the Darkness Is Harsh, 1954; Mr. Fuller's Revolt, 1954; Youth Eternal, 1955; The Outward Sign, 1958; Passion Play, 1962; The Graveyard Heart, 1964; Horseman, 1962; The Teachers Rode a Wheel of Fire, 1962; Moonless in Byzantium, 1962; On the Road to Sploenoba, 1963; Final Dining, 1963; The Borgia Hand, 1963; Nine Starships Waiting, 1963; Circe Has Her Problems, 1963; The Malatesta Collection, 1963; The Stainless Steel Leech – writing as Harrison Denmark, 1963; The Doors of His Face, the Lamps of His Mouth, 1965; A Thing of Terrible Beauty – writing as Harrison Denmark, 1963; Monologue for Two – writing as Harrison Denmark, 1963; Threshold of the Prophet, 1963; A Museum Piece, 1963; Mine is the Kingdom – writing as Harrison Denmark, 1963; King Solomon's Ring, 1963; The Misfit, 1963; The Great Slow Kings, 1963; Collector's Fever, 1964; The Night Has 999 Eyes, 1964; He Who Shapes, 1965; Sundry Notes on Dybology and Suchlike – an essay, 1964; And Call Me Roger: The Literary Life of Roger Zelazny, Part 1 – an essay by Christopher S. Kovacs, 2009; Conditional Benefit, 1953; Hand of the Master, 2009; The Great Selchie of San Francisco Bay, 2009; and Studies in Saviory, 2009; along with an assortment of poetry.

90. Power & Light: The Collected Stories of Roger Zelazny. Edited by David G. Grubbs, Christopher S. Kovacs and Ann Crimmins. Published by NESFA Press, Framingham, Massachusetts, 2009. Hardcover. This contains: Notes throughout by Christopher S. Kovacs; A Word from the Editors by David G. Grubbs, Christopher S. Kovacs and Ann Crimmins; Lyricism and Warmth – an essay by Kristine Kathryn Rusch; A Singular Being – an essay by Walter Jon Williams; A Word from **Theodore Sturgeon** and **Frederik Pohl** – an essay; The Furies, 1965; Lucifer, 1964; The Salvation of Faust, 1964; The New Pleasure, 1964; The Monster and the Maiden, 1964; For a Breath I Tarry, 1966; Passage to Dilfar, 1965; Thelinde's Song, 1965; The Bells of Shoredan, 1966; A Knight for Merytha, 1967; The Injured, 1965; Devil Car, 1965; Of Time and the Yan, 1965; The Drawing, 1965; This Moment of the Storm, 1966; Comes Now the Power, 1966; Divine Madness, 1966; But Not the Herald, 1965; Late, Late Show, 1966; Love is an Imaginary Number, 1966; The Keys to December, 1966; The House of the Hanged Man, 1966; Death and the Executioner – later Lord of Light, 1967; Auto-da-Fe, 1967; The Juan's Thousandth, 2009; There Shall Be No Moon, 2009; Through a Glass, Greenly, 2009; Time of Night in the 7th Room, 2009; ...And Call Me Conrad – Part 1 of 2, 1965; ...And Call Me Conrad – Part 2 of 2, 1965; Guest of Honor Speech, Ozarkon 2 – an essay, 1967; On Writing and Stories – an essay, 1967; Shadows – an essay, 1967; and And Call Me Roger: The Literary Life of Roger Zelazny, Part 2 – an essay by Christopher S. Kovacs; along with an assortment of poetry.

91. This Mortal Mountain: The Collected Stories of Roger Zelazny. Edited by David G. Grubbs, Christopher S. Kovacs and Ann Crimmins. Published by NESFA Press, Framingham, Massachusetts, 2009. Hardcover. This contains: Notes throughout by Christopher S. Kovacs; A Word from the Editors by David G. Grubbs, Christopher S. Kovacs and Ann Crimmins; Of Meetings and Partings – an essay by Neil Gaiman; On Roger Zelazny – an essay by David G. Hartwell; This Mortal Mountain, 1967; The Man Who Loved the Faioli, 1967; Angel, Dark Angel, 1967; The Hounds of Sorrow, 2009; The Window Washer, 2009; Damnation Alley, 1967; The Last Inn on the Road – written with Dannie Plachta, 1967; A Hand Across the Galaxy, 1967; A Word from **Philip K. Dick** – an essay; The Insider, 2009; Heritage, 1968; He That Moves, 1968; Corrida, 1968; Dismal Light, 1968; Song of the Blue Baboon, 1968; A Word from **Frederik Pohl** – an essay; Stowaway,

1968; Here There Be Dragons, 1992; Way Up High, 1992; The Steel General – Excerpt, 1969; Come to Me Not in Winter's White – written with Harlan Ellison, 1969; A Word from Harlan Ellison – an essay; The Year of the Good Seed – written with Dannie Plachta, 1969; The Man at the Corner of Now and Forever, 1970; My Lady of the Diodes, 1970; Alas! Alas! This Woeful Fate, 1971; Sun's Trophy Stirring, 1971; Add Infinite Item, 1971; The Game of Blood and Dust, 1975; The Force That Through the Circuit Drives the Current, 1976; No Award, 1977; Is There a Demon Lover in the House?, 1977; The Engine at Heartspring's Center, 1974; Tomorrow Stuff – an essay, 2009; Short Fiction and How It Got That Way – an essay, 1971; Self-interview – an essay, 2009; The Genre: A Geological Survey – an essay, 1973; A Burnt-out Case? – an essay, 1978; Ideas, Digressions and Daydreams: The Amazing Science Fiction Magazine – an essay, 1976; Musings on Lord of Light – an essay, 1977; And Call Me Roger: The Literary Life of Roger Zelazny, Part 3 – an essay by Christopher S. Kovacs; Guns of Avalon: Deleted Sex Scene, 2009; Bridge of Ashes – outline, 2009; and Doorways in the Sand – a summary, 2009; along with an assortment of poetry.

92. Last Exit to Babylon: The Collected Stories of Roger Zelazny. Edited by David G. Grubbs, Christopher S. Kovacs and Ann Crimmins. Published by NESFA Press, Framingham, Massachusetts, 2009. Hardcover. This contains: Notes throughout by Christopher S. Kovacs; A Word from the Editors by David G. Grubbs, Christopher S. Kovacs and Ann Crimmins; The Prince of Amber – an essay by Joe Haldeman; What I Didn't Learn from Reading Roger Zelazny – an essay by Steven Brust; My Name Is Legion – Précis – an essay by Roger Zelazny, 2009; The Eve of RUMOKO, 1969; Kjwalll'kje'k'koothailll'kje'k, 1973; Home is the Hangman, 1975; Stand Pat, Ruby Stone, 1978; Go Starless in the Night, 1979; Halfjack, 1979; The Last Defender of Camelot, 1979; Fire and/or Ice, 1980; Exuent Omnes, 1980; A Very Good Year, 1979; The Places of Aache, 1980; A City Divided, 1982; The White Beast, 1979; Tower of Ice, 1981; The George Business, 1980; The Naked Matador, 1981; Walpurgisnacht, 1981; The Last of the Wild Ones, 1981; The Horse of Lir, 1981; Recital, 1981; And I Only Am Escaped to Tell Thee, 1981; Shadowjack, 1978; Shadowjack: Character Outline, 1983; Unicorn Variation, 1981; Some Science Fiction Parameters: A Biased View – an essay, 1975; Black Is the Color and None Is the Number – an essay, 2009; The Parts That Are Only Glimpsed: Three Reflexes – an essay, 2009; Future Crime – an essay, 1979; A Number of Princes in Amber – an essay, 1980; The Balance Between Art and Commerce – an essay, 1985; Amber and the Amberites – an essay, 1988; and And Call Me Roger: The Literary Life of Roger Zelazny, Part 4 – an essay by Christopher S. Kovacs; along with an assortment of poetry.

93. Nine Black Doves: The Collected Stories of Roger Zelazny. Edited by David G. Grubbs, Christopher S. Kovacs and Ann Crimmins. Published by NESFA Press, Framingham, Massachusetts, 2009. Hardcover. This contains: Notes throughout by Christopher S. Kovacs; A Word from the Editors by David G. Grubbs, Christopher S. Kovacs and Ann Crimmins; Considering Cows – an essay by Melinda Snodgrass; The Two Rogers – an essay by George R. R. Martin; Permafrost, 1986; Itself Surprised, 1984; Mana from Heaven, 1983; Devil and the Dancer, 1982; Garden of Blood, 1979; Dilvish, the Damned, 1982; LOKI 7281, 1984; Dreadsong, 1985; Dayblood, 1985; The Bands of Titan, 1986; Night Kings, 1986; Quest's End, 1987; The Sleeper, 1987; Ashes to Ashes, 1987; Deadboy Donner and the Filstone Cup, 1988; Kalifriki of the Thread, 1989; The Deadliest Game, 1990; 24 Vies of Mt. Fuji by Hokusai, 1985; Constructing a Science Fiction Novel – an essay, 1984; The Process of Composing – an essay, 1984; Science Fiction Writing at Length – an essay, 1991; Fantasy and Science Fiction: A Writer's View – an essay, 1985; Beyond the Idea – an essay, 1988; And Call Me Roger: The Literary Life of Roger Zelazny, Part 5 – an essay by Christopher S. Kovacs; Head Count, 2009; Coils – outline, 2009; Alien Speedway – outline, 2009; and The Ahriman Factor – outline, 2009; along with an assortment of poetry.

94. The Road to Amber: The Collected Stories of Roger Zelazny. Edited by David G. Grubbs, Christopher S. Kovacs and Ann Crimmins. Published by NESFA Press, Framingham, Massachusetts, 2009. Hardcover. This contains: Notes throughout by Christopher S. Kovacs; A Word from the Editors by David G. Grubbs, Christopher S. Kovacs and Ann Crimmins; Roger Zelazny – an essay by Jane Lindskold; Remembering Roger – an essay by Gerald Hausman; The Trickster – an essay by Gardner Dozois; Godson, 1994; Godson: A Play in Three Acts, 2009; Come Back to the Killing Ground, Alice, My Love, 1992; Prince of the Powers of This World, 1993; The Long Crawl of Hugh Glass, 1995; Tunnel Vision, 1994; Epithalamium, 1995; Prelude the First – Forever After, 1995; Prelude the Second – Forever After, 1995; Prelude the Third – Forever After, 1995; Prelude the Fourth – Forever After – 1995; Postlude – Forever After, 1995; Lady of Steel, 1995; The Three Descents of Jeremy Baker, 1995; The Sleeper: Character Outline, 2009; Concerto for Siren and Serotonin, 1988; The Long Sleep, 1993; A Word from George R. R. Martin – an essay; Prolog to Trumps of Doom, 1985; The Road to Amber, 1996; The Great Amber Questionnaire – an essay written with Ken St. Andre, 1978; A Secret of Amber – finished by Ed Greenwood, 2005; The Salesman's Tale, 1994; Blue Horse, Dancing Mountains, 1995; The Shrouding and the Guisel, 1994; Coming to a Cord, 1995; Hall of Mirrors, 1996; On Writing Horror After Reading Clive Barker – an essay, 1990; When It Comes It's Wonderful: Art Versus Craft in Writing – an essay, 1995; Warriors and Dreams – an essay, 1995; And Call Me Roger: The Literary Life of Roger Zelazny, Part 6 – an essay by Christopher S. Kovacs; Sandow's Shadow – an outline, 2009; Shadowland – an outline, 2009; Dysonized Biologicals – an outline, 2009; Donnerjack of Virtu: A Fable for the Machine Age – an outline, 2009; A Zelazny Timeline – an essay by Christopher S. Kovacs, Alice N. S. Lewis and David G. Grubbs; Z-world – an essay by Michael Whelan; The Quintessential Roger Zelazny – an essay by David G. Grubbs, Christopher S. Kovacs and Ann Crimmins; Isle of Regret – an essay by Trent Zelazny; and In Memoriam: Roger Zelazny, Lord of Light – an essay by George R. R. Martin; along with an assortment of poetry.

***

Roger Zelazny

ANTHOLOGIES

1. Nebula Award Stories 3. Published by Doubleday & Company, Garden City, New York, 1968. Hardcover. Herein: Introduction by **Roger Zelazny**; The Cloud Sculptors of Coral D by J. G. Ballard, 1967; Pretty Maggie Moneyeyes by Harlan Ellison, 1967; Mirror of Ice by Gary Wright, 1967; Aye and Gomorrah by **Samuel R. Delany**, 1967; Gonna Roll the Bones by **Fritz Leiber**, 1967; Behold the Man by **Michael Moorcock**, 1966; and Weyr Search by **Anne McCaffrey**, 1967.

2. Forever After. Published by Baen Books, New York City, 1995. Softcover. All from 1995, this contains: Arts and Sciences: The Gar Quithnick Story by Michael A. Stackpole; A Very Offensive Weapon; and Forever Afterword by David Drake; Wanted: Guardian by Robert Lynn Asprin; Domino's Tale by Jane Lindskold; and a series of Preludes by Roger Zelazny.

3. Wheel of Fortune. Published by Avonova, New York City, 1995. Softcover. All new work for 1995, this contains: Introduction by Roger Zelazny; Butterfly Wings by Nina Kiriki Hoffman; Kangaroo Straight by Jane M. Lindskold; Last Man Out by Dean Wesley Smith; The Casino Mirago by Gahan Wilson; The Vig by John DeChancie; Atlantic City Blues – a poem by Joe Haldeman, 1995; and Lines Composed on a Noisy Plane to Atlantic City by Joe Haldeman; Pipeline to Paradise by Nelson Bond; The Oddskeeper's Daughter by William Browning Spencer; Caution Merge by Jeff Bredenberg; The Unbolted by Kathe Koja and Barry N. Malzberg; Crapshoot by Larry Segriff; Dice with the Universe by Paul Dellinger; A Bigger Game by Don Webb; The Bataan Gamble by Thomas M. K. Stratman; Tyger Tyger Purring Loud by Gerald Hausman; A Round of Cards with the General by Karen Haber; Tip Off by Michael A. Stackpole; Elvis Bearpaw's Luck by William Sanders; The Tootsie Roll Factor by Richard A. Lupoff; and Blue Horse Dancing Mountains by Roger Zelazny.

4. Warriors of Blood and Dream. With Martin H. Greenberg. Published by Avonova, New York City, 1995. Softcover. All work from 1995. Herein: A Small Circle - an essay by Kazuaki Tanahashi; Sand Man by Steven Barnes; Heart of the Moment by Larry Segriff; Shapeshifter Finals by Jeffrey A. Carver; Guardian Angel by Victor Milan; Blood Duty by Michael A. Stackpole; Easy Living by Richard A. Lupoff; Fearless by Dave Smeds; The Seventh Martial Art by Jane Lindskold; Broadway Johnny by Walter Jon Williams; Master of Misery by Joe R. Lansdale; Eye of the Falcon by Gerald Hausman; Listen by Joel Richards; and True Grits by Jack C. Haldeman II.

5. The Williamson Effect. Published by Tor Books – Tom Doherty Associates, New York City, 1996. Hardcover. All new work. Herein: The Mayor of Mare Trang by **Frederik Pohl**; Before the Legion by Paul Dellinger; Inside Passage by **Poul Anderson**; Risk Assessment by Ben Bova; Emancipation by Pati Nagle; Thinkertoy by John Brunner; The Bad Machines by Fred Saberhagen; The Human Ingredient by Jeff Bredenberg; Child of the Night by Jane Lindskold; A Certain Talent by David Weber; Nonstop to Portales by **Connie Willis**; No Folded Hands by **Andre Norton**; Darker Than You Wrote by Mike Resnick; Words That Never Were: The Last Adventure of the Legion of Time by John J. Miller; Williamson's World - a poem by Scott E. Green; Near Portales... Freedom Shouts – a poem by Scott E. Green; and A World in Love with Change – an essay by David Brin.

***

RELATED

1. Roger Zelazny: Starmont Reader's Guide 2. By Carl B. Yoke. Published by Starmont, West Linn, Oregon, 1979. Softcover.

2. Roger Zelazny: A Primary and Secondary Bibliography. By Joseph L. Sanders. Published by G. K. Hall, Boston, Massachusetts, 1980. Hardcover.

3. Amber Dreams: A Roger Zelazny Bibliography. By Daniel Levack. Published by Underwood/Miller, San Francisco, California, 1983. Hardcover.

4. Roger Zelazny. By Theodore Krulik. Published by Ungar Publishing, New York City, 1986. Hardcover.

5. Seven No-Trump – A Crossroads Adventure in the World of Roger Zelazny's Amber. By Neil Randall. Published by Tor Books – Tom Doherty Associates, New York City, 1988. Softcover.

6. Roger Zelazny: Master of Amber – A Working Bibliography. By Phil Stephensen-Payne. Published by Galactic Central Publications, Leeds, England, 1991. Softcover.

7. A Checklist of Roger Zelazny. By Christopher P. Stephens. Published by Ultramarine, Hastings-on-Hudson, New York, 1993. Softcover.

8. Lord of the Fantastic – Stories in Honor of Roger Zelazny. Edited by Martin H. Greenberg. Published by Avon Books, New York City, 1998. Softcover. Herein: The Outling by Andre Norton; Arroyo de Oro by Pati Nagle; Calling Pittsburgh by Steven Brust; The Somehow Not Yet Dead by Nina Kiriki Hoffman; Ki'rin and the Blue and White Tiger by Jane M. Lindskold; Mad Jack by Jennifer Roberson; Movers and Shakers by Paul Dellinger; The Halfway House at the Heart of Darkness by William Browning Spencer; Only the End of the World Again by Neil Gaiman; Slow Symphonies of Mass and Time by Gregory Benford; Asgard Unlimited by Michael A. Stackpole; Wherefore the Rest is Silence by Gerald Hausman; Lethe by Walter Jon Williams; The Story Roger Never Told by Jack Williamson; If I Take the Wings of Morning by Katharine Eliska Kimbriel; The Eryx by Robert Sheckley; Southern Discomfort by Jack C. Haldeman II; Suicide Kings by John J. Miller; Changing of the Guard by Robert Wayne McCoy and Thomas F. Monteleone; The Flying Dutchman by John Varley; Ninekiller and the Neterw by William Sanders; Call Me Titan by Robert Silverberg; and Back in the Real World by Bradley H. Sinor.

9. Roger Zelazny. By Carl B. Yoke. Published by Wildside Press, United States, 2007. Softcover.

APPENDIX: The Futurians

Isaac Asimov
Elise Balter
James Blish
Hannes Bok
Daniel Burford
Chester Cohen
Rosalind Cohen
Harry Dockweiler
Jack Gillespie
Virginia Kidd
Damon Knight
Cyril Kornbluth
Mary Byers

Walter Kubilius
David Kyle
Herman Leventman
Robert A. W. Lowndes
Judith Merril
John Michel
Frederik Pohl
Leslie Perri - Doris Baumgardt
Jack Rubinson
Arthur W. Saha
Larry Shaw
Richard Wilson
Donald A. Wollheim

BIBLIOGRAPHY

Online Sources:

The Science Fiction Hall of Fame.
Internet Movie Database.
The Internet Speculative Fiction Database.
Wikipedia.

Books:

Ackerman, Forrest J. FORREST J. ACKERMAN'S WORLD OF SCIENCE FICTION. Preface by **A. E. van Vogt**. Foreword by John Landis. General Publishing, Los Angeles, 1997.

Aldiss, Brian W.; Harrison, Harry. HELL'S CARTOGRAPHERS - Some Personal Histories of Science Fiction Writers. Harper and Row, New York, 1975.

Aldiss, Brian; Wingrove, David. TRILLION YEAR SPREE - The History of Science Fiction. Paladin - Grafton Books, London, 1988.

Ash, Brian. WHO'S WHO IN SCIENCE FICTION. Sphere Books, London, 1977.

Ashley, Mike. THE AMAZING STORY. Amazing Stories, TSR Inc., Lake Geneva, Wisconsin, 1992. Printed in six parts, starting in January and running into the June issue.

Asimov, Isaac. IN MEMORY YET GREEN: The Autobiography of Isaac Asimov 1920 - 1954. Doubleday and Company, Garden City, New York, 1979.

Asimov, Isaac. IN JOY STILL FELT: The Autobiography of Isaac Asimov 1954 - 1978. Doubleday and Company, Garden City, New York, 1980.

Asimov, Isaac. ASIMOV ON SCIENCE FICTION. Doubleday and Company, Garden City, New York, 1981.

Asimov, Isaac. I. ASIMOV: A Memoir. Doubleday and Company, Garden City, New York, 1994.

Asimov, Isaac. YOURS, ISAAC ASIMOV. Edited by Stan Asimov. Doubleday and Company, Garden City, New York, 1995.

Bailey, J. O. PILGRIMS THROUGH SPACE AND TIME - Trends and Patterns in Scientific and Utopian Fiction. Argus Books, New York, 1947.

Barron, Neil. ANATOMY OF WONDER - Science Fiction. R. R. Bowker, New York, 1976.

Bleiler, Everett F.; Bleiler, Richard J. SCIENCE FICTION: The Early Years. The Kent State University Press, Kent, Ohio, 1990.

Bleiler, Everett F. SCIENCE FICTION: The Gernsback Years - A complete coverage of the genre magazines Amazing, Astounding, Wonder, and others from 1926 through 1936. The Kent State University Press, Kent, Ohio, 1998.

Bretnor, Reginald (editor). SCIENCE FICTION Today and Tomorrow: A Discursive Symposium. Harper and Row, New York, 1974.

Cassiday, Bruce (editor). MODERN MYSTERY, FANTASY AND SCIENCE FICTION WRITERS. The Continuum Publishing Company, New York, 1993.

Clute, John; Nicholls, Peter. THE ENCYCLOPEDIA OF SCIENCE FICTION. St. Martin's Press, New York, 1993.

Clute, John; Grant, John. THE ENCYCLOPEDIA OF FANTASY. St. Martin's Press, New York, 1997.

Coren, Michael. THE INVISIBLE MAN: The Life and Liberties of H. G. Wells. Random House, Toronto, 1993.

Curry, L. W. SCIENCE FICTION AND FANTASY AUTHORS - A Bibliography of First Printings of Their Fiction. G. K. Hall, Boston, Massachusetts, 1979.

Davin, Eric Leif. PIONEERS OF WONDER - Conversations with the Founders of Science Fiction. Prometheus Books, Amherst, New York, 1999.

Del Rey, Lester. THE WORLD OF SCIENCE FICTION - The History of a Subculture. Del Rey - Ballantine Books, New York, 1979.

Dickson, Lovat. H. G. WELLS - His Turbulent Life and Times. Pelican Books, Middlesex, England, 1972.

Disch, Thomas M. THE DREAMS OUR STUFF IS MADE OF - How Science Fiction Conquered the World. Touchstone - Simon and Schuster, New York, 2000.

Dozois, Gardner; Lee, Tina; Schmidt, Stanley; Strock, Ian Randal; Williams, Sheila. (editors). WRITING SCIENCE FICTION AND FANTASY - 20 Dynamic Essays by Today's Top Professionals. St. Martin's Press, New York, 1991.

Erardi, Glenn. COLLECTING EDGAR RICE BURROUGHS. Schiffer Publishing, Atglen, Pennsylvania, 2000.

Eshbach, Lloyd Arthur (editor). OF WORLDS BEYOND - A Symposium. Dennis Dobson, London, 1965.

Fulton, Roger; Betancourt, John. THE SCI-FI CHANNEL ENCYCLOPEDIA OF TV SCIENCE FICTION. Warner Books, New York, 1998.

Gunn, James. ALTERNATE WORLDS - The Illustrated History of Science Fiction. Foreword by Isaac Asimov. Prentice Hall Inc., Englewood Cliffs, New Jersey, 1975.

Gunn, James. ISAAC ASIMOV - The Foundations of Science Fiction. Oxford University Press, New York, 1982.

Gunn, James (editor). THE NEW ENCYCLOPEDIA OF SCIENCE FICTION. Viking, New York, 1988.
Harbottle, Philip; Holland, Stephen. VULTURES OF THE VOID: A History of British Science Fiction Publishing 1946 - 1956. The Borgo Press, San Bernardino, California, 1992.

Hardy, Phil. SCIENCE FICTION - The Complete Film Sourcebook. Foreword by Michael Haggiard. William Morrow and Company, New York, 1984.

Hartwell, David. AGE OF WONDERS - Exploring the World of Science Fiction. Walker and Company, New York, 1984.

Holdstock, Robert (editor). ENCYCLOPEDIA OF SCIENCE FICTION. Foreword by Isaac Asimov. Octopus Books, London, 1978.

Jaffery, Sheldon; Cook Fred. WEIRD TALES. Bowling Green State University Popular Press, Bowling Green, Ohio, 1985.

Knight, Damon. THE FUTURIANS. John Day, New York, 1977.

Lentz, Harris M. III. SCIENCE FICTION, HORROR & FANTASY FILM AND TELEVISION CREDITS. McFarland & Company, Jefferson, North Carolina, 1983.

Lundwall, Sam J. SCIENCE FICTION: What It's All About. Ace Books, New York, 1971.

Moskowitz, Sam (editor). UNDER THE MOONS OF MARS - A History and Anthology of "The Scientific Romance" in the Munsey Magazines 1912 - 1920. Holt, Reinhart and Winston, New York, 1970.

Murray, Terry A. SCIENCE FICTION MAGAZINE STORY INDEX 1926 - 1995. McFarland & Company, Jefferson, North Carolina, 1999.

Naha, Ed. THE SCIENCE FICTIONARY - An A - Z Guide to the World of SF Authors, Films and TV Shows. Wideview Books, United States, 1980.

Nicholls, Peter. THE SCIENCE FICTION ENCYCLOPEDIA. Doubleday & Company, Garden City, New York, 1979.

Panshin, Alexei; Panshin, Cory. SF IN DIMENSION - A Book of Explorations. Advent Publishers, Chicago, 1976.

Philmus, Robert M. INTO THE UNKNOWN - The Evolution of Science Fiction from Francis Godwin to H. G. Wells. University of California Press, Berkeley, California, 1983.

Platt, Charles. DREAM MAKERS: The Uncommon People Who Write Science Fiction - Interviews. Berkley Books, New York, 1980.

Platt, Charles. DREAM MAKERS - Volume II: The Uncommon Men and Women Who Write Science Fiction - Interviews. Berkley Books, New York, 1983.

Pohl, Frederik. THE SCIENCE FICTION ROLE OF HONOR. Random House, New York, 1975.

Pohl, Frederik. THE WAY THE FUTURE WAS - A Memoir. Del Rey - Ballantine Books, New York, 1978.

Pollock, Dale. SKYWALKING - The Life and Films of George Lucas. Harmony Books, New York, 1983.

Rose, Lois; Rose, Stephen. THE SHATTERED RING - Science Fiction and the Quest for Meaning. John Knox Press, Richmond, Virginia, 1970.

Scholes, Robert; Rabkin, Eric S. SCIENCE FICTION - History Science Vision. Oxford University Press, New York, 1977.

Searles, Baird; Last, Martin; Meacham, Beth; Franklin, Michael. A READER'S GUIDE TO SCIENCE FICTION. Foreword by Samuel R. Delaney. Avon Books, New York, 1979.

Searles, Baird; Meacham, Beth; Franklin, Michael. A READER'S GUIDE TO FANTASY. Foreword by Poul Anderson. Avon Books, New York, 1982.

Silverberg, Robert. ROBERT SILVERBERG'S WORLDS OF WONDER - Exploring the Craft of Science Fiction. Warner Books, New York, 1987.

Suvin, Darko. METAMORPHOSES OF SCIENCE FICTION - On the Poetics and History of a Literary Genre. Yale University Press, New Haven, Connecticut, 1979.

Tuck, Donald H. THE ENCYCLOPEDIA OF SCIENCE FICTION AND FANTASY. Advent Publishers, Chicago, 1974.

Tymn, Marshall B.; Zahorski, Kenneth J.; Boyer, Robert H. FANTASY LITERATURE - A Core Collection and Reference Guide. R. R. Bowker Company, New York, 1979.

Weaver, Tom. SCIENCE FICTION AND FANTASY FILM FLASHBACKS - Conversations with 24 Actors, Writers, Producers and Directors from the Golden Age. McFarland and Company, Jefferson, North Carolina, 2004.

Wells, Stuart W. III. THE SCIENCE FICTION HEROIC FANTASY AUTHOR INDEX. Purple Unicorn Books, Duluth, Minnesota, 1978.

Williamson, Jack. WONDER'S CHILD: My Life in Science Fiction. Bluejay Books, New York, 1984.

Wingrove, David (editor). THE SCIENCE FICTION SOURCE BOOK. Foreword by **Brian W. Aldiss**. Van Nostrand Reinhold, New York, 1984.

Wright, Gene. WHO'S WHO & WHAT'S WHAT IN SCIENCE FICTION - Film, Television, Radio & Theater: A Fact-Packed A-Z Encyclopedia. Introduction by Isaac Asimov. Bonanza Books, New York, 1985.

Wynorski, Jim. THEY CAME FROM OUTER SPACE - 12 Classic Science Fiction Tales that Became Major Motion Pictures. Introduction by **Ray Bradbury**. Doubleday and Company, Garden City, New York, 1980.